W. SOMERSET MAUGHAM

LIBRARY OF ESSENTIAL WRITERS

W. SOMERSET MAUGHAM

◆

FIVE NOVELS

◆

COMPLETE AND UNABRIDGED

Liza of Lambeth • Mrs. Craddock •
The Explorer • Of Human Bondage •
The Moon and Sixpence

BARNES & NOBLE
NEW YORK

Compilation © 2006 by Barnes & Noble Publishing, Inc.

Introduction by Philip Holden © 2006 by Barnes & Noble Publishing, Inc.

All rights reserved. No part of this publication may be reproduced, stored in a retrieval system, or transmitted, in any form or by any means, electronic, mechanical, photocopying, recording, or otherwise, without prior written permission from the publisher.

Cover design by Allison Saltzman

2006 Barnes & Noble Publishing

ISBN-13: 978-0-7607-8274-3
ISBN-10: 0-7607-8274-1

Printed and bound in China

1 3 5 7 9 10 8 6 4 2

Contents

Introduction	VII
Liza of Lambeth	1
Mrs. Craddock	91
The Explorer	317
Of Human Bondage	497
The Moon and Sixpence	1091

Introduction

W. SOMERSET MAUGHAM ENJOYED ONE OF THE LONGEST AND MOST VARIED LITERARY careers of any writer in the English language. His first novel was published when Queen Victoria was still on the throne, and he was still producing controversial new writing in the 1960s, having achieved critical and popular success in three different genres: drama, the novel, and the short story. Maugham's career is remarkable for more than just its length and variety; he was a versatile prose writer whose craftsmanship exerted a strong influence on authors as disparate as George Orwell and V. S. Naipaul. The novels collected here show Maugham during the first half of his literary career, and include both his masterpiece *Of Human Bondage*, and the book that first brought him popular success, *The Moon and Sixpence*. They range in setting from the slums of South London to the South Pacific island of Tahiti, yet each illustrates the sardonic vision and narrative skill that would make Maugham one of the most prolific and best-selling writers in the English language.

William Somerset Maugham was born in Paris in 1874 to a British lawyer and his wife, and spent his childhood in France. His mother died when he was eight, and he lost his father to stomach cancer two years later. Responsibility for young Willie's upbringing thus fell to his uncle, Henry MacDonald Maugham, a Church of England clergyman who lived in Kent, in the southeast of England. At ten, Maugham went to England for the first time; his uncle immediately dismissed his French nurse, and a year later sent him off to the harsh environment of King's School in Canterbury. Maugham hated the restrictive atmosphere of the English boarding school, and at sixteen left to study German and attend university classes in Heidelberg, spending a year and a half in a bohemian environment in which he cultivated a passionate interest in philosophy, literature, and the arts. Returning to England, he trained as a doctor in London from 1892 to 1897.

The social deprivation Maugham witnessed as an obstetrics clerk at Saint Thomas's Hospital in South London provided background material for the gritty realism of his first novel, *Liza of Lambeth* (1897). Maugham's first foray in prose fiction was influenced by contemporary accounts of working class life by writers such as Arthur Morrison, but scenes such as the conclusion of the novel, which relate the predicament of the unmarried Liza Kemp, pregnant by a married man, are clearly drawn from his own London experiences. *Liza* made a strong impact on critics and the reading public. In a reader's report, writer and critic Edward Garnett praised it as a "very clever and realistic study" but warned that book reviewers might object to the strong language and unflinchingly realistic description of working class life. He was proved right. The *Academy* condemned the work as "a sordid story of vulgar seduction," while *The National Review* characterized it as "gratuitously brutal." The novel was even the subject of a condemnatory Sunday sermon at Westminster Abbey. As Maugham was to come to know well later in his career, controversy sells books, and *Liza of Lambeth* soon went into its second printing.

In the second novel collected here, *Mrs. Craddock*, written in 1899 but not published until 1902, Maugham also drew on biographical material, reaching back beyond his time at Saint Thomas's hospital to his teenage years in Kent. Place names in the novel are transparent adaptations of real ones. Whitstable, where Maugham lived with his clergyman uncle and his wife after he was orphaned, becomes, with rather wicked irony, "Blackstable," while the first two syllables of Canterbury are transposed in the name of the fictional town "Tercanbury." The parsimonious curate Mr. Glover is a direct if rather jaundiced portrait of Maugham's uncle Henry. Yet the protagonist of *Mrs. Craddock*, Bertha Leys, loving life but married to the stolid and uninspiring Edward Craddock, is drawn not from Maugham's life but from fiction. In temperament and situation, if not in eventual fate, she resembles the protagonist of one of Maugham's favorite novels, Gustave Flaubert's *Madame Bovary*. Indeed, the resemblance of the titles is not coincidental: in both Maugham's and Flaubert's novels, the protagonists find themselves defined and restricted by the roles their husbands expect them to play.

Mrs. Craddock was largely well-received, although it also courted controversy. Heinemann, the novel's publisher, initially objected to the explicitness of Maugham's descriptions of Bertha's passion for her husband and lover, and only consented to publish the novel if a key passage was deleted. The setting of *Mrs. Craddock* is very different from *Liza of Lambeth*, yet there are important thematic continuities. Both novels feature women protagonists struggling against an uncaring social order, and both contain controversial passages in which a woman expresses sexual desire for a man. Maugham's sympathy with the position of women in Victorian and Edwardian England, and indeed his frequent use of a female point of view, may represent a strategy to work through a dilemma in his own life: his closeted homosexuality. Deeply influenced as a young man by the public hysteria surrounding the 1895 trials and conviction of homosexual writer Oscar Wilde for "committing acts of gross indecency with other male persons," Maugham would never discuss his sexuality publicly, yet it emerges surreptitiously in many of his works.

The third novel collected here, *The Explorer*, was published in 1907. The narrative begins in the same social milieu as *Mrs. Craddock* but quickly moves beyond provincial England by introducing the imperialist Alec MacKenzie, and following his developing relationship with Lucy Allerton, the impoverished daughter of a country gentry family fallen on hard times, and his adventures in the wilds of East Africa. In writing *The Explorer* Maugham again showed commercial acumen, following in the literary footsteps of popular writers such as Henry Rider Haggard and Rudyard Kipling in dramatizing deeds of manly adventure on the imperial frontier. The novel, however, also develops elements present in the earlier fiction. In Lucy, Maugham again creates a woman who must contend with social forces beyond her control, and the narrative's contrast between the character-building dangers of exploration in Africa and the pettiness of domestic English society also allows an acerbic critique of the latter. The opposition between a corrupt, hypocritical, and repressed Europe and other, putatively more natural and open societies in Asia, Africa, and the South Pacific would indeed become a staple of much of Maugham's later fiction.

Both *Mrs. Craddock* and *The Explorer* contain extended scenes of witty dialogue with little accompanying description, hinting at Maugham's other preoccupation while writing them: the theatre. After the breakthrough success of *Lady Frederick* (written in 1903 but not staged until 1907), Maugham quickly became one of the most popular playwrights in the Edwardian era: in 1909 he achieved the unusual distinction of having four plays being performed at the same time in London's West End, and his success would continue until the closing of London theatres after the beginning of World War I in 1914. In his personal life, Maugham also took a new direction, embarking on a series of heterosexual liaisons which culminated in a relationship with Syrie Wellcome, the estranged wife of the pharmaceutical company head and philanthropist Henry Wellcome. Syrie and Maugham had a daughter, Liza, and he was named as respondent when Wellcome brought divorce proceedings against his wife in 1915. The couple wed in 1917 after Syrie's divorce, but it was largely a marriage of mutual convenience for both parties. In 1914, while volunteering in the Ambulance Corps in France, Maugham had met the young American Gerald Haxton, who was to become the central love interest of his life and his companion until Gerald's early death in 1944.

Maugham's most important early novel, *Of Human Bondage* (1915), was published during these turbulent years. He had first drafted the manuscript, originally titled "The Artistic Temperament of Stephen Carey," years before, and an early version was rejected by publishers in 1899. As Maugham himself noted, his revision of the manuscript over a decade after it was first written enriched it substantially, giving him a more mature and critical perspective on the autobiographical material it contains.

Of Human Bondage commences in a manner similar to many Victorian novels, such as Charles Dickens's *David Copperfield*, as a *Bildungsroman*, the account of a young man's growth, education, and movement out into the world. Much of the early material is autobiographical: Maugham's protagonist, now named Philip Carey, is an orphan sent by his clergyman uncle to boarding school, where he develops an intense attachment to another boy named Rose. Even here there is some embroidering of the raw materials of life: Maugham's stammer is replaced by the more concrete disability of Philip's club foot. As Philip reaches maturity, the optimistic narrative trajectory of the *Bildungsroman* begins to unravel. He becomes trapped in a humiliating and abusive relationship with the waitress Mildred Rogers, and although he emerges from it into the prospect of marriage with the wholesome Sally Athelny, the ending seems contrived given the agonies of anguish and disillusionment he has suffered.

If Maugham's novel reflects many of the larger social and interpersonal insecurities that haunted the Edwardian world, it also represents his own internal struggles. Mildred is androgynous in appearance, and may be a displaced portrait of a male lover—possibly Harry Philips, Maugham's companion during his time in Paris early in the twentieth century. Despite these strategies of concealment, the novel arguably still shows Maugham at his most naked and emotionally honest, and is devoid of the elaborate narrative frames that create ironic distance in much of his later work. However, the disruption of publishing and critical networks during the First World War meant that *Of Human Bondage,* despite its thematic depth, did not initially receive the recognition that Maugham's later fiction would attract. American novelist Theodore Dreiser was almost alone in recognizing its worth, praising it as a great realist work of art which dealt unflinchingly with the degradation of human beings in modern urban society. Certainly Maugham remained uniquely attached to the novel: biographer Jeffrey Meyers notes that when the author was asked to make a recording of the first chapter thirty years after its publication, Maugham found himself overwhelmed by the emotions it raised, and was unable to finish.

The last of the novels collected here, *The Moon and Sixpence,* was published in 1919, and arose from a trip that Maugham and Gerald Haxton made to the South Pacific two years earlier, apparently under the aegis of the British Secret Intelligence Service. Maugham borrows heavily from the life of the French postimpressionist painter Paul Gauguin in creating his protagonist, Charles Strickland, a seemingly inoffensive middle-aged English stockbroker who deserts his family to devote himself to painting, traveling first to Paris where he learns his craft, and then on to Tahiti, where he produces his greatest work, but eventually dies. Like the young narrator of his novel, Maugham combed Tahiti for traces of Gauguin, and even succeeded in locating and buying one of his remaining paintings, *Eve in Paradise*, at a bargain price. Some differences between Gauguin's and Strickland's life were no doubt dictated by literary propriety: the syphilis that caused Gauguin's death is transmuted into leprosy in the novel. Others changes seem more personal to Maugham himself, in particular his continued exploration of the theme of the emotional cruelty in unbalanced relationships in which one lover loves more than the other. This subject reprises his concerns in *Of Human Bondage*, but also perhaps reflects his tempestuous relationship with Gerald.

In portraying the South Pacific as a place permitting an Edenic reclamation of human nature now corrupted by civilization in Europe, Maugham draws on a long tradition of exotic travel writing by figures such as French travel writer Pierre Loti. Much of the design of *The Moon and Sixpence*, however, in which a jejeune narrator encounters and later traces the path of a flawed but heroic figure whom he is moved by yet cannot fully comprehend, is drawn from Joseph Conrad's novella *Heart of Darkness*. Just as in Conrad's text, so in Maugham's the narrator returns to England at the conclusion of the novel to interview his protagonist's beloved. Unlike Kurtz's intended, however, Mrs. Strickland has recovered from her husband's abandonment well enough to participate in the growing commercialization of his works, fabricating details of their marriage and admiring the essentially "decorative" nature of her husband's art. The conclusion of the novel thus again expresses Maugham's disillusionment with the superficial hypocrisy of European civilization in contrast with a Tahiti which, like Africa in The Explorer, permits an unnerving yet invigorating encounter with the dark recesses of human nature.

The popularity of *The Moon and Sixpence*, published when its author was 45, cemented Maugham's commercial success as a novelist, but it also attracted criticism from a new angle. New Zealand writer Katherine Mansfield was not alone in noting that the novel left her "strangely unsatisfied": Maugham's fiction would from now on be frequently critiqued as middlebrow, lacking the formal experimentation or thematic range of his modernist contemporaries. Yet the author's popularity grew as his critical reputation waned, and *The Moon and Sixpence* served as the prelude to a career writing fiction that would span four more decades.

In the 1920s and 1930s, Maugham achieved his greatest fame as the writer of some of the most widely-read short stories in the English language, while maintaining a steady output of popular novels. He is perhaps best remembered for his short stories set in the South Pacific and Southeast Asia, so much so that British Malaya of the 1920s and 1930s is now often thought of as "Maugham country." Although Maugham had little knowledge of Asian cultures, collections such as *The Trembling of a Leaf* (1921), *The Casuarina Tree* (1926), and *Ah King* (1933), containing such famous stories as "Rain" and "The Letter," skillfully dramatized the hypocrisies of the ruling elites of colonial societies. At the same time, Maugham's Ashenden stories, based on his experiences in Switzerland working for British Intelligence during World War I, pioneered the genre of espionage fiction. Maugham continued writing during and after the Second World War. His most popular novel, *The Razor's Edge*, which is set in India and Chicago, was not published until 1944, just after his seventieth birthday, and his last book, *Purely for My Pleasure*, was published in 1962, when its author was eighty-eight years old. Maugham died in Nice, France on December 16, 1965, a little more than a month before his ninety-second birthday.

"Sometimes people carry to such perfection the mask they have assumed," Maugham wrote in *The Moon and Sixpence*, "that in due course they actually become the person they seem." Maugham's novels, with their transformation of autobiographical material into fiction, and indeed his own construction of a public personality as an urbane man of letters, might be seen as a mask which eventually became more compelling than the reality underneath. Yet the author's complex and frequently unhappy life produced an ironic literary vision which has captivated successive generations of readers. In a new millennium, Maugham's novels and short stories are still widely read; more so, indeed than those of many of his more illustrious contemporaries.

PHILIP HOLDEN

Philip Holden is the author of *Orienting Masculinity, Orienting Nation: W. Somerset Maugham's Exotic Fiction*, and has published widely on colonial fiction in English. He is associate professor in the Department of English Language and Literature at the National University of Singapore.

LIZA OF LAMBETH

Chapter I

It was the first Saturday afternoon in August; it had been broiling hot all day, with a cloudless sky, and the sun had been beating down on the houses so that the top rooms were like ovens; but now with the approach of evening it was cooler, and everyone in Vere Street was out-of-doors.

Vere Street, Lambeth, is a short, straight street leading out of the Westminster Bridge Road; it has forty houses on one side and forty houses on the other, and these eighty houses are very much more like one another than ever peas are like peas, or young ladies like young ladies. They are newish, three-storied buildings of dingy grey brick with slate roofs, and they are perfectly flat, without a bow-window or even a projecting cornice or window-sill to break the straightness of the line from one end of the street to the other.

This Saturday afternoon the street was full of life: no traffic came down Vere Street, and the cemented space between the pavements was given up to children. Several games of cricket were being played by wildly excited boys, using coats for wickets, an old tennis-ball or a bundle of rags tied together for a ball, and, generally, an old broomstick for bat. The wicket was so large and the bat so small that the man in was always getting bowled, when heated quarrels would arise, the batter absolutely refusing to go out and the bowler absolutely insisting on going in. The girls were more peaceable; they were chiefly employed in skipping, and only abused one another mildly when the rope was not properly turned or the skipper did not jump sufficiently high. Worst off of all were the very young children, for there had been no rain for weeks, and the street was as dry and clean as a covered court, and, in the lack of mud to wallow in, they sat about the road, disconsolate as poets. The number of babies was prodigious; they sprawled about everywhere, on the pavement, round the doors, and about their mothers' skirts. The grown-ups were gathered round the open doors; there were usually two women squatting on the doorstep, and two or three more seated on either side on chairs; they were invariably nursing babies, and most of them showed clear signs that the present object of the maternal care would be soon ousted by a new arrival. Men were less numerous, but such as there were leant against the walls, smoking, or sat on the sills of the ground-floor windows. It was the dead season in Vere Street as much as in Belgravia, and really if it had not been for babies just come or just about to come, and an opportune murder in a neighbouring doss-house, there would have been nothing whatever to talk about. As it was, the little groups talked quietly, discussing the atrocity or the merits of the local midwives, comparing the circumstances of their various confinements.

"You'll be 'avin' your little trouble soon, eh, Polly?" asked one good lady of another.

"Oh, I reckon I've got another two months ter go yet," answered Polly.

"Well," said a third, "I wouldn't 'ave thought you'd go so long by the look of yer!"

"I 'ope you'll have it easier this time, my dear," said a very stout old person, a woman of great importance.

"She said she wasn't goin' to 'ave no more, when the last one come." This remark came from Polly's husband.

"Ah," said the stout old lady, who was in the business, and boasted vast experience. "That's wot they all says; but, Lor' bless yer, they don't mean it."

"Well, I've got three, and I'm not goin' to 'ave no more bli'me if I will; 'tain't good enough—that's wot I says."

"You're abaht right there, ole gal," said Polly, "My word, 'Arry, if you 'ave any more I'll git a divorce, that I will."

At that moment an organ-grinder turned the corner and came down the street.

"Good biz; 'ere's an organ!" cried half a dozen people at once.

The organ-man was an Italian, with a shock of black hair and a ferocious moustache. Drawing his organ to a favourable spot, he stopped, released his shoulder from the leather straps by which he dragged it, and cocking his large soft hat on the side of his head, began turning the handle. It was a lively tune, and in less than no time a little crowd had gathered round to listen, chiefly the young men and the maidens, for the married ladies were never in a fit state to dance, and therefore disinclined to trouble themselves to stand round the organ. There was a moment's hesitation at opening the ball; then one girl said to another—

"Come on, Florrie, you and me ain't shy; we'll begin, and bust it!"

The two girls took hold of one another, one acting gentleman, the other lady; three or four more pairs of girls immediately joined them, and they began a waltz. They held themselves very upright; and with an air of grave dignity which was quite impressive, glided slowly about, making their steps with the utmost precision, bearing themselves with sufficient decorum for a court ball. After a while the men began to itch for a turn, and two of them, taking hold of one another in the most approved fashion, waltzed round the circle with the gravity of judges.

All at once there was a cry: "There's Liza!" And several members of the group turned and called out: "Oo, look at Liza!"

The dancers stopped to see the sight, and the organ-grinder, having come to the end of his tune, ceased turning the handle and looked to see what was the excitement.

"Oo, Liza!" they called out. "Look at Liza; oo, I sy!"

It was a young girl of about eighteen, with dark eyes, and an enormous fringe, puffed-out and curled and frizzed, covering her whole forehead from side to side, and coming down to meet her eyebrows. She was dressed in brilliant violet, with great lappets of velvet, and she had on her head an enormous black hat covered with feathers.

"I sy, ain't she got up dossy?" called out the groups at the doors, as she passed.

"Dressed ter death, and kill the fashion; that's wot I calls it."

Liza saw what a sensation she was creating; she arched her back and lifted her head, and walked down the street, swaying her body from side to side, and swaggering along as though the whole place belonged to her.

" 'Ave yer bought the street, Bill?" shouted one youth; and then half a dozen burst forth at once, as if by inspiration—

"Knocked 'em in the Old Kent Road!"

It was immediately taken up by a dozen more, and they all yelled it out—

"Knocked 'em in the Old Kent Road. Yah, ah, knocked 'em in the Old Kent Road!"

"Oo, Liza!" they shouted; the whole street joined in, and they gave long, shrill, ear-piercing shrieks and strange calls, that rung down the street and echoed back again.

"Hextra special!" called out a wag.

"Oh, Liza! Oo! Ooo!" yells and whistles, and then it thundered forth again—

"Knocked 'em in the Old Kent Road!"

Liza put on the air of a conquering hero, and sauntered on, enchanted at the uproar. She stuck out her elbows and jerked her head on one side, and said to herself as she passed through the bellowing crowd—

"This is jam!"

"Knocked 'em in the Old Kent Road!"

When she came to the group round the barrel-organ, one of the girls cried out to her—

"Is that yer new dress, Liza?"

"Well, it don't look like my old one, do it?" said Liza.

"Where did yer git it?" asked another friend, rather enviously.

"Picked it up in the street, of course," scornfully answered Liza.

"I believe it's the same one as I saw in the pawnbroker's dahn the road," said one of the men, to teaze her.

"Thet's it; but wot was you doin' in there? Pledgin' yer shirt, or was it yer trousers?"

"Yah, I wouldn't git a second-'and dress at a pawnbroker's!"

"Garn!" said Liza indignantly. "I'll swipe yer over the snitch if yer talk ter me.

I got the mayterials in the West Hend, didn't I? And I 'ad it mide up by my Court Dressmiker, so you jolly well dry up, old jellybelly."

"Garn!" was the reply.

Liza had been so intent on her new dress and the comment it was exciting that she had not noticed the organ.

"Oo, I say, let's 'ave some dancin'," she said as soon as she saw it. "Come on, Sally," she added, to one of the girls, "you an' me'll dance togither. Grind away, old cock!"

The man turned on a new tune, and the organ began to play the Intermezzo from the *Cavalleria*; other couples quickly followed Liza's example, and they began to waltz round with the same solemnity as before; but Liza outdid them all; if the others were as stately as queens, she was as stately as an empress; the gravity and dignity with which she waltzed were something appalling, you felt that the minuet was a frolic in comparison; it would have been a fitting measure to tread round the grave of a *première danseuse*, or at the funeral of a professional humorist. And the graces she put on, the languor of the eyes, the contemptuous curl of the lips, the exquisite turn of the hand, the dainty arching of the foot! You felt there could be no questioning her right to the tyranny of Vere Street.

Suddenly she stopped short, and disengaged herself from her companion.

"Oh, I sy," she said, "this is too bloomin' slow; it gives me the sick."

That is not precisely what she said, but it is impossible always to give the exact unexpurgated words of Liza and the other personages of the story; the reader is therefore entreated with his thoughts to piece out the necessary imperfections of the dialogue.

"It's too bloomin' slow," she said again; "it gives me the sick. Let's 'ave somethin' a bit more lively than this 'ere waltz. You stand over there, Sally, an' we'll show 'em 'ow ter skirt dance."

They all stopped waltzing.

"Talk of the ballet at the Canterbury and the South London. You just wite till you see the ballet at Vere Street, Lambeth—we'll knock 'em!"

She went up to the organ-grinder.

"Na then, Italiano," she said to him, "you buck up; gives us a tune that's got some guts in it! See?"

She caught hold of his big hat and squashed it down over his eyes. The man grinned from ear to ear, and, touching the little catch at the side, began to play a lively tune such as Liza had asked for.

The men had fallen out, but several girls had put themselves in position, in couples, standing face to face; and immediately the music struck up, they began. They held up their skirts on each side, so as to show their feet, and proceeded to go through the difficult steps and motions of the dance. Liza was right; they could not have done it better in a trained ballet. But the best dancer of them all was Liza; she threw her whole soul into it; forgetting the stiff bearing which she had thought proper to the waltz, and casting off its elaborate graces, she gave herself up entirely to the present pleasure. Gradually the other couples stood aside, so that Liza and Sally were left alone. They paced it carefully, watching each other's steps, and as if by instinct performing corresponding movements, so as to make the whole a thing of symmetry.

"I'm abaht done," said Sally, blowing and puffing. "I've 'ad enough of it."

"Go on, Liza!" cried out a dozen voices when Sally stopped.

She gave no sign of having heard them other than calmly to continue her dance. She glided through the steps, and swayed about, and manipulated her skirt, all with the most charming grace imaginable; then, the music altering, she changed the style of her dancing, her feet moved more quickly, and did not keep so strictly to the ground. She was getting excited at the admiration of the onlookers and her dance grew wilder and more daring. She lifted her skirts higher, brought in new and more difficult movements into her improvisation, kicking up her legs she did the wonderful twist, backwards and forwards, of which the dancer is proud.

"Look at 'er legs!" cried one of the men.

"Look at 'er stockin's!" shouted another; and indeed they were remarkable, for Liza had chosen them of the same brilliant hue as her dress, and was herself most proud of the harmony.

Her dance became gayer: her feet scarcely touched the ground, she whirled round madly.

"Take care yer don't split!" cried out one of the wags, at a very audacious kick.

The words were hardly out of his mouth when Liza, with a gigantic effort, raised her foot and kicked off his hat. The feat was greeted with applause, and she went on, making turns and twists, flourishing her skirts, kicking higher and higher, and finally, amid a volley of shouts, fell on her hands and turned head over heels in a magnificent catharine-wheel; then scrambling to her feet again, she tumbled into the arms of a young man standing in the front of the ring.

"That's right, Liza," he said. "Give us a kiss, now," and promptly tried to take one.

"Git aht!" said Liza, pushing him away, not too gently.

"Yus, give us a kiss," cried another, running up to her.

"I'll smack yer in the fice!" said Liza, elegantly, as she dodged him.

"Ketch 'old on 'er, Bill," cried out a third, "an' we'll all kiss her."

"Na, you won't!" shrieked Liza, beginning to run.

"Come on," they cried, "we'll ketch 'er."

She dodged in and out, between their legs, under their arms, and then, getting clear of the little crowd, caught up her skirts so that they might not hinder her, and took to her heels along the street. A score of men set in chase, whistling, shouting, yelling; the people at the doors looked up to see the fun, and cried out to her as she dashed past; she ran like the wind. Suddenly a man from the side darted into the middle of the road, stood straight in her way, and before she knew where she was, she had jumped shrieking into his arms, and he, lifting her up to him, had imprinted two sounding kisses on her cheeks.

"Oh you—!" she said. Her expression was quite unprintable; nor can it be euphemized.

There was a shout of laughter from the bystanders and the young men in chase of her, and Liza, looking up, saw a big, bearded man whom she had never seen before. She blushed to the very roots of her hair, quickly extricated herself from his arms, and, amid the jeers and laughter of everyone, slid into the door of the nearest house and was lost to view.

Chapter II

LIZA AND HER MOTHER WERE HAVING SUPPER. MRS. KEMP WAS AN ELDERLY woman, short, and rather stout, with a red face, and grey hair brushed tight back over her forehead. She had been a widow for many years, and since her husband's death had lived with Liza in the ground-floor front room in which they were now sitting. Her husband had been a soldier, and from a grateful country she received a pension large enough to keep her from starvation, and by charring and doing such odd jobs as she could get she earned a little extra to supply herself with liquor. Liza was able to make her own living by working at a factory.

Mrs. Kemp was rather sulky this evening.

"Wot was yer doin' this afternoon, Liza?" she asked.

"I was in the street."

"You're always in the street when I want yer."

"I didn't know as 'ow yer wanted me, mother," answered Liza.

"Well, yer might 'ave come ter see! I might 'ave been dead, for all you knew."

Liza said nothing.

"My rheumatics was thet bad to-dy, thet I didn't know wot ter do with myself. The doctor said I was to be rubbed with that stuff 'e give me, but yer won't never do nothin' for me."

"Well, mother," said Liza, 'your rheumatics was all right yesterday."

"I know wot you was doin'; you was showin' off thet new dress of yours. Pretty waste of money thet is, instead of givin' it me ter sive up. An' for the matter of thet, I wanted a new dress far worse than you did. But, of course, I don't matter."

Liza did not answer, and Mrs. Kemp, having nothing more to say, continued her supper in silence.

It was Liza who spoke next.

"There's some new people moved in the street. 'Ave you seen 'em?" she asked.

"No, wot are they?"

"I dunno; I've seen a chap, a big chap with a beard. I think 'e lives up at the other end."

She felt herself blushing a little.

"No one any good you be sure," said Mrs. Kemp. "I can't swaller these new people as are comin' in; the street ain't wot it was when I fust come."

When they had done, Mrs. Kemp got up, and having finished her half-pint of beer, said to her daughter:

"Put the things awy, Liza. I'm just goin' round to see Mrs. Clayton; she's just 'ad twins, and she 'ad nine before these come. It's a pity the Lord don't see fit ter tike some on 'em—thet's wot I say."

After which pious remark Mrs. Kemp went out of the house and turned into another a few doors up.

Liza did not clear the supper things away as she was told, but opened the window and drew her chair to it. She leant on the sill, looking out into the street. The sun had set, and it was twilight, the sky was growing dark, bringing to view the twinkling stars; there was no breeze, but it was pleasantly and restfully cool. The good folk still sat at their doorsteps, talking as before on the same inexhaustible subjects, but a little subdued with the approach of night. The boys were still playing cricket, but they were mostly at the other end of the street, and their shouts were muffled before they reached Liza's ears.

She sat, leaning her head on her hands, breathing in the fresh air and feeling a certain exquisite sense of peacefulness which she was not used to. It was Saturday evening, and she thankfully remembered that there would be no factory on the morrow; she was glad to rest. Somehow she felt a little tired, perhaps it was through the excitement of the afternoon, and she enjoyed the quietness of the evening. It seemed so tranquil and still; the silence filled her with a strange delight, she felt as if she could sit there all through the night looking out into the cool, dark street, and up heavenwards at the stars. She was very happy, but yet at the same time experienced a strange new sensation of melancholy, and she almost wished to cry.

Suddenly a dark form stepped in front of the open window. She gave a little shriek.

" 'Oo's thet?" she asked, for it was quite dark, and she did not recognise the man standing in front of her.

"Me, Liza," was the answer.

"Tom?"

"Yus!"

It was a young man with light yellow hair and a little fair moustache, which made him appear almost boyish; he was light-complexioned, and blue-eyed, and had a frank and pleasant look mingled with a curious bashfulness that made him blush when people spoke to him.

"Wot's up?" asked Liza.

"Come aht for a walk, Liza, will yer?"

"No!" she answered, decisively.

"You promised ter yesterday, Liza."

"Yesterday an' ter-day's two different things," was her wise reply.

"Yus, come on, Liza."

"Na, I tell yer, I won't."

"I want ter talk ter yer, Liza." Her hand was resting on the window-sill, and he put his upon it. She quickly drew it back.

"Well, I don't want yer ter talk ter me."

But she did, for it was she who broke the silence.

"Say, Tom, 'oo are them new folk as 'as come into the street? It's a big chap with a brown beard."

"D'you mean the bloke as kissed yer this afternoon?"

Liza blushed again.

"Well, why shouldn't 'e kiss me?" she said, with some inconsequence.

"I never said as 'ow 'e shouldn't; I only arst yer if it was the sime."

"Yea, thet's 'oo I mean."

" 'Is nime is Blakeston—Jim Blakeston. I've only spoke to 'im once; he's took the two top rooms at No. 19 'ouse."

"Wot's 'e want two top rooms for?"

" 'Im? Oh, 'e's got a big family—five kids. Ain't yer seen 'is wife abaht the street? She's a big, fat woman, as does 'er 'air funny."

"I didn't know 'e 'ad a wife."

There was another silence; Liza sat thinking, and Tom stood at the window, looking at her.

"Won't yer come aht with me, Liza?" he asked, at last.

"Na, Tom," she said, a little more gently, "It's too lite."

"Liza," he said, blushing to the roots of his hair.

"Well?"

"Liza"—he couldn't go on, and stuttered in his shyness—"Liza, I—I—I loves yer, Liza."

"Garn awy!"

He was quite brave now, and took hold of her hand.

"Yer know, Liza, I'm earnin' twenty-three shillin's at the works now, an' I've got some furniture as mother left me when she was took."

The girl said nothing.

"Liza, will you 'ave me? I'll make yer a good 'usband, Liza, swop me bob, I will; an' yer know I'm not a drinkin' sort. Liza, will yer marry me?"

"Na, Tom," she answered quietly.

"Oh, Liza, won't you 'ave me?"

"Na, Tom, I can't."

"Why not? You've come aht walkin' with me ever since Whitsun."

"Ah, things is different now."

"You're not walkin' aht with anybody else, are you, Liza?" he asked, quickly.

"Na, not that."

"Well, why won't yer, Liza? Oh Liza, I do love yer; I've never loved anybody as I love you!"

"Oh, I can't, Tom!"

"There ain't no one else?"

"Na."

"Then why not?"

"I'm very sorry, Tom, but I don't love yer so as ter marry yer."

"Oh, Liza!"

She could not see the look upon his face, but she heard the agony in his voice; and, moved with sudden pity, she bent out, threw her arms round his neck, and kissed him on both cheeks.

"Never mind old chap!" she said. "I'm not worth troublin' abaht."

And quickly drawing back, she slammed the window to, and moved into the further part of the room.

Chapter III

THE FOLLOWING DAY WAS SUNDAY. LIZA, WHEN SHE WAS DRESSING HERSELF in the morning, felt the hardness of fate in the impossibility of eating one's cake and having it; she wished she had reserved her new dress and had still before her the sensation of a first appearance in it. With a sigh she put on her ordinary everyday working dress, and proceeded to get the breakfast ready, for her mother had been out late the previous night, celebrating the new arrivals in the street, and had the "rheumatics" this morning.

"Oo, my 'ead!" she was saying, as she pressed her hands on each side of her forehead. "I've got the neuralgy agin; wot shall I do? I dunno 'ow it is, but it always comes on Sunday mornings. Oo, an' my rheumatics, they give me sich a doin' in the night!"

"You'd better go to the 'orspital mother."

"Not I!" answered the worthy lady, with great decision. "You 'as a dozen young chaps messin' you abaht, and lookin' at yer, and then they tells yer ter leave off beer and spirrits. Well, wot I says, I says I can't do withaht my glass of beer." She thumped her pillow to emphasise the statement.

"Wot with the work I 'ave ter do, lookin' after you and the cookin' and gettin' everythin' ready and doin' all the 'ousework, and goin' aht charring besides—well, I says, if I don't 'ave a drop of beer, I says, ter pull me together, I should be under the turf in no time."

She munched her bread and butter and drank her tea.

"When you've done breakfast, Liza," she said, "you can give the grate a cleanin', an' my boots'd do with a bit of polishin'. Mrs. Tike, in the next 'ouse, 'll give yer some blackin'."

She remained silent for a bit, then said:

"I don't think I shall get up ter-day, Liza. My rheumatics is bad. You can put the room straight and cook the dinner."

"Arright, mother; you stay where you are, an' I'll do everythin' for yer."

"Well, it's only wot yer ought to do, considerin' all the trouble you've been ter me when you was young, and considerin' thet when you was born the doctor thought I never should get through it. Wot 'ave you done with your week's money, Liza?"

"Oh, I've put it awy," answered Liza, quietly.

"Where?" asked her mother.

"Where it'll be safe."

"Where's that?"

Liza was driven into a corner.

"Why d'you want ter know?" she asked.

"Why shouldn't I know; d'you think I want ter steal it from yer?"

"Na, not thet."

"Well, why won't you tell me?"

"Oh, a thing's sifer when only one person knows where it is."

This was a very discreet remark, but it set Mrs. Kemp in a whirlwind of passion. She raised herself and sat up in the bed, flourishing her clenched fist at her daughter.

"I know wot yer mean, you——you!" Her language was emphatic, her epithets picturesque, but too forcible for reproduction. "You think I'd steal it," she went on. "I know yer! D'yer think I'd go an' tike yer dirty money?"

"Well, mother," said Liza, "when I've told yer before, the money's perspired like."

"Wot d'yer mean?"

"It got less."

"Well, I can't 'elp thet, can I? Anyone can come in 'ere and tike the money."

"If it's 'idden awy, they can't, can they, mother?" said Liza.

Mrs. Kemp shook her fist.

"You dirty slut, you," she said, "yer think I tike yer money! Why, you ought ter give it me every week instead of savin' it up and spendin' it on all sorts of muck, while I 'ave ter grind my very bones down to keep yer."

"Yer know, mother, if I didn't 'ave a little bit saved up, we should be rather short when you're dahn in yer luck."

Mrs. Kemp's money always ran out on Tuesday, and Liza had to keep things going till the following Saturday.

"Oh, don't talk ter me!" proceeded Mrs. Kemp. "When I was a girl I give all my money ter my mother. She never 'ad ter ask me for nothin'. On Saturday when I come 'ome with my wiges, I give it 'er every farthin'. That's wot a daughter ought ter do. I can say this for myself, I be'aved by my mother like a gal should. None of your prodigal sons for me! She didn't 'ave ter ask me for three 'apence ter get a drop of beer."

Liza was wise in her generation; she held her tongue, and put on her hat.

"Now, you're goin' aht, and leavin' me; I dunno wot you get up to in the street with all those men. No good, I'll be bound. An' 'ere am I left alone, an' I might die for all you care."

In her sorrow at herself the old lady began to cry, and Liza slipped out of the room and into the street.

Leaning against the wall of the opposite house was Tom; he came towards her.

" 'Ulloa!" she said, as she saw him. "Wot are you doin' 'ere?"

"I was waitin' for you ter come aht, Liza," he answered.

She looked at him quickly.

"I ain't comin' aht with yer ter-day, if thet's wot yer mean," she said.

"I never thought of arskin' yer, Liza—after wot you said ter me last night."

His voice was a little sad, and she felt so sorry for him.

"But yer did want ter speak ter me, didn't yer, Tom?" she said, more gently.

"You've got a day off ter-morrow, ain't yer?"

"Bank 'Oliday. Yus! Why?"

"Why, 'cause they've got a drag startin' from the 'Red Lion' that's goin' down ter Chingford for the day—an' I'm goin'."

"Yus!" she said.

He looked at her doubtfully.

"Will yer come too, Liza? It'll be a regular beeno; there's only goin' ter be people in the street. Eh, Liza?"

"Na, I can't."

"Why not?"

"I ain't got—I ain't got the ooftish."

"I mean, won't yer come with me?"

"Na, Tom, thank yer; I can't do thet neither."

"Yer might as well, Liza; it wouldn't 'urt yer."

"Na, it wouldn't be right like; I can't come aht with yer, and then mean nothin'! It would be doin' yer aht of an outing."

"I don't see why," he said, very crestfallen.

"I can't go on keepin' company with you—after what I said last night."

"I shan't enjoy it a bit without you, Liza."

"You git somebody else, Tom. You'll do withaht me all right."

She nodded to him, and walked up the street to the house of her friend Sally. Having arrived in front of it, she put her hands to her mouth in trumpet form, and shouted:

" 'I! 'I! 'I! Sally!"

A couple of fellows standing by copied her.

" 'I! 'I! 'I! Sally!"

"Garn!" said Liza, looking round at them.

Sally did not appear and she repeated her call. The men imitated her, and half a dozen took it up, so that there was enough noise to wake the seven sleepers.

" 'I! 'I! 'I! Sally!"

A head was put out of a top window, and Liza, taking off her hat, waved it, crying:

"Come on dahn, Sally!"

"Arright, old gal!" shouted the other. "I'm comin'!"

"So's Christmas!" was Liza's repartee.

There was a clatter down the stairs, and Sally, rushing through the passage, threw herself on to her friend. They began fooling, in reminiscence of a melodrama they had lately seen together.

"Oh, my darlin' duck!" said Liza, kissing her and pressing her, with affected rapture, to her bosom.

"My sweetest sweet!" replied Sally, copying her.

"An' 'ow does your lidyship ter-day?"

"Oh!"—with immense languor—"fust class; and is your royal 'ighness quite well?"

"I deeply regret," answered Liza, 'but my royal 'ighness 'as got the collywobbles."

Sally was a small, thin girl, with sandy hair and blue eyes, and a very freckled complexion. She had an enormous mouth, with terrible, square teeth set wide apart, which looked as if they could masticate an iron bar. She was dressed like Liza, in a shortish black skirt and an old-fashioned bodice, green and grey and yellow with age; her sleeves were tucked up to the elbow, and she wore a singularly dirty apron, that had once been white.

"Wot 'ave you got yer 'air in them things for?" asked Liza, pointing to the curl-papers. "Goin' aht with yer young man ter-day?"

"No, I'm going ter stay 'ere all day."

"Wot for, then?"

"Why, 'Arry's going ter tike me ter Chingford ter-morrer."

"Oh? In the 'Red Lion' brake?"

"Yus. Are you goin'?"

"Na!"

"Not! Well, why don't you get round Tom? 'E'll tike yer, and jolly glad 'e'll be, too."

" 'E arst me ter go with 'im, but I wouldn't."

"Swop me bob—why not?"

"I ain't keeping company with 'im."

"Yer might 'ave gone with 'im all the sime."

"Na. You're goin' with 'Arry, ain't yer?"

"Yus!"

"An' you're goin' to 'ave 'im?"

"Right again!"

"Well, I couldn't go with Tom, and then throw 'im over."

"Well, you are a mug!"

The two girls had strolled down towards the Westminster Bridge Road, and Sally, meeting her young man, had gone to him. Liza walked back, wishing to get home in time to cook the dinner. But she went slowly, for she knew every dweller in the street, and as she passed the groups sitting at their doors, as on the previous evening, but this time mostly engaged in peeling potatoes or shelling peas, she stopped and had a little chat. Everyone liked her, and was glad to have her company. "Good old Liza," they would say, as she left them, "she's a rare good sort, ain't she?"

She asked after the aches and pains of all the old people, and delicately inquired after the babies, past and future; the children hung on to her skirts and asked her to play with them, and she would hold one end of the rope while tiny little ragged girls skipped, invariably entangling themselves after two jumps.

She had nearly reached home, when she heard a voice cry—

"Mornin'!"

She looked round and recognised the man whom Tom had told her was called Jim Blakeston. He was sitting on a stool at the door of one of the houses, playing with two young children, to whom he was giving rides on his knee. She remembered his heavy brown beard from the day before, and she had also an impression of great size; she noticed this morning that he was, in fact, a big man, tall and broad, and she saw besides that he had large, masculine features and pleasant brown eyes. She supposed him to be about forty.

"Mornin'!" he said again, as she stopped and looked at him.

Liza blushed scarlet, and was too confused to answer.

"Well, yer needn't look as if I was goin' ter eat yer up, 'cause I ain't," he said.

" 'Oo are you? I'm not afeard of yer."

"Wot are yer so bloomin' red abaht?" he asked pointedly.

"Well, I'm 'ot."

"You ain't shirty 'cause I kissed yer last night?"

"I'm not shirty; but it was pretty cool, considerin' like as I didn't know yer."

"Well, you run into my arms."

"Thet I didn't; you run aht and caught me."

"An' kissed yer before you could say 'Jack Robinson'." He laughed at the thought. "Well, Liza," he went on, "seein' as 'ow I kissed yer against yer will, the best thing you can do ter make it up is to kiss me not against yer will."

"Me?" said Liza, looking at him, open-mouthed. "Well you are a pill!"

The children began to clamour for the riding, which had been discontinued on Liza's approach.

"Are them your kids?" she asked.

"Yus; them's two on 'em."

" 'Ow many 'ave yer got?"

"Five; the eldest gal's fifteen, and the next one 'oo's a boy's twelve, and then there are these two and baby."

"Well, you've got enough for your money."

"Too many for me—and more comin'."

"Ah well," said Liza, laughing, "thet's your fault, ain't it?"

Then she bade him good-morning, and strolled off.

He watched her as she went, and saw half a dozen little boys surround her and beg her to join them in their game of cricket. They caught hold of her arms and skirts, and pulled her to their pitch.

"No, I can't," she said trying to disengage herself. "I've got the dinner ter cook."

"Dinner ter cook?" shouted one small boy. "Why, they always cooks the cats' meat at the shop."

"You little so-and-so!" said Liza, somewhat inelegantly, making a dash at him.

He dodged her and gave a whoop; then turning he caught her round the legs, and another boy catching hold of her round the neck they dragged her down, and all three struggled on the ground, rolling over and over; the other boys threw themselves on the top, so that there was a great heap of legs and arms and heads waving and bobbing up and down.

Liza extricated herself with some difficulty, and taking off her hat she began cuffing the boys with it, using all the time the most lively expressions. Then, having cleared the field, she retired victorious into her own house and began cooking the dinner.

Chapter IV

BANK HOLIDAY WAS A BEAUTIFUL DAY: THE CLOUDLESS SKY THREATENED A stifling heat for noontide, but early in the morning, when Liza got out of bed and threw open the window, it was fresh and cool. She dressed herself, wondering how she should spend her day; she thought of Sally going off to Chingford with her lover, and of herself remaining alone in the dull street with half the people away. She almost wished it were an ordinary work-day, and that there were no such things as bank holidays. And it seemed to be a little like two Sundays running, but with the second rather worse than the first. Her mother was still sleeping, and she was in no great hurry about getting the breakfast, but stood quietly looking out of the window at the house opposite.

In a little while she saw Sally coming along. She was arrayed in purple and fine linen—a very smart red dress, trimmed with velveteen, and a tremendous hat covered with feathers. She had reaped the benefit of keeping her hair in curl-papers since Saturday, and her sandy fringe stretched from ear to ear. She was in enormous spirits.

" 'Ulloa, Liza!" she called as soon as she saw her at the window.

Liza looked at her a little enviously.

" 'Ulloa!" she answered quietly.

"I'm just goin' to the 'Red Lion' to meet 'Arry."

"At what time d'yer start?"

"The brake leaves at 'alf-past eight sharp."

"Why, it's only eight; it's only just struck at the church. " 'Arry won't be there yet, will he?"

"Oh, 'e's sure ter be early. I couldn't wite. I've been witin' abaht since 'alf-past six. I've been up since five this morning."

"Since five! What 'ave you been doin'?"

"Dressin' myself and doin' my 'air. I woke up so early. I've been dreamin' all the night abaht it. I simply couldn't sleep."

"Well, you are a caution!" said Liza.

"Bust it, I don't go on the spree every day! Oh, I do 'ope I shall enjoy myself."

"Why, you simply dunno where you are!" said Liza, a little crossly.

"Don't you wish you was comin', Liza?" asked Sally.

"Na! I could if I liked, but I don't want ter."

"You are a coughdrop—thet's all I can say. Ketch me refusin' when I 'ave the chanst."

"Well, it's done now. I ain't got the chanst anymore." Liza said this with just a little regret in her voice.

"Come on dahn to the 'Red Lion,' Liza, and see us off," said Sally.

"No, I'm damned if I do!" answered Liza, with some warmth.

"You might as well. P'raps 'Arry won't be there, an' you can keep me company till 'e comes. An' you can see the 'orses."

Liza was really very anxious to see the brake and the horses and the people going; but she hesitated a little longer. Sally asked her once again. Then she said:

"Arright; I'll come with yer, and wite till the bloomin' old thing starts."

She did not trouble to put on a hat, but just walked out as she was, and accompanied Sally to the public-house which was getting up the expedition.

Although there was still nearly half an hour to wait, the brake was drawn up before the main entrance; it was large and long, with seats arranged crosswise, so that four people could sit on each; and it was drawn by two powerful horses, whose harness the coachman was now examining. Sally was not the first on the scene, for already half a dozen people had taken their places, but Harry had not yet arrived. The two girls stood by the public-house door, looking at the preparations. Huge baskets full of food were brought out and stowed away; cases of beer were hoisted up and put in every possible place—under the seats, under the driver's legs, and even beneath the brake. As more people came up, Sally began to get excited about Harry's non-appearance.

"I say, I wish 'e'd come!" she said. " 'E is lite."

Then she looked up and down the Westminster Bridge Road, to see if he was in view.

"Suppose 'e don't turn up! I will give it 'im when 'e comes for keepin' me witin' like this."

"Why, there's a quarter of an hour yet," said Liza, who saw nothing at all to get excited about.

At last Sally saw her lover, and rushed off to meet him. Liza was left alone, rather disconsolate at all this bustle and preparation. She was not sorry that she had refused Tom's invitation, but she did wish that she had conscientiously been able to accept it. Sally and her friend came up; attired in his Sunday best, he was a fit match for his lady-love—he wore a shirt and collar, unusual luxuries!—and he carried under his arm a concertina to make things merry on the way.

"Ain't you goin', Liza?" he asked in surprise at seeing her without a hat and with her apron on.

"Na," said Sally, "ain't she a soft? Tom said 'e'd tike 'er, an' she wouldn't."

"Well, I'm dashed!"

Then they climbed the ladder and took their seats, so that Liza was left alone again. More people had come along, and the brake was nearly full. Liza knew them all, but they were too busy taking their places to talk to her. At last Tom came. He saw her standing there and went up to her.

"Won't yer change yer mind, Liza, an' come along with us?"

"Na, Tom, I told yer I wouldn't—it's not right like." She felt she must repeat that to herself often.

"I shan't enjoy it a bit without you," he said.

"Well, I can't 'elp it!" she answered, somewhat sullenly.

At that moment a man came out of the public-house with a horn in his hand; her heart gave a great jump, for if there was anything she adored it was to drive along to the tootling of a horn. She really felt it was very hard lines that she must stay at home when all these people were going to have such a fine time; and they were all so merry, and she could picture to herself so well the delights of the drive and the picnic. She felt very much inclined to cry. But she mustn't go, and she wouldn't go: she repeated that to herself twice as the trumpeter gave a preliminary tootle.

Two more people hurried along, and when they came near Liza saw that they were Jim Blakeston and a woman whom she supposed to be his wife.

"Are you comin', Liza?" Jim said to her.

"No," she answered. "I didn't know you was goin'."

"I wish you was comin'," he replied; "we shall 'ave a game."

She could only just keep back the sobs; she so wished she were going. It did seem hard that she must remain behind; and all because she wasn't going to marry Tom. After all, she didn't see why that should prevent her; there really was no need to refuse for that. She began to think she had acted foolishly: it didn't do anyone any good that she refused to go out with Tom, and no one thought it anything specially fine that she should renounce her pleasure. Sally merely thought her a fool.

Tom was standing by her side, silent, and looking disappointed and rather unhappy. Jim said to her, in a low voice:

"I am sorry you're not comin'!"

It was too much. She did want to go so badly, and she really couldn't resist any longer. If Tom would only ask her once more, and if she could only change her mind reasonably and decently, she would accept; but he stood silent, and she had to speak herself. It was very undignified.

"Yer know, Tom," she said, "I don't want ter spoil your day."

"Well, I don't think I shall go alone; it 'ud be so precious slow."

Supposing he didn't ask her again! What should she do? She looked up at the clock on the front of the pub, and noticed that it only wanted five minutes to the half-hour. How terrible it would be if the brake started and he didn't ask her! Her heart beat violently against her chest, and in her agitation she fumbled with the corner of her apron.

"Well, what can I do, Tom dear?"

"Why, come with me, of course. Oh, Liza, do say yes."

She had got the offer again, and it only wanted a little seemly hesitation, and the thing was done.

"I should like ter, Tom," she said. "But d'you think it 'ud be arright?"

"Yus, of course it would. Come on, Liza!" In his eagerness he clasped her hand.

"Well," she remarked, looking down, "if it'd spoil your 'oliday—"

"I won't go if you don't—swop me bob, I won't!" he answered.

"Well, if I come, it won't mean that I'm keepin' company with you."

"Na, it won't mean anythin' you don't like."

"Arright!" she said.

"You'll come?" he could hardly believe her.

"Yus!" she answered, smiling all over her face.

"You're a good sort, Liza! I say, 'Arry, Liza's comin'!" he shouted.

"Liza? 'Oorray!" shouted Harry.

" 'S'at right, Liza?" called Sally.

And Liza feeling quite joyful and light of heart called back:

"Yus!"

" 'Oorray!" shouted Sally in answer.

"Thet's right, Liza," called Jim; and he smiled pleasantly as she looked at him.

"There's just room for you two 'ere," said Harry, pointing to the vacant places by his side.

"Arright!" said Tom.

"I must just go an' get a 'at an' tell mother," said Liza.

"There's just three minutes. Be quick!" answered Tom, and as she scampered off as hard as she could go, he shouted to the coachman, "Old 'ard; there's another passenger comin' in a minute."

"Arright, old cock," answered the coachman; "no 'urry!"

Liza rushed into the room, and called to her mother, who was still asleep:

"Mother! mother! I'm going to Chingford!"

Then tearing off her old dress she slipped into her gorgeous violet one; she kicked off her old ragged shoes and put on her new boots. She brushed her hair down and rapidly gave her fringe a twirl and a twist—it was luckily still moderately in curl from the previous Saturday—and putting on her black hat with all the feathers, she rushed along the street, and scrambling up the brake steps fell panting on Tom's lap.

The coachman cracked his whip, the trumpeter tootled his horn, and with a cry and a cheer from the occupants, the brake clattered down the road.

Chapter V

As soon as Liza had recovered herself she started examining the people on the brake; and first of all she took stock of the woman whom Jim Blakeston had with him.

"This is my missus!" said Jim, pointing to her with his thumb.

"You ain't been dahn in the street much, 'ave yer?" said Liza, by way of making the acquaintance.

"Na," answered Mrs. Blakeston, "my youngster's been dahn with the measles, an' I've 'ad my work cut out lookin' after 'im."

"Oh, an' is 'e all right now?"

"Yus, 'e's gettin' on fine, an' Jim wanted ter go ter Chingford ter-day, an' 'e says ter me, well, 'e says, 'You come along ter Chingford, too; it'll do you good.' An' 'e says, 'You can leave Polly'—she's my eldest, yer know—'you can leave Polly,' says 'e, 'ter look after the kids.' So I says, 'Well, I don't mind if I do,' says I."

Meanwhile Liza was looking at her. First she noticed her dress: she wore a black cloak and a funny, old-fashioned black bonnet; then examining the woman herself, she saw a middle-sized, stout person anywhere between thirty and forty years old. She had a large, fat face with a big mouth, and her hair was curiously done, parted in the middle and plastered down on each side of the head in little plaits. One could see that she was a woman of great strength, notwithstanding evident traces of hard work and much child-bearing.

Liza knew all the other passengers, and now that everyone was settled down and had got over the excitement of departure, they had time to greet one another. They were delighted to have Liza among them, for where she was there was no dulness. Her attention was first of all taken up by a young coster who had arrayed himself in the traditional costume—grey suit, tight trousers, and shiny buttons in profusion.

"Wot cheer, Bill!" she cried to him.

"Wot cheer, Liza!" he answered.

"You are got up dossy; you'll knock 'em."

"Na then, Liza Kemp," said his companion, turning round with mock indignation, "you let my Johnny alone. If you come gettin' round 'im I'll give you wot for."

"Arright, Clary Sharp, I don't want 'im," answered Liza. "I've got one of my own, an' thet's a good 'andful—ain't it, Tom?"

Tom was delighted, and, unable to find a repartee, in his pleasure gave Liza a great nudge with his elbow.

" 'Oo, I say," said Liza, putting her hand to her side. "Tike care of my ribs; you'll brike 'em."

"Them's not yer ribs," shouted a candid friend—"them's yer whale-bones yer afraid of breakin'."

"Garn!"

" 'Ave yer got whale-bones?" said Tom, with affected simplicity, putting his arm round her waist to feel.

"Na, then," she said, "keep off the grass!"

"Well, I only wanted ter know if you'd got any."

"Garn; yer don't git round me like thet."

He still kept as he was.

"Na then," she repeated, "tike yer 'and away. If yer touch me there you'll 'ave ter marry me."

"Thet's just wot I wants ter do, Liza!"

"Shut it!" she answered cruelly, and drew his arm away from her waist.

The horses scampered on, and the man behind blew his horn with vigour.

"Don't bust yerself, guv'nor!" said one of the passengers to him when he made a particularly discordant sound. They drove along eastwards, and as the hour grew later the streets became more filled and the traffic greater. At last they got on the road to Chingford, and caught up numbers of other vehicles going in the same direction—donkey-shays, pony-carts, tradesmen's carts, dog-carts, drags, brakes, every conceivable kind of wheel thing, all filled with people, the wretched donkey dragging along four solid ratepayers to the pair of stout horses easily managing a couple of score. They exchanged cheers and greetings as they passed, the "Red Lion" brake being noticeable above all for its uproariousness. As the day wore on the sun became hotter, and the road seemed more dusty and threw up a greater heat.

"I am getting 'ot!" was the common cry, and everyone began to puff and sweat.

The ladies removed their cloaks and capes, and the men, following their example, took off their coats and sat in their shirt-sleeves. Whereupon ensued much banter of a not particularly edifying kind respecting the garments which each person would like to remove—which showed that the innuendo of French farce is not so unknown to the upright, honest Englishman as might be supposed.

At last came in sight the half-way house, where the horses were to have a rest and a sponge down. They had been talking of it for the last quarter of a mile, and when at length it was observed on the top of a hill a cheer broke out, and some thirsty wag began to sing "Rule Britannia," whilst others burst forth with a different national ditty, "Beer, Glorious Beer!" They drew up before the pub entrance, and all climbed down as quickly as they could. The bar was besieged, and potmen and barmaids were quickly busy drawing beer and handing it over to the eager folk outside.

The Idyll of Corydon and Phyllis

Gallantry ordered that the faithful swain and the amorous shepherdess should drink out of one and the same pot.

" 'Urry up an' 'ave your whack," said Corydon, politely handing the foaming bowl for his fair one to drink from.

Phyllis, without replying, raised it to her lips and drank deep. The swain watched anxiously.

" 'Ere, give us a chanst!" he said, as the pot was raised higher and higher and its contents appeared to be getting less and less.

At this the amorous shepherdess stopped and handed the pot to her lover.

"Well, I'm dashed!" said Corydon, looking into it; and added, "I guess you know a thing or two." Then with courtly grace putting his own lips to the place where had been those of his beloved, finished the pint.

"Go' lumme!" remarked the shepherdess, smacking her lips, "that was somethin' like!" And she put out her tongue and licked her lips, and then breathed deeply.

The faithful swain having finished, gave a long sigh, and said:

"Well, I could do with some more!"

"For the matter of thet, I could do with a gargle!"

Thus encouraged, the gallant returned to the bar, and soon brought out a second pint.

"You 'ave fust pop," amorously remarked Phyllis, and he took a long drink and handed the pot to her.

She, with maiden modesty, turned it so as to have a different part to drink from; but he remarked as he saw her:

"You are bloomin' particular."

Then, unwilling to grieve him, she turned it back again and applied her ruby lips to the place where his had been.

"Now we shan't be long!" she remarked, as she handed him back the pot.

The faithful swain took out of his pocket a short clay pipe, blew through it, filled it, and began to smoke, while Phyllis sighed at the thought of the cool liquid gliding down her throat, and with the pleasing recollection gently stroked her stomach. Then Corydon spat, and immediately his love said:

"I can spit farther than thet."

"I bet yer yer can't."

She tried, and did. He collected himself and spat again, further than before, she followed him, and in this idyllic contest they remained till the tootling horn warned them to take their places.

At last they reached Chingford, and here the horses were taken out and the drag, on which they were to lunch, drawn up in a sheltered spot. They were all rather hungry, but as it was not yet feeding-time, they scattered to have drinks meanwhile. Liza and Tom, with Sally and her young man, went off together to the nearest public-house, and as they drank beer Harry, who was a great sportsman, gave them a graphic account of a prize-fight he had seen on the previous Saturday evening, which had been rendered specially memorable by one man being so hurt that he had died from the effects. It had evidently been a very fine affair, and Harry said that several swells from the West End had been present, and he related their ludicrous efforts to get in without being seen by anyone, and their terror when someone to frighten them called out "Copper!" Then Tom and he entered into a discussion on the subject of boxing, in which Tom, being a shy and undogmatic sort of person, was entirely worsted. After this they strolled back to the brake, and found things being prepared for luncheon; the hampers were brought out and emptied, and the bottles of beer in great profusion made many a thirsty mouth thirstier.

"Come along, lidies an' gentlemen—if you are gentlemen," shouted the coachman; 'the animals is now goin' ter be fed!"

"Garn awy," answered somebody, "we're not hanimals; we don't drink water."

"You're too clever," remarked the coachman; 'I can see you've just come from the board school."

As the former speaker was a lady of quite mature appearance, the remark was not without its little irony. The other man blew his horn by way of grace, at which Liza called out to him:

"Don't do thet; you'll bust, I know you will, an' if you bust you'll quite spoil my dinner!"

Then they all set to. Pork-pies, saveloys, sausages, cold potatoes, hard-boiled eggs, cold bacon, veal, ham, crabs and shrimps, cheese, butter, cold suet-puddings and treacle, gooseberry-tarts, cherry-tarts, butter, bread, more sausages, and yet again pork-pies! They devoured the provisions like ravening beasts, stolidly, silently, earnestly, in large mouthfuls which they shoved down their throats unmasticated. The intelligent foreigner seeing them thus dispose of their food would have understood why England is a great nation. He would have understood why Britons never, never will be slaves. They never stopped except to drink, and then at each gulp they emptied their glass; no heel-taps! And still they ate, and still they drank—but as all things must cease, they stopped at last, and a long sigh of content broke from their two-and-thirty throats.

Then the gathering broke up, and the good folk paired themselves and separated. Harry and his lady strolled off to secluded byways in the forest, so that they might discourse of their loves and digest their dinner. Tom had all the morning been waiting for this happy moment; he had counted on the expansive effect of a full stomach to thaw his Liza's coldness, and he had pictured himself sitting on the grass with his back against the trunk of a spreading chestnut-tree, with his arm round his Liza's waist, and her head resting affectionately on his manly bosom. Liza too had foreseen the separation into couples after dinner, and had been racking her brains to find a means of getting out of it.

"I don't want 'im slobberin' abaht me," she said; "it gives me the sick, all this kissin' an' cuddlin'!"

She scarcely knew why she objected to his caresses; but they bored her and made her cross. But luckily the blessed institution of marriage came to her rescue, for Jim and his wife naturally had no particular desire to spend the afternoon together, and Liza, seeing a little embarrassment on their part, proposed that they should go for a walk together in the forest.

Jim agreed at once, and with pleasure; but Tom was dreadfully disappointed. He hadn't the courage to say anything, but he glared at Blakeston. Jim smiled benignly at him, and Tom began to sulk. Then they began a funny walk through the woods. Jim tried to go on with Liza, and Liza was not at all disinclined to this, for she had come to the conclusion that Jim, notwithstanding his "cheek," was not " 'alf a bad sort." But Tom kept walking alongside of them, and as Jim slightly quickened his pace so as to get Liza on in front, Tom quickened his, and Mrs. Blakeston, who didn't want to be left behind, had to break into a little trot to keep up with them. Jim tried also to get Liza all to himself in the conversation, and let Tom see that he was out in the cold, but Tom would break in with cross, sulky remarks, just to make the others uncomfortable. Liza at last got rather vexed with him.

"Strikes me you got aht of bed the wrong way this mornin'," she said to him.

"Yer didn't think thet when yer said you'd come aht with me." He emphasised the "me."

Liza shrugged her shoulders.

"You give me the 'ump," she said. "If yer wants ter mike a fool of yerself, you can go elsewhere an' do it."

"I suppose yer want me ter go awy now," he said, angrily.

"I didn't say I did."

"Arright, Liza, I won't stay where I'm not wanted." And turning on his heel he marched off, striking through the underwood into the midst of the forest.

He felt extremely unhappy as he wandered on, and there was a choky feeling in his throat as he thought of Liza: she was very unkind and ungrateful, and he wished he had never come to Chingford. She might so easily have come for a walk with him instead of going with that beast of a Blakeston; she wouldn't ever do anything for him, and he hated her—but all the same he was a poor foolish thing in love, and he began to feel that perhaps he had been a little exacting and a little forward to take offence. And then he wished he had never said anything, and he wanted so much to see her and make it up. He made his way back to Chingford, hoping she would not make him wait too long.

Liza was a little surprised when Tom turned and left them.

"Wot 'as 'e got the needle abaht?" she said.

"Why, 'e's jealous," answered Jim, with a laugh.

"Tom jealous?"

"Yus; 'e's jealous of me."

"Well, 'e ain't got no cause ter be jealous of anyone—that 'e ain't!" said Liza, and continued by telling him all about Tom: how he had wanted to marry her and she wouldn't have him, and how she had only agreed to come to Chingford with him on the understanding that she should preserve her entire freedom. Jim listened sympathetically, but his wife paid no attention; she was doubtless engaged in thought respecting her household or her family.

When they got back to Chingford they saw Tom standing in solitude looking at them. Liza was struck by the woebegone expression on his face; she felt she had been cruel to him, and leaving the Blakestons went up to him.

"I say, Tom," she said, "don't tike on so; I didn't mean it."

He was bursting to apologise for his behaviour.

"Yer know, Tom," she went on, 'I'm rather 'asty, an' I'm sorry I said wot I did."

"Oh, Liza, you are good! You ain't cross with me?"

"Me? Na; it's you thet oughter be cross."

"You are a good sort, Liza!"

"You ain't vexed with me?"

"Give me Liza every time; that's wot I say," he answered, as his face lit up. "Come along an' 'ave tea, an' then we'll go for a donkey-ride."

The donkey-ride was a great success. Liza was a little afraid at first, so Tom walked by her side to take care of her; she screamed the moment the beast began to trot, and clutched hold of Tom to save herself from falling, and as he felt her hand on his shoulder, and heard her appealing cry, "Oh, do 'old me! I'm fallin'!" he felt that he had never in his life been so deliciously happy. The whole party joined in, and it was proposed that they should have races; but in the first heat, when the donkeys broke into a canter, Liza fell off into Tom's arms and the donkeys scampered on without her.

"I know wot I'll do," she said, when the runaway had been recovered, "I'll ride 'im straddlewyse."

"Garn!" said Sally, "yer can't with petticoats."

"Yus, I can; an' I will too!"

So another donkey was procured, this time with a man's saddle, and putting her foot in the stirrup, she cocked her leg over and took her seat triumphantly. Neither modesty nor bashfulness was to be reckoned among Liza's faults, and in this position she felt quite at ease.

"I'll git along arright now, Tom," she said; "you garn and git yerself a moke, and come an' jine in."

The next race was perfectly uproarious. Liza kicked and beat her donkey with all her might, shrieking and laughing the while, and finally came in winner by a length. After that they felt rather warm and dry, and repaired to the public-house to restore themselves and talk over the excitements of the racecourse.

When they had drunk several pints of beer Liza and Sally, with their respective adorers and the Blakestons, walked round to find other means of amusing themselves; they were arrested by a coconut-shy.

"Oh, let's 'ave a shy!" said Liza, excitedly, at which the unlucky men had to pull out their coppers, while Sally and Liza made ludicrously bad shots at the coconuts.

"It looks so bloomin' easy," said Liza, brushing up her hair, 'but I can't 'it the blasted thing. You 'ave a shot, Tom."

He and Harry were equally unskilful, but Jim got three coconuts running, and the proprietors of the show began to look on him with some concern.

"You are a dab at it," said Liza, in admiration.

They tried to induce Mrs. Blakeston to try her luck, but she stoutly refused.

"I don't 'old with such foolishness. It's wiste of money ter me," she said.

"Na then, don't crack on, old tart," remarked her husband, "let's go an' eat the coconuts."

There was one for each couple, and after the ladies had sucked the juice they divided them and added their respective shares to their dinners and teas. Supper came next. Again they fell to sausage-rolls, boiled eggs, and saveloys, and countless bottles of beer were added to those already drunk.

"I dunno 'ow many bottles of beer I've drunk—I've lost count," said Liza; whereat there was a general laugh.

They still had an hour before the brake was to start back, and it was then the concertinas came in useful. They sat down on the grass, and the concert was begun by Harry, who played a solo; then there was a call for a song, and Jim stood up and sang that ancient ditty, "O dem Golden Kippers, O." There was no shyness in the company, and Liza, almost without being asked, gave another popular comic song. Then there was more concertina playing, and another demand for a song. Liza turned to Tom, who was sitting quietly by her side.

"Give us a song, old cock," she said.

"I can't," he answered. "I'm not a singin' sort." At which Blakeston got up and offered to sing again.

"Tom is rather a soft," said Liza to herself, "not like that cove Blakeston."

They repaired to the public-house to have a few last drinks before the brake started, and when the horn blew to warn them, rather unsteadily, they proceeded to take their places.

Liza, as she scrambled up the steps, said, "Well, I believe I'm boozed."

The coachman had arrived at the melancholy stage of intoxication, and was sitting on his box holding his reins, with his head bent on his chest. He was thinking sadly of the long-lost days of his youth, and wishing he had been a better man.

Liza had no respect for such holy emotions, and she brought down her fist on the crown of his hat, and bashed it over his eyes.

"Na then, old jellybelly," she said, "wot's the good of 'avin' a fice as long as a kite?"

He turned round and smote her.

"Jellybelly yerself!" said he.

"Puddin' fice!" she cried.

"Kite fice!"

"Boss eye!"

She was tremendously excited, laughing and singing, keeping the whole company in an uproar. In her jollity she had changed hats with Tom, and he in her big feathers made her shriek with laughter. When they started they began to sing "For 'e's a jolly good feller," making the night resound with their noisy voices.

Liza and Tom and the Blakestons had got a seat together, Liza being between the two men. Tom was perfectly happy, and only wished that they might go on so forever. Gradually as they drove along they became quieter, their singing ceased, and they talked in undertones. Some of them slept; Sally and her young man were leaning up against one another, slumbering quite peacefully. The night was beautiful, the sky still blue, very dark, scattered over with countless brilliant stars, and Liza, as she looked up at the heavens, felt a certain emotion, as if she wished to be taken in someone's arms, or feel some strong man's caress; and there was in her heart a strange sensation as though it were growing big. She stopped speaking, and all four were silent. Then slowly she felt Tom's arm steal round her waist, cautiously, as though it were afraid of being there; this time both she and Tom were happy. But suddenly there was a movement on the other side of her, a hand was advanced along her leg, and her hand was grasped and gently pressed. It was Jim Blakeston. She started a little and began trembling so that Tom noticed it, and whispered:

"You're cold, Liza."

"Na, I'm not, Tom; it's only a sort of shiver thet went through me."

His arm gave her waist a squeeze, and at the same time the big rough hand pressed her little one. And so she sat between them till they reached the "Red Lion" in the Westminster Bridge Road, and Tom said to himself, "I believe she does care for me after all."

When they got down they all said good-night, and Sally and Liza, with their respective slaves and the Blakestons, marched off homewards. At the corner of Vere Street Harry said to Tom and Blakeston:

"I say, you blokes, let's go an' 'ave another drink before closin' time."

"I don't mind," said Tom, "after we've took the gals 'ome."

"Then we shan't 'ave time; it's just on closin' time now." answered Harry.

"Well, we can't leave 'em 'ere."

"Yus, you can," said Sally. "No one'll run awy with us."

Tom did not want to part from Liza, but she broke in with:

"Yus, go on, Tom. Sally an' me'll git along aright; an' you ain't got too much time."

"Yus, good-night, 'Arry," said Sally, to settle the matter.

"Good-night, old gal," he answered, "give us another slobber."

And she, not at all unwilling, surrendered herself to him, while he imprinted two sounding kisses on her cheeks.

"Good-night, Tom," said Liza, holding out her hand.

"Good-night, Liza," he answered, taking it, but looking very wistfully at her.

She understood, and with a kindly smile lifted up her face to him. He bent down, and taking her in his arms, kissed her passionately.

"You do kiss nice, Liza," he said, making the others laugh.

"Thanks for tikin' me aht, old man," she said as they parted.

"Arright, Liza," he answered, and added, almost to himself, "God bless yer!"

" 'Ulloa, Blakeston, ain't you comin'?" said Harry, seeing that Jim was walking off with his wife instead of joining him and Tom.

"Na," he answered, 'I'm goin' 'ome. I've got ter be up at five ter-morrer."

"You are a chap!" said Harry, disgustedly, strolling off with Tom to the pub, while the others made their way down the sleeping street.

The house where Sally lived came first, and she left them; then, walking a few yards more, they came to the Blakestons', and after a little talk at the door Liza bade the couple good-night, and was left to walk the rest of the way home. The street was perfectly silent, and the lamp-posts, far apart, threw a dim light which only served to make Lisa realise her solitude. There was such a difference between the street at midday, with its swarms of people, and now, when there was neither sound nor soul besides herself, that even she was struck by it. The regular line of houses on either side, with the even pavements and straight, cemented road, seemed to her like some desert place, as if everyone were dead, or a fire had raged and left it all desolate. Suddenly she heard a footstep; she started and looked back. It was a man hurrying behind her, and in a moment she had recognised Jim. He beckoned to her, and in a low voice called:

"Liza!"

She stopped till he had come up to her.

"Wot 'ave yer come aht again for?" she said.

"I've come aht ter say good-night to you, Liza," he answered.

"But yer said good-night a moment ago."

"I wanted to say it again—properly."

"Where's yer missus?"

"Oh, she's gone in. I said I was dry and was goin' ter 'ave a drink after all."

"But she'll know yer didn't go ter the pub."

"Na, she won't; she's gone straight upstairs to see after the kid. I wanted ter see yer alone, Liza."

"Why?"

He didn't answer, but tried to take hold of her hand. She drew it away quickly. They walked in silence till they came to Liza's house.

"Good-night," said Liza.

"Won't you come for a little walk, Liza?"

"Tike care no one 'ears you," she said, in a whisper, though why she whispered she did not know.

"Will yer?" he asked again.

"Na—you've got to get up at five."

"Oh, I only said thet not ter go inter the pub with them."

"So as yer might come 'ere with me?" asked Liza.

"Yus!"

"No, I'm not comin'. Good-night."

"Well, say good-night nicely."

"Wot d'yer mean?"

"Tom said you did kiss nice."

She looked at him without speaking, and in a moment he had clasped his arms round her, almost lifting her off her feet, and kissed her. She turned her face away.

"Give us yer lips, Liza," he whispered—"give us yer lips."

He turned her face without resistance and kissed her on the mouth.

At last she tore herself from him, and opening the door slid away into the house.

Chapter VI

NEXT MORNING ON HER WAY TO THE FACTORY LIZA CAME UP WITH SALLY. They were both of them rather stale and bedraggled after the day's outing; their fringes were ragged and untidily straying over their foreheads, their back hair, carelessly tied in a loose knot, fell over their necks and threatened completely to come down. Liza had not had time to put her hat on, and was holding it in her hand. Sally's was pinned on sideways, and she had to bash it down on her head every now and then to prevent its coming off. Cinderella herself was not more transformed than they were; but Cinderella even in her rags was virtuously tidy and patched up, while Sally had a great tear in her shabby dress, and Liza's stockings were falling over her boots.

"Wot cheer, Sal!" said Liza, when she caught her up.

"Oh, I 'ave got sich a 'ead on me this mornin'!" she remarked, turning round a pale face heavily lined under the eyes.

"I don't feel too chirpy neither," said Liza, sympathetically.

"I wish I 'adn't drunk so much beer," added Sally, as a pang shot through her head.

"Oh, you'll be arright in a bit," said Liza. Just then they heard the clock strike eight, and they began to run so that they might not miss getting their tokens and thereby their day's pay; they turned into the street at the end of which was the factory, and saw half a hundred women running like themselves to get in before it was too late.

All the morning Liza worked in a dead-and-alive sort of fashion, her head like a piece of lead with electric shocks going through it when she moved, and her tongue and mouth hot and dry. At last lunch-time came.

"Come on, Sal," said Liza, "I'm goin' to 'ave a glass o' bitter. I can't stand this no longer."

So they entered the public-house opposite, and in one draught finished their pots. Liza gave a long sigh of relief.

"That bucks you up, don't it?"

"I was dry! I ain't told yer yet, Liza, 'ave I? 'E got it aht last night."

"Who d'yer mean?"

"Why, 'Arry. 'E spit it aht at last."

"Arst yer ter nime the day?" said Liza, smiling.

"Thet's it."

"And did yer?"

"Didn't I jest!" answered Sally, with some emphasis. "I always told yer I'd git off before you."

"Yus!" said Liza, thinking.

"Yer know, Liza, you'd better tike Tom; 'e ain't a bad sort." She was quite patronising.

"I'm goin' ter tike 'oo I like; an' it ain't nobody's business but mine."

"Arright, Liza, don't get shirty over it; I don't mean no offence."

"What d'yer say it for then?"

"Well, I thought as seeing as yer'd gone aht with 'im yesterday thet yer meant ter after all."

" 'E wanted ter tike me; I didn't arsk 'im."

"Well, I didn't arsk my 'Arry, either."

"I never said yer did," replied Liza.

"Oh, you've got the 'ump, you 'ave!" finished Sally, rather angrily.

The beer had restored Liza: she went back to work without a headache, and, except for a slight languor, feeling no worse for the previous day's debauch. As she worked on she began going over in her mind the events of the preceding day, and she found entwined in all her thoughts the burly person of Jim Blakeston. She saw him walking by her side in the forest, presiding over the meals, playing the concertina, singing, joking; and finally, on the drive back, she felt the heavy form by her side, and the big, rough hand holding hers, while Tom's arm was round her waist. Tom! That was the first time he had entered her mind, and he sank into a shadow beside the other. Last of all she remembered the walk home from the pub, the good-nights, and the rapid footsteps as Jim caught her up, and the kiss. She blushed and looked up quickly to see whether any of the girls were looking at her; she could not help thinking of that moment when he took her in his arms; she still felt the roughness of his beard pressing on her mouth. Her heart seemed to grow larger in her breast, and she caught for breath as she threw back her head as if to receive his lips again. A shudder ran through her from the vividness of the thought.

"Wot are you shiverin' for, Liza?" asked one of the girls. "You ain't cold."

"Not much," answered Liza, blushing awkwardly on her meditations being broken into. "Why, I'm sweatin' so—I'm drippin' wet."

"I expect yer caught cold in the Faurest yesterday."

"I see your mash as I was comin' along this mornin'."

Liza stared a little.

"I ain't got one; 'oo d'yer mean, ay?"

"Yer only Tom, of course. 'E did look washed aht. Wot was yer doin' with 'im yesterday?"

" 'E ain't got nothin' ter do with me, 'e ain't."

"Garn; don't you tell me!"

The bell rang, and, throwing over their work, the girls trooped off, and after chattering in groups outside the factory gates for a while, made their way in different directions to their respective homes. Liza and Sally went along together.

"I sy, we are comin' aht!" cried Sally, seeing the advertisement of a play being acted at the neighbouring theatre.

"I should like ter see thet!" said Liza, as they stood arm in arm in front of the flaring poster. It represented two rooms and a passage in between; in one room a dead man was lying on the floor, while two others were standing horror-stricken, listening to a youth who was in the passage, knocking at the door.

"You see, they've killed 'im," said Sally, excitedly.

"Yus, any fool can see thet! an' the one ahtside, wot's 'e doin' of?"

"Ain't 'e beautiful? I'll git my 'Arry ter tike me, I will. I should like ter see it. 'E said 'e'd tike me to the ply."

They strolled on again, and Liza, leaving Sally, made her way to her mother's. She knew she must pass Jim's house, and wondered whether she would see him. But as she walked along the street she saw Tom coming the opposite way; with a sudden impulse she turned back so as not to meet him, and began walking the way she had come. Then thinking herself a fool for what she had done, she turned again and walked towards him. She wondered if she had seen her or noticed her movement, but when she looked down the street he was nowhere to be seen; he had not caught sight of her, and had evidently gone in to see a mate in one or other of the houses. She quickened her step, and passing the house where lived Jim, could not help looking up; he was standing at the door watching her, with a smile on his lips.

"I didn't see yer, Mr. Blakeston," she said, as he came up to her.

"Didn't yer? Well, I knew yer would; an' I was witin' for yer ter look up. I see yer before ter-day."

"Na, when?"

"I passed be'ind yer as you an' thet other girl was lookin' at the advertisement of thet ply."

"I never see yer."

"Na, I know yer didn't. I 'ear yer say, you says, 'I should like to see thet.' "

"Yus, an' I should too."

"Well, I'll tike yer."

"You?"

"Yus; why not?"

"I like thet; wot would yer missus sy?"

"She wouldn't know."

"But the neighbours would!"

"No they wouldn't; no one 'd see us."

He was speaking in a low voice so that people could not hear.

"You could meet me ahtside the theatre," he went on.

"Na, I couldn't go with you; you're a married man."

"Garn! wot's the matter—jest ter go ter the ply? An' besides, my missus can't come if she wanted; she's got the kids ter look after."

"I should like ter see it," said Liza, meditatively.

They had reached her house, and Jim said—

"Well, come aht this evenin' and tell me if yer will—eh, Liza?"

"Na, I'm not comin' aht this evening."

"Thet won't 'urt yer. I shall wite for yer."

" 'Tain't a bit of good your witing', 'cause I shan't come."

"Well, then, look 'ere, Liza; next Saturday night's the last night, an' I shall go to the theatre, any'ow. An' if you'll come, you just come to the door at 'alf-past six, an' you'll find me there. See?"

"Na, I don't," said Liza, firmly.

"Well, I shall expect yer."

"I shan't come, so you needn't expect." And with that she walked into the house and slammed the door behind her.

Her mother had not come in from her day's charing, and Liza set about getting her tea. She thought it would be rather lonely eating it alone, so pouring out a cup of tea and putting a little condensed milk into it, she cut a huge piece of bread and butter, and sat herself down outside on the doorstep. Another woman came downstairs, and seeing Liza, sat down by her side and began to talk.

"Why, Mrs. Stanley, wot 'ave yer done to your 'ead?" asked Liza, noticing a bandage round her forehead.

"I 'ad an accident last night," answered the woman, blushing uneasily.

"Oh, I am sorry! Wot did yer do to yerself?"

"I fell against the coal-scuttle and cut my 'ead open."

"Well, I never!"

"To tell yer the truth, I 'ad a few words with my old man. But one doesn't like them things to get abaht; yer won't tell anyone, will yer?"

"Not me!" answered Liza. "I didn't know yer husband was like thet."

"Oh, 'e's as gentle as a lamb when 'e's sober," said Mrs. Stanley, apologetically. "But, Lor' bless yer, when 'e's 'ad a drop too much 'e's a demond, an' there's no two ways abaht it."

"An' you ain't been married long neither?" said Liza.

"Na, not above eighteen months; ain't it disgriceful? Thet's wot the doctor at the 'orspital says ter me. I 'ad ter go ter the 'orspital. You should have seen 'ow it bled!—it bled all dahn' my fice, and went streamin' like a bust water-pipe. Well, it fair frightened my old man, an' I says ter 'im, 'I'll charge yer,' an' although I was bleedin' like a bloomin' pig I shook my fist at 'im, an' I says, 'I'll charge ye—see if I don't!' An' 'e says, 'Na,' says 'e, 'don't do thet, for God's sike, Kitie, I'll git three months.' 'An' serve yer damn well right!' says I, an' I went aht an' left 'im. But, Lor' bless yer, I wouldn't charge 'im! I know 'e don't mean it; 'e's as gentle as a lamb when 'e's sober." She smiled quite affectionately as she said this.

"Wot did yer do, then?" asked Liza.

"Well, as I wos tellin' yer, I went to the 'orspital, an' the doctor 'e says to me, 'My good woman,' says 'e, 'you might have been very seriously injured.' An' me not been married eighteen months! An' as I was tellin' the doctor all about it, 'Missus,' 'e says ter me, lookin' at me straight in the eyeball. 'Missus,' says 'e, ' 'ave you been drinkin'?' 'Drinkin'?' says I; 'no! I've 'ad a little drop, but as for drinkin'! Mind,' says I, 'I don't say I'm a teetotaler—I'm not; I 'ave my glass of beer, and I like it. I couldn't do withaht it, wot with the work I 'ave, I must 'ave somethin' ter keep me tergether. But as for drinkin' 'eavily! Well! I can say this, there ain't a soberer woman than myself in all London. Why, my fust 'usband never touched a drop. Ah, my fust 'usband, 'e was a beauty, 'e was.' "

She stopped the repetition of her conversation and addressed herself to Liza.

" 'E was thet different ter this one. 'E was a man as 'ad seen better days. 'E was a gentleman!" She mouthed the word and emphasised it with an expressive nod.

" 'E was a gentleman and a Christian. 'E'd been in good circumstances in 'is time; an' 'e was a man of education and a teetotaler for twenty-two years."

At that moment Liza's mother appeared on the scene.

"Good evenin', Mrs. Stanley," she said, politely.

"The sime ter you, Mrs. Kemp," replied that lady, with equal courtesy.

"An' 'ow is your poor 'ead?" asked Liza's mother, with sympathy.

"Oh, it's been achin' cruel. I've hardly known wot ter do with myself."

"I'm sure 'e ought ter be ashimed of 'imself for treatin' yer like thet."

"Oh, it wasn't 'is blows I minded so much, Mrs. Kemp," replied Mrs. Stanley, "an' don't you think it. It was wot 'e said ter me. I can stand a blow as well as any woman. I don't mind thet, an' when 'e don't tike a mean advantage of me I can stand up for myself an' give as good as I tike; an' many's the time I give my fust husband a black eye. But the language 'e used, an' the things 'e called me! It made me blush to the roots of my 'air; I'm not used ter bein' spoken ter like thet. I was in good circumstances when my fust 'usband was alive, 'e earned between two an' three pound a week, 'e did. As I said to 'im this mornin', ' 'Ow a gentleman can use sich language, I dunno.' "

" 'Usbands is cautions, 'owever good they are," said Mrs. Kemp, aphoristically. "But I mustn't stay aht 'ere in the night air."

" 'As yer rheumatism been troublin' yer litely?" asked Mrs. Stanley.

"Oh, cruel. Liza rubs me with embrocation every night, but it torments me cruel."

Mrs. Kemp then went into the house, and Liza remained talking to Mrs. Stanley; she too had to go in, and Liza was left alone. Some while she spent thinking of nothing, staring vacantly in front of her, enjoying the cool and quiet of the evening. But Liza could not be left alone long; several boys came along with a bat and a ball, and fixed upon the road just in front of her for their pitch. Taking off their coats they piled them up at the two ends, and were ready to begin.

"I say, old gal," said one of them to Liza, "come an' have a gime of cricket, will yer?"

"Na, Bob, I'm tired."

"Come on!"

"Na, I tell you I won't."

"She was on the booze yesterday, an' she ain't got over it," cried another boy.

"I'll swipe yer over the snitch!" replied Liza to him; and then on being asked again, said—

"Leave me alone, won't yer?"

"Liza's got the needle ter-night, thet's flat," commented a third member of the team.

"I wouldn't drink if I was you, Liza," added another, with mock gravity. "It's a bad 'abit ter git into," and he began rolling and swaying about like a drunken man.

If Liza had been "in form" she would have gone straight away and given the whole lot of them a sample of her strength; but she was only rather bored and vexed that they should disturb her quietness, so she let them talk. They saw she was not to be drawn, and leaving her, set to their game. She watched them for some time, but her thoughts gradually lost themselves, and insensibly her mind was filled with a burly form, and she was again thinking of Jim.

" 'E is a good sort ter want ter tike me ter the ply," she said to herself. "Tom never arst me!"

Jim had said he would come out in the evening; he ought to be here soon, she thought. Of course she wasn't going to the theatre with him, but she didn't mind talking to him; she rather enjoyed being asked to do a thing and refusing, and she would have liked another opportunity of doing so. But he didn't come and he had said he would!

"I say, Bill," she said at last to one of the boys who was fielding close beside her, "that there Blakeston—d'you know 'im?"

"Yus, rather; why, he works at the sime plice as me."

"Wot's 'e do with 'isself in the evening; I never see 'im abaht?"

"I dunno. I see 'im this evenin' go into the 'Red Lion.' I suppose 'e's there, but I dunno."

Then he wasn't coming. Of course she had told him she was going to stay indoors, but he might have come all the same—just to see.

"I know Tom 'ud 'ave come," she said to herself, rather sulkily.

"Liza! Liza!" she heard her mother's voice calling her.

"Arright, I'm comin'," said Liza.

"I've been witin' for you this last 'alf-hour ter rub me."

"Why didn't yer call?" asked Liza.

"I did call. I've been callin' this last I dunno 'ow long; it's give me quite a sore throat."

"I never 'eard yer."

"Na, yer didn't want ter 'ear me, did yer? Yer don't mind if I dies with rheumatics, do yer? I know."

Liza did not answer, but took the bottle, and, pouring some of the liniment on her hand, began to rub it into Mrs. Kemp's rheumatic joints, while the invalid kept complaining and grumbling at everything Liza did.

"Don't rub so 'ard, Liza; you'll rub all the skin off."

Then when Liza did it as gently as she could, she grumbled again.

"If you do it like thet, it won't do no good at all. You want ter sive yerself trouble—I know yer. When I was young girls didn't mind a little bit of 'ard work—but, law bless yer, you don't care abaht my rheumatics, do yer?"

At last she finished, and Liza went to bed by her mother's side.

Chapter VII

Two days passed, and it was Friday morning. Liza had got up early and strolled off to her work in good time, but she did not meet her faithful Sally on the way, nor find her at the factory when she herself arrived. The bell rang and all the girls trooped in, but still Sally did not come. Liza could not make it out, and was thinking she would be shut out, when just as the man who gave out the tokens for the day's work was pulling down the shutter in front of his window, Sally arrived, breathless and perspiring.

"Whew! Go' lumme, I am 'ot!" she said, wiping her face with her apron.

"I thought you wasn't comin'," said Liza.

"Well, I only just did it; I overslep' myself. I was aht lite last night."

"Were yer?"

"Me an' 'Arry went ter see the ply. Oh, Liza, it's simply spiffin'! I've never see sich a good ply in my life. Lor'! Why, it mikes yer blood run cold: they 'ang a man on the stige; oh, it mide me creep all over!"

And then she began telling Liza all about it—the blood and thunder, the shooting, the railway train, the murder, the bomb, the hero, the funny man—jumbling everything up in her excitement, repeating little scraps of dialogue—all wrong—gesticulating, getting excited and red in the face at the recollection. Liza listened rather crossly, feeling bored at the detail into which Sally was going: the piece really didn't much interest her.

"One 'ud think yer'd never been to a theatre in your life before," she said.

"I never seen anything so good, I can tell yer. You tike my tip, and git Tom ter tike yer."

"I don't want ter go; an' if I did I'd py for myself an' go alone."

"Cheese it! That ain't 'alf so good. Me an' 'Arry, we set together, 'im with 'is arm round my wiste and me oldin' 'is 'and. It was jam, I can tell yer!"

"Well, I don't want anyone sprawlin' me abaht; thet ain't my mark!"

"But I do like 'Arry; you dunno the little ways 'e 'as; an' we're goin' ter be married in three weeks now. 'Arry said, well, 'e says, 'I'll git a licence.' 'Na,' says I, ' 'ave the banns read aht in church; it seems more reg'lar like to 'ave banns; so they're goin' ter be read aht next Sunday. You'll come with me an' 'ear them, won't yer, Liza?"

"Yus, I don't mind."

On the way home Sally insisted on stopping in front of the poster and explaining to Liza all about the scene represented.

"Oh, you give me the sick with your 'Fital Card,' you do! I'm goin' 'ome." And she left Sally in the midst of her explanation.

"I dunno wot's up with Liza," remarked Sally to a mutual friend. "She's always got the needle, some'ow."

"Oh, she's barmy," answered the friend.

"Well, I do think she's a bit dotty sometimes—I do really," rejoined Sally.

Liza walked homewards, thinking of the play; at length she tossed her head impatiently.

"I don't want ter see the blasted thing; an' if I see that there Jim I'll tell 'im so; swop me bob, I will."

She did see him; he was leaning with his back against the wall of his house, smoking. Liza knew he had seen her, and as she walked by pretended not to have noticed him. To her disgust, he let her pass, and she was thinking he hadn't seen her after all, when she heard him call her name.

"Liza!"

She turned round and started with surprise—very well imitated. "I didn't see you was there!" she said.

"Why did yer pretend not ter notice me, as yer went past—eh, Liza?"

"Why, I didn't see yer."

"Garn! But you ain't shirty with me?"

"Wot 'ave I got to be shirty abaht?"

He tried to take her hand, but she drew it away quickly. She was getting used to the movement. They went on talking, but Jim did not mention the theatre; Liza was surprised, and wondered whether he had forgotten.

"Er—Sally went to the ply last night," she said, at last.

"Oh!" he said, and that was all.

She got impatient.

"Well, I'm off!" she said.

"Na, don't go yet; I want ter talk ter yer," he replied.

"Wot abaht? anythin' in partickler?" She would drag it out of him if she possibly could.

"Not thet I knows on," he said, smiling.

"Good-night!" she said, abruptly, turning away from him.

"Well, I'm damned if 'e ain't forgotten!" she said to herself, sulkily, as she marched home.

The following evening about six o'clock, it suddenly struck her that it was the last night of the "New and Sensational Drama."

"I do like thet Jim Blakeston," she said to herself; "fancy treatin' me like thet! You wouldn't catch Tom doin' sich a thing. Bli'me if I speak to 'im again, the———.

Now I shan't see it at all. I've a good mind ter go on my own 'ook. Fancy 'is forgettin' all abaht it, like thet!"

She was really quite indignant; though, as she had distinctly refused Jim's offer, it was rather hard to see why.

" 'E said 'e'd wite for me ahtside the doors; I wonder if 'e's there. I'll go an' see if 'e is, see if I don't—an' then if 'e's there, I'll go in on my own 'ook, jist ter spite 'im!"

She dressed herself in her best, and, so that the neighbours shouldn't see her, went up a passage between some model lodging-house buildings, and in this roundabout way got into the Westminster Bridge Road, and soon found herself in front of the theatre.

"I've been witin' for yer this 'alf-hour."

She turned round and saw Jim standing just behind her.

" 'Oo are you talkin' to? I'm not goin' to the ply with you. Wot d'yer tike me for, eh?"

" 'Oo are yer goin' with, then?"

"I'm goin' alone."

"Garn! don't be a bloomin' jackass!"

Liza was feeling very injured.

"Thet's 'ow you treat me! I shall go 'ome. Why didn't you come aht the other night?"

"Yer told me not ter."

She snorted at the ridiculous ineptitude of the reply.

"Why didn't you say nothin' abaht it yesterday?"

"Why, I thought you'd come if I didn't talk on it."

"Well, I think you're a——brute!" She felt very much inclined to cry.

"Come on, Liza, don't tike on; I didn't mean no offence." And he put his arm round her waist and led her to take their places at the gallery door. Two tears escaped from the corners of her eyes and ran down her nose, but she felt very relieved and happy, and let him lead her where he would.

There was a long string of people waiting at the door, and Liza was delighted to see a couple of niggers who were helping them to while away the time of waiting. The niggers sang and danced, and made faces, while the people looked on with appreciative gravity, like royalty listening to de Reszké, and they were very generous of applause and halfpence at the end of the performance. Then, when the niggers moved to the pit doors, paper boys came along offering *Tit-Bits* and "extra specials"; after that three little girls came round and sang sentimental songs and collected more halfpence. At last a movement ran through the serpent-like string of people, sounds were heard behind the door, everyone closed up, the men told the women to keep close and hold tight; there was a great unbarring and unbolting, the doors were thrown open, and, like a bursting river, the people surged in.

Half an hour more and the curtain went up. The play was indeed thrilling. Liza quite forgot her companion, and was intent on the scene; she watched the incidents breathlessly, trembling with excitement, almost beside herself at the celebrated hanging incident. When the curtain fell on the first act she sighed and mopped her face.

"See 'ow 'ot I am," she said to Jim, giving him her hand.

"Yus, you are!" he remarked, taking it.

"Leave go!" she said, trying to withdraw it from him.

"Not much," he answered, quite boldly.

"Garn! Leave go!" But he didn't, and she really did not struggle very violently.

The second act came, and she shrieked over the comic man; and her laughter rang higher than anyone else's, so that people turned to look at her, and said—

"She is enjoyin' 'erself."

Then when the murder came she bit her nails and the sweat stood on her forehead in great drops; in her excitement she even called out as loud as she could to the victim, "Look aht!" It caused a laugh and slackened the tension, for the whole house was holding its breath as it looked at the villains listening at the door, creeping silently forward, crawling like tigers to their prey.

Liza trembling all over, and in her terror threw herself against Jim, who put both his arms round her, and said—

"Don't be afride, Liza; it's all right."

At last the men sprang, there was a scuffle, and the wretch was killed; then came the scene depicted on the posters—the victim's son knocking at the door, on the inside of which were the murderers and the murdered man. At last the curtain came down, and the house in relief burst forth into cheers and cheers; the handsome hero in his top-hat was greeted thunderously; the murdered man, with his clothes still all disarranged, was hailed with sympathy; and the villains—the house yelled and hissed and booed, while the poor brutes bowed and tried to look as if they liked it.

"I am enjoyin' myself," said Liza, pressing herself quite close to Jim; "you are a good sort ter tike me—Jim."

He gave her a little hug, and it struck her that she was sitting just as Sally had done, and, like Sally, she found it "jam."

The *entr'actes* were short and the curtain was soon up again, and the comic man raised customary laughter by undressing and exposing his nether garments to the public view; then more tragedy, and the final act with its darkened room, its casting lots, and its explosion.

When it was all over and they had got outside Jim smacked his lips and said—

"I could do with a gargle; let's go onto thet pub there."

"I'm as dry as bone," said Liza; and so they went.

When they got in they discovered they were hungry, and seeing some appetising sausage-rolls, ate of them, and washed them down with a couple of pots of beer, then Jim lit his pipe and they strolled off. They had got quite near the Westminster Bridge Road when Jim suggested that they should go and have one more drink before closing time.

"I shall be tight," said Liza.

"Thet don't matter," answered Jim, laughing. "You ain't got ter go ter work in the mornin' an' you can sleep it aht."

"Arright, I don't mind if I do then; in for a penny, in for a pound."

At the pub door she drew back.

"I say, guv'ner," she said, "there'll be some of the coves from dahn our street, and they'll see us."

"Na, there won't be nobody there, don't yer 'ave no fear."

"I don't like ter go in for fear of it."

"Well, we ain't doin' no 'arm if they does see us, an' we can go into the private bar, an' you bet your boots there won't be no one there."

She yielded, and they went in.

"Two pints of bitter, please miss," ordered Jim.

"I say, 'old 'ard. I can't drink more than 'alf a pint," said Liza.

"Cheese it," answered Jim. "You can do with all you can get, I know."

At closing time they left and walked down the broad road which led homewards.

"Let's 'ave a little sit dahn," said Jim, pointing to an empty bench between two trees.

"Na, it's gettin' lite; I want ter be 'ome."

"It's such a fine night, it's a pity ter go in already"; and he drew her unresisting towards the seat. He put his arm round her waist.

"Un'and me, villin!" she said, in apt misquotation of the melodrama; but Jim only laughed, and she made no effort to disengage herself.

They sat there for a long while in silence; the beer had got to Liza's head, and the warm night air filled her with a double intoxication. She felt the arm round her waist, and the big, heavy form pressing against her side; she experienced again the curious sensation as if her heart were about to burst, and it choked her—a feeling so oppressive and painful it almost made her feel sick. Her hands began to tremble, and her breathing grew rapid, as though she were suffocating. Almost fainting, she swayed over towards the man, and a cold shiver ran through her from top to toe.

Jim bent over her, and, taking her in both arms, he pressed his lips to hers in a long, passionate kiss. At last, panting for breath, she turned her head away and groaned.

Then they again sat for a long while in silence, Liza full of a strange happiness, feeling as if she could laugh aloud hysterically, but restrained by the calm and silence of the night. Close behind struck a church clock—one!

"Bless my soul!" said Liza, starting, "there's one o'clock. I must get 'ome."

"It's so nice out 'ere; do sty, Liza." He pressed her closer to him. "Yer know, Liza, I love yer—fit ter kill."

"Na, I can't stay; come on." She got up from the seat, and pulled him up too. "Come on," she said.

Without speaking they went along, and there was no one to be seen either in front or behind them. He had not got his arm round her now, and they were walking side by side, slightly separated. It was Liza who spoke first.

"You'd better go dahn the road and by the church an' git into Vere Street the other end, an' I'll go through the passage, so thet no one shouldn't see us comin' together"; she spoke almost in a whisper.

"Arright, Liza," he answered, 'I'll do just as you tell me."

They came to the passage of which Liza spoke; it was a narrow way between blank walls, the backs of factories, and it led into the upper end of Vere Street. The entrance to it was guarded by two iron posts in the middle, so that horses or barrows should not be taken through.

They had just got to it when a man came out into the open road. Liza quickly turned her head away.

"I wonder if 'e see us," she said, when he had passed out of earshot. " 'E's lookin' back," she added.

"Why, 'oo is it?" asked Jim.

"It's a man aht of our street," she answered. "I dunno 'im, but I know where 'e lodges. D'yer think 'e sees us?"

"Na, 'e wouldn't know 'oo it was in the dark."

"But he looked round; all the street'll know it if he see us."

"Well, we ain't doin' no 'arm."

She stretched out her hand to say good-night.

"I'll come a wy with yer along the passage," said Jim.

"Na, you mustn't; you go straight round."

"But it's so dark; p'raps summat'll 'appen to yer."

"Not it! You go on 'ome an' leave me," she replied, and entering the passage, stood facing him with one of the iron pillars between them.

"Good-night, old cock," she said, stretching out her hand. He took it, and said—

"I wish yer wasn't goin' ter leave me, Liza."

"Garn! I must!" She tried to get her hand away from his, but he held it firm, resting it on the top of the pillar.

"Leave go my 'and," she said. He made no movement, but looked into her eyes steadily, so that it made her uneasy. She repented having come out with him. "Leave go my 'and." And she beat down on his with her closed fist.

"Liza!" he said, at last.

"Well, wot is it?" she answered, still thumping down on his hand with her fist.

"Liza," he said a whisper, "will yer?"

"Will I wot?" she said, looking down.

"You know, Liza. Sy, will yer?"

"Na," she said.

He bent over her and repeated—

"Will yer?"

She did not speak, but kept beating down on his hand.

"Liza," he said again, his voice growing hoarse and thick—"Liza, will yer?"

She still kept silence, looking away and continually bringing down her fist. He looked at her a moment, and she, ceasing to thump his hand, looked up at him with half-opened mouth. Suddenly he shook himself, and closing his fist gave her a violent, swinging blow in the stomach.

"Come on," he said.

And together they slid down into the darkness of the passage.

Chapter VIII

Mrs. Kemp was in the habit of slumbering somewhat heavily on Sunday mornings, or Liza would not have been allowed to go on sleeping as she did. When she woke she rubbed her eyes to gather her senses together, and gradually she remembered having gone to the theatre on the previous evening; then suddenly everything came back to her. She stretched out her legs and gave a long sigh of delight. Her heart was full; she thought of Jim, and the delicious sensation of love came over her. Closing her eyes, she imagined his warm kisses, and she lifted up her arms as if to put them round his neck and draw him down to her; she almost felt the rough beard on her face, and the strong heavy arms round her body. She smiled to herself and took a long breath; then, slipping back the sleeves of her night-dress, she looked at her own thin arms, just two pieces of bone with not a muscle on them, but very white and showing distinctly the interlacement of blue veins: she did not notice that her hands were rough, and red and dirty with the nails broken, and bitten to the quick. She got out of bed and looked at herself in the glass over the mantelpiece: with one hand she brushed back her hair and smiled at herself; her face was very small and thin, but the complexion was nice, clear and white, with a delicate tint of red on the cheeks, and her eyes were big and dark like her hair. She felt very happy.

She did not want to dress yet, but rather to sit down and think, so she twisted up her hair into a little knot, slipped a skirt over her night-dress, and sat on a chair near the window and began looking around. The decorations of the room had been centred on the mantelpiece; the chief ornament consisted of a pear and an apple, a pineapple, a bunch of grapes, and several fat plums, all very beautifully done in wax, as was the fashion about the middle of this most glorious reign. They were appropriately coloured—the apple blushing red, the grapes an inky black, emerald green leaves were scattered here and there to lend finish, and the whole was mounted on an ebonised stand covered with black velvet, and protected from dust and dirt by a beautiful glass cover bordered with red plush. Liza's eyes rested on this with approbation, and the pineapple quite made her mouth water. At either end of the mantelpiece were pink jars with blue flowers on the front; round the top in Gothic letters of gold was inscribed: "A Present from a Friend"—these were products of a later, but not less artistic age. The intervening spaces were taken up with little jars and cups and saucers—gold inside, with a view of a town outside, and surrounding them, "A Present from Clacton-on-Sea," or, alliteratively, "A Memento of Margate." Of these many were broken, but they had been mended with glue, and it is well known that pottery in the eyes of the connoisseur loses none of its value by a crack or two. Then there were portraits innumerable—little yellow cartes-de-visite in velvet frames, some of which were decorated with shells; they showed strange people with old-fashioned clothes, the women with bodices and sleeves fitting close to the figure, stern-featured females with hair carefully parted in the middle and plastered down on each side, firm chins and mouths, with small, pig-like eyes and wrinkled faces, and the men were uncomfortably clad in Sunday garments, very stiff and uneasy in their awkward postures, with large whiskers and shaved chins and upper lips and a general air of horny-handed toil. Then there were one or two daguerreotypes, little full-length figures framed in gold paper. There was one of Mrs. Kemp's father and one of her mother, and there were several photographs of betrothed or newly-married couples, the lady sitting down and the man standing behind her with his hand on the chair, or the man sitting and the woman with her hand on his shoulder. And from all sides of the room, standing on the mantelpiece, hanging above it, on the wall and over the bed, they stared full-face into the room, self-consciously fixed forever in their stiff discomfort.

The walls were covered with dingy, antiquated paper, and ornamented with coloured supplements from Christmas Numbers—there was a very patriotic picture of a soldier shaking the hand of a fallen comrade and waving his arm in defiance of a band of advancing Arabs; there was a "Cherry Ripe," almost black with age and dirt; there were two almanacks several years old, one with a coloured portrait of the Marquess of Lorne, very handsome and elegantly dressed, the object of Mrs. Kemp's adoration since her husband's demise; the other a Jubilee portrait of the Queen, somewhat losing in dignity by a moustache which Liza in an irreverent moment had smeared on with charcoal.

The furniture consisted of a wash-hand stand and a little deal chest of drawers, which acted as sideboard to such pots and pans and crockery as could not find room in the grate; and besides the bed there was nothing but two kitchen chairs and a lamp. Liza looked at it all and felt perfectly satisfied; she put a pin into one corner of the noble Marquess to prevent him from falling, fiddled about with the ornaments a little, and then started washing herself. After putting on her clothes she ate some bread and butter, swallowed a dishful of cold tea, and went out into the street.

She saw some boys playing cricket and went up to them.

"Let me ply," she said.

"Arright, Liza," cried half a dozen of them in delight; and the captain added: "You go an' scout over by the lamp-post."

"Go an' scout my eye!" said Liza, indignantly. "When I ply cricket I does the battin'."

"Na, you're not goin' ter bat all the time. 'Oo are you gettin' at?" replied the captain, who had taken advantage of his position to put himself in first, and was still at the wicket.

"Well, then I shan't ply," answered Liza.

"Garn, Ernie, let 'er go in!" shouted two or three members of the team.

"Well, I'm busted!" remarked the captain, as she took his bat. "You won't sty in long, I lay," he said, as he sent the old bowler fielding and took the ball himself. He was a young gentleman who did not suffer from excessive backwardness.

"Aht!" shouted a dozen voices as the ball went past Liza's bat and landed in the pile of coats which formed the wicket. The captain came forward to resume his innings, but Liza held the bat away from him.

"Garn!" she said; "thet was only a trial."

"You never said trial," answered the captain indignantly.

"Yus, I did," said Liza; "I said it just as the ball was comin'—under my breath."

"Well, I am busted!" repeated the captain.

Just then Liza saw Tom among the lookers-on, and as she felt very kindly disposed to the world in general that morning, she called out to him—

" 'Ulloa, Tom!" she said. "Come an' give us a ball; this chap can't bowl."

"Well, I got yer aht, any'ow," said that person.

"Ah, yer wouldn't 'ave got me aht plyin' square. But a trial ball—well, one don't ever know wot a trial ball's goin' ter do."

Tom began bowling very slowly and easily, so that Liza could swing her bat round and hit mightily; she ran well, too, and pantingly brought up her score to twenty. Then the fielders interposed.

"I sy, look 'ere, 'e's only givin' 'er lobs; 'e's not tryin' ter git 'er aht."

"You're spoilin' our gime."

"I don't care; I've got twenty runs—thet's more than you could do. I'll go aht now of my own accord, so there! Come on, Tom."

Tom joined her, and as the captain at last resumed his bat and the game went on, they commenced talking, Liza leaning against the wall of a house, while Tom stood in front of her, smiling with pleasure.

"Where 'ave you been 'idin' yerself, Tom? I ain't seen yer for I dunno 'ow long."

"I've been abaht as usual; an' I've seen you when you didn't see me."

"Well, yer might 'ave come up and said good mornin' when you see me."

"I didn't want ter force myself on yer, Liza."

"Garn! You are a bloomin' cuckoo. I'm blowed!"

"I thought yer didn't like me 'angin' round yer; so I kep' away."

"Why, yer talks as if I didn't like yer. Yer don't think I'd 'ave come aht bean-feastin' with yer if I 'adn't liked yer?"

Liza was really very dishonest, but she felt so happy this morning that she loved the whole world, and of course Tom came in with the others. She looked very kindly at him, and he was so affected that a great lump came in his throat and he could not speak.

Liza's eyes turned to Jim's house, and she saw coming out of the door a girl of about her own age; she fancied she saw in her some likeness to Jim.

"Say, Tom," she asked, "thet ain't Blakeston's daughter, is it?"

"Yus, thet's it."

"I'll go an' speak to 'er," said Liza, leaving Tom and going over the road.

"You're Polly Blakeston, ain't yer?" she said.

"Thet's me!" said the girl.

"I thought you was. Your dad, 'e says ter me, 'You dunno my daughter, Polly, do yer?' says 'e. 'Na,' says I, 'I don't.' 'Well,' says 'e, 'You can't miss 'er when you see 'er.' An' right enough I didn't."

"Mother says I'm all father, an' there ain't nothin' of 'er in me. Dad says it's lucky it ain't the other wy abaht, or 'e'd 'ave got a divorce."

They both laughed.

"Where are you goin' now?" asked Liza, looking at the slop-basin she was carrying.

"I was just goin' dahn into the road ter get some ice-cream for dinner. Father 'ad a bit of luck last night, 'e says, and 'e'd stand the lot of us ice-cream for dinner ter-day."

"I'll come with yer if yer like."

"Come on!" And, already friends, they walked arm in arm to the Westminster Bridge Road. Then they went along till they came to a stall where an Italian was selling the required commodity, and having had a taste apiece to see if they liked it, Polly planked down sixpence and had her basin filled with a poisonous-looking mixture of red and white ice-cream.

On the way back, looking up the street, Polly cried—

"There's father!"

Liza's heart beat rapidly and she turned red; but suddenly a sense of shame came over her, and casting down her head so that she might not see him, she said—

"I think I'll be off 'ome an' see 'ow mother's gettin' on." And before Polly could say anything she had slipped away and entered her own house.

Mother was not getting on at all well.

"You've come in at last, you——, you!" snarled Mrs. Kemp, as Liza entered the room.

"Wot's the matter, mother?"

"Matter! I like thet—matter indeed! Go an' matter yerself an' be mattered! Nice way ter treat an old woman like me—an' yer own mother, too!"

"Wot's up now?"

"Don't talk ter me; I don't want ter listen ter you. Leavin' me all alone, me with my rheumatics, an' the neuralgy! I've 'ad the neuralgy all the mornin', and my 'ead's been simply splittin', so thet I thought the bones 'ud come apart and all my brains go streamin' on the floor. An' when I wake up there's no one ter git my tea for me, an' I lay there witin' an' witin', an' at last I 'ad ter git up and mike it myself. And, my 'ead simply cruel! Why, I might 'ave been burnt ter death with the fire alight an' me asleep."

"Well, I am sorry, mother; but I went aht just for a bit, an' didn't think you'd wike. An' besides, the fire wasn't alight."

"Garn with yer! I didn't treat my mother like thet. Oh, you've been a bad daughter ter me—an' I 'ad more illness carryin' you than with all the other children put togither. You was a cross at yer birth, an' you've been a cross ever since. An' now in my old age, when I've worked myself ter the bone, yer leaves me to starve and burn to death." Here she began to cry, and the rest of her utterances was lost in sobs.

The dusk had darkened into night, and Mrs. Kemp had retired to rest with the dicky-birds. Liza was thinking of many things; she wondered why she had been unwilling to meet Jim in the morning.

"I was a bally fool," she said to herself.

It really seemed an age since the previous night, and all that had happened seemed very long ago. She had not spoken to Jim all day, and she had so much to say to him. Then, wondering whether he was about, she went to the window and looked out; but there was nobody there. She closed the window again and sat just beside it; the time went on, and she wondered whether he would come, asking herself whether he had been thinking of her as she of him; gradually her thoughts grew vague, and a kind of mist came over them. She nodded. Suddenly she roused herself with a start, fancying she had heard something; she listened again, and in a moment the sound was repeated, three or four gentle taps on the window. She opened it quickly and whispered—

"Jim."

"Thet's me," he answered; "come aht."

Closing the window, she went into the passage and opened the street door; it was hardly unlocked before Jim had pushed his way in; partly shutting it behind him, he took her in his arms and hugged her to his breast. She kissed him passionately.

"I thought yer'd come ter-night, Jim; summat in my 'eart told me so. But you 'ave been long."

"I wouldn't come before, 'cause I thought there'd be people abaht. Kiss us!" And again he pressed his lips to hers, and Liza nearly fainted with the delight of it.

"Let's go for a walk, shall we?" he said.

"Arright!" They were speaking in whispers. "You go into the road through the passage, an' I'll go by the street."

"Yus, thet's right," and kissing her once more, he slid out, and she closed the door behind him.

Then going back to get her hat, she came again into the passage, waiting behind the door till it might be safe for her to venture. She had not made up her mind to risk it, when she heard a key put in the lock, and she hardly had time to spring back to prevent herself from being hit by the opening door. It was a man, one of the upstairs lodgers.

" 'Ulloa!" he said, " 'oo's there?"

"Mr. 'Odges! Strikes me, you did give me a turn; I was just goin' aht." She blushed to her hair, but in the darkness he could see nothing.

"Good-night," she said, and went out.

She walked close along the sides of the houses like a thief, and the policeman as she passed him turned round and looked at her, wondering whether she was meditating some illegal deed. She breathed freely on coming into the open road, and seeing Jim skulking behind a tree, ran up to him, and in the shadows they kissed again.

Chapter IX

THUS BEGAN A TIME OF LOVE AND JOY. AS SOON AS HER WORK WAS OVER AND she had finished tea, Liza would slip out and at some appointed spot meet Jim. Usually it would be at the church, where the Westminster Bridge Road bends down to get to the river; and they would go off, arm in arm, till they came to some place where they could sit down and rest. Sometimes they would walk along the Albert Embankment to Battersea Park, and here sit on the benches, watching the children play. The female cyclist had almost abandoned Battersea for the parks on the other side of the river, but often enough one went by, and Liza, with the old-fashioned prejudice of her class, would look after the rider and make some remark about her, not seldom more forcible than ladylike. Both Jim and she liked children, and tiny, ragged urchins would gather round to have rides on the man's knees or mock fights with Liza.

They thought themselves far away from anyone in Vere Street, but twice, as they were walking along, they were met by people they knew. Once it was two workmen coming home from a job at Vauxhall: Liza did not see them till they were quite near; she immediately dropped Jim's arm, and they both cast their eyes to the ground as the men passed, like ostriches, expecting that if they did not look they would not be seen.

"D'you see 'em, Jim?" asked Liza, in a whisper, when they had gone by. "I wonder if they see us." Almost instinctively she turned round, and at the same moment one of the men turned too; then there was no doubt about it.

"Thet did give me a turn," she said.

"So it did me," answered Jim; 'I simply went 'ot all over."

"We was bally fools," said Liza; " 'we oughter 'ave spoken to 'em! D'you think they'll let aht?"

They heard nothing of it; when Jim afterwards met one of the men in a public-house he did not mention a meeting, and they thought that perhaps they had not been recognised. But the second time was worse.

It was on the Albert Embankment again. They were met by a party of four, all of whom lived in the street. Liza's heart sank within her, for there was no chance of escape; she thought of turning quickly and walking in the opposite direction, but there was not time, for the men had already seen them. She whispered to Jim—

"Back us up," and as they met she said to one of the men, " 'Ulloa there! Where are you off to?"

The men stopped, and one of them asked the question back:

"Where are you off to?"

"Me? Oh, I've just been to the 'orspital. One of the gals at our plice is queer, an' so I says ter myself, 'I'll go an' see 'er.' " She faltered a little as she began, but quickly gathered herself together, lying fluently and without hesitation.

"An' when I come aht," she went on, " 'oo should I see just passin' the 'orspital but this 'ere cove, an' 'e says to me, 'Wot cheer,' says 'e, 'I'm goin' ter Vaux'all, come an' walk a bit of the wy with us.' 'Arright,' says I, 'I don't mind if I do.' "

One man winked, and another said, "Go it, Liza!"

She fired up with the dignity of outraged innocence.

"Wot d'yer mean by thet?" she said; "d'yer think I'm kiddin'?"

"Kiddin'? no! You've only just come up from the country, ain't yer?"

"Think I'm kidding? What d'yer think I want ter kid for? Liars never believe anyone, thet's fact."

"Na then, Liza, don't be saucy."

"Saucy! I'll smack yer in the eye if yer sy much ter me. Come on," she said to Jim, who had been standing sheepishly by; and they walked away.

The men shouted, "Now we shan't be long!" and went off laughing.

After that they decided to go where there was no chance at all of their being seen. They did not meet till they got over Westminster Bridge, and thence they made their way into the Park; they would lie down on the grass in one another's arms, and thus spend the long summer evenings. After the heat of the day there would be a gentle breeze in the Park, and they would take in long breaths of the air; it seemed far away from London, it was so quiet and cool; and Liza, as she lay by Jim's side, felt her love for him overflowing to the rest of the world and enveloping mankind itself in a kind of grateful happiness. If it could only have lasted! They would stay and see the stars shine out dimly, one by one, from the blue sky, till it grew late and the blue darkened into black, and the stars glittered in thousands all above them. But as the nights grew cooler, they found it cold on the grass, and the time they had there seemed too short for the long journey they had to make; so, crossing the Bridge as before, they strolled along the Embankment till they came to a vacant bench, and there they would sit, with Liza nestling close up to her lover and his great arms around her. The rain of September made no difference to them; they went as usual to their seat beneath the trees, and Jim would take Liza on his knee, and, opening his coat, shelter her with it, while she, with her arms round his neck, pressed very close to him, and occasionally gave a little laugh of pleasure and delight. They hardly spoke at all through these evenings, for what had they to say to one another? Often without exchanging a word, they would sit for an hour with their faces touching, the one feeling on his cheek the hot breath from the other's mouth; while at the end of the time the only motion was an upraising of Liza's lips, a bending down of Jim's, so that they might meet and kiss. Sometimes Liza fell into a light doze, and Jim would sit very still for fear of waking her, and when she roused herself she would smile, while he bent down again and kissed her. They were very happy. But the hours passed by so quickly, that Big Ben striking twelve came upon them as a surprise, and unwillingly they got up and made their way homewards; their partings were never-ending—each evening Jim refused to let her go from his arms, and tears stood in his eyes at the thought of the separation.

"I'd give somethin'," he would say, "if we could be togither always."

"Never mind, old chap!" Liza would answer, herself half crying, "it can't be 'elped, so we must jolly well lump it."

But notwithstanding all their precautions people in Vere Street appeared to know. First of all Liza noticed that the women did not seem quite so cordial as before, and she often fancied they were talking of her; when she passed by they appeared to look at her, then say something or other, and perhaps burst out laughing; but when she approached they would immediately stop speaking, and keep silence in a rather awkward, constrained manner. For a long time she was unwilling to believe that there was any change in them, and Jim, who had observed nothing, persuaded her that it was all fancy. But gradually it became clearer, and Jim had to agree with her that somehow or other people had found out. Once when Liza had been talking to Polly, Jim's daughter, Mrs. Blakeston had called her, and when the girl had come to her mother Liza saw that she spoke angrily, and they both looked across at her. When Liza caught Mrs. Blakeston's eye she saw in her face a surly scowl, which almost frightened her; she wanted to brave it out, and stepped forward a little to go and speak with the woman, but Mrs. Blakeston, standing still, looked so angrily at her that she was afraid to. When she told Jim his face grew dark, and he said, "Blast the woman! I'll give 'er wot for if she says anythin' ter you."

"Don't strike 'er, wotever 'appens, will yer, Jim?" said Liza.

"She'd better tike care then!" he answered, and he told her that lately his wife had been sulking, and not speaking to him. The previous night, on coming home after the day's work and bidding her, "good evenin'," she had turned her back on him without answering.

"Can't you answer when you're spoke to?" he had said.

"Good evenin'," she had replied, sulkily, with her back still turned.

After that Liza noticed that Polly avoided her.

"Wot's up, Polly?" she said to her one day. "You never speaks now; 'ave you 'ad yer tongue cut aht?"

"Me? I ain't got nothin' ter speak abaht, thet I knows of," answered Polly, abruptly walking off. Liza grew very red and quickly looked to see if anyone had noticed the incident. A couple of youths, sitting on the pavement, had seen it, and she saw them nudge one another and wink.

Then the fellows about the street began to chaff her.

"You look pale," said one of a group to her one day.

"You're overworkin' yerself, you are," said another.

"Married life don't agree with Liza, thet's wot it is," added a third.

" 'Oo d'yer think yer gettin' at? I ain't married, an' never like ter be," she answered.

"Liza 'as all the pleasures of a 'usband an' none of the trouble."

"Bli'me if I know wot yer mean!" said Liza.

"Na, of course not; you don't know nothin', do yer?"

"Innocent as a bibe. Our Father which art in 'eaven!"

" 'Aven't been in London long, 'ave yer?"

They spoke in chorus, and Liza stood in front of them, bewildered, not knowing what to answer.

"Don't you mike no mistake abaht it, Liza knows a thing or two."

"O me darlin', I love yer fit to kill, but tike care your missus ain't round the corner." This was particularly bold, and they all laughed.

Liza felt very uncomfortable, and fiddled about with her apron, wondering how she should get away.

"Tike care yer don't git into trouble, thet's all," said one of the men, with burlesque gravity.

"Yer might give us a chanst, Liza; you come aht with me one evenin'. You oughter give us all a turn, jist ter show there's no ill-feelin'."

"Bli'me if I know wot yer all talkin' abaht. You're all barmy on the crumpet," said Liza, indignantly, and, turning her back on them, made for home.

Among other things that had happened was Sally's marriage. One Saturday a little procession had started from Vere Street, consisting of Sally, in a state of giggling excitement, her fringe magnificent after a whole week of curling-papers, clad in a perfectly new velveteen dress of the colour known as electric blue; and Harry, rather nervous and ill at ease in the unaccustomed restraint of a collar; these two walked arm in arm and were followed by Sally's mother and uncle, also arm in arm, and the procession was brought up by Harry's brother and a friend. They started with a flourish of trumpets and an old boot, and walked down the middle of Vere Street, accompanied by the neighbours' good wishes; but as they got into the Westminster Bridge Road and nearer to the church, the happy couple grew silent, and Harry began to perspire freely, so that his collar gave him perfect torture. There was a public-house just opposite the church and it was suggested that they should have a drink before going in. As it was a solemn occasion they went into the private bar, and there Sally's uncle, who was a man of means, ordered six pots of beer.

"Feel a bit nervous, 'Arry?" asked his friend.

"Na," said Harry, as if he had been used to getting married every day of his life; "bit warm, thet's all."

"Your very good 'ealth, Sally," said her mother, lifting her mug; "this is the last time as I shall ever address you as Miss."

"An' may she be as good a wife as you was," added Sally's uncle.

"Well, I don't think my old man ever 'ad no complaint ter mike abaht me. I did my duty by 'im, although it's me as says it," answered the good lady.

"Well, mates," said Harry's brother, "I reckon it's abaht time to go in. So 'ere's to the 'ealth of Mr. 'Enry Atkins, an' 'is future missus."

"An' God bless 'em!" said Sally's mother.

Then they went into the church, and as they solemnly walked up the aisle a pale-faced young curate came out of the vestry and down to the bottom of the chancel. The beer had had a calming effect on their troubled minds, and both Harry and Sally began to think it rather a good joke. They smiled on each other, and at those parts of the service which they thought suggestive violently nudged one another in the ribs. When the ring had to be produced, Harry fumbled about in different pockets, and his brother whispered:

"Swop me bob, 'e's gone and lorst it!"

However, all went right, and Sally having carefully pocketed the certificate, they went out and had another drink to celebrate the happy event.

In the evening Liza and several friends came into the couple's room, which they had taken in the same house as Sally had lived in before, and drank the health of the bride and bridegroom till they thought fit to retire.

Chapter X

IT WAS NOVEMBER. THE FINE WEATHER HAD QUITE GONE NOW, AND WITH IT much of the sweet pleasure of Jim and Liza's love. When they came out at night on the Embankment they found it cold and dreary; sometimes a light fog covered the river-banks, and made the lamps glow out dim and large; a light rain would be falling, which sent a chill into their very souls; foot passengers came along at rare intervals, holding up umbrellas, and staring straight in front of them as they hurried along in the damp and cold; a cab would pass rapidly by, splashing up the mud on each side. The benches were deserted, except, perhaps, for some poor homeless wretch who could afford no shelter, and, huddled up in a corner, with his head buried in his breast, was sleeping heavily, like a dead man. The wet mud made Liza's skirts cling about her feet, and the damp would come in and chill her legs and creep up her body, till she shivered, and for warmth pressed herself close against Jim. Sometimes they would go into the third-class waiting-rooms at Waterloo or Charing Cross and sit there, but it was not like the Park or the Embankment on summer nights; they had warmth, but the heat made their wet clothes steam and smell, and the gas flared in their eyes, and they hated the people perpetually coming in and out, opening the doors and letting in a blast of cold air; they hated the noise of the guards and porters shouting out the departure of the trains, the shrill whistling of the steam-engine, the hurry and bustle and confusion. About eleven o'clock, when the trains grew less frequent, they got some quietness; but then their minds were troubled, and they felt heavy, sad, and miserable.

One evening they had been sitting at Waterloo Station; it was foggy outside—a thick, yellow November fog, which filled the waiting-room, entering the lungs, and making the mouth taste nasty and the eyes smart. It was about half-past eleven, and the station was unusually quiet; a few passengers, in wraps and overcoats, were walking to and fro, waiting for the last train, and one or two porters were standing about yawning. Liza and Jim had remained for an hour in perfect silence, filled with a gloomy unhappiness, as of a great weight on their brains. Liza was sitting forward, with her elbows on her knees, resting her face on her hands.

"I wish I was straight," she said at last, not looking up.

"Well, why won't yer come along of me altogether, an' you'll be arright then?" he answered.

"Na, that's no go; I can't do thet." He had often asked her to live with him entirely, but she had always refused.

"You can come along of me, an' I'll tike a room in a lodgin' 'ouse in 'Olloway, an' we can live there as if we was married."

"Wot abaht yer work?"

"I can get work over the other side as well as I can 'ere. I'm abaht sick of the wy things is goin' on."

"So am I; but I can't leave mother."

"She can come too."

"Not when I'm not married. I shouldn't like 'er ter know as I'd—as I'd gone wrong."

"Well, I'll marry yer. Swop me bob, I wants ter badly enough."

"Yer can't; yer married already."

"Thet don't matter! If I give the missus so much a week aht of my screw, she'll sign a piper ter give up all clime ter me, an' then we can get spliced. One of the men as I works with done thet, an' it was arright."

Liza shook her head.

"Na, yer can't do thet now; it's bigamy; an' the cop tikes yer, an' yer gits twelve months' 'ard for it."

"But swop me bob, Liza, I can't go on like this. Yer knows the missus—well, there ain't no bloomin' doubt abaht it, she knows as you an' me are carryin' on, an' she mikes no bones abaht lettin' me see it."

"She don't do thet?"

"Well, she don't exactly sy it, but she sulks an' won't speak, an' then when I says anythin' she rounds on me an' calls me all the nimes she can think of. I'd give 'er a good 'idin', but some'ow I don't like ter! She mikes the plice a 'ell ter me, an' I'm not goin' ter stand it no longer!"

"You'll 'ave ter sit it, then; yer can't chuck it."

"Yus I can, an' I would if you'd come along of me. I don't believe you like me at all, Liza, or you'd come."

She turned towards him and put her arms round his neck.

"Yer know I do, old cock," she said. "I like yer better than anyone else in the world; but I can't go awy an' leave mother."

"Bli'me me if I see why; she's never been much ter you. She mikes yer slave awy ter pay the rent, an' all the money she earns she boozes."

"Thet's true, she ain't been wot yer might call a good mother ter me—but some'ow she's my mother, an' I don't like ter leave 'er on 'er own, now she's so old—an' she can't do much with the rheumatics. An' besides, Jim dear, it ain't only mother, but there's yer own kids, yer can't leave them."

He thought for a while, and then said:

"You're abaht right there, Liza; I dunno if I could get on without the kids. If I could only tike them an' you too, swop me bob, I should be 'appy."

Liza smiled sadly.

"So yer see, Jim, we're in a bloomin' 'ole, an' there ain't no way aht of it thet I can see."

He took her on his knees, and pressing her to him, kissed her very long and very lovingly.

"Well, we must trust ter luck," she said again, "p'raps somethin' 'll 'appen soon, an' everythin' 'll come right in the end—when we gets four balls of worsted for a penny."

It was past twelve, and separating, they went by different ways along the dreary, wet, deserted roads till they came to Vere Street.

The street seemed quite different to Liza from what it had been three months before. Tom, the humble adorer, had quite disappeared from her life. One day, three or four weeks after the August Bank Holiday, she saw him dawdling along the pavement, and it suddenly struck her that she had not seen him for a long time; but she had been so full of her happiness that she had been unable to think of anyone but Jim. She wondered at his absence, since before wherever she had been there was he certain to be also. She passed him, but to her astonishment he did not speak to her. She thought by some wonder he had not seen her, but she felt his gaze resting upon her. She turned back, and suddenly he dropped his eyes and looked down, walking on as if he had not seen her, but blushing furiously.

"Tom," she said, "why don't yer speak ter me."

He started and blushed more than ever.

"I didn't know yer was there," he stuttered.

"Don't tell me," she said, "wot's up?"

"Nothin' as I knows of," he answered, uneasily.

"I ain't offended yer, 'ave I, Tom?"

"Na, not as I knows of," he replied, looking very unhappy.

"You don't ever come my way now," she said.

"I didn't know as yer wanted ter see me."

"Garn! Yer knows I likes you as well as anybody."

"Yer likes so many people, Liza," he said, flushing.

"What d'yer mean?" said Liza, indignantly, but very red; she was afraid he knew now, and it was from him especially she would have been so glad to hide it.

"Nothin'," he answered.

"One doesn't say things like thet without any meanin', unless one's a blimed fool."

"You're right there, Liza," he answered. "I am a blimed fool." He looked at her a little reproachfully, she thought, and then he said "Good-bye," and turned away.

At first she was horrified that he should know of her love for Jim; but then she did not care. After all, it was nobody's business, and what did anything matter as long as she loved Jim and Jim loved her? Then she grew angry that Tom should suspect her; he could know nothing but that some of the men had seen her with Jim near Vauxhall, and it seemed mean that he should condemn her for that. Thenceforward, when she ran against Tom, she cut him; he never tried to speak to her, but as she passed him, pretending to look in front of her, she could see that he always blushed, and she fancied his eyes were very sorrowful. Then several weeks went by, and as she began to feel more and more lonely in the street, she regretted the quarrel; she cried a little as she thought that she had lost his faithful, gentle love, and she would have much liked to be friends with him again. If he had only made some advance she would have welcomed him so cordially, but she was too proud to go to him herself and beg him to forgive her—and then, how could he forgive her?

She had lost Sally too, for on her marriage Harry had made her give up the factory; he was a young man with principles worthy of a Member of Parliament, and he had said:

"A woman's plice is 'er 'ome, an' if 'er old man can't afford ter keep 'er without 'er workin' in a factory—well, all I can say is thet 'e'd better go an' git single."

"Quite right too," agreed his mother-in-law; "an' wot's more, she'll 'ave a baby ter look after soon, an' thet'll tike 'er all 'er time, an' there's no one as knows thet better than me, for I've 'ad twelve, ter sy nothin' of two stills an' one miss."

Liza quite envied Sally her happiness, for the bride was brimming over with song and laughter; her happiness overwhelmed her.

"I am 'appy," she said to Liza one day a few weeks after her marriage. "You dunno wot a good sort 'Arry is. 'E's just a darlin', an' there's no mistikin' it. I don't care wot other people sy, but wot I says is, there's nothin' like marriage. Never a cross word passes his lips, an' mother 'as all 'er meals with us, an' 'e says all the better. Well I'm thet 'appy I simply dunno if I'm standin' on my 'ead or on my 'eels."

But alas! it did not last too long. Sally was not so full of joy when next Liza met her, and one day her eyes looked very much as if she had been crying.

"Wot's the matter?" asked Liza, looking at her. "Wot 'ave yer been blubberin' abaht?"

"Me?" said Sally, getting very red. "Oh, I've got a bit of a toothache, an'—well, I'm rather a fool like, an' it 'urt so much that I couldn't 'elp cryin'."

Liza was not satisfied, but could get nothing further out of her. Then one day it came out. It was a Saturday night, the time when women in Vere Street weep. Liza went up into Sally's room for a few minutes on her way to the Westminster Bridge Road, where she was to meet Jim. Harry had taken the top back room, and Liza, climbing up the second flight of stairs, called out as usual:

"Wot ho, Sally!"

The door remained shut, although Liza could see that there was a light in the room; but on getting to the door she stood still, for she heard the sound of sobbing. She listened for a minute and then knocked; there was a little flurry inside, and someone called out:

" 'Oo's there?"

"Only me," said Liza, opening the door. As she did so she saw Sally rapidly wipe her eyes and put her handkerchief away. Her mother was sitting by her side, evidently comforting her.

"Wot's up, Sal?" asked Liza.

"Nothin'," answered Sally, with a brave little gasp to stop the crying, turning her face downwards so that Liza should not see the tears in her eyes; but they were too strong for her, and, quickly taking out her handkerchief, she hid her face in it and began to sob broken-heartedly. Liza looked at the mother in interrogation.

"Oh, it's thet man again!" said the lady, snorting and tossing her head.

"Not 'Arry!" asked Liza, in surprise.

"Not 'Arry—'oo is it if it ain't 'Arry? The villin!"

"Wot's 'e been doin', then?" asked Liza again.

"Beatin' 'er, that's wot 'e's been doin'! Oh, the villin, 'e oughter be ashimed of 'isself, 'e ought!"

"I didn't know 'e was like that!" said Liza.

"Didn't yer? I thought the 'ole street knew it by now," said Mrs. Cooper, indignantly. "Oh, 'e's a wrong 'un, 'e is."

"It wasn't 'is fault," put in Sally, amidst her sobs; "it's only because 'e's 'ad a little drop too much. 'E's arright when 'e's sober."

"A little drop too much! I should just think 'e 'ad, the beast! I'd give it 'im if I was a man. They're all like thet—'usbinds is all alike; they're arright when they're sober—sometimes—but when they've got the liquor in 'em, they're beasts, an' no mistike. I 'ad a 'usbind myself for five-an'-twenty years, an' I know 'em."

"Well, mother," sobbed Sally, "it was all my fault. I should 'ave come 'ome earlier."

"Na, it wasn't your fault at all. Just you look 'ere, Liza: this is wot 'e done an' call 'isself a man. Just because Sally'd gone aht to 'ave a chat with Mrs. McLeod in the next 'ouse, when she come in 'e start bangin' 'er abaht. An' me too, wot d'yer think of that!" Mrs. Cooper was quite purple with indignation.

"Yus," she went on, "thet's a man for yer. Of course I wasn't goin' ter stand there an' see my daughter bein' knocked abaht; it wasn't likely—was it? An' 'e rounds on me, an' 'e 'its me with 'is fist. Look 'ere." She pulled up her sleeves and showed two red and brawny arms. " 'E's bruised my arms; I thought 'e'd broken it at fust. If I 'adn't put my arm up, 'e'd 'ave got me on the 'ead, an' 'e might 'ave killed me. An' I says to 'im, 'If you touch me again, I'll go ter the police-station, thet I will!' Well, that frightened 'im a bit, an' then didn't I let 'im 'ave it! 'You call yerself a man,' says I, 'an' you ain't fit ter clean the drains aht.' You should 'ave 'eard the language 'e used. 'You dirty old woman,' says 'e, 'you go away; you're always interferin' with me.' Well, I don't like ter repeat wot 'e said, and thet's the truth. An' I says ter 'im, 'I wish yer'd never married my daughter, an' if I'd known you was like this I'd 'ave died sooner than let yer.' "

"Well, I didn't know 'e was like thet!" said Liza.

" 'E was arright at fust," said Sally.

"Yus, they're always arright at fust! But ter think it should 'ave come to this now, when they ain't been married three months, an' the first child not born yet! I think it's disgraceful."

Liza stayed a little while longer, helping to comfort Sally, who kept pathetically taking to herself all the blame of the dispute; and then, bidding her good-night and better luck, she slid off to meet Jim.

When she reached the appointed spot he was not to be found. She waited for some time, and at last saw him come out of the neighbouring pub.

"Good-night, Jim," she said as she came up to him.

"So you've turned up, 'ave yer?" he answered roughly, turning round.

"Wot's the matter, Jim?" she asked in a frightened way, for he had never spoken to her in that manner.

"Nice thing ter keep me witin' all night for yer to come aht."

She saw that he had been drinking, and answered humbly:

"I'm very sorry, Jim, but I went in to Sally, an' 'er bloke 'ad been knockin' 'er abaht, an' so I sat with 'er a bit."

"Knockin' 'er abaht, 'ad 'e? and serve 'er damn well right, too; an' there's many more as could do with a good 'idin'!"

Liza did not answer. He looked at her, and then suddenly said:

"Come in an' 'ave a drink."

"Na, I'm not thirsty; I don't want a drink," she answered.

"Come on," he said, angrily.

"Na, Jim, you've had quite enough already."

" 'Oo are you talkin' ter?" he said. "Don't come if yer don't want ter; I'll go an' 'ave one by myself."

"Na, Jim, don't." She caught hold of his arm.

"Yus I shall," he said, going towards the pub, while she held him back. "Let me go, can't yer! Let me go!" He roughly pulled his arm away from her. As she tried to catch hold of it again, he pushed her back, and in the little scuffle caught her a blow over the face.

"Oh!" she cried, "you did 'urt!"

He was sobered at once.

"Liza," he said. "I ain't 'urt yer?" She didn't answer, and he took her in his arms. "Liza, I ain't 'urt you, 'ave I? Say I ain't 'urt yer. I'm so sorry; I beg your pardon, Liza."

"Arright, old chap," she said, smiling charmingly on him. "It wasn't the blow that 'urt me much; it was the wy you was talkin'."

"I didn't mean it, Liza." He was so contrite, he could not humble himself enough. "I 'ad another bloomin' row with the missus ter-night, an' then when I didn't find you 'ere, an' I kept witin' an' witin'—well, I fair downright lost my 'air. An' I 'ad two or three pints of four 'alf, an'—well, I dunno—"

"Never mind, old cock, I can stand more than thet as long as yer loves me."

He kissed her and they were quite friends again. But the little quarrel had another effect which was worse for Liza. When she woke up next morning she noticed a slight soreness over the ridge of bone under the left eye, and on looking in the glass saw that it was black and blue and green. She bathed it, but it remained, and seemed to get more marked. She was terrified lest people should see it, and kept indoors all day; but next morning it was blacker than ever. She went to the factory with her hat over her eyes and her head bent down; she escaped observation, but on the way home she was not so lucky. The sharp eyes of some girls noticed it first.

"Wot's the matter with yer eye?" asked one of them.

"Me?" answered Liza, putting her hand up as if in ignorance. "Nothin' thet I knows of."

Two or three young men were standing by, and hearing the girl, looked up.

"Why, yer've got a black eye, Liza!"

"Me? I ain't got no black eye!"

"Yus you 'ave; 'ow d'yer get it?"

"I dunno," said Liza. "I didn't know I 'ad one."

"Garn! tell us another!" was the answer. "One doesn't git a black eye without knowin' 'ow they got it."

"Well, I did fall against the chest of drawers yesterday; I suppose I must 'ave got it then."

"Oh yes, we believe thet, don't we?"

"I didn't know 'e was so 'andy with 'is dukes, did you, Ted?" asked one man of another.

Liza felt herself grow red to the tips of her toes.

"Who?" she asked.

"Never you mind; nobody you know."

At that moment Jim's wife passed and looked at her with a scowl. Liza wished herself a hundred miles away, and blushed more violently than ever.

"Wot are yer blushin' abaht?" ingenuously asked one of the girls.

And they all looked from her to Mrs. Blakeston and back again. Someone said, " 'Ow abaht our Sunday boots on now?" And a titter went through them. Liza's nerve deserted her; she could think of nothing to say, and a sob burst from her. To hide the tears which were coming from her eyes she turned away and walked homewards. Immediately a great shout of laughter broke from the group, and she heard them positively screaming till she got into her own house.

Chapter XI

A FEW DAYS AFTERWARDS LIZA WAS TALKING WITH SALLY, WHO DID NOT seem very much happier than when Liza had last seen her.

" 'E ain't wot I thought 'e was," she said. "I don't mind sayin' thet; but 'e 'as a lot ter put up with; I expect I'm rather tryin' sometimes, an' 'e means well. P'raps 'e'll be kinder like when the biby's born."

"Cheer up, old gal," answered Liza, who had seen something of the lives of many married couples; "it won't seem so bad after yer gets used to it; it's a bit disappointin' at fust, but yer gits not ter mind it."

After a little Sally said she must go and see about her husband's tea. She said good-bye, and then rather awkwardly:

"Say, Liza, tike care of yerself!"

"Tike care of meself—why?" asked Liza, in surprise.

"Yer know wot I mean."

"Na, I'm darned if I do."

"Thet there Mrs. Blakeston, she's lookin' aht for you."

"Mrs. Blakeston!" Liza was startled.

"Yus; she says she's goin' ter give you somethin' if she can git 'old on yer. I should advise yer ter tike care."

"Me?" said Liza.

Sally looked away, so as not to see the other's face.

"She says as 'ow yer've been messin' abaht with 'er old man."

Liza didn't say anything, and Sally, repeating her good-bye, slid off.

Liza felt a chill run through her. She had several times noticed a scowl and a look of anger on Mrs. Blakeston's face, and she had avoided her as much as possible; but she had no idea that the woman meant to do anything to her. She was very frightened, a cold sweat broke out over her face. If Mrs. Blakeston got hold of her she would be helpless, she was so small and weak, while the other was strong and muscular. Liza wondered what she would do if she did catch her.

That night she told Jim, and tried to make a joke of it.

"I say, Jim, your missus—she says she's goin' ter give me socks if she catches me."

"My missus! 'Ow d'yer know?"

"She's been tellin' people in the street."

"Go' lumme," said Jim, furious, "if she dares ter touch a 'air of your 'ead, swop me dicky I'll give 'er sich a 'idin' as she never 'ad before! By God, give me the chanst, an' I would let 'er 'ave it; I'm bloomin' well sick of 'er sulks!" He clenched his fist as he spoke.

Liza was a coward. She could not help thinking of her enemy's threat; it got on her nerves, and she hardly dared go out for fear of meeting her; she would look nervously in front of her, quickly turning round if she saw in the distance anyone resembling Mrs. Blakeston. She dreamed of her at night; she saw the big, powerful form, the heavy, frowning face, and the curiously braided brown hair; and she would wake up with a cry and find herself bathed in sweat.

It was the Saturday afternoon following this, a chill November day, with the roads sloshy, and a grey, comfortless sky that made one's spirits sink. It was about three o'clock, and Liza was coming home from work; she got into Vere Street, and was walking quickly towards her house when she saw Mrs. Blakeston coming towards her. Her heart gave a great jump. Turning, she walked rapidly in the direction she had come; with a screw round of her eyes she saw that she was being followed, and therefore went straight out of Vere Street. She went right round, meaning to get into the street from the other end, and, unobserved, slip into her house, which was then quite close; but she dared not risk it immediately for fear Mrs. Blakeston should still be there; so she waited about for half an hour. It seemed an age. Finally, taking her courage in both hands, she turned the corner and entered Vere Street. She nearly ran into the arms of Mrs. Blakeston, who was standing close to the public-house door.

Liza gave a little cry, and the woman said, with a sneer:

"Yer didn't expect ter see me, did yer?"

Liza did not answer, but tried to walk past her. Mrs. Blakeston stepped forward and blocked her way.

"Yer seem ter be in a mighty fine 'urry," she said.

"Yus, I've got ter git 'ome," said Liza, again trying to pass.

"But supposin' I don't let yer?" remarked Mrs. Blakeston, preventing her from moving.

"Why don't yer leave me alone?" Liza said. "I ain't interferin' with you!"

"Not interferin' with me, aren't yer? I like thet!"

"Let me go by," said Liza. "I don't want ter talk ter you."

"Na, I know thet," said the other; "but I want ter talk ter you, an' I shan't let yer go until I've said wot I wants ter sy."

Liza looked round for help. At the beginning of the altercation the loafers about the public-house had looked up with interest, and gradually gathered round in a little circle. Passers-by had joined in, and a number of other people in the street, seeing the crowd, added themselves to it to see what was going on. Liza saw that all eyes were fixed on her, the men amused and excited, the women unsympathetic, rather virtuously indignant. Liza wanted to ask for help, but there were so many people, and they all seemed so much against her, that she had not the courage to. So, having surveyed the crowd, she turned her eyes to Mrs. Blakeston, and stood in front of her, trembling a little, and very white.

"Na, 'e ain't there," said Mrs. Blakeston, sneeringly, "so yer needn't look for 'im."

"I dunno wot yer mean," answered Liza, "an' I want ter go awy. I ain't done nothin' ter you."

"Not done nothin' ter me?" furiously repeated the woman. "I'll tell yer wot yer've done ter me—you've robbed me of my 'usbind, you 'ave. I never 'ad a word with my 'usbind until you took 'im from me. An' now it's all you with 'im. 'E's got no time for 'is wife an' family—it's all you. An' 'is money, too. I never git a penny of it; if it weren't for the little bit I 'ad saved up in the siving-bank, me an' my children 'ud be starvin' now! An' all through you!" She shook her fist at her.

"I never 'ad any money from anyone."

"Don' talk ter me; I know yer did. Yer dirty bitch! You oughter be ashimed of yourself tikin' a married man from 'is family, an' 'im old enough ter be yer father."

"She's right there!" said one or two of the onlooking women. "There can't be no good in 'er if she tikes somebody else's 'usbind."

"I'll give it yer!" proceeded Mrs. Blakeston, getting more hot and excited, brandishing her fist, and speaking in a loud voice, hoarse with rage. "Oh, I've been tryin' ter git 'old on yer this four weeks. Why, you're a prostitute—that's wot you are!"

"I'm not!" answered Liza indignantly.

"Yus, you are," repeated Mrs. Blakeston, advancing menacingly, so that Liza shrank back. "An' wot's more, 'e treats yer like one. I know 'oo give yer thet black eye; thet shows what 'e thinks of yer! An' serve yer bloomin' well right if 'e'd give yer one in both eyes!"

Mrs. Blakeston stood close in front of her, her heavy jaw protruded and the frown of her eyebrows dark and stern. For a moment she stood silent, contemplating Liza, while the surrounders looked on in breathless interest.

"Yer dirty little bitch, you!" she said at last. "Tike that!" and with her open hand she gave her a sharp smack on the cheek.

Liza started back with a cry and put her hand up to her face.

"An' tike thet!" added Mrs. Blakeston, repeating the blow. Then, gathering up the spittle in her mouth, she spat in Liza's face.

Liza sprang on her, and with her hands spread out like claws buried her nails in the woman's face and drew them down her cheeks. Mrs. Blakeston caught hold of her hair with both hands and tugged at it as hard as she could. But they were immediately separated.

" 'Ere, 'old 'ard!" said some of the men. "Fight it aht fair and square. Don't go scratchin' and maulin' like thet."

"I'll fight 'er; I don't mind!" shouted Mrs. Blakeston, tucking up her sleeves and savagely glaring at her opponent.

Liza stood in front of her, pale and trembling; as she looked at her enemy, and saw the long red marks of her nails, with blood coming from one or two of them, she shrank back.

"I don't want ter fight," she said, hoarsely.

"Na, I don't suppose yer do," hissed the other, "but yer'll damn well 'ave ter!"

"She's ever so much bigger than me; I've got no chanst," added Liza, tearfully.

"You should 'ave thought of thet before. Come on!" and with these words Mrs. Blakeston rushed upon her. She hit her with both fists one after the other. Liza did not try to guard herself, but imitating the woman's motion, hit out with her own fists; and for a minute or two they continued thus, raining blows on one another with the same wind-mill motion of the arms. But Liza could not stand against the other woman's weight; the blows came down heavy and rapid all over her face and head. She put up her hands to cover her face and turned her head away, while Mrs. Blakeston kept on hitting mercilessly.

"Time!" shouted some of the men—"Time!" and Mrs. Blakeston stopped to rest herself.

"It don't seem 'ardly fair to set them two on tergether. Liza's got no chanst against a big woman like thet," said a man among the crowd.

"Well, it's 'er own fault," answered a woman; "she didn't oughter mess about with 'er 'usbind."

"Well, I don't think it's right," added another man. "She's gettin' it too much."

"An' serve 'er right too!" said one of the women. "She deserves all she gets, an' a damn sight more inter the bargain."

"Quite right," put in a third; "a woman's got no right ter tike someone's 'usbind from 'er. An' if she does she's bloomin' lucky if she gits off with a 'idin'—thet's wot I think."

"So do I. But I wouldn't 'ave thought it of Liza. I never thought she was a wrong 'un."

"Pretty specimen she is!" said a little dark woman, who looked like a Jewess. "If she messed abaht with my old man, I'd stick 'er—I swear I would!"

"Now she's been carryin' on with one, she'll try an' git others—you see if she don't."

"She'd better not come round my 'ouse; I'll soon give 'er wot for."

Meanwhile Liza was standing at one corner of the ring, trembling all over and crying bitterly. One of her eyes was bunged up, and her hair, all dishevelled, was hanging down over her face. Two young fellows, who had constituted themselves her seconds, were standing in front of her, offering rather ironical comfort. One of them had taken the bottom corners of her apron and was fanning her with it, while the other was showing her how to stand and hold her arms.

"You stand up to 'er, Liza," he was saying; "there ain't no good funkin' it, you'll simply get it all the worse. You 'it 'er back. Give 'er one on the boko, like this—see; yer must show a bit of pluck, yer know."

Liza tried to check her sobs.

"Yus, 'it 'er 'ard, that's wot yer've got ter do," said the other. "An' if yer find she's gettin' the better on yer, you close on 'er and catch 'old of 'er 'air and scratch 'er."

"You've marked 'er with yer nails, Liza. By gosh, you did fly on her when she spat at yer! thet's the way ter do the job!"

Then turning to his fellow, he said—

"D'yer remember thet fight as old Mother Gregg 'ad with another woman in the street last year?"

"Na," he answered, "I never saw thet."

"It was a cawker; an' the cops come in and took 'em both off ter quod."

Liza wished the policemen would come and take her off; she would willingly have gone to prison to escape the fiend in front of her; but no help came.

"Time's up!" shouted the referee. "Fire away!"

"Tike care of the cops!" shouted a man.

"There's no fear abaht them," answered somebody else. "They always keeps out of the way when there's anythin' goin' on."

"Fire away!"

Mrs. Blakeston attacked Liza madly; but the girl stood up bravely, and as well as she could gave back the blows she received. The spectators grew tremendously excited.

"Got 'im again!" they shouted. "Give it 'er, Liza, thet's a good 'un!—'it 'er 'ard!"

"Two ter one on the old 'un!" shouted a sporting gentleman; but Liza found no backers.

"Ain't she standin' up well now she's roused?" cried someone.

"Oh, she's got some pluck in 'er, she 'as!"

"Thet's a knock-aht!" they shouted as Mrs. Blakeston brought her fist down on to Liza's nose; the girl staggered back, and blood began to flow. Then, losing all fear, mad with rage, she made a rush on her enemy, and rained down blows all over her nose and eyes and mouth. The woman recoiled at the sudden violence of the onslaught, and the men cried:

"By God, the little 'un's gettin' the best of it!"

But quickly recovering herself the woman closed with Liza, and dug her nails into her flesh. Liza caught hold of her hair and pulled with all her might, and turning her teeth on Mrs. Blakeston tried to bite her. And thus for a minute they swayed about, scratching, tearing, biting, sweat and blood pouring down their faces, and their eyes fixed on one another, bloodshot and full of rage. The audience shouted and cheered and clapped their hands.

"Wot the 'ell's up 'ere?"

"I sy, look there," said some of the women in a whisper. "It's the 'usbind!"

He stood on tiptoe and looked over the crowd.

"My Gawd," he said, "it's Liza!"

Then roughly pushing the people aside, he made his way through the crowd into the centre, and thrusting himself between the two women, tore them apart. He turned furiously on his wife.

"By Gawd, I'll give yer somethin' for this!"

And for a moment they all three stood silently looking at one another.

Another man had been attracted by the crowd, and he, too, pushed his way through.

"Come 'ome, Liza," he said.

"Tom!"

He took hold of her arm, and led her through the people, who gave way to let her pass. They walked silently through the street, Tom very grave, Liza weeping bitterly.

"Oh, Tom," she sobbed after a while, "I couldn't 'elp it!" Then, when her tears permitted, "I did love 'im so!"

When they got to the door she plaintively said, "Come in," and he followed her to her room. Here she sank on to a chair, and gave herself up to her tears.

Tom wetted the end of a towel and began wiping her face, grimy with blood and tears. She let him do it, just moaning amid her sobs:

"You are good ter me, Tom."

"Cheer up, old gal," he said, kindly, "it's all over now."

After a while the excess of crying brought its cessation. She drank some water, and then taking up a broken hand-glass she looked at herself, saying:

"I am a sight!" and proceeded to wind up her hair. "You 'ave been good ter me, Tom," she repeated, her voice still broken with sobs; and as he sat down beside her she took his hand.

"Na, I ain't," he answered; "it's only wot anybody 'ud 'ave done."

"Yer know, Tom," she said, after a little silence, "I'm so sorry I spoke cross like when I met yer in the street; you ain't spoke ter me since."

"Oh, thet's all over now, old lidy, we needn't think of thet."

"Oh, but I 'ave treated yer bad. I'm a regular wrong 'un, I am."

He pressed her hand without speaking.

"I say, Tom," she began, after another pause. "Did yer know thet—well, you know—before ter-day?"

He blushed as he answered—

"Yus."

She spoke very sadly and slowly.

"I thought yer did; yer seemed so cut up like when I used to meet yer. Yer did love me then, Tom, didn't yer?"

"I do now, dearie," he answered.

"Ah, it's too lite now," she sighed.

"D'yer know, Liza," he said, "I just abaht kicked the life aht of a feller 'cause 'e said you was messin' abaht with—with 'im."

"An' yer knew I was?"

"Yus—but I wasn't goin' ter 'ave anyone say it before me."

"They've all rounded on me except you, Tom. I'd 'ave done better if I'd tiken you when you arst me; I shouldn't be where I am now, if I 'ad."

"Well, won't yer now? Won't yer 'ave me now?"

"Me? After wot's 'appened?"

"Oh, I don't mind abaht thet. Thet don't matter ter me if you'll marry me. I fair can't live without yer, Liza—won't yer?"

She groaned.

"Na, I can't, Tom, it wouldn't be right."

"Why, not, if I don't mind?"

"Tom," she said, looking down, almost whispering, "I'm like that—you know!"

"Wot d'yer mean?"

She could scarcely utter the words:

"I think I'm in the family wy."

He paused a moment; then spoke again.

"Well—I don't mind, if yer'll only marry me."

"Na, I can't Tom," she said, bursting into tears; "I can't, but you are so good ter me; I'd do anythin' ter mike it up ter you."

She put her arms round his neck and slid on to his knees.

"Yer know, Tom, I couldn't marry yer now; but anythin' else—if yer wants me ter do anythin' else, I'll do it if it'll mike you 'appy."

He did not understand, but only said:

"You're a good gal, Liza," and bending down he kissed her gravely on the forehead.

Then with a sigh he lifted her down, and getting up left her alone. For a while she sat where he left her, but as she thought of all she had gone through her loneliness and misery overcame her, the tears welled forth, and throwing herself on the bed she buried her face in the pillows.

Jim stood looking at Liza as she went off with Tom, and his wife watched him jealously.

"It's 'er you're thinkin' abaht. Of course you'd 'ave liked ter tike 'er 'ome yerself, I know, an' leave me to shift for myself."

"Shut up!" said Jim, angrily turning upon her.

"I shan't shut up," she answered, raising her voice. "Nice 'usbind you are. Go' lumme, as good as they mike 'em! Nice thing ter go an' leave yer wife and children for a thing like thet! At your age, too! You oughter be ashimed of yerself. Why, it's like messin' abaht with your own daughter!"

"By God!"—he ground his teeth with rage—"if yer don't leave me alone, I'll kick the life aht of yer!"

"There!" she said, turning to the crowd—"there, see 'ow 'e treats me! Listen ter that! I've been 'is wife for twenty years, an' yer couldn't 'ave 'ad a better wife, an' I've bore 'im nine children, yet say nothin' of a miscarriage, an' I've got another comin', an' thet's 'ow 'e treats me! Nice 'usbind, ain't it?" She looked at him scornfully, then again at the surrounders as if for their opinion.

"Well, I ain't goin' ter stay 'ere all night; get aht of the light!" He pushed aside the people who barred his way, and the one or two who growled a little at his roughness, looking at his angry face, were afraid to complain.

"Look at 'im!" said his wife. " 'E's afraid, 'e is. See 'im skinkin' awy like a bloomin' mongrel with 'is tail between 'is legs. Ugh!" She walked just behind him, shouting and brandishing her arms.

"Yer dirty beast, you," she yelled; "ter go foolin' abaht with a little girl! Ugh! I wish yer wasn't my 'usbind; I wouldn't be seen drowned with yer, if I could 'elp it. Yer mike me sick ter look at yer."

The crowd followed them on both sides of the road, keeping at a discreet distance, but still eagerly listening.

Jim turned on her once or twice and said:

"Shut up!"

But it only made her more angry. "I tell yer I shan't shut up. I don't care 'oo knows it, you're a ———, you are! I'm ashimed the children should 'ave such a father as you. D'yer think I didn't know wot you was up ter them nights you was awy—courtin', yus, courtin'? You're a nice man, you are!"

Jim did not answer her, but walked on. At last he turned round to the people who were following, and said:

"Na then, wot d'you want 'ere? You jolly well clear, or I'll give some of you somethin'!"

They were mostly boys and women, and at his words they shrank back.

" 'E's afraid ter sy anythin' ter me," jeered Mrs. Blakeston. " 'E's a beauty!"

Jim entered his house, and she followed him till they came up into their room. Polly was giving the children their tea. They all started up as they saw their mother with her hair and clothes in disorder, blotches of dried blood on her face, and the long scratch-marks.

"Oh, mother," said Polly, "wot is the matter?"

" 'E's the matter," she answered, pointing to her husband. "It's through 'im I've got all this. Look at yer father, children; 'e's a father to be proud of, leavin' yer ter starve an' spendin' 'is wee's money on a dirty little strumpet."

Jim felt easier now he had not got so many strange eyes on him.

"Now, look 'ere," he said, "I'm not goin' ter stand this much longer, so just you tike care."

"I ain't frightened of yer. I know yer'd like ter kill me, but yer'll get strung up if you do."

"Na, I won't kill yer, but if I 'ave anymore of your sauce I'll do the next thing to it."

"Touch me if yer dare," she said; "I'll 'ave the law on you. An' I shouldn't mind 'ow many month's 'ard you got."

"Be quiet!" he said, and, closing his hand, gave her a heavy blow in the chest that made her stagger.

"Oh, you——!" she screamed.

She seized the poker, and in a fury of rage rushed at him.

"Would yer?" he said, catching hold of it and wrenching it from her grasp. He threw it to the end of the room and grappled with her. For a moment they swayed about from side to side, then with an effort he lifted her off her feet and threw her to the ground; but she caught hold of him and he came down on the top of her. She screamed as her head thumped down on the floor, and the children, who were standing huddled up in a corner, terrified, screamed too.

Jim caught hold of his wife's head and began beating it against the floor.

She cried out, "You're killing me! Help! help!"

Polly in terror ran up to her father, and tried to pull him off.

"Father, don't 'it 'er! Anythin' but thet—for God's sike!"

"Leave me alone," he said, "or I'll give you somethin' too."

She caught hold of his arm, but Jim, still kneeling on his wife, gave Polly a back-handed blow which sent her staggering back.

"Tike that!"

Polly ran out of the room, downstairs to the first-floor front, where two men and two women were sitting at tea.

"Oh, come an' stop father!" she cried. " 'E's killin' mother!"

"Why, wot's 'e doin'?"

"Oh, 'e's got 'er on the floor, an' 'e's bangin' 'er 'ead. 'E's payin' 'er aht for givin' Liza Kemp a 'idin'."

One of the women started up and said to her husband:

"Come on, John, you go an' stop it."

"Don't you, John," said the other man. "When a man's givin' 'is wife socks it's best not ter interfere."

"But 'e's killin' 'er," repeated Polly, trembling with fright.

"Garn!" rejoined the man; "she'll git over it; an' p'raps she deserves it, for all you know."

John sat undecided, looking now at Polly, now at his wife, and now at the other man.

"Oh, do be quick—for God's sike!" said Polly.

At that moment a sound as of something smashing was heard upstairs, and a woman's shriek. Mrs. Blakeston, in an effort to tear herself away from her husband, had knocked up against the wash-hand stand, and the whole thing had crashed down.

"Go on, John," said the wife.

"No, I ain't goin'; I shan't do no good, an' 'e'll only round on me."

"Well, you are a bloomin' lot of cowards, thet's all I can say," indignantly answered the wife. "But I ain't goin' ter see a woman murdered; I'll go an' stop 'im."

With that she ran upstairs and threw open the door. Jim was still kneeling on his wife, hitting her furiously, while she was trying to protect her head and face with her hands.

"Leave off!" shouted the woman.

Jim looked up. " 'Oo the devil are you?" he said.

"Leave off, I tell yer. Aren't yer ashimed of yerself, knockin' a woman abaht like that?" And she sprang at him, seizing his fist.

"Let go," he said, "or I'll give you a bit."

"Yer'd better not touch me," she said. "Yer dirty coward! Why, look at 'er, she's almost senseless."

Jim stopped and gazed at his wife. He got up and gave her a kick.

"Git up!" he said; but she remained huddled up on the floor, moaning feebly. The woman from downstairs went on her knees and took her head in her arms.

"Never mind, Mrs. Blakeston. 'E's not goin' ter touch yer. 'Ere, drink this little drop of water." Then turning to Jim, with infinite disdain, "Yer dirty blackguard, you! If I was a man I'd give you something for this."

Jim put on his hat and went out, slamming the door, while the woman shouted after him, "Good riddance!"

"Lord love yer," said Mrs. Kemp, "wot is the matter?"

She had just come in, and opening the door had started back in surprise at seeing Liza on the bed, all tears. Liza made no answer, but cried as if her heart were breaking. Mrs. Kemp went up to her and tried to look at her face.

"Don't cry, dearie; tell us wot it is."

Liza sat up and dried her eyes.

"I am so un'appy!"

"Wot 'ave yer been doin' ter yer fice? My!"

"Nothin'."

"Garn! Yer can't 'ave got a fice like thet all by itself."

"I 'ad a bit of a scrimmage with a woman dahn the street," sobbed out Liza.

"She 'as give yer a doin'; an' yer all upset—an' look at yer eye! I brought in a little bit of stike for ter-morrer's dinner; you just cut a bit off an' put it over yer optic, that'll soon put it right. I always used ter do thet myself when me an' your poor father 'ad words."

"Oh, I'm all over in a tremble; an' my 'ead, oo, my 'ead does feel bad!"

"I know wot yer want," remarked Mrs. Kemp, nodding her head, "an' it so 'appens as I've got the very thing with me." She pulled a medicine bottle out of her pocket, and taking out the cork smelt it. "Thet's good stuff; none of your firewater or your methylated spirit. I don't often indulge in sich things, but when I do I likes to 'ave the best."

She handed the bottle to Liza, who took a mouthful and gave it her back; she had a drink herself, and smacked her lips.

"Thet's good stuff. 'Ave a drop more."

"Na," said Liza, "I ain't used ter drinkin' spirits."

She felt dull and miserable, and a heavy pain throbbed through her head. If she could only forget!

"Na, I know you're not, but, bless your soul, thet won' 'urt yer. It'll do you no end of good. Why, often when I've been feelin' thet done up thet I didn't know wot ter do with myself, I've just 'ad a little drop of whisky or gin—I'm not partic'ler wot spirit it is—an' it's pulled me up wonderful."

Liza took another sip, a slightly longer one; it burned as it went down her throat, and sent through her a feeling of comfortable warmth.

"I really do think it's doin' me good," she said, wiping her eyes and giving a sigh of relief as the crying ceased.

"I knew it would. Tike my word for it, if people took a little drop of spirits in time, there'd be much less sickness abaht."

They sat for a while in silence, then Mrs. Kemp remarked:

"Yer know, Liza, it strikes me as 'ow we could do with a drop more. You not bein' in the 'abit of tikin' anythin' I only brought just this little drop for me; an' it ain't took us long ter finish thet up. But as you're an invalid like we'll git a little more this time; it's sure ter turn aht useful."

"But you ain't got nothin' ter put it in."

"Yus, I 'ave," answered Mrs. Kemp; "there's thet bottle as they gives me at the 'orspital. Just empty the medicine aht into the pile, an' wash it aht, an' I'll tike it round to the pub myself."

Liza, when she was left alone, began to turn things over in her mind. She did not feel so utterly unhappy as before, for the things she had gone through seemed further away.

"After all," she said, "it don't so much matter."

Mrs. Kemp came in.

" 'Ave a little drop more, Liza." she said.

"Well, I don't mind if I do. I'll get some tumblers, shall I? There's no mistike abaht it," she added, when she had taken a little, "it do buck yer up."

"You're right, Liza—you're right. An' you wanted it badly. Fancy you 'avin' a fight with a woman! Oh, I've 'ad some in my day, but then I wasn't a little bit of a thing like you is. I wish I'd been there, I wouldn't 'ave stood by an' looked on while my daughter was gettin' the worst of it; although I'm turned sixty-five, an' gettin' on for sixty-six, I'd 'ave said to 'er: 'If you touch my daughter you'll 'ave me ter deal with, so just look aht!' "

She brandished her glass, and that reminding her, she refilled it and Liza's.

"Ah, Liza," she remarked, "you're a chip of the old block. Ter see you settin' there an' 'avin' your little drop, it mikes me feel as if I was livin' a better life. Yer used ter be rather 'ard on me, Liza, 'cause I took a little drop on Saturday nights. An', mind, I don't sy I didn't tike a little drop too much sometimes—accidents will occur even in the best regulated of families; but wot I say is this—it's good stuff, I say, an' it don't 'urt yer."

"Buck up, old gal!" said Liza, filling the glasses, "no 'eel-taps. I feel like a new woman now. I was thet dahn in the dumps—well, I shouldn't 'ave cared if I'd been at the bottom of the river, an' thet's the truth."

"You don't sy so," replied her affectionate mother.

"Yus, I do, an' I mean it too, but I don't feel like thet now. You're right, mother, when you're in trouble there's nothin' like a bit of spirits."

"Well, if I don't know, I dunno 'oo does, for the trouble I've 'ad, it 'ud be enough to kill many women. Well, I've 'ad thirteen children, an' you can think wot thet was; everyone I 'ad I used ter sy I wouldn't 'ave no more—but one does, yer know. You'll 'ave a family someday, Liza, an' I shouldn't wonder if you didn't 'ave as many as me. We come from a very prodigal family, we do, we've all gone in ter double figures, except your Aunt Mary, who only 'ad three—but then she wasn't married, so it didn't count, like."

They drank each other's health. Everything was getting blurred to Liza; she was losing her head.

"Yus," went on Mrs. Kemp, "I've 'ad thirteen children an' I'm proud of it. As your poor dear father used ter sy, it shows as 'ow one's got the blood of a Briton in one. Your poor dear father, 'e was a great 'and at speakin', 'e was: 'e used ter speak at parliamentary meetin's—I really believe 'e'd 'ave been a Member of Parliament if 'e'd been alive now. Well, as I was sayin', your father 'e used ter sy, 'None of your small families for me, I don't approve of them,' says 'e. 'E was a man of very 'igh principles, an' by politics 'e was a Radical. 'No,' says 'e, when 'e got talkin', 'when a man can 'ave a family risin' into double figures, it shows 'e's got the backbone of a Briton in 'im. That's the stuff as 'as built up England's nime and glory! When one thinks of the mighty British Hempire,' says 'e, 'on which the sun never sets from mornin' till night, one 'as ter be proud of 'isself, an' one 'as ter do one's duty in thet walk of life in which it 'as pleased Providence ter set one—an' every man's fust duty is ter get as many children as 'e bloomin' well can.' Lord love yer— 'e could talk, I can tell yer."

"Drink up, mother," said Liza. "You're not 'alf drinkin'." She flourished the bottle. "I don't care a twopanny 'ang for all them blokes; I'm quite 'appy, an' I don't want anythin' else."

"I can see you're my daughter now," said Mrs. Kemp. "When yer used ter round on me I used ter think as 'ow if I 'adn't carried yer for nine months, it must 'ave been some mistike, an' yer wasn't my daughter at all. When you come ter think of it, a man 'e don't know if it's 'is child or somebody else's, but yer can't deceive a woman like thet. Yer couldn't palm off somebody else's kid on 'er."

"I am beginnin' ter feel quite lively," said Liza. "I dunno wot it is, but I feel as if I wanted to laugh till I fairly split my sides."

And she began to sing, "For 'e's a jolly good feller—for 'e's a jolly good feller!"

Her dress was all disarranged; her face covered with the scars of scratches, and clots of blood had fixed under her nose; her eye had swollen up so that it was nearly closed, and red; her hair was hanging over her face and shoulders, and she laughed stupidly and leered with heavy, sodden ugliness.

> *Disy, Disy! I can't afford a kerridge,*
> *But you'll look neat, on the seat*
> *Of a bicycle mide for two.*

She shouted out the tunes, beating time on the table, and her mother, grinning, with her thin, grey hair hanging dishevelled over her head, joined in with her weak, cracked voice:

> *Oh, dem golden kippers, oh!*

Then Liza grew more melancholy and broke into "Auld Lang Syne."

> *Should old acquaintance be forgot*
> *And never brought to mind?*
> • • • •
> *For old lang syne.*

Finally they both grew silent, and in a little while there came a snore from Mrs. Kemp; her head fell forward to her chest; Liza tumbled from her chair on to the bed, and sprawling across it fell asleep.

> *Although I am drunk and bad, be you kind,*
> *Cast a glance at this heart which is bewildered and distressed.*
> *O God, take away from my mind my cry and my complaint.*
> *Offer wine, and take sorrow from my remembrance.*
> *Offer wine!*

Chapter XII

About the middle of the night Liza woke; her mouth was hot and dry, and a sharp, cutting pain passed through her head as she moved. Her mother had evidently roused herself, for she was lying in bed by her side, partially undressed, with all the bedclothes rolled round her. Liza shivered in the cold night, and taking off some of her things—her boots, her skirt, and jacket—got right into bed; she tried to get some of the blanket from her mother, but as she pulled Mrs. Kemp gave a growl in her sleep and drew the clothes more tightly round her. So Liza put over herself her skirt and a shawl, which was lying over the end of the bed, and tried to go to sleep. But she could not; her head and hands were broiling hot, and she was terribly thirsty; when she lifted herself up to get a drink of water such a pang went through her head that she fell back on the bed groaning, and lay there with beating heart. And strange pains that she did not know, went through her. Then a cold shiver seemed to rise in the very marrow of her bones and run down every artery and vein, freezing the blood; her skin puckered up, and drawing up her legs she lay huddled together in a heap, the shawl wrapped tightly round her, and her teeth chattering. Shivering, she whispered:

"Oh, I'm so cold, so cold. Mother, give me some clothes; I shall die of the cold. Oh, I'm freezing!"

But after a while the cold seemed to give way, and a sudden heat seized her, flushing her face, making her break out into perspiration, so that she threw everything off and loosened the things about her neck.

"Give us a drink," she said. "Oh, I'd give anythin' for a little drop of water!"

There was no one to hear; Mrs. Kemp continued to sleep heavily, occasionally breaking out into a little snore.

Liza remained there, now shivering with cold, now panting for breath, listening to the regular, heavy breathing by her side, and in her pain she sobbed. She pulled at her pillow and said:

"Why can't I go to sleep? Why can't I sleep like 'er?"

And the darkness was awful; it was a heavy, ghastly blackness, that seemed palpable, so that it frightened her, and she looked for relief at the faint light glimmering through the window from a distant street-lamp. She thought the night would never end—the minutes seemed like hours, and she wondered how she should live through till morning. And strange pains that she did not know went through her.

Still the night went on, the darkness continued, cold and horrible, and her mother breathed loudly and steadily by her side.

At last with the morning sleep came; but the sleep was almost worse than the wakefulness, for it was accompanied by ugly, disturbing dreams. Liza thought she was going through the fight with her enemy, and Mrs. Blakeston grew enormous in size, and multiplied, so that every way she turned the figure confronted her. And she began running away, and she ran and ran till she found herself reckoning up an account she had puzzled over in the morning, and she did it backwards and forwards, upwards and downwards, starting here, starting there, and the figures got mixed up with other things, and she had to begin over again, and everything jumbled up, and her head whirled, till finally, with a start, she woke.

The darkness had given way to a cold, grey dawn, her uncovered legs were chilled to the bone, and by her side she heard again the regular, nasal breathing of the drunkard.

For a long while she lay where she was, feeling very sick and ill, but better than in the night. At last her mother woke.

"Liza!" she called.

"Yus, mother," she answered, feebly.

"Git us a cup of tea, will yer?"

"I can't, mother, I'm ill."

"Garn!" said Mrs. Kemp, in surprise. Then looking at her, "Swop me bob, wot's up with yer? Why, yer cheeks is flushed, an' yer forehead—it is 'ot! Wot's the matter with yer, gal?"

"I dunno," said Liza. "I've been thet bad all night, I thought I was goin' ter die."

"I know wot it is," said Mrs. Kemp, shaking her head; "the fact is, you ain't used ter drinkin', an' of course it's upset yer. Now me, why I'm as fresh as a disy. Tike my word, there ain't no good in teetotalism; it finds yer aht in the end, an' it's found you aht."

Mrs. Kemp considered it a judgment of Providence. She got up and mixed some whisky and water.

" 'Ere, drink this," she said. "When one's 'ad a drop too much at night, there's nothin' like havin' a drop more in the mornin' ter put one right. It just acts like magic."

"Tike it awy," said Liza, turning from it in disgust; "the smell of it gives me the sick. I'll never touch spirits again."

"Ah, that's wot we all says sometime in our lives, but we does, an' wot's more we can't do withaht it. Why, me, the 'ard life I've 'ad—" It is unnecessary to repeat Mrs. Kemp's repetitions.

Liza did not get up all day. Tom came to inquire after her, and was told she was very ill. Liza plaintively asked whether anyone else had been, and sighed a little when her mother answered no. But she felt too ill to think much or trouble much about anything. The fever came again as the day wore on, and the pains in her head grew worse. Her mother came to bed, and quickly went off to sleep, leaving Liza to bear her agony alone. She began to have frightful pains all over her, and she held her breath to prevent herself from crying out and waking her mother. She clutched the sheets in her agony, and at last, about six o'clock in the morning, she could bear it no longer, and in the anguish of labour screamed out, and woke her mother.

Mrs. Kemp was frightened out of her wits. Going upstairs she woke the woman who lived on the floor above her. Without hesitating, the good lady put on a skirt and came down.

"She's 'ad a miss," she said, after looking at Liza. "Is there anyone you could send to the 'orspital?"

"Na, I dunno 'oo I could get at this hour?"

"Well, I'll git my old man ter go."

She called her husband, and sent him off. She was a stout, middle-aged woman, rough-visaged and strong-armed. Her name was Mrs. Hodges.

"It's lucky you came ter me," she said, when she had settled down. "I go aht nursin', yer know, so I know all abaht it."

"Well, you surprise me," said Mrs. Kemp. "I didn't know as Liza was thet way. She never told me nothin' abaht it."

"D'yer know 'oo it is 'as done it?"

"Now you ask me somethin' I don't know," replied Mrs. Kemp. "But now I come ter think of it, it must be thet there Tom. 'E's been keepin' company with Liza. 'E's a single man, so they'll be able ter get married—thet's somethin'."

"It ain't Tom," feebly said Liza.

"Not 'im; 'oo is it, then?"

Liza did not answer.

"Eh?" repeated the mother; "'oo is it?"

Liza lay still without speaking.

"Never mind, Mrs. Kemp," said Mrs. Hodges, "don't worry 'er now; you'll be able ter find aht all abaht it when she gits better."

For a while the two women sat still, waiting the doctor's coming, and Liza lay gazing vacantly at the wall, panting for breath. Sometimes Jim crossed her mind, and she opened her mouth to call for him, but in her despair she restrained herself.

The doctor came.

"D'you think she's bad, doctor?" asked Mrs. Hodges.

"I'm afraid she is rather," he answered. "I'll come in again this evening."

"Oh, doctor," said Mrs. Kemp, as he was going, "could yer give me somethin' for my rheumatics? I'm a martyr to rheumatism, an' these cold days I 'ardly knows wot ter do with myself. An', doctor, could you let me 'ave some beef-tea? My 'usbind's dead, an' of course I can't do no work with my daughter ill like this, an' we're very short—"

The day passed, and in the evening Mrs. Hodges, who had been attending to her own domestic duties, came downstairs again. Mrs. Kemp was on the bed, sleeping.

"I was just 'avin' a little nap," she said to Mrs. Hodges, on waking.

"'Ow is the girl?" asked that lady.

"Oh," answered Mrs. Kemp, "my rheumatics 'as been thet bad I really 'aven't known wot ter do with myself; an' now Liza can't rub me I'm worse than ever. It is unfortunate thet she should get ill just now when I want so much attendin' ter myself; but there, it's just my luck!"

Mrs. Hodges went over and looked at Liza; she was lying just as when she left in the morning, her cheeks flushed, her mouth open for breath, and tiny beads of sweat stood on her forehead.

"'Ow are yer, ducky?" asked Mrs. Hodges; but Liza did not answer.

"It's my belief she's unconscious," said Mrs. Kemp. "I've been askin' 'er 'oo it was as done it, but she don't seem to 'ear wot I say. It's been a great shock ter me, Mrs. 'Odges."

"I believe you," replied that lady, sympathetically.

"Well, when you come in and said wot it was, yer might 'ave knocked me dahn with a feather. I knew no more than the dead wot 'ad 'appened."

"I saw at once wot it was," said Mrs. Hodges, nodding her head.

"Yus, of course you knew. I expect you've 'ad a great deal of practise one way an' another."

"You're right, Mrs. Kemp, you're right. I've been on the job now for nearly twenty years, an' if I don't know somethin' abaht it I ought."

"D'yer finds it pays well?"

"Well, Mrs. Kemp, tike it all in all, I ain't got no grounds for complaint. I'm in the 'abit of askin' five shillings, an' I will say this, I don't think it's too much for wot I do."

The news of Liza's illness had quickly spread, and more than once in the course of the day a neighbour had come to ask after her. There was a knock at the door now, and Mrs. Hodges opened it. Tom stood on the threshold asking to come in.

"Yus, you can come," said Mrs. Kemp.

He advanced on tiptoe, so as to make no noise, and for a while stood silently looking at Liza. Mrs. Hodges was by his side.

"Can I speak to 'er?" he whispered.

"She can't 'ear you."

He groaned.

"D'yer think she'll get arright?" he asked.

Mrs. Hodges shrugged her shoulders.

"I shouldn't like ter give an opinion," she said, cautiously.

Tom bent over Liza, and, blushing, kissed her; then, without speaking further, went out of the room.

"Thet's the young man as was courtin' 'er," said Mrs. Kemp, pointing over her shoulder with her thumb.

Soon after the doctor came.

"Wot do yer think of 'er, doctor?" said Mrs. Hodges, bustling forwards authoritatively in her position of midwife and sick-nurse.

"I'm afraid she's very bad."

"D'yer think she's goin' ter die?" she asked, dropping her voice to a whisper.

"I'm afraid so!"

As the doctor sat down by Liza's side Mrs. Hodges turned round and significantly nodded to Mrs. Kemp, who put her handkerchief to her eyes. Then she went outside to the little group waiting at the door.

"Wot does the doctor sy?" they asked, among them Tom.

" 'E says just wot I've been sayin' all along; I knew she wouldn't live."

And Tom burst out, "Oh, Liza!"

As she retired a woman remarked:

"Mrs. 'Odges is very clever, I think."

"Yus," remarked another, "she got me through my last confinement simply wonderful. If it come to choosin' between 'em I'd back Mrs. 'Odges against forty doctors."

"Ter tell yer the truth, so would I. I've never known 'er wrong yet."

Mrs. Hodges sat down beside Mrs. Kemp and proceeded to comfort her.

"Why don't yer tike a little drop of brandy ter calm yer nerves, Mrs. Kemp?" she said; "you want it."

"I was just feelin' rather faint, an' I couldn't 'elp thinkin' as 'w twopenneth of whisky 'ud do me good."

"Na, Mrs. Kemp," said Mrs. Hodges, earnestly, putting her hand on the other's arm. "You tike my tip—when you're queer there's nothin' like brandy for pullin' yer together. I don't object to whisky myself, but as a medicine yer can't beat brandy."

"Well, I won't set up myself as knowin' better than you Mrs. 'Odges; I'll do wot you think right."

Quite accidentally there was some in the room, and Mrs. Kemp poured it out for herself and her friend.

"I'm not in the 'abit of tikin' anythin' when I'm aht on business," she apologised, "but just ter keep you company I don't mind if I do."

"Your 'ealth, Mrs. 'Odges."

"Sime ter you, an' thank yer, Mrs. Kemp."

Liza lay still, breathing very quietly, her eyes closed. The doctor kept his fingers on her pulse.

"I've been very unfortunate of lite," remarked Mrs. Hodges, as she licked her lips; "this mikes the second death I've 'ad in the last ten days—women, I mean; of course I don't count bibies."

"Yer don't sy so."

"Of course the other one—well, she was only a prostitute, so it didn't so much matter. It ain't like another woman, is it?"

"Na, you're right."

"Still, one don't like 'em ter die, even if they are thet. One mustn't be too 'ard on 'em."

"Strikes me you've got a very kind 'eart, Mrs. 'Odges," said Mrs. Kemp.

"I 'ave thet; an' I often says it 'ud be better for my peace of mind an' my business if I 'adn't. I 'ave ter go through a lot, I do; but I can say this for myself, I always gives satisfaction, an' thet's somethin' as all lidies in my line can't say."

They sipped their brandy for a while.

"It's a great trial ter me that this should 'ave 'appened," said Mrs. Kemp, coming to the subject that had been disturbing her for some time. "Mine's always been a very respectable family, an' such a thing as this 'as never 'appened before. No, Mrs. 'Odges, I was lawfully married in church, an' I've got my marriage lines now ter show I was, an' thet one of my daughters should 'ave gone wrong in this way—well, I can't understand it. I give 'er a good education, an' she 'ad all the comforts of a 'ome. She never wanted for nothin'; I worked myself to the bone ter keep 'er in luxury, an' then thet she should go an' disgrace me like this!"

"I understand wot yer mean, Mrs. Kemp."

"I can tell you my family was very respectable; an' my 'usband, 'e earned twenty-five shillings a week, an' was in the sime plice seventeen years; an' 'is employers sent a beautiful wreath ter put on 'is coffin; an' they tell me they never 'ad such a good workman an' sich an 'onest man before. An' me! Well, I can sy this—I've done my duty by the girl, an' she's never learnt anythin' but good from me. Of course I ain't always been in wot yer might call flourishing circumstances, but I've always set her a good example, as she could tell yer so 'erself if she wasn't speechless."

Mrs. Kemp paused for a moment's reflection.

"As they sy in the Bible," she finished, "it's enough ter mike one's grey 'airs go dahn into the ground in sorrer. I can show yer my marriage certificate. Of course one doesn't like ter say much, because of course she's very bad; but if she got well I should 'ave given 'er a talkin' ter."

There was another knock.

"Do go an' see 'oo thet is; I can't, on account of my rheumatics."

Mrs. Hodges opened the door. It was Jim.

He was very white, and the blackness of his hair and beard, contrasting with the deathly pallor of his face, made him look ghastly. Mrs. Hodges stepped back.

" 'Oo's 'e?" she said, turning to Mrs. Kemp.

Jim pushed her aside and went up to the bed.

"Doctor, is she very bad?" he asked.

The doctor looked at him questioningly.

Jim whispered: "It was me as done it. She ain't goin' ter die, is she?"

The doctor nodded.

"O God! wot shall I do? It was my fault! I wish I was dead!"

Jim took the girl's head in his hands, and the tears burst from his eyes.

"She ain't dead yet, is she?"

"She's just living," said the doctor.

Jim bent down.

"Liza, Liza, speak ter me! Liza, say you forgive me! Oh, speak ter me!"

His voice was full of agony. The doctor spoke.

"She can't hear you."

"Oh, she must hear me! Liza! Liza!"

He sank on his knees by the bed-side.

They all remained silent: Liza lying stiller than ever, her breast unmoved by the feeble respiration, Jim looking at her very mournfully; the doctor grave, with his fingers on the pulse. The two women looked at Jim.

"Fancy it bein' 'im!" said Mrs. Kemp. "Strike me lucky, ain't 'e a sight!"

"You 'ave got 'er insured, Mrs. Kemp?" asked the midwife. She could bear the silence no longer.

"Trust me fur thet!" replied the good lady. "I've 'ad 'er insured ever since she was born. Why, only the other dy I was sayin' ter myself thet all thet money 'ad been wisted, but you see it wasn't; yer never know yer luck, you see!"

"Quite right, Mrs. Kemp; I'm a rare one for insurin'. It's a great thing. I've always insured all my children."

"The way I look on it is this," said Mrs. Kemp—"wotever yer do when they're alive, an' we all know as children is very tryin' sometimes, you should give them a good funeral when they dies. Thet's my motto, an' I've always acted up to it."

"Do you deal with Mr. Stearman?" asked Mrs. Hodges.

"No, Mrs. 'Odges, for undertikin' give me Mr. Footley every time. In the black line 'e's fust an' the rest nowhere!"

"Well, thet's very strange now—thet's just wot I think. Mr. Footley does 'is work well, an' 'e's very reasonable. I'm a very old customer of 'is, an' 'e lets me 'ave things as cheap as anybody."

"Does 'e indeed! Well Mrs. 'Odges, if it ain't askin' too much of yer, I should look upon it as very kind if you'd go an' mike the arrangements for Liza."

"Why, certainly, Mrs. Kemp. I'm always willin' ter do a good turn to anybody, if I can."

"I want it done very respectable," said Mrs. Kemp; "I'm not goin' ter stint for nothin' for my daughter's funeral. I like plumes, you know, although they is a bit extra."

"Never you fear, Mrs. Kemp, it shall be done as well as if it was for my own 'usbind, an' I can't say more than thet. Mr. Footley thinks a deal of me, 'e does! Why, only the other dy as I was goin' inter 'is shop 'e says, 'Good mornin', Mrs. 'Odges.' 'Good mornin', Mr. Footley,' says I. 'You've jest come in the nick of time,' says 'e. 'This gentleman an' myself,' pointin' to another gentleman as was standin' there, 'we was 'avin' a bit of an argument. Now you're a very intelligent woman, Mrs. 'Odges, and a good customer, too.' 'I can say thet for myself,' say I, 'I gives yer all the work I can.' 'I believe you,' says 'e. 'Well,' 'e says, 'now which do you think? Does hoak look better than helm, or does helm look better than hoak? Hoak *versus* helm, thet's the question.' 'Well, Mr. Footley,' says I, 'for my own private opinion, when you've got a nice brass plite in the middle, an' nice brass 'andles each end, there's nothin' like hoak.' 'Quite right,' says 'e, 'thet's wot I think; for coffins give me hoak any day, an' I 'ope,' says 'e, 'when the Lord sees fit ter call me to 'imself, I shall be put in a hoak coffin myself.' 'Amen,' says I."

"I like hoak," said Mrs. Kemp. "My poor 'usband 'e 'ad a hoak coffin. We did 'ave a job with 'im, I can tell yer. You know 'e 'ad dropsy, an' 'e swell up—oh, 'e did swell; 'is own mother wouldn't 'ave known 'im. Why, 'is leg swell up till it was as big round as 'is body, swop me bob, it did."

"Did it indeed!" ejaculated Mrs. Hodges.

"Yus, an' when 'e died they sent the coffin up. I didn't 'ave Mr. Footley at thet time; we didn't live 'ere then, we lived in Battersea, an' all our undertikin' was done by Mr. Brownin'; well, 'e sent the coffin up, an' we got my old man in, but we couldn't get the lid down, he was so swell up. Well, Mr. Brownin', 'e was a great big man, thirteen stone if 'e was a ounce. Well, 'e stood on the coffin, an' a young man 'e 'ad with 'im stood on it too, an' the lid simply wouldn't go dahn; so Mr. Brownin', 'e said, 'Jump on, missus,' so I was in my widow's weeds, yer know, but we 'ad ter git it dahn, so I stood on it, an' we all jumped, an' at last we got it to, an' screwed it; but, lor', we did 'ave a job; I shall never forget it."

Then all was silence. And a heaviness seemed to fill the air like a grey blight, cold and suffocating; and the heaviness was Death. They felt the presence in the room, and they dared not move, they dared not draw their breath. The silence was terrifying.

Suddenly a sound was heard—a loud rattle. It was from the bed and rang through the room, piercing the stillness.

The doctor opened one of Liza's eyes and touched it, then he laid on her breast the hand he had been holding, and drew the sheet over her head.

Jim turned away with a look of intense weariness on his face, and the two women began weeping silently. The darkness was sinking before the day, and a dim, grey light came through the window. The lamp spluttered out.

MRS. CRADDOCK

Epistle Dedicatory

DEAR MISS LEY—You will not consider it unflattering if I ask myself when exactly it was that I had the good fortune to make your acquaintance; for, though I am well aware the date is not far distant, I seem to have known you all my life. Was it really during the summer before last, at Naples? (I forget why you go habitually to winter resorts in the middle of August; the reasons you gave were ingenious but inconclusive—surely it is not to avoid your fellow-countrymen?) I was in the Gallery of Masterpieces, looking at the wonderful portrait-statue of Agrippina, when you, sitting beside me, asked some question. We began to talk—by the way, we never inquired if our respective families were desirable; you took my reputability for granted—and since then we have passed a good deal of time together; indeed, you have been seldom absent from my thoughts.

Now that we stand at a parting of ways (the phrase is hackneyed and you would loathe it), you must permit me to tell you what pleasure your regard has given me and how thoroughly I have enjoyed our intercourse, regretting always that inevitable circumstances made it so rare. I confess I stand in awe of you—this you will not believe, for you have often accused me of flippancy (I am not half so flippant as you); but your thin and mocking smile, after some remark of mine, continually makes me feel that I have said a foolish thing, than which in your eyes I know there is no greater crime.... You have told me that when an acquaintance has left a pleasant recollection, one should resist the temptation to renew it: altered time and surroundings create new impressions which cannot rival with the old, doubly idealised by novelty and absence. The maxim is hard, but therefore, perhaps, more likely to be true. Still, I cannot wish that the future may bring us nothing better than forgetfulness. It is certain that our paths are different, I shall be occupied with other work and you will be lost to me in the labyrinth of Italian hotels, wherein it pleases you, perversely, to hide your lights. I see no prospect of reunion (this sounds quite sentimental and you hate effusiveness. My letter is certainly over-full of parentheses); but I wish, notwithstanding and with all my heart, that someday you may consent to risk the experiment. What say you? I am, dear Miss Ley, very truly (don't laugh at me, I should like to say—affectionately)—Yours,

W. M.

Chapter I

THIS BOOK MIGHT BE CALLED ALSO *THE TRIUMPH OF LOVE*.
Bertha was looking out of window, at the bleakness of the day. The sky was sombre and the clouds heavy and low; the neglected carriage-drive was swept by the bitter wind, and the elm-trees that bordered it were bare of leaf, their naked branches shivering with horror of the cold. It was the end of November, and the day was utterly cheerless. The dying year seemed to have cast over all Nature the terror of death; the imagination would not bring to the wearied mind thoughts of the merciful sunshine, thoughts of the Spring coming as a maiden to scatter from her baskets the flowers and the green leaves.

Bertha turned round and looked at her aunt, cutting the leaves of a new *Spectator*. Wondering what books to get down from Mudie's, Miss Ley read the autumn lists and the laudatory expressions which the adroitness of publishers extracts from unfavourable reviews.

"You're very restless this afternoon, Bertha," she remarked, in answer to the girl's steady gaze.

"I think I shall walk down to the gate."

"You've already visited the gate twice in the last hour. Do you find in it something alarmingly novel?"

Bertha did not reply, but turned again to the window: the scene in the last two hours had fixed itself upon her mind with monotonous accuracy.

"What are you thinking about, Aunt Polly?" she asked suddenly, turning back to her aunt and catching the eyes fixed upon her.

"I was thinking that one must be very penetrative to discover a woman's emotions from the view of her back hair."

Bertha laughed: "I don't think I have any emotions to discover. I feel . . ." she sought for some way of expressing the sensation—"I feel as if I should like to take my hair down."

Miss Ley made no rejoinder, but looked again at her paper. She hardly wondered what her niece meant, having long ceased to be astonished at Bertha's ways and doings; indeed, her only surprise was that they never sufficiently corroborated the common opinion that Bertha was an independent young woman from whom anything might be expected. In the three years they had spent together since the death of Bertha's father the two women had learned to tolerate one another extremely well. Their mutual affection was mild and perfectly respectable, in every way becoming to fastidious persons bound together by ties of convenience and decorum.... Miss Ley, called to the deathbed of her brother in Italy, made Bertha's acquaintance over the dead man's grave, and the girl was then too old and of too independent character to accept a stranger's authority; nor had Miss Ley the smallest desire to exert authority over anyone. She was a very indolent woman, who wished nothing more than to leave people alone and be left alone by them. But if it was obviously her duty to take charge of an orphan niece, it was also an advantage that Bertha was eighteen, and, but for the conventions of decent society, could very well take charge of herself. Miss Ley was not unthankful to a merciful Providence on the discovery that her ward had every intention of going her own way, and none whatever of hanging about the skirts of a maiden aunt who was passionately devoted to her liberty.

They travelled on the Continent, seeing many churches, pictures, and cities, in the examination of which their chief aim appeared to be to conceal from one another the emotions they felt. Like the Red Indian who will suffer the most horrid tortures without wincing, Miss Ley would have thought it highly disgraceful to display feeling at some touching scene. She used polite cynicism as a cloak for sentimentality, laughing that she might not cry—and her want of originality herein, the old repetition of Grimaldi's doubleness, made her snigger at herself. She felt that tears were unbecoming and foolish.

"Weeping makes a fright even of a good-looking woman," she said, "but if she is ugly they make her simply repulsive."

Finally, letting her own flat in London, Miss Ley settled down with Bertha to cultivate rural delights at Court Leys, near Blackstable, in the county of Kent. The two ladies lived together with much harmony, although the demonstrations of their affection did not exceed a single kiss morning and night, given and received with almost equal indifference. Each had considerable respect for the other's abilities, and particularly for the wit which occasionally exhibited itself in little friendly sarcasms. But they were too clever to get on badly, and since they neither hated nor loved one another excessively, there was really no reason why they should not continue on the best of terms. The general result of their relations was that Bertha's restlessness on this particular day aroused in Miss Ley no more question than was easily answered by the warmth of her young blood; and her eccentric curiosity in respect of the gate on a very cold and unpleasant winter afternoon did not even cause a shrug of disapproval or an upraising of the eyelids in wonder.

Bertha put on a hat and walked out. The avenue of elm-trees, reaching from the façade of Court Leys in a straight line to the gates, had been once rather an imposing sight, but now announced clearly the ruin of an ancient house. Here and there a tree had died and fallen, leaving an unsightly gap, and one huge trunk still lay upon the ground after a terrific storm of the preceding year, left there to rot in the indifference of bailiffs and of tenants. On either side of the elms was a broad strip of meadow which once had been a well-kept lawn, but now was foul with docks and rank weeds; a few sheep nibbled the grass where a century ago fine ladies in hoops and gentlemen with periwigs had sauntered, discussing the wars and the last volumes of Mr. Richardson. Beyond was an ill-trimmed hedge, and then the broad fields of the Ley estate. . . . Bertha walked down, looking at the highway beyond the gate. It was a relief to feel no longer Miss Ley's cold eyes fixed upon her; she had emotions enough in her breast, they beat against one another like birds in a net struggling to get free; but not for worlds would Bertha have bidden anyone look in her heart full of expectation, of longings, of a hundred strange desires. She went out on the highroad that led from Blackstable to Tercanbury, she looked up and down with a tremor, and a quick beating of the heart. But the road was empty, swept by the winter wind, and she almost sobbed with disappointment.

She could not return to the house; a roof just then would stifle her, and the walls seemed like a prison: there was a certain pleasure in the biting wind that blew through her clothes and chilled her to the bone. The waiting was terrible. She entered the grounds and looked up the carriage-drive to the big white house which was hers. The very roadway was in need of repair, and the dead leaves that none troubled about rustled hither and thither in the gusts of wind. The house stood in its squareness without relation to any environment: built in the reign of George II., it seemed to have acquired no hold upon the land which bore it. With its plain front and many windows, the Doric portico exactly in the middle, it looked as if it were merely placed upon the ground as a house of cards is built upon the floor, with no foundations. The passing years had given it no beauty, and it stood now as for more than a century it had stood, a blot upon the landscape, vulgar and new. Surrounded by the fields, it had no garden but for a few beds planted about its feet, and in these the flowers, uncared for, had grown wild or withered away.

The day was declining and the lowering clouds seemed to shut out the light. Bertha gave up hope. But she looked once more down the hill and her heart gave a great thud against her chest; she felt herself blushing furiously. Her blood seemed to rush through the vessels with sudden rapidity, and in dismay at her want of composure she had an impulse to turn quickly and fly. She forgot the sickening expectation, the hours she had spent in looking for the figure that tramped up the hill.

Of course it was a man! He came nearer, a tall fellow of twenty-seven, massively set together, big boned, with long arms and legs, and a magnificent breadth of chest. Bertha recognised the costume that always pleased her, the knickerbockers and gaiters, the Norfolk-jacket of rough tweed, the white stock and the cap—

all redolent of the country which for his sake she was beginning to love, and all vigorously masculine. Even the huge boots which covered his feet gave her by their very size a thrill of pleasure; their dimensions suggested a certain firmness of character, a masterfulness, which were intensely reassuring. The style of dress fitted perfectly the background of brown road and of ploughed field. Bertha wondered if he knew that he was exceedingly picturesque as he climbed the hill.

"Afternoon, Miss Bertha."

He showed no sign of pausing, and the girl's heart sank at the thought that he might go on with only a commonplace word of greeting.

"I thought it was you I saw coming up the hill," she said, stretching out her hand.

He stopped and shook it; the touch of his big, firm fingers made her tremble. His hand was massive and hard as if it were hewn of stone. She looked up at him and smiled.

"Isn't it cold?" she said. It is terrible to be desirous of saying all sorts of passionate things, while convention debars you from any but the most commonplace.

"You haven't been walking at the rate of five miles an hour," he said, cheerily. "I've been into Blackstable to see about buying a nag."

He was the very picture of health; the winds of November were like summer breezes to him, and his face glowed with the pleasant cold. His cheeks were flushed and his eyes glistened. His vitality was intense, shining out upon others with almost a material warmth.

"Were you going out?" he asked.

"Oh no," Bertha replied, without strict regard to truth. "I just walked down to the gate and I happened to catch sight of you."

"I am very glad—I see you so seldom now, Miss Bertha."

"I wish you wouldn't call me *Miss Bertha*," she cried, "it sounds horrid." It was worse than that, it sounded almost menial. "When we were boy and girl we used to call each other by our Christian names."

He blushed a little and his modesty filled Bertha with delight.

"Yes, but when you came back six months ago, you had changed so much—I didn't dare; and besides, you called me Mr. Craddock."

"Well, I won't anymore," she said, laughing; "I'd much sooner call you Edward."

She did not add that the word seemed to her the most beautiful in the whole list of Christian names, nor that in the past few weeks she had already repeated it to herself a thousand times.

"It'll be like old days," he said. "D'you remember what fun we used to have when you were a little girl, before you went abroad with Mr. Ley?"

"I remember that you used to look upon me with great contempt because I *was* a little girl," she replied, laughing.

"Well, I was awfully frightened the first time I saw you again—with your hair up and long dresses."

"I'm not really very terrible."

For five minutes they had been looking into one another's eyes, and suddenly, without obvious reason, Craddock blushed. Bertha noticed it, and a strange little thrill went through her; she reddened too, and her dark eyes flashed even more brightly than before.

"I wish I didn't see you so seldom, Miss Bertha," he said.

"You have only yourself to blame, fair sir. You perceive the road that leads to my palace, and at the end you will certainly find a door."

"I'm rather afraid of your aunt."

It was on the tip of Bertha's tongue to say that faint heart never won fair lady, but for modesty's sake she refrained. Her spirits had suddenly gone up and she felt extraordinarily happy.

"Do you want to see me very badly?" she asked, her heart beating at quite an absurd rate.

Craddock blushed again and seemed to have some difficulty in finding a reply; his confusion and his ingenuous air were new enchantments to Bertha.

"If he only knew how I adored him!" she thought; but naturally she could not tell him in so many words.

"You've changed so much in these years," he said, "I don't understand you."

"You haven't answered my question."

"Of course I want to see you, Bertha," he said quickly, seeming to take his courage in both hands; "I want to see you always."

"Well," she said, with a charming smile, "I sometimes take a walk after dinner to the gate and observe the shadows of night."

"By Jove, I wish I'd known that before."

"Foolish creature!" said Bertha to herself with amusement, "he doesn't gather that this is the first night upon which I shall have done anything of the kind."

Chapter II

With swinging step Bertha returned to the house, and like a swarm of birds a hundred amorets flew about her head; Cupid leapt from tree to tree and shot his arrows into her willing heart; her imagination clothed the naked branches with tender green, and in her happiness the grey sky turned to azure.... It was the first time that Edward Craddock had shown his love in a manner which was unmistakable; if before, much had suggested that he was not indifferent, nothing had been absolutely convincing, and the doubt had caused her every imaginable woe. As for her, she made no effort to conceal it from herself; she was not ashamed, she loved him passionately, she worshipped the ground he trod on; she confessed boldly that he of all men was the one to make her happy; her life she would give into his strong and manly hands. She had made up her mind firmly that Craddock should lead her to the altar.

Times without number already had she fancied herself resting in his arms—in his strong arms—the very thought of which was a protection against all the ills of the world. Oh yes, she wanted him to take her in his arms and kiss her; in imagination she felt his lips upon hers, and the warmth of his breath made her faint with the anguish of love.

She asked herself how she could wait till the evening; how on earth was she to endure the slow passing of the hours? And she must sit opposite her aunt and pretend to read, or talk on this subject and on that. It was insufferable. Then, inconsequently, she asked herself if Edward knew that she loved him; he could not dream how intense was her desire.

"I'm sorry I'm late for tea," she said, on entering the drawing-room.

"My dear," said Miss Ley, "the buttered toast is probably horrid, but I don't see why you should not eat cake."

"I don't want anything to eat," cried Bertha, flinging herself on a chair.

"But you're dying with thirst," added Miss Ley, looking at her niece with sharp eyes. "Wouldn't you like your tea out of a breakfast cup?"

Miss Ley had come to the conclusion that the restlessness and the long absence could only be due to some masculine cause. Mentally she shrugged her shoulders, hardly wondering who the creature was.

"Of course," she thought, "it's certain to be someone quite ineligible. I hope they won't have a long engagement."

Miss Ley could not have supported for several months the presence of a bashful and love-sick swain. She found lovers invariably ridiculous. She watched Bertha drink six cups of tea: of course those shining eyes, the flushed cheeks and the breathlessness, indicated some amorous excitement; it amused her, but she thought it charitable and wise to pretend that she noticed nothing.

"After all it's no business of mine," she thought; "and if Bertha is going to get married at all, it would be much more convenient for her to do it before next quarter-day, when the Browns give up my flat."

Miss Ley sat on the sofa by the fireside, a woman of middle-size, very slight, with a thin and much wrinkled face. Of her features the mouth was the most noticeable, not large, with lips that were a little too thin; it was always so tightly compressed as to give her an air of great determination, but there was about the corners an expressive mobility, contradicting in rather an unusual manner the inferences which might be drawn from the rest of her person. She had a habit of fixing her cold eyes on people with a steadiness that was not a little embarrassing. They said Miss Ley looked as if she thought them great fools, and as a matter of fact that usually was her precise opinion. Her thin grey hair was very plainly done; and the extreme simplicity of her costume gave a certain primness, so that her favourite method of saying rather absurd things in the gravest and most decorous manner often disconcerted the casual stranger. She was a woman who, one felt, had never been handsome, but now, in middle-age, was distinctly prepossessing.

Young men thought her somewhat terrifying till they discovered that they were to her a constant source of amusement; while elderly ladies asserted that she was a little queer.

"You know, Aunt Polly," said Bertha, finishing her tea and getting up, "I think you should have been christened Martha or Matilda. I don't think Polly suits you."

"My dear, you need not remind me so pointedly that I'm forty-five and you need not smile in that fashion because you know that I'm really forty-seven. I say forty-five merely as a round number; in another year I shall call myself fifty. A woman never acknowledges such a nondescript age as forty-eight unless she is going to marry a widower with seventeen children."

"I wonder why you never married, Aunt Polly?" said Bertha, looking away.

Miss Ley smiled almost imperceptibly, finding Bertha's remark highly significant. "My dear," she said, "why should I? I had five hundred a year of my own. . . . Ah yes, I know it's not what might have been expected; I'm sorry for your sake that I had no hopeless amour. The only excuse for an old maid is, that she has pined thirty years for a lover who is buried under the snowdrops, or has married another."

Bertha made no answer; she was feeling that the world had turned good, and wanted to hear nothing that could suggest imperfections in human nature: suddenly there had come over the universe a Sunday-school air which appealed to her better self. Going upstairs she sat at the window, gazing towards the farm where lived her heart's desire. She wondered what Edward was doing! was he awaiting the night as anxiously as she? It gave her quite a pang that a sizeable hill should intervene between herself and him. During dinner she hardly spoke, and Miss Ley was mercifully silent. Bertha could not eat; she crumbled her bread and toyed with the various meats put before her. She looked at the clock a dozen times, and started absurdly when it struck the hour.

She did not trouble to make any excuse to Miss Ley, whom she left to think as she chose. The night was dark and cold; Bertha slipped out of the side-door with a delightful feeling of doing something venturesome. But her legs would scarcely carry her, she had a sensation that was entirely novel; never before had she experienced that utter weakness of the knees so that she feared to fall; her breathing was strangely oppressive, and her heart beat almost painfully. She walked down the carriage-drive scarcely knowing what she did. She had forced herself to wait indoors till the desire to go out became uncontrollable, and she dared not imagine her dismay if there was no one to meet her when she reached the gate. It would mean he did not love her; she stopped with a sob. Ought she not to wait longer? It was still early. But her impatience forced her on.

She gave a little cry. Craddock had suddenly stepped out of the darkness.

"Oh, I'm sorry," he said, "I frightened you. I thought you wouldn't mind my coming this evening. You're not angry?"

She could not answer; it was an immense load off her heart. She was extremely happy, for then he did love her; and he feared she was angry with him.

"I expected you," she whispered. What was the good of pretending to be modest and bashful? She loved him and he loved her. Why should she not tell him all she felt?

"It's so dark," he said, "I can't see you."

She was too deliriously happy to speak, and the only words she could have said were, *I love you, I love you*. She moved a step nearer so as to touch him. Why did he not open his arms and take her in them, and kiss her as she had dreamed that he would kiss her?

But he took her hand and the contact thrilled her; her knees were giving way, and she almost tottered.

"What's the matter?" he said. "Are you trembling?"

"I'm only a little cold." She was trying with all her might to speak naturally. Nothing came into her head to say.

"You've got nothing on," he said. "You must wear my coat." He began to take it off.

"No," she said, "then you'll be cold."

"Oh no, I shan't."

What he was doing seemed to her a marvel of unselfish kindness; she was beside herself with gratitude.

"It's awfully good of you, Edward," she whispered, almost tearfully.

When he put it round her shoulders, the touch of his hands made her lose the little self-control she had left. A curious spasm passed through her, and she pressed herself closer to him; at the same time his hands sank down, dropping the cloak, and encircled her waist. Then she surrendered herself entirely to his embrace and lifted her face to his. He bent down and kissed her. The kiss was such utter madness that she almost groaned. She could not tell if it was pain or pleasure. She flung her arms round his neck and drew him to her.

"What a fool I am," she said at last, with something between a sob and a laugh. She drew herself a little away, though not so violently as to make him withdraw the arm which so comfortably encircled her.

But why did he say nothing? Why did he not swear he loved her? Why did he not ask what she was so willing to grant? She rested her head on his shoulder.

"Do you like me at all, Bertha?" he asked. "I've been wanting to ask you almost ever since you came home."

"Can't you see?" She was reassured; she understood that it was only timidity that clogged his tongue. "You're so absurdly bashful."

"You know who I am, Bertha; and—" he hesitated.

"And what, foolish boy?" she nestled still more closely to him.

"And you're Miss Ley of Court Leys, while I'm just one of your tenants, with nothing whatever to my back."

"I've got very little," she said. "And if I had ten thousand a year, my only wish would be to lay it at your feet."

"Bertha, what d'you mean? Don't be cruel to me. You know what I want, but—"

"As far as I can make out," she said, laughing, "you want me to propose to you."

"Oh, Bertha, don't laugh at me. I love you; I want to ask you to marry me. But I haven't got anything to offer you, and I know I oughtn't—don't be angry with me, Bertha."

"But I love you with all my heart," she cried. "I want no better husband; you can give me happiness, and I want nothing else in the world."

Then he caught her again in his arms, quite passionately, and kissed her.

"Didn't you see that I loved you?" she whispered.

"I thought perhaps you did; but I wasn't sure, and I was afraid that you wouldn't think me good enough."

"Oh yes, I love you with all my heart. I never imagined it possible to love a person as I love you. Oh, Eddie, you don't know how happy you have made me."

He kissed her again, and again she flung her arms around his neck.

"Oughtn't you to be going in," he said at last; "what will Miss Ley think?"

"Oh no—not yet," she cried.

"How will you tell her? D'you think she'll like me? She'll try and make you give me up."

"Oh, I'm sure she'll love you; besides, what does it matter if she doesn't?—she isn't going to marry you."

"She can take you abroad again and then you may see someone you like better."

"But I'm twenty-one tomorrow, Edward—didn't you know? And I shall be my own mistress. I shan't leave Blackstable till I'm your wife."

They were walking slowly towards the house, whither he, in his anxiety lest she should stay cut too long, had guided her steps. They went arm in arm, and Bertha enjoyed her happiness.

"Dr. Ramsay is coming to luncheon tomorrow," she said, "and I shall tell them both that I'm going to be married to you."

"He won't like it," said Craddock, rather nervously.

"I'm sure I don't care. If you like it and I like it, the rest can think as they choose."

"I leave everything in your hands," he said.

They had arrived at the portico, and Bertha looked at it doubtfully.

"I suppose I ought to go in," she said, wishing Edward to persuade her to take one more turn round the garden.

"Yes, do," he said. "I'm so afraid you'll catch cold."

It was charming of him to be so solicitous about her health, and of course he was right. Everything he did and said was right; for the moment Bertha forgot her wayward nature, and wished suddenly to subject herself to his strong guidance. His very strength made her feel curiously weak.

"Good-night, my beloved," she whispered, passionately.

She could not tear herself away from him; it was utter madness. Their kisses never ended.

"Good-night!"

She watched him at last disappear into the darkness, and finally shut the door behind her.

Chapter III

With old and young great sorrow is followed by a sleepless night, and with the old great joy is as disturbing; but youth, I suppose, finds happiness more natural and its rest is not thereby disturbed. Bertha slept without dreams, and awaking, for the moment did not remember the occurrence of the previous day; but quickly it came back to her and she stretched herself with a sigh of great content. She lay in bed to contemplate her well-being. She could hardly realise that she had attained her dearest wish. God was very good, and gave His creatures what they asked; without words, from the fulness of her heart, she offered up thanks. It was quite extraordinary, after the maddening expectation, after the hopes and fears, the lover's pains which are nearly pleasure, at last to be satisfied. She had now nothing more to desire, for her happiness was complete. Ah yes, indeed, God was very good!

Bertha thought of the two months she had spent at Blackstable.... After the first excitement of getting into the house of her fathers she had settled down to the humdrum of country life; she spent the day wandering about the lanes or on the seashore watching the desolate sea; she read a great deal, and looked forward to the ampel time at her disposal to satisfy an immoderate desire for knowledge. She spent long hours in the library which her father had made, for it was only with falling fortunes that the family of Ley had taken to reading books; it had only applied itself to literature when it was too poor for any other pursuit. Bertha looked at the titles of the many volumes, receiving a certain thrill as she read over the great names of the past, and imagined the future delights that they would give her.

One day she was calling at the Vicarage and Edward Craddock happened to be there, lately returned from a short holiday. She had known him in days gone by— his father had been her father's tenant, and he still farmed the same land—but for eight years they had not seen one another, and now Bertha hardly recognised him. She thought him, however, a good-looking fellow in his knickerbockers and thick stockings, and was not displeased when he came up to speak, asking if she remembered him. He sat down and a certain pleasant odour of the farmyard was wafted over to Bertha, a mingled perfume of strong tobacco, of cattle and horses; she did not understand why it made her heart beat, but she inhaled it voluptuously and her eyes glittered. He began to talk, and his voice sounded like music in her ears; he looked at her and his eyes were large and grey, she found them highly sympathetic; he was clean-shaven, and his mouth was very attractive. She blushed and felt herself a fool. Bertha took pains to be as charming as possible; she knew her own dark eyes were beautiful, and fixed them upon his. When at last he bade her good-bye and shook hands, she blushed again; she was extraordinarily troubled, and as, with his rising, the strong masculine odour of the countryside reached her nostrils, her head whirled. She was very glad Miss Ley was not there to see her.

She walked home in the darkness trying to compose herself, for she could think of nothing but Edward Craddock. She recalled the past, trying to bring back to her memory incidents of their old acquaintance. At night she dreamed of him, and she dreamed he kissed her.

She awoke in the morning, thinking of Craddock, and felt it impossible to go through the day without seeing him. She thought of sending an invitation to luncheon or to tea, but hardly dared; and she did not want Miss Ley to see him yet. Then she remembered the farm; she would walk there, was it not hers? He would surely be working upon it. The god of love was propitious, and in a field she saw him, directing some operation. She trembled at the sight, her heart beat very quickly; and when, seeing her, he came forward with a greeting, she turned red and then white in the most compromising fashion. But he was very handsome as, with easy gait, he sauntered to the hedge; above all he was manly, and the pleasing thought passed through Bertha that his strength must be quite herculean. She barely concealed her admiration.

"Oh, I didn't know this was your farm," she said, shaking hands. "I was just walking at random."

"I should like to show you round, Miss Bertha."

Craddock opened the gate and took her to the sheds where he kept his carts, pointing out a couple of sturdy horses ploughing an adjacent field; he showed her his cattle, and poked the pigs to let her admire their excellent condition; he gave her sugar for his hunter, and took her to the sheep—explaining everything while she listened spell-bound. When, with great pride, Craddock showed her his machines and explained the use of the horse-tosser and the expense of the reaper, she thought that never in her life had she heard anything so enthralling. But above all Bertha wished to see the house in which he lived.

"D'you mind giving me a glass of water?" she said, "I'm so thirsty."

"Do come in," he answered, opening the door.

He led her to a little parlour with an oil-cloth on the floor. On the table, which took up most of the room, was a stamped, red cloth; the chairs and the sofa, covered with worn old leather, were arranged with the greatest possible stiffness. On the chimney-piece, along with pipes and tobacco-jars, were bright china vases with rushes in them, and in the middle a marble clock.

"Oh how pretty!" cried Bertha, with enthusiasm. "You must feel very lonely here by yourself."

"Oh no—I'm always out. Shall I get you some milk? It'll be better for you than water."

But Bertha saw a napkin laid on the table, a jug of beer, and some bread and cheese.

"Have I been keeping you from your lunch?" she asked. "I'm so sorry."

"It doesn't matter at all. I just have a little snack at eleven."

"Oh, may I have some too? I love bread and cheese, and I'm perfectly ravenous."

They sat opposite one another, seeing a great joke in the impromptu meal. The bread, which he cut in a great chunk, was delicious, and the beer, of course, was nectar. But afterwards, Bertha feared that Craddock must be thinking her somewhat odd.

"D'you think it's very eccentric of me to come and lunch with you in this way?"

"I think it's awfully good of you. Mr. Ley often used to come and have a snack with my father."

"Oh, did he?" said Bertha. Of course that made her proceeding quite natural. "But I really must go now. I shall get into awful trouble with Aunt Polly."

He begged her to take some flowers, and hastily cut a bunch a dahlias. She accepted them with the most embarrassing gratitude; and when they shook hands at parting, her heart went pit-a-pat again ridiculously.

Miss Ley inquired from whom she got her flowers.

"Oh," said Bertha coolly, "I happened to meet one of the tenants and he gave them to me."

"Hm," murmured Miss Ley, "it would be more to the purpose if they paid their rent."

Miss Ley presently left the room, and Bertha looked at the prim dahlias with a heart full of emotion. She gave a laugh.

"It's no good trying to hide it from myself," she murmured, "I'm head over ears in love."

She kissed the flowers and felt very glad. . . . She evidently was in that condition, since by the night Bertha had made up her mind to marry Edward Craddock or die. She lost no time, for less than a month had passed and their wedding-day was certainly in sight.

Miss Ley loathed all manifestations of feeling. Christmas, when everybody is supposed to take his neighbour to his bosom and harbour towards him a number of sentimental emotions, caused her such discomfort that she habitually buried herself for the time in some continental city where she knew no one, and could escape the overbrimming of other people's hearts. Even in summer Miss Ley could not see a holly-tree without a little shiver of disgust; her mind went immediately to the decorations of middle-class houses, the mistletoe hanging from a gas-chandelier, and the foolish old gentlemen who found amusement in kissing stray females. She was glad that Bertha had thought fit to refuse the display of enthusiasm from servants and impoverished tenants, which, on the attainment of her majority, her guardian had wished to arrange. Miss Ley could imagine that the festivities possible on such an occasion, the handshaking, the making of good cheer, and the obtrusive joviality of the country Englishman, might surpass even the tawdry rejoicings of Yuletide. But Bertha fortunately detested such things as sincerely as did Miss Ley herself, and suggested to the persons concerned that they could not oblige her more than by taking no notice of an event which really did not to her seem very significant.

But Dr. Ramsay's heartiness could not be entirely restrained; and he had also a fine old English sense of the fitness of things, that passion to act in a certain manner merely because in times past people have always so acted. He insisted on solemnly meeting Bertha to offer congratulations, a blessing, and some statement of his stewardship.

Bertha came downstairs when Miss Ley was already eating breakfast—a very feminine meal, consisting of nothing more substantial than a square inch of bacon and a morsel of dry toast. Miss Ley was really somewhat nervous, she was bothered by the necessity of referring to Bertha's natal day.

"That is one advantage of women," she told herself, "after twenty-five they gloss over their birthdays like improprieties. A man is so impressed with his cleverness in having entered the world at all that the anniversary always interests him; and the foolish creature thinks it interests other people as well."

But Bertha came into the room and kissed her.

"Good-morning, dear," said Miss Ley, and then, pouring out her niece's coffee, "our estimable cook has burnt the milk in honour of your majority; I trust she will not celebrate the occasion by getting drunk—at all events, till after dinner."

"I hope Dr. Ramsay won't enthuse too vigorously," replied Bertha, understanding Miss Ley's feeling.

"Oh, my dear, I tremble at the prospect of his jollity. He's a good man. I should think his principles were excellent, and I don't suppose he's more ignorant than most general practitioners; but his friendliness is sometimes painfully aggressive."

But Bertha's calm was merely external, her brain was in a whirl, and her heart beat with excitement. She was full of impatience to declare her news. Bertha had some sense of dramatic effect and looked forward a little to the scene when, the keys of her kingdom being handed to her, she made the announcement that she had already chosen a king to rule by her side. She felt also that between herself and

Miss Ley alone the necessary explanations would be awkward. Dr. Ramsay's outspoken bluffness made him easier to deal with; there is always a difficulty in conducting oneself with a person who ostentatiously believes that everyone should mind his own business and who, whatever her thoughts, takes more pleasure in the concealment than in the expression thereof. Bertha sent a note to Craddock, telling him to come at three o'clock to be introduced as the future lord and master of Court Leys.

Dr. Ramsay arrived and burst at once into a prodigious stream of congratulation, partly jocose, partly grave and sentimental, but entirely distasteful to the fastidiousness of Miss Ley. Bertha's guardian was a big, broad-shouldered man, with a mane of fair hair, now turning white; Miss Ley vowed he was the last person upon this earth to wear mutton-chop whiskers. He was very red cheeked, and by his size, joviality, and florid complexion, gave an idea of unalterable health. With his shaven chin and his loud-voiced burliness he looked like a yeoman of the old school, before bad times and the spread of education had made the farmer a sort of cross between the city clerk and the Newmarket trainer. Dr. Ramsay's frock coat and top-hat, notwithstanding the habit of many years, sat uneasily upon him with the air of Sunday clothes upon an agricultural labourer. Miss Ley, who liked to find absurd descriptions of people, or to hit upon an apt comparison, had never been able exactly to suit him; and that somewhat irritated her. In her eyes the only link that connected the doctor with humanity was a certain love of antiquities, which had filled his house with old snuff-boxes, china, and other precious things: humanity, Miss Ley took to be a small circle of persons, mostly feminine, middle-aged, unattached, and of independent means, who travelled on the continent, read good literature and abhorred the vast majority of their fellow-creatures, especially when these shrieked philanthropically, thrust their religion in your face, or cultivated their muscle with aggressive ardour!

Dr. Ramsay ate his luncheon with an appetite that Miss Ley thought must be a great source of satisfaction to his butcher. She asked politely after his wife, to whom she secretly objected for her meek submission to the doctor. Miss Ley made a practice of avoiding those women who had turned themselves into mere shadows of their lords, more especially when their conversation was of household affairs; and Mrs. Ramsay, except on Sundays, when her mind was turned to the clothes of the congregation, thought of nothing beyond her husband's enormous appetite and the methods of subduing it.

They returned to the drawing-room and Dr. Ramsay began to tell Bertha about the property, who this tenant was and the condition of that farm, winding up with the pitiful state of the times and the impossibility of getting rents.

"And now, Bertha, what are you thinking of doing?" he asked.

This was the opportunity for which Bertha had been looking.

"I?" she said quietly—"Oh, I intend to get married."

Dr. Ramsay, opening his mouth, threw back his head and laughed immoderately.

"Very good indeed," he cried. "Ha, ha!"

Miss Ley looked at him with uplifted eyebrows.

"Girls are coming on nowadays," he said, with much amusement. "Why, in my time, a young woman would have been all blushes and downcast glances. If anyone had talked of marriage she would have prayed Heaven to send an earthquake to swallow her up."

"Fiddlesticks!" said Miss Ley.

Bertha was looking at Dr. Ramsay with a smile that she with difficulty repressed, and Miss Ley caught the expression.

"So you intend to be married, Bertha?" said the doctor, again laughing.

"Yes."

"When?" asked Miss Ley, who did not take Bertha's remark as merely playful.

Bertha was looking out the window, wondering when Edward would arrive.

"When?" she repeated, turning round. "This day four weeks!"

"What!" cried Dr. Ramsay, jumping up. "You don't mean to say you've found someone! Are you engaged? Oh, I see, I see. You've been having a little joke with me. Why didn't you tell me that Bertha was engaged all the time, Miss Ley?"

"My good doctor," answered Miss Ley, with great composure, "until this moment I knew nothing whatever about it. . . . I suppose we ought to offer our congratulations; it's a blessing to get them all over on one day."

Dr. Ramsay looked from one to the other with perplexity.

"Well, upon my word," he said, "I don't understand."

"Neither do I," replied Miss Ley, "but I keep calm."

"It's very simple," said Bertha. "I got engaged last night, and as I say, I mean to be married exactly four weeks from today—to Mr. Craddock."

"What!" cried Dr. Ramsay, jumping up in astonishment and causing the floor to quake in the most dangerous way. "Craddock! What d'you mean? Which Craddock?"

"Edward Craddock," replied Bertha coolly, "of Bewlie's Farm."

"Brrh!!" Dr. Ramsay's exclamation cannot be transcribed, but it sounded horrid! "The scroundrel! It's absurd. You'll do nothing of the sort."

Bertha looked at him with a gentle smile, but did not trouble to answer.

"You're very emphatic, dear doctor," said Miss Ley. "Who is this gentleman?"

"He isn't a gentleman," said Dr. Ramsay, purple with vexation.

"He's going to be my husband, Dr. Ramsay," said Bertha, compressing her lips in the manner which with Miss Ley had become habitual; and turned to that lady: "I've known him all my life, and father was a great friend of his father's. He's a gentleman-farmer."

"The definition of which," said Dr. Ramsay, "is a man who's neither a farmer nor a gentleman."

"I forget what your father was?" said Bertha, who remembered perfectly well.

"My father was a farmer," replied Dr. Ramsay, with some heat, "and, thank God! he made no pretence of being a gentleman. He worked with his own hands; I've seen him often enough with a pitchfork, turning over a heap of manure, when no one else was handy."

"I see," said Bertha.

"But my father can have nothing to do with it; you can't marry him because he's been dead these thirty years, and you can't marry me because I've got a wife already."

Miss Ley, amused at the doctor's bluntness, concealed a smile; but Bertha, getting rather angry, thought him singularly rude.

"And what have you against him?" she asked.

"If you want to make a fool of yourself, he's got no right to encourage you. He knows he isn't a fit match for you."

"Why not, if I love him?"

"Why not!" shouted Dr. Ramsay. "Because he's the son of a farmer—like I am—and you're Miss Ley of Court Leys. Because a man in that position without fifty pounds to his back doesn't make love on the sly to a girl with a fortune."

"Five thousand acres which pay no rent," murmured Miss Ley, who was always in opposition.

"You have nothing whatever against him," retorted Bertha; "you told me yourself that he had the very best reputation."

"I didn't know you were asking me with a view to matrimony."

"I wasn't. I care nothing for his reputation. If he were drunken and idle and dissolute I'd marry him, because I love him."

"My dear Bertha," said Miss Ley, "the doctor will have an apoplectic fit if you say such things."

"You told me he was one of the best fellows you knew, Dr. Ramsay," said Bertha.

"I don't deny it," cried the doctor, and his red cheeks really had in them a purple tinge that was quite alarming. "He knows his business and he works hard, and he's straight and steady."

"Good heavens, Doctor," cried Miss Ley, "he must be a miracle of rural excellence. Bertha would surely never have fallen in love with him if he were faultless."

"If Bertha wanted an agent," Dr. Ramsay proceeded, "I could recommend no one better, but as for marrying him—"

"Does he pay his rent?" asked Miss Ley.

"He's one of the best tenants we've got," growled the doctor, somewhat annoyed by Miss Ley's frivolous interruptions.

"Of course in these bad times," added Miss Ley, who was determined not to allow Dr. Ramsay to play the heavy father with too much seriousness, "I suppose about the only resource of the respectable farmer is to marry his landlady."

"Here he is!" interrupted Bertha.

"Good God, is he coming here?" cried her guardian.

"I sent for him. Remember he is going to be my husband."

"I'm damned if he is!" said Dr. Ramsay.

Chapter IV

BERTHA THREW OFF HER TROUBLED LOOKS AND THE VEXATION WHICH THE argument had caused her. She blushed charmingly as the door opened, and with the entrance of the fairy prince her face was wreathed in smiles. She went towards him and took his hands.

"Aunt Polly," she said, "this is Mr. Edward Craddock. . . . Dr. Ramsay you know."

He shook hands with Miss Ley and looked at the doctor, who promptly turned his back on him. Craddock flushed, and sat down by Miss Ley.

"We were talking about you, dearest," said Bertha. The pause at his arrival had been disconcerting, and while Craddock was rather nervously thinking of something to say, Miss Ley made no effort to help him. "I have told Aunt Polly and Dr. Ramsay that we intend to be married four weeks from today."

This was the first that Craddock had heard of the date, but he showed no particular astonishment. He was, in fact, trying to recall the speech which he had composed for the occasion.

"I will try to be a good husband to your niece, Miss Ley," he began.

But that lady interrupted him: she had already come to the conclusion that he was a man likely to say on a given occasion the sort of thing which might be expected; and that, in her eyes, was a hideous crime.

"Oh yes, I have no doubt," she replied. "Bertha, as you know, is her own mistress, and responsible for her acts to no one."

Craddock was a little embarrassed; he had meant to express his sense of unworthiness and his desire to do his duty, also to make clear his own position, but Miss Ley's remark seemed to prohibit further explanation.

"Which is really very convenient," said Bertha, coming to his rescue, "because I have a mind to manage my life in my own way, without interference from anybody."

Miss Ley wondered whether the young man looked upon Bertha's statement as auguring complete tranquillity in the future, but Craddock seemed to see in it nothing ominous; he looked at Bertha with a grateful smile, and the glance which she returned was full of the most passionate devotion.

Since his arrival Miss Ley had been observing Craddock with great minuteness, and, being a woman, could not help finding some pleasure in the knowledge that Bertha was trying with anxiety to discover her judgment. Craddock's appearance was prepossessing. Miss Ley liked young men generally, and this was a very good-looking member of the species. His eyes were good, but otherwise there was nothing remarkable in the physiognomy—he looked healthy and good-tempered. Miss Ley noticed even that he did not bite his nails, and that his hands were strong and firm. There was really nothing to distinguish him from the common run of healthy young Englishmen, with good morals and fine physique; but the class is pleasant. Miss Ley's only wonder was that Bertha had chosen him rather than ten thousand others of the same variety, for that Bertha had chosen him somewhat actively there was in Miss Ley's mind not the shadow of a doubt.

Miss Ley turned to him.

"Has Bertha shown you our chickens?" she asked, calmly.

"No," he said, surprised at the question; "I hope she will."

"Oh, no doubt. You know I am quite ignorant of agriculture. Have you ever been abroad?"

"No, I stick to my own country," he replied; "it's good enough for me."

"I dare say it is," said Miss Ley, looking to the ground. "Bertha must certainly show you our chickens. They interest me because they're very like human beings—they're so stupid."

"I can't get mine to lay at all at this time of year," said Craddock.

"Of course I'm not an agriculturist," repeated Miss Ley, "but chickens amuse me."

Dr. Ramsay began to smile, and Bertha flushed angrily.

"You have never shown any interest in the chickens before, Aunt Polly."

"Haven't I, my dear? Don't you remember last night I remarked how tough was that one we had for dinner? . . . How long have you known Bertha, Mr. Craddock?"

"It seems all my life," he replied. "And I want to know her more."

This time Bertha smiled, and Miss Ley, though she felt certain the repartee was unintentional, was not displeased with it.

All this time Dr. Ramsay was not saying a word, and his behaviour aroused Bertha's anger.

"I have never seen you sit for five minutes in silence before, Dr. Ramsay," she said.

"I think what I have to say would scarcely please you, Miss Bertha."

Miss Ley was anxious that no altercation should disturb the polite discomfort of the meeting.

"You're thinking about those rents again, doctor," she said, and turning to Craddock: "The poor doctor is unhappy because half of our tenants say they cannot pay."

The poor doctor grunted and sniffed, and Miss Ley thought it was high time for the young man to take his leave. She looked at Bertha, who quickly understood, and getting up, said—

"Let us leave them alone, Eddie; I want to show you the house."

He rose with alacrity, evidently much relieved at the end of the ordeal. He shook Miss Ley's hand, and this time could not be restrained from making a little speech.

"I hope you're not angry with me for taking Bertha away from you. I hope I shall soon get to know you better, and that we shall become great friends."

Miss Ley was taken aback, but really thought his effort not bad. It might have been worse, and at all events he had kept out of it references to the Almighty and to his duty! Then Craddock turned to Dr. Ramsay, and went up to him with an outstretched hand that could not be refused.

"I should like to see you sometime, Dr. Ramsay," he said, looking at him steadily. "I fancy you want to have a talk with me, and I should like it too. When can you give me an appointment?"

Bertha flushed with pleasure at his frank words, and Miss Ley was pleased at the courage with which he had attacked the old curmudgeon.

"I think it would be a very good idea," said the doctor. "I can see you tonight at eight."

"Good! Good-bye, Miss Ley."

He went out with Bertha.

Miss Ley was not one of those persons who consider it indiscreet to form an opinion upon small evidence. Before knowing a man for five minutes she made up her mind about him, and liked nothing better than to impart her impression to any that asked her.

"Upon my word, doctor," she said, as soon as the door was shut, "he's not so terrible as I expected."

"I never said he was not good-looking," pointedly answered Dr. Ramsay, who was convinced that any and every woman was willing to make herself a fool with a handsome man.

Miss Ley smiled. "Good looks, my dear doctor, are three parts of the necessary equipment in the battle of life. You can't imagine the miserable existence of a really plain girl."

"Do you approve of Bertha's ridiculous idea?"

"To tell you the truth, I think it makes very little difference if you and I approve or not; therefore we'd much better take the matter quietly."

"You can do what you like, Miss Ley," replied the doctor very bluntly, "but I mean to stop the business."

"You won't, my dear doctor," said Miss Ley, smiling again. "I know Bertha so much better than you. I've lived with her for three years, and I've found constant entertainment in the study of her character. . . . Let me tell you how I first knew her. Of course you know that her father and I hadn't been on speaking terms for years. Having played ducks and drakes with his own money, he wanted to play the same silly game with mine; and as I strongly objected he flew into a violent passion, called me an ungrateful wretch, and nourished the grievance to the end of his days. Well, his health broke down after his wife's death, and he spent several years with Bertha wandering about the continent. She was educated as best could be, in half a dozen countries, and it's a marvel to me that she is not entirely ignorant or entirely vicious. She's a brilliant example in favour of the opinion that the human race is inclined to good rather than to evil."

Miss Ley smiled, for she was herself convinced of precisely the opposite.

"Well, one day," she proceeded, "I got a telegram, sent through my solicitors: 'Father dead, please come if convenient.—Bertha Ley.' It was addressed from Naples and I was in Florence. Of course I rushed down, taking nothing but a bag, a few yards of crape, and some smelling-salts. I was met at the station by Bertha, whom I hadn't seen for ten years; I saw a tall and handsome young woman, very self-possessed, and admirably gowned in the very latest fashion. I kissed her in a subdued way, proper to the occasion; and as we drove back, inquired when the funeral was to be, holding the smelling-salts in readiness for an outburst of weeping. 'Oh, it's all over,' she said. 'I didn't send my wire till everything was settled; I thought it would only upset you. I've given notice to the landlord of the villa and to the servants. There was really no need for you to come at all, only the doctor and the English parson seemed to think it rather queer of me to be here alone.' I used the smelling-salts myself! Imagine my emotion; I expected to find a hobbledehoy of a girl in hysterics, everything topsy-turvy and all sorts of horrid things to do; instead of which I found everything arranged perfectly well and the hobbledehoy rather disposed to manage me if I let her. At luncheon she looked at my travelling dress. 'I suppose you left Florence in a hurry,' she remarked. 'If you want to get anything black, you'd better go to my dressmaker; she's not bad. I must go there this afternoon myself to try some things on.' "

Miss Ley stopped and looked at the doctor to see the effect of her words. He said nothing.

"And the impression I gained then," she added, "has only been strengthened since. You'll be a very clever man if you prevent Bertha from doing a thing upon which she has set her mind."

"D'you mean to tell me that you're going to sanction the marriage?"

Miss Ley shrugged her shoulders. "My dear Dr. Ramsay, I tell you it won't make the least difference whether we bless or curse. And he seems an average sort of young man—let us be thankful that she's done no worse. He's not uneducated."

"No, he's not that. He spent ten years at Regis School, Tercanbury; so he ought to know something."

"What was exactly his father?"

"His father was the same as himself—a gentleman-farmer. He'd been educated at Regis School, as his son was. He knew most of the gentry, but he wasn't quite one of them; he knew all the farmers and he wasn't quite one of them either. And that's what they've been for generations, neither flesh, fowl, nor good red herring."

"It's those people that the newspapers tell us are the backbone of the country, Dr. Ramsay."

"Let 'em remain in their proper place then, in the back," said the doctor. "You can do as you please, Miss Ley; I'm going to put a stop to the business. After all, old Mr. Ley made me the girl's guardian, and though she is twenty-one I think it's my duty to see that she doesn't fall into the hands of the first penniless scamp who asks her to marry him."

"You can do as *you* please," retorted Miss Ley, who was a little bored. "You'll do no good with Bertha."

"I'm not going to Bertha; I'm going to Craddock direct, and I mean to give him a piece of my mind."

Miss Ley shrugged her shoulders. Dr. Ramsay evidently did not see who was the active party in the matter, and she did not feel it her duty to inform him.

"The question is," she said quietly, "can she marry anyone worse? I must say I'm quite relieved that Bertha doesn't want to marry a creature from Bayswater."

The doctor took his leave, and in a few minutes Bertha joined Miss Ley. The latter obviously intended to make no efforts to disturb the course of true love.

"You'll have to be thinking of ordering your trousseau, my dear," she said, with a dry smile.

"We're going to be married quite privately," answered Bertha. "We neither of us want to make a fuss."

"I think you're very wise. Of course most people, when they get married, fancy they're doing a very original thing. It never occurs to them that quite a number of persons have committed matrimony since Adam and Eve."

"I've asked Edward to luncheon tomorrow," said Bertha.

Chapter V

NEXT DAY, AFTER LUNCHEON, MISS LEY RETIRED TO THE DRAWING-ROOM and unpacked the books which had just arrived from Mudie. She looked through them, and read a page here and there to see what they were like, thinking meanwhile of the meal they had just finished. Edward Craddock had been somewhat nervous, sitting uncomfortably on his chair, too officious, perhaps, in handing things to Miss Ley, salt and pepper and the like, as he saw she wanted them. He evidently wished to make himself amiable. At the same time he was subdued, and not gaily enthusiastic as might be expected from a happy lover. Miss Ley could not help asking herself if he really loved her niece. Bertha was obviously without a doubt on the subject. She had been radiant, keeping her eyes all the while fixed upon the young man as if he were the most delightful and wonderful object she had ever seen. Miss Ley was surprised at the girl's expansiveness, contrasting with her old reserve. She seemed now not to care a straw if all the world saw her emotions. She was not only happy to be in love, she was proud also. Miss Ley laughed aloud at the doctor's idea that he could disturb the course of such passion. . . . But if Miss Ley, well aware that the watering-pots of reason could not put out those raging fires, had no intention of hindering the match, neither had she a desire to witness the preliminaries thereof; and after luncheon, remarking that she felt tired and meant to lie down, went into the drawing-room alone. It pleased her to think she could at the same time suit the lovers' pleasure and her own convenience.

She chose that book from the bundle which seemed most promising, and began to read. Presently the door was opened by a servant, and Miss Glover was announced. An expression of annoyance passed over Miss Ley's face but was immediately succeeded by one of mellifluous amiability.

"Oh, don't get up, dear Miss Ley," said the visitor, as her hostess slowly rose from the sofa.

Miss Ley shook hands and began to talk. She said she was delighted to see Miss Glover, thinking meanwhile that this estimable person's sense of etiquette was very tedious. The Glovers had dined at Court Leys during the previous week, and punctually seven days afterwards Miss Glover was paying a ceremonious call.

Miss Glover was a worthy person, but dull; and that Miss Ley could not forgive. Better ten thousand times, in her opinion, was it to be Becky Sharp and a monster of wickedness than Amelia and a monster of stupidity.

"*Pardon me, Madam, it is well known that Thackeray, in Amelia, gave us a type* of the pure-hearted, sweet-minded English maiden, whose qualities are the foundation of the greatness of Great Britain, and the superiority of the Anglo-Saxon race."

"I have no doubt that such was his intention. But why do you think novelists, when they draw the average English girl, should invariably produce an utter fool?"

"Madam, Madam, this is heresy."

"No, sir, it is merely a question—prompted by a desire for information."

"It must be their want of skill."

"I hope so."

Miss Glover was one of the best natured and most charitable creatures upon the face of the earth, a miracle of abnegation and unselfishness; but a person to be amused by her could have been only an absolute lunatic.

"She's really a dear kind thing," said Miss Ley of her, "and she does endless good in the parish—but she's really too dull: she's only fit for heaven!"

And the image passed through Miss Ley's mind, unsobered by advancing years, of Miss Glover, with her colourless hair hanging down her back, wings, and a golden harp, singing hymns in a squeaky voice, morning, noon, and night. Indeed, the general conception of paradisaical costume suited Miss Glover very ill. She was a woman of about eight and twenty, but might have been any age between one score and two; you felt that she had always been the same and that years would have no power over her strength of mind. She had no figure, and her clothes were so stiff and unyielding as to give an impression of armour. She was nearly always dressed in a tight black jacket of ribbed cloth that was evidently most durable, the plainest of skirts, and strong, really strong boots! Her hat was suited for all weathers and she had made it herself! She never wore a veil, and her skin was dry and hard, drawn so tightly over the bones as to give her face extraordinary angularity; over her prominent cheek-bones was a red flush, the colour of which was not uniformly suffused, but with the capillaries standing out distinctly, forming a network. Her nose and mouth were what is politely termed of a determined character, her pale blue eyes slightly protruded. Ten years of East Anglian winds had blown all the softness from her face, and their bitter fury seemed to have bleached even her hair. One could not tell if this was brown and had lost its richness, or gold from which the shimmer had vanished; and the roots sprang from the cranium with a curious apartness, so that Miss Ley always thought how easy in her case it would be for the Recording Angel to number the hairs. But notwithstanding the hard, uncompromising exterior which suggested extreme determination, Miss Glover was so bashful, so absurdly self-conscious, as to blush at every opportunity; and in the presence of a stranger to go through utter misery from inability to think of a single word to say. At the same time she had the tenderest of hearts, sympathetic, compassionate; she overflowed with love and pity for her fellow-creatures. She was also excessively sentimental!

"And how is your brother?" asked Miss Ley.

Mr. Glover was the Vicar of Leanham, which was about a mile from Court Leys on the Tercanbury Road, and for him Miss Glover had kept house since his appointment to the living.

"Oh, he's very well. Of course he's rather worried about the dissenters. You know they're putting up a new chapel in Leanham; it's perfectly dreadful."

"Mr. Craddock mentioned the fact at luncheon."

"Oh, was he lunching with you? I didn't know you knew him well enough for that."

"I suppose he's here now," said Miss Ley; "he's not been in to say good-bye."

Miss Glover looked at her with some want of intelligence. But it was not to be expected that Miss Ley could explain before making the affair a good deal more complicated.

"And how is Bertha?" asked Miss Glover, whose conversation was chiefly concerned with inquiries about mutual acquaintance.

"Oh, of course, she's in the seventh heaven of delight."

"Oh!" said Miss Glover, not understanding at all what Miss Ley meant.

She was somewhat afraid of the elder lady. Even though her brother Charles said he feared she was worldly, Miss Glover could not fail to respect a woman who had lived in London and on the continent, who had met Dean Farrar and seen Miss Marie Corelli.

"Of course," she said, "Bertha is young, and naturally high spirited."

"Well, I'm sure, I hope she'll be happy."

"You must be very anxious about her future, Miss Ley." Miss Glover found her hostess's observations simply cryptic, and, feeling foolish, blushed a fiery red.

"Not at all; she's her own mistress, and as able-bodied and as reasonably-minded as most young women. But, of course, it's a great risk."

"I'm very sorry, Miss Ley," said the vicar's sister, in such distress as to give her friend certain qualms of conscience, "but I really don't understand. What is a great risk?"

"Matrimony, my dear."

"Is Bertha going to be married? Oh, dear Miss Ley, let me congratulate you. How happy and proud you must be!"

"My dear Miss Glover, please keep calm. And if you want to congratulate anybody, congratulate Bertha—not me."

"But I'm so glad, Miss Ley. To think of dear Bertha getting married; Charles will be so pleased."

"It's to Mr. Edward Craddock," drily said Miss Ley, interrupting these transports.

"Oh!" Miss Glover's jaw dropped and she changed colour; then, recovering herself: "You don't say so!"

"You seem surprised, dear Miss Glover," said the elder lady, with a thin smile.

"I am surprised. I thought they scarcely knew one another; and besides—" Miss Glover stopped, with embarrassment.

"And besides what?" inquired Miss Ley, sharply.

"Well, Miss Ley, of course Mr. Craddock is a very good young man and I like him, but I shouldn't have thought him a suitable match for Bertha."

"It depends upon what you mean by a suitable match."

"I was always hoping Bertha would marry young Mr. Branderton of the Towers."

"Hm!" said Miss Ley, who did not like the neighbouring squire's mother, "I don't know what Mr. Branderton has to recommend him beyond the possession of four or five generations of particularly stupid ancestors and two or three thousand acres which he can neither let nor sell."

"Of course Mr. Craddock is a very worthy young man," added Miss Glover, who was afraid she had said too much. "If you approve of the match no one else can complain."

"I don't approve of the match, Miss Glover, but I'm not such a fool as to oppose it. Marriage is always a hopeless idiocy for a woman who has enough money of her own to live upon."

"It's an institution of the Church, Miss Ley," replied Miss Glover, rather severely.

"Is it?" retorted Miss Ley. "I always thought it was an arrangement to provide work for the judges in the Divorce Court."

To this Miss Glover very properly made no answer.

"Do you think they'll be happy together?"

"I think it very improbable," said Miss Ley.

"Well, don't you think it's your duty—excuse my mentioning it, Miss Ley—to do something?"

"My dear Miss Glover, I don't think they'll be more unhappy than most married couples; and one's greatest duty in this world is to leave people alone."

"There I cannot agree with you," said Miss Glover, bridling. "If duty was not more difficult than that there would be no credit in doing it."

"Ah, my dear, your idea of a happy life is always to do the disagreeable thing: mine is to gather the roses—with gloves on, so that the thorns should not prick me."

"That's not the way to win the battle, Miss Ley. We must all fight."

"My dear Miss Glover!" said Bertha's aunt.

She fancied it a little impertinent for a woman twenty years younger than herself to exhort her to lead a better life. But the picture of that poor, ill-dressed creature fighting with a devil, cloven-footed, betailed and behorned, was as pitiful as it was comic; and with difficulty Miss Ley repressed an impulse to argue and to startle a little her estimable friend.

But at that moment Dr. Ramsay came in. He shook hands with both ladies.

"I thought I'd look in to see how Bertha was," he said.

"Poor Mr. Craddock has another adversary," remarked Miss Ley. "Miss Glover thinks I ought to take the affair seriously."

"I do, indeed," said Miss Glover.

"Ever since I was a young girl," said Miss Ley, "I've been trying not to take things seriously, and I'm afraid now I'm hopelessly frivolous."

The contrast between this assertion and Miss Ley's prim manner was really funny, but Miss Glover saw only something quite incomprehensible.

"After all," added Miss Ley, "nine marriages out of ten are more or less unsatisfactory. You say young Branderton would have been more suitable; but really a string of ancestors is no particular assistance to matrimonial felicity, and otherwise I see no marked difference between him and Edward Craddock. Mr. Branderton has been to Eton and Oxford, but he conceals the fact with very great success. Practically he's just as much a gentleman-farmer as Mr. Craddock; but one family is working itself up and the other is working itself down. The Brandertons represent the past and the Craddocks the future; and though I detest reform and progress, so far as matrimony is concerned I prefer myself the man who founds a family to the man who ends it. But, good Heavens! you're making me sententious."

It was curious how opposition was making Miss Ley almost a champion of Edward Craddock.

"Well," said the doctor, in his heavy way, "I'm in favour of everyone sticking to his own class. Nowadays, whoever a man is he wants to be the next thing better; the labourer apes the tradesman, the tradesman apes the professional man."

"And the professional man is worst of all, dear doctor," said Miss Ley, "for he apes the noble lord, who seldom affords a very admirable example. And the amusing thing is that each set thinks itself quite as good as those above, while harbouring profound contempt for all below. In fact the only members of society who hold themselves in proper estimation are the servants. I always think that the domestics of gentlemen's houses in South Kensington are several degrees less odious than their masters."

This was not a subject which Miss Glover or Dr. Ramsay could discuss, and there was a momentary pause.

"What single point can you bring in favour of this marriage?" asked the doctor, suddenly.

Miss Ley looked at him as if she were thinking, then with a dry smile: "My dear doctor, Mr. Craddock is so matter of fact—the moon will never rouse him to poetic ecstasies."

"Miss Ley!" said the parson's sister, in a tone of entreaty.

Miss Ley glanced from one to the other. "Do you want my serious opinion?" she asked, rather more gravely than usual. "The girl loves him, my dear doctor. Marriage, after all, is such a risk that only passion makes it worthwhile."

Miss Glover looked up uneasily at the word *passion*.

"Yes, I know what you all think in England," said Miss Ley, catching the glance and its meaning. "You expect people to marry from every reason except the proper one—and that is the instinct of reproduction."

"Miss Ley!" exclaimed Miss Glover, blushing.

"Oh, you're old enough to take a sensible view of the matter," answered Miss Ley, somewhat brutally. "Bertha is merely the female attracted to the male, and that is the only decent foundation of marriage—the other way seems to me merely horrid. And what does it matter if the man is not of the same station, the instinct has nothing to do with the walk in life; if I'd ever been in love I shouldn't have cared if it was a pot-boy, I'd have married him—if he asked me."

"Well, upon my word!" said the doctor.

But Miss Ley was roused now, and interrupted him: "The particular function of a woman is to propagate her species; and if she's wise she'll choose a strong and healthy man to be the father of her children. I have no patience with those women who marry a man because he's got brains. What is the good of a husband who can make abstruse mathematical calculations? A woman wants a man with strong arms and the digestion of an ox."

"Miss Ley," broke in Miss Glover, "I'm not clever enough to argue with you, but I know you're wrong. I don't think I am right to listen to you; I'm sure Charles wouldn't like it."

"My dear, you've been brought up like the majority of English girls—that is, like a fool."

Poor Miss Glover blushed. "At all events I've been brought up to regard marriage as a holy institution. We're here upon earth to mortify the flesh, not to indulge it. I hope I shall never be tempted to think of such matters in the way you've suggested. If ever I marry I know that nothing will be further from me than carnal thoughts. I look upon marriage as a spiritual union in which it is my duty to love, honour, and obey my husband, to assist and sustain him, to live with him such a life that when the end comes we may be prepared for it."

"Fiddlesticks!" said Miss Ley.

"I should have thought you of all people," said Dr. Ramsay, "would object to Bertha marrying beneath her."

"They can't be happy," said Miss Glover.

"Why not? I used to know in Italy Lady Justitia Shawe, who married her footman. She made him take her name, and they drank like fishes. They lived for forty years in complete felicity, and when he drank himself to death poor Lady Justitia was so grieved that her next attack of *delirium tremens* carried her off. It was most pathetic."

"I can't think you look forward with pleasure to such a fate for your only niece, Miss Ley," said Miss Glover, who took everything seriously.

"I have another niece, you know," answered Miss Ley. "My sister, Mrs. Vaudrey, has three children."

But the doctor broke in: "Well, I don't think you need trouble yourselves about the matter, for I have authority to announce to you that the marriage of Bertha and young Craddock is broken off."

"What!" cried Miss Ley. "I don't believe it."

"You don't say so," ejaculated Miss Glover at the same moment. "Oh, I *am* relieved."

Dr. Ramsay rubbed his hands, beaming with delight. "I knew I should stop it," he said. "What do you think now, Miss Ley?"

He was evidently rejoicing over her discomfiture, and that lady became rather cross.

"How can I think anything till you explain yourself?" she asked.

"He came to see me last night—you remember he asked for an interview of his own accord—and I put the case before him. I talked to him, I told him that the marriage was impossible; and I said the Leanham and Blackstable people would call him a fortune-hunter. I appealed to him for Bertha's sake. He's an honest, straightforward fellow—I always said he was. I made him see he wasn't doing the straight thing, and at last he promised he'd break it off."

"He won't keep a promise of that sort," said Miss Ley.

"Oh, won't he!" cried the doctor. "I've known him all his life, and he'd rather die than break his word."

"Poor fellow!" said Miss Glover, "it must have pained him terribly."

"He bore it like a man."

Miss Ley pursed her lips till they practically disappeared. "And when is he supposed to carry out your ridiculous suggestion, Dr. Ramsay?" she asked.

"He told me he was lunching here today, and would take the opportunity to ask Bertha for his release."

"The man's a fool!" muttered Miss Ley to herself, but quite audibly.

"I think it's very noble of him," said Miss Glover, "and I shall make a point of telling him so."

"I wasn't thinking of Mr. Craddock," snapped Miss Ley.

Miss Glover looked at Dr. Ramsay to see how he took the rudeness; but at that moment the door was opened and Bertha walked in. Miss Ley caught her mood at a glance. Bertha was evidently not at all distressed; there were no signs of tears, but her cheeks showed more colour than usual, and her lips were firmly compressed; Miss Ley concluded that her niece was in a very pretty passion. However, she drove away the appearance of anger, and her face was full of smiles as she greeted her visitors.

"Miss Glover, how kind of you to come. How d'you do, Dr. Ramsay? . . . Oh, by the way, I think I must ask you—er—not to interfere in future with my private concerns."

"Dearest," broke in Miss Glover, "it's all for the best."

Bertha turned to her and the flush on her face deepened: "Ah, I see you've been discussing the matter. How good of you! Edward has been asking me to release him."

Dr. Ramsay nodded with satisfaction.

"But I refused!"

Dr. Ramsay sprang up, and Miss Glover, lifting her hands, cried: "Oh, dear! Oh, dear!" This was one of the rare occasions in her life upon which Miss Ley was known to laugh outright.

Bertha now was simply beaming with happiness. "He pretended that he wanted to break the engagement—but I utterly declined."

"D'you mean to say you wouldn't let him go when he asked you?" said the doctor.

"Did you think I was going to let my happiness be destroyed by you?" she asked, contemptuously. "I found out that you had been meddling, Dr. Ramsay. Poor boy, he thought his honour required him not to take advantage of my inexperience; I told him, what I've told him a thousand times, that I love him, and that I can't live without him. . . . Oh, I think you ought to be ashamed of yourself, Dr. Ramsay. What d'you mean by coming between me and Edward?"

Bertha said the last words passionately, breathing hard. Dr. Ramsay was taken aback, and Miss Glover, thinking such a manner of speech almost unlady-like, looked down. Miss Ley's sharp eyes played from one to the other.

"Do you think he really loves you?" said Miss Glover, at last. "It seems to me that if he had, he would not have been so ready to give you up."

Miss Ley smiled; it was certainly curious that a creature of quite angelic goodness should make so Machiavellian a suggestion.

"He offered to give me up because he loved me," said Bertha, proudly. "I adore him ten thousand times more for the suggestion."

"I have no patience with you," cried the doctor, unable to contain himself. "He's marrying you for your money."

Bertha gave a little laugh. She was standing by the fire and turned to the glass. . . . She looked at her hands, resting on the edge of the chimney-piece, small and exquisitely modelled, the fingers tapering, the nails of the softest pink. They were the gentlest hands in the world, made for caresses; and, conscious of their beauty, she wore no rings. With them Bertha was well satisfied. Then, raising her glance, she saw herself in the mirror: for a while she gazed into her dark eyes, flashing sometimes and at others conveying the burning messages of love. She looked at her ears—small, and pink like a shell; they made one feel that no materials were so grateful to the artist's hands as the materials which make up the body of man. Her hair was dark too, so abundant that she scarcely knew how to wear it, curling; one wanted to pass one's hands through it, imagining that its touch must be delightful. She put her fingers to one side, to arrange a stray lock: they might say what they liked, she thought, but her hair was good. Bertha wondered why she was so dark; her olive skin suggested, indeed, the south with its burning passion: she had the complexion of the fair women in Umbria, clear and soft beyond description. A painter once had said that her skin had in it all the colour of the setting sun, of the setting sun at its borders where the splendour mingles with the sky; it had an hundred mellow tints, cream and ivory, the palest yellow of the heart of roses and the faintest, the very faintest green, all flushed with radiant light. She looked at her full, red lips, almost passionately sensual. Bertha smiled at herself, and saw the even, glistening teeth; the scrutiny had made her blush, and the colour rendered still more exquisite the pallid, marvellous complexion. She turned slowly and faced the three persons looking at her.

"Do you think it impossible for a man to love me for myself? You are not flattering, dear doctor."

Miss Ley thought Bertha certainly very bold thus to challenge the criticism of two women, both unmarried; but she silenced it. Miss Ley's eyes went from the statuesque neck to the arms as finely formed, and to the figure.

"You're looking your best, my dear," she said, with a smile.

The doctor uttered an expression of annoyance: "Can you do nothing to hinder this madness, Miss Ley?"

"My dear Dr. Ramsay, I have trouble enough in arranging my own life; do not ask me to interfere with other people's."

Chapter VI

BERTHA SURRENDERED HERSELF COMPLETELY TO THE ENJOYMENT OF HER love. Her sanguine temperament never allowed her to do anything half-heartedly, and she took no care now to conceal her feelings; love was a great sea into which she boldly plunged, uncaring whether she would swim or sink.

"I am such a fool," she told Craddock, "I can't realise that anyone has loved before. I feel that the world is only now beginning."

She hated any separation from him. In the morning she existed for nothing but her lover's visit at luncheon time, and the walk back with him to his farm; then the afternoon seemed endless, and she counted the hours that must pass before she saw him again. But what bliss it was when, after his work was over, he arrived, and they sat side by side near the fire, talking; Bertha would have no other light than the fitful flaming of the coals, so that, but for the little space where they sat, the room was dark, and the redness of the fire threw on Edward's face a glow and weird shadows. She loved to look at him, at his clean-cut features, and into his grey eyes. Then her passion knew no restraint.

"Shut your eyes," she whispered, and she kissed the closed lids; she passed her lips slowly over his lips, and the soft contact made her shudder and laugh. She buried her face in his clothes, inhaling those masterful scents of the countryside which had always fascinated her.

"What have you been doing today, my dearest?"

"Oh, there's nothing much going on the farm just now. We've just been ploughing and root-carting."

It enchanted her to receive information on agricultural subjects, and she could have listened to him for hours. Every word that Edward spoke was charming and original. Bertha never took her eyes off him; she loved to see him speak, and often scarcely listened to what he said, merely watching the play of his expression. It puzzled him sometimes to catch her smile of intense happiness, when he was discussing the bush-drainage, for instance, of some field. However, she really took a deep interest in all his stock, and never failed to inquire after a bullock that was indisposed; it pleased her to think of the strong man among his beasts, and the thought gave a tautness to her own muscles. She determined to learn riding and tennis and golf, so that she might accompany him in his amusements; her own attainments seemed unnecessary and even humiliating. Looking at Edward Craddock she realised that man was indeed the lord of creation. She saw him striding over his fields with long steps, ordering his labourers here and there, able to direct their operations, fearless, brave, and free. It was astonishing how many excellent traits she derived from examination of his profile.

Then, talking of the men he employed, she could imagine no felicity greater than to have such a master.

"I should like to be a milkmaid on your farm," she said.

"I don't keep milkmaids," he replied. "I have a milkman; it's more useful."

"You dear old thing," she cried. "How matter of fact you are!"

She caught hold of his hands and looked at them.

"I'm rather frightened of you, sometimes," she said, laughing. "You're so strong. I feel so utterly weak and helpless beside you."

"Are you afraid I shall beat you?"

She looked up at him and then down at the strong hands.

"I don't think I should mind if you did. I think I should only love you more."

He burst out laughing and kissed her.

"I'm not joking," she said. "I understand now those women who love beasts of men. They say that some wives will stand anything from their husbands; they love them all the more because they're brutal. I think I'm like that; but I've never seen you in a passion, Eddie. What are you like when you're angry?"

"I never am angry."

"Miss Glover told me that you had the best temper in the world. I'm terrified at all these perfections."

"Don't expect too much from me, Bertha. I'm not a model man, you know."

Of course she kissed him when he made remarks of such absurd modesty.

"I'm very pleased," she answered; "I don't want perfection. Of course you've got faults, though I can't see them yet. But when I do, I know I shall only love you better. When a woman loves an ugly man, they say the ugliness only makes him more attractive and I shall love your faults as I love everything that is yours."

They sat for a while without speaking, and the silence was even more entrancing than the speech. Bertha wished she could remain thus forever, resting in his arms. She forgot that soon Craddock would develop a healthy appetite and demolish a substantial dinner.

"Let me look at your hands," she said.

She loved them too. They were large and roughly made, hard with work and exposure, ten times pleasanter, she thought, than the soft hands of the townsman. She felt them firm and intensely masculine. They reminded her of a hand in an Italian Museum, sculptured in porphyry, but for some reason left unfinished; and the lack of detail gave the same impression of massive strength. His hands, too, might have been those of a demi-god or of an hero. She stretched out the long, strong fingers. Craddock, knowing her very little, looked with wonder and amusement. She caught his glance, and with a smile bent down to kiss the upturned palms. She wanted to abase herself before the strong man, to be low and humble before him. She would have been his handmaiden, and nothing could have satisfied her so much as to perform for him the most menial services. She knew not how to show the immensity of her passion.

It pleased Bertha to walk into Blackstable with her lover and to catch the people's stares, knowing how much the marriage interested them. What did she care if they were surprised at her choosing Edward Craddock, whom they had known all his life? She was proud of him, proud to be his wife.

One day, when it was very warm for the time of year, she was resting on a stile, while Craddock stood by her side. They did not speak, but looked at one another in ecstatic happiness.

"Look," said Craddock, suddenly. "There's Arthur Branderton."

He glanced at Bertha, then from side to side uneasily, as if he wished to avoid a meeting.

"He's been away, hasn't he?" asked Bertha. "I wanted to meet him." She was quite willing that all the world should see them. "Good-afternoon, Arthur!" she called out, as the youth approached.

"Oh! is it you, Bertha? Hulloa, Craddock!" He looked at Edward, wondering what he did there with Miss Ley.

"We've just been walking into Leanham, and I was tired."

"Oh!" Young Branderton thought it queer that Bertha should take walks with Craddock.

Bertha burst out laughing. "Oh, he doesn't know, Edward! He's the only person in the county who hasn't heard the news."

"What news?" asked Branderton. "I've been in Yorkshire for the last week at my brother-in-law's."

"Mr. Craddock and I are going to be married."

"Are you, by Jove!" cried Branderton; he looked at Craddock and then, awkwardly, offered his congratulations. They could not help seeing his astonishment, and Craddock flushed, knowing it due to the fact that Bertha had consented to marry a penniless beggar like himself, a man of no family. "I hope you'll invite me to the wedding," said the young man to cover his confusion.

"Oh, it's going to be very quiet—there will only be ourselves, Dr. Ramsay, my aunt, and Edward's best man."

"Then mayn't I come?" asked Branderton.

Bertha looked quickly at Edward; it had caused her some uneasiness to think that he might be supported by a person of no great consequence in the place. After all she was Miss Ley; and she had already discovered that some of her lover's friends were not too desirable. Chance offered her means of surmounting the difficulty.

"I'm afraid it's impossible," she said, in answer to Branderton's appeal, "unless you can get Edward to offer you the important post of best man."

She succeeded in making the pair thoroughly uncomfortable. Branderton had no great wish to perform that office for Edward—"of course, Craddock is a very good fellow, and a fine sportsman, but not the sort of chap you'd expect a girl like Bertha Ley to marry." And Edward, understanding the younger man's feelings, was silent.

But Branderton had some knowledge of polite society, and broke the momentary pause.

"Who is going to be your best man, Craddock?" he asked; he could do nothing else.

"I don't know—I haven't thought of it."

But Branderton, catching Bertha's eye, suddenly understood her desire and the reason of it.

"Won't you have me?" he said quickly. "I dare say you'll find me intelligent enough to learn the duties."

"I should like it very much," answered Craddock. "It's very good of you."

Branderton looked at Bertha, and she smiled her thanks; he saw she was pleased.

"Where are you going for your honeymoon?" he asked now, to make conversation.

"I don't know," answered Craddock. "We've hardly had time to think of it yet."

"You certainly are very vague in all your plans."

He shook hands with them, receiving from Bertha a grateful pressure, and went off.

"Have you really not thought of our honeymoon, foolish boy?" asked Bertha.

"No!"

"Well, I have. I've made up my mind and settled it all. We're going to Italy, and I mean to show you Florence and Pisa and Siena. It'll be simply heavenly. We won't go to Venice, because it's too sentimental; self-respecting people can't make love in gondolas at the end of the nineteenth century. . . . Oh, I long to be with you in the South, beneath the blue sky and the countless stars of night."

"I've never been abroad before," he said, without much enthusiasm.

But her fire was quite enough for two. "I know, I shall have the pleasure of unfolding it all to you. I shall enjoy it more than I ever have before; it'll be so new to you. And we can stay six months if we like."

"Oh, I couldn't possibly," he cried. "Think of the farm."

"Oh, bother the farm. It's our honeymoon, *Sposo mio*."

"I don't think I could possibly stay away more than a fortnight."

"What nonsense! We can't go to Italy for a fortnight. The farm can get on without you."

"And in January and February too, when all the lambing is coming on."

He did not want to distress Bertha, but really half his lambs would die if he were not there to superintend their entrance into this wicked world.

"But you must go," said Bertha. "I've set my heart upon it."

He looked down for a while, rather unhappily.

"Wouldn't a month do?" he asked. "I'll do anything you really want, Bertha."

But his obvious dislike to the suggestion cut Bertha's heart. She was only inclined to be stubborn when she saw he might resist her; and his first word of surrender made her veer round penitently.

"What a selfish beast I am!" she said. "I don't want to make you miserable, Eddie. I thought it would please you to go abroad, and I'd planned it all so well. . . . But we won't go; I hate Italy. Let's just go up to town for a fortnight, like two country bumpkins."

"Oh, but you won't like that."

"Of course I shall. I like everything you like. D'you think I care where we go so long as I'm with you? . . . You're not angry with me, darling, are you?"

Mr. Craddock was good enough to intimate that he was not.

Miss Ley, much against her will, had been driven by Miss Glover into working for some charitable institution, and was knitting babies' socks (as the smallest garments she could make) when Bertha told her of the altered plan: she dropped a stitch! Miss Ley was too wise to say anything, but she wondered if the world were coming to an end; Bertha's schemes were shattered like brittle glass, and she really seemed delighted. A month ago opposition would have made Bertha traverse seas and scale precipices rather than abandon an idea that she had got into her head. Verily, love is a prestidigitator who can change the lion into the lamb as easily as a handkerchief into a flower-pot! Miss Ley began to admire Edward Craddock.

He, on his way home after leaving Bertha, was met by the Vicar of Leanham. Mr. Glover was a tall man, angular, fair, thin and red-cheeked—a somewhat feminine edition of his sister, but smelling in the most remarkable fashion of antiseptics; Miss Ley vowed he peppered his clothes with iodoform, and bathed daily in carbolic acid. He was strenuous and charitable, hated a Dissenter, and was over forty.

"Ah, Craddock, I wanted to see you."

"Not about the banns, Vicar, is it? We're going to be married by special licence."

Like many countrymen, Edward saw something funny in the clergy—one should not grudge it them, for it is the only jest in their lives—and he was given to treating the parson with more humour than he used in the other affairs of this world. The Vicar laughed; it is one of the best traits of the country clergy that they are willing to be amused with their parishioners' jocosity.

"The marriage is all settled then? You're a very lucky young man."

Craddock put his arm through Mr. Glover's with the unconscious friendliness that had gained him an hundred friends. "Yes, I am lucky," he said. "I know you people think it rather queer that Bertha and I should get married, but we're very much attached to one another, and I mean to do my best by her. You know I've never racketed about, Vicar, don't you?"

"Yes, my boy," said the Vicar, touched at Edward's confidence. "Everyone knows you're steady enough."

"Of course, she could have found men of much better social position than mine—but I'll try to make her happy. And I've got nothing to hide from her as some men have; I go to her almost as straight as she comes to me."

"That is a very fortunate thing to be able to say."

"I have never loved another woman in my life, and as for the rest—well, of course, I'm young and I've been up to town sometimes; but I always hated and loathed it. And the country and the hard work keep one pretty clear of anything nasty."

"I'm very glad to hear you say that," answered Mr. Glover. "I hope you'll be happy, and I think you will."

The Vicar felt a slight pricking of conscience, for at first his sister and himself had called the match a *mésalliance* (they pronounced the word vilely), and not till they learned it was inevitable did they begin to see that their attitude was a little wanting in charity. The two men shook hands.

"I hope you don't mind me spitting out these things to you, Vicar. I suppose it's your business in a sort of way. I've wanted to tell Miss Ley something of the kind; but somehow or other I can never get an opportunity."

Chapter VII

EXACTLY ONE MONTH AFTER HER TWENTY-FIRST BIRTHDAY, AS BERTHA HAD announced, the marriage took place; and the young couple started off to spend their honeymoon in London. Bertha, knowing she would not read, took with her notwithstanding a book, to wit the *Meditations of Marcus Aurelius*; and Edward, thinking that railway journeys were always tedious, bought for the occasion *The Mystery of the Six-fingered Woman*, the title of which attracted him. He was determined not to be bored, for, not content with his novel, he purchased at the station a *Sporting Times*.

"Oh," said Bertha, when the train had started, heaving a great sigh of relief, "I'm so glad to be alone with you at last. Now we shan't have anybody to worry us, and no one can separate us, and we shall be together for the rest of our lives."

Craddock put down the newspaper, which, from force of habit, he had opened after settling himself in his seat.

"I'm glad to have the ceremony over too."

"D'you know," she said, "I was terrified on the way to church; it occurred to me that you might not be there—that you might have changed your mind and fled."

He laughed. "Why on earth should I change my mind? That's a thing I never do."

"Oh, I can't sit solemnly opposite you as if we'd been married a century. Make room for me, boy."

She came over to his side and nestled close to him.

"Tell me you love me," she whispered.

"I love you very much."

He bent down and kissed his wife, then putting his arm around her waist drew her nearer to him. He was a little nervous, he would not really have been very sorry if some officious person had disregarded the *engaged* on the carriage and entered. He felt scarcely at home with Bertha, and was still bewildered by his change of fortune; there was, indeed, a vast difference between Court Leys and Bewlie's Farm.

"I'm so happy," said Bertha. "Sometimes I'm afraid. . . . D'you think it can last, d'you think we shall always be as happy? I've got everything I want in the world, and I'm absolutely and completely content." She was silent for a minute, caressing his hands. "You will always love me, Eddie, won't you—even when I'm old and horrible?"

"I'm not the sort of chap to alter."

"Oh, you don't know how I adore you," she cried passionately. "*My* love will never alter, it is too strong. To the end of my days I shall always love you with all my heart. I wish I could tell you what I feel."

Of late the English language had seemed quite incompetent for the expression of her manifold emotions.

They went to a far more expensive hotel than they could afford. Craddock had prudently suggested something less extravagant, but Bertha would not hear of it; as Miss Ley she had been unused to the second-rate, and she was too proud of her new name to take it to any but the best hotel in London.

The more Bertha saw of her husband's mind, the more it delighted her. She loved the simplicity and the naturalness of the man; she cast off like a tattered silken cloak the sentiments with which for years she had lived, and robed herself in the sturdy homespun which so well suited her lord and master. It was charming to see his naïve enjoyment of everything. To him all was fresh and novel; he would explode with laughter at the comic papers, and in the dailies continually find observations which struck him for their profound originality. He was the unspoiled child of nature; his mind free from the million perversities of civilisation. To know him was in Bertha's opinion an education in all the goodness and purity, the strength and virtue of the Englishman!

They went often to the theatre, and it pleased Bertha to watch her husband's simple enjoyment. The pathetic passages of a melodrama, which made Bertha's lips curl with semi-amused contempt, moved him to facile tears; and in the darkness he held her hand to comfort her, imagining that his wife enjoyed the same emotions as himself. Ah, she wished she could; she hated the education of foreign countries, which, in the study of pictures and palaces and strange peoples, had released her mind from its prison of darkness, yet had destroyed half her illusions; now she would far rather have retained the plain and unadorned illiteracy, the ingenuous ignorance of the typical and creamy English girl. What is the use of knowledge? Blessed are the poor in spirit: all that a woman really wants is purity and goodness, and perhaps a certain acquaintance with plain cooking.

But the lovers, the injured heroine and the wrongly suspected hero, had bidden one another a heartrending good-bye, and the curtain descended to rapturous applause. Edward cleared his throat and blew his nose.

"Isn't it splendid?" he said, turning to his wife.

"You dear thing!" she whispered.

It touched her to see how deeply he felt it all. How clean and big and simple and good must be his heart! She loved him ten times more because his emotions were easily aroused. Ah yes, she abhorred the cold cynicism of the worldly-wise who sneer at the burning tears of the simple minded.

The curtain rose on the next act, and in his eagerness to see what was about to happen, Edward immediately ceased to listen to what Bertha was in the middle of saying, and gave himself over to the play. The feelings of the audience having been sufficiently harrowed, the comic relief was turned on. The funny man made jokes about various articles of clothing, tumbling over tables and chairs; and it charmed Bertha again to see her husband's open-hearted hilarity. It tickled her immensely to hear his peals of unrestrained laughter; he put his head back, and, with his hands to his sides, simply roared.

"He has a charming character," she thought.

Craddock had the strictest notions of morality, and absolutely refused to take his wife to a music-hall; Bertha had seen abroad many sights, the like of which Edward did not dream, but she respected his innocence. It pleased her to see the firmness with which he upheld his principles, and it somewhat amused her to be treated like a little schoolgirl. They went to all the theatres; Edward, on his rare visits to London, had done his sight-seeing economically, and the purchase of stalls, the getting into dress-clothes, were new sensations which caused him great pleasure. Bertha liked to see her husband in evening dress; the black suited his florid style, and the white shirt with a high collar threw up his sunburned, weather-beaten face. He looked strong above all things, and manly; and he was her husband, never to be parted from her except by death: she adored him.

Craddock's interest in the stage was unflagging; he always wanted to know what was going to happen, and he was able to follow with the closest attention even the incomprehensible plot of a musical comedy. Nothing bored him. Even the most ingenuous find a little cloying the humours and the harmonies of a Gaiety burlesque; they are like toffee and butterscotch, delicacies for which we cannot understand our youthful craving. Bertha had learned something of music in lands where it is cultivated as a pleasure rather than as a duty, and the popular melodies with obvious refrains sent cold shivers down her back; but they stirred Craddock to the depths of his soul. He beat time to the swinging, vulgar tunes, and his face was transfigured when the band played a patriotic march with a great braying of brass and beating of drums. He whistled and hummed it for days afterwards.

"I love music," he told Bertha in the *entracte*. "Don't you?"

With a tender smile she confessed she did, and for fear of hurting Edward's feelings did not suggest that the music in question made her almost vomit. What mattered it if his taste in that respect were not beyond reproach; after all there was something to be said for the honest, homely melodies that touched the people's heart. It is only by a convention that the *Pastoral Symphony* is thought better art than *Tarara-boom-deay*. Perhaps, in two or three hundred years, when everything is done by electricity and everyone is equal, when we are all happy socialists, with good educations and better morals, Beethoven's complexity will be like a mass of wickedness, and only the plain, honest homeliness of the comic song will appeal to our simple feelings.

"When we get home," said Craddock, "I want you to play to me; I'm so fond of it."

"I shall love to," she murmured. She thought of the long winter evenings which they would spend at the piano, her husband by her side to turn the leaves, while to his astonished ears she unfolded the manifold riches of the great composers. She was convinced that his taste was really excellent.

"I have lots of music that my mother used to play," he said. "By Jove, I shall like to hear it again—some of those old tunes I can never hear often enough—*The Last Rose of Summer*, and *Home, Sweet Home*, and a lot more like that."

"By Jove, that show was ripping," said Craddock, when they were having supper; "I should like to see it again before we go back."

"We'll do whatever you like, my dearest."

"I think an evening like that does you good. It bucks me up; doesn't it you?"

"It does me good to see you amused," replied Bertha, diplomatically.

The performance had appeared to her vulgar, but in the face of her husband's enthusiasm she could only accuse herself of a ridiculous squeamishness. Why should she set herself up as a judge of these things? Was it not somewhat vulgar to find vulgarity in what gave such pleasure to the unsophisticated? She was like the *nouveau riche* who is distressed at the universal lack of gentility; but she was tired of analysis and subtlety, and all the concomitants of decadent civilisation.

"For goodness's sake," she thought, "let us be simple and easily amused."

She remembered the four young ladies who had appeared in flesh-coloured tights and nothing else worth mentioning, and danced a singularly ungraceful jig, which the audience, in its delight, had insisted on having twice repeated.

With no business to do and no friends to visit, there is some difficulty in knowing how to spend one's time in London. Bertha would have been content to sit all day with Edward in the private sitting-room, contemplating him and her extreme felicity. But Craddock had the fine energy of the Anglo-Saxon race, that desire to be always doing something which has made the English athletes, and missionaries, and members of Parliament.

After his first mouthful of breakfast he invariably asked, "What shall we do today?" And Bertha ransacked her brain and a *Baedeker* to find sights to visit, for to treat London as a foreign town and systematically to explore it was their only resource. They went to the Tower of London and gaped at the crowns and sceptres, at the insignia of the various orders; to Westminster Abbey and joined the party of Americans and country-folk who were being driven hither and thither by a black-robed verger; they visited the tombs of the kings and saw everything which it was their duty to see. Bertha developed a fine enthusiasm for the antiquities of London; she quite enjoyed the sensations of bovine ignorance with which the Cook's tourist surrenders himself into the hands of a custodian, looking as he is told and swallowing with open mouth the most unreliable information. Feeling herself more stupid, Bertha was conscious of a closer connection with her fellow-men. Edward did not like all things in an equal degree; pictures bored him (they were the only things that really did), and their visit to the National Gallery was not a success. Neither did the British Museum meet with his approval; for one thing, he had great difficulty in directing Bertha's attention so that her eyes should not wander to various naked statues which are exhibited there with no regard at all for the susceptibilities of modest persons. Once she stopped in front of a group that some shields and swords quite inadequately clothed, and remarked on their beauty. Edward looked about uneasily to see whether anyone noticed them, and agreeing briefly that they were fine figures, moved rapidly away to some less questionable object.

"I can't stand all this rot," he said, when they stood opposite the three goddesses of the Parthenon; "I wouldn't give twopence to come to this place again."

Bertha felt somewhat ashamed that she had a sneaking admiration for the statues in question.

"Now tell me," he said, "where is the beauty of those creatures without any heads?"

Bertha could not tell him, and he was triumphant. He was a dear, good boy and she loved him with all her heart!

The Natural History Museum, on the other hand, aroused Craddock to great enthusiasm. Here he was quite at home; no improprieties were there from which he must keep his wife, and animals were the sort of things that any man could understand. But they brought back to him strongly the country of East Kent and the life which it pleased him most to lead. London was all very well, but he did not feel at home, and it was beginning to pall upon him. Bertha also began talking of home and of Court Leys; she had always lived more in the future than in the present, and even in this, the time of her greatest happiness, looked forward to the days to come at Leanham, when complete felicity would indeed be hers.

She was contented enough now—it was only the eighth day of her married life, but she ardently wished to settle down and satisfy all her anticipations. They talked of the alterations they must make in the house, Craddock had already plans for putting the park in order, for taking over the Home Farm and working it himself.

"I wish we were home," said Bertha. "I'm sick of London."

"I don't think I should mind much if we'd got to the end of our fortnight," he replied.

Craddock had arranged with himself to stay in town fourteen days, and he could not alter his mind. It made him uncomfortable to change his plans and think out something new; he prided himself, moreover, on always doing the thing he had determined.

But a letter came from Miss Ley announcing that she had packed her trunks and was starting for the continent.

"Oughtn't we to ask her to stay on?" said Craddock. "It seems a bit rough to turn her out so quickly."

"You don't want to have her live with us, do you?" asked Bertha, in some dismay.

"No, rather not; but I don't see why you should pack her off like a servant with a month's notice."

"Oh, I'll ask her to stay," said Bertha, anxious to obey her husband's smallest wish; and obedience was easy, for she knew that Miss Ley would never dream of accepting the offer.

Bertha wished to see no one just then, least of all her aunt, feeling confusedly that her bliss would be diminished by the intrusion of an actor in her old life. Her emotions also were too intense for concealment, and she would have been ashamed to display them to Miss Ley's critical instinct. Bertha saw only discomfort in meeting the elder lady, with her calm irony and polite contempt for the things which on her husband's account Bertha most sincerely cherished.

But Miss Ley's reply showed perhaps that she guessed her niece's thoughts better than Bertha had given her credit for.

MY DEAREST BERTHA—I am much obliged to your husband for his politeness in asking me to stay at Court Leys; but I flatter myself you have too high an opinion of me to think me capable of accepting. Newly married people offer much matter for ridicule (which, they say, is the noblest characteristic of man, being the only one that distinguishes him from the brutes); but since I am a peculiarly self-denying creature, I do not avail myself of the opportunity. Perhaps in a year you will have begun to see one another's imperfections, and then, though less amusing, you will be more interesting. No, I am going to Italy—to hurl myself once more into that sea of pensions and second-rate hotels, wherein it is the fate of single women, with moderate incomes, to spend their lives; and I am taking with me a Baedeker, so that if ever I am inclined to think myself less foolish than the average man I may look upon its red cover and remember that I am but human. By the way, I hope you do not show your correspondence to your husband, least of all mine. A man can never understand a woman's epistolary communications, for he reads them with his own simple alphabet of twenty-six letters, whereas he requires one of at least fifty-two; and even that is little. It is madness for a happy pair to pretend to have no secrets from one another: it leads them into so much deception. If, however, as I suspect, you think it your duty to show Edward this note of mine, he will perhaps find it not unuseful for the elucidation of my character, in the study of which I myself have spent many entertaining years.

I give you no address so that you may not be in want of an excuse to leave this letter unanswered.—Your affectionate Aunt,

MARY LEY

Bertha impatiently tossed the letter to Edward.

"What does she mean?" he asked, when he had read it.

Bertha shrugged her shoulders. "She believes in nothing but the stupidity of other people. . . . Poor woman, she has never been in love! But we won't have any secrets from one another, Eddie. I know that you will never hide anything from me, and I—What can I do that is not at your telling?"

"It's a funny letter," he replied, looking at it again.

"But we're free now, darling," she said. "The house is ready for us; shall we go at once?"

"But we haven't been here a fortnight yet," he objected.

"What does it matter? We're both sick of London; let us go home and start our life. We're going to lead it for the rest of our days, so we'd better begin it quickly. Honeymoons are stupid things."

"Well, I don't mind. By Jove, fancy if we'd gone to Italy for six weeks."

"Oh, I didn't know what a honeymoon was like. I think I imagined something quite different."

"You see I was right, wasn't I?"

"Of course you were right," she answered, flinging her arms round his neck; "you're always right, my darling. . . . Ah! you can't think how I love you."

Chapter VIII

THE KENTISH COAST IS BLEAK AND GREY BETWEEN LEANHAM AND BLACK-stable; through the long winter months the winds of the North Sea sweep down upon it, bowing the trees before them; and from the murky waters perpetually arise the clouds, and roll up in heavy banks. It is a country that offers those who live there, what they give: sometimes the sombre colours and the silent sea express only restfulness and peace; sometimes the chill breezes send the blood racing through the veins; but also the solitude can answer the deepest melancholy, or the cheerless sky a misery which is more terrible than death. The moment's mood seems always reproduced in the surrounding scenes, and in them may be found, as it were, a synthesis of the emotions. Bertha stood upon the high-road which ran past Court Leys, and from the height looked down upon the lands which were hers. Close at hand the only habitations were a pair of humble cottages, from which time and rough weather had almost effaced the obtrusiveness of human handiwork. They stood away from the road, among fruit trees—a part of nature and not a blot upon it, as Court Leys had never ceased to be. All around were fields, great stretches of ploughed earth and meadows of coarse herbage. The trees were few, and stood out here and there in the distance, bent before the wind. Beyond was Blackstable, straggling grey houses with a border of new villas built for the Londoners who came in summer; and the sea was dotted with the smacks of the fishing town.

Bertha looked at the scene with sensations that she had never known; the heavy clouds hung above her, shutting out the whole world, and she felt an invisible barrier between herself and all other things. This was the land of her birth out of which she, and her fathers before her, had arisen; they had their day, and one by one returned whence they came and became again united with the earth. She had withdrawn from the pomps and vanities of life to live as her ancestors had lived, ploughing the land, sowing and reaping; but her children, the sons of the future, would belong to a new stock, stronger and fairer than the old. The Leys had gone down into the darkness of death, and her children would bear another name. All these things she gathered out of the brown fields and the grey sea mist. She was a little tired and the physical sensation caused a mental fatigue so that she felt in her suddenly the weariness of a family that had lived too long; she knew she was right to choose new blood to mix with the old blood of the Leys. It needed freshness and youth, the massive strength of her husband, to bring life to the decayed race. Her thoughts wandered to her father, the dilettante who wandered through Italy in search of beautiful things and emotions which his native country could not give him; of Miss Ley, whose attitude towards life was a shrug of the shoulders and a well-bred smile of contempt. Was not she, the last of them, wise? Feeling herself too weak to stand alone, she had taken a mate whose will and vitality would be a pillar of strength to her defaillance: her husband had still in his sinews the might of his mother, the Earth, a barbaric power which knew not the subtleties of weakness; he was the conqueror, and she was his handmaiden. But an umbrella was being waved at Mrs. Craddock from the bottom of the hill, and she smiled, recognising the masculine walk of Miss Glover.

Even from a distance the maiden's determination and strength of mind were apparent; she approached, her face redder even than usual after the climb, encased in the braided jacket that fitted her as severely as sardines are fitted in their tin.

"I was coming to see you, Bertha," she cried. "I heard you were back."

"We've been home several days, getting to rights."

Miss Glover shook Bertha's hand with much vigour, and together they walked back to the house, along the avenue bordered with leafless trees.

"Now, do tell me all about your honeymoon, I'm so anxious to hear everything."

But Bertha was not very communicative, she had an instinctive dislike to telling her private affairs, and never had any overpowering desire for sympathy.

"Oh, I don't think there's much to tell," she answered, when they were in the drawing-room and she was pouring out tea for her guest. "I suppose all honeymoons are more or less alike."

"You funny girl," said Miss Glover. "Didn't you enjoy it?"

"Yes," said Bertha, with a smile that was almost ecstatic; then after a little pause: "We had a very good time—we went to all the theatres."

Miss Glover felt that marriage had caused a difference in Bertha, and it made her nervous to realise the change. She looked uneasily at the married woman and occasionally blushed.

"And are you really happy?" she blurted out suddenly. Bertha smiled, and reddening, looked more charming than ever.

"Yes—I think I'm perfectly happy."

"Aren't you sure?" asked Miss Glover, who cultivated precision in every part of life and strongly disapproved of persons who did not know their own minds.

Bertha looked at her for a moment, as if considering the question.

"You know," she answered, at last, "happiness is never quite what one expected it to be. I hardly hoped for so much; but I didn't imagine it quite like it is."

"Ah, well, I think it's better not to go into these things," replied Miss Glover, a little severely, thinking the suggestion of analysis scarcely suitable in a young married woman. "We ought to take things as they are, and be thankful."

"Ought we?" said Bertha lightly, "I never do. . . . I'm never satisfied with what I have."

They heard the opening of the front-door and Bertha jumped up.

"There's Edward! I must go and see him. You don't mind, do you?"

She almost skipped out of the room; marriage, curiously enough, had dissipated the gravity of manner which had made people find so little girlishness about her. She seemed younger, lighter of heart.

"What a funny creature she is!" thought Miss Glover. "When she was a girl she had all the ways of a married woman, and now that she's really married she might be a schoolgirl."

The parson's sister was not certain whether the irresponsibility of Bertha was fit to her responsible position, whether her unusual bursts of laughter were proper to a mystic state demanding gravity.

"I hope she'll turn out all right," she sighed.

But Bertha impulsively rushed to her husband and kissed him. She helped him off with his coat.

"I'm so glad to see you again," she cried, laughing a little at her own eagerness; for it was only after luncheon that he had left her.

"Is anyone here?" he asked, noticing Miss Glover's umbrella. He returned his wife's embrace somewhat mechanically.

"Come and see," said Bertha, taking his arm and dragging him along. "You must be dying for tea, you poor thing."

"Miss Glover!" he said, shaking the lady's hand as energetically as she shook his. "How good of you to come and see us. I *am* glad to see you. You see we came home sooner than we expected—there's no place like the country, is there?"

"You're right there, Mr. Craddock; I can't bear London."

"Oh, you don't know it," said Bertha; "for you it's Aerated Bread shops, Exeter Hall, and Church Congresses."

"Bertha!" cried Edward, in a tone of surprise; he could not understand frivolity with Miss Glover.

That good creature was far too kind-hearted to take offence at any remark of Bertha's, and smiled grimly: she could smile in no other way.

"Tell me what you did in London. I can't get anything out of Bertha."

Craddock's mind was communicative, nothing pleased him more than to give people information, and he was always ready to share his knowledge with the world at large. He never picked up a fact without rushing to tell it to somebody else. Some persons when they know a thing immediately lose interest and it bores them to discuss it, but Craddock was not of these. Nor could repetition exhaust his eagerness to enlighten his fellows, he would tell an hundred people the news of the day and be as fresh as ever when it came to the hundred and first. Such a characteristic is undoubtedly a gift, useful in the highest degree to schoolmasters and politicians, but slightly tedious to their hearers. Craddock favoured his guest with a detailed account of all their adventures in London, the plays they had seen, the plots thereof and the actors who played them. He gave the complete list of the museums and churches and public buildings they had visited, while Bertha looked at him, smiling happily at his enthusiasm. She cared little what he spoke of, the mere sound of his voice was music in her ears, and she would have listened delightedly while he read aloud from end to end *Whitaker's Almanack:* that was a thing, by the way, which he was quite capable of doing. Edward corresponded far more with Miss Glover's conception of the newly married man than did Bertha with that of the newly married woman.

"He is a nice fellow," she said to her brother afterwards, when they were eating their supper of cold mutton, solemnly seated at either end of a long table.

"Yes," answered the Vicar, in his tired, patient voice, "I think he'll turn out a good husband."

Mr. Glover was patience itself, which a little irritated Miss Ley, who liked a man of spirit; and of that Mr. Glover had never a grain. He was resigned to everything; he was resigned to his food being badly cooked, to the perversity of human nature, to the existence of dissenters (almost), to his infinitesmal salary; he was resignation driven to death. Miss Ley said he was like those Spanish donkeys that one sees plodding along in a string, listlessly bearing over-heavy loads—patient, patient, patient. But not so patient as Mr. Glover; the donkey sometimes kicked, the Vicar of Leanham never.

"I do hope it will turn out well, Charles," said Miss Glover.

"I hope it will," he answered; then after a pause: "Did you ask them if they were coming to church tomorrow?" He helped himself to mashed potatoes, noticing long-sufferingly that they were burned again; the potatoes were always burned, but he made no comment.

"Oh, I quite forgot," said his sister, answering the question. "But I think they're sure to. Edward Craddock was always a regular attendant."

Mr. Glover made no reply, and they kept silence for the rest of the meal. Immediately afterwards the parson went into his study to finish the morrow's sermon, and Miss Glover took out of her basket her brother's woollen socks and began to darn them. She worked for more than an hour, thinking meanwhile of the Craddocks; she liked Edward better and better each time she saw him, and she felt he was a man who could be trusted. She upbraided herself a little for her disapproval of the marriage; her action was unchristian, and she asked herself whether it was not her duty to apologise to Bertha or to Craddock; the thought of doing something humiliating to her own self-respect attracted her wonderfully. But Bertha was different from other girls; Miss Glover, thinking of her, grew confused.

But a tick of the clock to announce an hour about to strike made her look up, and she saw it wanted but five minutes to ten.

"I had no idea it was so late."

She got up and tidily put away her work, then taking from the top of the harmonium the Bible and the big prayer-book which were upon it, placed them at the end of the table. She drew forward a chair for her brother, and sat patiently to await his coming. As the clock struck she heard the study-door open, and the Vicar walked in. Without a word he went to the books, and sitting down, found his place in the Bible.

"Are you ready?" she asked.

He looked up one moment over his spectacles. "Yes."

Miss Glover leant forward and rang the bell—the servant appeared with a basket of eggs, which she placed on the table. Mr. Glover looked at her till she was settled on her chair, and began the lesson. Afterwards the servant lit two candles and bade them good-night. Miss Glover counted the eggs.

"How many are there today?" asked the parson.

"Seven," she answered, dating them one by one, and entering the number in a book kept for the purpose.

"Are you ready?" now asked Mr. Glover.

"Yes, Charles," she said, taking one of the candles.

He put out the lamp, and with the other candle followed her upstairs. She stopped outside her door and bade him good-night; he kissed her coldly on the forehead and they went into their respective rooms.

There is always a certain flurry in a country-house on Sunday morning. There is in the air a feeling peculiar to the day, a state of alertness and expectation; for even when they are repeated for years, week by week, the preparations for church cannot be taken coolly. The odour of clean linen is unmistakable, everyone is highly starched and somewhat ill-at-ease; the members of the household ask one another if they're ready, they hunt for prayer-books; the ladies are never dressed in time and sally out at last, buttoning their gloves; the men stamp and fume and take out their watches. Edward, of course, wore a tail-coat and a top-hat, which is quite the proper costume for the squire to go to church in, and no one gave more thought to the proprieties than Edward. He held himself very upright, cultivating the slightly self-conscious gravity considered fit to the occasion.

"We shall be late, Bertha," he said. "It will look so bad—the first time we come to church since our marriage, too."

"My dear," said Bertha, "you may be quite certain that even if Mr. Glover is so indiscreet as to start, for the congregation the ceremony will not really begin till we appear."

They drove up in an old-fashioned brougham used only for going to church and to dinner-parties, and the word was immediately passed by the loungers at the porch to the devout within; there was a rustle of attention as Mr. and Mrs. Craddock walked up the aisle to the front pew which was theirs by right.

"He looks at home, don't he?" murmured the natives, for the behaviour of Edward interested them more than that of his wife, who was sufficiently above them to be almost a stranger.

Bertha sailed up with a royal unconsciousness of the eyes upon her; she was pleased with her personal appearance, and intensely proud of her good-looking husband. Mrs. Branderton, the mother of Craddock's best man, fixed her eye-glass upon her and stared as is the custom of great ladies in the suburbs. Mrs. Branderton was a woman who cultivated the mode in the depths of the country, a little, giggling, grey-haired creature who talked stupidly in a high, cracked voice and had her too juvenile bonnets straight from Paris. She was a gentlewoman, and this, of course, is a very fine thing to be. She was proud of it (in quite a nice way), and in the habit of saying that gentlefolk were gentlefolk; which, if you come to think of it, is a most profound remark.

"I mean to go and speak to the Craddocks afterwards," she whispered to her son. "It will have a good effect on the Leanham people; I wonder if poor Bertha feels it yet."

Mrs. Branderton had a self-importance which was almost sublime; it never occurred to her that there might be persons sufficiently ill-conditioned as to resent her patronage. She did it all in kindness—she showered advice upon all and sundry, besides soups and jellies upon the poor, to whom when they were ill she even sent her cook to read the Bible. She would have gone herself, only she strongly disapproved of familiarity with the lower classes, which made them independent and often rude. Mrs. Branderton knew without possibility of question that she and her equals were made of different clay from common-folk; but, being a gentlewoman, did not throw this fact in the latters' faces, unless, of course, they gave themselves airs, when she thought a straight talking-to did them good. Without any striking advantages of birth, money, or intelligence, Mrs. Branderton never doubted her right to direct the affairs and fashions, even the modes of thought of her neighbours; and by sheer force of self-esteem had caused them to submit for thirty years to her tyranny, hating her and yet looking upon her invitations to a bad dinner, as something quite desirable.

Mrs. Branderton had debated with herself how she should treat the Craddocks.

"I wonder if it's my duty to cut them," she said. "Edward Craddock is *not* the sort of man a Miss Ley ought to marry. But there are so few gentlefolk in the neighbourhood, and of course people do make marriages which they wouldn't have dreamed of twenty years ago. Even the best society is very mixed nowadays. Perhaps I'd better err on the side of mercy!"

Mrs. Branderton was a little pleased to think that the Leys required her support—as was proved by the request of her son's services at the wedding.

"The fact is gentlefolk are gentlefolk, and they must stand by one another in these days of pork-butchers and furniture people."

After the service, when the parishioners were standing about the churchyard, Mrs. Branderton sailed up to the Craddocks followed by Arthur, and in her high, cracked voice began to talk with Edward. She kept an eye on the Leanham people to see that her action was being duly noticed, speaking to Craddock in the manner a gentlewoman should adopt with a man whose gentility was a little doubtful. Of course he was very much pleased and flattered.

Chapter IX

SOME DAYS LATER, AFTER THE DUE PRELIMINARIES WHICH MRS. BRANDERTON would on no account have neglected, the Craddocks received an invitation to dinner. Bertha silently passed it to her husband.

"I wonder who she'll ask to meet us," he said.

"D'you want to go?" asked Bertha.

"Why, don't you? We've got no engagement, have we?"

"Have you ever dined there before?" said Bertha.

"No. I've been to tennis-parties and that sort of thing, but I've hardly set foot inside their house."

"Well, I think it's an impertinence of her to ask you now."

Edward opened his mouth wide: "What on earth d'you mean?"

"Oh, don't you see?" cried his wife, "they're merely asking you because you're my husband. It's humiliating."

"Nonsense!" replied Edward, laughing. "And if they are, what do I care?—I'm not so thin-skinned as that. Mrs. Branderton was very nice to me the other Sunday; it would be funny if we didn't accept."

"Did you think she was nice? Didn't you see that she was patronising you as if you were a groom. It made me boil with rage. I could hardly hold my tongue."

Edward laughed again. "I never noticed anything. It's just your fancy, Bertha."

"I'm not going to her horrid dinner-party."

"Then I shall go by myself," he replied, laughing.

Bertha turned white; it was as if she had received a sudden blow; but he was laughing, of course he did not mean what he said. She hurriedly agreed to all he asked.

"Of course if you want to go, Eddie, I'll come too. . . . It was only for your sake that I did not wish to."

"We must be neighbourly. I want to be friends with everybody."

She sat on the side of his chair, putting her arm round his neck. Edward patted her hand and she looked at him with eyes full of eager love, she bent down and kissed his hair. How foolish had been her sudden thought that he did not love her!

But Bertha had another reason for not wishing to go to Mrs. Branderton. She knew Edward would be bitterly criticised, and the thought made her wretched; they would talk of his appearance and manner, and wonder how they got on together. Bertha understood well enough the position Edward occupied in Leanham; the Brandertons and their like, knowing him all his life, had treated him as a mere acquaintance: for them he had been a person to whom you are civil, and that is all. This was the first occasion upon which he had been dealt with entirely as an equal; it was his introduction into what Mrs. Branderton was pleased to call the upper ten of Leanham. It did indeed make Bertha's blood boil; and it cut her to the heart to think that for years he had been used in so infamous a fashion: he did not seem to mind.

"If I were he," she said, "I'd rather die than go. They've ignored him always, and now they take him up as a favour to me."

But Edward appeared to have no pride; of course his character was charming, and he could bear ill will to no one. He neither resented the former neglect of the Brandertons nor their present impertinence.

"I wish I could make him understand."

Bertha passed the intervening week in a tremor of anxiety. She divined who the other guests would be. Would they laugh at him? Of course not openly; Mrs. Branderton, the least charitable of them all, prided herself upon her breeding; but Edward was shy, and among strangers awkward. To Bertha this was a charm rather than a defect; his half-bashful candour touched her, and she compared it favourably with the foolish worldliness of the imaginary man-about-town, whose dissipations she always opposed to her husband's virtues. But she knew that a spiteful tongue would find another name for what she called a delightful *naïveté*.

When at last the great day arrived, and they trundled off in the old-fashioned brougham, Bertha was thoroughly prepared to take mortal offence at the merest shadow of a slight offered to her husband. The Lord Chief Justice himself could not have been more careful of a company promoter's fair name than was Mrs. Craddock of her husband's susceptibilities; Edward, like the financier, treated the affair with indifference.

Mrs. Branderton had routed out the whole countryside for her show of gentlefolk. They had come from Blackstable and Tercanbury and Faversley, and from the seats and mansions which surrounded those places. Mrs. Mayston Ryle was there in a wonderful jete-black wig, and a voluminous dress of violet silk. Lady Wagget was there.

"Merely the widow of a city knight, my dear," said the hostess to Bertha, "but if she isn't distinguished, she's good; so one mustn't be too hard upon her."

General Hancock arrived with two fuzzy-haired daughters, who were dreadfully plain, but pretended not to know it. They had walked; and while the soldier toddled in, blowing like a grampus, the girls (whose united ages made the respectable total of sixty-five years) stayed behind to remove their boots and put on the shoes which they had brought in a bag. Then, in a little while, came the Dean, meek and somewhat talkative; Mr. Glover had been invited for his sake, and of course Charles' sister could not be omitted. She was looking almost festive in very shiny black satin.

"Poor dear," said Mrs. Branderton to another guest, "it's her only dinner dress; I've seen it for years. I'd willingly give her one of my old ones, only I'm afraid I should offend her by offering it. People in that class are so ridiculously sensitive."

Mr. Atthill Bacot was announced; he had once contested the seat, and ever after been regarded as an authority upon the nation's affairs. Mr. James Lycett and Mr. Molson came next, both red-faced squires with dogmatic opinions; they were alike as two peas, and it had been the local joke for thirty years that no one but their wives could tell them apart. Mrs. Lycett was thin and quiet and staid, wearing two little strips of lace on her hair to represent a cap; Mrs. Molson was so insignificant that no one had ever noticed what she was like. It was one of Mrs. Branderton's representative gatherings; moral excellence was joined to perfect gentility and the result could not fail to edify. She was herself in high spirits and her cracked voice rang high and shrill. She was conscious of a successful costume; she really had much taste, and her frock would have looked charming on a woman half her age. Thinking also that it was part of woman's duty to be amiable, Mrs. Branderton smiled and ogled at the old gentlemen in a way that quite alarmed them, and Mr. Atthill Bacot really thought she had designs upon his virtue.

The dinner just missed being eatable. Mrs. Branderton was a woman of fashion and disdained the solid fare of a country dinner-party—thick soup, fried soles, mutton cutlets, roast mutton, pheasant, Charlotte russe, and jellies. (The earlier dishes are variable according to season, but the Charlotte russe and the jelly are inevitable.) No, Mrs. Branderton said she must be a little more "distangay" than that, and provided her guests with clear soup, *entrees* from the Stores, a fluffy sweet which looked pretty and tasted horrid. The feast was extremely elegant, but it was not filling, which is unpleasant to elderly squires with large appetites.

"I never get enough to eat at the Brandertons," said Mr. Atthill Bacot, indignantly.

"Well, I know the old woman," replied Mr. Molson. Mrs. Branderton was the same age as himself, but he was rather a dog, and thought himself quite young enough to flirt with the least plain of the two Miss Hancocks. "I know her well, and I make a point of drinking a glass of sherry with a couple of eggs beaten up in it before I come."

"The wines are positively immoral," said Mrs. Mayston Ryle, who prided herself on her palate. "I'm always inclined to bring with me a flask with a little good whisky in it."

But if the food was not heavy the conversation was. It is an axiom of narration that truth should coincide with probability, and the realist is perpetually hampered by the wild exaggeration of actual facts; a verbatim report of the conversation at

Mrs. Branderton's dinner-party would read like a shrieking caricature. The anecdote reigned supreme. Mrs. Mayston Ryle was a specialist in the clerical anecdote; she successively related the story of Bishop Thorold and his white hands, the story of Bishop Wilberforce and the bloody shovel. (This somewhat shocked the ladies, but Mrs. Mayston Ryle could not spoil her point by the omission of a swear word.) The Dean gave an anecdote about himself, to which Mrs. Mayston Ryle retorted with one about the Archbishop of Canterbury and the tedious curate. Mr. Atthill Bacot gave political anecdotes, Mr. Gladstone and the table of the House of Commons, Dizzy and the agricultural labourer. The climax came when General Hancock gave his celebrated stories about the Duke of Wellington. Edward laughed heartily at them all.

Bertha's eyes were constantly upon her husband. She detested the thoughts that ran through her head, for that they should come to her at all was disparaging to him; but still she was horribly anxious. Was he not perfect, and handsome, and adorable? Why should she tremble before the opinion of a dozen stupid people? But she could not help it. However much she despised her neighbours, she could not prevent herself from being miserably affected by their judgment. And what did Edward feel? Was he as nervous as she? She could not bear the thought that he should suffer pain. It was an immense relief when Mrs. Branderton rose from the table. Bertha looked at Arthur holding open the door; she would have given anything to ask him to look after Edward, but dared not. She was terrified lest, to his humiliation, those old squires should pointedly ignore him.

On reaching the drawing-room Miss Glover found herself by Bertha's side, a little separated from the others, and the accident seemed designed by higher powers to give her an opportunity for the amends which she felt it her duty to make Mrs. Craddock for her former disparagement of Edward. She had been thinking the matter over, and considered an apology distinctly needful. But Miss Glover suffered terribly from nervousness, and the idea of broaching so delicate a subject caused her indescribable torture; yet the very unpleasantness of it reassured her, if speech was so disagreeable, it must obviously be her duty. But the words stuck in her throat, and she began talking of the weather. She reproached herself for cowardice; she set her teeth and grew scarlet.

"Bertha, I want to beg your pardon," she blurted out suddenly.

"What on earth for?" Bertha opened her eyes wide and looked at the poor woman with astonishment.

"I feel I've been unjust to your husband. I thought he wasn't a proper match for you, and I said things about him which I shouldn't even have thought. I'm very sorry. He's one of the best and kindest men I've ever seen, and I'm very glad you married him, and I'm sure you'll be very happy."

Tears came to Bertha's eyes as she laughed; she felt inclined to throw her arms round the grim Miss Glover's neck, for such a speech at that moment was very comforting.

"Of course I know you didn't mean what you said."

"Oh yes, I did, I'm sorry to say," replied Miss Glover, who could allow no extenuation to her own crime.

"I'd quite forgotten all about it; and I believe you'll soon be as madly in love with Edward as I am."

"My dear Bertha," replied Miss Glover, who never jested, "with your husband? You must be joking."

But Mrs. Branderton interrupted them with her high voice.

"Bertha, dear, I want to talk to you." Bertha, smiling, sat down beside her, and Mrs. Branderton proceeded in undertones.

"I must tell you, everyone has been saying you're the handsomest couple in the county, and we all think your husband is so nice."

"He laughed at all your jokes," replied Bertha.

"Yes," said Mrs. Branderton, looking upwards and sideways like a canary, "he has such a merry disposition. But I've always liked him, dear. I was telling Mrs. Mayston Ryle that I've known him intimately ever since he was born. I thought it would please you to know that we all think your husband is nice."

"I'm very much pleased. I hope Edward will be equally satisfied with all of you."

The Craddock's carriage came early, and Bertha offered to drive the Glovers home.

"I wonder if that lady has swallowed a poker," said Mr. Molson, as soon as the drawing-room door was closed.

The two Miss Hancocks went into shrieks of laughter at this sally, and even the Dean smiled gently.

"Where did she get her diamonds from?" said the elder Miss Hancock. "I thought they were as poor as church mice."

"The diamonds and the pictures are the only things they have left," said Mrs. Branderton; "her family always refused to sell them; though, of course, it's absurd for people in that position to have such jewels."

"*He's* a remarkably nice fellow," said Mrs. Mayston Ryle in her deep, authoritative voice; "but I agree with Mr. Molson, she's distinctly inclined to give herself airs."

"The Leys for generations have been as proud as turkey-cocks," added Mrs. Branderton.

"I shouldn't have thought Mrs. Craddock had much to be proud of now, at all events," said the elder Miss Hancock; she had no ancestors herself, and thought people who had were snobs.

"Perhaps she was a little nervous," said Lady Waggett, who, though not distinguished, was good. "I know when I was a bride I used to be all of a tremble when I went to dinner-parties."

"Nonsense," said Mrs. Mayston Ryle. "She was extremely self-possessed; I don't think it looks well for a young woman to have so much assurance. And I think she ought to be told that it's hardly well bred for a young married woman to leave a house before anybody else as if she were royalty, when there are present women of a certain age and of a position undoubtedly not inferior to her own."

"Oh, they're so newly married they like to be alone, poor things," said Lady Waggett. "I know I used to when I was first married to Sir Samuel."

"My dear Lady Waggett," answered Mrs. Mayston Ryle in tones of thunder, "the cases are not similar; Mrs. Craddock was a Miss Ley, and really should know something of the usages of good society."

"Well, what do you think she said to me?" said Mrs. Branderton, waving her thin arms. "I was telling her that we were all so pleased with her husband—I thought it would comfort her a little, poor thing—and she said she hoped he would be equally satisfied with us."

Mrs. Mayston Ryle for a moment was stupefied, but soon recovered.

"How very amusing," she cried, rising from her chair. "Ha! ha! She hopes Mr. Edward Craddock will be satisfied with Mrs. Mayston Ryle."

The two Miss Hancocks said "Ha! ha!" in chorus. Then, the great lady's carriage being announced, she bade the assembly good-night, and swept out with a great rustling of her violet silk. The party might now really be looked upon as concluded, and the others obediently flocked off.

When they had put the Glovers down, Bertha nestled close to her husband.

"I'm so glad it's all over," she whispered; "I'm only happy when I'm alone with you."

"It was a jolly evening, wasn't it," he said. "I thought they were all ripping."

"I'm so glad you enjoyed it, dear; I was afraid you'd be bored."

"Good heavens, that's the last thing I should be. It does one good to hear conversation like that now and then—it brightens one up."

Bertha started a little.

"Old Bacot is a very well informed man, isn't he? I shouldn't wonder if he was right in thinking that the government would go out at the end of their six years."

"He always leads one to believe that he's in the Prime Minister's confidence," said Bertha.

"And the General is a funny old chap," added Edward. "That was a good story he told about the Duke of Wellington."

Somehow this remark had a curious effect upon Bertha; she could not restrain herself, but burst suddenly into shrieks of hysterical laughter. Her husband, thinking she was laughing at the anecdote, burst also into peal upon peal.

"And the story about the Bishop's gaiters!" cried Edward, shouting with merriment.

The more he laughed, the more hysterical became Bertha; and as they drove through the silent night they screamed and yelled and shook with uncontrollable mirth.

Chapter X

AND SO THE CRADDOCKS BEGAN THEIR JOURNEY ALONG THE GREAT ROAD nowhither which is called the Road of Holy Matrimony. The spring came, and with it a hundred new delights; Bertha watched the lengthening days, the coloured crocus spring from the ground, the snowbells; the warm damp days of February brought the primroses and then the violets. February is a month of languors; the world's heart is heavy, listless of the unrest of April and the vigorous life of May. Throughout nature the seed is germinating and the pulse of all things throbs. The sea mists arose from the North Sea, and covered the Kentish land with a veil of moisture, white and almost transparent, so that through it the leafless trees were seen strangely distorted, their branches like long arms writhing to free themselves from the shackles of winter; the grass was very green in the marshes, and the young lambs frisked and gambolled, bleating to their mothers. Already the thrushes and the blackbirds were singing in the hedge-rows. March roared in boisterously, and the clouds, high above, swept across the sky before the tearing winds, sometimes heaped up in heavy masses and then blown asunder, flying westwards, tripping over one another's heels in their hurry. Nature was resting; holding her breath, as it were, before the great effort of birth.

Gradually Bertha came to know her husband better. At her marriage she had really known nothing but that she loved him; the senses only had spoken, she and he were merely puppets whom nature had thrown together and made attractive in one another's eyes, that the race might be continued. Bertha, desire burning within her like a fire, had flung herself into her husband's arms, loving as the beasts love—and as the gods. He was the man and she was the woman, and the world was a Garden of Eden, conjured up by the power of passion. But greater knowledge brought only greater love. Little by little, reading in Edward's mind, Bertha discovered to her delight an unexpected purity; it was with a feeling of curious happiness that she recognised his innocence. She saw that he had never loved before, that woman to him was a strange thing, a thing he had scarcely known. She was proud that her husband had come to her unsoiled by foreign embraces, the lips that kissed hers were clean; no speech on the subject had passed between them, and yet she felt certain of his extreme chastity. His soul was truly virginal.

And this being so, how could she fail to adore him! Bertha was only happy in her husband's company, and it was an exquisite pleasure for her to think that their bonds could not be sundered, that so long as they lived they would be always together, always inseparable. She followed him like a dog, with a subjection that was really touching; her pride had utterly vanished, and she desired to exist only in Edward, to fuse her character with his and be entirely one with him. She wanted him to be her only individuality, likening herself to ivy climbing to the oak-tree; for he was an oak-tree, a pillar of strength, and she was very weak. In the morning after breakfast she accompanied him on his walk around the farms, and only when her presence was impossible did she stay at home to look after her house. The attempt to read was hopeless, and she had thrown aside her books. Why should she read? Not for entertainment, since her husband was a perpetual occupation; and if she knew how to love, what other knowledge was useful? Often, left alone for a while, she would take up some volume, but her mind quickly wandered and she thought of Edward again, wishing to be with him.

Bertha's life was an exquisite dream, a dream which need never end; for her happiness was not of that boisterous sort which needs excursions and alarums, but equable and smooth; she dwelt in a paradise of rosy tints, in which were neither violent shadows nor glaring lights. She was in heaven, and the only link attaching her to earth was the weekly service at Leanham. There was a delightful humanity about the bare church with its pitch-pine, highly varnished pews, and the odours of hair-pomade and Reckitt's Blue. Edward was in his Sabbath garments, the organist made horrid sounds, and the village choir sang out of tune; Mr. Glover's mechanical delivery of the prayers cleverly extracted all beauty from them, and his sermon was intensely prosaic. Those two hours of church gave Bertha just the touch of earthliness which was necessary to make her realise that life was not entirely spiritual.

Now came April. The elms before Court Leys were beginning to burst into leaf; the green buds covered the branches like a delicate rain, a verdant haze that was visible from a little distance and vanished when one came near. The brown fields also clothed themselves with a summer garment; the clover sprang up green and luxurious, and the crops showed good promise for the future. There were days when the air was almost balmy, when the sun was warm and the heart leapt, certain at last that the spring was at hand. The warm and comfortable rain soaked into the ground; and from the branches continually hung the countless drops, glistening in the succeeding sun. The self-conscious tulip unfolded her petals and carpeted the ground with gaudy colour. The clouds above Leanham were lifted up and the world was stretched out in a greater circle. The birds now sang with no uncertain notes as in March, but from a full throat, filling the air; and in the hawthorn behind Court Leys the first nightingale poured out his richness. And the full scents of the earth rose up, the fragrance of the mould and of the rain, the perfumes of the sun and of the soft breezes.

But sometimes, without ceasing, it rained from morning till night, and then Edward rubbed his hands.

"I wish this would keep on for a week; it's just what the country wants."

One such day Bertha was lying on a sofa while Edward stood at the window, looking at the pattering rain. She thought of the November afternoon when she had stood at the same window considering the dreariness of the winter, but her heart full of hope and love.

"Come and sit down beside me, Eddie dear," she said. "I've hardly seen you all day."

"I've got to go out," he said, without turning round.

"Oh no, you haven't. Come here and sit down."

"I'll come for two minutes, while they're putting the trap in."

"Kiss me."

He kissed her and she laughed. "You funny boy, I don't believe you care about kissing me a bit."

He could not answer this, for at that moment the trap came to the door and he sprang up.

"Where are you going?"

"I'm driving over to see old Potts at Herne about some sheep."

"Is that all? Don't you think you might stay in for an afternoon when I ask you?"

"Why?" he replied. "There's nothing to do in here. Nobody is coming, I suppose."

"I want to be with you, Eddie," she said, plaintively.

He laughed. "I'm afraid I can't break an appointment just for that."

"Shall I come with you then?"

"What on earth for?" he asked, with surprise.

"I want to be with you; I hate being always separated from you."

"But we're not always separated. Hang it all, it seems to me that we're always together."

"You don't notice my absence as I notice yours," said Bertha in a low voice, looking down.

"But it's raining cats and dogs, and you'll get wet through, if you come."

"What do I care about that if I'm with you!"

"Then come by all means if you like."

"You don't care if I come or not; it's nothing to you."

"Well, I think it would be very silly of you to come in the rain. You bet, I shouldn't go if I could help it."

"Then go," she said. She kept back with difficulty the bitter words which were on the tip of her tongue.

"You're much better at home," said her husband, cheerfully. "I shall be in to tea at five. Ta-ta!"

He might have said a thousand things. He might have said that nothing would please him more than that she should accompany him, that the appointment could go to the devil and he would stay with her. But he went off, cheerfully whistling. He didn't care. Bertha's cheeks grew red with the humiliation of his refusal.

"He doesn't love me," she said, and suddenly burst into tears—the first tears of her married life, the first she had wept since her father's death; and they made her ashamed. She tried to control them, but could not and wept ungovernably. Edward's words seemed terribly cruel; she wondered how he could have said them.

"I might have expected it," she said; "he doesn't love me."

She grew angry with him, remembering the little coldnesses which had often pained her. Often he almost pushed her away when she came to caress him—because he had at the moment something else to occupy him; often he had left unanswered her protestations of undying affection. Did he not know that he cut her to the quick? When she said she loved him with all her heart, he wondered if the clock was wound up! Bertha brooded for two hours over her unhappiness, and, ignorant of the time, was surprised to hear the trap again at the door; her first impulse was to run and let Edward in, but she restrained herself. She was very angry. He entered, and shouting to her that he was wet and must change, pounded upstairs. Of course he had not noticed that for the first time since their marriage his wife had not met him in the hall when he came in—he never noticed anything.

Edward entered the room, his face glowing with the fresh air.

"By Jove, I'm glad you didn't come. The rain simply poured down. How about tea? I'm starving."

He thought of his tea when Bertha wanted apologies, humble excuses, a plea for pardon. He was as cheerful as usual and quite unconscious that his wife had been crying herself into a towering passion.

"Did you buy your sheep?" she said, in an indignant tone. She was anxious for Edward to notice her discomposure, so that she might reproach him for his sins; but he noticed nothing.

"Not much," he cried. "I wouldn't have given a fiver for the lot."

"You might as well have stayed with me, as I asked you."

"As far as business goes, I really might. But I dare say the drive across country did me good." He was a man who always made the best of things.

Bertha took up a book and began reading.

"Where's the paper?" asked Edward. "I haven't read the leading articles yet."

"I'm sure I don't know."

They sat till dinner, Edward methodically going through the *Standard*, column after column; Bertha turning over the pages of her book, trying to understand, but occupied the whole time only with her injuries. They ate the meal almost in silence, for Edward was not talkative. He merely remarked that soon they would be having new potatoes and that he had met Dr. Ramsay. Bertha answered in monosyllables.

"You're very quiet, Bertha," he remarked, later in the evening. "What's the matter?"

"Nothing!"

"Got a headache?"

"No!"

He made no more inquiries, satisfied that her silence was due to natural causes. He did not seem to notice that she was in any way different from usual. She held herself in as long as she could, but finally burst out, referring to his remark of an hour before.

"Do you care if I have a headache or not?" It was hardly a question so much as a taunt.

He looked up with surprise. "What's the matter?"

She looked at him and then, with a gesture of impatience, turned away. But coming to her, he put his arm round her waist.

"Aren't you well, dear?" he asked, with concern.

She looked at him again, but now her eyes were full of tears and she could not repress a sob.

"Oh, Eddie, be nice to me," she said, suddenly weakening.

"Do tell me what's wrong."

He put his arms round her and kissed her lips. The contact revived the passion which for an hour had lain a-dying, and she burst into tears.

"Don't be angry with me, Eddie," she sobbed; it was she who apologised and made excuses. "I've been horrid to you; I couldn't help it. You're not angry, are you?"

"What on earth for?" he asked, completely mystified.

"I was so hurt this afternoon because you didn't seem to care about me two straws. You must love me, Eddie; I can't live without it."

"You *are* silly," he said, laughing.

She dried her tears, smiling. His forgiveness comforted her and she felt now trebly happy.

Chapter XI

BUT EDWARD WAS CERTAINLY NOT AN ARDENT LOVER. BERTHA COULD NOT tell when first she had noticed his irresponsiveness; at the beginning she had known only that she loved her husband with all her heart, and her ardour had lit up his somewhat pallid attachment till it seemed to glow as fiercely as her own. Yet gradually she began to think that he made very little return for the wealth of affection which she lavished upon him. The causes of her dissatisfaction were scarcely explicable: a slight motion of withdrawal, an indifference to her feelings—little nothings which had seemed almost comic. Bertha at first likened Edward to the Hippolitus of *Phædra*, he was untamed and wild; the kisses of woman frightened him; his phlegm pleased her disguised as rustic savagery, and she said her passion should thaw the icicles in his heart. But soon she ceased to consider his passiveness amusing, sometimes she upbraided him, and often, when alone, she wept.

"I wonder if you realise what pain you cause me at times," said Bertha.

"Oh, I don't think I do anything of the kind."

"You don't see it. . . . When I kiss you, it is the most natural thing in the world for you to push me away, as if—almost as if you couldn't bear me."

"Nonsense!"

To himself Edward was the same now as when they were first married.

"Of course after four months of married life you can't expect a man to be the same as on his honeymoon. One can't always be making love and canoodling. Everything in its proper time and season," he added, with the unoriginal man's fondness for proverbial philosophy.

After the day's work he liked to read his *Standard* in peace, so when Bertha came up to him he put her gently aside.

"Leave me alone for a bit, there's a good girl."

"Oh, you don't love me," she cried then, feeling as if her heart would break.

He did not look up from his paper nor make reply; he was in the middle of a leading article.

"Why don't you answer?" she cried.

"Because you're talking nonsense."

He was the best-humoured of men, and Bertha's temper never disturbed his equilibrium. He knew that women felt a little irritable at times, but if a man gave 'em plenty of rope, they'd calm down after a bit.

"Women are like chickens," he told a friend. "Give 'em a good run, properly closed in with stout wire netting, so that they can't get into mischief, and when they cluck and cackle just sit tight and take no notice."

Marriage had made no great difference in Edward's life. He had always been a man of regular habits, and these he continued to cultivate. Of course he was more comfortable.

"There's no denying it: a fellow wants a woman to look after him," he told Dr. Ramsay, whom he sometimes met on the latter's rounds. "Before I was married I used to find my shirts wore out in no time, but now when I see a cuff getting a bit groggy I just give it to the Missis and she makes it as good as new."

"There's a good deal of extra work, isn't there, now you've taken on the Home Farm?"

"Oh, bless you, I enjoy it. Fact is, I can't get enough work to do. And it seems to me that if you want to make farming pay nowadays you must do it on a big scale."

All day Edward was occupied, if not on the farms, then with business at Blackstable, Tercanbury, and Faversley.

"I don't approve of idleness," he said. "They always say the devil finds work for idle hands to do, and upon my word I think there's a lot of truth in it."

Miss Glover, to whom this sentiment was addressed, naturally approved, and when Edward immediately afterwards went out, leaving her with Bertha, she said—

"What a good fellow your husband is! You don't mind my saying so, do you?"

"Not if it pleases you," said Bertha, drily.

"I hear praise of him from every side. Of course Charles has the highest opinion of him."

Bertha did not answer, and Miss Glover added, "You can't think how glad I am that you're so happy."

Bertha smiled. "You've got such a kind heart, Fanny."

The conversation dragged, and after five minutes of heavy silence Miss Glover rose to go. When the door was closed upon her, Bertha sank back in her chair, thinking. This was one of her unhappy days—Eddie had walked into Blackstable, and she had wished to accompany him.

"I don't think you'd better come with me," he said. "I'm in rather a hurry and I shall walk fast."

"I can walk fast too," she said, her face clouding over.

"No, you can't—I know what you call walking fast. If you like you can come and meet me on the way back."

"Oh, you do everything you can to hurt me. It looks as if you welcomed an opportunity of being cruel."

"How unreasonable you are, Bertha. Can't you see that I'm in a hurry, and I haven't got time to saunter along and chatter about the buttercups."

"Well, let's drive in."

"That's impossible. The mare isn't well, and the pony had a hard day yesterday; he must rest today."

"It's simply because you don't want me to come. It's always the same, day after day. You invent anything to get rid of me."

She burst into tears, knowing that what she said was unjust, but feeling notwithstanding extremely ill-used. Edward smiled with irritating good temper.

"You'll be sorry for what you've said when you've calmed down, and then you'll want me to forgive you."

She looked up, flushing. "You think I'm a child and a fool."

"No, I just think you're out of sorts today."

Then he went out, whistling, and she heard him give an order to the gardener in his usual manner, as cheerful as if nothing had happened. Bertha knew that he had already forgotten the little scene. Nothing affected his good humour. She might weep, she might tear her heart out (metaphorically), and bang it on the floor, Edward would not be perturbed; he would still be placid, good-tempered, forbearing. Hard words, he said, broke nobody's bones—"Women are like chickens, when they cluck and cackle sit tight and take no notice!"

On his return Edward appeared not to see that his wife was out of temper. His spirits were always equable, and he was an unobservant person. She answered him in monosyllables, but he chattered away, delighted at having driven a good bargain with a man in Blackstable. Bertha longed for him to remark upon her condition so that she might burst out with reproaches, but Edward was hopelessly dense—or else he saw and was unwilling to give her an opportunity to speak. Bertha, almost for the first time, was seriously angry with her husband and it frightened her—suddenly Edward seemed an enemy, and she wished to inflict some hurt upon him. She did not understand herself—what was going to happen next? Why wouldn't he say something so that she might pour forth her woes and then be reconciled! The day wore on and she preserved a sullen silence; her heart was beginning to ache terribly—the night came, and still Edward made no sign; she looked about for a chance of beginning the quarrel, but nothing offered. Bertha pretended to go to sleep and she did not give him the kiss, the never-ending kiss of lovers which they always exchanged. Surely he would notice it, surely he would ask what troubled her, and then she could at last bring him to his knees. But he said nothing; he was dog-tired after a hard day's work, and without a word went to sleep—in five minutes Bertha heard his heavy, regular breathing.

Then she broke down; she could never sleep without saying good-night to him, without the kiss of his lips.

"He's stronger than I," she said, "because he doesn't love me."

Bertha wept silently; she could not bear to be angry with her husband. She would submit to anything rather than pass the night in wrath, and the next day as unhappily as this. She was entirely humbled. At last, unable any longer to bear the agony, she woke him.

"Eddie, you've not said good-night to me."

"By Jove, I forgot all about it," he answered, sleepily. Bertha stifled a sob.

"Hulloa, what's the matter?" he said. "You're not crying just because I forgot to kiss you—I was awfully fagged, you know."

He really had noticed nothing whatever; while she was passing through utter distress he had been as happily self-satisfied as usual. But the momentary recurrence of Bertha's anger was quickly stilled. She could not afford now to be proud.

"You're not angry with me?" she said. "I can't sleep unless you kiss me."

"Silly girl!" he whispered.

"You do love me, don't you?"

"Yes."

He kissed her as she loved to be kissed, and in the delight of it her anger was quite forgotten.

"I can't live unless you love me. Oh, I wish I could make you understand how I love you. . . . We're friends again now, aren't we?"

"We haven't ever been otherwise."

Bertha gave a sigh of relief, and lay in his arms completely happy. A minute more and Edward's breathing told her that he had already fallen asleep; she dared not move for fear of waking him.

The summer brought Bertha new pleasures, and she set herself to enjoy the pastoral life which she had imagined. The elms of Court Leys now were dark with leaves; and the heavy, close-fitting verdure gave quite a stately look to the house. The elm is the most respectable of trees, over-pompous if anything, but perfectly well-bred; and the shade it casts is no ordinary shade, but solid and self-assured as befits the estate of a county family. The fallen trunk had been removed, and in the autumn young trees were to be planted in the vacant spaces. Edward had set himself with a will to put the place properly to rights. The spring had seen a new coat of paint on Court Leys, so that it looked spick and span as the suburban villa of a stockbroker. The beds which for years had been neglected, now were trim with the abominations of carpet bedding; squares of red geraniums contrasted with circles of yellow calcellarias; the overgrown boxwood was cut down to a just height; the hawthorn hedge was doomed, and Edward had arranged to enclose the grounds with a wooden pallisade and laurel bushes. The drive was decorated with several loads of gravel, so that is became a thing of pride to the successor of an ancient and lackadaisical race. Craddock had not reigned in their stead a fortnight before the grimy sheep were expelled from the lawns on either side of the avenue, and since then the grass had been industriously mown and rolled. Now a tennis-court had been marked out, which, as Edward said, made things look homely. Finally the iron gates were gorgeous in black and gold as suited the entrance to a gentleman's mansion, and the renovated lodge proved to all and sundry that Court Leys was in the hands of a man who knew what was what, and delighted in the proprieties.

Though Bertha abhorred all innovations, she had meekly accepted Edward's improvements: they formed an inexhaustible topic of conversation, and his enthusiasm always pleased her.

"By Jove," he said, rubbing his hands, "the changes will make your aunt simply jump, won't they?"

"They will indeed," said Bertha, smiling.

She shuddered a little at the prospect of Miss Ley's sarcastic praise.

"She'll hardly recognise the place; the house looks as good as new, and the grounds might have been laid out only half a dozen years ago. . . . Give me five years more and even you won't know your old home."

Miss Ley had at last accepted one of the invitations which Edward insisted should be showered upon her, and wrote to say she was coming down for a week. Edward was of course much pleased; as he said, he wanted to be friends with everybody, and it didn't seem natural that Bertha's only relative should make a point of avoiding them.

"It looks as if she didn't approve of our marriage, and it makes the people talk."

He met the good lady at the station, and somewhat to her disgust greeted her with effusion.

"Ah, here you are at last!" he bellowed, in his jovial way. "We thought you were never coming. Here, porter!" He raised his voice so that the platform shook and rumbled.

He seized both Miss Ley's hands, and the terrifying thought flashed through her head that he would kiss her before the assembled multitude.

"He's cultivating the airs of the country squire," she thought. "I wish he wouldn't."

He took the innumerable bags with which she travelled and scattered them among the attendants. He even tried to induce her to take his arm to the dog-cart, but this honour she stoutly refused.

"Now, will you come round to this side and I'll help you up. Your luggage will come on afterwards with the pony."

He was managing everything in a self-confident and masterful fashion; Miss Ley noticed that marriage had dispelled the shyness which had been in him rather an attractive feature. He was becoming bluff and hearty. Also he was filling out. Prosperity and a knowledge of greater importance had broadened his back and straightened his shoulders; he was quite three inches more round the chest than when she had first known him, and his waist had proportionately increased.

"If he goes on developing in this way," she thought, "the good man will be colossal by the time he's forty."

"Of course, Aunt Polly," he said, boldly dropping the respectful *Miss Ley*, which hitherto he had invariably used, though his new relative was not a woman whom most men would have ventured to treat familiarly. "Of course it's all rot about your leaving us in a week; you must stay a couple of months at least."

"It's very good of you, dear Edward," replied Miss Ley drily, "but I have other engagements."

"Then you must break them; I can't have people leave my house immediately they come."

Miss Ley raised her eyebrows and smiled; was it *his* house already? Dear me!

"My dear Edward," she answered, "I never stay anywhere longer than two days—the first day I talk to people, the second I let them talk to me, and the third I go. . . . I stay a week at hotels so as to go *en pension*, and get my washing properly aired."

"You're treating us like a hotel," said Edward, laughing.

"It's a great compliment: in private houses one gets so abominably waited on."

"Ah well, we'll say no more about it. But I shall have your trunk taken to the box-room and I keep the key of it."

Miss Ley gave the short, dry laugh which denoted that her interlocutor's remark had not amused her, but something in her own mind. Presently they arrived at Court Leys.

"D'you see all the differences since you were last here?" asked Edward, jovially.

Miss Ley looked round and pursed her lips.

"It's charming," she said.

"I knew it would make you sit up," he cried, laughing.

Bertha received her aunt in the hall and embraced her with the grave decorum which had always characterised their relations.

"How clever you are, Bertha," said Miss Ley; "you manage to preserve your beautiful figure."

Then she set herself solemnly to investigate the connubial bliss of the young couple.

Chapter XII

THE PASSION TO ANALYSE THE CASUAL FELLOW-CREATURE WAS THE MOST absorbing vice that Miss Ley possessed; and no ties of relationship or affection (the two go not invariably together) prevented her from exercising her talents in that direction. She observed Bertha and Edward during luncheon: Bertha was talkative, chattering with a vivacity that seemed suspicious, about the neighbours—Mrs. Branderton's new bonnets and new hair, Miss Glover's good works and Mr. Glover's visits to London; Edward was silent, except when he pressed Miss Ley to take a second helping. He ate largely, and the maiden lady noticed the enormous mouthfuls he took and the heartiness with which he drank his beer. Of course she drew conclusions; and she drew further conclusions, when, having devoured half a pound of cheese and taken a last drink of ale, he pushed back his chair and with a sort of low roar, reminding one of a beast of prey gorged with food, said—

"Ah, well, I suppose I must set about my work. There's no rest for the weary."

He pulled a new briar-wood pipe from his pocket, filled and lit it.

"I feel better now. . . . Well, so-long; I shall be in to tea."

Conclusions buzzed about Miss Ley, like midges on a summer's day. She drew them all the afternoon; she drew them all through dinner. Bertha was effusive too, unusually so; and Miss Ley asked herself a dozen times if this stream of chatter, these peals of laughter, proceeded from a light heart or from a base desire to deceive a middle-aged and inquiring aunt. After dinner, Edward, telling her that of course she was one of the family so he hoped she did not wish him to stand on ceremony, began to read the paper. When Bertha, at Miss Ley's request, played the piano, good manners made him put it aside, and he yawned a dozen times in a quarter of an hour.

"I mustn't play anymore," said Bertha, "or Eddie will go to sleep—won't you, darling?"

"I shouldn't wonder," he replied, laughing. "The fact is that the things Bertha plays when we've got company give me the fair hump!"

"Edward only consents to listen when I play 'The Blue Bells of Scotland' or 'Yankee Doodle'."

Bertha made the remark, smiling good-naturedly at her husband, but Miss Ley drew conclusions.

"I don't mind confessing that I can't stand all this foreign music. What I say to Bertha is—why can't you play English stuff?"

"If you must play at all," interposed his wife.

"After all's said and done 'The Blue Bells of Scotland' has got a tune about it that a fellow can get his teeth into."

"You see, there's the difference," said Bertha, strumming a few bars of 'Rule Britannia,' "it sets mine on edge."

"Well, I'm patriotic," retorted Edward. "I like the good, honest, homely English airs. I like 'em because they're English. I'm not ashamed to say that for me the best piece of music that's ever been written is 'God Save the Queen'."

"Which was written by a German, dear Edward," said Miss Ley, smiling.

"That's as it may be," said Edward, unabashed, "but the sentiment's English and that's all I care about."

"Hear! hear!" cried Bertha. "I believe Edward has aspirations towards a political career. I know I shall finish up as the wife of the local M.P."

"I'm patriotic," said Edward, "and I'm not ashamed to confess it."

"Rule Britannia," sang Bertha, "Britannia rules the waves, Britons never, never shall be slaves. Ta-ra-ra-boom-de-ay! Ta-ra-ra-boom-de-ay!"

"It's the same everywhere now," proceeded the orator. "We're choke full of foreigners and their goods. I think it's scandalous. English music isn't good enough for you—you get it from France and Germany. Where do you get your butter from? Brittany! Where d'you get your meat from? New Zealand!" This he said with great scorn, and Bertha punctuated the observation with a resounding chord. "And as far as the butter goes, it isn't butter—it's margarine. Where does your bread come from? America. Your vegetables from Jersey."

"Your fish from the sea," interposed Bertha.

"And so it is all along the line—the British farmer hasn't got a chance!"

To this speech Bertha played a burlesque accompaniment, which would have irritated a more sensitive man than Craddock; but he merely laughed good-naturedly.

"Bertha won't take these things seriously," he said, passing his hand affectionately over her hair.

She suddenly stopped playing, and his good-humour, joined with the loving gesture, filled her with remorse. Her eyes filled with tears.

"You are a dear, good thing," she faltered, "and I'm utterly horrid."

"Now don't talk stuff before Aunt Polly. You know she'll laugh at us."

"Oh, I don't care," said Bertha, smiling happily. She stood up and linked her arm with his. "Eddie's the best tempered person in the world—he's perfectly wonderful."

"He must be, indeed," said Miss Ley, "if you have preserved your faith in him after six months of marriage."

But the maiden lady had stored so many observations that she felt an urgent need to retire to the privacy of her bedchamber, and sort them. She kissed Bertha and held out her hand to Edward.

"Oh, if you kiss Bertha, you must kiss me too," said he, bending forward with a laugh.

"Upon my word!" said Miss Ley, somewhat taken aback; then as he was evidently insisting she embraced him on the cheek. She positively blushed.

The upshot of Miss Ley's investigations was that once again the hymeneal path had been found strewn with roses; and the idea crossed her head as she laid it on the pillow, that Dr. Ramsay would certainly come and crow over her: it was not in masculine human nature, she thought, to miss an opportunity of exulting over a vanquished foe.

"He'll vow that I was the direct cause of the marriage. The dear man, he'll be so pleased with my discomfiture that I shall never hear the last of it. He's sure to call tomorrow."

Indeed the news of Miss Ley's arrival had been by Edward industriously spread abroad, and promptly Mrs. Ramsay put on her blue velvet calling-dress, and in the doctor's brougham drove with him to Court Leys. The Ramsays found Miss Glover and the Vicar of Leanham already in possession of the field. Mr. Glover looked thinner and older than when Miss Ley had last seen him; he was more weary, meek and brow-beaten; Miss Glover never altered.

"The parish?" said the parson, in answer to Miss Ley's polite inquiry, "I'm afraid it's in a bad way. The dissenters have got a new chapel, you know—and they say the Salvation Army is going to set up 'barracks,' as they call them. It's a great pity the government doesn't step in: after all we are established by law and the law ought to protect us from encroachment."

"You don't believe in liberty of conscience?" asked Miss Ley.

"My dear Miss Ley," said the Vicar, in his tired voice, "everything has its limits. I should have thought there was in the Established Church enough liberty of conscience for anyone."

"Things are becoming dreadful in Leanham," said Miss Glover. "Practically all the tradesmen go to chapel now, and it makes it so difficult for us."

"Yes," replied the Vicar, with a weary sigh; "and as if we hadn't enough to put up with, I hear that Walker has ceased coming to church."

"Oh dear, oh dear!" said Miss Glover.

"Walker, the baker?" asked Edward.

"Yes; and now the only baker in Leanham who goes to church is Andrews."

"Well, we can't possibly deal with him, Charles," said Miss Glover, "his bread is too bad."

"My dear, we must," groaned her brother. "It would be against all my principles to deal with a tradesman who goes to chapel. You must tell Walker to send his book in, unless he will give an assurance that he'll come to church regularly."

"But Andrews's bread always gives you indigestion, Charles," cried Miss Glover.

"I must put up with it. If none of our martyrdoms were more serious than that, we should have no cause to complain."

"Well, it's quite easy to get your bread from Tercanbury," said Mrs. Ramsay, who was severely practical.

Mr. Glover and his sister threw up their hands in dismay.

"Then Andrews would go to chapel too. The only thing that keeps them at church, I'm sorry to say, is the Vicarage custom, or the hope of getting it."

Presently Miss Ley found herself alone with the parson's sister.

"You must be very glad to see Bertha again, Miss Ley."

"Now she's going to crow," thought the good lady. "Of course I am."

"And it must be such a relief to you to see how well it's all turned out."

Miss Ley looked sharply at Miss Glover, but saw no trace of irony.

"Oh, I think it's beautiful to see a married couple so thoroughly happy. It really makes me feel a better woman when I come here and see how those two worship one another."

"Of course the poor thing's a perfect idiot," thought Miss Ley. "Yes, it's very satisfactory," she said, drily.

She glanced round for Dr. Ramsay, looking forward, notwithstanding that she was on the losing side, to the tussle she foresaw. She had the instincts of a good fighter, and, even though defeat was inevitable, never avoided an encounter. The doctor approached.

"Well, Miss Ley. So you have come back to us. We're all delighted to see you."

"How cordial these people are," thought Miss Ley, somewhat crossly, thinking Dr. Ramsay's remark preliminary to coarse banter or to reproach. "Shall we take a turn in the garden; I'm sure you wish to quarrel with me."

"There's nothing I should like better—to walk in the garden, I mean: of course, no one could quarrel with so charming a person as yourself."

"He would never be so polite if he did not mean afterwards to be very rude," thought Miss Ley. "I'm glad you like the garden."

"Craddock has improved it so wonderfully. It's a perfect pleasure to look at all he's done."

This Miss Ley considered a gibe, and searched for a repartee, but finding none was silent: Miss Ley was a wise woman! They walked a few steps without a word, and then Dr. Ramsay suddenly burst out—

"Well, Miss Ley, you were right after all."

She stopped and looked at the speaker—he seemed quite serious.

"Yes," he said, "I don't mind acknowledging it. I was wrong. It's a great triumph for you, isn't it?"

He looked at her, and shook with good-tempered laughter.

"Is he making fun of me?" Miss Ley asked herself, with something not very distantly removed from agony. This was the first occasion upon which she had failed to understand not only the good doctor, but his inmost thoughts as well. "So you think the estate has been improved?" she said hurriedly.

"I can't make out how the man's done so much in so short a time. Why, just look at it!"

Miss Ley pursed her lips. "Even in its most dilapidated days Court Leys looked gentlemanly: now all this," she glanced round with upturned nose, "might be the country mansion of a pork-butcher."

"My dear Miss Ley, you must pardon my saying so, but the place wasn't even respectable."

"But it is now; that is my complaint. My dear doctor, in the old days, the passer-by could see that the owners of Court Leys were decent people; that they could not make both ends meet was a detail—it was possibly because they burnt one end too rapidly, which is the sign of a rather delicate mind." Miss Ley was mixing her metaphors. "And the passer-by moralised accordingly. For a gentleman there are only two decorous states, absolute poverty or overpowering wealth; the middle condition is vulgar. Now the passer-by sees thrift and careful management, the ends meet, but they do it aggressively, as if it were something to be proud about. Pennies are looked at before they are spent; and, good heavens! the Leys serve to point a moral and adorn a tale. The Leys, who gambled and squandered their substance, who bought diamonds when they hadn't bread, and pawned the diamonds to give the King a garden-party, now form the heading of a copy-book and the ideal of a market-gardener."

Miss Ley had the characteristics of the true phrase-maker, for so long as her period was well rounded, she did not mind how much nonsense it contained. Coming to the end of her tirade, she looked at the doctor for the signs of disapproval which she thought her right, but he merely laughed.

"I see you want to rub it in," he said.

"What on earth does the creature mean?" Miss Ley asked herself.

"I confess I did believe things would turn out badly," the doctor proceeded. "And I couldn't help thinking he'd be tempted to play ducks and drakes with the whole property. Well, I don't mind frankly acknowledging that Bertha couldn't have chosen a better husband; he's a thoroughly good fellow; no one realised what he had in him, and there's no knowing how far he'll go."

A man would have expressed Miss Ley's feeling with a little whistle, but that lady merely raised her thin eyebrows. Then Dr. Ramsay shared the opinion of Miss Glover?

"And what precisely is the opinion of the county?" she asked. "Of that odious Mrs. Branderton, of Mrs. Ryle (she has no right to the *Mayston* at all), of the Hancocks, and the rest?"

"Edward Craddock has won golden opinions all round. Everyone likes him, and thinks well of him. No, I assure you, although I'm not so fond as all that of confessing I was wrong, he's the right man in the right place. It's extraordinary how people took up to him and respect him already. . . . I give you my word for it, Bertha has reason to congratulate herself—a girl doesn't pick up a husband like that every day of the week."

Miss Ley smiled; it was a great relief to find that she really was no more foolish than most people (so she modestly put it), for a doubt on the subject had given her some uneasiness.

"So everyone thinks they're as happy as turtle-doves?"

"Why, so they are," cried the doctor; "surely *you* don't think otherwise?"

Miss Ley never considered it a duty to dispel the error of her fellow-creatures, and whenever she had a little piece of knowledge, vastly preferred keeping it to herself.

"I?" she answered to the doctor's question. "I make a point of thinking with the majority—it's the only way to get a reputation for wisdom!" But Miss Ley, after all, was only human. "Which do you think is the predominant partner?" she asked, smiling drily.

"The man, as he should be," gruffly replied the doctor.

"Do you think he has more brains?"

"Ah, you're a feminist," said Dr. Ramsay, with great scorn.

"My dear doctor, my gloves are sixes, and perceive my shoes." She put out for the old gentleman's inspection a very pointed, high-heeled shoe, displaying at the same time the elaborate open-work of a silk stocking.

"Do you intend me to take that as an acknowledgment of the superiority of man?"

"Heavens, how argumentative you are!" Miss Ley laughed, for she was getting into her own particular element "I knew you wished to quarrel with me. Do you really want my opinion?"

"Yes."

"Well, it seems to me that if you take the very clever woman and set her beside an ordinary man, you prove nothing. That is how women mostly argue. We place George Eliot (who, by the way, had nothing of the woman but petticoats—and those not always) beside plain John Smith, and ask tragically if such a woman can be considered inferior to such a man. But that's silly! The question I've been asking myself for the last five-and-twenty years is, whether the average fool of a woman is a greater fool than the average fool of a man."

"And the answer?"

"Well, upon my word, I don't think there's much to choose between them."

"Then you haven't really an opinion on the subject at all?" cried the doctor.

"That is why I give it you."

"Hm!" grunted Dr. Ramsay. "And how does that apply to the Craddocks?"

"It doesn't apply to them. . . . I don't think Bertha is a fool."

"She couldn't be, having had the discretion to be born your niece, eh?"

"Why, doctor, you're growing quite pert."

They had finished the tour of the garden and Mrs. Ramsay was seen in the drawing-room, bidding Bertha good-bye.

"Now, seriously, Miss Ley," said the doctor, "they're quite happy, aren't they? Everyone thinks so."

"Everyone is always right," said Miss Ley.

"And what is your opinion?"

"Good heavens, what an insistent man it is! Well, Dr. Ramsay, all I would suggest is that—for Bertha, you know, the book of life is written throughout in italics; for Edward it is all in the big round hand of the copy-book headings. . . . Don't you think it will make the reading of the book somewhat difficult?"

Chapter XIII

WITH THE SUMMER EDWARD BEGAN TO TEACH BERTHA LAWN-TENNIS; and in the long evenings, when he had finished his work and changed into the flannels which suited him so well, they played innumerable sets. He prided himself upon his skill in this pursuit and naturally found it dull to play with a beginner; but he was very patient, hoping that eventually Bertha would acquire sufficient skill to give him a good game. To be doing something with her husband sufficiently amused Bertha. She liked him to correct her mistakes, to show her this stroke and that; she admired his good nature and his inexhaustible spirits. But her greatest delight was to lie on the long chair by the lawn when they had finished, and enjoy the feeling of exhaustion, gossiping of the little nothings which love made absorbingly interesting.

Miss Ley had been persuaded to prolong her stay. She had vowed to go at the end of her week; but Edward, in his high-handed fashion, had ordered the key of the box-room to be given him, and refused to surrender it.

"Oh no," he said, "I can't make people come here, but I can prevent them from going away. In this house everyone has to do as I tell them; isn't that so, Bertha?"

"If you say it, Edward," replied his wife.

Miss Ley gracefully acceded to her nephew's desire, which was the more easy, since the house was comfortable, she had really no pressing engagements, and her mind was set upon making further examination into the married life of her relations. It would have been a weakness, unworthy of her, to maintain her intention for consistence' sake.

Why for days together were Edward and Bertha the happiest lovers, and then suddenly why did Bertha behave almost brutally towards her husband, while he remained invariably good-tempered and amiable? The obvious reason was that some little quarrel had arisen, such as, since Adam and Eve, has troubled every married couple in the world; but the obvious reason was that which Miss Ley was least likely to credit. She never saw anything in the way of a disagreement, Bertha assented to all her husband's proposals; and with such docility on the one hand, such good-humour on the other, what on earth could form a bone of contention?

Miss Ley had discovered that when the green leaves of life are turning red and golden with approaching autumn, most pleasure can be obtained by a judicious mingling in simplicity of the gifts of nature and the resources of civilisation. She was satisfied to come in the evenings to the tennis-lawn and sit on a comfortable chair shaded by trees, and protected by a red parasol from the rays of the setting sun. She was not a woman to find distraction in needlework, and brought with her, therefore, a volume of Montaigne, her favourite writer. She read a page and then lifted her sharp eyes to the players. Edward was certainly very handsome—he looked so clean, and it was obvious to the most casual observer that he bathed himself daily: he was one of those men who carry the morning tub stamped on every line of their faces. You felt that Pear's Soap was as essential to him as his belief in the Conservative Party, Derby Day, and the Depression of Agriculture. As Bertha often said, his energy was superabundant. Notwithstanding his increasing size he was most agile, and perpetually did unnecessary feats of strength, such as jumping and hopping over the net, holding chairs with outstretched arm.

"If health and a good digestion are all that is necessary in a husband, Bertha certainly ought to be the most contented woman alive."

Miss Ley never believed so implicitly in her own theories that she was prevented from laughing at them. She had an impartial mind and saw the two sides of a question clearly enough to find little to choose between them; consequently she was able and willing to argue with equal force from either point of view.

The set was finished, and Bertha threw herself on a chair, panting.

"Find the balls, there's a dear," she cried.

Edward went off on the search, and Bertha looked at him with a delightful smile.

"He is such a good-tempered person," she said to Miss Ley. "Sometimes he makes me feel positively ashamed."

"He has all the virtues. Dr. Ramsay, the Glovers, even Mrs. Branderton, have been dinning his praise into my ears."

"Yes, they all like him. Arthur Branderton is always here, asking his advice about something or other. He's a dear, good thing."

"Who? Arthur Branderton?"

"No, of course not—Eddie."

Bertha took off her hat and stretched herself more comfortably on the long chair. Her hair was somewhat disarranged, and the rich locks wandered about her forehead and on the nape of her neck in a way that would have distracted any minor poet under seventy. Miss Ley looked at her niece's fine profile, and wondered again at the complexion, made up of the softest colours in the setting sun. Her eyes now were liquid with love, languorous with the shade of long lashes; and her full, sensual mouth was half open with a smile.

"Is my hair very untidy?" asked Bertha, catching Miss Ley's look and its meaning.

"No, I think it suits you when it is not done too severely."

"Edward hates it; he likes me to be prim. . . . And of course I don't care how I look so long as he's pleased. Don't you think he's very good-looking?" Then without waiting for an answer, she asked a second question.

"Do you think me a great fool for being so much in love, Aunt Polly?"

"My dear, it's surely the proper behaviour with one's lawful spouse."

Bertha's smile became a little sad as she replied—

"Edward seems to think it unusual." She followed him with her eyes, picking up the balls one by one, hunting among bushes: she was in the mood for confidences that afternoon. "You don't know how different everything has been since I fell in love. The world is fuller.... It's the only state worth living in." Edward advanced with the eight balls on his racket. "Come here and be kissed, Eddie," she cried.

"Not if I know it," he replied, laughing. "Bertha's a perfect terror. She wants me to spend my whole life in kissing her. . . . Don't you think it's unreasonable, Aunt Polly? My motto is: everything in its place and season."

"One kiss in the morning," said Bertha, "one kiss at night, will do to keep your wife quiet; and the rest of the time you can attend to your work and read your paper."

Again Bertha smiled charmingly, but Miss Ley saw no amusement in her eyes.

"Well, one can have too much of a good thing," said Edward, balancing his racket on the tip of his nose.

"Even of proverbial philosophy," remarked Bertha.

A few days later, his guest having definitely announced that she must go, Edward proposed a tennis-party as a parting honour. Miss Ley would gladly have escaped an afternoon of small-talk with the notabilities of Leanham, but Edward was determined to pay his aunt every attention, and his inner consciousness assured him that at least a small party was necessary to the occasion. They came, Mr. and Miss Glover, the Brandertons, the Hancocks, Mr. Atthill Bacot, the great politician (of the district). But Mr. Atthill Bacot was more than political, he was gallant, and he devoted himself to the entertainment of Miss Ley. He discussed with her the sins of the government and the incapacity of the army.

"More men, more guns!" he said. "An elementary education in common sense for the officers, and the rudiments of grammar if there's time!"

"Good heavens, Mr. Bacot, you mustn't say such things. I thought you were a Conservative."

"Madam, I stood for the constituency in '85. I may say that if a Conservative member could have got in, I should have been elected. But there are limits. Even the staunch Conservative will turn. Now look at General Hancock."

"Please don't talk so loud," said Miss Ley, with alarm, for Mr. Bacot had instinctively adopted his platform manner, and his voice could be heard through the whole garden.

"Look at General Hancock, I say," he repeated, taking no notice of the interruption. "Is that the sort of man whom you would wish to have the handling of ten thousand of your sons?"

"Oh, but be fair," cried Miss Ley, laughing. "They're not all such fools as poor General Hancock."

"I give you my word, madam, I think they are. . . . As far as I can make out, when a man has shown himself incapable of doing anything else they make him a general, just to encourage the others. I understand the reason. It's a great thing, of course, for parents sending their sons into the army to be able to say, 'Well, he may be a fool, but there's no reason why he shouldn't become a general.'"

"You wouldn't rob us of our generals," said Miss Ley; "they're so useful at tea-parties. In my young days the fool of the family was sent into the Church, but now, I suppose, he's sent into the army."

Mr. Bacot was about to make a very heated retort when Edward called to him—

"We want you to make up a set at tennis. Will you play with Miss Hancock against my wife and the General? Come on, Bertha."

"Oh no, I mean to sit out, Eddie," said Bertha, quickly. She saw that Edward was putting all the bad players into one set, so that they might be got rid of. "I'm not going to play."

"You must, or you'll disarrange the next lot. It's all settled; Miss Glover and I are going to take on Miss Jane Hancock and Arthur Branderton."

Bertha looked at him with eyes flashing angrily. Of course he did not notice her vexation. He preferred to play with Miss Glover, she told herself; the parson's sister played well, and for a good game he would never hesitate to sacrifice his wife's feelings. Besides Bertha, only Miss Glover and young Branderton were within earshot, and in his jovial, pleasant manner, Edward laughingly said—

"Bertha's such a duffer. Of course she's only just beginning. You don't mind playing with the General, do you, dear?"

Arthur Branderton laughed and Bertha smiled at the sally, but she reddened.

"I'm not going to play at all. I must see to the tea; and I dare say more people will be coming in presently."

"Oh, I forgot that," said Edward. "No; perhaps you oughtn't to play." And then putting his wife out of his thoughts, and linking his arm with young Branderton's, he sauntered off. "Come along, old chap; we must find some crock to make up the pat-ball set." Edward had such a charming, frank manner, one could not help liking him.

Bertha watched the two men go and turned very white.

"I must just go into the house a moment," she said to Miss Glover. "Go and entertain Mrs. Branderton, there's a dear." And precipitately she fled.

She ran to her room, and flinging herself on the bed, burst into a flood of tears. The humiliation seemed dreadful. She wondered how Eddie, whom she loved above all else in the world, could treat her so cruelly. What had she done? He knew—ah, yes, he knew well enough the happiness he could cause her—and he went out of his way to be brutal. She wept bitterly, and jealousy of Miss Glover (Miss Glover, of all people!) stabbed her to the heart.

"He doesn't love me," she moaned, her tears redoubling.

Presently there was a knock at the door.

"Who is it?" she cried.

The handle was turned and Miss Glover came in, red with nervousness.

"Forgive me for coming in, Bertha. But I thought you seemed unwell. Can't I do something for you?"

"Oh, I'm all right," said Bertha, drying her tears, "Only the heat upset me and I've got a headache."

"Shall I send Edward to you?"

"What do I want with Edward?" replied Bertha, petulantly. "I shall be all right in five minutes. I often have attacks like this."

"I'm sure he didn't mean to say anything unkind. He's kindness itself, I know."

Bertha flushed. "What on earth do you mean, Fanny? Who didn't say anything unkind?"

"I thought you were hurt by Edward's saying you were a duffer and a beginner."

"Oh, my dear, you must think me a fool." Bertha laughed hysterically. "It's quite true that I'm a duffer, I tell you it's only the weather. Why, if my feelings were hurt each time Eddie said a thing like that I should lead a miserable life."

"I wish you'd let me send him up to you," said Miss Glover, unconvinced.

"Good heavens! Why? See, I'm all right now." She washed her eyes and passed the powder-puff over her face. "My dear, it was only the sun."

With an effort she braced herself, and burst into a laugh joyful enough almost to deceive the Vicar's sister.

"Now, we must go down, or Mrs. Branderton will complain more than ever of my bad manners."

She put her arm round Miss Glover's waist and ran her down the stairs to the mingled terror and amazement of that good creature. For the rest of the afternoon, though her eyes never rested on Edward, she was perfectly charming—in the highest spirits, chattering incessantly, laughing; everyone noticed her good humour and commented upon her obvious felicity.

"It does one good to see a couple like that," said General Hancock, "just as happy as the day is long."

But the little scene had not escaped Miss Ley's sharp eyes, and she noticed with agony that Miss Glover had gone to Bertha. She could not stop her, being at the moment in the toils of Mrs. Branderton.

"Oh, these good people are too officious! Why can't she leave the girl alone to have it out with herself!"

But the explanation of everything now flashed across Miss Ley.

"What a fool I am!" she thought, and she was able to cogitate quite clearly while exchanging honeyed impertinences with Mrs. Branderton. "I noticed it the first day I saw them together. How could I ever forget it!" She shrugged her shoulders and murmured the maxim of La Rochefoucauld—

"Entre deux amants il-y-a toujours un qui aime, et un qui se laisse aimer."

And to this she added another, in the same language, which, knowing no original, she ventured to claim as her own; it seemed to summarise the situation.

"Celui qui aime a toujours tort."

Chapter XIV

BERTHA AND MISS LEY PASSED A TROUBLED NIGHT, WHILE EDWARD, OF course, after much exercise and a hearty dinner, slept the sleep of the just and of the pure at heart. Bertha was nursing her wrath; she had with difficulty brought herself to kiss her husband before, according to his habit, he turned his back upon her and began to snore. Miss Ley, with her knowledge of the difficulties in store for the couple, asked herself if she could do anything. But what could she do? They were reading the book of life in their separate ways, one in italics, the other in the big round letters of the copy-book; and how could she help them to find a common character? Of course the first year of married life is difficult, and the weariness of the flesh adds to the inevitable disillusionment. Every marriage has its moments of utter despair. The great danger is in the onlooker, who may pay to them too much attention and, by stepping in, render the difficulty permanent—cutting the knot instead of letting time undo it. Miss Ley's cogitations brought her not unnaturally to the course which most suited her temperament; she concluded that far and away the best plan was to attempt nothing, and let things right themselves as best they could. She did not postpone her departure, but, according to arrangement, went on the following day.

"Well, you see," said Edward, bidding her good-bye, "I told you that I should make you stay longer than a week."

"You're a wonderful person, Edward," said Miss Ley, drily. "I have never doubted it for an instant."

He was pleased seeing no irony in the compliment. Miss Ley took leave of Bertha with a suspicion of awkward tenderness that was quite unusual; she hated to show her feelings, and found it difficult, yet wanted to tell Bertha that if she was ever in difficulties she would always find in her an old friend and a true one. All she said was—

"If you want to do any shopping in London, I can always put you up, you know. And for the matter of that, I don't see why you shouldn't come and stay a month or so with me—if Edward can spare you. It will be a change."

When Miss Ley drove with Edward to the station, Bertha felt suddenly an extreme loneliness. Her aunt had been a barrier between herself and her husband, coming opportunely when, after the first months of mad passion, she was beginning to see herself linked to a man she did not know. A third person in the house had been a restraint. She looked forward already to the future with something like terror; her love for Edward was a bitter heartache. Oh yes, she loved him well, she loved him passionately; but he—he was fond of her, in his placid, calm way; it made her furious to think of it.

The weather was rainy, and for two days there was no question of tennis. On the third, however, the sun came out again, and the lawn was soon dry. Edward had driven over to Tercanbury, but returned towards evening.

"Hulloa!" he said, "you haven't got your tennis things on. You'd better hurry up."

This was the opportunity for which Bertha had been looking. She was tired of always giving way, of humbling herself; she wanted an explanation.

"You're very good," she said, "but I don't want to play tennis with you anymore."

"Why on earth not?"

She burst out furiously—"Because I'm sick and tired of being made a convenience by you. I'm too proud to be treated like that. Oh, don't look as if you didn't understand. You play with me because you've got no one else to play with. Isn't that so? That is how you are always with me. You prefer the company of the veriest fool in the world to mine. You seem to do everything you can to show your contempt for me."

"Why, what have I done now?"

"Oh, of course, you forget. You never dream that you are making me frightfully unhappy. Do you think I like to be treated before people as a sort of poor idiot that you can laugh and sneer at?"

Edward had never seen his wife so angry, and this time he was forced to pay her attention. She stood before him, at the end of her speech, with teeth clenched, her cheeks flaming.

"It's about the other day, I suppose. I saw at the time you were in a passion."

"And didn't care two straws."

"You're too silly," he said, with a laugh. "We couldn't play together when we had people here. They laugh at us as it is for being so devoted to one another."

"If they only knew how little you cared for me!"

"I might have managed a set with you later on, if you hadn't sulked and refused to play at all."

"It would never have occurred to you, I know you better than that. You're absolutely selfish."

"Come, come, Bertha," he cried good-humouredly, "that's a thing I've not been accused of before. No one has ever called me selfish."

"Oh no, they think you charming. They think because you're cheerful and even-tempered, because you're hail-fellow-well-met with everyone you know, that you've got such a nice character. If they knew you as well as I do, they'd understand it was merely because you're perfectly indifferent to them. You treat people as if they were your bosom friends, and then, five minutes after they've gone, you've forgotten all about them. . . . And the worst of it is, that I'm no more to you than anybody else."

"Oh, come, I don't think you can really find such awful things wrong with me."

"I've never known you sacrifice your slightest whim to gratify my most earnest desire."

"You can't expect me to do things which I think unreasonable."

"If you loved me, you'd not always be asking if the things I want are reasonable. I didn't think of reason when I married you."

Edward made no answer, which naturally added to Bertha's irritation. She was arranging flowers for the table, and broke off the stalks savagely. Edward, after a pause, went to the door.

"Where are you going?" she asked.

"Since you won't play, I'm just going to do a few serves for practice."

"Why don't you send for Miss Glover to come and play with you?"

A new idea suddenly came to him (they came at sufficiently rare intervals not to spoil his equanimity), but the absurdity of it made him laugh.

"Surely you're not jealous of her, Bertha?"

"I?" began Bertha, with tremendous scorn, and then changing her mind: "You prefer to play with her than to play with me."

He wisely ignored part of the charge. "Look at her and look at yourself. Do you think I could prefer her to you?"

"I think you're fool enough."

The words slipped out of Bertha's mouth almost before she knew she had said them, and the bitter, scornful tone added to their violence. They frightened her, and turning very white, she glanced at her husband.

"Oh, I didn't mean to say that, Eddie."

Fearing now that she had really wounded him, Bertha was entirely sorry; she would have given anything for the words to be unsaid. Edward was turning over the pages of a book, looking at it listlessly. She went up to him.

"I haven't offended you, have I, Eddie? I didn't mean to say that."

She put her arm in his; he did not answer.

"Don't be angry with me," she faltered again, and then breaking down, buried her face in his bosom. "I didn't mean what I said—I lost command over myself. You don't know how you humiliated me the other day. I haven't been able to sleep at night, thinking of it. . . . Kiss me."

He turned his face away, but she would not let him go; at last she found his lips.

"Say you're not angry with me."

"I'm not angry with you."

"Oh, I want your love so much, Eddie," she murmured. "Now more than ever. . . . I'm going to have a child."

Then in reply to his astonished exclamation—

"I wasn't certain till today. . . . Oh, Eddie, I'm so glad. I think it's what I wanted to make me happy."

"I'm glad too," he said.

"But you will be kind to me, Eddie—and not mind if I'm fretful and bad tempered. You know I can't help it, and I'm always sorry afterwards."

He kissed her as passionately as his cold nature allowed, and peace returned to Bertha's tormented heart.

Bertha had intended as long as possible to make a secret of her news; it was a comfort in her distress, and a bulwark against her increasing disillusionment. She was unable to reconcile herself to the discovery, seen as yet dimly, that Edward's cold temperament could not satisfy her ardent passions: love to her was a burning fire, a flame that absorbed the rest of life; love to him was a convenient and necessary institution of Providence, a matter about which there was as little need for excitement as about the ordering of a suit of clothes. Bertha's intense devotion for a while had obscured her husband's coolness, and she would not see that his temperament was to blame. She accused him of not loving her, and asked herself distractedly how to gain his affection; her pride was humiliated because her love was so much greater than his. For six months she had loved him blindly; and now, opening her eyes, she refused to look upon the naked fact, but insisted on seeing only what she wished.

Yet, the truth, elbowing itself through the crowd of her illusions, tormented her. She was afraid that Edward neither loved her nor had ever loved her; and she wavered uncertainly between the old passionate devotion and a new, equally passionate hatred. She told herself that she could not do things by halves; she must love or detest, but in either case, fiercely. And now the child made up for everything. Now it did not matter if Edward loved or not, it no longer pained her to realise how foolish had been her hopes, how quickly her ideal had been shattered. She felt that the infantine hands of her son were already breaking, one by one, the links that bound her to her husband. When she divined her pregnancy, she gave a cry not only of joy and pride, but also of exultation in her approaching freedom.

But when the suspicion was changed into a certainty, her feelings veered round; for her emotions were always unstable as the light winds of April. An extreme weakness made her long for the support and sympathy of her husband; she could not help telling him. In the hateful dispute of that very day, she had forced herself to say bitter things, but all the time she wished him to take her in his arms, saying he loved her. It needed so little to rekindle her dying affection; she wanted his help and she could not live without his love.

The weeks went on and Bertha was touched to see a change in Edward's behaviour, more noticeable after his past indifference. He looked upon her now as an invalid, and as such entitled to some consideration; he was really very kind-hearted, and during this time did everything for his wife that did not involve a sacrifice of his own convenience. When the doctor suggested some dainty to tempt her appetite, Edward was delighted to ride over to Tercanbury to fetch it; and in her presence he trod more softly and spoke in a gentler voice. After a while he used to insist on carrying Bertha up and downstairs, and though Dr. Ramsay assured them it was a quite unnecessary proceeding, Bertha would not allow Edward to give it up. It amused her to feel a little child in his strong arms, and she loved to nestle against his breast. Then, with winter, when it was too cold to drive out, Bertha would lie for long hours on a sofa by the window, looking at the line of elm-trees, now leafless again and melancholy, watching the heavy clouds that drove over from the sea: her heart was full of peace.

One day of the new year she was sitting as usual at her window when Edward came prancing up the drive on horseback. He stopped in front of her and waved his whip.

"What d'you think of my new horse?" he cried.

At that moment the animal began to cavort, and backed into a flower-bed. "Quiet, old fellow," cried Edward. "Now then, don't make a fuss; quiet!" The horse stood on its hind legs and laid its ears back viciously. Presently Edward dismounted and led him towards Bertha. "Isn't he a stunner? Just look at him."

He passed his hand down the beast's forelegs and stroked its sleek coat.

"I only gave thirty-five quid for it," he remarked. "I must just take him round to the stable and then I'll come in."

In a few minutes Edward joined his wife. The riding costume suited him well, and in his top-boots he had more than ever the appearance of the fox-hunting country squire, which had always been his ideal. He was in high spirits over the new purchase.

"It's the beast that threw Arthur Branderton when we were out last week.... Arthur's limping about now with a sprained ankle and a broken finger. He says the horse is the greatest devil he's ever ridden; he's frightened to use him again." Edward laughed scornfully.

"But you haven't bought him?" asked Bertha, with alarm.

"Of course I have," said Edward. "I couldn't miss a chance like that. Why, he's a perfect beauty—only he's got a temper, like we all have."

"But is he dangerous?"

"A bit—that's why I got him cheap. Arthur gave a hundred guineas for him, and he told me I could have him for seventy. 'No,' I said, 'I'll give you thirty-five—and take the risk of breaking my neck.' Well, he just had to accept my offer! the horse has got a bad name in the county, and he wouldn't get anyone to buy it in a hurry. A man has got to get up early if he wants to do me over a gee!"

By this time Bertha was frightened out of her wits.

"But, Eddie, you're not going to ride it—supposing something should happen. Oh, I wish you hadn't bought him."

"He's all right," said Craddock. "If anyone can ride him, I can—and, by Jove, I'm going to risk it. Why, if I bought him and then didn't use him, I'd never hear the last of it."

"To please me, Eddie, don't! What does it matter what people say? I'm so frightened. And now of all times you might do something to please me. It's not often I ask you to do me a favour."

"Well, when you ask for something reasonable, I always try my best to do it—but really, after I've paid thirty-five pounds for a horse, I can't cut him up for cat's meat."

"That means you'll always do anything for me so long as it doesn't interfere with your own likes and dislikes."

"Ah, well, we're all like that, aren't we? . . . Come, come, don't be nasty about it, Bertha."

He pinched her cheek good-naturedly—women, we all know, would like the moon if they could get it; and the fact that they can't doesn't prevent them from persistently asking for it. Edward sat down beside his wife, holding her hand.

"Now, tell us what you've been up to today. Has anyone been?"

Bertha sighed deeply. She had absolutely no influence over her husband. No prayers, no tears would stop him from doing a thing he had set his mind on—however much she argued he always managed to make her seem in the wrong, and then went his way rejoicing. But she had her child now.

"Thank God for that!" she murmured.

Chapter XV

CRADDOCK WENT OUT ON HIS NEW HORSE AND RETURNED TRIUMPHANTLY. "He was as quiet as a lamb," he said. "I could ride him with my arms tied behind my back; and as to jumping—he takes a five-barred gate in his stride."

Bertha was a little angry with him for having caused her such terror, angry with herself also for troubling.

"And it was rather lucky I had him today. Old Lord Philip Dirk was there, and he asked Branderton who I was. 'You tell him,' says he, 'that it isn't often I've seen a man ride as well as he does.' You should see Branderton, he isn't half glad at having let me take the beast for thirty-five quid. And Mr. Molson came up to me and said, 'I knew that horse would get into your hands before long, you're the only man in this part who can ride it—but if it don't break your neck, you'll be lucky.' "

He recounted with great satisfaction the compliments paid to him.

"We had a jolly good run today. . . . And how are you, dear, feeling comfy? Oh, I forgot to tell you—you know Rodgers, the huntsman, well, he said to me, 'That's a mighty fine hack you've got there, sir, but he takes some riding.'—'I know he does,' I said; 'but I flatter myself I know a thing or two more than most horses.' They all thought I should get rolled over before the day was out, but I just went slick at everything to show I wasn't frightened."

Then he gave details of the affair; and he had as great a passion for the meticulous as a German historian. He was one of those men who take infinite pains over trifles, flattering themselves that they never do things by halves. Bertha had a headache, and her husband bored her; she thought herself a great fool to be so concerned about his safety.

As the months wore on Miss Glover became very solicitous. The parson's sister looked upon birth as a mysteriously heart-fluttering business, which, however, modesty required decent people to ignore. She treated her friend in an absurdly self-conscious manner, and blushed like a peony when Bertha frankly referred to the coming event. The greatest torment of Miss Glover's life was that, as lady of the Vicarage, she had to manage the Maternity Bag, an institution to provide the infants of the needy with articles of raiment and their mothers with flannel petticoats. She could never, without much confusion, ask the necessary information of the beneficiaries in her charity; feeling that the whole thing ought not to be discussed at all, she kept her eyes averted, and acted generally so as to cause great indignation.

"Well," said one good lady, "I'd rather not 'ave her bag at all than be treated like that. Why, she treats you as if—well, as if you wasn't married."

"Yes," said another, "that's just what I complain of—I promise you I 'ad 'alf a mind to take my marriage lines out of my pocket an' show 'er. It ain't nothin' to be ashamed about—nice thing it would be after 'avin' sixteen, if I was bashful."

But of course the more unpleasant a duty was, the more zealously did Miss Glover perform it; she felt it right to visit Bertha with frequency, and manfully bore the young wife's persistence in referring to an unpleasant subject. She carried her heroism to the pitch of knitting socks for the forthcoming baby, although to do so made her heart palpitate uncomfortably; and when she was surprised at the work by her brother, her cheeks burned like two fires."

"Now, Bertha dear," she said one day, pulling herself together and straightening her back as she always did when she was mortifying the flesh. "Now, Bertha dear, I want to talk to you seriously."

Bertha smiled. "Oh don't, Fanny; you know how uncomfortably it makes you."

"I must," answered the good creature, gravely. "I know you'll think me ridiculous, but it's my duty."

"I shan't think anything of the kind," said Bertha, touched with her friend's humility.

"Well, you talk a great deal of—of what's going to happen"—Miss Glover blushed—"but I'm not sure if you are really prepared for it."

"Oh, is that all?" cried Bertha. "The nurse will be here in a fortnight, and Dr. Ramsay says she's a most reliable woman."

"I wasn't thinking of earthly preparations," said Miss Glover. "I was thinking of the other. Are you quite sure you're approaching the—the *thing*, in the right spirit?"

"What do you want me to do?"

"It isn't what I want you to do. It's what you ought to do. I'm nobody. But have you thought at all of the spiritual side of it?"

Bertha gave a sigh that was chiefly voluptuous. "I've thought that I'm going to have a son, that's mine and Eddie's; and I'm awfully thankful."

"Wouldn't you like me to read the Bible to you sometimes?"

"Good heavens, you talk as if I were going to die."

"One can never tell, dear Bertha," replied Miss Glover, sombrely; "I think you ought to be prepared. . . . 'In the midst of life we are in death'—one can never tell what may happen."

Bertha looked at her somewhat anxiously. She had been forcing herself of late to be cheerful, and had found it necessary to stifle a recurring presentiment of evil fortune. The Vicar's sister never realised that she was doing everything possible to make Bertha thoroughly unhappy.

"I brought my own Bible with me," she said. "Do you mind if I read you a chapter?"

"I should like it," said Bertha, and a cold shiver went through her.

"Have you got any preference for some particular part?" asked Miss Glover, extracting the book from a little black bag which she always carried.

On Bertha's answer that she had no preference, Miss Glover suggested opening the Bible at random, and reading on from the first line that crossed her eyes.

"Charles doesn't quite approve of it," she said; "he thinks it smacks of superstition. But I can't help doing it, and the early Protestants constantly did the same."

Miss Glover, having opened the book with closed eyes, began to read: *"The sons of Pharez! Hezron, and Hamul. And the sons of Zerah; Zimri, and Ethan, and Heman, and Calcol, and Dara; five of them in all."* Miss Glover cleared her throat. *"And the sons of Ethan; Asariah. The sons also of Hezron, that were born unto him; Jerahmeel, and Ram, and Chelubai. And Ram begat Amminadab; and Amminadab begat Nahshon, prince of the children of Judah."* She had fallen upon the genealogical table at the beginning of the Book of Chronicles. The chapter was very long, and consisted entirely of names, uncouth and difficult to pronounce; but Miss Glover shirked not one of them. With grave and somewhat high-pitched delivery, modelled on her brother's, she read out the bewildering list. Bertha looked at her in amazement.

"That's the end of the chapter," she said at last; "would you like me to read you another one?"

"Yes, I should like it very much; but I don't think the part you've hit on is quite to the point."

"My dear, I don't want to reprove you—that's not my duty—but all the Bible is to the point."

And as the time passed, Bertha quite lost her courage and was often seized by a panic fear. Suddenly, without obvious cause, her heart sank and she asked herself frantically how she could possibly get through it. She thought she was going to die, and wondered what would happen if she did. What would Edward do without her? Thinking of his bitter grief the tears came to her eyes, but her lips trembled with self-pity when the suspicion came that he would not be heartbroken: he was not a man to feel either grief or joy very poignantly. He would not weep; at the most his gaiety for a couple of days would be obscured, and then he would go about as before. She imagined him relishing the sympathy of his friends. In six months he would almost have forgotten her, and such memory as remained would not be extraordinarily pleasing. He would marry again; Edward loathed solitude, and next time doubtless he would choose a different sort of woman—one less remote from his ideal. Edward cared nothing for appearance, and Bertha imagined her successor plain as Miss Hancock or dowdy as Miss Glover; and the irony of it lay in the knowledge that either of those two would make a wife more suitable than she to his character, answering better to his conception of a helpmate.

Bertha fancied that Edward would willingly have given her beauty for some solid advantage, such as a knowledge of dressmaking; her taste, her arts and accomplishments, were nothing to him, and her impulsive passion was a positive defect. "Handsome is as handsome does," said he; he was a plain, simple man and he wanted a simple, plain wife.

She wondered if her death would really cause him much sorrow; Bertha's will gave him everything of which she was possessed, and he would spend it with a second wife. She was seized with insane jealousy.

"No, I won't die," she cried between her teeth, "I won't!"

But one day, while Edward was hunting, her morbid fancies took another turn. Supposing he should die? The thought was unendurable, but the very horror of it fascinated her; she could not drive away the scenes which, with strange distinctness, her imagination set before her. She was seated at the piano and heard suddenly a horse stop at the front-door—Edward was back early: but the bell rang; why should Edward ring? There was a murmur of voices without and Arthur Branderton came in. In her mind's eye she saw every detail most clearly. He was in his hunting clothes! Something had happened, and knowing what it was, Bertha was yet able to realise her terrified wonder, as one possibility and another rushed through her brain. He was uneasy, he had something to tell, but dared not say it; she looked at him, horror-stricken, and a faintness came over her so that she could hardly stand.

Bertha's heart beat quickly. She told herself it was absurd to let her imagination run away with her; but, notwithstanding, the pictures vividly proceeded: she seemed to assist at a ghastly play in which she was chief actor.

And what would she do when the fact was finally told her—that Edward was dead? She would faint or cry out.

"There's been an accident," said Branderton—"your husband is rather hurt."

Bertha put her hands to her eyes, the agony was dreadful.

"You mustn't upset yourself," he went on, trying to break it to her.

Then, rapidly passing over the intermediate details she found herself with her husband. He was dead, lying on the floor—and she pictured him to herself, she knew exactly how he would look; sometimes he slept so soundly, so quietly, that she was nervous and put her ear to his heart to know if it was beating. Now he was dead. Despair suddenly swept down upon her overpoweringly. Bertha tried again to shake off her fancies, she even went to the piano and played a few notes; but the morbid attraction was too strong for her and the scene went on. Now that he was dead, he could not check her passion, now he was helpless and she kissed him with all her love; she passed her hands through his hair, and stroked his face (he had hated this in life), she kissed his lips and his closed eyes.

The imagined grief was so poignant that Bertha burst into tears. She remained with the body, refusing to be separated from it—Bertha buried her face in the cushions so that nothing might disturb her illusion, she had ceased trying to drive it away. Ah, she loved him passionately, she had always loved him and could not live without him. She knew that she would shortly die—and she had been afraid of death. Ah, now it was welcome! She kissed his hands—he could not prevent her now—and with a little shudder opened his eyes; they were glassy, expressionless, immobile. Clinging to him, she sobbed in love and anguish. She would let none touch him but herself; it was a relief to perform the last offices for him who had been her whole life. She did not know that her love was so great.

She undressed the body and washed it; she washed the limbs one by one and sponged them, then very gently dried them with a towel. The touch of the cold flesh made her shudder voluptuously—she thought of him taking her in his strong arms, kissing her on the mouth. She wrapped him in the white shroud and surrounded him with flowers. They placed him in the coffin, and her heart stood still: she could not leave him. She passed with him all day and all night, looking ever at the quiet, restful face. Dr. Ramsay came and Miss Glover came, urging her to go away, but she refused. What was the care of her own health now, she had only wanted to live for him?

The coffin was closed, and she saw the gestures of the undertakers—she had seen her husband's face for the last time, her beloved: her heart was like a stone, and she beat her breast in pain.

Hurriedly now the pictures thronged upon her—the drive to the churchyard, the service, the coffin strewn with flowers, and finally the grave-side. They tried to keep her at home. What cared she for the silly, the abominable convention, which sought to prevent her from going to the funeral? Was it not her husband, the only light of her life, whom they were burying? They could not realise the horror of it, the utter despair. And distinctly, by the dimness of the winter day in her drawing-room at Court Leys, Bertha saw the lowering of the coffin, heard the rattle of earth thrown upon it.

What would her life be afterwards? She would try to live, she would surround herself with Edward's things, so that his memory might be always with her; the loneliness was appalling. Court Leys was empty and bare. She saw the endless succession of grey days; the seasons brought no change, and continually the clouds hung heavily above her; the trees were always leafless, and it was desolate. She could not imagine that travel would bring solace—the whole of life was blank, and what to her now were the pictures and churches, the blue skies of Italy? Her only happiness was to weep.

Then distractedly Bertha thought that she would kill herself, for life was impossible to endure. No life at all, the blankness of the grave, was preferable to the pangs gnawing continually at her heart. It would be easy to finish, with a little morphia to close the book of trouble; despair would give her courage, and the prick of the needle was the only pain. But her vision became dim, and she had to make an effort to retain it: her thoughts grew less coherent, travelling back to previous incidents, to the scene at the grave, to the voluptuous pleasure of washing the body.

It was all so vivid that the entrance of Edward came upon her as a surprise. But the relief was too great for words, it was the awakening from a horrible nightmare. When he came forward to kiss her, she flung her arms round his neck, her eyes moist with past tears, and pressed him passionately to her heart.

"Oh, thank God!" she cried.

"Hulloa, what's up now?"

"I don't know what's been the matter with me. . . . I've been so miserable, Eddie—I thought you were dead!"

"You've been crying!"

"It was so awful, I couldn't get the idea out of my head. . . . Oh, I should die also."

Bertha could scarcely realise that her husband was by her side in the flesh, alive and well.

"Would you be sorry if I died?" she asked him.

"But you're not going to do anything of the sort," he said, cheerily.

"Sometimes I'm so frightened, I don't believe I'll get over it."

He laughed at her, and his joyous tones were peculiarly comforting. She made him sit by her side and held his strong hands, the hands which to her were the visible signs of his powerful manhood. She stroked them and kissed the palms. She was quite broken with the past emotions; her limbs trembled and her eyes glistened with tears.

Chapter XVI

THE NURSE ARRIVED, BRINGING NEW APPREHENSION. SHE WAS AN OLD woman who, for twenty years, had helped the neighbouring gentry into the world; and she had a copious store of ghastly anecdote. In her mouth the terrors of birth were innumerable, and she told her stories with a cumulative art that was appalling. Of course, in her mind, she acted for the best; Bertha was nervous, and the nurse could imagine no better way of reassuring her than to give detailed accounts of patients who for days had been at death's door, given up by all the doctors, and yet had finally recovered.

Bertha's quick invention magnified the coming anguish till, for thinking of it, she could hardly sleep. The impossibility even to conceive it rendered it more formidable; she saw before her a long, long agony, and then death. She could not bear Edward to be out of her sight.

"Why, of course you'll get over it," he said. "I promise you it's nothing to make a fuss about."

He had bred animals for years and was quite used to the process which supplied him with veal, mutton, and beef, for the local butchers. It was a ridiculous fuss that human beings made over a natural and ordinary phenomenon.

"Oh, I'm so afraid of the pain. I feel certain that I shan't get over it—it's awful. I wish I hadn't got to go through it."

"Good heavens," cried the doctor, "one would think no one had ever had a baby before you."

"Oh, don't laugh at me. Can't you see how frightened I am! I have a presentiment that I shall die."

"I never knew a woman yet," said Dr. Ramsay, "who hadn't a presentiment that she would die, even if she had nothing worse that a finger-ache the matter with her."

"Oh, you can laugh," said Bertha. "I've got to go through it."

Another day passed, and the nurse said the doctor must be immediately sent for. Bertha had made Edward promise to remain with her all the time.

"I think I shall have courage if I can hold your hand," she said.

"Nonsense," said Dr. Ramsay, when Edward told him this, "I'm not going to have a man meddling about."

"I thought not," said Edward, "but I just promised, to keep her quiet."

"If you'll keep yourself quiet," answered the doctor, "that's all I shall expect."

"Oh, you needn't fear about me. I know all about these things—why, my dear doctor, I've brought a good sight more living things into the world than you have, I bet."

Edward, calm, self-possessed, unimaginative, was the ideal person for an emergency.

"There's no good my knocking about the house all the afternoon," he said. "I should only mope, and if I'm wanted I can always be sent for."

He left word that he was going to Bewlie's Farm to see a sick cow, about which he was very anxious.

"She's the best milker I've ever had. I don't know what I should do if anything went wrong with her. She gives her so-many pints a day, as regular as possible. She's brought in over and over again the money I gave for her."

He walked along with the free and easy step which Bertha so much admired, glancing now and then at the fields which bordered the highway. He stopped to examine the beans of a rival farmer.

"That soil's no good," he said, shaking his head. "It don't pay to grow beans on a patch like that."

When he arrived at Bewlie's Farm, Edward called for the labourer in charge of the invalid.

"Well, how's she going?"

"She ain't no better, squire."

"Bad job. . . . Has Thompson been to see her today?" Thompson was the vet.

" 'E can't make nothin' of it—'e thinks it's a habscess she's got, but I don't put much faith in Mister Thompson: 'is father was a labourer same as me, only 'e didn't 'ave to do with farming, bein' a bricklayer; and wot 'is son can know about cattle is beyond me altogether."

"Well, let's go and look at her," said Edward.

He strode over to the barn, followed by the labourer. The beast was standing in one corner, even more meditative than is usual with cows, hanging her head and humping her back. She seemed profoundly pessimistic.

"I should have thought Thompson could do something," said Edward.

" 'E says the butcher's the only thing for 'er," said the other, with great contempt.

Edward snorted indignantly. "Butcher indeed! I'd like to butcher him if I got the chance."

He went into the farm-house, which for years had been his home; but he was a practical, sensible fellow and it brought him no memories, no particular emotion.

"Well, Mrs. Jones," he said to the tenant's wife. "How's yourself?"

"Middlin', sir. And 'ow are you and Mrs. Craddock?"

"I'm all right—the Missus is having a baby, you know."

He spoke in the jovial, careless way which necessarily endeared him to the whole world.

"Bless my soul, is she indeed, sir—and I knew you when you was a boy! When d'you expect it?"

"I expect it every minute. Why, for all I know, I may be a happy father when I get back to tea."

"You take it pretty cool, governor," said Farmer Jones, who had known Edward in the days of his poverty.

"Me?" cried Edward, laughing. "I know all about this sort of thing, you see. Why, look at all the calves I've had—and mind you, I've not had an accident with a cow above twice, all the time I've gone in for breeding.... But I'd better be going to see how the Missus is getting on. Good-afternoon to you, Mrs. Jones."

"Now what I like about the squire," said Mrs. Jones, "is that there's no 'aughtiness in 'im. 'E ain't too proud to take a cup of tea with you, although 'e is the squire now."

" 'E's the best squire we've 'ad for thirty years," said Farmer Jones, "and, as you say, my dear, there's not a drop of 'aughtiness in 'im—which is more than you can say for his missus."

"Oh well, she's young-like," replied his wife. "They do say as 'ow 'e's the master, and I dare say 'e'll teach 'er better."

"Trust 'im for makin' 'is wife buckle under; 'e's not a man to stand nonsense from anybody."

Edward swung along the road, whirling his stick round, whistling, and talking to the dogs that accompanied him. He was of a hopeful disposition, and did not think it would be necessary to slaughter his best cow. He did not believe in the vet half so much as in himself, and his firm opinion was that she would recover. He walked up the avenue of Court Leys, looking at the young elms he had planted to fill the gaps; they were pretty healthy on the whole, and he was pleased with his work.

He went to Bertha's room and knocked at the door. Dr. Ramsay opened it, but with his burly frame barred the passage.

"Oh, don't be afraid," said Edward, "I don't want to come in. I know when I'm best out of the way.... How is she getting on?"

"Well, I'm afraid it won't be such an easy job as I thought," whispered the doctor; "but there's no reason to get alarmed."

"I shall be downstairs if you want me for anything."

"She was asking for you a good deal just now, but nurse told her it would upset you if you were there; so then she said, 'Don't let him come; I'll bear it alone.' "

"Oh, that's all right. In a time like this the husband is much better out of the way, I think."

Dr. Ramsay shut the door upon him.

"Sensible chap that," he said. "I like him better and better. Why, most men would be fussing about and getting hysterical, and Lord knows what."

"Was that Eddie?" asked Bertha, her voice trembling with recent agony.

"Yes; he came to see how you were."

"He isn't very much upset, is he? Don't tell him I'm very bad—it'll make him wretched. I'll bear it alone."

Edward, downstairs, told himself it was no use getting into a state, which was quite true, and taking the most comfortable chair in the room, settled down to read his paper. Before dinner he went to make more inquiries. Dr. Ramsay came out saying he had given Bertha opium, and for a while she was quiet.

"It's lucky you did it just at dinner time," said Edward, with a laugh. "We'll be able to have a snack together."

They sat down and began to eat. They rivalled one another in their appetites; and the doctor, liking Edward more and more, said it did him good to see a man who could eat well. But before they had reached the pudding, a message came from the nurse to say that Bertha was awake, and Dr. Ramsay regretfully left the table. Edward went on eating steadfastly. At last, with the happy sigh of the man conscious of virtue and a satisfied stomach, he lit his pipe and again settling himself in the arm-chair, shortly began to doze. The evening, however, was long, and he felt bored.

"It ought to be all over by now," he said. "I wonder if I need stay up?"

Dr. Ramsay seemed a little worried when Edward went to him a third time.

"I'm afraid it's a difficult case," he said. "It's most unfortunate. She's been suffering a good deal, poor thing."

"Well, is there anything I can do?" asked Edward.

"No, except to keep calm and not make a fuss."

"Oh, I shan't do that; you needn't fear. I will say that for myself, I have got nerve."

"You're splendid," said Dr. Ramsay. "I tell you I like to see a man keep his head so well through a job like this."

"Well, what I came to ask you was—is there any good in my sitting up? Of course I'll do it if anything can be done; but if not I may as well go to bed."

"Yes, I think you'd much better; I'll call you if you're wanted. I think you might come in and say a word or two to Bertha; it will encourage her."

Edward entered. Bertha was lying with staring, terrified eyes—eyes that seemed to have lately seen entirely new things, they shone glassily. Her face was whiter than ever, the blood had fled from her lips, and her cheeks were sunken: she looked as if she were dying. She greeted Edward with the faintest smile.

"How are you, little woman?" he asked.

His presence seemed to call her back to life, and a faint colour lit up her cheeks.

"I'm all right," she said, making an effort. "You mustn't worry yourself, dear."

"Been having a bad time?"

"No," she said, bravely. "I've not really suffered much—there's nothing for you to upset yourself about."

He went out, and she called Dr. Ramsay. "You haven't told him what I've gone through, have you? I don't want him to know."

"No, that's all right. I've told him to go to bed."

"Oh, I'm glad. He can't bear not to get his proper night's rest. . . . How long d'you think it will last—already I feel as if I'd been tortured forever, and it seems endless."

"Oh, it'll soon be over now, I hope."

"I'm sure I'm going to die," she whispered; "I feel that life is being gradually drawn out of me—I shouldn't mind if it weren't for Eddie. He'll be so cut up."

"What nonsense!" said the nurse, "you all say you're going to die."

Edward—dear, manly, calm, and pure-minded fellow as he was—went to bed quietly and soon was fast asleep. But his slumbers were somewhat troubled: generally he enjoyed the heavy dreamless sleep of the man who has no nerves and plenty of exercise. Tonight, however, he dreamed. He dreamed not only that one cow was sick, but that all his cattle had fallen ill—the cows stood about with gloomy eyes and humpbacks, surly and dangerous, evidently with their livers totally deranged; the oxen were "blown," and lay on their backs with legs kicking feebly in the air.

"You must send them all to the butcher's," said the vet; "there's nothing to be done with them."

"Good Lord deliver us," said Edward; "I shan't get four bob a stone for them."

But his dream was disturbed by a knock at the door, and Edward awoke to find Dr. Ramsay shaking him.

"Wake up, man—get up and dress quickly."

"What's the matter?" cried Edward, jumping out of bed and seizing his clothes. "What's the time?"

"It's half-past four. . . . I want you to go into Tercanbury for Dr. Spocref; Bertha is very bad."

"All right, I'll bring him back with me." Edward rapidly dressed himself.

"I'll go round and wake up the man to put the horse in."

"No, I'll do that myself; it'll take me half the time." He methodically laced his boots.

"Bertha is in no immediate danger. But I must have a consultation. I still hope we shall bring her through it."

"By Jove," said Edward, "I didn't know it was so bad as that."

"You need not get alarmed yet—the great thing is for you to keep calm and bring Spocref along as quickly as possible. It's not hopeless yet."

Edward, with all his wits about him, was soon ready and with equal rapidity set to harnessing the horse; he carefully lit the lamps, as the proverb, *more haste, less speed,* passed through his mind. In two minutes he was on the main road, and whipped up the horse. He went with a quick, steady trot through the silent night.

Dr. Ramsey, returning to the sick-room, thought what a splendid object was a man who could be relied upon to do anything, who never lost his head nor got excited. His admiration for Edward was growing by leaps and bounds.

Chapter XVII

EDWARD CRADDOCK WAS A STRONG MAN, ALSO UNIMAGINATIVE. DRIVING through the night to Tercanbury he did not give way to distressing thoughts, but easily kept his anxiety within proper bounds, and gave his whole attention to conducting the horse; he kept his eyes on the road in front of him, and the beast stepped out with swift, regular stride, rapidly passing the milestones. Edward rang Dr. Spocref up and gave him the note he carried. The doctor presently came down, an undersized man with a squeaky voice and a gesticulative manner. He looked upon Edward with suspicion.

"I suppose you're the husband?" he said, as they clattered down the street. "Would you like me to drive? I dare say you're rather upset."

"No—and don't want to be," answered Edward, with a laugh. He looked down a little upon people who lived in towns, and never trusted a man who was less than six feet high and burly in proportion!

"I'm rather nervous of anxious husbands who drive me at a breakneck pace in the middle of the night," said the doctor. "The ditches have an almost irresistible attraction for them."

"Well, I'm not nervous, doctor, so it doesn't matter twopence if you are."

When they reached the open country, Edward set the horse going at its fastest; he was somewhat amused at the doctor's desire to drive—absurd little man!

"Are you holding on tight?" he asked, with good-natured scorn.

"I see you can drive," said the doctor.

"It is not the first time I've had reins in my hands," replied Edward, modestly. "Here we are!"

He showed the specialist to the bed-room, and asked whether Dr. Ramsay required him further.

"No, I don't want you just now; but you'd better stay up to be ready, if anything happens. . . . I'm afraid Bertha is very bad indeed—you must be prepared for everything."

Edward retired to the next room and sat down. He was genuinely disturbed, but even now could not realise that Bertha was dying—his mind was sluggish, and he was unable to imagine the future. A more emotional man would have been white with fear, his heart beating painfully and his nerves quivering with a hundred anticipated terrors. He would have been quite useless; while Edward was fit for any emergency—he could have been trusted to drive another ten miles in search of some appliance, and, with perfect steadiness, to help in any necessary operation.

"You know," he said to Dr. Ramsay, "I don't want to get in your way; but if I should be any use in the room, you can trust me not to get flurried."

"I don't think there's anything you can do; the nurse is very trustworthy and capable."

"Women," said Edward, "get so excited; they always make fools of themselves if they possibly can."

But the night air had made Craddock sleepy, and after half an hour in the chair, trying to read a book, he dozed off. Presently, however, he awoke, and the first light of day filled the room with a grey coldness. He looked at his watch.

"By Jove, it's a long job," he said.

There was a knock at the door, and the nurse came in.

"Will you please come."

Dr. Ramsay met him in the passage. "Thank God, it's over. She's had a terrible time."

"Is she all right?"

"I think she's in no danger now—but I'm sorry to say we couldn't save the child."

A pang went through Edward's heart. "Is it dead?"

"It was still-born. I was afraid it was hopeless. You'd better go to Bertha now—she wants you. She doesn't know about the child."

Bertha was lying in an attitude of complete exhaustion: she lay on her back, with arms stretched in utter weakness by her sides. Her face was grey with past anguish, her eyes dull and lifeless, half closed; and her jaw hung almost as hangs the jaw of a corpse. She tried to form a smile as she saw Edward, but in her feebleness the lips scarcely moved.

"Don't try to speak, dear," said the nurse, seeing that Bertha was attempting words.

Edward bent down and kissed her, the faintest blush coloured her cheeks, and she began to cry; the tears stealthily glided down her cheeks.

"Come nearer to me, Eddie," she whispered.

He knelt beside her, suddenly touched. He took her hand, and the contact had a vivifying effect; she drew a long breath, and her lips formed a weary, weary smile.

"Thank God, it's over," she groaned, half whispering. "Oh, Eddie, darling, you can't think what I've gone through."

"Well, it's all over now."

"And you've been worrying too, Eddie. It encouraged me to think that you shared my trouble. You must go to sleep now. It was good of you to drive to Tercanbury for me."

"You mustn't talk," said Dr. Ramsay, coming back into the room, after seeing the specialist sent off.

"I'm better now," said Bertha, "since I've seen Eddie."

"Well, you must go to sleep."

"You've not told me yet if it's a boy or a girl; tell me, Eddie, you know."

Edward looked uneasily at the doctor.

"It's a boy," said Dr. Ramsay.

"I knew it would be," she murmured. An expression of ecstatic pleasure came into her face, chasing away the greyness of death. "I'm so glad. Have you seen it, Eddie?"

"Not yet."

"It's our child, isn't it? It's worth going through the pain to have a baby. I'm so happy."

"You must go to sleep now."

"I'm not a bit sleepy—and I want to see my boy."

"No, you can't see him now," said Dr. Ramsay, "he's asleep, and you mustn't disturb him."

"Oh, I should like to see him, just for one minute. You needn't wake him."

"You shall see him after you've been asleep," said the doctor, soothingly. "It'll excite you too much."

"Well, you go in and see him, Eddie, and kiss him, and then I'll go to sleep."

She seemed so anxious that at least its father should see his child, that the nurse led Edward into the next room. On a chest of drawers was lying something covered with a towel. This the nurse lifted, and Edward saw his child; it was naked and very small, hardly human, repulsive, yet very pitiful. The eyes were closed, the eyes that had never been opened. Edward looked at it for a minute.

"I promised I'd kiss it," he whispered.

He bent down and touched with his lips the white forehead; the nurse drew the towel over the body, and they went back to Bertha.

"Is he sleeping?" she asked.

"Yes."

"Did you kiss him?"

"Yes."

Bertha smiled. "Fancy your kissing baby before me."

But Dr. Ramsay's draught was taking its effect, and almost immediately Bertha fell into a pleasant sleep.

"Let's take a turn in the garden," said Dr. Ramsay. "I think I ought to be here when she wakes."

The air was fresh, scented with the spring flowers and the odour of the earth. Both men inspired it with relief after the close atmosphere of the sick-room. Dr. Ramsay put his arm in Edward's.

"Cheer up, my boy," he said. "You've borne it all magnificently. I've never seen a man go through a night like this better than you; and upon my word, you're as fresh as paint this morning."

"Oh, I'm all right," said Edward. "What's to be done about—about the baby?"

"I think she'll be able to bear it better after she's had a sleep. I really didn't dare say it was still-born. The shock would have been too much for her."

They went in and washed and ate, then waited for Bertha to wake. At last the nurse called them.

"You poor things," cried Bertha, as they entered the room. "Have you had no sleep at all? . . . I feel quite well now, and I want my baby. Nurse says it's sleeping and I can't have it—but I will. I want it to sleep with me, I want to look at my son."

Edward and the nurse looked at Dr. Ramsay, who for once was disconcerted.

"I don't think you'd better have him today, Bertha," he said. "It would upset you."

"Oh, but I must have my baby. Nurse, bring him to me at once."

Edward knelt down again by the bed-side and took her hands. "Now, Bertha, you mustn's be alarmed, but the baby's not well, and—"

"What d'you mean?" Bertha suddenly sprang up in the bed.

"Lie down. Lie down," cried Dr. Ramsay and the nurse, forcing her back on the pillow.

"What's the matter with him, doctor," she cried, in sudden terror.

"It's as Edward says, he's not well."

"Oh, he isn't going to die—after all I've gone through."

She looked from one to the other. "Oh, tell me; don't keep me in suspense. I can bear it, whatever it is."

Dr. Ramsay touched Edward, encouraging him.

"You must prepare yourself for bad news, darling. You know—"

"He isn't dead?" she shrieked.

"I'm awfully sorry, dear. . . . He was still-born."

"Oh, God!" groaned Bertha, it was a cry of despair. And then she burst into passionate weeping.

Her sobs were terrible, uncontrollable; it was her life that she was weeping away, her hope of happiness, all her desires and dreams. Her heart seemed breaking. She put her hands to her eyes, with a gesture of utter agony.

"Then I went through it all for nothing. . . . Oh, Eddie, you don't know the frightful pain of it—all night I thought I should die. . . . I would have given anything to be put out of my suffering. And it was all useless."

She sobbed still more irresistibly, quite crushed by the recollection of what she had gone through, and its futility.

"Oh, I wish I could die."

The tears were in Edward's eyes, and he kissed her hands.

"Don't give way, darling," he said, searching in vain for words to console her. His voice faltered and broke.

"Oh, Eddie," she said, "you're suffering just as much as I am. I forgot. . . . Let me see him now."

Dr. Ramsay made a sign to the nurse, and she fetched the dead child. She carried it to the bed-side and showed it to Bertha.

Bertha said nothing, and at last turned away; the nurse withdrew. Bertha's tears now had ceased, but her mouth was set into a hopeless woe.

"Oh, I loved him already so much."

Edward bent over. "Don't grieve, darling."

She put her arms round his neck as she had delighted to do. "Oh, Eddie, love me with all your heart. I want your love so badly."

Chapter XVIII

FOR DAYS BERTHA WAS OVERWHELMED WITH GRIEF. SHE THOUGHT ALWAYS OF the dead child that had never lived, and her heart ached. But above all she was tormented by the idea that all her pain had been futile; she had gone through so much, her sleep still was full of the past agony, and it had been utterly, utterly useless. Her body was mutilated so that she wondered it was possible for her to recover; she had lost her old buoyancy, that vitality which had been so enjoyable, and she felt like an old woman. Her sense of weariness was unendurable—she was so tired that it seemed to her impossible to get rest. She lay in bed, day after day, in a posture of hopeless fatigue, on her back, with arms stretched out alongside of her, the pillows supporting her head: all her limbs were singularly powerless.

Recovery was very slow, and Edward suggested sending for Miss Ley, but Bertha refused.

"I don't want to see anybody," she said; "I merely want to lie still and be quiet."

It bored her to speak with people, and even her affections, for the time, were dormant: she looked upon Edward as someone apart from her, his presence and absence gave no particular emotion. She was tired, and desired only to be left alone. All sympathy was unnecessary and useless, she knew that no one could enter into the bitterness of her sorrow, and she preferred to bear it alone.

Little by little, however, Bertha regained strength and consented to see the friends who called, some genuinely sorry, others impelled merely by a sense of duty or by a ghoul-like curiosity. Miss Glover, at this period, was a great trial; the good creature felt for Bertha the sincerest sympathy, but her feelings were one thing, her sense of right and wrong another. She did not think the young wife took her affliction with proper humility. Gradually a rebellious feeling had replaced the extreme prostration of the beginning, and Bertha raged at the injustice of her lot. Miss Glover came every day, bringing flowers and good advice; but Bertha was not docile, and refused to be satisfied with Miss Glover's pious consolations. When the good creature read the Bible, Bertha listened with a firmer closing of her lips, sullenly.

"Do you like me to read the Bible to you, dear?" asked the parson's sister once.

And Bertha, driven beyond her patience, could not as usual command her tongue.

"If it amuses you, dear," she answered, bitterly.

"Oh, Bertha, you're not taking it in the proper spirit—you're so rebellious, and it's wrong, it's utterly wrong."

"I can only think of my baby," said Bertha, hoarsely.

"Why don't you pray to God, dear—shall I offer a short prayer now, Bertha?"

"No, I don't want to pray to God—He's either impotent or cruel."

"Bertha," cried Miss Glover. "You don't know what you're saying. Oh, pray to God to melt your stubbornness; pray to God to forgive you."

"I don't want to be forgiven. I've done nothing that needs it. It's God who needs my forgiveness—not I His."

"You don't know what you're saying, Bertha," replied Miss Glover, very gravely and sorrowfully.

Bertha was still so ill that Miss Glover dared not press the subject, but she was grievously troubled. She asked herself whether she should consult her brother, to whom an absurd shyness prevented her from mentioning spiritual matters, unless necessity compelled. But she had immense faith in him, and to her he was a type of all that a Christian clergyman should be. Although her character was so much stronger than his, Mr. Glover always seemed to his sister a pillar of strength; and often in past times, when the flesh was more stubborn, had she found help and consolation in his very mediocre sermons. Finally, however, Miss Glover decided to speak to him, with the result that, for a week she avoided spiritual topics in her daily conversation with the invalid; then, Bertha having grown a little stronger, without previously mentioning the fact, she brought her brother to Court Leys.

Miss Glover went alone to Bertha's room, in her ardent sense of propriety fearing that Bertha, in bed, might not be costumed decorously enough for the visit of a clerical gentleman.

"Oh," she said, "Charles is downstairs and would like to see you so much. I thought I'd better come up first to see if you were—er—presentable."

Bertha was sitting up in bed, with a mass of cushions and pillows behind her—a bright red jacket contrasted with her dark hair and the pallor of her skin. She drew her lips together when she heard that the Vicar was below, and a slight frown darkened her forehead. Miss Glover caught sight of it.

"I don't think she likes your coming," said Miss Glover—to encourage him—when she fetched her brother, "but I think it's your duty."

"Yes, I think it's my duty," replied Mr. Glover, who liked the approaching interview as little as Bertha.

He was an honest man, oppressed by the inroads of dissent; but his ministrations were confined to the services in church, the collecting of subscriptions, and the visiting of the church-going poor. It was something new to be brought before a rebellious gentlewoman, and he did not quite know how to treat her.

Miss Glover opened the bed-room door for her brother and he entered, a cold wind laden with carbolic acid. She solemnly put a chair for him by the bed-side and another for herself at a little distance.

"Ring for the tea before you sit down, Fanny," said Bertha.

"I think, if you don't mind, Charles would like to speak to you first," said Miss Glover. "Am I not right, Charles?"

"Yes, dear."

"I took the liberty of telling him what you said to me the other day, Bertha."

Mrs. Craddock pursed her lips, but made no reply.

"I hope you're not angry with me for doing so, but I thought it my duty.... Now, Charles."

The Vicar of Leanham coughed.

"I can quite understand," he said, "that you must be most distressed at your affliction. It's a most unfortunate occurrence. I need not say that Fanny and I sympathise with you from the bottom of our hearts."

"We do indeed," said his sister.

Still Bertha did not answer and Miss Glover looked at her uneasily. The Vicar coughed again.

"But I always think that we should be thankful for the cross we have to bear. It is, as it were, a measure of the confidence that God places in us."

Bertha remained quite silent and Miss Glover saw that no good would come by beating about the bush.

"The fact is, Bertha," she said, breaking the awkward silence, "that Charles and I are very anxious that you should be churched. You don't mind our saying so, but we're both a great deal older than you are, and we think it will do you good. We do hope you'll consent to it; but, more than that, Charles is here as the clergyman of your parish, to tell you that it is your duty."

"I hope it won't be necessary for me to put it in that way, Mrs. Craddock."

Bertha paused a moment longer, and then asked for a prayer-book. Miss Glover gave a smile which for her was quite radiant.

"I've been wanting for a long time to make you a little present, Bertha," she said, "and it occurred to me that you might like a prayer-book with good large print. I've noticed in church that the book you generally use is so small that it must try your eyes, and be a temptation to you not to follow the service. So I've brought you one today, which it will give me very much pleasure if you will accept."

She produced a large volume, bound in gloomy black cloth, and redolent of the antiseptic odours which pervaded the Vicarage. The print was indeed large, but, since the society which arranged the publication insisted on the combination of cheapness with utility, the paper was abominable.

"Thank you very much," said Bertha, holding out her hand for the gift. "It's awfully kind of you."

"Shall I find you the *Churching of Women?*"

Bertha nodded, and presently the Vicar's sister handed her the book, open. She read a few lines and dropped it.

"I have no wish to 'give hearty thanks unto God,' " she said, looking almost fiercely at the worthy pair. "I'm very sorry to offend your prejudices, but it seems to me absurd that I should prostrate myself in gratitude to God."

"Oh, Mrs. Craddock, I trust you don't mean what you say," said the Vicar.

"This is what I told you, Charles," said Miss Glover. "I don't think Bertha is well, but still this seems to me dreadfully wicked."

Bertha frowned, finding it difficult to repress the sarcasm which rose to her lips; her forbearance was sorely tried. But Mr. Glover was a little undecided.

"We must be as thankful to God for the afflictions He sends as for the benefits," he said at last.

"I am not a worm to crawl upon the ground and give thanks to the foot that crushes me."

"I think that is blasphemous, Bertha," said Miss Glover.

"Oh, I have no patience with you, Fanny," said Bertha, raising herself, a flush lighting up her face. "Can you realise what I've gone through, the terrible pain of it? Oh, it was too awful. Even now when I think of it I almost scream."

"It is by suffering that we rise to our higher self," said Miss Glover. "Suffering is a fire that burns away the grossness of our material natures."

"What rubbish you talk," cried Bertha, passionately. "You can say that when you've never suffered. People say that suffering ennobles one; it's a lie, it only makes one brutal. . . . But I would have borne it—for the sake of my child. It was all useless—utterly useless. Dr. Ramsay told me the child had been dead the whole time. Oh, if God made me suffer like that, it's infamous. I wonder you're not ashamed to put it down to God. How can you imagine Him to be so stupid, so cruel! Why, even the vilest beast in the slums wouldn't cause a woman such frightful and useless agony for the mere pleasure of it."

Miss Glover sprang to her feet. "Bertha, your illness is no excuse for this. You must either be mad, or utterly depraved and wicked."

"No, I'm more charitable than you," cried Bertha. "I know there is no God."

"Then I, for one, can have nothing more to do with you." Miss Glover's cheeks were flaming, and a sudden indignation dispelled her habitual shyness.

"Fanny, Fanny!" cried her brother, "restrain yourself."

"Oh, this isn't a time to restrain one's self, Charles. It's one's duty to speak out sometimes. No, Bertha, if you're an athiest, I can have nothing more to do with you."

"She spoke in anger," said the Vicar. "It is not our duty to judge her."

"It's our duty to protest when the name of God is taken in vain, Charles. If you think Bertha's position excuses her blasphemies, Charles, then I think you ought to be ashamed of yourself.... But I'm not afraid to speak out. Yes, Bertha, I've known for a long time that you were proud and headstrong, but I thought time would change you. I have always had confidence in you, because I thought at the bottom you were good. But if you deny your Maker, Bertha, there can be no hope for you."

"Fanny, Fanny," murmured the Vicar.

"Let me speak, Charles; I think you're a bad and wicked woman—and I can no longer feel sorry for you, because everything that you have suffered I think you have thoroughly deserved. Your heart is absolutely hard, and I know nothing so thoroughly wicked as a hard-hearted woman."

"My dear Fanny," said Bertha, smiling, "we've both been absurdly melodramatic."

"I refuse to laugh at the subject. I see nothing ridiculous in it. Come, Charles, let us go, and leave her to her own thoughts."

But as Miss Glover bounded to the door the handle was turned from the outside and Mrs. Branderton came in. The position was awkward, and her appearance seemed almost providential to the Vicar, who could not fling out of the room like his sister, but also could not make up his mind to shake hands with Bertha, as if nothing had happened. Mrs. Branderton entered, all airs and graces, smirking and ogling, and the gew-gaws on her bran-new bonnet quivered with every movement.

"I told the servant I could find my way up alone, Bertha," she said. "I wanted so much to see you."

"Mr. and Miss Glover were just going. How kind of you to come!"

Miss Glover bounced out of the room with a smile at Mrs. Branderton that was almost ghastly; and Mr. Glover, meek, polite, and as antiseptic as ever, shaking hands with Mrs. Branderton, followed his sister.

"What queer people they are!" said Mrs. Branderton, standing at the window to see them come out of the front-door. "I really don't think they're quite human.... Why, she's walking on in front—she might wait for him—taking such long steps; and he's trying to catch her up. I believe they're having a race. Ha! ha! What ridiculous people! Isn't it a pity she will wear short skirts—my dear, her feet and ankles are positively awful. I believe they wear one another's boots indiscriminately.... And how are you, dear? I think you're looking much better."

Mrs. Branderton sat in such a position as to have full view of herself in a mirror.

"What nice looking-glasses you have in your room, my love. No woman can dress properly without them. Now, you've only got to look at poor Fanny Glover to know that she's so modest as never even to look at herself in the glass to put her hat on."

Mrs. Branderton chattered on, thinking that she was doing Bertha good. "A woman doesn't want one to be solemn when she's ill. I know when I have anything the matter, I like someone to talk to me about the fashions. I remember in my young days, when I was ill, I used to get old Mr. Crowhurst, the former vicar, to come and read the ladies' papers to me. He was such a nice old man, not a bit like a clergyman; and he used to say I was his only parishioner whom he really liked visiting. . . . I'm not tiring you, am I, dear?"

"Oh, dear, no!" said Bertha.

"Now I suppose the Glovers have been talking all sorts of stuff to you. Of course one has to put up with it, I suppose, because it sets a good example to the lower orders; but I must say I do think the clergy nowadays sometimes forget their place. I consider it most objectionable when they insist on talking religion with you, as if you were a common person. . . . But they're not nearly so nice as they used to be. In my young days the clergy were always gentlemen's sons—but then they weren't expected to trouble about the poor. I can quite understand that now a gentleman shouldn't like to become a clergyman; he has to mix with the lower classes, and they're growing more familiar every day."

But suddenly Bertha, without warning, burst into tears. Mrs. Branderton was flabbergasted!

"My dear, what is the matter? Where are your salts? Shall I ring the bell?"

Bertha, sobbing violently, begged Mrs. Branderton to take no notice of her. That fashionable creature had a sentimental heart, and would have been delighted to weep with Bertha; but she had several calls to make, and could not risk a disarrangement of her person. She was also curious, and would have given much to find out the cause of Bertha's outburst. She comforted herself, however, by giving the Hancocks, whose *At Home* day it was, a detailed account of the affair; and they, shortly afterwards, recounted it with sundry embellishments to Mrs. Mayston Ryle.

Mrs. Mayston Ryle, magnificently imposing as ever, snorted like a charger eager for battle.

"Mrs. Branderton sends *me* to sleep frequently," she said; "But I can quite understand that if the poor thing isn't well, Mrs. Branderton would make her cry. I never see her myself unless I'm in the most robust health, otherwise I know she'd simply make me howl."

"But I wonder what was the matter with poor Mrs. Craddock," said Miss Hancock.

"I don't know," answered Mrs. Mayston Ryle in her majestic manner. "But I'll find out. I dare say she only wants a little good society. *I* shall go and see her."

And she did!

Chapter XIX

But the apathy with which for weeks Bertha had looked upon all terrestrial concerns was passing away before her increasing strength. It had been due only to an utter physical weakness, of the same order as that merciful indifference to all earthly sympathies which gives ease to the final passage into the Unknown. The prospect of death would be unendurable if one did not know that the enfeebled body brought a like enfeeblement of spirit, dissolving the ties of this world: when the traveller must leave the hostel with the double gate, the wine he loved has lost its savour and the bread turned bitter in his mouth. Like useless gauds, Bertha had let fall the interests of life; her soul lay a-dying. Her soul was a lighted candle in a lantern, nickering in the wind so that its flame was hardly seen and the lantern was useless; but presently the wind of death was stilled, and the light shone out and filled the darkness.

With increasing strength the old passion returned; love came back like a conqueror, and Bertha knew that she had not done with life. In her loneliness she yearned for Edward's affection; for now he was all she had, and she stretched out her arms to him with a great desire. She blamed herself bitterly for her coldness, she wept at the idea of what he must have suffered. And she was ashamed that the love which she had thought eternal, should have been for a while destroyed. But a change had come over her. She did not now love her husband with the old blind passion, but with a new feeling added to it; for to him was transferred the tenderness which she had lavished on her dead child, and all the mother's spirit which must now, to her life's end, go unsatisfied. Her heart was like a house with empty chambers, and the fires of love raged through them triumphantly.

Bertha thought a little painfully of Miss Glover, but dismissed her with a shrug of the shoulders. The good creature had kept her resolve never again to come near Court Leys, and for days nothing had been heard of her.

"What does it matter?" cried Bertha. "So long as Eddie loves me, the rest of the world is nothing."

But her room gained now the aspect of a prison, so that she felt it impossible much longer to endure its dreadful monotony. Her bed was a bed of torture, and she fancied that so long as she remained stretched upon it, health would not return. She begged Dr. Ramsay to allow her to get up, but was always met with the same refusal, backed up by her husband's common sense. All she obtained was the dismissal of the nurse to whom she had taken a sudden and violent dislike. From no reasonable cause, Bertha found the mere presence of the poor woman unendurable, and her officious loquacity irritated her beyond measure. If she must remain in bed, Bertha preferred absolute solitude; the turn of her mind was becoming almost misanthropic.

The hours passed endlessly. From her pillow Bertha could see only the sky, now a metallic blue with dazzling clouds swaying heavily across, now grey, darkening the room. The furniture and the wall-paper forced themselves distastefully on her mind. Every detail was impressed on her consciousness as indelibly as the potter's mark on the clay.

Finally she made up her mind to get up, come what might. It was the Sunday after the quarrel with Miss Glover; Edward would be indoors and doubtless intended to spend most of the afternoon in her room, but she knew he disliked sitting there; the closeness, the odours of medicine, made his head ache. Her appearance in the drawing-room would be a delightful surprise. She would not tell him that she was getting up, but go downstairs and take him unawares. She got out of bed, but as she put her feet to the ground, had to cling to a chair; her legs were so weak that they hardly supported her, and her head reeled. But in a little while she gathered strength and slowly dressed herself, slowly and very difficultly; her weakness was almost pain. She had to sit down, and her hair was so wearisome to do that she was afraid she must give up the attempt and return to bed. But the thought of Edward's surprise upheld her—he had said how pleased he would be to have her downstairs with him. At last she was ready and went to the door, supporting herself on every object at hand. But what joy it was to be up again, to feel herself once more among the living—away from the grave of her bed!

She came to the top of the stairs and went down, leaning heavily on the banisters; she went one step at a time, as little children do, and laughed at herself. But the laugh changed almost into a groan, as in exhaustion she sank down and felt it impossible to go farther. Then the thought of Edward urged her on. She struggled to her feet, and persevered till she reached the bottom. Now she was outside the drawing-room, she heard Edward whistling within. She crept along, eager to make no sound; noiselessly she turned the handle and flung the door open.

"Eddie!"

He turned round with a cry. "Hulloa, what are you doing here?"

He came towards her, but showed not the great joy which she had expected.

"I wanted to surprise you. Aren't you glad to see me?"

"Yes, of course I am. But you oughtn't to have come without Dr. Ramsay's leave. And I didn't expect you today."

He led her to the sofa, and she lay down.

"I thought you'd be so pleased."

"Of course I am!"

He placed pillows under her, and covered her with a rug—little attentions which were exquisitely touching.

"You don't know how I struggled," she said. "I thought I should never get my things on, and then I almost tumbled down the stairs, I was so weak.... But I knew you must be lonely here, and you hate sitting in the bed-room."

"You oughtn't to have risked it. It may throw you back," he replied, gently. He looked at his watch. "You must only stay half an hour, and then I shall carry you up to bed."

Bertha gave a laugh, intending to permit nothing of the sort. It was so comfortable to lie on the sofa, with Edward by her side. She held his hands.

"I simply couldn't stay in the room any longer. It was so gloomy, with the rain pattering all day on the windows."

It was one of those days of late summer when the rain seems never ceasing, and the air is filled with the melancholy of nature, already conscious of the near decay.

"I was meaning to come up to you as soon as I'd finished my pipe."

Bertha was exhausted, and, keeping silence, pressed Edward's hand in acknowledgment of his kind intention. Presently he looked at his watch again.

"Your half-hour's nearly up. In five minutes I'm going to carry you to your room."

"Oh no, you're not," she replied playfully, taking his remark as humourous. "I'm going to stay till dinner."

"No, you can't possibly. It will be very bad for you.... To please me go back to bed now."

"Well, we'll split the difference and I'll go after tea."

"No, you must go now."

"Why, one would think you wanted to get rid of me!"

"I have to go out," said Edward.

"Oh no, you haven't—you're merely saying that to induce me to go upstairs. You fibber!"

"Let me carry you up now, there's a good girl."

"I won't, I won't, I won't."

"I shall have to leave you alone, Bertha. I didn't know you meant to get up today, and I have an engagement."

"Oh, but you can't leave me the first time I get up. What is it? You can write a note and break it."

"I'm awfully sorry," he replied. "But I'm afraid I can't do that. The fact is, I saw the Miss Hancocks after church, and they said they had to walk into Tercanbury this afternoon, and as it was so wet I offered to drive them in. I've promised to fetch them at three."

"You're joking," said Bertha; her eyes had suddenly become hard, and she was breathing fast.

Edward looked at her uneasily, "I didn't know you were going to get up, or I shouldn't have arranged to go out."

"Oh well, it doesn't matter," said Bertha, throwing off the momentary anger. "You can just write and say you can't come."

"I'm afraid I can't do that," he answered, gravely. "I've given my word and I can't break it."

"Oh, but it's infamous." Her wrath blazed out again. "Even you can't be so cruel as to leave me at such a time. I deserve some consideration—after all I've suffered. For weeks I lay at death's door, and at last when I'm a little better and come down—thinking to give you pleasure, you're engaged to drive the Misses Hancock into Tercanbury."

"Come, Bertha, be reasonable." Edward condescended to expostulate with his wife, though it was not his habit to humour her extravagances. "You see it's not my fault. Isn't it enough for you that I'm very sorry? I shall be back in an hour. Stay here, and then we'll spend the evening together."

"Why did you lie to me?"

"I haven't lied: I'm not given to that," said Edward, with natural satisfaction.

"You pretended it was for my health's sake that I must go upstairs. Isn't that a lie?"

"It was for your health's sake."

"You lie again. You wanted to get me out of the way, so that you might go to the Miss Hancocks without telling me."

"You ought to know me better than that by now."

"Why did you say nothing about them till you found it impossible to avoid."

Edward shrugged his shoulders good-humouredly. "Because I know how touchy you are."

"And yet you made them the offer."

"It came out almost unawares. They were grumbling about the weather, and without thinking, I said, 'I'll drive you over if you like.' And they jumped at it."

"You're so good-natured if anyone but your wife is concerned."

"Well, dear, I can't stay arguing. I shall be late already."

"You're not really going?" It had been impossible for Bertha to realise that Edward would carry out his intention.

"I must, my dear; it's my duty."

"You have more duty to me than to anyone else. . . . Oh, Eddie, don't go. You can't realise all it means to me."

"I must. I'm not going because I want to. I shall be back in an hour."

He bent down to kiss her, and she flung her arms round his neck, bursting into tears.

"Oh, please don't go—if you love me at all, if you've ever loved me.... Don't you see that you're destroying my love for you?"

"Now, don't be silly, there's a good girl."

He loosened her arms and walked away; but rising from the sofa she followed him and took his arm, beseeching him to stay.

"You see how unhappy I am; and you are all I have in the world now. For God's sake, stay, Eddie. It means more to me than you know."

She sank to the floor; she was kneeling before him.

"Come, get on to the sofa. All this is very bad for you."

He carried her to the couch, and then, to finish the scene, hurriedly left the room.

Bertha sprang up to follow him, but sank back as the door slammed, and burying her face in her hands, surrendered herself to a passion of tears. But humiliation and rage almost drove away her grief. She had knelt before her husband for a favour, and he had not granted it. Suddenly she abhorred him. The love, which had been a tower of brass, fell like a house of cards. She would not try now to conceal from herself the faults that stared her in the face. He cared only for himself: with him it was only self, self, self. Bertha found a bitter fascination in stripping her idol of the finery with which her madness had bedizened him; she saw him more accurately now, and he was utterly selfish. But most unbearable of all was her own extreme humiliation.

The rain poured down, unceasing, and the despair of nature ate into her soul. At last she was exhausted; and losing thought of time, lay half-unconscious, feeling at least no pain, her brain vacant and weary. When a servant came to ask if Miss Glover might see her, she hardly understood.

"Miss Glover doesn't usually stand on such ceremony," she said ill-temperedly, forgetting the incident of the previous week. "Ask her to come in."

The parson's sister came to the door and hesitated, growing red; the expression in her eyes was pained, and even frightened.

"May I come in, Bertha?"

"Yes."

She walked straight to the sofa, and fell on her knees.

"Oh, Bertha, please forgive me. I was wrong, and I've behaved wickedly to you."

"My dear Fanny," murmured Bertha, a smile breaking through her misery.

"I withdraw every word I said to you, Bertha; I can't understand how I said it. I humbly beg your forgiveness."

"There is nothing to forgive."

"Oh, yes, there is. Good heavens, I know! My conscience has been reproaching me ever since I was here, but I hardened my heart, and would not listen."

Poor Miss Glover could not really have hardened her heart, however much she tried.

"I knew I ought to come to you and beg your forgiveness, but I wouldn't. I've not slept a wink at night. I was afraid of dying, and if I'd been cut off in the midst of my wickedness, I should have been lost."

She spoke very quickly, finding it evidently a relief to express her trouble.

"I thought Charles would upbraid me, but he's never said a word. Oh, I wish he had, it would have been easier to bear than his sorrowful look. I know he's been worrying dreadfully, and I'm so sorry for him. I kept on saying I'd only done my duty, but in my heart I knew I had done wrong. Oh Bertha, and this morning I dared not take communion, I thought God would strike me for blasphemy. And I was afraid Charles would refuse me in front of the whole congregation. . . . It's the first Sunday since I was confirmed, that I've missed taking Holy Communion."

She buried her face in her hands, crying. Bertha heard her, almost listlessly; for her own trouble was overwhelming and she could not think of any other. Miss Glover raised her face, tear-stained and red; it was positively hideous, but notwithstanding, very pathetic.

"Then I couldn't bear it any longer," she said. "I thought if I begged your pardon I might be able to forgive myself. Oh, Bertha, please forget what I said, and forgive me. And I fancied that Edward would be here today, and the thought of exposing myself before him too was almost more than I could bear. But I knew the humiliation would be good for me. Oh, I was so thankful when Jane said he was out. . . . What can I do to earn your forgiveness?"

In her heart of hearts, Miss Glover desired some horrible penance which would thoroughly mortify her flesh.

"I have already forgotten all about it," said Bertha, smiling wearily. "If my forgiveness is worth anything, I forgive you entirely."

Miss Glover was a little pained at Bertha's manifest indifference, yet took it as a just punishment.

"And Bertha, let me say that I love you and admire you more than anyone after Charles. If you really think what you said the other day, I still love you and hope God will turn your heart. Charles and I will pray for you night and day, and soon I hope the Almighty will send you another child to take the place of the one you lost. Believe me, God is very good and merciful, and He will grant you what you wish."

Bertha gave a low cry of pain. "I can never have another child. . . . Dr. Ramsay told me it was impossible."

"Oh, Bertha, I didn't know."

Miss Glover took Bertha protectingly in her arms, crying, and kissed her like a little child.

But Bertha dried her eyes.

"Leave me now, Fanny, please. I'd rather be alone. But come and see me soon, and forgive me if I'm horrid. I'm very unhappy and I shall never be happy again."

A few minutes later, Edward returned—cheery, jovial, red-faced, and in the best of humours.

"Here we are again!" he shouted, like a clown in a harlequinade. "You see I've not been gone long and you haven't missed me a rap. Now, we'll have tea."

He kissed her and put her cushions right.

"By Jove, it does me good to see you down again. You must pour out the tea for me. . . . Now, confess; weren't you unreasonable to make such a fuss about my going away? And I couldn't help it, could I?"

Chapter XX

BUT THE LOVE WHICH HAD TAKEN SUCH DESPOTIC POSSESSION OF BERTHA'S nature could not be overthrown by any sudden means. When she recovered her health and was able to resume her habits, it blazed out again like a fire, momentarily subdued, which has gained new strength in its coercion. It dismayed her to think of her extreme loneliness; Edward was now her only mainstay and her only hope. She no longer sought to deny that his love was unlike hers; but his coldness was not always apparent; vehemently wishing to find a response to her ardour, she closed her eyes to all that did not too readily obtrude itself. She had such a consuming desire to find in Edward the lover of her dreams, that for certain periods she was indeed able to live in a fool's paradise, which was none the less grateful because at the bottom of her heart she had an aching suspicion of its true character.

But it seemed that the more passionately Bertha yearned for her husband's love, the more frequent became their differences. As time went on the calm between the storms was shorter, and every quarrel left its mark, and made Bertha more susceptible to affront. Realizing, finally, that Edward could not answer her demonstrations of affection, she became ten times more exacting; even the little tendernesses which at the beginning of her married life would have overjoyed her, now too much resembled alms thrown to an importunate beggar, to be received with anything but irritation. Their altercations proved conclusively that it does not require two persons to make a quarrel. Edward was a model of good-temper, and his equanimity was imperturbable. However cross Bertha was, Edward never lost his serenity. He imagined that she was troubling over the loss of her child, and that her health was not entirely restored: it had been his experience, especially with cows, that a difficult confinement frequently gave rise to some temporary change in disposition, so that the most docile animal in the world would suddenly develop an unexpected viciousness. He never tried to understand Bertha's varied moods; her passionate desire for love was to him as unreasonable as her outbursts of temper and the succeeding contrition. Now, Edward was always the same—contented equally with the universe at large and with himself; there was no shadow of a doubt about the fact that the world he lived in, the particular spot and period, were the very best possible; and that no existence could be more satisfactory than happily to cultivate one's garden. Not being analytic, he forbore to think about the matter; and if he had, would not have borrowed the phrases of M. de Voltaire, whom he had never heard of, and would have utterly abhorred as a Frenchman, a philosopher, and a wit. But the fact that Edward ate, drank, slept, and ate again, as regularly as the oxen on his farm, sufficiently proved that he enjoyed a happiness equal to theirs—and what more can a decent man want?

Edward had moreover that magnificent faculty of always doing right and of knowing it, which is said to be the most inestimable gift of the true Christian; but if his infallibility pleased himself and edified his neighbours, it did not fail to cause his wife the utmost annoyance. She would clench her hands and from her eyes shoot arrows of fire, when he stood in front of her, smilingly conscious of the justice of his own standpoint and the unreason of hers. And the worst of it was that in her saner moments Bertha had to confess that Edward's view was invariably right and she completely in the wrong. Her injustice appalled her, and she took upon her own shoulders the blame of all their unhappiness. Always, after a quarrel from which Edward had come with his usual triumph, Bertha's rage would be succeeded by a passion of remorse; and she could not find sufficient reproaches with which to castigate herself. She asked frantically how her husband could be expected to love her; and in a transport of agony and fear would take the first opportunity of throwing her arms around his neck and making the most abject apology. Then, having eaten the dust before him, having wept and humiliated herself, she would be for a week absurdly happy, under the impression that henceforward nothing short of an earthquake could disturb their blissful equilibrium. Edward was again the golden idol, clothed in the diaphanous garments of true love, his word was law and his deeds were perfect; Bertha was an humble worshipper, offering incense and devoutly grateful to the deity that forbore to crush her. It required very little for her to forget the slights and the coldness of her husband's affection: her love was like the tide covering a barren rock; the sea breaks into waves and is dispersed in foam, while the rock remains ever unchanged. This simile, by the way, would not have displeased Edward; when he thought at all, he liked to think how firm and steadfast he was.

At night, before going to sleep, it was Bertha's greatest pleasure to kiss her husband on the lips, and it mortified her to see how mechanically he replied to this embrace. It was always she who had to make the advance, and when, to try him, she omitted to do so, he promptly went off to sleep without even bidding her goodnight. Then she told herself that he must utterly despise her.

"Oh, it drives me mad to think of the devotion I waste on you," she cried. "I'm a fool! You are all in the world to me, and I, to you, am a sort of accident: you might have married anyone but me. If I hadn't come across your path you would infallibly have married somebody else."

"Well, so would you," he answered, laughing.

"I? Never! If I had not met you I should have married no one. My love isn't a bauble that I am willing to give to whomever chance throws in my way. My heart is one and indivisible; it would be impossible for me to love anyone but you.... When I think that to you I'm nothing more than any other woman might be, I'm ashamed."

"You do talk the most awful rot sometimes."

"Ah, that summarises your whole opinion. To you I'm merely a fool of a woman. I'm a domestic animal, a little more companionable than a dog, but on the whole, not so useful as a cow."

"I don't know what you want me to do more than I actually do. You can't expect me to be kissing and cuddling all the time. The honeymoon is meant for that, and a man who goes on honeymooning all his life, is an ass."

"Ah yes, with you love is kept out of sight all day, while you are occupied with the serious affairs of life, such as shearing sheep or hunting foxes; and after dinner it arises in your bosom, especially if you've had good things to eat, and is indistinguishable from the process of digestion. But for me love is everything, the cause and reason of life. Without love I should be non-existent."

"Well, you may love me," said Edward, "but, by Jove, you've got a jolly funny way of showing it.... But as far as I'm concerned, if you'll tell me what you want me to do, I'll try and do it."

"Oh, how can I tell you?" she cried, impatiently. "I do everything I can to make you love me and I can't. If you're a stock and a stone, how can I teach you to be the passionate lover? I want you to love me as I love you."

"Well, if you ask me for my opinion I should say it was rather a good job I don't. Why, the furniture would be smashed up in a week, if I were as violent as you."

"I shouldn't mind if you were violent if you loved me," replied Bertha, taking his remark with vehement seriousness. "I shouldn't care if you beat me; I should not mind how much you hurt me, if you did it because you loved me."

"I think a week of it would about sicken you of that sort of love, my dear."

"Anything would be preferable to your indifference."

"But God bless my soul, I'm not indifferent. Anyone would think I didn't care for you—or was gone on some other woman."

"I almost wish you were," answered Bertha. "If you loved anyone at all, I might have some hope of gaining your affection—but you're incapable of love."

"I don't know about that. I can say truly that after God and my honour, I treasure nothing in the world so much as you."

"You've forgotten your hunter," cried Bertha, scornfully.

"No, I haven't," answered Edward, with a certain gravity.

"What do you think I care for a position like that? You acknowledge that I am third—I would as soon be nowhere."

"I could not love you half so much, loved I not honour more," misquoted Edward.

"The man was a prig who wrote that. I want to be placed above your God and above your honour. The love I want is the love of the man who will lose everything, even his own soul, for the sake of a woman."

Edward shrugged his shoulders. "I don't know where you'll get that. My idea of love is that it's a very good thing in its place—but there's a limit to everything. There are other things in life."

"Oh yes, I know—there's duty and honour, and the farm, and fox-hunting, and the opinion of one's neighbours, and the dogs and the cat, and the new brougham, and a million other things. . . . What do you suppose you'd do if I had committed some crime and were likely to be imprisoned?"

"I don't want to suppose anything of the sort. You may be sure I'd do my duty."

"Oh, I'm sick of your duty. You din it into my ears morning, noon, and night. I wish to God you weren't so virtuous—you might be more human."

Edward found his wife's behaviour so extraordinary that he consulted Dr. Ramsay. The medical man had been for thirty years the recipient of marital confidences, and was sceptical as to the value of medicine in the cure of jealousy, talkativeness, incompatibility of temper, and the like diseases. He assured Edward that time was the only remedy by which all differences were reconciled; but after further pressing consented to send Bertha a bottle of harmless tonic, which it was his habit to give to all and sundry for most of the ills to which the flesh is heir. It would doubtless do Bertha no harm, and that is an important consideration to a general practitioner. Dr. Ramsay likewise advised Edward to keep calm and be confident that Bertha would eventually become the dutiful and submissive spouse whom it is every man's ideal to see by his fireside, when he wakes up from his after-dinner snooze.

Bertha's moods were certainly trying. No one could tell one day, how she would be the next; and this was peculiarly uncomfortable to a man who was willing to make the best of everything, but on the condition that he had time to get used to it. Sometimes she would be seized with melancholy, in the twilight of winter afternoons, for instance, when the mind is naturally led to a contemplation of the vanity of existence and the futility of all human endeavour. Edward, noticing she was pensive, a state which he detested, asked what were her thoughts; and half-dreamily she tried to express them.

"Good Lord deliver us!" he cried cheerily, "what rum things you do get into your little noddle. You must be out of sorts."

"It isn't that," she answered, smiling sadly.

"It's not natural for a woman to brood in that way. I think you ought to start taking that tonic again—but I dare say you're only tired and you'll think quite different in the morning."

Bertha made no answer. She suffered from the nameless pain of existence and he offered her—Iron and Quinine: when she required sympathy because her heart ached for the woes of her fellow-men, he poured Tincture of Nux Vomica down her throat. He could not understand, it was no use explaining that she found a savour in the tender contemplation of the evils of mankind. But the worst of it was that Edward was quite right—the brute, he always was! When the morning came, the melancholy had vanished, Bertha was left without a care, and the world did not even need rose-coloured spectacles to seem attractive. It was humiliating to find that her most beautiful thoughts, the ennobling emotions which brought home to her the charming fiction that all men are brothers, were due to mere physical exhaustion.

Some people have extraordinarily literal minds, they never allow for the play of imagination: life for them has no beer and skittles, and, far from being an empty dream, is a matter of extreme seriousness. Of such is the man who, when a woman tells him she feels dreadfully old, instead of answering that she looks absurdly young, replies that youth has its drawbacks and age its compensations! And of such was Edward. He could never realise that people did not mean exactly what they said. At first he had always consulted Bertha on the conduct of the estate; but she, pleased to be a nonentity in her own house, had consented to everything he suggested, and even begged him not to ask her. When she informed him that he was absolute lord not only of herself, but of all her worldly goods, it was not surprising that he should at last take her at her word.

"Women know nothing about farming," he said, "and it's best that I should have a free hand."

The result of his stewardship was all that could be desired; the estate was put into apple-pie order, and the farms paid rent for the first time since twenty years. The wandering winds, even the sun and the rain, seemed to conspire in favour of so clever and hard working a man; and fortune for once went hand in hand with virtue. Bertha constantly received congratulations from the surrounding squires on the admirable way in which Edward managed the place, and he, on his side, never failed to recount his triumphs and the compliments they occasioned.

But not only was Edward looked upon as master by his farm-hands and labourers; even the servants of Court Leys treated Bertha as a minor personage whose orders were only to be conditionally obeyed. Long generations of servitude have made the countryman peculiarly subtle in hierarchical distinctions; and there was a marked difference between his manner with Edward, on whom his livelihood depended, and his manner with Bertha, who shone only with a reflected light as the squire's missus.

At first this had only amused Bertha, but the most brilliant jest, constantly repeated, may lose its savour. More than once she had to speak sharply to a gardener who hesitated to do as he was bid, because his orders were not from the master. Her pride reviving with the decline of love, Bertha began to find the position intolerable; her mind was now very susceptible to affront, and she was desirous of an opportunity to show that after all she was still the mistress of Court Leys.

It soon came. For it chanced that some ancient lover of trees, unpractical as the Leys had ever been, had planted six beeches in a hedgerow, and these in course of time had grown into stately trees, the admiration of all beholders. But one day as Bertha walked along, a hideous gap caught her eye—one of the six beeches had disappeared. There had been no storm, it could not have fallen of itself. She went up, and found it cut down, and the men who had done the deed were already starting on another: a ladder was leaning against it, upon which stood a labourer attaching a line. No sight is more pathetic than an old tree levelled with the ground; and the space which it filled suddenly stands out with an unsightly emptiness. But Bertha was more angry than pained.

"What are you doing, Hodgkins? Who gave you orders to cut down this tree?"

"The squire, mum."

"Oh, it must be a mistake. Mr. Craddock never meant anything of the sort."

" 'E told us positive to take down this one and them others yonder. You can see his mark, mum."

"Nonsense. I'll talk to Mr. Craddock about it. Take that rope off and come down from the ladder. I forbid you to touch another tree."

The man on the ladder looked at her, but made no attempt to do as he was bid.

"The squire said most particular that we was to cut that tree down today."

"Will you have the goodness to do as I tell you?" said Bertha, reddening with anger. "Tell that man to unfasten the rope and come down. I forbid you to touch the tree."

The man Hodgkins repeated Bertha's order in a surly voice, and they all looked at her suspiciously, wishing to disobey but not daring—in case the squire should be angry.

"Well, I'll take no responsibility for it."

"Please hold your tongue and do what I tell you as quickly as possible."

She waited till the men had gathered up their various belongings and trooped off.

Chapter XXI

BERTHA WENT HOME, FUMING, KNOWING PERFECTLY WELL THAT EDWARD had really given the orders which she had countermanded, but glad of the chance to have a final settlement of rights. She did not see him for several hours.

"I say, Bertha," he said, when he came in, "why on earth did you stop those men cutting down the beeches on Carter's field? You've lost a whole half-day's work. I wanted to set them on something else tomorrow, now I shall have to leave it over till Thursday."

"I stopped them because I refuse to have the beeches cut down. They're the only ones in the place. I'm very much annoyed that even one should have gone without my knowing about it. You should have asked me before you did such a thing."

"My good girl, I can't come and ask you each time I want a thing done."

"Is the land mine or yours?"

"It's yours," answered Edward, laughing, "but I know better than you what ought to be done, and it's silly of you to interfere."

Bertha flushed. "In future, I wish to be consulted."

"You've told me fifty thousand times to do always as I think fit."

"Well, I've changed my mind."

"It's too late now," he laughed. "You made me take the reins in my own hands and I'm going to keep them."

Bertha in her anger hardly restrained herself from telling him she could send him away like a hired servant.

"I want you to understand, Edward, that I'm not going to have those trees cut down. You must tell the men you made a mistake."

"I shall tell them nothing of the sort. I'm not going to cut them all down—only three. We don't want them there—for one thing the shade damages the crops, and otherwise Carter's is one of our best fields. And then I want the wood."

"I care nothing about the crops, and if you want wood you can buy it. Those trees were planted nearly a hundred years ago, and I would sooner die than cut them down."

"The man who planted beeches in a hedgerow was about the silliest jackass I've ever heard of. Any tree's bad enough, but a beech of all things—why, it's drip, drip, drip, all the time, and not a thing will grow under them. That's the sort of thing that has been done all over the estate for years. It'll take me a lifetime to repair the blunders of your—of the former owners."

It is one of the curiosities of sentiment that its most abject slave rarely permits it to interfere with his temporal concerns; it appears as unusual for a man to sentimentalise in his own walk of life as for him to pick his own pocket. Edward, having passed all his days in contact with the earth, might have been expected to cherish a certain love of nature. The pathos of transpontine melodrama made him cough, and blow his nose; and in literature he affected the titled and consumptive heroine, and the soft-hearted, burly hero. But when it came to business, it was another matter—the sort of sentiment which asks a farmer to spare a sylvan glade for aesthetic reasons is absurd. Edward would have willingly allowed advertisement-mongers to put up boards on the most beautiful part of the estate, if thereby he could surreptitiously increase the profits of his farm.

"Whatever you may think of my people," said Bertha, "you will kindly pay attention to me. The land is mine, and I refuse to let you spoil it."

"It isn't spoiling it. It's the proper thing to do. You'll soon get used to not seeing the wretched trees—and I tell you I'm only going to take three down. I've given orders to cut the others tomorrow."

"D'you mean to say you're going to ignore me absolutely?"

"I'm going to do what's right; and if you don't approve of it, I'm very sorry, but I shall do it all the same."

"I shall give the men orders to do nothing of the kind."

Edward laughed. "Then you'll make an ass of yourself. You try giving them orders contrary to mine, and see what they do."

Bertha gave a cry. In her fury she looked round for something to throw; she would have liked to hit him; but he stood there, calm and self-possessed, quite amused.

"I think you must be mad," she said. "You do all you can to destroy my love for you."

She was in too great a passion for words. This was the measure of his affection; he must, indeed, utterly despise her; and this was the only result of the love she had humbly laid at his feet. She asked herself what she could do; she could do nothing—but submit. She knew as well as he that her orders would be disobeyed if they did not agree with his; and that he would keep his word she did not for a moment doubt. To do so was his pride. She did not speak for the rest of the day, but next morning when he was going out, asked what was his intention with regard to the trees.

"Oh, I thought you'd forgotten all about them," he replied. "I mean to do as I said."

"If you have the trees cut down, I shall leave you; I shall go to Aunt Polly's."

"And tell her that you wanted the moon, and I was so unkind as not to give it you?" he replied, smiling. "She'll laugh at you."

"You will find me as careful to keep my word as you."

Before luncheon she went out and walked to Carter's field. The men were still at work, but a second tree had gone, the third would doubtless fall in the afternoon. The men glanced at Bertha, and she thought they laughed; she stood looking at them for some while so that she might thoroughly digest the humiliation. Then she went home, and wrote to her aunt the following veracious letter:—

MY DEAR AUNT POLLY—I have been so seedy these last few weeks that Edward, poor dear, has been quite alarmed; and has been bothering me to come up to town to see a specialist. He's as urgent as if he wanted to get me out of the way, and I'm already half-jealous of my new parlour-maid, who has pink cheeks and golden hair—which is just the type that Edward really admires. I also think that Dr. Ramsay hasn't the ghost of an idea what is the matter with me, and not being particularly desirous to depart this life just yet, I think it will be discreet to see somebody who will at least change my medicine. I have taken gallons of iron and quinine, and I'm frightfully afraid that my teeth will go black. My own opinion, coinciding so exactly with Edward's (that horrid Mrs. Ryle calls us the humming-birds, meaning the turtledoves, her knowledge of natural history arouses dear Edward's contempt); I have gracefully acceded to his desire, and if you can put me up, will come at your earliest convenience.—Yours affectionately,

B. C.

P.S.—I shall take the opportunity of getting clothes (I am positively in rags), so you will have to keep me some little time.

Edward came in shortly afterwards, looking very much pleased. He glanced slily at Bertha, thinking himself so clever that he could scarcely help laughing: it was his habit to be most particular in his behaviour, or he would undoubtedly have put his tongue in his cheek.

"With women, my dear sir, you must be firm. When you're putting them to a fence, close your legs and don't check them; but mind you keep 'em under control or they'll lose their little heads. A man should always let a woman see that he's got her well in hand."

Bertha was silent, able to eat nothing for luncheon; she sat opposite her husband, wondering how he could gorge so disgracefully when she was angry and miserable. But in the afternoon her appetite returned, and, going to the kitchen, she ate so many sandwiches that at dinner she could again touch nothing. She hoped Edward would notice that she refused all food, and be properly alarmed and sorry. But he demolished enough for two, and never saw that his wife fasted.

At night Bertha went to bed and bolted herself in the room. Presently Edward came up and tried the door. Finding it closed, he knocked and cried to her to open. She did not answer. He knocked again more loudly and shook the handle.

"I want to have my room to myself," she cried out; "I'm ill. Please don't try to come in."

"What? Where am I to sleep?"

"Oh, you can sleep in one of the spare rooms."

"Nonsense!" he cried; and without further ado put his shoulder to the door: he was a strong man; one heave and the old hinges cracked. He entered, laughing.

"If you wanted to keep me out, you ought to have barricaded yourself up with the furniture."

Bertha was disinclined to treat the matter lightly. "If you come in," she said, "I shall go out."

"Oh no, you won't!" he said, dragging a big chest of drawers in front of the door.

Bertha got up and put on a yellow silk dressing-gown, which was really most becoming.

"I'll spend the night on the sofa then," she said. "I don't want to quarrel with you anymore or to make a scene. I have written to Aunt Polly, and the day after to-morrow I shall go to London."

"I was going to suggest that a change of air would do you good. I think your nerves are a bit groggy."

"It's very good of you to take an interest in my nerves," she replied, with a scornful glance, settling herself on the sofa.

"Are you really going to sleep there?" he said, getting into bed.

"It looks like it."

"You'll find it awfully cold. But I dare say you'll think better of it in an hour. I'm going to turn the light out. Good-night!"

Bertha did not answer, and in a few minutes she was angrily listening to his snores. Could he really be asleep? It was infamous that he slept so calmly.

"Edward," she called.

There was no answer, but she could not bring herself to believe that he was sleeping. She could never even close her eyes. He must be pretending—to annoy her. She wanted to touch him, but feared that he would burst out laughing. She felt indeed horribly cold, and piled rugs and dresses over her. It required great fortitude not to sneak back to bed. She was unhappy and thirsty. Nothing is so disagreeable as the water in toilet-bottles, with the glass tasting of tooth-wash; but she gulped some down, though it almost made her sick, and then walked about the room, turning over her manifold wrongs. Edward slept on insufferably. She made a noise to wake him, but he did not stir; she knocked down a table with a clatter sufficient to disturb the dead, but her husband was insensible. Then she looked at the bed, wondering whether she dared lie down for an hour, and trust to waking before him. She was so cold that she determined to risk it, feeling certain that she would not sleep long; she walked to the bed.

"Coming to bed after all?" said Edward, in a sleepy voice.

She stopped, and her heart rose to her mouth. "I was coming for my pillow," she replied indignantly, thanking her stars that he had not spoken a minute later.

She returned to the sofa, and eventually making herself very comfortable, fell asleep. In this blissful condition she continued till the morning, and when she awoke Edward was drawing up the blinds.

"Slept well?" he asked.

"I haven't slept a wink."

"Oh, what a crammer. I've been looking at you for the last hour!"

"I've had my eyes closed for about ten minutes, if that's what you mean."

Bertha was quite justly annoyed that her husband should have caught her napping soundly—it robbed her proceeding of half its effect. Moreover, Edward was as fresh as a bird, while she felt old and haggard, and hardly dared look at herself in the glass.

In the middle of the morning came a telegram from Miss Ley, telling Bertha to come whenever she liked—hoping Edward would come too! Bertha left it in a conspicuous place so that he could not fail to see it.

"So you're really going?" he said.

"I told you I was as able to keep my word as you."

"Well, I think it'll do you no end of good. How long will you stay?"

"How do I know! Perhaps for ever."

"That's a big word—though it has only two syllables."

It cut Bertha to the heart that Edward should be so indifferent—he could not care for her at all. He seemed to think it natural that she should leave him, pretending it was good for her health. Oh, what did she care about her health! As she made the needful preparations her courage failed her, and she felt it impossible to go. Tears came as she thought of the difference between their present state and the ardent love of a year before. She would have welcomed the poorest excuse that forced her to stay, and yet saved her self-respect. If Edward would only express grief at the parting, it might not be too late. But her boxes were packed and her train fixed; he told Miss Glover that his wife was going away for a change of air, and regretted that his farm prevented him from accompanying her. The trap was brought to the door, and Edward jumped up, taking his seat. Now there was no hope, and go she must. She wished for courage to tell Edward that she could not leave him, but was afraid. They drove along in silence; Bertha waited for her husband to speak, daring to say nothing herself, lest he should hear the tears in her voice. At last she made an effort.

"Are you sorry I'm going?"

"I think it's for your good—and I don't want to stand in the way of that."

Bertha asked herself what love a man had for his wife, who could bear her out of his sight, no matter what the necessity. She stifled a sigh.

They reached the station and he took her ticket. They waited in silence for the train, and Edward bought *Punch* and *The Sketch* from a newspaper boy. The horrible train steamed up; Edward helped her into a carriage, and the tears in her eyes now could not be concealed. She put out her lips.

"Perhaps for the last time," she whispered.

Chapter XXII

72 Eliot Mansions, Chelsea, S.W.
April 18.

DEAR EDWARD—I think we were wise to part. We were too unsuited to one another, and our difficulties could only have increased. The knot of marriage between two persons of differing temperaments is so intricate that it can only be cut: you may try to unravel it, and think you are succeeding, but another turn shows you that the tangle is only worse than ever. Even time is powerless. Some things are impossible; you cannot heap water up like stones, you cannot measure one man by another man's rule. I am certain we were wise to separate. I see that if we had continued to live together our quarrels would have perpetually increased. It is horrible to look back upon those vulgar brawls—we wrangled like fishwives. I cannot understand how my mouth could have uttered such things.

It is very bitter to look back and compare my anticipations with what has really happened. Did I expect too much from life? Ah me, I only expected that my husband would love me. It is because I asked so little that I have received nothing. In this world you must ask much, you must spread your praises abroad, you must trample underfoot those who stand in your path, you must take up all the room you can or you will be elbowed away; you must be irredeemably selfish, or you will be a thing of no account, a frippery that man plays with and flings aside.

Of course I expected the impossible, I was not satisfied with the conventional unity of marriage; I wanted to be really one with you. Oneself is the whole world, and all other people are merely strangers. At first in my vehement desire, I used to despair because I knew you so little; I was heartbroken at the impossibility of really understanding you, of getting right down into your heart of hearts. Never, to the best of my knowledge, have I seen your veritable self; you are nearly as much a stranger to me as if I had known you but an hour. I bared my soul to you, concealing nothing—there is in you a man I do not know and have never seen. We are so absolutely different, I don't know a single thing that we have in common; often when we have been talking and fallen into silence, our thoughts, starting from the same standpoint, have travelled in contrary directions, and on speaking again, we found how widely they had diverged. I hoped to know you to the bottom of your soul. Oh, I hoped that we should be united, so as to have but one soul between us; and yet on the most commonplace occasion, I can never know your thoughts. Perhaps it might have been different if we had had children; they might have formed between us a truer link, and perhaps in the delight of them I should have forgotten my impracticable dreams. But fate was against us, I come from a rotten stock. It is written in the book that the Leys should depart from the sight of men, and return to their mother the earth, to be incorporated with her; and who knows in the future what may be our lot! I like to think that in the course of ages I may be the wheat on a fertile plain, or the smoke from a fire of brambles on the common. I wish I could be buried in the open fields, rather than in the grim coldness of a churchyard, so that I might anticipate the change, and return more quickly to the life of nature.

Believe me, separation was the only possible outcome. I loved you too passionately to be content with the cold regard which you gave me. Oh, of course I was exacting, and tyrannical, and unkind; I can confess all my faults now; my only excuse is that I was very unhappy. For all the pain I have caused you, I beg you to forgive me. We may as well part friends, and I freely forgive you for all you have made me suffer. Now I can afford also to tell you how near I was to not carrying out my intention. Yesterday and this morning I scarcely held back my tears; the parting seemed too hard, I felt I could not leave you. If you had asked me not to go, if you had even shown the smallest sign of regretting my departure, I think I should have broken down. Yes, I can tell you now, that I would have given anything to stay. Alas! I am so weak. In the train I cried bitterly. It is the first time we have been apart since our marriage, the first time that we have slept under different roofs. But now the worst is over. I have taken the step, and I shall adhere to what I have done. I am sure I have acted for the best. I see no harm in our writing to one another occasionally if it pleases you to receive letters from me. I think I had better not see you, at all events for some time. Perhaps when we are both a good deal older we may, I without danger, see one another now and then; but not yet. I should be afraid to see your face.

Aunt Polly has no suspicion. I can assure you it has been an effort to laugh and talk during the evening, and I was glad to get to my room. Now it is past midnight and I am still writing to you. I felt I ought to let you know my thoughts, and I can tell them more easily by letter than by word of mouth. Does it not show how separated in heart we have become, that I should hesitate to say to you what I think— and I had hoped to have my heart always open to you. I fancied that I need never conceal a thing, nor hesitate to show you every emotion and every thought.— Good-bye.

BERTHA

72 Eliot Mansions, Chelsea, S.W.
April 23.

MY POOR EDWARD—You say you hope I shall soon get better and come back to Court Leys. You misunderstand my meaning so completely that I almost laughed.

It is true I was out of spirits and tired when I wrote—but that was not the reason of my letter. Cannot you conceive emotions not entirely due to one's physical condition? You cannot understand me, you never have; and yet I would not take up the vulgar and hackneyed position of a *femme incomprise*. There is nothing to understand about me. I am very simple and unmysterious. I only wanted love, and you could not give it me. No, our parting is final and irrevocable. What can you want me back for? You have Court Leys and your farms. Everyone likes you in the neighbourhood; I was the only bar to your complete happiness. Court Leys I freely give you for my life; until you came it brought in nothing, and the income now arising from it is entirely due to your efforts; you earn it and I beg you to keep it. For me the small income I have from my mother is sufficient.

Aunt Polly still thinks I am on a visit, and constantly speaks of you. I throw dust in her eyes, but I cannot hope to keep her in ignorance for long. At present I am engaged in periodically seeing the doctor for an imaginary ill, and getting one or two new things.

Shall we write to one another once a week? I know writing is a trouble to you; but I do not wish you to forget me altogether. If you like, I will write to you every Sunday, and you may answer or not as you please.

BERTHA

P.S.—Please do not think of any *rapprochement*. I am sure you will eventually see that we are both much happier apart.

72 Eliot Mansions, Chelsea, S.W.
May 15.

MY DEAR EDDIE—I was pleased to get your letter. I am a little touched at your wanting to see me. You suggest coming to town—perhaps it is fortunate that I shall be no longer here. If you had expressed such a wish before, much might have gone differently.

Aunt Polly having let her flat to friends, goes to Paris for the rest of the season. She starts tonight, and I have offered to accompany her. I am sick of London. I do not know whether she suspects anything, but I notice that now she never mentions your name. She looked a little sceptical the other day when I explained that I had long wished to go to Paris, and that you were having the inside of Court Leys painted. Fortunately, however, she makes it a practice not to inquire into other people's business, and I can rest assured that she will never ask me a single question.

Forgive the shortness of this letter, but I am very busy, packing.—Your affectionate wife,

BERTHA

41 Rue des Ecoliers, Paris,
May 16.

My dearest Eddie—I have been unkind to you. It is nice of you to want to see me, and my repugnance to it was perhaps unnatural. On thinking it over, I cannot think it will do any harm if we should see one another. Of course, I can never come back to Court Leys—there are some chains that having broken you can never weld together; and no fetters are so intolerable as the fetters of love. But if you want to see me I will put no obstacle in your way; I will not deny that I also should like to see you. I am farther away now, but if you care for me at all you will not hesitate to make the short journey.

We have here a very nice apartment, in the Latin Quarter, away from the rich people and the tourists. I do not know which is more vulgar, the average tripper or the part of Paris which he infests: I must say they become one another to a nicety. I loathe the shoddiness of the boulevards, with their gaudy cafés over-gilt and over-sumptuous, and their crowds of ill-dressed foreigners. But if you come I can show you a different Paris—a restful and old-fashioned Paris, theatres to which tourists do not go; gardens full of pretty children and nursemaids with long ribbons to their caps. I can take you down innumerable grey streets with funny shops, in old churches where you see people actually praying; and it is all very quiet and calming to the nerves. And I can take you to the Louvre at hours when there are few visitors, and show you beautiful pictures and statues that have come from Italy and Greece, where the gods have their home to this day. Come, Eddie.—Your ever loving wife,

Bertha

41 Rue des Ecoliers, Paris,
May 25.

My dearest Eddie—I am disappointed that you will not come. I should have thought, if you wanted to see me, you could have found time to leave the farms for a few days. But perhaps it is really better that we should not meet. I cannot conceal from you that sometimes I long for you dreadfully. I forget all that has happened, and desire with all my heart to be with you once more. What a fool I am! I know that we can never meet again, and you are never absent from my thoughts. I look forward to your letters almost madly, and your handwriting makes my heart beat as if I were a schoolgirl. Oh, you don't know how your letters disappoint me, they are so cold; you never say what I want you to say. It would be madness if we came together—I can only preserve my love to you by not seeing you. Does that sound horrible? And yet I would give anything to see you once more. I cannot help asking you to come here. It is not so very often I have asked you anything. Do come. I will meet you at the station, and you will have no trouble or bother—everything is perfectly simple, and Cook's Interpreters are everywhere. I'm sure you would enjoy yourself so much.—If you love me, come.

BERTHA

Court Leys, Blackstable, Kent,
May 30.

MY DEAREST BERTHA—Sorry I haven't answered yours of 25th inst. before, but I've been up to my eyes in work. You wouldn't think there could be so much to do on a farm at this time of year, unless you saw it with your own eyes. I can't possibly get away to Paris, and besides I can't stomach the French. I don't want to see their capital, and when I want a holiday, London's good enough for me. You'd better come back here, people are asking after you, and the place seems all topsy-turvy without you. Love to Aunt P.—In haste, your affectionate husband,

E. CRADDOCK

41 Rue des Ecoliers, Paris,
June 1.

MY DEAREST, DEAREST EDDIE—You don't know how disappointed I was to get your letter and how I longed for it. Whatever you do, don't keep me waiting so long for an answer. I imagined all sorts of things—that you were ill or dying. I was on the point of wiring. I want you to promise me that if you are ever ill, you will let me know. If you want me urgently I shall be pleased to come. But do not think that I can ever come back to Court Leys for good. Sometimes I feel ill and weak and I long for you, but I know I must not give way. I'm sure, for your good as well as for mine, I must never risk the unhappiness of our old life again. It was too degrading. With firm mind and the utmost resolution I swear that I will never, never return to Court Leys.—Your affectionate and loving wife,

BERTHA

TELEGRAM

Gare du Nord, 9:50 a.m., June 2.
Craddock, Court Leys, Blackstable.

Arriving 7:25 tonight.

—BERTHA

41 Rue des Ecoliers, Paris.

MY DEAR YOUNG FRIEND—I am perturbed. Bertha, as you know, has for the last six weeks lived with me, for reasons the naturalness of which aroused my strongest suspicions. No one, I thought, would need so many absolutely conclusive motives to do so very simple a thing. I resisted the temptation to write to Edward (her husband—a nice man, but stupid!) to ask for an explanation, fearing that the reasons given me were the right ones (although I could not believe it); in which case I should have made myself ridiculous. Bertha in London pretended to go to a physician, but never was seen to take medicine, and I am certain no well-established specialist would venture to take two guineas from a *malade imaginaire* and not administer copious drugs. She accompanied me to Paris, ostensibly to get dresses, but has behaved as if their fit were of no more consequence than a change of ministry. She has taken great pains to conceal her emotions and thereby made them the more conspicuous. I cannot tell you how often she has gone through the various stages from an almost hysterical elation to an equal despondency. She has mused as profoundly as was fashionable for the young ladies of fifty years ago (we were all young ladies then—not girls!); she has played Tristan and Isolde to the distraction of myself; she has snubbed an amorous French artist to the distraction of his wife; finally she has wept, and after weeping over-powdered her eyes, which in a pretty woman is an infallible sign of extreme mental prostration.

This morning when I got up I found at my door the following message: *"Don't think me an utter fool, but I couldn't stand another day away from Edward. Leaving by the 10 o'clock train.—B."* Now at 10:30 she had an appointment at Paquin's to try on the most ravishing dinner-dress you could imagine.

I will not insult you by drawing inferences from all these facts: I know you would much sooner draw them yourself, and I have a sufficiently good opinion of you to be certain that they will coincide with mine.—Yours very sincerely,

MARY LEY

P.S.—I am sending this to await you at Seville. Remember me to Mrs. J.

Chapter XXIII

BERTHA'S RELIEF WAS UNMISTAKABLE WHEN SHE LANDED ON ENGLISH SOIL; AT last she was near Edward, and she had been extremely sea-sick. Though it was less than thirty miles from Dover to Blackstable the communications were so bad that it was necessary to wait for hours at the port, or take the boat-train to London and then come sixty miles down again. Bertha was exasperated at the delay, forgetting that she was now (thank Heaven!) in a free country, where the railways were not run for the convenience of passengers, but the passengers necessary evils to create dividends for an ill-managed company. Bertha's impatience was so great that she felt it impossible to wait at Dover; she preferred to go the extra hundred miles and save herself ten minutes rather than spend the afternoon in the dreary waiting-room, or wandering about the town. The train seemed to crawl; and her restlessness became quite painful as she recognised the Kentish country, the fat meadows with trim hedges, the portly trees, and the general air of prosperity.

Bertha's thoughts were full of Edward, and he was the whole cause of her impatience. She had hoped, against her knowledge of him, that he would meet her at Dover, and it had been a disappointment not to see him. Then she thought he might have come to London, though not explaining to herself how he could possibly have divined that she would be there. Her heart beat absurdly when she saw a back which might have been Edward's. Still later, she comforted herself with the idea that he would certainly be at Faversley, which was the next station to Blackstable. When they reached that place she put her head out of window, looking along the platform—but he was nowhere.

"He might have come as far this," she thought.

Now, the train steaming on, she recognised the country more precisely, the desolate marsh and the sea—the line ran almost at the water's edge; the tide was out, leaving a broad expanse of shining mud, over which the seagulls flew, screeching. Then the houses were familiar, cottages beaten by wind and weather, the *Jolly Sailor*, where in the old days many a smuggled keg of brandy had been hidden on its way to the cathedral city of Tercanbury. The coastguard station was passed, a long building, trim and low. Finally they rattled across the bridge over the High Street; and the porters with their Kentish drawl, called out, "Blackstable, Blackstable."

Bertha's emotions were always uncontrolled, and so powerful as sometimes to unfit her for action: now she had hardly strength to open the carriage-door.

"At last!" she cried, with a gasp of relief.

She had never adored her husband so passionately as then, and her love was a physical sensation that turned her faint. The arrival of the moment so anxiously awaited left her half-frightened; she was of those who eagerly look for an opportunity and then can scarcely seize it.

Bertha's heart was so full that she was afraid of bursting into tears when she at last she should see Edward walking towards her; she had pictured the scene so often, her husband advancing with his swinging stride, waving his stick, the dogs in front, rushing towards her and barking furiously. The two porters waddled with their seaman's walk to the van to get out the luggage; people were stepping from the carriages. Next to her a pasty-faced clerk descended, in a dingy black, with a baby in his arms; and he was followed by a haggard wife with another baby and innumerable parcels. A labourer sauntered down the platform, three or four sailors, and a couple of infantrymen. They all surged for the wicket, at which stood the ticket-collector. The porters got out the boxes, and the train steamed off; an irascible city man was swearing volubly because his luggage had gone to Margate. (It's a free country, thank Heaven!) The station-master, in a decorated hat and a self-satisfied air, strolled up to see what was the matter. Bertha looked along the platform wildly. Edward was not there.

The station-master passed, and nodded patronisingly.

"Have you seen Mr. Craddock?" she asked.

"No, I can't say I have. But I think there's a carriage below for you."

Bertha began to tremble. A porter asked whether he should take her boxes; she nodded, unable to speak. She went down and found the brougham at the station-door; the coachman touched his hat and gave her a note.

DEAR BERTHA—Awfully sorry I can't come to meet you. I never expected you, so accepted an invitation of Lord Philip Dirk to a tennis tournament, and a ball afterwards. He's going to sleep me, so I shan't be back till tomorrow. Don't get in a wax. See you in the morning.

E. C.

Bertha got into the carriage and huddled herself into one corner so that none should see her. At first she scarcely understood; she had spent the last hours at such a height of excitement that the disappointment deprived her of the power of thinking. She never took things reasonably, and was now stunned; what had happened seemed impossible. It was so callous that Edward should go to a tennis-tournament when she was coming home—looking forward eagerly to seeing him. And it was no ordinary home-coming; it was the first time she had ever left him; and then she had gone, hating him, as she thought, for good. But her absence having revived her love, she had returned, yearning for reconciliation. And he was not there; he acted as though she had been to town for a day's shopping.

"Oh, God, what a fool I was to come!"

Suddenly she thought of going away there and then—would it not be easier? She felt she could not see him. But there were no trains: the London, Chatham, and Dover Railway has perhaps saved many an elopement. But he must have known how bitterly disappointed she would be, and the idea flashed through her that he would leave the tournament and come home. Perhaps he was already at Court Leys, waiting; she took fresh courage, and looked at the well-remembered scene. He might be at the gate. Oh, what joy it would be, what a relief! But they came to the gate, and he was not there; they drove to the portico, and he was not there. Bertha went into the house expecting to find him in the hall or in the drawing-room, not having heard the carriage, but he was nowhere to be found. And the servants corroborated his letter.

The house was empty, chill, and inhospitable; the rooms had an uninhabited air, the furniture was primly rearranged, and Edward had caused antimacassars to be placed on the chairs. These Bertha, to the housemaids' surprise, took off one by one, and, without a word, threw into the empty fireplace. And still she thought it incredible that Edward should stay away. She sat down to dinner, expecting him every moment; she sat up very late, feeling sure that eventually he would come. But still he came not.

"I wish to God I'd stayed away."

Her thoughts went back to the struggle of the last few weeks. Pride, anger, reason, everything had been on one side, and only love on the other; and love had conquered. The recollection of Edward had been seldom absent from her, and her dreams had been filled with his image. His letters had caused her an indescribable thrill, the mere sight of his handwriting had made her tremble, and she wanted to see him; she woke up at night with his kisses on her lips. She begged him to come, and he would not or could not. At last the yearning grew beyond control; and that very morning, not having received the letter she awaited, she had resolved to throw off all pretence of resentment, and come. What did she care if Miss Ley laughed, or if Edward scored a victory in the struggle—she could not live without him. He still was her life and her love.

"Oh, God, I wish I hadn't come."

She remembered how she had prayed that Edward might love her as she wished to be loved, beseeching God to grant her happiness. The passionate rebellion after her child's death had ceased insensibly, and in her misery, in her loneliness, she had found a new faith. Belief with some comes and goes without reason:

with them it is a matter not of conviction, but rather of sensibility; and Bertha found prayer easier in Catholic churches than in the cheerless meeting-houses she had been used to. She could not utter stated words at stated hours in a meaningless chorus; the crowd caused her to shut away her emotions, and her heart could expand only in solitude. In Paris she had found quiet chapels, open at all hours, to which she could go for rest when the sun without was over-dazzling; and in the evening, the dimness, the fragrance of old incense, and the silence, were very restful. Then the only light came from the tapers, burning in gratitude or in hope, throwing a fitful, mysterious glimmer; and Bertha prayed earnestly for Edward and for herself.

But Edward would not let himself be loved, and her efforts all were useless. Her love was a jewel that he valued not at all, that he flung aside and cared not if he lost. But she as too unhappy, too broken in spirit, to be angry. What was the use of anger? She knew that Edward would see nothing extraordinary in what he had done. He would return, confident, well-pleased with himself after a good night's rest, and entirely unaware that she had been grievously hurt.

"I suppose the injustice is on my side. I am too exacting. I can't help it."

She only knew one way to love, and that, it appeared was a foolish way. "Oh, I wish I could go away again now—forever."

She got up and ate a solitary breakfast, busying herself afterwards in the house. Edward had left word that he would be in to luncheon, and was it not his pride to keep his word? But all her impatience had gone; Bertha felt now no particular anxiety to see him. She was on the point of going out—the air was warm and balmy—but did not, in case Edward should return and be disappointed at her absence.

"What a fool I am to think of his feelings! If I'm not in, he'll just go about his work and think nothing more of me till I appear."

But, notwithstanding, she stayed. He arrived at last, and she did not hurry to meet him; she was putting things away in her bed-room, and continued though she heard his voice below. The difference was curious between her intense and almost painful expectation of the previous day and this present unconcern. She turned as he came in, but did not move towards him.

"So you've come back? Did you enjoy yourself?"

"Yes, rather. But I say, it's ripping to have you home. You weren't in a wax at my not being here?"

"Oh no," she said, smiling. "I didn't mind at all."

"That's all right. Of course I'd never been to Lord Philip's before, and I couldn't wire the last minute to say that my wife was coming home and I had to meet her."

"Of course not; it would have made you appear too absurd."

"But I was jolly sick, I can tell you. If you'd only let me know a week ago that you were coming, I should have refused the invitation."

"My dear Edward, I'm so unpractical, I never know my own mind, and I'm always doing things on the spur of the moment, to my own inconvenience and other people's. And I should never have expected you to deny yourself anything for my sake."

Bertha, perplexed, almost dismayed, looked at her husband with astonishment. She scarcely recognised him. In the three years of their common life Bertha had noticed no change in him, and with her great faculty for idealisation, had carried in her mind always his image, as he appeared when first she saw him, the slender, manly youth of eight-and-twenty. Miss Ley had discerned alterations, and spiteful feminine tongues had said that he was going off dreadfully. But his wife had seen nothing. And the separation had given further opportunities to her fantasy. In absence she had thought of him as the handsomest of men, delighting over his clear features, his fair hair, his inexhaustible youth and strength. The plains facts would have disappointed her even if Edward had retained the looks of his youth, but seeing now as well the other changes, the shock was extreme. It was a different man she saw, almost a stranger. Craddock did not wear well; though but thirty-one, he looked much older. He had broadened and put on flesh, his features had lost their delicacy, and the red of his cheeks was growing coarse. He wore his clothes in a slovenly fashion, and had fallen into a lumbering walk as if his boots were always heavy with clay; and there was in him, besides, the heartiness and intolerant joviality of the prosperous farmer. Edward's good looks had given Bertha the keenest pleasure, and now, rushing, as was her habit, to the other extreme, she found him almost ugly. This was an exaggeration, for though he was no longer the slim youth of her first acquaintance, he was still, in a heavy, massive way, better looking than the majority of men.

Edward kissed her with marital calm, and the propinquity wafted to Bertha's nostrils the strong scents of the farmyard, which, no matter what his clothes, hung perpetually about him. She turned away, hardly concealing a little shiver of disgust. Yet they were the same masculine odours as once had made her nearly faint with desire.

Chapter XXIV

BERTHA'S IMAGINATION SELDOM PERMITTED HER TO SEE THINGS IN ANYTHING but a false light; sometimes they were pranked out in the glamour of the ideal, while at others the process was quite reversed. It was astonishing that so short a break should have destroyed the habit of three years; but the fact was plain that Edward had become a stranger, so that she felt it irksome to share the same room with him. She saw him now with jaundiced eyes, and told herself that at last she had discovered his true colours. Poor Edward was paying heavily because the furtive years had robbed him of his locks and given him in exchange a superabundance of fat; because responsibility, the east wind, and good living, had taken the edge off his features and turned his cheeks plethoric.

Bertha's love, indeed, had finally disappeared as suddenly as it had arisen, and she began seriously to loathe her husband. She had acquired a certain part of Miss Ley's analytic faculty, which now she employed with destructive effect upon Edward's character. Her absence had increased the danger to Edward in another way, for the air of Paris had exhilarated her and sharpened her wits so that her alertness to find fault was doubled and her impatience with the commonplace and the stupid, extreme. And Bertha soon found that her husband's mind was not only commonplace, but common. His ignorance no longer seemed touching, but merely shameful; his prejudices no longer amusing but contemptible. She was indignant at having humbled herself so abjectly before a man of such narrowness of mind, of such insignificant character. She could not conceive how she had ever passionately loved him. He was bound in by the stupidest routine. It irritated her beyond measure to see the regularity with which he went through the varying processes of his toilet. She was indignant with his presumption, and self-satisfaction, and conscious rectitude. Edward's taste was contemptible in books, in pictures, and in music; and his pretentions to judge upon such matters filled Bertha with scorn. At first his deficiencies had not affected her, and later she consoled herself with the obvious truism that a man may be ignorant of all the arts, and yet have every virtue under the sun. But now she was less charitable. Bertha wondered that because her husband could read and write as well as most board-scholars, he should feel himself competent to judge books—even without reading them. Of course it was most unreasonable to blame the poor man for a foible common to the vast majority of mankind. Everyone who can hold a pen is confident of his ability to criticise, and to criticise superciliously. It never occurs to the average citizen that, to speak modestly, almost as much art is needed to write a book as to adulterate a pound of tea;

nor that the author has busied himself with style and contrast, characterisation, light and shade, and many other things to which the practice of haberdashery, greengrocery, company-promotion, or pork-butchery, is no great key.

One day, Edward, coming in, caught sight of the yellow paper-cover of a French book that Bertha was reading.

"What, at it again?" said he. "You read too much; it's not good for people to be always reading."

"Is that your opinion?"

"My idea is that a woman oughtn't to stuff her head with books. You'd be much better out in the open air or doing something useful."

"Is that your opinion?"

"Well, I should like to know why you're always reading?"

"Sometimes to instruct myself; always to amuse myself."

"Much instruction you'll get out of an indecent French novel."

Bertha without answering handed him the book and showed the title; they were the letters of *Madame de Sévigné*.

"Well?" he said.

"You're no wiser, dear Edward?" she asked, with a smile: such a question in such a tone, revenged her for much. "You're none the wiser? I'm afraid you're very ignorant. You see I'm not reading a novel, and it is not indecent. They are the letters of a mother to her daughter, models of epistolary style and feminine wisdom."

Bertha purposely spoke in rather formal and elaborate a manner.

"Oh," said Edward, somewhat mystified; feeling that he had been confounded, but certain, none the less, that he was in the right. Bertha smiled provokingly.

"Of course," he said, "I've got no objection to your reading if it amuses you."

"It's very good of you to say so."

"I don't pretend to have any book-learning: I'm a practical man, and it's not required. In my business you find that the man who reads books, comes a mucker!"

"You seem to think that ignorance is creditable."

"It's better to have a good and pure heart, Bertha, and a clean mind, than any amount of learning."

"It's better to have a grain of wit than a collection of moral saws."

"I don't know what you mean by that, but I'm quite content to be as I am, and I don't want to know a single foreign language. English is quite good enough for me."

"So long as you're a good sportsman and wash yourself regularly, you think you've performed the whole duty of man."

"If there's one chap I can't stick, it's a measly bookworm."

"I prefer him to the hybrid of a professional cricketer and a Turkish-bath man."

"Does that mean me?"

"You can take it to yourself if you like," said Bertha, smiling, "or apply it to a whole class. . . . Do you mind if I go on reading?"

Bertha took up her book; but Edward was the more argumentatively inclined since he saw he had not so far got the better of the contest.

"Well, what I must say is, if you want to read, why can't you read English books? Surely there are enough. I think English people ought to stick to their own country. I don't pretend to have read any French books, but I've never heard anybody deny, that at all events the great majority are indecent, and not the sort of thing a woman should read."

"It's always incautious to judge from common report," answered Bertha, without looking up.

"And now that the French are always behaving so badly to us, I should like to see every French book in the kingdom put into a huge bonfire. I'm sure it would be all the better for we English people. What we want now is purity and reconstitution of the national life. I'm in favour of English morals, and English homes, English mothers, and English habits."

"What always astounds me, dear, is that though you invariably read the *Standard* you always talk like the *Family Herald!*"

Bertha paid no further attention to Edward, who thereupon began to talk with his dogs. Like most frivolous persons he found silence onerous, and Bertha thought it disconcerted him by rendering evident even to himself, the vacuity of his mind. He talked with every animate thing, with the servants, with his pets, with the cat and the birds; he could not read even a newspaper without making a running commentary upon it.

It was only a substantial meal that could induce even a passing taciturity. Sometimes his unceasing chatter irritated Bertha so intensely that she was obliged to beg him, for heaven's sake, to hold his tongue. Then he would look up, with a good-natured laugh.

"Was I making a row? Sorry; I didn't know it."

He remained quiet for ten minutes and then began to hum some obvious melody, than which there is no more detestable habit.

Indeed the points of divergence between the pair were innumerable. Edward was a person who had the courage of his opinions, and these he held with a firmness equal to his lack of knowledge. He disliked also whatever was not clear to his somewhat narrow intelligence, and was inclined to think it immoral. Music, for instance, in his opinion was an English art, carried to the highest pitch in certain very simple melodies of his childhood. Bertha played the piano well and sang with a cultivated voice, but Edward objected to her performances because, whether she sang or whether she played, there was never a rollicking tune that a fellow could get his teeth into. It must be confessed that Bertha exaggerated, and that when a dull musical afternoon was given in the neighbourhood, she took a malicious pleasure in playing some long recitative form of a Wagner opera, which no one could make head or tail of.

On such an occasion at the Glovers, the eldest Miss Hancock turned to Edward and remarked upon his wife's admirable playing. Edward was a little annoyed, because everyone had vigorously applauded, and to him the sounds had been quite meaningless.

"Well, I'm a plain man," he said, "and I don't mind confessing that I never can understand the stuff Bertha plays."

"Oh, Mr. Craddock, not even Wagner?" said Miss Hancock, who had been as bored as Edward, but would not for worlds have confessed it; holding the contrary modest opinion, that the only really admirable things are those you can't understand.

Bertha looked at him, remembering her dream that they should sit at the piano together in the evening and play for hour after hour: as a matter of fact, he had always refused to budge from his chair and had gone to sleep regularly.

"My idea of music is like Dr. Johnson's," said Edward, looking round for approval.

"Is Saul also among the prophets?" murmured Bertha.

"When I hear a difficult piece I wish it was impossible."

"You forget, dear," said Bertha, smiling sweetly, "that Dr. Johnson was a very ill-mannered old man whom dear Fanny would not have allowed in her drawing-room for one minute."

"You sing now, Edward," said Miss Glover; "we've not heard you for ever so long."

"Oh, bless you," he retorted, "my singing's too old fashioned. My songs have all got a tune in them and some feeling—they're only fit for the kitchen."

"Oh, please give us 'Ben Bolt'," said Miss Hancock, "we're all so fond of it."

Edward's repertory was limited, and everyone knew his songs by heart.

"Anything to oblige," he said.

He was, as a matter of fact, fond of singing, and applause was always grateful to his ears.

"Shall I accompany you, dear?" said Bertha.

> *Oh! don't you remember sweet Alice, Ben Bolt,*
> *Sweet Alice with hai-air so brow-own;*
> *She wept with delight when you gave her a smile,*
> *And trembled with fe-ar at your frown.*

Once upon a time Bertha had found a subtle charm in these pleasing sentiments and in the honest melody which adorned them; but it was not to be wondered if constant repetition had left her a little callous. Edward sang the ditty with a simple, homely style—which is the same as saying, with no style at all—and he employed therein much pathos. But Bertha's spirit was not forgiving, she owed him some return for the gratuitous attack on her playing; and the idea came to her to improve upon the accompaniment with little trills and flourishes which amused her immensely, but quite disconcerted her husband. Finally, just when his voice was growing flat with emotion over the grey-haired schoolmaster who had died, she wove in the strains of the "Blue Bells of Scotland" and "God Save the Queen", so that Edward broke down. For once his even temper was disturbed.

"I say, I can't sing if you go playing the fool. You spoil the whole thing."

"I'm very sorry," laughed Bertha. "I forgot what I was doing. Let's begin all over again."

"No, I'm not going to sing anymore. You spoil the whole thing."

"Mrs. Craddock has no heart," said Miss Hancock.

"I don't think it's fair to laugh at an old song like this," said Edward. "After all anyone can sneer. . . . My idea of music is something that stirs one's heart—I'm not a sentimental chap, but 'Ben Bolt' almost brings the tears to my eyes every time I sing it."

Bertha with difficulty abstained from retorting that sometimes she also felt inclined to weep—especially when he sang out of tune. Everyone looked at her, as if she had behaved very badly, while she calmly smiled at Edward. But she was not amused. On the way home she asked him if he knew why she had spoiled his song.

"I'm sure I don't know—unless you were in one of your beastly tempers. I suppose you're sorry now."

"Not at all," she answered, laughing. "I thought you were rude to me just before, and I wanted to punish you a little. Sometimes you're really too supercilious. . . . And besides that, I object to being found fault with in public. You will have the goodness in future to keep your strictures till we are alone."

"I should have thought you could stand a bit of good-natured chaff by now."

"Oh, I can, dear Edward. Only, perhaps, you may have noticed that I am fairly quick at defending myself."

"What d'you mean by that?"

"Merely that I can be horrid when I like, and you will be wise not to expose yourself to a public snub."

Edward had never heard from his wife a threat so calmly administered, and it somewhat impressed him.

But as a general rule, Bertha checked the sarcasm which constantly rose to her tongue. She treasured in her heart the wrath and hatred which her husband occasioned, feeling that it was a satisfaction at last to be free from love of him. Looking back, the fetters which had bound her were intolerably heavy. And it was a sweet revenge, although he knew nothing of it, to strip the idol of his ermine cloak, and of his crown, and the gewgaws of his sovereignty. In his nakedness he was a pitiable figure.

Edward of all this was totally unconscious. He was like a lunatic reigning in a madhouse over an imaginary kingdom; he did not see the curl of Bertha's lips upon some foolish remark of his, nor the contempt with which she treated him. And since she was a great deal less exacting, he found himself far happier than before. The ironic philosopher might find some cause for moralising in the fact that it was not till Bertha began to hate Edward that he found marriage entirely satisfactory. He told himself that his wife's stay abroad had done her no end of good, and made her far more amenable to reason. Mr. Craddock's principles, of course, were quite right; he had given her plenty of run and ignored her cackle, and now she had come home to roost. There is nothing like a knowledge of farming, and an acquaintance with the habits of domestic animals, to teach a man how to manage his wife.

Chapter XXV

IF THE GODS, WHO SCATTER WIT IN SUNDRY UNEXPECTED PLACES, SO THAT IT is sometimes found beneath the bishop's mitre and, once in a thousand years, beneath a king's crown, had given Edward two-pennyworth of that commodity, he would undoubtedly have been a great as well as a good man. Fortune smiled upon him uninterruptedly; he enjoyed the envy of his neighbours; he farmed with profit, and, having tamed the rebellious spirit of his wife, he rejoiced in domestic felicity. And it must be noticed that he was rewarded only according to his deserts. He walked with upright spirit and contented mind along the path which it had pleased a merciful Providence to set before him. He was lighted on the way by a strong Sense of Duty, by the Principles which he had acquired at his Mother's Knee, and by a Conviction of his own Merit. Finally, a deputation waited on him to propose that he should stand for the County Council election which was shortly to be held. He had been unofficially informed of the project, and received Mr. Atthill Bacot with seven committee men, in his frock-coat and a manner full of responsibility. He told them he could do nothing rashly, must consider the matter, and would inform them of his decision. But Edward had already made up his mind to accept, and having shown the deputation to the door, went to Bertha.

"Things are looking up," he said, having given her the details. The Blackstable district for which Edward was invited to stand, being composed chiefly of fishermen, was intensely Radical. "Old Bacot said I was the only Moderate candidate who'd have a chance."

Bertha was too much astonished to reply. She had so poor an opinion of her husband that she could not understand why on earth they should make him such an offer. She turned over in her mind possible reasons.

"It's a ripping thing for me, isn't it?"

"But you're not thinking of accepting?"

"Not? Of course I am. What do *you* think!" This was not an inquiry, but an exclamation.

"You've never gone in for politics; you've never made a speech in your life."

She thought he would make an abject fool of himself, and for her sake, as well as for his, decided to prevent him from standing. "He's too ignorant!" she thought.

"What! I've made speeches at cricket dinners; you set me on my legs and I'll say something."

"But this is different—you know nothing about the County Council."

"All you have to do is to look after steam-rollers and get glandered horses killed. I know all about it."

There is nothing so difficult as to persuade men that they are not omniscient. Bertha, exaggerating the seriousness of the affair, thought it charlantry to undertake a post without knowledge and without capacity. Fortunately that is not the opinion of the majority, or the government of this enlightened country could not proceed.

"I should have thought you'd be glad to see me get a lift in the world," said Edward, somewhat offended that his wife did not fall down and worship.

"I don't want you to make a fool of yourself, Edward. You've told me often that you don't go in for book-learning; and it can't hurt your feelings when I say that you're utterly ignorant. I don't think it's honest to take a position you're not competent to fill."

"Me—not competent?" cried Edward, with surprise. "That's a good one! Upon my word, I'm not given to boasting, but I must say I think myself competent to do most things.... You just ask old Bacot what he thinks of me, and that'll open your eyes. The fact is, everyone appreciates me but you: but they say a man's never a hero to his valet."

"Your proverb is most apt, dear Edward.... But I have no intention of thwarting you in any of your plans. I only thought you did not know what you were going in for, and that I might save you from some humiliation."

"Humiliation, where? Pooh, you think I shan't get elected. Well, look here, I bet you any money you like that I shall come out top of the poll."

Next day Edward wrote to Mr. Bacot expressing pleasure that he was able to fall in with the views of the Conservative Association; and Bertha, who knew that no argument could turn him from his purpose, determined to coach him, so that he should not make too arrant a fool of himself. Her fears were proportionate to her estimate of Edward's ability! She sent to London for pamphlets and blue-books on the rights and duties of the County Council, and begged Edward to read them. But in his self-confident manner he pooh-poohed her, and laughed when she read them herself so as to be able to teach him.

"I don't want to know all that rot," he cried. "All a man wants is gumption. Why, d'you suppose a man who goes in for parliament knows anything about politics? Of course he doesn't."

Bertha was indignant that her husband should be so well satisfied in his illiteracy, and that he stoutly refused to learn. It is only when a man knows a good deal that he discovers how unfathomable is his ignorance. Edward, knowing so little, was convinced that there was little to know, and consequently felt quite assured that he knew all which was necessary. He might more easily have been persuaded that the moon was made of green cheese than that he lacked the very rudiments of knowledge.

The County Council elections in London were also being held at that time, and Bertha, hoping to give Edward useful hints, diligently read the oratory which they occasioned. But he refused to listen.

"I don't want to crib other men's stuff. I'm going to talk on my own."

"Why don't you write out a speech and get it by heart?"

Bertha fancied that so she might influence him a little and spare herself and him the humiliation of utter ridicule.

"Old Bacot says when he makes a speech, he always trusts to the spur of the moment. He says that Fox made his best speeches when he was blind drunk."

"D'you know who Fox was?" asked Bertha.

"Some old buffer or other who made speeches."

The day arrived when Edward for the first time was to address his constituents, in the Blackstable town-hall; and for a week past placards had been pasted on every wall and displayed in every shop, announcing the glad news. Mr. Bacot came to Court Leys, rubbing his hands.

"We shall have a full house. It'll be a big success. The hall will hold four hundred people and I think there won't be standing room. I dare say you'll have to address an overflow meeting at the Forresters Hall afterwards."

"I'll address any number of meetings you like," replied Edward.

Bertha grew more and more nervous. She anticipated a horrible collapse; they did not know—as she did—how limited was Edward's intelligence! She wanted to stay at home so as to avoid the ordeal, but Mr. Bacot had reserved for her a prominent seat on the platform.

"Are you nervous, Eddie?" she said, feeling more kindly disposed to him from his approaching trial.

"Me, nervous? What have I got to be nervous about?"

The hall was indeed crammed with the most eager, smelly, enthusiastic crowd Bertha had ever seen. The gas-jets flared noisily, throwing crude lights on the people, sailors, tradesmen, labourers, and boys. On the platform, in a semicircle like the immortal gods, sat the notabilities of the neighbourhood, Conservatives to the backbone. Bertha looked round with apprehension, but tried to calm herself with the thought that they were stupid people and she had no cause to tremble before them.

Presently the Vicar took the chair and in a few well-chosen words introduced Mr. Craddock.

"Mr. Craddock, like good wine, needs no bush. You all know him, and an introduction is superfluous. Still it is customary on such an occasion to say a few words on behalf of the candidate, and I have great pleasure, &c., &c. . . ."

Now Edward rose to his feet, and Bertha's blood ran cold. She dared not look at the audience. He advanced with his hands in his pockets—he had insisted on dressing himself up in a frock-coat and the most dismal pepper-and-salt trousers.

"Mr. Chairman, Ladies and Gentlemen—Unaccustomed to public speaking as I am . . ."

Bertha looked up with a start. Could a man at the end of the nineteenth century, seriously begin an oration with those words! But he was not joking; he went on gravely, and, looking around, Bertha caught not the shadow of a smile. Edward was not in the least nervous, he quickly got into the swing of his speech—and it was terrible! He introduced every hackneyed phrase he knew, he mingled slang incongruously with pompous language; and his silly jokes, chestnuts of great antiquity, made Bertha writhe and shudder. She wondered that he could go on with such self-possession. Did he not see that he was making himself perfectly absurd! She dared not look up for fear of catching the sniggers of Mrs. Branderton and of the Hancocks: "One sees what he was before he married Miss Ley. Of course he's a quite uneducated man. . . . I wonder his wife did not prevent him from making such an exhibition of himself. The grammar of it, my dear; and the jokes, and the stories!!!"

Bertha clenched her hands, furious because the flush of shame would not leave her cheeks. The speech was even worse than she had expected. He used the longest words, and, getting entangled in his own verbosity, was obliged to leave his sentence unfinished. He began a period with an elaborate flourish and waddled in confusion to the tamest commonplace: he was like a man who set out to explore the Andes and then, changing his mind, took a stroll in the Burlington Arcade. How long would it be, asked Bertha, before the audience broke into jeers and hisses? She blessed them for their patience. And what would happen afterwards? Would Mr. Bacot ask Edward to withdraw from the candidature? And supposing Edward refused, would it be necessary to tell him that he was really too great a fool? Bertha saw already the covert sneers of her neighbours.

"Oh, I wish he'd finish!" she muttered between her teeth. The agony, the humiliation of it, were unendurable.

But Edward was still talking, and gave no signs of an approaching termination. Bertha thought miserably that he had always been long-winded: if he would only sit down quickly the failure might not be irreparable. He made a vile pun and everyone cried, Oh! Oh! Bertha shivered and set her teeth; she must bear it to the end now—why wouldn't he sit down? Then Edward told an agricultural story, and the audience shouted with laughter. A ray of hope came to Bertha: perhaps his absolute vulgarity might save him with the vulgar people who formed the great body of the audience. But what must the Brandertons, and the Molsons, and the Hancocks, and all the rest of them, be saying? They must utterly despise him.

But worse was to follow. Edward came to his peroration, and a few remarks on current politics (of which he was entirely ignorant) brought him to his Country, England, Home and Beauty. He turned the tap of patriotism full on; it gurgled in a stream. He blew the penny trumpets of English purity, and the tin whistles of the British Empire, and he beat the big drum of the Great Anglo-Saxon Race. He thanked God he was an Englishman, and not as others are. Tommy Atkins, and Jack Tar, and Mr. Rudyard Kipling, danced a jig to the strains of the "British Grenadiers"; and Mr. Joseph Chamberlain executed a pas seul to the air of "Yankee Doodle." Lastly, he waved the Union Jack.

The hideous sentimentality, and the bad taste and the commonness made Bertha ashamed: it was horrible to think how ignoble must be the mind of a man who could foul his mouth with the expression of such sentiments.

Finally Edward sat down. For one moment the audience were silent—for the shortest instant; and then with one throat, broke into thunderous applause. It was no perfunctory clapping of hands; they rose as one man, and shouted and yelled with enthusiasm.

"Good old Teddy," cried a voice. And then the air was filled with: "For he's a jolly good fellow." Mrs. Branderton stood on a chair and waved her handkerchief; Miss Glover clapped her hands as if she were no longer an automaton.

"Wasn't it perfectly splendid?" she whispered to Bertha.

Everyone on the platform was in a frenzy of delight. Mr. Bacot warmly shook Edward's hand. Mrs. Mayston Ryle fanned herself desperately. The scene may well be described, in the language of journalists, as one of unparalleled enthusiasm. Bertha was dumbfoundered.

Mr. Bacot jumped to his feet.

"I must congratulate Mr. Craddock on his excellent speech. I am sure it comes as a surprise to all of us that he should prove such a fluent speaker, with such a fund of humour and—er—and common sense. And what is more valuable than these, his last words have proved to us that his heart—his heart, gentlemen—is in the right place, and that is saying a great deal. In fact I know nothing better to be said of a man than that his heart is in the right place. You know me, ladies and gentlemen, I have made many speeches to you since I had the honour of standing for the constituency in '85, but I must confess I couldn't make a better speech myself than the one you have just heard."

"You could—you could!" cried Edward, modestly.

"No, Mr. Craddock, no; I assert deliberately, and I mean it, that I could not do better myself. From my shoulders I let fall the mantle, and give it—"

Here Mr. Bacot was interrupted by the stentorian voice of the landlord of the *Pig and Whistle* (a rabid Conservative).

"Three cheers for good old Teddie!"

"That's right, my boys," repeated Mr. Bacot, for once taking an interruption in good part, "Three cheers for good old Teddy!"

The audience opened its mighty mouth and roared, and then burst again into, "For he's a jolly good fellow!" Arthur Branderton, when the tumult was subsiding, rose from his chair and called for more cheers. The object of all this enthusiasm sat calmly, with a well-satisfied look on his face, taking it all with his usual modest complacency. At last the meeting broke up, with cheers, and "God save the Queen," and "He's a jolly good fellow." The committee and the personal friends of the Craddocks retired to the side-room for light refreshment.

The ladies clustered round Edward, congratulating him. Arthur Branderton came to Bertha.

"Ripping speech, wasn't it?" he said. "I had no idea he could jaw like that. By Jove, it simply stirred me right through."

Before Bertha could answer, Mrs. Mayston Ryle sailed in.

"Where's the man?" she cried, in her loud tones. "Where is he? Show him to me.... My dear Mr. Craddock, your speech was perfect. I say it."

"And in such good taste," said Miss Hancock, her eyes glowing. "How proud you must be of your husband, Mrs. Craddock!"

"There's no chance for the Radicals now," said the Vicar, rubbing his hands.

"Oh, Mr. Craddock, let me come near you," cried Mrs. Branderton. "I've been trying to get at you for twenty minutes.... You've simply extinguished the horrid Radicals; I couldn't help crying, you were so pathetic."

"One may say what one likes," whispered Miss Glover to her brother, "but there's nothing in the world so beautiful as sentiment. I felt my heart simply bursting."

"Mr. Craddock," added Mrs. Mayston Ryle, "you've pleased me! Where's your wife, that I may tell her so?"

"It's the best speech we've ever had down here," cried Mrs. Branderton.

"That's the only true thing I've heard you say for twenty years, Mrs. Branderton," replied Mrs. Mayston Ryle, looking very hard at Mr. Atthill Bacot.

Chapter XXVI

WHEN LORD ROSEBERRY MAKES A SPEECH, EVEN THE JOURNALS OF HIS own party report him in the first person and at full length; and this is said to be the politician's supreme ambition. Having reached such distinction, there is nothing left him but an honourable death and a public funeral in Westminster Abbey. Now, the *Blackstable Times* accorded this honour to Edward's first effort; it was printed with numberless *I*'s peppered boldly over it; the grammar was corrected, and the stops inserted, just as for the most important orators. Edward bought a dozen copies and read the speech right through in each, to see that his sentiments were correctly expressed, and that there were no misprints. He gave it to Bertha, and stood over her while she read.

"Looks well, don't it?" he said.

"Splendid!"

"By the way, is Aunt Polly's address 72 Eliot Mansions?"

"Yes. Why?"

Her jaw fell as she saw him roll up half a dozen copies of the *Blackstable Times* and address the wrapper.

"I'm sure she'd like to read my speech. And it might hurt her feelings if she heard about it and I'd not sent her the report."

"Oh, I'm sure she'd like to see it very much. But if you send six copies you'll have none left—for other people."

"Oh, I can easily get more. The editor chap told me I could have a thousand if I liked. I'm sending her six, because I dare say she'd like to forward some to her friends."

By return of post came Miss Ley's reply.

MY DEAR EDWARD—I perused all six copies of your speech with the greatest interest; and I think you will agree with me that it is high proof of its merit that I was able to read it the sixth time with as unflagging attention as the first. The peroration, indeed, I am convinced that no acquaintance could stale. It is so true that "every Englishman has a mother" (supposing, of course, that an untimely death has not robbed him of her). It is curious how one does not realise the truth of some things till they are pointed out; when one's only surprise is at not having seen then before. I hope it will not offend you if I suggest that Bertha's handiwork seems to me not invisible in some of the sentiments (especially in that passage about the

Union Jack). Did you really write the whole speech yourself? Come, now, confess that Bertha helped you.—Yours very sincerely,

MARY LEY

Edward read the letter and tossed it, laughing, to Bertha.

"What cheek her suggesting that you helped me! I like that."

"I'll write at once and tell her that it was all your own."

Bertha still could hardly believe genuine the admiration which her husband excited. Knowing his extreme incapacity, she was astounded that the rest of the world should think him an uncommonly clever fellow. To her his pretensions were merely ridiculous; she marvelled that he should venture to discuss, with dogmatic glibness, subjects of which he knew nothing; but she marvelled still more that people should be impressed thereby: he had an astonishing faculty of concealing his ignorance.

At last the polling-day arrived, and Bertha waited anxiously at Court Leys for the result. Edward eventually appeared, radiant.

"What did I tell you?" said he.

"I see you've got in."

"Got in isn't the word for it! What did I tell you, eh? My dear girl, I've simply knocked 'em all into a cocked hat. I got double the number of votes that the other chap did, and it's the biggest poll they've ever had. . . . Aren't you proud that your hubby should be a County Councillor? I tell you I shall be an M.P. before I die."

"I congratulate you—with all my heart," said Bertha drily; but trying to be enthusiastic.

Edward in his excitement did not observe her coolness. He was walking up and down the room concocting schemes—asking himself how long it would be before Miles Campbell, the member, was confronted by the inevitable dilemma of the unopposed M.P., one horn of which is the Kingdom of Heaven, and the other—the House of Lords.

Presently he stopped. "I'm not a vain man," he remarked, "but I must say I don't think I've done badly."

Edward, for a while, was somewhat overwhelmed by his own greatness, but the opinion came to his rescue that the rewards were only according to his deserts; and presently he entered energetically into the not very arduous duties of the County Councillor.

Bertha continually expected to hear something to his disadvantage; but, on the contrary, everything seemed to proceed very satisfactorily; and Edward's aptitude for business, his keenness in making a bargain, his common sense, were heralded abroad in a manner that should have been most gratifying to his wife.

But as a matter of fact these constant praises exceedingly disquieted Bertha. She asked herself uneasily whether she was doing him an injustice. Was he really so clever; had he indeed the virtues which common report ascribed to him? Perhaps she was prejudiced; or perhaps—he was cleverer than she. This thought came like a blow, for she had never doubted that her intellect was superior to Edward's. Their respective knowledge was not comparable: she occupied herself with ideas that Edward did not conceive; his mind was ever engaged in the utterest trivialities. He never interested himself in abstract things, and his conversation was tedious, as only the absence of speculation could make it. It was extraordinary that everyone but herself should so highly estimate his intelligence. Bertha knew that his mind was paltry and his ignorance phenomenal: his pretentiousness made him a charlatan. One day he came to her, his head full of a new idea.

"I say, Bertha, I've been thinking it over and it seems a pity that your name should be dropped entirely. And it sounds funny that people called Craddock should live at Court Leys."

"D'you think so? I don't know how you can remedy it—unless you think of advertising for tenants with a more suitable name."

"Well, I was thinking it wouldn't be a bad idea, and it would have a good effect on the county, if we took your name again."

He looked at Bertha, who stared at him icily, but answered nothing.

"I've talked to old Bacot about it and he thinks it would be just the thing; so I think we'd better do it."

"I suppose you're going to consult me on the subject."

"That's what I'm doing now."

"Do you think of calling yourself Ley-Craddock or Craddock-Ley, or dropping the Craddock altogether?"

"Well, to tell you the truth, I hadn't gone so far as that yet."

Bertha gave a little scornful laugh. "I think the idea is perfectly ridiculous."

"I don't see that; I think it would be rather an improvement."

"Really, Edward, if I was not ashamed to take your name, I don't think that *you* need be ashamed to keep it."

"I say, I think you might be reasonable—you're always standing in my way."

"I have no wish to do that. If you think my name will add to your importance, use it by all means. . . . You may call yourself Tompkins for all I care."

"What about you?"

"Oh I—I shall continue to call myself Craddock."

"I do think it's rough. You never do anything to help me."

"I am sorry you're dissatisfied. But you forget that you have impressed one ideal on me for years: you have always given me to understand that your pattern female animal was the common or domestic cow."

Edward did not understand what Bertha meant, and it occurred to him dimly that it was perhaps not altogether proper.

"You know, Edward, I always regret that you didn't marry Fanny Glover. You would have suited one another admirably. And I think she would have worshipped you as you desire to be worshipped. I'm sure she would not have objected to your calling yourself Glover."

"I shouldn't have wanted to take her name. That's no better than Craddock. The only thing in Ley is that it's an old county name, and has belonged to your people."

"That is why I don't choose that you should use it."

Chapter XXVII

TIME PASSED SLOWLY, SLOWLY. BERTHA WRAPPED HER PRIDE ABOUT HER like a cloak, but sometimes it seemed too heavy to bear and she nearly fainted. The restraint which she imposed upon herself was often intolerable; anger and hatred seethed within her, but she forced herself to preserve the smiling face which people had always seen. She suffered intensely from her loneliness of spirit, she had not a soul to whom she could tell her unhappiness. It is terrible to have no means of expressing oneself, to keep imprisoned always the anguish that gnaws at one's heart-strings. It is well enough for the writer, he can find solace in his words, he can tell his secret and yet not betray it: but the woman has only silence.

Bertha loathed Edward now with such angry, physical repulsion that she could not bear his touch; and everyone she knew, was his admiring friend. How could she tell Fanny Glover that Edward was a fool who bored her to death, when Fanny Glover thought him the best and most virtuous of mankind? She was annoyed that in the universal estimation Edward should have eclipsed her so entirely: once his only importance lay in the fact that he was her husband, but now the positions were reversed. She found it very irksome thus to shine with reflected light, and at the same time despised herself for the petty jealousy. She could not help remembering that Court Leys was hers, and that if she chose she could send Edward away like a hired servant.

At last she felt it impossible longer to endure his company; he made her stupid and vulgar; she was ill and weak, and she utterly despaired. She made up her mind to go away again, this time for ever.

"If I stay, I shall kill myself."

For two days Edward had been utterly miserable; a favourite dog had died, and he was brought to the verge of tears. Bertha watched him contemptuously.

"You are more affected over the death of a wretched poodle than you have ever been over a pain of mine."

"Oh, don't rag me now, there's a good girl. I can't bear it."

"Fool!" muttered Bertha, under her breath.

He went about with hanging head and melancholy face, telling everyone the particulars of the beast's demise, in a voice quivering with emotion.

"Poor fellow!" said Miss Glover. "He has such a good heart."

Bertha could hardly repress the bitter invective that rose to her lips. If people knew the coldness with which he had met her love, the indifference he had shown to her tears and to her despair! She despised herself when she remembered the utter self-abasement of the past.

"He made me drink the cup of humiliation to the very dregs."

From the height of her disdain she summed him up for the thousandth time. It was inexplicable that she had been subject to a man so paltry in mind, so despicable in character. It made her blush with shame to think how servile had been her love.

Dr. Ramsay, who was visiting Bertha for some trivial ill, happened to come in when she was engaged with such thoughts.

"Well," he said, as soon as he had taken breath. "And how is Edward today?"

"Good heavens, how should I know?" she cried, beside herself, the words slipping out unawares after the long constraint.

"Hulloa, what's this? Have the turtle-doves had a tiff at last?"

"Oh, I'm sick of continually hearing Edward's praises. I'm sick of being treated as an appendage to him."

"What's the matter with you, Bertha?" said the doctor, bursting into a shout of laughter. "I always thought nothing pleased you more than to hear how much we all liked your husband."

"Oh, my good doctor, you must be blind or an utter fool. I thought everyone knew by now that I loathe my husband."

"What?" shouted Dr. Ramsay; then thinking Bertha was unwell: "Come, come, I see you want a little medicine, my dear. You're out of sorts, and like all women you think the world is consequently coming to an end."

Bertha sprang from the sofa. "D'you think I should speak like this if I hadn't good cause? Don't you think I'd conceal my humiliation if I could? Oh, I've hidden it long enough; now I must speak. Oh God, I can hardly help screaming with pain when I think of all I've suffered and hidden. I've never said a word to anyone but you, and now I can't help it. I tell you I loathe and abhor my husband and I utterly despise him. I can't live with him anymore, and I want to go away."

Dr. Ramsay opened his mouth and fell back in his chair; he looked at Bertha as if he expected her to have a fit. "You're not serious?"

Bertha stamped her foot impatiently. "Of course I'm serious. Do you think I'm a fool too? We've been miserable for years, and it can't go on. If you knew what I've had to suffer when everyone has congratulated me, and said how pleased they were to see me so happy. Sometimes I've had to dig my nails in my hands to prevent myself from crying out the truth."

Bertha walked up and down the room, letting herself go at last. The tears were streaming down her cheeks, but she took no notice of them. She was giving full vent to her passionate hatred.

"Oh, I've tried to love him. You know how I loved him once—how I adored him. I would have laid down my life for him with pleasure. I would have done anything he asked me; I used to search for the smallest indication of his wishes so that I might carry them out. It overjoyed me to think that I was his abject slave. But he's destroyed every vestige of my love, and now I only despise him, I utterly despise him. Oh, I've tried to love him, but he's too great a fool."

The last words Bertha said with such force that Dr. Ramsay was startled.

"My dear Bertha!"

"Oh, I know you all think him wonderful. I've had his praises thrown at me for years. But you don't know what a man really is till you've lived with him, till you've seen him in every mood and in every circumstance. I know him through and through, and he's a fool. You can't conceive how stupid, how utterly brainless he is. . . . He bores me to death!"

"Come now, you don't mean what you say. You're exaggerating as usual. You must expect to have little quarrels now and then; upon my word, I think it took me twenty years to get used to my wife."

"Oh, for God's sake, don't be sententious," Bertha interrupted, fiercely. "I've had enough moralising in these five years. I might have loved Edward better if he hadn't been so moral. He's thrown his virtues in my face till I'm sick of them. He's made every goodness ugly to me, till I sigh for vice just for a change. Oh, you can't imagine how frightfully dull is a really good man. Now I want to be free, I tell you I can't stand it anymore."

Bertha again walked up and down the room excitedly.

"Upon my word," cried Dr. Ramsay, "I can't make head or tail of it."

"I didn't expect you would. I knew you'd only moralise."

"What d'you want me to do? Shall I speak to him?"

"No! No! I've spoken to him endlessly. It's no good. D'you suppose your speaking to him will make him love me? He's incapable of it; all he can give me is esteem and affection—good God, what do I want with esteem! It requires a certain intelligence to love, and he hasn't got it. I tell you he's a fool. Oh, when I think that I'm shackled to him for the rest of my life, I feel I could kill myself."

"Come now, he's not such a fool as all that. Everyone agrees that he's a very smart man of business. And I can't help saying that I've always thought you did uncommonly well when you insisted on marrying him."

"It was all your fault," cried Bertha. "If you hadn't opposed me, I might not have married so quickly. Oh, you don't know how I've regretted it. . . . I wish I could see him dead at my feet."

Dr. Ramsay whistled. His mind worked somewhat slowly, and he was becoming confused with the overthrow of his cherished opinions, and the vehemence with which the unpleasant operation was conducted.

"I didn't know things were like this."

"Of course you didn't!" said Bertha, scornfully. "Because I smiled and hid my sorrow, you thought I was happy. When I look back on the wretchedness I've gone through, I wonder that I can ever have borne it."

"I can't believe that this is very serious. You'll be of a different mind tomorrow, and wonder that such things ever entered your head. You mustn't mind an old chap like me telling you that you're very headstrong and impulsive. After all, Edward is a fine fellow, and I can't believe that he would willingly hurt your feelings."

"Oh, for heaven's sake don't give me more of Edward's praises."

"I wonder if you're a little jealous of the way he's got on?" asked the doctor, looking at her sharply.

Bertha blushed, for she had asked herself the same question, and much scorn was needed to refute it.

"I? My dear doctor, you forget! Oh, don't you understand that it isn't a passing whim? It's dreadfully serious to me—I've borne the misery till I can bear it no longer. You must help me to get away. If you have any of your old affection for me, do what you can. I want to go away; but I don't want to have any more rows with Edward; I just want to leave him quietly. It's no good trying to make him understand that we're incompatible. He thinks that it's enough for my happiness just to be his wife. He's of iron, and I am pitifully weak. . . . I used to think myself so strong!"

"Am I to take it that you're absolutely serious? Do you want to take the extreme step of separating from your husband?"

"It's an extreme step that I've taken before. Last time I went with a flourish of trumpets, but now I want to go without any fuss at all. I still loved Edward then, but I have even ceased to hate him. Oh, I knew I was a fool to come back, but I couldn't help it. He asked me to return, and I did."

"Well, I don't know what I can do for you. I can't help thinking that if you wait a little things will get better."

"I can't wait any longer. I've waited too long. I'm losing my whole life."

"Why don't you go away for a few months, and then you can see? Miss Ley is going to Italy for the winter as usual, isn't she? Upon my word, I think it would do you good to go too."

"I don't mind what I do so long as I can get away. I'm suffering too much."

"Have you thought that Edward will miss you?" asked Dr. Ramsay, gravely.

"No, he won't. Good heavens, don't you think I know him by now? I know him through and through. And he's callous, and selfish, and stupid. And he's making me like himself. . . . Oh, Dr. Ramsay, please help me."

"Does Miss Ley know?" asked the doctor, remembering what she had told him on her visit to Court Leys.

"No, I'm sure she doesn't. She thinks we adore one another. And I don't want her to know. I'm such a coward now. Years ago I never cared a straw for what anyone in the world thought of me; but my spirit is utterly broken. Oh, get me away from here, Dr. Ramsay, get me away."

She burst into tears, weeping as she had been long unaccustomed to do; she was utterly exhausted after the outburst of all that for years she had kept hid.

"I'm still so young, and I almost feel an old woman. Sometimes I should like to lie down and die, and have done with it all."

A month later Bertha was in Rome. But at first she was hardly able to realise the change in her condition. Her life at Court Leys had impressed itself upon her with such ghastly distinctness that she could not imagine its cessation. She was like a prisoner so long immured that freedom dazes him, and he looks for his chains, and cannot understand that he is free.

The relief was so great that Bertha could not believe it true, and she lived in fear that her vision would be disturbed, and that she would find herself again within the prison walls of Court Leys. It was a dream that she wandered in sunlit places, where the air was scented with violets and with roses. The people were unreal, the models lounging on the steps of the Piazza di Spagna, the ragged urchins, quaintly costumed and importunate, the silver speech that caressed the air. How could she believe that life was true when it gave blue sky and sunshine, so that the heart thrilled with joy; when it gave rest, and peace, and the most delightful idleness? Real life was gloomy and strenuous; its setting a Georgian mansion, surrounded by desolate, wind-swept fields. In real life everyone was very virtuous and very dull; the ten commandments hedged one round with the menace of hell-fire and eternal damnation, a dungeon more terrible because it had not walls, nor bars and bolts.

But beyond these gloomy stones with their harsh *Thou shalt not* is a land of fragrance and of light, where the sunbeams send the blood running gaily through the veins; where the flowers give their perfume freely to the air, in token that riches must be spent and virtue must be squandered; where the amorets flutter here and there on the spring breezes, unknowing whither they go, uncaring. It is a land of olive-trees and of pleasant shade, and the sea kisses the shore gently to show the youths how they must kiss the maidens. There dark eyes flash lambently, telling the traveller he need not fear, since love may be had for the asking. Blood is warm, and hands linger with grateful pressure in hands, and red lips ask for the kisses that are so sweet to give. There the flesh and the spirit walk side by side, and each is well satisfied with the other. Ah, give me the sunshine of this blissful country, and a garden of roses, and the murmur of a pleasant brook; give me a shady bank, and wine, and books, and the coral lips of Amaryllis, and I will live in complete felicity—for at least ten days.

To Bertha the life in Rome seemed like a play. Miss Leys left her much freedom, and she wandered alone in strange places. She went often to the market and spent the morning among the booths, looking at a thousand things she did not want to buy; she fingered rich silks and antique bits of silver, smiling at the compliments of a friendly dealer. The people bustled around her, talking volubly, intensely alive, and yet, in her inability to understand that what she saw was true, they seemed but puppets. She went to the galleries, to the Sistine Chapel or to the Stanze of Raphael; and, lacking the hurry of the tourist and his sense of duty, she would spend a whole morning in front of one picture, or in a corner of some old church, weaving with the sight before her the fantasies of her imagination.

And when she felt the need of her fellow-men, Bertha went to the Pincio and mingled with the throng that listened to the band. But the Franciscan monk in his brown cowl, standing apart, was a figure of some romantic play; and the soldiers in gay uniforms, the Bersaglieri with the bold cock's feathers in their hats, were the chorus of a comic opera. And there were black-robed priests, some old and fat, taking the sun and smoking cigarettes, at peace with themselves and with the world; others young and restless, the flesh unsubdued shining out of their dark eyes. And everyone seemed as happy as the children who romped and scampered with merry cries.

But gradually the shadows of the past fell away and Bertha was able more consciously to appreciate the beauty and the life that surrounded her. And knowing it transitory she set herself to enjoy it as best she could. Care and youth are with difficulty yoked together, and merciful time wraps in oblivion the most gruesome misery. Bertha stretched out her arms to embrace the wonders of the living world, and she put away the dreadful thought that it must end so quickly. In the spring she spent long hours in the gardens that surround the city, where the remains of ancient Rome mingled exotically with the half tropical luxuriance, and called forth new and subtle emotions. The flowers grew in the sarcophagi with a wild exuberance, wantoning, it seemed, in mockery of the tomb from which they sprang. Death is hideous, but life is always triumphant; the rose and the hyacinth arise from man's decay; and the dissolution of man is but the signal of other birth: and the world goes on, beautiful and ever new, revelling in its vigour.

Bertha went to the Villa Medici and sat where she could watch the light glowing on the mellow facade of the old palace, and Syrinx peeping between the reeds: the students saw her and asked who was the beautiful woman who sat so long and so unconscious of the eyes that looked at her. She went to the Villa Doria-Pamphili, majestic and pompous, the fitting summer-house of princes in gorgeous clothes, of bishops and of cardinals. And the ruins of the Palatine with its cypress-trees sent her thought back and back, and she pictured to herself the glory of bygone power.

But the wildest garden of all, the garden of the Mattei, pleased her best. Here were a greater fertility and a greater abandonment; the distance and the difficulty of access kept strangers away, and Bertha could wander through it as if it were her own. She thought she had never enjoyed such exquisite moments as were given her by its solitude and its silence. Sometimes a troop of scarlet seminarists sauntered along the grass-grown avenues, vivid colour against the verdure.

Then she went home, tired and happy, and sat at her open window and watched the dying sun. The sun set over St. Peter's, and the mighty cathedral was transfigured into a temple of fire and gold; the dome was radiant, formed no longer of solid stones, but of light and sunshine—it was the crown of a palace of Hyperion. Then, as the sun fell to the horizon, St. Peter's stood out in darkness, stood out in majestic profile against the splendour of heaven.

Chapter XXVIII

BUT AFTER EASTER MISS LEY PROPOSED THAT THEY SHOULD TRAVEL SLOWLY back to England. Bertha had dreaded the suggestion, not only because she regretted to leave Rome, but still more because it rendered necessary some explanation. The winter had passed comfortably enough with the excuse of indifferent health, but now some other reason must be found to account for the continued absence from her husband's side; and Bertha's racked imagination gave her nothing. She was determined, however, under no circumstances, to return to Court Leys: after such happy freedom the confinement of body and soul would be doubly intolerable.

Edward had been satisfied with the pretext and had let Bertha go without a word. As he said, he was not the man to stand in his wife's way when her health required her to leave him; and he could peg along all right by himself. Their letters had been fairly frequent, but on Bertha's side a constant effort. She was always telling herself that the only rational course was to make Edward a final statement of her intentions, and then break off all communication. But the dread of fuss and bother, and of endless explanation, restrained her; and she compromised by writing as seldom as possible and adhering to the merest trivialities. She was surprised once or twice, when she had delayed her answer, to receive from him a second letter, asking with some show of anxiety why she did not write.

Miss Ley had never mentioned Edward's name and Bertha surmised that she knew much of the truth. But she kept her own counsel: blessed are they who mind their own business and hold their tongues! Miss Ley, indeed, was convinced that some catastrophe had occurred, but true to her habit of allowing people to work out their lives in their own way, without interference, took care to seem unobservant; which was really very noble, for she prided herself on nothing more than on her talent for observation.

"The most difficult thing for a wise woman to do," she said, "is to pretend to be a foolish one!"

Finally, she guessed Bertha's present difficulty; and it seemed easily surmountable.

"I wish you'd come back to London with me instead of going to Court Leys," she said. "You've never had a London season, have you? On the whole I think it's amusing: the opera is very good and sometimes you see people who are quite well dressed."

Bertha did not answer, and Miss Ley, seeing her wish to accept and at the same time her hesitation, suggested that she should come for a few weeks, well knowing that a woman's visit is apt to spin itself out for an indeterminate time.

"I'm sorry I shan't have room for Edward too," said Miss Ley, smiling drily, "but my flat is very small, you know."

They had been settled a few days in the flat at Eliot Mansions, when Bertha, coming in to breakfast one morning, found Miss Ley in a great state of suppressed amusement. She was quivering like an uncoiled spring; and she pecked at her toast and at her egg in a bird-like manner, which Bertha knew could only mean that someone had made a fool of himself, to the great entertainment of her aunt. Bertha began to laugh.

"Good Heavens," she cried, "what has happened?"

"My dear—a terrible catastrophe." Miss Ley repressed a smile, but her eyes gleamed and danced as though she were a young woman. "You don't know Gerald Vaudrey, do you? But you know who he is."

"I believe he's a cousin of mine."

Bertha's father, who made a practice of quarrelling with all his relations, had found in General Vaudrey a brother-in-law as irascible as himself; so that the two families had never been on speaking terms.

"I've just had a letter from his mother to say that he's been—er, philandering rather violently with her maid, and they're all in despair. The maid has been sent away in hysterics, his mother and his sister are in tears, and the General's in a passion and says he won't have the boy in his house another day. And the little wretch is only nineteen. Disgraceful, isn't it?"

"Disgraceful!" said Bertha, smiling, "I wonder what there is in a French maid that small boys should invariably make love to her."

"Oh, my dear, if you only saw my sister's maid. She's forty if she's a day, and her complexion is like parchment very much the worse for wear. . . . But the awful part of it is that your Aunt Betty beseeches me too look after the boy. He's going to Florida in a month, and meanwhile he's to stay in London. Now, what I want to know, is how am I to keep a dissolute infant out of mischief. Is it the sort of thing that one would expect of me?"

Miss Ley waved her arms with comic desperation.

"Oh, but it'll be great fun. We'll reform him together. We'll lead him on a path where French maids are not to be met at every turn and corner."

"My dear, you don't know what he is. He's an utter young scamp. He was expelled from Rugby. He's been to half a dozen crammers, because they wanted him to go to Sandhurst, but he utterly refused to work; and he's been ploughed in every exam he's gone in for—even for the militia. So now his father has given him five hundred pounds and told him to go to the devil."

"How rude! But why should the poor boy go to Florida?"

"I suggested that. I know some people who've got an orange plantation there. And I dare say that the view of several miles of orange blossom will suggest to him that promiscuous flirtation may have unpleasant results."

"I think I shall like him," said Bertha.

"I have no doubt you will; he's an utter scamp and rather pretty."

Next day, when Bertha was in the drawing-room, reading, Gerald Vaudrey was shown in. She smiled to reassure him and put out her hand in the friendliest manner; she thought he must be a little confused at meeting a stranger instead of Miss Ley, and unhappy in his disgrace.

"You don't know who I am?" she said.

"Oh yes, I do," he replied, with a very pleasant smile. "The slavey told me Aunt Polly was out, but that you were here."

"I'm glad you didn't go away."

"I thought I shouldn't frighten you, you know."

Bertha opened her eyes. He was certainly not at all shy, though he looked even younger than nineteen. He was a nice boy, very slight and not so tall as Bertha, with a small, quite girlish face. He had a tiny, pretty nose, and a pink and white freckled complexion. His hair was dark and curly, he wore it somewhat long, evidently aware that it was beautiful; and his handsome green eyes had a charming expression. His sensual mouth was always smiling.

"What a nice boy!" thought Bertha. "I'm sure I shall like him."

He began to talk as if he had known her all his life, and she was entertained by the contrast between his innocent appearance and his disreputable past. He looked about the room with boyish ease and stretched himself comfortably in a big arm-chair.

"Hulloa, that's new since I was here last!" he said, pointing to an Italian bronze.

"Have you been here often?"

"Rather! I used to come here whenever it got too hot for me at home. It's no good scrapping with your governor, because he's got the ooftish—it's a jolly unfair advantage that fathers have, but they always take it. So when the old chap flew into a passion, I used to say, 'I won't argue with you. If you can't treat me like a gentleman, I shall go away for a week.' And I used to come here. Aunt Polly always gave me five quid, and said, 'Don't tell me how you spend it, because I shouldn't approve; but come again when you want some more.' She's is a ripper, ain't she!"

"I'm sorry she's not in."

"I'm rather glad, because I can have a long talk with you till she comes. I've never seen you before, so I have such a lot to say."

"Have you?" said Bertha, laughing. "That's rather unusual in young men."

He looked so absurdly young that Bertha could not help treating him as a schoolboy; and she was amused at his communicativeness. She wanted him to tell her his escapades, but was afraid to ask.

"Are you very hungry?" She thought that boys always had appetites. "Would you like some tea?"

"I'm starving."

She poured him out a cup, and taking it and three jam sandwiches, he sat on a footstool at her feet. He made himself quite at home.

"You've never seen my Vaudrey cousins, have you?" he asked, with his mouth full. "I can't stick 'em at any price, they're such frumps. I'll tell 'em all about you; it'll make them beastly sick."

Bertha raised her eyebrows. "And do you object to frumps?"

"I simply loathe them. At the last tutor's I was at, the old chap's wife was the most awful old geezer you ever saw. So I wrote and told my mater that I was afraid my morals were being corrupted."

"And did she take you away?"

"Well, by a curious coincidence, the old chap wrote the very same day, and told the pater if he didn't remove me he'd give me the shoot. So I sent in my resignation, and told him his cigars were poisonous, and cleared out."

"Don't you think you'd better sit on a chair?" said Bertha, "You must be very uncomfortable on that footstool."

"Oh no, not at all. After a Turkey carpet and a dining-room table, there's nothing so comfy as a footstool. A chair always makes me feel respectable—and dull."

Bertha thought Gerald rather a nice name.

"How long are you staying in London?"

"Oh, only a month, worse luck. Then I've got to go to the States to make my fortune and reform."

"I hope you will."

"Which? One can't do both at once, you know. You make your money first, and you reform afterwards, if you've got time. But whatever happens, it'll be a good sight better than sweating away at an everlasting crammer's. If there is one man I can't stick at any price it's the army crammer."

"You have a large experience of them, I understand."

"I wish you didn't know all my past history. Now I shan't have the sport of telling you."

"I don't think it would be edifying."

"Oh yes, it would. It would show you how virtue is downtrodden (that's me), and how vice is triumphant. I'm awfully unlucky; people sort of conspire together to look at my actions from the wrong point of view. I've had jolly rough luck all through. First I was bunked from Rugby. Well, that wasn't my fault. I was quite willing to stay, and I'm blowed if I was worse than anybody else. The pater blackguarded me for six weeks, and said I was bringing his grey hairs with sorrow to the grave. Well, you know, he's simply awfully bald; so at last I couldn't help saying that I didn't know where his grey hairs were going to, but it didn't much look as if he meant to accompany them. So, after that, he sent me to a crammer who played poker. Well, he skinned me of every shilling I'd got, and then wrote and told the pater I was an immoral young dog, and corrupting his house."

"I think we'd better change the subject, Gerald," said Bertha.

"Oh, but you must have the sequel. The next place I went to, I found none of the other fellows knew poker; so of course I thought it a sort of merciful interposition of Providence to help me to recoup myself. I told 'em not to lay up treasures in this world, and walloped in thirty quid in four days; then the old thingamygig (I forget his name, but he was a parson) told me I was making his place into a gambling-hell, and that he wouldn't have me another day in his house. So off I toddled, and I stayed at home for six months. That gave me the fair hump, I can tell you."

The conversation was disturbed by the entrance of Miss Ley.

"You see we've made friends," said Bertha.

"Gerald always does that with everybody. He's the most gregarious person. How are you, Lothario?"

"Flourishing, my Belinda," he replied, flinging his arms round Miss Ley's neck to her great delight and pretended indignation.

"You're irrepressible," she said. "I expected to find you in sackcloth and ashes, penitent and silent."

"My dear Aunt Polly, ask me to do anything you like, except to repent and to hold my tongue."

"You know your mother has asked me to look after you."

"I like being looked after—and is Bertha going to help?"

"I've been thinking it over," added Miss Ley. "And the only way I can think to keep you out of mischief is to make you spend your evenings with me. So you'd better go home now and dress. I know there's nothing you like better than changing your clothes."

Meanwhile Bertha observed with astonishment that Gerald was simply devouring her with his eyes. It was impossible not to see his evident admiration.

"The boy must be mad," she thought, but could not help feeling a little flattered.

"He's been telling me some dreadful stories," she said to Miss Ley, when he had gone. "I hope they're not true."

"Oh, I think you must take all Gerald says with a grain of salt. He exaggerates dreadfully, and all boys like to seem Byronic. So do most men, for the matter of that!"

"He looks so young. I can't believe that he's really very naughty."

"Well, my dear, there's no doubt about his mother's maid. The evidence is of the—most conclusive order. I know I should be dreadfully angry with him, but everyone is so virtuous now-a-days that a change is quite refreshing. And he's so young, he may reform. Englishmen start galloping to the devil, but as they grow older they nearly always change horses and amble along gently to respectability, a wife, and seventeen children."

"I like the contrast of his green eyes and his dark hair."

"My dear, it can't be denied that he's made to capture the feminine heart. I never try to resist him myself. He's so extremely convincing when he tells you some outrageous fib."

Bertha went to her room and looked at herself in the glass, then put on her most becoming dinner-dress.

"Good gracious," said Miss Ley. "You've not put that on for Gerald? You'll turn the boy's head, he's dreadfully susceptible."

"It's the first one I came across," replied Bertha, innocently.

Chapter XXIX

"You've quite captured Gerald's heart," said Miss Ley to Bertha a day or two later. "He's confided to me that he thinks you 'perfectly stunning.'"

"He's a very nice boy," said Bertha, laughing.

The youth's outspoken admiration could not fail to increase her liking; and she was amused by the stare of his green eyes, which, with a woman's peculiar sense, she felt even when her back was turned. They followed her; they rested on her hair and on her beautiful hands; when she wore a low dress they burned themselves on her neck and breast; she felt them travel along her arms, and embrace her figure. They were the most caressing, smiling eyes, but with a certain mystery in their emerald depths. Bertha did not neglect to put herself in positions wherein Gerald could see her to advantage; and when he looked at her hands she could not be expected to withdraw them as though she were ashamed. Few Englishmen see anything in a woman, but her face; and it seldom occurs to them that her hand has the most delicate outlines, all grace and gentleness, with tapering fingers and rosy nails; they never look for the thousand things it has to say.

"Don't you know it's very rude to stare like that," said Bertha, with a smile, turning round suddenly.

"I beg your pardon, I didn't know you were looking."

"I wasn't, but I saw you all the same."

She smiled at him most engagingly and she saw a sudden flame leap into his eyes. A married woman is always gratified by the capture of a youth's fickle heart: it is an unsolicited testimonial to her charms, and has the great advantage of being completely free from danger. She tells herself that there is no better training for a boy than to fall in love with a really nice woman a good deal older than himself. It teaches him how to behave and keeps him from getting into mischief: how often have callow youths been know to ruin their lives by falling into the clutches of some horrid adventuress with yellow hair and painted cheeks! Since she is old enough to be his mother, the really nice woman thinks there can be no harm in flirting with the poor boy, and it seems to please him: so she makes him fetch and carry, and dazzles him, and drives him quite distracted, till his youthful fickleness comes to the rescue and he falls passionately enamoured of a barmaid—when, of course, she calls him an ungrateful and low-minded wretch, regrets she was so mistaken in his character, and tells him never to come near her again.

This of course only refers to the women that men fall in love with; it is well known that the others have the strictest views on the subject, and would sooner die than trifle with anyone's affections.

Gerald had the charming gift of becoming intimate with people at the shortest notice, and a cousin is an agreeable relation (especially when she's pretty), with whom it is easy to get on. The relationship is not so close as to warrant chronic disagreeableness, and close enough to permit personalities, which are the most amusing part of conversation.

Within a week Gerald took to spending his whole day with Bertha, and she found the London season much more amusing than she had expected. She looked back with distaste to her only two visits to town. One had been her honeymoon, and the other the first separation from her husband: it was odd that in retrospect both seem equally dreary. Edward had almost disappeared from her thoughts, and she exulted like a captive free from chains. Her only annoyance was his often-expressed desire to see her. Why could he not leave her alone, as she left him? He was perpetually asking when she would return to Court Leys; and she had to invent excuses to prevent his coming to London. She loathed the idea of seeing him again.

But she put aside these thoughts when Gerald came to fetch her, sometimes for a bicycle ride in Battersea Park, sometimes to spend an hour in one of the museums. It is no wonder that the English are a populous race when one observes how many are the resorts supplied by the munificence of governing bodies for the express purpose of philandering. On a hot day what spot can be more enchanting than the British Museum, cool, silent, and roomy, with harmless statues which tell no tales, and afford matter for conversation to break an awkward pause?

The parks also are eminently suited for those whose fancy turns to thoughts of Platonic love. Hyde Park is the fitting scene for an idyll in which Corydon wears patent-leather boots and a top-hat, while Phyllis has an exquisite frock which suits her perfectly. The well-kept lawns, the artificial water and the trim paths, give a mock rurality which is infinitely amusing to persons who do not wish to take things too seriously. Here, in the summer mornings, Gerald and Bertha spent much time. It pleased her to listen to his chatter, and to look into his green eyes; he was such a very nice boy, and seemed so much attached to her! Besides, he was only in London for a month, and, quite secure in his departure, she could afford to let him fall a little in love.

"Are you sorry you're going away so soon?" she asked.

"I shall be miserable at leaving you."

"It's nice of you to say so."

Bit by bit she extracted from him his discreditable history. Bertha was possessed by a curiosity to know details, which she elicited artfully, making him confess his iniquities that she might pretend to be angry. It gave her a curious thrill, partly of admiration, to think that he was such a depraved young person, and she looked at him with a sort of amused wonder. He was very different from the virtuous Edward. A child-like innocence shone out of his handsome eyes, and yet he had already tasted the wine of many emotions. Bertha felt somewhat envious of the sex which gave opportunity, and the spirit which gave power, to seize life boldly, and wring from it all it had to offer.

"I ought to refuse to speak to you anymore," she said. "I ought to be ashamed of you."

"But you're not. That's why you're such a ripper."

How could she be angry with a boy who adored her? His very perversity fascinated her. Here was a man who would never hesitate to go to the devil for a woman, and Bertha was pleased at the compliment to her sex.

One evening Miss Ley was dining out, and Gerald asked Bertha to come to dinner with him, and then to the opera. She refused, thinking of the expense; but he was so eager, and she really so anxious to go, that finally she consented.

"Poor boy, he's going away so soon, I may as well be nice to him."

Gerald arrived in high spirits, looking even more boyish than usual.

"I'm really afraid to go out with you," said Bertha. "People will think you're my son. 'Dear me, who'd have thought she was forty!'"

"What rot!" He looked at her beautiful gown. Like all really nice women, Bertha was extremely careful to be always well dressed. "By Jove, you are a stunner!"

"My dear child, I'm old enough to be your mother."

They drove off—to a restaurant which Gerald, boy-like, had chosen, because common report pronounced it the dearest in London. Bertha was much amused by the bustle, the glitter of women in diamonds, the busy waiters gliding to and fro, the glare of the electric light: and her eyes rested with approval on the handsome boy in front of her. She could not keep in check the recklessness with which he insisted on ordering the most expensive things; and when they arrived at the opera, she found he had a box.

"Oh, you wretch," she cried. "You must be utterly ruined."

"Oh, I've got five hundred quid," he replied, laughing. "I must blue some of it."

"But why on earth did you get a box?"

"I remembered that you hated any other part of the theatre."

"But you promised to get cheap seats."

"And I wanted to be alone with you."

He was by nature a flatterer; and few women could withstand the cajolery of his green eyes, and of his charming smile.

"He must be very fond of me," thought Bertha, as they drove home, and she put her arm in his to express her thanks and her appreciation.

"It's very nice of you to have been so good to me. I always thought you were a nice boy."

"I'd do more than that for you."

He would have given the rest of his five hundred pounds for one kiss. She knew it, and was pleased, but gave him no encouragement, and for once he was bashful. They separated at her doorstep with the quietest handshake.

"It's awfully kind of you to have come."

He appeared immensely grateful to her. Her conscience pricked her now that he had spent so much money; but she liked him all the more.

Gerald's month was nearly over, and Bertha was astonished that he occupied her thoughts so much. She did not know that she was so fond of him.

"I wish he weren't going," she said, and then quickly: "but of course it's much better that he should!"

At that moment the boy appeared.

"This day week you'll be on the sea, Gerald," she said. "Then you'll be sorry for all your iniquities."

"No!" he answered, sitting in the position he most affected, at Bertha's feet.

"No—which?"

"I shan't be sorry," he replied, with a smile, "and I'm not going away."

"What d'you mean?"

"I've altered my plans. The man I'm going to said I could start at the beginning of the month or a fortnight later."

"But why?" It was a foolish question, because she knew.

"I had nothing to stay for. Now I have, that's all."

Bertha looked at him, and caught his shining eyes fixed intently upon her. She became grave.

"You're not angry?" he asked, changing his tone. "I thought you wouldn't mind. I don't want to leave you."

He looked at her so earnestly and tears came to his eyes, Bertha could not help being touched.

"I'm very glad that you should stay, dear. I didn't want you to go so soon. We've been such good friends."

She passed her fingers through his curly hair and over his ears; but he started, and shivered.

"Don't do that," he said, pushing her hand away.

"Why not?" she cried, laughing. "Are you frightened of me?"

And caressingly she passed her hand over his ears again.

"Oh, you don't know what pain that gives me."

He sprang up, and to her astonishment Bertha saw that he was pale and trembling.

"I feel I shall go mad when you touch me."

Suddenly she saw the burning passion in his eyes; it was love that made him tremble. Bertha gave a little cry, and a curious sensation pressed her heart. Then without warning, the boy seized her hands and falling on his knees before her, kissed them repeatedly. His hot breath made Bertha tremble too, and the kisses burned themselves into her flesh. She snatched her hands away.

"I've wanted to do that so long," he whispered.

She was too deeply moved to answer, but stood looking at him.

"You must be mad, Gerald." She pretended to laugh.

"Bertha!"

They stood very close together; he was about to put his arms round her. And for an instant she had an insane desire to let him do what he would, to let him kiss her lips as he had kissed her hands; and she wanted to kiss his mouth, and the curly hair, and his cheeks soft as a girl's. But she recovered herself.

"Oh, it's absurd! Don't be silly, Gerald."

He could not speak; he looked at her, his green eyes sparkling with desire.

"I love you."

"My dear boy, do you want me to succeed your mother's maid?"

"Oh!" he gave a groan and turned red.

"I'm glad you're staying on. You'll be able to see Edward, who's coming to town. You've never met my husband, have you?"

His lips twitched, and he seemed to struggle to compose himself. Then he threw himself on a chair and buried his face in his hands. He seemed so little, so young—and he loved her. Bertha looked at him for a moment, and tears came to her eyes. She called herself brutal, and put her hand on his shoulder.

"Gerald!" He did not look up. "Gerald, I didn't mean to hurt your feelings. I'm sorry for what I said."

She bent down and drew his hands away from his face.

"Are you cross with me?" he asked, almost tearfully.

"No," she answered, caressingly. "But you mustn't be silly, dearest. You know I'm old enough to be your mother."

He did not seem consoled, and she felt still that she had been horrid. She took his face between her hands and kissed his lips. And, as if he were a little child, she kissed away the tear-drops that shone in his eyes.

Chapter XXX

BERTHA STILL FELT ON HER HANDS GERALD'S PASSIONATE KISSES, LIKE LITTLE patches of fire; and on her lips was still the touch of his boyish mouth. What magic current had passed from him to her that she should feel this sudden happiness? It was enchanting to think that Gerald loved her; she remembered how his eyes had sparkled, how his voice had grown hoarse so that he could hardly speak: ah, those were the signs of real love, of the love that is mighty and triumphant. Bertha put her hands to her heart with a rippling laugh of pure joy—for she was beloved. The kisses tingled on her fingers so that she looked at them with surprise, she seemed almost to see a mark of burning. She was very grateful to him, she wanted to take his head in her hands and kiss his hair and his boyish eyes and again the soft lips. She told herself that she would be a mother to him.

The day following he had come to her almost shyly, afraid that she would be angry, and the bashfulness contrasting with his usual happy audacity, had charmed her. It flattered her extremely to think that he was her humble slave, to see the pleasure he took in doing as she bade; but she could hardly believe it true that he loved her, and she wished to reassure herself. It gave her a queer thrill to see him turn white when she held his hand, to see him tremble when she leaned on his arm. She stroked his hair and was delighted with the anguish in his eyes.

"Don't do that," he cried. "Please. You don't know how it hurts."

"I was hardly touching you," she replied, laughing.

She saw in his eyes glistening tears—they were tears of passion, and she could scarcely restrain a cry of triumph. At last she was loved as she wished, she gloried in her power: here at last was one who would not hesitate to lose his soul for her sake. She was intensely grateful. But her heart grew cold when she thought it was too late, that it was no good: he was only a boy, and she was married and—nearly thirty.

But even then, why should she attempt to stop him? If it was the love she dreamed of, nothing could destroy it. And there was no harm; Gerald said nothing to which she might not listen, and he was so much younger than she, he was going in less than a month and it would all be over. Why should she not enjoy the modest crumbs that the gods let fall from their table—it was little enough, in all conscience! How foolish is he who will not bask in the sun of St. Martin's summer, because it heralds the winter as surely as the east wind!

They spent the whole day together to Miss Ley's amusement, who for once did not use her sharp eyes to much effect.

"I'm so thankful to you, Bertha, for looking after the lad. His mother ought to be eternally grateful to you for keeping him out of mischief."

"I'm very glad if I have," said Bertha, "he's such a nice boy, and I'm so fond of him. I should be very sorry if he got into trouble . . . I'm rather anxious about him afterwards."

"My dear, don't be; because he's certain to get into scrapes—it's his nature—but it's likewise his nature to get out of them. He'll swear eternal devotion to half a dozen fair damsels, and ride away rejoicing, while they are left to weep upon one another's bosoms. It's some men's nature to break women's hearts."

"I think he's only a little wild: he means no harm."

"These sort of people never do; that's what makes their wrong-doing so much more fatal."

"And he's so affectionate."

"My dear, I shall really believe that you're in love with him."

"I am," said Bertha. "Madly!"

The plain truth is often the surest way to hoodwink people, more especially when it is told unconsciously. Women of fifty have an irritating habit of treating as contemporaries all persons of their own sex who are over twenty-five, and it never struck Miss Ley that Bertha might look upon Gerald as anything but a little boy.

But Edward could no longer be kept in the country. Bertha was astonished that he should wish to see her, and a little annoyed, for now of all times his presence would be importunate. She did not wish to have her dream disturbed, she knew it was nothing else; it was a mere spring day of happiness in the long winter of life. She looked at Gerald now with a heavy heart and could not bear to think of the future. How empty would existence be without that joyous smile; above all, without that ardent passion! This love was wonderful; it surrounded her like a mystic fire and lifted her up so that she seemed to walk on air. But things always come too late or come by halves. Why should all her passion have been squandered and flung to the winds, so that now when a beautiful youth offered her his virgin heart, she had nothing to give in exchange? Bertha told herself that though she was extremely fond of Gerald, of course she did not love him; he was a mere boy!

She was a little nervous at the meeting between him and Edward; she wondered what they would think of one another, and she watched—Gerald! Edward came in like a country breeze, obstreperously healthy, jovial, large, and somewhat bald. Miss Ley trembled lest he should knock her china over as he went round the room. He kissed her on one cheek, and Bertha on the other.

"Well, how are you all?—And this is my young cousin, eh? How are you? Pleased to meet you."

He wrung Gerald's hand, towering over him, beaming good-naturedly; then sat in a chair much too small for him, which creaked and grumbled at his weight. There are few sensations more amusing for a woman than to look at the husband she has once adored and think how very unnecessary he is; but it is apt to make conversation a little difficult. Miss Ley soon carried Gerald off, thinking that husband and wife should enjoy a little of that isolation to which marriage had indissolubly doomed them. Bertha had been awaiting, with great discomfort, the necessary ordeal. She had nothing to tell Edward, and was much afraid that he would be sentimental.

"Where are you staying?" she asked.

"Oh, I'm putting up at the *Inns of Court*—I always go there."

"I thought you might care to go to the theatre tonight. I've got a box, so that Aunt Polly and Gerald can come too."

"I'm game for anything you like."

"You always were the best-tempered man," said Bertha, smiling gently.

"You don't seem to care very much for my society, all the same."

Bertha looked up quickly. "What makes you think that?"

"Well, you're a precious long time coming back to Court Leys," he replied, laughing.

Bertha was relieved, for evidently he was not taking the matter seriously. She had not the courage to say that she meant never to return: the endless explanation, his wonder, the impossibility of making him understand, were more than she could bear.

"When are you coming back? We all miss you, like anything."

"Do you?" she said. "I really don't know. We'll see after the season."

"What? Aren't you coming for another couple of months?"

"I don't think Blackstable suits me very well. I'm always ill there."

"Oh, nonsense. It's the finest air in England. Death-rate practically *nil*."

"D'you think our life was very happy, Edward?"

She looked at him anxiously to see how he would take the tentative remark: but he was only astonished.

"Happy? Yes, rather. Of course we had our little tiffs. All people do. But they were chiefly at first, the road was a bit rough and we hadn't got our tyres properly blown out. I'm sure I've got nothing to complain about."

"That of course is the chief thing," said Bertha.

"You look as well as anything now. I don't see why you shouldn't come back."

"Well, we'll see later. We shall have plenty of time to talk it over."

She was afraid to speak the words on the tip of her tongue; it would be easier by correspondence.

"I wish you'd give some fixed date—so that I could have things ready, and tell people."

"It depends upon Aunt Polly; I really can't say for certain. I'll write to you."

They kept silence for a moment and then an idea seized Bertha.

"What d'you say to going to the Natural History Museum? Don't you remember, we went there on our honeymoon? I'm sure it would amuse you to see it again."

"Would you like to go?" asked Edward.

"I'm sure it would amuse you," she replied.

Next day while Bertha was shopping with her husband, Gerald and Miss Ley sat alone.

"Are you very disconsolate without Bertha?" she asked.

"Utterly miserable!"

"That's very rude to me, dear boy."

"I'm awfully sorry, but I can never be polite to more than one person at a time: and I've been using up all my good manners on—Mr. Craddock."

"I'm glad you like him," replied Miss Ley, smiling.

"I don't!"

"He's a very worthy man."

"If I hadn't seen Bertha for six months, I shouldn't take her off at once to see bugs."

"Perhaps it was Bertha's suggestion."

"She must find Mr. Craddock precious dull if she prefers blackbeetles and stuffed kangaroos."

"You shouldn't draw such rapid conclusions, my friend."

"D'you think she's fond of him?"

"My dear Gerald, what a question! Is it not her duty to love, honour, and obey him?"

"If I were a woman I could never honour a man who was bald."

"His locks are somewhat scanty; but he has a strong sense of duty."

"I know that," shouted Gerald. "It oozes out of him whenever he gets hot, just like gum."

"He's a County Councillor, and he makes speeches about the Union Jack, and he's virtuous."

"I know that too. He simply reeks of the ten commandments: they stick out all over him, like almonds in a tipsy cake."

"My dear Gerald, Edward is a model; he is the typical Englishman as he flourishes in the country, upright and honest, healthy, dogmatic, moral—rather stupid. I esteem him enormously, and I ought to like him much better than you, who are a disgraceful scamp."

"I wonder why you don't."

"Because I'm a wicked old woman; and I've learnt by long experience that people generally keep their vices to themselves, but insist on throwing their virtues in your face. And if you don't happen to have any of your own, you get the worst of the encounter."

"I think that's what is so comfortable in you, Aunt Polly, that you're not obstreperously good. You're charity itself."

"My dear Gerald," said Miss Ley, putting up an admonishing forefinger, "women are by nature spiteful and intolerant; when you find one who exercises charity, it proves that she wants it very badly herself."

Miss Ley was glad that Edward could not stay more than two days, for she was always afraid of surprising him. Nothing is more tedious than to talk with persons who treat your most obvious remarks as startling paradoxes; and Edward suffered likewise from that passion for argument, which is the bad talker's substitute for conversation. People who cannot talk are always proud of their dialectic: they want to modify your tritest observations, and even if you suggest that the day is fine insist on arguing it out.

Bertha, in her husband's presence, had suffered singular discomfort; it had been such a constraint that she found it an effort to talk with him, and she had to rack her brain for subjects of conversation. Her heart was perceptibly lightened when she returned from Victoria after seeing him off, and it gave her a thrill of pleasure to hear Gerald jump up when she came in. He ran towards her with glowing eyes.

"Oh, I'm so glad. I've hardly had a chance of speaking to you these last two days."

"We have the whole afternoon before us."

"Let's go for a walk, shall we?"

Bertha agreed, and like two schoolfellows they sallied out. The day was sunny and warm, and they wandered by the river. The banks of the Thames about Chelsea have a pleasing trimness, a levity which is infinitely grateful after the sedateness of the rest of London. The embankments, in spite of their novelty, recall the days when the huge city was a great, straggling village, when the sedan-chair was a means of locomotion, and ladies wore patches and hoops; when epigram was the fashion and propriety was not.

Presently, as they watched the gleaming water, a penny steamboat approached the adjoining stage, and gave Bertha an idea.

"Would you like to take me to Greenwich?" she cried. "Aunt Polly's dining out; we can have dinner at the *Ship* and come back by train."

"By Jove, it will be ripping."

They bolted down the gangway and took their tickets; the boat started, and Bertha, panting, sank on a seat. She felt a little reckless, pleased with herself, and amused to see Gerald's unmeasured delight.

"I feel as if we were eloping," she said, with a laugh; "I'm sure Aunt Polly will be dreadfully shocked."

The boat went on, stopping every now and then to take in passengers. They came to the tottering wharves of Millbank, and then to the footstool turrets of St. John's, the eight red blocks of St. Thomas's Hospital, and the Houses of Parliament. They passed Westminster Bridge, and the massive strength of New Scotland Yard, the hotels and public buildings which line the Victoria Embankment, the Temple Gardens; and opposite this grandeur, on the Surrey side, were the dingy warehouses and factories of Lambeth. At London Bridge Bertha found new interest in the varying scene; she stood in the bows with Gerald by her side, not speaking; they were happy in being near one another. The traffic became denser and the boat more crowded—with artisans, clerks, noisy girls, going eastwards to Rotherhithe and Deptford. Great merchantmen lay by the riverside, or slowly made their way downstream under the Tower Bridge; and then the broad waters were crowded with every imaginable craft, with lazy barges as picturesque with their red sails as the fishing-boats of Venice, with little tugs, puffing and blowing, with ocean tramps, and with huge packets. And as they passed in the penny steamer they had swift pictures of groups of naked boys wallowing in the Thames mud or diving from the side of an anchored coal-barge. A new atmosphere enveloped them now. Grey warehouses which lined the river, and the factories, announced the commerce of a mighty nation; and the spirit of Charles Dickens gave to the passing scenes a fresh delight. How could they be prosaic when the great master had described them? An amiable stranger put names to the various places.

"Look, there's Wapping Old Stairs."

And the words thrilled Bertha like poetry. They passed innumerable wharves and docks, London Dock, John Cooper's wharves, and William Gibbs's wharves (who are John Cooper and William Gibbs?), Limehouse Basin, and West India Dock. Then with a great turn of the river they entered Limehouse Reach; and soon the noble lines of the hospital, the immortal monument of Inigo Jones, came into view, and they landed at Greenwich Pier.

Chapter XXXI

THEY STOOD FOR A WHILE ON A TERRACE OVERLOOKING THE RIVER BY THE side of the hospital. Immediately below, a crowd of boys were bathing, animated and noisy, chasing and ducking one another, running to and fro with many cries, and splashing in the mud.

The river was stretched more widely before them. The sun played on its yellow wavelets so that they shone with a glitter of gold. A tug grunted past with a long tail of barges, and a huge East Indiaman glided noiselessly by. In the late afternoon there was over the scene an old-time air of ease and spaciousness. The stately flood carried the mind away, so that the onlooker followed it in thought, and went down, as it broadened, with its crowd of traffic, till presently a sea-smell reached the nostrils, and the river, ever majestic, flowed into the sea. And the ships went east and west and south, bearing their merchandise to the uttermost parts of the earth, to southern, summer lands of palm-trees and dark-skinned peoples, bearing the name and wealth of England. The Thames became an emblem of the power of the mighty empire, and those who watched felt stronger in its strength, and proud of their name and of the undiminished glory of their race.

But Gerald looked sadly.

"In a very little while it must take me away from you, Bertha."

"But think of the freedom and the vastness. Sometimes in England one seems oppressed by the lack of room; one can hardly breathe."

"It's the thought of leaving you."

She put her hand on his arm caressingly; and then, to take him from his sadness, suggested that they should walk.

Greenwich is half London, half country town; and the unexpected union gives it a peculiar fascination. If the wharves and docks of London still preserve the spirit of Charles Dickens, here it is the happy breeziness of Captain Marryat which fills the imagination. Those tales of a freer life and of the sea-breezes come back amid the grey streets, still peopled with the vivid characters of *Poor Jack*. In the park, by the side of the labourers, navvies from the neighbouring docks, asleep on the grass, or watching the boys play a primitive cricket, may be seen fantastic old persons who would have delighted the grotesque pen of the seaman-novelist.

Bertha and Gerald sat beneath the trees, looking at the people, till it grew late, and then wandered back to the *Ship* for dinner. It amused them immensely to sit in the old coffee-room and be waited on by a black waiter, who extolled absurdly the various dishes.

"We won't be economical today," cried Bertha. "I feel utterly reckless."

"It takes all the fun away if one counts the cost."

"Well, for once let us be foolish and forget the morrow."

And they drank champagne, which to women and boys is the acme of dissipation and magnificence. Presently Gerald's green eyes flashed more brightly, and Bertha reddened before their ardent gaze.

"I shall never forget today, Bertha," said Gerald. "As long as I live I shall look back upon it with regret."

"Oh, don't think that it must come to an end, or we shall both be miserable."

"You are the most beautiful woman I've ever seen."

Bertha laughed, showing her exquisite teeth, and was glad that her own knowledge told her she looked her best.

"But come on the terrace again and smoke there. We'll watch the sunset."

They sat alone, and the sun was already sinking. The heavy western clouds were a rich and vivid red, and over the river the bricks and mortar stood out in ink-black masses. It was a sunset that singularly fitted the scene, combining in audacious colour with the river's strength. The murky wavelets danced like little flames of fire.

Bertha and the youth sat silently, very happy, but with the regret gnawing at their hearts that their hour of joy would have no morrow. The night fell, and one by one the stars shone out. The river flowed noiselessly, restfully; and around them twinkled the lights of the riverside towns. They did not speak, but Bertha knew the boy thought of her, and desired to hear him say so.

"What are you thinking of, Gerald?"

"What should I be thinking of, but you—and that I must leave you."

Bertha could not help the exquisite pleasure that his words gave: it was so delicious to be really loved, and she knew his love was real. She turned her face, so that he saw her dark eyes, darker in the night.

"I wish I hadn't made a fool of myself before," he whispered. "I feel it was all horrible; you've made me so ashamed."

"Oh, Gerald, you're not remembering what I said the other day? I didn't mean to hurt you. I've been so sorry ever since."

"I wish you loved me. Oh, Bertha, don't stop me now. I've kept it in so long, and I can't anymore. I don't want to go away without telling you."

"Oh, my dear Gerald, don't," said Bertha, her voice almost breaking. "It's no good, and we shall both be dreadfully unhappy. My dear, you don't know how much older I am than you. Even if I wasn't married, it would be impossible for us to love one another."

"But I love you with all my heart."

He seized her hands and pressed them, and she made no effort to resist.

"Don't you love me at all?" he asked.

Bertha did not answer, and he bent nearer to look into her eyes. Then leaving her hands, he flung his arms about her and pressed her to his heart.

"Bertha, Bertha!" He kissed her passionately. "Oh, Bertha, say you love me. It would make me so happy."

"My dearest," she whispered, and taking his head in her hand, she kissed him.

But the kiss that she had received fired her blood and she could not resist now from doing as she had wished. She kissed him on the lips, and on the eyes, and she kissed his curly hair. But at last she tore herself away, and sprang to her feet.

"What fools we are! Let's go to the station, Gerald; it's growing late."

"Oh, Bertha, don't go yet."

"We must. I daren't stay."

He tried to take her in his arms, begging her eagerly to remain.

"Please don't, Gerald," she said. "Don't ask me, you make me too unhappy. Don't you see how hopeless it is? What is the use of our loving one another? You're going away in a week and we shall never meet again. And even if you were staying, I'm married and I'm twenty-six and you're only nineteen. My dearest, we should only make ourselves ridiculous."

"But I can't go away. What do I care if you're older than I? And it's nothing if you're married: you don't care for your husband and he doesn't care two straws for you."

"How do you know?"

"Oh, I saw it. I felt so sorry for you."

"You dear boy!" murmured Bertha, almost crying. "I've been dreadfully unhappy. It's true, Edward never loved me—and he didn't treat me very well. Oh, I can't understand how I ever cared for him."

"I'm glad."

"I would never allow myself to fall in love again. I suffered too much."

"But I love you with all my heart, Bertha; don't you see it? Oh, this isn't like what I've felt before; it's something quite new and different. I can't live without you, Bertha. Oh, let me stay."

"It's impossible. Come away now, dearest; we've been here too long."

"Kiss me again."

Bertha, half smiling, half in tears, put her arms round his neck and kissed the soft, boyish lips.

"You are good to me," he whispered.

Then they walked to the station in silence; and eventually reached Chelsea. At the flat-door Bertha held out her hand and Gerald looked at her with a sadness that almost broke her heart, then he just touched her fingers and turned away.

But when Bertha was alone in her room, she threw herself down and burst into tears. For she knew at last that she loved him; Gerald's kisses still burned on her lips and the touch of his hands was tremulous on her arms. Suddenly she knew that she had deceived herself; it was more than friendship that held her heart as in a vice; it was more than affection; it was eager, vehement love.

For a moment she was overjoyed, but quickly remembered that she was married, that she was years older than he—to a boy nineteen a women of twenty-six must appear almost middle-aged. She seized a glass and looked at herself; she took it to the light so that the test might be more searching, and scrutinised her face for wrinkles and for crow's feet, the signs of departing youth.

"It's absurd," she said. "I'm making an utter fool of myself."

Gerald only thought he loved her, in a week he would be enamoured of some girl he met on the steamer. But thinking of his love, Bertha could not doubt that now at all events it was real; she knew better than anyone what love was. She exulted to think that his was the real love, and compared it with her husband's pallid flame. Gerald loved her with all his heart, with all his soul; he trembled with desire at her touch and his passion was an agony that blanched his cheek. She could not mistake the eager longing of his eyes. Ah, that was the love she wanted—the love that kills and the love that engenders. How could she regret that he loved her? She stood up, stretching out her arms in triumph, and in the empty room, her lips formed the words—

"Come, my beloved, come—for I love you!"

But the morning brought an intolerable depression. Bertha saw then the utter futility of her love: her marriage, his departure, made it impossible; the disparity of age made it even grotesque. But she could not dull the aching of her heart, she could not stop her tears.

Gerald arrived at midday and found her alone. He approached almost timidly.

"You've been crying, Bertha."

"I've been very unhappy," she said. "Oh, please, Gerald, forget our idiocy of yesterday. Don't say anything to me that I mustn't hear."

"I can't help loving you."

"Don't you see that it's all utter madness!"

She was angry with herself for loving him, angry with Gerald because he had aroused in her a passion that made her despise herself. It seemed horrible and unnatural that she should be willing to throw herself into the arms of a dissolute boy, and it lowered her in her own estimation. He caught the expression of her eyes, and something of its meaning.

"Oh, don't look at me like that, Bertha. You look as if you almost hated me."

She answered gravely, "I love you with all my heart, Gerald; and I'm ashamed."

"How can you!" he cried, with such pain in his voice that Bertha could not bear it.

"The whole thing is awful," she groaned. "For God's sake let us try to forget it. I've only succeeded in making you entirely wretched. The only remedy is to part quickly."

"I can't leave you, Bertha. Let me stay."

"It's impossible. You must go, now more than ever."

They were interrupted by the appearance of Miss Ley, who began to talk; but to her surprise neither Bertha nor Gerald showed their usual vivacity.

"What is the matter with you both today?" she asked. "You're unusually attentive to my observations."

"I'm rather tired," said Bertha, "and I have a headache."

Miss Ley looked at Bertha more closely, and fancied that she had been crying; Gerald also seemed profoundly miserable. Surely. . . . Then the truth dawned upon her, and she could hardly repress her astonishment.

"Good Heavens!" she thought, "I must have been blind. How lucky he's going in a week!"

Miss Ley now remembered a dozen occurrences which had escaped her notice, and was absolutely confounded.

"Upon my word," she thought, "I don't believe you can put a woman of seventy for five minutes in company of a boy of fourteen without their getting into mischief."

The week to Gerald and to Bertha passed with terrible quickness. They scarcely had a moment alone, for Miss Ley, under pretence of making much of her nephew, arranged little pleasure parties, so that all three might be continually together.

"We must spoil you a little before you go; and the harm it does you will be put right by the rocking of the boat."

And though Bertha was in a torment, she had strength to avoid any further encounter with Gerald. She dared not see him alone, and was grateful to Miss Ley for putting obstacles in the way. She knew that her love was impossible, but also that it was beyond control. It made her completely despise herself. Bertha had been a little proud of her uprightness, of her liberty from any degrading emotion. And that other love to her husband had been such an intolerable slavery, that when it died away the sense of freedom seemed the most delicious thing in life. She had vowed that never under any circumstance would she expose herself to the suffering that she had once endured. But this new passion had taken her unawares, and before she knew the danger Bertha found herself bound and imprisoned. She tried to reason away the infatuation, but without advantage; Gerald was never absent from her thoughts. Love had come upon her like the sudden madness with which the gods of old afflicted those that had incensed them. It was an insane fire in the blood, irresistible for all the horror it aroused, as that passion which distracted Phædra for Theseus' son.

The temptation came to bid Gerald stay. If he remained in England they might give rein to their passion and let it die of itself; and that might be the only way to kill it. Yet Bertha dared not. And it was terrible to think that he loved her, and she must continually distress him. She looked into his eyes, fancying she saw there the grief of a breaking heart; and his sorrow was more than she could bear. Then a greater temptation beset her. There is one way in which a woman can bind a man to her for ever, there is one tie that is indissoluble; her very flesh cried out, and she trembled at the thought that she could give Gerald the inestimable gift of her person. Then he might go, but that would have passed between them which could not be undone; they might be separated by ten thousand miles, but they would always be joined together. How else could she prove to him her wonderful love, how else could she show her immeasurable gratitude? The temptation was mighty, incessantly recurring; and she was very weak. It assailed her with all the violence of her fervid imagination. She drove it away with anger, she loathed it with all her heart—but she could not stifle the appalling hope that it might prove too strong.

Chapter XXXII

At last Gerald had but one day more. A longstanding engagement of Bertha and Miss Ley forced him to take leave of them early, for he started from London at seven in the morning.

"I'm dreadfully sorry that you can't spend your last evening with us," said Miss Ley. "But the Trevor-Joneses will never forgive us if we don't go to their dinner-party."

"Of course it was my fault for not finding out before, when I sailed."

"What are you going to do with yourself this evening, you wretch?"

"Oh, I'm going to have one last unholy bust."

"I'm afraid you're very glad that for one night we can't look after you."

In a little while Miss Ley, looking at her watch, told Bertha that it was time to dress. Gerald got up, and kissing Miss Ley, thanked her for her kindness.

"My dear boy, please don't sentimentalise. And you're not going for ever. You're sure to make a mess of things and come back—the Leys always do."

Then Gerald turned to Bertha and held out his hand.

"You've been awfully good to me," he said, smiling; but there was in his eyes a steadfast look, which seemed trying to make her understand something. "We've had some ripping times together."

"I hope you won't forget me entirely. We've certainly kept you out of mischief."

Miss Ley watched them, admiring their composure. She thought they took the parting very well.

"I dare say it was nothing but a little flirtation and not very serious. Bertha's so much older than he and so sensible that she's most unlikely to have made a fool of herself."

But she had to fetch the gift which she had prepared for Gerald.

"Wait just one moment, Gerald," she said. "I want to get something."

She left the room and immediately the boy bent forward.

"Don't go out tonight, Bertha. I must see you again."

Before Bertha could reply, Miss Ley called from the hall.

"Good-bye," said Gerald, aloud.

"Good-bye, I hope you'll have a nice journey."

"Here's a little present for you, Gerald," said Miss Ley, when he was outside. "You're dreadfully extravagant, and as that's the only virtue you have, I feel I ought to encourage it. And if you want money at any time, I can always scrape together a few guineas, you know."

She put into his hand two fifty-pound notes and then, as if she were ashamed of herself, bundled him out of doors. She went to her room; and having rather seriously inconvenienced herself for the next six months, for an entirely unworthy object, she began to feel remarkably pleased. In an hour Miss Ley returned to the drawing-room to wait for Bertha, who presently came in, dressed—but ghastly pale.

"Oh, Aunt Polly, I simply can't come tonight. I've got a racking headache; I can scarcely see. You must tell them that I'm sorry, but I'm too ill."

She sank on a chair and put her hand to her forehead, groaning with pain. Miss Ley lifted her eyebrows; the affair was evidently more serious that she thought. However, the danger now was over; it would ease Bertha to stay at home and cry it out. She thought it brave of her even to have dressed.

"You'll get no dinner," she said. "There's nothing in the place."

"Oh, I want nothing to eat."

Miss Ley expressed her concern, and promising to make the excuses, went away. Bertha started up when she heard the door close and went to the window. She looked round for Gerald, fearing he might be already there; he was incautious and eager: but if Miss Ley saw him, it would be fatal. The hansom drove away and Bertha breathed more freely. She could not help it; she too felt that she must see him. If they had to part, it could not be under Miss Ley's cold eyes.

She waited at the window, but he did not come. Why did he delay? He was wasting their few precious minutes; it was already past eight. She walked up and down the room and looked again, but still he was not in sight. She fancied that while she watched he would not come, and forced herself to read. But how could she! Again she looked out of window; and this time Gerald was there. He stood in the porch of the opposite house, looking up; and immediately he saw her, crossed the street. She went to the door and opened it gently, as he came upstairs.

He slipped in as if he were a thief, and on tiptoe they entered the drawing-room.

"Oh, it's so good of you," he said. "I couldn't leave you like that. I knew you'd stay."

"Why have you been so long? I thought you were never coming."

"I dared not risk it before. I was afraid something might happen to stop Aunt Polly."

"I said I had a headache. I dressed so that she might suspect nothing."

The night was falling and they sat together in the dimness. Gerald took her hands and kissed them.

"This week has been awful. I've never had the chance of saying a word to you. My heart has been breaking."

"My dearest."

"I wondered if you were sorry I was going."

She looked at him and tried to smile; already she could not trust herself to speak.

"Every day I thought you would tell me to stop and you never did—and now it's too late. Oh, Bertha, if you loved me you wouldn't send me away."

"I think I love you too much. Don't you see it's better that we should part?"

"I daren't think of tomorrow."

"You are so young; in a little while you'll fall in love with someone else. Don't you see that I'm old?"

"But I love you. Oh, I wish I could make you believe me. Bertha, Bertha, I can't leave you. I love you too much."

"For God's sake don't talk like that. It's hard enough to bear already—don't make it harder."

The night had fallen, and through the open window the summer breeze came in, and the softness of the air was like a kiss. They sat side by side in silence, the boy holding Bertha's hand; they could not speak, for words were powerless to express what was in their hearts. But presently a strange intoxication seized them, and the mystery of passion wrapped them about invisibly. Bertha felt the trembling of Gerald's hand, and it passed to hers. She shuddered and tried to withdraw, but he would not let it go. The silence now became suddenly intolerable: Bertha tried to speak, but her throat was dry, and she could utter no word.

A weakness came to her limbs and her heart beat painfully. Her eye crossed with Gerald's, and they both looked instantly aside, as if caught in some crime. Bertha began to breathe more quickly. Gerald's intense desire burned itself into her soul; she dared not move. She tried to implore God's help, but she could not. The temptation which all the week had terrified her returned with double force—the temptation which she abhorred, but to which she had a horrible longing not to resist.

And now she asked what it mattered. Her strength was dwindling, and Gerald had but to say a word. And now she wished him to say the word; he loved her, and she loved him passionately. She gave way; she no longer wished to resist. She turned her face to Gerald; she leaned towards him with parted lips.

"Bertha," he whispered, and they were nearly in one another's arms.

But a fine sound pierced the silence; they started back and listened. They heard a key put into the front-door, and the door was opened.

"Take care," whispered Bertha, and pushed Gerald away.

"It's Aunt Polly."

Bertha pointed to the electric switch, and understanding, Gerald turned on the light. He looked round instinctively for some way of escape, but Bertha, with a woman's quick invention, sprang to the door and flung it open.

"Is that you, Aunt Polly?" she cried. "How fortunate you came back; Gerald is here to bid us definitely good-bye."

"He makes as many farewells as a *prima donna*," said Miss Ley.

She came in, somewhat breathless, with two spots of red upon her cheeks.

"I thought you wouldn't mind if I came here to wait till you returned," said Gerald. "And I found Bertha."

"How funny that our thoughts should have been identical," said Miss Ley. "It occurred to me that you might come, and so I hurried home as quickly as I could."

"You're quite out of breath," said Bertha.

Miss Ley sank on a chair, exhausted. As she was eating her fish and talking to a neighbour, it suddenly dawned upon her that Bertha's indisposition was assumed.

"Oh, what a fool I am! They've hoodwinked me as if I were a child. . . . Good heavens, what are they doing now?"

The dinner seemed interminable, but immediately afterwards she took leave of her astonished hostess and gave the cabman orders to drive furiously. She arrived, inveighing against the deceitfulness of the human race. She had never run up the stairs so quickly.

"How is your headache, Bertha?"

"Thanks, it's much better. Gerald has driven it away."

This time Miss Ley's good-bye to the precocious youth was rather chilly; she was devoutly thankful that his boat sailed next morning.

"I'll show you out, Gerald," said Bertha. "Don't trouble, Aunt Polly—you must be dreadfully tired."

They went into the hall and Gerald put on his coat. He stretched out his hand to Bertha without speaking, but she, with a glance at the drawing-room, beckoned to him to follow her, and slid out of the front-door. There was no one on the stairs. She flung her arms round his neck and pressed her lips to his. She did not try to hide her passion now; she clasped him to her heart, and their very souls flew to their lips and mingled. Their kiss was rapture, madness; it was an ecstasy beyond description, their senses were powerless to contain their pleasure. Bertha felt herself about to die. In the bliss, in the agony, her spirit failed and she tottered; Gerald pressed her more closely to him.

But there was a sound of someone climbing the stairs. She tore herself away.

"Good-bye, for ever," she whispered, and slipping in, closed the door between them.

She sank down half fainting, but, in fear, struggled to her feet and dragged herself to her room. Her cheeks were glowing and her limbs trembled, the kiss still thrilled her whole being. Oh, now it was too late for prudence! What did she care for her marriage; what did she care that Gerald was younger that she! She loved him, she loved him insanely; the present was there with its infinite joy, and if the future brought misery, it was worth suffering. She could not let him go; he was hers—she stretched out her arms to take him in her embrace. She would surrender everything. She would bid him stay; she would follow him to the end of the earth. It was too late now for reason.

She walked up and down her room excitedly. She looked at the door; she had a mad desire to go to him now—to abandon everything for his sake. Her honour, her happiness, her station, were only precious because she could sacrifice them for him. He was her life and her love, he was her body and her soul. She listened at the door; Miss Ley would be watching, and she dared not go.

"I'll wait," said Bertha.

She tried to sleep, but could not. The thought of Gerald distracted her. She dozed, and his presence became more distinct. He seemed to be in the room and she cried: "At last, my dearest, at last!" She awoke and stretched out her hands to him; she could not realise that she had dreamed, that nothing was there.

Then the day came, dim and grey at first, but brightening with the brilliant summer morning; the sun shone in her window, and the sunbeams danced in the room. Now the moments were very few, she must make up her mind quickly—and the sunbeams spoke of life, and happiness, and the glory of the unknown. Oh, what a fool she was to waste her life, to throw away her chance of happiness—how weak not to grasp the love thrown in her way! She thought of Gerald packing his things, getting off, of the train speeding through the summer country. Her love was irresistible. She sprang up, and bathed, and dressed. It was past six when she slipped out of the room and made her way downstairs. The street was empty as in the night; but the sky was blue and the air fresh and sweet, she took a long breath and felt curiously elated. She walked till she found a cab, and told the driver to go quickly to Euston. The cab crawled along, and she was in an agony of impatience. Supposing she arrived too late? She told the man to hurry.

The Liverpool train was fairly full; but Bertha walking up the crowded platform quickly saw Gerald. He sprang towards her.

"Bertha you've come. I felt certain you wouldn't let me go without seeing you."

He took her hands and looked at her with eyes full of love.

"I'm so glad you've come," he said at last. "I want—I want to beg your pardon."

"What do you mean?" whispered Bertha, and suddenly she felt a dreadful fear which gripped her heart with unendurable pain.

"I've been thinking of you all night, and I'm dreadfully ashamed of myself. I must tell you how sorry I am that I've caused you unhappiness. I was selfish and brutal; I only thought of myself. I forgot how much you had to lose. Please forgive me, Bertha."

"Oh, Gerald, Gerald."

"I shall always be grateful to you, Bertha. I know I've been a beast, but now I'm going to turn over a new leaf. You see, you have reformed me after all."

He tried to smile in his old, light-hearted manner; but it was a very poor attempt. Bertha looked at him. She wished to say that she loved him with all her heart, and was ready to accompany him to the world's end; but the words stuck in her throat.

"I don't know what has happened to me," he said, "but I seem to see everything now so differently. Of course it is much better that I'm going away; but it's dreadfully hard."

An inspector came to look at the tickets. "Is the lady going?"

"No," said Gerald; and then, when the man had passed: "You won't forget me, Bertha, will you? You won't think badly of me; I lost my head. I didn't realise till last night that I wanted to do you the most frightful wrong. I didn't understand that I should have ruined you and your whole life."

At last Bertha forced herself to speak. The time was flying, and she could not understand what was passing in Gerald's mind.

"If you only knew how much I love you!" she cried.

He had but to ask her to go and she would go. But he did not ask. Was he repenting already? Was his love already on the wane? Bertha tried to make herself speak again, but could not. Why did he not repeat that he could not live without her!

"Take your seats, please! Take your seats, please!"

A guard ran along the platform. "Jump in, sir. Right behind!"

"Good-bye," said Gerald. "May I write to you?"

She shook her head. It was too late now.

"Jump in, sir. Jump in."

Gerald kissed her quickly and got into the carriage.

"Right away!"

The guard blew his whistle and waved a flag, and the train puffed slowly out of the station.

Chapter XXXIII

MISS LEY WAS MUCH ALARMED WHEN SHE GOT UP AND FOUND THAT BERTHA had flown.

"Upon my word, I think that Providence is behaving scandalously. Am I not a harmless middle-aged woman who mind my own business; what have I done to deserve these shocks?"

She suspected that her niece had gone to the station; but the train started at seven, and it was ten o'clock. She positively jumped when it occurred to her that Bertha might have—eloped: and like a swarm of abominable little demons came thoughts of the scenes she must undergo if such were the case, the writing of the news to Edward, his consternation, the comfort which she must administer, the fury of Gerald's father, the hysterics of his mother.

"She can't have done anything so stupid," she cried in distraction. "But if women can make fools of themselves, they always do!"

Miss Ley was extraordinarily relieved when at last she heard Bertha come in and go to her room.

Bertha for a long time had stood motionless on the platform, staring haggardly before her, stupefied. The excitement of the previous hours was followed by utter blankness; Gerald was speeding to Liverpool, and she was still in London. She walked out of the station, and turned towards Chelsea. The streets were endless, and she was already tired; almost fainting, she dragged herself along. She did not know the way, and wandered hopelessly, barely conscious. In Hyde Park she sat down to rest, feeling utterly exhausted; but the weariness of her body relieved the terrible aching of her heart. She walked on after a while; it never occurred to her to take a cab, and eventually she came to Eliot Mansions. The sun had grown hot, and burned the crown of her head with ghastly torture. Bertha crawled upstairs to her room, and throwing herself on the bed, burst into tears of bitter anguish. She wept desperately, and clenched her hands.

"Oh," she cried at last, "I dare say he was as worthless as the other."

Miss Ley sent to inquire if she would eat, but Bertha now really had a bad headache, and could touch nothing. All day she spent in agony, hardly able to think—despairing. Sometimes she reproached herself for denying Gerald when he asked her to let him stay, she had wilfully lost the happiness that was within her reach: and then, with a revulsion of feeling, she repeated that he was worthless. The dreary hours passed, and when night came Bertha scarcely had strength to undress; and not till the morning did she get rest. But the early post brought a letter from Edward, repeating his wish that she should return to Court Leys. She read it listlessly.

"Perhaps it's the best thing to do," she groaned.

She hated London now and the flat; the rooms must be horribly bare without the joyous presence of Gerald. To return to Court Leys seemed the only course left to her, and there at least she would have quiet and solitude. She thought almost with longing of the desolate shore, the marshes and the dreary sea; she wanted rest and silence. But if she went, she had better go at once; to stay in London was only to prolong her woe.

Bertha rose, and dressed, and went to Miss Ley; her face was deathly pale, and her eyes heavy and red with weeping. In exhaustion she made no attempt to hide her condition.

"I'm going down to Court Leys today, Aunt Polly. I think it's the best thing I can do."

"Edward will be very pleased to see you."

"I think he will."

Miss Ley hesitated, looking at Bertha.

"You know, Bertha," she said, after a pause, "in this world it's very difficult to know what to do. One struggles to know good from evil—but really they're often so very much alike. . . . I always think those people fortunate who are content to stand, without question, by the ten commandments, knowing exactly how to conduct themselves, and propped up by the hope of Paradise on the one hand, and by the fear of a cloven-footed devil with pincers, on the other. . . . But we who answer *Why* to the crude *Thou Shalt Not*, are like sailors on a wintry sea without a compass. Reason and instinct say one thing, and convention says another. But the worst of it is that one's conscience has been reared on the Decalogue, and fostered on hell-fire—and one's conscience has the last word. I dare say it's cowardly, but it's certainly discreet, to take it into consideration. It's like lobster salad; it's not actually immoral to eat it, but it will very likely give you indigestion. . . . One has to be very sure of oneself to go against the ordinary view of things; and if one isn't, perhaps it's better not to run any risks, but just to walk along the same secure old road as the common herd. It's not exhilarating, it's not brave, and it's rather dull; but it's eminently safe."

Bertha sighed, but did not answer.

"You'd better tell Jane to pack your boxes," said Miss Ley. "Shall I wire to Edward?"

When Bertha had at last started, Miss Ley began to think.

"I wonder if I've done right," she murmured, uncertain as ever.

She was sitting on the piano-stool, and as she meditated, her fingers passed idly over the keys. Presently her ear detected the beginning of a well-known melody, and almost unconsciously she began to play the air of *Rigoletto*.

> *La Donna é mobile*
> *Qual piuma al vento.*

Miss Ley smiled. "The fact is that few women can be happy with only one husband. I believe that the only solution of the marriage question is legalised polyandry."

In the train at Victoria, Bertha remembered with relief that the cattle-market was held at Tercanbury that day, and Edward would not come home till the evening. She would have opportunity to settle herself in Court Leys without fuss or bother. Full of her painful thoughts, the journey passed quickly, and Bertha was surprised to find herself at Blackstable. She got out, wondering whether Edward would have sent a trap to meet her—but to her extreme surprise Edward himself was on the platform, and running up, helped her out of the carriage.

"Here you are at last!" he cried.

"I didn't expect you," said Bertha. "I thought you'd be at Tercanbury."

"I got your wire fortunately just as I was starting, so of course I didn't go."

"I'm sorry I prevented you."

"Why? I'm jolly glad. You didn't think I was going to the cattle-market when my missus was coming home?"

She looked at him with astonishment; his honest, red face glowed with the satisfaction he felt at seeing her.

"By Jove, this is ripping," he said, as they drove away. "I'm tired of being a grass-widower, I can tell you."

They came to Corstal Hill and he walked the horse.

"Just look behind you," he said, in an undertone. "Notice anything?"

"What?"

"Look at Parke's hat." Parke was the footman.

Bertha, looking again, observed a cockade.

"What d'you think of that, eh?" Edward was almost exploding with laughter. "I was elected chairman of the Urban District Council yesterday; that means I'm *ex-officio* J.P. So, as soon as I heard you were coming, I bolted off and got a cockade."

When they reached Court Leys, he helped Bertha out of the trap quite tenderly. She was taken aback to find the tea ready, flowers in the drawing-room, and everything possible done to make her comfortable.

"Are you tired?" asked Edward. "Lie down on the sofa and I'll give you your tea."

He waited on her and pressed her to eat, and was, in fact, unceasing in his attentions.

"By Jove, I am glad to see you here again."

His pleasure was obvious, and Bertha was somewhat touched.

"Are you too tired to come for a little walk in the garden? I want to show what I've done for you, and just now the place is looking its best."

He put a shawl round her shoulders, so that the evening air might not hurt her, and insisted on giving her his arm.

"Now, look here; I've planted rose-trees outside the drawing-room window; I thought you'd like to see them when you sat in your favourite place, reading."

He took her farther, to a place which offered a fine prospect of the sea.

"I've put a bench here, between those two trees, so that you might sit down sometimes, and look at the view."

"It's very kind of you to be so thoughtful. Shall we sit there now?"

"Oh, I think you'd better not. There's a good deal of dew, and I don't want you to catch cold."

For dinner Edward had ordered the dishes which he knew Bertha preferred, and he laughed joyously, as she expressed her pleasure. Afterwards when she lay on the sofa, he arranged the cushions so as to make her quite easy.

"Ah, my dear," she thought, "if you'd been half as kind three years ago you might have kept my love."

She wondered whether absence had increased his affection, or whether it was she who had altered. Was he not unchanging as the rocks, and she knew herself unstable as water, mutable as the summer winds. Had he always been kind and considerate; and had she, demanding a passion which it was not in him to feel, been blind to his deep tenderness? Expecting nothing from him now, she was astonished to find he had so much to offer. But she felt sorry if he loved her, for she could give nothing in return but complete indifference; she was even surprised to find herself so utterly callous.

At bedtime she bade him good-night, and kissed his cheek.

"I've had the red room arranged for me," she said.

There was no change in Blackstable. Bertha's friends still lived, for the death-rate of that fortunate place was their pride, and they could do nothing to increase it. Arthur Branderton had married a pretty, fair-haired girl, nicely bred, and properly insignificant; but the only result of that was to give his mother a new topic of conversation. Bertha, resuming her old habits, had difficulty in realising that she had been long away. She set herself to forget Gerald, and was pleased to find the recollection of him not too importunate. A sentimentalist turned cynic has observed that a woman is only passionately devoted to her first lover, for afterwards it is love itself of which she is enamoured; and certainly the wounds of later attachments heal easily. Bertha was devoutly grateful to Miss Ley for her opportune return on Gerald's last night, and shuddered to think of what might otherwise have happened.

"It would have been too awful," she cried.

She could not understand what sudden madness had seized her, and the thought of the danger she had run, made Bertha's cheeks tingle. Her heart turned sick at the mere remembrance. She was thoroughly ashamed of that insane excursion to Euston, intent upon the most dreadful courses. She felt like a person who from the top of a tower has been so horribly tempted to throw himself down, that only the restraining hand of a bystander has saved him; and then afterwards from below shivers and sweats at the idea of his peril. But worse than the shame was the dread of ridicule; for the whole affair had been excessively undignified: she had run after a hobbledehoy years younger than herself, and had even fallen seriously in love with him. It was too grotesque. Bertha imagined the joy it must cause Miss Ley. She could not forgive Gerald that, on his account, she had made herself absurd. She saw that he was a fickle boy, prepared to philander with every woman he met; and at last told herself scornfully that she had never really cared for him.

But in a little while Bertha received a letter from America, forwarded by Miss Ley. She turned white as she recognised the handwriting: the old emotions came surging back, and she thought of Gerald's green eyes, and of his boyish lips; and she felt sick with love. She looked at the superscription, at the post mark; and then put the letter down.

"I told him not to write," she murmured.

A feeling of anger seized her that the sight of a letter from Gerald should bring her such pain. She almost hated him now; and yet with all her heart she wished to kiss the paper and every word that was written upon it. But the sheer violence of her emotions made her set her teeth, as it were, against giving way.

"I won't read it," she said.

She wanted to prove to herself that she had strength; and this temptation at least she was determined to resist. Bertha lit a candle and took the letter in her hand to burn it, but then put it down again. That would settle the matter too quickly, and she wanted rather to prolong the trial so as to receive full assurance of her fortitude. With a strange pleasure at the pain she was preparing for herself, Bertha placed the letter on the chimneypiece of her room, prominently, so that whenever she went in or out, she could not fail to see it. Wishing to punish herself, her desire was to make the temptation as distressing as possible.

She watched the unopened envelope for a month and sometimes the craving to open it was almost irresistible; sometimes she awoke in the middle of the night, thinking of Gerald, and told herself she must know what he said. Ah, how well she could imagine it! He vowed he loved her and he spoke of the kiss she had given him on that last day, and he said it was dreadfully hard to be without her. Bertha looked at the letter, clenching her hands so as not to seize it and tear it open; she had to hold herself forcibly back from covering it with kisses. But at last she conquered all desire, she was able to look at the handwriting indifferently; she scrutinised her heart and found no trace of emotion. The trial was complete.

"Now it can go," she said.

Again she lit a candle, and held the letter to the flame till it was all consumed; and she gathered up the ashes, putting them in her hand, and blew them out of the window. She felt that by that act she had finished with the whole thing, and Gerald was definitely gone out of her life.

But rest did not yet come to Bertha's troubled soul. At first she found her life fairly tolerable; but she had now no emotions to distract her and the routine of her day was unvarying. The weeks passed and the months; the winter came upon her, more dreary than she had ever known it; the country became insufferably dull. The days were grey and cold, and the clouds so low that she could almost touch them. The broad fields which once had afforded such inspiring thoughts were now merely tedious, and all the rural sights sank into her mind with a pitiless monotony; day after day, month after month, she saw the same things. She was bored to death.

Sometimes Bertha wandered to the seashore and looked across the desolate waste of water; she longed to travel as her eyes and her mind travelled, south, south to the azure skies, to the lands of beauty and of sunshine beyond the greyness. Fortunately she did not know that she was looking almost directly north, and that if she really went on and on as she desired, would reach no southern lands of pleasure, but merely the North Pole!

She walked along the beach, among the countless shells; and not content with present disquietude, tortured herself with anticipation of the future. She could only imagine that it would bring an increase of this frightful ennui, and her head ached as she looked forward to the dull monotony of her life. She went home, and groaned as she entered the house, thinking of the tiresome evening. Invariably after dinner they played piquet. Edward liked to conduct his life on the most mechanical lines, and regularly, as the clock struck nine, he said: "Shall we have a little game?" Bertha fetched the cards while he arranged the chairs. They played six hands. Edward added up the score and chuckled when he won. Bertha put the cards away, her husband replaced the chairs; and so it went on night after night, automatically.

Bertha was seized with the intense restlessness of utter boredom. She would walk up and down her room in a fever of almost physical agony. She would sit at the piano, and cease playing after half a dozen bars—music seemed as futile as everything else; she had done everything so often. She tried to read, but could hardly bring herself to begin a new volume, and the very sight of the printed pages was distasteful: the works of information told her things she did not want to know, the novels related deeds of persons in whom she took no interest. She read a few pages and threw down the book in disgust. Then she went out again—anything seemed preferable to what she actually was doing—she walked rapidly, but the motion, the country, the very atmosphere about her, were wearisome; and almost immediately she returned. Bertha was forced to take the same walks day after day; and the deserted roads, the trees, the hedges, the fields, impressed themselves on her mind with a dismal insistency. Then she was driven to go out merely for exercise, and walked a certain number of miles, trying to get them done quickly. The winds of the early year blew that season more persistently than ever, and they impeded her steps, and chilled her to the bone.

Sometimes Bertha paid visits, and the restraint she had to put upon herself relieved her for the moment, but no sooner was the door closed behind her than she felt more desperately bored than ever.

Yearning suddenly for society, she would send out invitations for some function; then felt it inexpressibly irksome to make preparations, and she loathed and abhorred her guests. For a long time she refused to see anyone, protesting her feeble health; and sometimes in the solitude she thought she would go mad. She turned to prayer as the only refuge of those who cannot act, but she only half believed, and therefore found no comfort. She accompanied Miss Glover on her district visiting, but she disliked the poor, and their chatter seemed hopelessly inane. The ennui made her head ache, and she put her hand to her temples, pressing them painfully; she felt she could take great wisps of her hair and tear it out.

She threw herself on her bed and wept in the agony of boredom. Edward once found her thus, and asked what was the matter.

"Oh, my head aches, so that I feel I could kill myself."

He sent for Ramsay, but Bertha knew the doctor's remedies were absurd and useless. She imagined that there was no remedy for her ill—not even time—no remedy but death.

She knew the terrible distress of waking in the morning with the thought that still another day must be gone through; she knew the relief of bed-time with the thought that she would enjoy a few hours of unconsciousness. She was racked with the imagination of the future's frightful monotony: night would follow day, and day would follow night, the months passing one by one and the years slowly, slowly.

They say that life is short. To those who look back perhaps it is; but to those who look forward it is long, horribly long—endless. Sometimes Bertha felt it impossible to endure. She prayed that she might fall asleep at night and never awake. How happy must be the lives of those who can look forward to eternity! To Bertha the idea was merely ghastly; she desired nothing but the long rest, the rest of an endless sleep, the dissolution into nothing.

Once in desperation she wished to kill herself, but was afraid. People say that suicide requires no courage. Fools! They cannot realise the horror of the needful preparation, the anticipation of the pain, the terrible fear that one may regret when it is too late, when life is ebbing away. And there is the dread of the unknown. And there is the dread of hell-fire—absurd and revolting, yet so engrained that no effort is able entirely to destroy it. Notwithstanding reason and argument there is still the numbing fear that the ghastly fables of our childhood may after all be true, the fear of a jealous God who will doom His wretched creatures to unending torture.

Chapter XXXIV

But if the human soul, or the heart, or the mind—call it what you will—is an instrument upon which countless melodies may be played, it is capable of responding for very long to no single one. Time dulls the most exquisite emotions, softens the most heartrending grief. The story is old of the philosopher who sought to console a woman in distress by the account of tribulations akin to hers, and upon losing his only son was sent by her a list of all kings similarly bereaved. He read it, acknowledged its correctness, but wept none the less. Three months later the philosopher and the lady were surprised to find one another quite gay, and erected a fine monument to Time with the inscription: *A celui qui console.*

When Bertha vowed that life had lost all savour, that her ennui was unending, she exaggerated as usual, and almost grew angry on discovering that existence could be more supportable than she supposed.

One gets used to all things. It is only very misanthropic persons who pretend that they cannot accustom themselves to the stupidity of their fellows; for, after a while, one gets hardened to the most desperate bores, and monotony even ceases to be quite monotonous. Accommodating herself to circumstances, Bertha found life less tedious; it was a calm river, and presently she came to the conclusion that it ran more easily without the cascades and waterfalls, the eddies, whirlpools and rocks, which had disturbed its course. The man who can still dupe himself with illusions has a future not lacking in brightness.

The summer brought a certain variety, and Bertha found amusement in things which before had never interested her. She went to sheltered parts to see if favourite wild flowers had begun to blow: her love of liberty made her prefer the hedge-roses to the pompous blooms of the garden, the buttercups and daisies of the field to the prim geranium, and the calcellaria. Time fled and she was surprised to find the year pass imperceptibly. She began to read with greater zest, and in her favourite seat, on the sofa by the window, spent long hours of pleasure. She read as fancy prompted her, without a plan, because she wished and not because she ought (how can they say that England is decadent when its young ladies are so strenuous!). She obtained pleasure by contrasting different writers, gaining emotions from the gravity of one and the frivolity of the next. She went from the latest novel to the *Orlando Furioso,* from the *Euphues* of John Lyly (most entertaining and whimsical of books!) to the passionate corruption of Verlaine. With a lifetime before her, the length of books was no hindrance, and she started boldly upon the eight volumes of the *Decline and Fall,* upon the many tomes of St. Simon: and she never hesitated to put them aside after a hundred pages.

Bertha found reality tolerable when it was merely a background, a foil to the fantastic happenings of old books. She looked at the green trees, and the song of birds mingled agreeably with her thoughts still occupied, perhaps, with the Dolorous Knight of La Mancha, with Manon Lescaut, or with the joyous band that wanders through the *Decameron.* With greater knowledge came greater curiosity, and she forsook the broad highroads of literature for the mountain pathways of some obscure poet, for the bridle-tracks of the Spanish picaroon. She found unexpected satisfaction in the half-forgotten masterpieces of the past, in poets not quite divine whom fashion had left on one side, in the playwrights, and novelists, and essayists, whose remembrance lives only with the bookworm. It is a relief sometimes to look away from the bright sun of perfect achievement; and the writers who appealed to their age and not to posterity, have by contrast a subtle charm. Undazzled by their splendour, one may discern more easily their individualities and the spirit of their time; they have pleasant qualities not always found among their betters, and there is even a certain pathos in their incomplete success.

In music also Bertha developed a taste for the half-known, the half archaic. It suited the Georgian drawing-room with its old pictures, with its Chippendale and chintz, to play the simple melodies of Couperin and Rameau; the rondos, the gavottes, the sonatinas in powder and patch, which delighted the rococo lords and ladies of a past century.

Living away from the present, in an artificial paradise, Bertha was almost completely happy. She found indifference to the whole world a trusty armour: life was easy without love or hate, hope or despair, without ambition, desire of change, or tumultuous passion. So bloom the flowers; unconscious, uncaring, the bud bursts from the enclosing leaf, and opens to the sunshine, squanders its perfume to the breeze and there is none to see its beauty—and then it dies.

Bertha found it possible to look back upon the past years with something like amusement. It seemed now melodramatic to have loved the simple Edward with such violence, and she was able even to smile at the contrast between her vivid expectations and the flat reality. Gerald was a pleasantly sentimental memory; she did not wish to see him again, but thought of him often, idealising him till he became unsubstantial as a character in a favourite book. Her winter in Italy also formed the motive of some of her most delightful thoughts, and she determined never to spoil the impression by another visit. She had advanced a good deal in the art of life when she realised that pleasure came by surprise, that happiness was a spirit which descended unawares, and seldom when it was sought.

Edward had fallen into a life of such activity that his time was entirely taken up. He had added largely to the Ley estate, and, with the second-rate man's belief that you must do a thing yourself to have it well done, kept the farms under his immediate supervision. He was an important member of all the rural bodies: he was on the School Board, on the Board of Guardians, on the County Council; he was chairman of the Urban District Council, president of the Leanham cricket club, president of the Faversley football club; patron of the Blackstable regatta; he was on the committee of the Tercanbury dog-show, and an enthusiastic supporter of the Mid-Kent Agricultural Exhibition. He was a pillar of the Blackstable Conservative Association, a magistrate, and a churchwarden. Finally he was an ardent Freemason, and flew over Kent to attend the meetings of the half-dozen lodges of which he was a member. But the amount of work did not disturb him.

"Lord bless you," he said, "I love work. You can't give me too much. If there's anything to be done, come to me and I'll do it, and say thank you for giving me the chance."

Edward had always been even-tempered, but now his good-nature was quite angelic. It became a byword. His success was according to his deserts, and to have him concerned in a matter was an excellent insurance. He was always jovial and gay, contented with himself and with the world at large; he was a model squire, landlord, farmer, conservative, man, Englishman. He did everything thoroughly, and his energy was such that he made a point of putting into every concern twice as much work as it really needed. He was busy from morning till night (as a rule quite unnecessarily), and he gloried in it.

"It shows I'm an excellent woman," said Bertha to Miss Glover, "to support his virtues with equanimity."

"My dear, I think you ought to be very proud and happy. He's an example to the whole county. If he were my husband, I should be grateful to God."

"I have much to be thankful for," murmured Bertha.

Since he let her go her own way and she was only too pleased that he should go his, there was really no possibility of difference, and Edward, wise man, came to the conclusion that he had effectually tamed his wife. He thought, with good-humoured scorn, that he had been quite right when he likened women to chickens, animals which, to be happy, required no more than a good run, well fenced in, where they could scratch about to their heart's content.

"Feed 'em regularly, and let 'em cackle; and there you are!"

It is always satisfactory when experience verifies the hypothesis of your youth.

One year, remembering by accident their wedding-day, Edward gave his wife a bracelet; and feeling benevolent in consequence, and having dined well, he patted her hand and remarked:—

"Time does fly, doesn't it?"

"I have heard people say so," she replied, smiling.

"Well, who'd have thought we'd been married eight years! it doesn't seem above eighteen months to me. And we've got on very well, haven't we?"

"My dear Edward, you are such a model husband. It quite embarrasses me sometimes."

"Ha, ha! that's a good one. But I can say this for myself, I do try to do my duty. Of course at first we had our little tiffs—people have to get used to one another, and one can't expect to have all plain sailing just at once. But for years now—well, ever since you went to Italy, I think, we've been as happy as the day is long, haven't we?"

"Yes, dear."

"When I look back at the little rumpuses we used to have, upon my word, I wonder what they were all about."

"So do I." And this Bertha said quite truthfully.

"I suppose it was just the weather."

"I dare say."

"Ah, well—all's well that ends well."

"My dear Edward, you're a philosopher."

"I don't know about that—but I think I'm a politician; which reminds me that I've not read about the new men-of-war in today's paper. What I've been agitating about for years is more ships and more guns—I'm glad to see the Government have taken my advice at last."

"It's very satisfactory, isn't it? It will encourage you to persevere. And, of course, it nice to know that the Cabinet read your speeches in the *Blackstable Times*."

"I think it would be a good sight better for the country if those in power paid more attention to provincial opinion. It's men like me who really know the feeling of the nation. You might get me the paper, will you—it's in the dining-room."

It seemed quite natural to Edward that Bertha should wait upon him: it was the duty of a wife. She handed him the *Standard*, and he began to read; he yawned once or twice.

"Lord, I am sleepy."

Presently he could not keep his eyes open, the paper dropped from his hand, and he sank back in his chair with legs outstretched, his hands resting comfortably on his stomach. His head lolled to one side and his jaw dropped, and he began to snore. Bertha read. After a while he woke with a start.

"Bless me, I do believe I've been asleep," he cried. "Well, I'm dead tired, I think I shall go to bed. I suppose you won't come up yet?"

"Not just yet."

"Well, don't stay up too late, there's a good girl, it's not good for you; and put the lights out properly when you come."

She turned to him her cheek, which he kissed, stifling a yawn; then he rolled upstairs.

"There's one advantage in Edward," murmured Bertha. "No one could accuse him of being uxorious."

Mariage à la mode.

Bertha's solitary walk was to the sea. The shore between Blackstable and the Medway was extraordinarily wild. At distant intervals were the long, low buildings of the coastguard stations; and the clean, pink walls, the neat railings, the well-kept gravel, contrasted rather surprisingly with the surrounding desolation. One could walk for miles without meeting a soul, and the country spread out from the sea, low and flat and marshy. The beach was of countless shells of every possible variety, which crumbled under foot; while here and there were great banks of seaweed and bits of wood or rope, the jetsam of a thousand tides. In one spot, a few yards out but high and dry at low water, were the remains of an old hulk, whose wooden ribs stood out weirdly like the skeleton of some huge sea-beast. And then all round was the lonely sea, with never a ship nor a fishing-smack in sight. In winter it was as if a spirit of solitude, like a mystic shroud, had descended upon the shore and upon the desert waters.

Then, in the melancholy, in the dreariness, Bertha found a subtle fascination. The sky was a threatening heavy cloud, low down; and the wind tore along shouting, screaming, and whistling: there was panic in the turbulent sea, murky and yellow, and the waves leaped up, one at the other's heels, and beat down on the beach with an angry roar. It was desolate, desolate; the sea was so merciless that the very sight appalled one: it was a wrathful power, beating forwards, ever wrathfully beating forwards, roaring with pain when the chains that bound it wrenched it back; and after each desperate effort it shrank with a yell of anguish. And the seagulls swayed above the waves in their melancholy flight, rising and falling with the wind.

Bertha loved also the calm of winter, when the sea-mist and the mist of heaven were one; when the sea was silent and heavy, and the solitary gull flew screeching over the grey waters, screeching mournfully. She loved the calm of summer when the sky was cloudless and infinite. Then she spent long hours, lying at the water's edge, delighted with the solitude and with her absolute peace. The sea, placid as a lake, unmoved by the lightest ripple, was a looking-glass reflecting the glory of heaven; and it turned to fire when the sun sank in the west; it was a sea of molten copper, red, brilliant, so that the eyes were dazzled. A troop of seagulls slept on the water; and there were hundreds of them, motionless and silent; one arose now and then, and flew for a moment with heavy wing, and sank down, and all was still.

Once the coolness was so tempting that Bertha could not resist it. Timidly, rapidly, she slipped off her clothes and looking round to see that there was really no one in sight, stepped in. The wavelets about her feet made her shiver a little, and then with a splash, stretching out her arms, she ran forward, and half fell, half dived into the water. Now it was delightful; she rejoiced in the freedom of her limbs, for it was an unknown pleasure to swim unhampered by costume. It gave a fine sense of power, and the salt water, lapping round her, was wonderfully exhilarating. She wanted to sing aloud in the joy of her heart. Diving below the surface, she came up with a shake of the head and a little cry of delight; then her hair was loosened and with a motion it all came tumbling about her shoulders and trailed out in its ringlets over the water.

She swam out, a fearless swimmer; and it gave her a feeling of strength and independence to have the deep waters all about her, the deep calm sea of summer; she turned on her back and floated, trying to look the sun in the face. The sea glimmered with the sunbeams and the sky was dazzling. Then, returning, Bertha floated again, quite near the shore; it amused her to lie on her back, rocked by the tiny waves, and to sink her ears so that she could hear the shingle rub together curiously with the ebb and flow of the tide. She shook out her long hair and it stretched about her like an aureole.

She exulted in her youth—in her youth? Bertha felt no older than when she was eighteen, and yet—she was thirty. The thought made her wince; for she had never realised the passage of the years, she had never imagined that her youth was waning. Did people think her already old? The sickening fear came to her that she resembled Miss Hancock, attempting by archness and by an assumption of frivolity, to persuade her neighbours that she was juvenile. Bertha asked herself whether she was ridiculous when she rolled in the water like a young girl: you cannot act the mermaid with crow's feet about your eyes, with wrinkles round your mouth. In a panic she dressed herself, and going home, flew to a looking-glass. She scrutinised her features as she had never done before, searching anxiously for the signs she feared to see; she looked at her neck and at her eyes: her skin was as smooth as ever, her teeth as perfect. She gave a sigh of relief.

"I see no difference."

Then, doubly to reassure herself, a fantastic idea seized Bertha to dress as though she were going to a great ball; she wished to see herself to all advantage.

She chose the most splendid gown she had, and took out her jewels. The Leys had sold every vestige of their old magnificence, but their diamonds, with characteristic obstinacy, they had invariably declined to part with; and they lay aside, year after year unused, the stones in their old settings, dulled with dust and neglect. The moisture still in Bertha's hair was an excuse to do it capriciously, and she placed in it the beautiful tiara which her grandmother had worn in the Regency. On her shoulders she wore two ornaments exquisitely set in gold-work, purloined by a great-uncle in the Peninsular War from the saint of a Spanish church. She slipped a string of pearls round her neck, bracelets on her arms, and fastened a glistening row of stars to her bosom. Knowing she had beautiful hands, Bertha disdained to wear rings, but now she covered her fingers with diamonds and emeralds and sapphires.

Finally she stood before the looking-glass, and gave a laugh of pleasure. She was not old yet.

But when she sailed into the drawing-room, Edward jumped up in surprise.

"Good Lord!" he cried. "What on earth's up! Have we got people coming to dinner?"

"My dear, if we had, I should not have dressed like this."

"You're got up as if the Prince of Wales were coming. And I'm only in knickerbockers. It's not our wedding-day?"

"No."

"Then I should like to know why you've dressed yourself up like that."

"I thought it would please you," she said, smiling.

"I wish you'd told me—I'd have dressed too. Are you sure no one's coming?"

"Quite sure."

"Well, I think I ought to dress. It would look so queer if someone turned up."

"If anyone does, I promise you I'll fly."

They went in to dinner, Edward feeling very uncomfortable, and keeping his ear alert for the front-door bell. They ate their soup, and then were set on the table—the remains of a cold leg of mutton and mashed potatoes. Bertha looked for a moment blankly, and then, leaning back, burst into peal upon peal of laughter.

"Good Lord, what is the matter now?" asked Edward.

Nothing is more annoying than to have people violently hilarious over a joke that you cannot see.

Bertha held her sides and tried to speak.

"I've just remembered that I told the servants they might go out tonight, there's a circus at Blackstable; and I said we'd just eat up the odds and ends."

"I don't see any joke in that."

And really there was none, but Bertha laughed again immoderately.

"I suppose there are some pickles," said Edward.

Bertha repressed her gaiety and began to eat.

"That is my whole life," she murmured under her breath, "to eat cold mutton and mashed potatoes in a ball-dress and all my diamonds."

Chapter XXXV

BUT IN THE WINTER OF THAT VERY YEAR EDWARD, WHILE HUNTING, HAD AN accident. For years he had made a practice of riding unmanageable horses, and he never heard of a vicious beast without wishing to try it. He knew that he was a fine rider, and since he was never shy of parading his powers, nor loath to taunt others on the score of inferior skill or courage, he preferred difficult animals. It gratified him to see people point to him and say, "There's a good rider": and his best joke with some person on a horse that pulled or refused, was to cry: "You don't seem friends with your gee; would you like to try mine?" And then, touching its sides with his spurs, he set it prancing. He was merciless with the cautious hunters who looked for low parts of a hedge or tried to get through a gate instead of over it; and when anyone said a jump was dangerous, Edward with a laugh promptly went for it, shouting as he did so—

"I wouldn't try it if I were you. You might fall off."

He had just bought a roan for a mere song, because it jumped uncertainly, and had a trick of swinging a foreleg as it rose. He took it out on the earliest opportunity, and the first two hedges and a ditch the horse cleared easily. Edward thought that once again he had got for almost nothing a hunter that merely wanted riding properly to behave like a lamb. They rode on, and came to a post and rail fence.

"Now, my beauty, this'll show what you're made of."

He took the horse up in a canter, and pressed his legs; the horse did not rise, but swerved round suddenly.

"No, you don't," said Edward, taking him back.

He dug his spurs in, and the horse cantered up, and refused again. This time Edward grew angry. Arthur Branderton came flying by, and having many old scores to pay, laughed loudly.

"Why don't you get down and walk over?" he shouted, as he passed Edward and took the jump.

"I'll either get over or break my neck," said Edward, setting his teeth.

But he did neither. He set the roan at the jump for the fourth time, hitting him with his crop; the beast rose, and then letting the fore-leg swing, came down with a crash.

Edward fell heavily, and for a minute was stunned. When he recovered consciousness, he found someone pouring brandy down his neck.

"Is the horse hurt?" he asked, not thinking of himself.

"No; he's all right. How d'you feel?"

A young surgeon was in the field, and rode up. "What's the matter? Anyone injured?"

"No," said Edward, struggling to his feet, somewhat annoyed at the exhibition he thought he was making of himself. "One would think none of you fellows had ever seen a man come down before. I've seen most of you come off often enough."

He walked up to the horse, and put his foot in the stirrup.

"You'd better go home, Craddock," said the surgeon. "I expect you're a bit shaken up."

"Go home be damned. Confound!" As he tried to mount, Edward felt a pain at the top of his chest. "I believe I've broken something."

The surgeon went up and helped him off with his coat. He twisted Edward's arm.

"Does that hurt?"

"A bit."

"You've broken your collar-bone," said the surgeon, after a moment's examination.

"I thought I'd smashed something. How long will it take to mend?"

"Only three weeks. You needn't be alarmed."

"I'm not alarmed, but I suppose I shall have to give up hunting for at least a month."

Edward was driven to Dr. Ramsay, who bandaged him and sent him back to Court Leys. Bertha was surprised to see him in a dogcart. Edward by now had recovered his good temper, and explained the occurrence, laughing.

"It's nothing to make a fuss about. Only I'm bandaged up so that I feel like a mummy, and I don't know how I'm going to get a bath. That's what worries me."

Next day Arthur Branderton came to see him. "You've found your match at last, Craddock."

"Me? Not much! I shall be all right in a month, and then out I go again."

"I wouldn't ride him again, if I were you. It's not worth it. With that trick of his of swinging his leg, you'll break your neck."

"Bah," said Edward, scornfully. "The horse hasn't been built that I can't ride."

"You're a good weight now, and your bones aren't as supple as when you were twenty. The next fall you have will be a bad one."

"Rot, man! One would think I was eighty; I've never funked a horse yet, and I'm not going to begin now."

Branderton shrugged his shoulders, and said nothing more at the time, but afterwards spoke to Bertha privately.

"You know, I think, if I were you, I'd persuade Edward to get rid of that horse. I don't think he ought to ride it again. It's not safe. However well he rides, it won't save him if the beast has got a bad trick."

Bertha had in this particular great faith in her husband's skill. Whatever he could not do, he was certainly one of the finest riders in the county; but she spoke to him notwithstanding.

"Pooh, that's all rot!" he said. "I tell you what, on the 11th of next month we go over pretty well the same ground; and I'm going out, and I swear he's going over that post and rail in Coulter's field."

"You're very incautious."

"No, I'm not. I know exactly what a horse can do. And I know that horse can jump if he wants to, and by George, I'll make him. Why, if I funked it now I could never ride again. When a chap gets to be near forty and has a bad fall, the only thing is to go for it again at once, or he'll lose his nerve and never get it back. I've seen that over and over again."

Miss Glover later on, when Edward's bandages were removed and he was fairly well, begged Bertha to use her influence with him.

"I've heard he's a most dangerous horse, Bertha, I think it would be madness for Edward to ride him."

"I've begged him to sell it, but he merely laughs at me," said Bertha. "He's extremely obstinate and I have very little power over him."

"Aren't you dreadfully frightened?"

Bertha laughed. "No, I'm really not. You know he always has ridden dangerous horses and he's never come to any harm. When we were first married I used to go through agonies. Every time he hunted I used to think he'd be brought home dead on a stretcher. But he never was, and I calmed down by degrees."

"I wonder you could."

"My dear, no one can keep on being frightfully agitated for ten years. People who live on volcanoes forget all about it; and you'd soon get used to sitting on barrels of gunpowder if you had no arm-chair."

"Never!" said Miss Glover, with conviction, seeing a vivid picture of herself in such a position.

Miss Glover was unaltered. Time passed over her head powerlessly; she still looked anything between five-and-twenty and forty, her hair was no more washed-out, her figure in its armour of black cloth was as juvenile as ever; and not a new idea nor a thought had entered her mind. She was like Alice's queen, who ran at the top of her speed and remained in the same place; but with Miss Glover the process was reversed: the world moved on, apparently faster and faster as the century drew near its end, but she remained fixed—an incarnation of the eighteen-eighties.

The day before the 11th arrived. The hounds were to meet at the *Share and Coulter,* as when Edward had been thrown. He sent for Dr. Ramsay to assure

Bertha that he was quite fit; and after the examination, brought him into the drawing-room.

"Dr. Ramsay says my collar-bone is stronger than ever."

"But I don't think he ought to ride the roan notwithstanding. Can't you persuade Edward not to, Bertha?"

Bertha looked from the doctor to Edward, smiling. "I've done my best."

"Bertha knows better than to bother," said Edward. "She don't think much of me as a churchwarden, but when a horse is concerned, she does trust me; don't you, dear?"

"I really do."

"There," said Edward, much pleased, "that's what I call a good wife."

Next day the horse was brought round and Bertha filled Edward's flask.

"You'll bury me nicely if I break my neck, won't you?" he said, laughing. "You'll order a handsome tombstone."

"My dear, you'll never come to a violent end. I feel certain you will die in your bed when you're a hundred and two, with a crowd of descendants weeping round you. You're just that sort of man."

"Ha, ha!" he laughed. "I don't know where the descendants are coming in."

"I have a presentiment that I am doomed to make way for Fanny Glover. I'm sure there's a fatality about it. I've felt for years that you will eventually marry her, and it's horrid of me to have kept you waiting so long—especially as she pines for you, poor thing."

Edward laughed again. "Well, good-bye!"

"Good-bye. Remember me to Mrs. Arthur."

She stood at the window to see him mount, and as he flourished his crop at her, she waved her hand.

The winter day closed in and Bertha, interested in the novel she was reading, was surprised to hear the clock strike five. She wondered that Edward had not yet come in, and ringing for tea and the lamps, had the curtains drawn. He could not now be long.

"I wonder if he's had another fall," she said, with a smile. "He really ought to give up hunting, he's getting too fat."

She decided to wait no longer, but poured out her tea and arranged herself so that she could get at the scones and see comfortably to read. Then she heard a carriage drive up. Who could it be?

"What bores these people are to call at this time!"

As the bell was rung, Bertha put down her book to receive the visitor. But no one was shown in; there was a confused sound of voices without. Could something have happened to Edward after all? She sprang to her feet and walked half across the room. She heard an unknown voice in the hall.

"Where shall we take it?"

It. What was *it*—a corpse? Bertha felt a coldness travel through all her body, she put her hand on a chair, so that she might steady herself if she felt faint. The door was opened slowly by Arthur Branderton, and he closed it quickly behind him.

"I'm awfully sorry, but there's been an accident. Edward is rather hurt."

She looked at him, growing pale, but found nothing to answer.

"You must nerve yourself, Bertha. I'm afraid he's very bad. You'd better sit down."

He hesitated, and she turned to him with sudden anger.

"If he's dead, why don't you tell me?"

"I'm awfully sorry. We did all we could. He fell at the same post and rail fence as the other day. I think he must have lost his nerve. I was close by him, I saw him rush at it blindly, and then pull just as the horse was rising. They came down with a crash."

"Is he dead?"

"Yes."

Bertha did not feel faint. She was a little horrified at the clearness with which she was able to understand Arthur Branderton. She seemed to feel nothing at all. The young man looked at her as if he expected that she would weep or swoon.

"Would you like me to send my wife to you?"

"No, thanks."

Bertha understood quite well that her husband was dead, but the news seemed to make no impression upon her. She heard it unmoved, as though it referred to a stranger. She found herself wondering what young Branderton thought of her unconcern.

"Won't you sit down," he said, taking her arm and leading her to a chair. "Shall I get you some brandy?"

"I'm all right, thanks. You need not trouble about me—Where is he?"

"I told them to take him upstairs. Shall I send Ramsay's assistant to you? He's here."

"No," she said, in a low voice. "I want nothing. Have they taken him up already?"

"Yes, but I don't think you ought to go to him. It will upset you dreadfully."

"I'll go to my room. Do you mind if I leave you? I should prefer to be alone."

Branderton held the door open and Bertha walked out, her face very pale, but showing not the least trace of emotion. Branderton walked to Leanham Vicarage to send Miss Glover to Court Leys, and then home, where he told his wife that the wretched widow was stunned by the shock.

Bertha locked herself in her room. She heard the hum of voices in the house, Dr. Ramsay came to her door, but she refused to open; then all was quite still.

She was aghast at the blankness of her heart, the tranquility was so inhuman that she wondered if she was going mad; she felt no emotion whatever. Bertha repeated to herself that Edward was killed; he was lying quite near at hand, dead—and she felt no grief. She remembered her anguish years before when she thought of his death; and now that it had taken place she did not faint, she did not weep, she was untroubled. Bertha had hidden herself to conceal her tears from strange eyes, and the tears came not. After her sudden suspicion was confirmed, she had experienced no emotion whatever; she was horrified that the tragic death affected her so little. She walked to the window and looked out, trying to gather her thoughts, trying to make herself care; but she was almost indifferent.

"I must be frightfully cruel," she muttered.

Then the idea came of what her friends would say when they saw her calm self-possession. She tried to weep, but her eyes remained dry.

There was a knock at the door, and Miss Glover's voice, broken with tears, "Bertha, Bertha, wont you let me in? It's me—Fanny."

Bertha sprang to her feet, but did not answer.

Miss Glover called again, and her voice was choked with sobs. Why could Fanny Glover weep for Edward's death, who was a stranger, when she, Bertha, remained insensible?

"Bertha!"

"Yes."

"Open the door for me. Oh, I'm so sorry for you. Please let me in."

Bertha looked wildly at the door, she dared not let Miss Glover come.

"I can see no one now," she cried, hoarsely. "Don't ask me."

"I think I could comfort you."

"I want to be alone."

Miss Glover was silent for a minute, crying audibly.

"Shall I wait downstairs? You can ring if you want me. Perhaps you'll see me later."

Bertha wished to tell her to go away, but dared not.

"Do as you like," she said.

There was silence again, an unearthly silence more trying than hideous din. It was a silence that tightened the nerves and made them horribly sensitive: one dared not breathe for fear of breaking it.

And one thought came to Bertha, assailing her like a devil tormenting. She cried out in horror, for this was more odious than anything; it was simply intolerable. She threw herself on her bed and buried her face in her pillow to drive it away. For shame, she put her hands to her ears so as not to hear the invisible fiends that whispered it silently.

She was free.

She quailed before the thought, but could not crush it. "Has it come to this!" she murmured.

And then came back the recollection of the beginnings of her love. She recalled the passion that had thrown her blindly into Edward's arms, her bitter humiliation when she realised that he could not respond to her ardour; her love was a fire playing ineffectually upon a rock of basalt. She recalled the hatred which followed the disillusion, and finally the indifference. It was the same indifference that chilled her heart now.

Her life seemed all wasted when she compared her mad desire for happiness with the misery she had actually endured. Bertha's many hopes stood out like phantoms, and she looked at them despairingly. She had expected so much and secured so little. She felt a terrible pain at her heart as she considered all she had gone through. Her strength fell away, and overcome by her own self-pity, she sank to her knees and burst into tears.

"Oh, God!" she cried, "what have I done that I should have been so unhappy?"

She sobbed aloud, not caring to restrain her grief. Miss Glover, good soul, was waiting outside the room, in case Bertha wanted her, crying silently. She knocked again when she heard the impetuous sobs within.

"Oh, Bertha, do let me in. You're tormenting yourself so much more because you won't see anybody."

Bertha dragged herself to her feet and undid the door. Miss Glover entered, and throwing off all reserve in her overwhelming sympathy, clasped Bertha to her heart.

"Oh, my dear, my dear, it's utterly dreadful; I'm so sorry for you. I don't know what to say. I can only pray."

Bertha sobbed unrestrainedly—not because Edward was dead.

"All you have now is God," said Miss Glover.

At last Bertha tore herself away and dried her eyes.

"Don't try and be too brave, Bertha," compassionately said the Vicar's sister. "It will do you good to cry. He was such a good, kind man, and he loved you so devotedly."

Bertha looked at her in silence.

"I must be horribly cruel," she thought.

"Do you mind if I stay here tonight, dear," added Miss Glover. "I've sent word to Charles."

"Oh, no, please don't. If you care for me, Fanny, let me be alone. I don't want to be unkind, but I can't bear to see anyone."

Miss Glover was deeply pained. "I don't want to be in the way. If you really wish me to go, I'll go."

"I feel if I can't be alone, I shall go mad."

"Would you like to see Charles?"

"No, dear. Don't be angry. Don't think me unkind or ungrateful, but I want nothing but to be left entirely by myself."

Chapter XXXVI

ALONE IN HER ROOM ONCE MORE, MEMORIES OF THE PAST CROWDED UPON her. The last years fled from her mind and Bertha saw vividly again the first days of her love, the visit to Edward at his farm, the night at the gate of Court Leys when he asked her to marry him. She recalled the rapture with which she had flung herself into his arms. Forgetting the real Edward who had just died, she remembered the tall strong youth who had made her faint with love; and her passion returned, overwhelming. On the chimney-piece stood a photograph of Edward as he was then; it had been before her for years, but she had never noticed it. She took it and pressed it to her heart, and kissed it. A thousand things came back and she saw him again standing before her as he was, manly, strong, so that she felt his love a protection against all the world.

But what was the use now?

"I should be mad if I began to love him again when it is too late."

Bertha was appalled by the regret which she felt rising within her, a devil that wrung her heart in an iron grip. Oh, she could not risk the possibility of grief, she had suffered too much and she must kill in herself the springs of pain. She dared not leave things which in future years might be the foundations of a new idolatry. Her only chance of peace was to destroy everything that might recall him.

She seized the photograph and without daring to look again, withdrew it from the frame and rapidly tore it in pieces. She looked round the room.

"I mustn't leave anything," she muttered.

She saw on a table an album containing pictures of Edward at all ages, the child with long curls, the urchin in knickerbockers, the schoolboy, the lover of her heart. She had persuaded him to be photographed in London during their honeymoon, and he was there in half a dozen different positions. Bertha thought her heart would break as she destroyed them one by one, and it needed all the strength she had to prevent her from covering them with passionate kisses. Her fingers ached with the tearing, but in a little while they were all in fragments in the fireplace. Then, desperately, she added the letters Edward had written to her; and applied a match. She watched them curl and frizzle and burn; and presently they were ashes.

She sank on a chair, exhausted by the effort, but quickly roused herself. She drank some water, nerving herself for a more terrible ordeal; for she knew that on the next few hours depended her future peace.

By now the night was late, a stormy night with the wind howling through the leafless trees. Bertha started when it beat against the windows with a scream that was nearly human. A fear seized her of what she was about to do, but she was driven by a greater fear. She took a candle, and opening the door, listened. There was no one; the wind roared with its long monotonous voice, and the branches of a tree beating against a window in the passage gave a ghastly tap-tap, as if unseen spirits were near.

The living, in the presence of death, feel that the whole air is full of something new and terrible. A greater sensitiveness perceives an inexplicable feeling of something present, or of some horrible thing happening invisibly. Bertha walked to her husband's room and for a while dared not enter. At last she opened the door, she lit the candles on the chimney-piece and on the dressing-table, then went to the bed. Edward was lying on his back, with a handkerchief bound round his jaw to hold it up, his hands crossed in front.

Bertha stood in front of the corpse and looked. The impression of the young man passed away, and she saw him as in truth he was, stout, red-faced, with the venules of his cheeks standing out distinctly in a purple network; the sides of his face were prominent as of late years they had become; and he had little side whiskers. His skin was lined already and rough, the hair over the front of his head was scanty, and the scalp was visible, shiny and white. The hands which once had delighted her by their strength, so that she compared them with the porphyry hands of an unfinished statue, now were repellent in their coarseness. For a long time their touch had a little disgusted her. This was the image Bertha wished to impress upon her mind. It was a stranger lying dead before her, a man to whom she was indifferent.

At last turning away, she went out and returned to her own room.

Three days later was the funeral. All the morning wreaths and crosses of beautiful flowers had poured in, and now there was a crowd in the drive in front of Court Leys. The Blackstable Freemasons (Lodge No. 31,899), of which Edward at his death was Worshipful Master, had signified their intention of attending, and lined the road, two and two, in white gloves and aprons. There were likewise representatives of the Tercanbury Lodge (4169), of the Provincial Grand Lodge, the Mark Masons, and the Knights Templars. The Blackstable Unionist Association sent one hundred Conservatives, who walked two and two after the Freemasons. There were a few words as to precedence between Brother G. W. Hancock (P.W.M.), who led the Blackstable Lodge (31,899), and Mr. Atthill Bacot, who marched at the head of the politicians; but it was finally settled in favour of the Lodge, as the older established body. Then came the members of the Local District Council, of which Edward had been chairman, and after these the carriages of the gentry. Mrs. Mayston Ryle sent a landau and pair, but Mrs. Branderton, the Molsons, and the rest, only sent broughams. It needed a prodigious amount of generalship to marshal these forces, and Arthur Branderton lost his temper because the Conservatives would start before they were wanted to.

"Ah," said Brother A. W. Rogers (the landlord of the *Pig and Whistle*), "they want Craddock here now. He was the best organiser I've ever seen; he'd have got the procession into working order and the funeral over by this time."

The last carriage disappeared, and Bertha, alone at length, lay down by the window on the sofa. She was devoutly grateful to the old convention which prevented the widow's attendance at the funeral.

She looked with tired and listless eyes at the long avenue of elm-trees, bare of leaf. The sky was grey and the clouds heavy and low. Bertha now was a pale woman of thirty, still beautiful, with curling, abundant hair; but her dark eyes had under them still darker lines, and their fire was half gone. Between her brows was a little vertical line, and her lips had lost the joyousness of youth, the corners of her mouth turned down with a melancholy expression. The face was thin and extremely pale; but what chiefly struck one was that she seemed so utterly weary. Her features remained singularly immobile, and there was in her eyes an apathy that was very painful. Her eyes said that she had loved and found love wanting, that she had been a mother and that her child had died, and that now she desired nothing very strongly but to be left in peace.

Bertha was indeed tired out, in body and mind, tired of love and hate, tired with friendship and knowledge, tired with the passing years. Her thought wandered to the future and she decided to leave Blackstable, and let Court Leys, so that in no moment of weakness might she be tempted to return. And first she intended to travel, wishing to live in places where she was unknown, so as more easily to forget the past. Bertha's memory brought back Italy, the land of those who suffer in unfulfilled desire, the lotus land. She would go there and she would go farther, ever towards the sun; for now she had no ties on earth, and at last, at last she was free.

The melancholy day closed in the great clouds hanging overhead darkened with approaching night. Bertha remembered how ready in her girlhood she had been to pour herself out to the world. Feeling intense fellowship with all human beings, she wished to throw herself into their arms, thinking that they would be outstretched to receive her. Her life seemed to overflow into the lives of others, becoming one with theirs as the water of rivers becomes one with the sea. But very soon the power she had felt of doing all this departed; she recognised a barrier between herself and human kind, and felt that they were strangers. Hardly understanding the impossibility of what she desired, she placed all her love, all her faculty of expansion, on one person, on Edward, making a final effort, as it were, to break the barrier of consciousness and unite her soul with his. She drew him towards her with all her might, Edward the man, seeking to know him in the depths of his heart, yearning to lose herself in him. But at last she saw that what she had striven for was unattainable. *I myself stand on one side and the rest of the world on the other.* There is an abyss between, that no power can cross, a strange barrier more insuperable than a mountain of fire. Not even the most devoted lovers know the essentials of one another's selves. However ardent their passion, however intimate their union, they are always strangers; scarcely more to one another than chance acquaintance.

And when she discovered this, with many tears and after bitter heartache, Bertha retired into herself. But soon she found solace. In her silence she built a world of her own, and kept it from the eyes of every living soul, knowing that none could understand it. And then all ties were irksome, all earthly attachments unnecessary.

Confusedly thinking these things, Bertha's thoughts reverted to Edward.

"If I had been keeping a diary of my emotions, I should close it today, with the words, 'My husband has broken his neck.'"

But she was pained at her own callousness.

"Poor fellow," she murmured. "He was honest and kind and forbearing. He did all he could, and tried always to act like a gentleman. He was very useful in the world, and, in his own way, he was fond of me. His only fault was that I loved him—and ceased to love him."

By her side lay the book she had read while waiting for Edward when he was hunting. Bertha had put it on the table open, face-downwards, when she rose from the sofa to receive the expected visitor; and it had remained as she left it. She was tired of thinking; and taking it now, began to read quietly.

THE EXPLORER

TO
My Dear Mrs. G. W. Steevens

Chapter I

THE SEA WAS VERY CALM. THERE WAS NO SHIP IN SIGHT, AND THE SEA-GULLS were motionless upon its even greyness. The sky was dark with lowering clouds, but there was no wind. The line of the horizon was clear and delicate. The shingly beach, no less deserted, was thick with tangled seaweed, and the innumerable shells crumbled under the feet that trod them. The breakwaters, which sought to prevent the unceasing encroachment of the waves, were rotten with age and green with the sea-slime. It was a desolate scene, but there was a restfulness in its melancholy; and the great silence, the suave monotony of colour, might have given peace to a heart that was troubled. They could not assuage the torment of the woman who stood alone upon that spot. She did not stir; and, though her gaze was steadfast, she saw nothing. Nature has neither love nor hate, and with indifference smiles upon the light at heart and to the heavy brings a deeper sorrow. It is a great irony that the old Greek, so wise and prudent, who fancied that the gods lived utterly apart from human passions, divinely unconscious in their high palaces of the grief and joy, the hope and despair, of the turbulent crowd of men, should have gone down to posterity as the apostle of brutish pleasure.

But the silent woman did not look for solace. She had a vehement pride which caused her to seek comfort only in her own heart; and when, against her will, heavy tears rolled down her cheeks, she shook her head impatiently. She drew a long breath and set herself resolutely to change her thoughts.

But they were too compelling, and she could not drive from her mind the memories that absorbed it. Her fancy, like a homing bird, hovered with light wings about another coast; and the sea she looked upon reminded her of another sea. The Solent. From her earliest years that sheet of water had seemed an essential part of her life, and the calmness at her feet brought back to her irresistibly the scenes she knew so well. But the rippling waves washed the shores of Hampshire with a persuasive charm that they had not elsewhere, and the broad expanse of it, lacking the illimitable majesty of the open sea, could be loved like a familiar thing. Yet there was in it, too, something of the salt freshness of the ocean, and, as the eye followed its course, the heart could exult with a sense of freedom. Sometimes, in the dusk of a winter afternoon, she remembered the Solent as desolate as the Kentish sea before her; but her imagination presented it to her more often with the ships, outward bound or homeward bound, that passed continually. She loved them all. She loved the great liners that sped across the ocean, unmindful of wind or weather, with their freight of passengers; and at night, when she recognised them only by the long row of lights, they fascinated her by the mystery of their thousand souls going out strangely into the unknown. She loved the little panting ferries that carried the good folk of the neighbourhood across the water to buy their goods in Southampton, or to sell the produce of their farms; she was intimate with their sturdy skippers, and she delighted in their airs of self-importance. She loved the fishing boats that went out in all weathers, and the neat yachts that fled across the bay with such a dainty grace. She loved the great barques and the brigantines that came in with a majestic ease, all their sails set to catch the remainder of the breeze; they were like wonderful, stately birds, and her soul rejoiced at the sight of them. But best of all she loved the tramps that plodded with a faithful, grim tenacity from port to port; often they were squat and ugly, battered by the tempest, dingy and ill-painted; but her heart went out to them. They touched her because their fate seemed so inglorious. No skipper, new to his craft, could ever admire the beauty of their lines, nor look up at the swelling canvas and exult he knew not why; no passengers would boast of their speed or praise their elegance. They were honest merchantmen, laborious, trustworthy, and of good courage, who took foul weather and peril in the day's journey and made no outcry. And with a sure instinct she saw the romance in the humble course of their existence and the beauty of an unboasting performance of their duty; and often, as she watched them, her fancy glowed with the thought of the varied merchandise they carried, and their long sojourning in foreign parts. There was a subtle charm in them because they went to Southern seas and white cities with tortuous streets, silent under the blue sky.

Striving still to free herself of a passionate regret, the lonely woman turned away and took a path that led across the marshes. But her heart sank, for she seemed to recognise the flats, the shallow dykes, the coastguard station, which she had known all her life. Sheep were grazing here and there, and two horses, put out to grass, looked at her listlessly as she passed. A cow heavily whisked its tail. To the indifferent, that line of Kentish coast, so level and monotonous, might be merely dull, but to her it was beautiful. It reminded her of the home she would never see again.

And then her thoughts, which had wandered around the house in which she was born, ever touching the fringe as it were, but never quite settling with the full surrender of attention, gave themselves over to it entirely.

Hamlyn's Purlieu had belonged to the Allertons for three hundred years, and the recumbent effigy, in stone, of the founder of the family's fortunes, with his two wives in ruffs and stiff martingales, was to be seen in the chancel of the parish church. It was the work of an Italian sculptor, lured to England in company of the craftsmen who made the lady-chapel of Westminster Abbey; and the renaissance delicacy of its work was very grateful in the homely English church. And for three hundred years the Allertons had been men of prudence, courage, and worth, so that the walls of the church by now were filled with the lists of the virtues and their achievements. They had intermarried with the great families of the neighbourhood, and with the help of these marble tablets you might have made out a roll of all that was distinguished in Hampshire. The Maddens of Brise, the Fletchers of Horton Park, the Daunceys of Malden Hall, the Garrods of Penda, had all, in the course of time, given daughters to the Allertons of Hamlyn's Purlieu; and the Allertons of Hamlyn's Purlieu had given in exchange richly dowered maidens to the Garrods of Penda, the Daunceys of Malden Hall, the Fletchers of Horton Park, and the Maddens of Brise.

And with each generation the Allertons grew prouder. The peculiar situation of their lands distinguished them a little from their neighbours; for, whereas the Garrods, the Daunceys, and the Fletchers lived within walking distance of each other, and Madden of Brise, because of his rank and opulence the most distinguished person in the county, within six or seven miles, Hamlyn's Purlieu was near the sea and separated by forest land from other places. The seclusion in which its owners were thus forced to dwell differentiated their characters from those of the neighbouring gentlemen. They found much cause for self-esteem in the number of their acres, and, though many of these consisted of salt marshes, and more of wild heath, others were as good as any in Hampshire; and the grand total made a formidable array in works of reference. But they found greater reason still for self-congratulation in their culture. No pride is so great as the pride of intellect, and the Allertons never doubted that their neighbours were boors beside them. Whether it was due to the peculiar lie of the land on which they were born and bred, that led them to introspection, or whether it was due to some accident of inheritance, the Allertons had all an interest in the things of the mind which had never troubled the Fletchers or the Garrods of Penda, the Daunceys, or my lords Madden of Brise. They were as good sportsmen as the others, and hunted or shot with the best of them, but they read books as well, and had a subtlety of intelligence which was no less unexpected than pleasing. The fat squires of the county looked up to them as miracles of learning, and congratulated themselves over their port on possessing in their midst persons who combined, in such excellent proportions, gentle birth and a good seat in the saddle with adequate means and an encyclopedic knowledge. Everything conspired to give the Allertons a good opinion of themselves. They not only looked down from superior heights on the persons with whom they habitually came in contact—that is common enough—but these persons without question looked up to them.

The Allertons made the grand tour in a style befitting their dignity; and the letters which each son of the house wrote in turn, describing Paris, Vienna, Dresden,

Munich, and Rome, with the persons of consequence who entertained him, were preserved with scrupulous care among the family papers. They testified to an agreeable interest in the arts; and each of them had made a point of bringing back with him, according to the fashion of the day, beautiful things which he had purchased on his journey. Hamlyn's Purlieu, a fine stone house goodly to look upon, was thus filled with Italian pictures, French cabinets of delicate workmanship, bronzes of all kinds, tapestries, and old Eastern carpets. The gardens had been tended with a loving care, and there grew in them trees and flowers which were unknown to other parts of England. Each Allerton in his time cherished the place with a passionate pride, looking upon it as his greatest privilege that he could add a little to its beauty and hand on to his successor a more magnificent heritage.

But at length Hamlyn's Purlieu came into the hands of Fred Allerton; and the gods, blind for so long to the prosperity of this house, determined now, it seemed, to wreak their malice. Fred Allerton had many of the characteristics of his race, but in him they took a sudden turn which bore him swiftly to destruction. They had been marked always by his good looks, a persuasive manner, and a singular liberality of mind; and he was perhaps the handsomest, and certainly the most charming of them all. But the freedom from prejudice which had prevented the others from giving way too much to their pride had in him degenerated into a singular unscrupulousness. His parents died when he was twenty, and a year later he found himself master of a great estate. The times were hard then for those who depended upon their land, and Fred Allerton was not so rich as his forebears. But he flung himself extravagantly into the pursuit of pleasure. He was the only member of his family who had failed to reside habitually at Hamlyn's Purlieu. He seemed to take no interest in it, and except now and then to shoot, never came near his native county. He lived much in Paris, which in the early years of the third republic had still something of the wanton gaiety of the Empire; and here he soon grew notorious for his prodigality and his adventures. He was an unlucky man, and everything he did led to disaster. But this never impaired his cheerfulness. He boasted that he had lost money in every gambling hall in Europe, and vowed that he would give up racing in disgust if ever a horse of his won a race. His charm of manner was irresistible, and no one had more friends than he. His generosity was great, and he was willing to lend money to everyone who asked. But it is even more expensive to be a man whom everyone likes than to keep a stud, and Fred Allerton found himself in due course much in need of ready money. He did not hesitate to mortgage his lands, and till he came to the end of these resources also, continued gaily to lead a life of splendour.

At length he had raised on Hamlyn's Purlieu every penny that he could, and was crippled with debt besides; but he still rode a fine horse, lived in expensive chambers, dressed better than any man in London, and gave admirable dinners to all and sundry. He realised then that he could only retrieve his fortunes by a rich marriage. Fred Allerton was still a handsome man, and he knew from long experience how easy it was to say pleasant things to a woman. There was a peculiar light in his blue eyes which persuaded everyone of the goodness of his heart. He was amusing and full of spirits. He fixed upon a Miss Boulger, one of the two daughters of a Liverpool manufacturer, and succeeded after a surprisingly short time in assuring her of his passion. There was a convincing air of truth in all he said, and she returned his flame with readiness. It was clear to him that her sister was equally prepared to fall in love with him, and he regretted with diverting frankness to his more intimate friends that the laws of the land prevented him from marrying them both and acquiring two fortunes instead of one. He married the younger Miss Boulger, and on her dowry paid off the mortgages on Hamlyn's Purlieu, his own debts, and succeeded for several years in having an excellent time. The poor woman, happily blind to his defects, adored him with all her soul. She trusted him entirely with the management of her money and only regretted that the affairs connected with it kept him so much in town. With marriage and his new connection with commerce Fred Allerton had come to the conclusion that he had business abilities, and he occupied himself thenceforward with all manner of financial schemes. With unwearied enthusiasm he entered upon some new affair which was going to bring him untold wealth as soon as the last had finally sunk into the abyss of bankruptcy. Hamlyn's Purlieu had never known such gaieties as during the fifteen years of Mrs. Allerton's married life. All kinds of people were brought down by Fred; and the dignified dining-room, which for centuries had witnessed discussions, learned or flippant, on the merits of Greek and Latin authors, or the excellencies of Italian masters, now heard strange talk of stocks and shares, companies, syndicates, options and holdings. When Mrs. Allerton died suddenly she was entirely unconscious that her husband had squandered every penny of the money which had been settled on her children, had mortgaged once more the broad fields of his ancestors, and was head over ears in debt. She expired with his name upon her lips, and blessed the day on which she had first seen him. She had one son and one daughter. Lucy was a girl of fifteen when her mother died, and George, the boy, was ten.

It was Lucy, now a woman of twenty-five, who turned her back upon the Kentish sea and slowly walked across the marsh. And as she walked, the recollection of the ten years that had passed since then was placed before her as it were in a single flash.

At first her father had seemed the most wonderful being in the world, and she had worshipped him with all her childish heart. The love that bound her to her mother was pale in comparison, for Lucy could not divide her affections, giving part here, part there; her father, with his wonderful gift of sympathy, his indescribable charm, conquered her entirely. It was her greatest delight to be with him. She was entertained and exhilarated by his society, and she hated the men of business who absorbed so much of his time.

When Mrs. Allerton died George was sent to school, but Lucy, in charge of a governess, remained year in, year out, at Hamlyn's Purlieu with her books, her dogs, and her horses. And gradually, she knew not how, it was borne in upon her that the father who had seemed such a paragon of chivalry, was weak, unreliable, and shifty. She fought against the suspicions that poisoned her mind, charging herself bitterly with meanness of spirit, but one small incident after another brought the truth home to her. She recognised with a shiver of anguish that his standard of veracity was utterly different from hers. He was not very careful to keep his word. He was not scrupulous in money matters. With her, honesty, truthfulness, exactness in all affairs, were not only instinctive, but deliberate; for the pride of her birth was so great that she felt it incumbent upon her to be ten times more careful in these things than the ordinary run of men.

And then, from a word here and a word there, by horrified guesses and by a kind of instinctive surmise, she realised presently the whole truth of her father's life. She found out that Hamlyn's Purlieu was mortgaged for every penny it was worth, she found out that there was a bill of sale on the furniture, that money had been raised on the pictures; and, at last, that her mother's money, left in her father's trust to her and George, had been spent. And still Fred Allerton lived with prodigal magnificence.

It was only very gradually that Lucy discovered these things. There was no one whom she could consult, and she had to devise some mode of conduct by herself. It was all a matter of supposition, and she knew almost nothing for certain. She made up her mind that she would probe no deeper. But since such knowledge as she had came to her only by degrees, she was able the better to adapt her behaviour to it. The pride which for so long had been a characteristic of the Allertons, but had unaccountably missed Fred, in her enjoyed all its force; and what she knew now served only to augment it. It the ruin of her ideals she had nothing but that to cling to, and she cherished it with an unreasoning passion. She had a cult for the ancestors whose portraits looked down upon her in one room after another of Hamlyn's Purlieu, and from their names and the look of them, which was all that remained, she made them in her fancy into personalities whose influence might somehow counteract the weakness of her father. In them there was so much uprightness, strength, and simple goodness; the sum total of it must prevail in the long run against the unruly instincts of one man. And she loved her old home, with all its exquisite contents, with its rich gardens, its broad, fertile fields, above all with its wild heath and flat sea-marshes, she loved it with a hungry devotion, saddened and yet more vehement because her hold on it was jeopardised. She set the whole strength of her will on preserving the place for her brother. Her greatest desire was to fill him with the determination to reclaim it from the foreign hands that had some hold upon it, and to restore it to its ancient freedom.

Upon George were set all Lucy's hopes. He could restore the fallen fortunes of their race, and her part must be to train him to the glorious task. He was growing up, and she made up her mind to keep from him all knowledge of her father's weakness. To George he must seem to the last an honest gentleman.

Lucy transferred to her brother all the love which she had lavished on her father. She watched his growth fondly, interesting herself in his affairs, and seeking to be to him not only a sister, but the mother he had lost, and the father who was unworthy. When he was of a fit age she was that he was sent to Winchester. She followed his career with passion and entered eagerly into all his interests.

But if Lucy had lost her old love for her father, its place had been taken by a pitying tenderness; and she did all she could to conceal him from the charge in her feelings. It was easy when she was with him, for them it was impossible to resist his charm; and it was only afterwards, when he was no longer there to explain things away, that she could not crush the horror and resentment with which she regarded him. But of this no one knew anything; and she set herself deliberately not only to make such headway as she could in the tangle of their circumstances, but to conceal from everyone the actual state of things.

For presently Fred Allerton seemed no longer to have an inexhaustible supply of ready money, and Lucy had to resort to a very careful economy. She reduced expenses in every way she could, and when left alone in the house, she lived with the utmost frugality. She hated to ask her father for money, and since often he did not pay the allowance that was due to her, she was obliged to exercise a good deal of self-denial. As soon as she was old enough, Lucy had taken the household affairs into her own hands and had learned to conduct them in such a way as to hide from the world how difficult it was to make both ends meet. Now, feeling that things were approaching a crisis, she sold the horses and dismissed most of the servants. A great fear seized her that it would be impossible to keep Hamlyn's Purlieu, and she was stricken with panic. She was willing to make every sacrifice but that, and if she were only allowed to remain there, did not care how penuriously she lived.

But the struggle was growing harder. None knew what she had endured in her endeavour to keep their heads above water. And she had borne everything with perfect cheerfulness. Though she saw a good deal of the neighbouring gentry, connected with her by blood or long friendship, not one of them divined her great anxiety. She felt vaguely that they knew how things were going, but she held her head high and gave no one an opportunity to pity her. Her father was now absent from home more frequently and seemed to avoid being alone with her. They had never discussed the state of their affairs, for her assumed with Lucy a determined flippancy which prevented any serious conversation. On her twenty-first birthday he had made some facetious observation about the money of which she was now mistress, but had treated the manner with such an airy charm that she had felt unable to proceed with it. Nor did she wish to, for if he had spent her money nothing could be done, and it was better not to know for certain. Notwithstanding settlements and wills, she felt that it was really his to do what he liked with, and she made up her mind that nothing in her behaviour should be construed as a reproach.

At length the crash came.

She received a telegram one day—she was nearly twenty-three then—from Richard Lomas, an old friend of her mother's, to say that he was coming down for luncheon. She walked to the station to meet him. She was very fond of him, not only for his own sake, but because her mother had been fond of him, too; and the affection which had existed between them, drew her nearer to the mother whom she felt now she had a little neglected. Dick Lomas was a barrister, who, after contesting two seats unsuccessfully, had got into Parliament at the last general election and had made already a certain name for himself by the wittiness of his speeches and the bluntness of his common sense. He had neither the portentous gravity nor the dogmatic airs which afflicted most of his legal colleagues in the house. He was a man who had solved the difficulty of being sensible without tediousness and pointed without impertinence. He was wise enough not to speak too often, and if only he had not possessed a sense of humour—which his countrymen always regarded with suspicion in an English politician—he might have looked forward to a brilliant future. He was a wiry little man, with a sharp, good-humoured face and sparkling eyes. He carried his seven-and-thirty years with gaiety.

But on this occasion he was unusually grave. Lucy, already surprised at his sudden visit, divined at once from the uneasiness of his pleasant, grey eyes that something was amiss. Her heart began to beat more quickly. He forced himself to smile as he took her hand, congratulating her on the healthiness of her appearance; and they walked slowly from the station. Dick spoke of indifferent things, while Lucy distractedly turned over in her mind all that could have happened. Luncheon was ready for them, and Dick sat down with apparent gusto, praising emphatically the good things she set before him; but he ate as little as she did. He seemed impatient for the meal to end, but unwilling to enter upon the subject which oppressed him. They drank their coffee.

"Shall we go for a turn in the garden?" he suggested.

"Certainly."

After his last visit, Dick had sent down an old sundial which he had picked up in a shop in Westminster, and Lucy took him to the place which they had before decided needed just such an ornament. They discussed it at some length, but then silence fell suddenly upon them, and they walked side by side without a word. Dick slipped his arm through hers with a caressing motion, and Lucy, unused to any tenderness, felt a sob rise to her throat. They went in once more and stood in the drawing-room. From the walls looked down the treasures of the house. There was a portrait by Reynolds, and another by Hoppner, and there was a beautiful picture of the Grand Canal by Guardi, and there was a portrait by Goya of a General Allerton who had fought in the Peninsular War. Dick gave them a glance, and his blood tingled with admiration. He leaned against the fireplace.

"Your father asked me to come down and see you, Lucy. He was too worried to come himself."

Lucy looked at him with grave eyes, but made no reply.

"He's had some very bad luck lately. Your father is a man who prides himself on his business ability, but he has no more knowledge of such matters than a child. He's an imaginative man, and when some scheme appeals to his feelings for romance, he loses all sense of proportion."

Dick paused again. It was impossible to soften the blow, and he could only put it bluntly.

"He's been gambling on the Stock Exchange, and he's been badly let down. He was bulling a number of South American railways, and there's been a panic in the market. He's lost enormously. I don't know if any settlement can be made with his creditors, but if not he must go bankrupt. In any case, I'm afraid Hamlyn's Purlieu must be sold."

Lucy walked to the window and looked out. But she could see nothing. Her eyes were blurred with tears. She breathed quickly, trying to control herself.

"I've been expecting it for a long time," she said at last. "I've refused to face it, and I put the thought away from me, but I knew really that it must come to that."

"I'm very sorry," said Dick helplessly.

She turned on him fiercely, and the colour rose to her cheeks. But she restrained herself and left unsaid the bitter words that had come to her tongue. She made a pitiful gesture of despair. He felt how poor were his words of consolation, and how inadequate to her great grief, and he was silent.

"And what about George?" she asked.

George was then eighteen, and on the point of leaving Winchester. It had been arranged that he should go to Oxford at the beginning of the next term.

"Lady Kelsey has offered to pay his expenses at the 'Varsity," answered Dick, "and she wants you to go and stay with her for the present."

"Do you mean to say we're penniless?" asked Lucy, desperately.

"I think you cannot depend on your father for much regular assistance."

Lucy was silent again.

Lady Kelsey was the elder sister of Mrs. Allerton, and some time after that lady's marriage had accepted a worthy merchant whose father had been in partnership with hers; and he, after a prosperous career crowned by surrendering his seat in Parliament to a defeated cabinet-minister—a patriotic act for which he was rewarded with a knighthood—had died, leaving her well off and childless. She had but one other nephew, Robert Boulger, her brother's only son, but he was rich with all the inherited wealth of the firm of Boulger & Kelsey; and her affections were placed chiefly upon the children of the man whom she had loved devotedly and who had married her sister.

"I was hoping you would come up to town with me now," said Dick. "Lady Kelsey is expecting you, and I cannot bear to think of you by yourself here."

"I shall stay till the last moment."

Dick hesitated again. He had wished to keep back the full brutality of the blow, but sooner or later it must be given.

"The place is already sold. Your father accepted an offer from Jarrett—you remember him, he has been down here; he is your father's broker and chief creditor—and everything else is to go to Christy's at once."

"Then there is no more to be said."

She gave Dick her hand.

"You won't mind if I don't come to the station with you?"

"Won't you come up to London?" he asked again.

She shook her head.

"I want to be alone. Forgive me if I make you go so abruptly."

"My dear girl, it's very good of you to make sure that I don't miss my train," he smiled drily.

"Good-bye and thank you."

Chapter II

WHILE LUCY WANDERED BY THE SEASHORE, OCCUPIED WITH PAINFUL memories, her old friend Dick, too lazy to walk with her, sat in the drawing-room of Court Leys, talking to his hostess.

Mrs. Crowley was an American woman, who had married an Englishman, and on being left a widow, had continued to live in England. She was a person who thoroughly enjoyed life; and indeed there was every reason that she should do so, since she was young, pretty, and rich; she had a quick mind and an alert tongue. She was of diminutive size, so small that Dick Lomas, by no means a tall man, felt quite large by the side of her. Her figure was exquisite, and she had the smallest hands in the world. Her features were so good, regular and well-formed, her complexion so perfect, her agile grace so enchanting, that she did not seem a real person at all. She was too delicate for the hurly-burly of life, and it seemed improbable that she could be made of the ordinary clay from which human beings are manufactured. She had the artificial grace of those dainty, exquisite ladies in the *Embarquement pour Cithère* of the charming Watteau; and you felt that she was fit to saunter on that sunny strand, habited in satin of delicate colours, with a witty, decadent cavalier by her side. It was preposterous to talk to her of serious things, and nothing but an airy badinage seemed possible in her company.

Mrs. Crowley had asked Lucy and Dick Lomas to stay with her in the house she had just taken for a term of years. She had spent a week by herself to arrange things to her liking, and insisted that Dick should admire all she had done. After a walk round the park he vowed that he was exhausted and must rest till tea-time.

"Now tell me what made you take it. It's so far from anywhere."

"I met the owner in Rome last winter. It belongs to a Mrs. Craddock, and when I told her I was looking out for a house, she suggested that I should come and see this."

"Why doesn't she live in it herself?"

"Oh, I don't know. It appears that she was passionately devoted to her husband, and he broke his neck in the hunting-field, so she couldn't bear to live here anymore."

Mrs. Crowley looked round the drawing-room with satisfaction. At first it had borne the cheerless look of a house uninhabited, but she had quickly made it pleasant with flowers, photographs, and silver ornaments. The Sheraton furniture and the chintzes suited the style of her beauty. She felt that she looked in place in that comfortable room, and was conscious that her frock fitted her and the circumstances perfectly. Dick's eye wandered to the books that were scattered here and there.

"And have you put out these portentous works in order to improve your mind, or with the laudable desire of impressing me with the serious turn of your intellect?"

"You don't think I'm such a perfect fool as to try and impress an entirely flippant person like yourself?"

On the table at his elbow were a copy of the *Revue des Deux Mondes* and one of the *Fornightly Review*. He took up two books, and saw that one was the *Fröhliche Wissenchaft* of Nietzsche, who was then beginning to be read in English by the fashionable world and was on the eve of being discovered by men of letters, while the other was a volume of Mrs. Crowley's compatriot, William James.

"American women amaze me," said Dick, as he put them down. "They buy their linen at Doucet's and read Herbert Spencer with avidity. And what's more, they seem to like him. An Englishwoman can seldom read a serious book without feeling a prig, and as soon as she feels a prig she leaves off her corsets."

"I feel vaguely that you're paying me a compliment," returned Mrs. Crowley, "but it's so elusive that I can't quite catch it."

"The best compliments are those that flutter about your head like butterflies around a flower."

"I much prefer to fix them down on a board with a pin through their insides and a narrow strip of paper to hold down each wing."

It was October, but the autumn, late that year, had scarcely coloured the leaves, and the day was warm. Mrs. Crowley, however, was a chilly being, and a fire burned in the grate. She put another log on it and watched the merry crackle of the flames.

"It was very good of you to ask Lucy down here," said Dick, suddenly.

"I don't know why. I like her so much. And I felt sure she would fit the place. She looks a little like a Gainsborough portrait, doesn't she? And I like to see her in this Georgian house."

"She's not had much of a time since they sold the family place. It was a great grief to her."

"I feel such a pig to have here the things I bought at the sale."

When the contents of Hamlyn's Purlieu were sent to Christy's, Mrs. Crowley, recently widowed and without a home, had bought one or two pictures and some old chairs. She had brought these down to Court Leys, and was much tormented at the thought of causing Lucy a new grief.

"Perhaps she didn't recognise them," said Dick.

"Don't be so idiotic. Of course she recognised them. I saw her eyes fall on the Reynolds the very moment she came into the room."

"I'm sure she would rather you had them than any stranger."

"She's said nothing about them. You know, I'm very fond of her, and I admire her extremely, but she would be easier to get on with if she were less reserved. I never shall get into this English way of bottling up my feelings and sitting on them."

"It sounds a less comfortable way of reposing oneself than sitting in an arm-chair."

"I would offer to give Lucy back all the things I bought, only I'm sure she'd snub me."

"She doesn't mean to be unkind, but she's had a very hard life, and it's had its effect on her character. I don't think anyone knows what she's gone through during these ten years. She's borne the responsibilities of her whole family since she was fifteen, and if the crash didn't come sooner, it was owing to her. She's never been a girl, poor thing; she was a child, and then suddenly she was a woman."

"But has she never had any lovers?"

"I fancy that she's rather a difficult person to make love to. It would be a bold young man who whispered sweet nothings in her ear; they'd sound so very foolish."

"At all events there's Bobbie Boulger. I'm sure he's asked her to marry him scores of times."

Sir Robert Boulger had succeeded his father, the manufacturer, as second baronet; and had promptly placed his wealth and his personal advantages at Lucy's feet. His devotion to her was well known to his friends. They had all listened to the protestations of undying passion, which Lucy, with gentle humour, put smilingly aside. Lady Kelsey, his aunt and Lucy's, had done all she could to bring the pair together; and it was evident that from every point of view a marriage between them was desirable. He was not unattractive in appearance, his fortune was considerable, and his manners were good. He was a good-natured, pleasant fellow, with no great strength of character perhaps, but Lucy had enough of that for two; and with her to steady him, he had enough brains to make some figure in the world.

"I've never seen Mr. Allerton," remarked Mrs. Crowley, presently. "He must be a horrid man."

"On the contrary, he's the most charming creature I ever met, and I don't believe there's a man in London who can borrow a hundred pounds of you with a greater air of doing you a service. If you met him you'd fall in love with him before you'd got well into your favourite conversation on bimetallism."

"I've never discussed bimetallism in my life," protested Mrs. Crowley.

"All women do."

"What?"

"Fall in love with him. He knows exactly what to talk to them about, and he has the most persuasive voice you ever heard. I believe Lady Kelsey has been in love with him for five-and-twenty years. It's lucky they've not yet passed the deceased wife's sister's bill, or he would have married her and run through her money as he did his first wife's. He's still very good-looking, and there's such a transparent honesty about him that I promise you he's irresistible."

"And what has happened to him since the catastrophe?"

"Well, the position of an undischarged bankrupt is never particularly easy, though I've known men who've cavorted about in motors and given dinners at the *Carlton* when they were at that state, and seemed perfectly at peace with the world in general. But with Fred Allerton the proceedings before the Officer Receiver seem to have broken down the last remnants of his self-respect. He was glad to get rid of his children, and Lady Kelsey was only too happy to provide for them. Heaven only knows how he's lived during the last two years. He's still occupied with a variety of crack-brained schemes, and he's been to me more than once for money to finance them with."

"I hope you weren't such a fool as to give it."

"I wasn't. I flatter myself that I combined frankness with good-nature in the right proportion, and in the end he was always satisfied with the nimble fiver. But I'm afraid things are going harder with him. He has lost his old alert gaiety, and he's a little down at heel in character as well as in person. There's a furtive look about him, as though he were ready for undertakings that were not quite above board, and there's a shiftiness in his eye which makes his company a little disagreeable."

"You don't think he'd do anything dishonest?" asked Mrs. Crowley quickly.

"Oh, no. I don't believe he has the nerve to sail closer to the wind than the law allows, and really, at bottom, notwithstanding all I know of him, I think he's an honest man. It's only behind his back that I have any doubts about him; when he's face to face with me I succumb to his charm. I can believe nothing to his discredit."

At that moment they saw Lucy walking towards them. Dick Lomas got up and stood at the window. Mrs. Crowley, motionless, watched her from her chair. They were both silent. A smile of sympathy played on Mrs. Crowley's lips, and her heart went out to the girl who had undergone so much. A vague memory came back to her, and for a moment she was puzzled; but then she hit upon the idea that had hovered about her mind, and she remembered distinctly the admirable picture by John Furse at Millbank, which is called *Diana of the Uplands*. It had pleased her always, not only because of its beauty and the fine power of the painter, but because it seemed to her as it were a synthesis of the English spirit. Her nationality gave her an interest in the observation of this, and her wide, systematic reading the power to compare and analyse. This portrait of a young woman holding two hounds in leash, the wind of the northern moor on which she stands, blowing her skirts and outlining her lithe figure, seemed to Mrs. Crowley admirably to follow in the tradition of the eighteenth century. And as Reynolds and Gainsborough, with their elegant ladies in powdered hair and high-waisted gowns, standing in leafy, woodland scenes, had given a picture of England in the age of Reason, well-bred and beautiful, artificial and a little airless, so had Furse in this represented the England of today. It was an England that valued cleanliness above all things, of the body and of the spirit, an England that loved the open air and feared not the wildness of nature nor the violence of the elements. And Mrs. Crowley had lived long enough in the land of her fathers to know that this was a true England, simple and honest; narrow perhaps, and prejudiced, but strong, brave, and of great ideals. The girl who stood on that upland, looking so candidly out of her blue eyes, was a true descendant of the ladies that Sir Joshua painted, but she had a bath every morning, loved her dogs, and wore a short, serviceable skirt. With an inward smile, Mrs. Crowley acknowledged that she was probably bored by Emerson and ignorant of English literature; but for the moment she was willing to pardon these failings in her admiration for the character and all it typified.

Lucy came in, and Mrs. Crowley gave her a nod of welcome. She was fond of her fantasies and would not easily interrupt them. She noted that Lucy had just that frank look of *Diana and the Uplands*, and the delicate, sensitive face, refined with the good-breeding of centuries, but strengthened by an athletic life. Her skin was very clear. It had gained a peculiar freshness by exposure to all manner of weather. Her bright, fair hair was a little disarranged after her walk, and she went to the glass to set it right. Mrs. Crowley observed with delight the straightness of her nose and the delicate curve of her lips. She was tall and strong, but her figure was very slight; and there was a charming litheness about her which suggested the good horsewoman.

But what struck Mrs. Crowley most was that only the keenest observer could have told that she had endured more than other women of her age. A stranger would have delighted in her frank smile and the kindly sympathy of her eyes; and it was only if you knew the troubles she had suffered that you saw how much more womanly she was than girlish. There was a self-possession about her which came from the responsibilities she had borne so long, and an unusual reserve, unconsciously masked by a great charm of manner, which only intimate friends discerned, but which even to them was impenetrable. Mrs. Crowley, with her American impulsiveness, had tried in all kindliness to get through the barrier, but she had never succeeded. All Lucy's struggles, her heart-burnings and griefs, her sudden despairs and eager hopes, her tempestuous angers, took place in the bottom of her heart. She would have been as dismayed at the thought of others seeing them as she would have been at the thought of being discovered unclothed. Shyness and pride combined to make her hide her innermost feelings so that no one should venture to offer sympathy or commiseration.

"Do ring the bell for tea," said Mrs. Crowley to Lucy, as her turned away from the glass. "I can't get Mr. Lomas to amuse me till he's had some stimulating refreshment."

"I hope you like the tea I sent you," said Dick.

"Very much. Though I'm inclined to look upon it as a slight that you should send me down only just enough to last over your visit."

"I always herald my arrival in a country house by a little present of tea," said Dick. "The fact is it's the only good tea in the world. I sent my father to China for seven years to find it, and I'm sure you will agree that my father has not lived an ill-spent life."

The tea was brought and duly drunk. Mrs. Crowley asked Lucy how her brother was. He had been at Oxford for the last two years.

"I had a letter from him yesterday," the girl answered. "I think he's getting on very well. I hope he'll take his degree next year."

A happy brightness came into her eyes as she talked of him. She apologised, blushing, for her eagerness.

"You know, I've looked after George ever since he was ten, and I feel like a mother to him. It's only with the greatest difficulty I can prevent myself from telling you how he got through the measles, and how well he bore vaccination."

Lucy was very proud of her brother. She found a constant satisfaction in his good looks, and she loved the openness of his smile. She had striven with all her might to keep away from him the troubles that oppressed her, and had determined that nothing, if she could help it, should disturb his radiant satisfaction with the world. She knew that he was apt to lean on her, but though she chid herself sometimes for fostering the tendency, she could not really prevent the intense pleasure it gave her. He was young yet, and would soon enough grow into manly ways; it could not matter if now he depended upon her for everything. She rejoiced in the ardent affection which he gave her; and the implicit trust he placed in her, the complete reliance on her judgment, filled her with a proud humility. It made her feel stronger and better capable of affronting the difficulties of life. And Lucy, living much in the future, was pleased to see how beloved George was of all his friends. Everyone seemed willing to help him, and this seemed of good omen for the career which she had mapped out for him.

The recollection of him came to Lucy now as she had last seen him. They had been spending part of the summer with Lady Kelsey at her house on the Thames. George was going to Scotland to stay with friends, and Lucy, bound elsewhere, was leaving earlier in the afternoon. He came to see her off. She was touched, in her own sorrow at leaving him, by his obvious emotion. The tears were in his eyes as he kissed her on the platform. She saw him waving to her as the train sped towards London, slender and handsome, looking more boyish than ever in his whites; and she felt a thrill of gratitude because, with all her sorrows and regrets, she at least had him.

"I hope he's a good shot," she said inconsequently, as Mrs. Crowley handed her a cup of tea. "Of course it's in the family."

"Marvellous family!" said Dick, ironically. "You would be wiser to wish he had a good head for figures."

"But I hope he has that, too," she answered.

It had been arranged that George should go into the business in which Lady Kelsey still had a large interest. Lucy wanted him to make great sums of money, so that he might pay his father's debts, and perhaps buy back the house which her family had owned so long.

"I want him to be a clever man of business—since business is the only thing open to him now—and an excellent sportsman."

She was too shy to describe her ambition, but her fancy had already cast a glow over the calling which George was to adopt. There was in the family an innate tendency toward the more exquisite things of life, and this would colour his career. She hopes he would become a merchant prince after the pattern of those Florentines who have left an ideal for succeeding ages of the way in which commerce may be ennobled by a liberal view of life. Like them he could drive hard bargains and amass riches—she recognised that riches now were the surest means of power—but like them also he could love music and art and literature, cherishing the things of the soul with a careful taste, and at the same time excel in all sports of the field. Life then would be as full as a man's heart could wish; and this intermingling of interests might so colour it that he would lead the whole with a certain beauty and grandeur.

"I wish I were a man," she cried, with a bright smile. "It's so hard that I can do nothing but sit at home and spur others on. I want to do things myself."

Mrs. Crowley leaned back in her chair. She gave her skirt a little twist so that the line of her form should be more graceful.

"I'm so glad I'm a woman," she murmured. "I want none of the privileges of the sex which I'm delighted to call stronger. I want men to be noble and heroic and self-sacrificing; then they can protect me from a troublesome world, and look after me, and wait upon me. I'm an irresponsible creature with whom they can never be annoyed however exacting I am—it's only pretty thoughtlessness on my part—and they must never lose their tempers however I annoy—it's only nerves. Oh, no, I like to be a poor, weak woman."

"You're a monster of cynicism," cried Dick. "You use an imaginary helplessness with the brutality of a buccaneer, and your ingenuousness is a pistol you put to one's head, crying: your money or your life."

"You look very comfortable, dear Mr. Lomas," she retorted. "Would you mind very much if I asked you to put my footstool right for me?"

"I should mind immensely," he smiled, without moving.

"Oh, please do," she said, with a piteous little expression of appeal. "I'm so uncomfortable, and my foot's going to sleep. And you needn't be horrid to me."

"I didn't know you really meant it," he said, getting up obediently and doing what was required of him.

"I didn't," she answered, as soon as he had finished. "But I know you're a lazy creature, and I merely wanted to see if I could make you move when I'd warned you immediately before that—I was a womanly woman."

"I wonder if you'd make Alec MacKenzie do that?" laughed Dick, good-naturedly.

"Good heavens, I'd never try. Haven't you discovered that women know by instinct what men they can make fools of, and they only try their arts on them? They've gained their reputation for omnipotence only on account of their robust common-sense, which leads them only to attack fortresses which are already half demolished."

"That suggests to my mind that every woman is a Potiphar's wife, though every man isn't a Joseph," said Dick.

"Your remark is too blunt to be witty," returned Mrs. Crowley, "but it's not without its grain of truth."

Lucy, smiling, listened to the nonsense they talked. In their company she lost all sense of reality; Mrs. Crowley was so fragile, and Dick had such a whimsical gaiety, that she could not treat them as real persons. She felt herself a grown-up being assisting at some childish game in which preposterous ideas were bandied to and fro like answers in the game of consequence.

"I never saw people wander from the subject as you do," she protested. "I can't imagine what connection there is between whether Mr. MacKenzie would arrange Julia's footstool, and the profligacy of the female sex."

"Don't be so hard on us," said Mrs. Crowley. "I must work off my flippancy before he arrives, and then I shall be ready to talk imperially."

"When does Alec come?" asked Dick.

"Now, this very minute. I've sent a carriage to meet him at the station. You won't let him depress me, will you?"

"Why did you ask him if he affects you in that way?" asked Lucy, laughing.

"But I like him—at least I think I do—and in any case, I admire him, and I'm sure he's good for me. And Mr. Lomas wanted me to ask him, and he plays bridge extraordinary well. And I thought he would be interesting. The only thing I have against him is that never laughs when I say a clever thing, and looks so uncomfortably at me when I say a foolish one."

"I'm glad I laugh when you say a clever thing," said Dick.

"You don't. But you roar so heartily at your own jokes that if I hurry up and slip one in before you've done, I can often persuade myself that you're laughing at mine."

"And do you like Alec MacKenzie, Lucy?" asked Dick.

She paused for a moment before she answered, and hesitated.

'I don't know," she said. "Sometimes I think I rather dislike him. But I'm like Julia, I certainly admire him."

"I suppose he is rather alarming," said Dick. "He's difficult to know, and he's obviously impatient with other people's affectations. There's a certain grimness about him which disturbs you unless you know him intimately."

"He's your greatest friend, isn't he?"

"He is."

Dick paused for a little while.

"I've known him for twenty years now, and I look upon him as the greatest man I've ever set eyes on. I think it's an inestimable privilege to have been his friend."

"I've not noticed that you treated him with especial awe," said Mrs. Crowley.

"Heaven save us!" cried Dick. "I can only hold my own by laughing at him persistently."

"He bears it with unexampled good-nature."

"Have I ever told you how I made his acquaintance? It was in about fifty fathoms of water, and at least a thousand miles from land."

"What an inconvenient place for an introduction!"

"We were both very wet. I was a young fool in those days, and I was playing the giddy goat—I was just going up to Oxford, and my wise father had sent me to America on a visit to enlarge my mind—I fell overboard and was proceeding to drown, when Alec jumped in after me and held me up by the hair of my head."

"He'd have some difficulty in doing that now, wouldn't he?" suggested Mrs. Crowley, with a glance at Dick's thinning locks.

"And the odd thing is that he was absurdly grateful to me for letting myself be saved. He seemed to think I had done him an intentional service, and fallen into the Atlantic for the sole purpose of letting him pull me out."

Dick had scarcely said these words when they heard the carriage drive up to the door of Court Leys.

"There he is," cried Dick eagerly.

Mrs. Crowley's butler opened the door and announced the man they had been discussing. Alexander MacKenzie came in.

He was just under six feet nigh, spare and well-made. He did not at the first glance give you the impression of particular strength, but his limbs were well-knit, there was no superfluous flesh about him, and you felt immediately that he had great powers of endurance. His hair was dark and cut very close. His short beard and his moustache were red. They concealed the squareness of his chin and the determination of his mouth. His eyes were not large, but they rested on the object that attracted his attention with a peculiar fixity. When he talked to you he did not glance this way or that, but looked straight at you with a deliberate steadiness that was a little disconcerting. He walked with an easy swing, like a man in the habit of covering a vast number of miles each day, and there was in his manner a self-assurance which suggested that he was used to command. His skin was tanned by exposure to tropical suns.

Mrs. Crowley and Dick chattered light-heartedly, but it was clear that he had no power of small-talk, and after the first greetings he fell into silence; he refused tea, but Mrs. Crowley poured out a cup and handed it to him.

"You need not drink it, but I insist on your holding it in your hand. I hate people who habitually deny themselves things, and I can't allow you to mortify the flesh in my house."

Alec smiled gravely.

"Of course I will drink it if it pleases you," he answered. "I got in the habit in Africa of eating only two meals a day, and I can't get out of it now. But I'm afraid it's very inconvenient for my friends." He looked at Lomas, and though his mouth did not smile, a look came into his eyes, partly of tenderness, partly of amusement. "Dick, of course, eats far too much."

"Good heavens, I'm nearly the only person left in London who is completely normal. I eat my three square meals a day regularly, and I always have a comfortable tea into the bargain. I don't suffer from any disease. I'm in the best of health. I have no fads. I neither nibble nuts like a squirrel, nor grapes like a bird—I care nothing for all this jargon about pepsins and proteids and all the rest of it. I'm not a vegetarian, but a carnivorous animal; I drink when I'm thirsty, and I decidedly prefer my beverages to be alcoholic."

"I was thinking at luncheon today," said Mrs. Crowley, "that the pleasure you took in roast-beef and ale showed a singularly gross and unemotional nature."

"I adore good food as I adore all the other pleasant things of life, and because I have that gift I am able to look upon the future with equanimity."

"Why?" asked Alec.

"Because a love for good food is the only thing that remains with man when he grows old. Love? What is love when you are five-and-fifty and can no longer hide the disgraceful baldness of your pate. Ambition? What is ambition when you have discovered that honours are to the pushing and glory to the vulgar. Finally we must all reach an age when every passion seems vain, every desire not worth the trouble of achieving it; but then there still remain to the man with a good appetite three pleasures each day, his breakfast, his luncheon, and his dinner."

Alec's eyes rested on him quietly. He had never got out of the habit of looking upon Dick as a scatter-brained boy who talked nonsense for the fun of it; and his expression wore the amused disdain which one might have seen on a Saint Bernard when a toy-terrier was going through its tricks.

"Please say something," cried Dick, half-irritably.

"I supposed you say those things in order that I may contradict you. Why should I? They're perfectly untrue, and I don't agree with a single word you say. But if it amuses you to talk nonsense, I don't see why you shouldn't."

"My dear Alec, I wish you wouldn't use the mailed fist in your conversation. It's so very difficult to play a game with a spillikin on one side and a sledgehammer on the other."

Lucy, sitting back in her chair, quietly, was observing the new arrival. Dick had asked her and Mrs. Crowley to meet him at luncheon immediately after his arrival from Mombassa. This was two months ago now, and since then she had seen much of him. But she felt that she knew him little more than on that first day, and still she could not make up her mind whether she liked him or not. She was glad that they were staying together at Court Leys; it would give her an opportunity of really becoming acquainted with him, and there was no doubt that he was worth the trouble. The fire lit up his face, casting grim shadows upon it, so that it looked more than ever masterful and determined. He was unconscious that her eyes rested upon him. He was always unconscious of the attention he aroused.

Lucy hoped that she would induce him to talk of the work he had done, and the work upon which he was engaged. With her mind fixed always on great endeavorurs, his career interested her enormously; and it gained something mysterious as well because there were gaps in her knowledge of him which no one seemed able to fill. He knew few people in London, but was known in one way or another of many; and all who had come in contact with him were unanimous in their opinion. He was supposed to know Africa as no other man knew it. During fifteen years he had been through every part of it, and had traversed districts which the white man had left untouched. But he had never written of his experiences, partly from indifference to chronicle the results of his undertakings, partly from a natural secrecy which made him hate to recount his deeds to all and sundry. It seemed that reserve was a deep-rooted instinct with him, and he was inclined to keep to himself all that he discovered. But if on this account he was unknown to the great public, his work was appreciated very highly by specialists. He had read papers before the Geographical Society, (though it had been necessary to exercise much pressure to induce him to do so), which had excited profound interest; and occasionally letters appeared from him in *Nature*, or in one of the ethnographical publications, stating briefly some discovery he had made, or some observation which he thought necessary to record. He had been asked now and again to make reports to the Foreign Office upon matters pertaining to the countries he knew; and Lucy had heard his perspicacity praised in no measured terms by those in power.

She put together such facts as she knew of his career.

Alec MacKenzie was a man of considerable means. He belonged to an old Scotch family, and had a fine place in the Highlands, but his income depended chiefly upon a colliery in Lancashire. His parents died during his childhood, and his wealth was much increased by a long minority. Having inherited from an uncle a ranch in the West, his desire to see this occasioned his first voyage from England in the interval between leaving Eton and going up to Oxford; and it was then he made acquaintance with Richard Lomas, who had remained his most intimate friend. The unlikeness of the two men caused perhaps the strength of the tie between them, the strenuous vehemence of the one finding a relief in the gaiety of the other. Soon after leaving Oxford, Mackenzie made a brief expedition into Algeria to shoot, and the mystery of the great continent seized him. As sometimes a man comes upon a new place which seems extraordinarily familiar, so that he is almost convinced that in a past state he had known it intimately, Alec suddenly found himself at home in the immense distances of Africa. He felt a singular exhilaration when the desert was spread out before his eyes, and capacities which he had not suspected in himself awoke in him. He had never thought himself an ambitious man, but ambition seized him. He had never imagined himself subject to poetic emotion, but all at once a feeling of the poetry of an adventurous life welled up within him. And though he had looked upon romance with the scorn of his Scottish common sense, an irresistible desire of the romantic surged upon him, like the waves of some unknown, mystical sea.

When he returned to England a peculiar restlessness took hold of him. He was indifferent to the magnificence of the bag which was the pride of his companions. He felt himself cribbed and confined. He could not breathe the air of cities.

He began to read the marvelous records of African exploration, and his blood tingled at the magic of those pages. Mungo Park, a Scot like himself, had started the roll. His aim had been to find the source and trace the seaward course of the Niger. He took his life in his hands, facing boldly the perils of climate, savage pa-

The Explorer

gans, and jealous Mohammedans, and discovered the upper portions of that great river. On a second expedition he undertook to follow it to the sea. Of his party some died of disease, and some were slain by the natives. Not one returned; and the only trace of Mungo Park was a book, known to have been in his possession, found by British explorers in the hut of a native chief.

Then Alec MacKenzie read of the efforts to reach Timbuktu, which was the great object of ambition to the explorers of the nineteenth century. It exercised the same fascination over their minds as did El Dorado, with its golden city of Monoa, to the adventurers in the days of Queen Elizabeth. It was thought to be the capital of a powerful and wealthy state; and those ardent minds promised themselves all kinds of wonders when they should at last come upon it. But it was not the desire for gold that urged them on, rather an irresistible curiosity, and a pride in their own courage. One after another desperate attempt were made, and it was reached at last by another Scot, Alexander Gordon Laing. And his success was a symbol of all earthly endeavours, for the golden city of his dreams was no more than a poverty-stricken village.

One by one Alec studied the careers of these great men; and he saw that the best of them had not gone with half an army at theirs back, but almost alone, sometimes with not a single companion, and had depended for their success not upon the strength of their arms, but upon the strength of their character. Major Durham, an old Peninsular officer, was the first European to cross the Sahara. Captain Clapperton, with his servant, Richard Lander, was the first who traversed Africa from the Mediterranean to the Guinea Coast. And he died at his journey's end. And there was something fine in the devotion of Richard Lander, the faithful servant, who went on with his master's work and cleared up at last the great mystery of the Niger. And he, too, had no sooner done his work than he died, near the mouth of the river he had so long travelled on, of wounds inflicted by the natives. There was not one of those early voyagers who had escaped with his life. It was the work of desperate men that they undertook, but there was no recklessness in them. They counted the cost and took the risk; the fascination of the unknown was too great for them, and they reckoned death as nothing if they could accomplish that on which they had set out.

Two men above all attracted Alec MacKenzie's interest. One was Richard Burton, that mighty, enigmatic man, more admirable for what he was than for what he did; and the other was Livingstone, the greatest of African explorers. There was something very touching in the character of that gentle Scot. MacKenzie's enthusiasm was seldom very strong, but here was a man whom he would willingly have known; and he was strangely affected by the thought of his lonely death, and his grave in the midst of the Dark Continent he loved so well. On that, too, might have been written the epitaph which is on the tomb of Sir Christopher Wren.

Finally he studied the works of Henry M. Stanley. Here the man excited neither admiration nor affection, but a cold respect. No one could help recognising the greatness of his powers. He was a man of Napoleonic instinct, who suited his means to his end, and ruthlessly fought his way until he had achieved it. His books were full of interest, and they were practical. From them much could be learned, and Alec studied them with a thoroughness which was in his nature.

When he arose from this long perusal, his mind was made up. He had found his vocation.

He did not disclose his plans to any of his friends till they were mature, and meanwhile set about seeing the people who could give him information. At last he sailed for Zanzibar, and started on a journey which was to try his powers. In a month he fell ill, and it was thought at the mission to which his bearers brought him that he could not live. For ten weeks he was at death's door, but he would not give in to the enemy. He insisted in the end on being taken back to the coast, and here, as if by a personal effort of will, he recovered. The season had passed for his expedition, and he was obliged to return to England. Most men would have been utterly discouraged, but Alec was only strengthened in his determination. He personified in a way that deadly climate and would not allow himself to be beaten by it. His short experience had shown him what he needed, and as soon as he was back in England, he proceeded to acquire a smattering of medical knowledge, and some acquaintance with the sciences which were wanted by a traveller. He had immense powers of concentration, and in a year of tremendous labour acquired a working knowledge of botany and geology, and the elements of surveying; he learned how to treat the maladies which were likely to attack people in tropical districts, and enough surgery to set a broken limb or to conduct a simple operation. He felt himself ready now for a considerable undertaking; but this time he meant to start from Mombassa.

So far Lucy was able to go, partly from her own imaginings, and partly from what Dick had told her. He had given her the proceedings of the Royal Geographical Society, and here she found Alec MacKenzie's account of his wanderings during the five years that followed. The countries which he explored then, become afterwards British East Africa.

But the bell rang for dinner, and so interrupted her meditations.

Chapter III

THEY PLAYED BRIDGE IMMEDIATELY AFTERWARDS. MRS. CROWLEY LOOKED upon conversation as a fine art, which could not be pursued while the body was engaged in the process of digestion; and she was of opinion that a game of cards agreeably diverted the mind and prepared the intellect for the quips and cranks which might follow when the claims of the body were satisfied. Lucy drew Alec MacKenzie as her partner, and so was able to watch his play when her cards were on the table. He did not play lightly as did Dick, who kept up a running commentary the whole time, but threw his whole soul into the game and never for a moment relaxed his attention. He took no notice of Dick's facetious observations. Presently Lucy grew more interested in his playing than in the game; she was struck, not only by his great gift of concentration, but by his boldness. He had a curious faculty for knowing almost from the beginning of a hand where each card lay. She saw, also, that he was plainly most absorbed when he was playing both hands himself; he was a man who liked to take everything on his own shoulders, and the division of responsibility irritated him.

At the end of the rubber Dick flung himself back in his chair irritably.

"I can't make it out," he cried. "I play much better than you, and I hold better hands, and yet you get the tricks."

Dick was known to be an excellent player, and his annoyance was excusable.

"We didn't make a single mistake," he assured his partner, "and we actually had the odd in our hands, but not one of our finesses came off, and all his did." He turned to Alec. "How the dickens did you guess I had those two queens?"

"Because I've known you for twenty years," answered Alec, smiling. "I know that, though you're impulsive and emotional, you're not without shrewdness; I know that your brain acts very quickly and sees all kinds of remote contingencies; then you're so pleased at having noticed them that you act as if they were certain to occur. Given these data, I can tell pretty well what cards you have, after they've gone round two or three times."

"The knowledge you have of your opponents' cards is too uncanny," said Mrs. Crowley.

"I can tell a good deal from people's faces. You see, in Africa I have had a lot of experience; it's apparently so much easier for the native to lie than to tell the truth that you get into the habit of paying no attention to what he says, and a great deal to the way he looks."

While Mrs. Crowley made herself comfortable in the chair, which she had already chosen as her favourite, Dick went over to the fire and stood in front of it in such a way as effectually to prevent the others from getting any of its heat.

"What made you first take to exploration?" asked Mrs. Crowley suddenly.

Alec gave her that slow, scrutinising look of his, and answered, with a smile:

"I don't know. I had nothing to do and plenty of money."

"Not a bit of it," interrupted Dick. "A lunatic wanted to find out about some district that people had never been to, and it wouldn't have been any use to them if they had, because, if the natives didn't kill you, the climate made no bones about it. He came back crippled with fever, having failed in his attempt, and, after asserting that no one could get into the heart of Rofa's country and return alive, promptly gave up the ghost. So Alec immediately packed up his traps and made for the place."

"I proved the man was wrong," said Alec quietly. "I became great friends with Rofa, and he wanted to marry my sister, only I hadn't one."

"And if anyone said it was impossible to hop through Asia on one foot, you'd go and do it just to show it could be done," retorted Dick. "You have a passion for doing things because they're difficult or dangerous, and, if they're downright impossible, you chortle with joy."

"You make me really too melodramatic," smiled Alec.

"But that's just what you are. You're the most transpontine person I ever saw in my life." Dick turned to Lucy and Mrs. Crowley with a wave of the hand. "I call you to witness. When he was at Oxford, Alec was a regular dab at classics; he had a gift for writing verses in languages that no one except dons wanted to read, and everyone thought that he was going to be the most brilliant scholar of his day."

"This is one of Dick's favourite stories," said Alec. "It would be quite amusing if there were any truth in it."

But Dick would not allow himself to be interrupted.

"At mathematics, on the other hand, he was a perfect ass. You know, some people seem to have that part of their brains wanting that deals with figures, and Alec couldn't add two and two together without making a hexameter out of it. One day his tutor got in a passion with him and said he'd rather teach arithmetic to a brick wall. I happened to be present, and he was certainly very rude. He was a man who had a precious gift for making people feel thoroughly uncomfortable. Alec didn't say anything, but he looked at him; and, when he flies into a temper, he doesn't get red and throw things about like a pleasant, normal person—he merely becomes a little paler and stares at you."

"I beg you not to believe a single word he says," remonstrated Alec.

"Well, Alec threw over his classics. Everyone concerned reasoned with him; they appealed to his common sense; they were appealing to the most obstinate fool in Christendom. Alec had made up his mind to be a mathematician. For more than two years he worked ten hours a day at a subject he loathed; he threw his whole might into it and forced out of nature the gifts she had denied him, with the result that he got a first class. And much good it's done him."

Alec shrugged his shoulders.

"It wasn't that I cared for mathematics, but it taught me to conquer the one inconvenient word in the English language."

"And what the deuce is that?"

"I'm afraid it sounds very priggish," laughed Alec. "The word *impossible*."

Dick gave a little snort of comic rage.

"And it also gave you a ghastly pleasure in doing things that hurt you. Oh, if you'd only been born in the Middle Ages, what a fiendish joy you would have taken in mortifying your flesh, and in denying yourself everything that makes life so good to live! You're never thoroughly happy unless you're making yourself thoroughly miserable."

"Each time I come back to England I find that you talk more and greater nonsense, Dick," returned Alec drily.

"I'm one of the few persons now alive who can talk nonsense," answered his friend, laughing. "That's why I'm so charming. Everyone else is so deadly earnest."

He settled himself down to make a deliberate speech.

"I deplore the strenuousness of the world in general. There is an idea abroad that is praiseworthy to do things, and what they are is of no consequence so long as you do them. I hate the mad hurry of the present day to occupy itself. I wish I could persuade people of the excellence of leisure."

"One could scarcely accuse you of cultivating it yourself," said Lucy, smiling.

Dick looked at her for a moment thoughtfully.

"Do you know that I'm hard upon forty?"

"With the light behind, you might still pass for thirty-two," interrupted Mrs. Crowley.

He turned to her seriously.

"I haven't a grey hair on my head."

"I suppose your servant plucks them out every morning?"

"Oh, no, very rarely; one a month at the outside."

"I think I see one just beside the left temple."

He turned quickly to the glass.

"Dear me, how careless of Charles! I shall have to give him a piece of my mind."

"Come here, and let me take it out," said Mrs. Crowley.

"I will let you do nothing of the sort. I should consider it most familiar."

"You were giving us the gratuitous piece of information that you were nearly forty," said Alec.

"The thought came to me the other day with something of a shock, and I set about a scrutiny of the life I was leading. I've worked at the bar pretty hard for fifteen years now, and I've been in the House since the general election. I've been earning two thousand a year, I've got nearly four thousand of my own, and I've never spent much more than half my income. I wondered if it was worthwhile to spend eight hours a day settling the sordid quarrels of foolish people, and another eight hours in the farce of governing the nation."

"Why do you call it that?"

Dick Lomas shrugged his shoulders scornfully.

"Because it is. A few big-wigs rule the roost, and the rest of us are only there to delude the British people into the idea that they're a self-governing community."

"What is wrong with you is that you have no absorbing aim in politics," said Alec gravely.

"Pardon me, I am a suffragist of the most vehement type," answered Dick, with a thin smile.

"That's the last thing I should have expected you to be," said Mrs. Crowley, who dressed with admirable taste. "Why on earth have you taken to that?"

Dick shrugged his shoulders.

"No one can have been through a parliamentary election without discovering how unworthy, sordid, and narrow are the reasons for which men vote. There are very few who are alive to the responsibilities that have been thrust upon them. They are indifferent to the importance of the stakes at issue, but make their vote a matter of ignoble barter. The parliamentary candidate is at the mercy of faddists and cranks. Now, I think that women, when they have votes, will be a trifle more narrow, and they will give them for motives that are a little more sordid and a little more unworthy. It will reduce universal suffrage to the absurd, and then it may be possible to try something else."

Dick had spoken with a vehemence that was unusual to him. Alec watched him with a certain interest.

"And what conclusions have you come to?"

For a moment he did not answer, then he gave a deprecating smile.

"I feel that the step I want to take is momentous for me, though I am conscious that it can matter to nobody else whatever. There will be a general election in a few months, and I have made up my mind to inform the whips that I shall not stand again. I shall give up my chambers in Lincoln's Inn, put up the shutters, so to speak, and Mr. Richard Lomas will retire from active life."

"You wouldn't really do that?" cried Mrs. Crowley.

"Why not?"

"In a month complete idleness will simply bore you to death."

"I doubt it. Do you know, it seems to me that a great deal of nonsense is talked about the dignity of work. Work is a drug that dull people take to avoid the pangs of unmitigated boredom. It has been adorned with fine phrases, because it is a necessity to most men, and men always gild the pill they're obliged to swallow. Work is a sedative. It keeps people quiet and contented. It makes them good material for their leaders. I think the greatest imposture of Christian times is the sanctification of labour. You see, the early Christians were slaves, and it was necessary to show them that their obligatory toil was noble and virtuous. But when all is said and done, a man works to earn his bread and to keep his wife and children; it is a painful necessity, but there is nothing heroic in it. If people choose to put a higher value on the means than on the end, I can only pass with a shrug of the shoulders, and regret the paucity of their intelligence."

"It's really unfair to talk so much all at once," said Mrs. Crowley, throwing up her pretty hands.

But Dick would not be stopped.

"For my part I have neither wife nor child, and I have an income that is more than adequate. Why should I take the bread out of somebody else's mouth? And it's not on my own merit that I get briefs—men seldom do—I only get them because I happen to have at the back of me a very large firm of solicitors. And I can find nothing worthy in attending to these foolish disputes. In most cases it's six of one and half a dozen of the other, and each side is very unjust and pig-headed. No, the bar is a fair way of earning your living like another, but it's no more than that; and, if you can exist without, I see no reason why Quixotic motives of the dignity of human toil should keep you to it. I've already told you why I mean to give up my seat in Parliament."

"Have you realised that you are throwing over a career that may be very brilliant? You should get an under-secretaryship in the next government."

"That would only mean licking the boots of a few more men whom I despise."

"It's a very dangerous experiment that you're making."

Dick looked straight into Alec MacKenzie's eyes.

"And is it you who counsel me not to make it on that account?" he said, smiling. "Surely experiments are only amusing if they're dangerous."

"And to what is it precisely that you mean to devote your time?" asked Mrs. Crowley.

"I should like to make idleness a fine art," he laughed. "People, nowadays, turn up their noses at the dilettante. Well, I mean to be a dilettante. I want to devote myself to the graces of life. I'm forty, and for all I know I haven't so very many years before me: in the time that remains, I want to become acquainted with the world and all the graceful, charming things it contains."

Alec, fallen into deep thought, stared into the fire. Presently he took a long breath, rose from his chair, and drew himself to his full height.

"I suppose it's a life like another, and there is no one to say which is better and which is worse. But, for my part, I would rather go on till I dropped. There are ten thousand things I want to do. If I had ten lives I couldn't get through a tithe of what, to my mind, so urgently needs doing."

"And what do you suppose will be the end of it?" asked Dick.

"For me?"

Dick nodded, but did not otherwise reply. Alec smiled faintly.

"Well, I suppose the end of it will be death in some swamp, obscurely, worn out with disease and exposure; and my bearers will make off with my guns and my stores, and the jackals will do the rest."

"I think it's horrible," said Mrs. Crowley, with a shudder.

"I'm a fatalist. I've lived too long among people with whom it is the deepest rooted article of their faith, to be anything else. When my time comes, I cannot escape it." He smiled whimsically. "But I believe in quinine, too, and I think that the daily use of that admirable drug will make the thread harder to cut."

To Lucy it was an admirable study, the contrast between the man who threw his whole soul into a certain aim, which he pursued with a savage intensity, knowing that the end was a dreadful, lonely death; and the man who was making up his mind deliberately to gather what was beautiful in life, and to cultivate its graces as though it were a flower garden.

"And the worst of it is that it will all be the same in a hundred years," said Dick. "We shall both be forgotten long before then, you with your strenuousness, and I with my folly."

"And what conclusion do you draw from that?" asked Mrs. Crowley.

"Only that the psychological moment has arrived for a whisky and soda."

Chapter IV

There was some rough shooting on the estate which Mrs. Crowley had rented, and next day Dick went out to see what he could find. Alec refused to accompany him.

"I think shooting in England bores me a little," he said. "I have a prejudice against killing things unless I want to eat them, and these English birds are so tame that it seems to me rather like shooting chickens."

"I don't believe a word of it," said Dick, as he set out. "The fact is that you can't hit anything smaller than a hippopotamus, and you know that there is nothing here to suit you except Mrs. Crowley's cows."

After luncheon Alec MacKenzie asked Lucy if she would take a stroll with him. She was much pleased.

"Where would you like to go?" she asked.

"Let us walk by the sea."

She took him along a road called Joy Lane, which ran from the fishing town of Blackstable to a village called Waveney. The sea there had a peculiar vastness, and the salt smell of the breeze was pleasant to the senses. The flatness of the marsh seemed to increase the distances that surrounded them, and unconsciously Alec fell into a more rapid swing. It did not look as if he walked fast, but he covered the ground with the steady method of a man who has been used to long journeys, and it was good for Lucy that she was accustomed to much walking. At first they spoke of trivial things, but presently silence fell upon them. Lucy saw that he was immersed in thought, and she did not interrupt him. It amused her that, after asking her to walk with him, this odd man should take no pains to entertain her. Now and then he threw back his head with a strange, proud motion, and looked out to sea. The gulls, with their melancholy flight, were skimming upon the surface of the water. The desolation of that scene—it was the same which, a few days before, had rent poor Lucy's heart—appeared to enter his soul; but, strangely enough, it uplifted him, filling him with exulting thoughts. He quickened his pace, and Lucy, without a word, kept step with him. He seemed not to notice where they walked, and presently she led him away from the sea. They tramped along a winding road, between trim hedges and fertile fields; and the country had all the sweet air of Kent, with its easy grace and its comfortable beauty. They passed a caravan, with a shaggy horse browsing at the wayside, and a family of dinglers sitting around a fire of sticks. The sight curiously affected Lucy. The wandering life of those people, with no ties but to the ramshackle carriage which was their only home, their familiarity with the fields and with strange hidden places, filled her with a wild desire for freedom and for vast horizons. At last they came to the massive gates of Court Leys. An avenue of elms led to the house.

"Here we are," said Lucy, breaking the long silence.

"Already?" He seemed to shake himself. "I have to thank you for a pleasant stroll, and we've had a good talk, haven't we?"

"Have we?" she laughed. She saw his look of surprise. "For two hours you've not vouchsafed to make an observation."

"I'm so sorry," he said, reddening under his tan. "How rude you must have thought me! I've been alone so much that I've got out of the way of behaving properly."

"It doesn't matter at all," she smiled. "You must talk to me another time."

She was subtly flattered. She felt that, for him, it was a queer kind of compliment that he had paid her. Their silent walk, she did not know why, seemed to have created a bond between them; and it appeared that he felt it, too, for afterwards he treated her with a certain intimacy. He seemed to look upon her no longer as an acquaintance, but as a friend.

A day or two later, Mrs. Crowley having suggested that they should drive into Tercanbury to see the cathedral, MacKenzie asked her if she would allow him to walk.

He turned to Lucy.

"I hardly dare to ask if you will come with me," he said.

"It would please me immensely."

"I will try to behave better than last time."

"You need not," she smiled.

Dick, who had an objection to walking when it was possible to drive, set out with Mrs. Crowley in a trap. Alec waited for Lucy. She went round to the stable to fetch a dog to accompany them, and, as she came towards him, he looked at her. Alec was a man to whom most of his fellows were abstractions. He saw them and talked to them, noting their peculiarities, but they were seldom living persons to him. They were shadows, as it were, that had to be reckoned with, but they never became part of himself. And it came upon him now with a certain shock of surprise to notice Lucy. He felt suddenly a new interest in her. He seemed to see her for the first time, and her rare beauty strangely moved him. In her serge dress and her gauntlets, with a motor cap and a flowing veil, a stick in her hand, she seemed on a sudden to express the country through which for the last two or three days he had wandered. He felt an unexpected pleasure in her slim erectness and in her buoyant step. There was something very charming in her blue eyes.

He was seized with a great desire to talk. And, without thinking for an instant that what concerned him so intensely might be of no moment to her, he began forthwith upon the subject which was ever at his heart. But he spoke as his interest prompted, of each topic as it most absorbed him, starting with what he was now about and going back to what had first attracted his attention to that business; then telling his plans for the future, and to make them clear, finishing with the events that had led up to his determination. Lucy listened attentively, now and then asking a question; and presently the whole matter sorted itself in her mind, so that she was able to make a connected narrative of his life since the details of it had escaped from Dick's personal observation.

For some years Alec MacKenzie had travelled in Africa with no object beyond a great curiosity, and no ambition but that of the unknown. His first important expedition had been, indeed, occasioned by the failure of a fellow-explorer. He had undergone the common vicissitudes of African travel, illness and hunger, incredible difficulties of transit through swamps that seemed never ending, and tropical forest through which it was impossible to advance at the rate of more than one mile a day; he had suffered from the desertion of his bearers and the perfidy of native tribes. But at last he reached the country which had been the aim of his journey. He had to encounter then a savage king's determined hostility to the white man, and he had to keep a sharp eye on his followers who, in abject terror of the tribe he meant to visit, took every opportunity to escape into the bush. The barbarian chief sent him a warning that he would have him killed if he attempted to enter his capital. The rest of the story Alec told with an apologetic air, as if he were ashamed of himself, and he treated it with a deprecating humour that sought to minimise both the danger he had run and the courage he had displayed. On receiving the king's message, Alec MacKenzie took up a high tone, and returned the answer that he would come to the royal kraal before midday. He wanted to give the king no time to recover from his astonishment, and the messengers had scarcely delivered the reply before he presented himself, unarmed and unattended.

"What did you say to him?" asked Lucy.

"I asked him what the devil he meant by sending me such an impudent message," smiled Alec.

"Weren't you frightened?" said Lucy.

"Yes," he answered.

He paused for a moment, and, as though unconsciously he were calling back the mood which had then seized him, he began to walk more slowly.

"You see, it was the only thing to do. We'd about come to the end of our food, and we were bound to get some by hook or by crook. If we'd shown the white feather they would probably have set upon us without more ado. My own people were too frightened to make a fight of it, and we should have been wiped out like sheep. Then I had a kind of instinctive feeling that it would be all right. I didn't feel as if my time had come."

But, notwithstanding, for three hours his life had hung in the balance; and Lucy understood that it was only his masterful courage which had won the day and turned a sullen, suspicious foe into a warm ally.

He achieved the object of his expedition, discovered a new species of antelope of which he was able to bring back to the Natural History Museum a complete skeleton and two hides; took some geographical observations which corrected current errors, and made a careful examination of the country. When he had learned all that was possible, still on the most friendly terms with the ferocious ruler, he set out for Mombassa. He reached it in one month more than five years after he had left it.

The results of this journey had been small enough, but Alec looked upon it as his apprenticeship. He had found his legs, and believed himself fit for much greater undertakings. He had learned how to deal with natives, and was aware that he had a natural influence over them. He had confidence in himself. He had surmounted the difficulties of the climate, and felt himself more or less proof against fever and heat. He returned to the coast stronger than he had ever been in his life, and his enthusiasm for African travel increased tenfold. The siren had taken hold of him, and no escape now was possible.

He spent a year in England, and then went back to Africa. He had determined now to explore certain districts to the northeast of the great lakes. They were in the hinterland of British East Africa, and England had a vague claim over them; but no actual occupation had taken place, and they formed a series of independent states under Arab emirs. He went this time with a roving commission from the government, and authority to make treaties with the local chieftains. Spending six years in these districts, he made a methodical survey of the country, and was able to prepare valuable maps. He collected an immense amount of scientific material. He studied the manners and customs of the inhabitants, and made careful observations on the political state. He found the whole land distracted with incessant warfare, and broad tracts of country, fertile and apt for the occupation of white men, given over to desolation. It was then that he realised the curse of slave-raiding, the abolition of which was to become the great object of his future activity. His strength was small, and, anxious not to arouse at once the enmity of the Arab slavers, he had to use much diplomacy in order to establish himself in the country. He knew himself to be an object of intense suspicion, and he could not trust even the petty rulers who were bound to him by ties of gratitude and friendship. For some time the sultan of the most powerful state kept him in a condition bordering on captivity, and at one period his life was for a year in the greatest danger. He never knew from day to day whether he would see the setting on the sun. The Arab, though he treated him with honour, would not let him go; and, at last, Alec, seizing an opportunity when the sultan was engaged in battle with a brother who sought to usurp his sovereignty, fled for his life, abandoning his property, and saving only his notes, his specimens, and his guns.

When MacKenzie reached England, he laid before the Foreign Office the result of his studies. He pointed out the state of anarchy to which the constant slave-raiding had reduced this wealthy country, and implored those in authority, not only for the sake of humanity, but for the prestige of the country, to send an expedition which should stamp out the murderous traffic. He offered to accompany this in any capacity; and, so long as he had the chance of assisting in a righteous war, agreed to serve under any leader they chose. His knowledge of the country and his influence over its inhabitants were indispensable. He guaranteed that, if they gave him a certain number of guns with three British officers, the whole affair could be settled in a year.

But the government was crippled by the Boer War; and though, appreciating the strength of his arguments, it realised the necessity of intervention, was disinclined to enter upon fresh enterprises. These little expeditions in Africa had a way of developing into much more important affairs than first appeared. They had been taught bitter lessons before now, and could not risk, in the present state of things, even an insignificant rebuff. If they sent out a small party, which was defeated, it would be a great blow to the prestige of the country through Africa—the Arabs would carry the news to India—and it would be necessary, then, to despatch such a force that failure was impossible. To supply this there was neither money nor men.

Alec was put off with one excuse after another. To him it seemed that hindrances were deliberately set in his way, and in fact the relations of England with the rest of Europe made his small schemes appear an intolerable nuisance. At length he was met with a flat refusal.

But Alec MacKenzie could not rest with this, and opposition only made him more determined to carry his business through. He understood that it was hard at second-hand to make men realise that the state of things in that distant land. But he had seen horrors beyond description. He knew the ruthless cruelty of the slave-raiders, and in his ears rang, still, the cries of agony when a village was set on fire and attacked by the Arabs. Not once, nor twice, but many times he had left some tiny kraal nestling sweetly among its fields of maize, an odd, savage counterpart to the country hamlet described in prim, melodious numbers by the gentle Goldsmith: the little naked children were playing merrily; the women sat in groups grinding their corn and chattering; the men worked in fields or lounged idly about the hut doors. It was a charming scene. You felt that here, perhaps, one great mystery of life had been solved; for happiness was on every face, and the mere joy of living was a sufficient reason for existence. And, when he returned, the village was a pile of cinders, smoking still; here and there were lying the dead and wounded; on one side he recognised a chubby boy with a great spear wound in his body; on another was a woman with her face blown away by some clumsy gun; and there a man in the agony of death, streaming with blood, lay heaped upon the ground in horrible disorder. And the rest of the inhabitants had been hurried away pellmell on the cruel journey across country, brutally treated and half starved, till they could be delivered into the hands of the slave merchant.

Alec MacKenzie went to the Foreign Office once more. He was willing to take the whole business on himself, and asked only for a commission to raise troops at his expense. Timorous secretaries did not know into what difficulties this determined man might lead them, and if he went with the authority of an official, but none of his responsibilities, he might land them in grave complications. The spheres of influence of the continental powers must be respected, and at this time of all others it was necessary to be very careful of national jealousies. Alec MacKenzie was told that if he went he must go as a private person. No help could be given him, and the British Government would not concern itself, even indirectly, with his enterprise. Alec had expected the reply and was not dissatisfied. If the government would not undertake the matter itself, he preferred to manage it without the hindrance of official restraints. And so this solitary man made up his mind, single handed, to crush the slave traffic in a district larger than England, and to wage war, unassisted, with a dozen local chieftains and against twenty thousand fighting men. The attempt seemed Quixotic, but Alec had examined the risks and was willing to take them. He had on his side a thorough knowledge of the country, a natural power over the natives, and some skill in managing them. He was accustomed now to the diplomacy which was needful, and he was well acquainted with the local politics.

He did not think it would be hard to collect a force on the coast, and there were plenty of hardy, adventurous fellows who would volunteer to officer the native levies, if he had money to pay them. Ready money was essential, so he crossed the Atlantic and sold his estate in Texas; he made arrangements to raise a further sum, if necessary, on the income which his colliery in Lancashire brought him. He engaged a surgeon, whom he had known for some years, and could trust in an emergency, and then sailed for Zanzibar, where he expected to find white men willing to take service under him. At Mombassa he collected the bearers who had been with him during his previous expeditions, and, his fame among the natives being widely spread, he was able to take his pick of those best suited for his purpose. His party consisted altogether of over three hundred.

When he arrived upon the scene of his operations, everything for a time went well. He showed great skill in dividing his enemies. The petty rulers were filled with jealousy of one another and eager always to fall upon their friends, when slave-raiding for a season was unsuccessful. Alec's plan was to join two or three smaller states in an attack upon the most powerful of them all, to crush this completely, and then to take his old allies one by one, if they would not guarantee to give up their raids on peaceful tribes. His influence with the natives was such that he felt certain it was possible to lead them into action against their dreaded foes, the Arabs, if he was once able to give them confidence. Everything turned out as he had hoped.

The great state which had aimed at the hegemony of the whole district was defeated; and Alec, with the method habitual to him, set about organising each strip of territory which was reclaimed from the barbarism. He was able to hold in check the emirs who had fought with him, and a sharp lesson given to one who had broken faith with him, struck terror in the others. The land was regaining its old security. Alec trusted that in five years a man would be able to travel from end to end of it as safely as in England. But suddenly everything he had achieved was undone. As sometimes happens in countries of small civilisation, a leader arose from among the Arabs. None knew from where he sprang, and it was said that he had been a camel driver. He was called Mohammed the Lame, because a leg badly set after a fracture had left him halting, and he was a shrewd man, far-seeing, ruthless, and ambitious. With a few companions as desperate as himself, he attacked the capital of a small state in the North which was distracted by the death of its ruler, seized it, and proclaimed himself king.

In a year he had brought under his sway all those shadowy lands which border upon Abyssinia, and was leading a great rabble, made with the lust of conquest, fanatic with hatred of the Christian, upon the South. Consternation reigned among the tribes to whom MacKenzie was the only hope of salvation. He pointed out to the Arabs who had accepted his influence, that their safety, as well as his, lay in resistance to the Lame One; but the war cry of the Prophet prevailed against the call of reason, and he found that they were against him to a man. His native allies were faithful, with the fidelity of despair, and these he brought up against the enemy. A pitched battle was fought, but the issue was undecided. The losses were great on both sides, and Alec himself was badly wounded.

Fortunately the wet season was approaching, and Mohammed the Lame, with a wholesome respect for the white man who for the moment, at least, had checked his onward course, withdrew to the Northern regions where his power was more secure. Alec knew that he would resume the attack at the first opportunity, and he knew also that he had not the means to withstand a foe who was astute and capable. His only chance was to get back to the coast, return to England, and try again to interest the government in the undertaking; if they still refused help he determined to go out once more himself, taking this time Maxim guns and men capable of handling them. He knew that his departure would seem like flight, but he could not help that. He was obliged to go. His wound prevented him from walking, but he caused himself to be carried; and, firing his caravan with his own indomitable spirit, he reached the coast by forced marches.

His brief visit to England was already drawing to its close, and, in less than a month now, he proposed to set out for Africa once more. This time he meant to finish the work. If only his life were spared, he would crush forever the infamous trade which turned a paradise into a wilderness.

Alec stopped speaking as they entered the cathedral close, and they paused for a moment to look at the stately pile. The trim lawns that surrounded it, in a manner enhanced its serene majesty. They entered the nave. There was a vast and solemn stillness. And there was something subtly impressive in the naked space; it uplifted the heart, and one felt a kind of scorn for all that was mean and low. The soaring of the Gothic columns, with their straight simplicity, raised the thoughts to a nobler standard. And, though that place had been given for three hundred years to colder rites, the atmosphere of an earlier, more splendid faith seemed to cling to it. A vague odour of a spectral incense hung about the pillars, a sweet, sad smell, and the shadows of ghostly priests in vestments of gold, and with embroidered copes, wound in a long procession through the empty aisles.

Lucy was glad that they had come there, and the restful grandeur of the place fitted in with the emotions that had filled her mind during the walk from Blackstable. Her spirit was enlarged, and she felt that her own small worries were petty. The consciousness came to her that the man with whom she had been speaking was making history, and she was fascinated by the fulness of his life and the greatness of his undertakings. Her eyes were dazzled with the torrid African sun which had shone through his words, and she felt the horror of the primeval forest and the misery of the unending swamps. And she was proud because his outlook was so clear, because he bore his responsibilities so easily, because his plans were so vast. She looked at him. He was standing by her side, and his eyes were upon her. She felt the colour rise to her cheeks, she knew not why, and in embarrassment looked down.

By some chance they missed Dick Lomas and Mrs. Crowley. Neither was sorry. When they left the cathedral and started for home, they spoke for a while of indifferent things. It seemed that Alec's tongue was loosened, and he was glad of it. Lucy knew instinctively that he had never talked to anyone as he talked to her, and she was curiously flattered.

But it seemed to both of them that the conversation could not proceed on the strenuous level on which it had been during the walk into Tercanbury, and they fell upon a gay discussion of their common acquaintance. Alec was a man of strong passions, hating fools fiercely, and he had a sardonic manner of gibing at persons he despised, which caused Lucy much amusement.

He described interviews with the great ones of the land in a broadly comic spirit; and, when telling an amusing story, he had a way of assuming a Scottish drawl that added vastly to its humour.

Presently they began to speak of books. Being strictly limited as to number, he was obliged to choose for his expeditions works which could stand reading an indefinite number of times.

"I'm like a convict," he said. "I know Shakespeare by heart, and I've read Boswell's *Johnson* till I think you couldn't quote a line which I couldn't cap with the next."

But Lucy was surprised to hear that he read the Greek classics with enthusiasm. She had vaguely imagined that people recognised their splendour, but did not read them unless they were dons or schoolmasters, and it was strange to find anyone for whom they were living works. To Alec they were a deliberate inspiration. They strengthened his purpose and helped him to see life from the heroic point of view. He was not a man who cared much for music or for painting; his whole aesthetic desires were centred in the Greek poets and the historians. To him Thucydides was a true support, and he felt in himself something of the spirit which had animated the great Athenian. His blood ran faster as he spoke of him, and his cheeks flushed. He felt that one who lived constantly in such company could do nothing base. But he found all he needed, put together with a power that seemed almost divine, within the two covers that bound his Sophocles. The mere look of the Greek letters filled him with exultation. Here was all he wanted, strength and simplicity, and greatness of life, and beauty.

He forgot that Lucy did not know that dead language and could not share his enthusiasm. He broke suddenly into a chorus from the *Antigone:* the sonorous, lovely words issued from his lips, and Lucy, not understanding, but feeling vaguely the beauty of the sounds, thought that his voice had never been more fascinating. It gained now a peculiar and entrancing softness. She had never dreamed that it was capable of such tenderness.

At last they reached Court Leys and walked up the avenue that led to the house. They saw Dick hurrying towards them. They waved their hands, but he did not reply, and, when he approached, they saw that his face was white and anxious.

"Thank God, you've come at last! I couldn't make out what had come to you."

"What's the matter?"

The barrister, all his flippancy gone, turned to Lucy.

"Bobbie Boulger has come down. He wants to see you. Please come at once."

Lucy looked at him quickly. Sick with fear, she followed him into the drawing-room.

Chapter V

MRS. CROWLEY AND ROBERT BOULGER WERE STANDING BY THE FIRE, AND there was a peculiar agitation about them. They were silent, but it seemed to Lucy that they had been speaking of her. Mrs. Crowley impulsively seized her hands and kissed her. Lucy's first thought was that something had happened to her brother. Lady Kelsey's generous allowance had made it possible for him to hunt, and the thought flashed through her that some terrible accident had happened.

"Is anything the matter with George?" she asked, with a gasp of terror.

"No," answered Boulger.

The colour came to Lucy's cheeks as she felt a sudden glow of relief.

"Thank God," she murmured. "I was so frightened."

She gave him, now, a smile of welcome as she shook hands with him. It could be nothing so very dreadful after all.

Lucy's uncle, Sir George Boulger, had been for many years senior partner in the great firm of Boulger & Kelsey. After sitting in Parliament for the quarter of a century and voting assiduously for his party, he had been given a baronetcy on the celebration of Queen Victoria's second Jubilee, and had finished a prosperous life by dying of apoplexy at the opening of a park, which he was presenting to the nation. He had been a fine type of the wealthy merchant, far-sighted in business affairs and proud to serve his native city in every way open to him. His son, Robert, now reigned in his stead, but the firm had been made into a company, and the responsibility that he undertook, notwithstanding that the greater number of shares were in his hands, was much less. The partner who had been taken into the house on Sir Alfred Kelsey's death now managed the more important part of the business in Manchester, while Robert, brought up by his father to be a man of affairs, had taken charge of the London branch. Commerce was in his blood, and he settled down to work with praiseworthy energy. He had considerable shrewdness, and it was plain that he would eventually become as good a merchant as his father. He was little older than Lucy, but his fair hair and his clean-shaven face gave him a more youthful look. With his spruce air and well-made clothes, his conversation about hunting and golf, few would have imagined that he arrived regularly at his office at ten in the morning, and was as keen to make a good bargain as any of the men he came in contact with.

Lucy, though very fond of him, was mildly scornful of his Philistine outlook. He cared nothing for books, and the only form of art that appealed to him was the musical comedy. She treated him as a rule with pleasant banter and refused to take him seriously. It required a good deal of energy to keep their friendship on a light footing, for she knew that he had been in love with her since he was eighteen. She could not help feeling flattered, though on her side there was no more than the cousinly affection due to their having been thrown together all their lives, and she was aware that they were little suited to one another. He had proposed to her a dozen times, and she was obliged to use many devices to protect herself from his assiduity. It availed nothing to tell him that she did not love him. He was only too willing to marry her on whatever conditions she chose to make. Her friends and her relations were anxious that she should accept him. Lady Kelsey had reasoned with her. Here was a man whom she had known always and could trust utterly; he had ten thousand a year, an honest heart, and a kindly disposition. Her father, seeing in the match a resource in his constant difficulties, was eager that she should take the boy, and George, who was devoted to him, had put in his words, too. Bobbie had asked her to marry him when he was twenty-one, and again when she was twenty-one, when George went to Oxford, when her father went into bankruptcy, and when Hamlyn's Purlieu was sold. He had urged his own father to buy it, when it was known that a sale was inevitable, hoping that the possession of it would incline Lucy's heart towards him; but the first baronet was too keen a man of business to make an unprofitable investment for sentimental reasons. Bobbie had proposed for the last time when he succeeded to the baronetcy and a large fortune. Lucy recognised his goodness and the advantages of the match, but she did not care for him. She felt, too, that she needed a free hand to watch over her father and George. Even Mrs. Crowley's suggestion that with her guidance Robert Boulger might become a man of consequence, did not move her. Bobbie, on the other hand, had set all his heart on marrying his cousin. It was the supreme interest of his life, and he hoped that his patience would eventually triumph over every obstacle. He was willing to wait.

When Lucy's first alarm was stayed, it occurred to her that Bobbie had come once more to ask her the eternal question, but the anxious look in his eyes drove the idea away. His pleasant, boyish expression was overcast with gravity; Mrs. Crowley flung herself in a chair and turned her face away.

"I have something to tell you which is very terrible, Lucy," he said.

The effort he made to speak was noticeable. His voice was strained by the force with which he kept it steady.

"Would you like me to leave you?" asked Alec, who had accompanied Lucy into the drawing-room.

She gave him a glance. It seemed to her that whatever it was, his presence would help her to bear it.

"Do you wish to see me alone, Bobbie?"

"I've already told Dick and Mrs. Crowley."

"What is it?" she asked.

Bobbie gave Dick an appealing look. It seemed too hard that he should have to break the awful news to her. He had not the heart to give her so much pain. And yet he had hurried down to the country so that he might soften the blow by his words: he would not trust to the callous cruelty of a telegram. Dick saw the agitation which made his good-humoured mouth twitch with pain, and stepped forward.

"Your father has been arrested for fraud," he said gravely.

For a moment no one spoke. The silence was intolerable to Mrs. Crowley, and she inveighed inwardly against the British stolidity. She could not look at Lucy, but the others, full of sympathy, kept their eyes upon her. Mrs. Crowley wondered why she did not faint. It seemed to Lucy that an icy hand clutched her heart so that the blood was squeezed out of it. She made a determined effort to keep her clearness of mind.

"It's impossible," she said at last, quietly.

"He was arrested last night, and brought up at Bow Street Police Court this morning. He was remanded for a week."

Lucy felt tears well up to her eyes, but with all her strength she forced them back. She collected her thoughts.

"It was very good of you to come down and tell me," she said to Boulger gently.

"The magistrate agreed to accept bail in five thousand pounds. Aunt Alice and I have managed it between us."

"Is he staying with Aunt Alice now?"

"No, he wouldn't do that. He's gone to his flat in Shaftesbury Avenue."

Lucy's thoughts went to the lad who was dearest to her in the world, and her heart sank.

"Does George know?"

"Not yet."

Dick saw the relief that came into her face, and thought he divined what was in her mind.

"But he must be told at once," he said. "He's sure to see something about it in the papers. We had better wire to him to come to London immediately."

"Surely father could have shown in two minutes that the whole thing was a mistake."

Bobbie made a hopeless gesture. He saw the sternness of her eyes, and he had not the heart to tell her the truth. Mrs. Crowley began to cry.

"You don't understand, Lucy," said Dick. "I'm afraid it's a very serious charge. Your father will be committed for trial."

"You know just as well as I do that father can't have done anything illegal. He's weak and rash, but he's no more than that. He would as soon think of doing anything wrong as of flying to the moon. If in his ignorance of business he's committed some technical offence, he can easily show that it was unintentional."

"Whatever it is, he'll have to stand his trial at the Old Bailey," answered Dick gravely.

He saw that Lucy did not for a moment appreciate the gravity of her father's position. After the first shock of dismay she was disposed to think that there could be nothing in it. Robert Boulger saw there was nothing for it but to tell her everything.

"Your father and a man called Saunders have been running a bucketshop under the name of Vernon and Lawford. They were obliged to trade under different names, because Uncle Fred is an undischarged bankrupt, and Saunders is the sort of man who only uses his own name on the charge sheet of a police court."

"Do you know what a bucketshop is, Lucy?" asked Dick.

He did not wait for a reply, but explained that it was a term used to describe a firm of outside brokers whose dealings were more or less dishonest.

"The action is brought against the pair of them by a Mrs. Sabidon, who accuses them of putting to their own uses various sums amounting altogether to more than eight thousand pounds, which she intrusted to them to invest."

Now that the truth was out, Lucy quailed before it. The intense seriousness on the faces of Alec and Dick Lomas, the piteous anxiety of her cousin, terrified her.

"You don't think there's anything in it?" she asked quickly.

Robert did not know what to answer. Dick interrupted with wise advice.

"We'll hope for the best. The only thing to do is to go up to London at once and get the best legal advice."

But Lucy would not allow herself, even for a moment, to doubt her father. Now that she thought of the matter, she saw that it was absurd. She forced herself to give a laugh.

"I'm quite reassured. You don't think for a moment that father would deliberately steal somebody else's money. And it's nothing short of theft."

"At all events it's something that we've been able to get him released on bail. It will make it so much easier to arrange the defence."

A couple of hours later Lucy, accompanied by Dick Lomas and Bobbie, was on her way to London. Alec, thinking his presence would be a nuisance to them, arranged with Mrs. Crowley to leave by a later train; and, when the time came for him to start, his hostess suddenly announced that she would go with him. With her party thus broken up and her house empty, she could not bear to remain at Court Leys. She was anxious about Lucy and eager to be at hand if her help were needed.

* * *

A telegram had been sent to George, and it was supposed that he would arrive at Lady Kelsey's during the evening. Lucy wanted to tell him herself what had happened. But she could not wait till then to see her father, and persuaded Dick to drive with her from the station to Shaftesbury Avenue. Fred Allerton was not in. Lucy wanted to go into the flat and stay there till he came, but the porter had no key and did not know when he would return. Dick was much relieved. He was afraid that the excitement and the anxiety from which Fred Allerton had suffered, would have caused him to drink heavily; and he could not let Lucy see him the worse for liquor. He induced her, after leaving a note to say that she would call early next morning, to go quietly home. When they arrived at Charles Street, where was Lady Kelsey's house, they found a wire from George to say he could not get up to town till the following day.

To Lucy this had, at least, the advantage that she could see her father alone, and at the appointed hour she made her way once more to his flat. He took her in his arms and kissed her warmly. She succumbed at once to the cheeriness of his manner.

"I can only give you two minutes, darling," he said. "I'm full of business, and I have an appointment with my solicitor at eleven."

Lucy could not speak. She clung to her father, looking at him with anxious, sombre eyes; but he laughed and patted her hand.

"You mustn't make too much of all this, my love," he said brightly. "These little things are always liable to happen to a man of business; they are the perils of the profession, and we have to put up with them, just as kings and queens have to put up with bombshells."

"There's no truth in it, father?"

She did not want to ask that wounding question, but the words slipped from her lips against her will. He broke away from her.

"Truth? My dear child, what do you mean? You don't suppose I'm the man to rob the widow and the orphan? Of course, there's no truth in it."

"Oh, I'm so glad to hear that," she exclaimed, with a deep sigh of relief.

"Have they been frightening you?"

Lucy flushed under his frank look of amusement. She felt that there was a barrier between herself and him, the barrier that had existed for years, and there was something in his manner which filled her with unaccountable anxiety. She would not analyse that vague emotion. It was a dread to see what was so carefully hidden by that breezy reserve. She forced herself to go on.

"I know that you're often carried away by your fancies, and I thought you might have got into an ambiguous position."

"I can honestly say that no one can bring anything up against me," he answered. "But I do blame myself for getting mixed up with that man Saunders. I'm afraid there's no doubt that he's a wrong 'un—and heaven only knows what he's been up to—but for my own part I give you my solemn word of honour that I've done nothing, absolutely nothing, that I have the least reason to be ashamed of."

Lucy took his hand, and a charming smile lit up her face.

"Oh, father, you've made me so happy by saying that. Now I shall be able to tell George that there's nothing to worry about."

Their conversation was interrupted by the arrival of Dick. Fred Allerton greeted him heartily.

"You've just come in time to take Lucy home. I've got to go out. But look here, George is coming up, isn't he? Let us all lunch at the *Carlton* at two, and get Alice to come. We'll have a jolly little meal together."

Dick was astounded to see the lightness with which Allerton took the affair. He seemed unconscious of the gravity of his position and unmindful of the charge which was hanging over him. Dick was not anxious to accept the invitation, but Allerton would hear of no excuses. He wanted to have his friends gathered around him, and he needed relaxation after the boredom of spending a morning in his lawyer's office.

"Come on," he said. "I can't wait another minute."

He opened the door, and Lucy walked out. It seemed to Dick that Allerton was avoiding any chance of conversation with him. But no man likes to meet his creditor within four walls, and this disinclination might be due merely to the fact that Allerton owed him a couple of hundred pounds. But he meant to get in one or two words.

"Are you fixed up with a solicitor?" he asked.

"Do you think I'm a child, Dick?" answered the other. "Why, I've got the smartest man in the whole profession, Teddie Blakely—you know him, don't you?"

"Only by reputation," answered Dick drily. "I should think that was enough for most people."

Fred Allerton gave that peculiarly honest laugh of his, which was so attractive. Dick knew that the solicitor he mentioned was a man of evil odour, who had made a specialty of dealing with the most doubtful sort of commercial work, and his name had been prominent in every scandal for the last fifteen years. It was surprising that he had never followed any of his clients to the jail he richly deserved.

"I thought it no good going to one of the old crusted family solicitors. I wanted a man who knew the tricks of the trade."

They were walking down the stairs, while Lucy waited at the bottom. Dick stopped and turned round. He looked at Allerton keenly.

"You're not going to do a bolt, are you?"

Allerton's face lit up with amusement. He put his hands on Dick's shoulders.

"My dear old Dick, don't be such an ass. I don't know about Saunders—he's got a fishy sort of customer—but I shall come out of all this with flying colours. The prosecution hasn't a leg to stand on."

Allerton, reminding them that they were to lunch together, jumped into a cab. Lucy and Dick walked slowly back to Charles Street. Dick was very silent. He had not seen Fred Allerton for some time and was surprised to see that he had regained his old smartness. The flat had pretty things in it which testified to the lessee's taste and to his means, and the clothes he wore were new and well-cut. The invitation to the *Carlton* showed that he was in no want of ready money, and there was a general air of prosperity about him which gave Dick much to think of.

Lucy did not ask him to come in, since George, by now, must have arrived, and she wished to see him alone. They agreed to meet again at two. As she shook hands with Dick, Lucy told him what her father had said.

"I had a sleepless night," she said. "It was so stupid of me; I couldn't get it out of my head that father, unintentionally, had done something rash or foolish; but I've got his word of honour that nothing is the matter, and I feel as if a whole world of anxiety were suddenly lifted from my shoulders."

The party at the *Carlton* was very gay. Fred Allerton seemed in the best of spirits, and his good-humour was infectious. He was full of merry quips. Lucy had made as little of the affair as possible to George. Her eyes rested on him, as he sat opposite to her, and she felt happy and proud. Now and then he looked at her, and an affectionate smile came to his lips. She was delighted with his slim handsomeness. There was a guileless look in his blue eyes which was infinitely attractive. His mouth was beautifully modelled. She took an immense pride in the candour of soul which shone with so clear a light on his face, and she was affected as a stranger might have been by the exquisite charm of manner which he had inherited from his father. She wanted to have him to herself that evening and suggested that they should go to a play together. He accepted the idea eagerly, for he admired his sister with all his heart; he felt in himself a need for protection, and she was able to minister to this. He was never so happy as when he was by her side. He liked to tell her all he did, and, when she fired him with noble ambitions, he felt capable of anything.

They were absurdly light-hearted, as they started on their little jaunt. Lady Kelsey had slipped a couple of banknotes into George's hand and told them to have a good time. They dined at the *Carlton*, went to a musical comedy, which amused Lucy because her brother laughed so heartily—she was fascinated by his keen power of enjoyment—and finished by going to the *Savoy* for supper. For the moment all her anxieties seemed to fall from her, and the years of trouble were forgotten. She was as merry and as irresponsible as George. He was enchanted. He had never seen Lucy so tender and so gay; there was a new brilliancy in her eyes; and, without quite knowing what it was that differed, he found a soft mellowness in her laughter which filled him with an uncomprehended delight. Neither did Lucy know why the world on a sudden seemed fuller than it had ever done before, nor why the future smiled so kindly: it never occurred to her that she was in love.

When Lucy, exhausted but content, found herself at length in her room, she thanked God for the happiness of the evening. It was the last time she could do that for many weary years.

A few days later Allerton appeared again at the police court, and the magistrate, committing him for trial, declined to renew his bail. The prisoner was removed in custody.

Chapter VI

DURING THE FORTNIGHT THAT FOLLOWED, ALEC SPENT MUCH TIME WITH Lucy. Together, in order to cheat the hours that hung so heavily on her hands, they took long walks in Hyde Park, and, when Alec's business permitted, they went to the National Gallery. Then he took her to the Natural History Museum, and his conversation, in the face of the furred and feathered things from Africa, made the whole country vivid to her. Lucy was very grateful to him because he drew her mind away from the topic that constantly absorbed it. Though he never expressed his sympathy in so many words, she felt it in every inflection of his voice. His patience was admirable.

At last came the day fixed for the trial.

Fred Allerton insisted that neither Lucy nor George should come to the Old Bailey, and they were to await the verdict at Lady Kelsey's. Dick and Robert Boulger were subpoenaed as witnesses. In order that she might be put out of her suspense quickly, Lucy asked Alec MacKenzie to go into court and bring her the result as soon as it was known.

The morning passed with leaden feet.

After luncheon Mrs. Crowley came to sit with Lady Kelsey, and together they watched the minute hand go round the clock. Now the verdict might be expected at any moment. After some time Canon Spratte, the vicar of the church which Lady Kelsey attended, sent up to ask if he might see her; and Mrs. Crowley, thinking to distract her, asked him to come in. The Canon's breezy courtliness as a rule soothed Lady Kelsey's gravest troubles, but now she would not be comforted.

"I shall never get over it," she said, with a handkerchief to her eyes. "I shall never cease blaming myself. Nothing of all this would have happened, if it hadn't been for me."

Canon Spratte and Mrs. Crowley watched her without answering. She was a stout, amiable woman, who had clothed herself in black because the occasion was tragic. Grief had made her garrulous.

"Poor Fred came to me one day and said he must have eight thousand pounds at once. He told me his partner had cheated him, and it was a matter of life and death. But it was such a large sum, and I've given him so much already. After all, I've got to think of Lucy and George. They only have me to depend on, and I refused to give it. Oh, I'd have given every penny I own rather than have this horrible shame."

"You mustn't take it too much to heart, Lady Kelsey," said Mrs. Crowley. "It will soon be all over."

"Our ways have parted for some time now," said Canon Spratte, "but at one period I used to see a good deal of Fred Allerton. I can't tell you how distressed I was to hear of this terrible misfortune."

"He's always been unlucky," returned Lady Kelsey. "I only hope this will be a lesson to him. He's like a child in business matters. Oh, it's awful to think of my poor sister's husband standing in the felon's dock!"

"You must try not to think of it. I'm sure everything will turn out quite well. In another hour you'll have him with you again."

The Canon got up and shook hands with Lady Kelsey.

"It was so good of you to come," she said.

He turned to Mrs. Crowley, whom he liked because she was American, rich, and a widow.

"I'm grateful, too," she murmured, as she bade him farewell. "A clergyman always helps one so much to bear other people's misfortunes."

Canon Spratte smiled and made a mental note of the remark, which he thought would do very well from his own lips.

"Where is Lucy?" asked Mrs. Crowley, when he had gone.

Lady Kelsey threw up her hands with the feeling, half of amusement, half of annoyance, which a very emotional person has always for one who is self-restrained.

"She's sitting in her room, reading. She's been reading all day. Heaven only know how she can do it. I tried, and all the letters swam before my eyes. It drives me mad to see how calm she is."

They began to talk of the immediate future. Lady Kelsey had put a large sum at Lucy's disposal, and it was arranged that the two children should take their father to some place in the south of France where he could rest after the terrible ordeal.

"I don't know what they would all have done without you," said Mrs. Crowley. "You have been a perfect angel."

"Nonsense," smiled Lady Kelsey. "They're my only relations in the world, except Bobbie, who's very much too rich as it is, and I love Lucy and George as if they were my own children. What is the good of my money except to make them happy and comfortable?"

Mrs. Crowley remembered Dick's surmise that Lady Kelsey had loved Fred Allerton, and she wondered how much of the old feeling still remained. She felt a great pity for the kind, unselfish creature. Lady Kelsey started as she heard the street door slam. But it was only George who entered.

"Oh, George, where have you been? Why didn't you come in to luncheon?"

He looked pale and haggard. The strain of the last fortnight had told on him enormously, and it was plain that his excitement was almost unbearable.

"I couldn't eat anything. I've been walking about, waiting for the damned hours to pass. I wish I hadn't promised father not to go into court. Anything would have been better than this awful suspense. I saw the man who's defending him when they adjourned for luncheon, and he told me it was all right."

"Of course it's all right. You didn't imagine that your father would be found guilty."

"Oh, I knew he wouldn't have done a thing like that," said George impatiently. "But I can't help being frightfully anxious. The papers are awful. They've got huge placards out: *County gentleman of the Old Bailey. Society in a Bucket Shop.*"

George shivered with horror.

"Oh, it's awful!" he cried.

Lady Kelsey began to cry again, and Mrs. Crowley sat in silence, not knowing what to say. George walked about in agitation.

"But I know he's not guilty," moaned Lady Kelsey.

"If he's guilty or not he's ruined me," said George. "I can't go up to Oxford again after this. I don't know what the devil's to become of me. We're all utterly disgraced. Oh, how could he! How could he!"

"Oh, George, don't," said Lady Kelsey.

But George, with a weak man's petulance, could not keep back the bitter words that he had turned over in his heart so often since the brutal truth was told him.

"Wasn't it enough that he fooled away every penny he had, so that we're simply beggars, both of us, and we have to live on your charity? I should have though that would have satisfied him, without getting locked up for being connected in a beastly bucketshop swindle."

"George, how can you talk of your father like that!"

He gave a sort of sob and looked at her with wild eyes. But at that moment a cab drove up, and he sprang on to the balcony.

"It's Dick Lomas and Bobbie. They've come to tell us."

He ran to the door and opened it. They walked up the stairs.

"Well?" he cried. "Well?"

"It's not over yet. We left just as the judge was summing up."

"Damn you!" cried George, with an explosion of sudden fury.

"Steady, old man," said Dick.

"Why didn't you stay?" moaned Lady Kelsey.

"I couldn't," said Dick. "It was too awful."

"How was it going?"

"I couldn't make head or tail of it. My mind was in a whirl. I'm an hysterical old fool."

Mrs. Crowley went up to Lady Kelsey and kissed her.

"Why don't you go and lie down for a little while, dear," she said. "You look positively exhausted."

"I have a racking headache," groaned Lady Kelsey.

"Alec MacKenzie has promised to come here as soon as it's over. But you mustn't expect him for another hour."

"Yes, I'll go and lie down," said Lady Kelsey.

George, unable to master his impatience, flung open the window and stood on the balcony, watching for the cab that would bring the news.

"Go and talk to him, there's a good fellow," said Dick to Robert Boulger. "Cheer him up a bit."

"Yes, of course I will. It's rot to make a fuss now that it's nearly over. Uncle Fred will be here himself in an hour."

Dick looked at him without answering. When Robert had gone on to the balcony, he flung himself wearily in a chair.

"I couldn't stand it any longer," he said. "You can't imagine how awful it was to see that wretched man in the dock. He looked like a hunted beast, his face was all grey with fright, and once I caught his eyes. I shall never forget the look that was in them."

"But I thought he was bearing it so well," said Mrs. Crowley.

"You know, he's a man who's never looked the truth in the face. He never seemed to realise the gravity of the charges that were brought against him, and even when the magistrate refused to renew his bail, his confidence never deserted him. It was only today, when the whole thing was unrolled before him, that he appeared to understand. Oh, if you'd heard the evidence that was given! And then the pitiful spectacle of those two men trying to throw the blame on one another!"

A look of terror came into Mrs. Crowley's face.

"You don't think he's guilty?" she gasped.

Dick looked at her steadily, but did not answer.

"But Lucy's convinced that he'll be acquitted."

"I wonder."

"What on earth do you mean?"

Dick shrugged his shoulders.

"But he can't be guilty," cried Mrs. Crowley. "It's impossible."

Dick made an effort to drive away from his mind the dreadful fears that filled it.

"Yes, that's what I feel, too," he said. "With all his faults Fred Allerton can't have committed such a despicable crime. You've never met him, you don't know him; but I've known him intimately for twenty years. He couldn't have swindled that wretched woman out of every penny she had, knowing that it meant starvation to her. He couldn't have been so brutally cruel."

"Oh, I'm so glad to hear you say that."

Silence fell upon them for a while, and they waited. From the balcony they heard George talking rapidly, but they could not distinguish his words.

"I felt ashamed to stay in court and watch the torture of that unhappy man. I've dined with him times out of number; I've stayed at his house; I've ridden his horses. Oh, it was too awful."

He got up impatiently and walked up and down the room.

"It must be over by now. Why doesn't Alec come? He swore he'd bolt round the very moment the verdict was given."

"The suspense is dreadful," said Mrs. Crowley.

Dick stood still. He looked at the little American, but his eyes did not see her.

"There are some people who are born without a moral sense. They are as unable to distinguish between right and wrong as a man who is colour blind, between red and green."

"Why do you say that?" asked Mrs. Crowley.

He did not answer. She went up to him anxiously.

"Mr. Lomas, I can't bear it. You must tell me. Do *you* think he's guilty?"

He passed his hands over his eyes.

"The evidence was damnable."

At that moment George sprang into the room.

"There's Alec. He's just driving along in a cab."

"Thank God, thank God!" cried Mrs. Crowley. "If it had lasted longer I should have gone mad."

George went to the door.

"I must tell Miller. He has orders to let no one up."

He leaned over the banisters, as the bell of the front-door was rung.

"Miller, Miller, let Mr. MacKenzie in."

"Very good, sir," answered the butler.

Lucy had heard the cab drive up, and she came into the drawing-room with Lady Kelsey. The elder woman had broken down altogether and was sobbing distractedly. Lucy was very white, but otherwise quite composed. She shook hands with Dick and Mrs. Crowley.

"It was kind of you to come," she said.

"Oh, my poor Lucy," said Mrs. Crowley, with a sob in her voice.

Lucy smiled bravely.

"It's all over now."

Alec came in, and she walked eagerly towards him.

"Well? I was hoping you'd bring father with you. When is he coming?"

She stopped. She gave a gasp as she saw Alec's face. Though her cheeks were pale before, now their pallor was deathly.

"What is the matter?"

"Isn't it all right?" cried George.

Lucy put her hand on his arm to quieten him. It seemed that Alec could not find words. There was a horrible silence, but they all knew what he had to tell them.

"I'm afraid you must prepare yourself for a great unhappiness," he said.

"Where's father?" cried Lucy. "Where's father? Why didn't you bring him with you?"

With the horrible truth dawning upon her, she was losing her self-control. She made an effort. Alec would not speak, and she was obliged to question him. When the words came, her voice was hoarse and low.

"You've not told us what the verdict was."

"Guilty," he answered.

Then the colour flew back to her cheeks, and her eyes flashed with anger.

"But it's impossible. He was innocent. He swore that he hadn't done it. There must be some horrible mistake."

"I wish to God there were," said Alec.

"You don't think he's guilty?" she cried.

He did not answer, and for a moment they looked at one another steadily.

"What was the sentence?" she asked.

"The judge was dead against him. He made some very violent remarks as he passed it."

"Tell me what he said."

"Why should you wish to torture yourself?"

"I want to know."

"He seemed to think the fact that your father was a gentleman made the crime more odious, and the way in which he had induced that woman to part with her money made no punishment too severe. He sentenced him to seven years penal servitude."

George gave a cry and sinking into a chair, burst into tears. Lucy put her hand on his shoulder.

"Don't, George," she said. "You must bear up. Now we want all our courage, now more than ever."

"Oh, I can't bear it," he moaned.

She bent down and kissed him tenderly.

"Be brave, my dearest, be brave for my sake."

But he sobbed uncontrollably. It was a horribly painful sight. Dick took him by the arm and led him away. Lucy turned to Alec, who was standing where first he had stopped.

"I want to ask you a question. Will you answer me quite truthfully, whatever the pain you think it will cause me?"

"I will."

"You followed the trial from the beginning, you know all the details of it. Do *you* think my father is guilty?"

"What can it matter what I think?"

"I beg you to tell me."

Alec hesitated for a moment. His voice was very low.

"If I had been on the jury I'm afraid I should have had no alternative but to decide as they did."

Lucy bent her head, and heavy tears rolled down her cheeks.

Chapter VII

NEXT MORNING LUCY RECEIVED A NOTE FROM ALEC MACKENZIE, ASKING IF he might see her that day; he suggested calling upon her early in the afternoon and expressed the hope that he might find her alone. She sat in the library at Lady Kelsey's and waited for him. She held a book in her hands, but she could not read. And presently she began to weep. Ever since the dreadful news had reached her, Lucy had done her utmost to preserve her self-control, and all night she had lain with clenched hands to prevent herself from giving way. For George's sake and for her father's, she felt that she must keep her strength. But now the strain was too great for her; she was alone; the tears began to flow helplessly, and she made no effort to restrain them.

She had been allowed to see her father. Lucy and George had gone to prison, and she recalled now the details of the brief interview. The whole thing was horrible. She felt that her heart would break.

In the night indignation had seized Lucy. After reading accounts of the case in half a dozen papers she could not doubt that her father was justly condemned, and she was horrified at the baseness of the crime. His letters to the poor woman he had robbed, were read in court, and Lucy flushed as she thought of them. They were a tissue of lies, hypocritical and shameless. Lucy remembered the question she put to Alec and his answer.

But neither the newspapers nor Alec's words were needed to convince her of her father's guilt; in the very depths of her being, not withstanding the passion with which she reproached herself, she had been convinced of it. She would not acknowledge even to herself that she doubted him; and all her words, all her thoughts even, expressed a firm belief in his innocence; but a ghastly terror had lurked in some hidden recess of her consciousness. It haunted her soul like a mysterious shadow which there was no bodily shape to explain. The fear had caught her, as though with material hands, when first the news of his arrest was brought to Court Leys by Robert Boulger, and again at her father's flat in Shaftesbury Avenue, when she saw a secret shame cowering behind the good-humoured flippancy of his smile. Notwithstanding his charm of manner and the tenderness of his affection for his children, she had known that he was a liar and a rascal. She hated him.

But when Lucy saw him, still with the hunted look that Dick had noticed at the trial, so changed from when last they had met, her anger melted away, and she felt only pity. She reproached herself bitterly. How could she be so heartless when he was suffering? At first he could not speak. He looked from one to the other of his children silently, with appealing eyes; and he saw the utter wretchedness which was on George's face. George was ashamed to look at him and kept his eyes averted. Fred Allerton was suddenly grown old and bent; his poor face was sunken, and the skin had an ashy look like that of a dying man. He had already a cringing air, as if he must shrink away from his fellows. It was horrible to Lucy that she was not allowed to take him in her arms. He broke down utterly and sobbed.

"Oh, Lucy, you don't hate me?" he whispered.

"No, I've never loved you more than I love you now," she said.

And she said it truthfully. Her conscience smote her, and she wondered bitterly what she had left undone that might have averted this calamity.

"I didn't mean to do it," he said, brokenly.

Lucy looked at his poor, worried eyes. It seemed very cruel that she might not kiss them.

"I'd have paid her everything if she'd only have given me time. Luck was against me all through. I've been a bad father to both of you."

Lucy was able to tell him that Lady Kelsey would pay the eight thousand pounds the woman had lost. The good creature had thought of it even before Lucy made the suggestion. At all events none of them need have on his conscience the beggary of that unfortunate person.

"Alice was always a good soul," said Allerton. He clung to Lucy as though she were his only hope. "You won't forget me while I'm away, Lucy?"

"I'll come and see you whenever I'm allowed to."

"It won't be very long. I hope I shall die quickly."

"You mustn't do that. You must keep well and strong for my sake and George's. We shall never cease to love you, father."

"What's going to happen to George now?" he asked.

"We shall find something for him. You need not worry about him."

George flushed. He could find nothing to say. He was ashamed and angry. He wanted to get away quickly from that place of horror, and he was relieved when the warden told them it was time to go.

"Good-bye, George," said Fred Allerton.

"Good-bye."

He kept his eyes sullenly fixed on the ground. The look of despair in Allerton's face grew more intense. He saw that his son hated him. And it had been on him that all his light affection was placed. He had been very proud of the handsome boy. And now his son merely wanted to be rid of him. Bitter words rose to his lips, but his heart was too heavy to utter them, and they expressed themselves only in a sob.

"Forgive me for all I've done against you, Lucy."

"Have courage, father, we will never love you less."

He forced a sad smile to his lips. She included George in what she said, but he knew that she spoke only for herself. They went. And he turned away into the darkness.

Lucy's tears relieved her a little. They exhausted her, and so made her agony more easy to bear. It was necessary now to think of the future. Alec MacKenzie must be there soon. She wondered why he had written, and what he could have to say that mattered. She could only think of her father, and above all George. She dried her eyes, and with a deep sigh set herself methodically to consider the difficult problem.

When Alec came she rose gravely to receive him. For a moment he was overcome by her loveliness, and he gazed at her in silence. Lucy was a woman who was at her best in the tragic situations of life; her beauty was heightened by the travail of her soul, and the heaviness of her eyes gave a pathetic grandeur to her wan face. She advanced to meet sorrow with an unquailing glance, and Alec, who knew something of heroism, recognised the greatness of her heart. Of late he had been more than once to see that portrait of *Diana of the Uplands*, in which he, too, found the gracious healthiness of Lucy Allerton; but now she seemed like some sad queen, English to the very bones, who bore with a royal dignity an intolerable grief, and yet by the magnificence of her spirit turned into something wholly beautiful.

"You must forgive me for forcing myself upon you today," he said slowly. "But my time is very short, and I wanted to speak to you at once."

"It is very good of you to come." She was embarrassed, and did not know what exactly to say. "I am always very glad to see you."

He looked at her steadily, as though he were turning over in his mind her commonplace words. She smiled.

"I wanted to thank you for your great kindness to me during these two or three weeks. You've been very good to me, and you've helped me to bear all that—I've had to bear."

"I would do far more for you than that," he answered. Suddenly it flashed through her mind why he had come. Her heart gave a great beat against her chest. The though had never entered her head. She sat down and waited for him to speak. He did not move. There was a singular immobility about him when something absorbed his mind.

"I wrote and asked if I might see you alone, because I had something that I wanted to say to you. I've wanted to say it ever since we were at Court Leys together, but I was going away—heaven only knows when I shall come back, and perhaps something may happen to me—and I thought it was unfair to you to speak."

He paused. His eyes were fixed upon hers. She waited for him to go on.

"I wanted to ask you if you would marry me."

She drew a long breath. Her face kept its expression of intense gravity.

"It's very kind and chivalrous of you to suggest it. You mustn't think me ungrateful if I tell you I can't."

"Why not?" he asked quietly.

"I must look after my father. If it is any use I shall go and live near the prison."

"There is no reason why you should not do that if you married me."

She shook her head.

"No, I must be free. As soon as my father is released I must be ready to live with him. And I can't take an honest man's name. It looks as if I were running away from my own and taking shelter elsewhere."

She hesitated for a while, since it made her very shy to say what she had in mind. When she spoke it was in a low and trembling voice.

"You don't know how proud I was of my name and my family. For centuries they've been honest, decent people, and I felt that we'd had a part in the making of England. And now I feel utterly ashamed. Dick Lomas laughed at me because I was so proud of my family. I daresay I was stupid. I never paid much attention to rank and that kind of thing, but it did seem to me that family was different. I've seen my father, and he simply doesn't realise for a moment that he's done something horribly mean and shameful. There must be some taint in our nature. I couldn't marry you; I should be afraid that my children would inherit the rottenness of my blood."

He listened to what she said. Then he went up to her and put his hands on her shoulders. His calmness, and the steadiness of his voice seemed to quiete her.

"I think you will be able to help your father and George better if you are my wife. I'm afraid your position will be very difficult. Won't you give me the great happiness of helping you?"

"We must stand on our own feet. I'm very grateful, but you can do nothing for us."

"I'm very awkward and stupid, I don't know how to say what I want. I think I loved you from that first day at Court Leys. I did not understand then what had happened; I suddenly felt that something new and strange had come into my life. And day by day I loved you more, and then it took up my whole soul. I've never loved anyone but you. I never can love anyone but you. I've been looking for you all my life."

She could not stand the look of his eyes, and she cast hers down. He saw the exquisite shadow of her eyelashes on her cheek.

"But I didn't dare say anything to you then. Even if you had cared for me, it seemed unfair to bind you to me when I was starting on this expedition. But now I must speak. I go in a week. It would give me so much strength and courage if I knew that I had your love. I love you with all my heart."

She looked up at him now, and her eyes were shining with tears, but they were not the tears of a hopeless pain.

"I can't marry you now. It would be unfair to you. I owe myself entirely to my father."

He dropped his hands from her shoulders and stepped back.

"It must be as you will."

"But don't think I'm ungrateful," she said. "I'm so proud that I have your love. It seems to left me up from the depths. You don't know how much good you have done me."

"I wanted to help you, and you will let me do nothing for you."

On a sudden a thought flashed through her. She gave a little cry of amazement, for here was the solution of her greatest difficulty.

"Yes, you can do something for me. Will you take George with you?"

"George?"

He remained silent for a moment, while he considered the proposition.

"I can trust him in your hands. You will make a good and a strong man of him. Oh, won't you give him this chance of washing out the stain that is on our name?"

"Do you know that he will have to undergo hunger and thirst and every kind of hardship? It's not a picnic that I'm going on."

"I'm willing that he should undergo everything. The cause is splendid. His self-respect is wavering in the balance. If he gets to noble work he will feel himself a man."

"There will be a good deal of fighting. It has seemed foolish to dwell on the dangers that await me, but I do realise that they are greater than I have ever faced before. This time it is win or die."

"The dangers can be no greater than those his ancestors have taken cheerfully."

"He may be wounded or killed."

Lucy hesitated for an instant. The words she uttered came from unmoving lips.

"If he dies a brave man's death I can ask for nothing more."

Alec smiled at her infinite courage. He was immensely proud of her.

"Then tell him that I shall be glad to take him."

"May I call him now?"

Alec nodded. She rang the bell and told the servant who came that she wished to see her brother. George came in. The strain of the last fortnight, the horrible shock of his father's conviction, had told on him far more than on Lucy. He looked worn and ill. He was broken down with shame. The corners of his mouth drooped querulously, and his handsome face bore an expression of utter misery. Alec looked at him steadily. He felt infinite pity for his youth, and there was a charm of manner about him, a way of appealing for sympathy, which touched the strong man. He wondered what character the boy had. His heart went out to him, and he loved him already because he was Lucy's brother.

"George, Mr. MacKenzie has offered to take you with him to Africa," she said eagerly. "Will you go?"

"I'll go anywhere so long as I can get out of this beastly country," he answered wearily. "I feel people are looking at me in the street when I go out, and they're saying to one another: there's the son of that swindling rotter who was sentenced to seven years."

He wiped the palms of his hands with his handkerchief.

"I don't mind what I do. I can't go back to Oxford; no one would speak to me. There's nothing I can do in England at all. I wish to God I were dead."

"George, don't say that."

"It's all very well for you. You're a girl, and it doesn't matter. Do you suppose anyone would trust me with sixpence now? Oh, how could he? How could he?"

"You must try and forget it, George," said Lucy, gently.

The boy pulled himself together and gave Alec a charming smile.

"It's awfully ripping of you to take pity on me."

"I want you to know before you decide that you'll have to rough it all the time. It'll be hard and dangerous work."

"Well, as far as I'm concerned it's Hobson's choice, isn't it?" he answered, bitterly.

Alec held out his hand, with one of his rare, quiet smiles.

"I hope we shall pull well together and be good friends."

"And when you come back, George, everything will be over. I wish I were a man so that I might go with you. I wish I had your chance. You've got everything before you, George. I think no man has ever had such an opportunity. All our hope is in you. I want to be proud of you. All my self-respect depends on you. I want you to distinguish yourself, so that I may feel once more honest and strong and clean."

Her voice was trembling with a deep emotion, and George, quick to respond, flushed.

"I am a selfish beast," he cried. "I've been thinking of myself all the time. I've never given a thought to you."

"I don't want you to: I only want you to be brave and honest and steadfast."

The tears came to his eyes, and he put his arms around her neck. He nestled against her heart as a child might have done.

"It'll be awfully hard to leave you, Lucy."

"It'll be harder for me, dear, because you will be doing great and heroic things, while I shall be able only to wait and watch. But I want you to go." Her voice broke, and she spoke almost in a whisper. "And don't forget that you're going for my sake as well as for your own. If you did anything wrong or disgraceful it would break my heart."

"I swear to you that you'll never be ashamed of me, Lucy," he said.

She kissed him and smiled. Alec had watched them silently. His heart was very full.

"But we mustn't be silly and sentimental, or Mr. MacKenzie will think us a pair of fools." She looked at him gaily. "We're both very grateful to you."

"I'm afraid I'm starting almost at once," he said. "George must be ready in a week."

"George can be ready in twenty-four hours if need be," she answered.

The boy walked towards the window and lit a cigarette. He wanted to steady his nerves.

"I'm afraid I shall be able to see little of you during the next few days," said Alec. "I have a great deal to do, and I must run up to Lancashire for the week-end."

"I'm sorry."

"Won't you change your mind?"

She shook her head.

"No, I can't do that. I must have complete freedom."

"And when I come back?"

She smiled delightfully.

"When you come back, if you still care, ask me again."

"And the answer?"

"The answer perhaps will be different."

Chapter VIII

A WEEK LATER ALEC MACKENZIE AND GEORGE ALLERTON STARTED FROM Charing Cross. They were to go by P. & O. from Marseilles to Aden, and there catch a German boat which would take them to Mombassa. Lady Kelsey was far too distressed to see her nephew off; and Lucy was glad, since it gave her the chance of driving to the station alone with George. She found Dick Lomas and Mrs. Crowley already there. When the train steamed away, Lucy was standing a little apart from the others. She was quite still. She did not even wave her hand, and there was little expression on her face. Mrs. Crowley was crying cheerfully, and she dried her eyes with a tiny handkerchief. Lucy turned to her and thanked her for coming.

"Shall I drive you back in the carriage?" sobbed Mrs. Crowley.

"I think I'll take a cab, if you don't mind," Lucy answered quietly. "Perhaps you'll take Dick."

She did not bid them good-bye, but walked slowly away.

"How exasperating you people are!" cried Mrs. Crowley. "I wanted to throw myself in her arms and have a good cry on the platform. You have no heart."

Dick walked along by her side, and they got into Mrs. Crowley's carriage. She soliloquised.

"I thank God that I have emotions, and I don't mind if I do show them. I was the only person who cried. I knew I should cry, and I brought three handkerchiefs on purpose. Look at them." She pulled them out of her bag and thrust them into Dick's hand. "They're soaking."

"You say it with triumph," he smiled.

"I think you're all perfectly heartless. Those two boys were going away for heaven knows how long on a dangerous journey, and they may never come back, and you and Lucy said good-bye to them just as if they were going off for a day's golf. I was the only one who said I was sorry, and that we should miss them dreadfully. I hate this English coldness. When I go to America, it's ten to one nobody comes to see me off, and if anyone does he just nods and says 'Good-bye, I hope you'll have a jolly time.' "

"Next time you go I will come and hurl myself on the ground, and gnash my teeth and shriek at the top of my voice."

"Oh, yes, do. And then I'll cry all the way to Liverpool, and I shall have a racking headache and feel quite miserable and happy."

Dick meditated for a moment.

"You see, we have an instinctive horror of exhibiting our emotion. I don't know why it is, I supposed training or the inheritance of our sturdy fathers, but we're ashamed to let people see what we feel. But I don't know whether on that account our feelings are any the less keen. Don't you think there's a certain beauty in a grief that forbids itself all expression? You know, I admire Lucy tremendously, and as she came towards us on the platform I thought there was something very fine in her calmness."

"Fiddlesticks!" said Mrs. Crowley, sharply. "I should have liked her much better if she had clung to her brother and sobbed and had to be torn away."

"Did you notice that she left us without even shaking hands? It was a very small omission, but it meant that she was quite absorbed in her grief."

They reached Mrs. Crowley's tiny house in Norfolk Street, and she asked Dick to come in.

"Sit down and read the paper," she said, "while I go and powder my nose."

Dick made himself comfortable. He blessed the charming woman when a butler of imposing dimensions brought in all that was necessary to make a cocktail. Mrs. Crowley cultivated England like a museum specimen. She had furnished her drawing-room with Chippendale furniture of an exquisite pattern. No chintzes were so smartly calendared as hers, and on the walls were mezzotints of the ladies whom Sir Joshua had painted. The chimney-piece was adorned with Lowestoft china, and on the silver table was a collection of old English spoons. She had chosen her butler because he went so well with the house. His respectability was portentous, his gravity was never disturbed by the shadow of a smile; and Mrs. Crowley treated him as though he were a piece of decoration, with an impertinence that fascinated him. He looked upon her as an outlandish freak, but his heavy British heart was surrendered to her entirely, and he watched over her with a solicitude that amused and touched her.

Dick thought that the little drawing-room was very comfortable, and when Mrs. Crowley returned, after an unconscionable time at the toilet-table, he was in the happiest mood. She gave a rapid glance at the glasses.

"You're a perfect hero," she said. "You've waited till I came down to have your cocktail."

"Richard Lomas, madam, is the soul of courtesy," he replied, with a flourish. "Besides, base is the soul that drinks in the morning by himself. At night, in your slippers and without a collar, with a pipe in your mouth and a good book in your hand, a solitary glass of whisky and soda is eminently desirable; but the anteprandial cocktail needs the sparkle of conversation."

"You seem to be in excellent health," said Mrs. Crowley.

"I am. Why?"

"I saw in yesterday's paper that your doctor had ordered you to go abroad for the rest of the winter."

"My doctor received the two guineas, and I wrote the prescription," returned Dick. "Do you remember that I explained to you the other day at length my intention of retiring into private life?"

"I do. I strongly disapprove of it."

"Well, I was convinced that if I relinquished my duties without any excuse people would say I was mad and shut me up in a lunatic asylum. I invented a breakdown in my health, and everything is plain sailing. I've got a pair for the rest of the session, and at the general election the excellent Robert Boulger will step into my unworthy shoes."

"And supposing you regret the step you've taken?"

"In my youth I imagined, with the romantic fervour of my age, that in life everything was irreparable. That is a delusion. One of the greatest advantages of life is that hardly anything is. One can make ever so many fresh starts. The average man lives long enough for a good many experiments, and it's they that give life its savour."

"I don't approve of this flippant way you talk of life," said Mrs. Crowley severely. "It seems to me something infinitely serious and complicated."

"That is an illusion of moralists. As a matter of fact, it's merely what you make it. Mine is quite light and simple."

Mrs. Crowley looked at Dick reflectively.

"I wonder why you never married," she said.

"I can tell you easily. Because I have a considerable gift for repartee. I discovered in my early youth that men propose not because they want to marry, but because on certain occasions they are entirely at a loss for topics of conversation."

"It was a momentous discovery," she smiled.

"No sooner had I made it than I began to cultivate my powers of small-talk. I felt that my only chance was to be ready with appropriate subjects at the smallest notice, and I spent a considerable part of my last year at Oxford in studying the best masters."

"I never noticed that you were particularly brilliant," murmured Mrs. Crowley, raising her eyebrows.

"I never played for brilliancy, I played for safety. I flatter myself that when prattle was needed, I have never been found wanting. I have met the ingenuousness of sweet seventeen with a few observations on Free Trade, while the haggard effects of thirty have struggled in vain against a brief exposition of the higher philosophy."

"When people talk higher philosophy to me I make it a definite rule to blush," said Mrs. Crowley.

"The skittish widow of uncertain age has retired in disorder before a complete acquaintance with the Restoration dramatists, and I have frequently routed the serious spinster with religious leanings by my remarkable knowledge of the results of missionary endeavour in Central America. Once a dowager sought to ask me my intentions, but I flung at her astonished head an article from the Encyclopedia Brittanica. An America *divorcée* swooned when I poured into her shell-like ear a few facts about the McKinley Tariff. These are only my serious efforts. I need not tell you how often I have evaded a flash of the eyes by an epigram, or ignored a sigh by an apt quotation from the poets."

"I don't believe a word you say," retorted Mrs. Crowley. "I believe you never married for the simple reason that nobody would have you."

"Do me the justice to acknowledge that I'm the only man who's known you for ten days without being tempted by those coal-mines of yours in Pennsylvania to offer you his hand and heart."

"I don't believe the coal has anything to do with it," answered Mrs. Crowley. "I put it down entirely to my very considerable personal attractions."

Dick looked at the time and found that the cocktail had given him an appetite. He asked Mrs. Crowley if she would lunch with him, and gaily they set out for a fashionable restaurant. Neither of them gave a thought to Alec and George speeding towards the unknown, nor to Lucy shut up in her room, given over to utter misery.

For Lucy it was the first of many dreary days. Dick went to Naples, and enjoying his new-won idleness, did not even write to her. Mrs. Crowley, after deciding on a trip to Egypt, was called to America by the illness of a sister; and Lady Kelsey, unable to stand the rigour of a Northern winter, set out for Nice. Lucy refused to accompany her. Though she knew it would be impossible to see her father, she could not bear to leave England; she could not face the gay people who thronged the Riviera, while he was bound to degrading tasks. The luxury of her own life horrified her when she compared it with his hard fare; and she could not look upon the comfortable rooms she lived in, with their delicate refinements, without thinking of the bare cell to which he was confined. Lucy was glad to be alone.

She went nowhere, but passed her days in solitude, striving to acquire peace of mind; she took long walks in the parks with her dogs, and spent much time in the picture galleries. Without realising the effect they had upon her, she felt vaguely the calming influence of beautiful things; often she would sit in the National Gallery before some royal picture, and the joy of it would fill her soul with quiet relief. Sometimes she would go to those majestic statues that decorated the pediment of the Parthenon, and the tears welled up in her clear eyes as she thanked the gods for the graciousness of their peace. She did not often listen to music, for then she could remain no longer mistress of her emotions; the tumultuous sounds of a symphony, the final anguish of *Tristan,* made vain all her efforts at self-control; and when she got home, she could only throw herself on her bed and weep passionately.

In reading she found her greatest solace. Many things that Alec had said returned dimly to her memory; and she began to read the Greek writers who had so profoundly affected him. She found a translation of Euripides which gave her some impression of the original, and her constant mood was answered by those old, exquisite tragedies. The complexity of that great poet, his doubt, despair, and his love of beauty, spoke to her heart as no modern writer could; and in the study of those sad deeds, in which men seemed always playthings of the fates, she found a relief to her own keen sorrow. She did not reason it out with herself, but almost unconsciously the thought came to her that the slings and arrows of the gods could be transformed into beauty by resignation and courage. Nothing was irreparable but a man's own weakness, and even in shame, disaster, and poverty, it was possible to lead a life that was not without grandeur. The man who was beaten to the ground by an outrageous fortune might be a finer thing than the unseeing, cruel powers that conquered him.

It was in this wise that Lucy battled with the intolerable shame that oppressed her. In that quiet corner of Hampshire in which her early years had been spent, among the memories of her dead kindred, the pride of her race had grown to unreasonable proportions; and now in the reaction she was terrified lest its decadence was in her, too, and in George. She could do nothing but suffer whatever pain it pleased the gods to send; but George was a man. In him were placed all her hopes. But now and again wild panic seized her. Then the agony was too great to bear, and she pressed her hands to her eyes in order to drive away the hateful thought: what if George failed her? She knew well enough that he had his father's engaging ways and his father's handsome face; but his father had had a smile as frank and a charm as great. What if with the son, too, they betokened only insincerity and weakness? A malicious devil whispered in her ear that now and again she had averted her eyes in order not to see George do things she hated. But it was youth that drove him. She had taken care to keep from him knowledge of the sordid struggles that occupied her, and how could she wonder if he was reckless and uncaring? She would not doubt him, she could not doubt him, for if anything went wrong with him there was no hope left. She could only cease to believe in herself.

When Lucy was allowed to write to her father, she set herself to cheer him. The thought that over five years must elapse before she would have him by her side once more, paralysed her pen; but she would not allow herself to be discouraged.

And she sought to give courage to him. She wanted him to see that her love was undiminished, and that he could count on it. Presently she received a letter from him. After a few weeks, the unaccustomed food, the change of life, had told upon him; and a general breakdown in his health had driven him into the infirmary. Lucy was thankful for the respite which his illness afforded. It must be a little less dreary in a prison hospital than in a prison cell.

A letter came from George, and another from Alec. Alec's was brief, telling of their journey down the Red Sea and their arrival at Mombassa; it was abrupt and awkward, making no reference to his love, or to the engagement which she had almost promised to make when he returned. He began and ended quite formally. George, apparently in the best of spirits, wrote as he always did, in a boyish, inconsequent fashion. His letter was filled with slang and gave no news. There was little to show that it was written from Mombassa, on the verge of a dangerous expedition into the interior, rather than from Oxford on the eve of a football match. But she read them over and over again. They were very matter of fact, and she smiled as she thought of Julia Crowley's indignation if she had seen them.

From her recollection of Alec's words, Lucy tried to make out the scene that first met her brother's eyes. She seemed to stand by his side, leaning over the rail, as the ship approached the harbour. The sea was blue with a blue she had never seen, and the sky was like an inverted bowl of copper. The low shore, covered with bush, stretched away in the distance; a line of waves was breaking on the reef. They came in sight of the island of Mombassa, with the overgrown ruins of a battery that had once commanded the entrance; and there were white-roofed houses, with deep verandas, which stood in little clearings with coral cliffs below them. On the opposite shore thick groves of palm-trees rose with their singular, melancholy beauty. Then as the channel narrowed, they passed an old Portuguese fort which carried the mind back to the bold adventurers who had first sailed those distant seas, and directly afterwards a mass of white buildings that reached to the edge of the lapping waves. They saw the huts of the native town, wattled and thatched, nestling close together; and below them was a fleet of native craft. On the jetty was the African crowd, shouting and jostling, some half-naked, and some strangely clad, Arabs from across the sea, Swahilis, and here and there a native from the interior.

In course of time other letters came from George, but Alec wrote no more. The days passed slowly. Lady Kelsey returned from the Riviera. Dick came back from Naples to enjoy the pleasures of the London season. He appeared thoroughly to enjoy his idleness, signally falsifying the predictions of those who had told him that it was impossible to be happy without regular work. Mrs. Crowley settled down once more in her house in Norfolk Street. During her absence she had written reams by every post to Lucy, and Lucy had looked forward very much to seeing her again. The little American was almost the only one of her friends with whom she did not feel shy. The apartness which her nationality gave her, made Mrs. Crowley more easy to talk to. She was too fond of Lucy to pity her. The general election came before it was expected, and Robert Boulger succeeded to the seat which Dick Lomas was only too glad to vacate. Bobbie was very charming. He surrounded Lucy with a protecting care, and she could not fail to be touched by his entire devotion. When he thought she had recovered somewhat from the first blow of her father's sentence, he sent her a letter in which once more he besought her to marry him. She was grateful to him for having chosen that method of expressing himself, for it seemed possible in writing to tell him with greater tenderness that if she could not accept his love she deeply valued his affection.

It seemed to Lucy that the life she led in London, or at Lady Kelsey's house on the river, was no more than a dream. She was but a figure in the procession of shadow pictures cast on a sheet in a fair, and nothing that she did signified. Her spirit was away in the heart of Africa, and by a vehement effort of her fancy she sought to see what each day her friend and her brother were doing.

Now they had long left the railway and such civilisation as was to be found in the lands where white men had already made their mark. She knew the exultation which Alec felt, and the thrill of independence, when he left behind him all traces of it. He held himself more proudly because he knew that thenceforward he must rely on his own resources, and success or failure depended only on himself.

Often as she lay awake and saw the ghostly dawn steal across the sky, she seemed borne to the African camp, where the break of day, like a gust of wind in a field of ripe corn, brought a sudden stir among the sleepers. Alec had described to her so minutely the changing scene that she was able to bring it vividly before her eyes. She saw him come out of his tent, in heavy boots, buckling on his belt. He wore knee-breeches and a pith helmet, and he was more bronzed than when she had bidden him farewell. He gave the order to the headman of the caravan to take up the loads. At the word there was a rush from all parts of the camp; each porter seized his load, carrying it off to lash on his mat and his cooking-pot, and then, sitting upon it, ate a few grains of roasted maize or the remains of last night's game. And as the sun appeared above the horizon, Alec, as was his custom, led the way, followed by a few *askari*. A band of natives struck up a strange and musical chant, and the camp, but now a scene of busy life, was deserted. The smouldering fires dieed out with the rising sun, and the silent life of the forest replaced the chatter and the hum of human kind. Giant beetles came from every quarter and carried away pieces of offal; small shy beasts stole out to gnaw the white bones upon which savage teeth had left but little; a gaunt hyena, with suspicious looks, snatched at a bone and dashed back into the jungle. Vultures settled down heavily, and with the deliberate air sought out the foulest refuse.

Then Lucy followed Alec upon his march, with his fighting men and his long string of porters. They went along a narrow track, pushing their way through bushes and thorns, or tall rank grass, sometimes with difficulty forcing through elephant reeds which closed over their heads and showered the cold dew down on their faces. Sometimes they passed through villages, with rich soul and extensive population; sometimes they plunged into heavy forests of gigantic trees, festooned with creepers, where the silence was unbroken even by the footfall of the traveller on the bottomless carpet of leaves; sometimes they traversed vast swamps, hurrying to avoid the deadly fever, and sometimes scrub jungles, in which as far as the eye could reach was a forest of cactus and thorn bush. Sometimes they made their way through grassy uplands with trees as splendid as those of an English park, and sometimes they toiled painfully along a game-track that ran by the bank of a swift-rushing river.

At midday a halt was called. The caravan had opened out by them; men who were sick or had stopped to adjust a load, others who were weak or lazy, had lagged behind; but at last they were all there; and the rear guard, perhaps with George in charge of it, whose orders were on no account to allow a single man to remain behind them, reported that no one was missing. During the heat of noon they made fires and cooked food. Presently they set off once more and marched till sundown.

When they reached the place which had been fixed on for camping, a couple of shots were fired as signals; and soon the natives, men and women, began to stream in with little baskets of grain or flour, with potatoes and chickens, and perhaps a pot or two of honey. Very quickly the tents were pitched, the bed gear arranged, the loads counted and stacked. The party whose duty it was to construct the *zeriba* cut down boughts and dragged them in to form a fence. Each little band of men selected the site for their bivouac; one went off to collect materials to build the huts, another to draw water, a third for firewood and stones, on which to place the cooking-pot. At sunset the headmen blew his whistle and asked if all were present. A lusty chorus replied. He reported to his chief and received the orders for the next day's march.

Alec had told Lucy that from the cry that goes up in answer to the headman's whistle, you could always gauge the spirit of the men. If game had been shot, or from scarcity the caravan had come to a land of plenty, there was a perfect babel of voices. But if the march had been long and hard, or if food had been issued for a number of days, of which this was the last, isolated voices replied; and perhaps one, bolder than the rest, cried out: I am hungry.

Then Alec and George, and the others sat down to their evening meal, while the porters, in little parties, were grouped around their huge pots of porridge. A little chat, a smoke, an exchange of sporting anecdotes, and the white men turned in. And Alec, gazing on the embers of his camp fire was alone with his thoughts: the silence of the night was upon him, and he looked up at the stars that shone in their countless myriads in the blue African sky. Lucy got up and stood at her open window. She, too, looked up at the sky, and she thought that she saw the same stars as he did. Now in that last half-hour, free from the burden of the day, with everyone at rest, he could give himself over to his thoughts, and his thoughts surely were of her.

During the months that had passed since Alec left England, Lucy's love had grown. In her solitude there was nothing else to give brightness to her life, and little by little it filled her heart. Her nature was so strong that she could do nothing by half measures, and it was with a feeling of extreme relief that she surrendered herself to this overwhelming passion. It seemed to her that she was growing in a different direction. The yearning of her soul for someone on whom to lean was satisfied at last. Hitherto the only instincts that had been fostered in her were those that had been useful to her father and George; they had needed her courage and her self-reliance. It was very comfortable to depend entirely upon Alec's love. Here she could be weak, here she could find a greater strength which made own seem puny. Lucy's thoughts were absorbed in the man whom really she knew so little. She exulted in his unselfish striving and in his firmness of purpose, and when she compared herself with him she felt unworthy. She treasured every recollection she had of him. She went over in mind all that she had heard him say, and reconstructed the conversations they had had together. She walked where they once walked, remembering how the sky had looked on those days and what flowers then bloomed in the parks; she visited the galleries they had seen in one another's company, and stood before the pictures which he had lingered at. And notwithstanding all there was to torment and humiliate her, she was happy. Something had come into her life which made all else tolerable. It was easy to hear the extremity of grief when he loved her.

After a long time Dick received a letter from Alec. MacKenzie was not a good letter-writer. He had no gift of self-expression, and when he had a pen in his hand seemed to be seized with an invincible shyness. The letter was dry and wooden. It was dated from the last trading-station before he set out into the wild country which was to be the scene of his operations. It said that hitherto everything had gone well with him, and the white men, but for fever occasionally, were bearing the climate well. One, named Macinnery, had made a nuisance of himself, and had been sent back to the coast. Alec gave no reasons for this step. He had been busy making the final arrangements. A company had been formed, the North East African Trading Company, to exploit the commercial possibilities of these unworked districts, and a charter had been given them; but the unsettled state of the land had so hampered them that the directors had gladly accepted Alec's offer to join their forces with his, and the traders at their stations had been instructed to take service under to sixteen. He had drilled the Swahilis whom he had brought from the coast, and given them guns, so that he had now an armed force of four hundred men. He was collecting levies from the native tribes, and he gave the outlandish names of the chiefs, armed with spears, who were to accompany him. The power of Mohammed the Lame was on the wane; for, during the three months which Alec had spent in England, an illness had seized him, which the natives asserted was a magic spell cast on him by one of his wives; and a son of his, taking advantage of this, had revolted and fortified himself in a stockade. The dying Sultan had taken the field against him, and this division of forces made Alec's position immeasurably stronger.

Dick handed Lucy the letter, and watched her while she read it.

"He says nothing about George," he said.

"He's evidently quite well."

Though it seemed strange that Alec made no mention of the boy, Dick said no more. Lucy appeared to be satisfied, and that was the chief thing. But he could not rid his mind of a certain uneasiness. He had received with misgiving Lucy's plan that George should accompany Alec. He could not help wondering whether those frank blue eyes and that facile smile did not conceal a nature as shallow as Fred Allerton's. But, after all, it was the boy's only chance, and he must take it.

Then an immense silence followed. Alec disappeared into those unknown countries as a man disappears into the night, and no more was heard of him. None knew how he faced. Not even a rumour reached the coast of success or failure. When he had crossed the mountains that divided the British protectorate from the lands that were to all intents independent, he vanished with his followers from human ken. The months passed, and there was nothing. It was a year now since he had arrived at Mombassa, then it was a year since the last letter had come from him. It was only possible to guess that behind those gaunt rocks fierce battles were fought, new lands explored, and the slavers beaten back foot by foot. Dick sought to persuade himself that the silence was encouraging, for it seemed to him that if the expedition had been cut to pieces the rejoicing of the Arabs would have spread itself abroad, and some news of a disaster would have travelled through Somaliland to the coast, or been carried by traders to Zanzibar. He made frequent inquiries at the Foreign Office, but there, too, nothing was known. The darkness had fallen upon them.

But Lucy suffered neither from anxiety nor fear. She had an immense confidence in Alec, and she believed in his strength, his courage, and his star. He had told her that he would not return till he had accomplished his task, and she expected to hear nothing till he had brought it to a triumphant conclusion. She did her little to help him. For at length the directors of the North East African Trading Company, growing anxious, proposed to get a question asked in Parliament, or to start an outcry in the newspapers which should oblige the government to send out a force to relieve Alec if he were in difficulties, or avenge him if he were dead. But Lucy knew that there was nothing Alec dreaded more than official interference. He was convinced that if this work could be done at all, he alone could do it; and she influenced Robert Boulger and Dick Lomas to use such means as they could to prevent anything from being done. She was certain that all Alec needed was time and a free hand.

Chapter IX

But the monotonous round of Lucy's life, with its dreams and its fond imaginings, was interrupted by news of a different character. An official letter came to her from Parkhurst to say that the grave state of her father's health had decided the authorities to remit the rest of his sentence, and he would be set free the next day but one at eight o'clock in the morning. She knew not whether to feel relief or sorrow; for if she was thankful that the wretched man's torture was ended, she could not buy realise that his liberty was given him only because he was dying. Mercy had been shown him, and Fred Allerton, in sight of a freedom from which no human laws could bar him, was given up to die among those who loved him.

Lucy went down immediately to the Isle of Wight, and there engaged rooms in the house of a woman who had formerly served her at Hamlyn's Purlieu.

It was midwinter, and a cold drizzle was falling when she waited for him at the prison gates. Three years had passed since they had parted. She took him in her arms and kissed him silently. Her heart was too full for words. A carriage was waiting for them, and she drove to the lodging-house; breakfast was ready, and Lucy had seen that good things which he liked should be ready for him to eat. Fred Allerton looked wistfully at the clean table-cloth, and at the flowers and the dainty scones; but he shook his head. He did not speak, and the tears ran slowly down his cheeks. He sank wearily into a chair. Lucy tried to induce him to eat; she brought him a cup of tea, but he put it away. He looked at her with haggard, bloodshot eyes.

"Give me the flowers," he muttered.

They were his first words. There was a large bowl of daffodils in the middle of the table, and she took them out of the water, deftly dried their stalks, and gave them to him. He took them with trembling hands and pressed them to his heart, then he buried his face in them, and the tears ran afresh, bedewing the yellow flowers.

Lucy put her arm around her father's neck and placed her cheek against his.

"Don't, father," she whispered. "You must try and forget."

He leaned back, exhausted, and the pretty flowers fell at his feet.

"You know why they've let me out?" he said.

She kissed him, but did not answer.

"I'm so glad that we're together again," she murmured.

"It's because I'm going to die."

"No, you mustn't die. In a little while you'll get strong again. You have many years before you, and you'll be very happy."

He gave her a long, searching look; and when he spoke, his voice had a hollowness in it that was strangely terrifying.

"Do you think I want to live?"

The pain seemed almost greater than Lucy could bear, and for a moment she had to remain silent so that her voice might grow steady.

"You must live for my sake."

"Don't you hate me?" he asked.

"No, I love you more than I ever did. I shall never cease to love you."

"I suppose no one would marry you while I was in prison."

His remark was so inconsequent that Lucy found nothing to say. He gave a bitter, short laugh.

"I ought to have shot myself. Then people would have forgotten all about it, and you might have had a chance. Why didn't you marry Bobbie?"

"I haven't wanted to marry."

He was so tired that he could only speak a little at a time, and now he closed his eyes. Lucy thought that he was dozing, and began to pick up the fallen flowers. But he noticed what she was doing.

"Let me hold them," he moaned, with the pleading quaver of a sick child.

As she gave them to him once more, he took her hands and began to caress them.

"The only thing for me is to hurry up and finish with life. I'm in the way. Nobody wants me, and I shall only be a burden. I didn't want them to let me go. I wanted to die there quietly."

Lucy sighed deeply. She hardly recognised her father in the bent, broken man who was sitting beside her. He had aged very much and seemed now to be an old man, but it was a premature aging, and there was a horror in it as of a process contrary to nature. He was very thin, and his hands trembled constantly. Most of his teeth had gone; his cheeks were sunken, and he mumbled his words so that it was difficult to distinguish them. There was no light in his eyes, and his short hair was quite white. Now and again he was shaken with a racking cough, and this was followed by an attack of such pain in his heart that it was anguish even to watch it. The room was warm, but he shivered with cold and cowered over the roaring fire.

When the doctor whom Lucy had sent for, saw him, he could only shrug his shoulders.

"I'm afraid nothing can be done," he said. "His heart is all wrong, and he's thoroughly broken up."

"Is there no chance of recovery?"

"I'm afraid all we can do is to alleviate the pain."

"And how long can he live?"

"It's impossible to say. He may die tomorrow, he may last six months."

The doctor was an old man, and his heart was touched by the sight of Lucy's grief. He had seen more cases than one of this kind.

"He doesn't want to live. It will be a mercy when death releases him."

Lucy did not answer. When she returned to her father, she could not speak. He was apathetic and did not ask what the doctor had said. Lady Kelsey, hating the thought of Lucy and her father living amid the discomfort of furnished lodgings, had written to offer the use of her house in Charles Street; and Mrs. Crowley, in case they wanted complete solitude, had put Court Leys at their disposal. Lucy waited a few days to see whether her father grew stronger, but no change was apparent in him, and it seemed necessary at last to make some decision. She put before him the alternative plans, but he would have none of them.

"Then would you rather stay here?" she said.

He looked at the fire and did not answer. Lucy thought the sense of her question had escaped him, for often it appeared to her that his mind wandered. She was on the point of repeating it when he spoke.

"I want to go back to the Purlieu."

Lucy stifled a gasp of dismay. She stared at the wretched man. Had he forgotten? He thought that the house of his fathers was his still; and all that had parted him from it was gone from his memory. How could she tell him?

"I want to die in my own house," he faltered.

Lucy was in a turmoil of anxiety. She must make some reply. What he asked was impossible, and yet it was cruel to tell him the whole truth.

"There are people living there," she answered.

"Are there?" he said, indifferently.

He looked at the fire still. The silence was dreadful.

"When can we go?" he said at last. "I want to get there quickly."

Lucy hesitated.

"We shall have to go into rooms."

"I don't mind."

He seemed to take everything as a matter of course. It was clear that he had forgotten the catastrophe that had parted him from Hamlyn's Purlieu, and yet, strangely, he asked no questions. Lucy was tortured by the thought of revisiting the place she loved so well. She had been able to deaden her passionate regret only by keeping her mind steadfastly averted from all thought of it, and now she must actually go there. The old wounds would be opened. But it was impossible to refuse, and she set about making the necessary arrangements. The rector, who had been given the living by Fred Allerton, was an old friend, and Lucy knew that she could trust in his affection. She wrote and told him that her father was dying and had set his heart on seeing once more his old home. She asked him to find rooms in one of the cottages. She did not mind how small nor how humble they were. The rector answered by telegram. He begged Lucy to bring her father to stay with him. She would be more comfortable than in lodgings, and, since he was a bachelor, there was plenty of room in the large rectory. Lucy, immensely touched by his kindness, gratefully accepted the invitation.

Next day they took the short journey across the Solent.

The rector had been a don, and Fred Allerton had offered him the living in accordance with the family tradition that required a man of attainments to live in the neighbouring rectory. He had been there now for many years, a spare, grey-haired, gentle creature, who live the life of a recluse in that distant village, doing his duty exactly, but given over for the most part to his beloved books. He seldom went away. The monotony of his daily round was broken only by the occasional receipt of a parcel of musty volumes, which he had ordered to be bought for him at some sale. He was a man of varied learning, full of remote information, eccentric from his solitariness, but with a great sweetness of nature. His life was simple, and his wants were few.

In this house, in rooms lined from floor to ceiling with old books, Lucy and her father took up their abode. It seemed that Fred Allerton had been kept up only by the desire to get back to his native place, for he had no sooner arrived than he grew much worse. Lucy was busily occupied with nursing him and could give no time to the regrets which she had imagined would assail her. She spent long hours in her father's room; and while he dozed, half-comatose, the kindly parson sat by the window and read to her in a low voice from queer, forgotten works.

One day Allerton appeared to be far better. For a week he had wandered much in his mind, and more than once Lucy had suspected that the end was near; but now he was singularly lucid. He wanted to get up, and Lucy felt it would be brutal to balk any wish he had. He asked if he might go out. The day was fine and warm. It was February, and there was a feeling in the air as if the spring were at hand. In sheltered places the snowdrops and the crocuses gave the garden the blitheness of an Italian picture; and you felt that on that multi-coloured floor might fitly trip the delicate angels of Messer Peregino. The rector had an old pony-chaise, in which he was used to visit his parishioners, and in this all three drove out.

"Let us go down to the marshes," said Allerton.

They drove slowly along the winding road till they came to the broad salt marshes. Beyond glittered the placid sea. There was no wind. Near them a cow looked up from her grazing and lazily whisked her tail. Lucy's heart began to beat more quickly. She felt that her father, too, looked upon that scene as the most typical of his home. Other places had broad acres and fine trees, other places had forest land and purple heather, but there was something in those green flats that made them seem peculiarly their own. She took her father's hand, and silently their eyes looked onwards. A more peaceful look came into Fred Allerton's worn face, and the sigh that broke from him was not altogether of pain. Lucy prayed that it might still remain hidden from him that those fair, broad fields were his no longer.

That night she had an intuition that death was at hand. Fred Allerton was very silent. Since his release from prison he had spoken barely a dozen sentences a day, and nothing served to wake him from his lethargy. But there was a curious restlessness about him now, and he would not go to bed. He sat in an arm-chair, and begged them to draw it near the window. The sky was cloudless, and the moon shone brightly. Fred Allerton could see the great old elms that surrounded Hamlyn's Purlieu; and his eyes were fixed steadily upon them. Lucy saw them, too, and she thought sadly of the garden which she had loved so well, and of the dear trees which old masters of the place had tended so lovingly. Her heart filled when she thought of the grey stone house and its happy, spacious rooms.

Suddenly there was a sound, and she looked up quickly. Her father's head had fallen back, and he was breathing with a strange noisiness. She called her friend.

"I think the end has come at last," she said.

"Would you like me to fetch the doctor?"

"It will be useless."

The rector looked at the man's wan face, lit dimly by the light of the shaded lamp, and falling on his knees, began to recite the prayers for the dying. A shiver passed through Lucy. In the farmyard a cock crew, and in the distance another cock answered cheerily. Lucy put her hand on the good rector's shoulder.

"It's all over," she whispered.

She bent down and kissed her father's eyes.

A week later Lucy took a walk by the seashore. They had buried Fred Allerton three days before among her ancestors whom he had dishonoured. It was a lonely funeral, for Lucy had asked Robert Boulger, her only friend then in England, not to come; and she was the solitary mourner. The coffin was lowered into the grave, and the rector read the sad, beautiful words of the burial service. She could not grieve. Her father was at peace. She could only hope that his errors and his crimes would be soon forgotten; and perhaps those who had known him would remember then that he had been a charming friend, and a clever, sympathetic companion. It was little enough in all conscience that Lucy asked.

On the morrow she was leaving the roof of the hospitable parson. Surmising her wish to walk alone once more through the country which was so dear to her, he had not offered his company. Lucy's heart was full of sadness, but there was a certain peace in it, too; the peace of her father's death had entered into her, and she experienced a new feeling, the feeling of resignation.

Now her mind was set upon the future, and she was filled with hope. She stood by the water's edge, looking upon the sea as three years before, when she was staying at Court Leys, she had looked upon the sea that washed the shores of Kent. Many things had passed since then, and many griefs had fallen upon her; but for all that she was happier than then; since on that distant day—and it seemed ages ago—there had been scarcely a ray of brightness in her life, and now she had a great love which made every burden light.

Low clouds hung upon the sky, and on the horizon the greyness of the heavens mingled with the greyness of the sea. She looked into the distance with longing eyes. Now all her life was set upon that far-off corner of unknown Africa, where Alec and George were doing great deeds. She wondered what was the meaning of the silence which had covered them so long.

"Oh, if I could only see," she murmured.

She sent her spirit upon that vast journey, trying to pierce the realms of space, but her spirit came back baffled. She could not know what they were at.

If Lucy's love had been able to bridge the abyss that parted them, if in some miraculous way she had been able to see what actions they did at that time, she would have witnessed a greater tragedy than any which she had yet seen.

Chapter X

THE NIGHT WAS STORMY AND DARK. THE RAIN WAS FALLING, AND THE ground in Alec's camp was heavy with mud. The faithful Swahilis whom he had brought from the coast, chattered with cold around their fires; and the sentries shivered at their posts. It was a night that took the spirit out of a man and made all that he longed for seem vain and trifling. In Alec's tent the water was streaming. Great rats ran about boldly. The stout canvas bellied before each gust of wind, and the cordage creaked, so that one might have thought the whole thing would be blown clean away. The tent was unusually crowded, though there was in it nothing but Alec's bed, covered with a mosquito-curtain, a folding table, with a couple of garden chairs, and the cases which contained his more precious belongings. A small tarpaulin on the floor squelched as one walked on it.

On one of the chairs a man sat, asleep, with his face resting on his arms. His gun was on the table in front of him. It was Walker, a young man who had been freshly sent out to take charge of the North East Africa Company's most northerly station, and had joined Alec's expedition a year before, taking the place of an older man who had gone home on leave. He was a funny, fat person with a round face and a comic manner, the most unexpected sort of fellow to find in the wildest of African districts; and he was eminently unsuited for the life he led. He had come into a little money on attaining his majority, and this he had set himself resolutely to squander in every unprofitable way that occurred to him. When his last penny was spent he had been offered a post by a friend of his family's, who happened to be a director of the company, and had accepted it as his only refuge from starvation. Adversity had not been able to affect his happy nature. He was always cheerful no matter what difficulties he was in, and neither regretted the follies of his past nor repined over the hardships which had followed them. Alec had taken a great liking to him. A silent man himself, he found a certain relaxation in people like Dick Lomas and Walker who talked incessantly; and the young man's simplicity, his constant surprise at the difference between Africa and Mayfair, never ceased to divert him.

Presently Adamson came into the tent. He was the Scotch doctor who had already been Alec's companion on two of his expeditions; and there was a firm friendship between them. He was an Edinburgh man, with a slow drawl and a pawky humour, a great big fellow, far and away the largest of any of the whites; and his movements were no less deliberate than his conversation.

"Hulloa, there," he called out, as he came in.

Walker started to his feet as if he were shot and instinctively seized his gun.

"All right!" laughed the doctor, putting up his hand. "Don't shoot. It's only me."

Walker put down the gun and looked at the doctor with a blank face.

"Nerves are a bit groggy, aren't they?"

The fat, cheerful man recovered his wits and gave a short laugh.

"Why the dickens did you wake me up? I was dreaming—dreaming of a high-heeled boot and a neat ankle and the swirl of a white lace petticoat."

"Were you indeed?" said the doctor, with a slow smile. "Then it's as well I woke ye up in the middle of it before ye made a fool of yourself. I thought I'd better have a look at your arm."

"It's one of the most aesthetic sights I know."

"Your arm?" said the doctor, drily.

"No," answered Walker. "A pretty woman crossing Piccadilly at Swan & Edgar's. You are a savage, my good doctor, and a barbarian; you don't know the care and forethought, the hours of anxious meditation, it has needed to hold up that well-made skirt with the elegant grace that enchants you."

"I'm afraid you're a very immoral man, Walker," answered Adamson with his long drawl, smiling.

"Under the present circumstances I have to content myself with condemning the behaviour of the pampered and idle. Just now a camp-bed in a stuffy tent, with mosquitoes buzzing all around me, has allurements greater than those of youth and beauty. And I would not sacrifice my dinner to philander with Helen of Troy herself."

"You remind me considerably of the fox who said the grapes were sour."

Walker flung a tin plate at a rat that sat up on its hind legs and looked at him impudently.

"Nonsense. Give me a comfortable bed to sleep in, plenty to eat, tobacco to smoke; and Amaryllis may go hang."

Dr. Adamson smiled quietly. He found a certain grim humour in the contrast between the difficulties of their situation and Walker's flippant side.

"Well, let us look at this wound of yours," he said, getting back to his business. "Has it been throbbing?"

"Oh, it's not worth bothering about. It'll be as right as rain tomorrow."

"I'd better dress it all the same."

Walker took off his coat and rolled up his sleeve. The doctor removed the bandages and looked at the broad flesh wound. He put a fresh dressing on it.

"It looks as healthy as one can expect," he murmured. "It's odd what good recoveries men make here when you'd think that everything was against them."

"You must be pretty well done up, aren't you?" asked Walker, as he watched the doctor neatly cut the lint.

"Just about dropping. But I've a devil of a lot more work to do before I turn in."

"The thing that amuses me is to think that I came to Africa thinking I was going to have a rattling good time, plenty of shooting and practically nothing to do."

"You couldn't exactly describe it as a picnic, could you?" answered the doctor. "But I don't suppose any of us knew it would be such a tough job as it's turned out."

Walker put his disengaged hand on the doctor's arm.

"My friend, if ever I return to my native land I will never be such a crass and blithering idiot as to give way again to a spirit of adventure. I shall look out for something safe and quiet, and end my days as a wine-merchant's tout or an insurance agent."

"Ah, that's what we all say when we're out here. But when we're once home again, the recollection of the forest and the plains and the roasting sun and the mosquitoes themselves, come haunting us, and before we know what's up we've booked our passage back to this God-forsaken continent."

The doctor's words were followed by a silence, which was broken by Walker inconsequently.

"Do you ever think of rumpsteaks?" he asked.

The doctor stared at him blankly, and Walker went on, smiling.

"Sometimes, when we're matching under a sun that just about takes the roof of your head off, and we've had the scantiest and most uncomfortable breakfast possible, I have a vision."

"I would be able to bandage you better if you only gesticulated with one arm," said Adamson.

"I see the dining-room of my club, and myself seated at a little table by the window looking out on Piccadilly. And there's a spotless table-cloth, and all the accessories are spick and span. An obsequious menial brings me a rumpsteak, grilled to perfection, and so tender that it melts in the mouth. And he puts by my side a plate of crisp fried potatoes. Can't you smell them? And then a liveried flunky brings me a pewter tankard, and into it he pours a bottle, a large bottle, mind you, of foaming ale."

"You've certainly added considerably to our cheerfulness, my friend," said Adamson.

Walker gaily shrugged his fat shoulders.

"I've often been driven to appease the pangs of raging hunger with a careless epigram, and by the laborious composition of a limerick I have sought to deceive a most unholy thirst."

He liked that sentence and made up his mind to remember it for future use. The doctor paused for a moment, and then he looked gravely at Walker.

"Last night I thought that you'd made your last joke, old man; and that I had given my last dose of quinine."

"We were in rather a tight corner, weren't we?"

"This is the third expedition I've been with MacKenzie, and I assure you I've never been so certain that all was over with us."

Walker permitted himself a philosophical reflection.

"Funny thing death is, you know! When you think of it beforehand, it makes you squirm in your shoes, but when you've just got it face to face it seems to obvious that you forget to be afraid."

Indeed it was only by a miracle that any of them was alive, and they had all a curious, light-headed feeling from the narrowness of the escape. They had been fighting, with their backs to the wall, and each one had shown what he was made of. A few hours before things had been so serious that now, in the first moment of relief, they sought refuge instinctively in banter. But Dr. Adamson was a solid man, and he wanted to talk the matter out.

"If the Arabs hadn't hesitated to attack us just those ten minutes, we would have been simply wiped out."

"MacKenzie was all there, wasn't he?"

Walker had the shyness of his nationality in the exhibition of enthusiasm, and he could only express his admiration for the commander of the party in terms of slang.

"He was, my son," answered Adamson, drily. "My own impression is, he thought we were done for."

"What makes you think that?"

"Well, you see, I know him pretty well. When things are going smoothly and everything's flourishing, he's apt to be a bit irritable. He keeps rather to himself, and he doesn't say much unless you do something he don't approve of."

"And then, by Jove, he comes down on you like a thousand of bricks," Walker agreed heartily. He remembered observations which Alec on more than one occasion had made to recall him to a sense of his great insignificance. "It's not for nothing the natives call him *Thunder and Lightning*."

"But when things look black, his spirits go up like one o'clock," proceeded the doctor. "And the worse they are the more cheerful he is."

"I know. When you're starving with hunger, dead tired and soaked to the skin, and wish you could just lie down and die, MacKenzie simply bubbles over with good humour. It's a hateful characteristic. When I'm in a bad temper, I much prefer everyone else to be in a bad temper, too."

"These last three days he's been positively hilarious. Yesterday he was cracking jokes with the natives."

"Scotch jokes," said Walker. "I daresay they sound funny in an African dialect."

"I've never seen him more cheerful," continued the other, sturdily ignoring the gibe. "By the Lord Harry, said I to myself, the chief thinks we're in a devil of a bad way."

Walker stood up and stretched himself lazily.

"Thank heavens, it's all over now. We've none of us had any sleep for three days, and when I once get off I don't mean to wake up for a week."

"I must go and see the rest of my patients. Perkins has got a bad dose of fever this time. He was quite delirious a little while ago."

"By Jove, I'd almost forgotten."

People changed in Africa. Walker was inclined to be surprised that he was fairly happy, inclined to make a little jest when it occurred to him; and it had nearly slipped his memory that one of the whites had been killed the day before, while another was lying unconsciously with a bullet in his skull. A score of natives were dead, and the rest of them had escaped by the skin of their teeth.

"Poor Richardson," he said.

"We couldn't spare him," answered the doctor slowly. "The fates never choose the right man."

Walker looked at the brawny doctor, and his placid face was clouded. He knew to what the Scot referred and shrugged his shoulders. But the doctor went on.

"If we had to lose someone it would have been a damned sight better if that young cub Allerton had got the bullet which killed poor Richardson."

"He wouldn't have been much loss, would he?" said Walker, after a silence.

"MacKenzie has been very patient with him. If I'd been in his shoes I'd have sent him back to the coast when he sacked Macinnery."

Walker did not answer, and the doctor proceeded to moralise.

"It seems to me that some men have natures so crooked that with every chance in the world to go straight, they can't manage it. The only thing is to let them go to the devil as best they may."

At that moment Alec MacKenzie came in. He was dripping with rain and threw off his macintosh. His face lit up when he saw Walker and the doctor. Adamson was an old and trusted friend, and he knew that on him he could rely always.

"I've been going the round of the outlying sentries," he said.

It was unlike him to volunteer even so trivial a piece of information, and Adamson looked up at him.

"All serene?" he asked.

"Yes."

Alec's eyes rested on the doctor as though he were considering something strange about him. The doctor knew him well enough to suspect that something very grave had happened, but also he knew him too well to hazard an inquiry. Presently Alec spoke again.

"I've just seen a native messenger that Mindabi sent me."

"Anything important?"

"Yes."

Alec's answer was so curt that it was impossible to question him further. He turned to Walker.

"How's the arm?"

"Oh, that's nothing. It's only a scratch."

"You'd better not make too light of it. The smallest wound has a way of being troublesome in this country."

"He'll be all right in a day or two," said the doctor.

Alec sat down. For a minute he did not speak, but seemed plunged in thought. He passed his fingers through his beard, ragged now and longer than when he was in England.

"How are the others?" he asked suddenly, looking at Adamson.

"I don't think Thompson can last till the morning."

"I've just been in to see him."

Thompson was the man who had been shot through the head and had lain unconscious since the day before. He was an old gold-prospector, who had thrown in his lot with the expedition against the slavers.

"Perkins of course will be down for several days longer. And some of the natives are rather badly hurt. Those devils have got explosive bullets."

"Is there anyone in great danger?"

"No, I don't think so. There are two men who are in a bad way, but I think they'll pull through with rest."

"I see," said Alec, laconically.

He stared intently at the table, absently passing his hand across the gun which Walker had left there.

"I say, have you had anything to eat lately?" asked Walker, presently.

Alec shook himself out of his meditation and gave the young man one of his rare, bright smiles. It was plain that he made an effort to be gay.

"Good Lord, I quite forgot; I wonder when the dickens I had some food last. These Arabs have been keeping us so confoundedly busy."

"I don't believe you've had anything today. You must be devilish hungry."

"Now you mention it, I think I am," answered Alec, cheerfully. "And thirsty, by Jove! I wouldn't give my thirst for an elephant tusk."

"And to think there's nothing but tepid water to drink!" Walker exclaimed with a laugh.

"I'll go and tell the boy to bring you some food," said the doctor. "It's a rotten game to play tricks with your digestion like that."

"Stern man, the doctor, isn't he?" said Alec, with twinkling eyes. "It won't hurt me once in a way, and I shall enjoy it all the more now."

But when Adamson went to call the boy, Alec stopped him.

"Don't trouble. The poor devil's half dead with exhaustion. I told him he might sleep till I called him. I don't watch much, and I can easily get it myself."

Alec looked about and presently found a tin of meat and some ship biscuits. During the fighting it had been impossible to go out on the search for game, and there was neither variety nor plenty about their larder. Alec placed the food before him, sat down, and began to eat. Walker looked at him.

"Appetising, isn't it?" he said ironically.

"Splendid!"

"No wonder you get on so well with the natives. You have all the instincts of the primeval savage. You take food for the gross and bestial purpose of appeasing your hunger, and I don't believe you have the least appreciation for the delicacies of eating as a fine art."

"The meat's getting rather mouldy," answered Alec.

He ate notwithstanding with a good appetite. His thoughts went suddenly to Dick who at the hour which corresponded with that which now passed in Africa, was getting ready for one of the pleasant little dinners at the *Carlton* upon which he prided himself. And then he thought of the noisy bustle of Piccadilly at night, the carriages and 'buses that streamed to and fro, the crowded pavements, the gaiety of the lights.

"I don't know how we're going to feed everyone tomorrow," said Walker. "Things will be going pretty bad if we can't get some grain in from somewhere."

Alec pushed back his plate.

"I wouldn't worry about tomorrow's dinner if I were you," he said, with a low laugh.

"Why?" asked Walker.

"Because I think it's ten to one that we shall be as dead as doornails before sunrise."

The two men stared at him silently. Outside, the wind howled grimly, and the rain swept against the side of the tent.

"Is this one of your little jokes, MacKenzie?" said Walker at last.

"You have often observed that I joke with difficulty."

"But what's wrong now?" asked the doctor quickly.

Alec looked at him and chuckled quietly.

"You'll neither of you sleep in your beds tonight. Another sell for the mosquitoes, isn't it? I propose to break up the camp and start marching in an hour."

"I say, it's a bit thick after a day like this," said Walker. "We're all so done up that we shan't be able to go a mile."

"You will have had two hours rest."

Adamson rose heavily to his feet. He meditated for an appreciable time.

"Some of those fellows who are wounded can't possibly be moved," he said.

"They must."

"I won't answer for their lives."

"We must take the risk. Our only chance is to make a bold dash for it, and we can't leave the wounded here."

"I suppose there's going to be a deuce of a row," said Walker.

"There is."

"Your companions seldom have a chance to complain of the monotony of their existence," said Walker, grimly. "What are you going to do now?"

"At this moment I'm going to fill my pipe."

With a whimsical smile, Alec took his pipe from his pocket, knocked it out on his heel, filled and lit it. The doctor and Walker digested the information he had given them. It was Walker who spoke first.

"I gather from the general amiability of your demeanour that we're in rather a tight place."

"Tighter than any of your patent-leather boots, my friend."

Walker moved uncomfortably in his chair. He no longer felt sleepy. A cold shiver ran down his spine.

"Have we any chance of getting through?" he asked gravely.

It seemed to him that Alec paused an unconscionable time before he answered.

"There's always a chance," he said.

"I suppose we're going to do a bit more fighting?"

"We are."

Walker yawned loudly.

"Well, at all events there's some comfort in that. If I am going to be done out of my night's rest, I should like to take it out of someone."

Alec looked at him with approval. That was the frame of mind that pleased him. When he spoke again there was in his voice a peculiar charm that perhaps in part accounted for the power he had over his fellows. It inspired an extraordinary belief in him, so that anyone would have followed him cheerfully to certain death. And though his words were few and bald, he was so unaccustomed to take others into his confidence, that when he did so, ever so little, and in that tone, it seemed that he was putting his hearers under a singular obligation.

"If things turn out all right, we shall come near finishing the job, and there won't be much more slave-trading in this part of Africa."

"And if things don't turn out all right?"

"Why then, I'm afraid the tea tables of Mayfair will be deprived of your scintillating repartee forever."

Walker looked down at the ground. Strange thoughts ran through his head, and when he looked up again, with a shrug of the shoulders, there was a queer look in his eyes.

"Well, I've not had a bad time in my life," he said slowly. "I've loved a little, and I've worked and played. I've heard some decent music, I've looked at nice pictures, and I've read some thundering fine books. If I can only account for a few more of those damned scoundrels before I die, I shouldn't think I had much to complain of."

Alec smiled, but did not answer. A silence fell upon them. Walker's words brought to Alec the recollection of what had caused the trouble which now threatened them, and his lips tightened. A dark frown settled between his eyes.

"Well, I suppose I'd better go and get things straight," said the doctor. "I'll do what I can with those fellows and trust to Providence that they'll stand the jolting."

"What about Perkins?" asked Alec.

"Lord knows! I'll try and keep him quiet with choral."

"You needn't say anything about our striking camp. I don't propose that anyone should know till a quarter of an hour before we start."

"But that won't give them time."

"I've trained them often enough to get on the march quickly," rejoined Alec, with a curtness that allowed no rejoinder.

The doctor turned to go, and at the same moment George Allerton appeared.

Chapter XI

GEORGE ALLERTON HAD CHANGED SINCE HE LEFT ENGLAND. THE FLESH HAD fallen away from his bones, and his face was sallow. He had not stood the climate well. His expression had changed too, for there was a singular querulousness about his mouth, and his eyes were shifty and cunning. He had lost his good looks.

"Can I come in?" he said.

"Yes," answered Alec, and then turning to the doctor: "You might stay a moment, will you?"

"Certainly."

Adamson stood where he was, with his back to the flap that closed the tent. Alec looked up quickly.

"Didn't Selim tell you I wanted to speak to you?"

"That's why I've come," answered George.

"You've taken your time about it."

"I say, could you give me a drink of brandy? I'm awfully done up."

"There's no brandy left," answered Alec.

"Hasn't the doctor got some?"

"No."

There was a long pause. Adamson and Walker did not know what was the matter, but they saw that there was something serious. They had never seen Alec so cold, and the doctor, who knew him well, saw that he was very angry. Alec lifted his eyes again and looked at George slowly.

"Do you know anything about the death of that Turkana woman?" he asked abruptly.

George did not answer immediately.

"No. How should I?" he said presently.

"Come now, you must know something about it. Last Tuesday you came into camp and said the Turkana were very much excited."

"Oh, yes, I remember," answered George, unwillingly.

"Well?"

"I'm not very clear about it. The woman had been shot, hadn't she? One of the station boys had been playing the fool with her, and he seems to have shot her."

"Have you made no attempt to find out which of the station boys it was?"

"I haven't had time," said George, in a surly way. "We've all been worked off our legs during the last three days."

"Do you suspect no one?"

"I don't think so."

"Think a moment."

"The only man who might have done it is that big scoundrel we got on the coast, the Swahili beggar with one ear."

"What makes you think that?"

"He's been making an awful nuisance of himself, and I know he's been running after the women."

Alec did not take his eyes off George. Walker saw what was coming and looked down at the ground.

"You'll be surprised to hear that when the woman was found she wasn't dead."

George did not move, but his cheeks became if possible more haggard. He was horribly frightened.

"She didn't die for nearly an hour."

There was a very short silence. It seemed to George that they must hear the furious beating of his heart.

"Was she able to say anything?"

"She said you'd shot her."

"What a damned lie!"

"It appears that *you* were—playing the fool with her. I don't know why you quarrelled. You took out your revolver and fired point-blank."

George laughed.

"It's just like these beastly niggers to tell a stupid lie like that. You wouldn't believe them rather than me, would you? After all, my word's worth more than theirs."

Alec quietly took from his pocket the case of an exploded cartridge. It could only have fitted a revolver.

"This was found about two yards from the body and was brought to me this evening."

"I don't know what that proves."

"You know just as well as I do that none of the natives has a revolver. Beside ourselves only one or two of the servants have them."

George took his handkerchief from his pocket and wiped his face. His throat was horribly dry, and he could hardly breathe.

"Will you give me your revolver," said Alec, quietly.

"I haven't got it. I lost it this afternoon when we made that sortie. I didn't tell you as I thought you'd get in a wax about it."

"I saw you cleaning it less than an hour ago," said Alec, gravely.

George shrugged his shoulders pettishly.

"Perhaps it's in my tent. I'll go and see."

"Stop here," said Alec sharply.

"Look here, I'm not going to be ordered about like a dog. You've got no right to talk to me like that. I came out here of my own free will, and I won't let you treat me like a damned nigger."

"If you put your hand to your hip-pocket I think you'll find your revolver there."

"I'm not going to give it you," said George, his lips white with fear.

"Do you want me to come and take it from you myself?"

The two men stared at one another for a moment. Then George slowly put his hand to his pocket and took out the revolver. But a sudden impulse seized him. He raised it, quietly aimed at Alec, and fired. Walker was standing near him, and seeing the movement, instinctively beat up the boy's hand as pulled the trigger. In a moment the doctor had sprung forward and seizing him round the waist, thrown him backwards. The revolver fell from his hand. Alec had not moved.

"Let me go, damn you!" cried George, his voice shrill with rage.

"You need not hold him," said Alec.

It was second nature with them all to perform Alec's commands, and without thinking twice they dropped their hands. George sank cowering into a chair. Walker, bending down, picked up the revolver and gave it to Alec, who silently fitted into an empty chamber the cartridge that had been brought to him.

"You must see that it fits," he said. "Hadn't you better make a clean breast of it?"

George was utterly cowed. A sob broke from him.

"Yes, I shot her," he said brokenly. "She made a row and the devil got into me. I didn't know what I'd done till she screamed and I saw the blood."

He cursed himself for being such a fool as to throw the cartridge away. His first thought had been to have all the chambers filled.

"Do you remember that two months ago I hanged a man to the nearest tree because he'd murdered one of the natives?"

George sprang up in terror, and he began to tremble.

"You wouldn't do that to me."

A wild prayer went up in his heart that mercy might be shown him, and then bitter anger seized him because he had ever come out to that country.

"You need not be afraid," answered Alec coldly. "In any case I must preserve the native respect for the white man."

"I was half drunk when I saw the woman. I wasn't responsible for my actions."

"In any case the result is that the whole tribe has turned against us."

The chief was Alec's friend, and it was he who had sent him the exploded cartridge. The news came to Alec like a thunderclap, for the Turkana were the best part of his fighting force, and he had always placed the utmost reliance on their fidelity. The chief said that he could not hold in his young men, and not only must Alec cease to count upon them, but they would probably insist on attacking him openly. They had stirred up the neighbouring tribes against him and entered into communication with the Arabs. He had been just at the turning point and on the verge of a great success, but now all that had been done during three years was frustrated. The Arabs had seized the opportunity and suddenly assumed the offensive. The unexpectedness of their attack had nearly proved fatal to Alec's party, and since then they had all had to fight for bare life.

George watched Alec as he stared at the ground.

"I suppose the whole damned thing's my fault," he muttered.

Alec did not answer directly.

"I think we may take it for certain that the natives will go over to the slavers tomorrow, and then we shall be attacked on all sides. We can't hold out against God knows how many thousands. I've sent Rogers and Deacon to bring in all the Latukas, but heaven knows if they can arrive in time."

"And if they don't?"

Alec shrugged his shoulders, but did not speak. George's breathing came hurriedly, and a sob rose to his throat.

"What are you going to do to me, Alec?"

MacKenzie walked up and down, thinking of the gravity of their position. In a moment he stopped and looked at Walker.

"I daresay you have some preparations to make," he said.

Walker got up.

"I'll be off," he answered, with a slight smile.

He was glad to go, for it made him ashamed to watch the boy's humiliation. His own nature was so honest, his loyalty so unbending, that the sight of viciousness affected him with a physical repulsion, and he turned away from it as he would have done from the sight of some hideous ulcer. The doctor surmised that his presence too was undesired. Murmuring that he had no time to lose if he wanted to get his patients ready for a night march, he followed Walker out of the tent. George breathed more freely when he was alone with Alec.

"I'm sorry I did that silly thing just now," he said. "I'm glad I didn't hit you."

"It doesn't matter at all," smiled Alec. "I'd forgotten all about it."

"I lost my head. I didn't know what I was doing."

"You need not trouble about that. In Africa even the strongest of us are apt to lose our balance."

Alec filled his pipe again, and lighting it, blew heavy clouds of smoke into the damp air. His voice was softer when he spoke.

"Did you ever know that before we came away I asked Lucy to marry me?"

George did not answer. He stifled a sob, for the recollection of Lucy, the centre of his love and the mainspring of all that was decent in him, transfixed his heart with pain.

"She asked me to bring you here in the hope that you'd,"—Alec had some difficulty in expressing himself—"do something that would make people forget what happened to your father. She's very proud of her family. She feels that your good name is—besmirched, and she wanted you to give it a new lustre. I think that is the object she has most at heart in the world. It is as great as her love for you. The plan hasn't been much of a success, has it?"

"She ought to have known that I wasn't suited for this sort of life," answered George, bitterly.

"I saw very soon that you were weak and irresolute, but I thought I could put some backbone into you. I hoped for her sake to make something of you after all. Your intentions seemed good enough, but you never had the strength to carry them out." Alec had been watching the smoke that rose from his pipe, but now he looked at George. "I'm sorry if I seem to be preaching at you."

"Oh, do you think I care what anyone says to me now?"

Alec went on very gravely, but not unkindly.

"Then I found you were drinking. I told you that no one could stand liquor in this country, and you gave me your word of honour that you wouldn't touch it again."

"Yes, I broke it. I couldn't help myself. The temptation was too strong."

"When we came to the station at Munias, and I was laid up with fever, you and Macinnery took the opportunity to get into an ugly scrape with some native women. You knew that that was the one thing I would not stand. I have nothing to do with morality—everyone is free in these things to do as he chooses—but I do know that nothing causes more trouble with the natives, and I've made definite rules on the subject. If the culprits are Swahilis I flog them, and if they're whites I send them back to the coast. That's what I ought to have done with you, but it would have broken Lucy's heart."

"It was Macinnery's fault."

"It's because I thought Macinnery was chiefly to blame that I sent him back alone. I determined to give you another chance. It struck me that the feeling of authority might have some influence on you, and so, when I had to build a *boma* to guard the road down to the coast, I put the chief part of the stores in your care and left you in command. I need not remind you what happened there."

George looked down at the floor sulkily, and in default of excuses, kept silent. He felt a sullen resentment as he remembered Alec's anger. He had never seen him give way before or since to such a furious wrath, and he had seen Alec hold himself with all his strength so that he might not thrash him. Alec remembered too, and his voice once more grew hard and cold.

"I came to the conclusion that it was hopeless. You seemed to me rotten through and through."

"Like my father before me," sneered George, with a little laugh.

"I couldn't believe a word you said. You were idle and selfish. Above all you were loathsomely, wantonly cruel. I was aghast when I heard of the fiendish cruelty with which you'd used the wretched men whom I left with you. If I hadn't returned in the nick of time, they'd have killed you and looted all the stores."

"It would have upset you to lose the stores, wouldn't it?"

"Is that all you've got to say?"

"You always believed their stories rather than mine."

"It was difficult not to believe when a man showed me his back all torn and bleeding, and said you'd had him flogged because he didn't cook your food to your satisfaction."

"I did it in a moment of temper. A man's not responsible for what he does when he's got fever."

"It was too late to send you to the coast then, and I was obliged to take you on. And now the end has come. Your murder of that woman has put us all in deadly peril. Already to your charge lie the deaths of Richardson and Thompson and about twenty natives. We're as near destruction as we can possibly be; and if we're killed, tomorrow the one tribe that has remained friendly will be attacked and their villages burned. Men, women and children, will be put to the sword or sold into slavery."

George seemed at last to see the abyss into which he was plunged, and his resentment gave way to despair.

"What are you going to do?"

"We're far away from the coast, and I must take the law into my own hands."

"You're not going to kill me?" gasped George.

"No," said Alec scornfully.

Alec sat on the little camp table so that he might be quite near George.

"Are you fond of Lucy?" he asked gently.

George broke into a sob.

"O God, you know I am," he cried piteously. "Why do you remind me of her? I've made a rotten mess of everything, and I'm better out of the way. But think of the disgrace of it. It'll kill Lucy. And she was hoping I'd do so much."

He hid his face in his hands and sobbed brokenheartedly. Alec, strangely touched, put his hand on his shoulder.

"Listen to me," he said. "I've sent Deacon and Rogers to bring up as many Latukas as they can. If we can tide over tomorrow we may be able to inflict a crushing blow on the Arabs; but we must seize the ford over the river. The Arabs are holding it and our only chance is to make a sudden attack on them tonight before the natives join them. We shall be enormously outnumbered, but we may do some damage if we take them by surprise, and if we can capture the ford, Rogers and Deacon will be able to get across to us. We've lost Richardson and Thompson. Perkins is down with fever. That reduces the whites to Walker, and the doctor, Condamine, Mason, you and myself. I can trust the Swahilis, but they're the only natives I can trust. Now, I'm going to start marching straight for the ford. The Arabs will come out of their stockade in order to cut us off. In the darkness I mean to slip away with the rest of the white men and the Swahilis, I've found a short cut by which I can take them in the rear. They'll attack just as the ford is reached, and I shall fall upon them. Do you see?"

George nodded, but he did not understand at what Alec was driving. The words reached his ears vaguely, as though they came from a long way off.

"I want one white man to lead the Turkana, and that man will run the greatest possible danger. I'd go myself only the Swahilis won't fight unless I lead them. . . . Will you take that post?"

The blood rushed to George's head, and he felt his ears singing.

"I?"

"I could order you to go, but the job's too dangerous for me to force it on anyone. If you refuse I shall call the others together and ask someone to volunteer."

George did not answer.

"I won't hide from you that it means almost certain death. But there's no other way of saving ourselves. On the other hand, if you show perfect courage at the moment the Arabs attack and the Turkana find we've given them the slip, you may escape. If you do, I promise you that nothing shall be said of all that has happened here."

George sprang to his feet, and once more on his lips flashed the old, frank smile.

"All right! I'll do that. And I thank you with all my heart for giving me the chance."

Alec held out his hand, and he gave a sigh of relief.

"I'm glad you've accepted. Whatever happens you'll have done one brave action in your life."

George flushed. He wanted to speak, but hesitated.

"I should like to ask you a great favour," he said at last.

Alec waited for him to go on.

"You won't let Lucy know the mess I've made of things, will you? Let her think I've done all she wanted me to do."

"Very well," answered Alec gently.

"Will you give me your word of honour that if I'm killed you won't say anything that will lead anyone to suspect how I came by my death."

Alec looked at him silently. It flashed across his mind that it might be necessary under certain circumstances to tell the whole truth. George was greatly moved. He seemed to divine the reason of Alec's hesitation.

"I have no right to ask anything of you. Already you've done far more for me than I deserved. But it's for Lucy's sake that I implore you not to give me away."

Alec, standing entirely still, uttered the words slowly.

"I give you my word of honour that whatever happens and in whatever circumstances I find myself placed, not a word shall escape me that could lead Lucy to suppose that you hadn't been always and in every way upright, brave, and honourable. I will take all the responsibility of your present action."

"I'm awfully grateful to you."

Alec moved at last. The strain of their conversation was become almost intolerable. Alec's voice became cheerful and brisk.

"I think there's nothing more to be said. You must be ready to start in half an hour. Here's your revolver." There was a twinkle in his eyes as he continued: "Remember that you've discharged one chamber. You'd better put in another cartridge."

"Yes, I'll do that."

George nodded and went out. Alec's face at once lost the lightness which it had assumed a moment before. He knew that he had just done something which might separate him from Lucy forever. His love for her was now the only thing in the world to him, and he had jeopardised it for that worthless boy. He saw that all sorts of interpretations might be put upon his action, and he should have been free to speak the truth. But even if George had not exacted from him the promise of silence, he could never have spoken a word. He loved Lucy far too deeply to cause her such bitter pain. Whatever happened, she must think that George was a brave man, and had died in the performance of his duty. He knew her well enough to be sure that if death were dreadful, it was more tolerable than dishonour. He knew how keenly she had felt her disgrace, how it affected her like a personal uncleanness, and he knew that she had placed all her hopes in George. Her brother was rotten to the core, as rotten as her father. How could he tell her that? He was willing to make any sacrifice rather than allow her to have such knowledge. But if ever she knew that he had sent George to his death she would hate him. And if he lost her love he lost everything. He had thought of that before he answered: Lucy could do without love better than without self-respect.

But he had told George that if he had pluck he might get through. Would he show that last virtue of a blackguard—courage?

Chapter XII

IT WAS NOT TILL SIX MONTHS LATER THAT NEWS OF ALEC MACKENZIE'S EXPEDItion reached the outer world, and at the same time Lucy received a letter from him in which he told her that her brother was dead. That stormy night had been fatal to the light-hearted Walker and to George Allerton, but success had rewarded Alec's desperate boldness, and a blow had been inflicted on the slavers which subsequent events proved to be crushing. Alec's letter was grave and tender. He knew the extreme grief he must inflict upon Lucy, and he knew that words could not assuage it. It seemed to him that the only consolation he could offer was that the life which was so precious to her had been given for a worthy cause. Now that George had made up in the only way possible for the misfortune his criminal folly had brought upon them, Alec was determined to put out of his mind all that had gone before. It was right that the weakness which had ruined him should be forgotten, and Alec could dwell honestly on the boy's charm of manner, and on his passionate love for his sister.

The months followed one another, the dry season gave place to the wet, and at length Alec was able to say that the result he had striven for was achieved. Success rewarded his long efforts, and it was worth the time, the money, and the lives that it had cost. The slavers were driven out of a territory larger than the United Kingdom, treaties were signed with chiefs who had hitherto been independent, by which they accepted the suzerainty of Great Britain; and only one step remained, that the government should take over the rights of the company which had been given powers to open up the country, and annex the conquered district to the empire. It was to this that MacKenzie now set himself; and he entered into communication with the directors of the company and with the commissioner at Nairobi.

But it seemed as if the fates would snatch from him all enjoyment of the laurels he had won, for on their way towards Nairobi, Alec and Dr. Adamson were attacked by blackwater fever. For weeks Alec lay at the point of death. His fine constitution seemed to break at last, and he himself thought that the end was come. Condamine, one of the company's agents, took command of the party and received Alec's final instructions. Alec lay in his camp bed, with his faithful Swahili boy by his side to brush away the flies, waiting for the end. He would have given much to live till all his designs were accomplished, but that apparently was not to be. There was only one thing that troubled him. Would the government let the splendid gift he offered slip through their fingers? Now was the time to take formal possession of the territories which he had pacified: the prestige of the whites was at its height, and there were no difficulties to be surmounted. He impressed upon Condamine, whom he wished to be appointed sub-commissioner under a chief at Nairobi, the importance of making all this clear to the authorities. The post he suggested would have been pressed upon himself, but he had no taste for official restrictions, and his part of his work was done. So far as this went, his death was of little consequence.

And then he thought of Lucy. He wondered if she would understand what he had done. He could acknowledge now that she had cause to be proud of him. She would be sorry for his death. He did not think that she loved him, he did not expect it; but he was glad to have loved her, and he wished he could have told her how much the thought of her had been to him during these years of difficulty. It was very hard that he might not see her once more in order to thank her for all she had been to him. She had given his life a beauty it could never have had, and for this he was very grateful. But the secret of George's death would die with him; for Walker was dead, and Adamson, the only man left who could throw light upon it, might be relied on to hold his tongue. And Alec, losing strength each day, thought that perhaps it were well if he died.

But Condamine could not bear to see his chief thus perish. For four years that man had led them, and only his companions knew his worth. To his acquaintance he might seem hard and unsympathetic, he might repel by his taciturnity and anger by his sternness; but his comrades knew how eminent were his qualities. It was impossible for anyone to live with him continually without being conquered by his greatness. If his power with the natives was unparalleled, it was because they had taken his measure and found him sterling. And he had bound the whites to him by ties from which they could not escape. He asked no one to do anything which he was not willing to do himself. If any plan of his failed he took the failure upon himself; if it succeeded he attributed the success to those who had carried out his orders. If he demanded courage and endurance from others it was easy, since he showed them the way by his own example to be strong and brave. His honesty, justice, and forbearance made all who came in contact with him ashamed of their own weakness. They knew the unselfishness which considered the comfort of the meanest porter before his own; and his tenderness to those who were ill knew no bounds.

The Swahilis assumed an unaccustomed silence, and the busy, noisy camp was like a death chamber. When Alec's boy told them that his master grew each day weaker, they went about with tears running down their cheeks, and they would have wailed aloud, but that they knew he must not be disturbed. It seemed to Condamine that there was but one chance, and that was to hurry down, with forced marches, to the nearest station. There they would find a medical missionary to look after him and the comforts of civilisation which in the forest they so wofully lacked.

Alec was delirious when they moved him. It was fortunate that he could not be told of Adamson's death, which had taken place three days before. The good, strong Scotchman had succumbed at last to the African climate; and on this, his third journey, having surmounted all the perils that had surrounded him for so long, almost on the threshold of home, he had sunk and died. He was buried at the foot of a great tree, far down so that the jackals might not find him, and Condamine with a shaking voice read over him the burial service from an English prayer-book.

It seemed a miracle that Alec survived the exhaustion of the long tramp. He was jolted along elephant paths that led through the dense bush, up stony hills and down again to the beds of dried-up rivers. Each time Condamine looked at the pale, wan man who lay in the litter, it was with a horrible fear that he would be dead. They began marching before sunrise, swiftly, to cover as much distance as was possible before the sun grew hot; they marched again towards sunset when a grateful coolness refreshed the weary patient. They passed through interminable forests, where the majestic trees sheltered under their foliage a wealth of graceful, tender plants: from trunk and branch swung all manner of creepers, which bound the forest giants in fantastic bonds. They forded broad streams, with exquisite care lest the sick man should come to hurt; they tramped through desolate marshes where the ground sunk under their feet. And at last they reached the station. Alec was still alive.

For weeks the tender skill of the medical missionary and the loving kindness of his wife wrestled with death, and at length Alec was out of danger. His convalescence was very slow, and it looked often as though he would never entirely get back his health. But as soon as his mind regained its old activity, he resumed direction of the affairs which were so near his heart; and no sooner was his strength equal to it than he insisted on being moved to Nairobi, where he was in touch with civilisation, and, through the commissioner, could influence a supine government to accept the precious gift he offered. All this took many months, months of anxious waiting, months of bitter disappointment; but at length everything was done: the worthy Condamine was given the appointment that Alec had desired and set out once more for the interior; Great Britain took possession of the broad lands which Alec, by his skill, tact, perseverance and strength, had wrested from barbarism. His work was finished, and he could return to England.

Public attention had been called at last to the greatness of his achievement, to the dangers he had run and the difficulties he had encountered; and before he sailed, he learned that the papers were ringing with his praise. A batch of cablegrams reached him, including one from Dick Lomas and one from Robert Boulger, congratulating him on his success. Two foreign potentates, through their consuls at Mombassa, bestowed decorations upon him; scientific bodies of all countries conferred on him the distinctions which were in their power to give; chambers of commerce passed resolutions expressing their appreciation of his services; publishers telegraphed offers for the book which they surmised he would write; newspaper correspondents came to him for a preliminary account of his travels. Alec smiled grimly when he read that an Under-Secretary for Foreign Affairs had referred to him in a debate with honeyed words. No such enthusiasm had been aroused in England since Stanley returned from the journey which he afterwards described in *Darkest Africa*. When he left Mombassa the residents gave a dinner in his honour, and everyone who had the chance jumped up on his legs and made a speech. In short, after many years during which Alec's endeavours had been coldly regarded, when the government had been inclined to look upon him as a busybody, the tide turned; and he was in process of being made a national hero.

Alec made up his mind to come home the whole way by sea, thinking that the rest of the voyage would give his constitution a chance to get the better of the ills which still troubled him; and at Gibraltar he received a letter from Dick. One had reached him at Suez; but that was mainly occupied with congratulations, and there was a tenderness due to the fear that Alec had hardly yet recovered from his dangerous illness, which made it, though touching to Alec, not so characteristic as the second.

My Dear Alec:—I am delighted that you will return in the nick of time for the London season. You will put the noses of the Christian Scientists out of joint, and the New Theologians will argue no more in the columns of the halfpenny papers. For you are going to be the lion of the season. Comb your mane and have it neatly curled and scented, for we do not like our lions unkempt; and learn how to flap your tail; be sure you cultivate a proper roar because we expect to shiver delightfully in our shoes at the sight of you, and young ladies are already practising how to swoon with awe in your presence. We have come to the conclusion that you are a hero, and I, your humble servant, shine already with reflected glory because for twenty years I have had the privilege of your acquaintance. Duchesses, my dear boy, duchesses with strawberry leaves around their snowy brows, (like the French grocer I make a point of never believing a duchess is more than thirty,) ask me to tea so that they may hear me prattle of your childhood's happy days, and I have promised to bring you to lunch with them, Tompkinson, whom you once kicked at Eton, has written an article in *Blackwood* on the beauty of your character; by which I take it that the hardness of your boot has been a lasting memory to him. All your friends are proud of you, and we go about giving the uninitiated to understand hat nothing of all this would have happened except for our encouragement. You will be surprised to learn how many people are anxious to reward you for your services to the empire by asking you to dinner. So far as I am concerned, I am smiling in my sleeve; for I alone know what an exceedingly disagreeable person you are. You are not a hero in the least, but a pig-headed beat who conquers kingdoms to annoy quiet, self-respecting persons like myself who make a point of minding their own business.

Yours ever affectionately,
RICHARD LOMAS

Alec smiled when he read the letter. It had struck him that there would be some attempt on his return to make a figure of him, and he much feared that his arrival in Southampton would be followed by an attack of interviewers. He was coming in a slow German ship, and at the moment a P. and O., homeward bound, put in at Gibraltar. By taking it he could reach England one day earlier and give everyone who came to meet him the skip. Leaving his heavy luggage, he got a steward to pack up the things he used on the journey, and in a couple of hours, after an excursion on the shore to the offices of the company, found himself installed on the English boat.

But when the great ship entered the English Channel, Alec could scarcely bear his impatience. It would have astonished those who thought him unhuman if they had known the tumultuous emotions that rent his soul. His fellow-passengers never suspected that the bronzed, silent man who sought to make no acquaintance, was the explorer with whose name all Europe was ringing; and it never occurred to them that as he stood in the bow of the ship, straining his eyes for the first sight of England, his heart was so full that he would not have dared to speak. Each absence had intensified his love for that sea-girt land, and his eyes filled with tears of longing as he thought that soon now he would see it once more. He loved the murky waters of the English Channel because they bathed its shores, and he loved the strong west wind. The west wind seemed to him the English wind; it was the trusty wind of seafaring men, and he lifted his face to taste its salt buoyancy. He could not think of the white cliffs of England without a deep emotion; and when they passed the English ships, tramps outward bound or stout brigantines driving before the wind with their spreading sails, he saw the three-deckers of Trafalgar and the proud galleons of the Elizabethans. He felt a personal pride in those dead adventurers who were spiritual ancestors of his, and he was proud to be an Englishman because Frobisher and Effingham were English, and Drake and Raleigh and the glorious Nelson.

And then his pride in the great empire which had sprung from that small island, a greater Rome in a greater world, dissolved into love as his wandering thoughts took him to green meadows and rippling streams. Now at last he need no longer keep so tight a rein upon his fancy, but could allow it to wander at will; and he thought of the green hedgerows and the pompous elm-trees; he thought of the lovely wayside cottages with their simple flowers and of the winding roads that were so good to walk on. He was breathing the English air now, and his spirit was uplifted. He loved the grey soft mists of low-lying country, and he loved the smell of the heather as he stalked across the moorland. There was no river he knew that equalled the kindly Thames, with the fair trees of its banks and its quiet backwaters, where white swans gently moved amid the waterlilies. His thoughts went to Oxford, with its spires, bathed in a violet haze, and in imagination he sat in the old garden of his college, so carefully tended, so great with memories of the past. And he thought of London. There was a subtle beauty in its hurrying crowds, and there was beauty in the thronged traffic of its river: the streets had that indefinable hue which is the colour of London, and the sky had the gold and purple of an Italian brocade. Now in Piccadilly Circus, around the fountain sat the women who sold flowers; and the gaiety of their baskets, rich with roses and daffodils and tulips, yellow and red, mingled with the sombre tones of the houses, the dingy gaudiness of 'buses and the sunny greyness of the sky.

At last his thoughts went back to the outward voyage. George Allerton was with him then, and now he was alone. He had received no letter from Lucy since he wrote to tell her that George was dead. He understood her silence. But when he thought of George, his heart was bitter against fate because that young life had been so pitifully wasted. He remembered so well the eagerness with which he had south to bind George to him, his desire to gain the boy's affection; and he remembered the dismay with which he learned that he was worthless. The frank smile, the open countenance, the engaging eyes, meant nothing; the boy was truthless, crooked of nature, weak. Alec remembered how, refusing to acknowledge the faults that were so plain, he blamed the difficulty of his own nature; and, when it was impossible to overlook them, his earnest efforts to get the better of them. But the effect of Africa was too strong. Alec had seen many men lose their heads under the influence of that climate. The feeling of an authority that seemed so little limited, over a race that was manifestly inferior, the subtle magic of the hot sunshine, the vastness, the remoteness from civilization, were very at to throw a man off his balance. The French had coined a name for the distemper and called it *folie d'Afrique*. Men seemed to go made from a sense of power, to lose all the restraints which had kept them in the way of righteousness. It needed a strong head or a strong morality to avoid the danger, and George had neither. He succumbed. He lost all sense of shame, and there was no power to hold him. And it was more hopeless because nothing could keep him from drinking. When Macinnery had been dismissed for breaking Alec's most stringent law, things, notwithstanding George's promise of amendment, had only gone from bad to worse. Alec remembered how he had come back to the camp in which he had left George, to find the men mutinous, most of them on the point of deserting, and George drunk. He had flown then into such a rage that he could not control himself. He was ashamed to think of it. He had seized George by the shoulders and shaken him, shaken him as though he were a rat; and it was with difficulty that he prevented himself from thrashing him with his own hands.

And at last had come the final madness and the brutal murder. Alec set his mind to consider once more those hazardous days during which by George's folly they had been on the brink of destruction. George had met his death on that desperate march to the ford, and lacking courage, had died miserably. Alec threw back his head with a curious movement.

"I was right in all I did," he muttered.

George deserved to die, and he was unworthy to be lamented. And yet, at that moment, when he was approaching the shores which George, too, perhaps, had loved, Alec's heart was softened. He sighed deeply. It was fate. If George had inherited the wealth which he might have counted on, if his father had escaped that cruel end, he might have gone through life happily enough. He would have done no differently from his fellows. With the safeguards about him of a civilised state, his irresolution would have prevented him from going astray; and he would have been a decent country gentleman—selfish, weak, and insignificant perhaps, but not remarkably worse than his fellows—and when he died he might have been mourned by a loving wife and fond children.

Now he lay on the borders of an African swamp, unsepulchred, unwept; and Alec had to face Lucy, with the story in his heart that he had sworn on his honour not to tell.

Chapter XIII

ALEC'S FIRST VISIT WAS TO LUCY. NO ONE KNEW THAT HE HAD ARRIVED, AND after changing his clothes at the rooms in Pall Mall that he had taken for the summer, he walked to Charles Street. His heart leaped as he strolled up the hull of St. James Street, bright by a fortunate chance with the sunshine of a summer day; and he rejoiced in the gaiety of the well-dressed youths who sauntered down, bound for one or other of the clubs, taking off their hats with a rapid smile of recognition to charming women who sat in victorias or in electric cars. There was an air of opulence in the broad street, of a civilisation refined without brutality, which was very grateful to his eyes accustomed for so long to the wilderness of Africa.

The gods were favourable to his wishes that day, for Lucy was at home; she sat in the drawing-room, by the window, reading a novel. At her side were masses of flowers, and his first glimpse of her was against a great bowl of roses. The servant announced his name, and she sprang up with a cry. She flushed with excitement, and then the blood fled from her cheeks, and she became extraordinarily pale. Alec noticed that she was whiter and thinner than when last he had seen her; but she was more beautiful.

"I didn't expect you so soon," she faltered.

And then unaccountably tears came to her eyes. Falling back into her chair, she hid her face. Her heart began to beat painfully.

"You must forgive me," she said, trying to smile. "I can't help being very silly."

For days Lucy had lived in an agony of terror, fearing this meeting, and now it had come upon her unexpectedly. More than four years had passed since last they had seen one another, and they had been years of anxiety and distress. She was certain that she had changed, and looking with pitiful dread in the glass, she told herself that she was pale and dull. She was nearly thirty. There were lines about her eyes, and her mouth had a bitter droop. She had no mercy on herself. She would not minimise the ravages of time, and with a brutal frankness insisted on seeing herself as she might be in ten years, when an increasing leanness, emphasising the lines and increasing the prominence of her features, made her still more haggard. She was seized with utter dismay. He might have ceased to love her. His life had been so full, occupied with strenuous adventures, while hers had been used up in waiting, only in waiting. It was natural enough that the strength of her passion should only have increased, but it was natural too that his should have vanished before a more urgent preoccupation. And what had she to offer him now? She turned away from the glass because her tears blurred the images it presented; and if she looked forward to the first meeting with vehement eagerness, it was also with sickening dread.

And now she was so troubled that she could not adopt the attitude of civil friendliness which she had intended in order to show him that she made no claim upon him. She wanted to seem quite collected so that her behaviour should not lead him to think her heart at all affected, but she could only watch his eyes hungrily. She braced herself to restrain a wail of sorrow if she saw his disillusionment. He talked in order to give time for her to master her agitation.

"I was afraid there would be interviewers and boring people generally to meet me if I came by the boat by which I was expected, so I got into another, and I've arrived a day before my time."

She was calmer now, and though she did not speak, she looked at him with strained attention, hanging on his words.

He was very bronzed, thin after his recent illness, but he looked well and strong. His manner had the noble self-confidence which had delighted her of old, and he spoke with the quiet deliberation she loved. Now and then a faint inflection betrayed his Scottish birth.

"I felt that I owed my first visit to you. Can you ever forgive me that I have not brought George home to you?"

Lucy gave a sudden gasp. And with bitter self-reproach she realised that in the cruel joy of seeing Alec once more she had forgotten her brother. She was ashamed. It was but eighteen months since he had died, but twelve since the cruel news had reached her, and now, at this moment of all others, she was so absorbed in her love that no other feeling could enter her heart.

She looked down at her dress. Its half-mourning still betokened that she had lost one who was very dear to her, but the black and white was a mockery. She remembered in a flash the stunning grief which Alec's letter had brought her. It seemed at first there must be a mistake and that her tears were but part of a hateful dream. It was too monstrously unjust that the fates should have hit upon George. She had already suffered too much. And George was so young. It was very hard that a mere boy should be robbed of the precious jewel which is life. And when she realised that it was really true, her grief knew no bounds. All that she had hoped was come to nought, and now she could only despair. She bitterly regretted that she had ever allowed the boy to go on that fatal expedition, and she blamed herself because it was she who had arranged it. He must have died accusing her of his death. Her father was dead, and George was dead, and she was alone. Now she had only Alec; and then, like some poor stricken beast, her heart went out to him, crying for love, crying for protection. All her strength, the strength on which she had prided herself, was gone; and she felt utterly weak and utterly helpless. And her heart yearned for Alec, and the love which had hitherto been like a strong enduring light, now was a consuming fire.

But Alec's words brought the recollection of George back to her reproachful heart, and she saw the boy as she was always pleased to remember him, in his flannels, the open shirt displaying his fine white neck, with the Panama hat that suited him so well; and she saw again his pleasant blue eyes and his engaging smile. He was a picture of honest English manhood. There was a sob in her throat, and her voice trembled when she spoke.

"I told you that if he died a brave man's death I could ask no more."

She spoke in so low a tone that Alec could scarcely hear, but his pulse throbbed with pride at her courage. She went on, almost in a whisper.

"I suppose it was predestined that our family should come to an end in this way. I'm thankful that George so died that his ancestors need have felt no shame for him."

"You are very brave."

She shook her head slowly.

"No, it's not courage; it's despair. Sometimes, when I think what his father was, I'm thankful George is dead. For at least his end was heroic. He died in a noble cause, in the performance of his duty. Life would have been too hard for him to allow me to regret his end."

Alec watched her. He foresaw the words that she would say, and he waited for them.

"I want to thank you for all you did for him," she said, steadying her voice.

"You need not do that," he answered, gravely.

She was silent for a moment. Then she raised her eyes and looked at him steadily. Her voice now had regained its usual calmness.

"I want you to tell me that he did all I could have wished him to do."

To Alec it seemed that she must notice the delay of his answer. He had not expected that the question would be put to him so abruptly. He had no moral scruples about telling a deliberate lie, but it affected him with a physical distaste. It sickened him like nauseous water.

"Yes, I think he did."

"It's my only consolation that in the short time there was given to him, he did nothing that was small or mean, and that in everything he was honourable, upright, and just dealing."

"Yes, he was all that."

"And in his death?"

It seemed to Alec that something caught at his throat. The ordeal was more terrible than he expected.

"In his death he was without fear."

Lucy drew a deep breath of relief.

"Oh, thank God! Thank God! You don't know how much it means to me to hear all that from your own lips. I feel that in a manner his courage, above all his death, have redeemed my father's fault. It shows that we're not rotten to the core, and it gives me back my self-respect. I feel I can look the world in the face once more. I'm infinitely grateful to George. He's repaid me ten thousand times for all my love, and my care, and my anxiety."

"I'm very glad that it is not only grief I have brought you. I was afraid you would hate me."

Lucy blushed, and there was a new light in her eyes. It seemed that on a sudden she had cast away the load of her unhappiness.

"No, I could never do that."

At that moment they heard the sound of a carriage stopping at the door.

"There's Aunt Alice," said Lucy. "She's been lunching out."

"Then let me go," said Alec. "You must forgive me, but I feel that I want to see no one else today."

He rose, and she gave him her hand. He held it firmly.

"You haven't changed?"

"Don't," she cried.

She looked away, for once more the tears were coming to her eyes. She tried to laugh.

"I'm frightfully weak and emotional now. You'll utterly despise me."

"I want to see you again very soon," he said.

The words of Ruth came to her mind: *Why have I found grace in thine eyes, that thou shouldst take knowledge of me,* and her heart was very full. She smiled in her old charming way.

When he was gone she drew a long breath. It seemed that a new joy was come into her life, and on a sudden she felt a keen pleasure in all the beauty of the world. She turned to the great bowl of flowers which stood on a table by the chair in which she had been sitting, and burying her face in them, voluptuously inhaled their fragrance. She knew that he loved her still.

Chapter XIV

THE FICKLE ENGLISH WEATHER FOR ONCE BELIED ITS REPUTATION, AND THE whole month of May was warm and fine. It seemed that the springtime brought back Lucy's youth to her; and, surrendering herself with all her heart to her new happiness, she took a girlish pleasure in the gaieties of the season. Alec had said nothing yet, but she was assured of his love, and she gave herself up to him with all the tender strength of her nature. She was a little overwhelmed at the importance which he seemed to have acquired, but she was very proud as well. The great ones of the earth were eager to do him honour. Papers were full of his praise. And it delighted her because he came to her for protection from lionising friends. She began to go out much more; and with Alec, Dick Lomas, and Mrs. Crowley, went much to the opera and often to the play. They had charming little dinner parties at the *Carlton* and musing suppers at the *Savoy*. Alec did not speak much on these occasions. It pleased him to sit by and listen, with a placid face but smiling eyes, to the nonsense that Dick Lomas and the pretty American talked incessantly. And Lucy watched him. Every day she found something new to interest her in the strong, sunburned face; and sometimes their eyes met: then they smiled quietly. They were very happy.

One evening Dick asked the others to sup with him; and since Alec had a public dinner to attend, and Lucy was going to the play with Lady Kelsey, he took Julia Crowley to the opera. To make an even number he invited Robert Boulger to join them at the *Savoy*. After brushing his hair with the scrupulous thought his thinning locks compelled, Dick waited in the vestibule for Mrs. Crowley. Presently she came, looking very pretty in a gown of flowered brocade which made her vaguely resemble a shepherdess in an old French picture. With her diamond necklace and a tiara in her dark hair, she looked like a dainty princess playing fantastically at the simple life.

"I think people are too stupid," she broke out, as she joined Dick. "I've just met a woman who said to me: 'Oh, I hear you're going to America. Do go and call on my sister. She'll be so glad to see you.' 'I shall be delighted,' I said, 'but where does your sister live?' 'Jonesville, Ohio,' 'Good heavens,' I said, 'I live in New York, and what should I be doing in Jonesville, Ohio?'"

"Keep perfectly calm," said Dick.

"I shall not keep calm," she answered. "I hate to be obviously thought next door to a red Indian by a woman who's slab-sided and round-shouldered. And I'm sure she has dirty petticoats."

"Why?"

"English women do."

"What a monstrous libel!" cried Dick.

At that moment they saw Lady Kelsey come in with Lucy, and a moment later Alec and Robert Boulger joined them. They went in to supper and sat down.

"I hate Amelia," said Mrs. Crowley emphatically, as she laid her long white gloves by the side of her.

"I deplore the prejudice with which you regard a very jolly sort of a girl," answered Dick.

"Amelia has everything that I thoroughly object to in a woman. She has no figure, and her legs are much too long, and she doesn't wear corsets. In the daytime she has a weakness for picture hats, and she can't say boo to a goose."

"Who is Amelia?" asked Boulger.

"Amelia is Mr. Lomas' affianced wife," answered the lady, with a provoking glance at him.

"I didn't know you were going to be married, Dick," said Lady Kelsey, inclined to be a little hurt because nothing had been said to her of this.

"I'm not," he answered. "And I've never set eyes on Amelia yet. She is an imaginary character that Mrs. Crowley has invented as the sort of woman whom I would marry."

"I know Amelia," Mrs. Crowley went on. "She wears quantities of false hair, and she'll adore you. She's so meek and so quiet, and she thinks you such a marvel. But don't ask me to be nice to Amelia."

"My dear lady, Amelia wouldn't approve of you. She'd think you much too outspoken, and she wouldn't like your American accent. You must never forget that Amelia is the granddaughter of a baronet."

"I shall hold her up to Fleming as an awful warning of the woman whom I won't let him marry at any price. 'If you marry a woman like that, Fleming,' I shall say to him, 'I shan't leave you a penny. It shall all go to the University of Pennsylvania.'"

"If ever it is my good fortune to meet Fleming, I shall have great pleasure in kicking him hard," said Dick. "I think he's a most objectionable little beast."

"How can you be so absurd? Why, my dead Mr. Lomas, Fleming could take you up in one hand and throw you over a ten-foot wall."

"Fleming must be a sportsman," said Bobbie, who did not in the least know who they were talking about.

"He is," answered Mrs. Crowley. "He's been used to the saddle since he was three years old, and I've never seen the fence that would make him lift a hair. And he's the best swimmer at Harvard, and he's a wonderful shot—I wish you could see him shoot, Mr. MacKenzie—and he's a dear."

"Fleming's a prig," said Dick.

"I'm afraid you're too old for Fleming," said Mrs. Crowley, looking at Lucy. "If it weren't for that, I'd make him marry you."

"Is Fleming your brother, Mrs. Crowley?" asked Lady Kelsey.

"No, Fleming's my son."

"But you haven't got a son," retorted the elder lady, much mystified.

"No, I know I haven't; but Fleming would have been my son if I'd had one."

"You mustn't mind them, Aunt Alice," smiled Lucy gaily. "They argue by the hour about Amelia and Fleming, and neither of them exists; but sometimes they go into such details and grow so excited that I really begin to believe in them myself."

But Mrs. Crowley, though she appeared a light-hearted and thoughtless little person, had much common sense; and when their party was ended and she was giving Dick a lift in her carriage, she showed that, notwithstanding her incessant chatter, her eyes throughout the evening had been well occupied.

"Did you owe Bobbie a grudge that you asked him to supper?" she asked suddenly.

"Good heavens, no. Why?"

"I hope Fleming won't be such a donkey as you are when he's your age."

"I'm sure Amelia will be much more polite than you to the amiable, middle-aged gentleman who has the good fortune to be her husband."

"You might have noticed that the poor boy was eating his heart out with jealousy and mortification, and Lucy was too much absorbed in Alec to pay the very smallest attention to him."

"What *are* you talking about?"

Mrs. Crowley gave him a glance of amused disdain.

"Haven't you noticed that Lucy is desperately in love with Mr. MacKenzie, and it doesn't move her in the least that poor Bobbie has fetched and carried for her for ten years, done everything she deigned to ask, and been generally nice and devoted and charming?"

"You amaze me," said Dick. "It never struck me that Lucy was the kind of girl to fall in love with anyone. Poor thing. I'm so sorry."

"Why?"

"Because Alec wouldn't dream of marrying. He's not that sort of man."

"Nonsense. Every man is a marrying man if a woman really makes up her mind to it."

"Don't say that. You terrify me."

"You need not be in the least alarmed," answered Mrs. Crowley, coolly, "because I shall refuse you."

"It's very kind of you to reassure me," he answered, smiling. "But all the same I don't think I'll risk a proposal."

"My dear friend, your only safety is in immediate flight."

"Why?"

"It must be obvious to the meanest intelligence that you've been on the verge of proposing to me for the last four years."

"Nothing will induce me to be false to Amelia."

"I don't believe that Amelia really loves you."

"I never said she did; but I'm sure she's quite willing to marry me."

"I think that's detestably vain."

"Not at all. However old, ugly, and generally undesirable a man is, he'll find a heap of charming girls who are willing to marry him. Marriage is still the only decent means of livelihood for a really nice woman."

"Don't let's talk about Amelia; let's talk about me," said Mrs. Crowley.

"I don't think you're half so interesting."

"Then you'd better take Amelia to the play tomorrow night instead of me."

"I'm afraid she's already engaged."

"Nothing will induce me to play second fiddle to Amelia."

"I've taken the seats and ordered an exquisite dinner at the *Carlton*."

"What have you ordered?"

"*Potage bisque.*"

Mrs. Crowley made a little face.

"*Sole Normande.*"

She shrugged her shoulders.

"Wild duck."

"With an orange salad?"

"Yes."

"I don't positively dislike that."

"And I've ordered a *souffle* with an ice in the middle of it."

"I shan't come."

"Why?"

"You're not being really nice to me."

"I shouldn't have thought you kept very well abreast of dramatic art if you insist on marrying everyone who takes you to a theatre," he said.

"I was very nicely brought up," she answered demurely, as the carriage stopped at Dick's door.

She gave him a ravishing smile as he took leave of her. She knew that he was quite prepared to marry her, and she had come to the conclusion that she was willing to have him. Neither much wished to hurry the affair, and each was determined that he would only yield to save the other from a fancied desperation. Their lovemaking was pursued with a light heart.

At Whitsuntide the friends separated. Alec went up to Scotland to see his house and proposed afterwards to spend a week in Lancashire. He had always taken a keen interest in the colliery which brought him so large an income, and he wanted to examine into certain matters that required his attention. Mrs. Crowley went to Blackstable, where she still had Court Leys, and Dick, in order to satisfy himself that he was not really a day older, set out for Paris. But they all arranged to meet again on the day, immediately after the holidays, which Lady Kelsey, having persuaded Lucy definitely to renounce her life of comparative retirement, had fixed for a dance. It was the first ball she had given for many years, and she meant it to be brilliant. Lady Kelsey had an amiable weakness for good society, and Alec's presence would add lustre to the occasion. Meanwhile she went with Lucy to her little place on the river, and did not return till two days before the party. They were spent in a turmoil of agitation. Lady Kelsey passed sleepless nights, fearing at one moment that not a soul would appear, and at another that people would come in such numbers that there would not be enough for them to eat. The day arrived.

But then happened an event which none but Alec could in the least have expected; and he, since his return from Africa, had been so taken up with his love for Lucy, that the possibility of it had slipped his memory.

Fergus Macinnery, the man whom three years before he had dismissed ignominiously from his service, found a way to pay off an old score.

Of the people most nearly concerned in the matter, it was Lady Kelsey who had first news of it. The morning papers were brought into her *boudoir* with her breakfast, and as she poured out her coffee, she ran her eyes lazily down the paragraphs of the *Morning Post* in which are announced the comings and goings of society. Then she turned to the *Daily Mail*. Her attention was suddenly arrested. Staring at her, in the most prominent part of the page, was a column of printed matter headed: *The Death of George Allerton*. It was a letter, a column long, signed by Fergus Macinnery. Lady Kelsey read it with amazement and dismay. At first she could not follow it, and she read it again; now its sense was clear to her, and she was overcome with horror. In set words, mincing no terms, it accused Alec MacKenzie of sending George Allerton to his death in order to save himself. The words treachery and cowardice were used boldly. The dates were given, and the testimony of natives was adduced.

The letter adverted with scathing sarcasm to the rewards and congratulations which had fallen to MacKenzie as a result of his labours; and ended with a challenge to him to bring an action for criminal libel against the writer. At first the whole thing seemed monstrous to Lady Kelsey, it was shameful, shameful; but in a moment she found there was a leading article on the subject, and then she did not know what to believe. It referred to the letter in no measured terms: the writer observed that *prima facie* the case was very strong and called upon Alec to reply without delay. Big words were used, and there was much talk of a national scandal. An instant refutation was demanded. Lady Kelsey did not know what on earth to do, and her thoughts flew to the dance, the success of which would certainly be imperilled by these revelations. She must have help at once. This business, if it concerned the world in general, certainly concerned Lucy more than anyone. Ringing for her maid, she told her to get Dick Lomas on the telephone and ask him to come at once. While she was waiting, she heard Lucy come downstairs and knew that she meant to wish her good-morning. She hid the paper hurriedly.

When Lucy came in and kissed her, she said:

"What is the news this morning?"

"I don't think there is any," said Lady Kelsey, uneasily. "Only the *Post* has come; we shall really have to change our newsagent."

She waited with beating heart for Lucy to pursue the subject, but naturally enough the younger woman did not trouble herself. She talked to her aunt of the preparations for the party that evening, and then, saying that she had much to do, left her. She had no sooner gone than Lady Kelsey's maid came back to say that Lomas was out of town and not expected back till the evening. Distractedly Lady Kelsey sent messages to her nephew and to Mrs. Crowley. She still looked upon Bobbie as Lucy's future husband, and the little American was Lucy's greatest friend. They were both found. Boulger had gone down as usual to the city, but in consideration of Lady Kelsey's urgent request, set out at once to see her.

He had changed little during the last four years, and had still a boyish look on his round, honest face. To Mrs. Crowley he seemed always an embodiment of British philistinism; and if she liked him for his devotion to Lucy, she laughed at him for his stolidity. When he arrived, Mrs. Crowley was already with Lady Kelsey. She had known nothing of the terrible letter, and Lady Kelsey, thinking that perhaps it had escaped him too, went up to him with the *Daily Mail* in her hand.

"Have you seen the paper, Bobbie?" she asked excitedly. "What on earth are we to do?"

He nodded.

"What does Lucy say?" he asked.

"Oh, I've not let her see it. I told a horrid fib and said the newsagent had forgotten to leave it."

"But she must know," he answered gravely.

"Not today," protested Lady Kelsey. "Oh, it's too dreadful that this should happen today of all days. Why couldn't they wait till tomorrow? After all Lucy's troubles it seemed as if a little happiness was coming back into her life, and now this dreadful thing happens."

"What are you going to do?" asked Bobbie.

"What can I do?" said Lady Kelsey desperately. "I can't put the dance off. I wish I had the courage to write and ask Mr. MacKenzie not to come."

Bobbie made a slight gesture of impatience. It irritated him that his aunt should harp continually on the subject of this wretched dance. But for all that he tried to reassure her.

"I don't think you need be afraid of MacKenzie. He'll never venture to show his face."

"You don't mean to say you think there's any truth in the letter?" exclaimed Mrs. Crowley.

He turned and faced her.

"I've never read anything more convincing in my life."

Mrs. Crowley looked at him, and he returned her glance steadily.

Of those three it was only Lady Kelsey who did not know that Lucy was deeply in love with Alec MacKenzie.

"Perhaps you're inclined to be unjust to him," said Mrs. Crowley.

"We shall see if he has any answer to make," he answered coldly. "The evening papers are sure to get something out of him. The city is ringing with the story, and he must say something at once."

"It's quite impossible that there should be anything in it," said Mrs. Crowley. "We all know the circumstances under which George went out with him. It's inconceivable that he should have sacrificed him as callously as this man's letter makes out."

"We shall see."

"You never liked him, Bobbie," said Lady Kelsey.

"I didn't," he answered briefly.

"I wish I'd never thought of giving this horrid dance," she moaned.

Presently, however, they succeeded in calming Lady Kelsey. Though both thought it unwise, they deferred to her wish that everything should be hidden from Lucy till the morrow. Dick Lomas was arriving from Paris that evening, and it would be possible then to take his advice. When at last Mrs. Crowley left the elder woman to her own devices, her thoughts went to Alec. She wondered where he was, and if he already knew that his name was more prominently than ever before the public.

MacKenzie was travelling down from Lancashire. He was not a man who habitually read papers, and it was in fact only by chance that he saw a copy of the *Daily*

Mail. A fellow traveller had with him a number of papers, and offered one of them to Alec. He took it out of mere politeness. His thoughts were otherwise occupied, and he scanned it carelessly. Suddenly he saw the heading which had attracted Lady Kelsey's attention. He read the letter, and he read the leading article. No one who watched him could have guessed that what he read concerned him so nearly. His face remained impassive. Then, letting the paper fall to the ground, he began to think. Presently he turned to the amiable stranger who had given him the paper, and asked him if he had seen the letter.

"Awful thing, isn't it?" the man said.

Alec fixed upon him his dark, firm eyes. The man seemed an average sort of person, not without intelligence.

"What do you think of it?"

"Pity," he said. "I thought MacKenzie was a great man. I don't know what he can do now but shoot himself."

"Do you think there's any truth in it?"

"The letter's perfectly damning."

Alec did not answer. In order to break off the conversation he got up and walked into the corridor. He lit a cigar and watched the green fields that fled past them. For two hours he stood motionless. At last he took his seat again, with a shrug of the shoulders, and a scornful smile on his lips.

The stranger was asleep, with his head thrown back and his mouth slightly open. Alec wondered whether his opinion of the affair would be that of the majority. He thought Alec should shoot himself?

"I can see myself doing it," Alec muttered.

Chapter XV

A FEW HOURS LATER LADY KELSEY'S DANCE WAS IN FULL SWING, AND TO ALL appearances it was a great success. Many people were there, and everyone seemed to enjoy himself. On the surface, at all events, there was nothing to show that anything had occurred to disturb the evening's pleasure, and for most of the party the letter in the *Daily Mail* was no more than a welcome topic of conversation.

Presently Canon Spratte went into the smoking-room. He had on his arm, as was his amiable habit, the prettiest girl at the dance, Grace Vizard, a niece of that Lady Vizard who was a pattern of all the proprieties and a devout member of the Church of Rome. He found that Mrs. Crowley and Robert Boulger were already sitting there, and he greeted them courteously.

"I really must have a cigarette," he said, going up to the table on which were all the necessary things for refreshment.

"If you press me dreadfully I'll have one, too," said Mrs. Crowley, with a flash of her beautiful teeth.

"Don't press her," said Bobbie. "She's had six already, and in a moment she'll be seriously unwell."

"Well, I'll forego the pressing, but not the cagarette."

Canon Spratte gallantly handed her the box, and gave her a light.

"It's against all my principles, you know," he smiled.

"What is the use of principles except to give one an agreeable sensation of wickedness when one doesn't act up to them?"

The words were hardly out of her mouth when Dick and Lady Kelsey appeared.

"Dear Mrs. Crowley, you're as epigrammatic as a dramatist," he exclaimed. "Do you say such things from choice or necessity?"

He had arrived late, and this was the first time she had seen him since they had all gone their ways before Whitsun. He mixed himself a whisky and soda.

"After all, is there anything you know so thoroughly insufferable as a ball?" he said, reflectively, as he sipped it with great content.

"Nothing, if you ask me pointblank," said Lady Kelsey, smiling with relief because he took so flippantly the news she had lately poured into his ear. "But it's excessively rude of you to say so."

"I don't mind yours, Lady Kelsey, because I can smoke as much as I please, and keep away from the sex which is technically known as fair."

Mrs. Crowley felt the remark was directed to her.

"I'm sure you think us a vastly overrated institution, Mr. Lomas," she murmured.

"I venture to think the world was not created merely to give women an opportunity to wear Paris frocks."

"I'm rather pleased to hear you say that."

"Why?" asked Dick, on his guard.

"We're all so dreadfully tired of being goddesses. For centuries foolish men have set us up on a pedestal and vowed they were unworthy to touch the hem of our garments. And it *is* so dull."

"What a clever woman you are, Mrs. Crowley. You always say what you don't mean."

"You're really very rude."

"Now that impropriety is out of fashion, rudeness is the only short cut to a reputation for wit."

Canon Spratte did not like Dick. He thought he talked too much. It was fortunately easy to change the conversation.

"Unlike Mr. Lomas, I thoroughly enjoy a dance," he said, turning to Lady Kelsey. "My tastes are ingenuous, and I can only hope you've enjoyed your evening as much as your guests."

"I?" cried Lady Kelsey. "I've been suffering agonies." They all knew to what she referred, and the remark gave Boulger an opportunity to speak to Dick Lomas.

"I suppose you saw the *Mail* this morning?" he asked.

"I never read the papers except in August," answered Dick drily.

"When there's nothing in them?" asked Mrs. Crowley.

"Pardon me, I am an eager student of the sea-serpent and of the giant gooseberry."

"I should like to kick that man," said Bobbie, indignantly.

Dick smiled.

"My dear chap, Alec is a hardy Scot and bigger than you; I really shouldn't advise you to try."

"Of course you've heard all about this business?" said Canon Spratte.

"I've only just arrived from Paris. I knew nothing of it till Lady Kelsey told me."

"What do you think?"

"I don't think at all; I *know* there's not a word of truth in it. Since Alec arrived at Mombassa, he's been acclaimed by everyone, private and public, who had any right to an opinion. Of course it couldn't last. There was bound to be a reaction."

"Do you know anything of this man Macinnery?" asked Boulger.

"It so happens that I do. Alec found him half starving at Mombassa, and took him solely out of charity. But he was a worthless rascal and had to be sent back."

"He seems to me to give ample proof for every word he says," retorted Bobbie.

Dick shrugged his shoulders scornfully.

"As I've already explained to Lady Kelsey, whenever an explorer comes home there's someone to tell nasty stories about him. People forget that kid gloves are not much use in a tropical forest, and they grow very indignant when they hear that a man has used a little brute force to make himself respected."

"All that's beside the point," said Boulger, impatiently. "MacKenzie sent poor George into a confounded trap to save his own dirty skin."

"Poor Lucy!" moaned Lady Kelsey. "First her father died . . ."

"You're not going to count that as an overwhelming misfortune?" Dick interrupted. "We were unanimous in describing that gentleman's demise as an uncommon happy release."

"I was engaged to dine with him this evening," said Bobbie, pursuing his own bitter reflections. "I wired to say I had a headache and couldn't come."

"What will he think if he sees you here?" cried Lady Kelsey.

"He can think what he likes."

Canon Spratte felt that it was needful now to put in the decisive word which he always expected from himself. He rubbed his hands blandly.

"In this matter I must say I agree entirely with our friend Bobbie. I read the letter with the utmost care, and I could see no loophole of escape. Until Mr. MacKenzie gives a definite answer I can hardly help looking upon him as nothing less than a murderer. In these things I feel that one should have the courage of one's opinions. I saw him in Piccadilly this evening, and I cut him dead. Nothing will induce me to shake hands with a man on whom rests so serious an accusation."

"I hope to goodness he doesn't come," said Lady Kelsey.

Canon Spratte looked at his watch and gave her a reassuring smile.

"I think you may feel quite safe. It's really growing very late."

"You say that Lucy doesn't know anything about this?" asked Dick.

"No," said Lady Kelsey. "I wanted to give her this evening's enjoyment unalloyed."

Dick shrugged his shoulders again. He did not understand how Lady Kelsey expected no suggestion to reach Lucy of a matter which seemed a common topic of conversation. The pause which followed Lady Kelsey's words was not broken when Lucy herself appeared. She was accompanied by a spruce young man, to whom she turned with a smile.

"I thought we should find your partner here."

He went to Grace Vizard, and claiming her for the dance that was about to begin, took her away. Lucy went up to Lady Kelsey and leaned over the chair in which she sat.

"Are you growing very tired, my aunt?" she asked kindly.

"I can rest myself till supper time. I don't think anyone else will come now."

"Have you forgotten Mr. MacKenzie?"

Lady Kelsey looked up quickly, but did not reply. Lucy put her hand gently on her aunt's shoulder.

"My dear, it was charming of you to hide the paper from me this morning. But it wasn't very wise."

"Did you see that letter?" cried Lady Kelsey. "I so wanted you not to till tomorrow."

"Mr. MacKenzie very rightly thought I should know at once what was said about him and my brother. He sent me the paper himself this evening."

"Did he write to you?" asked Dick.

"No, he merely scribbled on a card: *I think you should read this.*"

No one answered. Lucy turned and faced them; her cheeks were pale, but she was very calm. She looked gravely at Robert Boulger, waiting for him to say what she knew was in his mind, so that she might express at once her utter disbelief in the charges that were brought against Alec. But he did not speak, and she was obliged to utter her defiant words without provocation.

"He thought it unnecessary to assure me that he hadn't betrayed the trust I put in him."

"Do you mean to say the letter left any doubt in your mind?" said Boulger.

"Why on earth should I believe the unsupported words of a subordinate who was dismissed for misbehaviour?"

"For my part, I can only say that I never read anything more convincing in my life."

"I could hardly believe him guilty of such a crime if he confessed it with his own lips."

Bobbie shrugged his shoulders. It was only with difficulty that he held back the cruel words that were on his lips. But as if Lucy read his thoughts, her cheeks flushed.

"I think it's infamous that you should all be ready to believe the worst," she said hotly, in a low voice that trembled with indigant anger. "You're all of you so petty, so mean, that you welcome the chance of spattering with mud a man who is so infinitely above you. You've not given him a chance to defend himself."

Bobbie turned very pale. Lucy had never spoken to him in such a way before, and wrath flamed up in his heart, wrath mixed with hopeless love. He paused for a moment to command himself.

"You don't know apparently that interviewers went to him from the evening papers, and he refused to speak."

"He has never consented to be interviewed. Why should you expect him now to break his rule?"

Bobbie was about to answer, when a sudden look of dismay on Lady Kelsey's face stopped him. He turned round and saw MacKenzie standing at the door. He came forward with a smile, holding out his hand, and addressed himself to Lady Kelsey.

"I thought I should find you here," he said.

He was perfectly collected. He glanced around the room with a smile of quiet amusement. A certain embarrassment seized the little party, and Lady Kelsey, as she shook hands with him, was at a loss for words.

"How do you do?" she faltered. "We've just been talking of you."

"Really?"

The twinkle in his eyes caused her to lose the remainder of her self-possession, and she turned scarlet.

"It's so late, we were afraid you wouldn't come. I should have been dreadfully disappointed."

"It's very kind of you to say so. I've been at the *Travellers*, reading various appreciations of my character."

A hurried look of alarm crossed Lady Kelsey's good-tempered face.

"Oh, I heard there was something about you in the papers," she answered.

"There's a good deal. I really had no idea the world was so interested in me."

"It's charming of you to come here tonight," the good lady smiled, beginning to feel more at ease. "I'm sure you hate dances."

"Oh, no, they interest me enormously. I remember, an African king once gave me a dance in my honour. Four thousand warriors in war-paint. I assure you it was a most impressive sight."

"My dear fellow," Dick chuckled, "if paint is the attraction, you really need not go much further than Mayfair."

The scene amused him. He was deeply interested in Alec's attitude, for he knew him well enough to be convinced that his discreet gaiety was entirely assumed. It was impossible to tell by it what course he meant to adopt; and at the same time there was about him a greater unapproachableness, which warned all and sundry that it would be wiser to attempt no advance. But for his own part he did not care; he meant to have a word with Alec at the first opportunity.

Alec's quiet eyes now rested on Robert Boulger.

"Ah, there's my little friend Bobbikins. I thought you had a headache?"

Lady Kelsey remembered her nephew's broken engagement and interposed quickly.

"I'm afraid Bobbie is dreadfully dissipated. He's not looking at all well."

"You shouldn't keep such late hours," said Alec, good-humouredly. "At your age one needs one's beauty sleep."

"It's very kind of you to take an interest in me," said Boulger, flushed with annoyance. "My headache has passed off."

"I'm very glad. What do you use—phenacetin?"

"It went away of its own accord after dinner," returned Bobbie frigidly, conscious that he was being laughed at, but unable to extricate himself.

"So you resolved to give the girls a treat by coming to Lady Kelsey's dance? How nice of you not to disappoint them!"

Alec turned to Alec, and they looked into one another's eyes.

"I sent you a paper this evening," he said gravely.

"It was very good of you."

There was a silence. All who were present felt that the moment was impressive, and it needed Canon Spratte's determination to allow none but himself to monopolise attention, to bring to an end a situation which might have proved awkward. He came forward and offered his arm to Lucy.

"I think this is my dance. May I take you in?"

He was trying to repeat the direct cut which he had given Alec earlier in the day. Alec looked at him.

"I saw you in Piccadilly this evening. You were dashing about like a young gazelle."

"I didn't see you," said the Canon, frigidly.

"I observed that you were deeply engrossed in the shop windows as I passed. How are you?"

He held out his hand. For a moment the Canon hesitated to take it, but Alec's gaze compelled him.

"How do you do?" he said.

He felt, rather than heard, Dick's chuckle, and reddening, offered his arm to Lucy.

"Won't you come, Mr. MacKenzie?" said Lady Kelsey, making the best of her difficulty.

"If you don't mind, I'll stay and smoke a cigarette with Dick Lomas. You know, I'm not a dancing man."

It seemed that Alec was giving Dick the opportunity he sought, and as soon as they found themselves alone, the sprightly little man attacked him.

"I suppose you know we were all beseeching Providence you'd have the grace to stay away tonight?" he said.

"I confess that I suspected it," smiled Alec. "I shouldn't have come, only I wanted to see Miss Allerton."

"This fellow Macinnery proposes to make things rather uncomfortable, I imagine."

"I made a mistake, didn't I?" said Alec, with a thin smile. "I should have dropped him in the river when I had no further use for him."

"What are you going to do?"

"Nothing."

Dick stared at him.

"Do you mean to say you're going to sit still and let them throw mud at you?"

"If they want to."

"But look here, Alec, what the deuce is the meaning of the whole thing?"

Alec looked at him quietly.

"If I had intended to take the world in general into my confidence, I wouldn't have refused to see the interviewers who came to me this evening."

"We've known one another for twenty years, Alec," said Dick.

"Then you may be quite sure that if I refuse to discuss this matter with you, it must be for excellent reasons."

Dick sprang up excitedly.

"But, good God! you must explain. You can't let a charge like this rest on you. After all, it's not Tom, Dick, or Harry that's concerned; it's Lucy's brother. You must speak."

"I've never yet discovered that I must do anything that I don't choose," answered Alec.

Dick flung himself into a chair. He knew that when Alec spoke in that fashion no power on earth could move him. The whole thing was entirely unexpected, and he was at a loss for words. He had not read the letter which was causing all the bother, and knew only what Lady Kelsey had told him. He had some hope that on a close examination various things would appear which must explain Alec's attitude; but at present it was incomprehensible.

"Has it occurred to you that Lucy is very much in love with you, Alec?" he said at last.

Alec did not answer. He made no movement.

"What will you do if this loses you her love?"

"I have counted the cost," said Alec, coldly.

He got up from his chair, and Dick saw that he did not wish to continue the discussion. There was a moment of silence, and then Lucy came in.

"I've given my partner away to a wall-flower," she said, with a faint smile. "I felt I must have a few words alone with you."

"I will make myself scarce," said Dick.

They waited till he was gone. Then Lucy turned feverishly to Alec.

"Oh, I'm so glad you've come. I wanted so much to see you."

"I'm afraid people have been telling you horrible things about me."

"They wanted to hide it from me."

"It never occurred to me that people *could* say such shameful things," he said gravely.

It tormented him a little because it had been so easy to care nothing for the world's adulation, and it was so hard to care as little for its censure. He felt very bitter.

He took Lucy's hand and made her sit on the sofa by his side.

"There's something I must tell you at once."

She looked at him without answering.

"I've made up my mind to give no answer to the charges that are brought against me."

Lucy looked up quickly, and their eyes met.

"I give you my word of honour that I've done nothing which I regret. I swear to you that what I did was right with regard to George, and if it were all to come again I would do exactly as I did before."

She did not answer for a long time.

"I never doubted you for a single moment," she said at last.

"That is all I care about." He looked down, and there was a certain shyness in his voice when he spoke again. "Today is the first time I've wanted to be assured that I was trusted; and yet I'm ashamed to want it."

"Don't be too hard upon yourself," she said gently. "You're so afraid of letting your tenderness appear."

He seemed to give earnest thought to what she said. Lucy had never seen him more grave.

"The only way to be strong is *never* to surrender to one's weakness. Strength is merely a habit. I want you to be strong, too. I want you never to doubt me whatever you hear said."

"I gave my brother into your hands, and I said that if he died a brave man's death, I could ask for no more. You told me that such a death was his."

"I thought of you always, and everything I did was for your sake. Every single act of mine during those four years in Africa has been done because I loved you."

It was the first time since his return that he had spoken of love. Lucy bent her head still lower.

"Do you remember, I asked you a question before I went away? You refused to marry me then, but you told me that if I asked again when I came back, the answer might be different."

"Yes."

"The hope bore me up in every difficulty and in every danger. And when I came back I dared not ask you at once; I was so afraid that you would refuse once more. And I didn't wish you to think yourself bound by a vague promise. But each day I loved you more passionately."

"I knew, and I was very grateful for your love."

"Yesterday I could have offered you a certain name. I only cared for the honours they gave me so that I might put them at your feet. But what can I offer you now?"

"You must love me always, Alec, for now I have only you."

"Are you sure that you will never believe that I am guilty of this crime?"

"Why can you say nothing in self-defence?"

"That I can't tell you either."

There was a silence between them. At last Alec spoke again.

"But perhaps it will be easier for you to believe in me than for others, because you know that I loved you, and I can't have done the odious thing of which that man accuses me."

"I will never believe it. I do not know what your reasons are for keeping all this to yourself, but I trust you, and I know that they are good. If you cannot speak, it is because greater interests hold you back. I love you, Alec, with all my heart, and if you wish me to be your wife I shall be proud and honoured."

He took her in his arms, and as he kissed her, she wept tears of happiness. She did not want to think. She wanted merely to surrender herself to his strength.

Chapter XVI

Lady Kelsey's devout hope that her party would finish without unpleasantness was singularly frustrated. Robert Boulger was irritated beyond endurance by the things Lucy had said to him; and Lucy besides, as if to drive him to distraction, had committed a peculiar indiscretion. In her determination to show the world in general, represented then by the two hundred people who were enjoying Lady Kelsey's hospitality, that she, the person most interested, did not for an instant believe what was said about Alec, Lucy had insisted on dancing with him. Alec thought it unwise thus to outrage conventional opinion, but he could not withstand her fiery spirit. Dick and Mrs. Crowley were partners at the time, and the disapproval which Lucy saw in their eyes, made her more vehement in her defiance. She had caught Bobbie's glance, too, and she flung back her head a little as she saw his livid anger.

Little by little Lady Kelsey's guests bade her farewell, and at three o'clock few were left. Lucy had asked Alec to remain till the end, and he and Dick had taken refuge in the smoking-room. Presently Boulger came in with two men, named Mallins and Carbery, whom Alec knew slightly. He glanced at Alec, and went up to the table on which were cigarettes and various things to drink. His companions had no idea that he was bent upon an explanation and had asked them of set purpose to come into that room.

"May we smoke here, Bobbie?" asked one of them, a little embarrassed at seeing Alec, but anxious to carry things off pleasantly.

"Certainly. Dick insisted that this room should be particularly reserved for that purpose."

"Lady Kelsey is the most admirable of all hostesses," said Dick lightly.

He took out his case and offered a cigarette to Alec. Alec took it.

"Give me a match, Bobbikins, that's a good boy," he said carelessly.

Boulger, with his back turned to Alec, took no notice of the request. He poured himself out some whisky, and raising the glass, deliberately examined how much there was in it. Alec smiled faintly.

"Bobbie, throw me over the matches," he repeated.

At that moment Lady Kelsey's butler came into the room with a salver, upon which he put the dirty glasses. Bobbie, his back still turned, looked up at the servant.

"Miller."

"Yes, sir."

"Mr. MacKenzie is asking for something."

"Yes, sir."

"You might give me a match, will you?" said Alec.

"Yes, sir."

The butler put the matches on his salver and took them over to Alec, who lit his cigarette.

"Thank you."

No one spoke till the butler left the room. Alec occupied himself idly in making smoke rings, and he watched them rise into the air. When they were alone he turned slowly to Boulger.

"I perceive that during my absence you have not added good manners to your other accomplishments," he said.

Boulger wheeled round and faced him.

"If you want things you can ask servants for them."

"Don't be foolish," smiled Alec, good-humouredly.

Alec's contemptuous manner robbed Boulger of his remaining self-control. He strode angrily to Alec.

"If you talk to me like that I'll knock you down."

Alec was lying stretched out on the sofa, and did not stir. He seemed completely unconcerned.

"You could hardly do that when I'm already lying on my back," he murmured.

Boulger clenched his fists. He gasped in the fury of his anger.

"Look here, MacKenzie, I'm not going to let you play the fool with me. I want to know what answer you have to make to Macinnery's accusation."

"Might I suggest that only Miss Allerton had the least right to receive answers to her questions? And she hasn't questioned me."

"I've given up trying to understand her attitude. If I were she, it would make me sick with horror to look at you. But after all I have the right to know something. George Allerton was my cousin."

Alec rose slowly from the sofa. He faced Boulger with an indifference which was peculiarly irritating.

"That is a fact upon which he did not vastly pride himself."

"Since this morning you've rested under a perfectly direct charge of causing his death in a dastardly manner. And you've said nothing in self-defence."

"I haven't."

"You've been given an opportunity of explaining yourself, and you haven't taken it."

"Quite true."

"What are you going to do?"

Alec had already been asked that question by Dick, and he returned the same answer.

"Nothing."

Bobbie looked at him for an instant. Then he shrugged his shoulders.

"In that case I can draw only one conclusion. There appears to be no means of bringing you to justice, but at least I can tell you what an indescribable blackguard I think you."

"All is over between us," smiled Alec, faintly amused at the young man's violence. "And shall I return your letters and your photographs?"

"I assure you that I'm not joking," answered Bobbie grimly.

"I have observed that you joke with difficulty. It's singular that though I'm Scotch and you are English, *I* should be able to see how ridiculous you are, while you're quite blind to your own absurdity."

"Come, Alec, remember he's only a boy," remonstrated Dick, who till now had been unable to interpose.

Boulger turned upon him angrily.

"I'm perfectly able to look after myself, Dick, and I'll thank you not to interfere." He looked again at Alec: "If Lucy's so indifferent to her brother's death that she's willing to keep up with you, that's her own affair."

Dick interrupted once more.

"For heaven's sake don't make a scene, Bobbie. How can you make such a fool of yourself?"

"Leave me alone, confound you!"

"Do you think this is quite the best place for an altercation?" asked Alec quietly. "Wouldn't you gain more notoriety if you attacked me in my club or at Church Parade on Sunday?"

"It's mere shameless impudence that you should come here tonight," cried Bobbie, his voice hoarse with passion. You're using these wretched women as a shield, because you know that as long as Lucy sticks to you, there are people who won't believe the story."

"I came for the same reason as yourself, dear boy. Because I was invited."

"You acknowledge that you have no defence."

"Pardon me, I acknowledge nothing and deny nothing."

"That won't do for me," said Boulger. "I want the truth, and I'm going to get it. I've got a right to know."

"Don't make such an ass of yourself," cried Alec, shortly.

"By God, I'll make you answer."

He went up to Alec furiously, as if he meant to seize him by the throat, but Alec, with a twist of the arm, hurled him backwards.

"I could break your back, you silly boy," he cried, in a voice low with anger.

With a cry of rage Bobbie was about to spring at Alec when Dick got in his way.

"For God's sake, let us have no scenes here. And you'll only get the worst of it, Bobbie. Alec could just crumple you up." He turned to the two men who stood behind, startled by the unexpectedness of the quarrel. "Take him away, Mallins, there's a good chap."

"Let me alone, you fool!" cried Bobbie.

"Come along, old man," said Mallins, recovering himself.

When his two friends had got Bobbie out of the room, Dick heaved a great sigh of relief.

"Poor Lady Kelsey!" he laughed, beginning to see the humour of the situation. "Tomorrow half London will be saying that you and Bobbie had a stand-up fight in her drawing-room."

Alec looked at him angrily. He was not a man of easy temper, and the effort he had put upon himself was beginning to tell.

"You really needn't have gone out of your way to infuriate the boy," said Dick.

Alec wheeled round wrathfully.

"The damned cubs," he said. "I should like to break their silly necks."

"You have an amiable character, Alec," retorted Dick.

Alec began to walk up and down excitedly. Dick had never seen him before in such a state.

"The position is growing confoundedly awkward," he said drily.

Then Alec burst out.

"They lick my boots till I loathe them, and then they turn against me like a pack of curs. Oh, I despise them, these silly boys who stay at home wallowing in their ease, while men work—work and conquer. Thank God, I've done with them now. They think one can fight one's way through Africa as easily as walk down Piccadilly. They think one goes through hardship and danger, illness and starvation, to be the lion of a dinner-party in Mayfair."

"I think you're unfair to them," answered Dick. "Can't you see the other side of the picture? You're accused of a particularly low act of treachery. Your friends were hoping that you'd be able to prove at once that it was an abominable lie, and for some reason which no one can make out, you refuse even to notice it."

"My whole life is proof that it's a lie."

"Don't you think you'd better change your mind and make a statement that can be sent to the papers?"

"No, damn you!"

Dick's good nature was imperturbable, and he was not in the least annoyed by Alec's vivacity.

"My dear chap, do calm down," he laughed.

Alec started at the sound of his mocking. He seemed again to become aware of himself. It was interesting to observe the quite visible effort he made to regain his self-control. In a moment he had mastered his excitement, and he turned to Dick with studied nonchalance.

"Do you think I look wildly excited?" he asked blandly.

Dick smiled.

"If you will permit me to say so, I think butter would have *no* difficulty in melting in your mouth," he replied.

"I never felt cooler in my life."

"Lucky man, with the thermometer at a hundred and two!"

Alec laughed and put his arm through Dick's.

"Perhaps we had better go home," he said.

"Your common sense is no less remarkable than your personal appearance," answered Dick gravely.

They had already bidden their hostess good-night, and getting their things, they set out to walk their different ways. When Dick got home he did not go to bed. He sat in an arm-chair, considering the events of the evening, and trying to find some way out of the complexity of his thoughts. He was surprised when the morning sun sent a bright ray of light into his room.

But Lady Kelsey was not yet at the end of her troubles. Bobbie, having got rid of his friends, went to her and asked if she would not come downstairs and drink a cup of soup. The poor lady, quite exhausted, thought him very considerate. One or two persons, with their coats on, were still in the room, waiting for their womenkind; and in the hall there was a little group of belated guests huddled around the door, while cabs and carriages were being brought up for them. There was about everything the lassitude which follows the gaiety of a dance. The waiters behind the tables were heavy-eyed. Lucy was bidding good-bye to one or two more intimate friends.

Lady Kelsey drank the hot soup with relief.

"My poor legs are dropping," she said. "I'm sure I'm far too tired to go to sleep."

"I want to talk to Lucy before I go," said Bobbie, abruptly.

"Tonight?" she asked in dismay.

"Yes, I want you to send her a message that you wish to see her in your *boudoir*."

"Why, what on earth's the matter?"

"She can't go on in this way. It's perfectly monstrous. Something must be done immediately."

Lady Kelsey understood what he was driving at. She knew how great was his love, and she, too, had seen his anger when Lucy danced with Alec MacKenzie. But the whole affair perplexed her utterly. She put down her cup.

"Can't you wait till tomorrow?" she asked nervously.

"I feel it ought to be settled at once."

"I think you're dreadfully foolish. You know how Lucy resents any interference with her actions."

"I shall bear her resentment with fortitude," he said, with great bitterness.

Lady Kelsey looked at him helplessly.

"What do you want me to do?" she asked.

"I want you to be present at our interview."

He turned to a servant and told him to ask Miss Allerton from Lady Kelsey if she would kindly come to the *boudoir*. He gave his arm to Lady Kelsey, and they went upstairs. In a moment Lucy appeared.

"Did you send for me, my aunt? I'm told you want to speak to me here."

"I asked Aunt Alice to beg you to come here," said Boulger. "I was afraid you wouldn't come if *I* asked you."

Lucy looked at him with raised eyebrows and answered lightly.

"What nonsense! I'm always delighted to enjoy your society."

"I wanted to speak to you about something, and I thought Aunt Alice should be present."

Lucy gave him a quick glance. He met it coolly.

"Is it so important that it can't wait till tomorrow?"

"I venture to think it's very important. And by now everybody has gone."

"I'm all attention," she smiled.

Boulger hesitated for a moment, then braced himself for the ordeal.

"I've told you often, Lucy, that I've been desperately in love with you for more years than I can remember," he said, flushing with nervousness.

"Surely you've not snatched me from my last chance of a cup of soup in order to make me a proposal of marriage?"

"I'm perfectly serious, Lucy."

"I assure you it doesn't suit you at all," she smiled.

"The other day I asked you again to marry me, just before Alec MacKenzie came back."

A softer light came into Lucy's eyes, and the bantering tones fell away from her voice.

"It was very charming of you," she said gravely. "You mustn't think that because I laugh at you a little, I'm not very grateful for your affection."

"You know how long he's cared for you, Lucy," said Lady Kelsey.

Lucy went up to him and very tenderly placed her hand on his arm.

"I'm immensely touched by your great devotion, Bobbie, and I know that I've done nothing to deserve it. I'm very sorry that I can't give you anything in return. One's not mistress of one's love. I can only hope—with all my heart—that you'll fall in love with some girl who cares for you. You don't know how much I want you to be happy."

Boulger drew back coldly. He would not allow himself to be touched, though the sweetness of her voice tore his heart-strings.

"Just now it's not my happiness that's concerned," he said. "When Alec MacKenzie came back I thought I saw why nothing that I could do, had the power to change the utter indifference with which you looked at me."

He paused a moment and coughed uneasily.

"I don't know why you think it necessary to say all this," said Lucy, in a low voice.

"I tried to resign myself. You've always worshipped strength, and I understood that you must think Alec MacKenzie very wonderful. I had little enough to offer you when I compared myself with him. I hoped against hope that you weren't in love with him."

"Well?"

"Except for that letter in this morning's paper I should never have dared to say anything to you again. But that changes everything."

He paused once more. Though he tried to seem so calm, his heart was beating furiously. He really loved Lucy with all his soul, and he was doing what seemed to him a plain duty.

"I ask you again if you'll be my wife."

"I don't understand what you mean," she said slowly.

"You can't marry Alec MacKenzie now."

Lucy flung back her head. She grew very pale.

"You have no right to talk to me like this," she said. "You really presume too much upon my good nature."

"I think I have some right. I'm the only man who's related to you at all, and I love you."

They saw that Lady Kelsey wanted to speak, and Lucy turned round to her.

"I think you should listen to him, Lucy. I'm growing old, and soon you'll be quite alone in the world."

The simple kindness of her words calmed the passions of the other two, and brought down the conversation to a gentler level.

"I'll try my best to make you a good husband, Lucy," said Bobbie, very earnestly. "I don't ask you to care for me; I only want to serve you."

"I can only repeat that I'm very grateful to you. But I can't marry you, and I shall never marry you."

Boulger's face grew darker, and he was silent.

"Are you going to continue to know Alec MacKenzie?" he said at length.

"You have no right to ask me such a question."

"If you'll take the advice of any unprejudiced person about that letter, you'll find that he'll say the same as I. There can be no shadow of a doubt that the man is guilty of a monstrous crime."

"I don't care what the evidence is," said Lucy. "I know he can't have done a shameful thing."

"But, good God, have you forgotten that it's your own brother whom he killed!" he cried hotly. "The whole country is up in arms against him, and you are quite indifferent."

"Oh, Bobbie, how can you say that?" she wailed, suddenly moved to the very depths of her being. "How can you be so cruel?"

He went up to her, and they stood face to face. He spoke very quickly, flinging the words at her with indignant anger.

"If you cared for George at all, you must wish to punish the man who caused his death. At least you can't continue to be his"—he stopped as he saw the agony in her eyes, and changed his words—"his greatest friend. It was your doing that George went to Africa at all. The least you can do is to take some interest in his death."

She put up her hands to her eyes, as though to drive away the sight of hateful things.

"Oh, why do you torment me?" she cried pitifully. "I tell you he isn't guilty."

"He's refused to answer anyone. I tried to get something out of him, but I couldn't, and I lost my temper. He might give you the truth if you asked him point-blank."

"I couldn't do that."

"Why not?"

"It's very strange that he should insist on this silence," said Lady Kelsey. "One would have thought if he had nothing to be ashamed of, he'd have nothing to hide."

"Do you believe that story, too?" asked Lucy.

"I don't know what to believe. It's so extraordinary. Dick says he knows nothing about it. If the man's innocent, why on earth doesn't he speak?"

"He knows I trust him," said Lucy. "He knows I'm proud to trust him. Do you think I would cause him the great pain of asking him questions?"

"Are you afraid he couldn't answer them?" asked Boulger.

"No, no, no."

"Well, just try. After all you owe as much as that to the memory of George. Try."

"But don't you see that if he won't say anything, it's because there are good reasons," she cried distractedly. "How do I know what interests are concerned in the matter, beside which the death of George is insignificant . . ."

"Do you look upon it so lightly as that?"

She turned away, bursting into tears. She was like a hunted beast. There seemed no escape from the taunting questions.

"I must show my faith in him," she sobbed.

"I think you're a little nervous to go into the matter too closely."

"I believe in him implicitly. I believe in him with all the strength I've got."

"Then surely it can make no difference if you ask him. There can be no reason for him not to trust you."

"Oh, why don't you leave me alone?" she wailed.

"I do think it's very unreasonable, Lucy," said Lady Kelsey. "He knows you're his friend. He can surely count on your discretion."

"If he refused to answer me it would mean nothing. You don't know him as I do. He's a man of extraordinary character. If he has made up his mind that for certain reasons which we don't know, he must preserve an entire silence, nothing whatever will move him. Why should he answer? I believe in him absolutely. I think he's the greatest and most honourable man I've ever known. I should feel happy and grateful to be allowed to wait on him."

"Lucy, what *do* you mean?" cried Lady Kelsey.

But now Lucy had cast off all reserve. She did not mind what she said.

"I mean that I care more for his little finger than for the whole world. I love him with all my heart. And that's why he can't be guilty of this horrible thing, because I've loved him for years, and he's known it. And he loves me, and he's loved me always."

She sank exhausted into a chair, gasping for breath. Boulger looked at her for a moment, and he turned sick with anguish. What he had only suspected before, he knew now from her own lips; and it was harder than ever to bear. Now everything seemed ended.

"Are you going to marry him?" he asked.

"Yes."

"In spite of everything?"

"In spite of everything," she answered defiantly.

Bobbie choked down the groan of despairing rage that forced its way to his throat. He watched her for a moment.

"Good God," he said at last, "what is there in the man that he should have made you forget love and honour and common decency!"

Lucy made no reply. But she buried her face in her hands and wept. She rocked to and fro with the violence of her tears.

Without another word Bobbie turned round and left them. Lady Kelsey heard the door slam as he went out into the silent street.

Chapter XVII

NEXT DAY ALEC WAS CALLED UP TO LANCASHIRE.
When he went out in the morning, he saw on the placards of the evening papers that there had been a colliery explosion, but, his mind absorbed in other things, he paid no attention to it; and it was a shock that, on opening a telegram which waited for him at his club, he found that the accident had occurred in his own mine. Thirty miners were entombed, and it was feared that they could not be saved. Immediately all thought of his own concerns fled from him, and sending for a time-table, he looked out for a train. He found one that he could just catch. He took a couple of telegram forms in the cab with him, and on one scribbled instructions to his servant to follow him at once with clothes; the other he wrote to Lucy.

He just caught the train and in the afternoon found himself at the mouth of the pit. There was a little crowd around it of weeping women. All efforts to save the wretched men appeared to be useless. Many had been injured, and the manager's house had been converted into a hospital. Alec found everyone stunned by the disaster, and the attempts at rescue had been carried on feebly. He set himself to work at once. He put heart into the despairing women. He brought up everyone who could be of the least use and inspired them with his own resourceful courage. The day was drawing to a close, but no time could be lost; and all night they toiled. Alec, in his shirt-sleeves, laboured as heartily as the strongest miner; he seemed to want neither rest nor food. With clenched teeth, silently, he fought a battle with death, and the prize was thirty living men. In the morning he refreshed himself with a bath, paid a hurried visit to the injured, and returned to the pit mouth.

He had no time to think of other things. He did not know that on this very morning another letter appeared in the *Daily Mail,* filling in the details of the case against him, adding one damning piece of evidence to another; he did not know that the papers, amazed and indignant at his silence, now were unanimous in their condemnation. It was made a party matter, and the radical organs used the scandal as a stick to beat the dying donkey which was then in power. A question was put down to be asked in the House.

Alec waged his good fight and neither knew nor cared that the bubble of his glory was pricked. Still the miners lived in the tomb, and forty-eight hours passed. Hope was failing in the stout hearts of those who laboured by his side, but Alec urged them to greater endeavours. And now nothing was needed but a dogged perseverance. His tremendous strength stood him in good stead, and he was able to work twenty hours on end. He did not spare himself. And he seemed able to call prodigies of endurance out of those who helped him; with that example it seemed easier to endure. And still they toiled unrestingly. But their hope was growing faint. Behind that wall thirty men were lying, hopeless, starving; and some perhaps were dead already. And it was terrible to think of the horrors that assailed them, the horror of rising water, the horror of darkness, and the gnawing pangs of hungry. Among them was a boy of fourteen. Alec had spoken to him by chance on one of the days he had recently spent there, and had been amused by his cheeky brightness. He was a blue-eyed lad with a laughing mouth. It was pitiful to think that all that joy of life should have been crushed by a blind, stupid disaster. His father had been killed, and his body, charred and disfigured, lay in the mortuary. The boy was imprisoned with his brother, a man older than himself, married, and the father of children. With angry vehemence Alec set to again. He would not be beaten.

At last they heard sounds, faint and muffled, but unmistakable. At all events some of them were still alive. The rescuers increased their efforts. Now it was only a question of hours. They were so near that it renewed their strength; all fatigue fell from them; it needed but a little courage.

At last!

With a groan of relief which tried hard to be a cheer, the last barrier was broken, and the prisoners were saved. They were brought out one by one, haggard with sunken eyes that blinked feebly in the sunlight; their faces were pale with the shadow of death, and they could not stand on their feet. The bright-eyed boy were carried out in Alec's strong arms, and he tried to make a jest of it; but the smile on his lips was changed into a sob, and hiding his face in Alec's breast, he cried from utter weakness. They carried out his brother, and he was dead. His wife was waiting for him at the pit's mouth, with her children by her side.

This commonplace incident, briefly referred to in the corner of a morning paper, made his own affairs strangely unimportant to Alec. Face to face with the bitter tragedy of women left husbandless, of orphaned children, and the grim horror of men cut off in the prime of their manhood, the agitation which his own conduct was causing fell out of view. He was harassed and anxious. Much business had to be done which would allow of no delay. It was necessary to make every effort to get the mine once more into working order; it was necessary to provide for those who had lost the breadwinner. Alec found himself assailed on all sides with matters of urgent importance, and he had not a moment to devote to his own affairs. When at length it was possible for him to consider himself at all, he felt that the accident had raised him out of the narrow pettiness which threatened to submerge his soul; he was at close quarters with malignant fate, and he had waged a desperate battle with the cruel blindness of chance. He could only feel an utter scorn for the people who bespattered him with base charges. For, after all, his conscience was free.

When he wrote to Lucy, it never struck him that it was needful to refer to the events that had preceded his departure from London, and his letter was full of the strenuous agony of the past days. He told her how they had fought hand to hand with death and had snatched the prey from his grasp. In a second letter he told her what steps he was taking to repair the damage that had been caused, and what he was doing for those who were in immediate need. He would have given much to be able to write down the feelings of passionate devotion with which Lucy filled him, but with the peculiar shyness which was natural to him, he could not bring himself to it. Of the accusation with which the world was ringing, he said never a word.

Lucy read his letters over and over again. She could not understand them, and they seemed strangely indifferent. At that distance from the scene of the disaster she could not realise its absorbing anxiety, and she was bitterly disappointed at Alec's absence. She wanted his presence so badly, and she had to bear alone, on her own shoulders, the full weight of her trouble. When Macinnery's second letter appeared, Lady Kelsey gave it to her without a word. It was awful. The whole thing was preposterous, but it hung together in a way that was maddening, and there was an air of truth about it which terrified her. And why should Alec insist on this impenetrable silence? She had offered herself the suggestion that political exigencies with regard to the states whose spheres of influence bordered upon the territory which Alec had conquered, demanded the strictest reserve; but this explanation soon appeared fantastic. She read all that was said in the papers and found that opinion was dead against Alec. Now that it was become a party matter, his own side defended him; but in a half-hearted way, which showed how poor the case was. And since all that could be urged in his favour, Lucy had already repeated to herself a thousand times, what was said against him seemed infinitely more conclusive than what was said for him. And then her conscience smote her. Those cruel words of Bobbie's came back to her, and she was overwhelmed with self-reproach when she considered that it was her own brother of whom was all this to-do. She must be utterly heartless or utterly depraved. And then with a despairing energy she cried out that she believed in Alec; he was incapable of a treacherous act.

At last she could bear it no longer, and she wired to him: *For God's sake come quickly.*

She felt that she could not endure another day of this misery. She waited for him, given over to the wildest fears; she was ashamed and humiliated. She counted the hours which must pass before he could arrive; surely he would not delay. All her self-possession had vanished, and she was like a child longing for the protecting arms that should enfold it.

At last he came. Lucy was waiting in the same room in which she had sat on their first meeting after his return to England. She sprang up, pale and eager, and flung herself passionately into his arms.

"Thank God, you've come," she said. "I thought the hours would never end."

He did not know what so vehemently disturbed her, but he kissed her tenderly, and on a sudden she felt strangely comforted. There was an extraordinary honesty about him which strengthened and consoled her. For a while she could not speak, but clung to him, sobbing.

"What is it?" he asked at length. "Why did you send for me?"

"I want your love. I want your love so badly."

It was inconceivable, the exquisite tenderness with which he caressed her. No one would have thought that dour man capable of such gentleness.

"I felt I must see you," she sobbed. "You don't know what tortures I've endured."

"Poor child."

He kissed her hair and her white, pained forehead.

"Why did you go away? You knew I wanted you."

"I'm very sorry."

"I've been horribly wretched. I didn't know I could suffer so much."

"Come and sit down and tell me all about it."

He led her to the sofa and made her sit beside him. His arms were around her, and she nestled close to him. For a moment she remained silent, enjoying the feeling of great relief after the long days of agony. She smiled lightly through her tears.

"The moment I'm with you I feel so confident and happy."

"Only when you're with me?"

He asked the question caressingly, in a low passionate voice that she had never heard from his lips before. She did not answer, but clung more closely to him. Smiling, he repeated the question.

"Only when you're with me, darling?"

"I've told Bobbie and my aunt that we're going to be married. They made me suffer so dreadfully. I had to tell them. I couldn't keep it back, they said such horrible things about you.

He did not answer for a moment.

"It's very natural."

"It's nothing to you," she cried desperately. "But to me. . . . Oh, you don't know what agony I had to endure."

"I'm glad you told them."

"Bobbie said I must be heartless and cruel. And it's true: George is nothing to me now when I think of you. My heart is so filled with my love for you that I haven't room for anything else."

"I hope my love will make up for all that you have lost. I want you to be happy."

She withdrew from his arms and leaned back, against the corner of the sofa. It was absolutely necessary to say what was gnawing at her heartstrings, but she felt ashamed and could not look at him.

"That wasn't the only reason I told them. I'm such a coward. I thought I was much braver."

"Why?"

Lucy felt on a sudden sick at heart. She began to tremble a little, and it was only by great strength of will that she forced herself to go on. She was horribly frightened. Her mouth was dry, and when at last the words came, her voice sounded unnatural.

"I wanted to burn my ships behind me. I wanted to reassure myself."

This time it was Alec who did not answer, for he understood now what was on her mind. His heart sank, since he saw already that he must lose her. But he had faced that possibility long ago in the heavy forests of Africa, and he had made up his mind that Lucy could do without love better than without self-respect.

He made a movement to get up, but quickly Lucy put out her hand. And then suddenly a fire seized him, and a vehement determination not to give way till the end.

"I don't understand you," he said quietly.

"Forgive me, dear," she said.

She held his hand in hers, and she spoke quickly.

"You don't know how terrible it is. I stand so dreadfully alone. Everyone is so bitter against you, and not a soul has a good word to say for you. It's all so extraordinary and so inexplicable. It seems as if I am the only person who isn't convinced that you caused poor George's death. Oh, how callous and utterly heartless people must think me!"

"Does it matter very much what people think?" he said gravely.

"I'm so ashamed of myself. I try to put the thoughts out of my head, but I can't. I simply can't. I've tried to be brave. I've refused to discuss the possibility of there being anything in those horrible charges. I wanted to talk to Dick—I know he was fond of you—but I didn't dare. It seemed treacherous to you, and I wouldn't let anyone see that it meant anything to me. The first letter wasn't so bad, but the second—oh, it looks so dreadfully true."

Alec gave her a rapid glance. This was the first he had heard of another communication to the paper. During the frenzied anxiety of those days at the colliery, he had time to attend to nothing but the pressing work of rescue. But he made no reply.

"I've read it over and over again, and I *can't* understand. When Bobbie says it's conclusive, I tell him it means nothing—but—don't you see what I mean? The uncertainty is more than I can bear."

She stopped suddenly, and now she looked at him. There was a pitiful appeal in her eyes.

"At the first moment I felt so absolutely sure of you."

"And now you don't?" he asked quietly.

She cast down her eyes once more, and a sob caught her breath.

"I trust you just as much as ever. I know it's impossible that you should have done a shameful deed. But there it stands in black and white, and you have nothing to say in answer."

"I know it's very difficult. That's why I asked you to believe in me."

"I do, Alec," she cried vehemently. "With all my soul. But have mercy on me. I'm not as strong as I thought. It's easy for you to stand alone. You're iron. You're a mountain of granite. But I'm a weak woman, pitifully weak."

He shook his head.

"Oh, no, you're not like other women."

"It was easy to be brave where my father was concerned, or George, but now it's so difficult. Love has changed me. I haven't the courage any more to withstand the opinion of all my fellows."

Alec got up and walked once or twice across the room. He seemed to be thinking deeply. Lucy fancied that he must hear the beating of her heart. He stopped in front of her. Her heart was wrung by the great pain that was in his voice.

"Don't you remember that only a few days ago I told you that I'd done nothing which I wouldn't do again? I gave you my word of honour that I could reproach myself for nothing."

"Oh, I know," she cried. "I'm so utterly ashamed of myself. But I can't bear the doubt."

"*Doubt.* You've said the word at last."

"I tell myself that I don't believe a word of these horrible charges. I repeat to myself: I'm certain, I'm certain that he's innocent."

She gathered strength in the desperation of her love, and now at the crucial moment she had all the courage she needed.

"And yet at the bottom of my heart there's the doubt. And I *can't* crush it."

She waited for him to answer, but he did not speak.

"I wanted to kill that bitter pain of suspicion. I thought if I stood up before them and cried out that my trust in you was so great, I was willing to marry you notwithstanding everything—I should at least have peace in my heart."

Alec went to the window and looked out. The westering sun slanted across the street. Carriages and motors were waiting at the door of the house opposite, and a little crowd of footmen clustered about the steps. They were giving a party, and through the open windows Alec could see a throng of women. The sky was very blue. He turned back to Lucy.

"Will you show me the second letter of which you speak?"

"Haven't you seen it?" she asked in astonishment.

"I was so busy, I had no time to look at the papers. I suppose no one thought it his business to draw my attention to it."

Lucy went into the second drawing-room, divided from that in which they sat by an archway, and brought him the copy of the *Daily Mail* for which he asked. She gave it, and he took it silently. He sat down and with attention read the letter through. He observed with bitter scorn the thoroughness with which Macinnery had set out the case against him. In this letter he filled up the gaps which had been left in the first, adding here and there details which gave a greater coherency to the whole; and his evidence had an air of truth, since he quoted the very words of porters and askari who had been on the expedition. It was wonderful what power had that small admixture of falsehood joined with what was admittedly true, to change the whole aspect of the case. Alec was obliged to confess that Lucy had good grounds for her suspicion. There was a specious look about the story, which would have made him credit it himself if some other man had been concerned. The facts were given with sufficient exactness, and the untruth lay only in the motives that were ascribed to him; but who could tell what another's motives were? Alec put the paper on the table, and leaning back, his face resting in his hand, thought deeply. He saw again that scene in the tent when the wind was howling outside and the rain falling, falling; he called George's white face, the madness that came over him when he fired at Alec, the humility of his submission. The earth covered the boy, his crime, and his weakness. It was not easy to save one's self at a dead man's expense. And he knew that George's strength and courage had meant more than her life to Lucy. How could he cause her the bitter pain? How could he tell her that her brother died because he was a coward and a rogue? How could he tell her the pitiful story of the boy's failure to redeem the good name that was so dear to her? And what proof could he offer of anything he said? Walker had been killed on the same night as George, poor Walker with his cheerfulness in difficulties and his buoyant spirits: his death too must be laid to the charge of George Allerton; Adamson had died of fever. Those two alone had any inkling of the truth; they could have told a story that would at least have thrown grave doubts upon Macinnery's. But Alec set his teeth; he did not want their testimony. Finally there was the promise. He had given his solemn oath, and the place and the moment made it seem more binding, that he would utter no word that should lead Lucy to suspect even for an instant that her brother had been untrue to the trust she had laid upon him. Alec was a man of scrupulous truthfulness, not from deliberately moral motives but from mere taste, and he could not have broken his promise for the great discomfort it would have caused him. But it was the least of the motives which influenced him. Even if George had exacted nothing, he would have kept silence. And then, at the bottom of his heart, was a fierce pride. He was conscious of the honesty of his motives, and he expected that Lucy should share his consciousness. She must believe what he said to her because he said it. He could not suffer the humiliation of defending himself, and he felt that her love could not be very great if she could really doubt him. And because he was very proud perhaps he was unjust. He did not know that he was putting upon her a trial which he should have asked no one to bear.

He stood up and faced Lucy.

"What is it precisely that you want me to do?" he asked.

"I want you to have mercy on me because I love you. Don't tell the world if you choose not to. But tell me the truth. I know you're incapable of lying. If I only have it from your own lips I shall believe. I want to be certain, certain."

"Don't you realise that I would never have asked you to marry me if my conscience hadn't been quite clear?" he said slowly. "Don't you see that the reasons I have for holding my tongue must be overwhelming, or I wouldn't stand-by calmly while my good name was torn from me shred by shred?"

"But I'm going to be your wife, and I love you, and I know you love me."

"I implore you not to insist, Lucy. Let us remember only that the past is gone and that we love one another. It is impossible for me to tell you anything."

"Oh, but you must now," she implored. "If anything has happened, if any part of the story is true, you must give me a chance of judging for myself."

"I'm very sorry. I can't."

"But you'll kill my love for you."

She sprang to her feet and pressed both hands to her heart.

"The doubt that lurked at the bottom of my soul, now fills me. How can you let me suffer such maddening torture?"

An expression of anguish passed across his calm eyes. He made a gesture of despair.

"I thought you trusted me."

"I'll be satisfied if you'll only tell me one thing." She put her hands to her head with a rapid, aimless movement that showed the extremity of her agitation. "Oh, what has love done with me?" she cried desperately. "I was so proud of my brother and so utterly devoted to him. But I loved you so much that there wasn't any room in my heart for the past. I forgot all my unhappiness and all my loss. And even now they seem so little to me beside your love that it's you I think of first. I want to know that I can love you freely. I'll be satisfied if you'll only tell me that when you sent George out that night, you didn't *know* he'd be killed."

Alec looked at her steadily. And once more he saw himself in the African tent amid the rain and the boisterous wind. At the time he sought to persuade himself that George had a chance of escape. He told him with his own lips that if he showed perfect self-confidence at the moment of danger he might save himself alive; but at the bottom of his heart he knew, he had known all along, that it was indeed death he was sending him to, for George had not the last virtue of a scoundrel, courage.

"Only say that, Alec," she repeated. "Say that's not true, and I'll believe you."

There was a silence. Lucy's heart beat against her breast like a caged bird. She waited in horrible suspense.

"But it is true," he said, very quietly.

Lucy did not answer. She stared at him with terrified eyes. Her brain reeled, and she feared that she was going to faint. She had to put forth all her strength to drive back the enveloping night that seemed to crowd upon her.

"It is true," he repeated.

She gave a gasp of pain.

"I don't understand. Oh, my dearest, don't treat me as a child. Have mercy on me. You must be serious now. It's a matter of life and death to both of us."

"I'm perfectly serious."

A frightful coldness appeared to seize her, and the tips of her fingers were strangely numbed.

"You knew that you were sending George into a death-trap? You knew that he could not escape alive?"

"Except by a miracle."

"And you don't believe in miracles?"

Alec made no answer. She looked at him with increasing horror. Her eyes were staring wildly. She repeated the question.

"And you don't believe in miracles?"

"No."

She was seized with all manner of conflicting emotions. They seemed to wage a tumultuous battle in the depths of her heart. She was filled with horror and dismay, bitter anger, remorse for her callous indifference to George's death; and at the same time she felt an overwhelming love for Alec. And how could she love him now?

"Oh, it can't be true," she cried. "It's infamous. Oh, Alec, Alec, Alec . . . O God, what shall I do."

Alec held himself upright. He set his teeth, and his heavy jaw seemed squarer than ever. There was a great sternness in his voice.

"I tell you that whatever I did was inevitable."

Lucy flushed at the sound of his voice, and anger and sudden hatred took the place of all other feelings.

"Then if it's true, the rest must be true. Why don't you acknowledge as well that you sacrificed my brother's life in order to save your own?"

But the mood passed quickly, and in a moment she was seized with dismay.

"Oh, it's awful. I can't realise it." She turned to him with a desperate appeal. "Haven't you anything to say at all? You know how much I loved my brother. You know how much it meant to me that he should love to wipe out all memory of my father's crime. All the future was centred upon him. You can't have sacrificed him callously."

Alec hesitated for an instant.

"I think I might tell you this," he said. "We were entrapped by the Arabs, and our only chance of escape entailed the death of one of us."

"So you chose my brother because you loved me."

Alec looked at her. There was an extraordinary sadness in his eyes, but she did not see it. He answered very gravely.

"You see, the fault was his. He had committed a grave error. It was not unjust that he should suffer for the catastrophe that he had brought about."

"At those times one doesn't think of justice. He was so young, so frank and honest. Wouldn't it have been nobler to give your life for his?"

"Oh, my dear," he answered, with all the gentleness that was in him, "you don't know how easy it is to give one's life, how much more difficult it is to be just than generous. How little you know me! Do you think I should have hesitated if the difficulty had been one that my death could solve? It was necessary that I should live. I had my work to do. I was bound by solemn treaties to the surrounding tribes. Even if that had been all, it would have been cowardly for me to die."

"It is easy to find excuses for not acting like a brave man." She flung the words at him with indignant scorn.

"I was indispensable," he answered. "The whites I took with me I chose as instruments, not as leaders. If I had died the expedition would have broken in pieces. It was my influence that held together such of the native tribes as remained faithful to us. I had given my word that I would not desert them till I had exterminated the slave-raiders. Two days after my death my force would have melted away, and the whites would have been helpless. Not one of them would have escaped. And then the country would have been given up, defenceless, to those cursed Arabs. Fire and sword would have come instead of the peace I promised; and the whole country would have been rendered desolate. I tell you that it was my duty to live till I had carried out my work."

Lucy drew herself up a little. She looked at him firmly, and said very quietly and steadily:

"You coward! You coward!"

"I knew at the time that what I did might cost me your love, and though you won't believe this, I did it for your sake."

"I wish I had a whip in my hand that I might slash you across the face."

For a moment he did not say anything. She was quivering with indignation and with contempt.

"You see, it has cost me your love," he said. "I suppose it was inevitable."

"I am ashamed that I ever loved you."

"Good-bye."

He turned round and walked slowly to the door. He held his head erect, and there was no sign of emotion on his face. But as soon as he was gone Lucy could keep her self-control no longer. She sank into a chair, and hiding her face, began to sob as though her poor tortured heart would break.

Chapter XVIII

ALEC WENT BACK TO LANCASHIRE NEXT DAY. MUCH WAS STILL REQUIRED BEfore the colliery could be put once more in proper order, and he was overwhelmed with work. Lucy was not so fortunate. She had nothing to do but to turn over in her mind the conversation they had had. She passed one sleepless night after another. She felt ill and wretched. She told Lady Kelsey that her engagement with MacKenzie was broken off, but gave no reason; and Lady Kelsey, seeing her white, tortured face, had not the heart to question her. Lucy never sought for the sympathy of others and chose rather to bear her troubles alone. The season was drawing to a close, and Lady Kelsey suggested that they should advance by a week or two the date of their departure for the country; but Lucy would do nothing to run away from her suffering.

"I don't know why you should alter your plans," she said quietly.

Lady Kelsey looked at her compassionately, but did not insist. She felt somehow that Lucy was of different clay from herself, and for all her exquisite gentleness, her equanimity and pleasant temper, she had never been able to get entirely at close quarters with her. She would have given much to see Lucy give way openly to her grief; and her arms would have been open to receive her, if her niece had only flung herself simply into them. But Lucy's spirit was broken. With the extreme reserve that was part of her nature, she put all her strength into the effort to behave in the world with decency; and dreading any attempt at commiseration, she forced herself to be no less cheerful than usual. The strain was hardly tolerable. She had set all her hopes of happiness upon Alec, and he had failed her. She thought more of her brother and her father than she had done of late, and she mourned for them both as though the loss she had sustained were quite recent. It seemed to her that the only thing now was to prevent herself from thinking of Alec, and with angry determination she changed her thoughts as soon as he came into them.

Presently something else occurred to her. She felt that she owed some reparation to Bobbie: he had seen the truth at once, and because he had pointed it out to her, as surely it was his duty to do, she had answered him with bitter words. He had shown himself extraordinarily kind, and she had been harsh and cruel. Perhaps he knew that she was no longer engaged to marry Alec MacKenzie, and he must guess the reason; but since the night of the dance he had not been near them. She looked upon what Alec had told her as addressed to her only, and she could not repeat it to all and sundry. When acquaintances had referred to the affair, her manner had shown them quickly that she did not intend to discuss it. But Robert Boulger was different. It seemed necessary, in consideration of all that had passed, that he should be told the little she knew; and then she thought also, seized on a sudden with a desire for self-sacrifice, that it was her duty perhaps to reward him for his long devotion. She might at least try to make him a good wife; and she could explain exactly how she felt towards him. There would be no deceit. Her life had no value now, and if it really meant so much to him to marry her, it was right that she should consent. And there was another thing: it would put an irrevocable barrier between herself and Alec.

Lady Kelsey was accustomed to ask a few people to luncheon every Tuesday, and Lucy suggested that they should invite Bobbie on one of these occasions. Lady Kelsey was much pleased, for she was fond of her nephew, and it pained her that she had not seen him. She had sent a line to tell him that Lucy was no longer engaged, but he had not answered. Lucy wrote the invitation herself.

MY DEAR BOBBIE:—Aunt Alice will be very glad if you can lunch with us on Tuesday at two. We are asking Dick, Julia Crowley, and Canon Spratte. If you can come, and I hope you will, it would be very kind of you to arrive a good deal earlier than the others; I want to talk to you about something.

Yours affectionately,
LUCY

He answered at once.

MY DEAR LUCY:—I will come with pleasure. I hope half-past one will suit you.

Your affectionate cousin,
ROBERT BOULGER

"Why haven't you been to see us?" she said, holding his hand, when at the appointed time he appeared.

"I thought you didn't much want to see me."

"I'm afraid I was very cruel and unkind to you last time you were here," she said.

"It doesn't matter at all," he said gently.

"I think I should tell you that I did as you suggested to me. I asked Alec MacKenzie pointblank, and he confessed that he was guilty of George's death."

"I'm very sorry," said Bobbie.

"Why?" she asked, looking up at him with tear-laden eyes.

"Because I know that you were very much in love with him," he answered.

Lucy flushed. But she had much more to say.

"I was very unjust to you on the night of that dance. You were right to speak to me as you did, and I was very foolish. I regret what I said, and I beg you to forgive me."

"There's nothing to forgive, Lucy," he said warmly. "What does it matter what you said? You know I love you."

"I don't know what I've done to deserve such love," she said. "You make me dreadfully ashamed of myself."

He took her hand, and she did not attempt to withdraw it.

"Won't you change your mind, Lucy?" he said earnestly.

"Oh, my dear, I don't love you. I wish I did. But I don't and I'm afraid I never can."

"Won't you marry me all the same?"

"Do you care for me so much as that?" she cried painfully.

"Perhaps you will learn to love me in time."

"Don't be so humble; you make me still more ashamed. Bobbie, I should like to make you happy if I thought I could. It seems very wonderful to me that you should want to have me. But I must be honest with you. I know that if I pretend I'm willing to marry you merely for your sake I'm deceiving myself. I want to marry you because I'm afraid. I want to crush my love for Alec. I want to make it impossible for me ever to weaken in my resolve. You see, I'm horrid and calculating, and it's very little I can offer you."

"I don't care why you're marrying me," he said. "I want you so badly."

"Oh, no, don't take me like that. Let me say first that if you really think me worth having, I will do my duty gladly. And if I have no love to give, I have a great deal of affection and a great deal of gratitude. I want you to be happy."

He went down on his knees and kissed her hands passionately.

"I'm so thankful," he murmured. "I'm so thankful."

Lucy bent down and gently kissed his hair. Two tears rolled heavily down her cheeks.

Five minutes later Lady Kelsey came in. She was delighted to see that her nephew and her niece were apparently once more on friendly terms; but she had no time to find out what had happened, for Canon Spratte was immediately announced. Lady Kelsey had heard that he was to be offered a vacant bishoprie, and she mourned over his disappearance from London. He was a spiritual mentor who exactly suited her, handsome, urbane, attentive notwithstanding her mature age, and well-connected. He was just the man to be a bishop. Then Mrs. Crowley appeared. They waited a little, and presently Dick was announced. He sauntered in jauntily, unaware that he had kept the others waiting a full quarter of an hour; and the party was complete.

No gathering could be tedious when Canon Spratte was present, and the conversation proceeded merrily. Mrs. Crowley looked ravishing in a summer frock, and since she addressed herself exclusively to the handsome parson it was no wonder that he was in good humour. She laughed appreciatively at his facile jests and gave him provoking glances of her bright eyes. He did not attept to conceal from her that he though American women the most delightful creatures in the world, and she made no secret of her opinion that ecclesiastical dignitaries were often fascinating. They paid one another outrageous compliments. It never struck the good man that these charms and graces were displayed only for the purpose of vexing a gentleman of forty, who was eating his luncheon irritably on the other side of her. She managed to avoid talking to Dick Lomas afterwards, but when she bade Lady Kelsey farewell, he rose also.

"Shall I drive you home?" he asked.

"I'm not going home, but if you like to drive me to Victoria Street, you may. I have an appointment there at four."

They went out, stepped into a cab, and quite coolly Dick told the driver to go to Hammersmith. He sat himself down by her side, with a smile of self-satisfaction.

"What on earth are you doing?" she cried.

"I want to have a talk to you."

"I'm sure that's charming of you," she answered, "but I shall miss my appointment."

"That's a matter of indifference to me."

"Don't bother about my feelings, will you?" she replied, satirically.

"I have no intention of doing so," he smiled.

Mrs. Crowley was obliged to laugh at the neatness with which he had entrapped her. Or had he fallen into the trap which she had set for him? She really did not quite know.

"If your object in thus abducting me was to talk, hadn't you better do so?" she asked. "I hope you will endeavour to be not only amusing but instructive."

"I wanted to point out to you that it is not civil pointedly to ignore a man who is sitting next to you at luncheon."

"Did I do that? I'm so sorry. But I know you're greedy, and I thought you'd be absorbed in the lobster mayonnaise."

"I'm beginning to think I dislike you rather than otherwise," he murmured reflectively.

"Ah, I suppose that is why you haven't been in to see me for so long."

"May I venture to remind you that I've called upon you three times during the last week."

"I've been out so much lately," she answered, with a little wave of her hand.

"Nonsense. Once I heard you playing scales in the drawing-room, and once I positively saw you peeping at me through the curtains."

"Why didn't you make a face at me?" she asked.

"You're not going to trouble to deny it?"

"It's perfectly true."

Dick could not help giving a little laugh. He didn't quite know whether he wanted to kiss Julia Crowley or to shake her.

"And may I ask why you've treated me in this abominable fashion?" he asked blandly.

She looked at him sideways from beneath her long eyelashes. Dick was a man who appreciated the artifices of civilisation in the fair sex, and he was pleased with her pretty hat and with the flounces of her muslin frock.

"Because I chose," she smiled.

He shrugged his shoulders and put on an air of resignation.

"Of course if you're going to make yourself systematically disagreeable unless I marry you, I suppose I must bow to the inevitable."

"I don't know if you have the least idea what you're talking about," she answered, raising her eyebrows. "I'm sure I haven't."

"I was merely asking you in a rather well-turned phrase to name the day. The lamb shall be ready for the slaughter."

"Is that a proposal of marriage?" she asked gaily.

"If not it must be its twin brother," he returned.

"I'm so glad you've told me, because if I'd met it in the street I should never have recognised it, and I should simply have cut it dead."

"You show as little inclination to answer a question as a cabinet minister in the House of Commons."

"Couldn't you infuse a little romance into it? You see, I'm American, and I have a certain taste for sentiment in the affairs of the heart."

"I should be charmed, only you must remember that I have no experience in these matters."

"That is visible to the naked eye," she retorted. "But I would suggest that it is only decent to go down on your bended knees."

"That sounds a perilous feat to perform in a hansom cab, and it would certainly attract an amount of attention from passing 'bus-drivers which would be embarrassing."

"You could never convince me of the sincerity of your passion unless you did something of the kind," she replied.

"I assure you that it is quite out of fashion. Lovers now-a-days are much too middle-aged, and their joints are creaky. Besides it ruins the trousers."

"I admit your last reason is overwhelming. No nice woman should ask a man to make his trousers baggy at the knees."

"How could she love him if they were!" exclaimed Dick.

"But at all events there can be no excuse for your not saying that you know you are utterly unworthy of me."

"Wild horses wouldn't induce me to make a statement which is so remote from the truth," he replied coolly. "I did it with my little hatchet."

"And of course you must threaten to commit suicide if I don't consent. That is only decent."

"Women are such sticklers for routine," he sighed. "They have no originality. They have a passion for commonplace, and in moments of emotion they fly with unerring instinct into the flamboyance of melodrama."

"I like to hear you use long words. It makes me feel so grown-up."

"By the way, how old are you?" he asked suddenly.

"Twenty-nine," she answered promptly.

"Nonsense. There is no such age."

"Pardon me," she protested gravely. "Upper parlour maids are always twenty-nine. But I deplore your tendency to digress."

"Am I digressing? I'm so sorry. What were we talking about?"

Julia giggled. She did not know where the cab was going, and she certainly did not care. She was thoroughly enjoying herself.

"You were taking advantage of my vast experience in such matters to learn how a man proposes to an eligible widow of great personal attractions."

"Your advice can't be very valuable, since you always refused the others."

"I didn't indeed," she replied promptly. "I made a point of accepting them all."

"That at all events is encouraging."

"Of course you may do it in your own way if you choose. But I must have a proposal in due form."

"My intelligence may be limited, but it seems to me that only four words are needed." He counted them out deliberately on his fingers. 'Will—you—marry—me?"

"That is both clear and simple." She pressed back the thumb which he had left untouched. "I reply in one: no."

He looked at her with every sign of astonishment.

"I beg your pardon?" he said.

"You heard me quite correctly," she smiled. "The reply is in the negative."

She resisted a mad, but inconvenient, temptation to dance a breakdown on the floor of the hansom.

"You're joking," said Dick calmly. "You're certainly joking."

"I will be a sister to you."

Dick reflected for a moment, and he rubbed his chin.

"The chance will never recur, you know," he remarked.

"I will bear the threat that is implied in that with fortitude."

He turned round and taking her hand, raised it to his lips.

"I thank you from the bottom of my heart," he said earnestly.

This puzzled her.

"The man's mad," she murmured to a constable who stood on the curb as they passed. "The man's nothing short of a raving lunatic."

"It is one of my most cherished convictions that a really nice woman is never so cruel as to marry a man she cares for. You have given me proof of esteem which I promise I will never forget."

Mrs. Crowley could not help laughing.

"You're much too flippant to marry anybody, and you're perfectly odious into the bargain."

"I will be a brother to you, Mrs. Crowley."

He opened the trap and told the cabman to drive back to Victoria Street, but at Hyde Park Corner he suggested that Mrs. Crowley might drop him so that he could take a stroll in the park. When he got out and closed the doors behind him, Julia leaned forward.

"Would you like some letters of introduction before you go?" she said.

"What for?"

"It is evident that unless your soul is dead to all the finer feelings, you will seek to assuage your sorrow by shooting grizzlies in the Rocky Mountains. I thought a few letters to my friends in New York might be useful to you."

"I'm sure that's very considerate of you, but I fancy it's scarcely the proper season. I was thinking of a week in Paris."

"Then pray send me a dozen pairs of black suède gloves," she retorted coolly. "Sixes."

"Is that your last word?" he asked lightly.

"Yes, why?"

"I thought you might mean six and a half."

He lifted his hat and was gone.

Chapter XIX

A FEW DAYS LATER, LADY KELSEY AND LUCY HAVING GONE ON THE RIVER, Julia Crowley went to Court Leys. When she came down to breakfast the day after her arrival, she found waiting for her six pairs of long suède gloves. She examined their size and their quality, smiled with amusement, and felt a little annoyed. She really had every intention of accepting Dick when he proposed to her, and she did not in the least know why she had refused him. The conversation had carried her away in her own despite. She loved a repartee and notwithstanding the consequences could never resist making any that occurred to her. It was very stupid of Dick to take her so seriously, and she was inclined to be cross with him. Of course he had only gone to Paris to tease, and in a week he would be back again. She knew that he was just as much in love with her as she was with him, and it was absurd of him to put on airs. She awaited the post each day impatiently, for she constantly expected a letter from him to say he was coming down to luncheon. She made up her mind about the *menu* of the pleasant little meal she would set before him, and in imagination rehearsed the scene in which she would at length succumb to his passionate entreaties. It was evidently discreet not to surrender with unbecoming eagerness. But no letter came. A week went by. She began to think that Dick had no sense of humour. A second week passed, and then a third. Perhaps it was because she had nothing to do that Master Dick absorbed a quite unmerited degree of her attention. It was very inconvenient and very absurd. She tormented herself with all sorts of reasons to explain his absence, and once or twice, like the spoiled child she was, she cried. But Mrs. Crowley was a sensible woman and soon made up her mind that if she could not love without the man—though heaven only knew why she wanted him—she had better take steps to secure his presence. It was the end of August now, and she was bored and lonely. She sent him a very untruthful telegram.

I have to be in town on Friday to see my lawyer. May I come to tea at five?

JULIA

His answer did not arrive for twenty-four hours, and then it was addressed from Homburg.

Regret immensely, but shall be away.

RICHARD LOMAS

Julia stamped her tiny foot with indignation and laughed with amusement at her own anger. It was monstrous that while she was leading the dullest existence imaginable, he should be enjoying the gaieties of a fashionable watering-place. She telegraphed once more.

Thanks very much. Shall expect to see you on Friday.

JULIA

She travelled up to town on the appointed day and went to her house in Norfolk Street to see that the journey had left no traces on her appearance. Mayfair seemed quite deserted, and half the windows were covered with newspapers to keep out the dust. It was very hot, and the sun beat down from a cloudless sky. The pavements were white and dazzling. Julia realised with pleasure that she was the only cool person in London, and the lassitude she saw in the passers-by added to her own self-satisfaction. The month at the seaside had given an added freshness to her perfection, and her charming gown had a breezy lightness that must be very grateful to a gentleman of forty lately returned from foreign parts. As she looked at herself in the glass, Mrs. Crowley reflected that she did not know anyone who had a figure half so good as hers.

When she drove up to Dick's house, she noticed that there were fresh flowers in the window boxes, and when she was shown into his drawing-room, the first thing that struck her was the scent of red roses which were in masses everywhere. The blinds were down, and after the baking street the dark coolness of the room was very pleasant. The tea was on a little table, waiting to be poured out. Dick of course was there to receive her. As she shook hands with him, she smothered a little titter of wild excitement.

"So you've come back," she said.

"I was just passing through town," he answered, with an airy wave of the hand.

"From where to where?"

"From Homburg to the Italian Lakes."

"Rather out of the way, isn't it?" she smiled.

"Not at all," he replied. "If I were going from Manchester to Liverpool, I should break the journey in London. That's one of my hobbies."

Julia laughed gaily, and as they both made a capital tea, they talked of all manner of trivial things. They were absurdly glad to see one another again, and each was ready to be amused at everything the other said. But the conversation would have been unintelligible to a listener, since they mostly talked together, and every now and then made a little scene when one insisted that the other should listen to what he was saying.

Suddenly Mrs. Crowley threw up her hands with a gesture of dismay.

"Oh, how stupid of me!" she cried. "I quite forgot to tell you why I telegraphed to you the other day."

"I know," he retorted.

"Do you? Why?"

"Because you're the most disgraceful flirt I ever saw in my life," he answered promptly.

She opened her eyes wide with a very good imitation of complete amazement.

"My dear Mr. Lomas, have you never contemplated yourself in a looking-glass?"

"You're not a bit repentant of the havoc you have wrought," he cried dramatically.

She did not answer, but looked at him with a smile so entirely delightful that he cried out irritably:

"I wish you wouldn't look like that."

"How am I looking?" she smiled.

"To my innocent and inexperienced gaze very much as if you wanted to be kissed."

"You brute!" she cried. "I'll never speak to you again."

"Why do you make such rash statements? You know you couldn't hold your tongue for two minutes together."

"What a libel! I never can get a word in edgeways when I'm with you," she returned. "You're such a chatterbox."

"I don't know why you put on that aggrieved air. You seem to forget that it's I who ought to be furious."

"On the contrary, you behaved very unkindly to me a month ago, and I'm only here today because I have a Christian disposition."

"You forget that for the last four weeks I've been laboriously piecing together the fragments of a broken heart," he answered.

"It was entirely your fault," she laughed. "If you hadn't been so certain I was going to accept you, I should never have refused. I couldn't resist the temptation of saying no, just to see how you took it."

"I flatter myself I took it very well."

"You didn't," she answered. "You showed an entire lack of humour. You might have known that a nice woman doesn't accept a man the first time he asks her. It was very silly of you to go to Homburg as if you didn't care. How was I to know that you meant to wait a month before asking me again?"

He looked at her for a moment calmly.

"I haven't the least intention of asking you again."

But it required much more than this to put Julia Crowley out of countenance.

"Then why on earth did you invite me to tea?"

"May I respectfully remind you that you invited yourself?" he protested.

"That's just like a man. He will go into irrelevant details," she answered.

"Now, don't be cross," he smiled.

"I shall be cross if I want to," she exclaimed, with a little stamp of her foot. "You're not being at all nice to me."

He looked at her thoughtfully for a moment, and his eyes twinkled.

"Do you know what I'd do if I were you?"

"No, what?"

"Well, *I* can't suffer the humiliation of another refusal. Why don't you propose to me?"

"What cheek!" she cried.

Their eyes met, and she smiled.

"What will you say if I do?"

"That entirely depends on how you do it."

"I don't know how," she murmured plaintively.

"Yes, you do," he insisted. "You gave me an admirable lesson. First you go on your bended knees, and then you say you're quite unworthy of me."

"You are the most spiteful creature I've ever known," she laughed. "You're just the sort of man who'd beat his wife."

"Every Saturday night regularly," he agreed.

She hesitated, looking at him.

"Well?" he said.

"I shan't," she answered.

"Then I shall continue to be a brother to you."

She got up and curtsied.

"Mr. Lomas, I am a widow, twenty-nine years of age, and extremely eligible. My maid is a treasure, and my dressmaker is charming. I'm clever enough to laugh at your jokes and not so learned as to know where they come from."

"Really you're very long winded. I said it all in four words."

"You evidently put it too briefly, since you were refused," she smiled.

She stretched out her hands, and he took them.

"I think I'll do it by post," she said. "It'll sound so much more becoming."

"You'd better get it over now."

"You know, I don't really want to marry you a bit. I'm only doing it to please you."

"I admire your unselfishness."

"You will say yes if I ask you?"

"I refuse to commit myself."

"Obstinate beast," she cried.

She curtsied once more, as well as she could since he was firmly holding her hands.

"Sir, I have the honour to demand your hand in marriage."

He bowed elaborately.

"Madam, I have much pleasure in acceding to your request."

Then he drew her towards him and put his arms around her.

"I never saw anyone make such a fuss about so insignificant a detail as marriage," she murmured.

"You have the softest lips I ever kissed," he said.

"I wish to goodness you'd be serious," she laughed. "I've got something very important to say to you."

"You're not going to tell me the story of your past life," he cried.

"No, I was thinking of my engagement ring. I make a point of having a cabochon emerald: I collect them."

"No sooner said than done," he cried.

He took a ring from his pocket and slipped it on her finger. She looked from it to him.

"You see, I know that you made a specialty of emeralds."

"Then you meant to ask me all the time?"

"I confess it to my shame: I did," he laughed.

"Oh, I wish I'd known that before."

"What would you have done?"

"I'd have refused you again, you silly."

Dick Lomas and Mrs. Crowley said nothing about their engagement to anyone, since it seemed to both that the marriage of a middle-aged gentleman and a widow of uncertain years could concern no one but themselves. The ceremony was duly performed in a deserted church on a warm September day, when there was not a soul in London. Mrs. Crowley was given away by her solicitor, and the verger signed the book. The happy pair went to Court Leys for a fortnight's honeymoon and at the beginning of October returned to London; they made up their minds that they would go to America later in the autumn.

"I want to show you off to all my friends in New York," said Julia, gaily.

"Do you think they'll like me?" asked Dick.

"Not at all. They'll say: That silly little fool Julia Crowley has married another beastly Britisher."

"That is more alliterative than polite," he retorted. "On the other hand my friends and relations are already saying: What on earth has poor Dick Lomas married an American for? We always thought he was very well-to-do."

They went into roars of laughter, for they were in that state of happiness when the whole world seemed the best of jokes, and they spent their days in laughing at one another and at things in general. Life was a pleasant thing, and they could not imagine why others should not take it as easily as themselves.

They had engaged rooms at the *Carlton* while they were furnishing a new house. Each had one already, but neither would live in the other's, and so it had seemed necessary to look out for a third. Julia vowed that there was an air of bachelordom about Dick's house which made it impossible for a married woman to inhabit; and Dick, on his side, refused to move into Julia's establishment on Norfolk Street, since it have him the sensation of being a fortune-hunter living on his wife's income. Besides, a new house gave an opportunity for extravagance which delighted both of them since they realised perfectly that the other advantage of having plenty of money was to spend it in unnecessary ways. They were a pair of light-hearted children, who refused firmly to consider the fact that they were more than twenty-five.

Lady Kelsey and Lucy had gone from the River to Spa, for the elder woman's health, and on their return Julia went to see them in order to receive their congratulations and display her extreme happiness. She came back thoughtfully. When she sat down to luncheon with Dick in their sitting-room at the hotel, he saw that she was disturbed. He asked her what was the matter.

"Lucy has broken off her engagement with Robert Boulger," she said.

"That young woman seems to make a specialty of breaking her engagements," he answered drily.

"I'm afraid she's still in love with Alec MacKenzie."

"Then why on earth did she accept Bobbie?"

"My dear boy, she only took him in a fit of temper. When that had cooled down she very wisely thought better of it."

"I can never sufficiently admire the reasonableness of your sex," said Dick, ironically.

Julia shrugged her pretty shoulders.

"Half the women I know merely married their husbands to spite somebody else. I assure you it's one of the commonest causes of matrimony."

"Then heaven save me from matrimony," cried Dick.

"It hasn't," she laughed.

But immediately she grew serious once more.

"Mr. MacKenzie was in Brussels while they were in Spa."

"I had a letter from him this morning."

"Lady Kelsey says that according to the papers he's going to Africa again. I think it's that which has upset Lucy. They made a great fuss about him in Brussels."

"Yes, he tells me that everything is fixed up, and he proposes to start quite shortly. He's going to do some work in the Congo Free State. They want to find a new waterway, and the King of the Belgians has given him a free hand."

"I suppose the King of the Belgians look upon one atrocity more or less with equanimity," said Julia.

They were silent for a minute or two, while each was occupied with his own thoughts.

"You saw him after Lucy broke off the engagement," said Julia, presently. "Was he very wretched?"

"He never said a word. I wanted to comfort him, but he never gave me a chance. He never even mentioned Lucy's name."

"Did he seem unhappy?"

"No. He was just the same as ever, impassive and collected."

"Really, he's inhuman," exclaimed Julia impatiently.

"He's an anomaly in this juvenile country," Dick agreed. "He's an ancient Roman who buys his clothes in Savile Row."

"Then he's very much in the way in England, and it's much better that he should go back to Africa."

"I suppose it is. Here he reminds one of an eagle caged with a colony of canaries."

Julia looked at her husband reflectively.

"I think you're the only friend who has stuck to him," she said.

"I wouldn't put it in that way. After all, I'm the only friend he ever had. It was not unnatural that a number of acquaintances should drop him when he got into hot water."

"It must have been a great help to find someone who believed in him notwithstanding everything."

"I'm afraid it sounds very immoral, but whatever his crimes were, I should never like Alec less. You see, he's so awfully good and kind to me, I can look on with fortitude while he plays football with the Ten Commandments."

Julia's emotions were always sudden, and the tears came to her eyes as she answered.

"I'm really beginning to think you a perfect angel, Dick."

"Don't say that," he retorted quickly. "It makes me feel so middle-aged. 'I'd much sooner be a young sinner than an elderly cherub.' "

Smiling, she stretched out her hand, and he held it for a moment.

"You know, though I can't help liking you, I don't in the least approve of you."

"Good heavens, why not?" he cried.

"Well, I was brought up to believe that a man should work, and you're disgracefully idle."

"Good heavens, to marry an American wife is the most arduous profession in the world," he cried. "One has to combine the energy of the Universal Provider with the patience of an ambassador at the Sublime Porte."

"You foolish creature," she laughed.

But her thoughts immediately reverted to Lucy. Her pallid, melancholy face still lingered in Julia's memory, and her heart was touched by the hopeless woe that dwelt in her beautiful eyes.

"I suppose there's no doubt that those stories about Alec MacKenzie were true?" she said, thoughtfully.

Dick gave her a quick glance. He wondered what was in her mind.

"I'll tell you what I think," he said. "Anyone who knows Alec as well as I do must be convinced that he did nothing from motives that were mean and paltry. To accuse him of cowardice is absurd—he's the bravest man I've ever known—and it's equally absurd to accuse him of weakness. But what I do think is this: Alec is not the man to stick at half measures, and he's taken desperately to heart the maxim which says that he who desires an end desires the means also. I think he might be very ruthless, and on occasion he might be stern to the verge of brutality. Reading between the lines of those letters that Macinnery sent to the *Daily Mail*, I have wondered if Alec, finding that someone must be sacrificed, didn't deliberately choose George Allerton because he was the least useful to him and could be best spared. Even in small undertakings like that they must be some men who are only food for powder. If Alec had found George worthless to him, no consideration for Lucy would have prevented him from sacrificing him."

"If that were so why didn't he say it outright?"

"Do you think it would have made things any better? The British public is sentimental; they will not understand that in warfare it is necessary sometimes to be inhuman. And how would it have served him with Lucy if he had confessed that he had used George callously as a pawn in his game that must be sacrificed to win some greater advantage?"

"It's all very horrible," shuddered Julia.

"And so far as the public goes, events have shown that he was right to keep silence. The agitation against him died down for want of matter, and though he is vaguely discredited, nothing is proved definitely against him. Public opinion is very fickle, and already people are beginning to forget, and as they forget they will think they have misjudged him. When it is announced that he has given his services to the King of the Belgians, ten to one there will be a reaction in his favour."

They got up from luncheon, and coffee was served to them. They lit their cigarettes. For some time they were silent.

"Lucy wants to see him before he goes," said Julia suddenly.

Dick looked at her and gave an impatient shrug of the shoulders.

"I suppose she wants to indulge a truly feminine passion for making scenes. She's made Alec quite wretched enough already."

"Don't be unkind to her, Dick," said Julia, tears welling up in her bright eyes. "You don't know how desperately unhappy she is. My heart bled to see her this morning."

"Darling, I'll do whatever you want me to," he said, leaning over her.

Julia's sense of the ridiculous was always next door to her sense of the pathetic.

"I don't know why you should kiss me because Lucy's utterly miserable," she said, with a little laugh.

And then, gravely, as she nestled in his encircling arm:

"Will you try and manage it? She hesitates to write to him."

"I'm not sure if I had not better leave you to impart the pleasing information yourself," he replied. "I've asked Alec to come here this afternoon."

"You're a selfish beast," she answered. "But in that case you must leave me alone with him, because I shall probably weep gallons of tears, and you'll only snigger at me."

"Bless your little heart! Let us put handkerchiefs in every conceivable place."

"On occasions like this I carry a bagful about with me."

Chapter XX

In the afternoon Alec arrived. Julia's tender heart was touched by the change wrought in him during the three months of his absence from town. At the first glance there was little difference in him. He was still cool and collected, with that air of expecting people to do his bidding which had always impressed her; and there was still about him a sensation of strength, which was very comfortable to weaker vessels. But her sharp eyes saw that he held himself together by an effort of will, and it was singularly painful to the onlooker. The strain had told on him, and there was in his haggard eyes, in the deliberate firmness of his mouth, a tension which suggested that he was almost at the end of his tether. He was sterner than before and more silent. Julia could see how deeply he had suffered, and his suffering had been greater because of his determination to conquer it at all costs. She longed to go to him and beg him not to be too hard upon himself. Things would have gone more easily with him, if he had allowed himself a little weakness. But he was softer too, and she no longer felt the slight awe which to her till then had often made intercourse difficult. His first words were full of an unexpected kindness.

"I'm so glad to be able to congratulate you," he said, holding her hand and smiling with that rare, sweet smile of his. "I was a little unhappy at leaving Dick; but now I leave him in your hands I'm perfectly content. He's the dearest, kindest old chap I've ever known."

"Shut up, Alec," cried Dick promptly. "Don't play the heavy father, or Julia will burst into tears. She loves having a good cry."

But Alec ignored the interruption.

"He'll be an admirable husband because he's been an admirable friend."

For the first time Julia thought Alec altogether wise and charming.

"I know he will," she answered happily. "And I'm only prevented from saying all I think of him by the fear that he'll become perfectly unmanageable."

"Spare me the chaste blushes which mantle my youthful brow, and pour out the tea, Julia," said Dick.

She laughed and proceeded to do as he requested.

"And are you really starting for Africa so soon?" Julia asked, when they were settled around the tea-table.

Alec threw back his head, and his face lit up.

"I am. Everything is fixed up; the bother of collecting supplies and getting porters has been taken off my shoulders, and all I have to do is to get along as quickly as possible."

"I wish to goodness you'd give up these horrible explorations," cried Dick. "They make the rest of us feel so abominably unadventurous."

"But they're the very breath of my nostrils," answered Alec. "You don't know the exhilaration of the daily dangers, the joy of treading where only the wild beasts have trodden before."

"I freely confess that I don't want to," said Dick.

Alec sprang up and stretched his legs. As he spoke all signs of lassitude disappeared, and he was seized with an excitement that was rarely seen in him.

"Already I can hardly bear my impatience when I think of the boundless country and the enchanting freedom. Here one grows so small, so mean; but in Africa everything is built to a nobler standard. There the man is really a man. There one knows what are will and strength and courage You don't know what it is to stand on the edge of some great plan and breathe the pure keen air after the terrors of the forest."

"The boundless plain of Hyde Park is enough for me," said Dick. "And the aspect of Piccadilly on a fine day in June gives me quite as many emotions as I want."

But Julia was moved by Alec's unaccustomed rhetoric, and she looked at him earnestly.

"But what will you gain by it now that your work is over—by all the danger and all the hardships?"

He turned his dark, solemn eyes upon her.

"Nothing. I want to gain nothing. Perhaps I shall discover some new species of antelope or some unknown plant. I may be fortunate enough to find a new waterway. That is all the reward I want. I love the sense of power and the mastery. What do you think I care for the tinsel rewards of kings and peoples!"

"I always said you were melodramatic," said Dick. "I never heard anything so transpontine."

"And the end of it?" asked Julia, almost in a whisper. "What will be the end?"

A faint smile played for an instant upon Alec's lips. He shrugged his shoulders.

"The end is death. But I shall die standing up. I shall go the last journey as I have gone every other."

He stopped, for he would not add the last two words. Julia said them for him.

"Without fear."

"For all the world like the wicked baronet," cried the mocking Dick. "Once aboard the lugger, and the gurl is mine."

Julia reflected for a little while. She did not want to resist the admiration with which Alec filled her. But she shuddered. He did not seem to fit in with the generality of men.

"Don't you want people to remember you?" she asked.

"Perhaps they will," he answered slowly. "Perhaps in a hundred years, in some flourishing town where I discovered nothing but wilderness, they will commission a second-rate sculptor to make a fancy statue of me. And I shall stand in front of the Stock Exchange, a convenient perch for birds, to look eternally upon the shabby deeds of human kind."

He gave a short, abrupt laugh, and his words were followed by silence. Julia gave Dick a glance which he took to be a signal that she wished to be alone with Alec.

"Forgive me if I leave you for one minute," he said.

He got up and left the room. The silence still continued, and Alec seemed immersed in thought. At last Julia answered him.

"And is that really all? I can't help thinking that at the bottom of your heart there is something that you've never told to a living soul."

He looked at her, and their eyes met. He felt suddenly her extraordinary sympathy and her passionate desire to help him. And as though the bonds of the flesh were loosened, it seemed to him that their very souls faced one another. The reserve which was his dearest habit fell away from him, and he felt an urgent desire to say that which a curious delicacy had prevented him from every betraying to callous ears.

"I daresay I shall never see you again, and perhaps it doesn't much matter what I say to you. You'll think me very silly, but I'm afraid I'm rather—patriotic. It's only we who live away from England who really love it. I'm so proud of my country, and I wanted so much to do something for it. Often in Africa I've thought of this dear England and longed not to die till I had done my work."

His voice shook a little, and he paused. It seemed to Julia that she saw the man for the first time, and she wished passionately that Lucy could hear those words of his which he spoke so shyly, and yet with such a passionate earnestness.

"Behind all the soldiers and the statesmen whose fame is imperishable there is a long line of men who've built up the empire piece by piece. Their names are forgotten, and only students know their history, but each one of them gave a province to his country. And I too have my place among them. Year after year I toiled, night and day, and at last I was able to hand over to the commissioner a broad tract of land, rich and fertile. After my death England will forget my faults and my mistakes; and I care nothing for the flouts and gibes with which she has repaid all my pain, for I have added another fair jewel to her crown. I don't want rewards; I only want the honour of serving this dear land of ours."

Julia went up to him and laid her hand gently on his arm.

"Why is it, when you're so nice really, that you do all you can to make people think you're utterly horrid?"

"Don't laugh at me because you've found out that at bottom I'm nothing more than a sentimental old woman."

"I don't want to laugh at you. But if I didn't think it would embarrass you so dreadfully, I should certainly kiss you."

He smiled and lifting her hand to his lips, lightly kissed it.

"I shall begin to think I'm a very wonderful woman if I've taught you to do such pretty things as that."

She made him sit down, and then she sat by his side.

"I'm very glad you came today. I wanted to talk to you. Will you be very angry if I say something to you?"

"I don't think so," he smiled.

"I want to speak to you about Lucy."

He drew himself suddenly together, and the expansion of his mood disappeared. He was once more the cold, reserved man of their habitual intercourse.

"I'd rather you didn't," he said briefly.

But Julia was not to be so easily put off.

"What would you do if she came here today?" she asked.

He turned round and looked at her sharply, then answered with great deliberation.

"I have always lived in polite society. I should never dream of outraging its conventions. If Lucy happened to come, you may be sure that I should be scrupulously polite."

"Is that all?" she cried.

He did not answer, and into his face came a wild fierceness that appalled her. She saw the effort he was making at self-control. She wished with all her heart that he would be less brave.

"I think you might not be so hard if you knew how desperately Lucy has suffered."

He looked at her again, and his eyes were filled with bitterness, with angry passion at the injustice of fate. Did she think that he had not suffered? Because he did not whine his misery to all and sundry, did she think he did not care? He sprang up and walked to the other end of the room. He did not want that woman, for all her kindness, to see his face. He was not the man to fall in and out of love with every pretty girl he met. All his life he had kept an ideal before his eyes. He turned to Julia savagely.

"You don't know what it meant to me to fall in love. I felt that I had lived all my life in a prison, and at last Lucy came and took me by the hand, and led me out. And for the first time I breathed the free air of heaven."

He stopped abruptly, clenching his jaws. He would not tell her how bitterly he had suffered for it, he would not tell her of his angry rebelliousness because all that pain should have come to him. He wanted nobody to know the depths of his agony and of his despair. But he would not give way. He felt that, if he did not keep a tight hold on himself, he would break down and shake with passionate sobbing. He felt a sudden flash of hatred for Julia because she sat there and watched his weakness. But as though she saw at what a crisis of emotion he was, Julia turned her eyes from him and looked down at the ground. She did not speak. She felt the effort he was making to master himself, and she was infinitely disturbed. She wanted to go to him and comfort him, but she knew he would repel her. He wanted to fight his battle unaided.

At last he continued, but when he spoke again, his voice was singularly broken. It was hoarse and low.

"My love was the last human weakness I had. It was right that I should drink that bitter cup. And I've drunk its very dregs. I should have known that I wasn't meant for happiness and a life of ease. I have other work to do in the world."

He paused for a moment, and his calmness was restored to him.

"And now that I've overcome this last temptation I am ready to do it."

"But haven't you any pity for yourself? Haven't you any thought for Lucy?"

"Must I tell you, too, that everything I did was for Lucy's sake? And still I love her with all my heart and soul."

There was no bitterness in his tone now; it was gentle and resigned. He had, indeed, won the battle. Julia's eyes were filled with tears, and she could not answer. He came forward and shook hands with her.

"You mustn't cry," he said, smiling. "You're one of those persons whose part it is to bring sunshine into the lives of those with less fortunate dispositions. You must always be happy and child-like."

"I've got lots of handkerchiefs, thanks," she sobbed, laughing the while.

"You must forget all the nonsense I've talked to you," he said.

He smiled once more and was gone.

Dick was sitting in his bed-room, reading an evening paper, and she flung herself sobbing into his arms.

"Oh, Dick, I've had such a lovely cry, and I'm so happy and so utterly wretched. And I'm sure I shall have a red nose."

"Darling, I've long discovered that you only weep because you're the only person in the world to whom it's thoroughly becoming."

"Don't be horrid and unsympathetic. I think Alec MacKenzie's a perfect dear. I wanted to kiss him, only I was afraid it would frighten him to death."

"I'm glad you didn't. He would have thought you a forward hussy."

"I wish I could have married him, too," cried Julia. "I'm sure he'd make a nice husband."

Chapter XXI

THE DAYS WENT BY, SPENT BY ALEC IN MAKING NECESSARY PREPARATIONS for his journey, spent by Lucy in sickening anxiety. The last two months had been passed by her in a conflict of emotions. Love had planted itself in her heart like a great forest tree, and none of the storms that had assailed it seemed to have power to shake its stubborn roots. Reason, common decency, shame, had lost their power. She had prayed God that a merciful death might free her from the dreadful uncertainty. She was spiritless and cowed. She despised herself for her weakness. And sometimes she rebelled against the fate that crushed her with such misfortunes; she had tried to do her duty always, acting humbly according to her lights, and yet everything she was concerned in crumbled away to powder at her touch. She, too, began to think that she was not meant for happiness. She knew that she ought to hate Alec, but she could not. She knew that his action should fill her with nameless horror, but against her will she could not believe that he was false and wicked. One thing she was determined on, and that was to keep her word to Robert Boulger; but he himself gave her back her freedom.

He came to her one day, and after a little casual conversation broke suddenly into the middle of things.

"Lucy, I want to ask you to release me from my engagement to you," he said.

Her heart gave a great leap against her breast, and she began to tremble. He went on.

"I'm ashamed to have to say it; I find that I don't love you enough to marry you."

She looked at him silently, and her eyes filled with tears. The brutality with which he spoke was so unnatural that it betrayed the mercifulness of his intention.

"If you think that, there is nothing more to be said," she answered.

He gave her a look of such bitterness that she felt it impossible to continue a pretence which deceived neither of them.

"I'm unworthy of your love," she cried. "I've made you desperately wretched."

"It doesn't matter about me," he said. "But there's no reason for you to be wretched, too."

"I'm willing to do whatever you wish, Bobbie."

"I can't marry you simply because you're sorry for me. I thought I could, but—it's asking too much of you. We had better say no more about it."

"I'm very sorry," she whispered.

"You see, you're still in love with Alec MacKenzie."

He said it, vainly longing for a denial; but he knew in his heart that no denial would come.

"I always shall be, notwithstanding everything. I can't help myself."

"No, it's fate."

She sprang to her feet with vehement passion.

"Oh, Bobbie, don't you think there's some chance that everything may be explained?"

He hesitated for a moment. It was very difficult to answer.

"It's only fair to tell you that now things have calmed down, there are a great many people who don't believe Macinnery's story. It appears that the man's a thorough blackguard, whom MacKenzie loaded with benefits."

"Do *you* still believe that Alec caused George's death?"

"Yes."

Lucy leaned back in her chair, resting her face on her hand. She seemed to reflect deeply.

"And you?" said Bobbie.

She gave him a long, earnest look. The colour came to her cheeks.

"No," she said firmly.

"Why not?" he asked.

"I have no reason except that I love him."

"What are you going to do?"

"I don't know."

Bobbie got up, kissed her gently, and went out. She did not see him again, and in a day or two she heard that he had gone away.

Lucy made up her mind that she must see Alec before he went, but a secret bashfulness prevented her from writing to him. She was afraid that he would refuse, and she could not force herself upon him if she knew definitely that he did not want to see her. But with all her heart she wanted to ask his pardon. It would not be so hard to continue with the dreary burden which was her life if she knew that he had a little pity for her. He could not fail to forgive her when he saw how broken she was.

But the days followed one another, and the date which Julia, radiant with her own happiness, had given her as that of his departure, was approaching.

Julia, too, was exercised in mind. After her conversation with Alec she could not ask him to see Lucy, for she knew what his answer would be. No arguments would move him. He did not want to give either Lucy or himself the pain which he foresaw an interview would cause, and his wounds were too newly-healed for him to run any risks. Julia resolved to take the matter into her own hands. Alec was starting next day, and he had promised to look in towards the evening to bid them good-bye. Julia wrote a note to Lucy, asking her to come also.

When she told Dick, he was aghast.

"But it's a monstrous thing to do," he cried. "You can't entrap the man in that way."

"I know it's monstrous," she answered. "But that's the only advantage of being an American in England, that one can do monstrous things. You look upon us as first cousins to the red Indians, and you expect anything from us. In America I have to mind my p's and q's. I mayn't smoke in public, I shouldn't dream of lunching in a restaurant alone with a man, and I'm the most conventional person in the most conventional society in the world; but here, because the English are under the delusion that New York society is free and easy, and that American woman have no restraint, I can kick over the traces, and no one will think it even odd."

"But, my dear, it's a mere matter of common decency."

"There are times when common decency is out of place," she replied.

"Alec will never forgive you."

"I don't care. I think he ought to see Lucy, and since he'd refuse if I asked him, I'm not going to give him the chance."

"What will you do if he just bows and walks off?"

"I have his assurance that he'll behave like a civilised man," she answered.

"I wash my hands of it," said Dick. "I think it's perfectly indefensible."

"I never said it wasn't," she agreed. "But you see, I'm only a poor, weak woman, and I'm not supposed to have any sense of honour or propriety. You must let me take what advantage I can of the disabilities of the weaker sex."

Dick smiled and shrugged his shoulders.

"Your blood be upon your own head," he answered.

"If I perish, I perish."

And so it came about that when Alec had been ten minutes in Julia's cosy sitting-room, Lucy was announced. Julia went up to her, greeting her effusively to cover the awkwardness of the moment. Alec grew very pale, but made no sign that he was disconcerted. Only Dick was troubled. He was obviously at a loss for words, and it was plain to see that he was out of temper.

"I'm so glad you were able to come," said Julia, in order to show Alec that she had been expecting Lucy.

Lucy gave a rapid glance, and the colour flew to her cheeks. He was standing up and came forward with outstretched hand.

"How do you do?" he said. "How is Lady Kelsey?"

"She's much better, thanks. We've been to Spa, you know, for her health."

Julia's heart beat quickly. She was much excited at this meeting; and it seemed to her strangely romantic, a sign of the civilization of the times, that these two people with raging passions afire in their hearts, should exchange the commonplaces of polite society, Alec, having recovered from his momentary confusion was extremely urbane.

"Somebody told me you'd gone abroad," he said. "Was it you, Dick? Dick is an admirable person, a sort of gazetteer for the world of fashion."

Dick fussily brought forward a chair for Lucy to sit in, and offered to disembarrass her of the jacket she was wearing.

"You must make my excuses for not leaving a card on Lady Kelsey before going away," said Alec. "I've been excessively busy."

"It doesn't matter at all," Lucy answered.

Julia glanced at him. She saw that he was determined to keep the conversation on the indifferent level which it might have occupied if Lucy had been nothing more than an acquaintance. There was a bantering tone in his voice which was an effective barrier to all feeling. For a moment she was nonplussed.

"London is an excellent place for showing one of how little importance one is in the world. One makes a certain figure, and perhaps is tempted to think oneself of some consequence. Then one goes away, and on returning is surprised to discover that nobody has ever noticed one's absence."

Lucy smiled faintly. Dick, recovering her good-humour, came at once to the rescue.

"You're overmodest, Alec. If you weren't, you might be a great man. Now, I make a point of telling my friends that I'm indispensable, and they take me at my word."

"You are a leaven of flippancy in the heavy dough of British righteousness," smiled Alec.

"It is true that the wise man only takes the unimportant quite seriously."

"For it is obvious that one needs more brains to do nothing with elegance than to be a cabinet minister," said Alec.

"You pay me a great compliment, Alec," cried Dick. "You repeat to my very face one of my favourite observations."

Julia looked at him steadily.

"Haven't I heard you say that only the impossible is worth doing?"

"Good heavens," he cried. "I must have been quoting the headings of a copy-book."

Lucy felt that she must say something. She had been watching Alec, and her heart was nearly breaking. She turned to Dick.

"Are you going down to Southampton?" she asked.

"I am, indeed," he answered. "I shall hide my face on Alec's shoulder and weep salt tears. It will be most affecting, because in moments of emotion I always burst into epigram."

Alec sprang to his feet. There was a bitterness in his face which was in odd contrast with Dick's light words.

"I loathe all solemn leave-takings," he said. "I prefer to part from people with a nod or a smile, whether I'm going forever or for a day to Brighton."

"I've always assured you that you're a monster of inhumanity," said Mrs. Lomas, laughing difficultly.

He turned to her with a grim smile.

"Dick has been imploring me for twenty years to take life flippantly. I have learned at last that things are only grave if you take them gravely, and that is desperately stupid. It's so hard to be serious without being absurd. That is the chief power of women, that life and death for them are merely occasions for which a change of costume, marriage a creation in white, and the worship of God an opportunity for a Paris bonnet."

Julia saw that he was determined to keep the conversation on a level of amiable persiflage, and with her lively sense of the ridiculous she could hardly repress a smile at the heaviness of his hand. Through all that he said pieced the bitterness of his heart, and his every word was contradicted by the vehemence of his tortured voice. She was determined, too, that the interview which she had brought about, uncomfortable as it had been to all of them, should not be brought to nothing; characteristically she went straight to the point. She stood up.

"I'm sure you two have things to say to one another that you would like to say alone."

She saw Alec's eyes grow darker as he saw himself cornered, but she was implacable.

"I have some letters to send off by the American mail, and I want Dick to look over them to see that I've spelt *honour* with a u and *traveller* with a double l."

Neither Alec nor Lucy answered, and the determined little woman took her husband firmly away. When they were left alone, neither spoke for a while.

"I've just realised that you didn't know I was coming today," said Lucy at last. "I had no idea that you were being entrapped. I would never have consented to that."

"I'm very glad to have an opportunity of saying good-bye to you," he answered.

He preserved the conversational manner of polite society, and it seemed to Lucy that she would never have the strength to get beyond.

"I'm so glad that Dick and Julia are happily married. They're very much in love with one another."

"I should have thought love was the worst possible foundation for marriage," he answered. "Love creates illusions, and marriage destroys them. True lovers should never marry."

Again silence fell upon them, and again Lucy broke it.

"You're going away tomorrow?"

"I am."

She looked at him, but he would not meet her eyes. He went over to the window and looked out upon the busy street.

"Are you very glad to go?"

"You can't think what a joy it is to look upon London for the last time. I long for the infinite surface of the clean and comfortable sea."

Lucy gave a stifled sob. Alec started a little, but he did not move. He still looked down upon the stream of cabs and 'buses, lit by the misty autumn sun.

"Is there no one you regret to leave, Alec?"

It tore his heart that she should use his name. To hear her say it had always been like a caress, and the word on her lips brought back once more the whole agony of his distress; but he would not allow his emotions to be seen. He turned round and faced her gravely. Now, for the first time, he did not hesitate to look at her. And while he spoke the words he set himself to speak, he noticed the exquisite oval of her face, her charming, soft hair, and her unhappy eyes.

"You see, Dick is married, and so I'm much best out of the way. When a man takes a wife, his bachelor friends are wise to depart from his life, gracefully, before he shows them that he needs their company no longer."

"And besides Dick?"

"I have few friends and no relations. I can't flatter myself that anyone will be much distressed at my departure."

"You must have no heart at all," she said, in a low, hoarse voice.

He clenched his teeth. He was bitterly angry with Julia because she had exposed him to this unspeakable torture.

"If I had I certainly should not bring it to the *Carlton Hotel*. That sentimental organ would be surely out of place in such a neighbourhood."

Lucy sprang to her feet.

"Oh, why do you treat me as if we were strangers? How can you be so cruel?"

"Flippancy is often the only refuge from an uncomfortable position," he answered gravely. "We should really be much wiser merely to discuss the weather."

"Are you angry because I came?"

"That would be very ungracious on my part. Perhaps it wasn't quite necessary that we should meet again."

"You've been acting all the time I've been here. Do you think I didn't see it was unreal, when you talked with such cynical indifference? I know you well enough to tell when you're hiding your real self behind a mask."

"If that is so, the influence is obvious that I wish my real self to be hidden."

"I would rather you cursed me than treat me with such cold politeness."

"I'm afraid you're rather difficult to please," he said.

Lucy went up to him passionately, but he drew back so that she might not touch him. Her outstretched hands dropped powerless to her side.

"Oh, you're of iron," she cried pitifully. "Alec, Alec, I couldn't let you go without seeing you once more. Even you would be satisfied if you knew what bitter anguish I've suffered. Even you would pity me. I don't want you to think too badly of me."

"Does it matter what I think? We shall be five thousand miles apart."

"You must utterly despise me."

He shook his head. And now his manner lost that affected calmness which had been so cruelly wounding. He could not now attempt to hide the pain that he was suffering. His voice trembled a little with his great emotion.

"I loved you far too much to do that. Believe me, with all my heart I wish you well. Now that the first bitterness is past I see that you did the only possible thing. I hope that you'll be very happy. Robert Boulger is an excellent fellow, and I'm sure he'll make you a much better husband than I should ever have done."

Lucy blushed to the roots of her hair. Her heart sank, and she did not seek to conceal her agitation.

"Did they tell you I was going to marry Robert Boulger?"

"Isn't it true?"

"Oh, how cruel of them, how frightfully cruel! I became engaged to him, but he gave me my release. He knew that notwithstanding everything, I loved you better than my life."

Alec looked down, but he did not say anything. He did not move.

"Oh, Alec, don't be utterly pitiless," she wailed. "Don't leave me without a single word of kindness."

"Nothing is changed, Lucy. You sent me away because I caused your brother's death."

She stood before him, her hands behind her back, and they looked into one another's eyes. Her words were steady and quiet. It seemed to give her an infinite relief to say them.

"I hated you then, and yet I couldn't crush the love that was in my heart. And it's because I was frightened of myself that I told Bobbie I'd marry him. But I couldn't. I was horrified because I cared for you still. It seemed such odious treachery to George, and yet love burnt up my heart. I used to try and drive you away from my thoughts, but every word you had ever said came back to me. Don't you remember, you told me that everything you did was for my sake? Those words hammered away on my heart as though it were an anvil. I struggled not to believe them, I said to myself that you had sacrificed George, coldly, callously, prudently, but my love told me it wasn't true. Your whole life stood on one side and only this hateful story on the other. You couldn't have grown into a different man in one single instant. I've learnt to know you better during these three months of utter misery, and I'm ashamed of what I did."

"Ashamed?"

"I came here today to tell you that I don't understand the reason of what you did; but I don't want to understand. I believe in you now with all my strength. I believe in you as better women than I believe in God. I know that whatever you did was right and just—because you did it."

Alec looked at her for a moment. Then he held out his hand.

"Thank God," he said. "I'm so grateful to you."

"Have you nothing more to say to me than that?"

"You see, it's come too late. Nothing much matters now, for tomorrow I go away forever."

"But you'll come back."

He gave a short, scornful laugh.

"They were so glad to give me that job on the Congo because no one else would take it. I'm going to a part of Africa from which Europeans seldom return."

"Oh, that's too horrible," she cried. "Don't go, dearest; I can't bear it."

"I must now. Everything is settled, and there can be no drawing back."

She let go hopelessly of his hand.

"Don't you care for me anymore?" she whispered.

He looked at her, but he did not answer. She turned away, and sinking into a chair, began to cry.

"Don't, Lucy," he said, his voice breaking suddenly. "Don't make it harder."

"Oh, Alec, Alec, don't you see how much I love you."

He leaned over her and gently stroked her hair.

"Be brave, darling," he whispered.

She looked up passionately, seizing both his hands.

"I can't live without you. I've suffered too much. If you cared for me at all, you'd stay."

"Though I love you with all my soul, I can't do otherwise now than go."

"Then take me with you," she cried eagerly. "Let me come too."

"You!"

"You don't know what I can do. With you to help me I can be very brave. Let me come, Alec."

"It's impossible. You don't know what you ask."

"Then let me wait for you. Let me wait till you come back."

"And if I never come back?"

"I will wait for you still."

He placed his hands on her shoulders and looked into her eyes, as though he were striving to see into the depths of her soul. She felt very weak. She could scarcely see him through her tears, but she tried to smile. Then without a word he slipped his arms around her. Sobbing in the ecstasy of her happiness, she let her head fall on his shoulder.

"You will have the courage to wait?" he said.

"I know you love me, and I trust you."

"Then have no fear; I will come back. My journey was only dangerous because I wanted to die. I want to live now, and I shall live."

"Oh, Alec, Alec, I'm so glad you love me."

Outside in the street the bells of the motor 'buses tinkled noisily, and there was an incessant roar of the traffic that rumbled heavily over the wooden pavements. There was a clatter of horses' hoofs, and the blowing of horns; the electric broughams whizzed past with an odd, metallic whirr.

OF HUMAN BONDAGE

Chapter I

THE DAY BROKE GREY AND DULL. THE CLOUDS HUNG HEAVILY, AND THERE was a rawness in the air that suggested snow. A woman servant came into a room in which a child was sleeping and drew the curtains. She glanced mechanically at the house opposite, a stucco house with a portico, and went to the child's bed.

"Wake up, Philip," she said.

She pulled down the bed-clothes, took him in her arms, and carried him downstairs. He was only half awake.

"Your mother wants you," she said.

She opened the door of a room on the floor below and took the child over to a bed in which a woman was lying. It was his mother. She stretched out her arms, and the child nestled by her side. He did not ask why he had been awakened. The woman kissed his eyes, and with thin, small hands felt the warm body through his white flannel nightgown. She pressed him closer to herself.

"Are you sleepy, darling?" she said.

Her voice was so weak that it seemed to come already from a great distance. The child did not answer, but smiled comfortably. He was very happy in the large, warm bed, with those soft arms about him. He tried to make himself smaller still as he cuddled up against his mother, and he kissed her sleepily. In a moment he closed his eyes and was fast asleep. The doctor came forwards and stood by the bed-side.

"Oh, don't take him away yet," she moaned.

The doctor, without answering, looked at her gravely. Knowing she would not be allowed to keep the child much longer, the woman kissed him again; and she passed her hand down his body till she came to his feet; she held the right foot in her hand and felt the five small toes; and then slowly passed her hand over the left one. She gave a sob.

"What's the matter?" said the doctor. "You're tired."

She shook her head, unable to speak, and the tears rolled down her cheeks. The doctor bent down.

"Let me take him."

She was too weak to resist his wish, and she gave the child up. The doctor handed him back to his nurse.

"You'd better put him back in his own bed."

"Very well, sir."

The little boy, still sleeping, was taken away. His mother sobbed now broken-heartedly.

"What will happen to him, poor child?"

The monthly nurse tried to quiet her, and presently, from exhaustion, the crying ceased. The doctor walked to a table on the other side of the room, upon which, under a towel, lay the body of a still-born child. He lifted the towel and looked. He was hidden from the bed by a screen, but the woman guessed what he was doing.

"Was it a girl or a boy?" she whispered to the nurse.

"Another boy."

The woman did not answer. In a moment the child's nurse came back. She approached the bed.

"Master Philip never woke up," she said.

There was a pause. Then the doctor felt his patient's pulse once more.

"I don't think there's anything I can do just now," he said. "I'll call again after breakfast."

"I'll show you out, sir," said the child's nurse.

They walked downstairs in silence. In the hall the doctor stopped.

"You've sent for Mrs. Carey's brother-in-law, haven't you?"

"Yes, sir."

"D'you know at what time he'll be here?"

"No, sir, I'm expecting a telegram."

"What about the little boy? I should think he'd be better out of the way."

"Miss Watkin said she'd take him, sir."

"Who's she?"

"She's his godmother, sir. D'you think Mrs. Carey will get over it, sir?"

The doctor shook his head.

Chapter II

IT WAS A WEEK LATER. PHILIP WAS SITTING ON THE FLOOR IN THE DRAWING-room at Miss Watkin's house in Onslow Gardens. He was an only child and used to amusing himself. The room was filled with massive furniture, and on each of the sofas were three big cushions. There was a cushion too in each armchair. All these he had taken and, with the help of the gilt rout chairs, light and easy to move, had made an elaborate cave in which he could hide himself from the Red Indians who were lurking behind the curtains. He put his ear to the floor and listened to the herd of buffaloes that raced across the prairie. Presently, hearing the door open, he held his breath so that he might not be discovered; but a violent hand pulled away a chair and the cushions fell down.

"You naughty boy, Miss Watkin *will* be cross with you."

"Hulloa, Emma!" he said.

The nurse bent down and kissed him, then began to shake out the cushions, and put them back in their places.

"Am I to come home?" he asked.

"Yes, I've come to fetch you."

"You've got a new dress on."

It was in eighteen-eighty-five, and she wore a bustle. Her gown was of black velvet, with tight sleeves and sloping shoulders, and the skirt had three large flounces. She wore a black bonnet with velvet strings. She hesitated. The question she had expected did not come, and so she could not give the answer she had prepared.

"Aren't you going to ask how your mamma is?" she said at length.

"Oh, I forgot. How is mamma?"

Now she was ready.

"Your mamma is quite well and happy."

"Oh, I am glad."

"Your mamma's gone away. You won't ever see her anymore."

Philip did not know what she meant.

"Why not?"

"Your mamma's in heaven."

She began to cry, and Philip, though he did not quite understand, cried too. Emma was a tall, big-boned woman, with fair hair and large features. She came from Devonshire and, notwithstanding her many years of service in London, had never lost the breadth of her accent. Her tears increased her emotion, and she pressed the little boy to her heart. She felt vaguely the pity of that child deprived of the only love in the world that is quite unselfish. It seemed dreadful that he must be handed over to strangers. But in a little while she pulled herself together.

"Your Uncle William is waiting in to see you," she said. "Go and say good-bye to Miss Watkin, and we'll go home."

"I don't want to say good-bye," he answered, instinctively anxious to hide his tears.

"Very well, run upstairs and get your hat."

He fetched it, and when he came down Emma was waiting for him in the hall. He heard the sound of voices in the study behind the dining-room. He paused. He knew that Miss Watkin and her sister were talking to friends, and it seemed to him—he was nine years old—that if he went in they would be sorry for him.

"I think I'll go and say good-bye to Miss Watkin."

"I think you'd better," said Emma.

"Go in and tell them I'm coming," he said.

He wished to make the most of his opportunity. Emma knocked at the door and walked in. He heard her speak.

"Master Philip wants to say good-bye to you, miss."

There was a sudden hush of the conversation, and Philip limped in. Henrietta Watkin was a stout woman, with a red face and dyed hair. In those days to dye the hair excited comment, and Philip had heard much gossip at home when his godmother's changed colour. She lived with an elder sister, who had resigned herself contentedly to old age. Two ladies, whom Philip did not know, were calling, and they looked at him curiously.

"My poor child," said Miss Watkin, opening her arms.

She began to cry. Philip understood now why she had not been in to luncheon and why she wore a black dress. She could not speak.

"I've got to go home," said Philip, at last.

He disengaged himself from Miss Watkin's arms, and she kissed him again. Then he went to her sister and bade her good-bye too. One of the strange ladies asked if she might kiss him, and he gravely gave her permission. Though crying, he keenly enjoyed the sensation he was causing; he would have been glad to stay a little longer to be made much of, but felt they expected him to go, so he said that Emma was waiting for him. He went out of the room. Emma had gone downstairs to speak with a friend in the basement, and he waited for her on the landing. He heard Henrietta Watkin's voice.

"His mother was my greatest friend. I can't bear to think that she's dead."

"You oughtn't to have gone to the funeral, Henrietta," said her sister. "I knew it would upset you."

Then one of the strangers spoke.

"Poor little boy, it's dreadful to think of him quite alone in the world. I see he limps."

"Yes, he's got a club-foot. It was such a grief to his mother."

Then Emma came back. They called a hansom, and she told the driver where to go.

Chapter III

WHEN THEY REACHED THE HOUSE MRS. CAREY HAD DIED IN—IT WAS IN a dreary, respectable street between Notting Hill Gate and High Street, Kensington—Emma led Philip into the drawing-room. His uncle was writing letters of thanks for the wreaths which had been sent. One of them, which had arrived too late for the funeral, lay in its cardboard box on the hall-table.

"Here's Master Philip," said Emma.

Mr. Carey stood up slowly and shook hands with the little boy. Then on second thoughts he bent down and kissed his forehead. He was a man of somewhat less than average height, inclined to corpulence, with his hair, worn long, arranged over the scalp so as to conceal his baldness. He was clean-shaven. His features were regular, and it was possible to imagine that in his youth he had been good-looking. On his watch-chain he wore a gold cross.

"You're going to live with me now, Philip," said Mr. Carey. "Shall you like that?"

Two years before Philip had been sent down to stay at the vicarage after an attack of chicken-pox; but there remained with him a recollection of an attic and a large garden rather than of his uncle and aunt.

"Yes."

"You must look upon me and your Aunt Louisa as your father and mother."

The child's mouth trembled a little, he reddened, but did not answer.

"Your dear mother left you in my charge."

Mr. Carey had no great ease in expressing himself. When the news came that his sister-in-law was dying, he set off at once for London, but on the way thought of nothing but the disturbance in his life that would be caused if her death forced him to undertake the care of her son. He was well over fifty, and his wife, to whom he had been married for thirty years, was childless; he did not look forward with any pleasure to the presence of a small boy who might be noisy and rough. He had never much liked his sister-in-law.

"I'm going to take you down to Blackstable tomorrow," he said.

"With Emma?"

The child put his hand in hers, and she pressed it.

"I'm afraid Emma must go away," said Mr. Carey.

"But I want Emma to come with me."

Philip began to cry, and the nurse could not help crying too. Mr. Carey looked at them helplessly.

"I think you'd better leave me alone with Master Philip for a moment."

"Very good, sir."

Though Philip clung to her, she released herself gently. Mr. Carey took the boy on his knee and put his arm round him.

"You mustn't cry," he said. "You're too old to have a nurse now. We must see about sending you to school."

"I want Emma to come with me," the child repeated.

"It costs too much money, Philip. Your father didn't leave very much, and I don't know what's become of it. You must look at every penny you spend."

Mr. Carey had called the day before on the family solicitor. Philip's father was a surgeon in good practice, and his hospital appointments suggested an established position; so that it was a surprise on his sudden death from blood-poisoning to find that he had left his widow little more than his life insurance and what could be got for the lease of their house in Bruton Street. This was six months ago; and Mrs. Carey, already in delicate health, finding herself with child, had lost her head and accepted for the lease the first offer that was made. She stored her furniture, and, at a rent which the parson thought outrageous, took a furnished house for a year, so that she might suffer from no inconvenience till her child was born. But she had never been used to the management of money, and was unable to adapt her expenditure to her altered circumstances. The little she had slipped through her fingers in one way and another, so that now, when all expenses were paid, not much more than two thousand pounds remained to support the boy till he was able to earn his own living. It was impossible to explain all this to Philip and he was sobbing still.

"You'd better go to Emma," Mr. Carey said, feeling that she could console the child better than anyone.

Without a word Philip slipped off his uncle's knee, but Mr. Carey stopped him.

"We must go tomorrow, because on Saturday I've got to prepare my sermon, and you must tell Emma to get your things ready today. You can bring all your toys. And if you want anything to remember your father and mother by you can take one thing for each of them. Everything else is going to be sold."

The boy slipped out of the room. Mr. Carey was unused to work, and he turned to his correspondence with resentment. On one side of the desk was a bundle of bills, and these filled him with irritation. One especially seemed preposterous. Immediately after Mrs. Carey's death Emma had ordered from the florist masses of white flowers for the room in which the dead woman lay. It was sheer waste of money. Emma took far too much upon herself. Even if there had been no financial necessity, he would have dismissed her.

But Philip went to her, and hid his face in her bosom, and wept as though his heart would break. And she, feeling that he was almost her own son—she had taken him when he was a month old—consoled him with soft words. She promised that she would come and see him sometimes, and that she would never forget him; and she told him about the country he was going to and about her own home in Devonshire—her father kept a turnpike on the high-road that led to Exeter, and there were pigs in the sty, and there was a cow, and the cow had just had a calf—till Philip forgot his tears and grew excited at the thought of his approaching journey. Presently she put him down, for there was much to be done, and he helped her to lay out his clothes on the bed. She sent him into the nursery to gather up his toys, and in a little while he was playing happily.

But at last he grew tired of being alone and went back to the bed-room, in which Emma was now putting his things into a big tin box; he remembered then that his uncle had said he might take something to remember his father and mother by. He told Emma and asked her what he should take.

"You'd better go into the drawing-room and see what you fancy."

"Uncle William's there."

"Never mind that. They're your own things now."

Philip went downstairs slowly and found the door open. Mr. Carey had left the room. Philip walked slowly round. They had been in the house so short a time that there was little in it that had a particular interest to him. It was a stranger's room, and Philip saw nothing that struck his fancy. But he knew which were his mother's things and which belonged to the landlord, and presently fixed on a little clock that he had once heard his mother say she liked. With this he walked again rather disconsolately upstairs. Outside the door of his mother's bed-room he stopped and listened. Though no one had told him not to go in, he had a feeling that it would be wrong to do so; he was a little frightened, and his heart beat uncomfortably; but at the same time something impelled him to turn the handle. He turned it very gently, as if to prevent anyone within from hearing, and then slowly pushed the door open. He stood on the threshold for a moment before he had the courage to enter. He was not frightened now, but it seemed strange. He closed the door behind him. The blinds were drawn, and the room, in the cold light of a January afternoon, was dark. On the dressing-table were Mrs. Carey's brushes and the hand-mirror. In a little tray were hairpins. There was a photograph of himself on the chimney-piece and one of his father. He had often been in the room when his mother was not in it, but now it seemed different. There was something curious in the look of the chairs. The bed was made as though someone were going to sleep in it that night, and in a case on the pillow was a night-dress.

Philip opened a large cupboard filled with dresses and, stepping in, took as many of them as he could in his arms and buried his face in them. They smelled of the scent his mother used. Then he pulled open the drawers, filled with his mother's things, and looked at them: there were lavender bags among the linen, and their scent was fresh and pleasant. The strangeness of the room left it, and it seemed to him that his mother had just gone out for a walk. She would be in presently and would come upstairs to have nursery tea with him. And he seemed to feel her kiss on his lips.

It was not true that he would never see her again. It was not true simply because it was impossible. He climbed up on the bed and put his head on the pillow. He lay there quite still.

Chapter IV

PHILIP PARTED FROM EMMA WITH TEARS, BUT THE JOURNEY TO BLACKSTABLE amused him, and, when they arrived, he was resigned and cheerful. Blackstable was sixty miles from London. Giving their luggage to a porter, Mr. Carey set out to walk with Philip to the vicarage; it took them little more than five minutes, and, when they reached it, Philip suddenly remembered the gate. It was red and five-barred: it swung both ways on easy hinges; and it was possible, though forbidden, to swing backwards and forwards on it. They walked through the garden to the front-door. This was only used by visitors and on Sundays, and on special occasions, as when the Vicar went up to London or came back. The traffic of the house took place through a side-door, and there was a back-door as well for the gardener and for beggars and tramps. It was a fairly large house of yellow brick, with a red roof, built about five-and-twenty years before in an ecclesiastical style. The front-door was like a church porch, and the drawing-room windows were gothic.

Mrs. Carey, knowing by what train they were coming, waited in the drawing-room and listened for the click of the gate. When she heard it she went to the door.

"There's Aunt Louisa," said Mr. Carey, when he saw her. "Run and give her a kiss."

Philip started to run, awkwardly, trailing his club-foot, and then stopped. Mrs. Carey was a little, shrivelled woman of the same age as her husband, with a face extraordinarily filled with deep wrinkles, and pale blue eyes. Her grey hair was arranged in ringlets according to the fashion of her youth. She wore a black dress, and her only ornament was a gold chain, from which hung a cross. She had a shy manner and a gentle voice.

"Did you walk, William?" she said, almost reproachfully, as she kissed her husband.

"I didn't think of it," he answered, with a glance at his nephew.

"It didn't hurt you to walk, Philip, did it?" she asked the child.

"No. I always walk."

He was a little surprised at their conversation. Aunt Louisa told him to come in, and they entered the hall. It was paved with red and yellow tiles, on which alternately were a Greek Cross and the Lamb of God. An imposing staircase led out of the hall. It was of polished pine, with a peculiar smell, and had been put in because fortunately, when the church was reseated, enough wood remained over. The balusters were decorated with emblems of the Four Evangelists.

"I've had the stove lighted as I thought you'd be cold after your journey," said Mrs. Carey.

It was a large black stove that stood in the hall and was only lighted if the weather was very bad and the Vicar had a cold. It was not lighted if Mrs. Carey had a cold. Coal was expensive. Besides, Mary Ann, the maid, didn't like fires all over the place. If they wanted all them fires they must keep a second girl. In the winter Mr. and Mrs. Carey lived in the dining-room so that one fire should do, and in the summer they could not get out of the habit, so the drawing-room was used only by Mr. Carey on Sunday afternoons for his nap. But every Saturday he had a fire in the study so that he could write his sermon.

Aunt Louisa took Philip upstairs and showed him into a tiny bed-room that looked out on the drive. Immediately in front of the window was a large tree, which Philip remembered now because the branches were so low that it was possible to climb quite high up it.

"A small room for a small boy," said Mrs. Carey. "You won't be frightened at sleeping alone?"

"Oh, no."

On his first visit to the vicarage he had come with his nurse, and Mrs. Carey had had little to do with him. She looked at him now with some uncertainty.

"Can you wash your own hands, or shall I wash them for you?"

"I can wash myself," he answered firmly.

"Well, I shall look at them when you come down to tea," said Mrs. Carey.

She knew nothing about children. After it was settled that Philip should come down to Blackstable, Mrs. Carey had thought much how she should treat him; she was anxious to do her duty; but now he was there she found herself just as shy of him as he was of her. She hoped he would not be noisy and rough, because her husband did not like rough and noisy boys. Mrs. Carey made an excuse to leave Philip alone, but in a moment came back and knocked at the door; she asked him, without coming in, if he could pour out the water himself. Then she went downstairs and rang the bell for tea.

The dining-room, large and well-proportioned, had windows on two sides of it, with heavy curtains of red rep; there was a big table in the middle; and at one end an imposing mahogany sideboard with a looking-glass in it. In one corner stood a harmonium. On each side of the fireplace were chairs covered in stamped leather, each with an antimacassar; one had arms and was called the husband, and the other had none and was called the wife. Mrs. Carey never sat in the arm-chair: she said she preferred a chair that was not too comfortable; there was always a lot to do, and if her chair had had arms she might not be so ready to leave it.

Mr. Carey was making up the fire when Philip came in, and he pointed out to his nephew that there were two pokers. One was large and bright and polished and unused, and was called the Vicar; and the other, which was much smaller and had evidently passed through many fires, was called the Curate.

"What are we waiting for?" said Mr. Carey.

"I told Mary Ann to make you an egg. I thought you'd be hungry after your journey."

Mrs. Carey thought the journey from London to Blackstable very tiring. She seldom travelled herself, for the living was only three hundred a year, and, when her husband wanted a holiday, since there was not money for two, he went by himself. He was very fond of Church Congresses and usually managed to go up to London once a year; and once he had been to Paris for the exhibition, and two or three times to Switzerland. Mary Ann brought in the egg, and they sat down. The chair was much too low for Philip, and for a moment neither Mr. Carey nor his wife knew what to do.

"I'll put some books under him," said Mary Ann.

She took from the top of the harmonium the large Bible and the prayer-book from which the Vicar was accustomed to read prayers, and put them on Philip's chair.

"Oh, William, he can't sit on the Bible," said Mrs. Carey, in a shocked tone. "Couldn't you get him some books out of the study?"

Mr. Carey considered the question for an instant.

"I don't think it matters this once if you put the prayer-book on the top, Mary Ann," he said. "The book of Common Prayer is the composition of men like ourselves. It has no claim to divine authorship."

"I hadn't thought of that, William," said Aunt Louisa.

Philip perched himself on the books, and the Vicar, having said grace, cut the top off his egg.

"There," he said, handing it to Philip, "you can eat my top if you like."

Philip would have liked an egg to himself, but he was not offered one, so took what he could.

"How have the chickens been laying since I went away?" asked the Vicar.

"Oh, they've been dreadful, only one or two a day."

"How did you like that top, Philip?" asked his uncle.

"Very much, thank you."

"You shall have another one on Sunday afternoon."

Mr. Carey always had a boiled egg at tea on Sunday, so that he might be fortified for the evening service.

Chapter V

Philip came gradually to know the people he was to live with, and by fragments of conversation, some of it not meant for his ears, learned a good deal both about himself and about his dead parents. Philip's father had been much younger than the Vicar of Blackstable. After a brilliant career at St. Luke's Hospital he was put on the staff, and presently began to earn money in considerable sums. He spent it freely. When the parson set about restoring his church and asked his brother for a subscription, he was surprised by receiving a couple of hundred pounds: Mr. Carey, thrifty by inclination and economical by necessity, accepted it with mingled feelings; he was envious of his brother because he could afford to give so much, pleased for the sake of his church, and vaguely irritated by a generosity which seemed almost ostentatious. Then Henry Carey married a patient, a beautiful girl but penniless, an orphan with no near relations, but of good family; and there was an array of fine friends at the wedding. The parson, on his visits to her when he came to London, held himself with reserve. He felt shy with her and in his heart he resented her great beauty: she dressed more magnificently than became the wife of a hardworking surgeon; and the charming furniture of her house, the flowers among which she lived even in winter, suggested an extravagance which he deplored. He heard her talk of entertainments she was going to; and, as he told his wife on getting home again, it was impossible to accept hospitality without making some return. He had seen grapes in the dining-room that must have cost at least eight shillings a pound; and at luncheon he had been given asparagus two months before it was ready in the vicarage garden. Now all he had anticipated was come to pass: the Vicar felt the satisfaction of the prophet who saw fire and brimstone consume the city which would not mend its way to his warning. Poor Philip was practically penniless, and what was the good of his mother's fine friends now? He heard that his father's extravagance was really criminal, and it was a mercy that Providence had seen fit to take his dear mother to itself: she had no more idea of money than a child.

When Philip had been a week at Blackstable an incident happened which seemed to irritate his uncle very much. One morning he found on the breakfast-table a small packet which had been sent on by post from the late Mrs. Carey's house in London. It was addressed to her. When the parson opened it he found a dozen photographs of Mrs. Carey. They showed the head and shoulders only, and her hair was more plainly done than usual, low on the forehead, which gave her an unusual look; the face was thin and worn, but no illness could impair the beauty of her features. There was in the large dark eyes a sadness which Philip did not remember. The first sight of the dead woman gave Mr. Carey a little shock, but this was quickly followed by perplexity. The photographs seemed quite recent, and he could not imagine who had ordered them.

"D'you know anything about these, Philip?" he asked.

"I remember mamma said she'd been taken," he answered. "Miss Watkin scolded her.... She said: I wanted the boy to have something to remember me by when he grows up."

Mr. Carey looked at Philip for an instant. The child spoke in a clear treble. He recalled the words, but they meant nothing to him.

"You'd better take one of the photographs and keep it in your room," said Mr. Carey. "I'll put the others away."

He sent one to Miss Watkin, and she wrote and explained how they came to be taken.

One day Mrs. Carey was lying in bed, but she was feeling a little better than usual, and the doctor in the morning had seemed hopeful; Emma had taken the child out, and the maids were downstairs in the basement; suddenly Mrs. Carey felt desperately alone in the world. A great fear seized her that she would not recover from the confinement which she was expecting in a fortnight. Her son was nine years old. How could he be expected to remember her? She could not bear to think that he would grow up and forget, forget her utterly; and she had loved him so passionately, because he was weakly and deformed, and because he was her child. She had no photographs of herself taken since her marriage, and that was ten years before. She wanted her son to know what she looked like at the end. He could not forget her then, not forget utterly. She knew that if she called her maid and told her she wanted to get up, the maid would prevent her, and perhaps send for the doctor, and she had not the strength now to struggle or argue. She got out of bed and began to dress herself. She had been on her back so long that her legs gave way beneath her, and then the soles of her feet tingled so that she could hardly bear to put them to the ground. But she went on. She was unused to doing her own hair and, when she raised her arms and began to brush it, she felt faint. She could never do it as her maid did. It was beautiful hair, very fine, and of a deep rich gold. Her eyebrows were straight and dark. She put on a black skirt, but chose the bodice of the evening-dress which she liked best: it was of a white damask which was fashionable in those days. She looked at herself in the glass. Her face was very pale, but her skin was clear: she had never had much colour, and this had always made the redness of her beautiful mouth emphatic. She could not restrain a sob. But she could not afford to be sorry for herself; she was feeling already desperately tired; and she put on the furs which Henry had given her the Christmas before—she had been so proud of them and so happy then—and slipped downstairs with beating heart. She got safely out of the house and drove to a photographer. She paid for a dozen photographs. She was obliged to ask for a glass of water in the middle of the sitting; and the assistant, seeing she was ill, suggested that she should come another day, but she insisted on staying till the end. At last it was finished, and she drove back again to the dingy little house in Kensington which she hated with all her heart. It was a horrible house to die in.

She found the front-door open, and when she drove up the maid and Emma ran down the steps to help her. They had been frightened when they found her room empty. At first they thought she must have gone to Miss Watkin, and the cook was sent round. Miss Watkin came back with her and was waiting anxiously in the drawing-room. She came downstairs now full of anxiety and reproaches; but the exertion had been more than Mrs. Carey was fit for, and when the occasion for firmness no longer existed she gave way. She fell heavily into Emma's arms and was carried upstairs. She remained unconscious for a time that seemed incredibly long to those that watched her, and the doctor, hurriedly sent for, did not come. It was next day, when she was a little better, that Miss Watkin got some explanation out of her. Philip was playing on the floor of his mother's bed-room, and neither of the ladies paid attention to him. He only understood vaguely what they were talking about, and he could not have said why those words remained in his memory.

"I wanted the boy to have something to remember me by when he grows up."

"I can't make out why she ordered a dozen," said Mr. Carey. "Two would have done."

Chapter VI

ONE DAY WAS VERY LIKE ANOTHER AT THE VICARAGE. Soon after breakfast Mary Ann brought in *The Times*. Mr. Carey shared it with two neighbours. He had it from ten till one, when the gardener took it over to Mr. Ellis at the Limes, with whom it remained till seven; then it was taken to Miss Brooks at the Manor House, who, since she got it late, had the advantage of keeping it. In summer Mrs. Carey, when she was making jam, often asked her for a copy to cover the pots with. When the Vicar settled down to his paper his wife put on her bonnet and went out to do the shopping. Philip accompanied her. Blackstable was a fishing village. It consisted of a high street in which were the shops, the bank, the doctor's house, and the houses of two or three coal-ship owners; round the little harbour were shabby streets in which lived fishermen and poor people; but since they went to chapel they were of no account. When Mrs. Carey passed the dissenting ministers in the street she stepped over to the other side to avoid meeting them, but if there was not time for this fixed her eyes on the pavement. It was a scandal to which the Vicar had never resigned himself that there were three chapels in the High Street: he could not help feeling that the law should have stepped in to prevent their erection. Shopping in Blackstable was not a simple matter; for dissent, helped by the fact that the parish church was two miles from the town, was very common; and it was necessary to deal only with churchgoers; Mrs. Carey knew perfectly that the vicarage custom might make all the difference to a tradesman's faith. There were two butchers who went to church, and they would not understand that the Vicar could not deal with both of them at once; nor were they satisfied with his simple plan of going for six months to one and for six months to the other. The butcher who was not sending meat to the vicarage constantly threatened not to come to church, and the Vicar was sometimes obliged to make a threat: it was very wrong of him not to come to church, but if he carried iniquity further and actually went to chapel, then of course, excellent as his meat was, Mr. Carey would be forced to leave him forever. Mrs. Carey often stopped at the bank to deliver a message to Josiah Graves, the manager, who was choir-master, treasurer, and churchwarden. He was a tall, thin man with a sallow face and a long nose; his hair was very white, and to Philip he seemed extremely old. He kept the parish accounts, arranged the treats for the choir and the schools; though there was no organ in the parish church, it was generally considered (in Blackstable) that the choir he led was the best in Kent; and when there was any ceremony, such as a visit from the Bishop for confirmation or from the Rural Dean to preach at the Harvest Thanksgiving, he made the necessary preparations. But he had no hesitation in doing all manner of things without more than a perfunctory consultation with the Vicar, and the Vicar, though always ready to be saved trouble, much resented the churchwarden's managing ways. He really seemed to look upon himself as the most important person in the parish. Mr. Carey constantly told his wife that if Josiah Graves did not take care he would give him a good rap over the knuckles one day; but Mrs. Carey advised him to bear with Josiah Graves: he meant well, and it was not his fault if he was not quite a gentleman. The Vicar, finding his comfort in the practice of a Christian virtue, exercised forbearance; but he revenged himself by calling the churchwarden Bismarck behind his back.

Once there had been a serious quarrel between the pair, and Mrs. Carey still thought of that anxious time with dismay. The Conservative candidate had announced his intention of addressing a meeting at Blackstable; and Josiah Graves, having arranged that it should take place in the Mission Hall, went to Mr. Carey and told him that he hoped he would say a few words. It appeared that the candidate had asked Josiah Graves to take the chair. This was more than Mr. Carey could put up with. He had firm views upon the respect which was due to the cloth, and it was ridiculous for a churchwarden to take the chair at a meeting when the Vicar was there. He reminded Josiah Graves that parson meant person, that is, the vicar was the person of the parish. Josiah Graves answered that he was the first to recognise the dignity of the church, but this was a matter of politics, and in his turn he reminded the Vicar that their Blessed Saviour had enjoined upon them to render unto Cæsar the things that were Cæsar's. To this Mr. Carey replied that the devil could quote scripture to his purpose, himself had sole authority over the Mission Hall, and if he were not asked to be chairman he would refuse the use of it for a political meeting. Josiah Graves told Mr. Carey that he might do as he chose, and for his part he thought the Wesleyan Chapel would be an equally suitable place. Then Mr. Carey said that if Josiah Graves set foot in what was little better than a heathen temple he was not fit to be churchwarden in a Christian parish. Josiah Graves thereupon resigned all his offices, and that very evening sent to the church for his cassock and surplice. His sister, Miss Graves, who kept house for him, gave up her secretaryship of the Maternity Club, which provided the pregnant poor with flannel, baby linen, coals, and five shillings. Mr. Carey said he was at last master in his own house. But soon he found that he was obliged to see to all sorts of things that he knew nothing about; and Josiah Graves, after the first moment of irritation, discovered that he had lost his chief interest in life. Mrs. Carey and Miss Graves were much distressed by the quarrel; they met after a discreet exchange of letters, and made up their minds to put the matter right: they talked, one to her husband, the other to her brother, from morning till night; and since they were persuading these gentlemen to do what in their hearts they wanted, after three weeks of anxiety a reconciliation was effected. It was to both their interests, but they ascribed it to a common love for their Redeemer. The meeting was held at the Mission Hall, and the doctor was asked to be chairman. Mr. Carey and Josiah Graves both made speeches.

When Mrs. Carey had finished her business with the banker, she generally went upstairs to have a little chat with his sister; and while the ladies talked of parish matters, the curate or the new bonnet of Mrs. Wilson—Mr. Wilson was the richest man in Blackstable, he was thought to have at least five hundred a year, and he had married his cook—Philip sat demurely in the stiff parlour, used only to receive visitors, and busied himself with the restless movements of goldfish in a bowl. The windows were never opened except to air the room for a few minutes in the morning, and it had a stuffy smell which seemed to Philip to have a mysterious connection with banking.

Then Mrs. Carey remembered that she had to go to the grocer, and they continued their way. When the shopping was done they often went down a side-street of little houses, mostly of wood, in which fishermen dwelled (and here and there a fisherman sat on his doorstep mending his nets, and nets hung to dry upon the doors), till they came to a small beach, shut in on each side by warehouses, but with a view of the sea. Mrs. Carey stood for a few minutes and looked at it, it was turbid and yellow, [and who knows what thoughts passed through her mind?] while Philip searched for flat stones to play ducks and drakes. Then they walked slowly back. They looked into the post office to get the right time, nodded to Mrs. Wigram the doctor's wife, who sat at her window sewing, and so got home.

Dinner was at one o'clock; and on Monday, Tuesday, and Wednesday it consisted of beef, roast, hashed, and minced, and on Thursday, Friday, and Saturday of mutton. On Sunday they ate one of their own chickens. In the afternoon Philip did his lessons. He was taught Latin and mathematics by his uncle who knew neither, and French and the piano by his aunt. Of French she was ignorant, but she knew the piano well enough to accompany the old-fashioned songs she had sung for thirty years. Uncle William used to tell Philip that when he was a curate his wife had known twelve songs by heart, which she could sing at a moment's notice whenever she was asked. She often sang still when there was a tea-party at the vicarage. There were few people whom the Careys cared to ask there, and their parties consisted always of the curate, Josiah Graves with his sister, Dr. Wigram and his wife. After tea Miss Graves played one or two of Mendelssohn's *Songs without Words,* and Mrs. Carey sang *When the Swallows Homeward Fly,* or *Trot, Trot, My Pony.*

But the Careys did not give tea-parties often; the preparations upset them, and when their guests were gone they felt themselves exhausted. They preferred to have tea by themselves, and after tea they played backgammon. Mrs. Carey arranged that her husband should win, because he did not like losing. They had cold supper at eight. It was a scrappy meal because Mary Ann resented getting anything ready after tea, and Mrs. Carey helped to clear away. Mrs. Carey seldom ate more than bread and butter, with a little stewed fruit to follow, but the Vicar had a slice of cold meat. Immediately after supper Mrs. Carey rang the bell for prayers, and then Philip went to bed. He rebelled against being undressed by Mary Ann and after a while succeeded in establishing his right to dress and undress himself. At nine o'clock Mary Ann brought in the eggs and the plate. Mrs. Carey wrote the date on each egg and put the number down in a book. She then took the plate-basket on her arm and went upstairs. Mr. Carey continued to read one of his old books, but as the clock struck ten he got up, put out the lamps, and followed his wife to bed.

When Philip arrived there was some difficulty in deciding on which evening he should have his bath. It was never easy to get plenty of hot water, since the kitchen boiler did not work, and it was impossible for two persons to have a bath on the same day. The only man who had a bathroom in Blackstable was Mr. Wilson, and it was thought ostentatious of him. Mary Ann had her bath in the kitchen on Monday night, because she liked to begin the week clean. Uncle William could not have his on Saturday, because he had a heavy day before him and he was always a little tired after a bath, so he had it on Friday. Mrs. Carey had hers on Thursday for the same reason. It looked as though Saturday were naturally indicated for Philip, but Mary Ann said she couldn't keep the fire up on Saturday night: what with all the cooking on Sunday, having to make pastry and she didn't know what all, she did not feel up to giving the boy his bath on Saturday night; and it was quite clear that he could not bath himself. Mrs. Carey was shy about bathing a boy, and of course the Vicar had his sermon. But the Vicar insisted that Philip should be clean and sweet for the Lord's Day. Mary Ann said she would rather go than be put upon—and after eighteen years she didn't expect to have more work given her, and they might show some consideration—and Philip said he didn't want anyone to bath him, but could very well bath himself. This settled it. Mary Ann said she was quite sure he wouldn't bath himself properly, and rather than he should go dirty—and not because he was going into the presence of the Lord, but because she couldn't abide a boy who wasn't properly washed—she'd work herself to the bone even if it was Saturday night.

Chapter VII

SUNDAY WAS A DAY CROWDED WITH INCIDENT. MR. CAREY WAS ACCUSTOMED to say that he was the only man in his parish who worked seven days a week. The household got up half an hour earlier than usual. No lying abed for a poor parson on the day of rest, Mr. Carey remarked as Mary Ann knocked at the door punctually at eight. It took Mrs. Carey longer to dress, and she got down to breakfast at nine, a little breathless, only just before her husband. Mr. Carey's boots stood in front of the fire to warm. Prayers were longer than usual, and the breakfast more substantial. After breakfast the Vicar cut thin slices of bread for the communion, and Philip was privileged to cut off the crust. He was sent to the study to fetch a marble paperweight, with which Mr. Carey pressed the bread till it was thin and pulpy, and then it was cut into small squares. The amount was regulated by the weather. On a very bad day few people came to church, and on a very fine one, though many came, few stayed for communion. There were most when it was dry enough to make the walk to church pleasant, but not so fine that people wanted to hurry away.

Then Mrs. Carey brought the communion plate out of the safe, which stood in the pantry, and the Vicar polished it with a chamois leather. At ten the fly drove up, and Mr. Carey got into his boots. Mrs. Carey took several minutes to put on her bonnet, during which the Vicar, in a voluminous cloak, stood in the hall with just such an expression on his face as would have become an early Christian about to be led into the arena. It was extraordinary that after thirty years of marriage his wife could not be ready in time on Sunday morning. At last she came, in black satin; the Vicar did not like colours in a clergyman's wife at any time, but on Sundays he was determined that she should wear black; now and then, in conspiracy with Miss Graves, she ventured a white feather or a pink rose in her bonnet, but the Vicar insisted that it should disappear; he said he would not go to church with the scarlet woman: Mrs. Carey sighed as a woman but obeyed as a wife. They were about to step into the carriage when the Vicar remembered that no one had given him his egg. They knew that he must have an egg for his voice, there were two women in the house, and no one had the least regard for his comfort. Mrs. Carey scolded Mary Ann, and Mary Ann answered that she could not think of everything. She hurried away to fetch an egg, and Mrs. Carey beat it up in a glass of sherry. The Vicar swallowed it at a gulp. The communion plate was stowed in the carriage, and they set off.

The fly came from *The Red Lion* and had a peculiar smell of stale straw. They drove with both windows closed so that the Vicar should not catch cold. The sexton was waiting at the porch to take the communion plate, and while the Vicar went to the vestry Mrs. Carey and Philip settled themselves in the vicarage pew. Mrs. Carey placed in front of her the sixpenny bit she was accustomed to put in the plate, and gave Philip threepence for the same purpose. The church filled up gradually and the service began.

Philip grew bored during the sermon, but if he fidgetted Mrs. Carey put a gentle hand on his arm and looked at him reproachfully. He regained interest when the final hymn was sung and Mr. Graves passed round with the plate.

When everyone had gone Mrs. Carey went into Miss Graves' pew to have a few words with her while they were waiting for the gentlemen, and Philip went to the vestry. His uncle, the curate, and Mr. Graves were still in their surplices. Mr. Carey gave him the remains of the consecrated bread and told him he might eat it. He had been accustomed to eat it himself, as it seemed blasphemous to throw it away, but Philip's keen appetite relieved him from the duty. Then they counted the money. It consisted of pennies, sixpences and threepenny bits. There were always two single shillings, one put in the plate by the Vicar and the other by Mr. Graves; and sometimes there was a florin. Mr. Graves told the Vicar who had given this. It was always a stranger to Blackstable, and Mr. Carey wondered who he was. But Miss Graves had observed the rash act and was able to tell Mrs. Carey that the stranger came from London, was married and had children. During the drive home Mrs. Carey passed the information on, and the Vicar made up his mind to call on him and ask for a subscription to the Additional Curates Society. Mr. Carey asked if Philip had behaved properly; and Mrs. Carey remarked that Mrs. Wigram had a new mantle, Mr. Cox was not in church, and somebody thought that Miss Phillips was engaged. When they reached the vicarage they all felt that they deserved a substantial dinner.

When this was over Mrs. Carey went to her room to rest, and Mr. Carey lay down on the sofa in the drawing-room for forty winks.

They had tea at five, and the Vicar ate an egg to support himself for evensong. Mrs. Carey did not go to this so that Mary Ann might, but she read the service through and the hymns. Mr. Carey walked to church in the evening, and Philip limped along by his side. The walk through the darkness along the country road strangely impressed him, and the church with all its lights in the distance, coming gradually nearer, seemed very friendly. At first he was shy with his uncle, but little by little grew used to him, and he would slip his hand in his uncle's and walk more easily for the feeling of protection.

They had supper when they got home. Mr. Carey's slippers were waiting for him on a footstool in front of the fire and by their side Philip's, one the shoe of a small boy, the other misshapen and odd. He was dreadfully tired when he went up to bed, and he did not resist when Mary Ann undressed him. She kissed him after she tucked him up, and he began to love her.

Chapter VIII

PHILIP HAD LED ALWAYS THE SOLITARY LIFE OF AN ONLY CHILD, AND HIS loneliness at the vicarage was no greater than it had been when his mother lived. He made friends with Mary Ann. She was a chubby little person of thirty-five, the daughter of a fisherman, and had come to the vicarage at eighteen; it was her first place and she had no intention of leaving it; but she held a possible marriage as a rod over the timid heads of her master and mistress. Her father and mother lived in a little house off Harbour Street, and she went to see them on her evenings out. Her stories of the sea touched Philip's imagination, and the narrow alleys round the harbour grew rich with the romance which his young fancy lent them. One evening he asked whether he might go home with her; but his aunt was afraid that he might catch something, and his uncle said that evil communications corrupted good manners. He disliked the fisher-folk, who were rough, uncouth, and went to chapel. But Philip was more comfortable in the kitchen than in the dining-room, and, whenever he could, he took his toys and played there. His aunt was not sorry. She did not like disorder, and though she recognised that boys must be expected to be untidy she preferred that he should make a mess in the kitchen. If he fidgeted his uncle was apt to grow restless and say it was high time he went to school. Mrs. Carey thought Philip very young for this, and her heart went out to the motherless child; but her attempts to gain his affection were awkward, and the boy, feeling shy, received her demonstrations with so much sullenness that she was mortified. Sometimes she heard his shrill voice raised in laughter in the kitchen, but when she went in, he grew suddenly silent, and he flushed darkly when Mary Ann explained the joke. Mrs. Carey could not see anything amusing in what she heard, and she smiled with constraint.

"He seems happier with Mary Ann than with us, William," she said, when she returned to her sewing.

"One can see he's been very badly brought up. He wants licking into shape."

On the second Sunday after Philip arrived an unlucky incident occurred. Mr. Carey had retired as usual after dinner for a little snooze in the drawing-room, but he was in an irritable mood and could not sleep. Josiah Graves that morning had objected strongly to some candlesticks with which the Vicar had adorned the altar. He had bought them second-hand in Tercanbury, and he thought they looked very well. But Josiah Graves said they were popish. This was a taunt that always aroused the Vicar. He had been at Oxford during the movement which ended in the secession from the Established Church of Edward Manning, and he felt a certain sympathy for the Church of Rome. He would willingly have made the service more ornate than had been usual in the low-church parish of Blackstable, and in his secret soul he yearned for processions and lighted candles. He drew the line at incense. He hated the word protestant. He called himself a Catholic. He was accustomed to say that Papists required an epithet, they were Roman Catholic; but the Church of England was Catholic in the best, the fullest, and the noblest sense of the term. He was pleased to think that his shaven face gave him the look of a priest, and in his youth he had possessed an ascetic air which added to the impression. He often related that on one of his holidays in Boulogne, one of those holidays upon which his wife for economy's sake did not accompany him, when he was sitting in a church, the *curé* had come up to him and invited him to preach a sermon. He dismissed his curates when they married, having decided views on the celibacy of the unbeneficed clergy. But when at an election the Liberals had written on his garden fence in large blue letters: This way to Rome, he had been very angry, and threatened to prosecute the leaders of the Liberal party in Blackstable. He made up his mind now that nothing Josiah Graves said would induce him to remove the candlesticks from the altar, and he muttered Bismarck to himself once or twice irritably.

Suddenly he heard an unexpected noise. He pulled the handkerchief off his face, got up from the sofa on which he was lying, and went into the dining-room. Philip was seated on the table with all his bricks around him. He had built a monstrous castle, and some defect in the foundation had just brought the structure down in noisy ruin.

"What are you doing with those bricks, Philip? You know you're not allowed to play games on Sunday."

Philip stared at him for a moment with frightened eyes, and, as his habit was, flushed deeply.

"I always used to play at home," he answered.

"I'm sure your dear mamma never allowed you to do such a wicked thing as that."

Philip did not know it was wicked; but if it was, he did not wish it to be supposed that his mother had consented to it. He hung his head and did not answer.

"Don't you know it's very, very wicked to play on Sunday? What d'you suppose it's called the day of rest for? You're going to church tonight, and how can you face your Maker when you've been breaking one of His laws in the afternoon?"

Mr. Carey told him to put the bricks away at once, and stood over him while Philip did so.

"You're a very naughty boy," he repeated. "Think of the grief you're causing your poor mother in heaven."

Philip felt inclined to cry, but he had an instinctive disinclination to letting other people see his tears, and he clenched his teeth to prevent the sobs from escaping. Mr. Carey sat down in his arm-chair and began to turn over the pages of a book. Philip stood at the window. The vicarage was set back from the high-road to Tercanbury, and from the dining-room one saw a semi-circular strip of lawn and then as far as the horizon green fields. Sheep were grazing in them. The sky was forlorn and grey. Philip felt infinitely unhappy.

Presently Mary Ann came in to lay the tea, and Aunt Louisa descended the stairs.

"Have you had a nice little nap, William?" she asked.

"No," he answered. "Philip made so much noise that I couldn't sleep a wink."

This was not quite accurate, for he had been kept awake by his own thoughts; and Philip, listening sullenly, reflected that he had only made a noise once, and there was no reason why his uncle should not have slept before or after. When Mrs. Carey asked for an explanation the Vicar narrated the facts.

"He hasn't even said he was sorry," he finished.

"Oh, Philip, I'm sure you're sorry," said Mrs. Carey, anxious that the child should not seem wickeder to his uncle than need be.

Philip did not reply. He went on munching his bread and butter. He did not know what power it was in him that prevented him from making any expression of regret. He felt his ears tingling, he was a little inclined to cry, but no word would issue from his lips.

"You needn't make it worse by sulking," said Mr. Carey.

Tea was finished in silence. Mrs. Carey looked at Philip surreptitiously now and then, but the Vicar elaborately ignored him. When Philip saw his uncle go upstairs to get ready for church he went into the hall and got his hat and coat, but when the Vicar came downstairs and saw him, he said:

"I don't wish you to go to church tonight, Philip. I don't think you're in a proper frame of mind to enter the House of God."

Philip did not say a word. He felt it was a deep humiliation that was placed upon him, and his cheeks reddened. He stood silently watching his uncle put on his broad hat and his voluminous cloak. Mrs. Carey as usual went to the door to see him off. Then she turned to Philip.

"Never mind, Philip, you won't be a naughty boy next Sunday, will you, and then your uncle will take you to church with him in the evening."

She took off his hat and coat, and led him into the dining-room.

"Shall you and I read the service together, Philip, and we'll sing the hymns at the harmonium. Would you like that?"

Philip shook his head decidedly. Mrs. Carey was taken aback. If he would not read the evening service with her she did not know what to do with him.

"Then what would you like to do until your uncle comes back?" she asked helplessly.

Philip broke his silence at last.

"I want to be left alone," he said.

"Philip, how can you say anything so unkind? Don't you know that your uncle and I only want your good? Don't you love me at all?"

"I hate you. I wish you was dead."

Mrs. Carey gasped. He said the words so savagely that it gave her quite a start. She had nothing to say. She sat down in her husband's chair; and as she thought of her desire to love the friendless, crippled boy and her eager wish that he should love her—she was a barren woman and, even though it was clearly God's will that she should be childless, she could scarcely bear to look at little children sometimes, her heart ached so—the tears rose to her eyes and one by one, slowly, rolled down her cheeks. Philip watched her in amazement. She took out her handkerchief, and now she cried without restraint. Suddenly Philip realised that she was crying because of what he had said, and he was sorry. He went up to her silently and kissed her. It was the first kiss he had ever given her without being asked. And the poor lady, so small in her black satin, shrivelled up and sallow, with her funny corkscrew curls, took the little boy on her lap and put her arms around him and wept as though her heart would break. But her tears were partly tears of happiness, for she felt that the strangeness between them was gone. She loved him now with a new love because he had made her suffer.

Chapter IX

ON THE FOLLOWING SUNDAY, WHEN THE VICAR WAS MAKING HIS PREPARAtions to go into the drawing-room for his nap—all the actions of his life were conducted with ceremony—and Mrs. Carey was about to go upstairs, Philip asked:

"What shall I do if I'm not allowed to play?"

"Can't you sit still for once and be quiet?"

"I can't sit still till tea-time."

Mr. Carey looked out of the window, but it was cold and raw, and he could not suggest that Philip should go into the garden.

"I know what you can do. You can learn by heart the collect for the day."

He took the prayer-book which was used for prayers from the harmonium, and turned the pages till he came to the place he wanted.

"It's not a long one. If you can say it without a mistake when I come in to tea you shall have the top of my egg."

Mrs. Carey drew up Philip's chair to the dining-room table—they had bought him a high chair by now—and placed the book in front of him.

"The devil finds work for idle hands to do," said Mr. Carey.

He put some more coals on the fire so that there should be a cheerful blaze when he came in to tea, and went into the drawing-room. He loosened his collar, arranged the cushions, and settled himself comfortably on the sofa. But thinking the drawing-room a little chilly, Mrs. Carey brought him a rug from the hall; she put it over his legs and tucked it round his feet. She drew the blinds so that the light should not offend his eyes, and since he had closed them already went out of the room on tiptoe. The Vicar was at peace with himself today, and in ten minutes he was asleep. He snored softly.

It was the Sixth Sunday after Epiphany, and the collect began with the words: *O God, whose blessed Son was manifested that he might destroy the works of the devil, and make us the sons of God, and heirs of Eternal life.* Philip read it through. He could make no sense of it. He began saying the words aloud to himself, but many of them were unknown to him, and the construction of the sentence was strange. He could not get more than two lines in his head. And his attention was constantly wandering: there were fruit-trees trained on the walls of the vicarage, and a long twig beat now and then against the window-pane; sheep grazed stolidly in the field beyond the garden. It seemed as though there were knots inside his brain. Then panic seized him that he would not know the words by tea-time, and he kept on whispering them to himself quickly; he did not try to understand, but merely to get them parrot-like into his memory.

Mrs. Carey could not sleep that afternoon, and by four o'clock she was so wide awake that she came downstairs. She thought she would hear Philip his collect so that he should make no mistakes when he said it to his uncle. His uncle then would be pleased; he would see that the boy's heart was in the right place. But when Mrs. Carey came to the dining-room and was about to go in, she heard a sound that made her stop suddenly. Her heart gave a little jump. She turned away and quietly slipped out of the front-door. She walked round the house till she came to the dining-room window and then cautiously looked in. Philip was still sitting on the chair she had put him in, but his head was on the table buried in his arms, and he was sobbing desperately. She saw the convulsive movement of his shoulders. Mrs. Carey was frightened. A thing that had always struck her about the child was that he seemed so collected. She had never seen him cry. And now she realised that his calmness was some instinctive shame of showing his feelings: he hid himself to weep.

Without thinking that her husband disliked being wakened suddenly, she burst into the drawing-room.

"William, William," she said. "The boy's crying as though his heart would break."

Mr. Carey sat up and disentangled himself from the rug about his legs.

"What's he got to cry about?"

"I don't know.... Oh, William, we can't let the boy be unhappy. D'you think it's our fault? If we'd had children we'd have known what to do."

Mr. Carey looked at her in perplexity. He felt extraordinarily helpless.

"He can't be crying because I gave him the collect to learn. It's not more than ten lines."

"Don't you think I might take him some picture books to look at, William? There are some of the Holy Land. There couldn't be anything wrong in that."

"Very well, I don't mind."

Mrs. Carey went into the study. To collect books was Mr. Carey's only passion, and he never went into Tercanbury without spending an hour or two in the second-hand shop; he always brought back four or five musty volumes. He never read them, for he had long lost the habit of reading, but he liked to turn the pages, look at the illustrations if they were illustrated, and mend the bindings. He welcomed wet days because on them he could stay at home without pangs of conscience and spend the afternoon with white of egg and a glue-pot, patching up the Russia leather of some battered quarto. He had many volumes of old travels, with steel engravings, and Mrs. Carey quickly found two which described Palestine. She coughed elaborately at the door so that Philip should have time to compose himself, she felt that he would be humiliated if she came upon him in the midst of his tears, then she rattled the door handle. When she went in Philip was poring over the prayer-book, hiding his eyes with his hands so that she might not see he had been crying.

"Do you know the collect yet?" she said.

He did not answer for a moment, and she felt that he did not trust his voice. She was oddly embarrassed.

"I can't learn it by heart," he said at last, with a gasp.

"Oh, well, never mind," she said. "You needn't. I've got some picture books for you to look at. Come and sit on my lap, and we'll look at them together."

Philip slipped off his chair and limped over to her. He looked down so that she should not see his eyes. She put her arms round him.

"Look," she said, "that's the place where our Blessed Lord was born."

She showed him an Eastern town with flat roofs and cupolas and minarets. In the foreground was a group of palm-trees, and under them were resting two Arabs and some camels. Philip passed his hand over the picture as if he wanted to feel the houses and the loose habiliments of the nomads.

"Read what it says," he asked.

Mrs. Carey in her even voice read the opposite page. It was a romantic narrative of some Eastern traveller of the thirties, pompous maybe, but fragrant with the emotion with which the East came to the generation that followed Byron and Chateaubriand. In a moment or two Philip interrupted her.

"I want to see another picture."

When Mary Ann came in and Mrs. Carey rose to help her lay the cloth. Philip took the book in his hands and hurried through the illustrations. It was with difficulty that his aunt induced him to put the book down for tea. He had forgotten his horrible struggle to get the collect by heart; he had forgotten his tears. Next day it was raining, and he asked for the book again. Mrs. Carey gave it him joyfully. Talking over his future with her husband she had found that both desired him to take orders, and this eagerness for the book which described places hallowed by the presence of Jesus seemed a good sign. It looked as though the boy's mind addressed itself naturally to holy things. But in a day or two he asked for more books. Mr. Carey took him into his study, showed him the shelf in which he kept illustrated works, and chose for him one that dealt with Rome. Philip took it greedily. The pictures led him to a new amusement. He began to read the page before and the page after each engraving to find out what it was about, and soon he lost all interest in his toys.

Then, when no one was near, he took out books for himself; and perhaps because the first impression on his mind was made by an Eastern town, he found his chief amusement in those which described the Levant. His heart beat with excitement at the pictures of mosques and rich palaces; but there was one, in a book on Constantinople, which peculiarly stirred his imagination. It was called the Hall of the Thousand Columns. It was a Byzantine cistern, which the popular fancy had endowed with fantastic vastness; and the legend which he read told that a boat was always moored at the entrance to tempt the unwary, but no traveller venturing into the darkness had ever been seen again. And Philip wondered whether the boat went on forever through one pillared alley after another or came at last to some strange mansion.

One day a good fortune befell him, for he hit upon Lane's translation of *The Thousand Nights and a Night.* He was captured first by the illustrations, and then he began to read, to start with, the stories that dealt with magic, and then the others; and those he liked he read again and again. He could think of nothing else. He forgot the life about him. He had to be called two or three times before he would come to his dinner. Insensibly he formed the most delightful habit in the world, the habit of reading: he did not know that thus he was providing himself with a refuge from all the distress of life; he did not know either that he was creating for himself an unreal world which would make the real world of every day a source of bitter disappointment. Presently he began to read other things. His brain was precocious. His uncle and aunt, seeing that he occupied himself and neither worried nor made a noise, ceased to trouble themselves about him. Mr. Carey had so many books that he did not know them, and as he read little he forgot the odd lots he had bought at one time and another because they were cheap. Haphazard among the sermons and homilies, the travels, the lives of the Saints, the Fathers, the histories of the church, were old-fashioned novels; and these Philip at last discovered. He chose them by their titles, and the first he read was *The Lancashire Witches,* and then he read *The Admirable Crichton,* and then many more. Whenever he started a book with two solitary travellers riding along the brink of a desperate ravine he knew he was safe.

The summer was come now, and the gardener, an old sailor, made him a hammock and fixed it up for him in the branches of a weeping willow. And here for long hours he lay, hidden from anyone who might come to the vicarage, reading, reading passionately. Time passed and it was July; August came: on Sundays the church was crowded with strangers, and the collection at the offertory often amounted to two pounds. Neither the Vicar nor Mrs. Carey went out of the garden much during this period; for they disliked strange faces, and they looked upon the visitors from London with aversion. The house opposite was taken for six weeks by a gentleman who had two little boys, and he sent in to ask if Philip would like to go and play with them; but Mrs. Carey returned a polite refusal. She was afraid that Philip would be corrupted by little boys from London. He was going to be a clergyman, and it was necessary that he should be preserved from contamination. She liked to see in him an infant Samuel.

Chapter X

THE CAREYS MADE UP THEIR MINDS TO SEND PHILIP TO KING'S SCHOOL AT Tercanbury. The neighbouring clergy sent their sons there. It was united by long tradition to the Cathedral: its headmaster was an honorary Canon, and a past headmaster was the Archdeacon. Boys were encouraged there to aspire to Holy Orders, and the education was such as might prepare an honest lad to spend his life in God's service. A preparatory school was attached to it, and to this it was arranged that Philip should go. Mr. Carey took him into Tercanbury one Thursday afternoon towards the end of September. All day Philip had been excited and rather frightened. He knew little of school life but what he had read in the stories of *The Boy's Own Paper*. He had also read *Eric, or Little by Little*.

When they got out of the train at Tercanbury, Philip felt sick with apprehension, and during the drive in to the town sat pale and silent. The high brick wall in front of the school gave it the look of a prison. There was a little door in it, which opened on their ringing; and a clumsy, untidy man came out and fetched Philip's tin trunk and his play-box. They were shown into the drawing-room; it was filled with massive, ugly furniture, and the chairs of the suite were placed round the walls with a forbidding rigidity. They waited for the headmaster.

"What's Mr. Watson like?" asked Philip, after a while.

"You'll see for yourself."

There was another pause. Mr. Carey wondered why the headmaster did not come. Presently Philip made an effort and spoke again.

"Tell him I've got a club-foot," he said.

Before Mr. Carey could speak the door burst open and Mr. Watson swept into the room. To Philip he seemed gigantic. He was a man of over six feet high, and broad, with enormous hands and a great red beard; he talked loudly in a jovial manner; but his aggressive cheerfulness struck terror in Philip's heart. He shook hands with Mr. Carey, and then took Philip's small hand in his.

"Well, young fellow, are you glad to come to school?" he shouted.

Philip reddened and found no word to answer.

"How old are you?"

"Nine," said Philip.

"You must say sir," said his uncle.

"I expect you've got a good lot to learn," the headmaster bellowed cheerily.

To give the boy confidence he began to tickle him with rough fingers. Philip, feeling shy and uncomfortable, squirmed under his touch.

"I've put him in the small dormitory for the present. . . . You'll like that, won't you?" he added to Philip. "Only eight of you in there. You won't feel so strange."

Then the door opened, and Mrs. Watson came in. She was a dark woman with black hair, neatly parted in the middle. She had curiously thick lips and a small round nose. Her eyes were large and black. There was a singular coldness in her appearance. She seldom spoke and smiled more seldom still. Her husband introduced Mr. Carey to her, and then gave Philip a friendly push towards her.

"This is a new boy, Helen, His name's Carey."

Without a word she shook hands with Philip and then sat down, not speaking, while the headmaster asked Mr. Carey how much Philip knew and what books he had been working with. The Vicar of Blackstable was a little embarrassed by Mr. Watson's boisterous heartiness, and in a moment or two got up.

"I think I'd better leave Philip with you now."

"That's all right," said Mr. Watson. "He'll be safe with me. He'll get on like a house on fire. Won't you, young fellow?"

Without waiting for an answer from Philip the big man burst into a great bellow of laughter. Mr. Carey kissed Philip on the forehead and went away.

"Come along, young fellow," shouted Mr. Watson. "I'll show you the schoolroom."

He swept out of the drawing-room with giant strides, and Philip hurriedly limped behind him. He was taken into a long, bare room with two tables that ran along its whole length; on each side of them were wooden forms.

"Nobody much here yet," said Mr. Watson. "I'll just show you the playground, and then I'll leave you to shift for yourself."

Mr. Watson led the way. Philip found himself in a large play-ground with high brick walls on three sides of it. On the fourth side was an iron railing through which you saw a vast lawn and beyond this some of the buildings of King's School. One small boy was wandering disconsolately, kicking up the gravel as he walked.

"Hulloa, Venning," shouted Mr. Watson. "When did you turn up?"

The small boy came forward and shook hands.

"Here's a new boy. He's older and bigger than you, so don't you bully him."

The headmaster glared amicably at the two children, filling them with fear by the roar of his voice, and then with a guffaw left them.

"What's your name?"

"Carey."

"What's your father?"

"He's dead."

"Oh! Does your mother wash?"

"My mother's dead, too."

Philip thought this answer would cause the boy a certain awkwardness, but Venning was not to be turned from his facetiousness for so little.

"Well, did she wash?" he went on.

"Yes," said Philip indignantly.

"She was a washerwoman then?"

"No, she wasn't."

"Then she didn't wash."

The little boy crowed with delight at the success of his dialectic. Then he caught sight of Philip's feet.

"What's the matter with your foot?"

Philip instinctively tried to withdraw it from sight. He hid it behind the one which was whole.

"I've got a club-foot," he answered.

"How did you get it?"

"I've always had it."

"Let's have a look."

"No."

"Don't then."

The little boy accompanied the words with a sharp kick on Philip's shin, which Philip did not expect and thus could not guard against. The pain was so great that it made him gasp, but greater than the pain was the surprise. He did not know why Venning kicked him. He had not the presence of mind to give him a black eye. Besides, the boy was smaller than he, and he had read in *The Boy's Own Paper* that it was a mean thing to hit anyone smaller than yourself. While Philip was nursing his shin a third boy appeared, and his tormentor left him. In a little while he noticed that the pair were talking about him, and he felt they were looking at his feet. He grew hot and uncomfortable.

But others arrived, a dozen together, and then more, and they began to talk about their doings during the holidays, where they had been, and what wonderful cricket they had played. A few new boys appeared, and with these presently Philip found himself talking. He was shy and nervous. He was anxious to make himself pleasant, but he could not think of anything to say. He was asked a great many questions and answered them all quite willingly. One boy asked him whether he could play cricket.

"No," answered Philip. "I've got a club-foot."

The boy looked down quickly and reddened. Philip saw that he felt he had asked an unseemly question. He was too shy to apologise and looked at Philip awkwardly.

Chapter XI

NEXT MORNING WHEN THE CLANGING OF A BELL AWOKE PHILIP HE LOOKED round his cubicle in astonishment. Then a voice sang out, and he remembered where he was.

"Are you awake, Singer?"

The partitions of the cubicle were of polished pitch-pine, and there was a green curtain in front. In those days there was little thought of ventilation, and the windows were closed except when the dormitory was aired in the morning.

Philip got up and knelt down to say his prayers. It was a cold morning, and he shivered a little; but he had been taught by his uncle that his prayers were more acceptable to God if he said them in his nightshirt than if he waited till he was dressed. This did not surprise him, for he was beginning to realise that he was the creature of a God who appreciated the discomfort of his worshippers. Then he washed. There were two baths for the fifty boarders, and each boy had a bath once a week. The rest of his washing was done in a small basin on a wash-stand, which with the bed and a chair, made up the furniture of each cubicle. The boys chatted gaily while they dressed. Philip was all ears. Then another bell sounded, and they ran downstairs. They took their seats on the forms on each side of the two long tables in the school-room; and Mr. Watson, followed by his wife and the servants, came in and sat down. Mr. Watson read prayers in an impressive manner, and the supplications thundered out in his loud voice as though they were threats personally addressed to each boy. Philip listened with anxiety. Then Mr. Watson read a chapter from the Bible, and the servants trooped out. In a moment the untidy youth brought in two large pots of tea and on a second journey immense dishes of bread and butter.

Philip had a squeamish appetite, and the thick slabs of poor butter on the bread turned his stomach, but he saw other boys scraping it off and followed their example. They all had potted meats and such like, which they had brought in their play-boxes; and some had "extras," eggs or bacon, upon which Mr. Watson made a profit. When he had asked Mr. Carey whether Philip was to have these, Mr. Carey replied that he did not think boys should be spoiled. Mr. Watson quite agreed with him—he considered nothing was better than bread and butter for growing lads—but some parents, unduly pampering their offspring, insisted on it.

Philip noticed that "extras" gave boys a certain consideration and made up his mind, when he wrote to Aunt Louisa, to ask for them.

After breakfast the boys wandered out into the play-ground. Here the day-boys were gradually assembling. They were sons of the local clergy, of the officers at the Depot, and of such manufacturers or men of business as the old town possessed. Presently a bell rang, and they all trooped into school. This consisted of a large, long room at opposite ends of which two undermasters conducted the second and third forms, and of a smaller one, leading out of it, used by Mr. Watson, who taught the first form. To attach the preparatory to the senior school these three classes were known officially, on speech days and in reports, as upper, middle, and lower second. Philip was put in the last. The master, a red-faced man with a pleasant voice, was called Rice; he had a jolly manner with boys, and the time passed quickly. Philip was surprised when it was a quarter to eleven and they were let out for ten minutes' rest.

The whole school rushed noisily into the play-ground. The new boys were told to go into the middle, while the others stationed themselves along opposite walls. They began to play *Pig in the Middle*. The old boys ran from wall to wall while the new boys tried to catch them: when one was seized and the mystic words said—one, two, three, and a pig for me—he became a prisoner and, turning sides, helped to catch those who were still free. Philip saw a boy running past and tried to catch him, but his limp gave him no chance; and the runners, taking their opportunity, made straight for the ground he covered. Then one of them had the brilliant idea of imitating Philip's clumsy run. Other boys saw it and began to laugh; then they all copied the first; and they ran round Philip, limping grotesquely, screaming in their treble voices with shrill laughter. They lost their heads with the delight of their new amusement, and choked with helpless merriment. One of them tripped Philip up and he fell, heavily as he always fell, and cut his knee. They laughed all the louder when he got up. A boy pushed him from behind, and he would have fallen again if another had not caught him. The game was forgotten in the entertainment of Philip's deformity. One of them invented an odd, rolling limp that struck the rest as supremely ridiculous, and several of the boys lay down on the ground and rolled about in laughter: Philip was completely scared. He could not make out why they were laughing at him. His heart beat so that he could hardly breathe, and he was more frightened than he had ever been in his life. He stood still stupidly while the boys ran round him, mimicking and laughing; they shouted to him to try and catch them; but he did not move. He did not want them to see him run anymore. He was using all his strength to prevent himself from crying.

Suddenly the bell rang, and they all trooped back to school. Philip's knee was bleeding, and he was dusty and dishevelled. For some minutes Mr. Rice could not control his form. They were excited still by the strange novelty, and

Philip saw one or two of them furtively looking down at his feet. He tucked them under the bench.

In the afternoon they went up to play football, but Mr. Watson stopped Philip on the way out after dinner.

"I suppose you can't play football, Carey?" he asked him.

Philip blushed self-consciously.

"No, sir."

"Very well. You'd better go up to the field. You can walk as far as that, can't you?"

Philip had no idea where the field was, but he answered all the same.

"Yes, sir."

The boys went in charge of Mr. Rice, who glanced at Philip and, seeing he had not changed, asked why he was not going to play.

"Mr. Watson said I needn't, sir," said Philip.

"Why?"

There were boys all round him, looking at him curiously, and a feeling of shame came over Philip. He looked down without answering. Others gave the reply.

"He's got a club-foot, sir."

"Oh, I see."

Mr. Rice was quite young; he had only taken his degree a year before; and he was suddenly embarrassed. His instinct was to beg the boy's pardon, but he was too shy to do so. He made his voice gruff and loud.

"Now then, you boys, what are you waiting about for? Get on with you."

Some of them had already started and those that were left now set off, in groups of two or three.

"You'd better come along with me, Carey," said the master. "You don't know the way, do you?"

Philip guessed the kindness, and a sob came to his throat.

"I can't go very fast, sir."

"Then I'll go very slow," said the master, with a smile.

Philip's heart went out to the red-faced, commonplace young man who said a gentle word to him. He suddenly felt less unhappy.

But at night when they went up to bed and were undressing, the boy who was called Singer came out of his cubicle and put his head in Philip's.

"I say, let's look at your foot," he said.

"No," answered Philip.

He jumped into bed quickly.

"Don't say no to me," said Singer. "Come on, Mason."

The boy in the next cubicle was looking round the corner, and at the words he slipped in. They made for Philip and tried to tear the bed-clothes off him, but he held them tightly.

"Why can't you leave me alone?" he cried.

Singer seized a brush and with the back of it beat Philip's hands clenched on the blanket. Philip cried out.

"Why don't you show us your foot quietly?"

"I won't."

In desperation Philip clenched his fist and hit the boy who tormented him, but he was at a disadvantage, and the boy seized his arm. He began to turn it.

"Oh, don't, don't," said Philip. "You'll break my arm."

"Stop still then and put out your foot."

Philip gave a sob and a gasp. The boy gave the arm another wrench. The pain was unendurable.

"All right. I'll do it," said Philip.

He put out his foot. Singer still kept his hand on Philip's wrist. He looked curiously at the deformity.

"Isn't it beastly?" said Mason.

Another came in and looked too.

"Ugh," he said, in disgust.

"My word, it is rum," said Singer, making a face. "Is it hard?"

He touched it with the tip of his forefinger, cautiously, as though it were something that had a life of its own. Suddenly they heard Mr. Watson's heavy tread on the stairs. They threw the clothes back on Philip and dashed like rabbits into their cubicles. Mr. Watson came into the dormitory. Raising himself on tiptoe he could see over the rod that bore the green curtain, and he looked into two or three of the cubicles. The little boys were safely in bed. He put out the light and went out.

Singer called out to Philip, but he did not answer. He had got his teeth in the pillow so that his sobbing should be inaudible. He was not crying for the pain they had caused him, nor for the humiliation he had suffered when they looked at his foot, but with rage at himself because, unable to stand the torture, he had put out his foot of his own accord.

And then he felt the misery of his life. It seemed to his childish mind that this unhappiness must go on forever. For no particular reason he remembered that cold morning when Emma had taken him out of bed and put him beside his mother. He had not thought of it once since it happened, but now he seemed to feel the warmth of his mother's body against his and her arms around him. Suddenly it seemed to him that his life was a dream, his mother's death, and the life at the vicarage, and these two wretched days at school, and he would awake in the morning and be back again at home. His tears dried as he thought of it. He was too unhappy, it must be nothing but a dream, and his mother was alive, and Emma would come up. presently and go to bed. He fell asleep.

But when he awoke next morning it was to the clanging of a bell, and the first thing his eyes saw was the green curtain of his cubicle.

Chapter XII

AS TIME WENT ON PHILIP'S DEFORMITY CEASED TO INTEREST. IT WAS ACcepted like one boy's red hair and another's unreasonable corpulence. But meanwhile he had grown horribly sensitive. He never ran if he could help it, because he knew it made his limp more conspicuous, and he adopted a peculiar walk. He stood still as much as he could, with his club-foot behind the other, so that it should not attract notice, and he was constantly on the look out for any reference to it. Because he could not join in the games which other boys played, their life remained strange to him; he only interested himself from the outside in their doings; and it seemed to him that there was a barrier between them and him. Sometimes they seemed to think that it was his fault if he could not play football, and he was unable to make them understand. He was left a good deal to himself. He had been inclined to talkativeness, but gradually he became silent. He began to think of the difference between himself and others.

The biggest boy in his dormitory, Singer, took a dislike to him, and Philip, small for his age, had to put up with a good deal of hard treatment. About half-way through the term a mania ran through the school for a game called Nibs. It was a game for two, played on a table or a form with steel pens. You had to push your nib with the finger-nail so as to get the point of it over your opponent's, while he manoeuvred to prevent this and to get the point of his nib over the back of yours; when this result was achieved you breathed on the ball of your thumb, pressed it hard on the two nibs, and if you were able then to lift them without dropping either, both nibs became yours. Soon nothing was seen but boys playing this game, and the more skilful acquired vast stores of nibs. But in a little while Mr. Watson made up his mind that it was a form of gambling, forbade the game, and confiscated all the nibs in the boys' possession. Philip had been very adroit, and it was with a heavy heart that he gave up his winnings; but his fingers itched to play still, and a few days later, on his way to the football field, he went into a shop and bought a pennyworth of J pens. He carried them loose in his pocket and enjoyed feeling them. Presently Singer found out that he had them. Singer had given up his nibs too, but he had kept back a very large one, called a Jumbo, which was almost unconquerable, and he could not resist the opportunity of getting Philip's Js out of him. Though Philip knew that he was at a disadvantage with his small nibs, he had an adventurous disposition and was willing to take the risk; besides, he was aware that Singer would not allow him to refuse. He had not played for a week and sat down to the game now with a thrill of excitement. He lost two of his small nibs quickly, and Singer was jubilant, but the third time by some chance the Jumbo slipped round and Philip was able to push his J across it. He crowed with triumph. At that moment Mr. Watson came in.

"What are you doing?" he asked.

He looked from Singer to Philip, but neither answered.

"Don't you know that I've forbidden you to play that idiotic game?"

Philip's heart beat fast. He knew what was coming and was dreadfully frightened, but in his fright there was a certain exultation. He had never been swished. Of course it would hurt, but it was something to boast about afterwards.

"Come into my study."

The headmaster turned, and they followed him side by side. Singer whispered to Philip:

"We're in for it."

Mr. Watson pointed to Singer.

"Bend over," he said.

Philip, very white, saw the boy quiver at each stroke, and after the third he heard him cry out. Three more followed.

"That'll do. Get up."

Singer stood up. The tears were streaming down his face. Philip stepped forward. Mr. Watson looked at him for a moment.

"I'm not going to cane you. You're a new boy. And I can't hit a cripple. Go away, both of you, and don't be naughty again."

When they got back into the school-room a group of boys, who had learned in some mysterious way what was happening, were waiting for them. They set upon Singer at once with eager questions. Singer faced them, his face red with the pain and marks of tears still on his cheeks. He pointed with his head at Philip, who was standing a little behind him.

"He got off because he's a cripple," he said angrily.

Philip stood silent and flushed. He felt that they looked at him with contempt.

"How many did you get?" one boy asked Singer.

But he did not answer. He was angry because he had been hurt.

"Don't ask me to play Nibs with you again," he said to Philip. "It's jolly nice for you. You don't risk anything."

"I didn't ask you."

"Didn't you!"

He quickly put out his foot and tripped Philip up. Philip was always rather unsteady on his feet, and he fell heavily to the ground.

"Cripple," said Singer.

For the rest of the term he tormented Philip cruelly, and, though Philip tried to keep out of his way, the school was so small that it was impossible; he tried being friendly and jolly with him; he abased himself so far as to buy him a knife; but though Singer took the knife he was not placated. Once or twice, driven beyond endurance, he hit and kicked the bigger boy, but Singer was so much stronger that Philip was helpless, and he was always forced after more or less torture to beg his pardon. It was that which rankled with Philip: he could not bear the humiliation of apologies, which were wrung from him by pain greater than he could bear. And what made it worse was that there seemed no end to his wretchedness; Singer was only eleven and would not go to the upper school till he was thirteen. Philip realised that he must live two years with a tormentor from whom there was no escape. He was only happy while he was working and when he got into bed. And often there recurred to him then that queer feeling that his life with all its misery was nothing but a dream, and that he would awake in the morning in his own little bed in London.

Chapter XIII

TWO YEARS PASSED, AND PHILIP WAS NEARLY TWELVE. HE WAS IN THE FIRST form, within two or three places of the top, and after Christmas when several boys would be leaving for the senior school he would be head boy. He had already quite a collection of prizes, worthless books on bad paper, but in gorgeous bindings decorated with the arms of the school: his position had freed him from bullying, and he was not unhappy. His fellows forgave him his success because of his deformity.

"After all, it's jolly easy for him to get prizes," they said, "there's nothing he *can* do but swat."

He had lost his early terror of Mr. Watson. He had grown used to the loud voice, and when the headmaster's heavy hand was laid on his shoulder Philip discerned vaguely the intention of a caress. He had the good memory which is more useful for scholastic achievements than mental power, and he knew Mr. Watson expected him to leave the preparatory school with a scholarship.

But he had grown very self-conscious. The new-born child does not realise that his body is more a part of himself than surrounding objects, and will play with his toes without any feeling that they belong to him more than the rattle by his side; and it is only by degrees, through pain, that he understands the fact of the body. And experiences of the same kind are necessary for the individual to become conscious of himself; but here there is the difference that, although everyone becomes equally conscious of his body as a separate and complete organism, everyone does not become equally conscious of himself as a complete and separate personality. The feeling of apartness from others comes to most with puberty, but it is not always developed to such a degree as to make the difference between the individual and his fellows noticeable to the individual. It is such as he, as little conscious of himself as the bee in a hive, who are the lucky in life, for they have the best chance of happiness: their activities are shared by all, and their pleasures are only pleasures because they are enjoyed in common; you will see them on Whit-Monday dancing on Hampstead Heath, shouting at a football match, or from club windows in Pall Mall cheering a royal procession. It is because of them that man has been called a social animal.

Philip passed from the innocence of childhood to bitter consciousness of himself by the ridicule which his club-foot had excited. The circumstances of his case were so peculiar that he could not apply to them the ready-made rules which acted well enough in ordinary affairs, and he was forced to think for himself. The many books he had read filled his mind with ideas which, because he only half understood them, gave more scope to his imagination. Beneath his painful shyness something was growing up within him, and obscurely he realised his personality. But at times it gave him odd surprises; he did things, he knew not why, and afterwards when he thought of them found himself all at sea.

There was a boy called Luard between whom and Philip a friendship had arisen, and one day, when they were playing together in the school-room, Luard began to perform some trick with an ebony pen-holder of Philip's.

"Don't play the giddy ox," said Philip. "You'll only break it."

"I shan't."

But no sooner were the words out of the boy's mouth than the pen-holder snapped in two. Luard looked at Philip with dismay.

"Oh, I say, I'm awfully sorry."

The tears rolled down Philip's cheeks, but he did not answer.

"I say, what's the matter?" said Luard, with surprise. "I'll get you another one exactly the same."

"It's not about the pen-holder I care," said Philip, in a trembling voice, "only it was given me by my mater, just before she died."

"I say, I'm awfully sorry, Carey."

"It doesn't matter. It wasn't your fault."

Philip took the two pieces of the pen-holder and looked at them. He tried to restrain his sobs. He felt utterly miserable. And yet he could not tell why, for he knew quite well that he had bought the pen-holder during his last holidays at Blackstable for one and twopence. He did not know in the least what had made him invent that pathetic story, but he was quite as unhappy as though it had been true. The pious atmosphere of the vicarage and the religious tone of the school had made Philip's conscience very sensitive; he absorbed insensibly the feeling about him that the Tempter was ever on the watch to gain his immortal soul; and though he was not more truthful than most boys he never told a lie without suffering from remorse. When he thought over this incident he was very much distressed, and made up his mind that he must go to Luard and tell him that the story was an invention. Though he dreaded humiliation more than anything in the world, he hugged himself for two or three days at the thought of the agonising joy of humiliating himself to the Glory of God. But he never got any further. He satisfied his conscience by the more comfortable method of expressing his repentance only to the Almighty. But he could not understand why he should have been so genuinely affected by the story he was making up. The tears that flowed down his grubby cheeks were real tears. Then by some accident of association there occurred to him that scene when Emma had told him of his mother's death, and, though he could not speak for crying, he had insisted on going in to say good-bye to the Misses Watkin so that they might see his grief and pity him.

Chapter XIV

THEN A WAVE OF RELIGIOSITY PASSED THROUGH THE SCHOOL. BAD LANGUAGE was no longer heard, and the little nastinesses of small boys were looked upon with hostility; the bigger boys, like the lords temporal of the Middle Ages, used the strength of their arms to persuade those weaker than themselves to virtuous courses.

Philip, his restless mind avid for new things, became very devout. He heard soon that it was possible to join a Bible League, and wrote to London for particulars. These consisted in a form to be filled up with the applicant's name, age, and school; a solemn declaration to be signed that he would read a set portion of Holy Scripture every night for a year; and a request for half a crown; this, it was explained, was demanded partly to prove the earnestness of the applicant's desire to become a member of the League, and partly to cover clerical expenses. Philip duly sent the papers and the money, and in return received a calendar worth about a penny, on which was set down the appointed passage to be read each day, and a sheet of paper on one side of which was a picture of the Good Shepherd and a lamb, and on the other, decoratively framed in red lines, a short prayer which had to be said before beginning to read.

Every evening he undressed as quickly as possible in order to have time for his task before the gas was put out. He read industriously, as he read always, without criticism, stories of cruelty, deceit, ingratitude, dishonesty, and low cunning. Actions which would have excited his horror in the life about him, in the reading passed through his mind without comment, because they were committed under the direct inspiration of God. The method of the League was to alternate a book of the Old Testament with a book of the New, and one night Philip came across these words of Jesus Christ:

If ye have faith, and doubt not, ye shall not only do this which is done to the fig-tree, but also if ye shall say unto this mountain. Be thou removed, and be thou cast into the sea; it shall be done.

And all this, whatsoever ye shall ask in prayer, believing, ye shall receive.

They made no particular impression on him, but it happened that two or three days later, being Sunday, the Canon in residence chose them for the text of his sermon. Even if Philip had wanted to hear this it would have been impossible, for the boys of King's School sit in the choir, and the pulpit stands at the corner of the transept so that the preacher's back is almost turned to them. The distance also is so great that it needs a man with a fine voice and a knowledge of elocution to make himself heard in the choir; and according to long usage the Canons of Tercanbury are chosen for their learning rather than for any qualities which might be of use in a cathedral church. But the words of the text, perhaps because he had read them so short a while before, came clearly enough to Philip's ears, and they seemed on a sudden to have a personal application. He thought about them through most of the sermon, and that night, on getting into bed, he turned over the pages of the Gospel and found once more the passage. Though he believed implicitly everything he saw in print, he had learned already that in the Bible things that said one thing quite clearly often mysteriously meant another. There was no one he liked to ask at school, so he kept the question he had in mind till the Christmas holidays, and then one day he made an opportunity. It was after supper and prayers were just finished. Mrs. Carey was counting the eggs that Mary Ann had brought in as usual and writing on each one the date. Philip stood at the table and pretended to turn listlessly the pages of the Bible.

"I say, Uncle William, this passage here, does it really mean that?"

He put his finger against it as though he had come across it accidentally.

Mr. Carey looked up over his spectacles. He was holding *The Blackstable Times* in front of the fire. It had come in that evening damp from the press, and the Vicar always aired it for ten minutes before he began to read.

"What passage is that?" he asked.

"Why, this about if you have faith you can remove mountains."

"If it says so in the Bible it is so, Philip," said Mrs. Carey gently, taking up the plate-basket.

Philip looked at his uncle for an answer.

"It's a matter of faith."

"D'you mean to say that if you really believed you could move mountains you could?"

"By the grace of God," said the Vicar.

"Now, say good-night to your uncle, Philip," said Aunt Louisa. "You're not wanting to move a mountain tonight, are you?"

Philip allowed himself to be kissed on the forehead by his uncle and preceded Mrs. Carey upstairs. He had got the information he wanted. His little room was icy, and he shivered when he put on his nightgown. But he always felt that his prayers were more pleasing to God when he said them under conditions of discomfort. The coldness of his hands and feet were an offering to the Almighty. And tonight he sank on his knees, buried his face in his hands, and prayed to God with all his might that He would make his club-foot whole. It was a very small thing beside the moving of mountains. He knew that God could do it if He wished, and his own faith was complete. Next morning, finishing his prayers with the same request, he fixed a date for the miracle.

"Oh, God, in Thy loving mercy and goodness, if it be Thy will, please make my foot all right on the night before I go back to school."

He was glad to get his petition into a formula, and he repeated it later in the dining-room during the short pause which the Vicar always made after prayers, before he rose from his knees. He said it again in the evening and again, shivering in his nightshirt, before he got into bed. And he believed. For once he looked forward with eagerness to the end of the holidays. He laughed to himself as he thought of his uncle's astonishment when he ran down the stairs three at a time; and after breakfast he and Aunt Louisa would have to hurry out and buy a new pair of boots. At school they would be astounded.

"Hulloa, Carey, what have you done with your foot?"

"Oh, it's all right now," he would answer casually, as though it were the most natural thing in the world.

He would be able to play football. His heart leaped as he saw himself running, running, faster than any of the other boys. At the end of the Easter term there were the sports, and he would be able to go in for the races; he rather fancied himself over the hurdles. It would be splendid to be like everyone else, not to be stared at curiously by new boys who did not know about his deformity, nor at the baths in summer to need incredible precautions, while he was undressing, before he could hide his foot in the water.

He prayed with all the power of his soul. No doubts assailed him. He was confident in the word of God. And the night before he was to go back to school he went up to bed tremulous with excitement. There was snow on the ground, and Aunt Louisa had allowed herself the unaccustomed luxury of a fire in her bedroom; but in Philip's little room it was so cold that his fingers were numb, and he had great difficulty in undoing his collar. His teeth chattered. The idea came to him that he must do something more than usual to attract the attention of God, and he turned back the rug which was in front of his bed so that he could kneel on the bare boards; and then it struck him that his nightshirt was a softness that might displease his Maker, so he took it off and said his prayers naked. When he got into bed he was so cold that for some time he could not sleep, but when he did, it was so soundly that Mary Ann had to shake him when she brought in his hot water next morning. She talked to him while she drew the curtains, but he did not answer; he had remembered at once that this was the morning for the miracle. His heart was filled with joy and gratitude. His first instinct was to put down his hand and feel the foot which was whole now, but to do this seemed to doubt the goodness of God. He knew that his foot was well. But at last he made up his mind, and with the toes of his right foot he just touched his left. Then he passed his hand over it.

He limped downstairs just as Mary Ann was going into the dining-room for prayers, and then he sat down to breakfast.

"You're very quiet this morning, Philip," said Aunt Louisa presently.

"He's thinking of the good breakfast he'll have at school tomorrow," said the Vicar.

When Philip answered, it was in a way that always irritated his uncle, with something that had nothing to do with the matter in hand. He called it a bad habit of wool-gathering.

"Supposing you'd asked God to do something," said Philip, "and really believed it was going to happen, like moving a mountain, I mean, and you had faith, and it didn't happen, what would it mean?"

"What a funny boy you are!" said Aunt Louisa. "You asked about moving mountains two or three weeks ago."

"It would just mean that you hadn't got faith," answered Uncle William.

Philip accepted the explanation. If God had not cured him, it was because he did not really believe. And yet he did not see how he could believe more than he did. But perhaps he had not given God enough time. He had only asked Him for nineteen days. In a day or two he began his prayer again, and this time he fixed upon Easter. That was the day of His Son's glorious resurrection, and God in His happiness might be mercifully inclined. But now Philip added other means of attaining his desire: he began to wish, when he saw a new moon or a dappled horse, and he looked out for shooting stars; during exeat they had a chicken at the vicarage, and he broke the lucky bone with Aunt Louisa and wished again, each time that his foot might be made whole. He was appealing unconsciously to gods older to his race than the God of Israel. And he bombarded the Almighty with his prayer, at odd times of the day, whenever it occurred to him, in identical words always, for it seemed to him important to make his request in the same terms. But presently the feeling came to him that this time also his faith would not be great enough. He could not resist the doubt that assailed him. He made his own experience into a general rule.

"I suppose no one ever has faith enough," he said.

It was like the salt which his nurse used to tell him about: you could catch any bird by putting salt on his tail; and once he had taken a little bag of it into Kensington Gardens. But he could never get near enough to put the salt on a bird's tail. Before Easter he had given up the struggle. He felt a dull resentment against his uncle for taking him in. The text which spoke of the moving of mountains was just one of those that said one thing and meant another. He thought his uncle had been playing a practical joke on him.

Chapter XV

THE KING'S SCHOOL AT TERCANBURY, TO WHICH PHILIP WENT WHEN HE was thirteen, prided itself on its antiquity. It traced its origin to an abbey school, founded before the Conquest, where the rudiments of learning were taught by Augustine monks; and, like many another establishment of this sort, on the destruction of the monasteries it had been reorganised by the officers of King Henry VIII and thus acquired its name. Since then, pursuing its modest course, it had given to the sons of the local gentry and of the professional people of Kent an education sufficient to their needs. One or two men of letters, beginning with a poet, than whom only Shakespeare had a more splendid genius, and ending with a writer of prose whose view of life has affected profoundly the generation of which Philip was a member, had gone forth from its gates to achieve fame; it had produced one or two eminent lawyers, but eminent lawyers are common, and one or two soldiers of distinction; but during the three centuries since its separation from the monastic order it had trained especially men of the church, bishops, deans, canons, and above all country clergymen: there were boys in the school whose fathers, grandfathers, great-grandfathers, had been educated there and had all been rectors of parishes in the diocese of Tercanbury; and they came to it with their minds made up already to be ordained. But there were signs notwithstanding that even there changes were coming; for a few, repeating what they had heard at home, said that the Church was no longer what it used to be. It wasn't so much the money; but the class of people who went in for it weren't the same; and two or three boys knew curates whose fathers were tradesmen: they'd rather go out to the Colonies (in those days the Colonies were still the last hope of those who could get nothing to do in England) than be a curate under some chap who wasn't a gentleman. At King's School, as at Blackstable Vicarage, a tradesman was anyone who was not lucky enough to own land (and here a fine distinction was made between the gentleman farmer and the landowner), or did not follow one of the four professions to which it was possible for a gentleman to belong. Among the day-boys, of whom there were about a hundred and fifty, sons of the local gentry and of the men stationed at the *dépôt*, those whose fathers were engaged in business were made to feel the degradation of their state.

The masters had no patience with modern ideas of education, which they read of sometimes in *The Times* or *The Guardian,* and hoped fervently that King's School would remain true to its old traditions. The dead languages were taught with such thoroughness that an old boy seldom thought of Homer or Virgil in after life without a qualm of boredom; and though in the common-room at dinner one or two bolder spirits suggested that mathematics were of increasing importance, the general feeling was that they were a less noble study than the classics. Neither German nor chemistry was taught, and French only by the form-masters; they could keep order better than a foreigner, and, since they knew the grammar as well as any Frenchman, it seemed unimportant that none of them could have got a cup of coffee in the restaurant at Boulogne unless the waiter had known a little English. Geography was taught chiefly by making boys draw maps, and this was a favourite occupation, especially when the country dealt with was mountainous: it was possible to waste a great deal of time in drawing the Andes or the Apennines. The masters, graduates of Oxford or Cambridge, were ordained and unmarried; if by chance they wished to marry they could only do so by accepting one of the smaller livings at the disposal of the Chapter; but for many years none of them had cared to leave the refined society of Tercanbury, which owing to the cavalry *dépôt* had a martial as well as an ecclesiastical tone, for the monotony of life in a country rectory; and they were now all men of middle age.

The headmaster, on the other hand, was obliged to be married, and he conducted the school till age began to tell upon him. When he retired he was rewarded with a much better living than any of the undermasters could hope for, and an honorary Canonry.

But a year before Philip entered the school a great change had come over it. It had been obvious for some time that Dr. Fleming, who had been headmaster for the quarter of a century, was become too deaf to continue his work to the greater glory of God; and when one of the livings on the outskirts of the city fell vacant, with a stipend of six hundred a year, the Chapter offered it to him in such a manner as to imply that they thought it high time for him to retire. He could nurse his ailments comfortably on such an income. Two or three curates who had hoped for preferment told their wives it was scandalous to give a parish that needed a young, strong, and energetic man to an old fellow who knew nothing of parochial work, and had feathered his nest already; but the mutterings of the unbeneficed clergy do not reach the ears of a cathedral Chapter. And as for the parishioners they had nothing to say in the matter, and therefore nobody asked for their opinion. The Wesleyans and the Baptists both had chapels in the village.

When Dr. Fleming was thus disposed of it became necessary to find a successor. It was contrary to the traditions of the school that one of the lower-masters should be chosen. The common-room was unanimous in desiring the election of Mr. Watson, headmaster of the preparatory school; he could hardly be described as already a master of King's School, they had all known him for twenty years, and there was no danger that he would make a nuisance of himself. But the Chapter sprang a surprise on them. It chose a man called Perkins. At first nobody knew who Perkins was, and the name favourably impressed no one; but before the shock of it had passed away, it was realised that Perkins was the son of Perkins the linen-draper. Dr. Fleming informed the masters just before dinner, and his manner showed his consternation. Such of them as were dining in, ate their meal almost in silence, and no reference was made to the matter till the servants had left the room. Then they set to. The names of those present on this occasion are unimportant, but they had been known to generations of schoolboys as Sighs, Tar, Winks, Squirts, and Pat.

They all knew Tom Perkins. The first thing about him was that he was not a gentleman. They remembered him quite well. He was a small, dark boy, with untidy black hair and large eyes. He looked like a gipsy. He had come to the school as a day-boy, with the best scholarship on their endowment, so that his education had cost him nothing. Of course he was brilliant. At every Speech-Day he was loaded with prizes. He was their show-boy, and they remembered now bitterly their fear that he would try to get some scholarship at one of the larger public schools and so pass out of their hands. Dr. Fleming had gone to the linen-draper his father—they all remembered the shop, Perkins and Cooper, in St. Catherine's Street—and said he hoped Tom would remain with them till he went to Oxford. The school was Perkins and Cooper's best customer, and Mr. Perkins was only too glad to give the required assurance. Tom Perkins continued to triumph, he was the finest classical scholar that Dr. Fleming remembered, and on leaving the school took with him the most valuable scholarship they had to offer. He got another at Magdalen and settled down to a brilliant career at the University. The school magazine recorded the distinctions he achieved year after year, and when he got his double first Dr. Fleming himself wrote a few words of eulogy on the front page. It was with greater satisfaction that they welcomed his success, since Perkins and Cooper had fallen upon evil days: Cooper drank like a fish, and just before Tom Perkins took his degree the linen-drapers filed their petition in bankruptcy.

In due course Tom Perkins took Holy Orders and entered upon the profession for which he was so admirably suited. He had been an assistant master at Wellington and then at Rugby.

But there was quite a difference between welcoming his success at other schools and serving under his leadership in their own. Tar had frequently given him lines, and Squirts had boxed his ears. They could not imagine how the Chapter had made such a mistake. No one could be expected to forget that he was the son of a bankrupt linen-draper, and the alcoholism of Cooper seemed to increase the disgrace. It was understood that the Dean had supported his candidature with zeal, so the Dean would probably ask him to dinner; but would the pleasant little dinners in the precincts ever be the same when Tom Perkins sat at the table? And what about the *dépôt?* He really could not expect officers and gentlemen to receive him as one of themselves. It would do the school incalculable harm. Parents would be dissatisfied, and no one could be surprised if there were wholesale withdrawals. And then the indignity of calling him Mr. Perkins! The masters thought by way of protest of sending in their resignations in a body, but the uneasy fear that they would be accepted with equanimity restrained them.

"The only thing is to prepare ourselves for changes," said Sighs, who had conducted the fifth form for five-and-twenty years with unparallelled incompetence.

And when they saw him they were not reassured. Dr. Fleming invited them to meet him at luncheon. He was now a man of thirty-two, tall and lean, but with the same wild and unkempt look they remembered on him as a boy. His clothes, ill-made and shabby, were put on untidily. His hair was as black and as long as ever, and he had plainly never learned to brush it; it fell over his forehead with every gesture, and he had a quick movement of the hand with which he pushed it back from his eyes. He had a black moustache and a beard which came high up on his face almost to the cheek-bones. He talked to the masters quite easily, as though he had parted from them a week or two before; he was evidently delighted to see them. He seemed unconscious of the strangeness of the position and appeared not to notice any oddness in being addressed as Mr. Perkins.

When he bade them good-bye, one of the masters, for something to say, remarked that he was allowing himself plenty of time to catch his train.

"I want to go round and have a look at the shop," he answered cheerfully.

There was a distinct embarrassment. They wondered that he could be so tactless, and to make it worse Dr. Fleming had not heard what he said. His wife shouted it in his ear.

"He wants to go round and look at his father's old shop."

Only Tom Perkins was unconscious of the humiliation which the whole party felt. He turned to Mrs. Fleming.

"Who's got it now, d'you know?"

She could hardly answer. She was very angry.

"It's still a linen-draper's," she said bitterly. "Grove is the name. We don't deal there anymore."

"I wonder if he'd let me go over the house."

"I expect he would if you explain who you are."

It was not till the end of dinner that evening that any reference was made in the common-room to the subject that was in all their minds. Then it was Sighs who asked:

"Well, what did you think of our new head?"

They thought of the conversation at luncheon. It was hardly a conversation; it was a monologue. Perkins had talked incessantly. He talked very quickly, with a flow of easy words and in a deep, resonant voice. He had a short, odd little laugh which showed his white teeth. They had followed him with difficulty, for his mind darted from subject to subject with a connection they did not always catch. He talked of pedagogics, and this was natural enough; but he had much to say of modern theories in Germany which they had never heard of and received with misgiving. He talked of the classics, but he had been to Greece, and he discoursed of archaeology; he had once spent a winter digging; they could not see how that helped a man to teach boys to pass examinations. He talked of politics. It sounded odd to them to hear him compare Lord Beaconsfield with Alcibiades. He talked of Mr. Gladstone and Home Rule. They realised that he was a Liberal. Their hearts sank. He talked of German philosophy and of French fiction. They could not think a man profound whose interests were so diverse.

It was Winks who summed up the general impression and put it into a form they all felt conclusively damning. Winks was the master of the upper third, a weak-kneed man with drooping eyelids. He was too tall for his strength, and his movements were slow and languid. He gave an impression of lassitude, and his nickname was eminently appropriate.

"He's very enthusiastic," said Winks.

Enthusiasm was ill-bred. Enthusiasm was ungentlemanly. They thought of the Salvation Army with its braying trumpets and its drums. Enthusiasm meant change. They had goose-flesh when they thought of all the pleasant old habits which stood in imminent danger. They hardly dared to look forward to the future.

"He looks more of a gipsy than ever," said one, after a pause.

"I wonder if the Dean and Chapter knew that he was a Radical when they elected him," another observed bitterly.

But conversation halted. They were too much disturbed for words.

When Tar and Sighs were walking together to the Chapter House on Speech-Day a week later, Tar, who had a bitter tongue, remarked to his colleague:

"Well, we've seen a good many Speech-Days here, haven't we? I wonder if we shall see another."

Sighs was more melancholy even than usual.

"If anything worth having comes along in the way of a living I don't mind when I retire."

Chapter XVI

A YEAR PASSED, AND WHEN PHILIP CAME TO THE SCHOOL THE OLD MASTERS were all in their places; but a good many changes had taken place notwithstanding their stubborn resistance, none the less formidable because it was concealed under an apparent desire to fall in with the new head's ideas. Though the form-masters still taught French to the lower school, another master had come, with a degree of doctor of philology from the University of Heidelberg and a record of three years spent in a French *lycée*, to teach French to the upper forms and German to anyone who cared to take it up instead of Greek. Another master was engaged to teach mathematics more systematically than had been found necessary hitherto. Neither of these was ordained. This was a real revolution, and when the pair arrived the older masters received them with distrust. A laboratory had been fitted up, army classes were instituted; they all said the character of the school was changing. And heaven only knew what further projects Mr. Perkins turned in that untidy head of his. The school was small as public schools go, there were not more than two hundred boarders; and it was difficult for it to grow larger, for it was huddled up against the Cathedral; the precincts, with the exception of a house in which some of the masters lodged, were occupied by the cathedral clergy; and there was no more room for building. But Mr. Perkins devised an elaborate scheme by which he might obtain sufficient space to make the school double its present size. He wanted to attract boys from London. He thought it would be good for them to be thrown in contact with the Kentish lads, and it would sharpen the country wits of these.

"It's against all our traditions," said Sighs, when Mr. Perkins made the suggestion to him. "We've rather gone out of our way to avoid the contamination of boys from London."

"Oh, what nonsense!" said Mr. Perkins.

No one had ever told the form-master before that he talked nonsense, and he was meditating an acid reply, in which perhaps he might insert a veiled reference to hosiery, when Mr. Perkins in his impetuous way attacked him outrageously.

"That house in the Precincts—if you'd only marry I'd get the Chapter to put another couple of stories on, and we'd make dormitories and studies, and your wife could help you."

The elderly clergyman gasped. Why should he marry? He was fifty-seven, a man couldn't marry at fifty-seven. He couldn't start looking after a house at his time of life. He didn't want to marry. If the choice lay between that and the country living he would much sooner resign. All he wanted now was peace and quietness.

"I'm not thinking of marrying," he said.

Mr. Perkins looked at him with his dark, bright eyes, and if there was a twinkle in them poor Sighs never saw it.

"What a pity! Couldn't you marry to oblige me? It would help me a great deal with the Dean and Chapter when I suggest rebuilding your house."

But Mr. Perkins' most unpopular innovation was his system of taking occasionally another man's form. He asked it as a favour, but after all it was a favour which could not be refused, and as Tar, otherwise Mr. Turner, said, it was undignified for all parties. He gave no warning, but after morning prayers would say to one of the masters:

"I wonder if you'd mind taking the Sixth today at eleven. We'll change over, shall we?"

They did not know whether this was usual at other schools, but certainly it had never been done at Tercanbury. The results were curious. Mr. Turner, who was the first victim, broke the news to his form that the headmaster would take them for Latin that day, and on the pretence that they might like to ask him a question or two so that they should not make perfect fools of themselves, spent the last quarter of an hour of the history lesson in construing for them the passage of Livy which had been set for the day; but when he rejoined his class and looked at the paper on which Mr. Perkins had written the marks, a surprise awaited him; for the two boys at the top of the form seemed to have done very ill, while others who had never distinguished themselves before were given full marks. When he asked Eldridge, his cleverest boy, what was the meaning of this the answer came sullenly:

"Mr. Perkins never gave us any construing to do. He asked me what I knew about General Gordon."

Mr. Turner looked at him in astonishment. The boys evidently felt they had been hardly used, and he could not help agreeing with their silent dissatisfaction. He could not see either what General Gordon had to do with Livy. He hazarded an inquiry afterwards.

"Eldridge was dreadfully put out because you asked him what he knew about General Gordon," he said to the headmaster, with an attempt at a chuckle.

Mr. Perkins laughed.

"I saw they'd got to the agrarian laws of Caius Gracchus, and I wondered if they knew anything about the agrarian troubles in Ireland. But all they knew about Ireland was that Dublin was on the Liffey. So I wondered if they'd ever heard of General Gordon."

Then the horrid fact was disclosed that the new head had a mania for general information. He had doubts about the utility of examinations on subjects which had been crammed for the occasion. He wanted common sense.

Sighs grew more worried every month; he could not get the thought out of his head that Mr. Perkins would ask him to fix a day for his marriage; and he hated the attitude the head adopted towards classical literature. There was no doubt that he was a fine scholar, and he was engaged on a work which was quite in the right tradition: he was writing a treatise on the trees in Latin literature; but he talked of it flippantly, as though it were a pastime of no great importance, like billiards, which engaged his leisure but was not to be considered with seriousness. And Squirts, the master of the middle third, grew more ill-tempered every day.

It was in his form that Philip was put on entering the school. The Rev. B. B. Gordon was a man by nature ill-suited to be a schoolmaster: he was impatient and choleric. With no one to call him to account, with only small boys to face him, he had long lost all power of self-control. He began his work in a rage and ended it in a passion. He was a man of middle height and of a corpulent figure; he had sandy hair, worn very short and now growing grey, and a small bristly moustache. His large face, with indistinct features and small blue eyes, was naturally red, but during his frequent attacks of anger it grew dark and purple. His nails were bitten to the quick, for while some trembling boy was construing he would sit at his desk shaking with the fury that consumed him, and gnaw his fingers. Stories, perhaps exaggerated, were told of his violence, and two years before there had been some excitement in the school when it was heard that one father was threatening a prosecution: he had boxed the ears of a boy named Walters with a book so violently that his hearing was affected and the boy had to be taken away from the school. The boy's father lived in Tercanbury, and there had been much indignation in the city, the local paper had referred to the matter; but Mr. Walters was only a brewer, so the sympathy was divided. The rest of the boys, for reasons best known to themselves, though they loathed the master, took his side in the affair, and, to show their indignation that the school's business had been dealt with outside, made things as uncomfortable as they could for Walters' younger brother, who still remained. But Mr. Gordon had only escaped the country living by the skin of his teeth, and he had never hit a boy since. The right the masters possessed to cane boys on the hand was taken away from them, and Squirts could no longer emphasise his anger by beating his desk with the cane. He never did more now than take a boy by the shoulders and shake him. He still made a naughty or refractory lad stand with one arm stretched out for anything from ten minutes to half an hour, and he was as violent as before with his tongue.

No master could have been more unfitted to teach things to so shy a boy as Philip. He had come to the school with fewer terrors than he had when first he went to Mr. Watson's. He knew a good many boys who had been with him at the preparatory school. He felt more grown-up, and instinctively realised that among the larger numbers his deformity would be less noticeable. But from the first day Mr. Gordon struck terror in his heart; and the master, quick to discern the boys who were frightened of him, seemed on that account to take a peculiar dislike to him. Philip had enjoyed his work, but now he began to look upon the hours passed in school with horror. Rather than risk an answer which might be wrong and excite a storm of abuse from the master, he would sit stupidly silent, and when it came towards his turn to stand up and construe he grew sick and white with apprehension. His happy moments were those when Mr. Perkins took the form. He was able to gratify the passion for general knowledge which beset the headmaster; he had read all sorts of strange books beyond his years, and often Mr. Perkins, when a question was going round the room, would stop at Philip with a smile that filled the boy with rapture, and say:

"Now, Carey, you tell them."

The good marks he got on these occasions increased Mr. Gordon's indignation. One day it came to Philip's turn to translate, and the master sat there glaring at him and furiously biting his thumb. He was in a ferocious mood. Philip began to speak in a low voice.

"Don't mumble," shouted the master.

Something seemed to stick in Philip's throat.

"Go on. Go on. Go on."

Each time the words were screamed more loudly. The effect was to drive all he knew out of Philip's head, and he looked at the printed page vacantly. Mr. Gordon began to breathe heavily.

"If you don't know why don't you say so? Do you know it or not? Did you hear all this construed last time or not? Why don't you speak? Speak, you blockhead, speak!"

The master seized the arms of his chair and grasped them as though to prevent himself from falling upon Philip. They knew that in past days he often used to seize boys by the throat till they almost choked. The veins in his forehead stood out and his face grew dark and threatening. He was a man insane.

Philip had known the passage perfectly the day before, but now he could remember nothing.

"I don't know it," he gasped.

"Why don't you know it? Let's take the words one by one. We'll soon see if you don't know it."

Philip stood silent, very white, trembling a little, with his head bent down on the book. The master's breathing grew almost stertorous.

"The headmaster says you're clever. I don't know how he sees it. General information." He laughed savagely. "I don't know what they put you in this form for. Blockhead."

He was pleased with the word, and he repeated it at the top of his voice.

"Blockhead! Blockhead! Club-footed blockhead!"

That relieved him a little. He saw Philip redden suddenly. He told him to fetch the Black Book. Philip put down his Cæsar and went silently out. The Black Book was a sombre volume in which the names of boys were written with their misdeeds, and when a name was down three times it meant a caning. Philip went to the headmaster's house and knocked at his study-door. Mr. Perkins was seated at his table.

"May I have the Black Book, please, sir."

"There it is," answered Mr. Perkins, indicating its place by a nod of his head. "What have you been doing that you shouldn't?"

"I don't know, sir."

Mr. Perkins gave him a quick look, but without answering went on with his work. Philip took the book and went out. When the hour was up, a few minutes later, he brought it back.

"Let me have a look at it," said the headmaster. "I see Mr. Gordon has black-booked you for 'gross impertinence.' What was it?"

"I don't know, sir. Mr. Gordon said I was a club-footed blockhead."

Mr. Perkins looked at him again. He wondered whether there was sarcasm behind the boy's reply, but he was still much too shaken. His face was white and his eyes had a look of terrified distress. Mr. Perkins got up and put the book down. As he did so he took up some photographs.

"A friend of mine sent me some pictures of Athens this morning," he said casually. "Look here, there's the Acropolis."

He began explaining to Philip what he saw. The ruin grew vivid with his words. He showed him the theatre of Dionysus and explained in what order the people sat, and how beyond they could see the blue Aegean. And then suddenly he said:

"I remember Mr. Gordon used to call me a gipsy counter-jumper when I was in his form."

And before Philip, his mind fixed on the photographs, had time to gather the meaning of the remark, Mr. Perkins was showing him a picture of Salamis, and with his finger, a finger of which the nail had a little black edge to it, was pointing out how the Greek ships were placed and how the Persian.

Chapter XVII

PHILIP PASSED THE NEXT TWO YEARS WITH COMFORTABLE MONOTONY. HE was not bullied more than other boys of his size; and his deformity, withdrawing him from games, acquired for him an insignificance for which he was grateful. He was not popular, and he was very lonely. He spent a couple of terms with Winks in the Upper Third. Winks, with his weary manner and his drooping eyelids, looked infinitely bored. He did his duty, but he did it with an abstracted mind. He was kind, gentle, and foolish. He had a great belief in the honour of boys; he felt that the first thing to make them truthful was not to let it enter your head for a moment that it was possible for them to lie. "Ask much," he quoted, "and much shall be given to you." Life was easy in the Upper Third. You knew exactly what lines would come to your turn to construe, and with the crib that passed from hand to hand you could find out all you wanted in two minutes; you could hold a Latin Grammar open on your knees while questions were passing round; and Winks never noticed anything odd in the fact that the same incredible mistake was to be found in a dozen different exercises. He had no great faith in examinations, for he noticed that boys never did so well in them as in form: it was disappointing, but not significant. In due course they were moved up, having learned little but a cheerful effrontery in the distortion of truth, which was possibly of greater service to them in after life than an ability to read Latin at sight.

Then they fell into the hands of Tar. His name was Turner; he was the most vivacious of the old masters, a short man with an immense belly, a black beard turning now to grey, and a swarthy skin. In his clerical dress there was indeed something in him to suggest the tar-barrel; and though on principle he gave five hundred lines to any boy on whose lips he overheard his nickname, at dinner-parties in the precincts he often made little jokes about it. He was the most worldly of the masters; he dined out more frequently than any of the others, and the society he kept was not so exclusively clerical. The boys looked upon him as rather a dog. He left off his clerical attire during the holidays and had been seen in Switzerland in gay tweeds. He liked a bottle of wine and a good dinner, and having once been seen at the Café Royal with a lady who was very probably a near relation, was thenceforward supposed by generations of schoolboys to indulge in orgies the circumstantial details of which pointed to an unbounded belief in human depravity.

Mr. Turner reckoned that it took him a term to lick boys into shape after they had been in the Upper Third; and now and then he let fall a sly hint, which showed that he knew perfectly what went on in his colleague's form. He took it good-humouredly. He looked upon boys as young ruffians who were more apt to be truthful if it was quite certain a lie would be found out, whose sense of honour was peculiar to themselves and did not apply to dealings with masters, and who were least likely to be troublesome when they learned that it did not pay. He was proud of his form and as eager at fifty-five that it should do better in examinations than any of the others as he had been when he first came to the school. He had the choler of the obese, easily roused and as easily calmed, and his boys soon discovered that there was much kindliness beneath the invective with which he constantly assailed them. He had no patience with fools, but was willing to take much trouble with boys whom he suspected of concealing intelligence behind their wilfulness. He was fond of inviting them to tea; and, though vowing they never got a look in with him at the cakes and muffins, for it was the fashion to believe that his corpulence pointed to a voracious appetite, and his voracious appetite to tapeworms, they accepted his invitations with real pleasure.

Philip was now more comfortable, for space was so limited that there were only studies for boys in the upper school, and till then he had lived in the great hall in which they all ate and in which the lower forms did preparation in a promiscuity which was vaguely distasteful to him. Now and then it made him restless to be with people and he wanted urgently to be alone. He set out for solitary walks into the country. There was a little stream, with pollards on both sides of it, that ran through green fields, and it made him happy, he knew not why, to wander along its banks. When he was tired he lay face-downward on the grass and watched the eager scurrying of minnows and of tadpoles. It gave him a peculiar satisfaction to saunter round the precincts. On the green in the middle they practised at nets in the summer, but during the rest of the year it was quiet: boys used to wander round sometimes arm in arm, or a studious fellow with abstracted gaze walked slowly, repeating to himself something he had to learn by heart. There was a colony of rooks in the great elms, and they filled the air with melancholy cries. Along one side lay the Cathedral with its great central tower, and Philip, who knew as yet nothing of beauty, felt when he looked at it a troubling delight which he could not understand. When he had a study (it was a little square room looking on a slum, and four boys shared it), he bought a photograph of that view of the Cathedral, and pinned it up over his desk. And he found himself taking a new interest in what he saw from the window of the Fourth Form room. It looked on to old lawns, carefully tended, and fine trees with foliage dense and rich. It gave him an odd feeling in his heart, and he did not know if it was pain or pleasure. It was the first dawn of the aesthetic emotion. It accompanied other changes. His voice broke. It was no longer quite under his control, and queer sounds issued from his throat.

Then he began to go to the classes which were held in the headmaster's study, immediately after tea, to prepare boys for confirmation. Philip's piety had not stood the test of time, and he had long since given up his nightly reading of the Bible; but now, under the influence of Mr. Perkins, with this new condition of the body which made him so restless, his old feelings revived, and he reproached himself bitterly for his backsliding. The fires of Hell burned fiercely before his mind's eye. If he had died during that time when he was little better than an infidel he would have been lost; he believed implicitly in pain everlasting, he believed in it much more than in eternal happiness; and he shuddered at the dangers he had run.

Since the day on which Mr. Perkins had spoken kindly to him, when he was smarting under the particular form of abuse which he could least bear, Philip had conceived for his headmaster a dog-like adoration. He racked his brains vainly for some way to please him. He treasured the smallest word of commendation which by chance fell from his lips. And when he came to the quiet little meetings in his house he was prepared to surrender himself entirely. He kept his eyes fixed on Mr. Perkins' shining eyes, and sat with mouth half open, his head a little thrown forward so as to miss no word. The ordinariness of the surroundings made the matters they dealt with extraordinarily moving. And often the master, seized himself by the wonder of his subject, would push back the book in front of him, and with his hands clasped together over his heart, as though to still the beating, would talk of the mysteries of their religion. Sometimes Philip did not understand, but he did not want to understand, he felt vaguely that it was enough to feel. It seemed to him then that the headmaster, with his black, straggling hair and his pale face, was like those prophets of Israel who feared not to take kings to task; and when he thought of the Redeemer he saw Him only with the same dark eyes and those wan cheeks.

Mr. Perkins took this part of his work with great seriousness. There was never here any of that flashing humour which made the other masters suspect him of flippancy. Finding time for everything in his busy day, he was able at certain intervals to take separately for a quarter of an hour or twenty minutes the boys whom he was preparing for confirmation. He wanted to make them feel that this was the first consciously serious step in their lives; he tried to grope into the depths of their souls; he wanted to instil in them his own vehement devotion. In Philip, notwithstanding his shyness, he felt the possibility of a passion equal to his own. The boy's temperament seemed to him essentially religious. One day he broke off suddenly from the subject on which he had been talking.

"Have you thought at all what you're going to be when you grow up?" he asked.

"My uncle wants me to be ordained," said Philip.

"And you?"

Philip looked away. He was ashamed to answer that he felt himself unworthy.

"I don't know any life that's so full of happiness as ours. I wish I could make you feel what a wonderful privilege it is. One can serve God in every walk, but we stand nearer to Him. I don't want to influence you, but if you made up your mind—oh, at once—you couldn't help feeling that joy and relief which never desert one again."

Philip did not answer, but the headmaster read in his eyes that he realised already something of what he tried to indicate.

"If you go on as you are now you'll find yourself head of the school one of these days, and you ought to be pretty safe for a scholarship when you leave. Have you got anything of your own?"

"My uncle says I shall have a hundred a year when I'm twenty-one."

"You'll be rich. I had nothing."

The headmaster hesitated a moment, and then, idly drawing lines with a pencil on the blotting paper in front of him, went on.

"I'm afraid your choice of professions will be rather limited. You naturally couldn't go in for anything that required physical activity."

Philip reddened to the roots of his hair, as he always did when any reference was made to his club-foot. Mr. Perkins looked at him gravely.

"I wonder if you're not oversensitive about your misfortune. Has it ever struck you to thank God for it?"

Philip looked up quickly. His lips tightened. He remembered how for months, trusting in what they told him, he had implored God to heal him as He had healed the Leper and made the Blind to see.

"As long as you accept it rebelliously it can only cause you shame. But if you looked upon it as a cross that was given you to bear only because your shoulders were strong enough to bear it, a sign of God's favour, then it would be a source of happiness to you instead of misery."

He saw that the boy hated to discuss the matter and he let him go.

But Philip thought over all that the headmaster had said, and presently, his mind taken up entirely with the ceremony that was before him, a mystical rapture seized him. His spirit seemed to free itself from the bonds of the flesh and he seemed to be living a new life. He aspired to perfection with all the passion that was in him. He wanted to surrender himself entirely to the service of God, and he made up his mind definitely that he would be ordained. When the great day arrived, his soul deeply moved by all the preparation, by the books he had studied and above all by the overwhelming influence of the head, he could hardly contain himself for fear and joy. One thought had tormented him. He knew that he would have to walk alone through the chancel, and he dreaded showing his limp thus obviously, not only to the whole school, who were attending the service, but also to the strangers, people from the city or parents who had come to see their sons confirmed. But when the time came he felt suddenly that he could accept the humiliation joyfully; and as he limped up the chancel, very small and insignificant beneath the lofty vaulting of the Cathedral, he offered consciously his deformity as a sacrifice to the God who loved him.

Chapter XVIII

BUT PHILIP COULD NOT LIVE LONG IN THE RAREFIED AIR OF THE HILLTOPS. What had happened to him when first he was seized by the religious emotion happened to him now. Because he felt so keenly the beauty of faith, because the desire for self-sacrifice burned in his heart with such a gem-like glow, his strength seemed inadequate to his ambition. He was tired out by the violence of his passion. His soul was filled on a sudden with a singular aridity. He began to forget the presence of God which had seemed so surrounding; and his religious exercises, still very punctually performed, grew merely formal. At first he blamed himself for this falling away, and the fear of hell-fire urged him to renewed vehemence; but the passion was dead, and gradually other interests distracted his thoughts.

Philip had few friends. His habit of reading isolated him: it became such a need that after being in company for some time he grew tired and restless; he was vain of the wider knowledge he had acquired from the perusal of so many books, his mind was alert, and he had not the skill to hide his contempt for his companions' stupidity. They complained that he was conceited; and, since he excelled only in matters which to them were unimportant, they asked satirically what he had to be conceited about. He was developing a sense of humour, and found that he had a knack of saying bitter things, which caught people on the raw; he said them because they amused him, hardly realising how much they hurt, and was much offended when he found that his victims regarded him with active dislike. The humiliations he suffered when first he went to school had caused in him a shrinking from his fellows which he could never entirely overcome; he remained shy and silent. But though he did everything to alienate the sympathy of other boys he longed with all his heart for the popularity which to some was so easily accorded. These from his distance he admired extravagantly; and though he was inclined to be more sarcastic with them than with others, though he made little jokes at their expense, he would have given anything to change places with them. Indeed he would gladly have changed places with the dullest boy in the school who was whole of limb. He took to a singular habit. He would imagine that he was some boy whom he had a particular fancy for; he would throw his soul, as it were, into the other's body, talk with his voice and laugh with his laugh; he would imagine himself doing all the things the other did. It was so vivid that he seemed for a moment really to be no longer himself. In this way he enjoyed many intervals of fantastic happiness.

At the beginning of the Christmas term which followed on his confirmation Philip found himself moved into another study. One of the boys who shared it was called Rose. He was in the same form as Philip, and Philip had always looked upon him with envious admiration. He was not good-looking; though his large hands and big bones suggested that he would be a tall man, he was clumsily made; but his eyes were charming, and when he laughed (he was constantly laughing) his face wrinkled all round them in a jolly way. He was neither clever nor stupid, but good enough at his work and better at games. He was a favourite with masters and boys, and he in his turn liked everyone.

When Philip was put in the study he could not help seeing that the others, who had been together for three terms, welcomed him coldly. It made him nervous to feel himself an intruder; but he had learned to hide his feelings, and they found him quiet and unobtrusive. With Rose, because he was as little able as anyone else to resist his charm, Philip was even more than usually shy and abrupt; and whether on account of this, unconsciously bent upon exerting the fascination he knew was his only by the results, or whether from sheer kindness of heart, it was Rose who first took Philip into the circle. One day, quite suddenly, he asked Philip if he would walk to the football field with him. Philip flushed.

"I can't walk fast enough for you," he said.

"Rot. Come on."

And just before they were setting out some boy put his head in the study-door and asked Rose to go with him.

"I can't," he answered. "I've already promised Carey."

"Don't bother about me," said Philip quickly. "I shan't mind."

"Rot," said Rose.

He looked at Philip with those good-natured eyes of his and laughed. Philip felt a curious tremor in his heart.

In a little while, their friendship growing with boyish rapidity, the pair were inseparable. Other fellows wondered at the sudden intimacy, and Rose was asked what he saw in Philip.

"Oh, I don't know," he answered. "He's not half a bad chap really."

Soon they grew accustomed to the two walking into chapel arm in arm or strolling round the precincts in conversation; wherever one was the other could be found also, and, as though acknowledging his proprietorship, boys who wanted Rose would leave messages with Carey. Philip at first was reserved. He would not let himself yield entirely to the proud joy that filled him; but presently his distrust of the fates gave way before a wild happiness. He thought Rose the most wonderful fellow he had ever seen. His books now were insignificant; he could not bother about them when there was something infinitely more important to occupy him.

Rose's friends used to come in to tea in the study sometimes or sit about when there was nothing better to do—Rose liked a crowd and the chance of a rag—and they found that Philip was quite a decent fellow. Philip was happy.

When the last day of term came he and Rose arranged by which train they should come back, so that they might meet at the station and have tea in the town before returning to school. Philip went home with a heavy heart. He thought of Rose all through the holidays, and his fancy was active with the things they would do together next term. He was bored at the vicarage, and when on the last day his uncle put him the usual question in the usual facetious tone:

"Well, are you glad to be going back to school?"

Philip answered joyfully:

"Rather."

In order to be sure of meeting Rose at the station he took an earlier train than he usually did, and he waited about the platform for an hour. When the train came in from Faversham, where he knew Rose had to change, he ran along it excitedly. But Rose was not there. He got a porter to tell him when another train was due, and he waited; but again he was disappointed; and he was cold and hungry, so he walked, through side-streets and slums, by a short cut to the school. He found Rose in the study, with his feet on the chimney-piece, talking eighteen to the dozen with half a dozen boys who were sitting on whatever there was to sit on. He shook hands with Philip enthusiastically, but Philip's face fell, for he realised that Rose had forgotten all about their appointment.

"I say, why are you so late?" said Rose. "I thought you were never coming."

"You were at the station at half-past four," said another boy. "I saw you when I came."

Philip blushed a little. He did not want Rose to know that he had been such a fool as to wait for him.

"I had to see about a friend of my people's," he invented readily. "I was asked to see her off."

But his disappointment made him a little sulky. He sat in silence, and when spoken to answered in monosyllables. He was making up his mind to have it out with Rose when they were alone. But when the others had gone Rose at once came over and sat on the arm of the chair in which Philip was lounging.

"I say, I'm jolly glad we're in the same study this term. Ripping, isn't it?"

He seemed so genuinely pleased to see Philip that Philip's annoyance vanished. They began as if they had not been separated for five minutes to talk eagerly of the thousand things that interested them.

Chapter XIX

At first Philip had been too grateful for Rose's friendship to make any demands on him. He took things as they came and enjoyed life. But presently he began to resent Rose's universal amiability; he wanted a more exclusive attachment, and he claimed as a right what before he had accepted as a favour. He watched jealously Rose's companionship with others; and though he knew it was unreasonable could not help sometimes saying bitter things to him. If Rose spent an hour playing the fool in another study, Philip would receive him when he returned to his own with a sullen frown. He would sulk for a day, and he suffered more because Rose either did not notice his ill-humour or deliberately ignored it. Not seldom Philip, knowing all the time how stupid he was, would force a quarrel, and they would not speak to one another for a couple of days. But Philip could not bear to be angry with him long, and even when convinced that he was in the right, would apologise humbly. Then for a week they would be as great friends as ever. But the best was over, and Philip could see that Rose often walked with him merely from old habit or from fear of his anger; they had not so much to say to one another as at first, and Rose was often bored. Philip felt that his lameness began to irritate him.

Towards the end of the term two or three boys caught scarlet fever, and there was much talk of sending them all home in order to escape an epidemic; but the sufferers were isolated, and since no more were attacked it was supposed that the outbreak was stopped. One of the stricken was Philip. He remained in hospital through the Easter holidays, and at the beginning of the summer term was sent home to the vicarage to get a little fresh air. The Vicar, notwithstanding medical assurance that the boy was no longer infectious, received him with suspicion; he thought it very inconsiderate of the doctor to suggest that his nephew's convalescence should be spent by the seaside, and consented to have him in the house only because there was nowhere else he could go.

Philip went back to school at half-term. He had forgotten the quarrels he had had with Rose, but remembered only that he was his greatest friend. He knew that he had been silly. He made up his mind to be more reasonable. During his illness Rose had sent him in a couple of little notes, and he had ended each with the words: "Hurry up and come back." Philip thought Rose must be looking forward as much to his return as he was himself to seeing Rose.

He found that owing to the death from scarlet fever of one of the boys in the Sixth there had been some shifting in the studies and Rose was no longer in his. It was a bitter disappointment. But as soon as he arrived he burst into Rose's study. Rose was sitting at his desk, working with a boy called Hunter, and turned round crossly as Philip came in.

"Who the devil's that?" he cried. And then, seeing Philip: "Oh, it's you."

Philip stopped in embarrassment.

"I thought I'd come in and see how you were."

"We were just working."

Hunter broke into the conversation.

"When did you get back?"

"Five minutes ago."

They sat and looked at him as though he was disturbing them. They evidently expected him to go quickly. Philip reddened.

"I'll be off. You might look in when you've done," he said to Rose.

"All right."

Philip closed the door behind him and limped back to his own study. He felt frightfully hurt. Rose, far from seeming glad to see him, had looked almost put out. They might never have been more than acquaintances. Though he waited in his study, not leaving it for a moment in case just then Rose should come, his friend never appeared; and next morning when he went into prayers he saw Rose and Hunter swinging along arm in arm. What he could not see for himself others told him. He had forgotten that three months is a long time in a schoolboy's life, and though he had passed them in solitude Rose had lived in the world. Hunter had stepped into the vacant place. Philip found that Rose was quietly avoiding him. But he was not the boy to accept a situation without putting it into words; he waited till he was sure Rose was alone in his study and went in.

"May I come in?" he asked.

Rose looked at him with an embarrassment that made him angry with Philip.

"Yes, if you want to."

"It's very kind of you," said Philip sarcastically.

"What d'you want?"

"I say, why have you been so rotten since I came back?"

"Oh, don't be an ass," said Rose.

"I don't know what you see in Hunter."

"That's my business."

Philip looked down. He could not bring himself to say what was in his heart. He was afraid of humiliating himself. Rose got up.

"I've got to go to the Gym," he said.

When he was at the door Philip forced himself to speak.

"I say, Rose, don't be a perfect beast."

"Oh, go to hell."

Rose slammed the door behind him and left Philip alone. Philip shivered with rage. He went back to his study and turned the conversation over in his mind. He hated Rose now, he wanted to hurt him, he thought of biting things he might have said to him. He brooded over the end to their friendship and fancied that others were talking of it. In his sensitiveness he saw sneers and wonderings in other fellows' manner when they were not bothering their heads with him at all. He imagined to himself what they were saying.

"After all, it wasn't likely to last long. I wonder he ever stuck Carey at all. Blighter!"

To show his indifference he struck up a violent friendship with a boy called Sharp whom he hated and despised. He was a London boy, with a loutish air, a heavy fellow with the beginnings of a moustache on his lip and bushy eyebrows that joined one another across the bridge of his nose. He had soft hands and manners too suave for his years. He spoke with the suspicion of a cockney accent. He was one of those boys who are too slack to play games, and he exercised great ingenuity in making excuses to avoid such as were compulsory. He was regarded by boys and masters with a vague dislike, and it was from arrogance that Philip now sought his society. Sharp in a couple of terms was going to Germany for a year. He hated school, which he looked upon as an indignity to be endured till he was old enough to go out into the world. London was all he cared for, and he had many stories to tell of his doings there during the holidays. From his conversation—he spoke in a soft, deep-toned voice—there emerged the vague rumour of the London streets by night. Philip listened to him at once fascinated and repelled. With his vivid fancy he seemed to see the surging throng round the pit-door of theatres, and the glitter of cheap restaurants, bars where men, half drunk, sat on high stools talking with barmaids; and under the street lamps the mysterious passing of dark crowds bent upon pleasure. Sharp lent him cheap novels from Holywell Row, which Philip read in his cubicle with a sort of wonderful fear.

Once Rose tried to effect a reconciliation. He was a good-natured fellow, who did not like having enemies.

"I say, Carey, why are you being such a silly ass? It doesn't do you any good cutting me and all that."

"I don't know what you mean," answered Philip.

"Well, I don't see why we shouldn't talk."

"You bore me," said Philip.

"Please yourself."

Rose shrugged his shoulders and left him. Philip was very white, as he always became when he was moved, and his heart beat violently. When Rose went away he felt suddenly sick with misery. He did not know why he had answered in that fashion. He would have given anything to be friends with Rose. He hated to have quarrelled with him, and now that he saw he had given him pain he was very sorry. But at the moment he had not been master of himself. It seemed that some devil had seized him, forcing him to say bitter things against his will, even though at the time he wanted to shake hands with Rose and meet him more than half-way. The desire to wound had been too strong for him. He had wanted to revenge himself for the pain and the humiliation he had endured. It was pride: it was folly too, for he knew that Rose would not care at all, while he would suffer bitterly. The thought came to him that he would go to Rose, and say:

"I say, I'm sorry I was such a beast. I couldn't help it. Let's make it up."

But he knew he would never be able to do it. He was afraid that Rose would sneer at him. He was angry with himself, and when Sharp came in a little while afterwards he seized upon the first opportunity to quarrel with him. Philip had a fiendish instinct for discovering other people's raw spots, and was able to say things that rankled because they were true. But Sharp had the last word.

"I heard Rose talking about you to Mellor just now," he said. "Mellor said: why didn't you kick him? It would teach him manners. And Rose said: I didn't like to. Damned cripple."

Philip suddenly became scarlet. He could not answer, for there was a lump in his throat that almost choked him.

Chapter XX

PHILIP WAS MOVED INTO THE SIXTH, BUT HE HATED SCHOOL NOW WITH ALL his heart, and, having lost his ambition, cared nothing whether he did ill or well. He awoke in the morning with a sinking heart because he must go through another day of drudgery. He was tired of having to do things because he was told; and the restrictions irked him, not because they were unreasonable, but because they were restrictions. He yearned for freedom. He was weary of repeating things that he knew already and of the hammering away, for the sake of a thick-witted fellow, at something that he understood from the beginning.

With Mr. Perkins you could work or not as you chose. He was at once eager and abstracted. The Sixth Form room was in a part of the old abbey which had been restored, and it had a Gothic window: Philip tried to cheat his boredom by drawing this over and over again; and sometimes out of his head he drew the great tower of the Cathedral or the gateway that led into the precincts. He had a knack for drawing. Aunt Louisa during her youth had painted in water colours, and she had several albums filled with sketches of churches, old bridges, and picturesque cottages. They were often shown at the vicarage tea-parties. She had once given Philip a paint-box as a Christmas present, and he had started by copying her pictures. He copied them better than anyone could have expected, and presently he did little pictures of his own. Mrs. Carey encouraged him. It was a good way to keep him out of mischief, and later on his sketches would be useful for bazaars. Two or three of them had been framed and hung in his bed-room.

But one day, at the end of the morning's work, Mr. Perkins stopped him as he was lounging out of the form-room.

"I want to speak to you, Carey."

Philip waited. Mr. Perkins ran his lean fingers through his beard and looked at Philip. He seemed to be thinking over what he wanted to say.

"What's the matter with you, Carey?" he said abruptly.

Philip, flushing, looked at him quickly. But knowing him well by now, without answering, he waited for him to go on.

"I've been dissatisfied with you lately. You've been slack and inattentive. You seem to take no interest in your work. It's been slovenly and bad."

"I'm very sorry, sir," said Philip.

"Is that all you have to say for yourself?"

Philip looked down sulkily. How could he answer that he was bored to death?

"You know, this term you'll go down instead of up. I shan't give you a very good report."

Philip wondered what he would say if he knew how the report was treated. It arrived at breakfast, Mr. Carey glanced at it indifferently, and passed it over to Philip.

"There's your report. You'd better see what it says," he remarked, as he ran his fingers through the wrapper of a catalogue of second-hand books.

Philip read it.

"Is it good?" asked Aunt Louisa.

"Not so good as I deserve," answered Philip, with a smile, giving it to her.

"I'll read it afterwards when I've got my spectacles," she said.

But after breakfast Mary Ann came in to say the butcher was there, and she generally forgot.

Mr. Perkins went on.

"I'm disappointed with you. And I can't understand. I know you *can* do things if you want to, but you don't seem to want to anymore. I was going to make you a monitor next term, but I think I'd better wait a bit."

Philip flushed. He did not like the thought of being passed over. He tightened his lips.

"And there's something else. You must begin thinking of your scholarship now. You won't get anything unless you start working very seriously."

Philip was irritated by the lecture. He was angry with the headmaster, and angry with himself.

"I don't think I'm going up to Oxford," he said.

"Why not? I thought your idea was to be ordained."

"I've changed my mind."

"Why?"

Philip did not answer. Mr. Perkins, holding himself oddly as he always did, like a figure in one of Perugino's pictures, drew his fingers thoughtfully through his beard. He looked at Philip as though he were trying to understand and then abruptly told him he might go.

Apparently he was not satisfied, for one evening, a week later, when Philip had to go into his study with some papers, he resumed the conversation; but this time he adopted a different method: he spoke to Philip not as a schoolmaster with a boy but as one human being with another. He did not seem to care now that Philip's work was poor, that he ran small chance against keen rivals of carrying off the scholarship necessary for him to go to Oxford: the important matter was his changed intention about his life afterwards. Mr. Perkins set himself to revive his eagerness to be ordained. With infinite skill he worked on his feelings, and this was easier since he was himself genuinely moved. Philip's change of mind caused him bitter distress, and he really thought he was throwing away his chance of happiness in life for he knew not what. His voice was very persuasive. And Philip, easily moved by the emotion of others, very emotional himself notwithstanding a placid exterior—his face, partly by nature but also from the habit of all these years at school, seldom except by his quick flushing showed what he felt—Philip was deeply touched by what the master said. He was very grateful to him for the interest he showed, and he was conscience-stricken by the grief which he felt his behaviour caused him. It was subtly flattering to know that with the whole school to think about Mr. Perkins should trouble with him, but at the same time something else in him, like another person standing at his elbow, clung desperately to two words.

"I won't. I won't. I won't."

He felt himself slipping. He was powerless against the weakness that seemed to well up in him; it was like the water that rises up in an empty bottle held over a full basin; and he set his teeth, saying the words over and over to himself.

"I won't. I won't. I won't."

At last Mr. Perkins put his hand on Philip's shoulder.

"I don't want to influence you," he said. "You must decide for yourself. Pray to Almighty God for help and guidance."

When Philip came out of the headmaster's house there was a light rain falling. He went under the archway that led to the precincts, there was not a soul there, and the rooks were silent in the elms. He walked round slowly. He felt hot, and the rain did him good. He thought over all that Mr. Perkins had said, calmly now that he was withdrawn from the fervour of his personality, and he was thankful he had not given way.

In the darkness he could but vaguely see the great mass of the Cathedral: he hated it now because of the irksomeness of the long services which he was forced to attend. The anthem was interminable, and you had to stand drearily while it was being sung; you could not hear the droning sermon, and your body twitched because you had to sit still when you wanted to move about. Then Philip thought of the two services every Sunday at Blackstable. The church was bare and cold, and there was a smell all about one of pomade and starched clothes. The curate preached once and his uncle preached once. As he grew up he had learned to know his uncle; Philip was downright and intolerant, and he could not understand that a man might sincerely say things as a clergyman which he never acted up to as a man. The deception outraged him. His uncle was a weak and selfish man, whose chief desire it was to be saved trouble.

Mr. Perkins had spoken to him of the beauty of a life dedicated to the service of God. Philip knew what sort of lives the clergy led in the corner of East Anglia which was his home. There was the Vicar of Whitestone, a parish a little way from Blackstable: he was a bachelor and to give himself something to do had lately taken up farming: the local paper constantly reported the cases he had in the county court against this one and that, labourers he would not pay their wages to or tradesmen whom he accused of cheating him; scandal said he starved his cows, and there was much talk about some general action which should be taken against him. Then there was the Vicar of Ferne, a bearded, fine figure of a man: his wife had been forced to leave him because of his cruelty, and she had filled the neighbourhood with stories of his immorality. The Vicar of Surle, a tiny hamlet by the sea, was to be seen every evening in the public-house a stone's throw from his vicarage; and the churchwardens had been to Mr. Carey to ask his advice. There was not a soul for any of them to talk to except small farmers or fishermen; there were long winter evenings when the wind blew, whistling drearily through the leafless trees, and all around they saw nothing but the bare monotony of ploughed fields; and there was poverty, and there was lack of any work that seemed to matter; every kink in their characters had free play; there was nothing to restrain them; they grew narrow and eccentric: Philip knew all this, but in his young intolerance he did not offer it as an excuse. He shivered at the thought of leading such a life; he wanted to get out into the world.

Chapter XXI

Mr. Perkins soon saw that his words had had no effect on Philip, and for the rest of the term ignored him. He wrote a report which was vitriolic. When it arrived and Aunt Louisa asked Philip what it was like, he answered cheerfully.

"Rotten."

"Is it?" said the Vicar. "I must look at it again."

"Do you think there's any use in my staying on at Tercanbury? I should have thought it would be better if I went to Germany for a bit."

"What has put that in your head?" said Aunt Louisa.

"Don't you think it's rather a good idea?"

Sharp had already left King's School and had written to Philip from Hanover. He was really starting life, and it made Philip more restless to think of it. He felt he could not bear another year of restraint.

"But then you wouldn't get a scholarship."

"I haven't a chance of getting one anyhow. And besides, I don't know that I particularly want to go to Oxford."

"But if you're going to be ordained, Philip?" Aunt Louisa exclaimed in dismay.

"I've given up that idea long ago."

Mrs. Carey looked at him with startled eyes, and then, used to self-restraint, she poured out another cup of tea for his uncle. They did not speak. In a moment Philip saw tears slowly falling down her cheeks. His heart was suddenly wrung because he caused her pain. In her tight black dress, made by the dressmaker down the street, with her wrinkled face and pale tired eyes, her grey hair still done in the frivolous ringlets of her youth, she was a ridiculous but strangely pathetic figure. Philip saw it for the first time.

Afterwards, when the Vicar was shut up in his study with the curate, he put his arms round her waist.

"I say, I'm sorry you're upset, Aunt Louisa," he said. "But it's no good my being ordained if I haven't a real vocation, is it?"

"I'm so disappointed, Philip," she moaned. "I'd set my heart on it. I thought you could be your uncle's curate, and then when our time came—after all, we can't last forever, can we?—you might have taken his place."

Philip shivered. He was seized with panic. His heart beat like a pigeon in a trap beating with its wings. His aunt wept softly, her head upon his shoulder.

"I wish you'd persuade Uncle William to let me leave Tercanbury. I'm so sick of it."

But the Vicar of Blackstable did not easily alter any arrangements he had made, and it had always been intended that Philip should stay at King's School till he was eighteen, and should then go to Oxford. At all events he would not hear of Philip leaving then, for no notice had been given and the term's fee would have to be paid in any case.

"Then will you give notice for me to leave at Christmas?" said Philip, at the end of a long and often bitter conversation.

"I'll write to Mr. Perkins about it and see what he says."

"Oh, I wish to goodness I were twenty-one. It is awful to be at somebody else's beck and call."

"Philip, you shouldn't speak to your uncle like that," said Mrs. Carey gently.

"But don't you see that Perkins will want me to stay? He gets so much a head for every chap in the school."

"Why don't you want to go to Oxford?"

"What's the good if I'm not going into the Church?"

"You can't go into the Church: you're in the Church already," said the Vicar.

"Ordained then," replied Philip impatiently.

"What are you going to be, Philip?" asked Mrs. Carey.

"I don't know. I've not made up my mind. But whatever I am, it'll be useful to know foreign languages. I shall get far more out of a year in Germany than by staying on at that hole."

He would not say that he felt Oxford would be little better than a continuation of his life at school. He wished immensely to be his own master. Besides he would be known to a certain extent among old schoolfellows, and he wanted to get away from them all. He felt that his life at school had been a failure. He wanted to start fresh.

It happened that his desire to go to Germany fell in with certain ideas which had been of late discussed at Blackstable. Sometimes friends came to stay with the doctor and brought news of the world outside; and the visitors spending August by the sea had their own way of looking at things. The Vicar had heard that there were people who did not think the old-fashioned education so useful nowadays as it had been in the past, and modern languages were gaining an importance which they had not had in his own youth. His own mind was divided, for a younger brother of his had been sent to Germany when he failed in some examination, thus creating a precedent but since he had there died of typhoid it was impossible to look upon the experiment as other than dangerous. The result of innumerable conversations was that Philip should go back to Tercanbury for another term, and then should leave.

With this agreement Philip was not dissatisfied. But when he had been back a few days the headmaster spoke to him.

"I've had a letter from your uncle. It appears you want to go to Germany, and he asks me what I think about it."

Philip was astounded. He was furious with his guardian for going back on his word.

"I thought it was settled, sir," he said.

"Far from it. I've written to say I think it the greatest mistake to take you away."

Philip immediately sat down and wrote a violent letter to his uncle. He did not measure his language. He was so angry that he could not get to sleep till quite late that night, and he awoke in the early morning and began brooding over the way they had treated him. He waited impatiently for an answer. In two or three days it came. It was a mild, pained letter from Aunt Louisa, saying that he should not write such things to his uncle, who was very much distressed. He was unkind and unchristian. He must know they were only trying to do their best for him, and they were so much older than he that they must be better judges of what was good for him. Philip clenched his hands. He had heard that statement so often, and he could not see why it was true; they did not know the conditions as he did, why should they accept it as self-evident that their greater age gave them greater wisdom? The letter ended with the information that Mr. Carey had withdrawn the notice he had given.

Philip nursed his wrath till the next half-holiday. They had them on Tuesdays and Thursdays, since on Saturday afternoons they had to go to a service in the Cathedral. He stopped behind when the rest of the Sixth went out.

"May I go to Blackstable this afternoon, please, sir?" he asked.

"No," said the headmaster briefly.

"I wanted to see my uncle about something very important."

"Didn't you hear me say no?"

Philip did not answer. He went out. He felt almost sick with humiliation, the humiliation of having to ask and the humiliation of the curt refusal. He hated the headmaster now. Philip writhed under that despotism which never vouchsafed a reason for the most tyrannous act. He was too angry to care what he did, and after dinner walked down to the station, by the back ways he knew so well, just in time to catch the train to Blackstable. He walked into the vicarage and found his uncle and aunt sitting in the dining-room.

"Hulloa, where have you sprung from?" said the Vicar.

It was very clear that he was not pleased to see him. He looked a little uneasy.

"I thought I'd come and see you about my leaving. I want to know what you mean by promising me one thing when I was here, and doing something different a week after."

He was a little frightened at his own boldness, but he had made up his mind exactly what words to use, and, though his heart beat violently, he forced himself to say them.

"Have you got leave to come here this afternoon?"

"No. I asked Perkins and he refused. If you like to write and tell him I've been here you can get me into a really fine old row."

Mrs. Carey sat knitting with trembling hands. She was unused to scenes and they agitated her extremely.

"It would serve you right if I told him," said Mr. Carey.

"If you like to be a perfect sneak you can. After writing to Perkins as you did you're quite capable of it."

It was foolish of Philip to say that, because it gave the Vicar exactly the opportunity he wanted.

"I'm not going to sit still while you say impertinent things to me," he said with dignity.

He got up and walked quickly out of the room into his study. Philip heard him shut the door and lock it.

"Oh, I wish to God I were twenty-one. It is awful to be tied down like this."

Aunt Louisa began to cry quietly.

"Oh, Philip, you oughtn't to have spoken to your uncle like that. Do please go and tell him you're sorry."

"I'm not in the least sorry. He's taking a mean advantage. Of course it's just waste of money keeping me on at school, but what does he care? It's not his money. It was cruel to put me under the guardianship of people who know nothing about things."

"Philip."

Philip in his voluble anger stopped suddenly at the sound of her voice. It was heart-broken. He had not realised what bitter things he was saying.

"Philip, how can you be so unkind? You know we are only trying to do our best for you, and we know that we have no experience; it isn't as if we'd had any children of our own: that's why we consulted Mr. Perkins." Her voice broke. "I've tried to be like a mother to you. I've loved you as if you were my own son."

She was so small and frail, there was something so pathetic in her old-maidish air, that Philip was touched. A great lump came suddenly in his throat and his eyes filled with tears.

"I'm so sorry," he said. "I didn't mean to be beastly."

He knelt down beside her and took her in his arms, and kissed her wet, withered cheeks. She sobbed bitterly, and he seemed to feel on a sudden the pity of that wasted life. She had never surrendered herself before to such a display of emotion.

"I know I've not been what I wanted to be to you, Philip, but I didn't know how. It's been just as dreadful for me to have no children as for you to have no mother."

Philip forgot his anger and his own concerns, but thought only of consoling her, with broken words and clumsy little caresses. Then the clock struck, and he had to bolt off at once to catch the only train that would get him back to Tercanbury in time for call-over. As he sat in the corner of the railway carriage he saw that he had done nothing. He was angry with himself for his weakness. It was despicable to have allowed himself to be turned from his purpose by the pompous airs of the Vicar and the tears of his aunt. But as the result of he knew not what conversations between the couple another letter was written to the headmaster. Mr. Perkins read it with an impatient shrug of the shoulders. He showed it to Philip. It ran:

DEAR MR. PERKINS—Forgive me for troubling you again about my ward, but both his Aunt and I have been uneasy about him. He seems very anxious to leave school, and his Aunt thinks he is unhappy. It is very difficult for us to know what to do as we are not his parents. He does not seem to think he is doing very well and he feels it is wasting his money to stay on. I should be very much obliged if you would have a talk to him, and if he is still of the same mind perhaps it would be better if he left at Christmas as I originally intended.

Yours very truly,
WILLIAM CAREY

Philip gave him back the letter. He felt a thrill of pride in his triumph. He had got his own way, and he was satisfied. His will had gained a victory over the wills of others.

"It's not much good my spending half an hour writing to your uncle if he changes his mind the next letter he gets from you," said the headmaster irritably.

Philip said nothing, and his face was perfectly placid; but he could not prevent the twinkle in his eyes. Mr. Perkins noticed it and broke into a little laugh.

"You've rather scored, haven't you?" he said.

Then Philip smiled outright. He could not conceal his exultation.

"Is it true that you're very anxious to leave?"

"Yes, sir."

"Are you unhappy here?"

Philip blushed. He hated instinctively any attempt to get into the depths of his feelings.

"Oh, I don't know, sir."

Mr. Perkins, slowly dragging his fingers through his beard, looked at him thoughtfully. He seemed to speak almost to himself.

"Of course schools are made for the average. The holes are all round, and whatever shape the pegs are they must wedge in somehow. One hasn't time to bother about anything but the average." Then suddenly he addressed himself to Philip: "Look here, I've got a suggestion to make to you. It's getting on towards the end of the term now. Another term won't kill you, and if you want to go to Germany you'd better go after Easter than after Christmas. It'll be much pleasanter in the spring than in midwinter. If at the end of the next term you still want to go I'll make no objection. What d'you say to that?"

"Thank you very much, sir."

Philip was so glad to have gained the last three months that he did not mind the extra term. The school seemed less of a prison when he knew that before Easter he would be free from it forever. His heart danced within him. That evening in chapel he looked round at the boys, standing according to their forms, each in his due place, and he chuckled with satisfaction at the thought that soon he would never see them again. It made him regard them almost with a friendly feeling. His eyes rested on Rose. Rose took his position as a monitor very seriously: he had quite an idea of being a good influence in the school; it was his turn to read the lesson that evening, and he read it very well. Philip smiled when he thought that he would be rid of him forever, and it would not matter in six months whether Rose was tall and straight-limbed; and where would the importance be that he was a monitor and captain of the eleven? Philip looked at the masters in their gowns. Gordon was dead, he had died of apoplexy two years before, but all the rest were there. Philip knew now what a poor lot they were, except Turner perhaps, there was something of a man in him; and he writhed at the thought of the subjection in which they had held him. In six months they would not matter either. Their praise would mean nothing to him, and he would shrug his shoulders at their censure.

Philip had learned not to express his emotions by outward signs, and shyness still tormented him, but he had often very high spirits; and then, though he limped about demurely, silent and reserved, it seemed to be hallooing in his heart. He seemed to himself to walk more lightly. All sorts of ideas danced through his head, fancies chased one another so furiously that he could not catch them; but their coming and their going filled him with exhilaration. Now, being happy, he was able to work, and during the remaining weeks of the term set himself to make up for his long neglect. His brain worked easily, and he took a keen pleasure in the activity of his intellect. He did very well in the examinations that closed the term. Mr. Perkins made only one remark: he was talking to him about an essay he had written, and, after the usual criticisms, said:

"So you've made up your mind to stop playing the fool for a bit, have you?"

He smiled at him with his shining teeth, and Philip, looking down, gave an embarrassed smile.

The half dozen boys who expected to divide between them the various prizes which were given at the end of the summer term had ceased to look upon Philip as a serious rival, but now they began to regard him with some uneasiness. He told no one that he was leaving at Easter and so was in no sense a competitor, but left them to their anxieties. He knew that Rose flattered himself on his French, for he had spent two or three holidays in France; and he expected to get the Dean's Prize for English essay; Philip got a good deal of satisfaction in watching his dismay when he saw how much better Philip was doing in these subjects than himself. Another fellow, Norton, could not go to Oxford unless he got one of the scholarships at the disposal of the school. He asked Philip if he was going in for them.

"Have you any objection?" asked Philip.

It entertained him to think that he held someone else's future in his hand. There was something romantic in getting these various rewards actually in his grasp, and then leaving them to others because he disdained them. At last the breaking-up day came, and he went to Mr. Perkins to bid him good-bye.

"You don't mean to say you really want to leave?"

Philip's face fell at the headmaster's evident surprise.

"You said you wouldn't put any objection in the way, sir," he answered.

"I thought it was only a whim that I'd better humour. I know you're obstinate and headstrong. What on earth d'you want to leave for now? You've only got another term in any case. You can get the Magdalen scholarship easily; you'll get half the prizes we've got to give."

Philip looked at him sullenly. He felt that he had been tricked; but he had the promise, and Perkins would have to stand by it.

"You'll have a very pleasant time at Oxford. You needn't decide at once what you're going to do afterwards. I wonder if you realise how delightful the life is up there for anyone who has brains."

"I've made all my arrangements now to go to Germany, sir," said Philip.

"Are they arrangements that couldn't possibly be altered?" asked Mr. Perkins, with his quizzical smile. "I shall be very sorry to lose you. In schools the rather stupid boys who work always do better than the clever boy who's idle, but when the clever boy works—why then, he does what you've done this term."

Philip flushed darkly. He was unused to compliments, and no one had ever told him he was clever. The headmaster put his hand on Philip's shoulder.

"You know, driving things into the heads of thick-witted boys is dull work, but when now and then you have the chance of teaching a boy who comes half-way towards you, who understands almost before you've got the words out of your mouth, why, then teaching is the most exhilarating thing in the world."

Philip was melted by kindness; it had never occurred to him that it mattered really to Mr. Perkins whether he went or stayed. He was touched and immensely flattered. It would be pleasant to end up his school-days with glory and then go to Oxford: in a flash there appeared before him the life which he had heard described from boys who came back to play in the O.K.S. match or in letters from the University read out in one of the studies. But he was ashamed; he would look such a fool in his own eyes if he gave in now; his uncle would chuckle at the success of the headmaster's ruse. It was rather a come-down from the dramatic surrender of all these prizes which were in his reach, because he disdained to take them, to the plain, ordinary winning of them. It only required a little more persuasion, just enough to save his self-respect, and Philip would have done anything that Mr. Perkins wished; but his face showed nothing of his conflicting emotions. It was placid and sullen.

"I think I'd rather go, sir," he said.

Mr. Perkins, like many men who manage things by their personal influence, grew a little impatient when his power was not immediately manifest. He had a great deal of work to do, and could not waste more time on a boy who seemed to him insanely obstinate.

"Very well, I promised to let you if you really wanted it, and I keep my promise. When do you go to Germany?"

Philip's heart beat violently. The battle was won, and he did not know whether he had not rather lost it.

"At the beginning of May, sir," he answered.

"Well, you must come and see us when you get back."

He held out his hand. If he had given him one more chance Philip would have changed his mind, but he seemed to look upon the matter as settled. Philip walked out of the house. His school-days were over, and he was free; but the wild exultation to which he had looked forward at that moment was not there. He walked round the precincts slowly, and a profound depression seized him. He wished now that he had not been foolish. He did not want to go, but he knew he could never bring himself to go to the headmaster and tell him he would stay. That was a humiliation he could never put upon himself. He wondered whether he had done right. He was dissatisfied with himself and with all his circumstances. He asked himself dully whether whenever you got your way you wished afterwards that you hadn't.

Chapter XXII

Philip's uncle had an old friend, called Miss Wilkinson, who lived in Berlin. She was the daughter of a clergyman, and it was with her father, the rector of a village in Lincolnshire, that Mr. Carey had spent his last curacy; on his death, forced to earn her living, she had taken various situations as a governess in France and Germany. She had kept up a correspondence with Mrs. Carey, and two or three times had spent her holidays at Blackstable Vicarage, paying as was usual with the Careys' unfrequent guests a small sum for her keep. When it became clear that it was less trouble to yield to Philip's wishes than to resist them, Mrs. Carey wrote to ask her for advice. Miss Wilkinson recommended Heidelberg as an excellent place to learn German in and the house of Frau Professor Erlin as a comfortable home. Philip might live there for thirty marks a week, and the Professor himself, a teacher at the local high school, would instruct him.

Philip arrived in Heidelberg one morning in May. His things were put on a barrow and he followed the porter out of the station. The sky was bright blue, and the trees in the avenue through which they passed were thick with leaves; there was something in the air fresh to Philip, and mingled with the timidity he felt at entering on a new life, among strangers, was a great exhilaration. He was a little disconsolate that no one had come to meet him, and felt very shy when the porter left him at the front-door of a big white house. An untidy lad let him in and took him into a drawing-room. It was filled with a large suite covered in green velvet, and in the middle was a round table. On this in water stood a bouquet of flowers tightly packed together in a paper frill like the bone of a mutton chop, and carefully spaced round it were books in leather bindings. There was a musty smell.

Presently, with an odour of cooking, the Frau Professor came in, a short, very stout woman with tightly dressed hair and a red face; she had little eyes, sparkling like beads, and an effusive manner. She took both Philip's hands and asked him about Miss Wilkinson, who had twice spent a few weeks with her. She spoke in German and in broken English. Philip could not make her understand that he did not know Miss Wilkinson. Then her two daughters appeared. They seemed hardly young to Philip, but perhaps they were not more than twenty-five: the elder, Thekla, was as short as her mother, with the same, rather shifty air, but with a pretty face and abundant dark hair; Anna, her younger sister, was tall and plain, but since she had a pleasant smile Philip immediately preferred her. After a few minutes of polite conversation the Frau Professor took Philip to his room and left him. It was in a turret, looking over the tops of the trees in the Anlage; and the bed was in an alcove, so that when you sat at the desk it had not the look of a bed-room at all. Philip unpacked his things and set out all his books. He was his own master at last.

A bell summoned him to dinner at one o'clock, and he found the Frau Professor's guests assembled in the drawing-room. He was introduced to her husband, a tall man of middle age with a large fair head, turning now to grey, and mild blue eyes. He spoke to Philip in correct, rather archaic English, having learned it from a study of the English classics, not from conversation; and it was odd to hear him use words colloquially which Philip had only met in the plays of Shakespeare. Frau Professor Erlin called her establishment a family and not a pension; but it would have required the subtlety of a metaphysician to find out exactly where the difference lay. When they sat down to dinner in a long dark apartment that led out of the drawing-room, Philip, feeling very shy, saw that there were sixteen people. The Frau Professor sat at one end and carved. The service was conducted, with a great clattering of plates, by the same clumsy lout who had opened the door for him; and though he was quick, it happened that the first persons to be served had finished before the last had received their appointed portions. The Frau Professor insisted that nothing but German should be spoken, so that Philip, even if his bashfulness had permitted him to be talkative, was forced to hold his tongue. He looked at the people among whom he was to live. By the Frau Professor sat several old ladies, but Philip did not give them much of his attention. There were two young girls, both fair and one of them very pretty, whom Philip heard addressed as Fräulein Hedwig and Fräulein Cäcilie. Fräulein Cäcilie had a long pig-tail hanging down her back. They sat side by side and chattered to one another, with smothered laughter: now and then they glanced at Philip and one of them said something in an undertone; they both giggled, and Philip blushed awkwardly, feeling that they were making fun of him. Near them sat a Chinaman, with a yellow face and an expansive smile, who was studying Western conditions at the University. He spoke so quickly, with a queer accent, that the girls could not always understand him, and then they burst out laughing. He laughed too, good-humouredly, and his almond eyes almost closed as he did so. There were two or three American men, in black coats, rather yellow and dry of skin: they were theological students; Philip heard the twang of their New England accent through their bad German, and he glanced at them with suspicion; for he had been taught to look upon Americans as wild and desperate barbarians.

Afterwards, when they had sat for a little on the stiff green velvet chairs of the drawing-room, Fräulein Anna asked Philip if he would like to go for a walk with them.

Philip accepted the invitation. They were quite a party. There were the two daughters of the Frau Professor, the two other girls, one of the American students, and Philip. Philip walked by the side of Anna and Fräulein Hedwig. He was a little fluttered. He had never known any girls. At Blackstable there were only the farmers' daughters and the girls of the local tradesmen. He knew them by name and by sight, but he was timid, and he thought they laughed at his deformity. He accepted willingly the difference which the Vicar and Mrs. Carey put between their own exalted rank and that of the farmers. The doctor had two daughters, but they were both much older than Philip and had been married to successive assistants while Philip was still a small boy. At school there had been two or three girls of more boldness than modesty whom some of the boys knew; and desperate stories, due in all probability to the masculine imagination, were told of intrigues with them; but Philip had always concealed under a lofty contempt the terror with which they filled him. His imagination and the books he had read had inspired in him a desire for the Byronic attitude; and he was torn between a morbid self-consciousness and a conviction that he owed it to himself to be gallant. He felt now that he should be bright and amusing, but his brain seemed empty and he could not for the life of him think of anything to say. Fräulein Anna, the Frau Professor's daughter, addressed herself to him frequently from a sense of duty, but the other said little: she looked at him now and then with sparkling eyes, and sometimes to his confusion laughed outright. Philip felt that she thought him perfectly ridiculous. They walked along the side of a hill among pine-trees, and their pleasant odour caused Philip a keen delight. The day was warm and cloudless. At last they came to an eminence from which they saw the valley of the Rhine spread out before them under the sun. It was a vast stretch of country, sparkling with golden light, with cities in the distance; and through it meandered the silver ribband of the river. Wide spaces are rare in the corner of Kent which Philip knew, the sea offers the only broad horizon, and the immense distance he saw now gave him a peculiar, an indescribable thrill. He felt suddenly elated. Though he did not know it, it was the first time that he had experienced, quite undiluted with foreign emotions, the sense of beauty. They sat on a bench, the three of them, for the others had gone on, and while the girls talked in rapid German, Philip, indifferent to their proximity, feasted his eyes.

"By Jove, I am happy," he said to himself unconsciously.

Chapter XXIII

PHILIP THOUGHT OCCASIONALLY OF THE KING'S SCHOOL AT TERCANBURY, and laughed to himself as he remembered what at some particular moment of the day they were doing. Now and then he dreamed that he was there still, and it gave him an extraordinary satisfaction, on awaking, to realise that he was in his little room in the turret. From his bed he could see the great cumulus clouds that hung in the blue sky. He revelled in his freedom. He could go to bed when he chose and get up when the fancy took him. There was no one to order him about. It struck him that he need not tell any more lies.

It had been arranged that Professor Erlin should teach him Latin and German; a Frenchman came every day to give him lessons in French; and the Frau Professor had recommended for mathematics an Englishman who was taking a philological degree at the University. This was a man named Wharton. Philip went to him every morning. He lived in one room on the top floor of a shabby house. It was dirty and untidy, and it was filled with a pungent odour made up of many different stinks. He was generally in bed when Philip arrived at ten o'clock, and he jumped out, put on a filthy dressing-gown and felt slippers, and, while he gave instruction, ate his simple breakfast. He was a short man, stout from excessive beer drinking, with a heavy moustache and long, unkempt hair. He had been in Germany for five years and was become very Teutonic. He spoke with scorn of Cambridge where he had taken his degree and with horror of the life which awaited him when, having taken his doctorate in Heidelberg, he must return to England and a pedagogic career. He adored the life of the German University with its happy freedom and its jolly companionships. He was a member of a *Burschenschaft*, and promised to take Philip to a *Kneipe*. He was very poor and made no secret that the lessons he was giving Philip meant the difference between meat for his dinner and bread and cheese. Sometimes after a heavy night he had such a headache that he could not drink his coffee, and he gave his lesson with heaviness of spirit. For these occasions he kept a few bottles of beer under the bed, and one of these and a pipe would help him to bear the burden of life.

"A hair of the dog that bit him," he would say as he poured out the beer, carefully so that the foam should not make him wait too long to drink.

Then he would talk to Philip of the University, the quarrels between rival corps, the duels, and the merits of this and that professor. Philip learned more of life from him than of mathematics. Sometimes Wharton would sit back with a laugh and say:

"Look here, we've not done anything today. You needn't pay me for the lesson."

"Oh, it doesn't matter," said Philip.

This was something new and very interesting, and he felt that it was of greater import than trigonometry, which he never could understand. It was like a window on life that he had a chance of peeping through, and he looked with a wildly beating heart.

"No, you can keep your dirty money," said Wharton.

"But how about your dinner?" said Philip, with a smile, for he knew exactly how his master's finances stood.

Wharton had even asked him to pay him the two shillings which the lesson cost once a week rather than once a month, since it made things less complicated.

"Oh, never mind my dinner. It won't be the first time I've dined off a bottle of beer, and my mind's never clearer than when I do."

He dived under the bed (the sheets were grey with want of washing), and fished out another bottle. Philip, who was young and did not know the good things of life, refused to share it with him, so he drank alone.

"How long are you going to stay here?" asked Wharton.

Both he and Philip had given up with relief the pretence of mathematics.

"Oh, I don't know. I suppose about a year. Then my people want me to go to Oxford."

Wharton gave a contemptuous shrug of the shoulders. It was a new experience for Philip to learn that there were persons who did not look upon that seat of learning with awe.

"What d'you want to go there for? You'll only be a glorified schoolboy. Why don't you matriculate here? A year's no good. Spend five years here. You know, there are two good things in life, freedom of thought and freedom of action. In France you get freedom of action: you can do what you like and nobody bothers, but you must think like everybody else. In Germany you must do what everybody else does, but you may think as you choose. They're both very good things. I personally prefer freedom of thought. But in England you get neither: you're ground down by convention. You can't think as you like and you can't act as you like. That's because it's a democratic nation. I expect America's worse."

He leaned back cautiously, for the chair on which he sat had a ricketty leg, and it was disconcerting when a rhetorical flourish was interrupted by a sudden fall to the floor.

"I ought to go back to England this year, but if I can scrape together enough to keep body and soul on speaking terms I shall stay another twelve months. But then I shall have to go. And I must leave all this"—he waved his arm round the dirty garret, with its unmade bed, the clothes lying on the floor, a row of empty beer bottles against the wall, piles of unbound, ragged books in every corner—"for some provincial university where I shall try and get a chair of philology. And I shall play tennis and go to tea-parties." He interrupted himself and gave Philip, very neatly dressed, with a clean collar on and his hair well-brushed, a quizzical look. "And, my God! I shall have to wash."

Philip reddened, feeling his own spruceness an intolerable reproach; for of late he had begun to pay some attention to his toilet, and he had come out from England with a pretty selection of ties.

The summer came upon the country like a conqueror. Each day was beautiful. The sky had an arrogant blue which goaded the nerves like a spur. The green of the trees in the Anlage was violent and crude; and the houses, when the sun caught them, had a dazzling white which stimulated till it hurt. Sometimes on his way back from Wharton Philip would sit in the shade on one of the benches in the Anlage, enjoying the coolness and watching the patterns of light which the sun, shining through the leaves, made on the ground. His soul danced with delight as gaily as the sunbeams. He revelled in those moments of idleness stolen from his work. Sometimes he sauntered through the streets of the old town. He looked with awe at the students of the corps, their cheeks gashed and red, who swaggered about in their coloured caps. In the afternoons he wandered about the hills with the girls in the Frau Professor's house, and sometimes they went up the river and had tea in a leafy beer-garden. In the evenings they walked round and round the Stadtgarten, listening to the band.

Philip soon learned the various interests of the household. Fräulein Thekla, the professor's elder daughter, was engaged to a man in England who had spent twelve months in the house to learn German, and their marriage was to take place at the end of the year. But the young man wrote that his father, an india-rubber merchant who lived in Slough, did not approve of the union, and Fräulein Thekla was often in tears. Sometimes she and her mother might be seen, with stern eyes and determined mouths, looking over the letters of the reluctant lover. Thekla painted in water colour, and occasionally she and Philip, with another of the girls to keep them company, would go out and paint little pictures. The pretty Fräulein Hedwig had amorous troubles too. She was the daughter of a merchant in Berlin and a dashing hussar had fallen in love with her, a *von* if you please; but his parents opposed a marriage with a person of her condition, and she had been sent to Heidelberg to forget him. She could never, never do this, and corresponded with him continually, and he was making every effort to induce an exasperating father to change his mind. She told all this to Philip with pretty sighs and becoming blushes, and showed him the photograph of the gay lieutenant. Philip liked her best of all the girls at the Frau Professor's, and on their walks always tried to get by her side. He blushed a great deal when the others chaffed him for his obvious preference. He made the first declaration in his life to Fräulein Hedwig, but unfortunately it was an accident, and it happened in this manner. In the evenings when they did not go out, the young women sang little songs in the green velvet drawing-room, while Fräulein Anna, who always made herself useful, industriously accompanied. Fräulein Hedwig's favourite song was called *Ich liebe dich*, I love you; and one evening after she had sung this, when Philip was standing with her on the balcony, looking at the stars, it occurred to him to make some remark about it. He began:

"*Ich liebe dich.*"

His German was halting, and he looked about for the word he wanted. The pause was infinitesimal, but before he could go on Fräulein Hedwig said:

"*Ach, Herr Carey, Sie müssen mir nicht du sagen*—you mustn't talk to me in the second person singular."

Philip felt himself grow hot all over, for he would never have dared to do anything so familiar, and he could think of nothing on earth to say. It would be ungallant to explain that he was not making an observation, but merely mentioning the title of a song.

"*Entschuldigen Sie,*" he said. "I beg your pardon."

"It does not matter," she whispered.

She smiled pleasantly, quietly took his hand and pressed it, then turned back into the drawing-room.

Next day he was so embarrassed that he could not speak to her, and in his shyness did all that was possible to avoid her. When he was asked to go for the usual walk he refused because, he said, he had work to do. But Fräulein Hedwig seized an opportunity to speak to him alone.

"Why are you behaving in this way?" she said kindly. "You know, I'm not angry with you for what you said last night. You can't help it if you love me. I'm flattered. But although I'm not exactly engaged to Hermann I can never love anyone else, and I look upon myself as his bride."

Philip blushed again, but he put on quite the expression of a rejected lover.

"I hope you'll be very happy," he said.

Chapter XXIV

PROFESSOR ERLIN GAVE PHILIP A LESSON EVERY DAY. HE MADE OUT A LIST OF books which Philip was to read till he was ready for the final achievement of *Faust*, and meanwhile, ingeniously enough, started him on a German translation of one of the plays by Shakespeare which Philip had studied at school. It was the period in Germany of Goethe's highest fame. Notwithstanding his rather condescending attitude towards patriotism he had been adopted as the national poet, and seemed since the war of seventy to be one of the most significant glories of national unity. The enthusiastic seemed in the wildness of the *Walpurgisnacht* to hear the rattle of artillery at Gravelotte. But one mark of a writer's greatness is that different minds can find in him different inspirations; and Professor Erlin, who hated the Prussians, gave his enthusiastic admiration to Goethe because his works, Olympian and sedate, offered the only refuge for a sane mind against the onslaughts of the present generation. There was a dramatist whose name of late had been much heard at Heidelberg, and the winter before one of his plays had been given at the theatre amid the cheers of adherents and the hisses of decent people. Philip heard discussions about it at the Frau Professor's long table, and at these Professor Erlin lost his wonted calm: he beat the table with his fist, and drowned all opposition with the roar of his fine deep voice. It was nonsense and obscene nonsense. He forced himself to sit the play out, but he did not know whether he was more bored or nauseated. If that was what the theatre was coming to, then it was high time the police stepped in and closed the playhouses. He was no prude and could laugh as well as anyone at the witty immorality of a farce at the Palais Royal, but here was nothing but filth. With an emphatic gesture he held his nose and whistled through his teeth. It was the ruin of the family, the uprooting of morals, the destruction of Germany.

"*Aber, Adolf,*" said the Frau Professor from the other end of the table. "Calm yourself."

He shook his fist at her. He was the mildest of creatures and ventured upon no action of his life without consulting her.

"No, Helene, I tell you this," he shouted. "I would sooner my daughters were lying dead at my feet than see them listening to the garbage of that shameless fellow."

The play was *The Doll's House* and the author was Henrik Ibsen.

Professor Erlin classed him with Richard Wagner, but of him he spoke not with anger but with good-humoured laughter. He was a charlatan but a successful charlatan, and in that was always something for the comic spirit to rejoice in.

"*Verrückter Kerl!* A madman!" he said.

He had seen *Lohengrin* and that passed muster. It was dull but no worse. But *Siegfried!* When he mentioned it Professor Erlin leaned his head on his hand and bellowed with laughter. Not a melody in it from beginning to end! He could imagine Richard Wagner sitting in his box and laughing till his sides ached at the sight of all the people who were taking it seriously. It was the greatest hoax of the nineteenth century. He lifted his glass of beer to his lips, threw back his head, and drank till the glass was empty. Then wiping his mouth with the back of his hand, he said:

"I tell you young people that before the nineteenth century is out Wagner will be as dead as mutton. Wagner! I would give all his works for one opera by Donizetti."

Chapter XXV

THE ODDEST OF PHILIP'S MASTERS WAS HIS TEACHER OF FRENCH. MONSIEUR Ducroz was a citizen of Geneva. He was a tall old man, with a sallow skin and hollow cheeks; his grey hair was thin and long. He wore shabby black clothes, with holes at the elbows of his coat and frayed trousers. His linen was very dirty. Philip had never seen him in a clean collar. He was a man of few words, who gave his lesson conscientiously but without enthusiasm, arriving as the clock struck and leaving on the minute. His charges were very small. He was taciturn, and what Philip learned about him he learned from others: it appeared that he had fought with Garibaldi against the Pope, but had left Italy in disgust when it was clear that all his efforts for freedom, by which he meant the establishment of a republic, tended to no more than an exchange of yokes; he had been expelled from Geneva for it was not known what political offences. Philip looked upon him with puzzled surprise; for he was very unlike his idea of the revolutionary: he spoke in a low voice and was extraordinarily polite; he never sat down till he was asked to; and when on rare occasions he met Philip in the street took off his hat with an elaborate gesture; he never laughed, he never even smiled. A more complete imagination than Philip's might have pictured a youth of splendid hope, for he must have been entering upon manhood in 1848 when kings, remembering their brother of France, went about with an uneasy crick in their necks; and perhaps that passion for liberty which passed through Europe, sweeping before it what of absolutism and tyranny had reared its head during the reaction from the revolution of 1789, filled no breast with a hotter fire. One might fancy him, passionate with theories of human equality and human rights, discussing, arguing, fighting behind barricades in Paris, flying before the Austrian cavalry in Milan, imprisoned here, exiled from there, hoping on and upborne ever with the word which seemed so magical, the word Liberty; till at last, broken with disease and starvation, old, without means to keep body and soul together but such lessons as he could pick up from poor students, he found himself in that little neat town under the heel of a personal tyranny greater than any in Europe. Perhaps his taciturnity hid a contempt for the human race which had abandoned the great dreams of his youth and now wallowed in sluggish ease; or perhaps these thirty years of revolution had taught him that men are unfit for liberty, and he thought that he had spent his life in the pursuit of that which was not worth the finding. Or maybe he was tired out and waited only with indifference for the release of death.

One day Philip, with the bluntness of his age, asked him if it was true he had been with Garibaldi. The old man did not seem to attach any importance to the question. He answered quite quietly in as low a voice as usual.

"*Oui, monsieur.*"

"They say you were in the Commune?"

"Do they? Shall we get on with our work?"

He held the book open and Philip, intimidated, began to translate the passage he had prepared.

One day Monsieur Ducroz seemed to be in great pain. He had been scarcely able to drag himself up the many stairs to Philip's room; and when he arrived sat down heavily, his sallow face drawn, with beads of sweat on his forehead, trying to recover himself.

"I'm afraid you're ill," said Philip.

"It's of no consequence."

But Philip saw that he was suffering, and at the end of the hour asked whether he would not prefer to give no more lessons till he was better.

"No," said the old man, in his even low voice. "I prefer to go on while I am able."

Philip, morbidly nervous when he had to make any reference to money, reddened.

"But it won't make any difference to you," he said. "I'll pay for the lessons just the same. If you wouldn't mind I'd like to give you the money for next week in advance."

Monsieur Ducroz charged eighteen pence an hour. Philip took a ten-mark piece out of his pocket and shyly put it on the table. He could not bring himself to offer it as if the old man were a beggar.

"In that case I think I won't come again till I'm better." He took the coin and, without anything more than the elaborate bow with which he always took his leave, went out.

"*Bonjour, monsieur.*"

Philip was vaguely disappointed. Thinking he had done a generous thing, he had expected that Monsieur Ducroz would overwhelm him with expressions of gratitude. He was taken aback to find that the old teacher accepted the present as though it were his due. He was so young, he did not realise how much less is the sense of obligation in those who receive favours than in those who grant them. Monsieur Ducroz appeared again five or six days later. He tottered a little more and was very weak, but seemed to have overcome the severity of the attack. He was no more communicative than he had been before. He remained mysterious, aloof, and dirty. He made no reference to his illness till after the lesson; and then, just as he was leaving, at the door, which he held open, he paused. He hesitated, as though to speak were difficult.

"If it hadn't been for the money you gave me I should have starved. It was all I had to live on."

He made his solemn, obsequious bow, and went out. Philip felt a little lump in his throat. He seemed to realise in a fashion the hopeless bitterness of the old man's struggle, and how hard life was for him when to himself it was so pleasant.

Chapter XXVI

PHILIP HAD SPENT THREE MONTHS IN HEIDELBERG WHEN ONE MORNING THE Frau Professor told him that an Englishman named Hayward was coming to stay in the house, and the same evening at supper he saw a new face. For some days the family had lived in a state of excitement. First, as the result of heaven knows what scheming, by dint of humble prayers and veiled threats, the parents of the young Englishman to whom Fräulein Thekla was engaged had invited her to visit them in England, and she had set off with an album of water colours to show how accomplished she was and a bundle of letters to prove how deeply the young man had compromised himself. A week later Fräulein Hedwig with radiant smiles announced that the lieutenant of her affections was coming to Heidelberg with his father and mother. Exhausted by the importunity of their son and touched by the dowry which Fräulein Hedwig's father offered, the lieutenant's parents had consented to pass through Heidelberg to make the young woman's acquaintance. The interview was satisfactory and Fräulein Hedwig had the satisfaction of showing her lover in the Stadtgarten to the whole of Frau Professor Erlin's household. The silent old ladies who sat at the top of the table near the Frau Professor were in a flutter, and when Fräulein Hedwig said she was to go home at once for the formal engagement to take place, the Frau Professor, regardless of expense, said she would give a *Maibowle*. Professor Erlin prided himself on his skill in preparing this mild intoxicant, and after supper the large bowl of hock and soda, with scented herbs floating in it and wild strawberries, was placed with solemnity on the round table in the drawing-room. Fräulein Anna teazed Philip about the departure of his lady-love, and he felt very uncomfortable and rather melancholy. Fräulein Hedwig sang several songs, Fräulein Anna played the *Wedding March*, and the Professor sang *Die Wacht am Rhein*. Amid all this jollification Philip paid little attention to the new arrival. They had sat opposite one another at supper, but Philip was chattering busily with Fräulein Hedwig, and the stranger, knowing no German, had eaten his food in silence. Philip, observing that he wore a pale blue tie, had on that account taken a sudden dislike to him. He was a man of twenty-six, very fair, with long, wavy hair through which he passed his hand frequently with a careless gesture. His eyes were large and blue, but the blue was very pale, and they looked rather tired already. He was clean-shaven, and his mouth, notwithstanding its thin lips, was well-shaped. Fräulein Anna took an interest in physiognomy, and she made Philip notice afterwards how finely shaped was his skull, and how weak was the lower part of his face. The head, she remarked, was the head of a thinker, but the jaw lacked character. Fräulein Anna, foredoomed to a spinster's life, with her high cheek-bones and large misshapen nose, laid great stress upon character. While they talked of him he stood a little apart from the others, watching the noisy party with a good-humoured but faintly supercilious expression. He was tall and slim. He held himself with a deliberate grace. Weeks, one of the American students, seeing him alone, went up and began to talk to him. The pair were oddly contrasted: the American very neat in his black coat and pepper-and-salt trousers, thin and dried-up, with something of ecclesiastical unction already in his manner; and the Englishman in his loose tweed suit, large-limbed and slow of gesture.

Philip did not speak to the new-comer till next day. They found themselves alone on the balcony of the drawing-room before dinner. Hayward addressed him.

"You're English, aren't you?"

"Yes."

"Is the food always as bad as it was last night?"

"It's always about the same."

"Beastly, isn't it?"

"Beastly."

Philip had found nothing wrong with the food at all, and in fact had eaten it in large quantities with appetite and enjoyment, but he did not want to show himself a person of so little discrimination as to think a dinner good which another thought execrable.

Fräulein Thekla's visit to England made it necessary for her sister to do more in the house, and she could not often spare the time for long walks; and Fräulein Cäcilie, with her long plait of fair hair and her little snub-nosed face, had of late shown a certain disinclination for society. Fräulein Hedwig was gone, and Weeks, the American who generally accompanied them on their rambles, had set out for a tour of South Germany. Philip was left a good deal to himself. Hayward sought his acquaintance; but Philip had an unfortunate trait: from shyness or from some atavistic inheritance of the cave-dweller, he always disliked people on first acquaintance; and it was not till he became used to them that he got over his first impression. It made him difficult of access. He received Hayward's advances very shyly, and when Hayward asked him one day to go for a walk he accepted only because he could not think of a civil excuse. He made his usual apology, angry with himself for the flushing cheeks he could not control, and trying to carry it off with a laugh.

"I'm afraid I can't walk very fast."

"Good heavens, I don't walk for a wager. I prefer to stroll. Don't you remember the chapter in *Marius* where Pater talks of the gentle exercise of walking as the best incentive to conversation?"

Philip was a good listener; though he often thought of clever things to say, it was seldom till after the opportunity to say them had passed; but Hayward was communicative; anyone more experienced than Philip might have thought he liked to hear himself talk. His supercilious attitude impressed Philip. He could not help admiring, and yet being awed by, a man who faintly despised so many things which Philip had looked upon as almost sacred. He cast down the fetish of exercise, damning with the contemptuous word pot-hunters all those who devoted themselves to its various forms; and Philip did not realise that he was merely putting up in its stead the other fetish of culture.

They wandered up to the castle, and sat on the terrace that overlooked the town. It nestled in the valley along the pleasant Neckar with a comfortable friendliness. The smoke from the chimneys hung over it, a pale blue haze; and the tall roofs, the spires of the churches, gave it a pleasantly mediaeval air. There was a homeliness in it which warmed the heart. Hayward talked of *Richard Feverel* and *Madame Bovary*, of Verlaine, Dante, and Matthew Arnold. In those days Fitzgerald's translation of Omar Khayyam was known only to the elect, and Hayward repeated it to Philip. He was very fond of reciting poetry, his own and that of others, which he did in a monotonous sing-song. By the time they reached home Philip's distrust of Hayward was changed to enthusiastic admiration.

They made a practice of walking together every afternoon, and Philip learned presently something of Hayward's circumstances. He was the son of a country judge, on whose death some time before he had inherited three hundred a year. His record at Charterhouse was so brilliant that when he went to Cambridge the Master of Trinity Hall went out of his way to express his satisfaction that he was going to that college. He prepared himself for a distinguished career. He moved in the most intellectual circles; he read Browning with enthusiasm and turned up his well-shaped nose at Tennyson; he knew all the details of Shelley's treatment of Harriet; he dabbled in the history of art (on the walls of his rooms were reproductions of pictures by G. F. Watts, Burne-Jones, and Botticelli); and he wrote not without distinction verses of a pessimistic character. His friends told one another that he was a man of excellent gifts, and he listened to them willingly when they prophesied his future eminence. In course of time he became an authority on art and literature. He came under the influence of Newman's *Apologia*; the picturesqueness of the Roman Catholic faith appealed to his aesthetic sensibility; and it was only the fear of his father's wrath (a plain, blunt man of narrow ideas, who read Macaulay) which prevented him from "going over." When he only got a pass degree his friends were astonished; but he shrugged his shoulders and delicately insinuated that he was not the dupe of examiners. He made one feel that a first class was ever so slightly vulgar. He described one of the vivas with tolerant humour; some fellow in an outrageous collar was asking him questions in logic; it was infinitely tedious, and suddenly he noticed that he wore elastic-sided boots: it was grotesque and ridiculous; so he withdrew his mind and thought of the Gothic beauty of the Chapel at King's. But he had spent some delightful days at Cambridge; he had given better dinners than anyone he knew; and the conversation in his rooms had been often memorable. He quoted to Philip the exquisite epigram:

"They told me, Herakleitus, they told me you were dead."

And now, when he related again the picturesque little anecdote about the examiner and his boots, he laughed.

"Of course it was folly," he said, "but it was a folly in which there was something fine."

Philip, with a little thrill, thought it magnificent.

Then Hayward went to London to read for the Bar. He had charming rooms in Clement's Inn, with panelled walls, and he tried to make them look like his old rooms at the Hall. He had ambitions that were vaguely political, he described himself as a Whig, and he was put up for a club which was of Liberal but gentlemanly flavour. His idea was to practise at the Bar (he chose the Chancery side as less brutal), and get a seat for some pleasant constituency as soon as the various promises made him were carried out; meanwhile he went a great deal to the opera, and made acquaintance with a small number of charming people who admired the things that he admired. He joined a dining-club of which the motto was, The Whole, The Good, and The Beautiful. He formed a platonic friendship with a lady some years older than himself, who lived in Kensington Square; and nearly every afternoon he drank tea with her by the light of shaded candles, and talked of George Meredith and Walter Pater. It was notorious that any fool could pass the examinations of the Bar Council, and he pursued his studies in a dilatory fashion. When he was ploughed for his final he looked upon it as a personal affront. At the same time the lady in Kensington Square told him that her husband was coming home from India on leave, and was a man, though worthy in every way, of a commonplace mind, who would not understand a young man's frequent visits. Hayward felt that life was full of ugliness, his soul revolted from the thought of affronting again the cynicism of examiners, and he saw something rather splendid in kicking away the ball which lay at his feet. He was also a good deal in debt: it was difficult to live in London like a gentleman on three hundred a year; and his heart yearned for the Venice and Florence which John Ruskin had so magically described. He felt that he was unsuited to the vulgar bustle of the Bar, for he had discovered that it was not sufficient to put your name on a door to get briefs; and modern politics seemed to lack nobility. He felt himself a poet. He disposed of his rooms in Clement's Inn and went to Italy. He had spent a winter in Florence and a winter in Rome, and now was passing his second summer abroad in Germany so that he might read Goethe in the original.

Hayward had one gift which was very precious. He had a real feeling for literature, and he could impart his own passion with an admirable fluency. He could throw himself into sympathy with a writer and see all that was best in him, and then he could talk about him with understanding. Philip had read a great deal, but he had read without discrimination everything that he happened to come across, and it was very good for him now to meet someone who could guide his taste. He borrowed books from the small lending library which the town possessed and began reading all the wonderful things that Hayward spoke of. He did not read always with enjoyment but invariably with perseverance. He was eager for self-improvement. He felt himself very ignorant and very humble. By the end of August, when Weeks returned from South Germany, Philip was completely under Hayward's influence. Hayward did not like Weeks. He deplored the American's black coat and pepper-and-salt trousers, and spoke with a scornful shrug of his New England conscience. Philip listened complacently to the abuse of a man who had gone out of his way to be kind to him, but when Weeks in his turn made disagreeable remarks about Hayward he lost his temper.

"Your new friend looks like a poet," said Weeks, with a thin smile on his careworn, bitter mouth.

"He is a poet."

"Did he tell you so? In America we should call him a pretty fair specimen of a waster."

"Well, we're not in America," said Philip frigidly.

"How old is he? Twenty-five? And he does nothing but stay in pensions and write poetry."

"You don't know him," said Philip hotly.

"Oh yes, I do: I've met a hundred and forty-seven of him."

Weeks' eyes twinkled, but Philip, who did not understand American humour, pursed his lips and looked severe. Weeks to Philip seemed a man of middle age, but he was in point of fact little more than thirty. He had a long, thin body and the scholar's stoop; his head was large and ugly; he had pale scanty hair and an earthy skin; his thin mouth and thin, long nose, and the great protuberance of his frontal bones, gave him an uncouth look. He was cold and precise in his manner, a bloodless man, without passion; but he had a curious vein of frivolity which disconcerted the serious-minded among whom his instincts naturally threw him. He was studying theology in Heidelberg, but the other theological students of his own nationality looked upon him with suspicion. He was very unorthodox, which frightened them; and his freakish humour excited their disapproval.

"How can you have known a hundred and forty-seven of him?" asked Philip seriously.

"I've met him in the Latin Quarter in Paris, and I've met him in pensions in Berlin and Munich. He lives in small hotels in Perugia and Assisi. He stands by the dozen before the Botticellis in Florence, and he sits on all the benches of the Sistine Chapel in Rome. In Italy he drinks a little too much wine, and in Germany he drinks a great deal too much beer. He always admires the right thing whatever the right thing is, and one of these days he's going to write a great work. Think of it, there are a hundred and forty-seven great works reposing in the bosoms of a hundred and forty-seven great men, and the tragic thing is that not one of those hundred and forty-seven great works will ever be written. And yet the world goes on."

Weeks spoke seriously, but his grey eyes twinkled a little at the end of his long speech, and Philip flushed when he saw that the American was making fun of him.

"You do talk rot," he said crossly.

Chapter XXVII

WEEKS HAD TWO LITTLE ROOMS AT THE BACK OF FRAU ERLIN'S HOUSE, and one of them, arranged as a parlour, was comfortable enough for him to invite people to sit in. After supper, urged perhaps by the impish humour which was the despair of his friends in Cambridge, Mass., he often asked Philip and Hayward to come in for a chat. He received them with elaborate courtesy and insisted on their sitting in the only two comfortable chairs in the room. Though he did not drink himself, with a politeness of which Philip recognised the irony, he put a couple of bottles of beer at Hayward's elbow, and he insisted on lighting matches whenever in the heat of argument Hayward's pipe went out. At the beginning of their acquaintance Hayward, as a member of so celebrated a university, had adopted a patronising attitude towards Weeks, who was a graduate of Harvard; and when by chance the conversation turned upon the Greek tragedians, a subject upon which Hayward felt he spoke with authority, he had assumed the air that it was his part to give information rather than to exchange ideas. Weeks had listened politely, with smiling modesty, till Hayward finished; then he asked one or two insidious questions, so innocent in appearance that Hayward, not seeing into what a quandary they led him, answered blandly; Weeks made a courteous objection, then a correction of fact, after that a quotation from some little known Latin commentator, then a reference to a German authority; and the fact was disclosed that he was a scholar. With smiling ease, apologetically, Weeks tore to pieces all that Hayward had said; with elaborate civility he displayed the superficiality of his attainments. He mocked him with gentle irony. Philip could not help seeing that Hayward looked a perfect fool, and Hayward had not the sense to hold his tongue; in his irritation, his self-assurance undaunted, he attempted to argue: he made wild statements and Weeks amicably corrected them; he reasoned falsely and Weeks proved that he was absurd: Weeks confessed that he had taught Greek Literature at Harvard. Hayward gave a laugh of scorn.

"I might have known it. Of course you read Greek like a schoolmaster," he said. "I read it like a poet."

"And do you find it more poetic when you don't quite know what it means? I thought it was only in revealed religion that a mistranslation improved the sense."

At last, having finished the beer, Hayward left Weeks' room hot and dishevelled; with an angry gesture he said to Philip:

"Of course the man's a pedant. He has no real feeling for beauty. Accuracy is the virtue of clerks. It's the spirit of the Greeks that we aim at. Weeks is like that fellow who went to hear Rubinstein and complained that he played false notes. False notes! What did they matter when he played divinely?"

Philip, not knowing how many incompetent people have found solace in these false notes, was much impressed.

Hayward could never resist the opportunity which Weeks offered him of regaining ground lost on a previous occasion, and Weeks was able with the greatest ease to draw him into a discussion. Though he could not help seeing how small his attainments were beside the American's, his British pertinacity, his wounded vanity (perhaps they are the same thing), would not allow him to give up the struggle. Hayward seemed to take a delight in displaying his ignorance, self-satisfaction, and wrongheadedness. Whenever Hayward said something which was illogical, Weeks in a few words would show the falseness of his reasoning, pause for a moment to enjoy his triumph, and then hurry on to another subject as though Christian charity impelled him to spare the vanquished foe. Philip tried sometimes to put in something to help his friend, and Weeks gently crushed him, but so kindly, differently from the way in which he answered Hayward, that even Philip, outrageously sensitive, could not feel hurt. Now and then, losing his calm as he felt himself more and more foolish, Hayward became abusive, and only the American's smiling politeness prevented the argument from degenerating into a quarrel. On these occasions when Hayward left Weeks' room he muttered angrily:

"Damned Yankee!"

That settled it. It was a perfect answer to an argument which had seemed unanswerable.

Though they began by discussing all manner of subjects in Weeks' little room eventually the conversation always turned to religion: the theological student took a professional interest in it, and Hayward welcomed a subject in which hard facts need not disconcert him; when feeling is the gauge you can snap your angers at logic, and when your logic is weak that is very agreeable. Hayward found it difficult to explain his beliefs to Philip without a great flow of words; but it was clear (and this fell in with Philip's idea of the natural order of things), that he had been brought up in the church by law established. Though he had now given up all idea of becoming a Roman Catholic, he still looked upon that communion with sympathy. He had much to say in its praise, and he compared favourably its gorgeous ceremonies with the simple services of the Church of England. He gave Philip Newman's *Apologia* to read, and Philip, finding it very dull, nevertheless read it to the end.

"Read it for its style, not for its matter," said Hayward.

He talked enthusiastically of the music at the Oratory, and said charming things about the connection between incense and the devotional spirit. Weeks listened to him with his frigid smile.

"You think it proves the truth of Roman Catholicism that John Henry Newman wrote good English and that Cardinal Manning has a picturesque appearance?"

Hayward hinted that he had gone through much trouble with his soul. For a year he had swum in a sea of darkness. He passed his fingers through his fair, waving hair and told them that he would not for five hundred pounds endure again those agonies of mind. Fortunately he had reached calm waters at last.

"But what *do* you believe?" asked Philip, who was never satisfied with vague statements.

"I believe in the Whole, the Good, and the Beautiful."

Hayward with his loose large limbs and the fine carriage of his head looked very handsome when he said this, and he said it with an air.

"Is that how you would describe your religion in a census paper?" asked Weeks, in mild tones.

"I hate the rigid definition: it's so ugly, so obvious. If you like I will say that I believe in the church of the Duke of Wellington and Mr. Gladstone."

"That's the Church of England," said Philip.

"Oh wise young man!" retorted Hayward, with a smile which made Philip blush, for he felt that in putting into plain words what the other had expressed in a paraphrase, he had been guilty of vulgarity. "I belong to the Church of England. But I love the gold and the silk which clothe the priest of Rome, and his celibacy, and the confessional, and purgatory; and in the darkness of an Italian cathedral, incense-laden and mysterious, I believe with all my heart in the miracle of the Mass. In Venice I have seen a fisherwoman come in, barefoot, throw down her basket of fish by her side, fall on her knees, and pray to the Madonna; and that I felt was the real faith, and I prayed and believed with her. But I believe also in Aphrodite and Apollo and the Great God Pan."

He had a charming voice, and he chose his words as he spoke; he uttered them almost rhythmically. He would have gone on, but Weeks opened a second bottle of beer.

"Let me give you something to drink."

Hayward turned to Philip with the slightly condescending gesture which so impressed the youth.

"Now are you satisfied?" he asked.

Philip, somewhat bewildered, confessed that he was.

"I'm disappointed that you didn't add a little Buddhism," said Weeks. "And I confess I have a sort of sympathy for Mahomet, I regret that you should have left him out in the cold."

Hayward laughed, for he was in a good humour with himself that evening, and the ring of his sentences still sounded pleasant in his ears. He emptied his glass.

"I didn't expect you to understand me," he answered. "With your cold American intelligence you can only adopt the critical attitude. Emerson and all that sort of thing. But what is criticism? Criticism is purely destructive; anyone can destroy, but not everyone can build up. You are a pedant, my dear fellow. The important thing is to construct: I am constructive; I am a poet."

Weeks looked at him with eyes which seemed at the same time to be quite grave and yet to be smiling brightly.

"I think, if you don't mind my saying so, you're a little drunk."

"Nothing to speak of," answered Hayward cheerfully. "And not enough for me to be unable to overwhelm you in argument. But come, I have unbosomed my soul; now tell us what your religion is."

Weeks put his head on one side so that he looked like a sparrow on a perch.

"I've been trying to find that out for years. I think I'm a Unitarian."

"But that's a dissenter," said Philip.

He could not imagine why they both burst into laughter, Hayward uproariously, and Weeks with a funny chuckle.

"And in England dissenters aren't gentlemen, are they?" asked Weeks.

"Well, if you ask me point-blank, they're not," replied Philip rather crossly.

He hated being laughed at, and they laughed again.

"And will you tell me what a gentleman is?" asked Weeks.

"Oh, I don't know; everyone knows what it is."

"Are you a gentleman?"

No doubt had ever crossed Philip's mind on the subject, but he knew it was not a thing to state of oneself.

"If a man tells you he's a gentleman you can bet your boots he isn't," he retorted.

"Am I a gentleman?"

Philip's truthfulness made it difficult for him to answer, but he was naturally polite.

"Oh, well, you're different," he said. "You're American, aren't you?"

"I suppose we may take it that only Englishmen are gentlemen," said Weeks gravely.

Philip did not contradict him.

"Couldn't you give me a few more particulars?" asked Weeks.

Philip reddened, but, growing angry, did not care if he made himself ridiculous.

"I can give you plenty." He remembered his uncle's saying that it took three generations to make a gentleman: it was a companion proverb to the silk purse and the sow's ear. "First of all he's the son of a gentleman, and he's been to a public school, and to Oxford or Cambridge."

"Edinburgh wouldn't do, I suppose?" asked Weeks.

"And he talks English like a gentleman, and he wears the right sort of things, and if he's a gentleman he can always tell if another chap's a gentleman."

It seemed rather lame to Philip as he went on, but there it was: that was what he meant by the word, and everyone he had ever known had meant that too.

"It is evident to me that I am not a gentleman," said Weeks. "I don't see why you should have been so surprised because I was a dissenter."

"I don't quite know what a Unitarian is," said Philip.

Weeks in his odd way again put his head on one side: you almost expected him to twitter.

"A Unitarian very earnestly disbelieves in almost everything that anybody else believes, and he has a very lively sustaining faith in he doesn't quite know what."

"I don't see why you should make fun of me," said Philip. "I really want to know."

"My dear friend, I'm not making fun of you. I have arrived at that definition after years of great labour and the most anxious, nerve-racking study."

When Philip and Hayward got up to go, Weeks handed Philip a little book in a paper cover.

"I suppose you can read French pretty well by now. I wonder if this would amuse you."

Philip thanked him and, taking the book, looked at the title. It was Renan's *Vie de Jésus*.

Chapter XXVIII

IT OCCURRED NEITHER TO HAYWARD NOR TO WEEKS THAT THE CONVERSATIONS which helped them to pass an idle evening were being turned over afterwards in Philip's active brain. It had never struck him before that religion was a matter upon which discussion was possible. To him it meant the Church of England, and not to believe in its tenets was a sign of wilfulness which could not fail of punishment here or hereafter. There was some doubt in his mind about the chastisement of unbelievers. It was possible that a merciful judge, reserving the flames of hell for the heathen—Mahommedans, Buddhists, and the rest—would spare Dissenters and Roman Catholics (though at the cost of how much humiliation when they were made to realise their error!), and it was also possible that He would be pitiful to those who had had no chance of learning the truth—this was reasonable enough, though such were the activities of the Missionary Society there could not be many in this condition—but if the chance had been theirs and they had neglected it (in which category were obviously Roman Catholics and Dissenters), the punishment was sure and merited. It was clear that the miscreant was in a parlous state. Perhaps Philip had not been taught it in so many words, but certainly the impression had been given him that only members of the Church of England had any real hope of eternal happiness.

One of the things that Philip had heard definitely stated was that the unbeliever was a wicked and a vicious man; but Weeks, though he believed in hardly anything that Philip believed, led a life of Christian purity. Philip had received little kindness in his life, and he was touched by the American's desire to help him: once when a cold kept him in bed for three days, Weeks nursed him like a mother. There was neither vice nor wickedness in him, but only sincerity and lovingkindness. It was evidently possible to be virtuous and unbelieving.

Also Philip had been given to understand that people adhered to other faiths only from obstinacy or self-interest: in their hearts they knew they were false; they deliberately sought to deceive others. Now, for the sake of his German he had been accustomed on Sunday mornings to attend the Lutheran service, but when Hayward arrived he began instead to go with him to Mass. He noticed that, whereas the Protestant church was nearly empty and the congregation had a listless air, the Jesuit on the other hand was crowded and the worshippers seemed to pray with all their hearts. They had not the look of hypocrites. He was surprised at the contrast; for he knew of course that the Lutherans, whose faith was closer to that of the Church of England, on that account were nearer the truth than the Roman

Catholics. Most of the men—it was largely a masculine congregation—were South Germans; and he could not help saying to himself that if he had been born in South Germany he would certainly have been a Roman Catholic. He might just as well have been born in a Roman Catholic country as in England; and in England as well in a Wesleyan, Baptist, or Methodist family as in one that fortunately belonged to the church by law established. He was a little breathless at the danger he had run. Philip was on friendly terms with the little Chinaman who sat at table with him twice each day. His name was Sung. He was always smiling, affable, and polite. It seemed strange that he should frizzle in hell merely because he was a Chinaman; but if salvation was possible whatever a man's faith was, there did not seem to be any particular advantage in belonging to the Church of England.

Philip, more puzzled than he had ever been in his life, sounded Weeks. He had to be careful, for he was very sensitive to ridicule; and the acidulous humour with which the American treated the Church of England disconcerted him. Weeks only puzzled him more. He made Philip acknowledge that those South Germans whom he saw in the Jesuit church were every bit as firmly convinced of the truth of Roman Catholicism as he was of that of the Church of England, and from that he led him to admit that the Mahommedan and the Buddhist were convinced also of the truth of their respective religions. It looked as though knowing that you were right meant nothing; they all knew they were right. Weeks had no intention of undermining the boy's faith, but he was deeply interested in religion, and found it an absorbing topic of conversation. He had described his own views accurately when he said that he very earnestly disbelieved in almost everything that other people believed. Once Philip asked him a question, which he had heard his uncle put when the conversation at the vicarage had fallen upon some mildly rationalistic work which was then exciting discussion in the newspapers.

"But why should you be right and all those fellows like St. Anselm and St. Augustine be wrong?"

"You mean that they were very clever and learned men, while you have grave doubts whether I am either?" asked Weeks.

"Yes," answered Philip uncertainly, for put in that way his question seemed impertinent.

"St. Augustine believed that the earth was flat and that the sun turned round it."

"I don't know what that proves."

"Why, it proves that you believe with your generation. Your saints lived in an age of faith, when it was practically impossible to disbelieve what to us is positively incredible."

"Then how d'you know that we have the truth now?"

"I don't."

Philip thought this over for a moment, then he said:

"I don't see why the things we believe absolutely now shouldn't be just as wrong as what they believed in the past."

"Neither do I."

"Then how can you believe anything at all?"

"I don't know."

Philip asked Weeks what he thought of Hayward's religion.

"Men have always formed gods in their own image," said Weeks. "He believes in the picturesque."

Philip paused for a little while, then he said:

"I don't see why one should believe in God at all."

The words were no sooner out of his mouth than he realised that he had ceased to do so. It took his breath away like a plunge into cold water. He looked at Weeks with startled eyes. Suddenly he felt afraid. He left Weeks as quickly as he could. He wanted to be alone. It was the most startling experience that he had ever had. He tried to think it all out; it was very exciting, since his whole life seemed concerned (he thought his decision on this matter must profoundly affect its course) and a mistake might lead to eternal damnation; but the more he reflected the more convinced he was; and though during the next few weeks he read books, aids to scepticism, with eager interest it was only to confirm him in what he felt instinctively. The fact was that he had ceased to believe not for this reason or the other, but because he had not the religious temperament. Faith had been forced upon him from the outside. It was a matter of environment and example. A new environment and a new example gave him the opportunity to find himself. He put off the faith of his childhood quite simply, like a cloak that he no longer needed. At first life seemed strange and lonely without the belief which, though he never realised it, had been an unfailing support. He felt like a man who has leaned on a stick and finds himself forced suddenly to walk without assistance. It really seemed as though the days were colder and the nights more solitary. But he was upheld by the excitement; it seemed to make life a more thrilling adventure; and in a little while the stick which he had thrown aside, the cloak which had fallen from his shoulders, seemed an intolerable burden of which he had been eased. The religious exercises which for so many years had been forced upon him were part and parcel of religion to him. He thought of the collects and epistles which he had been made to learn by heart, and the long services at the Cathedral through which he had sat when every limb itched with the desire for movement; and he remembered those walks at night through muddy roads to the parish church at Blackstable, and the coldness of that bleak building; he sat with his feet like ice, his fingers numb and heavy, and all around was the sickly odour of pomatum. Oh, he had been so bored! His heart leaped when he saw he was free from all that.

He was surprised at himself because he ceased to believe so easily, and, not knowing that he felt as he did on account of the subtle workings of his inmost nature, he ascribed the certainty he had reached to his own cleverness. He was unduly pleased with himself. With youth's lack of sympathy for an attitude other than its own he despised not a little Weeks and Hayward because they were content with the vague emotion which they called God and would not take the further step which to himself seemed so obvious. One day he went alone up a certain hill so that he might see a view which, he knew not why, filled him always with wild exhilaration. It was autumn now, but often the days were cloudless still, and then the sky seemed to glow with a more splendid light: it was as though nature consciously sought to put a fuller vehemence into the remaining days of fair weather. He looked down upon the plain, a-quiver with the sun, stretching vastly before him: in the distance were the roofs of Mannheim and ever so far away the dimness of Worms. Here and there a more piercing glitter was the Rhine. The tremendous spaciousness of it was glowing with rich gold. Philip, as he stood there, his heart beating with sheer joy, thought how the tempter had stood with Jesus on a high mountain and shown him the kingdoms of the earth. To Philip, intoxicated with the beauty of the scene, it seemed that it was the whole world which was spread before him, and he was eager to step down and enjoy it. He was free from degrading fears and free from prejudice. He could go his way without the intolerable dread of hell-fire. Suddenly he realised that he had lost also that burden of responsibility which made every action of his life a matter of urgent consequence. He could breathe more freely in a lighter air. He was responsible only to himself for the things he did. Freedom! He was his own master at last. From old habit, unconsciously he thanked God that he no longer believed in Him.

Drunk with pride in his intelligence and in his fearlessness, Philip entered deliberately upon a new life. But his loss of faith made less difference in his behaviour than he expected. Though he had thrown on one side the Christian dogmas it never occurred to him to criticise the Christian ethics; he accepted the Christian virtues, and indeed thought it fine to practise them for their own sake, without a thought of reward or punishment. There was small occasion for heroism in the Frau Professor's house, but he was a little more exactly truthful than he had been, and he forced himself to be more than commonly attentive to the dull, elderly ladies who sometimes engaged him in conversation. The gentle oath, the violent adjective, which are typical of our language and which he had cultivated before as a sign of manliness, he now elaborately eschewed.

Having settled the whole matter to his satisfaction he sought to put it out of his mind, but that was more easily said than done; and he could not prevent the regrets nor stifle the misgivings which sometimes tormented him. He was so young and had so few friends that immortality had no particular attractions for him, and he was able without trouble to give up belief in it; but there was one thing which made him wretched; he told himself that he was unreasonable, he tried to laugh himself out of such pathos; but the tears really came to his eyes when he thought that he would never see again the beautiful mother whose love for him had grown more precious as the years since her death passed on. And sometimes, as though the influence of innumerable ancestors, God-fearing and devout, were working in him unconsciously, there seized him a panic fear that perhaps after all it was all true, and there was, up there behind the blue sky, a jealous God who would punish in everlasting flames the atheist. At these times his reason could offer him no help, he imagined the anguish of a physical torment which would last endlessly, he felt quite sick with fear and burst into a violent sweat. At last he would say to himself desperately:

"After all, it's not my fault. I can't force myself to believe. If there is a God after all and he punishes me because I honestly don't believe in Him I can't help it."

Chapter XXIX

WINTER SET IN. WEEKS WENT TO BERLIN TO ATTEND THE LECTURES OF Paulssen, and Hayward began to think of going South. The local theatre opened its doors. Philip and Hayward went to it two or three times a week with the praiseworthy intention of improving their German, and Philip found it a more diverting manner of perfecting himself in the language than listening to sermons. They found themselves in the midst of a revival of the drama. Several of Ibsen's plays were on the repertory for the winter; Sudermann's *Die Ehre* was then a new play, and on its production in the quiet university town caused the greatest excitement; it was extravagantly praised and bitterly attacked; other dramatists followed with plays written under the modern influence, and Philip witnessed a series of works in which the vileness of mankind was displayed before him. He had never been to a play in his life till then (poor touring companies sometimes came to the Assembly Rooms at Blackstable, but the Vicar, partly on account of his profession, partly because he thought it would be vulgar, never went to see them) and the passion of the stage seized him. He felt a thrill the moment he got into the little, shabby, ill-lit theatre. Soon he came to know the peculiarities of the small company, and by the casting could tell at once what were the characteristics of the persons in the drama; but this made no difference to him. To him it was real life. It was a strange life, dark and tortured, in which men and women showed to remorseless eyes the evil that was in their hearts: a fair face concealed a depraved mind; the virtuous used virtue as a mask to hide their secret vice, the seeming-strong fainted within with their weakness; the honest were corrupt, the chaste were lewd. You seemed to dwell in a room where the night before an orgy had taken place: the windows had not been opened in the morning; the air was foul with the dregs of beer, and stale smoke, and flaring gas. There was no laughter. At most you sniggered at the hypocrite or the fool: the characters expressed themselves in cruel words that seemed wrung out of their hearts by shame and anguish.

Philip was carried away by the sordid intensity of it. He seemed to see the world again in another fashion, and this world too he was anxious to know. After the play was over he went to a tavern and sat in the bright warmth with Hayward to eat a sandwich and drink a glass of beer. All round were little groups of students, talking and laughing; and here and there was a family, father and mother, a couple of sons and a girl; and sometimes the girl said a sharp thing, and the father leaned back in his chair and laughed, laughed heartily. It was very friendly and innocent. There was a pleasant homeliness in the scene, but for this Philip had no eyes. His thoughts ran on the play he had just come from.

"You do feel it's life, don't you?" he said excitedly. "You know, I don't think I can stay here much longer. I want to get to London so that I can really begin. I want to have experiences. I'm so tired of preparing for life: I want to live it now."

Sometimes Hayward left Philip to go home by himself. He would never exactly reply to Philip's eager questioning, but with a merry, rather stupid laugh, hinted at a romantic amour; he quoted a few lines of Rossetti, and once showed Philip a sonnet in which passion and purple, pessimism and pathos, were packed together on the subject of a young lady called Trude. Hayward surrounded his sordid and vulgar little adventures with a glow of poetry, and thought he touched hands with Pericles and Pheidias because to describe the object of his attentions he used the word *hetaira* instead of one of those, more blunt and apt, provided by the English language. Philip in the daytime had been led by curiosity to pass through the little street near the old bridge, with its neat white houses and green shutters, in which according to Hayward the Fräulein Trude lived; but the women, with brutal faces and painted cheeks, who came out of their doors and cried out to him, filled him with fear; and he fled in horror from the rough hands that sought to detain him. He yearned above all things for experience and felt himself ridiculous because at his age he had not enjoyed that which all fiction taught him was the most important thing in life; but he had the unfortunate gift of seeing things as they were, and the reality which was offered him differed too terribly from the ideal of his dreams.

He did not know how wide a country, arid and precipitous, must be crossed before the traveller through life comes to an acceptance of reality. It is an illusion that youth is happy, an illusion of those who have lost it; but the young know they are wretched, for they are full of the truthless ideals which have been instilled into them, and each time they come in contact with the real they are bruised and wounded. It looks as if they were victims of a conspiracy; for the books they read, ideal by the necessity of selection, and the conversation of their elders, who look back upon the past through a rosy haze of forgetfulness, prepare them for an unreal life. They must discover for themselves that all they have read and all they have been told are lies, lies, lies; and each discovery is another nail driven into the body on the cross of life. The strange thing is that each one who has gone through that bitter disillusionment adds to it in his turn, unconsciously, by the power within him which is stronger than himself. The companionship of Hayward was the worst possible thing for Philip. He was a man who saw nothing for himself, but only through a literary atmosphere, and he was dangerous because he had deceived himself into sincerity. He honestly mistook his sensuality for romantic emotion, his vacillation for the artistic temperament, and his idleness for philosophic calm. His mind, vulgar in its effort at refinement, saw everything a little larger than life size, with the outlines blurred, in a golden mist of sentimentality. He lied and never knew that he lied, and when it was pointed out to him said that lies were beautiful. He was an idealist.

Chapter XXX

PHILIP WAS RESTLESS AND DISSATISFIED. HAYWARD'S POETIC ALLUSIONS TROUbled his imagination, and his soul yearned for romance. At least that was how he put it to himself.

And it happened that an incident was taking place in Frau Erlin's house which increased Philip's preoccupation with the matter of sex. Two or three times on his walks among the hills he had met Fräulein Cäcilie wandering by herself. He had passed her with a bow, and a few yards further on had seen the Chinaman. He thought nothing of it; but one evening on his way home, when night had already fallen, he passed two people walking very close together. Hearing his footstep, they separated quickly, and though he could not see well in the darkness he was almost certain they were Cäcilie and Herr Sung. Their rapid movement apart suggested that they had been walking arm in arm. Philip was puzzled and surprised. He had never paid much attention to Fräulein Cäcilie. She was a plain girl, with a square face and blunt features. She could not have been more than sixteen, since she still wore her long fair hair in a plait. That evening at supper he looked at her curiously; and, though of late she had talked little at meals, she addressed him.

"Where did you go for your walk today, Herr Carey?" she asked.

"Oh, I walked up towards the Königstuhl."

"I didn't go out," she volunteered. "I had a headache."

The Chinaman, who sat next to her, turned round.

"I'm so sorry," he said. "I hope it's better now."

Fräulein Cäcilie was evidently uneasy, for she spoke again to Philip.

"Did you meet many people on the way?"

Philip could not help reddening when he told a downright lie.

"No. I don't think I saw a living soul."

He fancied that a look of relief passed across her eyes.

Soon, however, there could be no doubt that there was something between the pair, and other people in the Frau Professor's house saw them lurking in dark places. The elderly ladies who sat at the head of the table began to discuss what was now a scandal. The Frau Professor was angry and harassed. She had done her best to see nothing. The winter was at hand, and it was not as easy a matter then as in the summer to keep her house full. Herr Sung was a good customer: he had two rooms on the ground floor, and he drank a bottle of Moselle at each meal. The Frau Professor charged him three marks a bottle and made a good profit. None of her other guests drank wine, and some of them did not even drink beer. Neither did she wish to lose Fräulein Cäcilie, whose parents were in business in South America and paid well for the Frau Professor's motherly care; and she knew that if she wrote to the girl's uncle, who lived in Berlin, he would immediately take her away. The Frau Professor contented herself with giving them both severe looks at table and, though she dared not be rude to the Chinaman, got a certain satisfaction out of incivility to Cäcilie. But the three elderly ladies were not content. Two were widows, and one, a Dutchwoman, was a spinster of masculine appearance; they paid the smallest possible sum for their pension, and gave a good deal of trouble, but they were permanent and therefore had to be put up with. They went to the Frau Professor and said that something must be done; it was disgraceful, and the house was ceasing to be respectable. The Frau Professor tried obstinacy, anger, tears, but the three old ladies routed her, and with a sudden assumption of virtuous indignation she said that she would put a stop to the whole thing.

After luncheon she took Cäcilie into her bed-room and began to talk very seriously to her; but to her amazement the girl adopted a brazen attitude; she proposed to go about as she liked; and if she chose to walk with the Chinaman she could not see it was anybody's business but her own. The Frau Professor threatened to write to her uncle.

"Then Onkel Heinrich will put me in a family in Berlin for the winter, and that will be much nicer for me. And Herr Sung will come to Berlin too."

The Frau Professor began to cry. The tears rolled down her coarse, red, fat cheeks; and Cäcilie laughed at her.

"That will mean three rooms empty all through the winter," she said.

Then the Frau Professor tried another plan. She appealed to Fräulein Cäcilie's better nature: she was kind, sensible, tolerant; she treated her no longer as a child, but as a grown woman. She said that it wouldn't be so dreadful, but a Chinaman, with his yellow skin and flat nose, and his little pig's eyes! That's what made it so horrible. It filled one with disgust to think of it.

"*Bitte, bitte,*" said Cäcilie, with a rapid intake of the breath. "I won't listen to anything against him."

"But it's not serious?" gasped Frau Erlin.

"I love him. I love him. I love him."

"*Gott im Himmel!*"

The Frau Professor stared at her with horrified surprise; she had thought it was no more than naughtiness on the child's part, and innocent folly; but the passion in her voice revealed everything. Cäcilie looked at her for a moment with flaming eyes, and then with a shrug of her shoulders went out of the room.

Frau Erlin kept the details of the interview to herself, and a day or two later altered the arrangement of the table. She asked Herr Sung if he would not come and sit at her end, and he with his unfailing politeness accepted with alacrity. Cäcilie took the change indifferently. But as if the discovery that the relations between them were known to the whole household made them more shameless, they made no secret now of their walks together, and every afternoon quite openly set out to wander about the hills. It was plain that they did not care what was said of them. At last even the placidity of Professor Erlin was moved, and he insisted that his wife should speak to the Chinaman. She took him aside in his turn and expostulated; he was ruining the girl's reputation, he was doing harm to the house, he must see how wrong and wicked his conduct was; but she was met with smiling denials; Herr Sung did not know what she was talking about, he was not paying any attention to Fräulein Cäcilie, he never walked with her; it was all untrue, every word of it.

"*Ach*, Herr Sung, how can you say such things? You've been seen again and again."

"No, you're mistaken. It's untrue."

He looked at her with an unceasing smile, which showed his even, little white teeth. He was quite calm. He denied everything. He denied with bland effrontery. At last the Frau Professor lost her temper and said the girl had confessed she loved him. He was not moved. He continued to smile.

"Nonsense! Nonsense! It's all untrue."

She could get nothing out of him. The weather grew very bad; there was snow and frost, and then a thaw with a long succession of cheerless days, on which walking was a poor amusement. One evening when Philip had just finished his German lesson with the Herr Professor and was standing for a moment in the drawing-room, talking to Frau Erlin, Anna came quickly in.

"Mamma, where is Cäcilie?" she said.

"I suppose she's in her room."

"There's no light in it."

The Frau Professor gave an exclamation, and she looked at her daughter in dismay. The thought which was in Anna's head had flashed across hers.

"Ring for Emil," she said hoarsely.

This was the stupid lout who waited at table and did most of the housework. He came in.

"Emil, go down to Herr Sung's room and enter without knocking. If anyone is there say you came in to see about the stove."

No sign of astonishment appeared on Emil's phlegmatic face.

He went slowly downstairs. The Frau Professor and Anna left the door open and listened. Presently they heard Emil come up again, and they called him.

"Was anyone there?" asked the Frau Professor.

"Yes, Herr Sung was there."

"Was he alone?"

The beginning of a cunning smile narrowed his mouth.

"No, Fräulein Cäcilie was there."

"Oh, it's disgraceful," cried the Frau Professor.

Now he smiled broadly.

"Fräulein Cäcilie is there every evening. She spends hours at a time there."

Frau Professor began to wring her hands.

"Oh, how abominable! But why didn't you tell me?"

"It was no business of mine," he answered, slowly shrugging his shoulders.

"I suppose they paid you well. Go away. Go."

He lurched clumsily to the door.

"They must go away, mamma," said Anna.

"And who is going to pay the rent? And the taxes are falling due. It's all very well for you to say they must go away. If they go away I can't pay the bills." She turned to Philip, with tears streaming down her face. "*Ach*, Herr Carey, you will not say what you have heard. If Fräulein Forster—" this was the Dutch spinster—"if Fräulein Forster knew she would leave at once. And if they all go we must close the house. I cannot afford to keep it."

"Of course I won't say anything."

"If she stays, I will not speak to her," said Anna.

That evening at supper Fräulein Cäcilie, redder than usual, with a look of obstinacy on her face, took her place punctually; but Herr Sung did not appear, and for a while Philip thought he was going to shirk the ordeal. At last he came, very smiling, his little eyes dancing with the apologies he made for his late arrival. He insisted as usual on pouring out the Frau Professor a glass of his Moselle, and he offered a glass to Fräulein Forster. The room was very hot, for the stove had been alight all day and the windows were seldom opened. Emil blundered about, but succeeded somehow in serving everyone quickly and with order. The three old ladies sat in silence, visibly disapproving: the Frau Professor had scarcely recovered from her tears; her husband was silent and oppressed. Conversation languished. It seemed to Philip that there was something dreadful in that gathering which he had sat with so often; they looked different under the light of the two hanging lamps from what they had ever looked before; he was vaguely uneasy. Once he caught Cäcilie's eye, and he thought she looked at him with hatred and contempt. The room was stifling. It was as though the beastly passion of that pair troubled them all; there was a feeling of Oriental depravity; a faint savour of joss-sticks, a mystery of hidden vices, seemed to make their breath heavy. Philip could feel the beating of the arteries in his forehead. He could not understand what strange emotion distracted him; he seemed to feel something infinitely attractive, and yet he was repelled and horrified.

For several days things went on. The air was sickly with the unnatural passion which all felt about them, and the nerves of the little household seemed to grow exasperated. Only Herr Sung remained unaffected; he was no less smiling, affable, and polite than he had been before: one could not tell whether his manner was a triumph of civilisation or an expression of contempt on the part of the Oriental for the vanquished West. Cäcilie was flaunting and cynical. At last even the Frau Professor could bear the position no longer. Suddenly panic seized her; for Professor Erlin with brutal frankness had suggested the possible consequences of an intrigue which was now manifest to everyone, and she saw her good name in Heidelberg and the repute of her house ruined by a scandal which could not possibly be hidden. For some reason, blinded perhaps by her interests, this possibility had never occurred to her; and now, her wits muddled by a terrible fear, she could hardly be prevented from turning the girl out of the house at once. It was due to Anna's good sense that a cautious letter was written to the uncle in Berlin suggesting that Cäcilie should be taken away.

But having made up her mind to lose the two lodgers, the Frau Professor could not resist the satisfaction of giving rein to the ill-temper she had curbed so long. She was free now to say anything she liked to Cäcilie.

"I have written to your uncle, Cäcilie, to take you away. I cannot have you in my house any longer."

Her little round eyes sparkled when she noticed the sudden whiteness of the girl's face.

"You're shameless. Shameless," she went on.

She called her foul names.

"What did you say to my uncle Heinrich, Frau Professor?" the girl asked, suddenly falling from her attitude of flaunting independence.

"Oh, he'll tell you himself. I expect to get a letter from him tomorrow."

Next day, in order to make the humiliation more public, at supper she called down the table to Cäcilie.

"I have had a letter from your uncle, Cäcilie. You are to pack your things tonight, and we will put you in the train tomorrow morning. He will meet you himself in Berlin at the Central Bahnhof."

"Very good, Frau Professor."

Herr Sung smiled in the Frau Professor's eyes, and notwithstanding her protests insisted on pouring out a glass of wine for her. The Frau Professor ate her supper with a good appetite. But she had triumphed unwisely. Just before going to bed she called the servant.

"Emil, if Fräulein Cäcilie's box is ready you had better take it downstairs tonight. The porter will fetch it before breakfast."

The servant went away and in a moment came back.

"Fräulein Cäcilie is not in her room, and her bag has gone."

With a cry the Frau Professor hurried along: the box was on the floor, strapped and locked; but there was no bag, and neither hat nor cloak. The dressing-table was empty. Breathing heavily, the Frau Professor ran downstairs to the Chinaman's rooms, she had not moved so quickly for twenty years, and Emil called out after her to beware she did not fall; she did not trouble to knock, but burst in. The rooms were empty. The luggage had gone, and the door into the garden, still open, showed how it had been got away. In an envelope on the table were notes for the money due on the month's board and an approximate sum for extras. Groaning, suddenly overcome by her haste, the Frau Professor sank obesely on to a sofa. There could be no doubt. The pair had gone off together. Emil remained stolid and unmoved.

Chapter XXXI

HAYWARD, AFTER SAYING FOR A MONTH THAT HE WAS GOING SOUTH NEXT day and delaying from week to week out of inability to make up his mind to the bother of packing and the tedium of a journey, had at last been driven off just before Christmas by the preparations for that festival. He could not support the thought of a Teutonic merry-making. It gave him gooseflesh to think of the season's aggressive cheerfulness, and in his desire to avoid the obvious he determined to travel on Christmas Eve.

Philip was not sorry to see him off, for he was a downright person and it irritated him that anybody should not know his own mind. Though much under Hayward's influence, he would not grant that indecision pointed to a charming sensitiveness; and he resented the shadow of a sneer with which Hayward looked upon his straight ways. They corresponded. Hayward was an admirable letter-writer, and knowing his talent took pains with his letters. His temperament was receptive to the beautiful influences with which he came in contact, and he was able in his letters from Rome to put a subtle fragrance of Italy. He thought the city of the ancient Romans a little vulgar, finding distinction only in the decadence of the Empire; but the Rome of the Popes appealed to his sympathy, and in his chosen words, quite exquisitely, there appeared a Rococo beauty. He wrote of old church music and the Alban Hills, and of the languor of incense and the charm of the streets by night, in the rain, when the pavements shone and the light of the street lamps was mysterious. Perhaps he repeated these admirable letters to various friends. He did not know what a troubling effect they had upon Philip; they seemed to make his life very humdrum. With the spring Hayward grew dithyrambic. He proposed that Philip should come down to Italy. He was wasting his time at Heidelberg. The Germans were gross and life there was common: how could the soul come to her own in that prim landscape? In Tuscany the spring was scattering flowers through the land, and Philip was nineteen; let him come and they could wander through the mountain towns of Umbria. Their names sang in Philip's heart. And Cäcilie too, with her lover, had gone to Italy. When he thought of them Philip was seized with a restlessness he could not account for. He cursed his fate because he had no money to travel, and he knew his uncle would not send him more than the fifteen pounds a month which had been agreed upon. He had not managed his allowance very well. His pension and the price of his lessons left him very little over, and he had found going about with Hayward expensive. Hayward had often suggested excursions, a visit to the play, or a bottle of wine, when Philip had come to the end of his month's money; and with the folly of his age he had been unwilling to confess he could not afford an extravagance.

Luckily Hayward's letters came seldom, and in the intervals Philip settled down again to his industrious life. He had matriculated at the university and attended one or two courses of lectures. Kuno Fischer was then at the height of his fame and during the winter had been lecturing brilliantly on Schopenhauer. It was Philip's introduction to philosophy. He had a practical mind and moved uneasily amid the abstract; but he found an unexpected fascination in listening to metaphysical disquisitions; they made him breathless; it was a little like watching a tight-rope dancer doing perilous feats over an abyss; but it was very exciting. The pessimism of the subject attracted his youth; and he believed that the world he was about to enter was a place of pitiless woe and of darkness. That made him none the less eager to enter it; and when, in due course, Mrs. Carey, acting as the correspondent for his guardian's views, suggested that it was time for him to come back to England, he agreed with enthusiasm. He must make up his mind now what he meant to do. If he left Heidelberg at the end of July they could talk things over during August, and it would be a good time to make arrangements.

The date of his departure was settled, and Mrs. Carey wrote to him again. She reminded him of Miss Wilkinson, through whose kindness he had gone to Frau Erlin's house at Heidelberg, and told him that she had arranged to spend a few weeks with them at Blackstable. She would be crossing from Flushing on such and such a day, and if he travelled at the same time he could look after her and come on to Blackstable in her company. Philip's shyness immediately made him write to say that he could not leave till a day or two afterwards. He pictured himself looking out for Miss Wilkinson, the embarrassment of going up to her and asking if it were she (and he might so easily address the wrong person and be snubbed), and then the difficulty of knowing whether in the train he ought to talk to her or whether he could ignore her and read his book.

At last he left Heidelberg. For three months he had been thinking of nothing but the future; and he went without regret. He never knew that he had been happy there. Fräulein Anna gave him a copy of *Der Trompeter von Säckingen* and in return he presented her with a volume of William Morris. Very wisely neither of them ever read the other's present.

Chapter XXXII

Philip was surprised when he saw his uncle and aunt. He had never noticed before that they were quite old people. The Vicar received him with his usual, not unamiable indifference. He was a little stouter, a little balder, a little greyer. Philip saw how insignificant he was. His face was weak and self-indulgent. Aunt Louisa took him in her arms and kissed him; and tears of happiness flowed down her cheeks. Philip was touched and embarrassed; he had not known with what a hungry love she cared for him.

"Oh, the time has seemed long since you've been away, Philip," she cried.

She stroked his hands and looked into his face with glad eyes.

"You've grown. You're quite a man now."

There was a very small moustache on his upper lip. He had bought a razor and now and then with infinite care shaved the down off his smooth chin.

"We've been so lonely without you." And then shyly, with a little break in her voice, she asked: "You are glad to come back to your home, aren't you?"

"Yes, rather."

She was so thin that she seemed almost transparent, the arms she put round his neck were frail bones that reminded you of chicken bones, and her faded face was oh! so wrinkled. The grey curls which she still wore in the fashion of her youth gave her a queer, pathetic look; and her little withered body was like an autumn leaf, you felt it might be blown away by the first sharp wind. Philip realised that they had done with life, these two quiet little people: they belonged to a past generation, and they were waiting there patiently, rather stupidly, for death; and he, in his vigour and his youth, thirsting for excitement and adventure, was appalled at the waste. They had done nothing, and when they went it would be just as if they had never been. He felt a great pity for Aunt Louisa, and he loved her suddenly because she loved him.

Then Miss Wilkinson, who had kept discreetly out of the way till the Careys had had a chance of welcoming their nephew, came into the room.

"This is Miss Wilkinson, Philip," said Mrs. Carey.

"The prodigal has returned," she said, holding out her hand. "I have brought a rose for the prodigal's button-hole."

With a gay smile she pinned to Philip's coat the flower she had just picked in the garden. He blushed and felt foolish. He knew that Miss Wilkinson was the daughter of his Uncle William's last rector, and he had a wide acquaintance with the daughters of clergymen. They wore ill-cut clothes and stout boots. They were generally dressed in black, for in Philip's early years at Blackstable homespuns had not reached East Anglia, and the ladies of the clergy did not favour colours. Their hair was done very untidily, and they smelled aggressively of starched linen. They considered the feminine graces unbecoming and looked the same whether they were old or young. They bore their religion arrogantly. The closeness of their connection with the church made them adopt a slightly dictatorial attitude to the rest of mankind.

Miss Wilkinson was very different. She wore a white muslin gown stamped with gay little bunches of flowers, and pointed, high-heeled shoes, with open-work stockings. To Philip's inexperience it seemed that she was wonderfully dressed; he did not see that her frock was cheap and showy. Her hair was elaborately dressed, with a neat curl in the middle of the forehead: it was very black, shiny and hard, and it looked as though it could never be in the least disarranged. She had large black eyes and her nose was slightly aquiline; in profile she had somewhat the look of a bird of prey, but full face she was prepossessing. She smiled a great deal, but her mouth was large and when she smiled she tried to hide her teeth, which were big and rather yellow. But what embarrassed Philip most was that she was heavily powdered; he had very strict views on feminine behaviour and did not think a lady ever powdered; but of course Miss Wilkinson was a lady because she was a clergyman's daughter, and a clergyman was a gentleman.

Philip made up his mind to dislike her thoroughly. She spoke with a slight French accent; and he did not know why she should, since she had been born and bred in the heart of England. He thought her smile affected, and the coy sprightliness of her manner irritated him. For two or three days he remained silent and hostile, but Miss Wilkinson apparently did not notice it. She was very affable. She addressed her conversation almost exclusively to him, and there was something flattering in the way she appealed constantly to his sane judgment. She made him laugh too, and Philip could never resist people who amused him: he had a gift now and then of saying neat things; and it was pleasant to have an appreciative listener. Neither the Vicar nor Mrs. Carey had a sense of humour, and they never laughed at anything he said. As he grew used to Miss Wilkinson, and his shyness left him, he began to like her better; he found the French accent picturesque; and at a garden-party which the doctor gave she was very much better dressed than anyone else. She wore a blue foulard with large white spots, and Philip was tickled at the sensation it caused.

"I'm certain they think you're no better than you should be," he told her, laughing.

"It's the dream of my life to be taken for an abandoned hussy," she answered.

One day when Miss Wilkinson was in her room he asked Aunt Louisa how old she was.

"Oh, my dear, you should never ask a lady's age; but she's certainly too old for you to marry."

The Vicar gave his slow, obese smile.

"She's no chicken, Louisa," he said. "She was nearly grown up when we were in Lincolnshire, and that was twenty years ago. She wore a pigtail hanging down her back."

"She may not have been more than ten," said Philip.

"She was older than that," said Aunt Louisa.

"I think she was nearer twenty," said the Vicar.

"Oh no, William. Sixteen or seventeen at the outside."

"That would make her well over thirty," said Philip.

At that moment Miss Wilkinson tripped downstairs, singing a song by Benjamin Goddard. She had put her hat on, for she and Philip were going for a walk, and she held out her hand for him to button her glove. He did it awkwardly. He felt embarrassed but gallant. Conversation went easily between them now, and as they strolled along they talked of all manner of things. She told Philip about Berlin, and he told her of his year in Heidelberg. As he spoke, things which had appeared of no importance gained a new interest: he described the people at Frau Erlin's house; and to the conversations between Hayward and Weeks, which at the time seemed so significant, he gave a little twist, so that they looked absurd. He was flattered at Miss Wilkinson's laughter.

"I'm quite frightened of you," she said. "You're so sarcastic."

Then she asked him playfully whether he had not had any love affairs at Heidelberg. Without thinking, he frankly answered that he had not; but she refused to believe him.

"How secretive you are!" she said. "At your age is it likely?"

He blushed and laughed.

"You want to know too much," he said.

"Ah, I thought so," she laughed triumphantly. "Look at him blushing."

He was pleased that she should think he had been a sad dog, and he changed the conversation so as to make her believe he had all sorts of romantic things to conceal. He was angry with himself that he had not. There had been no opportunity.

Miss Wilkinson was dissatisfied with her lot. She resented having to earn her living and told Philip a long story of an uncle of her mother's, who had been expected to leave her a fortune but had married his cook and changed his will. She hinted at the luxury of her home and compared her life in Lincolnshire, with horses to ride and carriages to drive in, with the mean dependence of her present state. Philip was a little puzzled when he mentioned this afterwards to Aunt Louisa, and she told him that when she knew the Wilkinsons they had never had anything more than a pony and a dog-cart; Aunt Louisa had heard of the rich uncle, but as he was married and had children before Emily was born she could never have had much hope of inheriting his fortune. Miss Wilkinson had little good to say of Berlin, where she was now in a situation. She complained of the vulgarity of German life, and compared it bitterly with the brilliance of Paris, where she had spent a number of years. She did not say how many. She had been governess in the family of a fashionable portrait-painter, who had married a Jewish wife of means, and in their house she had met many distinguished people. She dazzled Philip with their names. Actors from the *Comédie Française* had come to the house frequently, and Coquelin, sitting next her at dinner, had told her he had never met a foreigner who spoke such perfect French. Alphonse Daudet had come also, and he had given her a copy of *Sappho:* he had promised to write her name in it, but she had forgotten to remind him. She treasured the volume none the less and she would lend it to Philip. Then there was Maupassant. Miss Wilkinson with a rippling laugh looked at Philip knowingly. What a man, but what a writer! Hayward had talked of Maupassant, and his reputation was not unknown to Philip.

"Did he make love to you?" he asked.

The words seemed to stick funnily in his throat, but he asked them nevertheless. He liked Miss Wilkinson very much now, and was thrilled by her conversation, but he could not imagine anyone making love to her.

"What a question!" she cried. "Poor Guy, he made love to every woman he met. It was a habit that he could not break himself of."

She sighed a little, and seemed to look back tenderly on the past.

"He was a charming man," she murmured.

A greater experience than Philip's would have guessed from these words the probabilities of the encounter: the distinguished writer invited to luncheon *en famille,* the governess coming in sedately with the two tall girls she was teaching; the introduction:

"Notre Miss Anglaise."

"Mademoiselle."

And the luncheon during which the *Miss Anglaise* sat silent while the distinguished writer talked to his host and hostess.

But to Philip her words called up much more romantic fancies.

"Do tell me all about him," he said excitedly.

"There's nothing to tell," she said truthfully, but in such a manner as to convey that three volumes would scarcely have contained the lurid facts. "You mustn't be curious."

She began to talk of Paris. She loved the boulevards and the Bois. There was grace in every street, and the trees in the Champs Élysées had a distinction which trees had not elsewhere. They were sitting on a stile now by the high-road, and Miss Wilkinson looked with disdain upon the stately elms in front of them. And the theatres: the plays were brilliant, and the acting was incomparable. She often went with Madame Foyot, the mother of the girls she was educating, when she was trying on clothes.

"Oh, what a misery to be poor!" she cried. "These beautiful things, it's only in Paris they know how to dress, and not to be able to afford them! Poor Madame Foyot, she had no figure. Sometimes the dressmaker used to whisper to me: 'Ah, Mademoiselle, if she only had your figure.'"

Philip noticed then that Miss Wilkinson had a robust form, and was proud of it.

"Men are so stupid in England. They only think of the face. The French, who are a nation of lovers, know how much more important the figure is."

Philip had never thought of such things before, but he observed now that Miss Wilkinson's ankles were thick and ungainly. He withdrew his eyes quickly.

"You should go to France. Why don't you go to Paris for a year? You would learn French, and it would—*déniaiser* you."

"What is that?" asked Philip.

She laughed slyly.

"You must look it out in the dictionary. Englishmen do not know how to treat women. They are so shy. Shyness is ridiculous in a man. They don't know how to make love. They can't even tell a woman she is charming without looking foolish."

Philip felt himself absurd. Miss Wilkinson evidently expected him to behave very differently; and he would have been delighted to say gallant and witty things, but they never occurred to him; and when they did he was too much afraid of making a fool of himself to say them.

"Oh, I loved Paris," sighed Miss Wilkinson. "But I had to go to Berlin. I was with the Foyots till the girls married, and then I could get nothing to do, and I had the chance of this post in Berlin. They're relations of Madame Foyot, and I accepted. I had a tiny apartment in the Rue Bréda, on the *cinquième:* it wasn't at all respectable. You know about the Rue Bréda—*ces dames,* you know."

Philip nodded, not knowing at all what she meant, but vaguely suspecting, and anxious she should not think him too ignorant.

"But I didn't care. *Je suis libre, n'est-ce-pas?*" She was very fond of speaking French, which indeed she spoke well. "Once I had such a curious adventure there."

She paused a little and Philip pressed her to tell it.

"You wouldn't tell me yours in Heidelberg," she said.

"They were so unadventurous," he retorted.

"I don't know what Mrs. Carey would say if she knew the sort of things we talk about together."

"You don't imagine I shall tell her."

"Will you promise?"

When he had done this, she told him how an art-student who had a room on the floor above her—but she interrupted herself.

"Why don't you go in for art? You paint so prettily."

"Not well enough for that."

"That is for others to judge. *Je m'y connais,* and I believe you have the making of a great artist."

"Can't you see Uncle William's face if I suddenly told him I wanted to go to Paris and study art?"

"You're your own master, aren't you?"

"You're trying to put me off. Please go on with the story."

Miss Wilkinson, with a little laugh, went on. The art-student had passed her several times on the stairs, and she had paid no particular attention. She saw that he had fine eyes, and he took off his hat very politely. And one day she found a letter slipped under her door. It was from him. He told her that he had adored her for months, and that he waited about the stairs for her to pass. Oh, it was a charming letter! Of course she did not reply, but what woman could help being flattered? And next day there was another letter! It was wonderful, passionate, and touching. When next she met him on the stairs she did not know which way to look. And every day the letters came, and now he begged her to see him. He said he would come in the evening, *vers neuf heures,* and she did not know what to do. Of course it was impossible, and he might ring and ring, but she would never open the door; and then while she was waiting for the tinkling of the bell, all nerves, suddenly he stood before her. She had forgotten to shut the door when she came in.

"C'était une fatalité."

"And what happened then?" asked Philip.

"That is the end of the story," she replied, with a ripple of laughter.

Philip was silent for a moment. His heart beat quickly, and strange emotions seemed to be hustling one another in his heart. He saw the dark staircase and the chance meetings, and he admired the boldness of the letters—oh, he would never have dared to do that—and then the silent, almost mysterious entrance. It seemed to him the very soul of romance.

"What was he like?"

"Oh, he was handsome. *Charmant garcon.*"

"Do you know him still?"

Philip felt a slight feeling of irritation as he asked this.

"He treated me abominably. Men are always the same. You're heartless, all of you."

"I don't know about that," said Philip, not without embarrassment.

"Let us go home," said Miss Wilkinson.

Chapter XXXIII

PHILIP COULD NOT GET MISS WILKINSON'S STORY OUT OF HIS HEAD. IT WAS clear enough what she meant even though she cut it short, and he was a little shocked. That sort of thing was all very well for married women, he had read enough French novels to know that in France it was indeed the rule, but Miss Wilkinson was English and unmarried; her father was a clergyman. Then it struck him that the art-student probably was neither the first nor the last of her lovers, and he gasped: he had never looked upon Miss Wilkinson like that; it seemed incredible that anyone should make love to her. In his ingenuousness he doubted her story as little as he doubted what he read in books, and he was angry that such wonderful things never happened to him. It was humiliating that if Miss Wilkinson insisted upon his telling her of his adventures in Heidelberg he would have nothing to tell. It was true that he had some power of invention, but he was not sure whether he could persuade her that he was steeped in vice; women were full of intuition, he had read that, and she might easily discover that he was fibbing. He blushed scarlet as he thought of her laughing up her sleeve.

Miss Wilkinson played the piano and sang in a rather tired voice; but her songs, Massenet, Benjamin Goddard, and Augusta Holmès, were new to Philip; and together they spent many hours at the piano. One day she wondered if he had a voice and insisted on trying it. She told him he had a pleasant baritone and offered to give him lessons. At first with his usual bashfulness he refused, but she insisted, and then every morning at a convenient time after breakfast she gave him an hour's lesson. She had a natural gift for teaching, and it was clear that she was an excellent governess. She had method and firmness. Though her French accent was so much part of her that it remained, all the mellifluousness of her manner left her when she was engaged in teaching. She put up with no nonsense. Her voice became a little peremptory, and instinctively she suppressed inattention and corrected slovenliness. She knew what she was about and put Philip to scales and exercises.

When the lesson was over she resumed without effort her seductive smiles, her voice became again soft and winning, but Philip could not so easily put away the pupil as she the pedagogue; and this impression conflicted with the feelings her stories had aroused in him. He looked at her more narrowly. He liked her much better in the evening than in the morning. In the morning she was rather lined and the skin of her neck was just a little rough. He wished she would hide it, but the weather was very warm just then and she wore blouses which were cut low. She was very fond of white; in the morning it did not suit her. At night she often looked very attractive, she put on a gown which was almost a dinner-dress, and she wore a chain of garnets round her neck; the lace about her bosom and at her elbows gave her a pleasant softness, and the scent she wore (at Blackstable no one used anything but *Eau de Cologne,* and that only on Sundays or when suffering from a sick headache) was troubling and exotic. She really looked very young then.

Philip was much exercised over her age. He added twenty and seventeen together, and could not bring them to a satisfactory total. He asked Aunt Louisa more than once why she thought Miss Wilkinson was thirty-seven: she didn't look more than thirty, and everyone knew that foreigners aged more rapidly than English women; Miss Wilkinson had lived so long abroad that she might almost be called a foreigner. He personally wouldn't have thought her more than twenty-six.

"She's more than that," said Aunt Louisa.

Philip did not believe in the accuracy of the Careys' statements. All they distinctly remembered was that Miss Wilkinson had not got her hair up the last time they saw her in Lincolnshire. Well, she might have been twelve then: it was so long ago and the Vicar was always so unreliable. They said it was twenty years ago, but people used round figures, and it was just as likely to be eighteen years, or seventeen. Seventeen and twelve were only twenty-nine, and hang it all, that wasn't old, was it? Cleopatra was forty-eight when Antony threw away the world for her sake.

It was a fine summer. Day after day was hot and cloudless; but the heat was tempered by the neighbourhood of the sea, and there was a pleasant exhilaration in the air, so that one was excited and not oppressed by the August sunshine. There was a pond in the garden in which a fountain played; water lilies grew in it and gold fish sunned themselves on the surface. Philip and Miss Wilkinson used to take rugs and cushions there after dinner and lie on the lawn in the shade of a tall hedge of roses. They talked and read all the afternoon. They smoked cigarettes, which the Vicar did not allow in the house; he thought smoking a disgusting habit, and used frequently to say that it was disgraceful for anyone to grow a slave to a habit. He forgot that he was himself a slave to afternoon tea.

One day Miss Wilkinson gave Philip *La Vie de Bohème.* She had found it by accident when she was rummaging among the books in the Vicar's study. It had been bought in a lot with something Mr. Carey wanted and had remained undiscovered for ten years.

Philip began to read Murger's fascinating, ill-written, absurd masterpiece, and fell at once under its spell. His soul danced with joy at that picture of starvation which is so good-humoured, of squalor which is so picturesque, of sordid love which is so romantic, of bathos which is so moving. Rodolphe and Mimi, Musette and Schaunard! They wander through the grey streets of the Latin Quarter, finding refuge now in one attic, now in another, in their quaint costumes of Louis

Philippe, with their tears and their smiles, happy-go-lucky and reckless. Who can resist them? It is only when you return to the book with a sounder judgment that you find how gross their pleasures were, how vulgar their minds; and you feel the utter worthlessness, as artists and as human beings, of that gay procession. Philip was enraptured.

"Don't you wish you were going to Paris instead of London?" asked Miss Wilkinson, smiling at his enthusiasm.

"It's too late now even if I did," he answered.

During the fortnight he had been back from Germany there had been much discussion between himself and his uncle about his future. He had refused definitely to go to Oxford, and now that there was no chance of his getting scholarships even Mr. Carey came to the conclusion that he could not afford it. His entire fortune had consisted of only two thousand pounds, and though it had been invested in mortgages at five per cent, he had not been able to live on the interest. It was now a little reduced. It would be absurd to spend two hundred a year, the least he could live on at a university, for three years at Oxford which would lead him no nearer to earning his living. He was anxious to go straight to London. Mrs. Carey thought there were only four professions for a gentleman, the Army, the Navy, the Law, and the Church. She had added medicine because her brother-in-law practised it, but did not forget that in her young days no one ever considered the doctor a gentleman. The first two were out of the question, and Philip was firm in his refusal to be ordained. Only the law remained. The local doctor had suggested that many gentlemen now went in for engineering, but Mrs. Carey opposed the idea at once.

"I shouldn't like Philip to go into trade," she said.

"No, he must have a profession," answered the Vicar.

"Why not make him a doctor like his father?"

"I should hate it," said Philip.

Mrs. Carey was not sorry. The Bar seemed out of the question, since he was not going to Oxford, for the Careys were under the impression that a degree was still necessary for success in that calling; and finally it was suggested that he should become articled to a solicitor. They wrote to the family lawyer, Albert Nixon, who was co-executor with the Vicar of Blackstable for the late Henry Carey's estate, and asked him whether he would take Philip. In a day or two the answer came back that he had not a vacancy, and was very much opposed to the whole scheme; the profession was greatly overcrowded, and without capital or connections a man had small chance of becoming more than a managing clerk; he suggested, however, that Philip should become a chartered accountant. Neither the Vicar nor his wife knew in the least what this was, and Philip had never heard of anyone being a chartered accountant; but another letter from the solicitor explained that the growth of modern businesses and the increase of companies had led to the formation of many firms of accountants to examine the books and put into the financial affairs of their clients an order which old-fashioned methods had lacked. Some years before a Royal Charter had been obtained, and the profession was becoming every year more respectable, lucrative, and important. The chartered accountants whom Albert Nixon had employed for thirty years happened to have a vacancy for an articled pupil, and would take Philip for a fee of three hundred pounds. Half of this would be returned during the five years the articles lasted in the form of salary. The prospect was not exciting, but Philip felt that he must decide on something, and the thought of living in London over-balanced the slight shrinking he felt. The Vicar of Blackstable wrote to ask Mr. Nixon whether it was a profession suited to a gentleman; and Mr. Nixon replied that, since the Charter, men were going into it who had been to public schools and a university; moreover, if Philip disliked the work and after a year wished to leave, Herbert Carter, for that was the accountant's name, would return half the money paid for the articles. This settled it, and it was arranged that Philip should start work on the fifteenth of September.

"I have a full month before me," said Philip.

"And then you go to freedom and I to bondage," returned Miss Wilkinson.

Her holidays were to last six weeks, and she would be leaving Blackstable only a day or two before Philip.

"I wonder if we shall ever meet again," she said.

"I don't know why not."

"Oh, don't speak in that practical way. I never knew anyone so unsentimental."

Philip reddened. He was afraid that Miss Wilkinson would think him a milksop: after all she was a young woman, sometimes quite pretty, and he was getting on for twenty; it was absurd that they should talk of nothing but art and literature. He ought to make love to her. They had talked a good deal of love. There was the art-student in the Rue Bréda, and then there was the painter in whose family she had lived so long in Paris: he had asked her to sit for him, and had started to make love to her so violently that she was forced to invent excuses not to sit to him again. It was clear enough that Miss Wilkinson was used to attentions of that sort. She looked very nice now in a large straw hat: it was hot that afternoon, the hottest day they had had, and beads of sweat stood in a line on her upper lip. He called to mind Fräulein Cäcilie and Herr Sung. He had never thought of Cäcilie in an amorous way, she was exceedingly plain; but now, looking back, the affair seemed very romantic. He had a chance of romance too. Miss Wilkinson was practically French, and that added zest to a possible adventure. When he thought of it at night in bed, or when he sat by himself in the garden reading a book, he was thrilled by it; but when he saw Miss Wilkinson it seemed less picturesque.

At all events, after what she had told him, she would not be surprised if he made love to her. He had a feeling that she must think it odd of him to make no sign: perhaps it was only his fancy, but once or twice in the last day or two he had imagined that there was a suspicion of contempt in her eyes.

"A penny for your thoughts," said Miss Wilkinson, looking at him with a smile.

"I'm not going to tell you," he answered.

He was thinking that he ought to kiss her there and then. He wondered if she expected him to do it; but after all he didn't see how he could without any preliminary business at all. She would just think him mad, or she might slap his face; and perhaps she would complain to his uncle. He wondered how Herr Sung had started with Fräulein Cäcilie. It would be beastly if she told his uncle: he knew what his uncle was, he would tell the doctor and Josiah Graves; and he would look a perfect fool. Aunt Louisa kept on saying that Miss Wilkinson was thirty-seven if she was a day; he shuddered at the thought of the ridicule he would be exposed to; they would say she was old enough to be his mother.

"Twopence for your thoughts," smiled Miss Wilkinson.

"I was thinking about you," he answered boldly.

That at all events committed him to nothing.

"What were you thinking?"

"Ah, now you want to know too much."

"Naughty boy!" said Miss Wilkinson.

There it was again! Whenever he had succeeded in working himself up she said something which reminded him of the governess. She called him playfully a naughty boy when he did not sing his exercises to her satisfaction. This time he grew quite sulky.

"I wish you wouldn't treat me as if I were a child."

"Are you cross?"

"Very."

"I didn't mean to."

She put out her hand and he took it. Once or twice lately when they shook hands at night he had fancied she slightly pressed his hand, but this time there was no doubt about it.

He did not quite know what he ought to say next. Here at last was his chance of an adventure, and he would be a fool not to take it; but it was a little ordinary, and he had expected more glamour. He had read many descriptions of love, and he felt in himself none of that uprush of emotion which novelists described; he was not carried off his feet in wave upon wave of passion; nor was Miss Wilkinson the ideal: he had often pictured to himself the great violet eyes and the alabaster skin of some lovely girl, and he had thought of himself burying his face in the rippling masses of her auburn hair. He could not imagine himself burying his face in Miss Wilkinson's hair, it always struck him as a little sticky. All the same it would be very satisfactory to have an intrigue, and he thrilled with the legitimate pride he would enjoy in his conquest. He owed it to himself to seduce her. He made up his mind to kiss Miss Wilkinson; not then, but in the evening; it would be easier in the dark, and after he had kissed her the rest would follow. He would kiss her that very evening. He swore an oath to that effect.

He laid his plans. After supper he suggested that they should take a stroll in the garden. Miss Wilkinson accepted, and they sauntered side by side. Philip was very nervous. He did not know why, but the conversation would not lead in the right direction; he had decided that the first thing to do was to put his arm round her waist; but he could not suddenly put his arm round her waist when she was talking of the regatta which was to be held next week. He led her artfully into the darkest parts of the garden, but having arrived there his courage failed him. They sat on a bench, and he had really made up his mind that here was his opportunity when Miss Wilkinson said she was sure there were earwigs and insisted on moving. They walked round the garden once more, and Philip promised himself he would take the plunge before they arrived at that bench again; but as they passed the house, they saw Mrs. Carey standing at the door.

"Hadn't you young people better come in? I'm sure the night air isn't good for you."

"Perhaps we had better go in," said Philip. "I don't want you to catch cold."

He said it with a sigh of relief. He could attempt nothing more that night. But afterwards, when he was alone in his room, he was furious with himself. He had been a perfect fool. He was certain that Miss Wilkinson expected him to kiss her, otherwise she wouldn't have come into the garden. She was always saying that only Frenchmen knew how to treat women. Philip had read French novels. If he had been a Frenchman he would have seized her in his arms and told her passionately that he adored her; he would have pressed his lips on her *nuque*. He did not know why Frenchmen always kissed ladies on the *nuque*. He did not himself see anything so very attractive in the nape of the neck. Of course it was much easier for Frenchmen to do these things; the language was such an aid; Philip could never help feeling that to say passionate things in English sounded a little absurd. He wished now that he had never undertaken the siege of Miss Wilkinson's virtue; the first fortnight had been so jolly, and now he was wretched; but he was determined not to give in, he would never respect himself again if he did, and he made up his mind irrevocably that the next night he would kiss her without fail.

Next day when he got up he saw it was raining, and his first thought was that they would not be able to go into the garden that evening. He was in high spirits at breakfast. Miss Wilkinson sent Mary Ann in to say that she had a headache and would remain in bed. She did not come down till tea-time, when she appeared in a becoming wrapper and a pale face; but she was quite recovered by supper, and the meal was very cheerful. After prayers she said she would go straight to bed, and she kissed Mrs. Carey. Then she turned to Philip.

"Good gracious!" she cried. "I was just going to kiss you too."

"Why don't you?" he said.

She laughed and held out her hand. She distinctly pressed his.

The following day there was not a cloud in the sky, and the garden was sweet and fresh after the rain. Philip went down to the beach to bathe and when he came home ate a magnificent dinner. They were having a tennis-party at the vicarage in the afternoon and Miss Wilkinson put on her best dress. She certainly knew how to wear her clothes, and Philip could not help noticing how elegant she looked beside the curate's wife and the doctor's married daughter. There were two roses in her waistband. She sat in a garden chair by the side of the lawn, holding a red parasol over herself, and the light on her face was very becoming. Philip was fond of tennis. He served well and as he ran clumsily played close to the net: notwithstanding his club-foot he was quick, and it was difficult to get a ball past him. He was pleased because he won all his sets. At tea he lay down at Miss Wilkinson's feet, hot and panting.

"Flannels suit you," she said. "You look very nice this afternoon."

He blushed with delight.

"I can honestly return the compliment. You look perfectly ravishing."

She smiled and gave him a long look with her black eyes.

After supper he insisted that she should come out.

"Haven't you had enough exercise for one day?"

"It'll be lovely in the garden tonight. The stars are all out."

He was in high spirits.

"D'you know, Mrs. Carey has been scolding me on your account?" said Miss Wilkinson, when they were sauntering through the kitchen-garden. "She says I mustn't flirt with you."

"Have you been flirting with me? I hadn't noticed it."

"She was only joking."

"It was very unkind of you to refuse to kiss me last night."

"If you saw the look your uncle gave me when I said what I did!"

"Was that all that prevented you?"

"I prefer to kiss people without witnesses."

"There are no witnesses now."

Philip put his arm round her waist and kissed her lips. She only laughed a little and made no attempt to withdraw. It had come quite naturally. Philip was very proud of himself. He said he would, and he had. It was the easiest thing in the world. He wished he had done it before. He did it again.

"Oh, you mustn't," she said.

"Why not?"

"Because I like it," she laughed.

Chapter XXXIV

Next day after dinner they took their rugs and cushions to the fountain, and their books; but they did not read. Miss Wilkinson made herself comfortable and she opened the red sun-shade. Philip was not at all shy now, but at first she would not let him kiss her.

"It was very wrong of me last night," she said. "I couldn't sleep, I felt I'd done so wrong."

"What nonsense!" he cried. "I'm sure you slept like a top."

"What do you think your uncle would say if he knew?"

"There's no reason why he should know."

He leaned over her, and his heart went pit-a-pat.

"Why d'you want to kiss me?"

He knew he ought to reply: "Because I love you." But he could not bring himself to say it.

"Why do you think?" he asked instead.

She looked at him with smiling eyes and touched his face with the tips of her fingers.

"How smooth your face is," she murmured.

"I want shaving awfully," he said.

It was astonishing how difficult he found it to make romantic speeches. He found that silence helped him much more than words. He could look inexpressible things. Miss Wilkinson sighed.

"Do you like me at all?"

"Yes, awfully."

When he tried to kiss her again she did not resist. He pretended to be much more passionate than he really was, and he succeeded in playing a part which looked very well in his own eyes.

"I'm beginning to be rather frightened of you," said Miss Wilkinson.

"You'll come out after supper, won't you?" he begged.

"Not unless you promise to behave yourself."

"I'll promise anything."

He was catching fire from the flame he was partly simulating, and at tea-time he was obstreperously merry. Miss Wilkinson looked at him nervously.

"You mustn't have those shining eyes," she said to him afterwards. "What will your Aunt Louisa think?"

"I don't care what she thinks."

Miss Wilkinson gave a little laugh of pleasure. They had no sooner finished supper than he said to her:

"Are you going to keep me company while I smoke a cigarette?"

"Why don't you let Miss Wilkinson rest?" said Mrs. Carey. "You must remember she's not as young as you."

"Oh, I'd like to go out, Mrs. Carey," she said, rather acidly.

"After dinner walk a mile, after supper rest a while," said the Vicar.

"Your aunt is very nice, but she gets on my nerves sometimes," said Miss Wilkinson, as soon as they closed the side-door behind them.

Philip threw away the cigarette he had just lighted, and flung his arms round her. She tried to push him away.

"You promised you'd be good, Philip."

"You didn't think I was going to keep a promise like that?"

"Not so near the house, Philip," she said. "Supposing someone should come out suddenly?"

He led her to the kitchen-garden where no one was likely to come, and this time Miss Wilkinson did not think of earwigs. He kissed her passionately. It was one of the things that puzzled him that he did not like her at all in the morning, and only moderately in the afternoon, but at night the touch of her hand thrilled him. He said things that he would never have thought himself capable of saying; he could certainly never have said them in the broad light of day; and he listened to himself with wonder and satisfaction.

"How beautifully you make love," she said.

That was what he thought himself.

"Oh, if I could only say all the things that burn my heart!" he murmured passionately.

It was splendid. It was the most thrilling game he had ever played; and the wonderful thing was that he felt almost all he said. It was only that he exaggerated a little. He was tremendously interested and excited in the effect he could see it had on her. It was obviously with an effort that at last she suggested going in.

"Oh, don't go yet," he cried.

"I must," she muttered. "I'm frightened."

He had a sudden intuition what was the right thing to do then.

"I can't go in yet. I shall stay here and think. My cheeks are burning. I want the night-air. Good-night."

He held out his hand seriously, and she took it in silence. He thought she stifled a sob. Oh, it was magnificent! When, after a decent interval during which he had been rather bored in the dark garden by himself, he went in he found that Miss Wilkinson had already gone to bed.

After that things were different between them. The next day and the day after Philip showed himself an eager lover. He was deliciously flattered to discover that Miss Wilkinson was in love with him: she told him so in English, and she told him so in French. She paid him compliments. No one had ever informed him before that his eyes were charming and that he had a sensual mouth. He had never bothered much about his personal appearance, but now, when occasion presented, he looked at himself in the glass with satisfaction. When he kissed her it was wonderful to feel the passion that seemed to thrill her soul. He kissed her a good deal, for he found it easier to do that than to say the things he instinctively felt she expected of him. It still made him feel a fool to say he worshipped her. He wished there were someone to whom he could boast a little, and he would willingly have discussed minute points of his conduct. Sometimes she said things that were enigmatic, and he was puzzled. He wished Hayward had been there so that he could ask him what he thought she meant, and what he had better do next. He could not make up his mind whether he ought to rush things or let them take their time. There were only three weeks more.

"I can't bear to think of that," she said. "It breaks my heart. And then perhaps we shall never see one another again."

"If you cared for me at all, you wouldn't be so unkind to me," he whispered.

"Oh, why can't you be content to let it go on as it is? Men are always the same. They're never satisfied."

And when he pressed her, she said:

"But don't you see it's impossible. How can we here?"

He proposed all sorts of schemes, but she would not have anything to do with them.

"I daren't take the risk. It would be too dreadful if your aunt found out."

A day or two later he had an idea which seemed brilliant.

"Look here, if you had a headache on Sunday evening and offered to stay at home and look after the house, Aunt Louisa would go to church."

Generally Mrs. Carey remained in on Sunday evening in order to allow Mary Ann to go to church, but she would welcome the opportunity of attending evensong.

Philip had not found it necessary to impart to his relations the change in his views on Christianity which had occurred in Germany; they could not be expected to understand; and it seemed less trouble to go to church quietly. But he only went in the morning. He regarded this as a graceful concession to the prejudices of society and his refusal to go a second time as an adequate assertion of free thought.

When he made the suggestion, Miss Wilkinson did not speak for a moment, then shook her head.

"No, I won't," she said.

But on Sunday at tea-time she surprised Philip.

"I don't think I'll come to church this evening," she said suddenly. "I've really got a dreadful headache."

Mrs. Carey, much concerned, insisted on giving her some "drops" which she was herself in the habit of using. Miss Wilkinson thanked her, and immediately after tea announced that she would go to her room and lie down.

"Are you sure there's nothing you'll want?" asked Mrs. Carey anxiously.

"Quite sure, thank you."

"Because, if there isn't, I think I'll go to church. I don't often have the chance of going in the evening."

"Oh yes, do go."

"I shall be in," said Philip. "If Miss Wilkinson wants anything, she can always call me."

"You'd better leave the drawing-room door open, Philip, so that if Miss Wilkinson rings, you'll hear."

"Certainly," said Philip.

So after six o'clock Philip was left alone in the house with Miss Wilkinson. He felt sick with apprehension. He wished with all his heart that he had not suggested the plan; but it was too late now; he must take the opportunity which he had made. What would Miss Wilkinson think of him if he did not! He went into the hall and listened. There was not a sound. He wondered if Miss Wilkinson really had a headache. Perhaps she had forgotten his suggestion. His heart beat painfully. He crept up the stairs as softly as he could, and he stopped with a start when they creaked. He stood outside Miss Wilkinson's room and listened; he put his hand on the knob of the door-handle. He waited. It seemed to him that he waited for at least five minutes, trying to make up his mind; and his hand trembled. He would willingly have bolted, but he was afraid of the remorse which he knew would seize him. It was like getting on the highest diving-board in a swimming-bath; it looked nothing from below, but when you got up there and stared down at the water your heart sank; and the only thing that forced you to dive was the shame of coming down meekly by the steps you had climbed up. Philip screwed up his courage. He turned the handle softly and walked in. He seemed to himself to be trembling like a leaf.

Miss Wilkinson was standing at the dressing-table with her back to the door, and she turned round quickly when she heard it open.

"Oh, it's you. What d'you want?"

She had taken off her skirt and blouse, and was standing in her petticoat. It was short and only came down to the top of her boots; the upper part of it was black, of some shiny material, and there was a red flounce. She wore a camisole of white calico with short arms. She looked grotesque. Philip's heart sank as he stared at her; she had never seemed so unattractive; but it was too late now. He closed the door behind him and locked it.

Chapter XXXV

Philip woke early next morning. His sleep had been restless; but when he stretched his legs and looked at the sunshine that slid through the Venetian blinds, making patterns on the floor, he sighed with satisfaction. He was delighted with himself. He began to think of Miss Wilkinson. She had asked him to call her Emily, but, he knew not why, he could not; he always thought of her as Miss Wilkinson. Since she chid him for so addressing her, he avoided using her name at all. During his childhood he had often heard a sister of Aunt Louisa, the widow of a naval officer, spoken of as Aunt Emily. It made him uncomfortable to call Miss Wilkinson by that name, nor could he think of any that would have suited her better. She had begun as Miss Wilkinson, and it seemed inseparable from his impression of her. He frowned a little: somehow or other he saw her now at her worst; he could not forget his dismay when she turned round and he saw her in her camisole and the short petticoat; he remembered the slight roughness of her skin and the sharp, long lines on the side of the neck. His triumph was short-lived. He reckoned out her age again, and he did not see how she could be less than forty. It made the affair ridiculous. She was plain and old. His quick fancy showed her to him, wrinkled, haggard, made-up, in those frocks which were too showy for her position and too young for her years. He shuddered; he felt suddenly that he never wanted to see her again; he could not bear the thought of kissing her. He was horrified with himself. Was that love?

He took as long as he could over dressing in order to put back the moment of seeing her, and when at last he went into the dining-room it was with a sinking heart. Prayers were over, and they were sitting down at breakfast.

"Lazy bones," Miss Wilkinson cried gaily.

He looked at her and gave a little gasp of relief. She was sitting with her back to the window. She was really quite nice. He wondered why he had thought such things about her. His self-satisfaction returned to him.

He was taken aback by the change in her. She told him in a voice thrilling with emotion immediately after breakfast that she loved him; and when a little later they went into the drawing-room for his singing lesson and she sat down on the music-stool she put up her face in the middle of a scale and said:

"*Embrasse-moi.*"

When he bent down she flung her arms round his neck. It was slightly uncomfortable, for she held him in such a position that he felt rather choked.

"*Ah, je t'aime. Je t'aime. Je t'aime,*" she cried, with her extravagantly French accent. Philip wished she would speak English.

"I say, I don't know if it's struck you that the gardener's quite likely to pass the window any minute."

"*Ah, je m'en fiche du jardinier. Je m'en refiche, et je m'en contrefiche.*"

Philip thought it was very like a French novel, and he did not know why it slightly irritated him.

At last he said:

"Well, I think I'll tootle along to the beach and have a dip."

"Oh, you're not going to leave me this morning—of all mornings?"

Philip did not quite know why he should not, but it did not matter.

"Would you like me to stay?" he smiled.

"Oh, you darling! But no, go. Go. I want to think of you mastering the salt sea waves, bathing your limbs in the broad ocean."

He got his hat and sauntered off.

"What rot women talk!" he thought to himself.

But he was pleased and happy and flattered. She was evidently frightfully gone on him. As he limped along the high street of Blackstable he looked with a tinge of superciliousness at the people he passed. He knew a good many to nod to, and as he gave them a smile of recognition he thought to himself, if they only knew! He did want someone to know very badly. He thought he would write to Hayward, and in his mind composed the letter. He would talk of the garden and the roses, and the little French governess, like an exotic flower amongst them, scented and perverse: he would say she was French, because—well, she had lived in France so long that she almost was, and besides it would be shabby to give the whole thing away too exactly, don't you know; and he would tell Hayward how he had seen her first in her pretty muslin dress and of the flower she had given him. He made a delicate idyl of it: the sunshine and the sea gave it passion and magic, and the stars added poetry, and the old vicarage garden was a fit and exquisite setting. There was something Meredithian about it: it was not quite Lucy Feverel and not quite Clara Middleton; but it was inexpressibly charming. Philip's heart beat quickly. He was so delighted with his fancies that he began thinking of them again as soon as he crawled back, dripping and cold, into his bathing-machine. He thought of the object of his affections. She had the most adorable little nose and large brown eyes—he would describe her to Hayward—and masses of soft brown hair, the sort of hair it was delicious to bury your face in, and a skin which was like ivory and sunshine, and her cheek was like a red, red rose. How old was she? Eighteen perhaps, and he called her Musette. Her laughter was like a rippling brook, and her voice was so soft, so low, it was the sweetest music he had ever heard.

"What *are* you thinking about?"

Philip stopped suddenly. He was walking slowly home.

"I've been waving at you for the last quarter of a mile. You *are* absent-minded."

Miss Wilkinson was standing in front of him, laughing at his surprise.

"I thought I'd come and meet you."

"That's awfully nice of you," he said.

"Did I startle you?"

"You did a bit," he admitted.

He wrote his letter to Hayward all the same. There were eight pages of it.

The fortnight that remained passed quickly, and though each evening, when they went into the garden after supper, Miss Wilkinson remarked that one day more had gone, Philip was in too cheerful spirits to let the thought depress him. One night Miss Wilkinson suggested that it would be delightful if she could exchange her situation in Berlin for one in London. Then they could see one another constantly. Philip said it would be very jolly, but the prospect aroused no enthusiasm in him; he was looking forward to a wonderful life in London, and he preferred not to be hampered. He spoke a little too freely of all he meant to do, and allowed Miss Wilkinson to see that already he was longing to be off.

"You wouldn't talk like that if you loved me," she cried.

He was taken aback and remained silent.

"What a fool I've been," she muttered.

To his surprise he saw that she was crying. He had a tender heart, and hated to see anyone miserable.

"Oh, I'm awfully sorry. What have I done? Don't cry."

"Oh, Philip, don't leave me. You don't know what you mean to me. I have such a wretched life, and you've made me so happy."

He kissed her silently. There really was anguish in her tone, and he was frightened. It had never occurred to him that she meant what she said quite, quite seriously.

"I'm awfully sorry. You know I'm frightfully fond of you. I wish you would come to London."

"You know I can't. Places are almost impossible to get, and I hate English life."

Almost unconscious that he was acting a part, moved by her distress, he pressed her more and more. Her tears vaguely flattered him, and he kissed her with real passion.

But a day or two later she made a real scene. There was a tennis-party at the vicarage, and two girls came, daughters of a retired major in an Indian regiment who had lately settled in Blackstable. They were very pretty, one was Philip's age and the other was a year or two younger. Being used to the society of young men (they were full of stories of hill-stations in India, and at that time the stories of Rudyard Kipling were in every hand) they began to chaff Philip gaily; and he, pleased with the novelty—the young ladies at Blackstable treated the Vicar's nephew with a certain seriousness—was gay and jolly. Some devil within him prompted him to start a violent flirtation with them both, and as he was the only young man there, they were quite willing to meet him half-way. It happened that they played tennis quite well and Philip was tired of pat-ball with Miss Wilkinson (she had only begun to play when she came to Blackstable), so when he arranged the sets after tea he suggested that Miss Wilkinson should play against the curate's wife, with the curate as her partner; and he would play later with the new-comers. He sat down by the elder Miss O'Connor and said to her in an undertone:

"We'll get the duffers out of the way first, and then we'll have a jolly set afterwards."

Apparently Miss Wilkinson overheard him, for she threw down her racket, and, saying she had a headache, went away. It was plain to everyone that she was offended. Philip was annoyed that she should make the fact public. The set was arranged without her, but presently Mrs. Carey called him.

"Philip, you've hurt Emily's feelings. She's gone to her room and she's crying."

"What about?"

"Oh, something about a duffer's set. Do go to her, and say you didn't mean to be unkind, there's a good boy."

"All right."

He knocked at Miss Wilkinson's door, but receiving no answer went in. He found her lying face downwards on her bed, weeping. He touched her on the shoulder.

"I say, what on earth's the matter?"

"Leave me alone. I never want to speak to you again."

"What have I done? I'm awfully sorry if I've hurt your feelings. I didn't mean to. I say, do get up."

"Oh, I'm so unhappy. How could you be cruel to me? You know I hate that stupid game. I only play because I want to play with you."

She got up and walked towards the dressing-table, but after a quick look in the glass sank into a chair. She made her handkerchief into a ball and dabbed her eyes with it.

"I've given you the greatest thing a woman can give a man—oh, what a fool I was—and you have no gratitude. You must be quite heartless. How could you be so cruel as to torment me by flirting with those vulgar girls. We've only got just over a week. Can't you even give me that?"

Philip stood over her rather sulkily. He thought her behaviour childish. He was vexed with her for having shown her ill-temper before strangers.

"But you know I don't care twopence about either of the O'Connors. Why on earth should you think I do?"

Miss Wilkinson put away her handkerchief. Her tears had made marks on her powdered face, and her hair was somewhat disarranged. Her white dress did not suit her very well just then. She looked at Philip with hungry, passionate eyes.

"Because you're twenty and so's she," she said hoarsely. "And I'm old."

Philip reddened and looked away. The anguish of her tone made him feel strangely uneasy. He wished with all his heart that he had never had anything to do with Miss Wilkinson.

"I don't want to make you unhappy," he said awkwardly. "You'd better go down and look after your friends. They'll wonder what has become of you."

"All right."

He was glad to leave her.

The quarrel was quickly followed by a reconciliation, but the few days that remained were sometimes irksome to Philip. He wanted to talk of nothing but the future, and the future invariably reduced Miss Wilkinson to tears. At first her weeping affected him, and feeling himself a beast he redoubled his protestations of undying passion; but now it irritated him: it would have been all very well if she had been a girl, but it was silly of a grown-up woman to cry so much. She never ceased reminding him that he was under a debt of gratitude to her which he could never repay. He was willing to acknowledge this since she made a point of it, but he did not really know why he should be any more grateful to her than she to him. He was expected to show his sense of obligation in ways which were rather a nuisance: he had been a good deal used to solitude, and it was a necessity to him sometimes; but Miss Wilkinson looked upon it as an unkindness if he was not always at her beck and call. The Miss O'Connors asked them both to tea, and Philip would have liked to go, but Miss Wilkinson said she only had five days more and wanted him entirely to herself. It was flattering, but a bore. Miss Wilkinson told him stories of the exquisite delicacy of Frenchmen when they stood in the same relation to fair ladies as he to Miss Wilkinson. She praised their courtesy, their passion for self-sacrifice, their perfect tact. Miss Wilkinson seemed to want a great deal.

Philip listened to her enumeration of the qualities which must be possessed by the perfect lover, and he could not help feeling a certain satisfaction that she lived in Berlin.

"You will write to me, won't you? Write to me every day. I want to know everything you're doing. You must keep nothing from me."

"I shall be awfully busy" he answered. "I'll write as often as I can."

She flung her arms passionately round his neck. He was embarrassed sometimes by the demonstrations of her affection. He would have preferred her to be more passive. It shocked him a little that she should give him so marked a lead: it did not tally altogether with his prepossessions about the modesty of the feminine temperament.

At length the day came on which Miss Wilkinson was to go, and she came down to breakfast, pale and subdued, in a serviceable travelling dress of black and white check. She looked a very competent governess. Philip was silent too, for he did not quite know what to say that would fit the circumstance; and he was terribly afraid that, if he said something flippant, Miss Wilkinson would break down before his uncle and make a scene. They had said their last good-bye to one another in the garden the night before, and Philip was relieved that there was now no opportunity for them to be alone. He remained in the dining-room after breakfast in case Miss Wilkinson should insist on kissing him on the stairs. He did not want Mary Ann, now a woman hard upon middle age with a sharp tongue, to catch them in a compromising position. Mary Ann did not like Miss Wilkinson and called her an old cat. Aunt Louisa was not very well and could not come to the station, but the Vicar and Philip saw her off. Just as the train was leaving she leaned out and kissed Mr. Carey.

"I must kiss you too, Philip," she said.

"All right," he said, blushing.

He stood up on the step and she kissed him quickly. The train started, and Miss Wilkinson sank into the corner of her carriage and wept disconsolately. Philip as he walked back to the vicarage felt a distinct sensation of relief.

"Well, did you see her safely off?" asked Aunt Louisa, when they got in.

"Yes, she seemed rather weepy. She insisted on kissing me and Philip."

"Oh, well, at her age it's not dangerous." Mrs. Carey pointed to the sideboard. "There's a letter for you, Philip. It came by the second post."

It was from Hayward and ran as follows:

MY DEAR BOY—I answer your letter at once. I ventured to read it to a great friend of mine, a charming woman whose help and sympathy have been very precious to me, a woman withal with a real feeling for art and literature; and we agreed that it was charming. You wrote from your heart and you do not know the delightful naïveté which is in every line. And because you love you write like a poet. Ah, dear boy, that is the real thing: I felt the glow of your young passion, and your prose was musical from the sincerity of your emotion. You must be happy! I wish I could have been present unseen in that enchanted garden while you wandered hand in hand, like Daphnis and Chloe, amid the flowers. I can see you, my Daphnis, with the light of young love in your eyes, tender, enraptured, and ardent; while Chloe in your arms, so young and soft and fresh, vowing she would ne'er consent—consented. Roses and violets and honeysuckle! Oh, my friend, I envy you. It is so good to think that your first love should have been pure poetry. Treasure the moments, for the immortal gods have given you the Greatest Gift of All, and it will be a sweet, sad memory till your dying day. You will never again enjoy that careless rapture. First love is best love; and she is beautiful and you are young, and all the world is yours. I felt my pulse go faster when with your adorable simplicity you told me that you buried your face in her long hair. I am sure that it is that exquisite chestnut which seems just touched with gold. I would have you sit under a leafy tree side by side, and read together *Romeo and Juliet*; and then I would have you fall on your knees and on my behalf kiss the ground on which her foot has left its imprint; then tell her it is the homage of a poet to her radiant youth and to your love for her.

Yours always,
G. ETHERIDGE HAYWARD

"What damned rot!" said Philip, when he finished the letter.

Miss Wilkinson oddly enough had suggested that they should read *Romeo and Juliet* together; but Philip had firmly declined. Then, as he put the letter in his pocket, he felt a queer little pang of bitterness because reality seemed so different from the ideal.

Chapter XXXVI

A FEW DAYS LATER PHILIP WENT TO LONDON. THE CURATE HAD RECOMmended rooms in Barnes, and these Philip engaged by letter at fourteen shillings a week. He reached them in the evening; and the landlady, a funny little old woman with a shrivelled body and a deeply wrinkled face, had prepared high tea for him. Most of the sitting-room was taken up by the sideboard and a square table; against one wall was a sofa covered with horsehair, and by the fireplace an arm-chair to match: there was a white antimacassar over the back of it, and on the seat, because the springs were broken, a hard cushion.

After having his tea he unpacked and arranged his books, then he sat down and tried to read; but he was depressed. The silence in the street made him slightly uncomfortable, and he felt very much alone.

Next day he got up early. He put on his tail-coat and the tall hat which he had worn at school; but it was very shabby, and he made up his mind to stop at the Stores on his way to the office and buy a new one. When he had done this he found himself in plenty of time and so walked along the Strand. The office of Messrs. Herbert Carter & Co. was in a little street off Chancery Lane, and he had to ask his way two or three times. He felt that people were staring at him a great deal, and once he took off his hat to see whether by chance the label had been left on. When he arrived he knocked at the door; but no one answered, and looking at his watch he found it was barely half-past nine; he supposed he was too early. He went away and ten minutes later returned to find an office-boy, with a long nose, pimply face, and a Scotch accent, opening the door. Philip asked for Mr. Herbert Carter. He had not come yet.

"When will he be here?"

"Between ten and half-past."

"I'd better wait," said Philip.

"What are you wanting?" asked the office-boy.

Philip was nervous, but tried to hide the fact by a jocose manner.

"Well, I'm going to work here if you have no objection."

"Oh, you're the new articled clerk? You'd better come in. Mr. Goodworthy'll be here in a while."

Philip walked in, and as he did so saw the office-boy—he was about the same age as Philip and called himself a junior clerk—look at his foot. He flushed and, sitting down, hid it behind the other. He looked round the room. It was dark and very dingy. It was lit by a skylight. There were three rows of desks in it and against them high stools. Over the chimney-piece was a dirty engraving of a prize-fight. Presently a clerk came in and then another; they glanced at Philip and in an undertone asked the office-boy (Philip found his name was Macdougal) who he was. A whistle blew, and Macdougal got up.

"Mr. Goodworthy's come. He's the managing clerk. Shall I tell him you're here?"

"Yes, please," said Philip.

The office-boy went out and in a moment returned.

"Will you come this way?"

Philip followed him across the passage and was shown into a room, small and barely furnished, in which a little, thin man was standing with his back to the fireplace. He was much below the middle height, but his large head, which seemed to hang loosely on his body, gave him an odd ungainliness. His features were wide and flattened, and he had prominent, pale eyes; his thin hair was sandy; he wore whiskers that grew unevenly on his face, and in places where you would have expected the hair to grow thickly there was no hair at all. His skin was pasty and yellow. He held out his hand to Philip, and when he smiled showed badly decayed teeth. He spoke with a patronising and at the same time a timid air, as though he sought to assume an importance which he did not feel. He said he hoped Philip would like the work; there was a good deal of drudgery about it, but when you got used to it, it was interesting; and one made money, that was the chief thing, wasn't it? He laughed with his odd mixture of superiority and shyness.

"Mr. Carter will be here presently," he said. "He's a little late on Monday mornings sometimes. I'll call you when he comes. In the meantime I must give you something to do. Do you know anything about book-keeping or accounts?"

"I'm afraid not," answered Philip.

"I didn't suppose you would. They don't teach you things at school that are much use in business, I'm afraid." He considered for a moment. "I think I can find you something to do."

He went into the next room and after a little while came out with a large cardboard box. It contained a vast number of letters in great disorder, and he told Philip to sort them out and arrange them alphabetically according to the names of the writers.

"I'll take you to the room in which the articled clerk generally sits. There's a very nice fellow in it. His name is Watson. He's a son of Watson, Crag, and Thompson—you know—the brewers. He's spending a year with us to learn business."

Mr. Goodworthy led Philip through the dingy office, where now six or eight clerks were working, into a narrow room behind. It had been made into a separate apartment by a glass partition, and here they found Watson sitting back in a chair, reading *The Sportsman*. He was a large, stout young man, elegantly dressed, and he looked up as Mr. Goodworthy entered. He asserted his position by calling the managing clerk Goodworthy. The managing clerk objected to the familiarity, and pointedly called him Mr. Watson, but Watson, instead of seeing that it was a rebuke, accepted the title as a tribute to his gentlemanliness.

"I see they've scratched Rigoletto," he said to Philip, as soon as they were left alone.

"Have they?" said Philip, who knew nothing about horse-racing.

He looked with awe upon Watson's beautiful clothes. His tail-coat fitted him perfectly, and there was a valuable pin artfully stuck in the middle of an enormous tie. On the chimney-piece rested his tall hat; it was saucy and bell-shaped and shiny. Philip felt himself very shabby. Watson began to talk of hunting—it was such an infernal bore having to waste one's time in an infernal office, he would only be able to hunt on Saturdays—and shooting: he had ripping invitations all over the country and of course he had to refuse them. It was infernal luck, but he wasn't going to put up with it long; he was only in this internal hole for a year, and then he was going into the business, and he would hunt four days a week and get all the shooting there was.

"You've got five years of it, haven't you?" he said, waving his arm round the tiny room.

"I suppose so," said Philip.

"I daresay I shall see something of you. Carter does our accounts, you know."

Philip was somewhat overpowered by the young gentleman's condescension. At Blackstable they had always looked upon brewing with civil contempt, the Vicar made little jokes about the beerage, and it was a surprising experience for Philip to discover that Watson was such an important and magnificent fellow. He had been to Winchester and to Oxford, and his conversation impressed the fact upon one with frequency. When he discovered the details of Philip's education his manner became more patronising still.

"Of course, if one doesn't go to a public school those sort of schools are the next best thing, aren't they?"

Philip asked about the other men in the office.

"Oh, I don't bother about them much, you know," said Watson. "Carter's not a bad sort. We have him to dine now and then. All the rest are awful bounders."

Presently Watson applied himself to some work he had in hand, and Philip set about sorting his letters. Then Mr. Goodworthy came in to say that Mr. Carter had arrived. He took Philip into a large room next door to his own. There was a big desk in it, and a couple of big arm-chairs; a Turkey carpet adorned the floor, and the walls were decorated with sporting prints. Mr. Carter was sitting at the desk and got up to shake hands with Philip. He was dressed in a long frock coat. He looked like a military man; his moustache was waxed, his grey hair was short and neat, he held himself upright, he talked in a breezy way, he lived at Enfield. He was very keen on games and the good of the country. He was an officer in the Hertfordshire Yeomanry and chairman of the Conservative Association. When he was told that a local magnate had said no one would take him for a City man, he felt that he had not lived in vain. He talked to Philip in a pleasant, off-hand fashion. Mr. Goodworthy would look after him. Watson was a nice fellow, perfect gentleman, good sportsman—did Philip hunt? Pity, *the* sport for gentlemen. Didn't have much chance of hunting now, had to leave that to his son. His son was at Cambridge, he'd sent him to Rugby, fine school Rugby, nice class of boys there, in a couple of years his son would be articled, that would be nice for Philip, he'd like his son, thorough sportsman. He hoped Philip would get on well and like the work, he mustn't miss his lectures, they were getting up the tone of the profession, they wanted gentlemen in it. Well, well, Mr. Goodworthy was there. If he wanted to know anything Mr. Goodworthy would tell him. What was his handwriting like? Ah well, Mr. Goodworthy would see about that.

Philip was overwhelmed by so much gentlemanliness: in East Anglia they knew who were gentlemen and who weren't, but the gentlemen didn't talk about it.

Chapter XXXVII

At first the novelty of the work kept Philip interested. Mr. Carter dictated letters to him, and he had to make fair copies of statements of accounts.

Mr. Carter preferred to conduct the office on gentlemanly lines; he would have nothing to do with typewriting and looked upon shorthand with disfavour: the office-boy knew shorthand, but it was only Mr. Goodworthy who made use of his accomplishment. Now and then Philip with one of the more experienced clerks went out to audit the accounts of some firm: he came to know which of the clients must be treated with respect and which were in low water. Now and then long lists of figures were given him to add up. He attended lectures for his first examination. Mr. Goodworthy repeated to him that the work was dull at first, but he would grow used to it. Philip left the office at six and walked across the river to Waterloo. His supper was waiting for him when he reached his lodgings and he spent the evening reading. On Saturday afternoons he went to the National Gallery. Hayward had recommended to him a guide which had been compiled out of Ruskin's works, and with this in hand he went industriously through room after room: he read carefully what the critic had said about a picture and then in a determined fashion set himself to see the same things in it. His Sundays were difficult to get through. He knew no one in London and spent them by himself. Mr. Nixon, the solicitor, asked him to spend a Sunday at Hampstead, and Philip passed a happy day with a set of exuberant strangers; he ate and drank a great deal, took a walk on the heath, and came away with a general invitation to come again whenever he liked; but he was morbidly afraid of being in the way, so waited for a formal invitation. Naturally enough it never came, for with numbers of friends of their own the Nixons did not think of the lonely, silent boy whose claim upon their hospitality was so small. So on Sundays he got up late and took a walk along the tow-path. At Barnes the river is muddy, dingy, and tidal; it has neither the graceful charm of the Thames above the locks nor the romance of the crowded stream below London Bridge. In the afternoon he walked about the common; and that is grey and dingy too; it is neither country nor town; the gorse is stunted; and all about is the litter of civilisation. He went to a play every Saturday night and stood cheerfully for an hour or more at the gallery-door. It was not worthwhile to go back to Barnes for the interval between the closing of the Museum and his meal in an A. B. C. shop, and the time hung heavily on his hands. He strolled up Bond Street or through the Burlington Arcade, and when he was tired went and sat down in the Park or in wet weather in the public library in St. Martin's Lane. He looked at the people walking about and envied them because they had friends; sometimes his envy turned to hatred because they were happy and he was miserable. He had never imagined that it was possible to be so lonely in a great city. Sometimes when he was standing at the gallery-door the man next to him would attempt a conversation; but Philip had the country boy's suspicion of strangers and answered in such a way as to prevent any further acquaintance. After the play was over, obliged to keep to himself all he thought about it, he hurried across the bridge to Waterloo. When he got back to his rooms, in which for economy no fire had been lit, his heart sank. It was horribly cheerless. He began to loathe his lodgings and the long solitary evenings he spent in them. Sometimes he felt so lonely that he could not read, and then he sat looking into the fire hour after hour in bitter wretchedness.

He had spent three months in London now, and except for that one Sunday at Hampstead had never talked to anyone but his fellow-clerks. One evening Watson asked him to dinner at a restaurant and they went to a music-hall together; but he felt shy and uncomfortable. Watson talked all the time of things he did not care about, and while he looked upon Watson as a Philistine he could not help admiring him. He was angry because Watson obviously set no store on his culture, and with his way of taking himself at the estimate at which he saw others held him he began to despise the acquirements which till then had seemed to him not unimportant. He felt for the first time the humiliation of poverty. His uncle sent him fourteen pounds a month and he had had to buy a good many clothes. His evening suit cost him five guineas. He had not dared tell Watson that it was bought in the Strand. Watson said there was only one tailor in London.

"I suppose you don't dance," said Watson, one day, with a glance at Philip's club-foot.

"No," said Philip.

"Pity. I've been asked to bring some dancing men to a ball. I could have introduced you to some jolly girls."

Once or twice, hating the thought of going back to Barnes, Philip had remained in town, and late in the evening wandered through the West End till he found some house at which there was a party. He stood among the little group of shabby people, behind the footmen, watching the guests arrive, and he listened to the music that floated through the window. Sometimes, notwithstanding the cold, a couple came on to the balcony and stood for a moment to get some fresh air; and Philip, imagining that they were in love with one another, turned away and limped along the street with a heavy hurt. He would never be able to stand in that man's place. He felt that no woman could ever really look upon him without distaste for his deformity.

That reminded him of Miss Wilkinson. He thought of her without satisfaction. Before parting they had made an arrangement that she should write to Charing Cross Post Office till he was able to send her an address, and when he went there he found three letters from her. She wrote on blue paper with violet ink, and she wrote in French. Philip wondered why she could not write in English like a sensible woman, and her passionate expressions, because they reminded him of a French novel, left him cold. She upbraided him for not having written, and when he answered he excused himself by saying that he had been busy. He did not quite know how to start the letter. He could not bring himself to use *dearest* or *darling*, and he hated to address her as Emily, so finally he began with the word *dear*. It looked odd, standing by itself, and rather silly, but he made it do. It was the first love letter he had ever written, and he was conscious of its tameness; he felt that he should say all sorts of vehement things, how he thought of her every minute of the day and how he longed to kiss her beautiful hands and how he trembled at the thought of her red lips, but some inexplicable modesty prevented him; and instead he told her of his new rooms and his office. The answer came by return of post, angry, heart-broken, reproachful: how could he be so cold? Did he not know that she hung on his letters? She had given him all that a woman could give, and this was her reward. Was he tired of her already? Then, because he did not reply for several days, Miss Wilkinson bombarded him with letters. She could not bear his unkindness, she waited for the post, and it never brought her his letter, she cried herself to sleep night after night, she was looking so ill that everyone remarked on it: if he did not love her why did he not say so? She added that she could not live without him, and the only thing was for her to commit suicide. She told him he was cold and selfish and ungrateful. It was all in French, and Philip knew that she wrote in that language to show off, but he was worried all the same. He did not want to make her unhappy. In a little while she wrote that she could not bear the separation any longer, she would arrange to come over to London for Christmas. Philip wrote back that he would like nothing better, only he had already an engagement to spend Christmas with friends in the country, and he did not see how he could break it. She answered that she did not wish to force herself on him, it was quite evident that he did not wish to see her; she was deeply hurt, and she never thought he would repay with such cruelty all her kindness. Her letter was touching, and Philip thought he saw marks of her tears on the paper; he wrote an impulsive reply saying that he was dreadfully sorry and imploring her to come; but it was with relief that he received her answer in which she said that she found it would be impossible for her to get away. Presently when her letters came his heart sank: he delayed opening them, for he knew what they would contain, angry reproaches and pathetic appeals; they would make him feel a perfect beast, and yet he did not see with what he had to blame himself. He put off his answer from day to day, and then another letter would come, saying she was ill and lonely and miserable.

"I wish to God I'd never had anything to do with her," he said.

He admired Watson because he arranged these things so easily. The young man had been engaged in an intrigue with a girl who played in touring companies, and his account of the affair filled Philip with envious amazement. But after a time Watson's young affections changed, and one day he described the rupture to Philip.

"I thought it was no good making any bones about it so I just told her I'd had enough of her," he said.

"Didn't she make an awful scene?" asked Philip.

"The usual thing, you know, but I told her it was no good trying on that sort of thing with me."

"Did she cry?"

"She began to, but I can't stand women when they cry, so I said she'd better hook it."

Philip's sense of humour was growing keener with advancing years.

"And did she hook it?" he asked smiling.

"Well, there wasn't anything else for her to do, was there?"

Meanwhile the Christmas holidays approached. Mrs. Carey had been ill all through November, and the doctor suggested that she and the Vicar should go to Cornwall for a couple of weeks round Christmas so that she should get back her strength. The result was that Philip had nowhere to go, and he spent Christmas Day in his lodgings. Under Hayward's influence he had persuaded himself that the festivities that attend this season were vulgar and barbaric, and he made up his mind that he would take no notice of the day; but when it came, the jollity of all around affected him strangely. His landlady and her husband were spending the day with a married daughter, and to save trouble Philip announced that he would take his meals out. He went up to London towards mid-day and ate a slice of turkey and some Christmas pudding by himself at Gatti's, and since he had nothing to do afterwards went to Westminster Abbey for the afternoon service. The streets were almost empty, and the people who went along had a preoccupied look; they did not saunter but walked with some definite goal in view, and hardly anyone was alone. To Philip they all seemed happy. He felt himself more solitary than he had ever done in his life. His intention had been to kill the day somehow in the streets and then dine at a restaurant, but he could not face again the sight of cheerful people, talking, laughing, and making merry; so he went back to Waterloo, and on his way through the Westminster Bridge Road bought some ham and a couple of mince pies and went back to Barnes. He ate his food in his lonely little room and spent the evening with a book. His depression was almost intolerable.

When he was back at the office it made him very sore to listen to Watson's account of the short holiday. They had had some jolly girls staying with them, and after dinner they had cleared out the drawing-room and had a dance.

"I didn't get to bed till three and I don't know how I got there then. By George, I was squiffy."

At last Philip asked desperately:

"How does one get to know people in London?"

Watson looked at him with surprise and with a slightly contemptuous amusement.

"Oh, I don't know, one just knows them. If you go to dances you soon get to know as many people as you can do with."

Philip hated Watson, and yet he would have given anything to change places with him. The old feeling that he had had at school came back to him, and he tried to throw himself into the other's skin, imagining what life would be if he were Watson.

Chapter XXXVIII

AT THE END OF THE YEAR THERE WAS A GREAT DEAL TO DO. PHILIP WENT TO various places with a clerk named Thompson and spent the day monotonously calling out items of expenditure, which the other checked; and sometimes he was given long pages of figures to add up. He had never had a head for figures, and he could only do this slowly. Thompson grew irritated at his mistakes. His fellow-clerk was a long, lean man of forty, sallow, with black hair and a ragged moustache; he had hollow cheeks and deep lines on each side of his nose. He took a dislike to Philip because he was an articled clerk. Because he could put down three hundred guineas and keep himself for five years Philip had the chance of a career; while he, with his experience and ability, had no possibility of ever being more than a clerk at thirty-five shillings a week. He was a cross-grained man, oppressed by a large family, and he resented the superciliousness which he fancied he saw in Philip. He sneered at Philip because he was better educated than himself, and he mocked at Philip's pronunciation; he could not forgive him because he spoke without a cockney accent, and when he talked to him sarcastically exaggerated his aitches. At first his manner was merely gruff and repellent, but as he discovered that Philip had no gift for accountancy he took pleasure in humiliating him; his attacks were gross and silly, but they wounded Philip, and in self-defence he assumed an attitude of superiority which he did not feel.

"Had a bath this morning?" Thompson said when Philip came to the office late, for his early punctuality had not lasted.

"Yes, haven't you?"

"No, I'm not a gentleman, I'm only a clerk. I have a bath on Saturday night."

"I suppose that's why you're more than usually disagreeable on Monday."

"Will you condescend to do a few sums in simple addition today? I'm afraid it's asking a great deal from a gentleman who knows Latin and Greek."

"Your attempts at sarcasm are not very happy."

But Philip could not conceal from himself that the other clerks, ill-paid and uncouth, were more useful than himself. Once or twice Mr. Goodworthy grew impatient with him.

"You really ought to be able to do better than this by now," he said. "You're not even as smart as the office-boy."

Philip listened sulkily. He did not like being blamed, and it humiliated him, when, having been given accounts to make fair copies of, Mr. Goodworthy was not satisfied and gave them to another clerk to do. At first the work had been tolerable from its novelty, but now it grew irksome; and when he discovered that he had no aptitude for it, he began to hate it. Often, when he should have been doing something that was given him, he wasted his time drawing little pictures on the office note-paper. He made sketches of Watson in every conceivable attitude, and Watson was impressed by his talent. It occurred to him to take the drawings home, and he came back next day with the praises of his family.

"I wonder you didn't become a painter," he said. "Only of course there's no money in it."

It chanced that Mr. Carter two or three days later was dining with the Watsons, and the sketches were shown him. The following morning he sent for Philip. Philip saw him seldom and stood in some awe of him.

"Look here, young fellow, I don't care what you do out of office-hours, but I've seen those sketches of yours and they're on office-paper, and Mr. Goodworthy tells me you're slack. You won't do any good as a chartered accountant unless you look alive. It's a fine profession, and we're getting a very good class of men in it, but it's a profession in which you have to . . ." he looked for the termination of his phrase, but could not find exactly what he wanted, so finished rather tamely, "in which you have to look alive."

Perhaps Philip would have settled down but for the agreement that if he did not like the work he could leave after a year and get back half the money paid for his articles. He felt that he was fit for something better than to add up accounts, and it was humiliating that he did so ill something which seemed contemptible. The vulgar scenes with Thompson got on his nerves. In March Watson ended his year at the office and Philip, though he did not care for him, saw him go with regret. The fact that the other clerks disliked them equally, because they belonged to a class a little higher than their own, was a bond of union. When Philip thought that he must spend over four years more with that dreary set of fellows his heart sank. He had expected wonderful things from London and it had given him nothing. He hated it now. He did not know a soul, and he had no idea how he was to get to know anyone. He was tired of going everywhere by himself. He began to feel that he could not stand much more of such a life. He would lie in bed at night and think of the joy of never seeing again that dingy office or any of the men in it, and of getting away from those drab lodgings.

A great disappointment befell him in the spring. Hayward had announced his intention of coming to London for the season, and Philip had looked forward very much to seeing him again. He had read so much lately and thought so much that his mind was full of ideas which he wanted to discuss, and he knew nobody who was willing to interest himself in abstract things. He was quite excited at the thought of talking his fill with someone, and he was wretched when Hayward wrote to say that the spring was lovelier than ever he had known it in Italy, and he could not bear to tear himself away. He went on to ask why Philip did not come. What was the use of squandering the days of his youth in an office when the world was beautiful? The letter proceeded.

I wonder you can bear it. I think of Fleet Street and Lincoln's Inn now with a shudder of disgust. There are only two things in the world that make life worth living, love and art. I cannot imagine you sitting in an office over a ledger, and do you wear a tall hat and an umbrella and a little black bag? My feeling is that one should look upon life as an adventure, one should burn with the hard, gem-like flame, and one should take risks, one should expose oneself to danger. Why do you not go to Paris and study art? I always thought you had talent.

The suggestion fell in with the possibility that Philip for some time had been vaguely turning over in his mind. It startled him at first, but he could not help thinking of it, and in the constant rumination over it he found his only escape from the wretchedness of his present state. They all thought he had talent; at Heidelberg they had admired his water colours, Miss Wilkinson had told him over and over again that they were charming; even strangers like the Watsons had been struck by his sketches. *La Vie de Bohème* had made a deep impression on him. He had brought it to London and when he was most depressed he had only to read a few pages to be transported into those charming attics where Rodolphe and the rest of them danced and loved and sang. He began to think of Paris as before he had thought of London, but he had no fear of a second disillusion; he yearned for romance and beauty and love, and Paris seemed to offer them all. He had a passion for pictures, and why should he not be able to paint as well as anybody else? He wrote to Miss Wilkinson and asked her how much she thought he could live on in Paris. She told him that he could manage easily on eighty pounds a year, and she enthusiastically approved of his project. She told him he was too good to be wasted in an office. Who would be a clerk when he might be a great artist, she asked dramatically, and she besought Philip to believe in himself: that was the great thing. But Philip had a cautious nature. It was all very well for Hayward to talk of taking risks, he had three hundred a year in gilt-edged securities; Philip's entire fortune amounted to no more than eighteen-hundred pounds. He hesitated.

Then it chanced that one day Mr. Goodworthy asked him suddenly if he would like to go to Paris. The firm did the accounts for a hotel in the Faubourg St. Honoré, which was owned by an English company, and twice a year Mr. Goodworthy and a clerk went over. The clerk who generally went happened to be ill, and a press of work prevented any of the others from getting away. Mr. Goodworthy thought of Philip because he could best be spared, and his articles gave him some claim upon a job which was one of the pleasures of the business. Philip was delighted.

"You'll 'ave to work all day," said Mr. Goodworthy, "but we get our evenings to ourselves, and Paris is Paris." He smiled in a knowing way. "They do us very well at the hotel, and they give us all our meals, so it don't cost one anything. That's the way I like going to Paris, at other people's expense."

When they arrived at Calais and Philip saw the crowd of gesticulating porters his heart leaped.

"This is the real thing," he said to himself.

He was all eyes as the train sped through the country; he adored the sand dunes, their colour seemed to him more lovely than anything he had ever seen; and he was enchanted with the canals and the long lines of poplars. When they got out of the Gare du Nord, and trundled along the cobbled streets in a ramshackle, noisy cab, it seemed to him that he was breathing a new air so intoxicating that he could hardly restrain himself from shouting aloud. They were met at the door of the hotel by the manager, a stout, pleasant man, who spoke tolerable English; Mr. Goodworthy was an old friend and he greeted them effusively; they dined in his private room with his wife, and to Philip it seemed that he had never eaten anything so delicious as the *beefsteak aux pommes,* nor drunk such nectar as the *vin ordinaire,* which were set before them.

To Mr. Goodworthy, a respectable householder with excellent principles, the capital of France was a paradise of the joyously obscene. He asked the manager next morning what there was to be seen that was "thick." He thoroughly enjoyed these visits of his to Paris; he said they kept you from growing rusty. In the evenings, after their work was over and they had dined, he took Philip to the Moulin Rouge and the Folies Bergères. His little eyes twinkled and his face wore a sly, sensual smile as he sought out the pornographic. He went into all the haunts which were specially arranged for the foreigner, and afterwards said that a nation could come to no good which permitted that sort of thing. He nudged Philip when at some revue a woman appeared with practically nothing on, and pointed out to him the most strapping of the courtesans who walked about the hall. It was a vulgar Paris that he showed Philip, but Philip saw it with eyes blinded with illusion. In the early morning he would rush out of the hotel and go to the Champs Élysées, and stand at the Place de la Concorde. It was June, and Paris was silvery with the delicacy of the air. Philip felt his heart go out to the people. Here he thought at last was romance.

They spent the inside of a week there, leaving on Sunday, and when Philip late at night reached his dingy rooms in Barnes his mind was made up; he would surrender his articles, and go to Paris to study art; but so that no one should think him unreasonable he determined to stay at the office till his year was up. He was to have his holiday during the last fortnight in August, and when he went away he would tell Herbert Carter that he had no intention of returning. But though Philip could force himself to go to the office every day he could not even pretend to show any interest in the work. His mind was occupied with the future. After the middle of July there was nothing much to do and he escaped a good deal by pretending he had to go to lectures for his first examination. The time he got in this way he spent in the National Gallery. He read books about Paris and books about painting. He was steeped in Ruskin. He read many of Vasari's lives of the painters. He liked that story of Correggio, and he fancied himself standing before some great masterpiece and crying: *Anch 'io son' pittore*. His hesitation had left him now, and he was convinced that he had in him the makings of a great painter.

"After all, I can only try," he said to himself. "The great thing in life is to take risks."

At last came the middle of August. Mr. Carter was spending the month in Scotland, and the managing clerk was in charge of the office. Mr. Goodworthy had seemed pleasantly disposed to Philip since their trip to Paris, and now that Philip knew he was so soon to be free, he could look upon the funny little man with tolerance.

"You're going for your holiday tomorrow, Carey?" he said to him in the evening.

All day Philip had been telling himself that this was the last time he would ever sit in that hateful office.

"Yes, this is the end of my year."

"I'm afraid you've not done very well. Mr. Carter's very dissatisfied with you."

"Not nearly so dissatisfied as I am with Mr. Carter," returned Philip cheerfully.

"I don't think you should speak like that, Carey."

"I'm not coming back. I made the arrangement that if I didn't like accountancy Mr. Carter would return me half the money I paid for my articles and I could chuck it at the end of a year."

"You shouldn't come to such a decision hastily."

"For ten months I've loathed it all, I've loathed the work, I've loathed the office, I loathe Loudon. I'd rather sweep a crossing than spend my days here."

"Well, I must say, I don't think you're very fitted for accountancy."

"Good-bye," said Philip, holding out his hand. "I want to thank you for your kindness to me. I'm sorry if I've been troublesome. I knew almost from the beginning I was no good."

"Well, if you really do make up your mind it is good-bye. I don't know what you're going to do, but if you're in the neighbourhood at any time come in and see us."

Philip gave a little laugh.

"I'm afraid it sounds very rude, but I hope from the bottom of my heart that I shall never set eyes on any of you again."

Chapter XXXIX

THE VICAR OF BLACKSTABLE WOULD HAVE NOTHING TO DO WITH THE scheme which Philip laid before him. He had a great idea that one should stick to whatever one had begun. Like all weak men he laid an exaggerated stress on not changing one's mind.

"You chose to be an accountant of your own free will," he said.

"I just took that because it was the only chance I saw of getting up to town. I hate London, I hate the work, and nothing will induce me to go back to it."

Mr. and Mrs. Carey were frankly shocked at Philip's idea of being an artist. He should not forget, they said, that his father and mother were gentlefolk, and painting wasn't a serious profession; it was Bohemian, disreputable, immoral. And then Paris!

"So long as I have anything to say in the matter, I shall not allow you to live in Paris," said the Vicar firmly.

It was a sink of iniquity. The scarlet woman and she of Babylon flaunted their vileness there; the cities of the plain were not more wicked.

"You've been brought up like a gentleman and Christian, and I should be false to the trust laid upon me by your dead father and mother if I allowed you to expose yourself to such temptation."

"Well, I know I'm not a Christian and I'm beginning to doubt whether I'm a gentleman," said Philip.

The dispute grew more violent. There was another year before Philip took possession of his small inheritance, and during that time Mr. Carey proposed only to give him an allowance if he remained at the office. It was clear to Philip that if he meant not to continue with accountancy he must leave it while he could still get back half the money that had been paid for his articles. The Vicar would not listen. Philip, losing all reserve, said things to wound and irritate.

"You've got no right to waste my money," he said at last. "After all it's my money, isn't it? I'm not a child. You can't prevent me from going to Paris if I make up my mind to. You can't force me to go back to London."

"All I can do is to refuse you money unless you do what I think fit."

"Well, I don't care, I've made up my mind to go to Paris. I shall sell my clothes, and my books, and my father's jewellery."

Aunt Louisa sat by in silence, anxious and unhappy: she saw that Philip was beside himself, and anything she said then would but increase his anger. Finally the Vicar announced that he wished to hear nothing more about it and with dignity left the room. For the next three days neither Philip nor he spoke to one another. Philip wrote to Hayward for information about Paris, and made up his mind to set out as soon as he got a reply. Mrs. Carey turned the matter over in her mind incessantly; she felt that Philip included her in the hatred he bore her husband, and the thought tortured her. She loved him with all her heart. At length she spoke to him; she listened attentively while he poured out all his disillusionment of London and his eager ambition for the future.

"I may be no good, but at least let me have a try. I can't be a worse failure than I was in that beastly office. And I feel that I *can* paint. I know I've got it in me."

She was not so sure as her husband that they did right in thwarting so strong an inclination. She had read of great painters whose parents had opposed their wish to study, the event had shown with what folly; and after all it was just as possible for a painter to lead a virtuous life to the glory of God as for a chartered accountant.

"I'm so afraid of your going to Paris," she said piteously. "It wouldn't be so bad if you studied in London."

"If I'm going in for painting I must do it thoroughly, and it's only in Paris that you can get the real thing."

At his suggestion Mrs. Carey wrote to the solicitor, saying that Philip was discontented with his work in London, and asking what he thought of a change. Mr. Nixon answered as follows:

DEAR MRS. CAREY—I have seen Mr. Herbert Carter, and I am afraid I must tell you that Philip has not done so well as one could have wished. If he is very strongly set against the work, perhaps it is better that he should take the opportunity there is now to break his articles. I am naturally very disappointed, but as you know you can take a horse to the water, but you can't make him drink.

Yours very sincerely,
ALBERT NIXON

The letter was shown to the Vicar, but served only to increase his obstinacy. He was willing enough that Philip should take up some other profession, he suggested his father's calling, medicine, but nothing would induce him to pay an allowance if Philip went to Paris.

"It's a mere excuse for self-indulgence and sensuality," he said.

"I'm interested to hear you blame self-indulgence in others," retorted Philip acidly.

But by this time an answer had come from Hayward, giving the name of a hotel where Philip could get a room for thirty francs a month and enclosing a note of introduction to the *massière* of a school. Philip read the letter to Mrs. Carey and told her he proposed to start on the first of September.

"But you haven't got any money?" she said.

"I'm going into Tercanbury this afternoon to sell the jewellery."

He had inherited from his father a gold watch and chain, two or three rings, some links, and two pins. One of them was a pearl and might fetch a considerable sum.

"It's a very different thing, what a thing's worth and what it'll fetch," said Aunt Louisa.

Philip smiled, for this was one of his uncle's stock phrases.

"I know, but at the worst I think I can get a hundred pounds on the lot, and that'll keep me till I'm twenty-one."

Mrs. Carey did not answer, but she went upstairs, put on her little black bonnet, and went to the bank. In an hour she came back. She went to Philip, who was reading in the drawing-room, and handed him an envelope.

"What's this?" he asked.

"It's a little present for you," she answered, smiling shyly.

He opened it and found eleven five-pound notes and a little paper sack bulging with sovereigns.

"I couldn't bear to let you sell your father's jewellery. It's the money I had in the bank. It comes to very nearly a hundred pounds."

Philip blushed, and, he knew not why, tears suddenly filled his eyes.

"Oh, my dear, I can't take it," he said. "It's most awfully good of you, but I couldn't bear to take it."

When Mrs. Carey was married she had three hundred pounds, and this money, carefully watched, had been used by her to meet any unforeseen expense, any urgent charity, or to buy Christmas and birthday presents for her husband and for Philip. In the course of years it had diminished sadly, but it was still with the Vicar a subject for jesting. He talked of his wife as a rich woman and he constantly spoke of the "nest egg."

"Oh, please take it, Philip. I'm so sorry I've been extravagant, and there's only that left. But it'll make me so happy if you'll accept it."

"But you'll want it," said Philip.

"No, I don't think I shall. I was keeping it in case your uncle died before me. I thought it would be useful to have a little something I could get at immediately if I wanted it, but I don't think I shall live very much longer now."

"Oh, my dear, don't say that. Why, of course you're going to live forever. I can't possibly spare you."

"Oh, I'm not sorry." Her voice broke and she hid her eyes, but in a moment, drying them, she smiled bravely. "At first, I used to pray to God that He might not take me first, because I didn't want your uncle to be left alone, I didn't want him to have all the suffering, but now I know that it wouldn't mean so much to your uncle as it would mean to me. He wants to live more than I do, I've never been the wife he wanted, and I daresay he'd marry again if anything happened to me. So I should like to go first. You don't think it's selfish of me, Philip, do you? But I couldn't bear it if he went."

Philip kissed her wrinkled, thin cheek. He did not know why the sight he had of that overwhelming love made him feel strangely ashamed. It was incomprehensible that she should care so much for a man who was so indifferent, so selfish, so grossly self-indulgent; and he divined dimly that in her heart she knew his indifference and his selfishness, knew them and loved him humbly all the same.

"You will take the money, Philip?" she said, gently stroking his hand. "I know you can do without it, but it'll give me so much happiness. I've always wanted to do something for you. You see, I never had a child of my own, and I've loved you as if you were my son. When you were a little boy, though I knew it was wicked, I used to wish almost that you might be ill, so that I could nurse you day and night. But you were only ill once and then it was at school. I should so like to help you. It's the only chance I shall ever have. And perhaps someday when you're a great artist you won't forget me, but you'll remember that I gave you your start."

"It's very good of you," said Philip. "I'm very grateful."

A smile came into her tired eyes, a smile of pure happiness.

"Oh, I'm so glad."

Chapter XL

A FEW DAYS LATER MRS. CAREY WENT TO THE STATION TO SEE PHILIP OFF. She stood at the door of the carriage, trying to keep back her tears. Philip was restless and eager. He wanted to be gone.

"Kiss me once more," she said.

He leaned out of the window and kissed her. The train started, and she stood on the wooden platform of the little station, waving her handkerchief till it was out of sight. Her heart was dreadfully heavy, and the few hundred yards to the vicarage seemed very, very long. It was natural enough that he should be eager to go, she thought, he was a boy and the future beckoned to him; but she—she clenched her teeth so that she should not cry. She uttered a little inward prayer that God would guard him, and keep him out of temptation, and give him happiness and good fortune.

But Philip ceased to think of her a moment after he had settled down in his carriage. He thought only of the future. He had written to Mrs. Otter, the *massière* to whom Hayward had given him an introduction, and had in his pocket an invitation to tea on the following day. When he arrived in Paris he had his luggage put on a cab and trundled off slowly through the gay streets, over the bridge, and along the narrow ways of the Latin Quarter. He had taken a room at the Hôtel des Deux Écoles, which was in a shabby street off the Boulevard du Montparnasse; it was convenient for Amitrano's School at which he was going to work. A waiter took his box up five flights of stairs, and Philip was shown into a tiny room, fusty from unopened windows, the greater part of which was taken up by a large wooden bed with a canopy over it of red rep; there were heavy curtains on the windows of the same dingy material; the chest of drawers served also as a washing-stand; and there was a massive wardrobe of the style which is connected with the good King Louis Philippe. The wall-paper was discoloured with age; it was dark grey, and there could be vaguely seen on it garlands of brown leaves. To Philip the room seemed quaint and charming.

Though it was late he felt too excited to sleep and, going out, made his way into the boulevard and walked towards the light. This led him to the station; and the square in front of it, vivid with arc-lamps, noisy with the yellow trams that seemed to cross it in all directions, made him laugh aloud with joy. There were cafés all round, and by chance, thirsty and eager to get a nearer sight of the crowd, Philip installed himself at a little table outside the Café de Versailles. Every other table was taken, for it was a fine night; and Philip looked curiously at the people, here little family groups, there a knot of men with odd-shaped hats and beards talking loudly and gesticulating; next to him were two men who looked like painters with women who Philip hoped were not their lawful wives; behind him he heard Americans loudly arguing on art. His soul was thrilled. He sat till very late, tired out but too happy to move, and when at last he went to bed he was wide awake; he listened to the manifold noise of Paris.

Next day about tea-time he made his way to the Lion de Belfort, and in a new street that led out of the Boulevard Raspail found Mrs. Otter. She was an insignificant woman of thirty, with a provincial air and a deliberately lady-like manner; she introduced him to her mother. He discovered presently that she had been studying in Paris for three years and later that she was separated from her husband. She had in her small drawing-room one or two portraits which she had painted, and to Philip's inexperience they seemed extremely accomplished.

"I wonder if I shall ever be able to paint as well as that," he said to her.

"Oh, I expect so," she replied, not without self-satisfaction. "You can't expect to do everything all at once, of course."

She was very kind. She gave him the address of a shop where he could get a portfolio, drawing-paper, and charcoal.

"I shall be going to Amitrano's about nine tomorrow, and if you'll be there then I'll see that you get a good place and all that sort of thing."

She asked him what he wanted to do, and Philip felt that he should not let her see how vague he was about the whole matter.

"Well, first I want to learn to draw," he said.

"I'm so glad to hear you say that. People always want to do things in such a hurry. I never touched oils till I'd been here for two years, and look at the result."

She gave a glance at the portrait of her mother, a sticky piece of painting that hung over the piano.

"And if I were you, I would be very careful about the people you get to know. I wouldn't mix myself up with any foreigners. I'm very careful myself."

Philip thanked her for the suggestion, but it seemed to him odd. He did not know that he particularly wanted to be careful.

"We live just as we would if we were in England," said Mrs. Otter's mother, who till then had spoken little. "When we came here we brought all our own furniture over."

Philip looked round the room. It was filled with a massive suite, and at the window were the same sort of white lace curtains which Aunt Louisa put up at the vicarage in summer. The piano was draped in Liberty silk and so was the chimney-piece. Mrs. Otter followed his wandering eye.

"In the evening when we close the shutters one might really feel one was in England."

"And we have our meals just as if we were at home," added her mother. "A meat breakfast in the morning and dinner in the middle of the day."

When he left Mrs. Otter Philip went to buy drawing materials; and next morning at the stroke of nine, trying to seem self-assured, he presented himself at the school. Mrs. Otter was already there, and she came forward with a friendly smile. He had been anxious about the reception he would have as a *nouveau*, for he had read a good deal of the rough joking to which a new-comer was exposed at some of the studios; but Mrs. Otter had reassured him.

"Oh, there's nothing like that here," she said. "You see, about half our students are ladies, and they set a tone to the place."

The studio was large and bare, with grey walls, on which were pinned the studies that had received prizes. A model was sitting in a chair with a loose wrap thrown over her, and about a dozen men and women were standing about, some talking and others still working on their sketch. It was the first rest of the model.

"You'd better not try anything too difficult at first," said Mrs. Otter. "Put your easel here. You'll find that's the easiest pose."

Philip placed an easel where she indicated, and Mrs. Otter introduced him to a young woman who sat next to him.

"Mr. Carey—Miss Price. Mr. Carey's never studied before, you won't mind helping him a little just at first, will you?" Then she turned to the model. *"La Pose."*

The model threw aside the paper she had been reading, *La Petite République*, and sulkily, throwing off her gown, got on to the stand. She stood, squarely on both feet, with her hands clasped behind her head.

"It's a stupid pose," said Miss Price. "I can't imagine why they chose it."

When Philip entered, the people in the studio had looked at him curiously, and the model gave him an indifferent glance, but now they ceased to pay attention to him. Philip, with his beautiful sheet of paper in front of him, stared awkwardly at the model. He did not know how to begin. He had never seen a naked woman before. She was not young and her breasts were shrivelled. She had colourless, fair hair that fell over her forehead untidily, and her face was covered with large freckles. He glanced at Miss Price's work. She had only been working on it two days, and it looked as though she had had trouble; her paper was in a mess from constant rubbing out, and to Philip's eyes the figure looked strangely distorted.

"I should have thought I could do as well as that," he said to himself.

He began on the head, thinking that he would work slowly downwards, but, he could not understand why, he found it infinitely more difficult to draw a head from the model than to draw one from his imagination. He got into difficulties. He glanced at Miss Price. She was working with vehement gravity. Her brow was wrinkled with eagerness, and there was an anxious look in her eyes. It was hot in the studio, and drops of sweat stood on her forehead. She was a girl of twenty-six, with a great deal of dull gold hair; it was handsome hair, but it was carelessly done, dragged back from her forehead and tied in a hurried knot. She had a large face, with broad, flat features and small eyes; her skin was pasty, with a singular unhealthiness of tone, and there was no colour in the cheeks. She had an unwashed air and you could not help wondering if she slept in her clothes. She was serious and silent. When the next pause came, she stepped back to look at her work.

"I don't know why I'm having so much bother," she said. "But I mean to get it right." She turned to Philip. "How are you getting on?"

"Not at all," he answered, with a rueful smile.

She looked at what he had done.

"You can't expect to do anything that way. You must take measurements. And you must square out your paper."

She showed him rapidly how to set about the business. Philip was impressed by her earnestness, but repelled by her want of charm. He was grateful for the hints she gave him and set to work again. Meanwhile other people had come in, mostly men, for the women always arrived first, and the studio for the time of year (it was early yet) was fairly full. Presently there came in a young man with thin, black hair, an enormous nose, and a face so long that it reminded you of a horse. He sat down next to Philip and nodded across him to Miss Price.

"You're very late," she said. "Are you only just up?"

"It was such a splendid day, I thought I'd lie in bed and think how beautiful it was out."

Philip smiled, but Miss Price took the remark seriously.

"That seems a funny thing to do, I should have thought it would be more to the point to get up and enjoy it."

"The way of the humourist is very hard," said the young man gravely.

He did not seem inclined to work. He looked at his canvas; he was working in colour, and had sketched in the day before the model who was posing. He turned to Philip.

"Have you just come out from England?"

"Yes."

"How did you find your way to Amitrano's?"

"It was the only school I knew of."

"I hope you haven't come with the idea that you will learn anything here which will be of the smallest use to you."

"It's the best school in Paris," said Miss Price. "It's the only one where they take art seriously."

"Should art be taken seriously?" the young man asked; and since Miss Price replied only with a scornful shrug, he added: "But the point is, all schools are bad. They are academical, obviously. Why this is less injurious than most is that the teaching is more incompetent than elsewhere. Because you learn nothing. . . ."

"But why d'you come here then?" interrupted Philip.

"I see the better course, but do not follow it. Miss Price, who is cultured, will remember the Latin of that."

"I wish you would leave me out of your conversation, Mr. Clutton," said Miss Price brusquely.

"The only way to learn to paint," he went on, imperturbable, "is to take a studio, hire a model, and just fight it out for yourself."

"That seems a simple thing to do," said Philip.

"It only needs money," replied Clutton.

He began to paint, and Philip looked at him from the corner of his eye. He was long and desperately thin; his huge bones seemed to protrude from his body; his elbows were so sharp that they appeared to jut out through the arms of his shabby coat. His trousers were frayed at the bottom, and on each of his boots was a clumsy patch. Miss Price got up and went over to Philip's easel.

"If Mr. Clutton will hold his tongue for a moment, I'll just help you a little," she said.

"Miss Price dislikes me because I have humour," said Clutton, looking meditatively at his canvas, "but she detests me because I have genius."

He spoke with solemnity, and his colossal, misshapen nose made what he said very quaint. Philip was obliged to laugh, but Miss Price grew darkly red with anger.

"You're the only person who has ever accused you of genius."

"Also I am the only person whose opinion is of the least value to me."

Miss Price began to criticise what Philip had done. She talked glibly of anatomy and construction, planes and lines, and of much else which Philip did not understand. She had been at the studio a long time and knew the main points which the masters insisted upon, but though she could show what was wrong with Philip's work she could not tell him how to put it right.

"It's awfully kind of you to take so much trouble with me," said Philip.

"Oh, it's nothing," she answered, flushing awkwardly. "People did the same for me when I first came, I'd do it for anyone."

"Miss Price wants to indicate that she is giving you the advantage of her knowledge from a sense of duty rather than on account of any charms of your person," said Clutton.

Miss Price gave him a furious look, and went back to her own drawing. The clock struck twelve, and the model with a cry of relief stepped down from the stand.

Miss Price gathered up her things.

"Some of us go to Gravier's for lunch," she said to Philip, with a look at Clutton. "I always go home myself."

"I'll take you to Gravier's if you like," said Clutton.

Philip thanked him and made ready to go. On his way out Mrs. Otter asked him how he had been getting on.

"Did Fanny Price help you?" she asked. "I put you there because I know she can do it if she likes. She's a disagreeable, ill-natured girl, and she can't draw herself at all, but she knows the ropes, and she can be useful to a new-comer if she cares to take the trouble."

On their way down the street Clutton said to him:

"You've made an impression on Fanny Price. You'd better look out."

Philip laughed. He had never seen anyone on whom he wished less to make an impression. They came to the cheap little restaurant at which several of the students ate, and Clutton sat down at a table at which three or four men were already seated. For a franc, they got an egg, a plate of meat, cheese, and a small bottle of wine. Coffee was extra. They sat on the pavement, and yellow trams passed up and down the boulevard with a ceaseless ringing of bells.

"By the way, what's your name?" said Clutton, as they took their seats.

"Carey."

"Allow me to introduce an old and trusted friend, Carey by name," said Clutton gravely. "Mr. Flanagan, Mr. Lawson."

They laughed and went on with their conversation. They talked of a thousand things, and they all talked at once. No one paid the smallest attention to anyone else. They talked of the places they had been to in the summer, of studios, of the various schools; they mentioned names which were unfamiliar to Philip, Monet, Manet, Renoir, Pissarro, Degas. Philip listened with all his ears, and though he felt a little out of it, his heart leaped with exultation. The time flew. When Clutton got up he said:

"I expect you'll find me here this evening if you care to come. You'll find this about the best place for getting dyspepsia at the lowest cost in the Quarter."

Chapter XLI

PHILIP WALKED DOWN THE BOULEVARD DU MONTPARNASSE. IT WAS NOT AT all like the Paris he had seen in the spring during his visit to do the accounts of the Hôtel St. Georges—he thought already of that part of his life with a shudder—but reminded him of what he thought a provincial town must be. There was an easy-going air about it, and a sunny spaciousness which invited the mind to day-dreaming. The trimness of the trees, the vivid whiteness of the houses, the breadth, were very agreeable; and he felt himself already thoroughly at home. He sauntered along, staring at the people; there seemed an elegance about the most ordinary, workmen with their broad red sashes and their wide trousers, little soldiers in dingy, charming uniforms. He came presently to the Avenue de l'Observatoire, and he gave a sigh of pleasure at the magnificent, yet so graceful, vista. He came to the gardens of the Luxembourg: children were playing, nurses with long ribbons walked slowly two by two, busy men passed through with satchels under their arms, youths strangely dressed. The scene was formal and dainty; nature was arranged and ordered, but so exquisitely, that nature unordered and unarranged seemed barbaric. Philip was enchanted. It excited him to stand on that spot of which he had read so much; it was classic ground to him; and he felt the awe and the delight which some old don might feel when for the first time he looked on the smiling plain of Sparta.

As he wandered he chanced to see Miss Price sitting by herself on a bench. He hesitated, for he did not at that moment want to see anyone, and her uncouth way seemed out of place amid the happiness he felt around him; but he had divined her sensitiveness to affront, and since she had seen him thought it would be polite to speak to her.

"What are you doing here?" she said, as he came up.

"Enjoying myself. Aren't you?"

"Oh, I come here every day from four to five. I don't think one does any good if one works straight through."

"May I sit down for a minute?" he said.

"If you want to."

"That doesn't sound very cordial," he laughed.

"I'm not much of a one for saying pretty things."

Philip, a little disconcerted, was silent as he lit a cigarette.

"Did Clutton say anything about my work?" she asked suddenly.

"No, I don't think he did," said Philip.

"He's no good, you know. He thinks he's a genius, but he isn't. He's too lazy, for one thing. Genius is an infinite capacity for taking pains. The only thing is to peg away. If one only makes up one's mind badly enough to do a thing one can't help doing it."

She spoke with a passionate strenuousness which was rather striking. She wore a sailor hat of black straw, a white blouse which was not quite clean, and a brown skirt. She had no gloves on, and her hands wanted washing. She was so unattractive that Philip wished he had not begun to talk to her. He could not make out whether she wanted him to stay or go.

"I'll do anything I can for you," she said all at once, without reference to anything that had gone before. "I know how hard it is."

"Thank you very much," said Philip, then in a moment: "Won't you come and have tea with me somewhere?"

She looked at him quickly and flushed. When she reddened her pasty skin acquired a curiously mottled look, like strawberries and cream that had gone bad.

"No, thanks. What d'you think I want tea for? I've only just had lunch."

"I thought it would pass the time," said Philip.

"If you find it long you needn't bother about me, you know. I don't mind being left alone."

At that moment two men passed, in brown velveteens, enormous trousers, and basque caps. They were young, but both wore beards.

"I say, are those art-students?" said Philip. "They might have stepped out of the *Vie de Bohème*."

"They're Americans," said Miss Price scornfully. "Frenchmen haven't worn things like that for thirty years, but the Americans from the Far West buy those clothes and have themselves photographed the day after they arrive in Paris. That's about as near to art as they ever get. But it doesn't matter to them, they've all got money."

Philip liked the daring picturesqueness of the Americans' costume; he thought it showed the romantic spirit. Miss Price asked him the time.

"I must be getting along to the studio," she said. "Are you going to the sketch classes?"

Philip did not know anything about them, and she told him that from five to six every evening a model sat, from whom anyone who liked could go and draw at the cost of fifty centimes. They had a different model every day, and it was very good practice.

"I don't suppose you're good enough yet for that. You'd better wait a bit."

"I don't see why I shouldn't try. I haven't got anything else to do."

They got up and walked to the studio. Philip could not tell from her manner whether Miss Price wished him to walk with her or preferred to walk alone. He remained from sheer embarrassment, not knowing how to leave her; but she would not talk; she answered his questions in an ungracious manner.

A man was standing at the studio door with a large dish into which each person as he went in dropped his half franc. The studio was much fuller than it had been in the morning, and there was not the preponderance of English and Americans; nor were women there in so large a proportion. Philip felt the assemblage was more the sort of thing he had expected. It was very warm, and the air quickly grew fetid. It was an old man who sat this time, with a vast grey beard, and Philip tried to put into practice the little he had learned in the morning; but he made a poor job of it; he realised that he could not draw nearly as well as he thought. He glanced enviously at one or two sketches of men who sat near him, and wondered whether he would ever be able to use the charcoal with that mastery. The hour passed quickly. Not wishing to press himself upon Miss Price he sat down at some distance from her, and at the end, as he passed her on his way out, she asked him brusquely how he had got on.

"Not very well," he smiled.

"If you'd condescended to come and sit near me I could have given you some hints. I suppose you thought yourself too grand."

"No, it wasn't that. I was afraid you'd think me a nuisance."

"When I do that I'll tell you sharp enough."

Philip saw that in her uncouth way she was offering him help.

"Well, tomorrow I'll just force myself upon you."

"I don't mind," she answered.

Philip went out and wondered what he should do with himself till dinner. He was eager to do something characteristic. *Absinthe!* Of course it was indicated, and so, sauntering towards the station, he seated himself outside a café and ordered it. He drank with nausea and satisfaction. He found the taste disgusting, but the moral effect magnificent; he felt every inch an art-student; and since he drank on an empty stomach his spirits presently grew very high. He watched the crowds, and felt all men were his brothers. He was happy. When he reached Gravier's the table at which Clutton sat was full, but as soon as he saw Philip limping along he called out to him. They made room. The dinner was frugal, a plate of soup, a dish of meat, fruit, cheese, and half a bottle of wine; but Philip paid no attention to what he ate. He took note of the men at the table. Flanagan was there again: he was an American, a short, snub-nosed youth with a jolly face and a laughing mouth. He wore a Norfolk jacket of bold pattern, a blue stock round his neck, and a tweed cap of fantastic shape. At that time impressionism reigned in the Latin Quarter, but its victory over the older schools was still recent; and Carolus-Duran, Bouguereau, and their like were set up against Manet, Monet, and Degas. To appreciate these was still a sign of grace. Whistler was an influence strong with the English and his compatriots, and the discerning collected Japanese prints. The old masters were tested by new standards. The esteem in which Raphael had been for centuries held was a matter of derision to wise young men. They offered to give all his works for Velasquez' head of Philip IV in the National Gallery. Philip found that a discussion on art was raging. Lawson, whom he had met at luncheon, sat opposite to him. He was a thin youth with a freckled face and red hair. He had very bright green eyes. As Philip sat down he fixed them on him and remarked suddenly:

"Raphael was only tolerable when he painted other people's pictures. When he painted Peruginos or Pinturicchios he was charming; when he painted Raphaels he was," with a scornful shrug, "Raphael."

Lawson spoke so aggressively that Philip was taken aback, but he was not obliged to answer because Flanagan broke in impatiently.

"Oh, to hell with art!" he cried. "Let's get ginny."

"You were ginny last night, Flanagan," said Lawson.

"Nothing to what I mean to be tonight," he answered. "Fancy being in Pa-ris and thinking of nothing but art all the time." He spoke with a broad Western accent. "My, it is good to be alive." He gathered himself together and then banged his fist on the table. "To hell with art, I say."

"You not only say it, but you say it with tiresome iteration," said Clutton severely.

There was another American at the table. He was dressed like those fine fellows whom Philip had seen that afternoon in the Luxembourg. He had a handsome face, thin, ascetic, with dark eyes; he wore his fantastic garb with the dashing air of a buccaneer. He had a vast quantity of dark hair which fell constantly over his eyes, and his most frequent gesture was to throw back his head dramatically to get some long wisp out of the way. He began to talk of the *Olympia* by Manet, which then hung in the Luxembourg.

"I stood in front of it for an hour today, and I tell you it's not a good picture."

Lawson put down his knife and fork. His green eyes flashed fire, he gasped with rage; but he could be seen imposing calm upon himself.

"It's very interesting to hear the mind of the untutored savage," he said. "Will you tell us why it isn't a good picture?"

Before the American could answer someone else broke in vehemently.

"D'you mean to say you can look at the painting of that flesh and say it's not good?"

"I don't say that. I think the right breast is very well painted."

"The right breast be damned," shouted Lawson. "The whole thing's a miracle of painting."

He began to describe in detail the beauties of the picture, but at this table at Gravier's they who spoke at length spoke for their own edification. No one listened to him. The American interrupted angrily.

"You don't mean to say you think the head's good?"

Lawson, white with passion now, began to defend the head; but Clutton, who had been sitting in silence with a look on his face of good-humoured scorn, broke in.

"Give him the head. We don't want the head. It doesn't affect the picture."

"All right, I'll give you the head," cried Lawson. "Take the head and be damned to you."

"What about the black line?" cried the American, triumphantly pushing back a wisp of hair which nearly fell in his soup. "You don't see a black line round objects in nature."

"Oh, God, send down fire from heaven to consume the blasphemer," said Lawson. "What has nature got to do with it? No one knows what's in nature and what isn't! The world sees nature through the eyes of the artist. Why, for centuries it saw horses jumping a fence with all their legs extended, and by Heaven, sir, they were extended. It saw shadows black until Monet discovered they were coloured, and by Heaven, sir, they were black. If we choose to surround objects with a black line, the world will see the black line, and there will be a black line; and if we paint grass red and cows blue, it'll see them red and blue, and, by Heaven, they will be red and blue."

"To hell with art," murmured Flanagan. "I want to get ginny."

Lawson took no notice of the interruption.

"Now look here, when *Olympia* was shown at the Salon, Zola—amid the jeers of the philistines and the hisses of the *pompiers*, the academicians, and the public, Zola said: 'I look forward to the day when Manet's picture will hang in the Louvre opposite the *Odalisque* of Ingres, and it will not be the *Odalisque* which will gain by comparison.' It'll be there. Every day I see the time grow nearer. In ten years the *Olympia* will be in the Louvre."

"Never," shouted the American, using both hands now with a sudden desperate attempt to get his hair once for all out of the way. "In ten years that picture will be dead. It's only a fashion of the moment. No picture can live that hasn't got something which that picture misses by a million miles."

"And what is that?"

"Great art can't exist without a moral element."

"Oh God!" cried Lawson furiously. "I knew it was that. He wants morality." He joined his hands and held them towards heaven in supplication. "Oh, Christopher Columbus, Christopher Columbus, what did you do when you discovered America?"

"Ruskin says . . ."

But before he could add another word, Clutton rapped with the handle of his knife imperiously on the table.

"Gentlemen," he said in a stern voice, and his huge nose positively wrinkled with passion, "a name has been mentioned which I never thought to hear again in decent society. Freedom of speech is all very well, but we must observe the limits of common propriety. You may talk of Bouguereau if you will: there is a cheerful disgustingness in the sound which excites laughter; but let us not sully our chaste lips with the names of J. Ruskin, G. F. Watts, or E. B. Jones."

"Who was Ruskin anyway?" asked Flanagan.

"He was one of the great Victorians. He was a master of English style."

"Ruskin's style—a thing of shreds and purple patches," said Lawson. "Besides, damn the Great Victorians. Whenever I open a paper and see Death of a Great Victorian, I thank Heaven there's one more of them gone. Their only talent was longevity, and no artist should be allowed to live after he's forty; by then a man has done his best work, all he does after that is repetition. Don't you think it was the greatest luck in the world for them that Keats, Shelley, Bonnington, and Byron died early? What a genius we should think Swinburne if he had perished on the day the first series of *Poems and Ballads* was published!"

The suggestion pleased, for no one at the table was more than twenty-four, and they threw themselves upon it with gusto. They were unanimous for once. They elaborated. Someone proposed a vast bonfire made out of the works of the Forty Academicians into which the Great Victorians might be hurled on their fortieth birthday. The idea was received with acclamation. Carlyle and Ruskin, Tennyson, Browning, G. F. Watts, E. B. Jones, Dickens, Thackeray, they were hurried into the flames; Mr. Gladstone, John Bright, and Cobden; there was a moment's discussion about George Meredith, but Matthew Arnold and Emerson were given up cheerfully. At last came Walter Pater.

"Not Walter Pater," murmured Philip.

Lawson stared at him for a moment with his green eyes and then nodded.

"You're quite right, Walter Pater is the only justification for Mona Lisa. D'you know Cronshaw? He used to know Pater."

"Who's Cronshaw?" asked Philip.

"Cronshaw's a poet. He lives here. Let's go to the Lilas."

La Closerie des Lilas was a café to which they often went in the evening after dinner, and here Cronshaw was invariably to be found between the hours of nine at night and two in the morning. But Flanagan had had enough of intellectual conversation for one evening, and when Lawson made his suggestion, turned to Philip.

"Oh gee, let's go where there are girls," he said. "Come to the Gaîtê Montparnasse, and we'll get ginny."

"I'd rather go and see Cronshaw and keep sober," laughed Philip.

Chapter XLII

THERE WAS A GENERAL DISTURBANCE. FLANAGAN AND TWO OR THREE MORE went on to the music-hall, while Philip walked slowly with Clutton and Lawson to the Closerie des Lilas.

"You must go to the Gaîté Montparnasse," said Lawson to him. "It's one of the loveliest things in Paris. I'm going to paint it one of these days."

Philip, influenced by Hayward, looked upon music-halls with scornful eyes, but he had reached Paris at a time when their artistic possibilities were just discovered. The peculiarities of lighting, the masses of dingy red and tarnished gold, the heaviness of the shadows and the decorative lines, offered a new theme; and half the studios in the Quarter contained sketches made in one or other of the local theatres. Men of letters, following in the painters' wake, conspired suddenly to find artistic value in the turns; and red-nosed comedians were lauded to the skies for their sense of character; fat female singers, who had bawled obscurely for twenty years, were discovered to possess inimitable drollery; there were those who found an aesthetic delight in performing dogs; while others exhausted their vocabulary to extol the distinction of conjurers and trick-cyclists. The crowd too, under another influence, was become an object of sympathetic interest. With Hayward, Philip had disdained humanity in the mass; he adopted the attitude of one who wraps himself in solitariness and watches with disgust the antics of the vulgar; but Clutton and Lawson talked of the multitude with enthusiasm. They described the seething throng that filled the various fairs of Paris, the sea of faces, half seen in the glare of acetylene, half hidden in the darkness, and the blare of trumpets, the hooting of whistles, the hum of voices. What they said was new and strange to Philip. They told him about Cronshaw.

"Have you ever read any of his work?"

"No," said Philip.

"It came out in *The Yellow Book*."

They looked upon him, as painters often do writers, with contempt because he was a layman, with tolerance because he practised an art, and with awe because he used a medium in which themselves felt ill-at-ease.

"He's an extraordinary fellow. You'll find him a bit disappointing at first, he only comes out at his best when he's drunk."

"And the nuisance is," added Clutton, "that it takes him a devil of a time to get drunk."

When they arrived at the café Lawson told Philip that they would have to go in. There was hardly a bite in the autumn air, but Cronshaw had a morbid fear of draughts and even in the warmest weather sat inside.

"He knows everyone worth knowing," Lawson explained. "He knew Pater and Oscar Wilde, and he knows Mallarmé and all those fellows."

The object of their search sat in the most sheltered corner of the café, with his coat on and the collar turned up. He wore his hat pressed well down on his forehead so that he should avoid cold air. He was a big man, stout but not obese, with a round face, a small moustache, and little, rather stupid eyes. His head did not seem quite big enough for his body. It looked like a pea uneasily poised on an egg. He was playing dominoes with a Frenchman, and greeted the new-comers with a quiet smile; he did not speak, but as if to make room for them pushed away the little pile of saucers on the table which indicated the number of drinks he had already consumed. He nodded to Philip when he was introduced to him, and went on with the game. Philip's knowledge of the language was small, but he knew enough to tell that Cronshaw, although he had lived in Paris for several years, spoke French execrably.

At last he leaned back with a smile of triumph.

"*Je vous ai battu,*" he said, with an abominable accent. "*Garçong!*"

He called the waiter and turned to Philip.

"Just out from England? See any cricket?"

Philip was a little confused at the unexpected question.

"Cronshaw knows the averages of every first-class cricketer for the last twenty years," said Lawson, smiling.

The Frenchman left them for friends at another table, and Cronshaw, with the lazy enunciation which was one of his peculiarities, began to discourse on the relative merits of Kent and Lancashire. He told them of the last test match he had seen and described the course of the game wicket by wicket.

"That's the only thing I miss in Paris," he said, as he finished the *bock* which the waiter had brought. "You don't get any cricket."

Philip was disappointed, and Lawson, pardonably anxious to show off one of the celebrities of the Quarter, grew impatient. Cronshaw was taking his time to wake up that evening, though the saucers at his side indicated that he had at least made an honest attempt to get drunk. Clutton watched the scene with amusement. He fancied there was something of affectation in Cronshaw's minute knowledge of cricket; he liked to tantalise people by talking to them of things that obviously bored them; Clutton threw in a question.

"Have you seen Mallarmé lately?"

Cronshaw looked at him slowly, as if he were turning the inquiry over in his mind, and before he answered rapped on the marble table with one of the saucers.

"Bring my bottle of whiskey," he called out. He turned again to Philip. "I keep my own bottle of whiskey. I can't afford to pay fifty centimes for every thimbleful."

The waiter brought the bottle, and Cronshaw held it up to the light.

"They've been drinking it. Waiter, who's been helping himself to my whiskey?"

"Mais personne, Monsieur Cronshaw."

"I made a mark on it last night, and look at it."

"Monsieur made a mark, but he kept on drinking after that. At that rate Monsieur wastes his time in making marks."

The waiter was a jovial fellow and knew Cronshaw intimately. Cronshaw gazed at him.

"If you give me your word of honour as a nobleman and a gentleman that nobody but I has been drinking my whiskey, I'll accept your statement."

This remark, translated literally into the crudest French, sounded very funny, and the lady at the *comptoir* could not help laughing.

"Il est impayable," she murmured.

Cronshaw, hearing her, turned a sheepish eye upon her; she was stout, matronly, and middle-aged; and solemnly kissed his hand to her. She shrugged her shoulders.

"Fear not, madam," he said heavily. "I have passed the age when I am tempted by forty-five and gratitude."

He poured himself out some whiskey and water, and slowly drank it. He wiped his mouth with the back of his hand.

"He talked very well."

Lawson and Clutton knew that Cronshaw's remark was an answer to the question about Mallarmé. Cronshaw often went to the gatherings on Tuesday evenings when the poet received men of letters and painters, and discoursed with subtle oratory on any subject that was suggested to him. Cronshaw had evidently been there lately.

"He talked very well, but he talked nonsense. He talked about art as though it were the most important thing in the world."

"If it isn't, what are we here for?" asked Philip.

"What you're here for I don't know. It is no business of mine. But art is a luxury. Men attach importance only to self-preservation and the propagation of their species. It is only when these instincts are satisfied that they consent to occupy themselves with the entertainment which is provided for them by writers, painters, and poets."

Cronshaw stopped for a moment to drink. He had pondered for twenty years the problem whether he loved liquor because it made him talk or whether he loved conversation because it made him thirsty.

Then he said: "I wrote a poem yesterday."

Without being asked he began to recite it, very slowly, marking the rhythm with an extended forefinger. It was possibly a very fine poem, but at that moment a young woman came in. She had scarlet lips, and it was plain that the vivid colour of her cheeks was not due to the vulgarity of nature; she had blackened her eyelashes and eyebrows, and painted both eyelids a bold blue, which was continued to a triangle at the corner of the eyes. It was fantastic and amusing. Her dark hair was done over her ears in the fashion made popular by Mlle. Cléo de Merode. Philip's eyes wandered to her, and Cronshaw, having finished the recitation of his verses, smiled upon him indulgently.

"You were not listening," he said.

"Oh yes, I was."

"I do not blame you, for you have given an apt illustration of the statement I just made. What is art beside love? I respect and applaud your indifference to fine poetry when you can contemplate the meretricious charms of this young person."

She passed by the table at which they were sitting, and he took her arm.

"Come and sit by my side, dear child, and let us play the divine comedy of love."

"*Fichez-moi la paix,*" she said, and pushing him on one side continued her perambulation.

"Art," he continued, with a wave of the hand, "is merely the refuge which the ingenious have invented, when they were supplied with food and women, to escape the tediousness of life."

Cronshaw filled his glass again, and began to talk at length. He spoke with rotund delivery. He chose his words carefully. He mingled wisdom and nonsense in the most astounding manner, gravely making fun of his hearers at one moment, and at the next playfully giving them sound advice. He talked of art, and literature, and life. He was by turns devout and obscene, merry and lachrymose. He grew remarkably drunk, and then he began to recite poetry, his own and Milton's, his own and Shelley's, his own and Kit Marlowe's.

At last Lawson, exhausted, got up to go home.

"I shall go too," said Philip.

Clutton, the most silent of them all, remained behind listening, with a sardonic smile on his lips, to Cronshaw's maunderings. Lawson accompanied Philip to his hotel and then bade him good-night. But when Philip got to bed he could not sleep. All these new ideas that had been flung before him carelessly seethed in his brain. He was tremendously excited. He felt in himself great powers. He had never before been so self-confident.

"I know I shall be a great artist," he said to himself. "I feel it in me."

A thrill passed through him as another thought came, but even to himself he would not put it into words:

"By George, I believe I've got genius."

He was in fact very drunk, but as he had not taken more than one glass of beer, it could have been due only to a more dangerous intoxicant than alcohol.

Chapter XLIII

ON TUESDAYS AND FRIDAYS MASTERS SPENT THE MORNING AT AMITRANO'S, criticising the work done. In France the painter earns little unless he paints portraits and is patronised by rich Americans; and men of reputation are glad to increase their incomes by spending two or three hours once a week at one of the numerous studios where art is taught. Tuesday was the day upon which Michel Rollin came to Amitrano's. He was an elderly man, with a white beard and a florid complexion, who had painted a number of decorations for the State, but these were an object of derision to the students he instructed: he was a disciple of Ingres, impervious to the progress of art and angrily impatient with that *tas de farceurs* whose names were Manet, Degas, Monet, and Sisley; but he was an excellent teacher, helpful, polite, and encouraging. Foinet, on the other hand, who visited the studio on Fridays, was a difficult man to get on with. He was a small, shrivelled person, with bad teeth and a bilious air, an untidy grey beard, and savage eyes; his voice was high and his tone sarcastic. He had had pictures bought by the Luxembourg, and at twenty-five looked forward to a great career; but his talent was due to youth rather than to personality, and for twenty years he had done nothing but repeat the landscape which had brought him his early success. When he was reproached with monotony, he answered:

"Corot only painted one thing. Why shouldn't I?"

He was envious of everyone else's success, and had a peculiar, personal loathing of the impressionists; for he looked upon his own failure as due to the mad fashion which had attracted the public, *sale bête,* to their works. The genial disdain of Michel Rollin, who called them impostors, was answered by him with vituperation, of which *crapule* and *canaille* were the least violent items; he amused himself with abuse of their private lives, and with sardonic humour, with blasphemous and obscene detail, attacked the legitimacy of their births and the purity of their conjugal relations: he used an Oriental imagery and an Oriental emphasis to accentuate his ribald scorn. Nor did he conceal his contempt for the students whose work he examined. By them he was hated and feared; the women by his brutal sarcasm he reduced often to tears, which again aroused his ridicule; and he remained at the studio, notwithstanding the protests of those who suffered too bitterly from his attacks, because there could be no doubt that he was one of the best masters in Paris. Sometimes the old model who kept the school ventured to remonstrate with him, but his expostulations quickly gave way before the violent insolence of the painter to abject apologies.

It was Foinet with whom Philip first came in contact. He was already in the studio when Philip arrived. He went round from easel to easel, with Mrs. Otter, the *massière*, by his side to interpret his remarks for the benefit of those who could not understand French. Fanny Price, sitting next to Philip, was working feverishly. Her face was sallow with nervousness, and every now and then she stopped to wipe her hands on her blouse; for they were hot with anxiety. Suddenly she turned to Philip with an anxious look, which she tried to hide by a sullen frown.

"D'you think it's good?" she asked, nodding at her drawing.

Philip got up and looked at it. He was astounded; he felt she must have no eye at all; the thing was hopelessly out of drawing.

"I wish I could draw half as well myself," he answered.

"You can't expect to, you've only just come. It's a bit too much to expect that you should draw as well as I do. I've been here two years."

Fanny Price puzzled Philip. Her conceit was stupendous. Philip had already discovered that everyone in the studio cordially disliked her; and it was no wonder, for she seemed to go out of her way to wound people.

"I complained to Mrs. Otter about Foinet," she said now. "The last two weeks he hasn't looked at my drawings. He spends about half an hour on Mrs. Otter because she's the *massière*. After all I pay as much as anybody else, and I suppose my money's as good as theirs. I don't see why I shouldn't get as much attention as anybody else."

She took up her charcoal again, but in a moment put it down with a groan.

"I can't do any more now. I'm so frightfully nervous."

She looked at Foinet, who was coming towards them with Mrs. Otter. Mrs. Otter, meek, mediocre, and self-satisfied, wore an air of importance. Foinet sat down at the easel of an untidy little Englishwoman called Ruth Chalice. She had the fine black eyes, languid but passionate, the thin face, ascetic but sensual, the skin like old ivory, which under the influence of Burne-Jones were cultivated at that time by young ladies in Chelsea. Foinet seemed in a pleasant mood; he did not say much to her, but with quick, determined strokes of her charcoal pointed out her errors. Miss Chalice beamed with pleasure when he rose. He came to Clutton, and by this time Philip was nervous too, but Mrs. Otter had promised to make things easy for him. Foinet stood for a moment in front of Clutton's work, biting his thumb silently, then absent-mindedly spat out upon the canvas the little piece of skin which he had bitten off.

"That's a fine line," he said at last, indicating with his thumb what pleased him. "You're beginning to learn to draw."

Clutton did not answer, but looked at the master with his usual air of sardonic indifference to the world's opinion.

"I'm beginning to think you have at least a trace of talent."

Mrs. Otter, who did not like Clutton, pursed her lips. She did not see anything out of the way in his work. Foinet sat down and went into technical details. Mrs. Otter grew rather tired of standing. Clutton did not say anything, but nodded now and then, and Foinet felt with satisfaction that he grasped what he said and the reasons of it; most of them listened to him, but it was clear they never understood. Then Foinet got up and came to Philip.

"He only arrived two days ago," Mrs. Otter hurried to explain. "He's a beginner. He's never studied before."

"*Ça se voit,*" the master said. "One sees that."

He passed on, and Mrs. Otter murmured to him:

"This is the young lady I told you about."

He looked at her as though she were some repulsive animal, and his voice grew more rasping.

"It appears that you do not think I pay enough attention to you. You have been complaining to the *massière*. Well, show me this work to which you wish me to give attention."

Fanny Price coloured. The blood under her unhealthy skin seemed to be of a strange purple. Without answering she pointed to the drawing on which she had been at work since the beginning of the week. Foinet sat down.

"Well, what do you wish me to say to you? Do you wish me to tell you it is good? It isn't. Do you wish me to tell you it is well drawn? It isn't. Do you wish me to say it has merit? It hasn't. Do you wish me to show you what is wrong with it? It is all wrong. Do you wish me to tell you what to do with it? Tear it up. Are you satisfied now?"

Miss Price became very white. She was furious because he had said all this before Mrs. Otter. Though she had been in France so long and could understand French well enough, she could hardly speak two words.

"He's got no right to treat me like that. My money's as good as anyone else's. I pay him to teach me. That's not teaching me."

"What does she say? What does she say?" asked Foinet.

Mrs. Otter hesitated to translate, and Miss Price repeated in execrable French.

"*Je vous paye pour m'apprendre.*"

His eyes flashed with rage, he raised his voice and shook his fist.

"*Mais, nom de Dieu*, I can't teach you. I could more easily teach a camel." He turned to Mrs. Otter. "Ask her, does she do this for amusement, or does she expect to earn money by it?"

"I'm going to earn my living as an artist," Miss Price answered.

"Then it is my duty to tell you that you are wasting your time. It would not matter that you have no talent, talent does not run about the streets in these days, but you have not the beginning of an aptitude. How long have you been here? A child of five after two lessons would draw better than you do. I only say one thing to you, give up this hopeless attempt. You're more likely to earn your living as a *bonne à tout faire* than as a painter. Look."

He seized a piece of charcoal, and it broke as he applied it to the paper. He cursed, and with the stump drew great firm lines. He drew rapidly and spoke at the same time, spitting out the words with venom.

"Look, those arms are not the same length. That knee, it's grotesque. I tell you a child of five. You see, she's not standing on her legs. That foot!"

With each word the angry pencil made a mark, and in a moment the drawing upon which Fanny Price had spent so much time and eager trouble was unrecognisable, a confusion of lines and smudges. At last he flung down the charcoal and stood up.

"Take my advice, Mademoiselle, try dressmaking." He looked at his watch. "It's twelve. *À la semaine prochaine, messieurs.*"

Miss Price gathered up her things slowly. Philip waited behind after the others to say to her something consolatory. He could think of nothing but:

"I say, I'm awfully sorry. What a beast that man is!"

She turned on him savagely.

"Is that what you're waiting about for? When I want your sympathy I'll ask for it. Please get out of my way."

She walked past him, out of the studio, and Philip, with a shrug of the shoulders, limped along to Gravier's for luncheon.

"It served her right," said Lawson, when Philip told him what had happened. "Ill-tempered slut."

Lawson was very sensitive to criticism and, in order to avoid it, never went to the studio when Foinet was coming.

"I don't want other people's opinion of my work," he said. "I know myself if it's good or bad."

"You mean you don't want other people's bad opinion of your work," answered Clutton dryly.

In the afternoon Philip thought he would go to the Luxembourg to see the pictures, and walking through the garden he saw Fanny Price sitting in her accustomed seat. He was sore at the rudeness with which she had met his well-meant attempt to say something pleasant, and passed as though he had not caught sight of her. But she got up at once and came towards him.

"Are you trying to cut me?" she said.

"No, of course not. I thought perhaps you didn't want to be spoken to."

"Where are you going?"

"I wanted to have a look at the Manet, I've heard so much about it."

"Would you like me to come with you? I know the Luxembourg rather well. I could show you one or two good things."

He understood that, unable to bring herself to apologise directly, she made this offer as amends.

"It's awfully kind of you. I should like it very much."

"You needn't say yes if you'd rather go alone," she said suspiciously.

"I wouldn't."

They walked towards the gallery. Caillebotte's collection had lately been placed on view, and the student for the first time had the opportunity to examine at his ease the works of the impressionists. Till then it had been possible to see them only at Durand-Ruel's shop in the Rue Lafitte (and the dealer, unlike his fellows in England, who adopt towards the painter an attitude of superiority, was always pleased to show the shabbiest student whatever he wanted to see), or at his private house, to which it was not difficult to get a card of admission on Tuesdays, and where you might see pictures of world-wide reputation. Miss Price led Philip straight up to Manet's *Olympia*. He looked at it in astonished silence.

"Do you like it?" asked Miss Price.

"I don't know," he answered helplessly.

"You can take it from me that it's the best thing in the gallery except perhaps Whistler's portrait of his mother."

She gave him a certain time to contemplate the masterpiece and then took him to a picture representing a railway-station.

"Look, here's a Monet," she said. "It's the Gare St. Lazare."

"But the railway lines aren't parallel," said Philip.

"What does that matter?" she asked, with a haughty air.

Philip felt ashamed of himself. Fanny Price had picked up the glib chatter of the studios and had no difficulty in impressing Philip with the extent of her knowledge. She proceeded to explain the pictures to him, superciliously but not without insight, and showed him what the painters had attempted and what he must look for. She talked with much gesticulation of the thumb, and Philip, to whom all she said was new, listened with profound but bewildered interest. Till now he had worshipped Watts and Burne-Jones. The pretty colour of the first, the affected drawing of the second, had entirely satisfied his aesthetic sensibilities. Their vague idealism, the suspicion of a philosophical idea which underlay the titles they gave their pictures, accorded very well with the functions of art as from his diligent perusal of Ruskin he understood it; but here was something quite different: here was no moral appeal; and the contemplation of these works could help no one to lead a purer and a higher life. He was puzzled.

At last he said: "You know, I'm simply dead. I don't think I can absorb anything more profitably. Let's go and sit down on one of the benches."

"It's better not to take too much art at a time," Miss Price answered.

When they got outside he thanked her warmly for the trouble she had taken.

"Oh, that's all right," she said, a little ungraciously. "I do it because I enjoy it. We'll go to the Louvre tomorrow if you like, and then I'll take you to Durand-Ruel's."

"You're really awfully good to me."

"You don't think me such a beast as the most of them do."

"I don't," he smiled.

"They think they'll drive me away from the studio; but they won't; I shall stay there just exactly as long as it suits me. All that this morning, it was Lucy Otter's doing, I know it was. She always has hated me. She thought after that I'd take myself off. I daresay she'd like me to go. She's afraid I know too much about her."

Miss Price told him a long, involved story, which made out that Mrs. Otter, a humdrum and respectable little person, had scabrous intrigues. Then she talked of Ruth Chalice, the girl whom Foinet had praised that morning.

"She's been with every one of the fellows at the studio. She's nothing better than a street-walker. And she's dirty. She hasn't had a bath for a month, I know it for a fact."

Philip listened uncomfortably. He had heard already that various rumours were in circulation about Miss Chalice; but it was ridiculous to suppose that Mrs. Otter, living with her mother, was anything but rigidly virtuous. The woman walking by his side with her malignant lying positively horrified him.

"I don't care what they say. I shall go on just the same. I know I've got it in me. I feel I'm an artist. I'd sooner kill myself than give it up. Oh, I shan't be the first they've all laughed at in the schools and then he's turned out the only genius of the lot. Art's the only thing I care for, I'm willing to give my whole life to it. It's only a question of sticking to it and pegging away"

She found discreditable motives for everyone who would not take her at her own estimate of herself. She detested Clutton. She told Philip that his friend had no talent really; it was just flashy and superficial; he couldn't compose a figure to save his life. And Lawson:

"Little beast, with his red hair and his freckles. He's so afraid of Foinet that he won't let him see his work. After all, I don't funk it, do I? I don't care what Foinet says to me, I know I'm a real artist."

They reached the street in which she lived, and with a sigh of relief Philip left her.

Chapter XLIV

BUT NOTWITHSTANDING WHEN MISS PRICE ON THE FOLLOWING SUNDAY OFfered to take him to the Louvre Philip accepted. She showed him Mona Lisa. He looked at it with a slight feeling of disappointment, but he had read till he knew by heart the jewelled words with which Walter Pater has added beauty to the most famous picture in the world; and these now he repeated to Miss Price.

"That's all literature," she said, a little contemptuously. "You must get away from that."

She showed him the Rembrandts, and she said many appropriate things about them. She stood in front of the *Disciples at Emmaus*.

"When you feel the beauty of that," she said, "you'll know something about painting."

She showed him the *Odalisque* and *La Source* of Ingres. Fanny Price was a peremptory guide, she would not let him look at the things he wished, and attempted to force his admiration for all she admired. She was desperately in earnest with her study of art, and when Philip, passing in the Long Gallery a window that looked out on the Tuileries, gay, sunny, and urbane, like a picture by Raffaëlli, exclaimed:

"I say, how jolly! Do let's stop here a minute."

She said, indifferently: "Yes, it's all right. But we've come here to look at pictures."

The autumn air, blithe and vivacious, elated Philip; and when towards mid-day they stood in the great court-yard of the Louvre, he felt inclined to cry like Flanagan: To Hell with art.

"I say, do let's go to one of those restaurants in the Boul' Mich' and have a snack together, shall we?" he suggested.

Miss Price gave him a suspicious look.

"I've got my lunch waiting for me at home," she answered.

"That doesn't matter. You can eat it tomorrow. Do let me stand you a lunch."

"I don't know why you want to."

"It would give me pleasure," he replied, smiling.

They crossed the river, and at the corner of the Boulevard St. Michel there was a restaurant.

"Let's go in there."

"No, I won't go there, it looks too expensive."

She walked on firmly, and Philip was obliged to follow. A few steps brought them to a smaller restaurant, where a dozen people were already lunching on the pavement under an awning; on the window was announced in large white letters: *Déjeuner 1.25, vin compris.*

"We couldn't have anything cheaper than this, and it looks quite all right."

They sat down at a vacant table and waited for the omelette which was the first article on the bill of fare. Philip gazed with delight upon the passersby. His heart went out to them. He was tired but very happy.

"I say, look at that man in the blouse. Isn't he ripping!"

He glanced at Miss Price, and to his astonishment saw that she was looking down at her plate, regardless of the passing spectacle, and two heavy tears were rolling down her cheeks.

"What on earth's the matter?" he exclaimed.

"If you say anything to me I shall get up and go at once," she answered.

He was entirely puzzled, but fortunately at that moment the omelette came. He divided it in two and they began to eat. Philip did his best to talk of indifferent things, and it seemed as though Miss Price were making an effort on her side to be agreeable; but the luncheon was not altogether a success. Philip was squeamish, and the way in which Miss Price ate took his appetite away. She ate noisily, greedily, a little like a wild beast in a menagerie, and after she had finished each course rubbed the plate with pieces of bread till it was white and shining, as if she did not wish to lose a single drop of gravy. They had Camembert cheese, and it disgusted Philip to see that she ate rind and all of the portion that was given her. She could not have eaten more ravenously if she were starving.

Miss Price was unaccountable, and having parted from her on one day with friendliness he could never tell whether on the next she would not be sulky and uncivil; but he learned a good deal from her: though she could not draw well herself, she knew all that could be taught, and her constant suggestions helped his progress. Mrs. Otter was useful to him too, and sometimes Miss Chalice criticised his work; he learned from the glib loquacity of Lawson and from the example of Clutton. But Fanny Price hated him to take suggestions from anyone but herself, and when he asked her help after someone else had been talking to him she would refuse with brutal rudeness. The other fellows, Lawson, Clutton, Flanagan, chaffed him about her.

"You be careful, my lad," they said, "she's in love with you."

"Oh, what nonsense," he laughed.

The thought that Miss Price could be in love with anyone was preposterous. It made him shudder when he thought of her uncomeliness, the bedraggled hair and the dirty hands, the brown dress she always wore, stained and ragged at the hem:

he supposed she was hard up, they were all hard up, but she might at least be clean; and it was surely possible with a needle and thread to make her skirt tidy.

Philip began to sort his impressions of the people he was thrown in contact with. He was not so ingenuous as in those days which now seemed so long ago at Heidelberg, and, beginning to take a more deliberate interest in humanity, he was inclined to examine and to criticise. He found it difficult to know Clutton any better after seeing him every day for three months than on the first day of their acquaintance. The general impression at the studio was that he was able; it was supposed that he would do great things, and he shared the general opinion; but what exactly he was going to do neither he nor anybody else quite knew. He had worked at several studios before Amitrano's, at Julian's, the Beaux Arts, and MacPherson's, and was remaining longer at Amitrano's than anywhere because he found himself more left alone. He was not fond of showing his work, and unlike most of the young men who were studying art neither sought nor gave advice. It was said that in the little studio in the Rue Campagne Première, which served him for work-room and bed-room, he had wonderful pictures which would make his reputation if only he could be induced to exhibit them. He could not afford a model but painted still life, and Lawson constantly talked of a plate of apples which he declared was a masterpiece. He was fastidious, and, aiming at something he did not quite fully grasp, was constantly dissatisfied with his work as a whole: perhaps a part would please him, the forearm or the leg and foot of a figure, a glass or a cup in a still-life; and he would cut this out and keep it, destroying the rest of the canvas; so that when people invited themselves to see his work he could truthfully answer that he had not a single picture to show. In Brittany he had come across a painter whom nobody else had heard of, a queer fellow who had been a stockbroker and taken up painting at middle age, and he was greatly influenced by his work. He was turning his back on the impressionists and working out for himself painfully an individual way not only of painting but of seeing. Philip felt in him something strangely original.

At Gravier's where they ate, and in the evening at the Versailles or at the Closerie des Lilas Clutton was inclined to taciturnity. He sat quietly, with a sardonic expression on his gaunt face, and spoke only when the opportunity occurred to throw in a witticism. He liked a butt and was most cheerful when someone was there on whom he could exercise his sarcasm. He seldom talked of anything but painting, and then only with the one or two persons whom he thought worthwhile. Philip wondered whether there was in him really anything: his reticence, the haggard look of him, the pungent humour, seemed to suggest personality, but might be no more than an effective mask which covered nothing.

With Lawson on the other hand Philip soon grew intimate. He had a variety of interests which made him an agreeable companion. He read more than most of the students and though his income was small, loved to buy books. He lent them willingly; and Philip became acquainted with Flaubert and Balzac, with Verlaine, Heredia, and Villiers de l'Isle Adam. They went to plays together and sometimes to the gallery of the Opéra Comique. There was the Odéon quite near them, and Philip soon shared his friend's passion for the tragedians of Louis XIV and the sonorous Alexandrine. In the Rue Taitbout were the Concerts Rouge, where for seventy-five centimes they could hear excellent music and get into the bargain something which it was quite possible to drink: the seats were uncomfortable, the place was crowded, the air thick with caporal horrible to breathe, but in their young enthusiasm they were indifferent. Sometimes they went to the Bal Bullier. On these occasions Flanagan accompanied them. His excitability and his roisterous enthusiasm made them laugh. He was an excellent dancer, and before they had been ten minutes in the room he was prancing round with some little shop-girl whose acquaintance he had just made.

The desire of all of them was to have a mistress. It was part of the paraphernalia of the art-student in Paris. It gave consideration in the eyes of one's fellows. It was something to boast about. But the difficulty was that they had scarcely enough money to keep themselves, and though they argued that Frenchwomen were so clever it cost no more to keep two than one, they found it difficult to meet young women who were willing to take that view of the circumstances. They had to content themselves for the most part with envying and abusing the ladies who received protection from painters of more settled respectability than their own. It was extraordinary how difficult these things were in Paris. Lawson would become acquainted with some young thing and make an appointment; for twenty-four hours he would be all in a flutter and describe the charmer at length to everyone he met; but she never by any chance turned up at the time fixed. He would come to Gravier's very late, ill-tempered, and exclaim:

"Confound it, another rabbit! I don't know why it is they don't like me. I suppose it's because I don't speak French well, or my red hair. It's too sickening to have spent over a year in Paris without getting hold of anyone."

"You don't go the right way to work," said Flanagan.

He had a long and enviable list of triumphs to narrate, and though they took leave not to believe all he said, evidence forced them to acknowledge that he did not altogether lie. But he sought no permanent arrangement. He only had two years in Paris: he had persuaded his people to let him come and study art instead of going to college; but at the end of that period he was to return to Seattle and go into his father's business. He had made up his mind to get as much fun as possible into the time, and demanded variety rather than duration in his love affairs.

"I don't know how you get hold of them," said Lawson furiously.

"There's no difficulty about that, sonny," answered Flanagan. "You just go right in. The difficulty is to get rid of them. That's where you want tact."

Philip was too much occupied with his work, the books he was reading, the plays he saw, the conversation he listened to, to trouble himself with the desire for female society. He thought there would be plenty of time for that when he could speak French more glibly.

It was more than a year now since he had seen Miss Wilkinson, and during his first weeks in Paris he had been too busy to answer a letter she had written to him just before he left Blackstable. When another came, knowing it would be full of reproaches and not being just then in the mood for them, he put it aside, intending to open it later; but he forgot and did not run across it till a month afterwards, when he was turning out a drawer to find some socks that had no holes in them. He looked at the unopened letter with dismay. He was afraid that Miss Wilkinson had suffered a good deal, and it made him feel a brute; but she had probably got over the suffering by now, at all events the worst of it. It suggested itself to him that women were often very emphatic in their expressions. These did not mean so much as when men used them. He had quite made up his mind that nothing would induce him ever to see her again. He had not written for so long that it seemed hardly worthwhile to write now. He made up his mind not to read the letter.

"I daresay she won't write again," he said to himself. "She can't help seeing the thing's over. After all, she was old enough to be my mother; she ought to have known better."

For an hour or two he felt a little uncomfortable. His attitude was obviously the right one, but he could not help a feeling of dissatisfaction with the whole business. Miss Wilkinson, however, did not write again; nor did she, as he absurdly feared, suddenly appear in Paris to make him ridiculous before his friends. In a little while he clean forgot her.

Meanwhile he definitely forsook his old gods. The amazement with which at first he had looked upon the works of the impressionists, changed to admiration; and presently he found himself talking as emphatically as the rest on the merits of Manet, Monet, and Degas. He bought a photograph of a drawing by Ingres of the *Odalisque* and a photograph of the *Olympia*. They were pinned side by side over his washing-stand so that he could contemplate their beauty while he shaved. He knew now quite positively that there had been no painting of landscape before Monet; and he felt a real thrill when he stood in front of Rembrandt's *Disciples at Emmaus* or Velasquez' *Lady with the Flea-bitten Nose*. That was not her real name, but by that she was distinguished at Gravier's to emphasise the picture's beauty notwithstanding the somewhat revolting peculiarity of the sitter's appearance.

With Ruskin, Burne-Jones, and Watts, he had put aside his bowler hat and the neat blue tie with white spots which he had worn on coming to Paris; and now disported himself in a soft, broad-brimmed hat, a flowing black cravat, and a cape of romantic cut. He walked along the Boulevard du Montparnasse as though he had known it all his life, and by virtuous perseverance he had learned to drink absinthe without distaste. He was letting his hair grow, and it was only because Nature is unkind and has no regard for the immortal longings of youth that he did not attempt a beard.

Chapter XLV

PHILIP SOON REALISED THAT THE SPIRIT WHICH INFORMED HIS FRIENDS WAS Cronshaw's. It was from him that Lawson got his paradoxes; and even Clutton, who strained after individuality, expressed himself in the terms he had insensibly acquired from the older man. It was his ideas that they bandied about at table, and on his authority they formed their judgments. They made up for the respect with which unconsciously they treated him by laughing at his foibles and lamenting his vices.

"Of course, poor old Cronshaw will never do any good," they said. "He's quite hopeless."

They prided themselves on being alone in appreciating his genius; and though, with the contempt of youth for the follies of middle age, they patronised him among themselves, they did not fail to look upon it as a feather in their caps if he had chosen a time when only one was there to be particularly wonderful. Cronshaw never came to Gravier's. For the last four years he had lived in squalid conditions with a woman whom only Lawson had once seen, in a tiny apartment on the sixth floor of one of the most dilapidated houses on the Quai des Grands Augustins: Lawson described with gusto the filth, the untidiness, the litter.

"And the stink nearly blew your head off."

"Not at dinner, Lawson," expostulated one of the others.

But he would not deny himself the pleasure of giving picturesque details of the odours which met his nostril. With a fierce delight in his own realism he described the woman who had opened the door for him. She was dark, small, and fat, quite young, with black hair that seemed always on the point of coming down. She wore a slatternly blouse and no corsets. With her red cheeks, large sensual mouth, and shining, lewd eyes, she reminded you of the *Bohèmienne* in the Louvre by Franz Hals. She had a flaunting vulgarity which amused and yet horrified. A scrubby, unwashed baby was playing on the floor. It was known that the slut deceived Cronshaw with the most worthless ragamuffins of the Quarter, and it was a mystery to the ingenuous youths who absorbed his wisdom over a café table that Cronshaw with his keen intellect and his passion for beauty could ally himself to such a creature. But he seemed to revel in the coarseness of her language and would often report some phrase which reeked of the gutter. He referred to her ironically as *la fille de mon concierge*. Cronshaw was very poor. He earned a bare subsistence by writing on the exhibitions of pictures for one or two English papers, and he did a certain amount of translating. He had been on the staff of an English paper in Paris, but had been dismissed for drunkenness; he still however did odd jobs for it, describing sales at the Hotel Drouot or the revues at music-halls. The life of Paris had got into his bones, and he would not change it, notwithstanding its squalor, drudgery, and hardship, for any other in the world. He remained there all through the year, even in summer when everyone he knew was away, and felt himself only at ease within a mile of the Boulevard St. Michel. But the curious thing was that he had never learned to speak French passably, and he kept in his shabby clothes bought at *La Belle Jardinière* an ineradicably English appearance.

He was a man who would have made a success of life a century and a half ago when conversation was a passport to good company and inebriety no bar.

"I ought to have lived in the eighteen hundreds," he said himself. "What I want is a patron. I should have published my poems by subscription and dedicated them to a nobleman. I long to compose rhymed couplets upon the poodle of a countess. My soul yearns for the love of chamber-maids and the conversation of bishops."

He quoted the romantic Rolla,

"Je suis venu trop tard dans un monde trop vieux."

He liked new faces, and he took a fancy to Philip, who seemed to achieve the difficult feat of talking just enough to suggest conversation and not too much to prevent monologue. Philip was captivated. He did not realise that little that Cronshaw said was new. His personality in conversation had a curious power. He had a beautiful and a sonorous voice, and a manner of putting things which was irresistible to youth. All he said seemed to excite thought, and often on the way home Lawson and Philip would walk to and from one another's hotels, discussing some point which a chance word of Cronshaw had suggested. It was disconcerting to Philip, who had a youthful eagerness for results, that Cronshaw's poetry hardly came up to expectation. It had never been published in a volume, but most of it had appeared in periodicals; and after a good deal of persuasion Cronshaw brought down a bundle of pages torn out of *The Yellow Book*, *The Saturday Review*, and other journals, on each of which was a poem. Philip was taken aback to find that most of them reminded him either of Henley or of Swinburne. It needed the splendour of Cronshaw's delivery to make them personal. He expressed his disappointment to Lawson, who carelessly repeated his words; and next time Philip went to the Closerie des Lilas the poet turned to him with his sleek smile:

"I hear you don't think much of my verses."

Philip was embarrassed.

"I don't know about that," he answered. "I enjoyed reading them very much."

"Do not attempt to spare my feelings," returned Cronshaw, with a wave of his fat hand. "I do not attach any exaggerated importance to my poetical works. Life is there to be lived rather than to be written about. My aim is to search out the manifold experience that it offers, wringing from each moment what of emotion it presents. I look upon my writing as a graceful accomplishment which does not absorb but rather adds pleasure to existence. And as for posterity—damn posterity."

Philip smiled, for it leaped to one's eyes that the artist in life had produced no more than a wretched daub. Cronshaw looked at him meditatively and filled his glass. He sent the waiter for a packet of cigarettes.

"You are amused because I talk in this fashion and you know that I am poor and live in an attic with a vulgar trollop who deceives me with hair-dressers and *garçons de café*; I translate wretched books for the British public, and write articles upon contemptible pictures which deserve not even to be abused. But pray tell me what is the meaning of life?"

"I say, that's rather a difficult question. Won't you give the answer yourself?"

"No, because it's worthless unless you yourself discover it. But what do you suppose you are in the world for?"

Philip had never asked himself, and he thought for a moment before replying.

"Oh, I don't know: I suppose to do one's duty, and make the best possible use of one's faculties, and avoid hurting other people."

"In short, to do unto others as you would they should do unto you?"

"I suppose so."

"Christianity."

"No, it isn't," said Philip indignantly. "It has nothing to do with Christianity. It's just abstract morality."

"But there's no such thing as abstract morality."

"In that case, supposing under the influence of liquor you left your purse behind when you leave here and I picked it up, why do you imagine that I should return it to you? It's not the fear of the police."

"It's the dread of hell if you sin and the hope of Heaven if you are virtuous."

"But I believe in neither."

"That may be. Neither did Kant when he devised the Categorical Imperative. You have thrown aside a creed, but you have preserved the ethic which was based upon it. To all intents you are a Christian still, and if there is a God in Heaven you will undoubtedly receive your reward. The Almighty can hardly be such a fool as the churches make out. If you keep His laws I don't think He can care a packet of pins whether you believe in Him or not."

"But if I left my purse behind you would certainly return it to me," said Philip.

"Not from motives of abstract morality, but only from fear of the police."

"It's a thousand to one that the police would never find out."

"My ancestors have lived in a civilised state so long that the fear of the police has eaten into my bones. The daughter of my *concierge* would not hesitate for a moment. You answer that she belongs to the criminal classes; not at all, she is merely devoid of vulgar prejudice."

"But then that does away with honour and virtue and goodness and decency and everything," said Philip.

"Have you ever committed a sin?"

"I don't know, I suppose so," answered Philip.

"You speak with the lips of a dissenting minister. I have never committed a sin."

Cronshaw in his shabby great-coat, with the collar turned up, and his hat well down on his head, with his red fat face and his little gleaming eyes, looked extraordinarily comic; but Philip was too much in earnest to laugh.

"Have you never done anything you regret?"

"How can I regret when what I did was inevitable?" asked Cronshaw in return.

"But that's fatalism."

"The illusion which man has that his will is free is so deeply rooted that I am ready to accept it. I act as though I were a free agent. But when an action is performed it is clear that all the forces of the universe from all eternity conspired to cause it, and nothing I could do could have prevented it. It was inevitable. If it was good I can claim no merit; if it was bad I can accept no censure."

"My brain reels," said Philip.

"Have some whiskey," returned Cronshaw, passing over the bottle. "There's nothing like it for clearing the head. You must expect to be thick-witted if you insist upon drinking beer."

Philip shook his head, and Cronshaw proceeded:

"You're not a bad fellow, but you won't drink. Sobriety disturbs conversation. But when I speak of good and bad . . ." Philip saw he was taking up the thread of his discourse, "I speak conventionally. I attach no meaning to those words. I refuse to make a hierarchy of human actions and ascribe worthiness to some and ill-repute to others. The terms vice and virtue have no signification for me. I do not confer praise or blame: I accept. I am the measure of all things. I am the centre of the world."

"But there are one or two other people in the world," objected Philip.

"I speak only for myself. I know them only as they limit my activities. Round each of them too the world turns, and each one for himself is the centre of the universe. My right over them extends only as far as my power. What I can do is the only limit of what I may do. Because we are gregarious we live in society, and society holds together by means of force, force of arms (that is the policeman) and force of public opinion (that is Mrs. Grundy). You have society on one hand and the individual on the other: each is an organism striving for self-preservation. It is might against might. I stand alone, bound to accept society and not unwilling, since in return for the taxes I pay it protects me, a weakling, against the tyranny of another stronger than I am; but I submit to its laws because I must; I do not acknowledge their justice: I do not know justice, I only know power. And when I have paid for the policeman who protects me and, if I live in a country where conscription is in force, served in the army which guards my house and land from the invader, I am quits with society: for the rest I counter its might with my wiliness. It makes laws for its self-preservation, and if I break them it imprisons or kills me: it has the might to do so and therefore the right. If I break the laws I will accept the vengeance of the state, but I will not regard it as punishment nor shall I feel myself convicted of wrong-doing. Society tempts me to its service by honours and riches and the good opinion of my fellows; but I am indifferent to their good opinion, I despise honours and I can do very well without riches."

"But if everyone thought like you things would go to pieces at once."

"I have nothing to do with others, I am only concerned with myself. I take advantage of the fact that the majority of mankind are led by certain rewards to do things which directly or indirectly tend to my convenience."

"It seems to me an awfully selfish way of looking at things," said Philip.

"But are you under the impression that men ever do anything except for selfish reasons?"

"Yes."

"It is impossible that they should. You will find as you grow older that the first thing needful to make the world a tolerable place to live in is to recognise the inevitable selfishness of humanity. You demand unselfishness from others, which is a preposterous claim that they should sacrifice their desires to yours. Why should they? When you are reconciled to the fact that each is for himself in the world you will ask less from your fellows. They will not disappoint you, and you will look upon them more charitably. Men seek but one thing in life—their pleasure."

"No, no, no!" cried Philip.

Cronshaw chuckled.

"You rear like a frightened colt, because I use a word to which your Christianity ascribes a deprecatory meaning. You have a hierarchy of values; pleasure is at the bottom of the ladder, and you speak with a little thrill of self-satisfaction of duty, charity, and truthfulness. You think pleasure is only of the senses; the wretched slaves who manufactured your morality despised a satisfaction which they had small means of enjoying. You would not be so frightened if I had spoken of happiness instead of pleasure: it sounds less shocking, and your mind wanders from the sty of Epicurus to his garden. But I will speak of pleasure, for I see that men aim at that, and I do not know that they aim at happiness. It is pleasure that lurks in the practice of every one of your virtues. Man performs actions because they are good for him, and when they are good for other people as well they are thought virtuous: if he finds pleasure in giving alms he is charitable; if he finds pleasure in helping others he is benevolent; if he finds pleasure in working for society he is public-spirited; but it is for your private pleasure that you give twopence to a beggar as much as it is for my private pleasure that I drink another whiskey and soda. I, less of a humbug than you, neither applaud myself for my pleasure nor demand your admiration."

"But have you never known people do things they didn't want to instead of things they did?"

"No. You put your question foolishly. What you mean is that people accept an immediate pain rather than an immediate pleasure. The objection is as foolish as your manner of putting it. It is clear that men accept an immediate pain rather than an immediate pleasure, but only because they expect a greater pleasure in the future. Often the pleasure is illusory, but their error in calculation is no refutation of the rule. You are puzzled because you cannot get over the idea that pleasures are only of the senses; but, child, a man who dies for his country dies because he likes it as surely as a man eats pickled cabbage because he likes it. It is a law of creation. If it were possible for men to prefer pain to pleasure the human race would have long since become extinct."

"But if all that is true," cried Philip, "what is the use of anything? If you take away duty and goodness and beauty why are we brought into the world?"

"Here comes the gorgeous East to suggest an answer," smiled Cronshaw.

He pointed to two persons who at that moment opened the door of the café, and, with a blast of cold air, entered. They were Levantines, itinerant vendors of cheap rugs, and each bore on his arm a bundle. It was Sunday evening, and the café was very full. They passed among the tables, and in that atmosphere heavy and discoloured with tobacco smoke, rank with humanity, they seemed to bring an air of mystery. They were clad in European, shabby clothes, their thin great-coats were threadbare, but each wore a tarbouch. Their faces were grey with cold. One was of middle age, with a black beard, but the other was a youth of eighteen, with a face deeply scarred by small-pox and with one eye only. They passed by Cronshaw and Philip.

"Allah is great, and Mahomet is his prophet," said Cronshaw impressively.

The elder advanced with a cringing smile, like a mongrel used to blows. With a sidelong glance at the door and a quick surreptitious movement he showed a pornographic picture.

"Are you Masr-ed-Deen, the merchant of Alexandria, or is it from far Bagdad that you bring your goods, O, my uncle; and yonder one-eyed youth, do I see in him one of the three kings of whom Scheherazade told stories to her lord?"

The pedlar's smile grew more ingratiating, though he understood no word of what Cronshaw said, and like a conjurer he produced a sandalwood box.

"Nay, show us the priceless web of Eastern looms," quoth Cronshaw. "For I would point a moral and adorn a tale."

The Levantine unfolded a table-cloth, red and yellow, vulgar, hideous, and grotesque.

"Thirty-five francs," he said.

"O, my uncle, this cloth knew not the weavers of Samarkand, and those colours were never made in the vats of Bokhara."

"Twenty-five francs," smiled the pedlar obsequiously.

"Ultima Thule was the place of its manufacture, even Birmingham the place of my birth."

"Fifteen francs," cringed the bearded man.

"Get thee gone, fellow," said Cronshaw. "May wild asses defile the grave of thy maternal grandmother."

Imperturbably, but smiling no more, the Levantine passed with his wares to another table. Cronshaw turned to Philip.

"Have you ever been to the Cluny, the museum? There you will see Persian carpets of the most exquisite hue and of a pattern the beautiful intricacy of which delights and amazes the eye. In them you will see the mystery and the sensual beauty of the East, the roses of Hafiz and the wine-cup of Omar; but presently you will see more. You were asking just now what was the meaning of life. Go and look at those Persian carpets, and one of these days the answer will come to you."

"You are cryptic," said Philip.

"I am drunk," answered Cronshaw.

Chapter XLVI

PHILIP DID NOT FIND LIVING IN PARIS AS CHEAP AS HE HAD BEEN LED TO BElieve and by February had spent most of the money with which he started. He was too proud to appeal to his guardian, nor did he wish Aunt Louisa to know that his circumstances were straitened, since he was certain she would make an effort to send him something from her own pocket, and he knew how little she could afford to. In three months he would attain his majority and come into possession of his small fortune. He tided over the interval by selling the few trinkets which he had inherited from his father.

At about this time Lawson suggested that they should take a small studio which was vacant in one of the streets that led out of the Boulevard Raspail. It was very cheap. It had a room attached, which they could use as a bed-room; and since Philip was at the school every morning Lawson could have the undisturbed use of the studio then; Lawson, after wandering from school to school, had come to the conclusion that he could work best alone, and proposed to get a model in three or four days a week. At first Philip hesitated on account of the expense, but they reckoned it out; and it seemed (they were so anxious to have a studio of their own that they calculated pragmatically) that the cost would not be much greater than that of living in a hotel. Though the rent and the cleaning by the *concierge* would come to a little more, they would save on the *petit déjeuner,* which they could make themselves. A year or two earlier Philip would have refused to share a room with anyone, since he was so sensitive about his deformed foot, but his morbid way of looking at it was growing less marked: in Paris it did not seem to matter so much, and, though he never by any chance forgot it himself, he ceased to feel that other people were constantly noticing it.

They moved in, bought a couple of beds, a washing-stand, a few chairs, and felt for the first time the thrill of possession. They were so excited that the first night they went to bed in what they could call a home they lay awake talking till three in the morning; and next day found lighting the fire and making their own coffee, which they had in pyjamas, such a jolly business that Philip did not get to Amitrano's till nearly eleven. He was in excellent spirits. He nodded to Fanny Price.

"How are you getting on?" he asked cheerily.

"What does that matter to you?" she asked in reply.

Philip could not help laughing.

"Don't jump down my throat. I was only trying to make myself polite."

"I don't want your politeness."

"D'you think it's worthwhile quarrelling with me too?" asked Philip mildly. "There are so few people you're on speaking terms with, as it is."

"That's my business, isn't it?"

"Quite."

He began to work, vaguely wondering why Fanny Price made herself so disagreeable. He had come to the conclusion that he thoroughly disliked her. Everyone did. People were only civil to her at all from fear of the malice of her tongue; for to their faces and behind their backs she said abominable things. But Philip was feeling so happy that he did not want even Miss Price to bear ill-feeling towards him. He used the artifice which had often before succeeded in banishing her ill-humour.

"I say, I wish you'd come and look at my drawing. I've got in an awful mess."

"Thank you very much, but I've got something better to do with my time."

Philip stared at her in surprise, for the one thing she could be counted upon to do with alacrity was to give advice. She went on quickly in a low voice, savage with fury.

"Now that Lawson's gone you think you'll put up with me. Thank you very much. Go and find somebody else to help you. I don't want anybody else's leavings."

Lawson had the pedagogic instinct; whenever he found anything out he was eager to impart it; and because he taught with delight he taught with profit. Philip, without thinking anything about it, had got into the habit of sitting by his side; it never occurred to him that Fanny Price was consumed with jealousy, and watched his acceptance of someone else's tuition with ever-increasing anger.

"You were very glad to put up with me when you knew nobody here," she said bitterly, "and as soon as you made friends with other people you threw me aside, like an old glove"—she repeated the stale metaphor with satisfaction—"like an old glove. All right, I don't care, but I'm not going to be made a fool of another time."

There was a suspicion of truth in what she said, and it made Philip angry enough to answer what first came into his head.

"Hang it all, I only asked your advice because I saw it pleased you."

She gave a gasp and threw him a sudden look of anguish. Then two tears rolled down her cheeks. She looked frowsy and grotesque. Philip, not knowing what on earth this new attitude implied, went back to his work. He was uneasy and conscience-stricken; but he would not go to her and say he was sorry if he had caused her pain, because he was afraid she would take the opportunity to snub him. For two or three weeks she did not speak to him, and, after Philip had got over the discomfort of being cut by her, he was somewhat relieved to be free from so difficult a friendship. He had been a little disconcerted by the air of proprietorship she assumed over him. She was an extraordinary woman. She came every day to the studio at eight o'clock, and was ready to start working when the model was in position; she worked steadily, talking to no one, struggling hour after hour with difficulties she could not overcome, and remained till the clock struck twelve. Her work was hopeless. There was not in it the smallest approach even to the mediocre achievement at which most of the young persons were able after some months to arrive. She wore every day the same ugly brown dress, with the mud of the last wet day still caked on the hem and with the raggedness, which Philip had noticed the first time he saw her, still unmended.

But one day she came up to him, and with a scarlet face asked whether she might speak to him afterwards.

"Of course, as much as you like," smiled Philip. "I'll wait behind at twelve."

He went to her when the day's work was over.

"Will you walk a little bit with me?" she said, looking away from him with embarrassment.

"Certainly."

They walked for two or three minutes in silence.

"D'you remember what you said to me the other day?" she asked then on a sudden.

"Oh, I say, don't let's quarrel," said Philip. "It really isn't worthwhile."

She gave a quick, painful inspiration.

"I don't want to quarrel with you. You're the only friend I had in Paris. I thought you rather liked me. I felt there was something between us. I was drawn towards you—you know what I mean, your club-foot."

Philip reddened and instinctively tried to walk without a limp. He did not like anyone to mention the deformity. He knew what Fanny Price meant. She was ugly and uncouth, and because he was deformed there was between them a certain sympathy. He was very angry with her, but he forced himself not to speak.

"You said you only asked my advice to please me. Don't you think my work's any good?"

"I've only seen your drawing at Amitrano's. It's awfully hard to judge from that."

"I was wondering if you'd come and look at my other work. I've never asked anyone else to look at it. I should like to show it to you."

"It's awfully kind of you. I'd like to see it very much."

"I live quite near here," she said apologetically. "It'll only take you ten minutes."

"Oh, that's all right," he said.

They were walking along the boulevard, and she turned down a side-street, then led him into another, poorer still, with cheap shops on the ground floor, and at last stopped. They climbed flight after flight of stairs. She unlocked a door, and they went into a tiny attic with a sloping roof and a small window. This was closed and the room had a musty smell. Though it was very cold there was no fire and no sign that there had been one. The bed was unmade. A chair, a chest of drawers which served also as a wash-stand, and a cheap easel, were all the furniture. The place would have been squalid enough in any case, but the litter, the untidiness, made the impression revolting. On the chimney-piece, scattered over with paints and brushes, were a cup, a dirty plate, and a tea-pot.

"If you'll stand over there I'll put them on the chair so that you can see them better."

She showed him twenty small canvases, about eighteen by twelve. She placed them on the chair, one after the other, watching his face; he nodded as he looked at each one.

"You do like them, don't you?" she said anxiously, after a bit.

"I just want to look at them all first," he answered. "I'll talk afterwards."

He was collecting himself. He was panic-stricken. He did not know what to say. It was not only that they were ill-drawn, or that the colour was put on amateurishly by someone who had no eye for it; but there was no attempt at getting the values, and the perspective was grotesque. It looked like the work of a child of five, but a child would have had some naïveté and might at least have made an attempt to put down what he saw; but here was the work of a vulgar mind chock full of recollections of vulgar pictures. Philip remembered that she had talked enthusiastically about Monet and the Impressionists, but here were only the worst traditions of the Royal Academy.

"There," she said at last, "that's the lot."

Philip was no more truthful than anybody else, but he had a great difficulty in telling a thundering, deliberate lie, and he blushed furiously when he answered:

"I think they're most awfully good."

A faint colour came into her unhealthy cheeks, and she smiled a little.

"You needn't say so if you don't think so, you know. I want the truth."

"But I do think so."

"Haven't you got any criticism to offer? There must be some you don't like as well as others."

Philip looked round helplessly. He saw a landscape, the typical picturesque "bit" of the amateur, an old bridge, a creeper-clad cottage, and a leafy bank.

"Of course I don't pretend to know anything about it," he said. "But I wasn't quite sure about the values of that."

She flushed darkly and taking up the picture quickly turned its back to him.

"I don't know why you should have chosen that one to sneer at. It's the best thing I've ever done. I'm sure my values are all right. That's a thing you can't teach anyone, you either understand values or you don't."

"I think they're all most awfully good," repeated Philip.

She looked at them with an air of self-satisfaction.

"I don't think they're anything to be ashamed of."

Philip looked at his watch.

"I say, it's getting late. Won't you let me give you a little lunch?"

"I've got my lunch waiting for me here."

Philip saw no sign of it, but supposed perhaps the *concierge* would bring it up when he was gone. He was in a hurry to get away. The mustiness of the room made his head ache.

Chapter XLVII

IN MARCH THERE WAS ALL THE EXCITEMENT OF SENDING IN TO THE SALON. Clutton, characteristically, had nothing ready, and he was very scornful of the two heads that Lawson sent; they were obviously the work of a student, straightforward portraits of models, but they had a certain force; Clutton, aiming at perfection, had no patience with efforts which betrayed hesitancy, and with a shrug of the shoulders told Lawson it was an impertinence to exhibit stuff which should never have been allowed out of his studio; he was not less contemptuous when the two heads were accepted. Flanagan tried his luck too, but his picture was refused. Mrs. Otter sent a blameless *Portrait de ma Mère,* accomplished and second-rate; and was hung in a very good place.

Hayward, whom Philip had not seen since he left Heidelberg, arrived in Paris to spend a few days in time to come to the party which Lawson and Philip were giving in their studio to celebrate the hanging of Lawson's pictures. Philip had been eager to see Hayward again, but when at last they met, he experienced some disappointment. Hayward had altered a little in appearance: his fine hair was thinner, and with the rapid wilting of the very fair, he was becoming wizened and colourless; his blue eyes were paler than they had been, and there was a muzziness about his features. On the other hand, in mind he did not seem to have changed at all, and the culture which had impressed Philip at eighteen aroused somewhat the contempt of Philip at twenty-one. He had altered a good deal himself, and regarding with scorn all his old opinions of art, life, and letters, had no patience with anyone who still held them. He was scarcely conscious of the fact that he wanted to show off before Hayward, but when he took him round the galleries he poured out to him all the revolutionary opinions which himself had so recently adopted. He took him to Manet's *Olympia* and said dramatically:

"I would give all the old masters except Velasquez, Rembrandt, and Vermeer for that one picture."

"Who was Vermeer?" asked Hayward.

"Oh, my dear fellow, don't you know Vermeer? You're not civilised. You mustn't live a moment longer without making his acquaintance. He's the one old master who painted like a modern."

He dragged Hayward out of the Luxembourg and hurried him off to the Louvre.

"But aren't there any more pictures here?" asked Hayward, with the tourist's passion for thoroughness.

"Nothing of the least consequence. You can come and look at them by yourself with your Baedeker."

When they arrived at the Louvre Philip led his friend down the Long Gallery.

"I should like to see *The Gioconda*," said Hayward.

"Oh, my dear fellow, it's only literature," answered Philip.

At last, in a small room, Philip stopped before *The Lacemaker* of Vermeer van Delft.

"There, that's the best picture in the Louvre. It's exactly like a Manet."

With an expressive, eloquent thumb Philip expatiated on the charming work. He used the jargon of the studios with overpowering effect.

"I don't know that I see anything so wonderful as all that in it," said Hayward.

"Of course it's a painter's picture," said Philip. "I can quite believe the layman would see nothing much in it."

"The what?" said Hayward.

"The layman."

Like most people who cultivate an interest in the arts, Hayward was extremely anxious to be right. He was dogmatic with those who did not venture to assert themselves, but with the self-assertive he was very modest. He was impressed by Philip's assurance, and accepted meekly Philip's implied suggestion that the painter's arrogant claim to be the sole possible judge of painting has anything but its impertinence to recommend it.

A day or two later Philip and Lawson gave their party. Cronshaw, making an exception in their favour, agreed to eat their food; and Miss Chalice offered to come and cook for them. She took no interest in her own sex and declined the suggestion that other girls should be asked for her sake. Clutton, Flanagan, Potter, and two others made up the party. Furniture was scarce, so the model stand was used as a table, and the guests were to sit on portmanteaux if they liked, and if they didn't on the floor. The feast consisted of a *pot-au-feu*, which Miss Chalice had made, of a leg of mutton roasted round the corner and brought round hot and savoury (Miss Chalice had cooked the potatoes, and the studio was redolent of the carrots she had fried; fried carrots were her specialty); and this was to be followed by *poires flambées*, pears with burning brandy, which Cronshaw had volunteered to make. The meal was to finish with an enormous *fromage de Brie*, which stood near the window and added fragrant odours to all the others which filled the studio. Cronshaw sat in the place of honour on a Gladstone bag, with his legs curled under him like a Turkish bashaw, beaming good-naturedly on the young people who surrounded him. From force of habit, though the small studio with the stove lit was very hot, he kept on his great-coat, with the collar turned up, and his bowler hat: he looked with satisfaction on the four large *fiaschi* of Chianti which stood in front of him in a row, two on each side of a bottle of whiskey; he said it reminded him of a slim fair Circassian guarded by four corpulent eunuchs. Hayward in order to put the rest of them at their ease had clothed himself in a tweed suit and a Trinity Hall tie. He looked grotesquely British. The others were elaborately polite to him, and during the soup they talked of the weather and the political situation. There was a pause while they waited for the leg of mutton, and Miss Chalice lit a cigarette.

"Rapunzel, Rapunzel, let down your hair," she said suddenly.

With an elegant gesture she untied a ribbon so that her tresses fell over her shoulders. She shook her head.

"I always feel more comfortable with my hair down."

With her large brown eyes, thin, ascetic face, her pale skin, and broad forehead, she might have stepped out of a picture by Burne-Jones. She had long, beautiful hands, with fingers deeply stained by nicotine. She wore sweeping draperies, mauve and green. There was about her the romantic air of High Street, Kensington. She was wantonly aesthetic; but she was an excellent creature, kind and good-natured; and her affectations were but skin-deep. There was a knock at the door, and they all gave a shout of exultation. Miss Chalice rose and opened. She took the leg of mutton and held it high above her, as though it were the head of John the Baptist on a platter; and, the cigarette still in her mouth, advanced with solemn, hieratic steps.

"Hail, daughter of Herodias," cried Cronshaw.

The mutton was eaten with gusto, and it did one good to see what a hearty appetite the pale-faced lady had. Clutton and Potter sat on each side of her, and everyone knew that neither had found her unduly coy. She grew tired of most people in six weeks, but she knew exactly how to treat afterwards the gentlemen who had laid their young hearts at her feet. She bore them no ill-will, though having loved them she had ceased to do so, and treated them with friendliness but without familiarity. Now and then she looked at Lawson with melancholy eyes. The *poires flambées* were a great success, partly because of the brandy, and partly because Miss Chalice insisted that they should be eaten with the cheese.

"I don't know whether it's perfectly delicious, or whether I'm just going to vomit," she said, after she had thoroughly tried the mixture.

Coffee and cognac followed with sufficient speed to prevent any untoward consequence, and they settled down to smoke in comfort. Ruth Chalice, who could do nothing that was not deliberately artistic, arranged herself in a graceful attitude by Cronshaw and just rested her exquisite head on his shoulder. She looked into the dark abyss of time with brooding eyes, and now and then with a long meditative glance at Lawson she sighed deeply.

* * *

Then came the summer, and restlessness seized these young people. The blue skies lured them to the sea, and the pleasant breeze sighing through the leaves of the plane-trees on the boulevard drew them towards the country. Everyone made plans for leaving Paris; they discussed what was the most suitable size for the canvases they meant to take; they laid in stores of panels for sketching; they argued about the merits of various places in Brittany. Flanagan and Potter went to Concarneau; Mrs. Otter and her mother, with a natural instinct for the obvious, went to Pont-Aven; Philip and Lawson made up their minds to go to the forest of Fontainebleau, and Miss Chalice knew of a very good hotel at Moret where there was lots of stuff to paint; it was near Paris, and neither Philip nor Lawson was indifferent to the railway fare. Ruth Chalice would be there, and Lawson had an idea for a portrait of her in the open air. Just then the Salon was full of portraits of people in gardens, in sunlight, with blinking eyes and green reflections of sunlit leaves on their faces. They asked Clutton to go with them, but he preferred spending the summer by himself. He had just discovered Cézanne, and was eager to go to Provence; he wanted heavy skies from which the hot blue seemed to drip like beads of sweat, and broad white dusty roads, and pale roofs out of which the sun had burned the colour, and olive-trees grey with heat.

The day before they were to start, after the morning class, Philip, putting his things together, spoke to Fanny Price.

"I'm off tomorrow," he said cheerfully.

"Off where?" she said quickly. "You're not going away?" Her face fell.

"I'm going away for the summer. Aren't you?"

"No, I'm staying in Paris. I thought you were going to stay too. I was looking forward. . . ."

She stopped and shrugged her shoulders.

"But won't it be frightfully hot here? It's awfully bad for you."

"Much you care if it's bad for me. Where are you going?"

"Moret."

"Chalice is going there. You're not going with her?"

"Lawson and I are going. And she's going there too. I don't know that we're actually going together."

She gave a low guttural sound, and her large face grew dark and red.

"How filthy! I thought you were a decent fellow. You were about the only one here. She's been with Clutton and Potter and Flanagan, even with old Foinet—that's why he takes so much trouble about her—and now two of you, you and Lawson. It makes me sick."

"Oh, what nonsense! She's a very decent sort. One treats her just as if she were a man."

"Oh, don't speak to me, don't speak to me."

"But what can it matter to you?" asked Philip. "It's really no business of yours where I spend my summer."

"I was looking forward to it so much," she gasped, speaking it seemed almost to herself. "I didn't think you had the money to go away, and there wouldn't have been anyone else here, and we could have worked together, and we'd have gone to see things." Then her thoughts flung back to Ruth Chalice. "The filthy beast," she cried. "She isn't fit to speak to."

Philip looked at her with a sinking heart. He was not a man to think girls were in love with him; he was too conscious of his deformity, and he felt awkward and clumsy with women; but he did not know what else this outburst could mean. Fanny Price, in the dirty brown dress, with her hair falling over her face, sloppy, untidy, stood before him; and tears of anger rolled down her cheeks. She was repellent. Philip glanced at the door, instinctively hoping that someone would come in and put an end to the scene.

"I'm awfully sorry," he said.

"You're just the same as all of them. You take all you can get, and you don't even say thank you. I've taught you everything you know. No one else would take any trouble with you. Has Foinet ever bothered about you? And I can tell you this—you can work here for a thousand years and you'll never do any good. You haven't got any talent. You haven't got any originality. And it's not only me—they all say it. You'll never be a painter as long as you live."

"That is no business of yours either, is it?" said Philip, flushing.

"Oh, you think it's only my temper. Ask Clutton, ask Lawson, ask Chalice. Never, never, never. You haven't got it in you."

Philip shrugged his shoulders and walked out. She shouted after him.

"Never, never, never."

Moret was in those days an old-fashioned town of one street at the edge of the forest of Fontainebleau, and the *Ecu d'Or* was a hotel which still had about it the decrepit air of the *Ancien Régime*. It faced the winding river, the Loing; and Miss Chalice had a room with a little terrace overlooking it, with a charming view of the old bridge and its fortified gateway. They sat here in the evenings after dinner, drinking coffee, smoking, and discussing art. There ran into the river, a little way off, a narrow canal bordered by poplars, and along the banks of this after their day's work they often wandered. They spent all day painting. Like most of their generation they were obsessed by the fear of the picturesque, and they turned their backs on the obvious beauty of the town to seek subjects which were devoid of a prettiness they despised. Sisley and Monet had painted the canal with its poplars, and they felt a desire to try their hands at what was so typical of France; but they were frightened of its formal beauty, and set themselves deliberately to avoid it. Miss Chalice, who had a clever dexterity which impressed Lawson notwithstanding his contempt for feminine art, started a picture in which she tried to circumvent the commonplace by leaving out the tops of the trees; and Lawson had the brilliant idea of putting in his foreground a large blue advertisement of *chocolat Menier* in order to emphasise his abhorrence of the chocolate box.

Philip began now to paint in oils. He experienced a thrill of delight when first he used that grateful medium. He went out with Lawson in the morning with his little box and sat by him painting a panel; it gave him so much satisfaction that he did not realise he was doing no more than copy; he was so much under his friend's influence that he saw only with his eyes. Lawson painted very low in tone, and they both saw the emerald of the grass like dark velvet, while the brilliance of the sky turned in their hands to a brooding ultramarine. Through July they had one fine day after another; it was very hot; and the heat, searing Philip's heart, filled him with languor; he could not work; his mind was eager with a thousand thoughts. Often he spent the mornings by the side of the canal in the shade of the poplars, reading a few lines and then dreaming for half an hour. Sometimes he hired a rickety bicycle and rode along the dusty road that led to the forest, and then lay down in a clearing. His head was full of romantic fancies. The ladies of Watteau, gay and insouciant, seemed to wander with their cavaliers among the great trees, whispering to one another careless, charming things, and yet somehow oppressed by a nameless fear.

They were alone in the hotel but for a fat Frenchwoman of middle age, a Rabelaisian figure with a broad, obscene laugh. She spent the day by the river patiently fishing for fish she never caught, and Philip sometimes went down and talked to her. He found out that she had belonged to a profession whose most notorious member for our generation was Mrs. Warren, and having made a competence she now lived the quiet life of the *bourgeoise*. She told Philip lewd stories.

"You must go to Seville," she said—she spoke a little broken English. "The most beautiful women in the world."

She leered and nodded her head. Her triple chin, her large belly, shook with inward laughter.

It grew so hot that it was almost impossible to sleep at night. The heat seemed to linger under the trees as though it were a material thing. They did not wish to leave the starlit night, and the three of them would sit on the terrace of Ruth Chalice's room, silent, hour after hour, too tired to talk any more, but in voluptuous enjoyment of the stillness. They listened to the murmur of the river. The church clock struck one and two and sometimes three before they could drag themselves to bed. Suddenly Philip became aware that Ruth Chalice and Lawson were lovers. He divined it in the way the girl looked at the young painter, and in his air of possession; and as Philip sat with them he felt a kind of effluence surrounding them, as though the air were heavy with something strange. The revelation was a shock. He had looked upon Miss Chalice as a very good fellow and he liked to talk to her, but it had never seemed to him possible to enter into a closer relationship. One Sunday they had all gone with a tea-basket into the forest, and when they came to a glade which was suitably sylvan, Miss Chalice, because it was idyllic, insisted on taking off her shoes and stockings. It would have been very charming only her feet were rather large and she had on both a large corn on the third toe. Philip felt it made her proceeding a little ridiculous. But now he looked upon her quite differently; there was something softly feminine in her large eyes and her olive skin; he felt himself a fool not to have seen that she was attractive. He thought he detected in her a touch of contempt for him, because he had not had the sense to see that she was there, in his way, and in Lawson a suspicion of superiority. He was envious of Lawson, and he was jealous, not of the individual concerned, but of his love. He wished that he was standing in his shoes and feeling with his heart. He was troubled, and the fear seized him that love would pass him by. He wanted a passion to seize him, he wanted to be swept off his feet and borne powerless in a mighty rush he cared not whither. Miss Chalice and Lawson seemed to him now somehow different, and the constant companionship with them made him restless. He was dissatisfied with himself. Life was not giving him what he wanted, and he had an uneasy feeling that he was losing his time.

The stout Frenchwoman soon guessed what the relations were between the couple, and talked of the matter to Philip with the utmost frankness.

"And you," she said, with the tolerant smile of one who had fattened on the lust of her fellows, "have you got a *petite amie?*"

"No," said Philip, blushing.

"And why not? *C'est de votre age.*"

He shrugged his shoulders. He had a volume of Verlaine in his hands, and he wandered off. He tried to read, but his passion was too strong. He thought of the stray amours to which he had been introduced by Flanagan, the sly visits to houses in a *cul-de-sac*, with the drawing-room in Utrecht velvet, and the mercenary graces of painted women. He shuddered. He threw himself on the grass, stretching his limbs like a young animal freshly awaked from sleep; and the rippling water, the poplars gently tremulous in the faint breeze, the blue sky, were almost more than he could bear. He was in love with love. In his fancy he felt the kiss of warm lips on his, and around his neck the touch of soft hands. He imagined himself in the arms of Ruth Chalice, he thought of her dark eyes and the wonderful texture of her skin; he was mad to have let such a wonderful adventure slip through his fingers. And if Lawson had done it why should not he? But this was only when he did not see her, when he lay awake at night or dreamed idly by the side of the canal; when he saw her he felt suddenly quite different; he had no desire to take her in his arms, and he could not imagine himself kissing her. It was very curious. Away from her he thought her beautiful, remembering only her magnificent eyes and the creamy pallor of her face; but when he was with her he saw only that she was flat-chested and that her teeth were slightly decayed; he could not forget the corns on her toes. He could not understand himself. Would he always love only in absence and be prevented from enjoying anything when he had the chance by that deformity of vision which seemed to exaggerate the revolting?

He was not sorry when a change in the weather, announcing the definite end of the long summer, drove them all back to Paris.

Chapter XLVIII

WHEN PHILIP RETURNED TO AMITRANO'S HE FOUND THAT FANNY PRICE was no longer working there. She had given up the key of her locker. He asked Mrs. Otter whether she knew what had become of her; and Mrs. Otter, with a shrug of the shoulders, answered that she had probably gone back to England. Philip was relieved. He was profoundly bored by her ill-temper. Moreover she insisted on advising him about his work, looked upon it as a slight when he did not follow her precepts, and would not understand that he felt himself no longer the duffer he had been at first. Soon he forgot all about her. He was working in oils now and he was full of enthusiasm. He hoped to have something done of sufficient importance to send to the following year's Salon. Lawson was painting a portrait of Miss Chalice. She was very paintable, and all the young men who had fallen victims to her charm had made portraits of her. A natural indolence, joined with a passion for picturesque attitude, made her an excellent sitter; and she had enough technical knowledge to offer useful criticisms. Since her passion for art was chiefly a passion to live the life of artists, she was quite content to neglect her own work. She liked the warmth of the studio, and the opportunity to smoke innumerable cigarettes; and she spoke in a low, pleasant voice of the love of art and the art of love. She made no clear distinction between the two.

Lawson was painting with infinite labour, working till he could hardly stand for days and then scraping out all he had done. He would have exhausted the patience of anyone but Ruth Chalice. At last he got into a hopeless muddle.

"The only thing is to take a new canvas and start fresh," he said. "I know exactly what I want now, and it won't take me long."

Philip was present at the time, and Miss Chalice said to him:

"Why don't you paint me too? You'll be able to learn a lot by watching Mr. Lawson."

It was one of Miss Chalice's delicacies that she always addressed her lovers by their surnames.

"I should like it awfully if Lawson wouldn't mind."

"I don't care a damn," said Lawson.

It was the first time that Philip set about a portrait, and he began with trepidation but also with pride. He sat by Lawson and painted as he saw him paint. He profited by the example and by the advice which both Lawson and Miss Chalice freely gave him. At last Lawson finished and invited Clutton in to criticise. Clutton had only just come back to Paris. From Provence he had drifted down to Spain, eager to see Velasquez at Madrid, and thence he had gone to Toledo. He stayed there three months, and he was returned with a name new to the young men: he had wonderful things to say of a painter called El Greco, who it appeared could only be studied in Toledo.

"Oh yes, I know about him," said Lawson, "he's the old master whose distinction it is that he painted as badly as the moderns."

Clutton, more taciturn than ever, did not answer, but he looked at Lawson with a sardonic air.

"Are you going to show us the stuff you've brought back from Spain?" asked Philip.

"I didn't paint in Spain, I was too busy."

"What did you do then?"

"I thought things out. I believe I'm through with the Impressionists; I've got an idea they'll seem very thin and superficial in a few years. I want to make a clean sweep of everything I've learnt and start fresh. When I came back I destroyed everything I'd painted. I've got nothing in my studio now but an easel, my paints, and some clean canvases."

"What are you going to do?"

"I don't know yet. I've only got an inkling of what I want."

He spoke slowly, in a curious manner, as though he were straining to hear something which was only just audible. There seemed to be a mysterious force in him which he himself did not understand, but which was struggling obscurely to find an outlet. His strength impressed you. Lawson dreaded the criticism he asked for and had discounted the blame he thought he might get by affecting a contempt for any opinion of Clutton's; but Philip knew there was nothing which would give him more pleasure than Clutton's praise. Clutton looked at the portrait for some time in silence, then glanced at Philip's picture, which was standing on an easel.

"What's that?" he asked.

"Oh, I had a shot at a portrait too."

"The sedulous ape," he murmured.

He turned away again to Lawson's canvas. Philip reddened but did not speak.

"Well, what d'you think of it?" asked Lawson at length.

"The modelling's jolly good," said Clutton. "And I think it's very well drawn."

"D'you think the values are all right?"

"Quite."

Lawson smiled with delight. He shook himself in his clothes like a wet dog.

"I say, I'm jolly glad you like it."

"I don't. I don't think it's of the smallest importance."

Lawson's face fell, and he stared at Clutton with astonishment: he had no notion what he meant, Clutton had no gift of expression in words, and he spoke as though it were an effort. What he had to say was confused, halting, and verbose; but Philip knew the words which served as the text of his rambling discourse. Clutton, who never read, had heard them first from Cronshaw; and though they had made small impression, they had remained in his memory; and lately, emerging on a sudden, had acquired the character of a revelation: a good painter had two chief objects to paint, namely, man and the intention of his soul. The Impressionists had been occupied with other problems, they had painted man admirably, but they had troubled themselves as little as the English portrait painters of the eighteenth century with the intention of his soul.

"But when you try to get that you become literary," said Lawson, interrupting. "Let me paint the man like Manet, and the intention of his soul can go to the devil."

"That would be all very well if you could beat Manet at his own game, but you can't get anywhere near him. You can't feed yourself on the day before yesterday, it's ground which has been swept dry. You must go back. It's when I saw the Grecos that I felt one could get something more out of portraits than we knew before."

"It's just going back to Ruskin," cried Lawson.

"No—you see, he went for morality: I don't care a damn for morality: teaching doesn't come in, ethics and all that, but passion and emotion. The greatest portrait painters have painted both, man and the intention of his soul; Rembrandt and El Greco; it's only the second-raters who've only painted man. A lily of the valley would be lovely even if it didn't smell, but it's more lovely because it has perfume. That picture"—he pointed to Lawson's portrait—"Well, the drawing's all right and so's the modelling all right, but just conventional; it ought to be drawn and modelled so that you know the girl's a lousy slut. Correctness is all very well: El Greco made his people eight feet high because he wanted to express something he couldn't get any other way."

"Damn El Greco," said Lawson, "what's the good of jawing about a man when we haven't a chance of seeing any of his work?"

Clutton shrugged his shoulders, smoked a cigarette in silence, and went away. Philip and Lawson looked at one another.

"There's something in what he says," said Philip.

Lawson stared ill-temperedly at his picture.

"How the devil is one to get the intention of the soul except by painting exactly what one sees?"

About this time Philip made a new friend. On Monday morning models assembled at the school in order that one might be chosen for the week, and one day a young man was taken who was plainly not a model by profession. Philip's attention was attracted by the manner in which he held himself: when he got on to the stand he stood firmly on both feet, square, with clenched hands, and with his head defiantly thrown forward; the attitude emphasised his fine figure; there was no fat on him, and his muscles stood out as though they were of iron. His head, close-cropped, was well-shaped, and he wore a short beard; he had large, dark eyes and heavy eyebrows. He held the pose hour after hour without appearance of fatigue. There was in his mien a mixture of shame and of determination. His air of passionate energy excited Philip's romantic imagination, and when, the sitting ended, he saw him in his clothes, it seemed to him that he wore them as though he were a king in rags. He was uncommunicative, but in a day or two Mrs. Otter told Philip that the model was a Spaniard and that he had never sat before.

"I suppose he was starving," said Philip.

"Have you noticed his clothes? They're quite neat and decent, aren't they?"

It chanced that Potter, one of the Americans who worked at Amitrano's, was going to Italy for a couple of months, and offered his studio to Philip. Philip was pleased. He was growing a little impatient of Lawson's peremptory advice and wanted to be by himself. At the end of the week he went up to the model and on the pretence that his drawing was not finished asked whether he would come and sit to him one day.

"I'm not a model," the Spaniard answered. "I have other things to do next week."

"Come and have luncheon with me now, and we'll talk about it," said Philip, and as the other hesitated, he added with a smile: "It won't hurt you to lunch with me."

With a shrug of the shoulders the model consented, and they went off to a *crémerie*. The Spaniard spoke broken French, fluent but difficult to follow, and Philip managed to get on well enough with him. He found out that he was a writer. He had come to Paris to write novels and kept himself meanwhile by all the expedients possible to a penniless man: he gave lessons, he did any translations he could get hold of, chiefly business documents, and at last had been driven to make money by his fine figure. Sitting was well paid, and what he had earned during the last week was enough to keep him for two more; he told Philip, amazed, that he could live easily on two francs a day; but it filled him with shame that he was obliged to show his body for money, and he looked upon sitting as a degradation which only hunger could excuse. Philip explained that he did not want him to sit for the figure, but only for the head; he wished to do a portrait of him which he might send to the next Salon.

"But why should you want to paint me?" asked the Spaniard.

Philip answered that the head interested him, he thought he could do a good portrait.

"I can't afford the time. I grudge every minute that I have to rob from my writing."

"But it would only be in the afternoon. I work at the school in the morning. After all, it's better to sit to me than to do translations of legal documents."

There were legends in the Latin Quarter of a time when students of different countries lived together intimately, but this was long since passed, and now the various nations were almost as much separated as in an Oriental city. At Julian's and at the Beaux Arts a French student was looked upon with disfavour by his fellow-countrymen when he consorted with foreigners, and it was difficult for an Englishman to know more than quite superficially any native inhabitants of the city in which he dwelled. Indeed, many of the students after living in Paris for five years knew no more French than served them in shops and lived as English a life as though they were working in South Kensington.

Philip, with his passion for the romantic, welcomed the opportunity to get in touch with a Spaniard; he used all his persuasiveness to overcome the man's reluctance.

"I'll tell you what I'll do," said the Spaniard at last. "I'll sit to you, but not for money, for my own pleasure."

Philip expostulated, but the other was firm, and at length they arranged that he should come on the following Monday at one o'clock. He gave Philip a card on which was printed his name: Miguel Ajuria.

Miguel sat regularly, and though he refused to accept payment he borrowed fifty francs from Philip every now and then: it was a little more expensive than if Philip had paid for the sittings in the usual way; but gave the Spaniard a satisfactory feeling that he was not earning his living in a degrading manner. His nationality made Philip regard him as a representative of romance, and he asked him about Seville and Granada, Velasquez and Calderon. But Miguel had no patience with the grandeur of his country. For him, as for so many of his compatriots, France was the only country for a man of intelligence and Paris the centre of the world.

"Spain is dead," he cried. "It has no writers, it has no art, it has nothing."

Little by little, with the exuberant rhetoric of his race, he revealed his ambitions. He was writing a novel which he hoped would make his name. He was under the influence of Zola, and he had set his scene in Paris. He told Philip the story at length. To Philip it seemed crude and stupid; the naïve obscenity—*c'est la vie, mon cher, c'est la vie*, he cried—the naïve obscenity served only to emphasise the conventionality of the anecdote. He had written for two years, amid incredible hardships, denying himself all the pleasures of life which had attracted him to Paris, fighting with starvation for art's sake, determined that nothing should hinder his great achievement. The effort was heroic.

"But why don't you write about Spain?" cried Philip. "It would be so much more interesting. You know the life."

"But Paris is the only place worth writing about. Paris is life."

One day he brought part of the manuscript, and in his bad French, translating excitedly as he went along so that Philip could scarcely understand, he read passages. It was lamentable. Philip, puzzled, looked at the picture he was painting: the mind behind that broad brow was trivial; and the flashing, passionate eyes saw nothing in life but the obvious. Philip was not satisfied with his portrait, and at the end of a sitting he nearly always scraped out what he had done. It was all very well to aim at the intention of the soul: who could tell what that was when people seemed a mass of contradictions? He liked Miguel, and it distressed him to realise that his magnificent struggle was futile: he had everything to make a good writer but talent. Philip looked at his own work. How could you tell whether there was anything in it or whether you were wasting your time? It was clear that the will to achieve could not help you and confidence in yourself meant nothing. Philip thought of Fanny Price; she had a vehement belief in her talent; her strength of will was extraordinary.

"If I thought I wasn't going to be really good, I'd rather give up painting," said Philip. "I don't see any use in being a second-rate painter."

Then one morning when he was going out, the *concierge* called out to him that there was a letter. Nobody wrote to him but his Aunt Louisa and sometimes Hayward, and this was a handwriting he did not know. The letter was as follows:

Please come at once when you get this. I couldn't put up with it any more. Please come yourself. I can't bear the thought that anyone else should touch me. I want you to have everything.

F. PRICE

I have not had anything to eat for three days.

Philip felt on a sudden sick with fear. He hurried to the house in which she lived. He was astonished that she was in Paris at all. He had not seen her for months and imagined she had long since returned to England. When he arrived he asked the *concierge* whether she was in.

"Yes, I've not seen her go out for two days."

Philip ran upstairs and knocked at the door. There was no reply. He called her name. The door was locked, and on bending down he found the key was in the lock.

"Oh, my God, I hope she hasn't done something awful," he cried aloud.

He ran down and told the porter that she was certainly in the room. He had had a letter from her and feared a terrible accident. He suggested breaking open the door. The porter, who had been sullen and disinclined to listen, became alarmed; he could not take the responsibility of breaking into the room; they must go for the *commissaire de police*. They walked together to the *bureau*, and then they fetched a locksmith. Philip found that Miss Price had not paid the last quarter's rent: on New Year's Day she had not given the *concierge* the present which old-established custom led him to regard as a right. The four of them went upstairs, and they knocked again at the door. There was no reply. The locksmith set to work, and at last they entered the room. Philip gave a cry and instinctively covered his eyes with his hands. The wretched woman was hanging with a rope round her neck, which she had tied to a hook in the ceiling fixed by some previous tenant to hold up the curtains of the bed. She had moved her own little bed out of the way and had stood on a chair, which had been kicked away. It was lying on its side on the floor. They cut her down. The body was quite cold.

Chapter XLIX

THE STORY WHICH PHILIP MADE OUT IN ONE WAY AND ANOTHER WAS TERrible. One of the grievances of the women-students was that Fanny Price would never share their gay meals in restaurants, and the reason was obvious: she had been oppressed by dire poverty. He remembered the luncheon they had eaten together when first he came to Paris and the ghoulish appetite which had disgusted him: he realised now that she ate in that manner because she was ravenous. The *concierge* told him what her food had consisted of. A bottle of milk was left for her every day and she brought in her own loaf of bread; she ate half the loaf and drank half the milk at mid-day when she came back from the school, and consumed the rest in the evening. It was the same day after day. Philip thought with anguish of what she must have endured. She had never given anyone to understand that she was poorer than the rest, but it was clear that her money had been coming to an end, and at last she could not afford to come any more to the studio. The little room was almost bare of furniture, and there were no other clothes than the shabby brown dress she had always worn. Philip searched among her things for the address of some friend with whom he could communicate. He found a piece of paper on which his own name was written a score of times. It gave him a peculiar shock. He supposed it was true that she had loved him; he thought of the emaciated body, in the brown dress, hanging from the nail in the ceiling; and he shuddered. But if she had cared for him why did she not let him help her? He would so gladly have done all he could. He felt remorseful because he had refused to see that she looked upon him with any particular feeling, and now these words in her letter were infinitely pathetic: *I can't bear the thought that anyone else should touch me.* She had died of starvation.

Philip found at length a letter signed: *your loving brother, Albert*. It was two or three weeks old, dated from some road in Surbiton, and refused a loan of five pounds. The writer had his wife and family to think of, he didn't feel justified in lending money, and his advice was that Fanny should come back to London and try to get a situation. Philip telegraphed to Albert Price, and in a little while an answer came:

"*Deeply distressed. Very awkward to leave my business. Is presence essential? Price.*"

Philip wired a succinct affirmative, and next morning a stranger presented himself at the studio.

"My name's Price," he said, when Philip opened the door.

He was a commonish man in black with a band round his bowler hat; he had something of Fanny's clumsy look; he wore a stubbly moustache, and had a cockney accent. Philip asked him to come in. He cast sidelong glances round the studio while Philip gave him details of the accident and told him what he had done.

"I needn't see her, need I?" asked Albert Price. "My nerves aren't very strong, and it takes very little to upset me."

He began to talk freely. He was a rubber-merchant, and he had a wife and three children. Fanny was a governess, and he couldn't make out why she hadn't stuck to that instead of coming to Paris.

"Me and Mrs. Price told her Paris was no place for a girl. And there's no money in art—never 'as been."

It was plain enough that he had not been on friendly terms with his sister, and he resented her suicide as a last injury that she had done him. He did not like the idea that she had been forced to it by poverty; that seemed to reflect on the family. The idea struck him that possibly there was a more respectable reason for her act.

"I suppose she 'adn't any trouble with a man, 'ad she? You know what I mean, Paris and all that. She might 'ave done it so as not to disgrace herself."

Philip felt himself reddening and cursed his weakness. Price's keen little eyes seemed to suspect him of an intrigue.

"I believe your sister to have been perfectly virtuous," he answered acidly. "She killed herself because she was starving."

"Well, it's very 'ard on her family, Mr. Carey. She only 'ad to write to me. I wouldn't have let my sister want."

Philip had found the brother's address only by reading the letter in which he refused a loan; but he shrugged his shoulders: there was no use in recrimination. He hated the little man and wanted to have done with him as soon as possible. Albert Price also wished to get through the necessary business quickly so that he could get back to London. They went to the tiny room in which poor Fanny had lived. Albert Price looked at the pictures and the furniture.

"I don't pretend to know much about art," he said. "I suppose these pictures would fetch something, would they?"

"Nothing," said Philip.

"The furniture's not worth ten shillings."

Albert Price knew no French and Philip had to do everything. It seemed that it was an interminable process to get the poor body safely hidden away under ground: papers had to be obtained in one place and signed in another; officials had to be seen. For three days Philip was occupied from morning till night. At last he and Albert Price followed the hearse to the cemetery at Montparnasse.

"I want to do the thing decent," said Albert Price, "but there's no use wasting money."

The short ceremony was infinitely dreadful in the cold grey morning. Half a dozen people who had worked with Fanny Price at the studio came to the funeral, Mrs. Otter because she was *massière* and thought it her duty, Ruth Chalice because she had a kind heart, Lawson, Clutton, and Flanagan. They had all disliked her during her life. Philip, looking across the cemetery crowded on all sides with monuments, some poor and simple, others vulgar, pretentious, and ugly, shuddered. It was horribly sordid. When they came out Albert Price asked Philip to lunch with him. Philip loathed him now and he was tired; he had not been sleeping well, for he dreamed constantly of Fanny Price in the torn brown dress, hanging from the nail in the ceiling; but he could not think of an excuse.

"You take me somewhere where we can get a regular slap-up lunch. All this is the very worst thing for my nerves."

"Lavenue's is about the best place round here," answered Philip.

Albert Price settled himself on a velvet seat with a sigh of relief. He ordered a substantial luncheon and a bottle of wine.

"Well, I'm glad that's over," he said.

He threw out a few artful questions, and Philip discovered that he was eager to hear about the painter's life in Paris. He represented it to himself as deplorable, but he was anxious for details of the orgies which his fancy suggested to him. With sly winks and discreet sniggering he conveyed that he knew very well that there was a great deal more than Philip confessed. He was a man of the world, and he knew a thing or two. He asked Philip whether he had ever been to any of those places in Montmartre which are celebrated from Temple Bar to the Royal Exchange. He would like to say he had been to the Moulin Rouge. The luncheon was very good and the wine excellent. Albert Price expanded as the processes of digestion went satisfactorily forwards.

"Let's 'ave a little brandy," he said when the coffee was brought, "and blow the expense."

He rubbed his hands.

"You know, I've got 'alf a mind to stay over tonight and go back tomorrow. What d'you say to spending the evening together?"

"If you mean you want me to take you round Montmartre tonight, I'll see you damned," said Philip.

"I suppose it wouldn't be quite the thing."

The answer was made so seriously that Philip was tickled.

"Besides it would be rotten for your nerves," he said gravely.

Albert Price concluded that he had better go back to London by the four o'clock train, and presently he took leave of Philip.

"Well, good-bye, old man," he said. "I tell you what, I'll try and come over to

Paris again one of these days and I'll look you up. And then we won't 'alf go on the razzle."

Philip was too restless to work that afternoon, so he jumped on a bus and crossed the river to see whether there were any pictures on view at Durand-Ruel's. After that he strolled along the boulevard. It was cold and wind-swept. People hurried by wrapped up in their coats, shrunk together in an effort to keep out of the cold, and their faces were pinched and careworn. It was icy underground in the cemetery at Montparnasse among all those white tombstones. Philip felt lonely in the world and strangely home-sick. He wanted company. At that hour Cronshaw would be working, and Clutton never welcomed visitors; Lawson was painting another portrait of Ruth Chalice and would not care to be disturbed. He made up his mind to go and see Flanagan. He found him painting, but delighted to throw up his work and talk. The studio was comfortable, for the American had more money than most of them, and warm; Flanagan set about making tea. Philip looked at the two heads that he was sending to the Salon.

"It's awful cheek my sending anything," said Flanagan, "but I don't care, I'm going to send. D'you think they're rotten?"

"Not so rotten as I should have expected," said Philip.

They showed in fact an astounding cleverness. The difficulties had been avoided with skill, and there was a dash about the way in which the paint was put on which was surprising and even attractive. Flanagan, without knowledge or technique, painted with the loose brush of a man who has spent a lifetime in the practice of the art.

"If one were forbidden to look at any picture for more than thirty seconds you'd be a great master, Flanagan," smiled Philip.

These young people were not in the habit of spoiling one another with excessive flattery.

"We haven't got time in America to spend more than thirty seconds in looking at any picture," laughed the other.

Flanagan, though he was the most scatter-brained person in the world, had a tenderness of heart which was unexpected and charming. Whenever anyone was ill he installed himself as sick-nurse. His gaiety was better than any medicine. Like many of his countrymen he had not the English dread of sentimentality which keeps so tight a hold on emotion; and, finding nothing absurd in the show of feeling, could offer an exuberant sympathy which was often grateful to his friends in distress. He saw that Philip was depressed by what he had gone through and with unaffected kindliness set himself boisterously to cheer him up. He exaggerated the Americanisms which he knew always made the Englishmen laugh and poured out a breathless stream of conversation, whimsical, high-spirited, and jolly. In due course they went out to dinner and afterwards to the Gaîté Montparnasse, which was Flanagan's favourite place of amusement. By the end of the evening he was in his most extravagant humour. He had drunk a good deal, but any inebriety from which he suffered was due much more to his own vivacity than to alcohol. He proposed that they should go to the Bal Bullier, and Philip, feeling too tired to go to bed, willingly enough consented. They sat down at a table on the platform at the side, raised a little from the level of the floor so that they could watch the dancing, and drank a bock. Presently Flanagan saw a friend and with a wild shout leaped over the barrier on to the space where they were dancing. Philip watched the people. Bullier was not the resort of fashion. It was Thursday night and the place was crowded. There were a number of students of the various faculties, but most of the men were clerks or assistants in shops; they wore their everyday clothes, ready-made tweeds or queer tail-coats, and their hats, for they had brought them in with them, and when they danced there was no place to put them but their heads. Some of the women looked like servant-girls, and some were painted hussies, but for the most part they were shop-girls. They were poorly-dressed in cheap imitation of the fashions on the other side of the river. The hussies were got up to resemble the music-hall artiste or the dancer who enjoyed notoriety at the moment; their eyes were heavy with black and their cheeks impudently scarlet. The hall was lit by great white lights, low down, which emphasised the shadows on the faces; all the lines seemed to harden under it, and the colours were most crude. It was a sordid scene. Philip leaned over the rail, staring down, and he ceased to hear the music. They danced furiously. They danced round the room, slowly, talking very little, with all their attention given to the dance. The room was hot, and their faces shone with sweat. It seemed to Philip that they had thrown off the guard which people wear on their expression, the homage to convention, and he saw them now as they really were. In that moment of abandon they were strangely animal: some were foxy and some were wolf-like; and others had the long, foolish face of sheep. Their skins were sallow from the unhealthy life they led and the poor food they ate. Their features were blunted by mean interests, and their little eyes were shifty and cunning. There was nothing of nobility in their bearing, and you felt that for all of them life was a long succession of petty concerns and sordid thoughts. The air was heavy with the musty smell of humanity. But they danced furiously as though impelled by some strange power within them, and it seemed to Philip that they were driven forward by a rage for enjoyment. They were seeking desperately to escape from a world of horror. The desire for pleasure which Cronshaw said was the only motive of human action urged them blindly on, and the very vehemence of the desire seemed to rob it of all pleasure. They were hurried on by a great wind, helplessly, they knew not why and they knew not whither. Fate seemed to tower above them, and they danced as though everlasting darkness were beneath their feet. Their silence was vaguely alarming. It was as if life terrified them and robbed them of power of speech so that the shriek which was in their hearts died at their throats. Their eyes were haggard and grim; and notwithstanding the beastly lust that disfigured them, and the meanness of their faces, and the cruelty, notwithstanding the stupidness which was worst of all, the anguish of those fixed eyes made all that crowd terrible and pathetic. Philip loathed them, and yet his heart ached with the infinite pity which filled him.

He took his coat from the cloak-room and went out into the bitter coldness of the night.

Chapter L

PHILIP COULD NOT GET THE UNHAPPY EVENT OUT OF HIS HEAD. WHAT TROUbled him most was the uselessness of Fanny's effort. No one could have worked harder than she, nor with more sincerity; she believed in herself with all her heart; but it was plain that self-confidence meant very little, all his friends had it, Miguel Ajuria among the rest; and Philip was shocked by the contrast between the Spaniard's heroic endeavour and the triviality of the thing he attempted. The unhappiness of Philip's life at school had called up in him the power of self-analysis; and this vice, as subtle as drug-taking, had taken possession of him so that he had now a peculiar keenness in the dissection of his feelings. He could not help seeing that art affected him differently from others. A fine picture gave Lawson an immediate thrill. His appreciation was instinctive. Even Flanagan felt certain things which Philip was obliged to think out. His own appreciation was intellectual. He could not help thinking that if he had in him the artistic temperament (he hated the phrase, but could discover no other) he would feel beauty in the emotional, unreasoning way in which they did. He began to wonder whether he had anything more than a superficial cleverness of the hand which enabled him to copy objects with accuracy. That was nothing. He had learned to despise technical dexterity. The important thing was to feel in terms of paint. Lawson painted in a certain way because it was his nature to, and through the imitativeness of a student sensitive to every influence, there pierced individuality. Philip looked at his own portrait of Ruth Chalice, and now that three months had passed he realised that it was no more than a servile copy of Lawson. He felt himself barren. He painted with the brain, and he could not help knowing that the only painting worth anything was done with the heart.

He had very little money, barely sixteen hundred pounds, and it would be necessary for him to practise the severest economy. He could not count on earning anything for ten years. The history of painting was full of artists who had earned nothing at all. He must resign himself to penury; and it was worthwhile if he produced work which was immortal; but he had a terrible fear that he would never be more than second-rate. Was it worthwhile for that to give up one's youth, and the gaiety of life, and the manifold chances of being? He knew the existence of foreign painters in Paris enough to see that the lives they led were narrowly provincial. He knew some who had dragged along for twenty years in the pursuit of a fame which always escaped them till they sunk into sordidness and alcoholism. Fanny's suicide had aroused memories, and Philip heard ghastly stories of the way in which one person or another had escaped from despair. He remembered the scornful advice which the master had given poor Fanny: it would have been well for her if she had taken it and given up an attempt which was hopeless.

Philip finished his portrait of Miguel Ajuria and made up his mind to send it to the Salon. Flanagan was sending two pictures, and he thought he could paint as well as Flanagan. He had worked so hard on the portrait that he could not help feeling it must have merit. It was true that when he looked at it he felt that there was something wrong, though he could not tell what; but when he was away from it his spirits went up and he was not dissatisfied. He sent it to the Salon and it was refused. He did not mind much, since he had done all he could to persuade himself that there was little chance that it would be taken, till Flanagan a few days later rushed in to tell Lawson and Philip that one of his pictures was accepted. With a blank face Philip offered his congratulations, and Flanagan was so busy congratulating himself that he did not catch the note of irony which Philip could not prevent from coming into his voice. Lawson, quicker-witted, observed it and looked at Philip curiously. His own picture was all right, he knew that a day or two before, and he was vaguely resentful of Philip's attitude. But he was surprised at the sudden question which Philip put him as soon as the American was gone.

"If you were in my place would you chuck the whole thing?"

"What *do* you mean?"

"I wonder if it's worthwhile being a second-rate painter. You see, in other things, if you're a doctor or if you're in business, it doesn't matter so much if you're mediocre. You make a living and you get along. But what is the good of turning out second-rate pictures?"

Lawson was fond of Philip and, as soon as he thought he was seriously distressed by the refusal of his picture, he set himself to console him. It was notorious that the Salon had refused pictures which were afterwards famous; it was the first time Philip had sent, and he must expect a rebuff; Flanagan's success was explicable, his picture was showy and superficial: it was just the sort of thing a languid jury would see merit in. Philip grew impatient; it was humiliating that Lawson should think him capable of being seriously disturbed by so trivial a calamity and would not realise that his dejection was due to a deep-seated distrust of his powers.

Of late Clutton had withdrawn himself somewhat from the group who took their meals at Gravier's, and lived very much by himself. Flanagan said he was in love with a girl, but Clutton's austere countenance did not suggest passion; and Philip thought it more probable that he separated himself from his friends so that he might grow clear with the new ideas which were in him. But that evening, when the others had left the restaurant to go to a play and Philip was sitting alone, Clutton came in and ordered dinner. They began to talk, and finding Clutton more loquacious and less sardonic than usual, Philip determined to take advantage of his good humour.

"I say I wish you'd come and look at my picture," he said. "I'd like to know what you think of it."

"No, I won't do that."

"Why not?" asked Philip, reddening.

The request was one which they all made of one another, and no one ever thought of refusing. Clutton shrugged his shoulders.

"People ask you for criticism, but they only want praise. Besides, what's the good of criticism? What does it matter if your picture is good or bad?"

"It matters to me."

"No. The only reason that one paints is that one can't help it. It's a function like any of the other functions of the body, only comparatively few people have got it. One paints for oneself: otherwise one would commit suicide. Just think of it, you spend God knows how long trying to get something on to canvas, putting the sweat of your soul into it, and what is the result? Ten to one it will be refused at the Salon; if it's accepted, people glance at it for ten seconds as they pass; if you're lucky some ignorant fool will buy it and put it on his walls and look at it as little as he looks at his dining-room table. Criticism has nothing to do with the artist. It judges objectively, but the objective doesn't concern the artist."

Clutton put his hands over his eyes so that he might concentrate his mind on what he wanted to say.

"The artist gets a peculiar sensation from something he sees, and is impelled to express it and, he doesn't know why, he can only express his feeling by lines and colours. It's like a musician; he'll read a line or two, and a certain combination of notes presents itself to him: he doesn't know why such and such words call forth in him such and such notes; they just do. And I'll tell you another reason why criticism is meaningless: a great painter forces the world to see nature as he sees it; but in the next generation another painter sees the world in another way, and then the public judges him not by himself but by his predecessor. So the Barbizon people taught our fathers to look at trees in a certain manner, and when Monet came along and painted differently, people said: But trees aren't like that. It never struck them that trees are exactly how a painter chooses to see them. We paint from within outwards—if we force our vision on the world it calls us great painters; if we don't it ignores us; but *we* are the same. We don't attach any meaning to greatness or to smallness. What happens to our work afterwards is unimportant; we have got all we could out of it while we were doing it."

There was a pause while Clutton with voracious appetite devoured the food that was set before him. Philip, smoking a cheap cigar, observed him closely. The ruggedness of the head, which looked as though it were carved from a stone refractory to the sculptor's chisel, the rough mane of dark hair, the great nose, and the massive bones of the jaw, suggested a man of strength; and yet Philip wondered whether perhaps the mask concealed a strange weakness. Clutton's refusal to show his work might be sheer vanity: he could not bear the thought of anyone's criticism, and he would not expose himself to the chance of a refusal from the Salon; he wanted to be received as a master and would not risk comparisons with other work which might force him to diminish his own opinion of himself. During the eighteen months Philip had known him Clutton had grown more harsh and bitter; though he would not come out into the open and compete with his fellows, he was indignant with the facile success of those who did. He had no patience with Lawson, and the pair were no longer on the intimate terms upon which they had been when Philip first knew them.

"Lawson's all right," he said contemptuously, "he'll go back to England, become a fashionable portrait painter, earn ten thousand a year and be an A. R. A. before he's forty. Portraits done by hand for the nobility and gentry!"

Philip, too, looked into the future, and he saw Clutton in twenty years, bitter, lonely, savage, and unknown; still in Paris, for the life there had got into his bones, ruling a small *cénacle* with a savage tongue, at war with himself and the world, producing little in his increasing passion for a perfection he could not reach; and perhaps sinking at last into drunkenness. Of late Philip had been captivated by an idea that since one had only one life it was important to make a success of it, but he did not count success by the acquiring of money or the achieving of fame; he did not quite know yet what he meant by it, perhaps variety of experience and the making the most of his abilities. It was plain anyway that the life which Clutton seemed destined to was failure. Its only justification would be the painting of imperishable masterpieces. He recollected Cronshaw's whimsical metaphor of the Persian carpet; he had thought of it often; but Cronshaw with his faun-like humour had refused to make his meaning clear: he repeated that it had none unless one discovered it for oneself. It was this desire to make a success of life which was at the bottom of Philip's uncertainty about continuing his artistic career. But Clutton began to talk again.

"D'you remember my telling you about that chap I met in Brittany? I saw him the other day here. He's just off to Tahiti. He was broke to the world. He was a *brasseur d'affaires,* a stockbroker I suppose you call it in English; and he had a wife and family, and he was earning a large income. He chucked it all to become a painter. He just went off and settled down in Brittany and began to paint. He hadn't got any money and did the next best thing to starving."

"And what about his wife and family?" asked Philip.

"Oh, he dropped them. He left them to starve on their own account."

"It sounds a pretty low-down thing to do."

"Oh, my dear fellow, if you want to be a gentleman you must give up being an artist. They've got nothing to do with one another. You hear of men painting potboilers to keep an aged mother—well, it shows they're excellent sons, but it's no excuse for bad work. They're only tradesmen. An artist would let his mother go to the work-house. There's a writer I know over here who told me that his wife died in childbirth. He was in love with her and he was mad with grief, but as he sat at the bed-side watching her die he found himself making mental notes of how she looked and what she said and the things he was feeling. Gentlemanly, wasn't it?"

"But is your friend a good painter?" asked Philip.

"No, not yet, he paints just like Pissarro. He hasn't found himself, but he's got a sense of colour and a sense of decoration. But that isn't the question. It's the feeling, and that he's got. He's behaved like a perfect cad to his wife and children, he's always behaving like a perfect cad; the way he treats the people who've helped him—and sometimes he's been saved from starvation merely by the kindness of his friends—is simply beastly. He just happens to be a great artist."

Philip pondered over the man who was willing to sacrifice everything, comfort, home, money, love, honour, duty, for the sake of getting on to canvas with paint the emotion which the world gave him. It was magnificent, and yet his courage failed him.

Thinking of Cronshaw recalled to him the fact that he had not seen him for a week, and so, when Clutton left him, he wandered along to the café in which he was certain to find the writer. During the first few months of his stay in Paris Philip had accepted as gospel all that Cronshaw said, but Philip had a practical outlook and he grew impatient with the theories which resulted in no action. Cronshaw's slim bundle of poetry did not seem a substantial result for a life which was sordid. Philip could not wrench out of his nature the instincts of the middle-class from which he came; and the penury, the hack work which Cronshaw did to keep body and soul together, the monotony of existence between the slovenly attic and the café table, jarred with his respectability. Cronshaw was astute enough to know that the young man disapproved of him, and he attacked his philistinism with an irony which was sometimes playful but often very keen.

"You're a tradesman," he told Philip, "you want to invest life in consols so that it shall bring you in a safe three per cent. I'm a spendthrift, I run through my capital. I shall spend my last penny with my last heartbeat."

The metaphor irritated Philip, because it assumed for the speaker a romantic attitude and cast a slur upon the position which Philip instinctively felt had more to say for it than he could think of at the moment.

But this evening Philip, undecided, wanted to talk about himself. Fortunately it was late already and Cronshaw's pile of saucers on the table, each indicating a drink, suggested that he was prepared to take an independent view of things in general.

"I wonder if you'd give me some advice," said Philip suddenly.

"You won't take it, will you?"

Philip shrugged his shoulders impatiently.

"I don't believe I shall ever do much good as a painter. I don't see any use in being second-rate. I'm thinking of chucking it."

"Why shouldn't you?"

Philip hesitated for an instant.

"I suppose I like the life."

A change came over Cronshaw's placid, round face. The corners of the mouth were suddenly depressed, the eyes sunk dully in their orbits; he seemed to become strangely bowed and old.

"This?" he cried, looking round the café in which they sat. His voice really trembled a little.

"If you can get out of it, do while there's time."

Philip stared at him with astonishment, but the sight of emotion always made him feel shy, and he dropped his eyes. He knew that he was looking upon the tragedy of failure. There was silence. Philip thought that Cronshaw was looking upon his own life; and perhaps he considered his youth with its bright hopes and the disappointments which wore out the radiancy; the wretched monotony of pleasure, and the black future. Philip's eyes rested on the little pile of saucers, and he knew that Cronshaw's were on them too.

Chapter LI

TWO MONTHS PASSED.

It seemed to Philip, brooding over these matters, that in the true painters, writers, musicians, there was a power which drove them to such complete absorption in their work as to make it inevitable for them to subordinate life to art. Succumbing to an influence they never realised, they were merely dupes of the instinct that possessed them, and life slipped through their fingers unlived. But he had a feeling that life was to be lived rather than portrayed, and he wanted to search out the various experiences of it and wring from each moment all the emotion that it offered. He made up his mind at length to take a certain step and abide by the result, and, having made up his mind, he determined to take the step at once. Luckily enough the next morning was one of Foinet's days, and he resolved to ask him point-blank whether it was worth his while to go on with the study of art. He had never forgotten the master's brutal advice to Fanny Price. It had been sound. Philip could never get Fanny entirely out of his head. The studio seemed strange without her, and now and then the gesture of one of the women working there or the tone of a voice would give him a sudden start, reminding him of her: her presence was more noticeable now she was dead than it had ever been during her life; and he often dreamed of her at night, waking with a cry of terror. It was horrible to think of all the suffering she must have endured.

Philip knew that on the days Foinet came to the studio he lunched at a little restaurant in the Rue d'Odessa, and he hurried his own meal so that he could go and wait outside till the painter came out. Philip walked up and down the crowded street and at last saw Monsieur Foinet walking, with bent head, towards him; Philip was very nervous, but he forced himself to go up to him.

"*Pardon, monsieur,* I should like to speak to you for one moment."

Foinet gave him a rapid glance, recognised him, but did not smile a greeting.

"Speak," he said.

"I've been working here nearly two years now under you. I wanted to ask you to tell me frankly if you think it worthwhile for me to continue."

Philip's voice was trembling a little. Foinet walked on without looking up. Philip, watching his face, saw no trace of expression upon it.

"I don't understand."

"I'm very poor. If I have no talent I would sooner do something else."

"Don't you know if you have talent?"

"All my friends know they have talent, but I am aware some of them are mistaken."

Foinet's bitter mouth outlined the shadow of a smile, and he asked:

"Do you live near here?"

Philip told him where his studio was. Foinet turned round.

"Let us go there? You shall show me your work."

"Now?" cried Philip.

"Why not?"

Philip had nothing to say. He walked silently by the master's side. He felt horribly sick. It had never struck him that Foinet would wish to see his things there and then; he meant, so that he might have time to prepare himself, to ask him if he would mind coming at some future date or whether he might bring them to Foinet's studio. He was trembling with anxiety. In his heart he hoped that Foinet would look at his picture, and that rare smile would come into his face, and he would shake Philip's hand and say: "*Pas mal.* Go on, my lad. You have talent, real talent." Philip's heart swelled at the thought. It was such a relief, such a joy! Now he could go on with courage; and what did hardship matter, privation, and disappointment, if he arrived at last? He had worked very hard, it would be too cruel if all that industry were futile. And then with a start he remembered that he had heard Fanny Price say just that. They arrived at the house, and Philip was seized with fear. If he had dared he would have asked Foinet to go away. He did not want to know the truth. They went in and the *concierge* handed him a letter as they passed. He glanced at the envelope and recognised his uncle's handwriting. Foinet followed him up the stairs. Philip could think of nothing to say; Foinet was mute, and the silence got on his nerves. The professor sat down; and Philip without a word placed before him the picture which the Salon had rejected; Foinet nodded but did not speak; then Philip showed him the two portraits he had made of Ruth Chalice, two or three landscapes which he had painted at Moret, and a number of sketches.

"That's all," he said presently, with a nervous laugh.

Monsieur Foinet rolled himself a cigarette and lit it.

"You have very little private means?" he asked at last.

"Very little," answered Philip, with a sudden feeling of cold at his heart. "Not enough to live on."

"There is nothing so degrading as the constant anxiety about one's means of livelihood. I have nothing but contempt for the people who despise money. They are hypocrites or fools. Money is like a sixth sense without which you cannot make a complete use of the other five. Without an adequate income half the possibilities of life are shut off. The only thing to be careful about is that you do not pay more than a shilling for the shilling you earn. You will hear people say that poverty is the best spur to the artist. They have never felt the iron of it in their flesh. They do not know how mean it makes you. It exposes you to endless humiliation, it cuts your wings, it eats into your soul like a cancer. It is not wealth one asks for, but just enough to preserve one's dignity, to work unhampered, to be generous, frank, and independent. I pity with all my heart the artist, whether he writes or paints, who is entirely dependent for subsistence upon his art."

Philip quietly put away the various things which he had shown.

"I'm afraid that sounds as if you didn't think I had much chance."

Monsieur Foinet slightly shrugged his shoulders.

"You have a certain manual dexterity. With hard work and perseverance there is no reason why you should not become a careful, not incompetent painter. You would find hundreds who painted worse than you, hundreds who painted as well. I see no talent in anything you have shown me. I see industry and intelligence. You will never be anything but mediocre."

Philip obliged himself to answer quite steadily.

"I'm very grateful to you for having taken so much trouble. I can't thank you enough."

Monsieur Foinet got up and made as if to go, but he changed his mind and, stopping, put his hand on Philip's shoulder.

"But if you were to ask me my advice, I should say: take your courage in both hands and try your luck at something else. It sounds very hard, but let me tell you this: I would give all I have in the world if someone had given me that advice when I was your age and I had taken it."

Philip looked up at him with surprise. The master forced his lips into a smile, but his eyes remained grave and sad.

"It is cruel to discover one's mediocrity only when it is too late. It does not improve the temper."

He gave a little laugh as he said the last words and quickly walked out of the room.

Philip mechanically took up the letter from his uncle. The sight of his handwriting made him anxious, for it was his aunt who always wrote to him. She had been ill for the last three months, and he had offered to go over to England and see her; but she, fearing it would interfere with his work, had refused. She did not want him to put himself to inconvenience; she said she would wait till August and then she hoped he would come and stay at the vicarage for two or three weeks. If by any chance she grew worse she would let him know, since she did not wish to die without seeing him again. If his uncle wrote to him it must be because she was too ill to hold a pen. Philip opened the letter. It ran as follows:

My dear Philip—I regret to inform you that your dear Aunt departed this life early this morning. She died very suddenly, but quite peacefully. The change for the worse was so rapid that we had no time to send for you. She was fully prepared for the end and entered into rest with the complete assurance of a blessed resurrection and with resignation to the divine will of our blessed Lord Jesus Christ. Your Aunt would have liked you to be present at the funeral so I trust you will come as soon as you can. There is naturally a great deal of work thrown upon my shoulders and I am very much upset. I trust that you will be able to do everything for me.

Your affectionate uncle,
William Carey

Chapter LII

NEXT DAY PHILIP ARRIVED AT BLACKSTABLE. SINCE THE DEATH OF HIS mother he had never lost anyone closely connected with him; his aunt's death shocked him and filled him also with a curious fear; he felt for the first time his own mortality. He could not realise what life would be for his uncle without the constant companionship of the woman who had loved and tended him for forty years. He expected to find him broken down with hopeless grief. He dreaded the first meeting; he knew that he could say nothing which would be of use. He rehearsed to himself a number of apposite speeches.

He entered the vicarage by the side-door and went into the dining-room. Uncle William was reading the paper.

"Your train was late," he said, looking up.

Philip was prepared to give way to his emotion, but the matter-of-fact reception startled him. His uncle, subdued but calm, handed him the paper.

"There's a very nice little paragraph about her in *The Blackstable Times*," he said.

Philip read it mechanically.

"Would you like to come up and see her?"

Philip nodded and together they walked upstairs. Aunt Louisa was lying in the middle of the large bed, with flowers all round her.

"Would you like to say a short prayer?" said the Vicar.

He sank on his knees, and because it was expected of him Philip followed his example. He looked at the little shrivelled face. He was only conscious of one emotion: what a wasted life! In a minute Mr. Carey gave a cough, and stood up. He pointed to a wreath at the foot of the bed.

"That's from the Squire," he said. He spoke in a low voice as though he were in church, but one felt that, as a clergyman, he found himself quite at home. "I expect tea is ready."

They went down again to the dining-room. The drawn blinds gave a lugubrious aspect. The Vicar sat at the end of the table at which his wife had always sat and poured out the tea with ceremony. Philip could not help feeling that neither of them should have been able to eat anything, but when he saw that his uncle's appetite was unimpaired he fell to with his usual heartiness. They did not speak for a while. Philip set himself to eat an excellent cake with the air of grief which he felt was decent.

"Things have changed a great deal since I was a curate," said the Vicar presently. "In my young days the mourners used always to be given a pair of black gloves and a piece of black silk for their hats. Poor Louisa used to make the silk into dresses. She always said that twelve funerals gave her a new dress."

Then he told Philip who had sent wreaths; there were twenty-four of them already; when Mrs. Rawlingson, wife of the Vicar at Ferne, had died she had had thirty-two; but probably a good many more would come the next day; the funeral would start at eleven o'clock from the vicarage, and they should beat Mrs. Rawlingson easily. Louisa never liked Mrs. Rawlingson.

"I shall take the funeral myself. I promised Louisa I would never let anyone else bury her."

Philip looked at his uncle with disapproval when he took a second piece of cake. Under the circumstances he could not help thinking it greedy.

"Mary Ann certainly makes capital cakes. I'm afraid no one else will make such good ones."

"She's not going?" cried Philip, with astonishment.

Mary Ann had been at the vicarage ever since he could remember. She never forgot his birthday, but made a point always of sending him a trifle, absurd but touching. He had a real affection for her.

"Yes," answered Mr. Carey. "I didn't think it would do to have a single woman in the house."

"But, good heavens, she must be over forty."

"Yes, I think she is. But she's been rather troublesome lately, she's been inclined to take too much on herself, and I thought this was a very good opportunity to give her notice."

"It's certainly one which isn't likely to recur," said Philip.

He took out a cigarette, but his uncle prevented him from lighting it.

"Not till after the funeral, Philip," he said gently.

"All right," said Philip.

"It wouldn't be quite respectful to smoke in the house so long as your poor Aunt Louisa is upstairs."

Josiah Graves, churchwarden and manager of the bank, came back to dinner at the vicarage after the funeral. The blinds had been drawn up, and Philip, against his will, felt a curious sensation of relief. The body in the house had made him uncomfortable: in life the poor woman had been all that was kind and gentle; and yet, when she lay upstairs in her bed-room, cold and stark, it seemed as though she cast upon the survivors a baleful influence. The thought horrified Philip.

He found himself alone for a minute or two in the dining-room with the churchwarden.

"I hope you'll be able to stay with your uncle a while," he said. "I don't think he ought to be left alone just yet."

"I haven't made any plans," answered Philip. "If he wants me I shall be very pleased to stay."

By way of cheering the bereaved husband the churchwarden during dinner talked of a recent fire at Blackstable which had partly destroyed the Wesleyan chapel.

"I hear they weren't insured," he said, with a little smile.

"That won't make any difference," said the Vicar. "They'll get as much money as they want to rebuild. Chapel people are always ready to give money."

"I see that Holden sent a wreath."

Holden was the dissenting minister, and, though for Christ's sake who died for both of them, Mr. Carey nodded to him in the street, he did not speak to him.

"I think it was very pushing," he remarked. "There were forty-one wreaths. Yours was beautiful. Philip and I admired it very much."

"Don't mention it," said the banker.

He had noticed with satisfaction that it was larger than anyone's else. It had looked very well. They began to discuss the people who attended the funeral. Shops had been closed for it, and the churchwarden took out of his pocket the notice which had been printed: *Owing to the funeral of Mrs. Carey this establishment will not be opened till one o'clock.*

"It was my idea," he said.

"I think it was very nice of them to close," said the Vicar. "Poor Louisa would have appreciated that."

Philip ate his dinner. Mary Ann had treated the day as Sunday, and they had roast chicken and a gooseberry tart.

"I suppose you haven't thought about a tombstone yet?" said the churchwarden.

"Yes, I have. I thought of a plain stone cross. Louisa was always against ostentation."

"I don't think one can do much better than a cross. If you're thinking of a text, what do you say to: *With Christ, which is far better?*"

The Vicar pursed his lips. It was just like Bismarck to try and settle everything himself. He did not like that text; it seemed to cast an aspersion on himself.

"I don't think I should put that. I much prefer: *The Lord has given and the Lord has taken away.*"

"Oh, do you? That always seems to me a little indifferent."

The Vicar answered with some acidity, and Mr. Graves replied in a tone which the widower thought too authoritative for the occasion. Things were going rather far if he could not choose his own text for his own wife's tombstone. There was a pause, and then the conversation drifted to parish matters. Philip went into the garden to smoke his pipe. He sat on a bench, and suddenly began to laugh hysterically.

A few days later his uncle expressed the hope that he would spend the next few weeks at Blackstable.

"Yes, that will suit me very well," said Philip.

"I suppose it'll do if you go back to Paris in September."

Philip did not reply. He had thought much of what Foinet said to him, but he was still so undecided that he did not wish to speak of the future. There would be something fine in giving up art because he was convinced that he could not excel; but unfortunately it would seem so only to himself: to others it would be an admission of defeat, and he did not want to confess that he was beaten. He was an obstinate fellow, and the suspicion that his talent did not lie in one direction made him inclined to force circumstances and aim notwithstanding precisely in that direction. He could not bear that his friends should laugh at him. This might have prevented him from ever taking the definite step of abandoning the study of painting, but the different environment made him on a sudden see things differently. Like many another he discovered that crossing the Channel makes things which had seemed important singularly futile. The life which had been so charming that he could not bear to leave it now seemed inept; he was seized with a distaste for the cafés, the restaurants with their ill-cooked food, the shabby way in which they all lived. He did not care any more what his friends thought about him: Cronshaw with his rhetoric, Mrs. Otter with her respectability, Ruth Chalice with her affectations, Lawson and Clutton with their quarrels; he felt a revulsion from them all. He wrote to Lawson and asked him to send over all his belongings. A week later they arrived. When he unpacked his canvases he found himself able to examine his work without emotion. He noticed the fact with interest. His uncle was anxious to see his pictures. Though he had so greatly disapproved of Philip's desire to go to Paris, he accepted the situation now with equanimity. He was interested in the life of students and constantly put Philip questions about it. He was in fact a little proud of him because he was a painter, and when people were present made attempts to draw him out. He looked eagerly at the studies of models which Philip showed him. Philip set before him his portrait of Miguel Ajuria.

"Why did you paint him?" asked Mr. Carey.

"Oh, I wanted a model, and his head interested me."

"As you haven't got anything to do here I wonder you don't paint me."

"It would bore you to sit."

"I think I should like it."

"We must see about it."

Philip was amused at his uncle's vanity. It was clear that he was dying to have his portrait painted. To get something for nothing was a chance not to be missed. For two or three days he threw out little hints. He reproached Philip for laziness, asked him when he was going to start work, and finally began telling everyone he met that Philip was going to paint him. At last there came a rainy day, and after breakfast Mr. Carey said to Philip:

"Now, what d'you say to starting on my portrait this morning?" Philip put down the book he was reading and leaned back in his chair.

"I've given up painting," he said.

"Why?" asked his uncle in astonishment.

"I don't think there's much object in being a second-rate painter, and I came to the conclusion that I should never be anything else."

"You surprise me. Before you went to Paris you were quite certain that you were a genius."

"I was mistaken," said Philip.

"I should have thought now you'd taken up a profession you'd have the pride to stick to it. It seems to me that what you lack is perseverance."

Philip was a little annoyed that his uncle did not even see how truly heroic his determination was.

" 'A rolling stone gathers no moss,' " proceeded the clergyman. Philip hated that proverb above all, and it seemed to him perfectly meaningless. His uncle had repeated it often during the arguments which had preceded his departure from business. Apparently it recalled that occasion to his guardian.

"You're no longer a boy, you know; you must begin to think of settling down. First you insist on becoming a chartered accountant, and then you get tired of that and you want to become a painter. And now if you please you change your mind again. It points to . . ."

He hesitated for a moment to consider what defects of character exactly it indicated, and Philip finished the sentence.

"Irresolution, incompetence, want of foresight, and lack of determination."

The Vicar looked up at his nephew quickly to see whether he was laughing at him. Philip's face was serious, but there was a twinkle in his eyes which irritated him. Philip should really be getting more serious. He felt it right to give him a rap over the knuckles.

"Your money matters have nothing to do with me now. You're your own master; but I think you should remember that your money won't last forever, and the unlucky deformity you have doesn't exactly make it easier for you to earn your living."

Philip knew by now that whenever anyone was angry with him his first thought was to say something about his club-foot. His estimate of the human race was determined by the fact that scarcely anyone failed to resist the temptation. But he had trained himself not to show any sign that the reminder wounded him. He had even acquired control over the blushing which in his boyhood had been one of his torments.

"As you justly remark," he answered, "my money matters have nothing to do with you and I am my own master."

"At all events you will do me the justice to acknowledge that I was justified in my opposition when you made up your mind to become an art-student."

"I don't know so much about that. I daresay one profits more by the mistakes one makes off one's own bat than by doing the right thing on somebody's else advice. I've had my fling, and I don't mind settling down now."

"What at?"

Philip was not prepared for the question, since in fact he had not made up his mind. He had thought of a dozen callings.

"The most suitable thing you could do is to enter your father's profession and become a doctor."

"Oddly enough that is precisely what I intend."

He had thought of doctoring among other things, chiefly because it was an occupation which seemed to give a good deal of personal freedom, and his experience of life in an office had made him determine never to have anything more to do with one; his answer to the Vicar slipped out almost unawares, because it was in the nature of a repartee. It amused him to make up his mind in that accidental way, and he resolved then and there to enter his father's old hospital in the autumn.

"Then your two years in Paris may be regarded as so much wasted time?"

"I don't know about that. I had a very jolly two years, and I learned one or two useful things."

"What?"

Philip reflected for an instant, and his answer was not devoid of a gentle desire to annoy.

"I learned to look at hands, which I'd never looked at before. And instead of just looking at houses and trees I learned to look at houses and trees against the sky. And I learned also that shadows are not black but coloured."

"I suppose you think you're very clever. I think your flippancy is quite inane."

Chapter LIII

TAKING THE PAPER WITH HIM MR. CAREY RETIRED TO HIS STUDY. PHILIP changed his chair for that in which his uncle had been sitting (it was the only comfortable one in the room), and looked out of the window at the pouring rain. Even in that sad weather there was something restful about the green fields that stretched to the horizon. There was an intimate charm in the landscape which he did not remember ever to have noticed before. Two years in France had opened his eyes to the beauty of his own countryside.

He thought with a smile of his uncle's remark. It was lucky that the turn of his mind tended to flippancy. He had begun to realise what a great loss he had sustained in the death of his father and mother. That was one of the differences in his life which prevented him from seeing things in the same way as other people. The love of parents for their children is the only emotion which is quite disinterested. Among strangers he had grown up as best he could, but he had seldom been used with patience or forbearance. He prided himself on his self-control. It had been whipped into him by the mockery of his fellows. Then they called him cynical and callous. He had acquired calmness of demeanour and under most circumstances an unruffled exterior, so that now he could not show his feelings. People told him he was unemotional; but he knew that he was at the mercy of his emotions: an accidental kindness touched him so much that sometimes he did not venture to speak in order not to betray the unsteadiness of his voice. He remembered the bitterness of his life at school, the humiliation which he had endured, the banter which had made him morbidly afraid of making himself ridiculous; and he remembered the loneliness he had felt since, faced with the world, the disillusion and the disappointment caused by the difference between what it promised to his active imagination and what it gave. But notwithstanding he was able to look at himself from the outside and smile with amusement.

"By Jove, if I weren't flippant, I should hang myself," he thought cheerfully.

His mind went back to the answer he had given his uncle when he asked him what he had learned in Paris. He had learned a good deal more than he told him. A conversation with Cronshaw had stuck in his memory, and one phrase he had used, a commonplace one enough, had set his brain working.

"My dear fellow," Cronshaw said, "there's no such thing as abstract morality."

When Philip ceased to believe in Christianity he felt that a great weight was taken from his shoulders; casting off the responsibility which weighed down every action, when every action was infinitely important for the welfare of his immortal soul, he experienced a vivid sense of liberty. But he knew now that this was an illusion. When he put away the religion in which he had been brought up, he had kept unimpaired the morality which was part and parcel of it. He made up his mind therefore to think things out for himself. He determined to be swayed by no prejudices. He swept away the virtues and the vices, the established laws of good and evil, with the idea of finding out the rules of life for himself. He did not know whether rules were necessary at all. That was one of the things he wanted to discover. Clearly much that seemed valid seemed so only because he had been taught it from his earliest youth. He had read a number of books, but they did not help him much, for they were based on the morality of Christianity; and even the writers who emphasised the fact that they did not believe in it were never satisfied till they had framed a system of ethics in accordance with that of the Sermon on the Mount. It seemed hardly worthwhile to read a long volume in order to learn that you ought to behave exactly like everybody else. Philip wanted to find out how he ought to behave, and he thought he could prevent himself from being influenced by the opinions that surrounded him. But meanwhile he had to go on living, and, until he formed a theory of conduct, he made himself a provisional rule.

"Follow your inclinations with due regard to the policeman round the corner."

He thought the best thing he had gained in Paris was a complete liberty of spirit, and he felt himself at last absolutely free. In a desultory way he had read a good deal of philosophy, and he looked forward with delight to the leisure of the next few months. He began to read at haphazard. He entered upon each system with a little thrill of excitement, expecting to find in each some guide by which he could rule his conduct; he felt himself like a traveller in unknown countries and as he pushed forward the enterprise fascinated him; he read emotionally, as other men read pure literature, and his heart leaped as he discovered in noble words what himself had obscurely felt. His mind was concrete and moved with difficulty in regions of the abstract; but, even when he could not follow the reasoning, it gave him a curious pleasure to follow the tortuosities of thoughts that threaded their nimble way on the edge of the incomprehensible. Sometimes great philosophers seemed to have nothing to say to him, but at others he recognised a mind with which he felt himself at home. He was like the explorer in Central Africa who comes suddenly upon wide uplands, with great trees in them and stretches of meadow, so that he might fancy himself in an English park. He delighted in the robust common sense of Thomas Hobbes; Spinoza filled him with awe, he had never before come in contact with a mind so noble, so unapproachable and austere; it reminded him of that statue by Rodin, *L'Âge d'Airain*, which he passionately admired; and then there was Hume: the scepticism of that charming philosopher touched a kindred note in Philip; and, revelling in the lucid style which seemed able to put complicated thought into simple words, musical and measured, he read as he might have read a novel, a smile of pleasure on his lips. But in none could he find exactly what he wanted. He had read somewhere that every man was born a Platonist, an Aristotelian, a Stoic, or an Epicurean; and the history of George Henry Lewes (besides telling you that philosophy was all moonshine) was there to show that the thought of each philospher was inseparably connected with the man he was. When you knew that you could guess to a great extent the philosophy he wrote. It looked as though you did not act in a certain way because you thought in a certain way, but rather that you thought in a certain way because you were made in a certain way. Truth had nothing to do with it. There was no such thing as truth. Each man was his own philosopher, and the elaborate systems which the great men of the past had composed were only valid for the writers.

The thing then was to discover what one was and one's system of philosophy would devise itself. It seemed to Philip that there were three things to find out: man's relation to the world he lives in, man's relation with the men among whom he lives, and finally man's relation to himself. He made an elaborate plan of study.

The advantage of living abroad is that, coming in contact with the manners and customs of the people among whom you live, you observe them from the outside and see that they have not the necessity which those who practise them believe. You cannot fail to discover that the beliefs which to you are self-evident to the foreigner are absurd. The year in Germany, the long stay in Paris, had prepared Philip to receive the sceptical teaching which came to him now with such a feeling of relief. He saw that nothing was good and nothing was evil; things were merely adapted to an end. He read *The Origin of Species*. It seemed to offer an explanation of much that troubled him. He was like an explorer now who has reasoned that certain natural features must present themselves, and, beating up a broad river, finds here the tributary that he expected, there the fertile, populated plains, and further on the mountains. When some great discovery is made the world is surprised afterwards that it was not accepted at once, and even on those who acknowledge its truth the effect is unimportant. The first readers of *The Origin of Species* accepted it with their reason; but their emotions, which are the ground of conduct, were untouched. Philip was born a generation after this great book was published, and much that horrified its contemporaries had passed into the feeling of the time, so that he was able to accept it with a joyful heart. He was intensely moved by the grandeur of the struggle for life, and the ethical rule which it suggested seemed to fit in with his predispositions. He said to himself that might was right. Society stood on one side, an organism with its own laws of growth and self-preservation, while the individual stood on the other. The actions which were to the advantage of society it termed virtuous and those which were not it called vicious. Good and evil meant nothing more than that. Sin was a prejudice from which the free man should rid himself. Society had three arms in its contest with the individual, laws, public opinion, and conscience: the first two could be met by guile, guile is the only weapon of the weak against the strong: common opinion put the matter well when it stated that sin consisted in being found out; but conscience was the traitor within the gates; it fought in each heart the battle of society, and caused the individual to throw himself, a wanton sacrifice, to the prosperity of his enemy. For it was clear that the two were irreconcilable, the state and the individual conscious of himself. *That* uses the individual for its own ends, trampling upon him if he thwarts it, rewarding him with medals, pensions, honours, when he serves it faithfully; *this*, strong only in his independence, threads his way through the state, for convenience' sake, paying in money or service for certain benefits, but with no sense of obligation; and, indifferent to the rewards, asks only to be left alone. He is the independent traveller, who uses Cook's tickets because they save trouble, but looks with good-humoured contempt on the personally conducted parties. The free man can do no wrong. He does everything he likes—if he can. His power is the only measure of his morality. He recognises the laws of the state and he can break them without sense of sin, but if he is punished he accepts the punishment without rancour. Society has the power.

But if for the individual there was no right and no wrong, then it seemed to Philip that conscience lost its power. It was with a cry of triumph that he seized the knave and flung him from his breast. But he was no nearer to the meaning of life than he had been before. Why the world was there and what men had come into existence for at all was as inexplicable as ever. Surely there must be some reason. He thought of Cronshaw's parable of the Persian Carpet. He offered it as a solution of the riddle, and mysteriously he stated that it was no answer at all unless you found it out for yourself.

"I wonder what the devil he meant," Philip smiled.

And so, on the last day of September, eager to put into practice all these new theories of life, Philip, with sixteen hundred pounds and his club-foot, set out for the second time to London to make his third start in life.

Chapter LIV

THE EXAMINATION PHILIP HAD PASSED BEFORE HE WAS ARTICLED TO A CHARtered accountant was sufficient qualification for him to enter a medical school. He chose St. Luke's because his father had been a student there, and before the end of the summer session had gone up to London for a day in order to see the secretary. He got a list of rooms from him, and took lodgings in a dingy house which had the advantage of being within two minutes' walk of the hospital.

"You'll have to arrange about a part to dissect," the secretary told him. "You'd better start on a leg; they generally do; they seem to think it easier."

Philip found that his first lecture was in anatomy, at eleven, and about half-past ten he limped across the road, and a little nervously made his way to the Medical School. Just inside the door a number of notices were pinned up, lists of lectures, football fixtures, and the like; and these he looked at idly, trying to seem at his ease. Young men and boys dribbled in and looked for letters in the rack, chatted with one another, and passed downstairs to the basement, in which was the students' reading-room. Philip saw several fellows with a desultory, timid look dawdling around, and surmised that, like himself, they were there for the first time. When he had exhausted the notices he saw a glass door which led into what was apparently a museum, and having still twenty minutes to spare he walked in. It was a collection of pathological specimens. Presently a boy of about eighteen came up to him.

"I say, are you first year?" he said.

"Yes," answered Philip.

"Where's the lecture-room, d'you know? It's getting on for eleven."

"We'd better try to find it."

They walked out of the museum into a long, dark corridor, with the walls painted in two shades of red, and other youths walking along suggested the way to them. They came to a door marked Anatomy Theatre. Philip found that there were a good many people already there. The seats were arranged in tiers, and just as Philip entered an attendant came in, put a glass of water on the table in the well of the lecture-room and then brought in a pelvis and two thigh-bones, right and left. More men entered and took their seats and by eleven the theatre was fairly full. There were about sixty students. For the most part they were a good deal younger than Philip, smooth-faced boys of eighteen, but there were a few who were older than he: he noticed one tall man, with a fierce red moustache, who might have been thirty; another little fellow with black hair, only a year or two younger; and there was one man with spectacles and a beard which was quite grey.

The lecturer came in, Mr. Cameron, a handsome man with white hair and clean-cut features. He called out the long list of names. Then he made a little speech. He spoke in a pleasant voice, with well-chosen words, and he seemed to take a discreet pleasure in their careful arrangement. He suggested one or two books which they might buy and advised the purchase of a skeleton. He spoke of anatomy with enthusiasm: it was essential to the study of Surgery; a knowledge of it added to the appreciation of art. Philip pricked up his ears. He heard later that Mr. Cameron lectured also to the students at the Royal Academy. He had lived many years in Japan, with a post at the University of Tokyo, and he flattered himself on his appreciation of the beautiful.

"You will have to learn many tedious things," he finished, with an indulgent smile, "which you will forget the moment you have passed your final examination, but in anatomy it is better to have learned and lost than never to have learned at all."

He took up the pelvis which was lying on the table and began to describe it. He spoke well and clearly.

At the end of the lecture the boy who had spoken to Philip in the pathological museum and sat next to him in the theatre suggested that they should go to the dissecting-room. Philip and he walked along the corridor again, and an attendant told them where it was. As soon as they entered Philip understood what the acrid smell was which he had noticed in the passage. He lit a pipe. The attendant gave a short laugh.

"You'll soon get used to the smell. I don't notice it myself."

He asked Philip's name and looked at a list on the board.

"You've got a leg—number four."

Philip saw that another name was bracketed with his own.

"What's the meaning of that?" he asked.

"We're very short of bodies just now. We've had to put two on each part."

The dissecting-room was a large apartment painted like the corridors, the upper part a rich salmon and the dado a dark terra-cotta. At regular intervals down the long sides of the room, at right angles with the wall, were iron slabs, grooved like meat-dishes; and on each lay a body. Most of them were men. They were very dark from the preservative in which they had been kept, and the skin had almost the look of leather. They were extremely emaciated. The attendant took Philip up to one of the slabs. A youth was standing by it.

"Is your name Carey?" he asked.

"Yes."

"Oh, then we've got this leg together. It's lucky it's a man, isn't it?"

"Why?" asked Philip.

"They generally always like a male better," said the attendant. "A female's liable to have a lot of fat about her."

Philip looked at the body. The arms and legs were so thin that there was no shape in them, and the ribs stood out so that the skin over them was tense. A man of about forty-five with a thin, grey beard, and on his skull scanty, colourless hair: the eyes were closed and the lower jaw sunken. Philip could not feel that this had ever been a man, and yet in the row of them there was something terrible and ghastly.

"I thought I'd start at two," said the young man who was dissecting with Philip.

"All right, I'll be here then."

He had bought the day before the case of instruments which was needful, and now he was given a locker. He looked at the boy who had accompanied him into the dissecting-room and saw that he was white.

"Make you feel rotten?" Philip asked him.

"I've never seen anyone dead before."

They walked along the corridor till they came to the entrance of the school. Philip remembered Fanny Price. She was the first dead person he had ever seen, and he remembered how strangely it had affected him. There was an immeasurable distance between the quick and the dead: they did not seem to belong to the same species; and it was strange to think that but a little while before they had spoken and moved and eaten and laughed. There was something horrible about the dead, and you could imagine that they might cast an evil influence on the living.

"What d'you say to having something to eat?" said his new friend to Philip.

They went down into the basement, where there was a dark room fitted up as a restaurant, and here the students were able to get the same sort of fare as they might have at an aerated bread shop. While they ate (Philip had a scone and butter and a cup of chocolate), he discovered that his companion was called Dunsford. He was a fresh-complexioned lad, with pleasant blue eyes and curly, dark hair, large-limbed, slow of speech and movement. He had just come from Clifton.

"Are you taking the Conjoint?" he asked Philip.

"Yes, I want to get qualified as soon as I can."

"I'm taking it too, but I shall take the F. R. C. S. afterwards. I'm going in for surgery."

Most of the students took the curriculum of the Conjoint Board of the College of Surgeons and the College of Physicians; but the more ambitious or the more industrious added to this the longer studies which led to a degree from the University of London. When Philip went to St. Luke's changes had recently been made in the regulations, and the course took five years instead of four as it had done for those who registered before the autumn of 1892. Dunsford was well up in his plans and told Philip the usual course of events. The "first conjoint" examination consisted of Biology, Anatomy, and Chemistry; but it could be taken in sections, and most fellows took their biology three months after entering the school. This science had been recently added to the list of subjects upon which the student was obliged to inform himself, but the amount of knowledge required was very small.

When Philip went back to the dissecting-room, he was a few minutes late, since he had forgotten to buy the loose sleeves which they wore to protect their shirts, and he found a number of men already working. His partner had started on the minute and was busy dissecting out cutaneous nerves. Two others were engaged on the second leg, and more were occupied with the arms.

"You don't mind my having started?"

"That's all right, fire away," said Philip.

He took the book, open at a diagram of the dissected part, and looked at what they had to find.

"You're rather a dab at this," said Philip.

"Oh, I've done a good deal of dissecting before, animals, you know, for the Pre Sci."

There was a certain amount of conversation over the dissecting-table, partly about the work, partly about the prospects of the football season, the demonstrators, and the lectures. Philip felt himself a great deal older than the others. They were raw schoolboys. But age is a matter of knowledge rather than of years; and Newson, the active young man who was dissecting with him, was very much at home with his subject. He was perhaps not sorry to show off, and he explained very fully to Philip what he was about. Philip, notwithstanding his hidden stores of wisdom, listened meekly. Then Philip took up the scalpel and the tweezers and began working while the other looked on.

"Ripping to have him so thin," said Newson, wiping his hands. "The blighter can't have had anything to eat for a month."

"I wonder what he died of," murmured Philip.

"Oh, I don't know, any old thing, starvation chiefly, I suppose. . . . I say, look out, don't cut that artery."

"It's all very fine to say, don't cut that artery," remarked one of the men working on the opposite leg. "Silly old fool's got an artery in the wrong place."

"Arteries always are in the wrong place," said Newson. "The normal's the one thing you practically never get. That's why it's called the normal."

"Don't say things like that," said Philip, "or I shall cut myself."

"If you cut yourself," answered Newson, full of information, "wash it at once with antiseptic. It's the one thing you've got to be careful about. There was a chap here last year who gave himself only a prick, and he didn't bother about it, and he got septicaemia."

"Did he get all right?"

"Oh no, he died in a week. I went and had a look at him in the P. M. room."

Philip's back ached by the time it was proper to have tea, and his luncheon had been so light that he was quite ready for it. His hands smelled of that peculiar odour which he had first noticed that morning in the corridor. He thought his muffin tasted of it too.

"Oh, you'll get used to that," said Newson. "When you don't have the good old dissecting-room stink about, you feel quite lonely."

"I'm not going to let it spoil my appetite," said Philip, as he followed up the muffin with a piece of cake.

Chapter LV

PHILIP'S IDEAS OF THE LIFE OF MEDICAL STUDENTS, LIKE THOSE OF THE PUBlic at large, were founded on the pictures which Charles Dickens drew in the middle of the nineteenth century. He soon discovered that Bob Sawyer, if he ever existed, was no longer at all like the medical student of the present.

It is a mixed lot which enters upon the medical profession, and naturally there are some who are lazy and reckless. They think it is an easy life, idle away a couple of years; and then, because their funds come to an end or because angry parents refuse any longer to support them, drift away from the hospital. Others find the examinations too hard for them; one failure after another robs them of their nerve; and, panic-stricken, they forget as soon as they come into the forbidding buildings of the Conjoint Board the knowledge which before they had so pat. They remain year after year, objects of good-humoured scorn to younger men: some of them crawl through the examination of the Apothecaries Hall; others become nonqualified assistants, a precarious position in which they are at the mercy of their employer; their lot is poverty, drunkenness, and Heaven only knows their end. But for the most part medical students are industrious young men of the middle-class with a sufficient allowance to live in the respectable fashion they have been used to; many are the sons of doctors who have already something of the professional manner; their career is mapped out: as soon as they are qualified they propose to apply for a hospital appointment, after holding which (and perhaps a trip to the Far East as a ship's doctor), they will join their father and spend the rest of their days in a country practice. One or two are marked out as exceptionally brilliant: they will take the various prizes and scholarships which are open each year to the deserving, get one appointment after another at the hospital, go on the staff, take a consulting-room in Harley Street, and, specialising in one subject or another, become prosperous, eminent, and titled.

The medical profession is the only one which a man may enter at any age with some chance of making a living. Among the men of Philip's year were three or four who were past their first youth: one had been in the Navy, from which according to report he had been dismissed for drunkenness; he was a man of thirty, with a red face, a brusque manner, and a loud voice. Another was a married man with two children, who had lost money through a defaulting solicitor; he had a bowed look as if the world were too much for him; he went about his work silently, and it was plain that he found it difficult at his age to commit facts to memory. His mind worked slowly. His effort at application was painful to see.

Philip made himself at home in his tiny rooms. He arranged his books and hung on the walls such pictures and sketches as he possessed. Above him, on the drawing-room floor, lived a fifth-year man called Griffiths; but Philip saw little of him, partly because he was occupied chiefly in the wards and partly because he had been to Oxford. Such of the students as had been to a university kept a good deal together: they used a variety of means natural to the young in order to impress upon the less fortunate a proper sense of their inferiority; the rest of the students found their Olympian serenity rather hard to bear. Griffiths was a tall fellow, with a quantity of curly red hair and blue eyes, a white skin and a very red mouth; he was one of those fortunate people whom everybody liked, for he had high spirits and a constant gaiety. He strummed a little on the piano and sang comic songs with gusto; and evening after evening, while Philip was reading in his solitary room, he heard the shouts and the uproarious laughter of Griffiths' friends above him. He thought of those delightful evenings in Paris when they would sit in the studio, Lawson and he, Flanagan and Clutton, and talk of art and morals, the love affairs of the present, and the fame of the future. He felt sick at heart. He found that it was easy to make a heroic gesture, but hard to abide by its results. The worst of it was that the work seemed to him very tedious. He had got out of the habit of being asked questions by demonstrators. His attention wandered at lectures. Anatomy was a dreary science, a mere matter of learning by heart an enormous number of facts; dissection bored him; he did not see the use of dissecting out laboriously nerves and arteries when with much less trouble you could see in the diagrams of a book or in the specimens of the pathological museum exactly where they were.

He made friends by chance, but not intimate friends, for he seemed to have nothing in particular to say to his companions. When he tried to interest himself in their concerns, he felt that they found him patronising. He was not of those who can talk of what moves them without caring whether it bores or not the people they talk to. One man, hearing that he had studied art in Paris, and fancying himself on his taste, tried to discuss art with him; but Philip was impatient of views which did not agree with his own; and, finding quickly that the other's ideas were conventional, grew monosyllabic. Philip desired popularity but could bring himself to make no advances to others. A fear of rebuff prevented him from affability, and he concealed his shyness, which was still intense, under a frigid taciturnity. He was going through the same experience as he had done at school, but here the freedom of the medical students' life made it possible for him to live a good deal by himself.

It was through no effort of his that he became friendly with Dunsford, the fresh-complexioned, heavy lad whose acquaintance he had made at the beginning of the session. Dunsford attached himself to Philip merely because he was the first person he had known at St. Luke's. He had no friends in London, and on Saturday nights he and Philip got into the habit of going together to the pit of a music-hall or the gallery of a theatre. He was stupid, but he was good-humoured and never took offence; he always said the obvious thing, but when Philip laughed at him merely smiled. He had a very sweet smile. Though Philip made him his butt, he liked him; he was amused by his candour and delighted with his agreeable nature: Dunsford had the charm which himself was acutely conscious of not possessing.

They often went to have tea at a shop in Parliament Street, because Dunsford admired one of the young women who waited. Philip did not find anything attractive in her. She was tall and thin, with narrow hips and the chest of a boy.

"No one would look at her in Paris," said Philip scornfully.

"She's got a ripping face," said Dunsford.

"What *does* the face matter?"

She had the small regular features, the blue eyes, and the broad low brow, which the Victorian painters, Lord Leighton, Alma Tadema, and a hundred others, induced the world they lived in to accept as a type of Greek beauty. She seemed to have a great deal of hair: it was arranged with peculiar elaboration and done over the forehead in what she called an Alexandra fringe. She was very anaemic. Her thin lips were pale, and her skin was delicate, of a faint green colour, without a touch of red even in the cheeks. She had very good teeth. She took great pains to prevent her work from spoiling her hands, and they were small, thin, and white. She went about her duties with a bored look.

Dunsford, very shy with women, had never succeeded in getting into conversation with her; and he urged Philip to help him.

"All I want is a lead," he said, "and then I can manage for myself."

Philip, to please him, made one or two remarks, but she answered with monosyllables. She had taken their measure. They were boys, and she surmised they were students. She had no use for them. Dunsford noticed that a man with sandy hair and a bristly moustache, who looked like a German, was favoured with her attention whenever he came into the shop; and then it was only by calling her two or three times that they could induce her to take their order. She used the clients whom she did not know with frigid insolence, and when she was talking to a friend was perfectly indifferent to the calls of the hurried. She had the art of treating women who desired refreshment with just that degree of impertinence which irritated them without affording them an opportunity of complaining to the management. One day Dunsford told him her name was Mildred. He had heard one of the other girls in the shop address her.

"What an odious name," said Philip.

"Why?" asked Dunsford. "I like it."

"It's so pretentious."

It chanced that on this day the German was not there, and, when she brought the tea, Philip, smiling, remarked:

"Your friend's not here today."

"I don't know what you mean," she said coldly.

"I was referring to the nobleman with the sandy moustache. Has he left you for another?"

"Some people would do better to mind their own business," she retorted.

She left them, and, since for a minute or two there was no one to attend to, sat down and looked at the evening paper which a customer had left behind him.

"You are a fool to put her back up," said Dunsford.

"I'm really quite indifferent to the attitude of her vertebrae," replied Philip.

But he was piqued. It irritated him that when he tried to be agreeable with a woman she should take offence. When he asked for the bill, he hazarded a remark which he meant to lead further.

"Are we no longer on speaking terms?" he smiled.

"I'm here to take orders and to wait on customers. I've got nothing to say to them, and I don't want them to say anything to me."

She put down the slip of paper on which she had marked the sum they had to pay, and walked back to the table at which she had been sitting. Philip flushed with anger.

"That's one in the eye for you, Carey," said Dunsford, when they got outside.

"Ill-mannered slut," said Philip. "I shan't go there again."

His influence with Dunsford was strong enough to get him to take their tea elsewhere, and Dunsford soon found another young woman to flirt with. But the snub which the waitress had inflicted on him rankled. If she had treated him with civility he would have been perfectly indifferent to her; but it was obvious that she disliked him rather than otherwise, and his pride was wounded. He could not suppress a desire to be even with her. He was impatient with himself because he had so petty a feeling, but three or four days' firmness, during which he would not go to the shop, did not help him to surmount it; and he came to the conclusion that it would be least trouble to see her. Having done so he would certainly cease to think of her. Pretexting an appointment one afternoon, for he was not a little ashamed of his weakness, he left Dunsford and went straight to the shop which he had vowed never again to enter. He saw the waitress the moment he came in and sat down at one of her tables. He expected her to make some reference to the fact that he had not been there for a week, but when she came up for his order she said nothing. He had heard her say to other customers:

"You're quite a stranger."

She gave no sign that she had ever seen him before. In order to see whether she had really forgotten him, when she brought his tea, he asked:

"Have you seen my friend tonight?"

"No, he's not been in here for some days."

He wanted to use this as the beginning of a conversation, but he was strangely nervous and could think of nothing to say. She gave him no opportunity, but at once went away. He had no chance of saying anything till he asked for his bill.

"Filthy weather, isn't it?" he said.

It was mortifying that he had been forced to prepare such a phrase as that. He could not make out why she filled him with such embarrassment.

"It don't make much difference to me what the weather is, having to be in here all day."

There was an insolence in her tone that peculiarly irritated him. A sarcasm rose to his lips, but he forced himself to be silent.

"I wish to God she'd say something really cheeky," he raged to himself, "so that I could report her and get her sacked. It would serve her damned well right."

Chapter LVI

HE COULD NOT GET HER OUT OF HIS MIND. HE LAUGHED ANGRILY AT HIS own foolishness: it was absurd to care what an anaemic little waitress said to him; but he was strangely humiliated. Though no one knew of the humiliation but Dunsford, and he had certainly forgotten, Philip felt that he could have no peace till he had wiped it out. He thought over what he had better do. He made up his mind that he would go to the shop every day; it was obvious that he had made a disagreeable impression on her, but he thought he had the wits to eradicate it; he would take care not to say anything at which the most susceptible person could be offended. All this he did, but it had no effect. When he went in and said good-evening she answered with the same words, but when once he omitted to say it in order to see whether she would say it first, she said nothing at all. He murmured in his heart an expression which though frequently applicable to members of the female sex is not often used of them in polite society; but with an unmoved face he ordered his tea. He made up his mind not to speak a word, and left the shop without his usual good-night. He promised himself that he would not go anymore, but the next day at tea-time he grew restless. He tried to think of other things, but he had no command over his thoughts. At last he said desperately:

"After all there's no reason why I shouldn't go if I want to."

The struggle with himself had taken a long time, and it was getting on for seven when he entered the shop.

"I thought you weren't coming," the girl said to him, when he sat down.

His heart leaped in his bosom and he felt himself reddening. "I was detained. I couldn't come before."

"Cutting up people, I suppose?"

"Not so bad as that."

"You are a stoodent, aren't you?"

"Yes."

But that seemed to satisfy her curiosity. She went away and, since at that late hour there was nobody else at her tables, she immersed herself in a novelette. This was before the time of the sixpenny reprints. There was a regular supply of inexpensive fiction written to order by poor hacks for the consumption of the illiterate. Philip was elated; she had addressed him of her own accord; he saw the time approaching when his turn would come and he would tell her exactly what he thought of her. It would be a great comfort to express the immensity of his contempt. He looked at her. It was true that her profile was beautiful; it was extraordinary how

English girls of that class had so often a perfection of outline which took your breath away, but it was as cold as marble; and the faint green of her delicate skin gave an impression of unhealthiness. All the waitresses were dressed alike, in plain black dresses, with a white apron, cuffs, and a small cap. On a half-sheet of paper that he had in his pocket Philip made a sketch of her as she sat leaning over her book (she outlined the words with her lips as she read), and left it on the table when he went away. It was an inspiration, for next day, when he came in, she smiled at him.

"I didn't know you could draw," she said.

"I was an art-student in Paris for two years."

"I showed that drawing you left be'ind you last night to the manageress and she *was* struck with it. Was it meant to be me?"

"It was," said Philip.

When she went for his tea, one of the other girls came up to him.

"I saw that picture you done of Miss Rogers. It was the very image of her," she said.

That was the first time he had heard her name, and when he wanted his bill he called her by it.

"I see you know my name," she said, when she came.

"Your friend mentioned it when she said something to me about that drawing."

"She wants you to do one of her. Don't you do it. If you once begin you'll have to go on, and they'll all be wanting you to do them." Then without a pause, with peculiar inconsequence, she said: "Where's that young fellow that used to come with you? Has he gone away?"

"Fancy your remembering him," said Philip.

"He was a nice-looking young fellow."

Philip felt quite a peculiar sensation in his heart. He did not know what it was. Dunsford had jolly curling hair, a fresh complexion, and a beautiful smile. Philip thought of these advantages with envy.

"Oh, he's in love," said he, with a little laugh.

Philip repeated every word of the conversation to himself as he limped home. She was quite friendly with him now. When opportunity arose he would offer to make a more finished sketch of her, he was sure she would like that; her face was interesting, the profile was lovely, and there was something curiously fascinating about the chlorotic colour. He tried to think what it was like; at first he thought of pea soup; but, driving away that idea angrily, he thought of the petals of a yellow rosebud when you tore it to pieces before it had burst. He had no ill-feeling towards her now.

"She's not a bad sort," he murmured.

It was silly of him to take offence at what she had said; it was doubtless his own fault; she had not meant to make herself disagreeable: he ought to be accustomed by now to making at first sight a bad impression on people. He was flattered at the success of his drawing; she looked upon him with more interest now that she was aware of this small talent. He was restless next day. He thought of going to lunch at the tea-shop, but he was certain there would be many people there then, and Mildred would not be able to talk to him. He had managed before this to get out of having tea with Dunsford, and, punctually at half-past four (he had looked at his watch a dozen times), he went into the shop.

Mildred had her back turned to him. She was sitting down, talking to the German whom Philip had seen there every day till a fortnight ago and since then had not seen at all. She was laughing at what he said. Philip thought she had a common laugh, and it made him shudder. He called her, but she took no notice; he called her again; then, growing angry, for he was impatient, he rapped the table loudly with his stick. She approached sulkily.

"How d'you do?" he said.

"You seem to be in a great hurry."

She looked down at him with the insolent manner which he knew so well.

"I say, what's the matter with you?" he asked.

"If you'll kindly give your order I'll get what you want. I can't stand talking all night."

"Tea and toasted bun, please," Philip answered briefly.

He was furious with her. He had *The Star* with him and read it elaborately when she brought the tea.

"If you'll give me my bill now I needn't trouble you again," he said icily.

She wrote out the slip, placed it on the table, and went back to the German. Soon she was talking to him with animation. He was a man of middle height, with the round head of his nation and a sallow face; his moustache was large and bristling; he had on a tail-coat and grey trousers, and he wore a massive gold watch-chain. Philip thought the other girls looked from him to the pair at the table and exchanged significant glances. He felt certain they were laughing at him, and his blood boiled. He detested Mildred now with all his heart. He knew that the best thing he could do was to cease coming to the tea-shop, but he could not bear to think that he had been worsted in the affair, and he devised a plan to show her that he despised her. Next day he sat down at another table and ordered his tea from another waitress. Mildred's friend was there again and she was talking to him. She paid no attention to Philip, and so when he went out he chose a moment when she had to cross his path: as he passed he looked at her as though he had never seen her before. He repeated this for three or four days. He expected that presently she would take the opportunity to say something to him; he thought she would ask why he never came to one of her tables now, and he had prepared an answer charged with all the loathing he felt for her. He knew it was absurd to trouble, but he could not help himself. She had beaten him again. The German suddenly disappeared, but Philip still sat at other tables. She paid no attention to him. Suddenly he realised that what he did was a matter of complete indifference to her; he could go on in that way till doomsday, and it would have no effect.

"I've not finished yet," he said to himself.

The day after he sat down in his old seat, and when she came up said good-evening as though he had not ignored her for a week. His face was placid, but he could not prevent the mad beating of his heart. At that time the musical comedy had lately leaped into public favour, and he was sure that Mildred would be delighted to go to one.

"I say," he said suddenly, "I wonder if you'd dine with me one night and come to *The Belle of New York*. I'll get a couple of stalls."

He added the last sentence in order to tempt her. He knew that when the girls went to the play it was either in the pit, or, if some man took them, seldom to more expensive seats than the upper circle. Mildred's pale face showed no change of expression.

"I don't mind," she said.

"When will you come?"

"I get off early on Thursdays."

They made arrangements. Mildred lived with an aunt at Herne Hill. The play began at eight so they must dine at seven. She proposed that he should meet her in the second-class waiting-room at Victoria Station. She showed no pleasure, but accepted the invitation as though she conferred a favour. Philip was vaguely irritated.

Chapter LVII

PHILIP ARRIVED AT VICTORIA STATION NEARLY HALF AN HOUR BEFORE THE time which Mildred had appointed, and sat down in the second-class waiting-room. He waited and she did not come. He began to grow anxious, and walked into the station watching the incoming suburban trains; the hour which she had fixed passed, and still there was no sign of her. Philip was impatient. He went into the other waiting-rooms and looked at the people sitting in them. Suddenly his heart gave a great thud.

"There you are. I thought you were never coming."

"I like that after keeping me waiting all this time. I had half a mind to go back home again."

"But you said you'd come to the second-class waiting-room."

"I didn't say any such thing. It isn't exactly likely I'd sit in the second-class room when I could sit in the first, is it?"

Though Philip was sure he had not made a mistake, he said nothing, and they got into a cab.

"Where are we dining?" she asked.

"I thought of the Adelphi Restaurant. Will that suit you?"

"I don't mind where we dine."

She spoke ungraciously. She was put out by being kept waiting and answered Philip's attempt at conversation with monosyllables. She wore a long cloak of some rough, dark material and a crochet shawl over her head. They reached the restaurant and sat down at a table. She looked round with satisfaction. The red shades to the candles on the tables, the gold of the decorations, the looking-glasses, lent the room a sumptuous air.

"I've never been here before."

She gave Philip a smile. She had taken off her cloak; and he saw that she wore a pale blue dress, cut square at the neck; and her hair was more elaborately arranged than ever. He had ordered champagne and when it came her eyes sparkled.

"You are going it," she said.

"Because I've ordered fiz?" he asked carelessly, as though he never drank anything else.

"I *was* surprised when you asked me to do a theatre with you."

Conversation did not go very easily, for she did not seem to have much to say; and Philip was nervously conscious that he was not amusing her. She listened carelessly to his remarks, with her eyes on other diners, and made no pretence that she was interested in him. He made one or two little jokes, but she took them quite seriously. The only sign of vivacity he got was when he spoke of the other girls in the shop; she could not bear the manageress and told him all her misdeeds at length.

"I can't stick her at any price and all the air she gives herself. Sometimes I've got more than half a mind to tell her something she doesn't think I know anything about."

"What is that?" asked Philip.

"Well, I happen to know that she's not above going to Eastbourne with a man for the week-end now and again. One of the girls has a married sister who goes there with her husband, and she's seen her. She was staying at the same boarding-house, and she 'ad a wedding-ring on, and I know for one she's not married."

Philip filled her glass, hoping that champagne would make her more affable; he was anxious that his little jaunt should be a success. He noticed that she held her knife as though it were a pen-holder, and when she drank protruded her little finger. He started several topics of conversation, but he could get little out of her, and he remembered with irritation that he had seen her talking nineteen to the dozen and laughing with the German. They finished dinner and went to the play. Philip was a very cultured young man, and he looked upon musical comedy with scorn. He thought the jokes vulgar and the melodies obvious; it seemed to him that they did these things much better in France; but Mildred enjoyed herself thoroughly; she laughed till her sides ached, looking at Philip now and then when something tickled her to exchange a glance of pleasure; and she applauded rapturously.

"This is the seventh time I've been," she said, after the first act, "and I don't mind if I come seven times more."

She was much interested in the women who surrounded them in the stalls. She pointed out to Philip those who were painted and those who wore false hair.

"It is horrible, these West-end people," she said. "I don't know how they can do it." She put her hand to her hair. "Mine's all my own, every bit of it."

She found no one to admire, and whenever she spoke of anyone it was to say something disagreeable. It made Philip uneasy. He supposed that next day she would tell the girls in the shop that he had taken her out and that he had bored her to death. He disliked her, and yet, he knew not why, he wanted to be with her. On the way home he asked:

"I hope you've enjoyed yourself?"

"Rather."

"Will you come out with me again one evening?"

"I don't mind."

He could never get beyond such expressions as that. Her indifference maddened him.

"That sounds as if you didn't much care if you came or not."

"Oh, if you don't take me out some other fellow will. I need never want for men who'll take me to the theatre."

Philip was silent. They came to the station, and he went to the booking-office.

"I've got my season," she said.

"I thought I'd take you home as it's rather late, if you don't mind."

"Oh, I don't mind if it gives you any pleasure."

He took a single first for her and a return for himself.

"Well, you're not mean, I will say that for you," she said, when he opened the carriage-door.

Philip did not know whether he was pleased or sorry when other people entered and it was impossible to speak. They got out at Herne Hill, and he accompanied her to the corner of the road in which she lived.

"I'll say good-night to you here," she said, holding out her hand. "You'd better not come up to the door. I know what people are, and I don't want to have anybody talking."

She said good-night and walked quickly away. He could see the white shawl in the darkness. He thought she might turn round, but she did not. Philip saw which house she went into, and in a moment he walked along to look at it. It was a trim, common little house of yellow brick, exactly like all the other little houses in the street. He stood outside for a few minutes, and presently the window on the top floor was darkened. Philip strolled slowly back to the station. The evening had been unsatisfactory. He felt irritated, restless, and miserable.

When he lay in bed he seemed still to see her sitting in the corner of the railway carriage, with the white crochet shawl over her head. He did not know how he was to get through the hours that must pass before his eyes rested on her again. He thought drowsily of her thin face, with its delicate features, and the greenish pallor of her skin. He was not happy with her, but he was unhappy away from her. He wanted to sit by her side and look at her, he wanted to touch her, he wanted . . . the thought came to him and he did not finish it, suddenly he grew wide awake . . . he wanted to kiss the thin, pale mouth with its narrow lips. The truth came to him at last. He was in love with her. It was incredible.

He had often thought of falling in love, and there was one scene which he had pictured to himself over and over again. He saw himself coming into a ball-room; his eyes fell on a little group of men and women talking; and one of the women turned round. Her eyes fell upon him, and he knew that the gasp in his throat was in her throat too. He stood quite still. She was tall and dark and beautiful, with eyes like the night; she was dressed in white, and in her black hair shone diamonds; they stared at one another, forgetting that people surrounded them. He went straight up to her, and she moved a little towards him. Both felt that the formality of introduction was out of place. He spoke to her.

"I've been looking for you all my life," he said.

"You've come at last," she murmured.

"Will you dance with me?"

She surrendered herself to his outstretched hands and they danced. (Philip always pretended that he was not lame.) She danced divinely.

"I've never danced with anyone who danced like you," she said.

She tore up her programme, and they danced together the whole evening.

"I'm so thankful that I waited for you," he said to her. "I knew that in the end I must meet you."

People in the ball-room stared. They did not care. They did not wish to hide their passion. At last they went into the garden. He flung a light cloak over her shoulders and put her in a waiting cab. They caught the midnight train to Paris; and they sped through the silent, starlit night into the unknown.

He thought of this old fancy of his, and it seemed impossible that he should be in love with Mildred Rogers. Her name was grotesque. He did not think her pretty; he hated the thinness of her, only that evening he had noticed how the bones of her chest stood out in evening-dress; he went over her features one by one; he did not like her mouth, and the unhealthiness of her colour vaguely repelled him. She was common. Her phrases, so bald and few, constantly repeated, showed the emptiness of her mind; he recalled her vulgar little laugh at the jokes of the musical comedy; and he remembered the little finger carefully extended when she held her glass to her mouth; her manners like her conversation, were odiously genteel. He remembered her insolence; sometimes he had felt inclined to box her ears; and suddenly, he knew not why, perhaps it was the thought of hitting her or the recollection of her tiny, beautiful ears, he was seized by an uprush of emotion. He yearned for her. He thought of taking her in his arms, the thin, fragile body, and kissing her pale mouth; he wanted to pass his fingers down the slightly greenish cheeks. He wanted her.

He had thought of love as a rapture which seized one so that all the world seemed spring-like, he had looked forward to an ecstatic happiness; but this was not happiness; it was a hunger of the soul, it was a painful yearning, it was a bitter anguish, he had never known before. He tried to think when it had first come to him. He did not know. He only remembered that each time he had gone into the shop, after the first two or three times, it had been with a little feeling in the heart that was pain; and he remembered that when she spoke to him he felt curiously breathless. When she left him it was wretchedness, and when she came to him again it was despair.

He stretched himself in his bed as a dog stretches himself. He wondered how he was going to endure that ceaseless aching of his soul.

Chapter LVIII

PHILIP WOKE EARLY NEXT MORNING, AND HIS FIRST THOUGHT WAS OF MILdred. It struck him that he might meet her at Victoria Station and walk with her to the shop. He shaved quickly, scrambled into his clothes, and took a bus to the station. He was there by twenty to eight and watched the incoming trains. Crowds poured out of them, clerks and shop-people at that early hour, and thronged up the platform: they hurried along, sometimes in pairs, here and there a group of girls, but more often alone. They were white, most of them, ugly in the early morning, and they had an abstracted look; the younger ones walked lightly, as though the cement of the platform were pleasant to tread, but the others went as though impelled by a machine: their faces were set in an anxious frown.

At last Philip saw Mildred, and he went up to her eagerly.

"Good-morning," he said. "I thought I'd come and see how you were after last night."

She wore an old brown ulster and a sailor hat. It was very clear that she was not pleased to see him.

"Oh, I'm all right. I haven't got much time to waste."

"D'you mind if I walk down Victoria Street with you?"

"I'm none too early. I shall have to walk fast," she answered, looking down at Philip's club-foot.

He turned scarlet.

"I beg your pardon. I won't detain you."

"You can please yourself."

She went on, and he with a sinking heart made his way home to breakfast. He hated her. He knew he was a fool to bother about her; she was not the sort of woman who would ever care two straws for him, and she must look upon his deformity with distaste. He made up his mind that he would not go in to tea that afternoon, but, hating himself, he went. She nodded to him as he came in and smiled.

"I expect I was rather short with you this morning," she said. "You see, I didn't expect you, and it came like a surprise."

"Oh, it doesn't matter at all."

He felt that a great weight had suddenly been lifted from him. He was infinitely grateful for one word of kindness.

"Why don't you sit down?" he asked. "Nobody's wanting you just now."

"I don't mind if I do."

He looked at her, but could think of nothing to say; he racked his brains anxiously, seeking for a remark which should keep her by him; he wanted to tell her how much she meant to him; but he did not know how to make love now that he loved in earnest.

"Where's your friend with the fair moustache? I haven't seen him lately"

"Oh, he's gone back to Birmingham. He's in business there. He only comes up to London every now and again."

"Is he in love with you?"

"You'd better ask him," she said, with a laugh. "I don't know what it's got to do with you if he is."

A bitter answer leaped to his tongue, but he was learning self-restraint.

"I wonder why you say things like that," was all he permitted himself to say.

She looked at him with those indifferent eyes of hers.

"It looks as if you didn't set much store on me," he added.

"Why should I?"

"No reason at all."

He reached over for his paper.

"You are quick-tempered," she said, when she saw the gesture. "You do take offence easily."

He smiled and looked at her appealingly.

"Will you do something for me?" he asked.

"That depends what it is."

"Let me walk back to the station with you tonight."

"I don't mind."

He went out after tea and went back to his rooms, but at eight o'clock, when the shop closed, he was waiting outside.

"You are a caution," she said, when she came out. "I don't understand you."

"I shouldn't have thought it was very difficult," he answered bitterly.

"Did any of the girls see you waiting for me?"

"I don't know and I don't care."

"They all laugh at you, you know. They say you're spoony on me."

"Much you care," he muttered.

"Now then, quarrelsome."

At the station he took a ticket and said he was going to accompany her home.

"You don't seem to have much to do with your time," she said.

"I suppose I can waste it in my own way."

They seemed to be always on the verge of a quarrel. The fact was that he hated himself for loving her. She seemed to be constantly humiliating him, and for each snub that he endured he owed her a grudge. But she was in a friendly mood that evening, and talkative: she told him that her parents were dead; she gave him to understand that she did not have to earn her living, but worked for amusement.

"My aunt doesn't like my going to business. I can have the best of everything at home. I don't want you to think I work because I need to."

Philip knew that she was not speaking the truth. The gentility of her class made her use this pretence to avoid the stigma attached to earning her living.

"My family's very well-connected," she said.

Philip smiled faintly, and she noticed it.

"What are you laughing at?" she said quickly. "Don't you believe I'm telling you the truth?"

"Of course I do," he answered.

She looked at him suspiciously, but in a moment could not resist the temptation to impress him with the splendour of her early days.

"My father always kept a dog-cart, and we had three servants. We had a cook and a housemaid and an odd man. We used to grow beautiful roses. People used to stop at the gate and ask who the house belonged to, the roses were so beautiful. Of course it isn't very nice for me having to mix with them girls in the shop, it's not the class of person I've been used to, and sometimes I really think I'll give up business on that account. It's not the work I mind, don't think that; but it's the class of people I have to mix with."

They were sitting opposite one another in the train, and Philip, listening sympathetically to what she said, was quite happy. He was amused at her naïveté and slightly touched. There was a very faint colour in her cheeks. He was thinking that it would be delightful to kiss the tip of her chin.

"The moment you come into the shop I saw you was a gentleman in every sense of the word. Was your father a professional man?"

"He was a doctor."

"You can always tell a professional man. There's something about them, I don't know what it is, but I know at once."

They walked along from the station together.

"I say, I want you to come and see another play with me," he said.

"I don't mind," she said.

"You might go so far as to say you'd like to."

"Why?"

"It doesn't matter. Let's fix a day. Would Saturday night suit you?"

"Yes, that'll do."

They made further arrangements, and then found themselves at the corner of the road in which she lived. She gave him her hand, and he held it.

"I say, I do so awfully want to call you Mildred."

"You may if you like, I don't care."

"And you'll call me Philip, won't you?"

"I will if I can think of it. It seems more natural to call you Mr. Carey."

He drew her slightly towards him, but she leaned back.

"What are you doing?"

"Won't you kiss me good-night?" he whispered.

"Impudence!" she said.

She snatched away her hand and hurried towards her house.

Philip bought tickets for Saturday night. It was not one of the days on which she got off early and therefore she would have no time to go home and change; but she meant to bring a frock up with her in the morning and hurry into her clothes at the shop. If the manageress was in a good temper she would let her go at seven. Philip had agreed to wait outside from a quarter-past seven onwards. He looked forward to the occasion with painful eagerness, for in the cab on the way from the theatre to the station he thought she would let him kiss her. The vehicle gave every facility for a man to put his arm round a girl's waist (an advantage which the hansom had over the taxi of the present day), and the delight of that was worth the cost of the evening's entertainment.

But on Saturday afternoon when he went in to have tea, in order to confirm the arrangements, he met the man with the fair moustache coming out of the shop. He knew by now that he was called Miller. He was a naturalised German, who had anglicised his name, and he had lived many years in England. Philip had heard him speak, and, though his English was fluent and natural, it had not quite the intonation of the native. Philip knew that he was flirting with Mildred, and he was horribly jealous of him; but he took comfort in the coldness of her temperament, which otherwise distressed him; and, thinking her incapable of passion, he looked upon his rival as no better off than himself. But his heart sank now, for his first thought was that Miller's sudden appearance might interfere with the jaunt which he had so looked forward to. He entered, sick with apprehension. The waitress came up to him, took his order for tea, and presently brought it.

"I'm awfully, sorry" she said, with an expression on her face of real distress. "I shan't be able to come tonight after all."

"Why?" said Philip.

"Don't look so stern about it," she laughed. "It's not my fault. My aunt was taken ill last night, and it's the girl's night out so I must go and sit with her. She can't be left alone, can she?"

"It doesn't matter. I'll see you home instead."

"But you've got the tickets. It would be a pity to waste them."

He took them out of his pocket and deliberately tore them up.

"What are you doing that for?"

"You don't suppose I want to go and see a rotten musical comedy by myself, do you? I only took seats there for your sake."

"You can't see me home if that's what you mean?"

"You've made other arrangements."

"I don't know what you mean by that. You're just as selfish as all the rest of them. You only think of yourself. It's not my fault if my aunt's queer."

She quickly wrote out his bill and left him. Philip knew very little about women, or he would have been aware that one should accept their most transparent lies. He made up his mind that he would watch the shop and see for certain whether Mildred went out with the German. He had an unhappy passion for certainty. At seven he stationed himself on the opposite pavement. He looked about for Miller, but did not see him. In ten minutes she came out, she had on the cloak and shawl which she had worn when he took her to the Shaftesbury Theatre. It was obvious that she was not going home. She saw him before he had time to move away, started a little, and then came straight up to him.

"What are you doing here?" she said.

"Taking the air," he answered.

"You're spying on me, you dirty little cad. I thought you was a gentleman."

"Did you think a gentleman would be likely to take any interest in you?" he murmured.

There was a devil within him which forced him to make matters worse. He wanted to hurt her as much as she was hurting him.

"I suppose I can change my mind if I like. I'm not obliged to come out with you. I tell you I'm going home, and I won't be followed or spied upon."

"Have you seen Miller today?"

"That's no business of yours. In point of fact I haven't, so you're wrong again."

"I saw him this afternoon. He'd just come out of the shop when I went in."

"Well, what if he did? I can go out with him if I want to, can't I? I don't know what you've got to say to it."

"He's keeping you waiting, isn't he?"

"Well, I'd rather wait for him than have you wait for me. Put that in your pipe and smoke it. And now p'raps you'll go off home and mind your own business in future."

His mood changed suddenly from anger to despair, and his voice trembled when he spoke.

"I say, don't be beastly with me, Mildred. You know I'm awfully fond of you.

I think I love you with all my heart. Won't you change your mind? I was looking forward to this evening so awfully. You see, he hasn't come, and he can't care twopence about you really. Won't you dine with me? I'll get some more tickets, and we'll go anywhere you like."

"I tell you I won't. It's no good you talking. I've made up my mind, and when I make up my mind I keep to it."

He looked at her for a moment. His heart was torn with anguish. People were hurrying past them on the pavement, and cabs and omnibuses rolled by noisily. He saw that Mildred's eyes were wandering. She was afraid of missing Miller in the crowd.

"I can't go on like this," groaned Philip. "It's too degrading. If I go now I go for good. Unless you'll come with me tonight you'll never see me again."

"You seem to think that'll be an awful thing for me. All I say is, good riddance to bad rubbish."

"Then good-bye."

He nodded and limped away slowly, for he hoped with all his heart that she would call him back. At the next lamp-post he stopped and looked over his shoulder. He thought she might beckon to him—he was willing to forget everything, he was ready for any humiliation—but she had turned away, and apparently had ceased to trouble about him. He realised that she was glad to be quit of him.

Chapter LIX

PHILIP PASSED THE EVENING WRETCHEDLY. HE HAD TOLD HIS LANDLADY THAT he would not be in, so there was nothing for him to eat, and he had to go to Gatti's for dinner. Afterwards he went back to his rooms, but Griffiths on the floor above him was having a party, and the noisy merriment made his own misery more hard to bear. He went to a music-hall, but it was Saturday night and there was standing-room only: after half an hour of boredom his legs grew tired and he went home. He tried to read, but he could not fix his attention; and yet it was necessary that he should work hard. His examination in biology was in little more than a fortnight, and, though it was easy, he had neglected his lectures of late and was conscious that he knew nothing. It was only a *viva*, however, and he felt sure that in a fortnight he could find out enough about the subject to scrape through. He had confidence in his intelligence. He threw aside his book and gave himself up to thinking deliberately of the matter which was in his mind all the time.

He reproached himself bitterly for his behaviour that evening. Why had he given her the alternative that she must dine with him or else never see him again? Of course she refused. He should have allowed for her pride. He had burned his ships behind him. It would not be so hard to bear if he thought that she was suffering now, but he knew her too well: she was perfectly indifferent to him. If he hadn't been a fool he would have pretended to believe her story; he ought to have had the strength to conceal his disappointment and the self-control to master his temper. He could not tell why he loved her. He had read of the idealisation that takes place in love, but he saw her exactly as she was. She was not amusing or clever, her mind was common; she had a vulgar shrewdness which revolted him, she had no gentleness nor softness. As she would have put it herself, she was on the make. What aroused her admiration was a clever trick played on an unsuspecting person; to "do" somebody always gave her satisfaction. Philip laughed savagely as he thought of her gentility and the refinement with which she ate her food; she could not bear a coarse word, so far as her limited vocabulary reached she had a passion for euphemisms, and she scented indecency everywhere; she never spoke of trousers but referred to them as nether garments; she thought it slightly indelicate to blow her nose and did it in a deprecating way. She was dreadfully anaemic and suffered from the dyspepsia which accompanies that ailing. Philip was repelled by her flat breast and narrow hips, and he hated the vulgar way in which she did her hair. He loathed and despised himself for loving her.

The fact remained that he was helpless. He felt just as he had felt sometimes in the hands of a bigger boy at school. He had struggled against the superior strength till his own strength was gone, and he was rendered quite powerless—he remembered the peculiar languor he had felt in his limbs, almost as though he were paralysed—so that he could not help himself at all. He might have been dead. He felt just that same weakness now. He loved the woman so that he knew he had never loved before. He did not mind her faults of person or of character, he thought he loved them too: at all events they meant nothing to him. It did not seem himself that was concerned; he felt that he had been seized by some strange force that moved him against his will, contrary to his interests; and because he had a passion for freedom he hated the chains which bound him. He laughed at himself when he thought how often he had longed to experience the overwhelming passion. He cursed himself because he had given way to it. He thought of the beginnings; nothing of all this would have happened if he had not gone into the shop with Dunsford. The whole thing was his own fault. Except for his ridiculous vanity he would never have troubled himself with the ill-mannered slut.

At all events the occurrences of that evening had finished the whole affair. Unless he was lost to all sense of shame he could not go back. He wanted passionately to get rid of the love that obsessed him; it was degrading and hateful. He must prevent himself from thinking of her. In a little while the anguish he suffered must grow less. His mind went back to the past. He wondered whether Emily Wilkinson and Fanny Price had endured on his account anything like the torment that he suffered now. He felt a pang of remorse.

"I didn't know then what it was like," he said to himself.

He slept very badly. The next day was Sunday, and he worked at his biology. He sat with the book in front of him, forming the words with his lips in order to fix his attention, but he could remember nothing. He found his thoughts going back to Mildred every minute, and he repeated to himself the exact words of the quarrel they had had. He had to force himself back to his book. He went out for a walk. The streets on the South side of the river were dingy enough on week-days, but there was an energy, a coming and going, which gave them a sordid vivacity; but on Sundays, with no shops open, no carts in the roadway, silent and depressed, they were indescribably dreary. Philip thought that day would never end. But he was so tired that he slept heavily, and when Monday came he entered upon life with determination. Christmas was approaching, and a good many of the students had gone into the country for the short holiday between the two parts of the winter session; but Philip had refused his uncle's invitation to go down to Blackstable. He had given the approaching examination as his excuse, but in point of fact he had been unwilling to leave London and Mildred. He had neglected his work so much that now he had only a fortnight to learn what the curriculum allowed three months for.

He set to work seriously. He found it easier each day not to think of Mildred. He congratulated himself on his force of character. The pain he suffered was no longer anguish, but a sort of soreness, like what one might be expected to feel if one had been thrown off a horse and, though no bones were broken, were bruised all over and shaken. Philip found that he was able to observe with curiosity the condition he had been in during the last few weeks. He analysed his feelings with interest. He was a little amused at himself. One thing that struck him was how little under those circumstances it mattered what one thought; the system of personal philosophy, which had given him great satisfaction to devise, had not served him. He was puzzled by this.

But sometimes in the street he would see a girl who looked so like Mildred that his heart seemed to stop beating. Then he could not help himself, he hurried on to catch her up, eager and anxious, only to find that it was a total stranger. Men came back from the country, and he went with Dunsford to have tea at an A.B.C. shop. The well-known uniform made him so miserable that he could not speak. The thought came to him that perhaps she had been transferred to another establishment of the firm for which she worked, and he might suddenly find himself face to face with her. The idea filled him with panic, so that he feared Dunsford would see that something was the matter with him: he could not think of anything to say; he pretended to listen to what Dunsford was talking about; the conversation maddened him; and it was all he could do to prevent himself from crying out to Dunsford for Heaven's sake to hold his tongue.

Then came the day of his examination. Philip, when his turn arrived, went forward to the examiner's table with the utmost confidence. He answered three or four questions. Then they showed him various specimens; he had been to very few lectures and, as soon as he was asked about things which he could not learn from books, he was floored. He did what he could to hide his ignorance, the examiner did not insist, and soon his ten minutes were over. He felt certain he had passed; but next day, when he went up to the examination buildings to see the result posted on the door, he was astounded not to find his number among those who had satisfied the examiners. In amazement he read the list three times. Dunsford was with him.

"I say, I'm awfully sorry you're ploughed," he said.

He had just inquired Philip's number. Philip turned and saw by his radiant face that Dunsford had passed.

"Oh, it doesn't matter a bit," said Philip. "I'm jolly glad you're all right. I shall go up again in July."

He was very anxious to pretend he did not mind, and on their way back along The Embankment insisted on talking of indifferent things. Dunsford good-naturedly wanted to discuss the causes of Philip's failure, but Philip was obstinately casual. He was horribly mortified; and the fact that Dunsford, whom he looked upon as a very pleasant but quite stupid fellow, had passed made his own rebuff harder to bear. He had always been proud of his intelligence, and now he asked himself desperately whether he was not mistaken in the opinion he held of himself. In the three months of the winter session the students who had joined in October had already shaken down into groups, and it was clear which were brilliant, which were clever or industrious, and which were "rotters." Philip was conscious that his failure was a surprise to no one but himself. It was tea-time, and he knew that a lot of men would be having tea in the basement of the Medical School: those who had passed the examination would be exultant, those who disliked him would look at him with satisfaction, and the poor devils who had failed would sympathise with him in order to receive sympathy. His instinct was not to go near the hospital for a week, when the affair would be no more thought of, but, because he hated so much to go just then, he went: he wanted to inflict suffering upon himself. He forgot for the moment his maxim of life to follow his inclinations with due regard for the policeman round the corner; or, if he acted in accordance with it, there must have been some strange morbidity in his nature which made him take a grim pleasure in self-torture.

But later on, when he had endured the ordeal to which he forced himself, going out into the night after the noisy conversation in the smoking-room, he was seized with a feeling of utter loneliness. He seemed to himself absurd and futile. He had an urgent need of consolation, and the temptation to see Mildred was irresistible. He thought bitterly that there was small chance of consolation from her; but he wanted to see her even if he did not speak to her; after all, she was a waitress and would be obliged to serve him. She was the only person in the world he cared for. There was no use in hiding that fact from himself. Of course it would be humiliating to go back to the shop as though nothing had happened, but he had not much self-respect left. Though he would not confess it to himself, he had hoped each day that she would write to him; she knew that a letter addressed to the hospital would find him; but she had not written: it was evident that she cared nothing if she saw him again or not. And he kept on repeating to himself:

"I must see her. I must see her."

The desire was so great that he could not give the time necessary to walk, but jumped in a cab. He was too thrifty to use one when it could possibly be avoided. He stood outside the shop for a minute or two. The thought came to him that perhaps she had left, and in terror he walked in quickly. He saw her at once. He sat down and she came up to him.

"A cup of tea and a muffin, please," he ordered.

He could hardly speak. He was afraid for a moment that he was going to cry.

"I almost thought you was dead," she said.

She was smiling. Smiling! She seemed to have forgotten completely that last scene which Philip had repeated to himself a hundred times.

"I thought if you'd wanted to see me you'd write," he answered.

"I've got too much to do to think about writing letters."

It seemed impossible for her to say a gracious thing. Philip cursed the fate which chained him to such a woman. She went away to fetch his tea.

"Would you like me to sit down for a minute or two?" she said, when she brought it.

"Yes."

"Where have you been all this time?"

"I've been in London."

"I thought you'd gone away for the holidays. Why haven't you been in then?"

Philip looked at her with haggard, passionate eyes.

"Don't you remember that I said I'd never see you again?"

"What are you doing now then?"

She seemed anxious to make him drink up the cup of his humiliation; but he knew her well enough to know that she spoke at random; she hurt him frightfully, and never even tried to. He did not answer.

"It was a nasty trick you played on me, spying on me like that. I always thought you was a gentleman in every sense of the word."

"Don't be beastly to me, Mildred. I can't bear it."

"You are a funny feller. I can't make you out."

"It's very simple. I'm such a blasted fool as to love you with all my heart and soul, and I know that you don't care twopence for me."

"If you had been a gentleman I think you'd have come next day and begged my pardon."

She had no mercy. He looked at her neck and thought how he would like to jab it with the knife he had for his muffin. He knew enough anatomy to make pretty certain of getting the carotid artery. And at the same time he wanted to cover her pale, thin face with kisses.

"If I could only make you understand how frightfully I'm in love with you."

"You haven't begged my pardon yet."

He grew very white. She felt that she had done nothing wrong on that occasion. She wanted him now to humble himself. He was very proud. For one instant he felt inclined to tell her to go to hell, but he dared not. His passion made him abject. He was willing to submit to anything rather than not see her.

"I'm very sorry, Mildred. I beg your pardon."

He had to force the words out. It was a horrible effort.

"Now you've said that I don't mind telling you that I wish I had come out with you that evening. I thought Miller was a gentleman, but I've discovered my mistake now. I soon sent him about his business."

Philip gave a little gasp.

"Mildred, won't you come out with me tonight? Let's go and dine somewhere."

"Oh, I can't. My aunt'll be expecting me home."

"I'll send her a wire. You can say you've been detained in the shop; she won't know any better. Oh, do come, for God's sake. I haven't seen you for so long, and I want to talk to you."

She looked down at her clothes.

"Never mind about that. We'll go somewhere where it doesn't matter how you're dressed. And we'll go to a music-hall afterwards. Please say yes. It would give me so much pleasure."

She hesitated a moment; he looked at her with pitifully appealing eyes.

"Well, I don't mind if I do. I haven't been out anywhere since I don't know how long."

It was with the greatest difficulty he could prevent himself from seizing her hand there and then to cover it with kisses.

Chapter LX

THEY DINED IN SOHO. PHILIP WAS TREMULOUS WITH JOY. IT WAS NOT ONE of the more crowded of those cheap restaurants where the respectable and needy dine in the belief that it is bohemian and the assurance that it is economical. It was a humble establishment, kept by a good man from Rouen and his wife, that Philip had discovered by accident. He had been attracted by the Gallic look of the window, in which was generally an uncooked steak on one plate and on each side two dishes of raw vegetables. There was one seedy French waiter, who was attempting to learn English in a house where he never heard anything but French; and the customers were a few ladies of easy virtue, a *ménage* or two, who had their own napkins reserved for them, and a few queer men who came in for hurried, scanty meals.

Here Mildred and Philip were able to get a table to themselves. Philip sent the waiter for a bottle of Burgundy from the neighbouring tavern, and they had a *potage aux herbes,* a steak from the window *aux pommes,* and an *omelette au kirsch*. There was really an air of romance in the meal and in the place. Mildred, at first a little reserved in her appreciation—"I never quite trust these foreign places, you never know what there is in these messed up dishes"—was insensibly moved by it.

"I like this place, Philip," she said. "You feel you can put your elbows on the table, don't you?"

A tall fellow came in, with a mane of grey hair and a ragged thin beard. He wore a dilapidated cloak and a wide-awake hat. He nodded to Philip, who had met him there before.

"He looks like an anarchist," said Mildred.

"He is, one of the most dangerous in Europe. He's been in every prison on the Continent and has assassinated more persons than any gentleman unhung. He always goes about with a bomb in his pocket, and of course it makes conversation a little difficult because if you don't agree with him he lays it on the table in a marked manner."

She looked at the man with horror and surprise, and then glanced suspiciously at Philip. She saw that his eyes were laughing. She frowned a little.

"You're getting at me."

He gave a little shout of joy. He was so happy. But Mildred didn't like being laughed at.

"I don't see anything funny in telling lies."

"Don't be cross."

He took her hand, which was lying on the table, and pressed it gently.

"You are lovely, and I could kiss the ground you walk on," he said.

The greenish pallor of her skin intoxicated him, and her thin white lips had an extraordinary fascination. Her anaemia made her rather short of breath, and she held her mouth slightly open. It seemed to add somehow to the attractiveness of her face.

"You do like me a bit, don't you?" he asked.

"Well, if I didn't I suppose I shouldn't be here, should I? You're a gentleman in every sense of the word, I will say that for you."

They had finished their dinner and were drinking coffee. Philip, throwing economy to the winds, smoked a threepenny cigar.

"You can't imagine what a pleasure it is to me just to sit opposite and look at you. I've yearned for you. I was sick for a sight of you."

Mildred smiled a little and faintly flushed. She was not then suffering from the dyspepsia which generally attacked her immediately after a meal. She felt more kindly disposed to Philip than ever before, and the unaccustomed tenderness in her eyes filled him with joy. He knew instinctively that it was madness to give himself into her hands; his only chance was to treat her casually and never allow her to see the untamed passions that seethed in his breast; she would only take advantage of his weakness; but he could not be prudent now: he told her all the agony he had endured during the separation from her; he told her of his struggles with himself, how he had tried to get over his passion, thought he had succeeded, and how he found out that it was as strong as ever. He knew that he had never really wanted to get over it. He loved her so much that he did not mind suffering. He bared his heart to her. He showed her proudly all his weakness.

Nothing would have pleased him more than to sit on in the cosy, shabby restaurant, but he knew that Mildred wanted entertainment. She was restless and, wherever she was, wanted after a while to go somewhere else. He dared not bore her.

"I say, how about going to a music-hall?" he said.

He thought rapidly that if she cared for him at all she would say she preferred to stay there.

"I was just thinking we ought to be going if we are going," she answered.

"Come on then."

Philip waited impatiently for the end of the performance. He had made up his mind exactly what to do, and when they got into the cab he passed his arm, as though almost by accident, round her waist. But he drew it back quickly with a little cry. He had pricked himself. She laughed.

"There, that comes of putting your arm where it's got no business to be," she said. "I always know when men try and put their arm round my waist. That pin always catches them."

"I'll be more careful."

He put his arm round again. She made no objection.

"I'm so comfortable," he sighed blissfully.

"So long as you're happy," she retorted.

They drove down St. James' Street into the Park, and Philip quickly kissed her. He was strangely afraid of her, and it required all his courage. She turned her lips to him without speaking. She neither seemed to mind nor to like it.

"If you only knew how long I've wanted to do that," he murmured.

He tried to kiss her again, but she turned her head away.

"Once is enough," she said.

On the chance of kissing her a second time he travelled down to Herne Hill with her, and at the end of the road in which she lived he asked her:

"Won't you give me another kiss?"

She looked at him indifferently and then glanced up the road to see that no one was in sight.

"I don't mind."

He seized her in his arms and kissed her passionately, but she pushed him away.

"Mind my hat, silly. You are clumsy," she said.

Chapter LXI

He saw her then every day. He began going to lunch at the shop, but Mildred stopped him: she said it made the girls talk; so he had to content himself with tea; but he always waited about to walk with her to the station; and once or twice a week they dined together. He gave her little presents, a gold bangle, gloves, handkerchiefs, and the like. He was spending more than he could afford, but he could not help it: it was only when he gave her anything that she showed any affection. She knew the price of everything, and her gratitude was in exact proportion with the value of his gift. He did not care. He was too happy when she volunteered to kiss him to mind by what means he got her demonstrativeness. He discovered that she found Sundays at home tedious, so he went down to Herne Hill in the morning, met her at the end of the road, and went to church with her.

"I always like to go to church once," she said. "It looks well, doesn't it?"

Then she went back to dinner, he got a scrappy meal at a hotel, and in the afternoon they took a walk in Brockwell Park. They had nothing much to say to one another, and Philip, desperately afraid she was bored (she was very easily bored), racked his brain for topics of conversation. He realised that these walks amused neither of them, but he could not bear to leave her, and did all he could to lengthen them till she became tired and out of temper. He knew that she did not care for him, and he tried to force a love which his reason told him was not in her nature: she was cold. He had no claim on her, but he could not help being exacting. Now that they were more intimate he found it less easy to control his temper; he was often irritable and could not help saying bitter things. Often they quarrelled, and she would not speak to him for a while; but this always reduced him to subjection, and he crawled before her. He was angry with himself for showing so little dignity. He grew furiously jealous if he saw her speaking to any other man in the shop, and when he was jealous he seemed to be beside himself. He would deliberately insult her, leave the shop and spend afterwards a sleepless night tossing on his bed, by turns angry and remorseful. Next day he would go to the shop and appeal for forgiveness.

"Don't be angry with me," he said. "I'm so awfully fond of you that I can't help myself."

"One of these days you'll go too far," she answered.

He was anxious to come to her home in order that the greater intimacy should give him an advantage over the stray acquaintances she made during her working-hours; but she would not let him.

"My aunt would think it so funny," she said.

He suspected that her refusal was due only to a disinclination to let him see her aunt. Mildred had represented her as the widow of a professional man (that was her formula of distinction), and was uneasily conscious that the good woman could hardly be called distinguished. Philip imagined that she was in point of fact the widow of a small tradesman. He knew that Mildred was a snob. But he found no means by which he could indicate to her that he did not mind how common the aunt was.

Their worst quarrel took place one evening at dinner when she told him that a man had asked her to go to a play with him. Philip turned pale, and his face grew hard and stern.

"You're not going?" he said.

"Why shouldn't I? He's a very nice gentlemanly fellow."

"I'll take you anywhere you like."

"But that isn't the same thing. I can't always go about with you. Besides he's asked me to fix my own day, and I'll just go one evening when I'm not going out with you. It won't make any difference to you."

"If you had any sense of decency, if you had any gratitude, you wouldn't dream of going."

"I don't know what you mean by gratitude. If you're referring to the things you've given me you can have them back. I don't want them."

Her voice had the shrewish tone it sometimes got.

"It's not very lively, always going about with you. It's always do you love me, do you love me, till I just get about sick of it."

(He knew it was madness to go on asking her that, but he could not help himself.

"Oh, I like you all right," she would answer.

"Is that all? I love you with all my heart."

"I'm not that sort, I'm not one to say much."

"If you knew how happy just one word would make me!"

"Well, what I always say is, people must take me as they find me, and if they don't like it they can lump it."

But sometimes she expressed herself more plainly still, and, when he asked the question, answered:

"Oh, don't go on at that again."

Then he became sulky and silent. He hated her.)

And now he said:

"Oh, well, if you feel like that about it I wonder you condescend to come out with me at all."

"It's not my seeking, you can be very sure of that, you just force me to."

His pride was bitterly hurt, and he answered madly.

"You think I'm just good enough to stand you dinners and theatres when there's no one else to do it, and when someone else turns up I can go to hell. Thank you, I'm about sick of being made a convenience."

"I'm not going to be talked to like that by anyone. I'll just show you how much I want your dirty dinner."

She got up, put on her jacket, and walked quickly out of the restaurant. Philip sat on. He determined he would not move, but ten minutes afterwards he jumped in a cab and followed her. He guessed that she would take a 'bus to Victoria, so that they would arrive about the same time. He saw her on the platform, escaped her notice, and went down to Herne Hill in the same train. He did not want to speak to her till she was on the way home and could not escape him.

As soon as she had turned out of the main street, brightly lit and noisy with traffic, he caught her up.

"Mildred," he called.

She walked on and would neither look at him nor answer. He repeated her name. Then she stopped and faced him.

"What d'you want? I saw you hanging about Victoria. Why don't you leave me alone?"

"I'm awfully sorry. Won't you make it up?"

"No, I'm sick of your temper and your jealousy. I don't care for you, I never have cared for you, and I never shall care for you. I don't want to have anything more to do with you."

She walked on quickly, and he had to hurry to keep up with her.

"You never make allowances for me," he said. "It's all very well to be jolly and amiable when you're indifferent to anyone. It's very hard when you're as much in love as I am. Have mercy on me. I don't mind that you don't care for me. After all you can't help it. I only want you to let me love you."

She walked on, refusing to speak, and Philip saw with agony that they had only a few hundred yards to go before they reached her house. He abased himself. He poured out an incoherent story of love and penitence.

"If you'll only forgive me this time I promise you you'll never have to complain of me in future. You can go out with whoever you choose. I'll be only too glad if you'll come with me when you've got nothing better to do."

She stopped again, for they had reached the corner at which he always left her.

"Now you can take yourself off. I won't have you coming up to the door."

"I won't go till you say you'll forgive me."

"I'm sick and tired of the whole thing."

He hesitated a moment, for he had an instinct that he could say something that would move her. It made him feel almost sick to utter the words.

"It is cruel, I have so much to put up with. You don't know what it is to be a cripple. Of course you don't like me. I can't expect you to."

"Philip, I didn't mean that," she answered quickly, with a sudden break of pity in her voice. "You know it's not true."

He was beginning to act now, and his voice was husky and low.

"Oh, I've felt it," he said.

She took his hand and looked at him, and her own eyes were filled with tears.

"I promise you it never made any difference to me. I never thought about it after the first day or two."

He kept a gloomy, tragic silence. He wanted her to think he was overcome with emotion.

"You know I like you awfully, Philip. Only you are so trying sometimes. Let's make it up."

She put up her lips to his, and with a sigh of relief he kissed her.

"Now are you happy again?" she asked.

"Madly."

She bade him good-night and hurried down the road. Next day he took her in a little watch with a brooch to pin on her dress. She had been hankering for it.

But three or four days later, when she brought him his tea, Mildred said to him:

"You remember what you promised the other night? You mean to keep that, don't you?"

"Yes."

He knew exactly what she meant and was prepared for her next words.

"Because I'm going out with that gentleman I told you about tonight."

"All right. I hope you'll enjoy yourself."

"You don't mind, do you?"

He had himself now under excellent control.

"I don't like it," he smiled, "but I'm not going to make myself more disagreeable than I can help."

She was excited over the outing and talked about it willingly. Philip wondered whether she did so in order to pain him or merely because she was callous. He was in the habit of condoning her cruelty by the thought of her stupidity. She had not the brains to see when she was wounding him.

"It's not much fun to be in love with a girl who has no imagination and no sense of humour," he thought, as he listened.

But the want of these things excused her. He felt that if he had not realised this he could never forgive her for the pain she caused him.

"He's got seats for the Tivoli," she said. "He gave me my choice and I chose that. And we're going to dine at the Café Royal. He says it's the most expensive place in London."

"He's a gentleman in every sense of the word," thought Philip, but he clenched his teeth to prevent himself from uttering a syllable.

Philip went to the Tivoli and saw Mildred with her companion, a smooth-faced young man with sleek hair and the spruce look of a commercial traveller, sitting in the second row of the stalls. Mildred wore a black picture hat with ostrich feathers in it, which became her well. She was listening to her host with that quiet smile which Philip knew; she had no vivacity of expression, and it required broad farce to excite her laughter; but Philip could see that she was interested and amused. He thought to himself bitterly that her companion, flashy and jovial, exactly suited her. Her sluggish temperament made her appreciate noisy people. Philip had a passion for discussion, but no talent for small-talk. He admired the easy drollery of which some of his friends were masters, Lawson for instance, and his sense of inferiority made him shy and awkward. The things which interested him bored Mildred. She expected men to talk about football and racing, and he knew nothing of either. He did not know the catchwords which only need be said to excite a laugh.

Printed matter had always been a fetish to Philip, and now, in order to make himself more interesting, he read industriously *The Sporting Times*.

Chapter LXII

PHILIP DID NOT SURRENDER HIMSELF WILLINGLY TO THE PASSION THAT CONsumed him. He knew that all things human are transitory and therefore that it must cease one day or another. He looked forward to that day with eager longing. Love was like a parasite in his heart, nourishing a hateful existence on his life's blood; it absorbed his existence so intensely that he could take pleasure in nothing else. He had been used to delight in the grace of St. James' Park, and often he sat and looked at the branches of a tree silhouetted against the sky, it was like a Japanese print; and he found a continual magic in the beautiful Thames with its barges and its wharfs; the changing sky of London had filled his soul with pleasant fancies. But now beauty meant nothing to him. He was bored and restless when he was not with Mildred. Sometimes he thought he would console his sorrow by looking at pictures, but he walked through the National Gallery like a sight-seer; and no picture called up in him a thrill of emotion. He wondered if he could ever care again for all the things he had loved. He had been devoted to reading, but now books were meaningless; and he spent his spare hours in the smoking-room of the hospital club, turning over innumerable periodicals. This love was a torment, and he resented bitterly the subjugation in which it held him; he was a prisoner and he longed for freedom.

Sometimes he awoke in the morning and felt nothing; his soul leaped, for he thought he was free; he loved no longer; but in a little while, as he grew wide awake, the pain settled in his heart, and he knew that he was not cured yet. Though he yearned for Mildred so madly he despised her. He thought to himself that there could be no greater torture in the world than at the same time to love and to contemn.

Philip, burrowing as was his habit into the state of his feelings, discussing with himself continually his condition, came to the conclusion that he could only cure himself of his degrading passion by making Mildred his mistress. It was sexual hunger that he suffered from, and if he could satisfy this he might free himself from the intolerable chains that bound him. He knew that Mildred did not care for him at all in that way. When he kissed her passionately she withdrew herself from him with instinctive distaste. She had no sensuality. Sometimes he had tried to make her jealous by talking of adventures in Paris, but they did not interest her; once or twice he had sat at other tables in the tea-shop and affected to flirt with the waitress who attended them, but she was entirely indifferent. He could see that it was no pretence on her part.

"You didn't mind my not sitting at one of your tables this afternoon?" he asked once, when he was walking to the station with her. "Yours seemed to be all full."

This was not a fact, but she did not contradict him. Even if his desertion meant nothing to her he would have been grateful if she had pretended it did. A reproach would have been balm to his soul.

"I think it's silly of you to sit at the same table every day. You ought to give the other girls a turn now and again."

But the more he thought of it the more he was convinced that complete surrender on her part was his only way to freedom. He was like a knight of old, metamorphosed by magic spells, who sought the potions which should restore him to his fair and proper form. Philip had only one hope. Mildred greatly desired to go to Paris. To her, as to most English people, it was the centre of gaiety and fashion: she had heard of the Magasin du Louvre, where you could get the very latest thing for about half the price you had to pay in London; a friend of hers had passed her honeymoon in Paris and had spent all day at the Louvre; and she and her husband, my dear, they never went to bed till six in the morning all the time they were there; the Moulin Rouge and I don't know what all. Philip did not care that if she yielded to his desires it would only be the unwilling price she paid for the gratification of her wish. He did not care upon what terms he satisfied his passion. He had even had a mad, melodramatic idea to drug her. He had plied her with liquor in the hope of exciting her, but she had no taste for wine; and though she liked him to order champagne because it looked well, she never drank more than half a glass. She liked to leave untouched a large glass filled to the brim.

"It shows the waiters who you are," she said.

Philip chose an opportunity when she seemed more than usually friendly. He had an examination in anatomy at the end of March. Easter, which came a week later, would give Mildred three whole days holiday.

"I say, why don't you come over to Paris then?" he suggested. "We'd have such a ripping time."

"How could you? It would cost no end of money."

Philip had thought of that. It would cost at least five-and-twenty pounds. It was a large sum to him. He was willing to spend his last penny on her.

"What does that matter? Say you'll come, darling."

"What next, I should like to know. I can't see myself going away with a man that I wasn't married to. You oughtn't to suggest such a thing."

"What does it matter?"

He enlarged on the glories of the Rue de la Paix and the garish splendour of the Folies Bergères. He described the Louvre and the Bon Marché. He told her about the Cabaret du Néant, the Abbaye, and the various haunts to which foreigners go. He painted in glowing colours the side of Paris which he despised. He pressed her to come with him.

"You know, you say you love me, but if you really loved me you'd want to marry me. You've never asked me to marry you."

"You know I can't afford it. After all, I'm in my first year, I shan't earn a penny for six years."

"Oh, I'm not blaming you. I wouldn't marry you if you went down on your bended knees to me."

He had thought of marriage more than once, but it was a step from which he shrank. In Paris he had come by the opinion that marriage was a ridiculous institution of the philistines. He knew also that a permanent tie would ruin him. He had middle-class instincts, and it seemed a dreadful thing to him to marry a waitress. A common wife would prevent him from getting a decent practice. Besides, he had only just enough money to last him till he was qualified; he could not keep a wife even if they arranged not to have children. He thought of Cronshaw bound to a vulgar slattern, and he shuddered with dismay. He foresaw what Mildred, with her genteel ideas and her mean mind, would become: it was impossible for him to marry her. But he decided only with his reason; he felt that he must have her whatever happened; and if he could not get her without marrying her he would do that; the future could look after itself. It might end in disaster; he did not care. When he got hold of an idea it obsessed him, he could think of nothing else, and he had a more than common power to persuade himself of the reasonableness of what he wished to do. He found himself overthrowing all the sensible arguments which had occurred to him against marriage. Each day he found that he was more passionately devoted to her; and his unsatisfied love became angry and resentful.

"By George, if I marry her I'll make her pay for all the suffering I've endured," he said to himself.

At last he could bear the agony no longer. After dinner one evening in the little restaurant in Soho, to which now they often went, he spoke to her.

"I say, did you mean it the other day that you wouldn't marry me if I asked you?"

"Yes, why not?"

"Because I can't live without you. I want you with me always. I've tried to get over it and I can't. I never shall now. I want you to marry me."

She had read too many novelettes not to know how to take such an offer.

"I'm sure I'm very grateful to you, Philip. I'm very much flattered at your proposal."

"Oh, don't talk rot. You will marry me, won't you?"

"D'you think we should be happy?"

"No. But what does that matter?"

The words were wrung out of him almost against his will. They surprised her.

"Well, you are a funny chap. Why d'you want to marry me then? The other day you said you couldn't afford it."

"I think I've got about fourteen hundred pounds left. Two can live just as cheaply as one. That'll keep us till I'm qualified and have got through with my hospital appointments, and then I can get an assistantship."

"It means you wouldn't be able to earn anything for six years. We should have about four pounds a week to live on till then, shouldn't we?"

"Not much more than three. There are all my fees to pay."

"And what would you get as an assistant?"

"Three pounds a week."

"D'you mean to say you have to work all that time and spend a small fortune just to earn three pounds a week at the end of it? I don't see that I should be any better off than I am now."

He was silent for a moment.

"D'you mean to say you won't marry me?" he asked hoarsely. "Does my great love mean nothing to you at all?"

"One has to think of oneself in those things, don't one? I shouldn't mind marrying, but I don't want to marry if I'm going to be no better off than what I am now. I don't see the use of it."

"If you cared for me you wouldn't think of all that."

"P'raps not."

He was silent. He drank a glass of wine in order to get rid of the choking in his throat.

"Look at that girl who's just going out," said Mildred. "She got them furs at the Bon Marché at Brixton. I saw them in the window last time I went down there."

Philip smiled grimly.

"What are you laughing at?" she asked. "It's true. And I said to my aunt at the time, I wouldn't buy anything that had been in the window like that, for everyone to know how much you paid for it."

"I can't understand you. You make me frightfully unhappy, and in the next breath you talk rot that has nothing to do with what we're speaking about."

"You are nasty to me," she answered, aggrieved. "I can't help noticing those furs, because I said to my aunt . . ."

"I don't care a damn what you said to your aunt," he interrupted impatiently.

"I wish you wouldn't use bad language when you speak to me Philip. You know I don't like it."

Philip smiled a little, but his eyes were wild. He was silent for a while. He looked at her sullenly. He hated, despised, and loved her.

"If I had an ounce of sense I'd never see you again," he said at last. "If you only knew how heartily I despise myself for loving you!"

"That's not a very nice thing to say to me," she replied sulkily.

"It isn't," he laughed. "Let's go to the Pavilion."

"That's what's so funny in you, you start laughing just when one doesn't expect you to. And if I make you that unhappy why d'you want to take me to the Pavilion? I'm quite ready to go home."

"Merely because I'm less unhappy with you than away from you."

"I should like to know what you really think of me."

He laughed outright.

"My dear, if you did you'd never speak to me again."

Chapter LXIII

PHILIP DID NOT PASS THE EXAMINATION IN ANATOMY AT THE END OF MARCH. He and Dunsford had worked at the subject together on Philip's skeleton, asking each other questions till both knew by heart every attachment and the meaning of every nodule and groove on the human bones; but in the examination room Philip was seized with panic, and failed to give right answers to questions from a sudden fear that they might be wrong. He knew he was ploughed and did not even trouble to go up to the building next day to see whether his number was up. The second failure put him definitely among the incompetent and idle men of his year.

He did not care much. He had other things to think of. He told himself that Mildred must have senses like anybody else, it was only a question of awakening them; he had theories about woman, the rip at heart, and thought that there must come a time with everyone when she would yield to persistence. It was a question of watching for the opportunity, keeping his temper, wearing her down with small attentions, taking advantage of the physical exhaustion which opened the heart to tenderness, making himself a refuge from the petty vexations of her work. He talked to her of the relations between his friends in Paris and the fair ladies they admired. The life he described had a charm, an easy gaiety, in which was no grossness. Weaving into his own recollections the adventures of Mimi and Rodolphe, of Musette and the rest of them, he poured into Mildred's ears a story of poverty made picturesque by song and laughter, of lawless love made romantic by beauty and youth. He never attacked her prejudices directly, but sought to combat them by the suggestion that they were suburban. He never let himself be disturbed by her inattention, nor irritated by her indifference. He thought he had bored her. By an effort he made himself affable and entertaining; he never let himself be angry, he never asked for anything, he never complained, he never scolded. When she made engagements and broke them, he met her next day with a smiling face; when she excused herself, he said it did not matter. He never let her see that she pained him. He understood that his passionate grief had wearied her, and he took care to hide every sentiment which could be in the least degree troublesome. He was heroic.

Though she never mentioned the change, for she did not take any conscious notice of it, it affected her nevertheless: she became more confidential with him; she took her little grievances to him, and she always had some grievance against the manageress of the shop, one of her fellow-waitresses, or her aunt; she was talkative enough now, and though she never said anything that was not trivial Philip was never tired of listening to her.

"I like you when you don't want to make love to me," she told him once.

"That's flattering for me," he laughed.

She did not realise how her words made his heart sink nor what an effort it needed for him to answer so lightly.

"Oh, I don't mind your kissing me now and then. It doesn't hurt me and it gives you pleasure."

Occasionally she went so far as to ask him to take her out to dinner, and the offer, coming from her, filled him with rapture.

"I wouldn't do it to anyone else," she said, by way of apology. "But I know I can with you."

"You couldn't give me greater pleasure," he smiled.

She asked him to give her something to eat one evening towards the end of April.

"All right," he said. "Where would you like to go afterwards?"

"Oh, don't let's go anywhere. Let's just sit and talk. You don't mind, do you?"

"Rather not."

He thought she must be beginning to care for him. Three months before the thought of an evening spent in conversation would have bored her to death. It was a fine day, and the spring added to Philip's high spirits. He was content with very little now.

"I say, won't it be ripping when the summer comes along," he said, as they drove along on the top of a 'bus to Soho—she had herself suggested that they should not be so extravagant as to go by cab. "We shall be able to spend every Sunday on the River. We'll take our luncheon in a basket."

She smiled slightly, and he was encouraged to take her hand. She did not withdraw it.

"I really think you're beginning to like me a bit," he smiled.

"You *are* silly, you know I like you, or else I shouldn't be here, should I?"

They were old customers at the little restaurant in Soho by now, and the *patronne* gave them a smile as they came in. The waiter was obsequious.

"Let me order the dinner tonight," said Mildred.

Philip, thinking her more enchanting than ever, gave her the menu, and she chose her favourite dishes. The range was small, and they had eaten many times all that the restaurant could provide. Philip was gay. He looked into her eyes, and he dwelled on every perfection of her pale cheek. When they had finished Mildred by way of exception took a cigarette. She smoked very seldom.

"I don't like to see a lady smoking," she said.

She hesitated a moment and then spoke.

"Were you surprised, my asking you to take me out and give me a bit of dinner tonight?"

"I was delighted."

"I've got something to say to you, Philip."

He looked at her quickly, his heart sank, but he had trained himself well.

"Well, fire away," he said, smiling.

"You're not going to be silly about it, are you? The fact is I'm going to get married."

"Are you?" said Philip.

He could think of nothing else to say. He had considered the possibility often and had imagined to himself what he would do and say. He had suffered agonies when he thought of the despair he would suffer, he had thought of suicide, of the mad passion of anger that would seize him; but perhaps he had too completely anticipated the emotion he would experience, so that now he felt merely exhausted. He felt as one does in a serious illness when the vitality is so low that one is indifferent to the issue and wants only to be left alone.

"You see, I'm getting on," she said. "I'm twenty-four and it's time I settled down."

He was silent. He looked at the *patronne* sitting behind the counter, and his eye dwelled on a red feather one of the diners wore in her hat. Mildred was nettled.

"You might congratulate me," she said.

"I might, mightn't I? I can hardly believe it's true. I've dreamt it so often. It rather tickles me that I should have been so jolly glad that you asked me to take you out to dinner. Whom are you going to marry?"

"Miller," she answered, with a slight blush.

"Miller?" cried Philip, astounded. "But you've not seen him for months."

"He came in to lunch one day last week and asked me then. He's earning very good money. He makes seven pounds a week now and he's got prospects."

Philip was silent again. He remembered that she had always liked Miller; he amused her; there was in his foreign birth an exotic charm which she felt unconsciously.

"I suppose it was inevitable," he said at last. "You were bound to accept the highest bidder. When are you going to marry?"

"On Saturday next. I have given notice."

Philip felt a sudden pang.

"As soon as that?"

"We're going to be married at a registry office. Emil prefers it."

Philip felt dreadfully tired. He wanted to get away from her. He thought he would go straight to bed. He called for the bill.

"I'll put you in a cab and send you down to Victoria. I daresay you won't have to wait long for a train."

"Won't you come with me?"

"I think I'd rather not if you don't mind."

"It's just as you please," she answered haughtily. "I suppose I shall see you at tea-time tomorrow?"

"No, I think we'd better make a full stop now. I don't see why I should go on making myself unhappy. I've paid the cab."

He nodded to her and forced a smile on his lips, then jumped on a 'bus and made his way home. He smoked a pipe before he went to bed, but he could hardly keep his eyes open. He suffered no pain. He fell into a heavy sleep almost as soon as his head touched the pillow.

Chapter LXIV

But about three in the morning Philip awoke and could not sleep again. He began to think of Mildred. He tried not to, but could not help himself. He repeated to himself the same thing time after time till his brain reeled. It was inevitable that she should marry: life was hard for a girl who had to earn her own living; and if she found someone who could give her a comfortable home she should not be blamed if she accepted. Philip acknowledged that from her point of view it would have been madness to marry him: only love could have made such poverty bearable, and she did not love him. It was no fault of hers; it was a fact that must be accepted like any other. Philip tried to reason with himself. He told himself that deep down in his heart was mortified pride; his passion had begun in wounded vanity, and it was this at bottom which caused now a great part of his wretchedness. He despised himself as much as he despised her. Then he made plans for the future, the same plans over and over again, interrupted by recollections of kisses on her soft pale cheek and by the sound of her voice with its trailing accent; he had a great deal of work to do, since in the summer he was taking Chemistry as well as the two examinations he had failed in. He had separated himself from his friends at the hospital, but now he wanted companionship. There was one happy occurrence: Hayward a fortnight before had written to say that he was passing through London and had asked him to dinner; but Philip, unwilling to be bothered, had refused. He was coming back for the season, and Philip made up his mind to write to him.

He was thankful when eight o'clock struck and he could get up. He was pale and weary. But when he had bathed, dressed, and had breakfast, he felt himself joined up again with the world at large; and his pain was a little easier to bear. He did not feel like going to lectures that morning, but went instead to the Army and Navy Stores to buy Mildred a wedding-present. After much wavering he settled on a dressing-bag. It cost twenty pounds, which was much more than he could afford, but it was showy and vulgar: he knew she would be aware exactly how much it cost; he got a melancholy satisfaction in choosing a gift which would give her pleasure and at the same time indicate for himself the contempt he had for her.

Philip had looked forward with apprehension to the day on which Mildred was to be married; he was expecting an intolerable anguish; and it was with relief that he got a letter from Hayward on Saturday morning to say that he was coming up early on that very day and would fetch Philip to help him to find rooms. Philip, anxious to be distracted, looked up a time-table and discovered the only train Hayward was likely to come by; he went to meet him, and the reunion of the friends was enthusiastic. They left the luggage at the station, and set off gaily. Hayward characteristically proposed that first of all they should go for an hour to the National Gallery; he had not seen pictures for some time, and he stated that it needed a glimpse to set him in tune with life. Philip for months had had no one with whom he could talk of art and books. Since the Paris days Hayward had immersed himself in the modern French versifiers, and, such a plethora of poets is there in France, he had several new geniuses to tell Philip about. They walked through the gallery pointing out to one another their favourite pictures; one subject led to another; they talked excitedly. The sun was shining and the air was warm.

"Let's go and sit in the Park," said Hayward. "We'll look for rooms after luncheon."

The spring was pleasant there. It was a day upon which one felt it good merely to live. The young green of the trees was exquisite against the sky; and the sky, pale and blue, was dappled with little white clouds. At the end of the ornamental water was the grey mass of the Horse Guards. The ordered elegance of the scene had the charm of an eighteenth-century picture. It reminded you not of Watteau, whose landscapes are so idyllic that they recall only the woodland glens seen in dreams, but of the more prosaic Jean-Baptiste Pater. Philip's heart was filled with lightness. He realised, what he had only read before, that art (for there was art in the manner in which he looked upon nature) might liberate the soul from pain.

They went to an Italian restaurant for luncheon and ordered themselves a *fiaschetto* of Chianti. Lingering over the meal they talked on. They reminded one another of the people they had known at Heidelberg, they spoke of Philip's friends in Paris, they talked of books, pictures, morals, life; and suddenly Philip heard a clock strike three. He remembered that by this time Mildred was married. He felt a sort of stitch in his heart, and for a minute or two he could not hear what Hayward was saying. But he filled his glass with Chianti. He was unaccustomed to alcohol and it had gone to his head. For the time at all events he was free from care. His quick brain had lain idle for so many months that he was intoxicated now with conversation. He was thankful to have someone to talk to who would interest himself in the things that interested him.

"I say don't let's waste this beautiful day in looking for rooms. I'll put you up tonight. You can look for rooms tomorrow or Monday."

"All right. What shall we do?" answered Hayward.

"Let's get on a penny steamboat and go down to Greenwich."

The idea appealed to Hayward, and they jumped into a cab which took them to Westminster Bridge. They got on the steamboat just as she was starting. Presently Philip, a smile on his lips, spoke.

"I remember when first I went to Paris, Clutton, I think it was, gave a long discourse on the subject that beauty is put into things by painters and poets. They create beauty. In themselves there is nothing to choose between the Campanile of Giotto and a factory chimney. And then beautiful things grow rich with the emotion that they have aroused in succeeding generations. That is why old things are more beautiful than modern. The *Ode on a Grecian Urn* is more lovely now than when it was written, because for a hundred years lovers have read it and the sick at heart taken comfort in its lines."

Philip left Hayward to infer what in the passing scene had suggested these words to him, and it was a delight to know that he could safely leave the inference. It was in sudden reaction from the life he had been leading for so long that he was now deeply affected. The delicate iridescence of the London air gave the softness of a pastel to the grey stone of the buildings; and in the wharves and storehouses there was the severity of grace of a Japanese print. They went further down; and the splendid channel, a symbol of the great empire, broadened, and it was crowded with traffic; Philip thought of the painters and the poets who had made all these things so beautiful, and his heart was filled with gratitude. They came to the Pool of London, and who can describe its majesty? The imagination thrills, and Heaven knows what figures people still its broad stream, Doctor Johnson with Boswell by his side, an old Pepys going on board a man-o'-war: the pageant of English history, and romance, and high adventure. Philip turned to Hayward with shining eyes.

"Dear Charles Dickens," he murmured, smiling a little at his own emotion.

"Aren't you rather sorry you chucked painting?" asked Hayward.

"No."

"I suppose you like doctoring?"

"No, I hate it, but there was nothing else to do. The drudgery of the first two years is awful, and unfortunately I haven't got the scientific temperament."

"Well, you can't go on changing professions."

"Oh, no. I'm going to stick to this. I think I shall like it better when I get into the wards. I have an idea that I'm more interested in people than in anything else in the world. And as far as I can see, it's the only profession in which you have your freedom. You carry your knowledge in your head; with a box of instruments and a few drugs you can make your living anywhere."

"Aren't you going to take a practice then?"

"Not for a good long time at any rate," Philip answered. "As soon as I've got through my hospital appointments I shall get a ship; I want to go to the East—the Malay Archipelago, Siam, China, and all that sort of thing—and then I shall take odd jobs. Something always comes along, cholera duty in India and things like that.

I want to go from place to place. I want to see the world. The only way a poor man can do that is by going in for the medical."

They came to Greenwich then. The noble building of Inigo Jones faced the river grandly.

"I say, look, that must be the place where Poor Jack dived into the mud for pennies," said Philip.

They wandered in the park. Ragged children were playing in it, and it was noisy with their cries: here and there old seamen were basking in the sun. There was an air of a hundred years ago.

"It seems a pity you wasted two years in Paris," said Hayward.

"Waste? Look at the movement of that child, look at the pattern which the sun makes on the ground, shining through the trees, look at that sky—why, I should never have seen that sky if I hadn't been to Paris."

Hayward thought that Philip choked a sob, and he looked at him with astonishment.

"What's the matter with you?"

"Nothing. I'm sorry to be so damned emotional, but for six months I've been starved for beauty."

"You used to be so matter of fact. It's very interesting to hear you say that."

"Damn it all, I don't want to be interesting," laughed Philip. "Let's go and have a stodgy tea."

Chapter LXV

Hayward's visit did Philip a great deal of good. Each day his thoughts dwelled less on Mildred. He looked back upon the past with disgust. He could not understand how he had submitted to the dishonour of such a love; and when he thought of Mildred it was with angry hatred, because she had submitted him to so much humiliation. His imagination presented her to him now with her defects of person and manner exaggerated, so that he shuddered at the thought of having been connected with her.

"It just shows how damned weak I am," he said to himself. The adventure was like a blunder that one had committed at a party so horrible that one felt nothing could be done to excuse it: the only remedy was to forget. His horror at the degradation he had suffered helped him. He was like a snake casting its skin and he looked upon the old covering with nausea. He exulted in the possession of himself once more; he realised how much of the delight of the world he had lost when he was absorbed in that madness which they called love; he had had enough of it; he did not want to be in love any more if love was that. Philip told Hayward something of what he had gone through.

"Wasn't it Sophocles," he asked, "who prayed for the time when he would be delivered from the wild beast of passion that devoured his heart-strings?"

Philip seemed really to be born again. He breathed the circumambient air as though he had never breathed it before, and he took a child's pleasure in all the facts of the world. He called his period of insanity six months' hard labour.

Hayward had only been settled in London a few days when Philip received from Blackstable, where it had been sent, a card for a private view at some picture gallery. He took Hayward, and, on looking at the catalogue, saw that Lawson had a picture in it.

"I suppose he sent the card," said Philip. "Let's go and find him, he's sure to be in front of his picture."

This, a profile of Ruth Chalice, was tucked away in a corner, and Lawson was not far from it. He looked a little lost, in his large soft hat and loose, pale clothes, amongst the fashionable throng that had gathered for the private view. He greeted Philip with enthusiasm, and with his usual volubility told him that he had come to live in London, Ruth Chalice was a hussy, he had taken a studio, Paris was played out, he had a commission for a portrait, and they'd better dine together and have a good old talk. Philip reminded him of his acquaintance with Hayward, and was entertained to see that Lawson was slightly awed by Hayward's elegant clothes and grand manner. They sat upon him better than they had done in the shabby little studio which Lawson and Philip had shared.

At dinner Lawson went on with his news. Flanagan had gone back to America. Clutton had disappeared. He had come to the conclusion that a man had no chance of doing anything so long as he was in contact with art and artists: the only thing was to get right away. To make the step easier he had quarrelled with all his friends in Paris. He developed a talent for telling them home truths, which made them bear with fortitude his declaration that he had done with that city and was settling in Gerona, a little town in the north of Spain which had attracted him when he saw it from the train on his way to Barcelona. He was living there now alone.

"I wonder if he'll ever do any good," said Philip.

He was interested in the human side of that struggle to express something which was so obscure in the man's mind that he was become morbid and querulous. Philip felt vaguely that he was himself in the same case, but with him it was the conduct of his life as a whole that perplexed him. That was his means of self-expression, and what he must do with it was not clear. But he had no time to continue with this train of thought, for Lawson poured out a frank recital of his affair with Ruth Chalice. She had left him for a young student who had just come from England, and was behaving in a scandalous fashion. Lawson really thought someone ought to step in and save the young man. She would ruin him. Philip gathered that Lawson's chief grievance was that the rupture had come in the middle of a portrait he was painting.

"Women have no real feeling for art," he said. "They only pretend they have." But he finished philosophically enough: "However, I got four portraits out of her, and I'm not sure if the last I was working on would ever have been a success."

Philip envied the easy way in which the painter managed his love affairs. He had passed eighteen months pleasantly enough, had got an excellent model for nothing, and had parted from her at the end with no great pang.

"And what about Cronshaw?" asked Philip.

"Oh, he's done for," answered Lawson, with the cheerful callousness of his youth. "He'll be dead in six months. He got pneumonia last winter. He was in the English hospital for seven weeks, and when he came out they told him his only chance was to give up liquor."

"Poor devil," smiled the abstemious Philip.

"He kept off for a bit. He used to go to the Lilas all the same, he couldn't keep away from that, but he used to drink hot milk, *avec de la fleur d'oranger,* and he was damned dull."

"I take it you did not conceal the fact from him."

"Oh, he knew it himself. A little while ago he started on whiskey again. He said he was too old to turn over any new leaves. He would rather be happy for six months and die at the end of it than linger on for five years. And then I think he's been awfully hard up lately. You see, he didn't earn anything while he was ill, and the slut he lives with has been giving him a rotten time."

"I remember, the first time I saw him I admired him awfully," said Philip. "I thought he was wonderful. It is sickening that vulgar, middle-class virtue should pay."

"Of course he was a rotter. He was bound to end in the gutter sooner or later," said Lawson.

Philip was hurt because Lawson would not see the pity of it. Of course it was cause and effect, but in the necessity with which one follows the other lay all tragedy of life.

"Oh, I'd forgotten," said Lawson. "Just after you left he sent round a present for you. I thought you'd be coming back and I didn't bother about it, and then I didn't think it worth sending on; but it'll come over to London with the rest of my things, and you can come to my studio one day and fetch it away if you want it."

"You haven't told me what it is yet."

"Oh, it's only a ragged little bit of carpet. I shouldn't think it's worth anything. I asked him one day what the devil he'd sent the filthy thing for. He told me he'd seen it in a shop in the Rue de Rennes and bought it for fifteen francs. It appears to be a Persian rug. He said you'd asked him the meaning of life and that was the answer. But he was very drunk."

Philip laughed.

"Oh yes, I know. I'll take it. It was a favourite wheeze of his. He said I must find out for myself, or else the answer meant nothing."

Chapter LXVI

PHILIP WORKED WELL AND EASILY; HE HAD A GOOD DEAL TO DO, SINCE HE was taking in July the three parts of the First Conjoint examination, two of which he had failed in before; but he found life pleasant. He made a new friend. Lawson, on the lookout for models, had discovered a girl who was understudying at one of the theatres, and in order to induce her to sit to him arranged a little luncheon-party one Sunday. She brought a chaperon with her; and to her Philip, asked to make a fourth, was instructed to confine his attentions. He found this easy, since she turned out to be an agreeable chatterbox with an amusing tongue. She asked Philip to go and see her; she had rooms in Vincent Square, and was always in to tea at five o'clock; he went, was delighted with his welcome, and went again. Mrs. Nesbit was not more than twenty-five, very small, with a pleasant, ugly face; she had very bright eyes, high cheek-bones, and a large mouth: the excessive contrasts of her colouring reminded one of a portrait by one of the modern French painters; her skin was very white, her cheeks were very red, her thick eyebrows, her hair, were very black. The effect was odd, a little unnatural, but far from unpleasing. She was separated from her husband and earned her living and her child's by writing penny novelettes. There were one or two publishers who made a specialty of that sort of thing, and she had as much work as she could do. It was ill-paid, she received fifteen pounds for a story of thirty thousand words; but she was satisfied.

"After all, it only costs the reader twopence," she said, "and they like the same thing over and over again. I just change the names and that's all. When I'm bored I think of the washing and the rent and clothes for baby, and I go on again."

Besides, she walked on at various theatres where they wanted supers and earned by this when in work from sixteen shillings to a guinea a week. At the end of her day she was so tired that she slept like a top. She made the best of her difficult lot. Her keen sense of humour enabled her to get amusement out of every vexatious circumstance. Sometimes things went wrong, and she found herself with no money at all; then her trifling possessions found their way to a pawnshop in the Vauxhall Bridge Road, and she ate bread and butter till things grew brighter. She never lost her cheerfulness.

Philip was interested in her shiftless life, and she made him laugh with the fantastic narration of her struggles. He asked her why she did not try her hand at literary work of a better sort, but she knew that she had no talent, and the abominable stuff she turned out by the thousand words was not only tolerably paid, but was the best she could do. She had nothing to look forward to but a continuation of the life she led. She seemed to have no relations, and her friends were as poor as herself.

"I don't think of the future," she said. "As long as I have enough money for three weeks' rent and a pound or two over for food I never bother. Life wouldn't be worth living if I worried over the future as well as the present. When things are at their worst I find something always happens."

Soon Philip grew in the habit of going in to tea with her every day, and so that his visits might not embarrass her he took in a cake or a pound of butter or some tea. They started to call one another by their Christian names. Feminine sympathy was new to him, and he delighted in someone who gave a willing ear to all his troubles. The hours went quickly. He did not hide his admiration for her. She was a delightful companion. He could not help comparing her with Mildred; and he contrasted with the one's obstinate stupidity, which refused interest to everything she did not know, the other's quick appreciation and ready intelligence. His heart sank when he thought that he might have been tied for life to such a woman as Mildred. One evening he told Norah the whole story of his love. It was not one to give him much reason for self-esteem, and it was very pleasant to receive such charming sympathy.

"I think you're well out of it," she said, when he had finished.

She had a funny way at times of holding her head on one side like an Aberdeen puppy. She was sitting in an upright chair, sewing, for she had no time to do nothing, and Philip had made himself comfortable at her feet.

"I can't tell you how heartily thankful I am it's all over," he sighed.

"Poor thing, you must have had a rotten time," she murmured, and by way of showing her sympathy put her hand on his shoulder.

He took it and kissed it, but she withdrew it quickly.

"Why did you do that?" she asked, with a blush.

"Have you any objection?"

She looked at him for a moment with twinkling eyes, and she smiled.

"No," she said.

He got up on his knees and faced her. She looked into his eyes steadily, and her large mouth trembled with a smile.

"Well?" she said.

"You know, you are a ripper. I'm so grateful to you for being nice to me. I like you so much."

"Don't be idiotic," she said.

Philip took hold of her elbows and drew her towards him. She made no resistance, but bent forward a little, and he kissed her red lips.

"Why did you do that?" she asked again.

"Because it's comfortable."

She did not answer, but a tender look came into her eyes, and she passed her hand softly over his hair.

"You know, it's awfully silly of you to behave like this. We were such good friends. It would be so jolly to leave it at that."

"If you really want to appeal to my better nature," replied Philip, "you'll do well not to stroke my cheek while you're doing it."

She gave a little chuckle, but she did not stop.

"It's very wrong of me, isn't it?" she said.

Philip, surprised and a little amused, looked into her eyes, and as he looked he saw them soften and grow liquid, and there was an expression in them that enchanted him. His heart was suddenly stirred, and tears came to his eyes.

"Norah, you're not fond of me, are you?" he asked, incredulously.

"You clever boy, you ask such stupid questions."

"Oh, my dear, it never struck me that you could be."

He flung his arms round her and kissed her, while she, laughing, blushing, and crying, surrendered herself willingly to his embrace.

Presently he released her and sitting back on his heels looked at her curiously.

"Well, I'm blowed!" he said.

"Why?"

"I'm so surprised."

"And pleased?"

"Delighted," he cried with all his heart, "and so proud and so happy and so grateful."

He took her hands and covered them with kisses. This was the beginning for Philip of a happiness which seemed both solid and durable. They became lovers but remained friends. There was in Norah a maternal instinct which received satisfaction in her love for Philip; she wanted someone to pet, and scold, and make a fuss of; she had a domestic temperament and found pleasure in looking after his health and his linen. She pitied his deformity, over which he was so sensitive, and her pity expressed itself instinctively in tenderness. She was young, strong, and healthy, and it seemed quite natural to her to give her love. She had high spirits and a merry soul. She liked Philip because he laughed with her at all the amusing things in life that caught her fancy, and above all she liked him because he was he.

When she told him this he answered gaily:

"Nonsense. You like me because I'm a silent person and never want to get a word in."

Philip did not love her at all. He was extremely fond of her, glad to be with her, amused and interested by her conversation. She restored his belief in himself and put healing ointments, as it were, on all the bruises of his soul. He was immensely flattered that she cared for him. He admired her courage, her optimism, her impudent defiance of fate; she had a little philosophy of her own, ingenuous and practical.

"You know, I don't believe in churches and parsons and all that," she said, "but I believe in God, and I don't believe He minds much about what you do as long as you keep your end up and help a lame dog over a stile when you can. And I think people on the whole are very nice, and I'm sorry for those who aren't."

"And what about afterwards?" asked Philip.

"Oh, well, I don't know for certain, you know," she smiled, "but I hope for the best. And anyhow there'll be no rent to pay and no novelettes to write."

She had a feminine gift for delicate flattery. She thought that Philip did a brave thing when he left Paris because he was conscious he could not be a great artist; and he was enchanted when she expressed enthusiastic admiration for him. He had never been quite certain whether this action indicated courage or infirmity of purpose. It was delightful to realise that she considered it heroic. She ventured to tackle him on a subject which his friends instinctively avoided.

"It's very silly of you to be so sensitive about your club-foot," she said. She saw him flush darkly, but went on. "You know, people don't think about it nearly as much as you do. They notice it the first time they see you, and then they forget about it."

He would not answer.

"You're not angry with me, are you?"

"No."

She put her arm round his neck.

"You know, I only speak about it because I love you. I don't want it to make you unhappy."

"I think you can say anything you choose to me," he answered, smiling. "I wish I could do something to show you how grateful I am to you."

She took him in hand in other ways. She would not let him be bearish and laughed at him when he was out of temper. She made him more urbane.

"You can make me do anything you like," he said to her once.

"D'you mind?"

"No, I want to do what you like."

He had the sense to realise his happiness. It seemed to him that she gave him all that a wife could, and he preserved his freedom; she was the most charming friend he had ever had, with a sympathy that he had never found in a man. The sexual relationship was no more than the strongest link in their friendship. It completed it, but was not essential. And because Philip's appetites were satisfied, he became more equable and easier to live with. He felt in complete possession of himself. He thought sometimes of the winter, during which he had been obsessed by a hideous passion, and he was filled with loathing for Mildred and with horror of himself.

His examinations were approaching, and Norah was as interested in them as he. He was flattered and touched by her eagerness. She made him promise to come at once and tell her the results. He passed the three parts this time without mishap, and when he went to tell her she burst into tears.

"Oh, I'm so glad, I was so anxious."

"You silly little thing," he laughed, but he was choking.

No one could help being pleased with the way she took it.

"And what are you going to do now?" she asked.

"I can take a holiday with a clear conscience. I have no work to do till the winter session begins in October."

"I suppose you'll go down to your uncle's at Blackstable?"

"You suppose quite wrong. I'm going to stay in London and play with you."

"I'd rather you went away."

"Why? Are you tired of me?"

She laughed and put her hands on his shoulders.

"Because you've been working hard, and you look utterly washed out. You want some fresh air and a rest. Please go."

He did not answer for a moment. He looked at her with loving eyes.

"You know, I'd never believe it of anyone but you. You're only thinking of my good. I wonder what you see in me."

"Will you give me a good character with my month's notice?" she laughed gaily.

"I'll say that you're thoughtful and kind, and you're not exacting; you never worry, you're not troublesome, and you're easy to please."

"All that's nonsense," she said, "but I'll tell you one thing: I'm one of the few persons I ever met who are able to learn from experience."

Chapter LXVII

PHILIP LOOKED FORWARD TO HIS RETURN TO LONDON WITH IMPATIENCE. During the two months he spent at Blackstable Norah wrote to him frequently, long letters in a bold, large hand, in which with cheerful humour she described the little events of the daily round, the domestic troubles of her landlady, rich food for laughter, the comic vexations of her rehearsals—she was walking on in an important spectacle at one of the London theatres—and her odd adventures with the publishers of novelettes. Philip read a great deal, bathed, played tennis, and sailed. At the beginning of October he settled down in London to work for the Second Conjoint examination. He was eager to pass it, since that ended the drudgery of the curriculum; after it was done with the student became an out-patients' clerk, and was brought in contact with men and women as well as with text-books. Philip saw Norah every day.

Lawson had been spending the summer at Poole, and had a number of sketches to show of the harbour and of the beach. He had a couple of commissions for portraits and proposed to stay in London till the bad light drove him away. Hayward, in London too, intended to spend the winter abroad, but remained week after week from sheer inability to make up his mind to go. Hayward had run to fat during the last two or three years—it was five years since Philip first met him in Heidelberg—and he was prematurely bald. He was very sensitive about it and wore his hair long to conceal the unsightly patch on the crown of his head. His only consolation was that his brow was now very noble. His blue eyes had lost their colour; they had a listless droop; and his mouth, losing the fulness of youth, was weak and pale. He still talked vaguely of the things he was going to do in the future, but with less conviction; and he was conscious that his friends no longer believed in him: when he had drank two or three glasses of whiskey he was inclined to be elegiac.

"I'm a failure," he murmured, "I'm unfit for the brutality of the struggle of life. All I can do is to stand aside and let the vulgar throng hustle by in their pursuit of the good things."

He gave you the impression that to fail was a more delicate, a more exquisite thing, than to succeed. He insinuated that his aloofness was due to distaste for all that was common and low. He talked beautifully of Plato.

"I should have thought you'd got through with Plato by now," said Philip impatiently.

"Would you?" he asked, raising his eyebrows.

He was not inclined to pursue the subject. He had discovered of late the effective dignity of silence.

"I don't see the use of reading the same thing over and over again," said Philip. "That's only a laborious form of idleness."

"But are you under the impression that you have so great a mind that you can understand the most profound writer at a first reading?"

"I don't want to understand him, I'm not a critic. I'm not interested in him for his sake but for mine."

"Why d'you read then?"

"Partly for pleasure, because it's a habit and I'm just as uncomfortable if I don't read as if I don't smoke, and partly to know myself. When I read a book I seem to read it with my eyes only, but now and then I come across a passage, perhaps only a phrase, which has a meaning for *me*, and it becomes part of me; I've got out of the book all that's any use to me, and I can't get anything more if I read it a dozen times. You see, it seems to me, one's like a closed bud, and most of what one reads and does has no effect at all; but there are certain things that have a peculiar significance for one, and they open a petal; and the petals open one by one; and at last the flower is there."

Philip was not satisfied with his metaphor, but he did not know how else to explain a thing which he felt and yet was not clear about.

"You want to do things, you want to become things," said Hayward, with a shrug of the shoulders. "It's so vulgar."

Philip knew Hayward very well by now. He was weak and vain, so vain that you had to be on the watch constantly not to hurt his feelings; he mingled idleness and idealism so that he could not separate them. At Lawson's studio one day he met a journalist, who was charmed by his conversation, and a week later the editor of a paper wrote to suggest that he should do some criticism for him. For forty-eight hours Hayward lived in an agony of indecision. He had talked of getting occupation of this sort so long that he had not the face to refuse outright, but the thought of doing anything filled him with panic. At last he declined the offer and breathed freely.

"It would have interfered with my work," he told Philip.

"What work?" asked Philip brutally.

"My inner life," he answered.

Then he went on to say beautiful things about Amiel, the professor of Geneva, whose brilliancy promised achievement which was never fulfilled; till at his death the reason of his failure and the excuse were at once manifest in the minute, wonderful journal which was found among his papers. Hayward smiled enigmatically.

But Hayward could still talk delightfully about books; his taste was exquisite and his discrimination elegant; and he had a constant interest in ideas, which made him an entertaining companion. They meant nothing to him really, since they never had any effect on him; but he treated them as he might have pieces of china in an auction-room, handling them with pleasure in their shape and their glaze, pricing them in his mind; and then, putting them back into their case, thought of them no more.

And it was Hayward who made a momentous discovery. One evening, after due preparation, he took Philip and Lawson to a tavern situated in Beak Street, remarkable not only in itself and for its history—it had memories of eighteenth-century glories which excited the romantic imagination—but for its snuff, which was the best in London, and above all for its punch. Hayward led them into a large, long room, dingily magnificent, with huge pictures on the walls of nude women: they were vast allegories of the school of Haydon; but smoke, gas, and the London atmosphere had given them a richness which made them look like old masters. The dark panelling, the massive, tarnished gold of the cornice, the mahogany tables, gave the room an air of sumptuous comfort, and the leather-covered seats along the wall were soft and easy. There was a ram's head on a table opposite the door, and this contained the celebrated snuff. They ordered punch. They drank it. It was hot rum punch. The pen falters when it attempts to treat of the excellence thereof; the sober vocabulary, the sparse epithet of this narrative, are inadequate to the task; and pompous terms, jewelled, exotic phrases rise to the excited fancy. It warmed the blood and cleared the head; it filled the soul with well-being; it disposed the mind at once to utter wit and to appreciate the wit of others; it had the vagueness of music and the precision of mathematics. Only one of its qualities was comparable to anything else: it had the warmth of a good heart; but its taste, its smell, its feel, were not to be described in words. Charles Lamb, with his infinite tact, attempting to, might have drawn charming pictures of the life of his day; Lord Byron in a stanza of Don Juan, aiming at the impossible, might have achieved the sublime; Oscar Wilde, heaping jewels of Ispahan upon brocades of Byzantium, might have created a troubling beauty. Considering it, the mind reeled under visions of the feasts of Elagabalus; and the subtle harmonies of Debussy mingled with the musty, fragrant romance of chests in which have been kept old clothes, ruffs, hose, doublets, of a forgotten generation, and the wan odour of lilies of the valley and the savour of Cheddar cheese.

Hayward discovered the tavern at which this priceless beverage was to be obtained by meeting in the street a man called Macalister who had been at Cambridge with him. He was a stockbroker and a philosopher. He was accustomed to go to the tavern once a week; and soon Philip, Lawson, and Hayward got into the habit of meeting there every Tuesday evening: change of manners made it now little frequented, which was an advantage to persons who took pleasure in conversation. Macalister was a big-boned fellow, much too short for his width, with a large, fleshy face and a soft voice. He was a student of Kant and judged everything from the standpoint of pure reason. He was fond of expounding his doctrines. Philip listened with excited interest. He had long come to the conclusion that nothing amused him more than metaphysics, but he was not so sure of their efficacy in the affairs of life. The neat little system which he had formed as the result of his meditations at Blackstable had not been of conspicuous use during his infatuation for Mildred. He could not be positive that reason was much help in the conduct of life. It seemed to him that life lived itself. He remembered very vividly the violence of the emotion which had possessed him and his inability, as if he were tied down to the ground with ropes, to react against it. He read many wise things in books, but he could only judge from his own experience (he did not know whether he was different from other people); he did not calculate the pros and cons of an action, the benefits which must befall him if he did it, the harm which might result from the omission; but his whole being was urged on irresistibly. He did not act with a part of himself but altogether. The power that possessed him seemed to have nothing to do with reason: all that reason did was to point out the methods of obtaining what his whole soul was striving for.

Macalister reminded him of the Categorical Imperative.

"Act so that every action of yours should be capable of becoming a universal rule of action for all men."

"That seems to me perfect nonsense," said Philip.

"You're a bold man to say that of anything stated by Emmanuel Kant," retorted Macalister.

"Why? Reverence for what somebody said is a stultifying quality: there's a damned sight too much reverence in the world. Kant thought things not because they were true, but because he was Kant."

"Well, what is your objection to the Categorical Imperative?"

(They talked as though the fate of empires were in the balance.)

"It suggests that one can choose one's course by an effort of will. And it suggests that reason is the surest guide. Why should its dictates be any better than those of passion? They're different. That's all."

"You seem to be a contented slave of your passions."

"A slave because I can't help myself, but not a contented one," laughed Philip.

While he spoke he thought of that hot madness which had driven him in pursuit of Mildred. He remembered how he had chafed against it and how he had felt the degradation of it.

"Thank God, I'm free from all that now," he thought.

And yet even as he said it he was not quite sure whether he spoke sincerely. When he was under the influence of passion he had felt a singular vigour, and his mind had worked with unwonted force. He was more alive, there was an excitement in sheer being, an eager vehemence of soul, which made life now a trifle dull. For all the misery he had endured there was a compensation in that sense of rushing, overwhelming existence.

But Philip's unlucky words engaged him in a discussion on the freedom of the will, and Macalister, with his well-stored memory, brought out argument after argument. He had a mind that delighted in dialectics, and he forced Philip to contradict himself; he pushed him into corners from which he could only escape by damaging concessions; he tripped him up with logic and battered him with authorities.

At last Philip said:

"Well, I can't say anything about other people. I can only speak for myself. The illusion of free will is so strong in my mind that I can't get away from it, but I believe it is only an illusion. But it is an illusion which is one of the strongest motives of my actions. Before I do anything I feel that I have choice, and that influences what I do; but afterwards, when the thing is done, I believe that it was inevitable from all eternity."

"What do you deduce from that?" asked Hayward.

"Why, merely the futility of regret. It's no good crying over spilt milk, because all the forces of the universe were bent on spilling it."

Chapter LXVIII

ONE MORNING PHILIP ON GETTING UP FELT HIS HEAD SWIM, AND GOING back to bed suddenly discovered he was ill. All his limbs ached and he shivered with cold. When the landlady brought in his breakfast he called to her through the open door that he was not well, and asked for a cup of tea and a piece of toast. A few minutes later there was a knock at his door, and Griffiths came in. They had lived in the same house for over a year, but had never done more than nod to one another in the passage.

"I say, I hear you're seedy," said Griffiths. "I thought I'd come in and see what was the matter with you."

Philip, blushing he knew not why, made light of the whole thing. He would be all right in an hour or two.

"Well, you'd better let me take your temperature," said Griffiths.

"It's quite unnecessary," answered Philip irritably.

"Come on."

Philip put the thermometer in his mouth. Griffiths sat on the side of the bed and chatted brightly for a moment, then he took it out and looked at it.

"Now, look here, old man, you must stay in bed, and I'll bring old Deacon in to have a look at you."

"Nonsense," said Philip. "There's nothing the matter. I wish you wouldn't bother about me."

"But it isn't any bother. You've got a temperature and you must stay in bed. You will, won't you?"

There was a peculiar charm in his manner, a mingling of gravity and kindliness, which was infinitely attractive.

"You've got a wonderful bed-side manner," Philip murmured, closing his eyes with a smile.

Griffiths shook out his pillow for him, deftly smoothed down the bed-clothes, and tucked him up. He went into Philip's sitting-room to look for a siphon, could not find one, and fetched it from his own room. He drew down the blind.

"Now, go to sleep and I'll bring the old man round as soon as he's done the wards."

It seemed hours before anyone came to Philip. His head felt as if it would split, anguish rent his limbs, and he was afraid he was going to cry. Then there was a knock at the door and Griffiths, healthy, strong, and cheerful, came in.

"Here's Doctor Deacon," he said.

The physician stepped forward, an elderly man with a bland manner, whom Philip knew only by sight. A few questions, a brief examination, and the diagnosis.

"What d'you make it?" he asked Griffiths, smiling.

"Influenza."

"Quite right."

Doctor Deacon looked round the dingy lodging-house room.

"Wouldn't you like to go to the hospital? They'll put you in a private ward, and you can be better looked after than you can here."

"I'd rather stay where I am," said Philip.

He did not want to be disturbed, and he was always shy of new surroundings. He did not fancy nurses fussing about him, and the dreary cleanliness of the hospital.

"I can look after him, sir," said Griffiths at once.

"Oh, very well."

He wrote a prescription, gave instructions, and left.

"Now you've got to do exactly as I tell you," said Griffiths. "I'm day-nurse and night-nurse all in one."

"It's very kind of you, but I shan't want anything," said Philip.

Griffiths put his hand on Philip's forehead, a large cool, dry hand, and the touch seemed to him good.

"I'm just going to take this round to the dispensary to have it made up, and then I'll come back."

In a little while he brought the medicine and gave Philip a dose. Then he went upstairs to fetch his books.

"You won't mind my working in your room this afternoon, will you?" he said, when he came down. "I'll leave the door open so that you can give me a shout if you want anything."

Later in the day Philip, awaking from an uneasy doze, heard voices in his sitting-room. A friend had come in to see Griffiths.

"I say, you'd better not come in tonight," he heard Griffiths saying.

And then a minute or two afterwards someone else entered the room and expressed his surprise at finding Griffiths there. Philip heard him explain.

"I'm looking after a second year's man who's got these rooms. The wretched blighter's down with influenza. No whist tonight, old man."

Presently Griffiths was left alone and Philip called him.

"I say, you're not putting off a party tonight, are you?" he asked.

"Not on your account. I must work at my surgery."

"Don't put it off. I shall be all right. You needn't bother about me."

"That's all right."

Philip grew worse. As the night came on he became slightly delirious, but towards morning he awoke from a restless sleep. He saw Griffiths get out of an armchair, go down on his knees, and with his fingers put piece after piece of coal on the fire. He was in pyjamas and a dressing-gown.

"What are you doing here?" he asked.

"Did I wake you up? I tried to make up the fire without making a row."

"Why aren't you in bed? What's the time?"

"About five. I thought I'd better sit up with you tonight. I brought an armchair in as I thought if I put a mattress down I should sleep so soundly that I shouldn't hear you if you wanted anything."

"I wish you wouldn't be so good to me," groaned Philip. "Suppose you catch it?"

"Then you shall nurse me, old man," said Griffiths, with a laugh.

In the morning Griffiths drew up the blind. He looked pale and tired after his night's watch, but was full of spirits.

"Now, I'm going to wash you," he said to Philip cheerfully.

"I can wash myself," said Philip, ashamed.

"Nonsense. If you were in the small ward a nurse would wash you, and I can do it just as well as a nurse."

Philip, too weak and wretched to resist, allowed Griffiths to wash his hands and face, his feet, his chest and back. He did it with charming tenderness, carrying on meanwhile a stream of friendly chatter; then he changed the sheet just as they did at the hospital, shook out the pillow, and arranged the bed-clothes.

"I should like Sister Arthur to see me. It would make her sit up. Deacon's coming in to see you early."

"I can't imagine why you should be so good to me," said Philip.

"It's good practice for me. It's rather a lark having a patient."

Griffiths gave him his breakfast and went off to get dressed and have something to eat. A few minutes before ten he came back with a bunch of grapes and a few flowers.

"You are awfully kind," said Philip.

He was in bed for five days.

Norah and Griffiths nursed him between them. Though Griffiths was the same age as Philip he adopted towards him a humourous, motherly attitude. He was a thoughtful fellow, gentle and encouraging; but his greatest quality was a vitality which seemed to give health to everyone with whom he came in contact. Philip was unused to the petting which most people enjoy from mothers or sisters and he was deeply touched by the feminine tenderness of this strong young man. Philip grew better. Then Griffiths, sitting idly in Philip's room, amused him with gay stories of amorous adventure. He was a flirtatious creature, capable of carrying on three or four affairs at a time; and his account of the devices he was forced to in order to keep out of difficulties made excellent hearing. He had a gift for throwing a romantic glamour over everything that happened to him. He was crippled with debts, everything he had of any value was pawned, but he managed always to be cheerful, extravagant, and generous. He was the adventurer by nature. He loved people of doubtful occupations and shifty purposes; and his acquaintance among the riff-raff that frequents the bars of London was enormous. Loose women, treating him as a friend, told him the troubles, difficulties, and successes of their lives; and card-sharpers, respecting his impecuniosity, stood him dinners and lent him five-pound notes. He was ploughed in his examinations time after time; but he bore this cheerfully, and submitted with such a charming grace to the parental expostulations that his father, a doctor in practice at Leeds, had not the heart to be seriously angry with him.

"I'm an awful fool at books," he said cheerfully, "but I *can't* work."

Life was much too jolly. But it was clear that when he had got through the exuberance of his youth, and was at last qualified, he would be a tremendous success in practice. He would cure people by the sheer charm of his manner.

Philip worshipped him as at school he had worshipped boys who were tall and straight and high of spirits. By the time he was well they were fast friends, and it was a peculiar satisfaction to Philip that Griffiths seemed to enjoy sitting in his little parlour, wasting Philip's time with his amusing chatter and smoking innumerable cigarettes. Philip took him sometimes to the tavern off Regent Street. Hayward found him stupid, but Lawson recognised his charm and was eager to paint him; he was a picturesque figure with his blue eyes, white skin, and curly hair. Often they discussed things he knew nothing about, and then he sat quietly, with a good-natured smile on his handsome face, feeling quite rightly that his presence was sufficient contribution to the entertainment of the company. When he discovered that Macalister was a stockbroker he was eager for tips; and Macalister, with his grave smile, told him what fortunes he could have made if he had bought certain stock at certain times. It made Philip's mouth water, for in one way and another he was spending more than he had expected, and it would have suited him very well to make a little money by the easy method Macalister suggested.

"Next time I hear of a really good thing I'll let you know," said the stockbroker. "They do come along sometimes. It's only a matter of biding one's time."

Philip could not help thinking how delightful it would be to make fifty pounds, so that he could give Norah the furs she so badly needed for the winter. He looked at the shops in Regent Street and picked out the articles he could buy for the money. She deserved everything. She made his life very happy.

Chapter LXIX

ONE AFTERNOON, WHEN HE WENT BACK TO HIS ROOMS FROM THE HOSPITAL to wash and tidy himself before going to tea as usual with Norah, as he let himself in with his latch-key, his landlady opened the door for him.

"There's a lady waiting to see you," she said.

"Me?" exclaimed Philip.

He was surprised. It would only be Norah, and he had no idea what had brought her.

"I shouldn't 'ave let her in, only she's been three times, and she seemed that upset at not finding you, so I told her she could wait."

He pushed past the explaining landlady and burst into the room. His heart turned sick. It was Mildred. She was sitting down, but got up hurriedly as he came in. She did not move towards him nor speak. He was so surprised that he did not know what he was saying.

"What the hell d'you want?" he asked.

She did not answer, but began to cry. She did not put her hands to her eyes, but kept them hanging by the side of her body. She looked like a housemaid applying for a situation. There was a dreadful humility in her bearing. Philip did not know what feelings came over him. He had a sudden impulse to turn round and escape from the room.

"I didn't think I'd ever see you again," he said at last.

"I wish I was dead," she moaned.

Philip left her standing where she was. He could only think at the moment of steadying himself. His knees were shaking. He looked at her, and he groaned in despair.

"What's the matter?" he said.

"He's left me—Emil."

Philip's heart bounded. He knew then that he loved her as passionately as ever. He had never ceased to love her. She was standing before him humble and unresisting. He wished to take her in his arms and cover her tear-stained face with kisses. Oh, how long the separation had been! He did not know how he could have endured it.

"You'd better sit down. Let me give you a drink."

He drew the chair near the fire and she sat in it. He mixed her whiskey and soda, and, sobbing still, she drank it. She looked at him with great, mournful eyes.

There were large black lines under them. She was thinner and whiter than when last he had seen her.

"I wish I'd married you when you asked me," she said.

Philip did not know why the remark seemed to swell his heart. He could not keep the distance from her which he had forced upon himself. He put his hand on her shoulder.

"I'm awfully sorry you're in trouble."

She leaned her head against his bosom and burst into hysterical crying. Her hat was in the way and she took it off. He had never dreamed that she was capable of crying like that. He kissed her again and again. It seemed to ease her a little.

"You were always good to me, Philip," she said. "That's why I knew I could come to you."

"Tell me what's happened."

"Oh, I can't, I can't," she cried out, breaking away from him.

He sank down on his knees beside her and put his cheek against hers.

"Don't you know that there's nothing you can't tell me? I can never blame you for anything."

She told him the story little by little, and sometimes she sobbed so much that he could hardly understand.

"Last Monday week he went up to Birmingham, and he promised to be back on Thursday, and he never came, and he didn't come on the Friday, so I wrote to ask what was the matter, and he never answered the letter. And I wrote and said that if I didn't hear from him by return I'd go up to Birmingham, and this morning I got a solicitor's letter to say I had no claim on him, and if I molested him he'd seek the protection of the law."

"But it's absurd," cried Philip. "A man can't treat his wife like that. Had you had a row?"

"Oh, yes, we'd had a quarrel on the Sunday, and he said he was sick of me, but he'd said it before, and he'd come back all right. I didn't think he meant it. He was frightened, because I told him a baby was coming. I kept it from him as long as I could. Then I had to tell him. He said it was my fault, and I ought to have known better. If you'd only heard the things he said to me! But I found out precious quick that he wasn't a gentleman. He left me without a penny. He hadn't paid the rent, and I hadn't got the money to pay it, and the woman who kept the house said such things to me—well, I might have been a thief the way she talked."

"I thought you were going to take a flat."

"That's what he said, but we just took furnished apartments in Highbury. He was that mean. He said I was extravagant, he didn't give me anything to be extravagant with."

She had an extraordinary way of mixing the trivial with the important. Philip was puzzled. The whole thing was incomprehensible.

"No man could be such a blackguard."

"You don't know him. I wouldn't go back to him now not if he was to come and ask me on his bended knees. I was a fool ever to think of him. And he wasn't earning the money he said he was. The lies he told me!"

Philip thought for a minute or two. He was so deeply moved by her distress that he could not think of himself.

"Would you like me to go to Birmingham? I could see him and try to make things up."

"Oh, there's no chance of that. He'll never come back now, I know him."

"But he must provide for you. He can't get out of that. I don't know anything about these things, you'd better go and see a solicitor."

"How can I? I haven't got the money."

"I'll pay all that. I'll write a note to my own solicitor, the sportsman who was my father's executor. Would you like me to come with you now? I expect he'll still be at his office."

"No, give me a letter to him. I'll go alone."

She was a little calmer now. He sat down and wrote a note. Then he remembered that she had no money. He had fortunately changed a cheque the day before and was able to give her five pounds.

"You are good to me, Philip," she said.

"I'm so happy to be able to do something for you."

"Are you fond of me still?"

"Just as fond as ever."

She put up her lips and he kissed her. There was a surrender in the action which he had never seen in her before. It was worth all the agony he had suffered.

She went away and he found that she had been there for two hours. He was extraordinarily happy.

"Poor thing, poor thing," he murmured to himself, his heart glowing with a greater love than he had ever felt before.

He never thought of Norah at all till about eight o'clock a telegram came. He knew before opening it that it was from her.

> Is anything the matter?
> NORAH

He did not know what to do nor what to answer. He could fetch her after the play, in which she was walking on, was over and stroll home with her as he sometimes did; but his whole soul revolted against the idea of seeing her that evening. He thought of writing to her, but he could not bring himself to address her as usual, *dearest Norah*. He made up his mind to telegraph.

> Sorry. Could not get away,
> PHILIP

He visualised her. He was slightly repelled by the ugly little face, with its high cheek-bones and the crude colour. There was a coarseness in her skin which gave him goose-flesh. He knew that his telegram must be followed by some action on his part, but at all events it postponed it.

Next day he wired again.

> *Regret, unable to come. Will write.*

Mildred had suggested coming at four in the afternoon, and he would not tell her that the hour was inconvenient. After all she came first. He waited for her impatiently. He watched for her at the window and opened the front-door himself.

"Well? Did you see Nixon?"

"Yes," she answered. "He said it wasn't any good. Nothing's to be done. I must just grin and bear it."

"But that's impossible," cried Philip.

She sat down wearily.

"Did he give any reasons?" he asked.

She gave him a crumpled letter.

"There's your letter, Philip. I never took it. I couldn't tell you yesterday, I really couldn't. Emil didn't marry me. He couldn't. He had a wife already and three children."

Philip felt a sudden pang of jealousy and anguish. It was almost more than he could bear.

"That's why I couldn't go back to my aunt. There's no one I can go to but you."

"What made you go away with him?" Philip asked, in a low voice which he struggled to make firm.

"I don't know. I didn't know he was a married man at first, and when he told me I gave him a piece of my mind. And then I didn't see him for months, and when he came to the shop again and asked me I don't know what came over me. I felt as if I couldn't help it. I had to go with him."

"Were you in love with him?"

"I don't know. I couldn't hardly help laughing at the things he said. And there was something about him—he said I'd never regret it, he promised to give me seven pounds a week—he said he was earning fifteen, and it was all a lie, he wasn't. And then I was sick of going to the shop every morning, and I wasn't getting on very well with my aunt; she wanted to treat me as a servant instead of a relation, said I ought to do my own room, and if I didn't do it nobody was going to do it for me. Oh, I wish I hadn't. But when he came to the shop and asked me I felt I couldn't help it."

Philip moved away from her. He sat down at the table and buried his face in his hands. He felt dreadfully humiliated.

"You're not angry with me, Philip?" she asked piteously.

"No," he answered, looking up but away from her, "only I'm awfully hurt."

"Why?"

"You see, I was so dreadfully in love with you. I did everything I could to make you care for me. I thought you were incapable of loving anyone. It's so horrible to know that you were willing to sacrifice everything for that bounder. I wonder what you saw in him."

"I'm awfully sorry, Philip. I regretted it bitterly afterwards, I promise you that."

He thought of Emil Miller, with his pasty, unhealthy look, his shifty blue eyes, and the vulgar smartness of his appearance; he always wore bright red knitted waistcoats. Philip sighed. She got up and went to him. She put her arm round his neck.

"I shall never forget that you offered to marry me, Philip."

He took her hand and looked up at her. She bent down and kissed him.

"Philip, if you want me still I'll do anything you like now. I know you're a gentleman in every sense of the word."

His heart stood still. Her words made him feel slightly sick.

"It's awfully good of you, but I couldn't."

"Don't you care for me any more?"

"Yes, I love you with all my heart."

"Then why shouldn't we have a good time while we've got the chance? You see, it can't matter now"

He released himself from her.

"You don't understand. I've been sick with love for you ever since I saw you, but now—that man. I've unfortunately got a vivid imagination. The thought of it simply disgusts me."

"You are funny," she said.

He took her hand again and smiled at her.

"You mustn't think I'm not grateful. I can never thank you enough, but you see, it's just stronger than I am."

"You are a good friend, Philip."

They went on talking, and soon they had returned to the familiar companionship of old days. It grew late. Philip suggested that they should dine together and go to a music-hall. She wanted some persuasion, for she had an idea of acting up to her situation, and felt instinctively that it did not accord with her distressed condition to go to a place of entertainment. At last Philip asked her to go simply to please him, and when she could look upon it as an act of self-sacrifice she accepted. She had a new thoughtfulness which delighted Philip. She asked him to take her to the little restaurant in Soho to which they had so often been; he was infinitely grateful to her, because her suggestion showed that happy memories were attached to it. She grew much more cheerful as dinner proceeded. The Burgundy from the public-house at the corner warmed her heart, and she forgot that she ought to preserve a dolorous countenance. Philip thought it safe to speak to her of the future.

"I suppose you haven't got a brass farthing, have you?" he asked, when an opportunity presented itself.

"Only what you gave me yesterday, and I had to give the landlady three pounds of that."

"Well, I'd better give you a tenner to go on with. I'll go and see my solicitor and get him to write to Miller. We can make him pay up something, I'm sure. If we can get a hundred pounds out of him it'll carry you on till after the baby comes."

"I wouldn't take a penny from him. I'd rather starve."

"But it's monstrous that he should leave you in the lurch like this."

"I've got my pride to consider."

It was a little awkward for Philip. He needed rigid economy to make his own money last till he was qualified, and he must have something over to keep him during the year he intended to spend as house physician and house surgeon either at his own or at some other hospital. But Mildred had told him various stories of Emil's meanness, and he was afraid to remonstrate with her in case she accused him too of want of generosity.

"I wouldn't take a penny piece from him. I'd sooner beg my bread. I'd have seen about getting some work to do long before now, only it wouldn't be good for me in the state I'm in. You have to think of your health, don't you?"

"You needn't bother about the present," said Philip. "I can let you have all you want till you're fit to work again."

"I knew I could depend on you. I told Emil he needn't think I hadn't got somebody to go to. I told him you was a gentleman in every sense of the word."

By degrees Philip learned how the separation had come about. It appeared that the fellow's wife had discovered the adventure he was engaged in during his periodical visits to London, and had gone to the head of the firm that employed him. She threatened to divorce him, and they announced that they would dismiss him if she did. He was passionately devoted to his children and could not bear the thought of being separated from them. When he had to choose between his wife and his mistress he chose his wife. He had been always anxious that there should be no child to make the entanglement more complicated; and when Mildred, unable longer to conceal its approach, informed him of the fact, he was seized with panic. He picked a quarrel and left her without more ado.

"When d'you expect to be confined?" asked Philip.

"At the beginning of March."

"Three months."

It was necessary to discuss plans. Mildred declared she would not remain in the rooms at Highbury, and Philip thought it more convenient too that she should be nearer to him. He promised to look for something next day. She suggested the Vauxhall Bridge Road as a likely neighbourhood.

"And it would be near for afterwards," she said.

"What do you mean?"

"Well, I should only be able to stay there about two months or a little more, and then I should have to go into a house. I know a very respectable place, where they have a most superior class of people, and they take you for four guineas a week and no extras. Of course the doctor's extra, but that's all. A friend of mine went there, and the lady who keeps it is a thorough lady. I mean to tell her that my husband's an officer in India and I've come to London for my baby, because it's better for my health."

It seemed extraordinary to Philip to hear her talking in this way. With her delicate little features and her pale face she looked cold and maidenly. When he thought of the passions that burned within her, so unexpected, his heart was strangely troubled. His pulse beat quickly.

Chapter LXX

PHILIP EXPECTED TO FIND A LETTER FROM NORAH WHEN HE GOT BACK TO his rooms, but there was nothing; nor did he receive one the following morning. The silence irritated and at the same time alarmed him. They had seen one another every day he had been in London since the previous June; and it must seem odd to her that he should let two days go by without visiting her or offering a reason for his absence; he wondered whether by an unlucky chance she had seen him with Mildred. He could not bear to think that she was hurt or unhappy, and he made up his mind to call on her that afternoon. He was almost inclined to reproach her because he had allowed himself to get on such intimate terms with her. The thought of continuing them filled him with disgust.

He found two rooms for Mildred on the second floor of a house in the Vauxhall Bridge Road. They were noisy, but he knew that she liked the rattle of traffic under her windows.

"I don't like a dead and alive street where you don't see a soul pass all day," she said. "Give me a bit of life."

Then he forced himself to go to Vincent Square. He was sick with apprehension when he rang the bell. He had an uneasy sense that he was treating Norah badly; he dreaded reproaches; he knew she had a quick temper, and he hated scenes: perhaps the best way would be to tell her frankly that Mildred had come back to him and his love for her was as violent as it had ever been; he was very sorry, but he had nothing to offer Norah any more. Then he thought of her anguish, for he knew she loved him; it had flattered him before, and he was immensely grateful; but now it was horrible. She had not deserved that he should inflict pain upon her. He asked himself how she would greet him now, and as he walked up the stairs all possible forms of her behaviour flashed across his mind. He knocked at the door. He felt that he was pale, and wondered how to conceal his nervousness.

She was writing away industriously, but she sprang to her feet as he entered.

"I recognised your step," she cried. "Where have you been hiding yourself, you naughty boy?"

She came towards him joyfully and put her arms round his neck. She was delighted to see him. He kissed her, and then, to give himself countenance, said he was dying for tea. She bustled the fire to make the kettle boil.

"I've been awfully busy," he said lamely.

She began to chatter in her bright way, telling him of a new commission she had to provide a novelette for a firm which had not hitherto employed her. She was to get fifteen guineas for it.

"It's money from the clouds. I'll tell you what we'll do, we'll stand ourselves a little jaunt. Let's go and spend a day at Oxford, shall we? I'd love to see the colleges."

He looked at her to see whether there was any shadow of reproach in her eyes; but they were as frank and merry as ever: she was overjoyed to see him. His heart sank. He could not tell her the brutal truth. She made some toast for him, and cut it into little pieces, and gave it him as though he were a child.

"Is the brute fed?" she asked.

He nodded, smiling; and she lit a cigarette for him. Then, as she loved to do, she came and sat on his knees. She was very light. She leaned back in his arms with a sigh of delicious happiness.

"Say something nice to me," she murmured.

"What shall I say?"

"You might by an effort of imagination say that you rather liked me."

"You know I do that."

He had not the heart to tell her then. He would give her peace at all events for that day, and perhaps he might write to her. That would be easier. He could not bear to think of her crying. She made him kiss her, and as he kissed her he thought of Mildred and Mildred's pale, thin lips. The recollection of Mildred remained with him all the time, like an incorporeal form, but more substantial than a shadow; and the sight continually distracted his attention.

"You're very quiet today," Norah said.

Her loquacity was a standing joke between them, and he answered:

"You never let me get a word in, and I've got out of the habit of talking."

"But you're not listening, and that's bad manners."

He reddened a little, wondering whether she had some inkling of his secret; he turned away his eyes uneasily. The weight of her irked him this afternoon, and he did not want her to touch him.

"My foot's gone to sleep," he said.

"I'm so sorry," she cried, jumping up. "I shall have to bant if I can't break myself of this habit of sitting on gentlemen's knees."

He went through an elaborate form of stamping his foot and walking about. Then he stood in front of the fire so that she should not resume her position. While she talked he thought that she was worth ten of Mildred; she amused him much more and was jollier to talk to; she was cleverer, and she had a much nicer nature. She was a good, brave, honest little woman; and Mildred, he thought bitterly, deserved none of these epithets. If he had any sense he would stick to Norah, she would make him much happier than he would ever be with Mildred: after all she loved him, and Mildred was only grateful for his help. But when all was said the important thing was to love rather than to be loved; and he yearned for Mildred with his whole soul. He would sooner have ten minutes with her than a whole afternoon with Norah, he prized one kiss of her cold lips more than all Norah could give him.

"I can't help myself," he thought. "I've just got her in my bones."

He did not care if she was heartless, vicious and vulgar, stupid and grasping, he loved her. He would rather have misery with the one than happiness with the other.

When he got up to go Norah said casually:

"Well, I shall see you tomorrow, shan't I?"

"Yes," he answered.

He knew that he would not be able to come, since he was going to help Mildred with her moving, but he had not the courage to say so. He made up his mind that he would send a wire. Mildred saw the rooms in the morning, was satisfied with them, and after luncheon Philip went up with her to Highbury. She had a trunk for her clothes and another for the various odds and ends, cushions, lamp-shades, photograph frames, with which she had tried to give the apartments a home-like air; she had two or three large cardboard boxes besides, but in all there was no more than could be put on the roof of a four-wheeler. As they drove through Victoria Street Philip sat well back in the cab in case Norah should happen to be passing. He had not had an opportunity to telegraph and could not do so from the post office in the Vauxhall Bridge Road, since she would wonder what he was doing in that neighbourhood; and if he was there he could have no excuse for not going into the neighbouring square where she lived. He made up his mind that he had better go in and see her for half an hour; but the necessity irritated him: he was angry with Norah, because she forced him to vulgar and degrading shifts. But he was happy to be with Mildred. It amused him to help her with the unpacking; and he experienced a charming sense of possession in installing her in these lodgings which he had found and was paying for. He would not let her exert herself. It was a pleasure to do things for her, and she had no desire to do what somebody else seemed desirous to do for her. He unpacked her clothes and put them away. She was not proposing to go out again, so he got her slippers and took off her boots. It delighted him to perform menial offices.

"You do spoil me," she said, running her fingers affectionately through his hair, while he was on his knees unbuttoning her boots.

He took her hands and kissed them.

"It is ripping to have you here."

He arranged the cushions and the photograph frames. She had several jars of green earthenware.

"I'll get you some flowers for them," he said.

He looked round at his work proudly.

"As I'm not going out any more I think I'll get into a tea-gown," she said. "Undo me behind, will you?"

She turned round as unconcernedly as though he were a woman. His sex meant nothing to her. But his heart was filled with gratitude for the intimacy her request showed. He undid the hooks and eyes with clumsy fingers.

"That first day I came into the shop I never thought I'd be doing this for you now," he said, with a laugh which he forced.

"Somebody must do it," she answered.

She went into the bed-room and slipped into a pale blue tea-gown decorated with a great deal of cheap lace. Then Philip settled her on a sofa and made tea for her.

"I'm afraid I can't stay and have it with you," he said regretfully. "I've got a beastly appointment. But I shall be back in half an hour."

He wondered what he should say if she asked him what the appointment was, but she showed no curiosity. He had ordered dinner for the two of them when he took the rooms, and proposed to spend the evening with her quietly. He was in such a hurry to get back that he took a tram along the Vauxhall Bridge Road. He thought he had better break the fact to Norah at once that he could not stay more than a few minutes.

"I say, I've got only just time to say how d'you do," he said, as soon as he got into her rooms. "I'm frightfully busy."

Her face fell.

"Why, what's the matter?"

It exasperated him that she should force him to tell lies, and he knew that he reddened when he answered that there was a demonstration at the hospital which he was bound to go to. He fancied that she looked as though she did not believe him, and this irritated him all the more.

"Oh, well, it doesn't matter," she said. "I shall have you all tomorrow."

He looked at her blankly. It was Sunday, and he had been looking forward to spending the day with Mildred. He told himself that he must do that in common decency; he could not leave her by herself in a strange house.

"I'm awfully sorry, I'm engaged tomorrow."

He knew this was the beginning of a scene which he would have given anything to avoid. The colour on Norah's cheeks grew brighter.

"But I've asked the Gordons to lunch"—they were an actor and his wife who were touring the provinces and in London for Sunday—"I told you about it a week ago."

"I'm awfully sorry, I forgot." He hesitated. "I'm afraid I can't possibly come. Isn't there somebody else you can get?"

"What are you doing tomorrow then?"

"I wish you wouldn't cross-examine me."

"Don't you want to tell me?"

"I don't in the least mind telling you, but it's rather annoying to be forced to account for all one's movements."

Norah suddenly changed. With an effort of self-control she got the better of her temper, and going up to him took his hands.

"Don't disappoint me tomorrow, Philip, I've been looking forward so much to spending the day with you. The Gordons want to see you, and we'll have such a jolly time."

"I'd love to if I could."

"I'm not very exacting, am I? I don't often ask you to do anything that's a bother. Won't you get out of your horrid engagement—just this once?"

"I'm awfully sorry, I don't see how I can," he replied sullenly.

"Tell me what it is," she said coaxingly.

He had had time to invent something.

"Griffiths' two sisters are up for the week-end and we're taking them out."

"Is that all?" she said joyfully. "Griffiths can so easily get another man."

He wished he had thought of something more urgent than that. It was a clumsy lie.

"No, I'm awfully sorry, I can't—I've promised and I mean to keep my promise."

"But you promised me too. Surely I come first."

"I wish you wouldn't persist," he said.

She flared up.

"You won't come because you don't want to. I don't know what you've been doing the last few days, you've been quite different."

He looked at his watch.

"I'm afraid I'll have to be going," he said.

"You won't come tomorrow?"

"No."

"In that case you needn't trouble to come again," she cried, losing her temper for good.

"That's just as you like," he answered.

"Don't let me detain you any longer," she added ironically.

He shrugged his shoulders and walked out. He was relieved that it had gone no worse. There had been no tears. As he walked along he congratulated himself on getting out of the affair so easily. He went into Victoria Street and bought a few flowers to take in to Mildred.

The little dinner was a great success. Philip had sent in a small pot of caviar, which he knew she was very fond of, and the landlady brought them up some cutlets with vegetables and a sweet. Philip had ordered Burgundy, which was her favourite wine. With the curtains drawn, a bright fire, and one of Mildred's shades on the lamp, the room was cosy.

"It's really just like home," smiled Philip.

"I might be worse off, mightn't I?" she answered.

When they finished, Philip drew two arm-chairs in front of the fire, and they sat down. He smoked his pipe comfortably. He felt happy and generous.

"What would you like to do tomorrow?" he asked.

"Oh, I'm going to Tulse Hill. You remember the manageress at the shop, well, she's married now, and she's asked me to go and spend the day with her. Of course she thinks I'm married too."

Philip's heart sank.

"But I refused an invitation so that I might spend Sunday with you."

He thought that if she loved him she would say that in that case she would stay with him. He knew very well that Norah would not have hesitated.

"Well, you were a silly to do that. I've promised to go for three weeks and more."

"But how can you go alone?"

"Oh, I shall say that Emil's away on business. Her husband's in the glove trade, and he's a very superior fellow."

Philip was silent, and bitter feelings passed through his heart. She gave him a sidelong glance.

"You don't grudge me a little pleasure, Philip? You see, it's the last time I shall be able to go anywhere for I don't know how long, and I had promised."

He took her hand and smiled.

"No, darling, I want you to have the best time you can. I only want you to be happy."

There was a little book bound in blue paper lying open, face downwards, on the sofa, and Philip idly took it up. It was a twopenny novelette, and the author was Courtenay Paget. That was the name under which Norah wrote.

"I do like his books," said Mildred. "I read them all. They're so refined."

He remembered what Norah had said of herself.

"I have an immense popularity among kitchen-maids. They think me so genteel."

Chapter LXXI

PHILIP, IN RETURN FOR GRIFFITHS' CONFIDENCES, HAD TOLD HIM THE DETAILS of his own complicated amours, and on Sunday morning, after breakfast when they sat by the fire in their dressing-gowns and smoked, he recounted the scene of the previous day. Griffiths congratulated him because he had got out of his difficulties so easily.

"It's the simplest thing in the world to have an affair with a woman," he remarked sententiously, "but it's a devil of a nuisance to get out of it."

Philip felt a little inclined to pat himself on the back for his skill in managing the business. At all events he was immensely relieved. He thought of Mildred enjoying herself in Tulse Hill, and he found in himself a real satisfaction because she was happy. It was an act of self-sacrifice on his part that he did not grudge her pleasure even though paid for by his own disappointment, and it filled his heart with a comfortable glow.

But on Monday morning he found on his table a letter from Norah. She wrote:

DEAREST—I'm sorry I was cross on Saturday. Forgive me and come to tea in the afternoon as usual. I love you.

YOUR NORAH

His heart sank, and he did not know what to do. He took the note to Griffiths and showed it to him.

"You'd better leave it unanswered," said he.

"Oh, I can't," cried Philip. "I should be miserable if I thought of her waiting and waiting. You don't know what it is to be sick for the postman's knock. I do, and I can't expose anybody else to that torture."

"My dear fellow, one can't break that sort of affair off without somebody suffering. You must just set your teeth to that. One thing is, it doesn't last very long."

Philip felt that Norah had not deserved that he should make her suffer; and what did Griffiths know about the degrees of anguish she was capable of? He remembered his own pain when Mildred had told him she was going to be married. He did not want anyone to experience what he had experienced then.

"If you're so anxious not to give her pain, go back to her," said Griffiths.

"I can't do that."

He got up and walked up and down the room nervously. He was angry with

Norah because she had not let the matter rest. She must have seen that he had no more love to give her. They said women were so quick at seeing those things.

"You might help me," he said to Griffiths.

"My dear fellow, don't make such a fuss about it. People do get over these things, you know. She probably isn't so wrapped up in you as you think, either. One's always rather apt to exaggerate the passion one's inspired other people with."

He paused and looked at Philip with amusement.

"Look here, there's only one thing you can do. Write to her, and tell her the thing's over. Put it so that there can be no mistake about it. It'll hurt her, but it'll hurt her less if you do the thing brutally than if you try half-hearted ways."

Philip sat down and wrote the following letter:

MY DEAR NORAH—I am sorry to make you unhappy, but I think we had better let things remain where we left them on Saturday. I don't think there's any use in letting these things drag on when they've ceased to be amusing. You told me to go and I went. I do not propose to come back. Good-bye.

PHILIP CAREY

He showed the letter to Griffiths and asked him what he thought of it. Griffiths read it and looked at Philip with twinkling eyes. He did not say what he felt.

"I think that'll do the trick," he said.

Philip went out and posted it. He passed an uncomfortable morning, for he imagined with great detail what Norah would feel when she received his letter. He tortured himself with the thought of her tears. But at the same time he was relieved. Imagined grief was more easy to bear than grief seen, and he was free now to love Mildred with all his soul. His heart leaped at the thought of going to see her that afternoon, when his day's work at the hospital was over.

When as usual he went back to his rooms to tidy himself, he had no sooner put the latch-key in his door than he heard a voice behind him.

"May I come in? I've been waiting for you for half an hour."

It was Norah. He felt himself blush to the roots of his hair. She spoke gaily. There was no trace of resentment in her voice and nothing to indicate that there was a rupture between them. He felt himself cornered. He was sick with fear, but he did his best to smile.

"Yes, do," he said.

He opened the door, and she preceded him into his sitting-room. He was nervous and, to give himself countenance, offered her a cigarette and lit one for himself. She looked at him brightly.

"Why did you write me such a horrid letter, you naughty boy? If I'd taken it seriously it would have made me perfectly wretched."

"It was meant seriously," he answered gravely.

"Don't be so silly. I lost my temper the other day, and I wrote and apologised. You weren't satisfied, so I've come here to apologise again. After all, you're your own master and I have no claims upon you. I don't want you to do anything you don't want to."

She got up from the chair in which she was sitting and went towards him impulsively, with outstretched hands.

"Let's make friends again, Philip. I'm so sorry if I offended you."

He could not prevent her from taking his hands, but he could not look at her.

"I'm afraid it's too late," he said.

She let herself down on the floor by his side and clasped his knees.

"Philip, don't be silly. I'm quick-tempered too and I can understand that I hurt you, but it's so stupid to sulk over it. What's the good of making us both unhappy? It's been so jolly, our friendship." She passed her fingers slowly over his hand. "I love you, Philip."

He got up, disengaging himself from her, and went to the other side of the room.

"I'm awfully sorry, I can't do anything. The whole thing's over."

"D'you mean to say you don't love me anymore?"

"I'm afraid so."

"You were just looking for an opportunity to throw me over and you took that one?"

He did not answer. She looked at him steadily for a time which seemed intolerable. She was sitting on the floor where he had left her, leaning against the armchair. She began to cry quite silently, without trying to hide her face, and the large tears rolled down her cheeks one after the other. She did not sob. It was horribly painful to see her. Philip turned away.

"I'm awfully sorry to hurt you. It's not my fault if I don't love you."

She did not answer. She merely sat there, as though she were overwhelmed, and the tears flowed down her cheeks. It would have been easier to bear if she had reproached him. He had thought her temper would get the better of her, and he was prepared for that. At the back of his mind was a feeling that a real quarrel, in which each said to the other cruel things, would in some way be a justification of his behaviour. The time passed. At last he grew frightened by her silent crying; he went into his bed-room and got a glass of water; he leaned over her.

"Won't you drink a little? It'll relieve you."

She put her lips listlessly to the glass and drank two or three mouthfuls. Then in an exhausted whisper she asked him for a handkerchief. She dried her eyes.

"Of course I knew you never loved me as much as I loved you," she moaned.

"I'm afraid that's always the case," he said. "There's always one who loves and one who lets himself be loved."

He thought of Mildred, and a bitter pain traversed his heart. Norah did not answer for a long time.

"I'd been so miserably unhappy, and my life was so hateful," she said at last.

She did not speak to him, but to herself. He had never heard her before complain of the life she had led with her husband or of her poverty. He had always admired the bold front she displayed to the world.

"And then you came along and you were so good to me. And I admired you because you were clever and it was so heavenly to have someone I could put my trust in. I loved you. I never thought it could come to an end. And without any fault of mine at all."

Her tears began to flow again, but now she was more mistress of herself, and she hid her face in Philip's handkerchief. She tried hard to control herself.

"Give me some more water," she said.

She wiped her eyes.

"I'm sorry to make such a fool of myself. I was so unprepared."

"I'm awfully sorry, Norah. I want you to know that I'm very grateful for all you've done for me."

He wondered what it was she saw in him.

"Oh, it's always the same," she sighed, "if you want men to behave well to you, you must be beastly to them; if you treat them decently they make you suffer for it."

She got up from the floor and said she must go. She gave Philip a long, steady look. Then she sighed.

"It's so inexplicable. What does it all mean?"

Philip took a sudden determination.

"I think I'd better tell you, I don't want you to think too badly of me, I want you to see that I can't help myself. Mildred's come back."

The colour came to her face.

"Why didn't you tell me at once? I deserved that surely."

"I was afraid to."

She looked at herself in the glass and set her hat straight.

"Will you call me a cab," she said. "I don't feel I *can* walk."

He went to the door and stopped a passing hansom; but when she followed him into the street he was startled to see how white she was. There was a heaviness in her movements as though she had suddenly grown older. She looked so ill that he had not the heart to let her go alone.

"I'll drive back with you if you don't mind."

She did not answer, and he got into the cab. They drove along in silence over the bridge, through shabby streets in which children, with shrill cries, played in the road. When they arrived at her door she did not immediately get out. It seemed as though she could not summon enough strength to her legs to move.

"I hope you'll forgive me, Norah," he said.

She turned her eyes towards him, and he saw that they were bright again with tears, but she forced a smile to her lips.

"Poor fellow, you're quite worried about me. You mustn't bother. I don't blame you. I shall get over it all right."

Lightly and quickly she stroked his face to show him that she bore no ill-feeling, the gesture was scarcely more than suggested; then she jumped out of the cab and let herself into her house.

Philip paid the hansom and walked to Mildred's lodgings. There was a curious heaviness in his heart. He was inclined to reproach himself. But why? He did not know what else he could have done. Passing a fruiterer's, he remembered that Mildred was fond of grapes. He was so grateful that he could show his love for her by recollecting every whim she had.

Chapter LXXII

For the next three months Philip went every day to see Mildred. He took his books with him and after tea worked, while Mildred lay on the sofa reading novels. Sometimes he would look up and watch her for a minute. A happy smile crossed his lips. She would feel his eyes upon her.

"Don't waste your time looking at me, silly. Go on with your work," she said.

"Tyrant," he answered gaily.

He put aside his book when the landlady came in to lay the cloth for dinner, and in his high spirits he exchanged chaff with her. She was a little cockney, of middle-age, with an amusing humour and a quick tongue. Mildred had become great friends with her and had given her an elaborate but mendacious account of the circumstances which had brought her to the pass she was in. The good-hearted little woman was touched and found no trouble too great to make Mildred comfortable. Mildred's sense of propriety had suggested that Philip should pass himself off as her brother. They dined together, and Philip was delighted when he had ordered something which tempted Mildred's capricious appetite. It enchanted him to see her sitting opposite him, and every now and then from sheer joy he took her hand and pressed it. After dinner she sat in the arm-chair by the fire, and he settled himself down on the floor beside her, leaning against her knees, and smoked. Often they did not talk at all, and sometimes Philip noticed that she had fallen into a doze. He dared not move then in case he woke her, and he sat very quietly, looking lazily into the fire and enjoying his happiness.

"Had a nice little nap?" he smiled, when she woke.

"I've not been sleeping," she answered. "I only just closed my eyes."

She would never acknowledge that she had been asleep. She had a phlegmatic temperament, and her condition did not seriously inconvenience her. She took a lot of trouble about her health and accepted the advice of anyone who chose to offer it. She went for a "constitutional" every morning that it was fine and remained out a definite time. When it was not too cold she sat in St. James' Park. But the rest of the day she spent quite happily on her sofa, reading one novel after another or chatting with the landlady; she had an inexhaustible interest in gossip, and told Philip with abundant detail the history of the landlady, of the lodgers on the drawing-room floor, and of the people who lived in the next house on either side. Now and then she was seized with panic; she poured out her fears to Philip about the pain of the confinement and was in terror lest she should die; she gave him a full account of the confinements of the landlady and of the lady on the drawing-room floor

(Mildred did not know her; "I'm one to keep myself to myself," she said, "I'm not one to go about with anybody.") and she narrated details with a queer mixture of horror and gusto; but for the most part she looked forward to the occurrence with equanimity.

"After all, I'm not the first one to have a baby, am I? And the doctor says I shan't have any trouble. You see, it isn't as if I wasn't well made."

Mrs. Owen, the owner of the house she was going to when her time came, had recommended a doctor, and Mildred saw him once a week. He was to charge fifteen guineas.

"Of course I could have got it done cheaper, but Mrs. Owen strongly recommended him, and I thought it wasn't worthwhile to spoil the ship for a coat of tar."

"If you feel happy and comfortable I don't mind a bit about the expense," said Philip.

She accepted all that Philip did for her as if it were the most natural thing in the world, and on his side he loved to spend money on her: each five-pound note he gave her caused him a little thrill of happiness and pride; he gave her a good many, for she was not economical.

"I don't know where the money goes to," she said herself, "it seems to slip through my fingers like water."

"It doesn't matter," said Philip. "I'm so glad to be able to do anything I can for you."

She could not sew well and so did not make the necessary things for the baby; she told Philip it was much cheaper in the end to buy them. Philip had lately sold one of the mortgages in which his money had been put; and now, with five hundred pounds in the bank waiting to be invested in something that could be more easily realised, he felt himself uncommonly well-to-do. They talked often of the future. Philip was anxious that Mildred should keep the child with her, but she refused: she had her living to earn, and it would be more easy to do this if she had not also to look after a baby. Her plan was to get back into one of the shops of the company for which she had worked before, and the child could be put with some decent woman in the country.

"I can find someone who'll look after it well for seven and sixpence a week. It'll be better for the baby and better for me."

It seemed callous to Philip, but when he tried to reason with her she pretended to think he was concerned with the expense.

"You needn't worry about that," she said. "I shan't ask *you* to pay for it."

"You know I don't care how much I pay."

At the bottom of her heart was the hope that the child would be still-born. She did no more than hint it, but Philip saw that the thought was there. He was shocked at first; and then, reasoning with himself, he was obliged to confess that for all concerned such an event was to be desired.

"It's all very fine to say this and that," Mildred remarked querulously, "but it's jolly difficult for a girl to earn her living by herself; it doesn't make it any easier when she's got a baby."

"Fortunately you've got me to fall back on," smiled Philip, taking her hand.

"You've been good to me, Philip."

"Oh, what rot!"

"You can't say I didn't offer anything in return for what you've done."

"Good heavens, I don't want a return. If I've done anything for you, I've done it because I love you. You owe me nothing. I don't want you to do anything unless you love me."

He was a little horrified by her feeling that her body was a commodity which she could deliver indifferently as an acknowledgment for services rendered.

"But I do want to, Philip. You've been so good to me."

"Well, it won't hurt for waiting. When you're all right again we'll go for our little honeymoon."

"You are naughty," she said, smiling.

Mildred expected to be confined early in March, and as soon as she was well enough she was to go to the seaside for a fortnight: that would give Philip a chance to work without interruption for his examination; after that came the Easter holidays, and they had arranged to go to Paris together. Philip talked endlessly of the things they would do. Paris was delightful then. They would take a room in a little hotel he knew in the Latin Quarter, and they would eat in all sorts of charming little restaurants; they would go to the play, and he would take her to music-halls. It would amuse her to meet his friends. He had talked to her about Cronshaw, she would see him; and there was Lawson, he had gone to Paris for a couple of months; and they would go to the Bal Bullier; there were excursions; they would make trips to Versailles, Chartres, Fontainebleau.

"It'll cost a lot of money," she said.

"Oh, damn the expense. Think how I've been looking forward to it. Don't you know what it means to me? I've never loved anyone but you. I never shall."

She listened to his enthusiasm with smiling eyes. He thought he saw in them a new tenderness, and he was grateful to her. She was much gentler than she used to be. There was in her no longer the superciliousness which had irritated him. She was so accustomed to him now that she took no pains to keep up before him any pretences. She no longer troubled to do her hair with the old elaboration, but just tied it in a knot; and she left off the vast fringe which she generally wore: the more careless style suited her. Her face was so thin that it made her eyes seem very large; there were heavy lines under them, and the pallor of her cheeks made their colour more profound. She had a wistful look which was infinitely pathetic. There seemed to Philip to be in her something of the Madonna. He wished they could continue in that same way always. He was happier than he had ever been in his life.

He used to leave her at ten o'clock every night, for she liked to go to bed early, and he was obliged to put in another couple of hours' work to make up for the lost evening. He generally brushed her hair for her before he went. He had made a ritual of the kisses he gave her when he bade her good-night; first he kissed the palms of her hands (how thin the fingers were, the nails were beautiful, for she spent much time in manicuring them), then he kissed her closed eyes, first the right one and then the left, and at last he kissed her lips. He went home with a heart overflowing with love. He longed for an opportunity to gratify the desire for self-sacrifice which consumed him.

Presently the time came for her to move to the nursing-home where she was to be confined. Philip was then able to visit her only in the afternoons. Mildred changed her story and represented herself as the wife of a soldier who had gone to India to join his regiment, and Philip was introduced to the mistress of the establishment as her brother-in-law.

"I have to be rather careful what I say," she told him, "as there's another lady here whose husband's in the Indian Civil."

"I wouldn't let that disturb me if I were you," said Philip. "I'm convinced that her husband and yours went out on the same boat."

"What boat?" she asked innocently.

"The Flying Dutchman."

Mildred was safely delivered of a daughter, and when Philip was allowed to see her the child was lying by her side. Mildred was very weak, but relieved that everything was over. She showed him the baby, and herself looked at it curiously.

"It's a funny-looking little thing, isn't it? I can't believe it's mine."

It was red and wrinkled and odd. Philip smiled when he looked at it. He did not quite know what to say; and it embarrassed him because the nurse who owned the house was standing by his side; and he felt by the way she was looking at him that, disbelieving Mildred's complicated story, she thought he was the father.

"What are you going to call her?" asked Philip.

"I can't make up my mind if I shall call her Madeleine or Cecilia."

The nurse left them alone for a few minutes, and Philip bent down and kissed Mildred on the mouth.

"I'm so glad it's all over happily, darling."

She put her thin arms round his neck.

"You have been a brick to me, Phil dear."

"Now I feel that you're mine at last. I've waited so long for you, my dear."

They heard the nurse at the door, and Philip hurriedly got up. The nurse entered. There was a slight smile on her lips.

Chapter LXXIII

THREE WEEKS LATER PHILIP SAW MILDRED AND HER BABY OFF TO BRIGHTON. She had made a quick recovery and looked better than he had ever seen her. She was going to a boarding-house where she had spent a couple of weekends with Emil Miller, and had written to say that her husband was obliged to go to Germany on business and she was coming down with her baby. She got pleasure out of the stories she invented, and she showed a certain fertility of invention in the working out of the details. Mildred proposed to find in Brighton some woman who would be willing to take charge of the baby. Philip was startled at the callousness with which she insisted on getting rid of it so soon, but she argued with common sense that the poor child had much better be put somewhere before it grew used to her. Philip had expected the maternal instinct to make itself felt when she had had the baby two or three weeks and had counted on this to help him persuade her to keep it; but nothing of the sort occurred. Mildred was not unkind to her baby; she did all that was necessary; it amused her sometimes, and she talked about it a good deal; but at heart she was indifferent to it. She could not look upon it as part of herself. She fancied it resembled its father already. She was continually wondering how she would manage when it grew older; and she was exasperated with herself for being such a fool as to have it at all.

"If I'd only known then all I do now," she said.

She laughed at Philip, because he was anxious about its welfare.

"You couldn't make more fuss if you was the father," she said. "I'd like to see Emil getting into such a stew about it."

Philip's mind was full of the stories he had heard of baby-farming and the ghouls who ill-treat the wretched children that selfish, cruel parents have put in their charge.

"Don't be so silly," said Mildred. "That's when you give a woman a sum down to look after a baby. But when you're going to pay so much a week it's to their interest to look after it well."

Philip insisted that Mildred should place the child with people who had no children of their own and would promise to take no other.

"Don't haggle about the price," he said. "I'd rather pay half a guinea a week than run any risk of the kid being starved or beaten."

"You're a funny old thing, Philip," she laughed.

To him there was something very touching in the child's helplessness. It was small, ugly, and querulous. Its birth had been looked forward to with shame and anguish. Nobody wanted it. It was dependent on him, a stranger, for food, shelter, and clothes to cover its nakedness.

As the train started he kissed Mildred. He would have kissed the baby too, but he was afraid she would laugh at him.

"You will write to me, darling, won't you? And I shall look forward to your coming back with oh! such impatience."

"Mind you get through your exam."

He had been working for it industriously, and now with only ten days before him he made a final effort. He was very anxious to pass, first to save himself time and expense, for money had been slipping through his fingers during the last four months with incredible speed; and then because this examination marked the end of the drudgery: after that the student had to do with medicine, midwifery, and surgery, the interest of which was more vivid than the anatomy and physiology with which he had been hitherto concerned. Philip looked forward with interest to the rest of the curriculum. Nor did he want to have to confess to Mildred that he had failed: though the examination was difficult and the majority of candidates were ploughed at the first attempt, he knew that she would think less well of him if he did not succeed; she had a peculiarly humiliating way of showing what she thought.

Mildred sent him a postcard to announce her safe arrival, and he snatched half an hour every day to write a long letter to her. He had always a certain shyness in expressing himself by word of mouth, but he found he could tell her, pen in hand, all sorts of things which it would have made him feel ridiculous to say. Profiting by the discovery he poured out to her his whole heart. He had never been able to tell her before how his adoration filled every part of him so that all his actions, all his thoughts, were touched with it. He wrote to her of the future, the happiness that lay before him, and the gratitude which he owed her. He asked himself (he had often asked himself before but had never put it into words) what it was in her that filled him with such extravagant delight; he did not know; he knew only that when she was with him he was happy, and when she was away from him the world was on a sudden cold and grey; he knew only that when he thought of her his heart seemed to grow big in his body so that it was difficult to breathe (as if it pressed against his lungs) and it throbbed, so that the delight of her presence was almost pain; his knees shook, and he felt strangely weak as though, not having eaten, he were tremulous from want of food. He looked forward eagerly to her answers. He did not expect her to write often, for he knew that letter-writing came difficultly to her; and he was quite content with the clumsy little note that arrived in reply to four of his. She spoke of the boarding-house in which she had taken a room, of the weather and the baby, told him she had been for a walk on the front with a lady-friend whom she had met in the boarding-house and who had taken such a fancy to baby, she was going to the theatre on Saturday night, and Brighton was filling up. It touched Philip because it was so matter-of-fact. The crabbed style, the formality of the matter, gave him a queer desire to laugh and to take her in his arms and kiss her.

He went into the examination with happy confidence. There was nothing in either of the papers that gave him trouble. He knew that he had done well, and though the second part of the examination was *viva voce* and he was more nervous, he managed to answer the questions adequately. He sent a triumphant telegram to Mildred when the result was announced.

When he got back to his rooms Philip found a letter from her, saying that she thought it would be better for her to stay another week in Brighton. She had found a woman who would be glad to take the baby for seven shillings a week, but she wanted to make inquiries about her, and she was herself benefiting so much by the sea-air that she was sure a few days more would do her no end of good. She hated asking Philip for money, but would he send some by return, as she had had to buy herself a new hat, she couldn't go about with her lady-friend always in the same hat, and her lady-friend was so dressy. Philip had a moment of bitter disappointment. It took away all his pleasure at getting through his examination.

"If she loved me one quarter as much as I love her she couldn't bear to stay away a day longer than necessary."

He put the thought away from him quickly; it was pure selfishness; of course her health was more important than anything else. But he had nothing to do now; he might spend the week with her in Brighton, and they could be together all day. His heart leaped at the thought. It would be amusing to appear before Mildred suddenly with the information that he had taken a room in the boarding-house. He looked out trains. But he paused. He was not certain that she would be pleased to see him; she had made friends in Brighton; he was quiet, and she liked boisterous joviality; he realised that she amused herself more with other people than with him. It would torture him if he felt for an instant that he was in the way. He was afraid to risk it. He dared not even write and suggest that, with nothing to keep him in town, he would like to spend the week where he could see her every day. She knew he had nothing to do; if she wanted him to come she would have asked him to. He dared not risk the anguish he would suffer if he proposed to come and she made excuses to prevent him.

He wrote to her next day, sent her a five-pound note, and at the end of his letter said that if she were very nice and cared to see him for the week-end he would be glad to run down; but she was by no means to alter any plans she had made. He awaited her answer with impatience. In it she said that if she had only known before she could have arranged it, but she had promised to go to a music-hall on the Saturday night; besides, it would make the people at the boarding-house talk if he stayed there. Why did he not come on Sunday morning and spend the day? They could lunch at the Metropole, and she would take him afterwards to see the very superior lady-like person who was going to take the baby.

Sunday. He blessed the day because it was fine. As the train approached Brighton the sun poured through the carriage window. Mildred was waiting for him on the platform.

"How jolly of you to come and meet me!" he cried, as he seized her hands.

"You expected me, didn't you?"

"I hoped you would. I say, how well you're looking."

"It's done me a rare lot of good, but I think I'm wise to stay here as long as I can. And there are a very nice class of people at the boarding-house. I wanted cheering up after seeing nobody all these months. It was dull sometimes."

She looked very smart in her new hat, a large black straw with a great many inexpensive flowers on it; and round her neck floated a long boa of imitation swansdown. She was still very thin, and she stooped a little when she walked (she had always done that), but her eyes did not seem so large; and though she never had any colour, her skin had lost the earthy look it had. They walked down to the sea. Philip, remembering he had not walked with her for months, grew suddenly conscious of his limp and walked stiffly in the attempt to conceal it.

"Are you glad to see me?" he asked, love dancing madly in his heart.

"Of course I am. You needn't ask that."

"By the way, Griffiths sends you his love."

"What cheek!"

He had talked to her a great deal of Griffiths. He had told her how flirtatious he was and had amused her often with the narration of some adventure which Griffiths under the seal of secrecy had imparted to him. Mildred had listened, with some pretence of disgust sometimes, but generally with curiosity; and Philip, admiringly, had enlarged upon his friend's good looks and charm.

"I'm sure you'll like him just as much as I do. He's so jolly and amusing, and he's such an awfully good sort."

Philip told her how, when they were perfect strangers, Griffiths had nursed him through an illness; and in the telling Griffiths' self-sacrifice lost nothing.

"You can't help liking him," said Philip.

"I don't like good-looking men," said Mildred. "They're too conceited for me."

"He wants to know you. I've talked to him about you an awful lot."

"What have you said?" asked Mildred.

Philip had no one but Griffiths to talk to of his love for Mildred, and little by little had told him the whole story of his connection with her. He described her to him fifty times. He dwelled amorously on every detail of her appearance, and Griffiths knew exactly how her thin hands were shaped and how white her face was, and he laughed at Philip when he talked of the charm of her pale, thin lips.

"By Jove, I'm glad I don't take things so badly as that," he said. "Life wouldn't be worth living."

Philip smiled. Griffiths did not know the delight of being so madly in love that it was like meat and wine and the air one breathed and whatever else was essential to existence. Griffiths knew that Philip had looked after the girl while she was having her baby and was now going away with her.

"Well, I must say you've deserved to get something," he remarked. "It must have cost you a pretty penny. It's lucky you can afford it."

"I can't," said Philip. "But what do I care!"

Since it was early for luncheon, Philip and Mildred sat in one of the shelters on the parade, sunning themselves, and watched the people pass. There were the Brighton shop-boys who walked in twos and threes, swinging their canes, and there were the Brighton shop-girls who tripped along in giggling bunches. They could tell the people who had come down from London for the day; the keen air gave a fillip to their weariness. There were many Jews, stout ladies in tight satin dresses and diamonds, little corpulent men with a gesticulative manner. There were middle-aged gentlemen spending a week-end in one of the large hotels, carefully dressed; and they walked industriously after too substantial a breakfast to give themselves an appetite for too substantial a luncheon: they exchanged the time of day with friends and talked of Dr. Brighton or London-by-the-Sea. Here and there a well-known actor passed, elaborately unconscious of the attention he excited: sometimes he wore patent leather boots, a coat with an astrakhan collar, and carried a silver-knobbed stick; and sometimes, looking as though he had come from a day's shooting, he strolled in knickerbockers, and ulster of Harris tweed, and a tweed hat on the back of his head. The sun shone on the blue sea, and the blue sea was trim and neat.

After luncheon they went to Hove to see the woman who was to take charge of the baby. She lived in a small house in a back street, but it was clean and tidy. Her name was Mrs. Harding. She was an elderly, stout person, with grey hair and a red, fleshy face. She looked motherly in her cap, and Philip thought she seemed kind.

"Won't you find it an awful nuisance to look after a baby?" he asked her.

She explained that her husband was a curate, a good deal older than herself, who had difficulty in getting permanent work, since vicars wanted young men to assist them; he earned a little now and then by doing locums when someone took a holiday or fell ill, and a charitable institution gave them a small pension; but her life was lonely, it would be something to do to look after a child, and the few shillings a week paid for it would help her to keep things going. She promised that it should be well fed.

"Quite the lady, isn't she?" said Mildred, when they went away.

They went back to have tea at the Metropole. Mildred liked the crowd and the band. Philip was tired of talking, and he watched her face as she looked with keen eyes at the dresses of the women who came in. She had a peculiar sharpness for reckoning up what things cost, and now and then she leaned over to him and whispered the result of her meditations.

"D'you see that aigrette there? That cost every bit of seven guineas."

Or: "Look at that ermine, Philip. That's rabbit, that is—that's not ermine." She laughed triumphantly. "I'd know it a mile off."

Philip smiled happily. He was glad to see her pleasure, and the ingenuousness of her conversation amused and touched him. The band played sentimental music.

After dinner they walked down to the station, and Philip took her arm. He told her what arrangements he had made for their journey to France. She was to come up to London at the end of the week, but she told him that she could not go away till the Saturday of the week after that. He had already engaged a room in a hotel in Paris. He was looking forward eagerly to taking the tickets.

"You won't mind going second-class, will you? We mustn't be extravagant, and it'll be all the better if we can do ourselves pretty well when we get there."

He had talked to her a hundred times of the Quarter. They would wander through its pleasant old streets, and they would sit idly in the charming gardens of the Luxembourg. If the weather was fine perhaps, when they had had enough of Paris, they might go to Fontainebleau. The trees would be just bursting into leaf. The green of the forest in spring was more beautiful than anything he knew; it was like a song, and it was like the happy pain of love. Mildred listened quietly. He turned to her and tried to look deep into her eyes.

"You do want to come, don't you?" he said.

"Of course I do," she smiled.

"You don't know how I'm looking forward to it. I don't know how I shall get through the next days. I'm so afraid something will happen to prevent it. It maddens me sometimes that I can't tell you how much I love you. And at last, at last . . ."

He broke off. They reached the station, but they had dawdled on the way, and Philip had barely time to say good-night. He kissed her quickly and ran towards the wicket as fast as he could. She stood where he left her. He was strangely grotesque when he ran.

Chapter LXXIV

THE FOLLOWING SATURDAY MILDRED RETURNED, AND THAT EVENING Philip kept her to himself. He took seats for the play, and they drank champagne at dinner. It was her first gaiety in London for so long that she enjoyed everything ingenuously. She cuddled up to Philip when they drove from the theatre to the room he had taken for her in Pimlico.

"I really believe you're quite glad to see me," he said.

She did not answer, but gently pressed his hand. Demonstrations of affection were so rare with her that Philip was enchanted.

"I've asked Griffiths to dine with us tomorrow," he told her.

"Oh, I'm glad you've done that. I wanted to meet him."

There was no place of entertainment to take her to on Sunday night, and Philip was afraid she would be bored if she were alone with him all day. Griffiths was amusing; he would help them to get through the evening; and Philip was so fond of them both that he wanted them to know and to like one another. He left Mildred with the words:

"Only six days more."

They had arranged to dine in the gallery at Romano's on Sunday, because the dinner was excellent and looked as though it cost a good deal more than it did. Philip and Mildred arrived first and had to wait some time for Griffiths.

"He's an unpunctual devil," said Philip. "He's probably making love to one of his numerous flames."

But presently he appeared. He was a handsome creature, tall and thin; his head was placed well on the body, it gave him a conquering air which was attractive; and his curly hair, his bold, friendly blue eyes, his red mouth, were charming. Philip saw Mildred look at him with appreciation, and he felt a curious satisfaction. Griffiths greeted them with a smile.

"I've heard a great deal about you," he said to Mildred, as he took her hand.

"Not so much as I've heard about you," she answered.

"Nor so bad," said Philip.

"Has he been blackening my character?"

Griffiths laughed, and Philip saw that Mildred noticed how white and regular his teeth were and how pleasant his smile.

"You ought to feel like old friends," said Philip. "I've talked so much about you to one another."

Griffiths was in the best possible humour, for, having at length passed his final examination, he was qualified, and he had just been appointed house-surgeon at a hospital in the North of London. He was taking up his duties at the beginning of May and meanwhile was going home for a holiday; this was his last week in town, and he was determined to get as much enjoyment into it as he could. He began to talk the gay nonsense which Philip admired because he could not copy it. There was nothing much in what he said, but his vivacity gave it point. There flowed from him a force of life which affected everyone who knew him; it was almost as sensible as bodily warmth. Mildred was more lively than Philip had ever known her, and he was delighted to see that his little party was a success. She was amusing herself enormously. She laughed louder and louder. She quite forgot the genteel reserve which had become second nature to her.

Presently Griffiths said:

"I say, it's dreadfully difficult for me to call you Mrs. Miller. Philip never calls you anything but Mildred."

"I daresay she won't scratch your eyes out if you call her that too," laughed Philip.

"Then she must call me Harry."

Philip sat silent while they chattered away and thought how good it was to see people happy. Now and then Griffiths teazed him a little, kindly, because he was always so serious.

"I believe he's quite fond of you, Philip," smiled Mildred.

"He isn't a bad old thing," answered Griffiths, and taking Philip's hand he shook it gaily.

It seemed an added charm in Griffiths that he liked Philip. They were all sober people, and the wine they had drunk went to their heads. Griffiths became more talkative and so boisterous that Philip, amused, had to beg him to be quiet. He had a gift for story-telling, and his adventures lost nothing of their romance and their laughter in his narration. He played in all of them a gallant, humourous part. Mildred, her eyes shining with excitement, urged him on. He poured out anecdote after anecdote. When the lights began to be turned out she was astonished.

"My word, the evening has gone quickly. I thought it wasn't more than half-past nine."

They got up to go and when she said good-bye, she added:

"I'm coming to have tea at Philip's room tomorrow. You might look in if you can."

"All right," he smiled.

On the way back to Pimlico Mildred talked of nothing but Griffiths. She was taken with his good looks, his well-cut clothes, his voice, his gaiety.

"I *am* glad you like him," said Philip. "D'you remember you were rather sniffy about meeting him?"

"I think it's so nice of him to be so fond of you, Philip. He is a nice friend for you to have."

She put up her face to Philip for him to kiss her. It was a thing she did rarely.

"I have enjoyed myself this evening, Philip. Thank you so much."

"Don't be so absurd," he laughed, touched by her appreciation so that he felt the moisture come to his eyes.

She opened her door and just before she went in, turned again to Philip.

"Tell Harry I'm madly in love with him," she said.

"All right," he laughed. "Good-night."

Next day, when they were having tea, Griffiths came in. He sank lazily into an arm-chair. There was something strangely sensual in the slow movements of his large limbs. Philip remained silent, while the others chattered away, but he was enjoying himself. He admired them both so much that it seemed natural enough for them to admire one another. He did not care if Griffiths absorbed Mildred's attention, he would have her to himself during the evening: he had something of the attitude of a loving husband, confident in his wife's affection, who looks on with amusement while she flirts harmlessly with a stranger. But at half-past seven he looked at his watch and said:

"It's about time we went out to dinner, Mildred."

There was a moment's pause, and Griffiths seemed to be considering.

"Well, I'll be getting along," he said at last. "I didn't know it was so late."

"Are you doing anything tonight?" asked Mildred.

"No."

There was another silence. Philip felt slightly irritated.

"I'll just go and have a wash," he said, and to Mildred he added: "Would you like to wash your hands?"

She did not answer him.

"Why don't you come and dine with us?" she said to Griffiths.

He looked at Philip and saw him staring at him sombrely.

"I dined with you last night," he laughed. "I should be in the way."

"Oh, that doesn't matter," insisted Mildred. "Make him come, Philip. He won't be in the way, will he?"

"Let him come by all means if he'd like to."

"All right, then," said Griffiths promptly. "I'll just go upstairs and tidy myself."

The moment he left the room Philip turned to Mildred angrily.

"Why on earth did you ask him to dine with us?"

"I couldn't help myself. It would have looked so funny to say nothing when he said he wasn't doing anything."

"Oh, what rot! And why the hell did you ask him if he was doing anything?"

Mildred's pale lips tightened a little.

"I want a little amusement sometimes. I get tired always being alone with you."

They heard Griffiths coming heavily down the stairs, and Philip went into his bed-room to wash. They dined in the neighbourhood in an Italian restaurant. Philip was cross and silent, but he quickly realised that he was showing to disadvantage in comparison with Griffiths, and he forced himself to hide his annoyance. He drank a good deal of wine to destroy the pain that was gnawing at his heart, and he set himself to talk. Mildred, as though remorseful for what she had said, did all she could to make herself pleasant to him. She was kindly and affectionate. Presently Philip began to think he had been a fool to surrender to a feeling of jealousy. After dinner when they got into a hansom to drive to a music-hall Mildred, sitting between the two men, of her own accord gave him her hand. His anger vanished. Suddenly, he knew not how, he grew conscious that Griffiths was holding her other hand. The pain seized him again violently, it was a real physical pain, and he asked himself, panic-stricken, what he might have asked himself before, whether Mildred and Griffiths were in love with one another. He could not see anything of the performance on account of the mist of suspicion, anger, dismay, and wretchedness which seemed to be before his eyes; but he forced himself to conceal the fact that anything was the matter; he went on talking and laughing. Then a strange desire to torture himself seized him, and he got up, saying he wanted to go and drink something. Mildred and Griffiths had never been alone together for a moment. He wanted to leave them by themselves.

"I'll come too," said Griffiths. "I've got rather a thirst on."

"Oh, nonsense, you stay and talk to Mildred."

Philip did not know why he said that. He was throwing them together now to make the pain he suffered more intolerable. He did not go to the bar, but up into the balcony, from where he could watch them and not be seen. They had ceased to look at the stage and were smiling into one another's eyes. Griffiths was talking with his usual happy fluency and Mildred seemed to hang on his lips. Philip's head began to ache frightfully. He stood there motionless. He knew he would be in the way if he went back. They were enjoying themselves without him, and he was suffering, suffering. Time passed, and now he had an extraordinary shyness about rejoining them. He knew they had not thought of him at all, and he reflected bitterly that he had paid for the dinner and their seats in the music-hall. What a fool they were making of him! He was hot with shame. He could see how happy they were without him. His instinct was to leave them to themselves and go home, but he had not his hat and coat, and it would necessitate endless explanations. He went back. He felt a shadow of annoyance in Mildred's eyes when she saw him, and his heart sank.

"You've been a devil of a time," said Griffiths, with a smile of welcome.

"I met some men I knew. I've been talking to them, and I couldn't get away. I thought you'd be all right together."

"I've been enjoying myself thoroughly," said Griffiths. "I don't know about Mildred."

She gave a little laugh of happy complacency. There was a vulgar sound in the ring of it that horrified Philip. He suggested that they should go.

"Come on," said Griffiths, "we'll both drive you home."

Philip suspected that she had suggested that arrangement so that she might not be left alone with him. In the cab he did not take her hand nor did she offer it, and he knew all the time that she was holding Griffiths'. His chief thought was that it was all so horribly vulgar. As they drove along he asked himself what plans they had made to meet without his knowledge, he cursed himself for having left them alone, he had actually gone out of his way to enable them to arrange things.

"Let's keep the cab," said Philip, when they reached the house in which Mildred was lodging. "I'm too tired to walk home."

On the way back Griffiths talked gaily and seemed indifferent to the fact that Philip answered in monosyllables. Philip felt he must notice that something was the matter. Philip's silence at last grew too significant to struggle against, and Griffiths, suddenly nervous, ceased talking. Philip wanted to say something, but he was so shy he could hardly bring himself to, and yet the time was passing and the opportunity would be lost. It was best to get at the truth at once. He forced himself to speak.

"Are you in love with Mildred?" he asked suddenly.

"I?" Griffiths laughed. "Is that what you've been so funny about this evening? Of course not. My dear old man."

He tried to slip his hand through Philip's arm, but Philip drew himself away. He knew Griffiths was lying. He could not bring himself to force Griffiths to tell him that he had not been holding the girl's hand. He suddenly felt very weak and broken.

"It doesn't matter to you, Harry," he said. "You've got so many women—don't take her away from me. It means my whole life. I've been so awfully wretched."

His voice broke, and he could not prevent the sob that was torn from him. He was horribly ashamed of himself.

"My dear old boy, you know I wouldn't do anything to hurt you. I'm far too fond of you for that. I was only playing the fool. If I'd known you were going to take it like that I'd have been more careful."

"Is that true?" asked Philip.

"I don't care a twopenny damn for her. I give you my word of honour."

Philip gave a sigh of relief. The cab stopped at their door.

Chapter LXXV

NEXT DAY PHILIP WAS IN A GOOD TEMPER. HE WAS VERY ANXIOUS NOT TO bore Mildred with too much of his society, and so had arranged that he should not see her till dinner-time. She was ready when he fetched her, and he chaffed her for her unwonted punctuality. She was wearing a new dress he had given her. He remarked on its smartness.

"It'll have to go back and be altered," she said. "The skirt hangs all wrong."

"You'll have to make the dressmaker hurry up if you want to take it to Paris with you."

"It'll be ready in time for that."

"Only three more whole days. We'll go over by the eleven o'clock, shall we?"

"If you like."

He would have her for nearly a month entirely to himself. His eyes rested on her with hungry adoration. He was able to laugh a little at his own passion.

"I wonder what it is I see in you," he smiled.

"That's a nice thing to say," she answered.

Her body was so thin that one could almost see her skeleton. Her chest was as flat as a boy's. Her mouth, with its narrow pale lips, was ugly, and her skin was faintly green.

"I shall give you Blaud's Pills in quantities when we're away," said Philip, laughing. "I'm going to bring you back fat and rosy."

"I don't want to get fat," she said.

She did not speak of Griffiths, and presently while they were dining Philip half in malice, for he felt sure of himself and his power over her, said:

"It seems to me you were having a great flirtation with Harry last night?"

"I told you I was in love with him," she laughed.

"I'm glad to know that he's not in love with you."

"How d'you know?"

"I asked him."

She hesitated a moment, looking at Philip, and a curious gleam came into her eyes.

"Would you like to read a letter I had from him this morning?"

She handed him an envelope and Philip recognised Griffiths' bold, legible writing. There were eight pages. It was well written, frank and charming; it was the letter of a man who was used to making love to women. He told Mildred that he loved her passionately, he had fallen in love with her the first moment he saw her; he did not want to love her, for he knew how fond Philip was of her, but he could not help himself. Philip was such a dear, and he was very much ashamed of himself, but it was not his fault, he was just carried away. He paid her delightful compliments. Finally he thanked her for consenting to lunch with him next day and said he was dreadfully impatient to see her. Philip noticed that the letter was dated the night before; Griffiths must have written it after leaving Philip, and had taken the trouble to go out and post it when Philip thought he was in bed.

He read it with a sickening palpitation of his heart, but gave no outward sign of surprise. He handed it back to Mildred with a smile, calmly.

"Did you enjoy your lunch?"

"Rather," she said emphatically.

He felt that his hands were trembling, so he put them under the table.

"You mustn't take Griffiths too seriously. He's just a butterfly, you know."

She took the letter and looked at it again.

"I can't help it either," she said, in a voice which she tried to make nonchalant. "I don't know what's come over me."

"It's a little awkward for me, isn't it?" said Philip.

She gave him a quick look.

"You're taking it pretty calmly, I must say."

"What do you expect me to do? Do you want me to tear out my hair in handfuls?"

"I knew you'd be angry with me."

"The funny thing is, I'm not at all. I ought to have known this would happen. I was a fool to bring you together. I know perfectly well that he's got every advantage over me; he's much jollier, and he's very handsome, he's more amusing, he can talk to you about the things that interest you."

"I don't know what you mean by that. If I'm not clever I can't help it, but I'm not the fool you think I am, not by a long way, I can tell you. You're a bit too superior for me, my young friend."

"D'you want to quarrel with me?" he asked mildly.

"No, but I don't see why you should treat me as if I was I don't know what."

"I'm sorry, I didn't mean to offend you. I just wanted to talk things over quietly. We don't want to make a mess of them if we can help it. I saw you were attracted by him and it seemed to me very natural. The only thing that really hurts me is that he should have encouraged you. He knew how awfully keen I was on you. I think it's rather shabby of him to have written that letter to you five minutes after he told me he didn't care twopence about you."

"If you think you're going to make me like him any the less by saying nasty things about him, you're mistaken."

Philip was silent for a moment. He did not know what words he could use to make her see his point of view. He wanted to speak coolly and deliberately, but he was in such a turmoil of emotion that he could not clear his thoughts.

"It's not worthwhile sacrificing everything for an infatuation that you know can't last. After all, he doesn't care for anyone more than ten days, and you're rather cold; that sort of thing doesn't mean very much to you."

"That's what you think."

She made it more difficult for him by adopting a cantankerous tone.

"If you're in love with him you can't help it. I'll just bear it as best I can. We get on very well together, you and I, and I've not behaved badly to you, have I? I've always known that you're not in love with me, but you like me all right, and when we get over to Paris you'll forget about Griffiths. If you make up your mind to put him out of your thoughts you won't find it so hard as all that, and I've deserved that you should do something for me."

She did not answer, and they went on eating their dinner. When the silence grew oppressive Philip began to talk of indifferent things. He pretended not to notice that Mildred was inattentive. Her answers were perfunctory, and she volunteered no remarks of her own. At last she interrupted abruptly what he was saying:

"Philip, I'm afraid I shan't be able to go away on Saturday. The doctor says I oughtn't to."

He knew this was not true, but he answered:

"When will you be able to come away?"

She glanced at him, saw that his face was white and rigid, and looked nervously away. She was at that moment a little afraid of him.

"I may as well tell you and have done with it, I can't come away with you at all."

"I thought you were driving at that. It's too late to change your mind now. I've got the tickets and everything."

"You said you didn't wish me to go unless I wanted it too, and I don't."

"I've changed my mind. I'm not going to have any more tricks played with me. You must come."

"I like you very much, Philip, as a friend. But I can't bear to think of anything else. I don't like you that way. I couldn't, Philip."

"You were quite willing to a week ago."

"It was different then."

"You hadn't met Griffiths?"

"You said yourself I couldn't help it if I'm in love with him."

Her face was set into a sulky look, and she kept her eyes fixed on her plate. Philip was white with rage. He would have liked to hit her in the face with his clenched fist, and in fancy he saw how she would look with a black eye. There were two lads of eighteen dining at a table near them, and now and then they looked at Mildred; he wondered if they envied him dining with a pretty girl; perhaps they were wishing they stood in his shoes. It was Mildred who broke the silence.

"What's the good of our going away together? I'd be thinking of him all the time. It wouldn't be much fun for you."

"That's my business," he answered.

She thought over all his reply implicated, and she reddened.

"But that's just beastly."

"What of it?"

"I thought you were a gentleman in every sense of the word."

"You were mistaken."

His reply entertained him, and he laughed as he said it.

"For God's sake don't laugh," she cried. "I can't come away with you, Philip. I'm awfully sorry. I know I haven't behaved well to you, but one can't force themselves."

"Have you forgotten that when you were in trouble I did everything for you? I planked out the money to keep you till your baby was born, I paid for your doctor and everything, I paid for you to go to Brighton, and I'm paying for the keep of your baby, I'm paying for your clothes, I'm paying for every stitch you've got on now."

"If you was a gentleman you wouldn't throw what you've done for me in my face."

"Oh, for goodness' sake, shut up. What d'you suppose I care if I'm a gentleman or not? If I were a gentleman I shouldn't waste my time with a vulgar slut like you. I don't care a damn if you like me or not. I'm sick of being made a blasted fool of. You're jolly well coming to Paris with me on Saturday or you can take the consequences."

Her cheeks were red with anger, and when she answered her voice had the hard commonness which she concealed generally by a genteel enunciation.

"I never liked you, not from the beginning, but you forced yourself on me, I always hated it when you kissed me. I wouldn't let you touch me now not if I was starving."

Philip tried to swallow the food on his plate, but the muscles of his throat refused to act. He gulped down something to drink and lit a cigarette. He was trembling in every part. He did not speak. He waited for her to move, but she sat in silence, staring at the white table-cloth. If they had been alone he would have flung his arms round her and kissed her passionately; he fancied the throwing back of her long white throat as he pressed upon her mouth with his lips. They passed an hour without speaking, and at last Philip thought the waiter began to stare at them curiously. He called for the bill.

"Shall we go?" he said then, in an even tone.

She did not reply, but gathered together her bag and her gloves. She put on her coat.

"When are you seeing Griffiths again?"

"Tomorrow," she answered indifferently.

"You'd better talk it over with him."

She opened her bag mechanically and saw a piece of paper in it. She took it out.

"Here's the bill for this dress," she said hesitatingly.

"What of it?"

"I promised I'd give her the money tomorrow."

"Did you?"

"Does that mean you won't pay for it after having told me I could get it?"

"It does."

"I'll ask Harry," she said, flushing quickly.

"He'll be glad to help you. He owes me seven pounds at the moment, and he pawned his microscope last week, because he was so broke."

"You needn't think you can frighten me by that. I'm quite capable of earning my own living."

"It's the best thing you can do. I don't propose to give you a farthing more."

She thought of her rent due on Saturday and the baby's keep, but did not say anything. They left the restaurant, and in the street Philip asked her:

"Shall I call a cab for you? I'm going to take a little stroll."

"I haven't got any money. I had to pay a bill this afternoon."

"It won't hurt you to walk. If you want to see me tomorrow I shall be in about tea-time."

He took off his hat and sauntered away. He looked round in a moment and saw that she was standing helplessly where he had left her, looking at the traffic. He went back and with a laugh pressed a coin into her hand.

"Here's two bob for you to get home with."

Before she could speak he hurried away.

Chapter LXXVI

NEXT DAY, IN THE AFTERNOON, PHILIP SAT IN HIS ROOM AND WONDERED whether Mildred would come. He had slept badly. He had spent the morning in the club of the Medical School, reading one newspaper after another. It was the vacation and few students he knew were in London, but he found one or two people to talk to, he played a game of chess, and so wore out the tedious hours. After luncheon he felt so tired, his head was aching so, that he went back to his lodgings and lay down; he tried to read a novel. He had not seen Griffiths. He was not in when Philip returned the night before; he heard him come back, but he did not as usual look into Philip's room to see if he was asleep; and in the morning Philip heard him go out early. It was clear that he wanted to avoid him. Suddenly there was a light tap at his door. Philip sprang to his feet and opened it. Mildred stood on the threshold. She did not move.

"Come in," said Philip.

He closed the door after her. She sat down. She hesitated to begin.

"Thank you for giving me that two shillings last night," she said.

"Oh, that's all right."

She gave him a faint smile. It reminded Philip of the timid, ingratiating look of a puppy that has been beaten for naughtiness and wants to reconcile himself with his master.

"I've been lunching with Harry," she said.

"Have you?"

"If you still want me to go away with you on Saturday, Philip, I'll come."

A quick thrill of triumph shot through his heart, but it was a sensation that only lasted an instant; it was followed by a suspicion.

"Because of the money?" he asked.

"Partly," she answered simply. "Harry can't do anything. He owes five weeks here, and he owes you seven pounds, and his tailor's pressing him for money. He'd pawn anything he could, but he's pawned everything already. I had a job to put the woman off about my new dress, and on Saturday there's the book at my lodgings, and I can't get work in five minutes. It always means waiting some little time till there's a vacancy."

She said all this in an even, querulous tone, as though she were recounting the injustices of fate, which had to be borne as part of the natural order of things. Philip did not answer. He knew what she told him well enough.

"You said partly," he observed at last.

"Well, Harry says you've been a brick to both of us. You've been a real good friend to him, he says, and you've done for me what p'raps no other man would have done. We must do the straight thing, he says. And he said what you said about him, that he's fickle by nature, he's not like you, and I should be a fool to throw you away for him. He won't last and you will, he says so himself."

"D'you *want* to come away with me?" asked Philip.

"I don't mind."

He looked at her, and the corners of his mouth turned down in an expression of misery. He had triumphed indeed, and he was going to have his way. He gave a little laugh of derision at his own humiliation. She looked at him quickly, but did not speak.

"I've looked forward with all my soul to going away with you, and I thought at last, after all that wretchedness, I was going to be happy . . ."

He did not finish what he was going to say. And then on a sudden, without warning, Mildred broke into a storm of tears. She was sitting in the chair in which Norah had sat and wept, and like her she hid her face on the back of it, towards the side where there was a little bump formed by the sagging in the middle, where the head had rested.

"I'm not lucky with women," thought Philip.

Her thin body was shaken with sobs. Philip had never seen a woman cry with such an utter abandonment. It was horribly painful, and his heart was torn. Without realising what he did, he went up to her and put his arms round her; she did not resist, but in her wretchedness surrendered herself to his comforting. He whispered to her little words of solace. He scarcely knew what he was saying, he bent over her and kissed her repeatedly.

"Are you awfully unhappy?" he said at last.

"I wish I was dead," she moaned. "I wish I'd died when the baby come."

Her hat was in her way, and Philip took it off for her. He placed her head more comfortably in the chair, and then he went and sat down at the table and looked at her.

"It is awful, love, isn't it?" he said. "Fancy anyone wanting to be in love."

Presently the violence of her sobbing diminished and she sat in the chair, exhausted, with her head thrown back and her arms hanging by her side. She had the grotesque look of one of those painters' dummies used to hang draperies on.

"I didn't know you loved him so much as all that," said Philip.

He understood Griffiths' love well enough, for he put himself in Griffiths' place and saw with his eyes, touched with his hands; he was able to think himself in Griffiths' body, and he kissed her with his lips, smiled at her with his smiling blue eyes. It was her emotion that surprised him. He had never thought her capable of passion, and this was passion: there was no mistaking it. Something seemed to give way in his heart; it really felt to him as though something were breaking, and he felt strangely weak.

"I don't want to make you unhappy. You needn't come away with me if you don't want to. I'll give you the money all the same."

She shook her head.

"No, I said I'd come, and I'll come."

"What's the good, if you're sick with love for him?"

"Yes, that's the word. I'm sick with love. I know it won't last, just as well as he does, but just now . . ."

She paused and shut her eyes as though she were going to faint. A strange idea came to Philip, and he spoke it as it came, without stopping to think it out.

"Why don't you go away with him?"

"How can I? You know we haven't got the money."

"I'll give you the money"

"You?"

She sat up and looked at him. Her eyes began to shine, and the colour came into her cheeks.

"Perhaps the best thing would be to get it over, and then you'd come back to me."

Now that he had made the suggestion he was sick with anguish, and yet the torture of it gave him a strange, subtle sensation. She stared at him with open eyes.

"Oh, how could we, on your money? Harry wouldn't think of it."

"Oh yes, he would, if you persuaded him."

Her objections made him insist, and yet he wanted her with all his heart to refuse vehemently.

"I'll give you a fiver, and you can go away from Saturday to Monday. You could easily do that. On Monday he's going home till he takes up his appointment at the North London."

"Oh, Philip, do you mean that?" she cried, clasping her hands. "If you could only let us go—I would love you so much afterwards, I'd do anything for you. I'm sure I shall get over it if you'll only do that. Would you really give us the money?"

"Yes," he said.

She was entirely changed now. She began to laugh. He could see that she was insanely happy. She got up and knelt down by Philip's side, taking his hands.

"You are a brick, Philip. You're the best fellow I've ever known. Won't you be angry with me afterwards?"

He shook his head, smiling, but with what agony in his heart!

"May I go and tell Harry now? And can I say to him that you don't mind? He won't consent unless you promise it doesn't matter. Oh, you don't know how I love him! And afterwards I'll do anything you like. I'll come over to Paris with you or anywhere on Monday."

She got up and put on her hat.

"Where are you going?"

"I'm going to ask him if he'll take me."

"Already?"

"D'you want me to stay? I'll stay if you like."

She sat down, but he gave a little laugh.

"No, it doesn't matter, you'd better go at once. There's only one thing: I can't bear to see Griffiths just now, it would hurt me too awfully. Say I have no ill-feeling towards him or anything like that, but ask him to keep out of my way."

"All right." She sprang up and put on her gloves. "I'll let you know what he says."

"You'd better dine with me tonight."

"Very well."

She put up her face for him to kiss her, and when he pressed his lips to hers she threw her arms round his neck.

"You are a darling, Philip."

She sent him a note a couple of hours later to say that she had a headache and could not dine with him. Philip had almost expected it. He knew that she was dining with Griffiths. He was horribly jealous, but the sudden passion which had seized the pair of them seemed like something that had come from the outside, as though a god had visited them with it, and he felt himself helpless. It seemed so natural that they should love one another. He saw all the advantages that Griffiths had over himself and confessed that in Mildred's place he would have done as Mildred did. What hurt him most was Griffiths' treachery; they had been such good friends, and Griffiths knew how passionately devoted he was to Mildred: he might have spared him.

He did not see Mildred again till Friday; he was sick for a sight of her by then; but when she came and he realised that he had gone out of her thoughts entirely, for they were engrossed in Griffiths, he suddenly hated her. He saw now why she and Griffiths loved one another, Griffiths was stupid, oh so stupid! he had known that all along, but had shut his eyes to it, stupid and empty-headed: that charm of his concealed an utter selfishness; he was willing to sacrifice anyone to his appetites. And how inane was the life he led, lounging about bars and drinking in music-halls, wandering from one light amour to another! He never read a book, he was blind to everything that was not frivolous and vulgar; he had never a thought that was fine: the word most common on his lips was smart; that was his highest praise for man or woman. Smart! It was no wonder he pleased Mildred. They suited one another.

Philip talked to Mildred of things that mattered to neither of them. He knew she wanted to speak of Griffiths, but he gave her no opportunity. He did not refer to the fact that two evenings before she had put off dining with him on a trivial excuse. He was casual with her, trying to make her think he was suddenly grown indifferent; and he exercised peculiar skill in saying little things which he knew would wound her; but which were so indefinite, so delicately cruel, that she could not take exception to them. At last she got up.

"I think I must be going off now," she said.

"I daresay you've got a lot to do," he answered.

She held out her hand, he took it, said good-bye, and opened the door for her. He knew what she wanted to speak about, and he knew also that his cold, ironical air intimidated her. Often his shyness made him seem so frigid that unintentionally he frightened people, and, having discovered this, he was able when occasion arose to assume the same manner.

"You haven't forgotten what you promised?" she said at last, as he held open the door.

"What is that?"

"About the money"

"How much d'you want?"

He spoke with an icy deliberation which made his words peculiarly offensive. Mildred flushed. He knew she hated him at that moment, and he wondered at the self-control by which she prevented herself from flying out at him. He wanted to make her suffer.

"There's the dress and the book tomorrow. That's all. Harry won't come, so we shan't want money for that."

Philip's heart gave a great thud against his ribs, and he let the door handle go. The door swung to.

"Why not?"

"He says we couldn't, not on your money."

A devil seized Philip, a devil of self-torture which was always lurking within him, and, though with all his soul he wished that Griffiths and Mildred should not go away together, he could not help himself; he set himself to persuade Griffiths through her.

"I don't see why not, if I'm willing," he said.

"That's what I told him."

"I should have thought if he really wanted to go he wouldn't hesitate."

"Oh, it's not that, he wants to all right. He'd go at once if he had the money."

"If he's squeamish about it I'll give *you* the money."

"I said you'd lend it if he liked, and we'd pay it back as soon as we could."

"It's rather a change for you going on your knees to get a man to take you away for a week-end."

"It is rather, isn't it?" she said, with a shameless little laugh.

It sent a cold shudder down Philip's spine.

"What are you going to do then?" he asked.

"Nothing. He's going home tomorrow. He must."

That would be Philip's salvation. With Griffiths out of the way he could get Mildred back. She knew no one in London, she would be thrown on to his society, and when they were alone together he could soon make her forget this infatuation. If he said nothing more he was safe. But he had a fiendish desire to break down their scruples, he wanted to know how abominably they could behave towards him; if he tempted them a little more they would yield, and he took a fierce joy at the thought of their dishonour. Though every word he spoke tortured him, he found in the torture a horrible delight.

"It looks as if it were now or never."

"That's what I told him," she said.

There was a passionate note in her voice which struck Philip. He was biting his nails in his nervousness.

"Where were you thinking of going?"

"Oh, to Oxford. He was at the 'Varsity there, you know. He said he'd show me the colleges."

Philip remembered that once he had suggested going to Oxford for the day, and she had expressed firmly the boredom she felt at the thought of sights.

"And it looks as if you'd have fine weather. It ought to be very jolly there just now."

"I've done all I could to persuade him."

"Why don't you have another try?"

"Shall I say you want us to go?"

"I don't think you must go as far as that," said Philip.

She paused for a minute or two, looking at him. Philip forced himself to look at her in a friendly way. He hated her, he despised her, he loved her with all his heart.

"I'll tell you what I'll do, I'll go and see if he can't arrange it. And then, if he says yes, I'll come and fetch the money tomorrow. When shall you be in?"

"I'll come back here after luncheon and wait."

"All right."

"I'll give you the money for your dress and your room now."

He went to his desk and took out what money he had. The dress was six guineas; there was besides her rent and her food, and the baby's keep for a week. He gave her eight pounds ten.

"Thanks very much," she said.

She left him.

Chapter LXXVII

AFTER LUNCHING IN THE BASEMENT OF THE MEDICAL SCHOOL PHILIP WENT back to his rooms. It was Saturday afternoon, and the landlady was cleaning the stairs.

"Is Mr. Griffiths in?" he asked.

"No, sir. He went away this morning, soon after you went out."

"Isn't he coming back?"

"I don't think so, sir. He's taken his luggage."

Philip wondered what this could mean. He took a book and began to read. It was Burton's *Journey to Meccah,* which he had just got out of the Westminster Public Library; and he read the first page, but could make no sense of it, for his mind was elsewhere; he was listening all the time for a ring at the bell. He dared not hope that Griffiths had gone away already, without Mildred, to his home in Cumberland. Mildred would be coming presently for the money. He set his teeth and read on; he tried desperately to concentrate his attention; the sentences etched themselves in his brain by the force of his effort, but they were distorted by the agony he was enduring. He wished with all his heart that he had not made the horrible proposition to give them money; but now that he had made it he lacked the strength to go back on it, not on Mildred's account, but on his own. There was a morbid obstinacy in him which forced him to do the thing he had determined. He discovered that the three pages he had read had made no impression on him at all; and he went back and started from the beginning: he found himself reading one sentence over and over again; and now it weaved itself in with his thoughts, horribly, like some formula in a nightmare. One thing he could do was to go out and keep away till midnight; they could not go then; and he saw them calling at the house every hour to ask if he was in. He enjoyed the thought of their disappointment. He repeated that sentence to himself mechanically. But he could not do that. Let them come and take the money, and he would know then to what depths of infamy it was possible for men to descend. He could not read any more now. He simply could not see the words. He leaned back in his chair, closing his eyes, and, numb with misery, waited for Mildred.

The landlady came in.

"Will you see Mrs. Miller, sir?"

"Show her in."

Philip pulled himself together to receive her without any sign of what he was feeling. He had an impulse to throw himself on his knees and seize her hands and beg her not to go; but he knew there was no way of moving her; she would tell Griffiths what he had said and how acted. He was ashamed.

"Well, how about the little jaunt?" he said gaily.

"We're going. Harry's outside. I told him you didn't want to see him, so he's kept out of your way. But he wants to know if he can come in just for a minute to say good-bye to you."

"No, I won't see him," said Philip.

He could see she did not care if he saw Griffiths or not. Now that she was there he wanted her to go quickly.

"Look here, here's the fiver. I'd like you to go now."

She took it and thanked him. She turned to leave the room.

"When are you coming back?" he asked.

"Oh, on Monday. Harry must go home then."

He knew what he was going to say was humiliating, but he was broken down with jealousy and desire.

"Then I shall see you, shan't I?"

He could not help the note of appeal in his voice.

"Of course. I'll let you know the moment I'm back."

He shook hands with her. Through the curtains he watched her jump into a four-wheeler that stood at the door. It rolled away. Then he threw himself on his bed and hid his face in his hands. He felt tears coming to his eyes, and he was angry with himself; he clenched his hands and screwed up his body to prevent them; but he could not; and great painful sobs were forced from him.

He got up at last, exhausted and ashamed, and washed his face. He mixed himself a strong whiskey and soda. It made him feel a little better. Then he caught sight of the tickets to Paris, which were on the chimney-piece, and, seizing them, with an impulse of rage he flung them in the fire. He knew he could have got the money back on them, but it relieved him to destroy them. Then he went out in search of someone to be with. The club was empty. He felt he would go mad unless he found someone to talk to; but Lawson was abroad; he went on to Hayward's rooms: the maid who opened the door told him that he had gone down to Brighton for the week-end. Then Philip went to a gallery and found it was just closing. He did not know what to do. He was distracted. And he thought of Griffiths and Mildred going to Oxford, sitting opposite one another in the train, happy. He went back to his rooms, but they filled him with horror, he had been so wretched in them; he tried once more to read Burton's book, but, as he read, he told himself again and again what a fool he had been; it was he who had made the suggestion that they should go away, he had offered the money, he had forced it upon them; he might have known what would happen when he introduced Griffiths to Mildred; his own vehement passion was enough to arouse the other's desire. By this time they had reached Oxford. They would put up in one of the lodging-houses in John Street; Philip had never been to Oxford, but Griffiths had talked to him about it so much that he knew exactly where they would go; and they would dine at the Clarendon: Griffiths had been in the habit of dining there when he went on the spree. Philip got himself something to eat in a restaurant near Charing Cross; he had made up his mind to go to a play, and afterwards he fought his way into the pit of a theatre at which one of Oscar Wilde's pieces was being performed. He wondered if Mildred and Griffiths would go to a play that evening: they must kill the evening somehow; they were too stupid, both of them to content themselves with conversation: he got a fierce delight in reminding himself of the vulgarity of their minds which suited them so exactly to one another. He watched the play with an abstracted mind, trying to give himself gaiety by drinking whiskey in each interval; he was unused to alcohol, and it affected him quickly, but his drunkenness was savage and morose. When the play was over he had another drink. He could not go to bed, he knew he would not sleep, and he dreaded the pictures which his vivid imagination would place before him. He tried not to think of them. He knew he had drunk too much. Now he was seized with a desire to do horrible, sordid things; he wanted to roll himself in gutters; his whole being yearned for beastliness; he wanted to grovel.

He walked up Piccadilly, dragging his club-foot, sombrely drunk, with rage and misery clawing at his heart. He was stopped by a painted harlot, who put her hand on his arm; he pushed her violently away with brutal words. He walked on a few steps and then stopped. She would do as well as another. He was sorry he had spoken so roughly to her. He went up to her.

"I say," he began.

"Go to hell," she said.

Philip laughed.

"I merely wanted to ask if you'd do me the honour of supping with me tonight."

She looked at him with amazement, and hesitated for a while. She saw he was drunk.

"I don't mind."

He was amused that she should use a phrase he had heard so often on Mildred's lips. He took her to one of the restaurants he had been in the habit of going to with Mildred. He noticed as they walked along that she looked down at his limb.

"I've got a club-foot," he said. "Have you any objection?"

"You are a cure," she laughed.

When he got home his bones were aching, and in his head there was a hammering that made him nearly scream. He took another whiskey and soda to steady himself, and going to bed sank into a dreamless sleep till mid-day.

Chapter LXXVIII

At last Monday came, and Philip thought his long torture was over. Looking out the trains he found that the latest by which Griffiths could reach home that night left Oxford soon after one, and he supposed that Mildred would take one which started a few minutes later to bring her to London. His desire was to go and meet it, but he thought Mildred would like to be left alone for a day; perhaps she would drop him a line in the evening to say she was back, and if not he would call at her lodgings next morning: his spirit was cowed. He felt a bitter hatred for Griffiths, but for Mildred, notwithstanding all that had passed, only a heart-rending desire. He was glad now that Hayward was not in London on Saturday afternoon when, distraught, he went in search of human comfort: he could not have prevented himself from telling him everything, and Hayward would have been astonished at his weakness. He would despise him, and perhaps be shocked or disgusted that he could envisage the possibility of making Mildred his mistress after she had given herself to another man. What did he care if it was shocking or disgusting? He was ready for any compromise, prepared for more degrading humiliations still, if he could only gratify his desire.

Towards the evening his steps took him against his will to the house in which she lived, and he looked up at her window. It was dark. He did not venture to ask if she was back. He was confident in her promise. But there was no letter from her in the morning, and, when about mid-day he called, the maid told him she had not arrived. He could not understand it. He knew that Griffiths would have been obliged to go home the day before, for he was to be best man at a wedding, and Mildred had no money. He turned over in his mind every possible thing that might have happened. He went again in the afternoon and left a note, asking her to dine with him that evening as calmly as though the events of the last fortnight had not happened. He mentioned the place and time at which they were to meet, and hoping against hope kept the appointment: though he waited for an hour she did not come. On Wednesday morning he was ashamed to ask at the house and sent a messenger-boy with a letter and instructions to bring back a reply; but in an hour the boy came back with Philip's letter unopened and the answer that the lady had not returned from the country. Philip was beside himself. The last deception was more than he could bear. He repeated to himself over and over again that he loathed Mildred, and, ascribing to Griffiths this new disappointment, he hated him so much that he knew what was the delight of murder: he walked about considering what a joy it would be to come upon him on a dark night and stick a knife into his throat, just about the carotid artery, and leave him to die in the street like a dog. Philip was out of his senses with grief and rage. He did not like whiskey, but he drank to stupefy himself. He went to bed drunk on the Tuesday and on the Wednesday night.

On Thursday morning he got up very late and dragged himself, blear-eyed and sallow, into his sitting-room to see if there were any letters. A curious feeling shot through his heart when he recognised the handwriting of Griffiths.

DEAR OLD MAN—I hardly know how to write to you and yet I feel I must write. I hope you're not awfully angry with me. I know I oughtn't to have gone away with Milly, but I simply couldn't help myself. She simply carried me off my feet and I would have done anything to get her. When she told me you had offered us the money to go I simply couldn't resist. And now it's all over I'm awfully ashamed of myself and I wish I hadn't been such a fool. I wish you'd write and say you're not angry with me, and I want you to let me come and see you. I was awfully hurt at your telling Milly you didn't want to see me. Do write me a line, there's a good chap, and tell me you forgive me. It'll ease my conscience. I thought you wouldn't mind or you wouldn't have offered the money. But I know I oughtn't to have taken it. I came home on Monday and Milly wanted to stay a couple of days at Oxford by herself. She's going back to London on Wednesday, so by the time you receive this letter you will have seen her and I hope everything will go off all right. Do write and say you forgive me. Please write at once.

Yours ever,
HARRY

Philip tore up the letter furiously. He did not mean to answer it. He despised Griffiths for his apologies, he had no patience with his prickings of conscience: one could do a dastardly thing if one chose, but it was contemptible to regret it afterwards. He thought the letter cowardly and hypocritical. He was disgusted at its sentimentality.

"It would be very easy if you could do a beastly thing," he muttered to himself, "and then say you were sorry, and that put it all right again."

He hoped with all his heart he would have the chance one day to do Griffiths a bad turn.

But at all events he knew that Mildred was in town. He dressed hurriedly, not waiting to shave, drank a cup of tea, and took a cab to her rooms. The cab seemed to crawl. He was painfully anxious to see her, and unconsciously he uttered a prayer to the God he did not believe in to make her receive him kindly. He only wanted to forget. With beating heart he rang the bell. He forgot all his suffering in the passionate desire to enfold her once more in his arms.

"Is Mrs. Miller in?" he asked joyously.

"She's gone," the maid answered.

He looked at her blankly.

"She came about an hour ago and took away her things."

For a moment he did not know what to say.

"Did you give her my letter? Did she say where she was going?"

Then he understood that Mildred had deceived him again. She was not coming back to him. He made an effort to save his face.

"Oh, well, I daresay I shall hear from her. She may have sent a letter to another address."

He turned away and went back hopeless to his rooms. He might have known that she would do this; she had never cared for him, she had made a fool of him from the beginning; she had no pity, she had no kindness, she had no charity. The only thing was to accept the inevitable. The pain he was suffering was horrible, he would sooner be dead than endure it; and the thought came to him that it would be better to finish with the whole thing: he might throw himself in the river or put his neck on a railway line; but he had no sooner set the thought into words than he rebelled against it. His reason told him that he would get over his unhappiness in time; if he tried with all his might he could forget her; and it would be grotesque to kill himself on account of a vulgar slut. He had only one life, and it was madness to fling it away. He *felt* that he would never overcome his passion, but he *knew* that after all it was only a matter of time.

He would not stay in London. There everything reminded him of his unhappiness. He telegraphed to his uncle that he was coming to Blackstable, and, hurrying to pack, took the first train he could. He wanted to get away from the sordid rooms in which he had endured so much suffering. He wanted to breathe clean air. He was disgusted with himself. He felt that he was a little mad.

Since he was grown up Philip had been given the best spare room at the vicarage. It was a corner-room and in front of one window was an old tree which blocked the view, but from the other you saw, beyond the garden and the vicarage field, broad meadows. Philip remembered the wall-paper from his earliest years. On the walls were quaint water colours of the early Victorian period by a friend of the Vicar's youth. They had a faded charm. The dressing-table was surrounded by stiff muslin. There was an old tall-boy to put your clothes in. Philip gave a sigh of pleasure; he had never realised that all those things meant anything to him at all. At the vicarage life went on as it had always done. No piece of furniture had been moved from one place to another; the Vicar ate the same things, said the same things, went for the same walk every day; he had grown a little fatter, a little more silent, a little more narrow. He had become accustomed to living without his wife and missed her very little. He bickered still with Josiah Graves. Philip went to see the churchwarden. He was a little thinner, a little whiter, a little more austere; he was autocratic still and still disapproved of candles on the altar. The shops had still a pleasant quaintness; and Philip stood in front of that in which things useful to seamen were sold, sea-boots and tarpaulins and tackle, and remembered that he had felt there in his childhood the thrill of the sea and the adventurous magic of the unknown.

He could not help his heart beating at each double knock of the postman in case there might be a letter from Mildred sent on by his landlady in London; but he knew that there would be none. Now that he could think it out more calmly he understood that in trying to force Mildred to love him he had been attempting the impossible. He did not know what it was that passed from a man to a woman, from a woman to a man, and made one of them a slave: it was convenient to call it the sexual instinct; but if it was no more than that, he did not understand why it should occasion so vehement an attraction to one person rather than another. It was irresistible: the mind could not battle with it; friendship, gratitude, interest, had no power beside it. Because he had not attracted Mildred sexually, nothing that he did had any effect upon her. The idea revolted him; it made human nature beastly; and he felt suddenly that the hearts of men were full of dark places. Because Mildred was indifferent to him he had thought her sexless; her anaemic appearance and thin lips, the body with its narrow hips and flat chest, the languor of her manner, carried out his supposition; and yet she was capable of sudden passions which made her willing to risk everything to gratify them. He had never understood her adventure with Emil Miller: it had seemed so unlike her, and she had never been able to explain it; but now that he had seen her with Griffiths he knew that just the same thing had happened then: she had been carried off her feet by an ungovernable desire. He tried to think out what those two men had which so strangely attracted her. They both had a vulgar facetiousness which tickled her simple sense of humour, and a certain coarseness of nature; but what took her perhaps was the blatant sexuality which was their most marked characteristic. She had a genteel refinement which shuddered at the facts of life, she looked upon the bodily functions as indecent, she had all sorts of euphemisms for common objects, she always chose an elaborate word as more becoming than a simple one: the brutality of these men was like a whip on her thin white shoulders, and she shuddered with voluptuous pain.

One thing Philip had made up his mind about. He would not go back to the lodgings in which he had suffered. He wrote to his landlady and gave her notice. He wanted to have his own things about him. He determined to take unfurnished rooms: it would be pleasant and cheaper; and this was an urgent consideration, for during the last year and a half he had spent nearly seven hundred pounds. He must make up for it now by the most rigid economy. Now and then he thought of the future with panic; he had been a fool to spend so much money on Mildred; but he knew that if it were to come again he would act in the same way. It amused him sometimes to consider that his friends, because he had a face which did not express his feelings very vividly and a rather slow way of moving, looked upon him as strong-minded, deliberate, and cool. They thought him reasonable and praised his common sense; but he knew that his placid expression was no more than a mask, assumed unconsciously, which acted like the protective colouring of butterflies; and himself was astonished at the weakness of his will. It seemed to him that he was swayed by every light emotion, as though he were a leaf in the wind, and when passion seized him he was powerless. He had no self-control. He merely seemed to possess it because he was indifferent to many of the things which moved other people.

He considered with some irony the philosophy which he had developed for himself, for it had not been of much use to him in the conjuncture he had passed through; and he wondered whether thought really helped a man in any of the critical affairs of life: it seemed to him rather that he was swayed by some power alien to and yet within himself, which urged him like that great wind of Hell which drove Paolo and Francesca ceaselessly on. He thought of what he was going to do and, when the time came to act, he was powerless in the grasp of instincts, emotions, he knew not what. He acted as though he were a machine driven by the two forces of his environment and his personality; his reason was someone looking on, observing the facts but powerless to interfere: it was like those gods of Epicurus, who saw the doings of men from their empyrean heights and had no might to alter one smallest particle of what occurred.

Chapter LXXIX

PHILIP WENT UP TO LONDON A COUPLE OF DAYS BEFORE THE SESSION BEGAN in order to find himself rooms. He hunted about the streets that led out of the Westminster Bridge Road, but their dinginess was distasteful to him; and at last he found one in Kennington which had a quiet and old-world air. It reminded one a little of the London which Thackeray knew on that side of the river, and in the Kennington Road, through which the great barouche of the Newcomes must have passed as it drove the family to the West of London, the plane-trees were bursting into leaf. The houses in the street which Philip fixed upon were two-storied, and in most of the windows was a notice to state that lodgings were to let. He knocked at one which announced that the lodgings were unfurnished, and was shown by an austere, silent woman four very small rooms, in one of which there was a kitchen range and a sink. The rent was nine shillings a week. Philip did not want so many rooms, but the rent was low and he wished to settle down at once. He asked the landlady if she could keep the place clean for him and cook his breakfast, but she replied that she had enough work to do without that; and he was pleased rather than otherwise because she intimated that she wished to have nothing more to do with him than to receive his rent. She told him that, if he inquired at the grocer's round the corner, which was also a post office, he might hear of a woman who would "do" for him.

Philip had a little furniture which he had gathered as he went along, an armchair that he had bought in Paris, and a table, a few drawings, and the small Persian rug which Cronshaw had given him. His uncle had offered a fold-up bed for which, now that he no longer let his house in August, he had no further use; and by spending another ten pounds Philip bought himself whatever else was essential. He spent ten shillings on putting a corn-coloured paper in the room he was making his parlour; and he hung on the walls a sketch which Lawson had given him of the Quai des Grands Augustins, and the photograph of the *Odalisque* by Ingres and Manet's *Olympia* which in Paris had been the objects of his contemplation while he shaved. To remind himself that he too had once been engaged in the practice of art, he put up a charcoal drawing of the young Spaniard Miguel Ajuria: it was the best thing he had ever done, a nude standing with clenched hands, his feet gripping the floor with a peculiar force, and on his face that air of determination which had been so impressive; and though Philip after the long interval saw very well the defects of his work its associations made him look upon it with tolerance. He wondered what had happened to Miguel. There is nothing so terrible as the pursuit of art by those who have no talent. Perhaps, worn out by exposure, starvation, disease, he had found an end in some hospital, or in an access of despair had sought death in the turbid Seine; but perhaps with his Southern instability he had given up the struggle of his own accord, and now, a clerk in some office in Madrid, turned his fervent rhetoric to politics and bull-fighting.

Philip asked Lawson and Hayward to come and see his new rooms, and they came, one with a bottle of whiskey, the other with a *paté de foie gras*; and he was delighted when they praised his taste. He would have invited the Scotch stockbroker too, but he had only three chairs, and thus could entertain only a definite number of guests. Lawson was aware that through him Philip had become very friendly with Norah Nesbit and now remarked that he had run across her a few days before.

"She was asking how you were."

Philip flushed at the mention of her name (he could not get himself out of the awkward habit of reddening when he was embarrassed), and Lawson looked at him quizzically. Lawson, who now spent most of the year in London, had so far surrendered to his environment as to wear his hair short and to dress himself in a neat serge suit and a bowler hat.

"I gather that all is over between you," he said.

"I've not seen her for months."

"She was looking rather nice. She had a very smart hat on with a lot of white ostrich feathers on it. She must be doing pretty well."

Philip changed the conversation, but he kept thinking of her, and after an interval, when the three of them were talking of something else, he asked suddenly:

"Did you gather that Norah was angry with me?"

"Not a bit. She talked very nicely of you."

"I've got half a mind to go and see her."

"She won't eat you."

Philip had thought of Norah often. When Mildred left him his first thought was of her, and he told himself bitterly that she would never have treated him so. His impulse was to go to her; he could depend on her pity; but he was ashamed: she had been good to him always, and he had treated her abominably.

"If I'd only had the sense to stick to her!" he said to himself, afterwards, when Lawson and Hayward had gone and he was smoking a last pipe before going to bed.

He remembered the pleasant hours they had spent together in the cosy sitting-room in Vincent Square, their visits to galleries and to the play, and the charming evenings of intimate conversation. He recollected her solicitude for his welfare and her interest in all that concerned him. She had loved him with a love that was kind and lasting, there was more than sensuality in it, it was almost maternal; he had always known that it was a precious thing for which with all his soul he should thank the gods. He made up his mind to throw himself on her mercy. She must have suffered horribly, but he felt she had the greatness of heart to forgive him: she was incapable of malice. Should he write to her? No. He would break in on her suddenly and cast himself at her feet—he knew that when the time came he would feel too shy to perform such a dramatic gesture, but that was how he liked to think of it—and tell her that if she would take him back she might rely on him forever. He was cured of the hateful disease from which he had suffered, he knew her worth, and now she might trust him. His imagination leaped forward to the future. He pictured himself rowing with her on the river on Sundays; he would take her to Greenwich, he had never forgotten that delightful excursion with Hayward, and the beauty of the Port of London remained a permanent treasure in his recollection; and on the warm summer afternoons they would sit in the Park together and talk: he laughed to himself as he remembered her gay chatter, which poured out like a brook bubbling over little stones, amusing, flippant, and full of character. The agony he had suffered would pass from his mind like a bad dream.

But when next day, about tea-time, an hour at which he was pretty certain to find Norah at home, he knocked at her door his courage suddenly failed him. Was it possible for her to forgive him? It would be abominable of him to force himself on her presence. The door was opened by a maid new since he had been in the habit of calling every day, and he inquired if Mrs. Nesbit was in.

"Will you ask her if she could see Mr. Carey?" he said. "I'll wait here."

The maid ran upstairs and in a moment clattered down again.

"Will you step up, please, sir. Second floor front."

"I know," said Philip, with a slight smile.

He went with a fluttering heart. He knocked at the door.

"Come in," said the well-known, cheerful voice.

It seemed to say come in to a new life of peace and happiness. When he entered Norah stepped forward to greet him. She shook hands with him as if they had parted the day before. A man stood up.

"Mr. Carey—Mr. Kingsford."

Philip, bitterly disappointed at not finding her alone, sat down and took stock of the stranger. He had never heard her mention his name, but he seemed to Philip to occupy his chair as though he were very much at home. He was a man of forty, clean-shaven, with long fair hair very neatly plastered down, and the reddish skin and pale, tired eyes which fair men get when their youth is passed. He had a large nose, a large mouth; the bones of his face were prominent, and he was heavily made; he was a man of more than average height, and broad-shouldered.

"I was wondering what had become of you," said Norah, in her sprightly manner. "I met Mr. Lawson the other day—did he tell you?—and I informed him that it was really high time you came to see me again."

Philip could see no shadow of embarrassment in her countenance, and he admired the ease with which she carried off an encounter of which himself felt the intense awkwardness. She gave him tea. She was about to put sugar in it when he stopped her.

"How stupid of me!" she cried. "I forgot."

He did not believe that. She must remember quite well that he never took sugar in his tea. He accepted the incident as a sign that her nonchalance was affected.

The conversation which Philip had interrupted went on, and presently he began to feel a little in the way. Kingsford took no particular notice of him. He talked fluently and well, not without humour, but with a slightly dogmatic manner: he was a journalist, it appeared, and had something amusing to say on every topic that was touched upon; but it exasperated Philip to find himself edged out of the conversation. He was determined to stay the visitor out. He wondered if he admired Norah. In the old days they had often talked of the men who wanted to flirt with her and had laughed at them together. Philip tried to bring back the conversation to matters which only he and Norah knew about, but each time the journalist broke in and succeeded in drawing it away to a subject upon which Philip was forced to be silent. He grew faintly angry with Norah, for she must see he was being made ridiculous; but perhaps she was inflicting this upon him as a punishment, and with this thought he regained his good humour. At last, however, the clock struck six, and Kingsford got up.

"I must go," he said.

Norah shook hands with him, and accompanied him to the landing. She shut the door behind her and stood outside for a couple of minutes. Philip wondered what they were talking about.

"Who is Mr. Kingsford?" he asked cheerfully, when she returned.

"Oh, he's the editor of one of Harmsworth's Magazines. He's been taking a good deal of my work lately."

"I thought he was never going."

"I'm glad you stayed. I wanted to have a talk with you." She curled herself into the large arm-chair, feet and all, in a way her small size made possible, and lit a cigarette. He smiled when he saw her assume the attitude which had always amused him.

"You look just like a cat."

She gave him a flash of her dark, fine eyes.

"I really ought to break myself of the habit. It's absurd to behave like a child when you're my age, but I'm comfortable with my legs under me."

"It's awfully jolly to be sitting in this room again," said Philip happily. "You don't know how I've missed it."

"Why on earth didn't you come before?" she asked gaily.

"I was afraid to," he said, reddening.

She gave him a look full of kindness. Her lips outlined a charming smile.

"You needn't have been."

He hesitated for a moment. His heart beat quickly.

"D'you remember the last time we met? I treated you awfully badly—I'm dreadfully ashamed of myself."

She looked at him steadily. She did not answer. He was losing his head; he seemed to have come on an errand of which he was only now realising the outrageousness. She did not help him, and he could only blurt out bluntly.

"Can you ever forgive me?"

Then impetuously he told her that Mildred had left him and that his unhappiness had been so great that he almost killed himself. He told her of all that had happened between them, of the birth of the child, and of the meeting with Griffiths, of his folly and his trust and his immense deception. He told her how often he had thought of her kindness and of her love, and how bitterly he had regretted throwing it away: he had only been happy when he was with her, and he knew now how great was her worth. His voice was hoarse with emotion. Sometimes he was so ashamed of what he was saying that he spoke with his eyes fixed on the ground. His face was distorted with pain, and yet he felt it a strange relief to speak. At last he finished. He flung himself back in his chair, exhausted, and waited. He had concealed nothing, and even, in his self-abasement, he had striven to make himself more despicable than he had really been. He was surprised that she did not speak, and at last he raised his eyes. She was not looking at him. Her face was quite white, and she seemed to be lost in thought.

"Haven't you got anything to say to me?"

She started and reddened.

"I'm afraid you've had a rotten time," she said. "I'm dreadfully sorry."

She seemed about to go on, but she stopped, and again he waited. At length she seemed to force herself to speak.

"I'm engaged to be married to Mr. Kingsford."

"Why didn't you tell me at once?" he cried. "You needn't have allowed me to humiliate myself before you."

"I'm sorry, I couldn't stop you. . . . I met him soon after you"—she seemed to search for an expression that should not wound him—"told me your friend had come back. I was very wretched for a bit, he was extremely kind to me. He knew someone had made me suffer, of course he doesn't know it was you, and I don't know what I should have done without him. And suddenly I felt I couldn't go on working, working, working; I was so tired, I felt so ill. I told him about my husband. He offered to give me the money to get my divorce if I would marry him as soon as I could. He had a very good job, and it wouldn't be necessary for me to do anything unless I wanted to. He was so fond of me and so anxious to take care of me. I was awfully touched. And now I'm very, very fond of him."

"Have you got your divorce then?" asked Philip.

"I've got the decree nisi. It'll be made absolute in July, and then we are going to be married at once."

For some time Philip did not say anything.

"I wish I hadn't made such a fool of myself," he muttered at length.

He was thinking of his long, humiliating confession. She looked at him curiously.

"You were never really in love with me," she said.

"It's not very pleasant being in love."

But he was always able to recover himself quickly, and, getting up now and holding out his hand, he said:

"I hope you'll be very happy. After all, it's the best thing that could have happened to you."

She looked a little wistfully at him as she took his hand and held it.

"You'll come and see me again, won't you?" she asked.

"No," he said, shaking his head. "It would make me too envious to see you happy."

He walked slowly away from her house. After all she was right when she said he had never loved her. He was disappointed, irritated even, but his vanity was more affected than his heart. He knew that himself. And presently he grew conscious that the gods had played a very good practical joke on him, and he laughed at himself mirthlessly. It is not very comfortable to have the gift of being amused at one's own absurdity.

Chapter LXXX

For the next three months Philip worked on subjects which were new to him. The unwieldy crowd which had entered the Medical School nearly two years before had thinned out: some had left the hospital, finding the examinations more difficult to pass than they expected, some had been taken away by parents who had not foreseen the expense of life in London, and some had drifted away to other callings. One youth whom Philip knew had devised an ingenious plan to make money; he had bought things at sales and pawned them, but presently found it more profitable to pawn goods bought on credit; and it had caused a little excitement at the hospital when someone pointed out his name in police-court proceedings. There had been a remand, then assurances on the part of a harassed father, and the young man had gone out to bear the White Man's Burden overseas. The imagination of another, a lad who had never before been in a town at all, fell to the glamour of music-halls and bar parlours; he spent his time among racing-men, tipsters, and trainers, and now was become a book-maker's clerk. Philip had seen him once in a bar near Piccadilly Circus in a tight-waisted coat and a brown hat with a broad, flat brim. A third, with a gift for singing and mimicry, who had achieved success at the smoking concerts of the Medical School by his imitation of notorious comedians, had abandoned the hospital for the chorus of a musical comedy. Still another, and he interested Philip because his uncouth manner and interjectional speech did not suggest that he was capable of any deep emotion, had felt himself stifle among the houses of London. He grew haggard in shut-in spaces, and the soul he knew not he possessed struggled like a sparrow held in the hand, with little frightened gasps and a quick palpitation of the heart: he yearned for the broad skies and the open, desolate places among which his childhood had been spent; and he walked off one day, without a word to anybody, between one lecture and another; and the next thing his friends heard was that he had thrown up medicine and was working on a farm.

Philip attended now lectures on medicine and on surgery. On certain mornings in the week he practised bandaging on out-patients glad to earn a little money, and he was taught auscultation and how to use the stethoscope. He learned dispensing. He was taking the examination in *Materia Medica* in July, and it amused him to play with various drugs, concocting mixtures, rolling pills, and making ointments. He seized avidly upon anything from which he could extract a suggestion of human interest.

He saw Griffiths once in the distance, but, not to have the pain of cutting him dead, avoided him. Philip had felt a certain self-consciousness with Griffiths' friends, some of whom were now friends of his, when he realised they knew of his quarrel with Griffiths and surmised they were aware of the reason. One of them, a very tall fellow, with a small head and a languid air, a youth called Ramsden, who was one of Griffiths' most faithful admirers, copied his ties, his boots, his manner of talking and his gestures, told Philip that Griffiths was very much hurt because Philip had not answered his letter. He wanted to be reconciled with him.

"Has he asked you to give me the message?" asked Philip.

"Oh, no, I'm saying this entirely on my own," said Ramsden. "He's awfully sorry for what he did, and he says you always behaved like a perfect brick to him. I know he'd be glad to make it up. He doesn't come to the hospital because he's afraid of meeting you, and he thinks you'd cut him."

"I should."

"It makes him feel rather wretched, you know."

"I can bear the trifling inconvenience that he feels with a good deal of fortitude," said Philip.

"He'll do anything he can to make it up."

"How childish and hysterical! Why should he care? I'm a very insignificant person, and he can do very well without my company. I'm not interested in him any more."

Ramsden thought Philip hard and cold. He paused for a moment or two, looking about him in a perplexed way.

"Harry wishes to God he'd never had anything to do with the woman."

"Does he?" asked Philip.

He spoke with an indifference which he was satisfied with. No one could have guessed how violently his heart was beating. He waited impatiently for Ramsden to go on.

"I suppose you've quite got over it now, haven't you?"

"I?" said Philip. "Quite."

Little by little he discovered the history of Mildred's relations with Griffiths. He listened with a smile on his lips, feigning an equanimity which quite deceived the dull-witted boy who talked to him. The week-end she spent with Griffiths at Oxford inflamed rather than extinguished her sudden passion; and when Griffiths went home, with a feeling that was unexpected in her she determined to stay in Oxford by herself for a couple of days, because she had been so happy in it. She felt that nothing could induce her to go back to Philip. He revolted her. Griffiths was taken aback at the fire he had aroused, for he had found his two days with her in the country somewhat tedious; and he had no desire to turn an amusing episode into a tiresome affair. She made him promise to write to her, and, being an honest, decent fellow, with natural politeness and a desire to make himself pleasant to everybody, when he got home he wrote her a long and charming letter. She answered it with reams of passion, clumsy, for she had no gift of expression, ill-written, and vulgar; the letter bored him, and when it was followed next day by another, and the day after by a third, he began to think her love no longer flattering but alarming. He did not answer; and she bombarded him with telegrams, asking him if he were ill and had received her letters; she said his silence made her dreadfully anxious. He was forced to write, but he sought to make his reply as casual as was possible without being offensive: he begged her not to wire, since it was difficult to explain telegrams to his mother, an old-fashioned person for whom a telegram was still an event to excite tremor. She answered by return of post that she must see him and announced her intention to pawn things (she had the dressing-case which Philip had given her as a wedding-present and could raise eight pounds on that) in order to come up and stay at the market town four miles from which was the village in which his father practised. This frightened Griffiths; and he, this time, made use of the telegraph wires to tell her that she must do nothing of the kind. He promised to let her know the moment he came up to London, and, when he did, found that she had already been asking for him at the hospital at which he had an appointment. He did not like this, and, on seeing her, told Mildred that she was not to come there on any pretext; and now, after an absence of three weeks, he found that she bored him quite decidedly; he wondered why he had ever troubled about her, and made up his mind to break with her as soon as he could. He was a person who dreaded quarrels, nor did he want to give pain; but at the same time he had other things to do, and he was quite determined not to let Mildred bother him. When he met her he was pleasant, cheerful, amusing, affectionate; he invented convincing excuses for the interval since last he had seen her; but he did everything he could to avoid her. When she forced him to make appointments he sent telegrams to her at the last moment to put himself off; and his landlady (the first three months of his appointment he was spending in rooms) had orders to say he was out when Mildred called. She would waylay him in the street and, knowing she had been waiting about for him to come out of the hospital for a couple of hours, he would give her a few charming, friendly words and bolt off with the excuse that he had a business engagement. He grew very skilful in slipping out of the hospital unseen. Once, when he went back to his lodgings at midnight, he saw a woman standing at the area railings and suspecting who it was went to beg a shake-down in Ramsden's rooms; next day the landlady told him that Mildred had sat crying on the doorsteps for hours, and she had been obliged to tell her at last that if she did not go away she would send for a policeman.

"I tell you, my boy," said Ramsden, "you're jolly well out of it. Harry says that if he'd suspected for half a second she was going to make such a blooming nuisance of herself he'd have seen himself damned before he had anything to do with her."

Philip thought of her sitting on that doorstep through the long hours of the night. He saw her face as she looked up dully at the landlady who sent her away.

"I wonder what she's doing now."

"Oh, she's got a job somewhere, thank God. That keeps her busy all day."

The last thing he heard, just before the end of the summer session, was that Griffiths' urbanity had given way at length under the exasperation of the constant persecution. He had told Mildred that he was sick of being pestered, and she had better take herself off and not bother him again.

"It was the only thing he could do," said Ramsden. "It was getting a bit too thick."

"Is it all over then?" asked Philip.

"Oh, he hasn't seen her for ten days. You know, Harry's wonderful at dropping people. This is about the toughest nut he's ever had to crack, but he's cracked it all right."

Then Philip heard nothing more of her at all. She vanished into the vast anonymous mass of the population of London.

Chapter LXXXI

AT THE BEGINNING OF THE WINTER SESSION PHILIP BECAME AN OUT-patients' clerk. There were three assistant-physicians who took out-patients, two days a week each, and Philip put his name down for Dr. Tyrell. He was popular with the students, and there was some competition to be his clerk. Dr. Tyrell was a tall, thin man of thirty-five, with a very small head, red hair cut short, and prominent blue eyes: his face was bright scarlet. He talked well in a pleasant voice, was fond of a little joke, and treated the world lightly. He was a successful man, with a large consulting practice and a knighthood in prospect. From commerce with students and poor people he had the patronising air, and from dealing always with the sick he had the healthy man's jovial condescension, which some consultants achieve as the professional manner. He made the patient feel like a boy confronted by a jolly schoolmaster; his illness was an absurd piece of naughtiness which amused rather than irritated.

The student was supposed to attend in the out-patients' room every day, see cases, and pick up what information he could; but on the days on which he clerked his duties were a little more definite. At that time the out-patients' department at St. Luke's consisted of three rooms, leading into one another, and a large, dark waiting-room with massive pillars of masonry and long benches. Here the patients waited after having been given their "letters" at mid-day; and the long rows of them, bottles and gallipots in hand, some tattered and dirty, others decent enough, sitting in the dimness, men and women of all ages, children, gave one an impression which was weird and horrible. They suggested the grim drawings of Daumier. All the rooms were painted alike, in salmon-colour with a high dado of maroon; and there was in them an odour of disinfectants, mingling as the afternoon wore on with the crude stench of humanity. The first room was the largest and in the middle of it were a table and an office chair for the physician; on each side of this were two smaller tables, a little lower: at one of these sat the house-physician and at the other the clerk who took the "book" for the day. This was a large volume in which were written down the name, age, sex, profession, of the patient and the diagnosis of his disease.

At half-past one the house-physician came in, rang the bell, and told the porter to send in the old patients. There were always a good many of these, and it was necessary to get through as many of them as possible before Dr. Tyrell came at two. The H.P. with whom Philip came in contact was a dapper little man, excessively conscious of his importance: he treated the clerks with condescension and patently resented the familiarity of older students who had been his contemporaries and did not use him with the respect he felt his present position demanded. He set about the cases. A clerk helped him. The patients streamed in. The men came first. Chronic bronchitis, "a nasty 'acking cough," was what they chiefly suffered from; one went to the H.P. and the other to the clerk, handing in their letters: if they were going on well the words *Rep 14* were written on them, and they went to the dispensary with their bottles or gallipots in order to have medicine given them for fourteen days more. Some old stagers held back so that they might be seen by the physician himself, but they seldom succeeded in this; and only three or four, whose condition seemed to demand his attention, were kept.

Dr. Tyrell came in with quick movements and a breezy manner. He reminded one slightly of a clown leaping into the arena of a circus with the cry: Here we are again. His air seemed to indicate: What's all this nonsense about being ill? I'll soon put that right. He took his seat, asked if there were any old patients for him to see, rapidly passed them in review, looking at them with shrewd eyes as he discussed their symptoms, cracked a joke (at which all the clerks laughed heartily) with the H.P., who laughed heartily too but with an air as if he thought it was rather impudent for the clerks to laugh, remarked that it was a fine day or a hot one, and rang the bell for the porter to show in the new patients.

They came in one by one and walked up to the table at which sat Dr. Tyrell. They were old men and young men and middle-aged men, mostly of the labouring class, dock labourers, draymen, factory hands, barmen; but some, neatly dressed, were of a station which was obviously superior, shop-assistants, clerks, and the like. Dr. Tyrell looked at these with suspicion. Sometimes they put on shabby clothes in order to pretend they were poor; but he had a keen eye to prevent what he regarded as fraud and sometimes refused to see people who, he thought, could well pay for medical attendance. Women were the worst offenders and they managed the thing more clumsily. They would wear a cloak and a skirt which were almost in rags, and neglect to take the rings off their fingers.

"If you can afford to wear jewellery you can afford a doctor. A hospital is a charitable institution," said Dr. Tyrell.

He handed back the letter and called for the next case.

"But I've got my letter."

"I don't care a hang about your letter; you get out. You've got no business to come and steal the time which is wanted by the really poor."

The patient retired sulkily, with an angry scowl.

"She'll probably write a letter to the papers on the gross mismanagement of the London hospitals," said Dr. Tyrell, with a smile, as he took the next paper and gave the patient one of his shrewd glances.

Most of them were under the impression that the hospital was an institution of the state, for which they paid out of the rates, and took the attendance they received as a right they could claim. They imagined the physician who gave them his time was heavily paid.

Dr. Tyrell gave each of his clerks a case to examine. The clerk took the patient into one of the inner rooms; they were smaller, and each had a couch in it covered with black horse-hair: he asked his patient a variety of questions, examined his lungs, his heart, and his liver, made notes of fact on the hospital letter, formed in his own mind some idea of the diagnosis, and then waited for Dr. Tyrell to come in. This he did, followed by a small crowd of students, when he had finished the men, and the clerk read out what he had learned. The physician asked him one or two questions, and examined the patient himself. If there was anything interesting to hear students applied their stethoscope: you would see a man with two or three to the chest, and two perhaps to his back, while others waited impatiently to listen. The patient stood among them a little embarrassed, but not altogether displeased to find himself the centre of attention: he listened confusedly while Dr. Tyrell discoursed glibly on the case. Two or three students listened again to recognise the murmur or the crepitation which the physician described, and then the man was told to put on his clothes.

When the various cases had been examined Dr. Tyrell went back into the large room and sat down again at his desk. He asked any student who happened to be standing near him what he would prescribe for a patient he had just seen. The student mentioned one or two drugs.

"Would you?" said Dr. Tyrell. "Well, that's original at all events. I don't think we'll be rash."

This always made the students laugh, and with a twinkle of amusement at his own bright humour the physician prescribed some other drug than that which the student had suggested. When there were two cases of exactly the same sort and the student proposed the treatment which the physician had ordered for the first, Dr. Tyrell exercised considerable ingenuity in thinking of something else. Sometimes, knowing that in the dispensary they were worked off their legs and preferred to give the medicines which they had all ready, the good hospital mixtures which had been found by the experience of years to answer their purpose so well, he amused himself by writing an elaborate prescription.

"We'll give the dispenser something to do. If we go on prescribing *mist: alb:* he'll lose his cunning."

The students laughed, and the doctor gave them a circular glance of enjoyment in his joke. Then he touched the bell and, when the porter poked his head in, said:

"Old women, please."

He leaned back in his chair, chatting with the H.P. while the porter herded along the old patients. They came in, strings of anaemic girls, with large fringes and pallid lips, who could not digest their bad, insufficient food; old ladies, fat and thin, aged prematurely by frequent confinements, with winter coughs; women with this, that, and the other, the matter with them. Dr. Tyrell and his house-physician got through them quickly. Time was getting on, and the air in the small room was growing more sickly. The physician looked at his watch.

"Are there many new women today?" he asked.

"A good few, I think," said the H.P.

"We'd better have them in. You can go on with the old ones."

They entered. With the men the most common ailments were due to the excessive use of alcohol, but with the women they were due to defective nourishment. By about six o'clock they were finished. Philip, exhausted by standing all the time, by the bad air, and by the attention he had given, strolled over with his fellow-clerks to the Medical School to have tea. He found the work of absorbing interest. There was humanity there in the rough, the materials the artist worked on; and Philip felt a curious thrill when it occurred to him that he was in the position of the artist and the patients were like clay in his hands. He remembered with an amused shrug of the shoulders his life in Paris, absorbed in colour, tone, values, Heaven knows what, with the aim of producing beautiful things: the directness of contact with men and women gave a thrill of power which he had never known. He found an endless excitement in looking at their faces and hearing them speak; they came in each with his peculiarity, some shuffling uncouthly, some with a little trip, others with heavy, slow tread, some shyly. Often you could guess their trades by the look of them. You learned in what way to put your questions so that they should be understood, you discovered on what subjects nearly all lied, and by what inquiries you could extort the truth notwithstanding. You saw the different way people took the same things. The diagnosis of dangerous illness would be accepted by one with a laugh and a joke, by another with dumb despair. Philip found that he was less shy with these people than he had ever been with others; he felt not exactly sympathy, for sympathy suggests condescension; but he felt at home with them. He found that he was able to put them at their ease, and, when he had been given a case to find out what he could about it, it seemed to him that the patient delivered himself into his hands with a peculiar confidence.

"Perhaps," he thought to himself, with a smile, "perhaps I'm cut out to be a doctor. It would be rather a lark if I'd hit upon the one thing I'm fit for."

It seemed to Philip that he alone of the clerks saw the dramatic interest of those afternoons. To the others men and women were only cases, good if they were complicated, tiresome if obvious; they heard murmurs and were astonished at abnormal livers; an unexpected sound in the lungs gave them something to talk about. But to Philip there was much more. He found an interest in just looking at them, in the shape of their heads and their hands, in the look of their eyes and the length of their noses. You saw in that room human nature taken by surprise, and often the mask of custom was torn off rudely, showing you the soul all raw. Sometimes you saw an untaught stoicism which was profoundly moving. Once Philip saw a man, rough and illiterate, told his case was hopeless; and, self-controlled himself, he wondered at the splendid instinct which forced the fellow to keep a stiff upper-lip before strangers. But was it possible for him to be brave when he was by himself, face to face with his soul, or would he then surrender to despair? Sometimes there was tragedy. Once a young woman brought her sister to be examined, a girl of eighteen, with delicate features and large blue eyes, fair hair that sparkled with gold when a ray of autumn sunshine touched it for a moment, and a skin of amazing beauty. The students' eyes went to her with little smiles. They did not often see a pretty girl in these dingy rooms. The elder woman gave the family history, father and mother had died of phthisis, a brother and a sister, these two were the only ones left. The girl had been coughing lately and losing weight. She took off her blouse and the skin of her neck was like milk. Dr. Tyrell examined her quietly, with his usual rapid method; he told two or three of his clerks to apply their stethoscopes to a place he indicated with his finger; and then she was allowed to dress. The sister was standing a little apart and she spoke to him in a low voice, so that the girl should not hear. Her voice trembled with fear.

"She hasn't got it, doctor, has she?"

"I'm afraid there's no doubt about it."

"She was the last one. When she goes I shan't have anybody."

She began to cry, while the doctor looked at her gravely; he thought she too had the type; she would not make old bones either. The girl turned round and saw her sister's tears. She understood what they meant. The colour fled from her lovely face and tears fell down her cheeks. The two stood for a minute or two, crying silently, and then the older, forgetting the indifferent crowd that watched them, went up to her, took her in her arms, and rocked her gently to and fro as if she were a baby.

When they were gone a student asked:

"How long d'you think she'll last, sir?"

Dr. Tyrell shrugged his shoulders.

"Her brother and sister died within three months of the first symptoms. She'll do the same. If they were rich one might do something. You can't tell these people to go to St. Moritz. Nothing can be done for them."

Once a man who was strong and in all the power of his manhood came because a persistent aching troubled him and his club-doctor did not seem to do him any good; and the verdict for him too was death, not the inevitable death that horrified and yet was tolerable because science was helpless before it, but the death which was inevitable because the man was a little wheel in the great machine of a complex civilisation, and had as little power of changing the circumstances as an automaton. Complete rest was his only chance. The physician did not ask impossibilities.

"You ought to get some very much lighter job."

"There ain't no light jobs in my business."

"Well, if you go on like this you'll kill yourself. You're very ill."

"D'you mean to say I'm going to die?"

"I shouldn't like to say that, but you're certainly unfit for hard work."

"If I don't work who's to keep the wife and the kids?"

Dr. Tyrell shrugged his shoulders. The dilemma had been presented to him a hundred times. Time was pressing and there were many patients to be seen.

"Well, I'll give you some medicine and you can come back in a week and tell me how you're getting on."

The man took his letter with the useless prescription written upon it and walked out. The doctor might say what he liked. He did not feel so bad that he could not go on working. He had a good job and he could not afford to throw it away.

"I give him a year," said Dr. Tyrell.

Sometimes there was comedy. Now and then came a flash of cockney humour, now and then some old lady, a character such as Charles Dickens might have drawn, would amuse them by her garrulous oddities. Once a woman came who was a member of the ballet at a famous music-hall. She looked fifty, but gave her age as twenty-eight. She was outrageously painted and ogled the students impudently with large black eyes; her smiles were grossly alluring. She had abundant self-confidence and treated Dr. Tyrell, vastly amused, with the easy familiarity with which she might have used an intoxicated admirer. She had chronic bronchitis, and told him it hindered her in the exercise of her profession.

"I don't know why I should 'ave such a thing, upon my word I don't. I've never 'ad a day's illness in my life. You've only got to look at me to know that."

She rolled her eyes round the young men, with a long sweep of her painted eyelashes, and flashed her yellow teeth at them. She spoke with a cockney accent, but with an affectation of refinement which made every word a feast of fun.

"It's what they call a winter cough," answered Dr. Tyrell gravely. "A great many middle-aged women have it."

"Well, I never! That is a nice thing to say to a lady. No one ever called me middle-aged before."

She opened her eyes very wide and cocked her head on one side, looking at him with indescribable archness.

"That is the disadvantage of our profession," said he. "It forces us sometimes to be ungallant."

She took the prescription and gave him one last, luscious smile.

"You will come and see me dance, dearie, won't you?"

"I will indeed."

He rang the bell for the next case.

"I am glad you gentlemen were here to protect me."

But on the whole the impression was neither of tragedy nor of comedy. There was no describing it. It was manifold and various; there were tears and laughter, happiness and woe; it was tedious and interesting and indifferent; it was as you saw it: it was tumultuous and passionate; it was grave; it was sad and comic; it was trivial; it was simple and complex; joy was there and despair; the love of mothers for their children, and of men for women; lust trailed itself through the rooms with leaden feet, punishing the guilty and the innocent, helpless wives and wretched children; drink seized men and women and cost its inevitable price; death sighed in these rooms; and the beginning of life, filling some poor girl with terror and shame, was diagnosed there. There was neither good nor bad there. There were just facts. It was life.

Chapter LXXXII

Towards the end of the year, when Philip was bringing to a close his three months as clerk in the out-patients' department, he received a letter from Lawson, who was in Paris.

Dear Philip—Cronshaw is in London and would be glad to see you. He is living at 43 Hyde Street, Soho. I don't know where it is, but I daresay you will be able to find out. Be a brick and look after him a bit. He is very down on his luck. He will tell you what he is doing. Things are going on here very much as usual. Nothing seems to have changed since you were here. Clutton is back, but he has become quite impossible. He has quarrelled with everybody. As far as I can make out he hasn't got a cent, he lives in a little studio right away beyond the Jardin des Plantes, but he won't let anybody see his work. He doesn't show anywhere, so one doesn't know what he is doing. He may be a genius, but on the other hand he may be off his head. By the way, I ran against Flanagan the other day. He was showing Mrs. Flanagan round the Quarter. He has chucked art and is now in popper's business. He seems to be rolling. Mrs. Flanagan is very pretty and I'm trying to work a portrait. How much would you ask if you were me? I don't want to frighten them, and then on the other hand I don't want to be such an ass as to ask £150 if they're quite willing to give £300.

Yours ever,
Frederick Lawson

Philip wrote to Cronshaw and received in reply the following letter. It was written on a half-sheet of common note-paper, and the flimsy envelope was dirtier than was justified by its passage through the post.

Dear Carey—Of course I remember you very well. I have an idea that I had some part in rescuing you from the Slough of Despond in which myself am hopelessly immersed. I shall be glad to see you. I am a stranger in a strange city and I am buffeted by the philistines. It will be pleasant to talk of Paris. I do not ask you to come and see me, since my lodging is not of a magnificence fit for the reception of an eminent member of Monsieur Purgon's profession, but you will find me eating modestly any evening between seven and eight at a restaurant yclept Au Bon Plaisir in Dean Street.

Your sincere
J. Cronshaw

Philip went the day he received this letter. The restaurant, consisting of one small room, was of the poorest class, and Cronshaw seemed to be its only customer. He was sitting in the corner, well away from draughts, wearing the same shabby great-coat which Philip had never seen him without, with his old bowler on his head.

"I eat here because I can be alone," he said. "They are not doing well; the only people who come are a few trollops and one or two waiters out of a job; they are giving up business, and the food is execrable. But the ruin of their fortunes is my advantage."

Cronshaw had before him a glass of absinthe. It was nearly three years since they had met, and Philip was shocked by the change in his appearance. He had been rather corpulent, but now he had a dried-up, yellow look: the skin of his neck was loose and wrinkled; his clothes hung about him as though they had been bought for someone else; and his collar, three or four sizes too large, added to the slatternliness of his appearance. His hands trembled continually. Philip remembered the handwriting which scrawled over the page with shapeless, haphazard letters. Cronshaw was evidently very ill.

"I eat little these days," he said. "I'm very sick in the morning. I'm just having some soup for my dinner, and then I shall have a bit of cheese."

Philip's glance unconsciously went to the absinthe, and Cronshaw, seeing it, gave him the quizzical look with which he reproved the admonitions of common sense.

"You have diagnosed my case, and you think it's very wrong of me to drink absinthe."

"You've evidently got cirrhosis of the liver," said Philip.

"Evidently."

He looked at Philip in the way which had formerly had the power of making him feel incredibly narrow. It seemed to point out that what he was thinking was distressingly obvious; and when you have agreed with the obvious what more is there to say? Philip changed the topic.

"When are you going back to Paris?"

"I'm not going back to Paris. I'm going to die."

The very naturalness with which he said this startled Philip. He thought of half a dozen things to say, but they seemed futile. He knew that Cronshaw was a dying man.

"Are you going to settle in London then?" he asked lamely.

"What is London to me? I am a fish out of water. I walk through the crowded streets, men jostle me, and I seem to walk in a dead city. I felt that I couldn't die in Paris. I wanted to die among my own people. I don't know what hidden instinct drew me back at the last."

Philip knew of the woman Cronshaw had lived with and the two draggle-tailed children, but Cronshaw had never mentioned them to him, and he did not like to speak of them. He wondered what had happened to them.

"I don't know why you talk of dying," he said.

"I had pneumonia a couple of winters ago, and they told me then it was a miracle that I came through. It appears I'm extremely liable to it, and another bout will kill me."

"Oh, what nonsense! You're not so bad as all that. You've only got to take precautions. Why don't you give up drinking?"

"Because I don't choose. It doesn't matter what a man does if he's ready to take the consequences. Well, I'm ready to take the consequences. You talk glibly of giving up drinking, but it's the only thing I've got left now. What do you think life would be to me without it? Can you understand the happiness I get out of my absinthe? I yearn for it; and when I drink it I savour every drop, and afterwards I feel my soul swimming in ineffable happiness. It disgusts you. You are a puritan and in your heart you despise sensual pleasures. Sensual pleasures are the most violent and the most exquisite. I am a man blessed with vivid senses, and I have indulged them with all my soul. I have to pay the penalty now, and I am ready to pay."

Philip looked at him for a while steadily.

"Aren't you afraid?"

For a moment Cronshaw did not answer. He seemed to consider his reply.

"Sometimes, when I'm alone." He looked at Philip. "You think that's a condemnation? You're wrong. I'm not afraid of my fear. It's folly, the Christian argument that you should live always in view of your death. The only way to live is to forget that you're going to die. Death is unimportant. The fear of it should never influence a single action of the wise man. I know that I shall die struggling for breath, and I know that I shall be horribly afraid. I know that I shall not be able to keep myself from regretting bitterly the life that has brought me to such a pass; but I disown that regret. I now, weak, old, diseased, poor, dying, hold still my soul in my hands, and I regret nothing."

"D'you remember that Persian carpet you gave me?" asked Philip.

Cronshaw smiled his old, slow smile of past days.

"I told you that it would give you an answer to your question when you asked me what was the meaning of life. Well, have you discovered the answer?"

"No," smiled Philip. "Won't you tell it me?"

"No, no, I can't do that. The answer is meaningless unless you discover it for yourself."

Chapter LXXXIII

CRONSHAW WAS PUBLISHING HIS POEMS. HIS FRIENDS HAD BEEN URGING HIM to do this for years, but his laziness made it impossible for him to take the necessary steps. He had always answered their exhortations by telling them that the love of poetry was dead in England. You brought out a book which had cost you years of thought and labour; it was given two or three contemptuous lines among a batch of similar volumes, twenty or thirty copies were sold, and the rest of the edition was pulped. He had long since worn out the desire for fame. That was an illusion like all else. But one of his friends had taken the matter into his own hands. This was a man of letters, named Leonard Upjohn, whom Philip had met once or twice with Cronshaw in the cafés of the Quarter. He had a considerable reputation in England as a critic and was the accredited exponent in this country of modern French literature. He had lived a good deal in France among the men who made the *Mercure de France* the liveliest review of the day, and by the simple process of expressing in English their point of view he had acquired in England a reputation for originality. Philip had read some of his articles. He had formed a style for himself by a close imitation of Sir Thomas Browne; he used elaborate sentences, carefully balanced, and obsolete, resplendent words: it gave his writing an appearance of individuality. Leonard Upjohn had induced Cronshaw to give him all his poems and found that there were enough to make a volume of reasonable size. He promised to use his influence with publishers. Cronshaw was in want of money. Since his illness he had found it more difficult than ever to work steadily; he made barely enough to keep himself in liquor; and when Upjohn wrote to him that this publisher and the other, though admiring the poems, thought it not worthwhile to publish them, Cronshaw began to grow interested. He wrote impressing upon Upjohn his great need and urging him to make more strenuous efforts. Now that he was going to die he wanted to leave behind him a published book, and at the back of his mind was the feeling that he had produced great poetry. He expected to burst upon the world like a new star. There was something fine in keeping to himself these treasures of beauty all his life and giving them to the world disdainfully when, he and the world parting company, he had no further use for them.

His decision to come to England was caused directly by an announcement from Leonard Upjohn that a publisher had consented to print the poems. By a miracle of persuasion Upjohn had persuaded him to give ten pounds in advance of royalties.

"In advance of royalties, mind you," said Cronshaw to Philip. "Milton only got ten pounds down."

Upjohn had promised to write a signed article about them, and he would ask his friends who reviewed to do their best. Cronshaw pretended to treat the matter with detachment, but it was easy to see that he was delighted with the thought of the stir he would make.

One day Philip went to dine by arrangement at the wretched eating-house at which Cronshaw insisted on taking his meals, but Cronshaw did not appear. Philip learned that he had not been there for three days. He got himself something to eat and went round to the address from which Cronshaw had first written to him. He had some difficulty in finding Hyde Street. It was a street of dingy houses huddled together; many of the windows had been broken and were clumsily repaired with strips of French newspaper; the doors had not been painted for years; there were shabby little shops on the ground floor, laundries, cobblers, stationers. Ragged children played in the road, and an old barrel-organ was grinding out a vulgar tune. Philip knocked at the door of Cronshaw's house (there was a shop of cheap sweetstuffs at the bottom), and it was opened by an elderly Frenchwoman in a dirty apron. Philip asked her if Cronshaw was in.

"Ah, yes, there is an Englishman who lives at the top, at the back. I don't know if he's in. If you want him you had better go up and see."

The staircase was lit by one jet of gas. There was a revolting odour in the house. When Philip was passing up a woman came out of a room on the first floor, looked at him suspiciously, but made no remark. There were three doors on the top landing. Philip knocked at one, and knocked again; there was no reply; he tried the handle, but the door was locked. He knocked at another door, got no answer, and tried the door again. It opened. The room was dark.

"Who's that?"

He recognised Cronshaw's voice.

"Carey. Can I come in?"

He received no answer. He walked in. The window was closed and the stink was overpowering. There was a certain amount of light from the arc-lamp in the street, and he saw that it was a small room with two beds in it, end to end; there was a washing-stand and one chair, but they left little space for anyone to move in. Cronshaw was in the bed nearest the window. He made no movement, but gave a low chuckle.

"Why don't you light the candle?" he said then.

Philip struck a match and discovered that there was a candlestick on the floor beside the bed. He lit it and put it on the washing-stand. Cronshaw was lying on his back immobile; he looked very odd in his nightshirt; and his baldness was disconcerting. His face was earthy and death-like.

"I say, old man, you look awfully ill. Is there anyone to look after you here?"

"George brings me in a bottle of milk in the morning before he goes to his work."

"Who's George?"

"I call him George because his name is Adolphe. He shares this palatial apartment with me."

Philip noticed then that the second bed had not been made since it was slept in. The pillow was black where the head had rested.

"You don't mean to say you're sharing this room with somebody else?" he cried.

"Why not? Lodging costs money in Soho. George is a waiter, he goes out at eight in the morning and does not come in till closing time, so he isn't in my way at all. We neither of us sleep well, and he helps to pass away the hours of the night by telling me stories of his life. He's a Swiss, and I've always had a taste for waiters. They see life from an entertaining angle."

"How long have you been in bed?"

"Three days."

"D'you mean to say you've had nothing but a bottle of milk for the last three days? Why on earth didn't you send me a line? I can't bear to think of you lying here all day long without a soul to attend to you."

Cronshaw gave a little laugh.

"Look at your face. Why, dear boy, I really believe you're distressed. You nice fellow."

Philip blushed. He had not suspected that his face showed the dismay he felt at the sight of that horrible room and the wretched circumstances of the poor poet. Cronshaw, watching Philip, went on with a gentle smile.

"I've been quite happy. Look, here are my proofs. Remember that I am indifferent to discomforts which would harass other folk. What do the circumstances of life matter if your dreams make you lord paramount of time and space?"

The proofs were lying on his bed, and as he lay in the darkness he had been able to place his hands on them. He showed them to Philip and his eyes glowed. He turned over the pages, rejoicing in the clear type; he read out a stanza.

"They don't look bad, do they?"

Philip had an idea. It would involve him in a little expense and he could not afford even the smallest increase of expenditure; but on the other hand this was a case where it revolted him to think of economy.

"I say, I can't bear the thought of your remaining here. I've got an extra room, it's empty at present, but I can easily get someone to lend me a bed. Won't you come and live with me for a while? It'll save you the rent of this."

"Oh, my dear boy, you'd insist on my keeping my window open."

"You shall have every window in the place sealed if you like."

"I shall be all right tomorrow. I could have got up today, only I felt lazy."

"Then you can very easily make the move. And then if you don't feel well at any time you can just go to bed, and I shall be there to look after you."

"If it'll please you I'll come," said Cronshaw, with his torpid not unpleasant smile.

"That'll be ripping."

They settled that Philip should fetch Cronshaw next day, and Philip snatched an hour from his busy morning to arrange the change. He found Cronshaw dressed, sitting in his hat and great-coat on the bed, with a small, shabby portmanteau, containing his clothes and books, already packed: it was on the floor by his feet, and he looked as if he were sitting in the waiting-room of a station. Philip laughed at the sight of him. They went over to Kennington in a four-wheeler, of which the windows were carefully closed, and Philip installed his guest in his own room. He had gone out early in the morning and bought for himself a second-hand bed-stead, a cheap chest of drawers, and a looking-glass. Cronshaw settled down at once to correct his proofs. He was much better.

Philip found him, except for the irritability which was a symptom of his disease, an easy guest. He had a lecture at nine in the morning, so did not see Cronshaw till the night. Once or twice Philip persuaded him to share the scrappy meal he prepared for himself in the evening, but Cronshaw was too restless to stay in, and preferred generally to get himself something to eat in one or other of the cheapest restaurants in Soho. Philip asked him to see Dr. Tyrell, but he stoutly refused; he knew a doctor would tell him to stop drinking, and this he was resolved not to do. He always felt horribly ill in the morning, but his absinthe at mid-day put him on his feet again, and by the time he came home, at midnight, he was able to talk with the brilliancy which had astonished Philip when first he made his acquaintance. His proofs were corrected; and the volume was to come out among the publications of the early spring, when the public might be supposed to have recovered from the avalanche of Christmas books.

Chapter LXXXIV

AT THE NEW YEAR PHILIP BECAME DRESSER IN THE SURGICAL OUT-PATIENTS' department. The work was of the same character as that which he had just been engaged on, but with the greater directness which surgery has than medicine; and a larger proportion of the patients suffered from those two diseases which a supine public allows, in its prudishness, to be spread broadcast. The assistant-surgeon for whom Philip dressed was called Jacobs. He was a short, fat man, with an exuberant joviality, a bald head, and a loud voice; he had a cockney accent, and was generally described by the students as an "awful bounder"; but his cleverness, both as a surgeon and as a teacher, caused some of them to overlook this. He had also a considerable facetiousness, which he exercised impartially on the patients and on the students. He took a great pleasure in making his dressers look foolish. Since they were ignorant, nervous, and could not answer as if he were their equal, this was not very difficult. He enjoyed his afternoons, with the home truths he permitted himself, much more than the students who had to put up with them with a smile. One day a case came up of a boy with a club-foot. His parents wanted to know whether anything could be done. Mr. Jacobs turned to Philip.

"You'd better take this case, Carey. It's a subject you ought to know something about."

Philip flushed, all the more because the surgeon spoke obviously with a humourous intention, and his brow-beaten dressers laughed obsequiously. It was in point of fact a subject which Philip, since coming to the hospital, had studied with anxious attention. He had read everything in the library which treated of talipes in its various forms. He made the boy take off his boot and stocking. He was fourteen, with a snub nose, blue eyes, and a freckled face. His father explained that they wanted something done if possible, it was such a hindrance to the kid in earning his living. Philip looked at him curiously. He was a jolly boy, not at all shy, but talkative and with a cheekiness which his father reproved. He was much interested in his foot.

"It's only for the looks of the thing, you know," he said to Philip. "I don't find it no trouble."

"Be quiet, Ernie," said his father. "There's too much gas about you."

Philip examined the foot and passed his hand slowly over the shapelessness of it. He could not understand why the boy felt none of the humiliation which always oppressed himself. He wondered why he could not take his deformity with that philosophic indifference. Presently Mr. Jacobs came up to him. The boy was sitting on the edge of a couch, the surgeon and Philip stood on each side of him; and in a semi-circle, crowding round, were students. With accustomed brilliancy Jacobs gave a graphic little discourse upon the club-foot: he spoke of its varieties and of the forms which followed upon different anatomical conditions.

"I suppose you've got talipes equinus?" he said, turning suddenly to Philip.

"Yes."

Philip felt the eyes of his fellow-students rest on him, and he cursed himself because he could not help blushing. He felt the sweat start up in the palms of his hands. The surgeon spoke with the fluency due to long practice and with the admirable perspicacity which distinguished him. He was tremendously interested in his profession. But Philip did not listen. He was only wishing that the fellow would get done quickly. Suddenly he realised that Jacobs was addressing him.

"You don't mind taking off your sock for a moment, Carey?"

Philip felt a shudder pass through him. He had an impulse to tell the surgeon to go to hell, but he had not the courage to make a scene. He feared his brutal ridicule. He forced himself to appear indifferent.

"Not a bit," he said.

He sat down and unlaced his boot. His fingers were trembling and he thought he should never untie the knot. He remembered how they had forced him at school to show his foot, and the misery which had eaten into his soul.

"He keeps his feet nice and clean, doesn't he?" said Jacobs, in his rasping, cockney voice.

The attendant students giggled. Philip noticed that the boy whom they were examining looked down at his foot with eager curiosity. Jacobs took the foot in his hands and said:

"Yes, that's what I thought. I see you've had an operation. When you were a child, I suppose?"

He went on with his fluent explanations. The students leaned over and looked at the foot. Two or three examined it minutely when Jacobs let it go.

"When you've quite done," said Philip, with a smile, ironically.

He could have killed them all. He thought how jolly it would be to jab a chisel (he didn't know why that particular instrument came into his mind) into their necks. What beasts men were! He wished he could believe in hell so as to comfort himself with the thought of the horrible tortures which would be theirs. Mr. Jacobs turned his attention to treatment. He talked partly to the boy's father and partly to the students. Philip put on his sock and laced his boot. At last the surgeon finished. But he seemed to have an afterthought and turned to Philip.

"You know, I think it might be worth your while to have an operation. Of course I couldn't give you a normal foot, but I think I can do something. You might think about it, and when you want a holiday you can just come into the hospital for a bit."

Philip had often asked himself whether anything could be done, but his distaste for any reference to the subject had prevented him from consulting any of the surgeons at the hospital. His reading told him that whatever might have been done when he was a small boy, and then treatment of talipes was not as skilful as in the present day, there was small chance now of any great benefit. Still it would be worthwhile if an operation made it possible for him to wear a more ordinary boot and to limp less. He remembered how passionately he had prayed for the miracle which his uncle had assured him was possible to omnipotence. He smiled ruefully.

"I was rather a simple soul in those days," he thought.

Towards the end of February it was clear that Cronshaw was growing much worse. He was no longer able to get up. He lay in bed, insisting that the window should be closed always, and refused to see a doctor; he would take little nourishment, but demanded whiskey and cigarettes: Philip knew that he should have neither, but Cronshaw's argument was unanswerable.

"I daresay they are killing me. I don't care. You've warned me, you've done all that was necessary: I ignore your warning. Give me something to drink and be damned to you."

Leonard Upjohn blew in two or three times a week, and there was something of the dead leaf in his appearance which made the word exactly descriptive of the manner of his appearance. He was a weedy-looking fellow of five-and-thirty, with long pale hair and a white face; he had the look of a man who lived too little in the open air. He wore a hat like a dissenting minister's. Philip disliked him for his patronising manner and was bored by his fluent conversation. Leonard Upjohn liked to hear himself talk. He was not sensitive to the interest of his listeners, which is the first requisite of the good talker; and he never realised that he was telling people what they knew already. With measured words he told Philip what to think of Rodin, Albert Samain, and Cæsar Franck. Philip's charwoman only came in for an hour in the morning, and since Philip was obliged to be at the hospital all day Cronshaw was left much alone. Upjohn told Philip that he thought someone should remain with him, but did not offer to make it possible.

"It's dreadful to think of that great poet alone. Why, he might die without a soul at hand."

"I think he very probably will," said Philip.

"How can you be so callous!"

"Why don't you come and do your work here every day, and then you'd be near if he wanted anything?" asked Philip drily.

"I? My dear fellow, I can only work in the surroundings I'm used to, and besides I go out so much."

Upjohn was also a little put out because Philip had brought Cronshaw to his own rooms.

"I wish you had left him in Soho," he said, with a wave of his long, thin hands. "There was a touch of romance in that sordid attic. I could even bear it if it were Wapping or Shoreditch, but the respectability of Kennington! What a place for a poet to die!"

Cronshaw was often so ill-humoured that Philip could only keep his temper by remembering all the time that this irritability was a symptom of the disease. Upjohn came sometimes before Philip was in, and then Cronshaw would complain of him bitterly. Upjohn listened with complacency.

"The fact is that Carey has no sense of beauty," he smiled. "He has a middle-class mind."

He was very sarcastic to Philip, and Philip exercised a good deal of self-control in his dealings with him. But one evening he could not contain himself. He had had a hard day at the hospital and was tired out. Leonard Upjohn came to him, while he was making himself a cup of tea in the kitchen, and said that Cronshaw was complaining of Philip's insistence that he should have a doctor.

"Don't you realise that you're enjoying a very rare, a very exquisite privilege? You ought to do everything in your power, surely, to show your sense of the greatness of your trust."

"It's a rare and exquisite privilege which I can ill afford," said Philip.

Whenever there was any question of money, Leonard Upjohn assumed a slightly disdainful expression. His sensitive temperament was offended by the reference.

"There's something fine in Cronshaw's attitude, and you disturb it by your importunity. You should make allowances for the delicate imaginings which you cannot feel."

Philip's face darkened.

"Let us go in to Cronshaw," he said frigidly.

The poet was lying on his back, reading a book, with a pipe in his mouth. The air was musty; and the room, notwithstanding Philip's tidying up, had the bedraggled look which seemed to accompany Cronshaw wherever he went. He took off his spectacles as they came in. Philip was in a towering rage.

"Upjohn tells me you've been complaining to him because I've urged you to have a doctor," he said. "I want you to have a doctor, because you may die any day, and if you hadn't been seen by anyone I shouldn't be able to get a certificate. There'd have to be an inquest and I should be blamed for not calling a doctor in."

"I hadn't thought of that. I thought you wanted me to see a doctor for my sake and not for your own. I'll see a doctor whenever you like."

Philip did not answer, but gave an almost imperceptible shrug of the shoulders. Cronshaw, watching him, gave a little chuckle.

"Don't look so angry, my dear. I know very well you want to do everything you can for me. Let's see your doctor, perhaps he can do something for me, and at any rate it'll comfort you." He turned his eyes to Upjohn. "You're a damned fool, Leonard. Why d'you want to worry the boy? He has quite enough to do to put up with me. You'll do nothing more for me than write a pretty article about me after my death. I know you."

Next day Philip went to Dr. Tyrell. He felt that he was the sort of man to be interested by the story, and as soon as Tyrell was free of his day's work he accompanied Philip to Kennington. He could only agree with what Philip had told him. The case was hopeless.

"I'll take him into the hospital if you like," he said. "He can have a small ward."

"Nothing would induce him to come."

"You know, he may die any minute, or else he may get another attack of pneumonia."

Philip nodded. Dr. Tyrell made one or two suggestions, and promised to come again whenever Philip wanted him to. He left his address. When Philip went back to Cronshaw he found him quietly reading. He did not trouble to inquire what the doctor had said.

"Are you satisfied now, dear boy?" he asked.

"I suppose nothing will induce you to do any of the things Tyrell advised?"

"Nothing," smiled Cronshaw.

Chapter LXXXV

About a fortnight after this Philip, going home one evening after his day's work at the hospital, knocked at the door of Cronshaw's room. He got no answer and walked in. Cronshaw was lying huddled up on one side, and Philip went up to the bed. He did not know whether Cronshaw was asleep or merely lay there in one of his uncontrollable fits of irritability. He was surprised to see that his mouth was open. He touched his shoulder. Philip gave a cry of dismay. He slipped his hand under Cronshaw's shirt and felt his heart; he did not know what to do; helplessly, because he had heard of this being done, he held a looking-glass in front of his mouth. It startled him to be alone with Cronshaw. He had his hat and coat still on, and he ran down the stairs into the street; he hailed a cab and drove to Harley Street. Dr. Tyrell was in.

"I say, would you mind coming at once? I think Cronshaw's dead."

"If he is it's not much good my coming, is it?"

"I should be awfully grateful if you would. I've got a cab at the door. It'll only take half an hour."

Tyrell put on his hat. In the cab he asked him one or two questions.

"He seemed no worse than usual when I left this morning," said Philip. "It gave me an awful shock when I went in just now. And the thought of his dying all alone. . . . D'you think he knew he was going to die?"

Philip remembered what Cronshaw had said. He wondered whether at that last moment he had been seized with the terror of death. Philip imagined himself in such a plight, knowing it was inevitable and with no one, not a soul, to give an encouraging word when the fear seized him.

"You're rather upset," said Dr. Tyrell.

He looked at him with his bright blue eyes. They were not unsympathetic. When he saw Cronshaw, he said:

"He must have been dead for some hours. I should think he died in his sleep. They do sometimes."

The body looked shrunk and ignoble. It was not like anything human. Dr. Tyrell looked at it dispassionately. With a mechanical gesture he took out his watch.

"Well, I must be getting along. I'll send the certificate round. I suppose you'll communicate with the relatives."

"I don't think there are any," said Philip.

"How about the funeral?"

"Oh, I'll see to that."

Dr. Tyrell gave Philip a glance. He wondered whether he ought to offer a couple of sovereigns towards it. He knew nothing of Philip's circumstances; perhaps he could well afford the expense; Philip might think it impertinent if he made any suggestion.

"Well, let me know if there's anything I can do," he said.

Philip and he went out together, parting on the doorstep, and Philip went to a telegraph office in order to send a message to Leonard Upjohn. Then he went to an undertaker whose shop he passed every day on his way to the hospital. His attention had been drawn to it often by the three words in silver lettering on a black cloth, which, with two model coffins, adorned the window: Economy, Celerity, Propriety. They had always diverted him. The undertaker was a little fat Jew with curly black hair, long and greasy, in black, with a large diamond ring on a podgy finger. He received Philip with a peculiar manner formed by the mingling of his natural blatancy with the subdued air proper to his calling. He quickly saw that Philip was very helpless and promised to send round a woman at once to perform the needful offices. His suggestions for the funeral were very magnificent; and Philip felt ashamed of himself when the undertaker seemed to think his objections mean. It was horrible to haggle on such a matter, and finally Philip consented to an expensiveness which he could ill afford.

"I quite understand, sir," said the undertaker, "you don't want any show and that—I'm not a believer in ostentation myself, mind you—but you want it done gentlemanly-like. You leave it to me, I'll do it as cheap as it can be done, 'aving regard to what's right and proper. I can't say more than that, can I?"

Philip went home to eat his supper, and while he ate the woman came along to lay out the corpse. Presently a telegram arrived from Leonard Upjohn.

Shocked and grieved beyond measure. Regret cannot come tonight. Dining out. With you early tomorrow. Deepest sympathy.   UPJOHN

In a little while the woman knocked at the door of the sitting-room.

"I've done now, sir. Will you come and look at 'im and see it's all right?"

Philip followed her. Cronshaw was lying on his back, with his eyes closed and his hands folded piously across his chest.

"You ought by rights to 'ave a few flowers, sir."

"I'll get some tomorrow."

She gave the body a glance of satisfaction. She had performed her job, and now she rolled down her sleeves, took off her apron, and put on her bonnet. Philip asked her how much he owed her.

"Well, sir, some give me two and sixpence and some give me five shillings."

Philip was ashamed to give her less than the larger sum. She thanked him with just so much effusiveness as was seemly in presence of the grief he might be supposed to feel, and left him. Philip went back into his sitting-room, cleared away the remains of his supper, and sat down to read Walsham's *Surgery*. He found it difficult. He felt singularly nervous. When there was a sound on the stairs he jumped, and his heart beat violently. That thing in the adjoining room, which had been a man and now was nothing, frightened him. The silence seemed alive, as if some mysterious movement were taking place within it; the presence of death weighed upon these rooms, unearthly and terrifying: Philip felt a sudden horror for what had once been his friend. He tried to force himself to read, but presently pushed away his book in despair. What troubled him was the absolute futility of the life which had just ended. It did not matter if Cronshaw was alive or dead. It would have been just as well if he had never lived. Philip thought of Cronshaw young; and it needed an effort of imagination to picture him slender, with a springing step, and with hair on his head, buoyant and hopeful. Philip's rule of life, to follow one's instincts with due regard to the policeman round the corner, had not acted very well there: it was because Cronshaw had done this that he had made such a lamentable failure of existence. It seemed that the instincts could not be trusted. Philip was puzzled, and he asked himself what rule of life was there, if that one was useless, and why people acted in one way rather than in another. They acted according to their emotions, but their emotions might be good or bad; it seemed just a chance whether they led to triumph or disaster. Life seemed an inextricable confusion. Men hurried hither and thither, urged by forces they knew not; and the purpose of it all escaped them; they seemed to hurry just for hurrying's sake.

Next morning Leonard Upjohn appeared with a small wreath of laurel. He was pleased with his idea of crowning the dead poet with this; and attempted, notwithstanding Philip's disapproving silence, to fix it on the bald head; but the wreath fitted grotesquely. It looked like the brim of a hat worn by a low comedian in a music-hall.

"I'll put it over his heart instead," said Upjohn.

"You've put it on his stomach," remarked Philip.

Upjohn gave a thin smile.

"Only a poet knows where lies a poet's heart," he answered.

They went back into the sitting-room, and Philip told him what arrangements he had made for the funeral.

"I hoped you've spared no expense. I should like the hearse to be followed by a long string of empty coaches, and I should like the horses to wear tall nodding plumes, and there should be a vast number of mutes with long streamers on their hats. I like the thought of all those empty coaches."

"As the cost of the funeral will apparently fall on me and I'm not over flush just now, I've tried to make it as moderate as possible."

"But, my dear fellow, in that case, why didn't you get him a pauper's funeral? There would have been something poetic in that. You have an unerring instinct for mediocrity."

Philip flushed a little, but did not answer; and next day he and Upjohn followed the hearse in the one carriage which Philip had ordered. Lawson, unable to come, had sent a wreath; and Philip, so that the coffin should not seem too neglected, had bought a couple. On the way back the coachman whipped up his horses. Philip was dog-tired and presently went to sleep. He was awakened by Upjohn's voice.

"It's rather lucky the poems haven't come out yet. I think we'd better hold them back a bit and I'll write a preface. I began thinking of it during the drive to the cemetery. I believe I can do something rather good. Anyhow I'll start with an article in *The Saturday*."

Philip did not reply, and there was silence between them. At last Upjohn said:

"I daresay I'd be wiser not to whittle away my copy. I think I'll do an article for one of the reviews, and then I can just print it afterwards as a preface."

Philip kept his eye on the monthlies, and a few weeks later it appeared. The article made something of a stir, and extracts from it were printed in many of the papers. It was a very good article, vaguely biographical, for no one knew much of Cronshaw's early life, but delicate, tender, and picturesque. Leonard Upjohn in his intricate style drew graceful little pictures of Cronshaw in the Latin Quarter, talking, writing poetry: Cronshaw became a picturesque figure, an English Verlaine; and Leonard Upjohn's coloured phrases took on a tremulous dignity, a more pathetic grandiloquence, as he described the sordid end, the shabby little room in Soho; and, with a reticence which was wholly charming and suggested a much greater generosity than modesty allowed him to state, the efforts he made to transport the poet to some cottage embowered with honeysuckle amid a flowering orchard. And the lack of sympathy, well-meaning but so tactless, which had taken the poet instead to the vulgar respectability of Kennington! Leonard Upjohn described Kennington with that restrained humour which a strict adherence to the vocabulary of Sir Thomas Browne necessitated. With delicate sarcasm he narrated the last weeks, the patience with which Cronshaw bore the well-meaning clumsiness of the young student who had appointed himself his nurse, and the pitifulness of that divine vagabond in those hopelessly middle-class surroundings. Beauty from ashes, he quoted from Isaiah. It was a triumph of irony for that outcast poet to die amid the trappings of vulgar respectability; it reminded Leonard Upjohn of Christ among the Pharisees, and the analogy gave him opportunity for an exquisite passage. And then he told how a friend—his good taste did not suffer him more than to hint subtly who the friend was with such gracious fancies—had laid a laurel wreath on the dead poet's heart; and the beautiful dead hands had seemed to rest with a voluptuous passion upon Apollo's leaves, fragrant with the fragrance of art, and more green than jade brought by swart mariners from the manifold, inexplicable China. And, an admirable contrast, the article ended with a description of the middle-class, ordinary, prosaic funeral of him who should have been buried like a prince or like a pauper. It was the crowning buffet, the final victory of Philistia over art, beauty, and immaterial things.

Leonard Upjohn had never written anything better. It was a miracle of charm, grace, and pity. He printed all Cronshaw's best poems in the course of the article, so that when the volume appeared much of its point was gone; but he advanced his own position a good deal. He was thenceforth a critic to be reckoned with. He had seemed before a little aloof; but there was a warm humanity about this article which was infinitely attractive.

Chapter LXXXVI

IN THE SPRING PHILIP, HAVING FINISHED HIS DRESSING IN THE OUT-PATIENTS' DEpartment, became an in-patients' clerk. This appointment lasted six months. The clerk spent every morning in the wards, first in the men's, then in the women's, with the house-physician; he wrote up cases, made tests, and passed the time of day with the nurses. On two afternoons a week the physician in charge went round with a little knot of students, examined the cases, and dispensed information. The work had not the excitement, the constant change, the intimate contact with reality, of the work in the out-patients' department; but Philip picked up a good deal of knowledge. He got on very well with the patients, and he was a little flattered at the pleasure they showed in his attendance on them. He was not conscious of any deep sympathy in their sufferings, but he liked them; and because he put on no airs he was more popular with them than others of the clerks. He was pleasant, encouraging, and friendly. Like everyone connected with hospitals he found that male patients were more easy to get on with than female. The women were often querulous and ill-tempered. They complained bitterly of the hard-worked nurses, who did not show them the attention they thought their right; and they were troublesome, ungrateful, and rude.

Presently Philip was fortunate enough to make a friend. One morning the house-physician gave him a new case, a man; and, seating himself at the bed-side, Philip proceeded to write down particulars on the "letter." He noticed on looking at this that the patient was described as a journalist: his name was Thorpe Athelny, an unusual one for a hospital patient, and his age was forty-eight. He was suffering from a sharp attack of jaundice, and had been taken into the ward on account of obscure symptoms which it seemed necessary to watch. He answered the various questions which it was Philip's duty to ask him in a pleasant, educated voice. Since he was lying in bed it was difficult to tell if he was short or tall, but his small head and small hands suggested that he was a man of less than average height. Philip had the habit of looking at people's hands, and Athelny's astonished him: they were very small, with long, tapering fingers and beautiful, rosy finger-nails; they were very smooth and except for the jaundice would have been of a surprising whiteness. The patient kept them outside the bed-clothes, one of them slightly spread out, the second and third fingers together, and, while he spoke to Philip, seemed to contemplate them with satisfaction. With a twinkle in his eyes Philip glanced at the man's face. Notwithstanding the yellowness it was distinguished; he had blue eyes, a nose of an imposing boldness, hooked, aggressive but not clumsy, and a small beard, pointed and grey: he was rather bald, but his hair had evidently been quite fine, curling prettily, and he still wore it long.

"I see you're a journalist," said Philip. "What papers d'you write for?"

"I write for all the papers. You cannot open a paper without seeing some of my writing."

There was one by the side of the bed and reaching for it he pointed out an advertisement. In large letters was the name of a firm well-known to Philip, Lynn and Sedley, Regent Street, London; and below, in type smaller but still of some magnitude, was the dogmatic statement: Procrastination is the Thief of Time. Then a question, startling because of its reasonableness: Why not order today? There was a repetition, in large letters, like the hammering of conscience on a murderer's heart: Why not? Then, boldly: Thousands of pairs of gloves from the leading markets of the world at astounding prices. Thousands of pairs of stockings from the most reliable manufacturers of the universe at sensational reductions. Finally the question recurred, but flung now like a challenging gauntlet in the lists: Why not order today?

"I'm the press representative of Lynn and Sedley." He gave a little wave of his beautiful hand. "To what base uses . . ."

Philip went on asking the regulation questions, some a mere matter of routine, others artfully devised to lead the patient to discover things which he might be expected to desire to conceal.

"Have you ever lived abroad?" asked Philip.

"I was in Spain for eleven years."

"What were you doing there?"

"I was secretary of the English water company at Toledo."

Philip remembered that Clutton had spent some months in Toledo, and the journalist's answer made him look at him with more interest; but he felt it would be improper to show this: it was necessary to preserve the distance between the hospital patient and the staff. When he had finished his examination he went on to other beds.

Thorpe Athelny's illness was not grave, and, though remaining very yellow, he soon felt much better: he stayed in bed only because the physician thought he should be kept under observation till certain reactions became normal. One day, on entering the ward, Philip noticed that Athelny, pencil in hand, was reading a book. He put it down when Philip came to his bed.

"May I see what you're reading?" asked Philip, who could never pass a book without looking at it.

Philip took it up and saw that it was a volume of Spanish verse, the poems of San Juan de la Cruz, and as he opened it a sheet of paper fell out. Philip picked it up and noticed that verse was written upon it.

"You're not going to tell me you've been occupying your leisure in writing poetry? That's a most improper proceeding in a hospital patient."

"I was trying to do some translations. D'you know Spanish?"

"No."

"Well, you know all about San Juan de la Cruz, don't you?"

"I don't indeed."

"He was one of the Spanish mystics. He's one of the best poets they've ever had. I thought it would be worthwhile translating him into English."

"May I look at your translation?"

"It's very rough," said Athelny, but he gave it to Philip with an alacrity which suggested that he was eager for him to read it.

It was written in pencil, in a fine but very peculiar handwriting, which was hard to read: it was just like black letter.

"Doesn't it take you an awful time to write like that? It's wonderful."

"I don't know why handwriting shouldn't be beautiful."

Philip read the first verse:

> *In an obscure night*
> *With anxious love inflamed*
> *O happy lot!*
> *Forth unobserved I went,*
> *My house being now at rest . . .*

Philip looked curiously at Thorpe Athelny. He did not know whether he felt a little shy with him or was attracted by him. He was conscious that his manner had been slightly patronising, and he flushed as it struck him that Athelny might have thought him ridiculous.

"What an unusual name you've got," he remarked, for something to say.

"It's a very old Yorkshire name. Once it took the head of my family a day's hard riding to make the circuit of his estates, but the mighty are fallen. Fast women and slow horses."

He was short-sighted and when he spoke looked at you with a peculiar intensity. He took up his volume of poetry.

"You should read Spanish," he said. "It is a noble tongue. It has not the mellifluousness of Italian, Italian is the language of tenors and organ-grinders, but it has grandeur: it does not ripple like a brook in a garden, but it surges tumultuous like a mighty river in flood."

His grandiloquence amused Philip, but he was sensitive to rhetoric; and he listened with pleasure while Athelny, with picturesque expressions and the fire of a real enthusiasm, described to him the rich delight of reading *Don Quixote* in the original and the music, romantic, limpid, passionate, of the enchanting Calderon.

"I must get on with my work," said Philip presently.

"Oh, forgive me, I forgot. I will tell my wife to bring me a photograph of Toledo, and I will show it you. Come and talk to me when you have the chance. You don't know what a pleasure it gives me."

During the next few days, in moments snatched whenever there was opportunity, Philip's acquaintance with the journalist increased. Thorpe Athelny was a good talker. He did not say brilliant things, but he talked inspiringly, with an eager vividness which fired the imagination; Philip, living so much in a world of make-believe, found his fancy teeming with new pictures. Athelny had very good manners. He knew much more than Philip, both of the world and of books; he was a much older man; and the readiness of his conversation gave him a certain superiority; but he was in the hospital a recipient of charity, subject to strict rules; and he held himself between the two positions with ease and humour. Once Philip asked him why he had come to the hospital.

"Oh, my principle is to profit by all the benefits that society provides. I take advantage of the age I live in. When I'm ill I get myself patched up in a hospital and I have no false shame, and I send my children to be educated at the board-school."

"Do you really?" said Philip.

"And a capital education they get too, much better than I got at Winchester. How else do you think I could educate them at all? I've got nine. You must come and see them all when I get home again. Will you?"

"I'd like to very much," said Philip.

Chapter LXXXVII

TEN DAYS LATER THORPE ATHELNY WAS WELL ENOUGH TO LEAVE THE HOSpital. He gave Philip his address, and Philip promised to dine with him at one o'clock on the following Sunday. Athelny had told him that he lived in a house built by Inigo Jones; he had raved, as he raved over everything, over the balustrade of old oak; and when he came down to open the door for Philip he made him at once admire the elegant carving of the lintel. It was a shabby house, badly needing a coat of paint, but with the dignity of its period, in a little street between Chancery Lane and Holborn, which had once been fashionable but was now little better than a slum: there was a plan to pull it down in order to put up handsome offices; meanwhile the rents were small, and Athelny was able to get the two upper floors at a price which suited his income. Philip had not seen him up before and was surprised at his small size; he was not more than five feet and five inches high. He was dressed fantastically in blue linen trousers of the sort worn by working men in France, and a very old brown velvet coat; he wore a bright red sash round his waist, a low collar, and for tie a flowing bow of the kind used by the comic Frenchman in the pages of *Punch*. He greeted Philip with enthusiasm. He began talking at once of the house and passed his hand lovingly over the balusters.

"Look at it, feel it, it's like silk. What a miracle of grace! And in five years the house-breaker will sell it for firewood."

He insisted on taking Philip into a room on the first floor, where a man in shirt-sleeves, a blousy woman, and three children were having their Sunday dinner.

"I've just brought this gentleman in to show him your ceiling. Did you ever see anything so wonderful? How are you, Mrs. Hodgson? This is Mr. Carey, who looked after me when I was in the hospital."

"Come in, sir," said the man. "Any friend of Mr. Athelny's is welcome. Mr. Athelny shows the ceiling to all his friends. And it don't matter what we're doing, if we're in bed or if I'm 'aving a wash, in 'e comes."

Philip could see that they looked upon Athelny as a little queer; but they liked him none the less and they listened open-mouthed while he discoursed with his impetuous fluency on the beauty of the seventeenth-century ceiling.

"What a crime to pull this down, eh, Hodgson? You're an influential citizen, why don't you write to the papers and protest?"

The man in shirt-sleeves gave a laugh and said to Philip:

"Mr. Athelny will 'ave his little joke. They do say these 'ouses are that insanitory, it's not safe to live in them."

"Sanitation be damned, give me art," cried Athelny. "I've got nine children and they thrive on bad drains. No, no, I'm not going to take any risks. None of your new-fangled notions for me! When I move from here I'm going to make sure the drains are bad before I take anything."

There was a knock at the door, and a little fair-haired girl opened it.

"Daddy, mummy says, do stop talking and come and eat your dinner."

"This is my third daughter," said Athelny, pointing to her with a dramatic forefinger. "She is called Maria del Pilar, but she answers more willingly to the name of Jane. Jane, your nose wants blowing."

"I haven't got a hanky, daddy."

"Tut, tut, child," he answered, as he produced a vast, brilliant bandanna, "what do you suppose the Almighty gave you fingers for?"

They went upstairs, and Philip was taken into a room with walls panelled in dark oak. In the middle was a narrow table of teak on trestle legs, with two supporting bars of iron, of the kind called in Spain *mesa de hieraje*. They were to dine there, for two places were laid, and there were two large arm-chairs, with broad flat arms of oak and leathern backs, and leathern seats. They were severe, elegant, and uncomfortable. The only other piece of furniture was a *bargueño*, elaborately ornamented with gilt iron-work, on a stand of ecclesiastical design roughly but very finely carved. There stood on this two or three lustre plates, much broken but rich in colour; and on the walls were old masters of the Spanish school in beautiful though dilapidated frames: though gruesome in subject, ruined by age and bad treatment, and second-rate in their conception, they had a glow of passion. There was nothing in the room of any value, but the effect was lovely. It was magnificent and yet austere. Philip felt that it offered the very spirit of old Spain. Athelny was in the middle of showing him the inside of the *bargueño*, with its beautiful ornamentation and secret drawers, when a tall girl, with two plaits of bright brown hair hanging down her back, came in.

"Mother says dinner's ready and waiting and I'm to bring it in as soon as you sit down."

"Come and shake hands with Mr. Carey, Sally." He turned to Philip. "Isn't she enormous? She's my eldest. How old are you, Sally?"

"Fifteen, father, come next June."

"I christened her Maria del Sol, because she was my first child and I dedicated her to the glorious sun of Castile; but her mother calls her Sally and her brother Pudding-Face."

The girl smiled shyly, she had even, white teeth, and blushed. She was well set-up, tall for her age, with pleasant grey eyes and a broad forehead. She had red cheeks.

"Go and tell your mother to come in and shake hands with Mr. Carey before he sits down."

"Mother says she'll come in after dinner. She hasn't washed herself yet."

"Then we'll go in and see her ourselves. He mustn't eat the Yorkshire pudding till he's shaken the hand that made it."

Philip followed his host into the kitchen. It was small and much overcrowded. There had been a lot of noise, but it stopped as soon as the stranger entered. There was a large table in the middle and round it, eager for dinner, were seated Athelny's children. A woman was standing at the oven, taking out baked potatoes one by one.

"Here's Mr. Carey, Betty," said Athelny.

"Fancy bringing him in here. What will he think?"

She wore a dirty apron, and the sleeves of her cotton dress were turned up above her elbows; she had curling pins in her hair. Mrs. Athelny was a large woman, a good three inches taller than her husband, fair, with blue eyes and a kindly expression; she had been a handsome creature, but advancing years and the bearing of many children had made her fat and blousy; her blue eyes had become pale, her skin was coarse and red, the colour had gone out of her hair. She straightened herself, wiped her hand on her apron, and held it out.

"You're welcome, sir," she said, in a slow voice, with an accent that seemed oddly familiar to Philip. "Athelny said you was very kind to him in the 'orspital."

"Now you must be introduced to the livestock," said Athelny. "That is Thorpe," he pointed to a chubby boy with curly hair, "he is my eldest son, heir to the title, estates, and responsibilities of the family. There is Athelstan, Harold, Edward." He pointed with his forefinger to three smaller boys, all rosy, healthy, and smiling, though when they felt Philip's smiling eyes upon them they looked shyly down at their plates. "Now the girls in order: Maria del Sol . . ."

"Pudding-Face," said one of the small boys.

"Your sense of humour is rudimentary, my son. Maria de los Mercedes, Maria del Pilar, Maria de la Concepcion, Maria del Rosario."

"I call them Sally, Molly, Connie, Rosie, and Jane," said Mrs. Athelny. "Now, Athelny, you go into your own room and I'll send you your dinner. I'll let the children come in afterwards for a bit when I've washed them."

"My dear, if I'd had the naming of you I should have called you Maria of the Soapsuds. You're always torturing these wretched brats with soap."

"You go first, Mr. Carey, or I shall never get him to sit down and eat his dinner."

Athelny and Philip installed themselves in the great monkish chairs, and Sally brought them in two plates of beef, Yorkshire pudding, baked potatoes, and cabbage. Athelny took sixpence out of his pocket and sent her for a jug of beer.

"I hope you didn't have the table laid here on my account," said Philip. "I should have been quite happy to eat with the children."

"Oh no, I always have my meals by myself. I like these antique customs. I don't think that women ought to sit down at table with men. It ruins conversation and I'm sure it's very bad for them. It puts ideas in their heads, and women are never at ease with themselves when they have ideas."

Both host and guest ate with a hearty appetite.

"Did you ever taste such Yorkshire pudding? No one can make it like my wife. That's the advantage of not marrying a lady. You noticed she wasn't a lady, didn't you?"

It was an awkward question, and Philip did not know how to answer it.

"I never thought about it," he said lamely.

Athelny laughed. He had a peculiarly joyous laugh.

"No, she's not a lady, nor anything like it. Her father was a farmer, and she's never bothered about aitches in her life. We've had twelve children and nine of them are alive. I tell her it's about time she stopped, but she's an obstinate woman, she's got into the habit of it now, and I don't believe she'll be satisfied till she's had twenty."

At that moment Sally came in with the beer, and, having poured out a glass for Philip, went to the other side of the table to pour some out for her father. He put his hand round her waist.

"Did you ever see such a handsome, strapping girl? Only fifteen and she might be twenty. Look at her cheeks. She's never had a day's illness in her life. It'll be a lucky man who marries her, won't it, Sally?"

Sally listened to all this with a slight, slow smile, not much embarrassed, for she was accustomed to her father's outbursts, but with an easy modesty which was very attractive.

"Don't let your dinner get cold, father," she said, drawing herself away from his arm. "You'll call when you're ready for your pudding, won't you?"

They were left alone, and Athelny lifted the pewter tankard to his lips. He drank long and deep.

"My word, is there anything better than English beer?" he said. "Let us thank God for simple pleasures, roast beef and rice pudding, a good appetite and beer. I was married to a lady once. My God! Don't marry a lady, my boy."

Philip laughed. He was exhilarated by the scene, the funny little man in his odd clothes, the panelled room and the Spanish furniture, the English fare: the whole thing had an exquisite incongruity.

"You laugh, my boy, you can't imagine marrying beneath you. You want a wife who's an intellectual equal. Your head is crammed full of ideas of comradeship.

Stuff and nonsense, my boy! A man doesn't want to talk politics to his wife, and what do you think I care for Betty's views upon the Differential Calculus? A man wants a wife who can cook his dinner and look after his children. I've tried both and I know. Let's have the pudding in."

He clapped his hands and presently Sally came. When she took away the plates, Philip wanted to get up and help her, but Athelny stopped him.

"Let her alone, my boy. She doesn't want you to fuss about, do you, Sally? And she won't think it rude of you to sit still while she waits upon you. She don't care a damn for chivalry, do you, Sally?"

"No, father," answered Sally demurely.

"Do you know what I'm talking about, Sally?"

"No, father. But you know mother doesn't like you to swear."

Athelny laughed boisterously. Sally brought them plates of rice pudding, rich, creamy, and luscious. Athelny attacked his with gusto.

"One of the rules of this house is that Sunday dinner should never alter. It is a ritual. Roast beef and rice pudding for fifty Sundays in the year. On Easter Sunday lamb and green peas, and at Michaelmas roast goose and apple sauce. Thus we preserve the traditions of our people. When Sally marries she will forget many of the wise things I have taught her, but she will never forget that if you want to be good and happy you must eat on Sundays roast beef and rice pudding."

"You'll call when you're ready for cheese," said Sally impassively.

"D'you know the legend of the halcyon?" said Athelny: Philip was growing used to his rapid leaping from one subject to another. "When the kingfisher, flying over the sea, is exhausted, his mate places herself beneath him and bears him along upon her stronger wings. That is what a man wants in a wife, the halcyon. I lived with my first wife for three years. She was a lady, she had fifteen hundred a year, and we used to give nice little dinner parties in our little red brick house in Kensington. She was a charming woman; they all said so, the barristers and their wives who dined with us, and the literary stockbrokers, and the budding politicians; oh, she was a charming woman. She made me go to church in a silk hat and a frock coat, she took me to classical concerts, and she was very fond of lectures on Sunday afternoon; and she sat down to breakfast every morning at eight-thirty, and if I was late breakfast was cold; and she read the right books, admired the right pictures, and adored the right music. My God, how that woman bored me! She is charming still, and she lives in the little red brick house in Kensington, with Morris papers and Whistler's etchings on the walls, and gives the same nice little dinner parties, with veal creams and ices from Gunter's, as she did twenty years ago."

Philip did not ask by what means the ill-matched couple had separated, but Athelny told him.

"Betty's not my wife, you know; my wife wouldn't divorce me. The children are bastards, every jack one of them, and are they any the worse for that? Betty was one of the maids in the little red brick house in Kensington. Four or five years ago I was on my uppers, and I had seven children, and I went to my wife and asked her to help me. She said she'd make me an allowance if I'd give Betty up and go abroad. Can you see me giving Betty up? We starved for a while instead. My wife said I loved the gutter. I've degenerated; I've come down in the world; I earn three pounds a week as press agent to a linen-draper, and every day I thank God that I'm not in the little red brick house in Kensington."

Sally brought in Cheddar cheese, and Athelny went on with his fluent conversation.

"It's the greatest mistake in the world to think that one needs money to bring up a family. You need money to make them gentlemen and ladies, but I don't want my children to be ladies and gentlemen. Sally's going to earn her living in another year. She's to be apprenticed to a dressmaker, aren't you, Sally? And the boys are going to serve their country. I want them all to go into the Navy; it's a jolly life and a healthy life, good food, good pay, and a pension to end their days on."

Philip lit his pipe. Athelny smoked cigarettes of Havana tobacco, which he rolled himself. Sally cleared away. Philip was reserved, and it embarrassed him to be the recipient of so many confidences. Athelny, with his powerful voice in the diminutive body, with his bombast, with his foreign look, with his emphasis, was an astonishing creature. He reminded Philip a good deal of Cronshaw. He appeared to have the same independence of thought, the same bohemianism, but he had an infinitely more vivacious temperament; his mind was coarser, and he had not that interest in the abstract which made Cronshaw's conversation so captivating. Athelny was very proud of the county family to which he belonged; he showed Philip photographs of an Elizabethan mansion, and told him:

"The Athelnys have lived there for seven centuries, my boy. Ah, if you saw the chimney-pieces and the ceilings!"

There was a cupboard in the wainscoting and from this he took a family tree. He showed it to Philip with child-like satisfaction. It was indeed imposing.

"You see how the family names recur, Thorpe, Athelstan, Harold, Edward; I've used the family names for my sons. And the girls, you see, I've given Spanish names to."

An uneasy feeling came to Philip that possibly the whole story was an elaborate imposture, not told with any base motive, but merely from a wish to impress, startle, and amaze. Athelny had told him that he was at Winchester; but Philip, sensitive to differences of manner, did not feel that his host had the characteristics of a man educated at a great public school. While he pointed out the great alliances which his ancestors had formed, Philip amused himself by wondering whether Athelny was not the son of some tradesman in Winchester, auctioneer or coal-merchant, and whether a similarity of surname was not his only connection with the ancient family whose tree he was displaying.

Chapter LXXXVIII

THERE WAS A KNOCK AT THE DOOR AND A TROOP OF CHILDREN CAME IN. They were clean and tidy now; their faces shone with soap, and their hair was plastered down; they were going to Sunday school under Sally's charge. Athelny joked with them in his dramatic, exuberant fashion, and you could see that he was devoted to them all. His pride in their good health and their good looks was touching. Philip felt that they were a little shy in his presence, and when their father sent them off they fled from the room in evident relief. In a few minutes Mrs. Athelny appeared. She had taken her hair out of the curling pins and now wore an elaborate fringe. She had on a plain black dress, a hat with cheap flowers, and was forcing her hands, red and coarse from much work, into black kid gloves.

"I'm going to church, Athelny," she said. "There's nothing you'll be wanting, is there?"

"Only your prayers, my Betty."

"They won't do you much good, you're too far gone for that," she smiled. Then, turning to Philip, she drawled: "I can't get him to go to church. He's no better than an atheist."

"Doesn't she look like Rubens' second wife?" cried Athelny. "Wouldn't she look splendid in a seventeenth-century costume? That's the sort of wife to marry, my boy. Look at her."

"I believe you'd talk the hind leg off a donkey, Athelny," she answered calmly.

She succeeded in buttoning her gloves, but before she went she turned to Philip with a kindly, slightly embarrassed smile.

"You'll stay to tea, won't you? Athelny likes someone to talk to, and it's not often he gets anybody who's clever enough."

"Of course he'll stay to tea," said Athelny. Then when his wife had gone: "I make a point of the children going to Sunday school, and I like Betty to go to church. I think women ought to be religious. I don't believe myself, but I like women and children to."

Philip, strait-laced in matters of truth, was a little shocked by this airy attitude.

"But how can you look on while your children are being taught things which you don't think are true?"

"If they're beautiful I don't much mind if they're not true. It's asking a great deal that things should appeal to your reason as well as to your sense of the aesthetic. I wanted Betty to become a Roman Catholic, I should have liked to see her converted in a crown of paper flowers, but she's hopelessly Protestant. Besides, religion is a matter of temperament; you will believe anything if you have the religious turn of mind, and if you haven't it doesn't matter what beliefs were instilled into you, you will grow out of them. Perhaps religion is the best school of morality. It is like one of those drugs you gentlemen use in medicine which carries another in solution: it is of no efficacy in itself, but enables the other to be absorbed. You take your morality because it is combined with religion; you lose the religion and the morality stays behind. A man is more likely to be a good man if he has learned goodness through the love of God than through a perusal of Herbert Spencer."

This was contrary to all Philip's ideas. He still looked upon Christianity as a degrading bondage that must be cast away at any cost; it was connected subconsciously in his mind with the dreary services in the cathedral at Tercanbury, and the long hours of boredom in the cold church at Blackstable; and the morality of which Athelny spoke was to him no more than a part of the religion which a halting intelligence preserved, when it had laid aside the beliefs which alone made it reasonable. But while he was meditating a reply Athelny, more interested in hearing himself speak than in discussion, broke into a tirade upon Roman Catholicism. For him it was an essential part of Spain; and Spain meant much to him, because he had escaped to it from the conventionality which during his married life he had found so irksome. With large gestures and in the emphatic tone which made what he said so striking, Athelny described to Philip the Spanish cathedrals with their vast dark spaces, the massive gold of the altar-pieces, and the sumptuous iron-work, gilt and faded, the air laden with incense, the silence: Philip almost saw the Canons in their short surplices of lawn, the acolytes in red, passing from the sacristy to the choir; he almost heard the monotonous chanting of vespers. The names which Athelny mentioned, Avila, Tarragona, Saragossa, Segovia, Cordova, were like trumpets in his heart. He seemed to see the great grey piles of granite set in old Spanish towns amid a landscape tawny, wild, and windswept.

"I've always thought I should love to go to Seville," he said casually, when Athelny, with one hand dramatically uplifted, paused for a moment.

"Seville!" cried Athelny. "No, no, don't go there. Seville: it brings to the mind girls dancing with castanets, singing in gardens by the Guadalquivir, bull-fights, orange-blossom, mantillas, *mantones de Manila*. It is the Spain of comic opera and Montmartre. Its facile charm can offer permanent entertainment only to an intelligence which is superficial. Théophile Gautier got out of Seville all that it has to offer. We who come after him can only repeat his sensations. He put large fat hands on the obvious and there is nothing but the obvious there; and it is all fingermarked and frayed. Murillo is its painter."

Athelny got up from his chair, walked over to the Spanish cabinet, let down the front with its great gilt hinges and gorgeous lock, and displayed a series of little drawers. He took out a bundle of photographs.

"Do you know El Greco?" he asked.

"Oh, I remember one of the men in Paris was awfully impressed by him."

"El Greco was the painter of Toledo. Betty couldn't find the photograph I wanted to show you. It's a picture that El Greco painted of the city he loved, and it's truer than any photograph. Come and sit at the table."

Philip dragged his chair forward, and Athelny set the photograph before him. He looked at it curiously, for a long time, in silence. He stretched out his hand for other photographs, and Athelny passed them to him. He had never before seen the work of that enigmatic master; and at the first glance he was bothered by the arbitrary drawing: the figures were extraordinarily elongated; the heads were very small; the attitudes were extravagant. This was not realism, and yet, and yet even in the photographs you had the impression of a troubling reality. Athelny was describing eagerly, with vivid phrases, but Philip only heard vaguely what he said. He was puzzled. He was curiously moved. These pictures seemed to offer some meaning to him, but he did not know what the meaning was. There were portraits of men with large, melancholy eyes which seemed to say you knew not what; there were long monks in the Franciscan habit or in the Dominican, with distraught faces, making gestures whose sense escaped you; there was an Assumption of the Virgin; there was a Crucifixion in which the painter by some magic of feeling had been able to suggest that the flesh of Christ's dead body was not human flesh only but divine; and there was an Ascension in which the Saviour seemed to surge up towards the empyrean and yet to stand upon the air as steadily as though it were solid ground: the uplifted arms of the Apostles, the sweep of their draperies, their ecstatic gestures, gave an impression of exultation and of holy joy. The background of nearly all was the sky by night, the dark night of the soul, with wild clouds swept by strange winds of hell and lit luridly by an uneasy moon.

"I've seen that sky in Toledo over and over again," said Athelny. "I have an idea that when first El Greco came to the city it was by such a night, and it made so vehement an impression upon him that he could never get away from it."

Philip remembered how Clutton had been affected by this strange master, whose work he now saw for the first time. He thought that Clutton was the most interesting of all the people he had known in Paris. His sardonic manner, his hostile aloofness, had made it difficult to know him; but it seemed to Philip, looking back, that there had been in him a tragic force, which sought vainly to express itself in painting. He was a man of unusual character, mystical after the fashion of a time that had no leaning to mysticism, who was impatient with life because he found himself unable to say the things which the obscure impulses of his heart suggested. His intellect was not fashioned to the uses of the spirit. It was not surprising that he felt a deep sympathy with the Greek who had devised a new technique to express the yearnings of his soul. Philip looked again at the series of portraits of Spanish gentlemen, with ruffles and pointed beards, their faces pale against the sober black of their clothes and the darkness of the background. El Greco was the painter of the soul; and these gentlemen, wan and wasted, not by exhaustion but by restraint, with their tortured minds, seem to walk unaware of the beauty of the world; for their eyes look only in their hearts, and they are dazzled by the glory of the unseen. No painter has shown more pitilessly that the world is but a place of passage. The souls of the men he painted speak their strange longings through their eyes: their senses are miraculously acute, not for sounds and odours and colour, but for the very subtle sensations of the soul. The noble walks with the monkish heart within him, and his eyes see things which saints in their cells see too, and he is unastounded. His lips are not lips that smile.

Philip, silent still, returned to the photograph of Toledo, which seemed to him the most arresting picture of them all. He could not take his eyes off it. He felt strangely that he was on the threshold of some new discovery in life. He was tremulous with a sense of adventure. He thought for an instant of the love that had consumed him: love seemed very trivial beside the excitement which now leaped in his heart. The picture he looked at was a long one, with houses crowded upon a hill; in one corner a boy was holding a large map of the town; in another was a classical figure representing the river Tagus; and in the sky was the Virgin surrounded by angels. It was a landscape alien to all Philip's notion, for he had lived in circles that worshipped exact realism; and yet here again, strangely to himself, he felt a reality greater than any achieved by the masters in whose steps humbly he had sought to walk. He heard Athelny say that the representation was so precise that when the citizens of Toledo came to look at the picture they recognised their houses. The painter had painted exactly what he saw, but he had seen with the eyes of the spirit. There was something unearthly in that city of pale grey. It was a city of the soul seen by a wan light that was neither that of night nor day. It stood on a green hill, but of a green not of this world, and it was surrounded by massive walls and bastions to be stormed by no machines or engines of man's invention, but by prayer and fasting, by contrite sighs and by mortifications of the flesh. It was a stronghold of God. Those grey houses were made of no stone known to masons, there was something terrifying in their aspect, and you did not know what men might live in them. You might walk through the streets and be unamazed to find them all deserted, and yet not empty; for you felt a presence invisible and yet manifest to every inner sense. It was a mystical city in which the imagination faltered like one who steps out of the light into darkness; the soul walked naked to and fro, knowing the unknowable, and conscious strangely of experience, intimate but inexpressible, of the absolute. And without surprise, in that blue sky, real with a reality that not the eye but the soul confesses, with its rack of light clouds driven by strange breezes, like the cries and the sighs of lost souls, you saw the Blessed Virgin with a gown of red and a cloak of blue, surrounded by winged angels. Philip felt that the inhabitants of that city would have seen the apparition without astonishment, reverent and thankful, and have gone their ways.

Athelny spoke of the mystical writers of Spain, of Teresa de Avila, San Juan de la Cruz, Fray Diego de Leon; in all of them was that passion for the unseen which Philip felt in the pictures of El Greco: they seemed to have the power to touch the incorporeal and see the invisible. They were Spaniards of their age, in whom were tremulous all the mighty exploits of a great nation: their fancies were rich with the glories of America and the green islands of the Caribbean Sea; in their veins was the power that had come from age-long battling with the Moor; they were proud, for they were masters of the world; and they felt in themselves the wide distances, the tawny wastes, the snow-capped mountains of Castile, the sunshine and the blue sky, and the flowering plains of Andalusia. Life was passionate and manifold, and because it offered so much they felt a restless yearning for something more; because they were human they were unsatisfied; and they threw this eager vitality of theirs into a vehement striving after the ineffable. Athelny was not displeased to find someone to whom he could read the translations with which for some time he had amused his leisure; and in his fine, vibrating voice he recited the canticle of the Soul and Christ her lover, the lovely poem which begins with the words *en una noche oscura*, and the *noche serena* of Fray Luis de Leon. He had translated them quite simply, not without skill, and he had found words which at all events suggested the rough-hewn grandeur of the original. The pictures of El Greco explained them, and they explained the pictures.

Philip had cultivated a certain disdain for idealism. He had always had a passion for life, and the idealism he had come across seemed to him for the most part a cowardly shrinking from it. The idealist withdrew himself, because he could not suffer the jostling of the human crowd; he had not the strength to fight and so called the battle vulgar; he was vain, and since his fellows would not take him at his own estimate, consoled himself with despising his fellows. For Philip his type was Hayward, fair, languid, too fat now and rather bald, still cherishing the remains of his good looks and still delicately proposing to do exquisite things in the uncertain future; and at the back of this were whiskey and vulgar amours of the street. It was in reaction from what Hayward represented that Philip clamoured for life as it stood; sordidness, vice, deformity, did not offend him; he declared that he wanted man in his nakedness; and he rubbed his hands when an instance came before him of meanness, cruelty, selfishness, or lust: that was the real thing. In Paris he had learned that there was neither ugliness nor beauty, but only truth: the search after beauty was sentimental. Had he not painted an advertisement of *chocolat Menier* in a landscape in order to escape from the tyranny of prettiness?

But here he seemed to divine something new. He had been coming to it, all hesitating, for some time, but only now was conscious of the fact; he felt himself on the brink of a discovery. He felt vaguely that here was something better than the realism which he had adored; but certainly it was not the bloodless idealism which stepped aside from life in weakness; it was too strong; it was virile; it accepted life in all its vivacity, ugliness and beauty, squalor and heroism; it was realism still; but it was realism carried to some higher pitch, in which facts were transformed by the more vivid light in which they were seen. He seemed to see things more profoundly through the grave eyes of those dead noblemen of Castile; and the gestures of the saints, which at first had seemed wild and distorted, appeared to have some mysterious significance. But he could not tell what that significance was. It was like a message which it was very important for him to receive, but it was given him in an unknown tongue, and he could not understand. He was always seeking for a meaning in life, and here it seemed to him that a meaning was offered; but it was obscure and vague. He was profoundly troubled. He saw what looked like the truth as by flashes of lightning on a dark, stormy night you might see a mountain range. He seemed to see that a man need not leave his life to chance, but that his will was powerful; he seemed to see that self-control might be as passionate and as active as the surrender to passion; he seemed to see that the inward life might be as manifold, as varied, as rich with experience, as the life of one who conquered realms and explored unknown lands.

Chapter LXXXIX

THE CONVERSATION BETWEEN PHILIP AND ATHELNY WAS BROKEN INTO BY a clatter up the stairs. Athelny opened the door for the children coming back from Sunday school, and with laughter and shouting they came in. Gaily he asked them what they had learned. Sally appeared for a moment, with instructions from her mother that father was to amuse the children while she got tea ready; and Athelny began to tell them one of Hans Andersen's stories. They were not shy children, and they quickly came to the conclusion that Philip was not formidable. Jane came and stood by him and presently settled herself on his knees. It was the first time that Philip in his lonely life had been present in a family circle: his eyes smiled as they rested on the fair children engrossed in the fairy tale. The life of his new friend, eccentric as it appeared at first glance, seemed now to have the beauty of perfect naturalness. Sally came in once more.

"Now then, children, tea's ready," she said.

Jane slipped off Philip's knees, and they all went back to the kitchen. Sally began to lay the cloth on the long Spanish table.

"Mother says, shall she come and have tea with you?" she asked. "I can give the children their tea."

"Tell your mother that we shall be proud and honoured if she will favour us with her company," said Athelny.

It seemed to Philip that he could never say anything without an oratorical flourish.

"Then I'll lay for her," said Sally.

She came back again in a moment with a tray on which were a cottage loaf, a slab of butter, and a jar of strawberry jam. While she placed the things on the table her father chaffed her. He said it was quite time she was walking out; he told Philip that she was very proud, and would have nothing to do with aspirants to that honour who lined up at the door, two by two, outside the Sunday school and craved the honour of escorting her home.

"You do talk, father," said Sally, with her slow, good-natured smile.

"You wouldn't think to look at her that a tailor's assistant has enlisted in the army because she would not say how d'you do to him and an electrical engineer, an electrical engineer, mind you, has taken to drink because she refused to share her hymn-book with him in church. I shudder to think what will happen when she puts her hair up."

"Mother'll bring the tea along herself," said Sally.

"Sally never pays any attention to me," laughed Athelny, looking at her with fond, proud eyes. "She goes about her business indifferent to wars, revolutions, and cataclysms. What a wife she'll make to an honest man!"

Mrs. Athelny brought in the tea. She sat down and proceeded to cut bread and butter. It amused Philip to see that she treated her husband as though he were a child. She spread jam for him and cut up the bread and butter into convenient slices for him to eat. She had taken off her hat; and in her Sunday dress, which seemed a little tight for her, she looked like one of the farmer's wives whom Philip used to call on sometimes with his uncle when he was a small boy. Then he knew why the sound of her voice was familiar to him. She spoke just like the people round Blackstable.

"What part of the country d'you come from?" he asked her.

"I'm a Kentish woman. I come from Ferne."

"I thought as much. My uncle's Vicar of Blackstable."

"That's a funny thing now," she said. "I was wondering in church just now whether you was any connection of Mr. Carey. Many's the time I've seen 'im. A cousin of mine married Mr. Barker of Roxley Farm, over by Blackstable Church, and I used to go and stay there often when I was a girl. Isn't that a funny thing now?"

She looked at him with a new interest, and a brightness came into her faded eyes. She asked him whether he knew Ferne. It was a pretty village about ten miles across country from Blackstable, and the Vicar had come over sometimes to Blackstable for the harvest thanksgiving. She mentioned names of various farmers in the neighbourhood. She was delighted to talk again of the country in which her youth was spent, and it was a pleasure to her to recall scenes and people that had remained in her memory with the tenacity peculiar to her class. It gave Philip a queer sensation too. A breath of the countryside seemed to be wafted into that panelled room in the middle of London. He seemed to see the fat Kentish fields with their stately elms; and his nostrils dilated with the scent of the air; it is laden with the salt of the North Sea, and that makes it keen and sharp.

Philip did not leave the Athelnys' till ten o'clock. The children came in to say good-night at eight and quite naturally put up their faces for Philip to kiss. His heart went out to them. Sally only held out her hand.

"Sally never kisses gentlemen till she's seen them twice," said her father.

"You must ask me again then," said Philip.

"You mustn't take any notice of what father says," remarked Sally, with a smile.

"She's a most self-possessed young woman," added her parent.

They had supper of bread and cheese and beer, while Mrs. Athelny was putting the children to bed; and when Philip went into the kitchen to bid her good-night (she had been sitting there, resting herself and reading *The Weekly Despatch*) she invited him cordially to come again.

"There's always a good dinner on Sundays so long as Athelny's in work," she said, "and it's a charity to come and talk to him."

On the following Saturday Philip received a postcard from Athelny saying that they were expecting him to dinner next day; but fearing their means were not such that Mr. Athelny would desire him to accept, Philip wrote back that he would only come to tea. He bought a large plum cake so that his entertainment should cost nothing. He found the whole family glad to see him, and the cake completed his conquest of the children. He insisted that they should all have tea together in the kitchen, and the meal was noisy and hilarious.

Soon Philip got into the habit of going to Athelny's every Sunday. He became a great favourite with the children, because he was simple and unaffected and because it was so plain that he was fond of them. As soon as they heard his ring at the door one of them popped a head out of window to make sure it was he, and then they all rushed downstairs tumultuously to let him in. They flung themselves into his arms. At tea they fought for the privilege of sitting next to him. Soon they began to call him Uncle Philip.

Athelny was very communicative, and little by little Philip learned the various stages of his life. He had followed many occupations, and it occurred to Philip that he managed to make a mess of everything he attempted. He had been on a tea plantation in Ceylon and a traveller in America for Italian wines; his secretaryship of the water company in Toledo had lasted longer than any of his employments; he had been a journalist and for some time had worked as police-court reporter for an evening paper; he had been sub-editor of a paper in the Midlands and editor of another on the Riviera. From all his occupations he had gathered amusing anecdotes, which he told with a keen pleasure in his own powers of entertainment. He had read a great deal, chiefly delighting in books which were unusual; and he poured forth his stores of abstruse knowledge with child-like enjoyment of the amazement of his hearers. Three or four years before abject poverty had driven him to take the job of press-representative to a large firm of drapers; and though he felt the work unworthy his abilities, which he rated highly, the firmness of his wife and the needs of his family had made him stick to it.

Chapter XC

When he left the Athelnys' Philip walked down Chancery Lane and along the Strand to get a 'bus at the top of Parliament Street. One Sunday, when he had known them about six weeks, he did this as usual, but he found the Kennington 'bus full. It was June, but it had rained during the day and the night was raw and cold. He walked up to Piccadilly Circus in order to get a seat; the 'bus waited at the fountain, and when it arrived there seldom had more than two or three people in it. This service ran every quarter of an hour, and he had some time to wait. He looked idly at the crowd. The public-houses were closing, and there were many people about. His mind was busy with the ideas Athelny had the charming gift of suggesting.

Suddenly his heart stood still. He saw Mildred. He had not thought of her for weeks. She was crossing over from the corner of Shaftesbury Avenue and stopped at the shelter till a string of cabs passed by. She was watching her opportunity and had no eyes for anything else. She wore a large black straw hat with a mass of feathers on it and a black silk dress; at that time it was fashionable for women to wear trains; the road was clear, and Mildred crossed, her skirt trailing on the ground, and walked down Piccadilly. Philip, his heart beating excitedly, followed her. He did not wish to speak to her, but he wondered where she was going at that hour; he wanted to get a look at her face. She walked slowly along and turned down Air Street and so got through into Regent Street. She walked up again towards the Circus. Philip was puzzled. He could not make out what she was doing. Perhaps she was waiting for somebody, and he felt a great curiosity to know who it was. She overtook a short man in a bowler hat, who was strolling very slowly in the same direction as herself; she gave him a sidelong glance as she passed. She walked a few steps more till she came to Swan and Edgar's, then stopped and waited, facing the road. When the man came up she smiled. The man stared at her for a moment, turned away his head, and sauntered on. Then Philip understood.

He was overwhelmed with horror. For a moment he felt such a weakness in his legs that he could hardly stand; then he walked after her quickly; he touched her on the arm.

"Mildred."

She turned round with a violent start. He thought that she reddened, but in the obscurity he could not see very well. For a while they stood and looked at one another without speaking. At last she said:

"Fancy seeing you!"

He did not know what to answer; he was horribly shaken; and the phrases that chased one another through his brain seemed incredibly melodramatic.

"It's awful," he gasped, almost to himself.

She did not say anything more, she turned away from him, and looked down at the pavement. He felt that his face was distorted with misery.

"Isn't there anywhere we can go and talk?"

"I don't want to talk," she said sullenly. "Leave me alone, can't you?"

The thought struck him that perhaps she was in urgent need of money and could not afford to go away at that hour.

"I've got a couple of sovereigns on me if you're hard up," he blurted out.

"I don't know what you mean. I was just walking along here on my way back to my lodgings. I expected to meet one of the girls from where I work."

"For God's sake don't lie now," he said.

Then he saw that she was crying, and he repeated his question.

"Can't we go and talk somewhere? Can't I come back to your rooms?"

"No, you can't do that," she sobbed. "I'm not allowed to take gentlemen in there. If you like I'll meet you tomorrow."

He felt certain that she would not keep an appointment. He was not going to let her go.

"No. You must take me somewhere now."

"Well, there is a room I know, but they'll charge six shillings for it."

"I don't mind that. Where is it?"

She gave him the address, and he called a cab. They drove to a shabby street beyond the British Museum in the neighbourhood of the Gray's Inn Road, and she stopped the cab at the corner.

"They don't like you to drive up to the door," she said.

They were the first words either of them had spoken since getting into the cab. They walked a few yards and Mildred knocked three times, sharply, at a door. Philip noticed in the fanlight a cardboard on which was an announcement that apartments were to let. The door was opened quietly, and an elderly, tall woman let them in. She gave Philip a stare and then spoke to Mildred in an undertone. Mildred led Philip along a passage to a room at the back. It was quite dark; she asked him for a match, and lit the gas; there was no globe, and the gas flared shrilly. Philip saw that he was in a dingy little bed-room with a suite of furniture painted to look like pine much too large for it; the lace curtains were very dirty; the grate was hidden by a large paper fan. Mildred sank on the chair which stood by the side of the chimney-piece. Philip sat on the edge of the bed. He felt ashamed. He saw now that Mildred's cheeks were thick with rouge, her eyebrows were blackened; but she looked thin and ill, and the red on her cheeks exaggerated the greenish pallor of her skin. She stared at the paper fan in a listless fashion. Philip could not think what to say, and he had a choking in his throat as if he were going to cry. He covered his eyes with his hands.

"My God, it is awful," he groaned.

"I don't know what you've got to fuss about. I should have thought you'd have been rather pleased."

Philip did not answer, and in a moment she broke into a sob.

"You don't think I do it because I like it, do you?"

"Oh, my dear," he cried. "I'm so sorry, I'm so awfully sorry."

"That'll do me a fat lot of good."

Again Philip found nothing to say. He was desperately afraid of saying anything which she might take for a reproach or a sneer.

"Where's the baby?" he asked at last.

"I've got her with me in London. I hadn't got the money to keep her on at Brighton, so I had to take her. I've got a room up Highbury way. I told them I was on the stage. It's a long way to have to come down to the West End every day, but it's a rare job to find anyone who'll let to ladies at all."

"Wouldn't they take you back at the shop?"

"I couldn't get any work to do anywhere. I walked my legs off looking for work. I did get a job once, but I was off for a week because I was queer, and when I went back they said they didn't want me anymore. You can't blame them either, can you? Them places, they can't afford to have girls that aren't strong."

"You don't look very well now," said Philip.

"I wasn't fit to come out tonight, but I couldn't help myself, I wanted the money. I wrote to Emil and told him I was broke, but he never even answered the letter."

"You might have written to me."

"I didn't like to, not after what happened, and I didn't want you to know I was in difficulties. I shouldn't have been surprised if you'd just told me I'd only got what I deserved."

"You don't know me very well, do you, even now?"

For a moment he remembered all the anguish he had suffered on her account, and he was sick with the recollection of his pain. But it was no more than recollection. When he looked at her he knew that he no longer loved her. He was very sorry for her, but he was glad to be free. Watching her gravely, he asked himself why he had been so besotted with passion for her.

"You're a gentleman in every sense of the word," she said. "You're the only one I've ever met." She paused for a minute and then flushed. "I hate asking you, Philip, but can you spare me anything?"

"It's lucky I've got some money on me. I'm afraid I've only got two pounds."

He gave her the sovereigns.

"I'll pay you back, Philip."

"Oh, that's all right," he smiled. "You needn't worry."

He had said nothing that he wanted to say. They had talked as if the whole thing were natural; and it looked as though she would go now, back to the horror of her life, and he would be able to do nothing to prevent it. She had got up to take the money, and they were both standing.

"Am I keeping you?" she asked. "I suppose you want to be getting home."

"No, I'm in no hurry," he answered.

"I'm glad to have a chance of sitting down."

Those words, with all they implied, tore his heart, and it was dreadfully painful to see the weary way in which she sank back into the chair. The silence lasted so long that Philip in his embarrassment lit a cigarette.

"It's very good of you not to have said anything disagreeable to me, Philip. I thought you might say I didn't know what all."

He saw that she was crying again. He remembered how she had come to him when Emil Miller had deserted her and how she had wept. The recollection of her suffering and of his own humiliation seemed to render more overwhelming the compassion he felt now.

"If I could only get out of it!" she moaned. "I hate it so. I'm unfit for the life, I'm not the sort of girl for that. I'd do anything to get away from it, I'd be a servant if I could. Oh, I wish I was dead."

And in pity for herself she broke down now completely. She sobbed hysterically, and her thin body was shaken.

"Oh, you don't know what it is. Nobody knows till they've done it."

Philip could not bear to see her cry. He was tortured by the horror of her position.

"Poor child," he whispered. "Poor child."

He was deeply moved. Suddenly he had an inspiration. It filled him with a perfect ecstasy of happiness.

"Look here, if you want to get away from it, I've got an idea. I'm frightfully hard up just now, I've got to be as economical as I can; but I've got a sort of little flat now in Kennington and I've got a spare room. If you like you and the baby can come and live there. I pay a woman three and sixpence a week to keep the place clean and to do a little cooking for me. You could do that and your food wouldn't come to much more than the money I should save on her. It doesn't cost any more to feed two than one, and I don't suppose the baby eats much."

She stopped crying and looked at him.

"D'you mean to say that you could take me back after all that's happened?"

Philip flushed a little in embarrassment at what he had to say.

"I don't want you to mistake me. I'm just giving you a room which doesn't cost me anything and your food. I don't expect anything more from you than that you should do exactly the same as the woman I have in does. Except for that I don't want anything from you at all. I daresay you can cook well enough for that."

She sprang to her feet and was about to come towards him.

"You are good to me, Philip."

"No, please stop where you are," he said hurriedly, putting out his hand as though to push her away.

He did not know why it was, but he could not bear the thought that she should touch him.

"I don't want to be anything more than a friend to you."

"You are good to me," she repeated. "You are good to me."

"Does that mean you'll come?"

"Oh, yes, I'd do anything to get away from this. You'll never regret what you've done, Philip, never. When can I come, Philip?"

"You'd better come tomorrow."

Suddenly she burst into tears again.

"What on earth are you crying for now?" he smiled.

"I'm so grateful to you. I don't know how I can ever make it up to you?"

"Oh, that's all right. You'd better go home now."

He wrote out the address and told her that if she came at half-past five he would be ready for her. It was so late that he had to walk home, but it did not seem a long way, for he was intoxicated with delight; he seemed to walk on air.

Chapter XCI

NEXT DAY HE GOT UP EARLY TO MAKE THE ROOM READY FOR MILDRED. HE told the woman who had looked after him that he would not want her anymore. Mildred came about six, and Philip, who was watching from the window, went down to let her in and help her to bring up the luggage: it consisted now of no more than three large parcels wrapped in brown paper, for she had been obliged to sell everything that was not absolutely needful. She wore the same black silk dress she had worn the night before, and, though she had now no rouge on her cheeks, there was still about her eyes the black which remained after a perfunctory wash in the morning: it made her look very ill. She was a pathetic figure as she stepped out of the cab with the baby in her arms. She seemed a little shy, and they found nothing but commonplace things to say to one another.

"So you've got here all right."

"I've never lived in this part of London before."

Philip showed her the room. It was that in which Cronshaw had died. Philip, though he thought it absurd, had never liked the idea of going back to it; and since Cronshaw's death he had remained in the little room, sleeping on a fold-up bed, into which he had first moved in order to make his friend comfortable. The baby was sleeping placidly.

"You don't recognise her, I expect," said Mildred.

"I've not seen her since we took her down to Brighton."

"Where shall I put her? She's so heavy I can't carry her very long."

"I'm afraid I haven't got a cradle," said Philip, with a nervous laugh.

"Oh, she'll sleep with me. She always does."

Mildred put the baby in an arm-chair and looked round the room. She recognised most of the things which she had known in his old diggings. Only one thing was new, a head and shoulders of Philip which Lawson had painted at the end of the preceding summer; it hung over the chimney-piece; Mildred looked at it critically.

"In some ways I like it and in some ways I don't. I think you're better looking than that."

"Things are looking up," laughed Philip. "You've never told me I was good-looking before."

"I'm not one to worry myself about a man's looks. I don't like good-looking men. They're too conceited for me."

Her eyes travelled round the room in an instinctive search for a looking-glass, but there was none; she put up her hand and patted her large fringe.

"What'll the other people in the house say to my being here?" she asked suddenly.

"Oh, there's only a man and his wife living here. He's out all day, and I never see her except on Saturday to pay my rent. They keep entirely to themselves. I've not spoken two words to either of them since I came."

Mildred went into the bed-room to undo her things and put them away. Philip tried to read, but his spirits were too high: he leaned back in his chair, smoking a cigarette, and with smiling eyes looked at the sleeping child. He felt very happy. He was quite sure that he was not at all in love with Mildred. He was surprised that the old feeling had left him so completely; he discerned in himself a faint physical repulsion from her; and he thought that if he touched her it would give him goose-flesh. He could not understand himself. Presently, knocking at the door, she came in again.

"I say, you needn't knock," he said. "Have you made the tour of the mansion?"

"It's the smallest kitchen I've ever seen."

"You'll find it large enough to cook our sumptuous repasts," he retorted lightly.

"I see there's nothing in. I'd better go out and get something."

"Yes, but I venture to remind you that we must be devilish economical."

"What shall I get for supper?"

"You'd better get what you think you can cook," laughed Philip.

He gave her some money and she went out. She came in half an hour later and put her purchases on the table. She was out of breath from climbing the stairs.

"I say, you are anaemic," said Philip. "I'll have to dose you with Blaud's Pills."

"It took me some time to find the shops. I bought some liver. That's tasty, isn't it? And you can't eat much of it, so it's more economical than butcher's meat."

There was a gas stove in the kitchen, and when she had put the liver on, Mildred came into the sitting-room to lay the cloth.

"Why are you only laying one place?" asked Philip. "Aren't you going to eat anything?"

Mildred flushed.

"I thought you mightn't like me to have my meals with you."

"Why on earth not?"

"Well, I'm only a servant, aren't I?"

"Don't be an ass. How can you be so silly?"

He smiled, but her humility gave him a curious twist in his heart. Poor thing!

He remembered what she had been when first he knew her. He hesitated for an instant.

"Don't think I'm conferring any benefit on you," he said. "It's simply a business arrangement, I'm giving you board and lodging in return for your work. You don't owe me anything. And there's nothing humiliating to you in it."

She did not answer, but tears rolled heavily down her cheeks. Philip knew from his experience at the hospital that women of her class looked upon service as degrading: he could not help feeling a little impatient with her; but he blamed himself, for it was clear that she was tired and ill. He got up and helped her to lay another place at the table. The baby was awake now, and Mildred had prepared some Mellin's Food for it. The liver and bacon were ready and they sat down. For economy's sake Philip had given up drinking anything but water, but he had in the house a half a bottle of whiskey, and he thought a little would do Mildred good. He did his best to make the supper pass cheerfully, but Mildred was subdued and exhausted. When they had finished she got up to put the baby to bed.

"I think you'll do well to turn in early yourself," said Philip. "You look absolute done up."

"I think I will after I've washed up."

Philip lit his pipe and began to read. It was pleasant to hear somebody moving about in the next room. Sometimes his loneliness had oppressed him. Mildred came in to clear the table, and he heard the clatter of plates as she washed up. Philip smiled as he thought how characteristic it was of her that she should do all that in a black silk dress. But he had work to do, and he brought his book up to the table. He was reading Osler's *Medicine*, which had recently taken the place in the students' favour of Taylor's work, for many years the text-book most in use. Presently Mildred came in, rolling down her sleeves. Philip gave her a casual glance, but did not move; the occasion was curious, and he felt a little nervous. He feared that Mildred might imagine he was going to make a nuisance of himself, and he did not quite know how without brutality to reassure her.

"By the way, I've got a lecture at nine, so I should want breakfast at a quarter-past eight. Can you manage that?"

"Oh, yes. Why, when I was in Parliament Street I used to catch the eight-twelve from Herne Hill every morning."

"I hope you'll find your room comfortable. You'll be a different woman tomorrow after a long night in bed."

"I suppose you work till late?"

"I generally work till about eleven or half-past."

"I'll say good-night then."

"Good-night."

The table was between them. He did not offer to shake hands with her. She shut the door quietly. He heard her moving about in the bed-room, and in a little while he heard the creaking of the bed as she got in.

Chapter XCII

THE FOLLOWING DAY WAS TUESDAY. PHILIP AS USUAL HURRIED THROUGH his breakfast and dashed off to get to his lecture at nine. He had only time to exchange a few words with Mildred. When he came back in the evening he found her seated at the window, darning his socks.

"I say, you are industrious," he smiled. "What have you been doing with yourself all day?"

"Oh, I gave the place a good cleaning and then I took baby out for a little."

She was wearing an old black dress, the same as she had worn as uniform when she served in the tea-shop; it was shabby, but she looked better in it than in the silk of the day before. The baby was sitting on the floor. She looked up at Philip with large, mysterious eyes and broke into a laugh when he sat down beside her and began playing with her bare toes. The afternoon sun came into the room and shed a mellow light.

"It's rather jolly to come back and find someone about the place. A woman and a baby make very good decoration in a room."

He had gone to the hospital dispensary and got a bottle of Blaud's Pills. He gave them to Mildred and told her she must take them after each meal. It was a remedy she was used to, for she had taken it off and on ever since she was sixteen.

"I'm sure Lawson would love that green skin of yours," said Philip. "He'd say it was so paintable, but I'm terribly matter of fact nowadays, and I shan't be happy till you're as pink and white as a milkmaid."

"I feel better already."

After a frugal supper Philip filled his pouch with tobacco and put on his hat. It was on Tuesdays that he generally went to the tavern in Beak Street, and he was glad that this day came so soon after Mildred's arrival, for he wanted to make his relations with her perfectly clear.

"Are you going out?" she said.

"Yes, on Tuesdays I give myself a night off. I shall see you tomorrow. Goodnight."

Philip always went to the tavern with a sense of pleasure. Macalister, the philosophic stockbroker, was generally there and glad to argue upon any subject under the sun; Hayward came regularly when he was in London; and though he and Macalister disliked one another they continued out of habit to meet on that one evening in the week. Macalister thought Hayward a poor creature, and sneered at his delicacies of sentiment: he asked satirically about Hayward's literary work and received with scornful smiles his vague suggestions of future masterpieces; their arguments were often heated; but the punch was good, and they were both fond of it; towards the end of the evening they generally composed their differences and thought each other capital fellows. This evening Philip found them both there, and Lawson also; Lawson came more seldom now that he was beginning to know people in London and went out to dinner a good deal. They were all on excellent terms with themselves, for Macalister had given them a good thing on the Stock Exchange, and Hayward and Lawson had made fifty pounds apiece. It was a great thing for Lawson, who was extravagant and earned little money: he had arrived at that stage of the portrait-painter's career when he was noticed a good deal by the critics and found a number of aristocratic ladies who were willing to allow him to paint them for nothing (it advertised them both, and gave the great ladies quite an air of patronesses of the arts); but he very seldom got hold of the solid philistine who was ready to pay good money for a portrait of his wife. Lawson was brimming over with satisfaction.

"It's the most ripping way of making money that I've ever struck," he cried. "I didn't have to put my hand in my pocket for sixpence."

"You lost something by not being here last Tuesday, young man," said Macalister to Philip.

"My God, why didn't you write to me?" said Philip. "If you only knew how useful a hundred pounds would be to me."

"Oh, there wasn't time for that. One has to be on the spot. I heard of a good thing last Tuesday, and I asked these fellows if they'd like to have a flutter. I bought them a thousand shares on Wednesday morning, and there was a rise in the afternoon so I sold them at once. I made fifty pounds for each of them and a couple of hundred for myself."

Philip was sick with envy. He had recently sold the last mortgage in which his small fortune had been invested and now had only six hundred pounds left. He was panic-stricken sometimes when he thought of the future. He had still to keep himself for two years before he could be qualified, and then he meant to try for hospital appointments, so that he could not expect to earn anything for three years at least. With the most rigid economy he would not have more than a hundred pounds left then. It was very little to have as a stand-by in case he was ill and could not earn money or found himself at any time without work. A lucky gamble would make all the difference to him.

"Oh, well, it doesn't matter," said Macalister. "Something is sure to turn up soon. There'll be a boom in South Africans again one of these days, and then I'll see what I can do for you."

Macalister was in the Kaffir market and often told them stories of the sudden fortunes that had been made in the great boom of a year or two back.

"Well, don't forget next time."

They sat on talking till nearly midnight, and Philip, who lived furthest off, was the first to go. If he did not catch the last tram he had to walk, and that made him very late. As it was he did not reach home till nearly half-past twelve. When he got upstairs he was surprised to find Mildred still sitting in his arm-chair.

"Why on earth aren't you in bed?" he cried.

"I wasn't sleepy."

"You ought to go to bed all the same. It would rest you."

She did not move. He noticed that since supper she had changed into her black silk dress.

"I thought I'd rather wait up for you in case you wanted anything."

She looked at him, and the shadow of a smile played upon her thin pale lips. Philip was not sure whether he understood or not. He was slightly embarrassed, but assumed a cheerful, matter-of-fact air.

"It's very nice of you, but it's very naughty also. Run off to bed as fast as you can, or you won't be able to get up tomorrow morning."

"I don't feel like going to bed."

"Nonsense," he said coldly.

She got up, a little sulkily, and went into her room. He smiled when he heard her lock the door loudly.

The next few days passed without incident. Mildred settled down in her new surroundings. When Philip hurried off after breakfast she had the whole morning to do the housework. They ate very simply, but she liked to take a long time to buy the few things they needed; she could not be bothered to cook anything for her dinner, but made herself some cocoa and ate bread and butter; then she took the baby out in the go-cart, and when she came in spent the rest of the afternoon in idleness. She was tired out, and it suited her to do so little. She made friends with Philip's forbidding landlady over the rent, which he left with Mildred to pay, and within a week was able to tell him more about his neighbours than he had learned in a year.

"She's a very nice woman," said Mildred. "Quite the lady. I told her we was married."

"D'you think that was necessary?"

"Well, I had to tell her something. It looks so funny me being here and not married to you. I didn't know what she'd think of me."

"I don't suppose she believed you for a moment."

"That she did, I lay. I told her we'd been married two years—I had to say that, you know, because of baby—only your people wouldn't hear of it, because you was only a student"—she pronounced it stoodent—"and so we had to keep it a secret, but they'd given way now and we were all going down to stay with them in the summer."

"You're a past mistress of the cock-and-bull story," said Philip.

He was vaguely irritated that Mildred still had this passion for telling fibs. In the last two years she had learned nothing. But he shrugged his shoulders.

"When all's said and done," he reflected, "she hasn't had much chance."

It was a beautiful evening, warm and cloudless, and the people of South London seemed to have poured out into the streets. There was that restlessness in the air which seizes the cockney sometimes when a turn in the weather calls him into the open. After Mildred had cleared away the supper she went and stood at the window. The street noises came up to them, noises of people calling to one another, of the passing traffic, of a barrel-organ in the distance.

"I suppose you must work tonight, Philip?" she asked him, with a wistful expression.

"I ought, but I don't know that I must. Why, d'you want me to do anything else?"

"I'd like to go out for a bit. Couldn't we take a ride on the top of a tram?"

"If you like."

"I'll just go and put on my hat," she said joyfully.

The night made it almost impossible to stay indoors. The baby was asleep and could be safely left; Mildred said she had always left it alone at night when she went out; it never woke. She was in high spirits when she came back with her hat on. She had taken the opportunity to put on a little rouge. Philip thought it was excitement which had brought a faint colour to her pale cheeks; he was touched by her childlike delight, and reproached himself for the austerity with which he had treated her. She laughed when she got out into the air. The first tram they saw was going towards Westminster Bridge and they got on it. Philip smoked his pipe, and they looked at the crowded street. The shops were open, gaily lit, and people were doing their shopping for the next day. They passed a music-hall called the Canterbury and Mildred cried out:

"Oh, Philip, do let's go there. I haven't been to a music-hall for months."

"We can't afford stalls, you know."

"Oh, I don't mind, I shall be quite happy in the gallery."

They got down and walked back a hundred yards till they came to the doors. They got capital seats for sixpence each, high up but not in the gallery, and the night was so fine that there was plenty of room. Mildred's eyes glistened. She enjoyed herself thoroughly. There was a simple-mindedness in her which touched

Philip. She was a puzzle to him. Certain things in her still pleased him, and he thought that there was a lot in her which was very good: she had been badly brought up, and her life was hard; he had blamed her for much that she could not help; and it was his own fault if he had asked virtues from her which it was not in her power to give. Under different circumstances she might have been a charming girl. She was extraordinarily unfit for the battle of life. As he watched her now in profile, her mouth slightly open and that delicate flush on her cheeks, he thought she looked strangely virginal. He felt an overwhelming compassion for her, and with all his heart he forgave her for the misery she had caused him. The smoky atmosphere made Philip's eyes ache, but when he suggested going she turned to him with beseeching face and asked him to stay till the end. He smiled and consented. She took his hand and held it for the rest of the performance. When they streamed out with the audience into the crowded street she did not want to go home; they wandered up the Westminster Bridge Road, looking at the people.

"I've not had such a good time as this for months," she said.

Philip's heart was full, and he was thankful to the fates because he had carried out his sudden impulse to take Mildred and her baby into his flat. It was very pleasant to see her happy gratitude. At last she grew tired and they jumped on a tram to go home; it was late now, and when they got down and turned into their own street there was no one about. Mildred slipped her arm through his.

"It's just like old times, Phil," she said.

She had never called him Phil before, that was what Griffiths called him; and even now it gave him a curious pang. He remembered how much he had wanted to die then; his pain had been so great that he had thought quite seriously of committing suicide. It all seemed very long ago. He smiled at his past self. Now he felt nothing for Mildred but infinite pity. They reached the house, and when they got into the sitting-room Philip lit the gas.

"Is the baby all right?" he asked.

"I'll just go in and see."

When she came back it was to say that it had not stirred since she left it. It was a wonderful child. Philip held out his hand.

"Well, good-night."

"D'you want to go to bed already?"

"It's nearly one. I'm not used to late hours these days," said Philip.

She took his hand and holding it looked into his eyes with a little smile.

"Phil, the other night in that room, when you asked me to come and stay here, I didn't mean what you thought I meant, when you said you didn't want me to be anything to you except just to cook and that sort of thing."

"Didn't you?" answered Philip, withdrawing his hand. "I did."

"Don't be such an old silly," she laughed.

He shook his head.

"I meant it quite seriously. I shouldn't have asked you to stay here on any other condition."

"Why not?"

"I feel I couldn't. I can't explain it, but it would spoil it all."

She shrugged her shoulders.

"Oh, very well, it's just as you choose. I'm not one to go down on my hands and knees for that, and chance it."

She went out, slamming the door behind her.

Chapter XCIII

NEXT MORNING MILDRED WAS SULKY AND TACITURN. SHE REMAINED IN HER room till it was time to get the dinner ready. She was a bad cook and could do little more than chops and steaks; and she did not know how to use up odds and ends, so that Philip was obliged to spend more money than he had expected. When she served up she sat down opposite Philip, but would eat nothing; he remarked on it; she said she had a bad headache and was not hungry. He was glad that he had somewhere to spend the rest of the day; the Athelnys were cheerful and friendly: it was a delightful and an unexpected thing to realise that everyone in that household looked forward with pleasure to his visit. Mildred had gone to bed when he came back, but next day she was still silent. At supper she sat with a haughty expression on her face and a little frown between her eyes. It made Philip impatient, but he told himself that he must be considerate to her; he was bound to make allowance.

"You're very silent," he said, with a pleasant smile.

"I'm paid to cook and clean, I didn't know I was expected to talk as well."

He thought it an ungracious answer, but if they were going to live together he must do all he could to make things go easily.

"I'm afraid you're cross with me about the other night," he said.

It was an awkward thing to speak about, but apparently it was necessary to discuss it.

"I don't know what you mean," she answered.

"Please don't be angry with me. I should never have asked you to come and live here if I'd not meant our relations to be merely friendly. I suggested it because I thought you wanted a home and you would have a chance of looking about for something to do."

"Oh, don't think I care."

"I don't for a moment," he hastened to say. "You mustn't think I'm ungrateful. I realise that you only proposed it for my sake. It's just a feeling I have, and I can't help it, it would make the whole thing ugly and horrid."

"You are funny" she said, looking at him curiously. "I can't make you out."

She was not angry with him now, but puzzled; she had no idea what he meant: she accepted the situation, she had indeed a vague feeling that he was behaving in a very noble fashion and that she ought to admire it; but also she felt inclined to laugh at him and perhaps even to despise him a little.

"He's a rum customer," she thought.

Life went smoothly enough with them. Philip spent all day at the hospital and worked at home in the evening except when he went to the Athelnys or to the tavern in Beak Street. Once the physician for whom he clerked asked him to a solemn dinner, and two or three times he went to parties given by fellow-students. Mildred accepted the monotony of her life. If she minded that Philip left her sometimes by herself in the evening she never mentioned it. Occasionally he took her to a music-hall. He carried out his intention that the only tie between them should be the domestic service she did in return for board and lodging. She had made up her mind that it was no use trying to get work that summer, and with Philip's approval determined to stay where she was till the autumn. She thought it would be easy to get something to do then.

"As far as I'm concerned you can stay on here when you've got a job if it's convenient. The room's there, and the woman who did for me before can come in to look after the baby."

He grew very much attached to Mildred's child. He had a naturally affectionate disposition, which had had little opportunity to display itself. Mildred was not unkind to the little girl. She looked after her very well and once when she had a bad cold proved herself a devoted nurse; but the child bored her, and she spoke to her sharply when she bothered; she was fond of her, but had not the maternal passion which might have induced her to forget herself. Mildred had no demonstrativeness, and she found the manifestations of affection ridiculous. When Philip sat with the baby on his knees, playing with it and kissing it, she laughed at him.

"You couldn't make more fuss of her if you was her father," she said. "You're perfectly silly with the child."

Philip flushed, for he hated to be laughed at. It was absurd to be so devoted to another man's baby, and he was a little ashamed of the overflowing of his heart. But the child, feeling Philip's attachment, would put her face against his or nestle in his arms.

"It's all very fine for you," said Mildred. "You don't have any of the disagreeable part of it. How would you like being kept awake for an hour in the middle of the night because her ladyship wouldn't go to sleep?"

Philip remembered all sorts of things of his childhood which he thought he had long forgotten. He took hold of the baby's toes.

"This little pig went to market, this little pig stayed at home."

When he came home in the evening and entered the sitting-room his first glance was for the baby sprawling on the floor, and it gave him a little thrill of delight to hear the child's crow of pleasure at seeing him. Mildred taught her to call him daddy, and when the child did this for the first time of her own accord, laughed immoderately.

"I wonder if you're that stuck on baby because she's mine," asked Mildred, "or if you'd be the same with anybody's baby."

"I've never known anybody else's baby, so I can't say," said Philip.

Towards the end of his second term as in-patients' clerk a piece of good fortune befell Philip. It was the middle of July. He went one Tuesday evening to the tavern in Beak Street and found nobody there but Macalister. They sat together, chatting about their absent friends, and after a while Macalister said to him:

"Oh, by the way, I heard of a rather good thing today, New Kleinfonteins; it's a gold mine in Rhodesia. If you'd like to have a flutter you might make a bit."

Philip had been waiting anxiously for such an opportunity, but now that it came he hesitated. He was desperately afraid of losing money. He had little of the gambler's spirit.

"I'd love to, but I don't know if I dare risk it. How much could I lose if things went wrong?"

"I shouldn't have spoken of it, only you seemed so keen about it," Macalister answered coldly.

Philip felt that Macalister looked upon him as rather a donkey.

"I'm awfully keen on making a bit," he laughed.

"You can't make money unless you're prepared to risk money."

Macalister began to talk of other things and Philip, while he was answering him, kept thinking that if the venture turned out well the stockbroker would be very facetious at his expense next time they met. Macalister had a sarcastic tongue.

"I think I will have a flutter if you don't mind," said Philip anxiously.

"All right. I'll buy you two hundred and fifty shares and if I see a half-crown rise I'll sell them at once."

Philip quickly reckoned out how much that would amount to, and his mouth watered; thirty pounds would be a godsend just then, and he thought the fates owed him something. He told Mildred what he had done when he saw her at breakfast next morning. She thought him very silly.

"I never knew anyone who made money on the Stock Exchange," she said. "That's what Emil always said, you can't expect to make money on the Stock Exchange, he said."

Philip bought an evening paper on his way home and turned at once to the money columns. He knew nothing about these things and had difficulty in finding the stock which Macalister had spoken of. He saw they had advanced a quarter. His heart leaped, and then he felt sick with apprehension in case Macalister had forgotten or for some reason had not bought. Macalister had promised to telegraph. Philip could not wait to take a tram home. He jumped into a cab. It was an unwonted extravagance.

"Is there a telegram for me?" he said, as he burst in.

"No," said Mildred.

His face fell, and in bitter disappointment he sank heavily into a chair.

"Then he didn't buy them for me after all. Curse him," he added violently. "What cruel luck! And I've been thinking all day of what I'd do with the money."

"Why, what were you going to do?" she asked.

"What's the good of thinking about that now? Oh, I wanted the money so badly."

She gave a laugh and handed him a telegram.

"I was only having a joke with you. I opened it."

He tore it out of her hands. Macalister had bought him two hundred and fifty shares and sold them at the half-crown profit he had suggested. The commission note was to follow next day. For one moment Philip was furious with Mildred for her cruel jest, but then he could only think of his joy.

"It makes such a difference to me," he cried. "I'll stand you a new dress if you like."

"I want it badly enough," she answered.

"I'll tell you what I'm going to do. I'm going to be operated upon at the end of July."

"Why, have you got something the matter with you?" she interrupted.

It struck her that an illness she did not know might explain what had so much puzzled her. He flushed, for he hated to refer to his deformity.

"No, but they think they can do something to my foot. I couldn't spare the time before, but now it doesn't matter so much. I shall start my dressing in October instead of next month. I shall only be in hospital a few weeks and then we can go away to the seaside for the rest of the summer. It'll do us all good, you and the baby and me."

"Oh, let's go to Brighton, Philip, I like Brighton, you get such a nice class of people there."

Philip had vaguely thought of some little fishing village in Cornwall, but as she spoke it occurred to him that Mildred would be bored to death there.

"I don't mind where we go as long as I get the sea."

He did not know why, but he had suddenly an irresistible longing for the sea. He wanted to bathe, and he thought with delight of splashing about in the salt water. He was a good swimmer, and nothing exhilarated him like a rough sea.

"I say, it will be jolly," he cried.

"It'll be like a honeymoon, won't it?" she said. "How much can I have for my new dress, Phil?"

Chapter XCIV

PHILIP ASKED MR. JACOBS, THE ASSISTANT-SURGEON FOR WHOM HE HAD dressed, to do the operation. Jacobs accepted with pleasure, since he was interested just then in neglected talipes and was getting together materials for a paper. He warned Philip that he could not make his foot like the other, but he thought he could do a good deal; and though he would always limp he would be able to wear a boot less unsightly than that which he had been accustomed to. Philip remembered how he had prayed to a God who was able to remove mountains for him who had faith, and he smiled bitterly.

"I don't expect a miracle," he answered.

"I think you're wise to let me try what I can do. You'll find a club-foot rather a handicap in practice. The layman is full of fads, and he doesn't like his doctor to have anything the matter with him."

Philip went into a "small ward," which was a room on the landing, outside each ward, reserved for special cases. He remained there a month, for the surgeon would not let him go till he could walk; and, bearing the operation very well, he had a pleasant enough time. Lawson and Athelny came to see him, and one day Mrs. Athelny brought two of her children; students whom he knew looked in now and again to have a chat; Mildred came twice a week. Everyone was very kind to him, and Philip, always surprised when anyone took trouble with him, was touched and grateful. He enjoyed the relief from care; he need not worry there about the future, neither whether his money would last out nor whether he would pass his final examinations; and he could read to his heart's content. He had not been able to read much of late, since Mildred disturbed him: she would make an aimless remark when he was trying to concentrate his attention, and would not be satisfied unless he answered; whenever he was comfortably settled down with a book she would want something done and would come to him with a cork she could not draw or a hammer to drive in a nail.

They settled to go to Brighton in August. Philip wanted to take lodgings, but Mildred said that she would have to do housekeeping, and it would only be a holiday for her if they went to a boarding-house.

"I have to see about the food every day at home, I get that sick of it I want a thorough change."

Philip agreed, and it happened that Mildred knew of a boarding-house at Kemp Town where they would not be charged more than twenty-five shillings a week each. She arranged with Philip to write about rooms, but when he got back to Kennington he found that she had done nothing. He was irritated.

"I shouldn't have thought you had so much to do as all that," he said.

"Well, I can't think of everything. It's not my fault if I forget, is it?"

Philip was so anxious to get to the sea that he would not wait to communicate with the mistress of the boarding-house.

"We'll leave the luggage at the station and go to the house and see if they've got rooms, and if they have we can just send an outside porter for our traps."

"You can please yourself," said Mildred stiffly.

She did not like being reproached, and, retiring huffily into a haughty silence, she sat by listlessly while Philip made the preparations for their departure. The little flat was hot and stuffy under the August sun, and from the road beat up a malodorous sultriness. As he lay in his bed in the small ward with its red, distempered walls he had longed for fresh air and the splashing of the sea against his breast. He felt he would go mad if he had to spend another night in London. Mildred recovered her good temper when she saw the streets of Brighton crowded with people making holiday, and they were both in high spirits as they drove out to Kemp Town. Philip stroked the baby's cheek.

"We shall get a very different colour into them when we've been down here a few days," he said, smiling.

They arrived at the boarding-house and dismissed the cab. An untidy maid opened the door and, when Philip asked if they had rooms, said she would inquire. She fetched her mistress. A middle-aged woman, stout and business-like, came downstairs, gave them the scrutinising glance of her profession, and asked what accommodation they required.

"Two single rooms, and if you've got such a thing we'd rather like a cot in one of them."

"I'm afraid I haven't got that. I've got one nice large double room, and I could let you have a cot."

"I don't think that would do," said Philip.

"I could give you another room next week. Brighton's very full just now, and people have to take what they can get."

"If it were only for a few days, Philip, I think we might be able to manage," said Mildred.

"I think two rooms would be more convenient. Can you recommend any other place where they take boarders?"

"I can, but I don't suppose they'd have room any more than I have."

"Perhaps you wouldn't mind giving me the address."

The house the stout woman suggested was in the next street, and they walked towards it. Philip could walk quite well, though he had to lean on a stick, and he was rather weak. Mildred carried the baby. They went for a little in silence, and then he saw she was crying. It annoyed him, and he took no notice, but she forced his attention.

"Lend me a hanky, will you? I can't get at mine with baby," she said in a voice strangled with sobs, turning her head away from him.

He gave her his handkerchief, but said nothing. She dried her eyes, and as he did not speak, went on.

"I might be poisonous."

"Please don't make a scene in the street," he said.

"It'll look so funny insisting on separate rooms like that. What'll they think of us?"

"If they knew the circumstances I imagine they'd think us surprisingly moral," said Philip.

She gave him a sidelong glance.

"You're not going to give it away that we're not married?" she asked quickly.

"No."

"Why won't you live with me as if we were married then?"

"My dear, I can't explain. I don't want to humiliate you, but I simply can't. I daresay it's very silly and unreasonable, but it's stronger than I am. I loved you so much that now . . ." he broke off. "After all, there's no accounting for that sort of thing."

"A fat lot you must have loved me!" she exclaimed.

The boarding-house to which they had been directed was kept by a bustling maiden lady, with shrewd eyes and voluble speech. They could have one double room for twenty-five shillings a week each, and five shillings extra for the baby, or they could have two single rooms for a pound a week more.

"I have to charge that much more," the woman explained apologetically, "because if I'm pushed to it I can put two beds even in the single rooms."

"I daresay that won't ruin us. What do you think, Mildred?"

"Oh, I don't mind. Anything's good enough for me," she answered.

Philip passed off her sulky reply with a laugh, and, the landlady having arranged to send for their luggage, they sat down to rest themselves. Philip's foot was hurting him a little, and he was glad to put it up on a chair.

"I suppose you don't mind my sitting in the same room with you," said Mildred aggressively.

"Don't let's quarrel, Mildred," he said gently.

"I didn't know you was so well off you could afford to throw away a pound a week."

"Don't be angry with me. I assure you it's the only way we can live together at all."

"I suppose you despise me, that's it."

"Of course I don't. Why should I?"

"It's so unnatural."

"Is it? You're not in love with me, are you?"

"Me? Who d'you take me for?"

"It's not as if you were a very passionate woman, you're not that."

"It's so humiliating," she said sulkily.

"Oh, I wouldn't fuss about that if I were you."

There were about a dozen people in the boarding-house. They ate in a narrow, dark room at a long table, at the head of which the landlady sat and carved. The food was bad. The landlady called it French cooking, by which she meant that the poor quality of the materials was disguised by ill-made sauces: plaice masqueraded as sole and New Zealand mutton as lamb. The kitchen was small and inconvenient, so that everything was served up lukewarm. The people were dull and pretentious; old ladies with elderly maiden daughters; funny old bachelors with mincing ways; pale-faced, middle-aged clerks with wives, who talked of their married daughters and their sons who were in a very good position in the Colonies. At table they discussed Miss Corelli's latest novel; some of them liked Lord Leighton better than Mr. Alma-Tadema, and some of them liked Mr. Alma-Tadema better than Lord Leighton. Mildred soon told the ladies of her romantic marriage with Philip; and he found himself an object of interest because his family, county people in a very good position, had cut him off with a shilling because he married while he was only a stoodent; and Mildred's father, who had a large place down Devonshire way, wouldn't do anything for them because she had married Philip. That was why they had come to a boarding-house and had not a nurse for the baby; but they had to have two rooms because they were both used to a good deal of accommodation and they didn't care to be cramped. The other visitors also had explanations of their presence: one of the single gentlemen generally went to the Metropole for his holiday, but he liked cheerful company and you couldn't get that at one of those expensive hotels; and the old lady with the middle-aged daughter was having her beautiful house in London done up and she said to her daughter: "Gwennie, my dear, we must have a cheap holiday this year," and so they had come there, though of course it wasn't at all the kind of thing they were used to. Mildred found them all very superior, and she hated a lot of common, rough people. She liked gentlemen to be gentlemen in every sense of the word.

"When people are gentlemen and ladies," she said, "I like them to be gentlemen and ladies."

The remark seemed cryptic to Philip, but when he heard her say it two or three times to different persons, and found that it aroused hearty agreement, he came to the conclusion that it was only obscure to his own intelligence. It was the first time that Philip and Mildred had been thrown entirely together. In London he did not see her all day, and when he came home the household affairs, the baby, the neighbours, gave them something to talk about till he settled down to work. Now he spent the whole day with her. After breakfast they went down to the beach; the morning went easily enough with a bathe and a stroll along the front; the evening, which they spent on the pier, having put the baby to bed, was tolerable, for there was music to listen to and a constant stream of people to look at (Philip amused himself by imagining who they were and weaving little stories about them; he had got into the habit of answering Mildred's remarks with his mouth only so that his thoughts remained undisturbed); but the afternoons were long and dreary. They sat on the beach. Mildred said they must get all the benefit they could out of Doctor Brighton, and he could not read because Mildred made observations frequently about things in general. If he paid no attention she complained.

"Oh, leave that silly old book alone. It can't be good for you always reading. You'll addle your brain, that's what you'll do, Philip."

"Oh, rot!" he answered.

"Besides, it's so unsociable."

He discovered that it was difficult to talk to her. She had not even the power of attending to what she was herself saying, so that a dog running in front of her or the passing of a man in a loud blazer would call forth a remark and then she would forget what she had been speaking of. She had a bad memory for names, and it irritated her not to be able to think of them, so that she would pause in the middle of some story to rack her brains. Sometimes she had to give it up, but it often occurred to her afterwards, and when Philip was talking of something she would interrupt him.

"Collins, that was it. I knew it would come back to me some time. Collins, that's the name I couldn't remember."

It exasperated him because it showed that she was not listening to anything he said, and yet, if he was silent, she reproached him for sulkiness. Her mind was of an order that could not deal for five minutes with the abstract, and when Philip gave way to his taste for generalising she very quickly showed that she was bored. Mildred dreamed a great deal, and she had an accurate memory for her dreams, which she would relate every day with prolixity.

One morning he received a long letter from Thorpe Athelny. He was taking his holiday in the theatrical way, in which there was much sound sense, which characterised him. He had done the same thing for ten years. He took his whole family to a hop-field in Kent, not far from Mrs. Athelny's home, and they spent three weeks hopping. It kept them in the open air, earned them money, much to Mrs. Athelny's satisfaction, and renewed their contact with mother earth. It was upon this that Athelny laid stress. The sojourn in the fields gave them a new strength; it was like a magic ceremony, by which they renewed their youth and the power of their limbs and the sweetness of the spirit: Philip had heard him say many fantastic, rhetorical, and picturesque things on the subject. Now Athelny invited him to come over for a day, he had certain meditations on Shakespeare and the musical glasses which he desired to impart, and the children were clamouring for a sight of Uncle Philip. Philip read the letter again in the afternoon when he was sitting with Mildred on the beach. He thought of Mrs. Athelny, cheerful mother of many children, with her kindly hospitality and her good humour; of Sally, grave for her years, with funny little maternal ways and an air of authority, with her long plait of fair hair and her broad forehead; and then in a bunch of all the others, merry, boisterous, healthy, and handsome. His heart went out to them. There was one quality which they had that he did not remember to have noticed in people before, and that was goodness. It had not occurred to him till now, but it was evidently the beauty of their goodness which attracted him. In theory he did not believe in it: if morality were no more than a matter of convenience good and evil had no meaning. He did not like to be illogical, but here was simple goodness, natural and without effort, and he thought it beautiful. Meditating, he slowly tore the letter into little pieces; he did not see how he could go without Mildred, and he did not want to go with her.

It was very hot, the sky was cloudless, and they had been driven to a shady corner. The baby was gravely playing with stones on the beach, and now and then she crawled up to Philip and gave him one to hold, then took it away again and placed it carefully down. She was playing a mysterious and complicated game known only to herself. Mildred was asleep. She lay with her head thrown back and her mouth slightly open; her legs were stretched out, and her boots protruded from her petticoats in a grotesque fashion. His eyes had been resting on her vaguely, but now he looked at her with peculiar attention. He remembered how passionately he had loved her, and he wondered why now he was entirely indifferent to her. The change in him filled him with dull pain. It seemed to him that all he had suffered had been sheer waste. The touch of her hand had filled him with ecstasy; he had desired to enter into her soul so that he could share every thought with her and every feeling; he had suffered acutely because, when silence had fallen between them, a remark of hers showed how far their thoughts had travelled apart, and he had rebelled against the unsurmountable wall which seemed to divide every personality from every other. He found it strangely tragic that he had loved her so madly and now loved her not at all. Sometimes he hated her. She was incapable of learning, and the experience of life had taught her nothing. She was as unmannerly as she had always been. It revolted Philip to hear the insolence with which she treated the hard-worked servant at the boarding-house.

Presently he considered his own plans. At the end of his fourth year he would be able to take his examination in midwifery, and a year more would see him qualified. Then he might manage a journey to Spain. He wanted to see the pictures which he knew only from photographs; he felt deeply that El Greco held a secret of peculiar moment to him; and he fancied that in Toledo he would surely find it out. He did not wish to do things grandly, and on a hundred pounds he might live for six months in Spain: if Macalister put him on to another good thing he could make that easily. His heart warmed at the thought of those old beautiful cities, and the tawny plains of Castile. He was convinced that more might be got out of life than offered itself at present, and he thought that in Spain he could live with greater intensity: it might be possible to practise in one of those old cities, there were a good many foreigners, passing or resident, and he should be able to pick up a living. But that would be much later; first he must get one or two hospital appointments; they gave experience and made it easy to get jobs afterwards. He wished to get a berth as ship's doctor on one of the large tramps that took things leisurely enough for a man to see something of the places at which they stopped. He wanted to go to the East; and his fancy was rich with pictures of Bangkok and Shanghai, and the ports of Japan: he pictured to himself palm-trees and skies blue and hot, dark-skinned people, pagodas; the scents of the Orient intoxicated his nostrils. His heart beat with passionate desire for the beauty and the strangeness of the world.

Mildred awoke.

"I do believe I've been asleep," she said. "Now then, you naughty girl, what have you been doing to yourself? Her dress was clean yesterday and just look at it now, Philip."

Chapter XCV

WHEN THEY RETURNED TO LONDON PHILIP BEGAN HIS DRESSING IN THE surgical wards. He was not so much interested in surgery as in medicine, which, a more empirical science, offered greater scope to the imagination. The work was a little harder than the corresponding work on the medical side. There was a lecture from nine till ten, when he went into the wards; there wounds had to be dressed, stitches taken out, bandages renewed: Philip prided himself a little on his skill in bandaging, and it amused him to wring a word of approval from a nurse. On certain afternoons in the week there were operations; and he stood in the well of the theatre, in a white jacket, ready to hand the operating surgeon any instrument he wanted or to sponge the blood away so that he could see what he was about. When some rare operation was to be performed the theatre would fill up, but generally there were not more than half a dozen students present, and then the proceedings had a cosiness which Philip enjoyed. At that time the world at large seemed to have a passion for appendicitis, and a good many cases came to the operating theatre for this complaint: the surgeon for whom Philip dressed was in friendly rivalry with a colleague as to which could remove an appendix in the shortest time and with the smallest incision.

In due course Philip was put on accident duty. The dressers took this in turn; it lasted three days, during which they lived in hospital and ate their meals in the common-room; they had a room on the ground floor near the casualty ward, with a bed that shut up during the day into a cupboard. The dresser on duty had to be at hand day and night to see to any casualty that came in. You were on the move all the time, and not more than an hour or two passed during the night without the clanging of the bell just above your head which made you leap out of bed instinctively. Saturday night was of course the busiest time and the closing of the public-houses the busiest hour. Men would be brought in by the police dead drunk and it would be necessary to administer a stomach-pump; women, rather the worse for liquor themselves, would come in with a wound on the head or a bleeding nose which their husbands had given them: some would vow to have the law on him, and others, ashamed, would declare that it had been an accident. What the dresser could manage himself he did, but if there was anything important he sent for the house-surgeon: he did this with care, since the house-surgeon was not vastly pleased to be dragged down five flights of stairs for nothing. The cases ranged from a cut finger to a cut throat. Boys came in with hands mangled by some machine, men were brought who had been knocked down by a cab, and children who had broken a limb while playing: now and then attempted suicides were carried in by the police: Philip saw a ghastly, wild-eyed man with a great gash from ear to ear, and he was in the ward for weeks afterwards in charge of a constable, silent, angry because he was alive, and sullen; he made no secret of the fact that he would try again to kill himself as soon as he was released. The wards were crowded, and the house-surgeon was faced with a dilemma when patients were brought in by the police: if they were sent on to the station and died there disagreeable things were said in the papers; and it was very difficult sometimes to tell if a man was dying or drunk. Philip did not go to bed till he was tired out, so that he should not have the bother of getting up again in an hour; and he sat in the casualty ward talking in the intervals of work with the night-nurse. She was a grey-haired woman of masculine appearance, who had been night-nurse in the casualty department for twenty years. She liked the work because she was her own mistress and had no sister to bother her. Her movements were slow, but she was immensely capable and she never failed in an emergency. The dressers, often inexperienced or nervous, found her a tower of strength. She had seen thousands of them, and they made no impression upon her: she always called them Mr. Brown; and when they expostulated and told her their real names, she merely nodded and went on calling them Mr. Brown. It interested Philip to sit with her in the bare room, with its two horse-hair couches and the flaring gas, and listen to her. She had long ceased to look upon the people who came in as human beings; they were drunks, or broken arms, or cut throats. She took the vice and misery and cruelty of the world as a matter of course; she found nothing to praise or blame in human actions: she accepted. She had a certain grim humour.

"I remember one suicide," she said to Philip, "who threw himself into the Thames. They fished him out and brought him here, and ten days later he developed typhoid fever from swallowing Thames water."

"Did he die?"

"Yes, he did all right. I could never make up my mind if it was suicide or not.... They're a funny lot, suicides. I remember one man who couldn't get any work to do and his wife died, so he pawned his clothes and bought a revolver; but he made a mess of it, he only shot out an eye and he got all right. And then, if you please, with an eye gone and a piece of his face blow away, he came to the conclusion that the world wasn't such a bad place after all, and he lived happily ever afterwards. Thing I've always noticed, people don't commit suicide for love, as you'd expect, that's just a fancy of novelists; they commit suicide because they haven't got any money. I wonder why that is."

"I suppose money's more important than love," suggested Philip.

Money was in any case occupying Philip's thoughts a good deal just then. He discovered the little truth there was in the airy saying which himself had repeated, that two could live as cheaply as one, and his expenses were beginning to worry him. Mildred was not a good manager, and it cost them as much to live as if they had eaten in restaurants; the child needed clothes, and Mildred boots, an umbrella, and other small things which it was impossible for her to do without. When they returned from Brighton she had announced her intention of getting a job, but she took no definite steps, and presently a bad cold laid her up for a fortnight. When she was well she answered one or two advertisements, but nothing came of it: either she arrived too late and the vacant place was filled, or the work was more than she felt strong enough to do. Once she got an offer, but the wages were only fourteen shillings a week, and she thought she was worth more than that.

"It's no good letting oneself be put upon," she remarked. "People don't respect you if you let yourself go too cheap."

"I don't think fourteen shillings is so bad," answered Philip, drily.

He could not help thinking how useful it would be towards the expenses of the household, and Mildred was already beginning to hint that she did not get a place because she had not got a decent dress to interview employers in. He gave her the dress, and she made one or two more attempts, but Philip came to the conclusion that they were not serious. She did not want to work. The only way he knew to make money was on the Stock Exchange, and he was very anxious to repeat the lucky experiment of the summer; but war had broken out with the Transvaal and nothing was doing in South Africans. Macalister told him that Redvers Buller would march into Pretoria in a month and then everything would boom. The only thing was to wait patiently. What they wanted was a British reverse to knock things down a bit, and then it might be worthwhile buying. Philip began reading assiduously the "city chat" of his favourite newspaper. He was worried and irritable. Once or twice he spoke sharply to Mildred, and since she was neither tactful nor patient she answered with temper, and they quarrelled. Philip always expressed his regret for what he had said, but Mildred had not a forgiving nature, and she would sulk for a couple of days. She got on his nerves in all sorts of ways; by the manner in which she ate, and by the untidiness which made her leave articles of clothing about their sitting-room: Philip was excited by the war and devoured the papers, morning and evening; but she took no interest in anything that happened. She had made the acquaintance of two or three people who lived in the street, and one of them had asked if she would like the curate to call on her. She wore a wedding-ring and called herself Mrs. Carey. On Philip's walls were two or three of the drawings which he had made in Paris, nudes, two of women and one of Miguel Ajuria, standing very square on his feet, with clenched fists. Philip kept them because they were the best things he had done, and they reminded him of happy days. Mildred had long looked at them with disfavour.

"I wish you'd take those drawings down, Philip," she said to him at last. "Mrs. Foreman, of number thirteen, came in yesterday afternoon, and I didn't know which way to look. I saw her staring at them."

"What's the matter with them?"

"They're indecent. Disgusting, that's what I call it, to have drawings of naked people about. And it isn't nice for baby either. She's beginning to notice things now."

"How can you be so vulgar?"

"Vulgar? Modest, I call it. I've never said anything, but d'you think I like having to look at those naked people all day long."

"Have you no sense of humour at all, Mildred?" he asked frigidly.

"I don't know what sense of humour's got to do with it. I've got a good mind to take them down myself. If you want to know what I think about them, I think they're disgusting."

"I don't want to know what you think about them, and I forbid you to touch them."

When Mildred was cross with him she punished him through the baby. The little girl was as fond of Philip as he was of her, and it was her great pleasure every morning to crawl into his room (she was getting on for two now and could walk pretty well), and be taken up into his bed. When Mildred stopped this the poor child would cry bitterly. To Philip's remonstrances she replied:

"I don't want her to get into habits."

And if then he said anything more she said:

"It's nothing to do with you what I do with my child. To hear you talk one would think you was her father. I'm her mother, and I ought to know what's good for her, oughtn't I?"

Philip was exasperated by Mildred's stupidity; but he was so indifferent to her now that it was only at times she made him angry. He grew used to having her about. Christmas came, and with it a couple of days holiday for Philip. He brought some holly in and decorated the flat, and on Christmas Day he gave small presents to Mildred and the baby. There were only two of them so they could not have a turkey, but Mildred roasted a chicken and boiled a Christmas pudding which she had bought at a local grocer's. They stood themselves a bottle of wine. When they had dined Philip sat in his arm-chair by the fire, smoking his pipe; and the unaccustomed wine had made him forget for a while the anxiety about money which was so constantly with him. He felt happy and comfortable. Presently Mildred came in to tell him that the baby wanted him to kiss her good-night, and with a smile he went into Mildred's bed-room. Then, telling the child to go to sleep, he turned down the gas and, leaving the door open in case she cried, went back into the sitting-room.

"Where are you going to sit?" he asked Mildred.

"You sit in your chair. I'm going to sit on the floor."

When he sat down she settled herself in front of the fire and leaned against his knees. He could not help remembering that this was how they had sat together in her rooms in the Vauxhall Bridge Road, but the positions had been reversed; it was he who had sat on the floor and leaned his head against her knee. How passionately he had loved her then! Now he felt for her a tenderness he had not known for a long time. He seemed still to feel twined round his neck the baby's soft little arms.

"Are you comfy?" he asked.

She looked up at him, gave a slight smile, and nodded. They gazed into the fire dreamily, without speaking to one another. At last she turned round and stared at him curiously.

"D'you know that you haven't kissed me once since I came here?" she said suddenly.

"D'you want me to?" he smiled.

"I suppose you don't care for me in that way anymore?"

"I'm very fond of you."

"You're much fonder of baby."

He did not answer, and she laid her cheek against his hand.

"You're not angry with me anymore?" she asked presently, with her eyes cast down.

"Why on earth should I be?"

"I've never cared for you as I do now. It's only since I passed through the fire that I've learnt to love you."

It chilled Philip to hear her make use of the sort of phrase she read in the penny novelettes which she devoured. Then he wondered whether what she said had any meaning for her: perhaps she knew no other way to express her genuine feelings than the stilted language of *The Family Herald*.

"It seems so funny our living together like this."

He did not reply for quite a long time, and silence fell upon them again; but at last he spoke and seemed conscious of no interval.

"You mustn't be angry with me. One can't help these things. I remember that I thought you wicked and cruel because you did this, that, and the other; but it was very silly of me. You didn't love me, and it was absurd to blame you for that. I thought I could make you love me, but I know now that was impossible. I don't know what it is that makes someone love you, but whatever it is, it's the only thing that matters, and if it isn't there you won't create it by kindness, or generosity, or anything of that sort."

"I should have thought if you'd loved me really you'd have loved me still."

"I should have thought so too. I remember how I used to think that it would last forever, I felt I would rather die than be without you, and I used to long for the time when you would be faded and wrinkled so that nobody cared for you anymore and I should have you all to myself."

She did not answer, and presently she got up and said she was going to bed. She gave a timid little smile.

"It's Christmas Day, Philip, won't you kiss me good-night?"

He gave a laugh, blushed slightly, and kissed her. She went to her bed-room and he began to read.

Chapter XCVI

THE CLIMAX CAME TWO OR THREE WEEKS LATER. MILDRED WAS DRIVEN BY Philip's behaviour to a pitch of strange exasperation. There were many different emotions in her soul, and she passed from mood to mood with facility. She spent a great deal of time alone and brooded over her position. She did not put all her feelings into words, she did not even know what they were, but certain things stood out in her mind, and she thought of them over and over again. She had never understood Philip, nor had very much liked him; but she was pleased to have him about her because she thought he was a gentleman. She was impressed because his father had been a doctor and his uncle was a clergyman. She despised him a little because she had made such a fool of him, and at the same time was never quite comfortable in his presence; she could not let herself go, and she felt that he was criticising her manners.

When she first came to live in the little rooms in Kennington she was tired out and ashamed. She was glad to be left alone. It was a comfort to think that there was no rent to pay; she need not go out in all weathers, and she could lie quietly in bed if she did not feel well. She had hated the life she led. It was horrible to have to be affable and subservient; and even now when it crossed her mind she cried with pity for herself as she thought of the roughness of men and their brutal language. But it crossed her mind very seldom. She was grateful to Philip for coming to her rescue, and when she remembered how honestly he had loved her and how badly she had treated him, she felt a pang of remorse. It was easy to make it up to him. It meant very little to her. She was surprised when he refused her suggestion, but she shrugged her shoulders: let him put on airs if he liked, she did not care, he would be anxious enough in a little while, and then it would be her turn to refuse; if he thought it was any deprivation to her he was very much mistaken. She had no doubt of her power over him. He was peculiar, but she knew him through and through. He had so often quarrelled with her and sworn he would never see her again, and then in a little while he had come on his knees begging to be forgiven. It gave her a thrill to think how he had cringed before her. He would have been glad to lie down on the ground for her to walk on him. She had seen him cry. She knew exactly how to treat him, pay no attention to him, just pretend you didn't notice his tempers, leave him severely alone, and in a little while he was sure to grovel. She laughed a little to herself, good-humouredly, when she thought how he had come and eaten dirt before her. She had had her fling now. She knew what men were and did not want to have anything more to do with them. She was quite ready to settle down with Philip. When all was said, he was a gentleman in every sense of the word, and that was something not to be sneezed at, wasn't it? Anyhow she was in no hurry, and she was not going to take the first step. She was glad to see how fond he was growing of the baby, though it tickled her a good deal; it was comic that he should set so much store on another man's child. He *was* peculiar and no mistake.

But one or two things surprised her. She had been used to his subservience: he was only too glad to do anything for her in the old days, she was accustomed to see him cast down by a cross word and in ecstasy at a kind one; he was different now, and she said to herself that he had not improved in the last year. It never struck her for a moment that there could be any change in his feelings, and she thought it was only acting when he paid no heed to her bad temper. He wanted to read sometimes and told her to stop talking: she did not know whether to flare up or to sulk, and was so puzzled that she did neither. Then came the conversation in which he told her that he intended their relations to be platonic, and, remembering an incident of their common past, it occurred to her that he dreaded the possibility of her being pregnant. She took pains to reassure him. It made no difference. She was the sort of woman who was unable to realise that a man might not have her own obsession with sex; her relations with men had been purely on those lines; and she could not understand that they ever had other interests. The thought struck her that Philip was in love with somebody else, and she watched him, suspecting nurses at the hospital or people he met out; but artful questions led her to the conclusion that there was no one dangerous in the Athelny household; and it forced itself upon her also that Philip, like most medical students, was unconscious of the sex of the nurses with whom his work threw him in contact. They were associated in his mind with a faint odour of iodoform. Philip received no letters, and there was no girl's photograph among his belongings. If he was in love with someone, he was very clever at hiding it; and he answered all Mildred's questions with frankness and apparently without suspicion that there was any motive in them.

"I don't believe he's in love with anybody else," she said to herself at last.

It was a relief, for in that case he was certainly still in love with her; but it made his behaviour very puzzling. If he was going to treat her like that why did he ask her to come and live at the flat? It was unnatural. Mildred was not a woman who conceived the possibility of compassion, generosity, or kindness. Her only conclusion was that Philip was queer. She took it into her head that the reasons for his conduct were chivalrous; and, her imagination filled with the extravagances of cheap fiction, she pictured to herself all sorts of romantic explanations for his delicacy. Her fancy ran riot with bitter misunderstandings, purifications by fire, snow-white souls, and death in the cruel cold of a Christmas night. She made up her mind that when they went to Brighton she would put an end to all his nonsense; they would be alone there, everyone would think them husband and wife, and there would be the pier and the band. When she found that nothing would induce Philip to share the same room with her, when he spoke to her about it with a tone in his voice she had never heard before, she suddenly realised that he did not want her. She was astounded. She remembered all he had said in the past and how desperately he had loved her. She felt humiliated and angry, but she had a sort of native insolence which carried her through. He needn't think she was in love with him, because she wasn't. She hated him sometimes, and she longed to humble him; but she found herself singularly powerless; she did not know which way to handle him. She began to be a little nervous with him. Once or twice she cried. Once or twice she set herself to be particularly nice to him; but when she took his arm while they walked along the front at night he made some excuse in a while to release himself, as though it were unpleasant for him to be touched by her. She could not make it out. The only hold she had over him was through the baby, of whom he seemed to grow fonder and fonder: she could make him white with anger by giving the child a slap or a push; and the only time the old, tender smile came back into his eyes was when she stood with the baby in her arms. She noticed it when she was being photographed like that by a man on the beach, and afterwards she often stood in the same way for Philip to look at her.

When they got back to London Mildred began looking for the work she had asserted was so easy to find; she wanted now to be independent of Philip; and she thought of the satisfaction with which she would announce to him that she was going into rooms and would take the child with her. But her heart failed her when she came into closer contact with the possibility. She had grown unused to the long hours, she did not want to be at the beck and call of a manageress, and her dignity revolted at the thought of wearing once more a uniform. She had made out to such of the neighbours as she knew that they were comfortably off: it would be a comedown if they heard that she had to go out and work. Her natural indolence asserted itself. She did not want to leave Philip, and so long as he was willing to provide for her, she did not see why she should. There was no money to throw away, but she got her board and lodging, and he might get better off. His uncle was an old man and might die any day, he would come into a little then, and even as things were, it was better than slaving from morning till night for a few shillings a week. Her efforts relaxed; she kept on reading the advertisement columns of the daily paper merely to show that she wanted to do something if anything that was worth her while presented itself. But panic seized her, and she was afraid that Philip would grow tired of supporting her. She had no hold over him at all now, and she fancied that he only allowed her to stay there because he was fond of the baby. She brooded over it all, and she thought to herself angrily that she would make him pay for all this someday. She could not reconcile herself to the fact that he no longer cared for her. She would make him. She suffered from pique, and sometimes in a curious fashion she desired Philip. He was so cold now that it exasperated her. She thought of him in that way incessantly. She thought that he was treating her very badly, and she did not know what she had done to deserve it. She kept on saying to herself that it was unnatural they should live like that. Then she thought that if things were different and she were going to have a baby, he would be sure to marry her. He was funny, but he was a gentleman in every sense of the word, no one could deny that. At last it became an obsession with her, and she made up her mind to force a change in their relations. He never even kissed her now, and she wanted him to: she remembered how ardently he had been used to press her lips. It gave her a curious feeling to think of it. She often looked at his mouth.

One evening, at the beginning of February, Philip told her that he was dining with Lawson, who was giving a party in his studio to celebrate his birthday; and he would not be in till late; Lawson had bought a couple of bottles of the punch they favoured from the tavern in Beak Street, and they proposed to have a merry evening. Mildred asked if there were going to be women there, but Philip told her there were not; only men had been invited; and they were just going to sit and talk and smoke: Mildred did not think it sounded very amusing; if she were a painter she would have half a dozen models about. She went to bed, but could not sleep, and presently an idea struck her; she got up and fixed the catch on the wicket at the landing, so that Philip could not get in. He came back about one, and she heard him curse when he found that the wicket was closed. She got out of bed and opened.

"Why on earth did you shut yourself in? I'm sorry I've dragged you out of bed."

"I left it open on purpose, I can't think how it came to be shut."

"Hurry up and get back to bed, or you'll catch cold."

He walked into the sitting-room and turned up the gas. She followed him in. She went up to the fire.

"I want to warm my feet a bit. They're like ice."

He sat down and began to take off his boots. His eyes were shining and his cheeks were flushed. She thought he had been drinking.

"Have you been enjoying yourself?" she asked, with a smile.

"Yes, I've had a ripping time."

Philip was quite sober, but he had been talking and laughing, and he was excited still. An evening of that sort reminded him of the old days in Paris. He was in high spirits. He took his pipe out of his pocket and filled it.

"Aren't you going to bed?" she asked.

"Not yet, I'm not a bit sleepy. Lawson was in great form. He talked sixteen to the dozen from the moment I got there till the moment I left."

"What did you talk about?"

"Heaven knows! Of every subject under the sun. You should have seen us all shouting at the tops of our voices and nobody listening."

Philip laughed with pleasure at the recollection, and Mildred laughed too. She was pretty sure he had drunk more than was good for him. That was exactly what she had expected. She knew men.

"Can I sit down?" she said.

Before he could answer she settled herself on his knees.

"If you're not going to bed you'd better go and put on a dressing-gown."

"Oh, I'm all right as I am." Then putting her arms round his neck, she placed her face against his and said: "Why are you so horrid to me, Phil?"

He tried to get up, but she would not let him.

"I do love you, Philip," she said.

"Don't talk damned rot."

"It isn't, it's true. I can't live without you. I want you."

He released himself from her arms.

"Please get up. You're making a fool of yourself and you're making me feel a perfect idiot."

"I love you, Philip. I want to make up for all the harm I did you. I can't go on like this, it's not in human nature."

He slipped out of the chair and left her in it.

"I'm very sorry, but it's too late."

She gave a heart-rending sob.

"But why? How can you be so cruel?"

"I suppose it's because I loved you too much. I wore the passion out. The thought of anything of that sort horrifies me. I can't look at you now without thinking of Emil and Griffiths. One can't help those things, I suppose it's just nerves."

She seized his hand and covered it with kisses.

"Don't," he cried.

She sank back into the chair.

"I can't go on like this. If you won't love me, I'd rather go away."

"Don't be foolish, you haven't anywhere to go. You can stay here as long as you like, but it must be on the definite understanding that we're friends and nothing more."

Then she dropped suddenly the vehemence of passion and gave a soft, insinuating laugh. She sidled up to Philip and put her arms round him. She made her voice low and wheedling.

"Don't be such an old silly. I believe you're nervous. You don't know how nice I can be."

She put her face against his and rubbed his cheek with hers. To Philip her smile was an abominable leer, and the suggestive glitter of her eyes filled him with horror. He drew back instinctively.

"I won't," he said.

But she would not let him go. She sought his mouth with her lips. He took her hands and tore them roughly apart and pushed her away.

"You disgust me," he said.

"Me?"

She steadied herself with one hand on the chimney-piece. She looked at him for an instant, and two red spots suddenly appeared on her cheeks. She gave a shrill, angry laugh.

"I disgust *you*."

She paused and drew in her breath sharply. Then she burst into a furious torrent of abuse. She shouted at the top of her voice. She called him every foul name she could think of. She used language so obscene that Philip was astounded; she was always so anxious to be refined, so shocked by coarseness, that it had never occurred to him that she knew the words she used now. She came up to him and thrust her face in his. It was distorted with passion, and in her tumultuous speech the spittle dribbled over her lips.

"I never cared for you, not once, I was making a fool of you always, you bored me, you bored me stiff, and I hated you, I would never have let you touch me only for the money, and it used to make me sick when I had to let you kiss me. We laughed at you, Griffiths and me, we laughed because you was such a mug. A mug! A mug!"

Then she burst again into abominable invective. She accused him of every mean fault; she said he was stingy, she said he was dull, she said he was vain, selfish; she cast virulent ridicule on everything upon which he was most sensitive. And at last she turned to go. She kept on, with hysterical violence, shouting at him an opprobrious, filthy epithet. She seized the handle of the door and flung it open. Then she turned round and hurled at him the injury which she knew was the only one that really touched him. She threw into the word all the malice and all the venom of which she was capable. She flung it at him as though it were a blow.

"Cripple!"

Chapter XCVII

PHILIP AWOKE WITH A START NEXT MORNING, CONSCIOUS THAT IT WAS LATE, and looking at his watch found it was nine o'clock. He jumped out of bed and went into the kitchen to get himself some hot water to shave with. There was no sign of Mildred, and the things which she had used for her supper the night before still lay in the sink unwashed. He knocked at her door.

"Wake up, Mildred. It's awfully late."

She did not answer, even after a second louder knocking, and he concluded that she was sulking. He was in too great a hurry to bother about that. He put some water on to boil and jumped into his bath which was always poured out the night before in order to take the chill off. He presumed that Mildred would cook his breakfast while he was dressing and leave it in the sitting-room. She had done that two or three times when she was out of temper. But he heard no sound of her moving, and realised that if he wanted anything to eat he would have to get it himself. He was irritated that she should play him such a trick on a morning when he had over-slept himself. There was still no sign of her when he was ready, but he heard her moving about her room. She was evidently getting up. He made himself some tea and cut himself a couple of pieces of bread and butter, which he ate while he was putting on his boots, then bolted downstairs and along the street into the main road to catch his tram. While his eyes sought out the newspaper shops to see the war news on the placards, he thought of the scene of the night before: now that it was over and he had slept on it, he could not help thinking it grotesque; he supposed he had been ridiculous, but he was not master of his feelings; at the time they had been overwhelming. He was angry with Mildred because she had forced him into that absurd position, and then with renewed astonishment he thought of her outburst and the filthy language she had used. He could not help flushing when he remembered her final jibe; but he shrugged his shoulders contemptuously. He had long known that when his fellows were angry with him they never failed to taunt him with his deformity. He had seen men at the hospital imitate his walk, not before him as they used at school, but when they thought he was not looking. He knew now that they did it from no wilful unkindness, but because man is naturally an imitative animal, and because it was an easy way to make people laugh: he knew it, but he could never resign himself to it.

He was glad to throw himself into his work. The ward seemed pleasant and friendly when he entered it. The sister greeted him with a quick, business-like smile.

"You're very late, Mr. Carey."

"I was out on the loose last night."

"You look it."

"Thank you."

Laughing, he went to the first of his cases, a boy with tuberculous ulcers, and removed his bandages. The boy was pleased to see him, and Philip chaffed him as he put a clean dressing on the wound. Philip was a favourite with the patients; he treated them good-humouredly; and he had gentle, sensitive hands which did not hurt them: some of the dressers were a little rough and happy-go-lucky in their methods. He lunched with his friends in the club-room, a frugal meal consisting of a scone and butter, with a cup of cocoa, and they talked of the war. Several men were going out, but the authorities were particular and refused everyone who had not had a hospital appointment. Someone suggested that, if the war went on, in a while they would be glad to take anyone who was qualified; but the general opinion was that it would be over in a month. Now that Roberts was there things would get all right in no time. This was Macalister's opinion too, and he had told Philip that they must watch their chance and buy just before peace was declared. There would be a boom then, and they might all make a bit of money. Philip had left with Macalister instructions to buy him stock whenever the opportunity presented itself. His appetite had been whetted by the thirty pounds he had made in the summer, and he wanted now to make a couple of hundred.

He finished his day's work and got on a tram to go back to Kennington. He wondered how Mildred would behave that evening. It was a nuisance to think that she would probably be surly and refuse to answer his questions. It was a warm evening for the time of year, and even in those grey streets of South London there was the languor of February; nature is restless then after the long winter months, growing things awake from their sleep, and there is a rustle in the earth, a forerunner of spring, as it resumes its eternal activities. Philip would have liked to drive on further, it was distasteful to him to go back to his rooms, and he wanted the air; but the desire to see the child clutched suddenly at his heart-strings, and he smiled to himself as he thought of her toddling towards him with a crow of delight. He was surprised, when he reached the house and looked up mechanically at the windows, to see that there was no light. He went upstairs and knocked, but got no answer. When Mildred went out she left the key under the mat and he found it there now. He let himself in and going into the sitting-room struck a match. Something had happened, he did not at once know what; he turned the gas on full and lit it; the room was suddenly filled with the glare and he looked round. He gasped. The whole place was wrecked. Everything in it had been wilfully destroyed. Anger seized him, and he rushed into Mildred's room. It was dark and empty. When he had got a light he saw that she had taken away all her things and the baby's (he had noticed on entering that the go-cart was not in its usual place on the landing, but thought Mildred had taken the baby out); and all the things on the washing-stand had been broken, a knife had been drawn cross-ways through the seats of the two chairs, the pillow had been slit open, there were large gashes in the sheets and the counterpane, the looking-glass appeared to have been broken with a hammer. Philip was bewildered. He went into his own room, and here too everything was in confusion. The basin and the ewer had been smashed, the looking-glass was in fragments, and the sheets were in ribands. Mildred had made a slit large enough to put her hand into the pillow and had scattered the feathers about the room. She had jabbed a knife into the blankets. On the dressing-table were photographs of Philip's mother, the frames had been smashed and the glass shivered. Philip went into the tiny kitchen. Everything that was breakable was broken, glasses, pudding-basins, plates, dishes.

It took Philip's breath away. Mildred had left no letter, nothing but this ruin to mark her anger, and he could imagine the set face with which she had gone about her work. He went back into the sitting-room and looked about him. He was so astonished that he no longer felt angry. He looked curiously at the kitchen-knife and the coal-hammer, which were lying on the table where she had left them. Then his eye caught a large carving-knife in the fireplace which had been broken. It must have taken her a long time to do so much damage. Lawson's portrait of him had been cut cross-ways and gaped hideously. His own drawings had been ripped in pieces; and the photographs, Manet's *Olympia* and the *Odalisque* of Ingres, the portrait of Philip IV, had been smashed with great blows of the coal-hammer. There were gashes in the table-cloth and in the curtains and in the two arm-chairs. They were quite ruined. On one wall over the table which Philip used as his desk was the little bit of Persian rug which Cronshaw had given him. Mildred had always hated it.

"If it's a rug it ought to go on the floor," she said, "and it's a dirty stinking bit of stuff, that's all it is."

It made her furious because Philip told her it contained the answer to a great riddle. She thought he was making fun of her. She had drawn the knife right through it three times, it must have required some strength, and it hung now in tatters. Philip had two or three blue and white plates, of no value, but he had bought them one by one for very small sums and liked them for their associations. They littered the floor in fragments. There were long gashes on the backs of his books, and she had taken the trouble to tear pages out of the unbound French ones. The little ornaments on the chimney-piece lay on the hearth in bits. Everything that it had been possible to destroy with a knife or a hammer was destroyed.

The whole of Philip's belongings would not have sold for thirty pounds, but most of them were old friends, and he was a domestic creature, attached to all those odds and ends because they were his; he had been proud of his little home, and on so little money had made it pretty and characteristic. He sank down now in despair. He asked himself how she could have been so cruel. A sudden fear got him on his feet again and into the passage, where stood a cupboard in which he kept his clothes. He opened it and gave a sigh of relief. She had apparently forgotten it and none of his things was touched.

He went back into the sitting-room and, surveying the scene, wondered what to do; he had not the heart to begin trying to set things straight; besides there was no food in the house, and he was hungry. He went out and got himself something to eat. When he came in he was cooler. A little pang seized him as he thought of the child, and he wondered whether she would miss him, at first perhaps, but in a week she would have forgotten him; and he was thankful to be rid of Mildred. He did not think of her with wrath, but with an overwhelming sense of boredom.

"I hope to God I never see her again," he said aloud.

The only thing now was to leave the rooms, and he made up his mind to give notice the next morning. He could not afford to make good the damage done, and he had so little money left that he must find cheaper lodgings still. He would be glad to get out of them. The expense had worried him, and now the recollection of Mildred would be in them always. Philip was impatient and could never rest till he had put in action the plan which he had in mind; so on the following afternoon he got in a dealer in second-hand furniture who offered him three pounds for all his goods damaged and undamaged; and two days later he moved into the house opposite the hospital in which he had had rooms when first he became a medical student. The landlady was a very decent woman. He took a bed-room at the top, which she let him have for six shillings a week; it was small and shabby and looked on the yard of the house that backed on to it, but he had nothing now except his clothes and a box of books, and he was glad to lodge so cheaply.

Chapter XCVIII

AND NOW IT HAPPENED THAT THE FORTUNES OF PHILIP CAREY, OF NO CONsequence to any but himself, were affected by the events through which his country was passing. History was being made, and the process was so significant that it seemed absurd it should touch the life of an obscure medical student. Battle after battle, Magersfontein, Colenso, Spion Kop, lost on the playing fields of Eton, had humiliated the nation and dealt the death-blow to the prestige of the aristocracy and gentry who till then had found no one seriously to oppose their assertion that they possessed a natural instinct of government. The old order was being swept away: history was being made indeed. Then the colossus put forth his strength, and, blundering again, at last blundered into the semblance of victory. Cronje surrendered at Paardeberg, Ladysmith was relieved, and at the beginning of March Lord Roberts marched into Bloemfontein.

It was two or three days after the news of this reached London that Macalister came into the tavern in Beak Street and announced joyfully that things were looking brighter on the Stock Exchange. Peace was in sight, Roberts would march into Pretoria within a few weeks, and shares were going up already. There was bound to be a boom.

"Now's the time to come in," he told Philip. "It's no good waiting till the public gets on to it. It's now or never."

He had inside information. The manager of a mine in South Africa had cabled to the senior partner of his firm that the plant was uninjured. They would start working again as soon as possible. It wasn't a speculation, it was an investment. To show how good a thing the senior partner thought it Macalister told Philip that he had bought five hundred shares for both his sisters; he never put them into anything that wasn't as safe as the Bank of England.

"I'm going to put my shirt on it myself," he said.

The shares were two and an eighth to a quarter. He advised Philip not to be greedy, but to be satisfied with a ten-shilling rise. He was buying three hundred for himself and suggested that Philip should do the same. He would hold them and sell when he thought fit. Philip had great faith in him, partly because he was a Scotsman and therefore by nature cautious, and partly because he had been right before. He jumped at the suggestion.

"I daresay we shall be able to sell before the account," said Macalister, "but if not, I'll arrange to carry them over for you."

It seemed a capital system to Philip. You held on till you got your profit, and you never even had to put your hand in your pocket. He began to watch the Stock Exchange columns of the paper with new interest. Next day everything was up a little, and Macalister wrote to say that he had had to pay two and a quarter for the shares. He said that the market was firm. But in a day or two there was a set-back. The news that came from South Africa was less reassuring, and Philip with anxiety saw that his shares had fallen to two; but Macalister was optimistic, the Boers couldn't hold out much longer, and he was willing to bet a top-hat that Roberts would march into Johannesburg before the middle of April. At the account Philip had to pay out nearly forty pounds. It worried him considerably, but he felt that the only course was to hold on: in his circumstances the loss was too great for him to pocket. For two or three weeks nothing happened; the Boers would not understand that they were beaten and nothing remained for them but to surrender: in fact they had one or two small successes, and Philip's shares fell half a crown more. It became evident that the war was not finished. There was a lot of selling. When Macalister saw Philip he was pessimistic.

"I'm not sure if the best thing wouldn't be to cut the loss. I've been paying out about as much as I want to in differences."

Philip was sick with anxiety. He could not sleep at night; he bolted his breakfast, reduced now to tea and bread and butter, in order to get over to the club reading-room and see the paper; sometimes the news was bad, and sometimes there was no news at all, but when the shares moved it was to go down. He did not know what to do. If he sold now he would lose altogether hard on three hundred and fifty pounds; and that would leave him only eighty pounds to go on with. He wished with all his heart that he had never been such a fool as to dabble on the Stock Exchange, but the only thing was to hold on; something decisive might happen any day and the shares would go up; he did not hope now for a profit, but he wanted to make good his loss. It was his only chance of finishing his course at the hospital. The summer session was beginning in May, and at the end of it he meant to take the examination in midwifery. Then he would only have a year more; he reckoned it out carefully and came to the conclusion that he could manage it, fees and all, on a hundred and fifty pounds; but that was the least it could possibly be done on.

Early in April he went to the tavern in Beak Street anxious to see Macalister. It eased him a little to discuss the situation with him; and to realise that numerous people beside himself were suffering from loss of money made his own trouble a little less intolerable. But when Philip arrived no one was there but Hayward, and no sooner had Philip seated himself than he said:

"I'm sailing for the Cape on Sunday."

"Are you!" exclaimed Philip.

Hayward was the last person he would have expected to do anything of the kind. At the hospital men were going out now in numbers; the Government was glad to get anyone who was qualified; and others, going out as troopers, wrote home that they had been put on hospital work as soon as it was learned that they were medical students. A wave of patriotic feeling had swept over the country, and volunteers were coming from all ranks of society.

"What are you going as?" asked Philip.

"Oh, in the Dorset Yeomanry. I'm going as a trooper."

Philip had known Hayward for eight years. The youthful intimacy which had come from Philip's enthusiastic admiration for the man who could tell him of art and literature had long since vanished; but habit had taken its place; and when Hayward was in London they saw one another once or twice a week. He still talked about books with a delicate appreciation. Philip was not yet tolerant, and sometimes Hayward's conversation irritated him. He no longer believed implicitly that nothing in the world was of consequence but art. He resented Hayward's contempt for action and success. Philip, stirring his punch, thought of his early friendship and his ardent expectation that Hayward would do great things; it was long since he had lost all such illusions, and he knew now that Hayward would never do anything but talk. He found his three hundred a year more difficult to live on now that he was thirty-five than he had when he was a young man; and his clothes, though still made by a good tailor, were worn a good deal longer than at one time he would have thought possible. He was too stout and no artful arrangement of his fair hair could conceal the fact that he was bald. His blue eyes were dull and pale. It was not hard to guess that he drank too much.

"What on earth made you think of going out to the Cape?" asked Philip.

"Oh, I don't know, I thought I ought to."

Philip was silent. He felt rather silly. He understood that Hayward was being driven by an uneasiness in his soul which he could not account for. Some power within him made it seem necessary to go and fight for his country. It was strange, since he considered patriotism no more than a prejudice, and, flattering himself on his cosmopolitanism, he had looked upon England as a place of exile. His countrymen in the mass wounded his susceptibilities. Philip wondered what it was that made people do things which were so contrary to all their theories of life. It would have been reasonable for Hayward to stand aside and watch with a smile while the barbarians slaughtered one another. It looked as though men were puppets in the hands of an unknown force, which drove them to do this and that; and sometimes they used their reason to justify their actions; and when this was impossible they did the actions in despite of reason.

"People are very extraordinary," said Philip. "I should never have expected you to go out as a trooper."

Hayward smiled, slightly embarrassed, and said nothing.

"I was examined yesterday," he remarked at last. "It was worthwhile undergoing the *gêne* of it to know that one was perfectly fit."

Philip noticed that he still used a French word in an affected way when an English one would have served. But just then Macalister came in.

"I wanted to see you, Carey," he said. "My people don't feel inclined to hold those shares anymore, the market's in such an awful state, and they want you to take them up."

Philip's heart sank. He knew that was impossible. It meant that he must accept the loss. His pride made him answer calmly.

"I don't know that I think that's worthwhile. You'd better sell them."

"It's all very fine to say that, I'm not sure if I can. The market's stagnant, there are no buyers."

"But they're marked down at one and an eighth."

"Oh yes, but that doesn't mean anything. You can't get that for them."

Philip did not say anything for a moment. He was trying to collect himself.

"D'you mean to say they're worth nothing at all?"

"Oh, I don't say that. Of course they're worth something, but you see, nobody's buying them now."

"Then you must just sell them for what you can get."

Macalister looked at Philip narrowly. He wondered whether he was very hard hit.

"I'm awfully sorry, old man, but we're all in the same boat. No one thought the war was going to hang on this way. I put you into them, but I was in myself too."

"It doesn't matter at all," said Philip. "One has to take one's chance."

He moved back to the table from which he had got up to talk to Macalister. He was dumbfounded; his head suddenly began to ache furiously; but he did not want them to think him unmanly. He sat on for an hour. He laughed feverishly at everything they said. At last he got up to go.

"You take it pretty coolly," said Macalister, shaking hands with him. "I don't suppose anyone likes losing between three and four hundred pounds."

When Philip got back to his shabby little room he flung himself on his bed, and gave himself over to his despair. He kept on regretting his folly bitterly; and though he told himself that it was absurd to regret, for what had happened was inevitable just because it had happened, he could not help himself. He was utterly miserable. He could not sleep. He remembered all the ways he had wasted money during the last few years. His head ached dreadfully.

The following evening there came by the last post the statement of his account. He examined his pass-book. He found that when he had paid everything he would have seven pounds left. Seven pounds! He was thankful he had been able to pay. It would have been horrible to be obliged to confess to Macalister that he had not the money. He was dressing in the eye-department during the summer session, and he had bought an ophthalmoscope off a student who had one to sell. He had not paid for this, but he lacked the courage to tell the student that he wanted to go back on his bargain. Also he had to buy certain books. He had about five pounds to go on with. It lasted him six weeks; then he wrote to his uncle a letter which he thought very business-like; he said that owing to the war he had had grave losses and could not go on with his studies unless his uncle came to his help. He suggested that the Vicar should lend him a hundred and fifty pounds paid over the next eighteen months in monthly instalments; he would pay interest on this and promised to refund the capital by degrees when he began to earn money. He would be qualified in a year and a half at the latest, and he could be pretty sure then of getting an assistantship at three pounds a week. His uncle wrote back that he could do nothing. It was not fair to ask him to sell out when everything was at its worst, and the little he had he felt that his duty to himself made it necessary for him to keep in case of illness. He ended the letter with a little homily. He had warned Philip time after time, and Philip had never paid any attention to him; he could not honestly say he was surprised; he had long expected that this would be the end of Philip's extravagance and want of balance. Philip grew hot and cold when he read this. It had never occurred to him that his uncle would refuse, and he burst into furious anger; but this was succeeded by utter blankness: if his uncle would not help him he could not go on at the hospital. Panic seized him and, putting aside his pride, he wrote again to the Vicar of Blackstable, placing the case before him more urgently; but perhaps he did not explain himself properly and his uncle did not realise in what desperate straits he was, for he answered that he could not change his mind; Philip was twenty-five and really ought to be earning his living. When he died Philip would come into a little, but till then he refused to give him a penny. Philip felt in the letter the satisfaction of a man who for many years had disapproved of his courses and now saw himself justified.

Chapter XCIX

PHILIP BEGAN TO PAWN HIS CLOTHES. HE REDUCED HIS EXPENSES BY EATING only one meal a day beside his breakfast; and he ate it, bread and butter and cocoa, at four so that it should last him till next morning. He was so hungry by nine o'clock that he had to go to bed. He thought of borrowing money from Lawson, but the fear of a refusal held him back; at last he asked him for five pounds. Lawson lent it with pleasure, but, as he did so, said:

"You'll let me have it back in a week or so, won't you? I've got to pay my framer, and I'm awfully broke just now."

Philip knew he would not be able to return it, and the thought of what Lawson would think made him so ashamed that in a couple of days he took the money back untouched. Lawson was just going out to luncheon and asked Philip to come too. Philip could hardly eat, he was so glad to get some solid food. On Sunday he was sure of a good dinner from Athelny. He hesitated to tell the Athelnys what had happened to him: they had always looked upon him as comparatively well-to-do, and he had a dread that they would think less well of him if they knew he was penniless.

Though he had always been poor, the possibility of not having enough to eat had never occurred to him; it was not the sort of thing that happened to the people among whom he lived; and he was as ashamed as if he had some disgraceful disease. The situation in which he found himself was quite outside the range of his experience. He was so taken aback that he did not know what else to do than to go on at the hospital; he had a vague hope that something would turn up; he could not quite believe that what was happening to him was true; and he remembered how during his first term at school he had often thought his life was a dream from which he would awake to find himself once more at home. But very soon he foresaw that in a week or so he would have no money at all. He must set about trying to earn something at once. If he had been qualified, even with a club-foot, he could have gone out to the Cape, since the demand for medical men was now great. Except for his deformity he might have enlisted in one of the yeomanry regiments which were constantly being sent out. He went to the secretary of the Medical School and asked if he could give him the coaching of some backward student; but the secretary held out no hope of getting him anything of the sort. Philip read the advertisement columns of the medical papers, and he applied for the post of unqualified assistant to a man who had a dispensary in the Fulham Road. When he went to see him, he saw the doctor glance at his club-foot; and on hearing that Philip was only in his fourth year at the hospital he said at once that his experience was insufficient: Philip understood that this was only an excuse; the man would not have an assistant who might not be as active as he wanted. Philip turned his attention to other means of earning money. He knew French and German and thought there might be some chance of finding a job as correspondence clerk; it made his heart sink, but he set his teeth; there was nothing else to do. Though too shy to answer the advertisements which demanded a personal application, he replied to those which asked for letters; but he had no experience to state and no recommendations: he was conscious that neither his German nor his French was commercial; he was ignorant of the terms used in business; he knew neither shorthand nor typewriting. He could not help recognising that his case was hopeless. He thought of writing to the solicitor who had been his father's executor, but he could not bring himself to, for it was contrary to his express advice that he had sold the mortgages in which his money had been invested. He knew from his uncle that Mr. Nixon thoroughly disapproved of him. He had gathered from Philip's year in the accountant's office that he was idle and incompetent.

"I'd sooner starve," Philip muttered to himself.

Once or twice the possibility of suicide presented itself to him; it would be easy to get something from the hospital dispensary, and it was a comfort to think that if the worst came to the worst he had at hand means of making a painless end of himself; but it was not a course that he considered seriously. When Mildred had left him to go with Griffiths his anguish had been so great that he wanted to die in order to get rid of the pain. He did not feel like that now. He remembered that the Casualty Sister had told him how people oftener did away with themselves for want of money than for want of love; and he chuckled when he thought that he was an exception. He wished only that he could talk his worries over with somebody, but he could not bring himself to confess them. He was ashamed. He went on looking for work. He left his rent unpaid for three weeks, explaining to his landlady that he would get money at the end of the month; she did not say anything, but pursed her lips and looked grim. When the end of the month came and she asked if it would be convenient for him to pay something on account, it made him feel very sick to say that he could not; he told her he would write to his uncle and was sure to be able to settle his bill on the following Saturday.

"Well, I 'ope you will, Mr. Carey, because I 'ave my rent to pay, and I can't afford to let accounts run on." She did not speak with anger, but with determination that was rather frightening. She paused for a moment and then said: "If you don't pay next Saturday, I shall 'ave to complain to the secretary of the 'ospital."

"Oh yes, that'll be all right."

She looked at him for a little and glanced round the bare room. When she spoke it was without any emphasis, as though it were quite a natural thing to say.

"I've got a nice 'ot joint downstairs, and if you like to come down to the kitchen you're welcome to a bit of dinner."

Philip felt himself redden to the soles of his feet, and a sob caught at his throat.

"Thank you very much, Mrs. Higgins, but I'm not at all hungry."

"Very good, sir."

When she left the room Philip threw himself on his bed. He had to clench his fists in order to prevent himself from crying.

Chapter C

SATURDAY. IT WAS THE DAY ON WHICH HE HAD PROMISED TO PAY HIS LANDlady. He had been expecting something to turn up all through the week. He had found no work. He had never been driven to extremities before, and he was so dazed that he did not know what to do. He had at the back of his mind a feeling that the whole thing was a preposterous joke. He had no more than a few coppers left, he had sold all the clothes he could do without; he had some books and one or two odds and ends upon which he might have got a shilling or two, but the landlady was keeping an eye on his comings and goings: he was afraid she would stop him if he took anything more from his room. The only thing was to tell her that he could not pay his bill. He had not the courage. It was the middle of June. The night was fine and warm. He made up his mind to stay out. He walked slowly along the Chelsea Embankment, because the river was restful and quiet, till he was tired, and then sat on a bench and dozed. He did not know how long he slept; he awoke with a start, dreaming that he was being shaken by a policeman and told to move on; but when he opened his eyes he found himself alone. He walked on, he did not know why, and at last came to Chiswick, where he slept again. Presently the hardness of the bench roused him. The night seemed very long. He shivered. He was seized with a sense of his misery; and he did not know what on earth to do: he was ashamed at having slept on the Embankment; it seemed peculiarly humiliating, and he felt his cheeks flush in the darkness. He remembered stories he had heard of those who did and how among them were officers, clergymen, and men who had been to universities: he wondered if he would become one of them, standing in a line to get soup from a charitable institution. It would be much better to commit suicide. He could not go on like that: Lawson would help him when he knew what straits he was in; it was absurd to let his pride prevent him from asking for assistance. He wondered why he had come such a cropper. He had always tried to do what he thought best, and everything had gone wrong. He had helped people when he could, he did not think he had been more selfish than anyone else, it seemed horribly unjust that he should be reduced to such a pass.

But it was no good thinking about it. He walked on. It was now light: the river was beautiful in the silence, and there was something mysterious in the early day; it was going to be very fine, and the sky, pale in the dawn, was cloudless. He felt very tired, and hunger was gnawing at his entrails, but he could not sit still; he was constantly afraid of being spoken to by a policeman. He dreaded the mortification of that. He felt dirty and wished he could have a wash. At last he found himself at

Hampton Court. He felt that if he did not have something to eat he would cry. He chose a cheap eating-house and went in; there was a smell of hot things, and it made him feel slightly sick: he meant to eat something nourishing enough to keep up for the rest of the day, but his stomach revolted at the sight of food. He had a cup of tea and some bread and butter. He remembered then that it was Sunday and he could go to the Athelnys; he thought of the roast beef and the Yorkshire pudding they would eat; but he was fearfully tired and could not face the happy, noisy family. He was feeling morose and wretched. He wanted to be left alone. He made up his mind that he would go into the gardens of the palace and lie down. His bones ached. Perhaps he would find a pump so that he could wash his hands and face and drink something; he was very thirsty; and now that he was no longer hungry he thought with pleasure of the flowers and the lawns and the great, leafy trees. He felt that there he could think out better what he must do. He lay on the grass, in the shade, and lit his pipe. For economy's sake he had for a long time confined himself to two pipes a day; he was thankful now that his pouch was full. He did not know what people did when they had no money. Presently he fell asleep. When he awoke it was nearly mid-day, and he thought that soon he must be setting out for London so as to be there in the early morning and answer any advertisements which seemed to promise. He thought of his uncle, who had told him that he would leave him at his death the little he had; Philip did not in the least know how much this was: it could not be more than a few hundred pounds. He wondered whether he could raise money on the reversion. Not without the old man's consent, and that he would never give.

"The only thing I can do is to hang on somehow till he dies."

Philip reckoned his age. The Vicar of Blackstable was well over seventy. He had chronic bronchitis, but many old men had that and lived on indefinitely. Meanwhile something must turn up; Philip could not get away from the feeling that his position was altogether abnormal; people in his particular station did not starve. It was because he could not bring himself to believe in the reality of his experience that he did not give way to utter despair. He made up his mind to borrow half a sovereign from Lawson. He stayed in the garden all day and smoked when he felt very hungry; he did not mean to eat anything until he was setting out again for London: it was a long way and he must keep up his strength for that. He started when the day began to grow cooler, and slept on benches when he was tired. No one disturbed him. He had a wash and brush up, and a shave at Victoria, some tea and bread and butter, and while he was eating this read the advertisement columns of the morning paper. As he looked down them his eye fell upon an announcement asking for a salesman in the "furnishing drapery" department of some well-known stores. He had a curious little sinking of the heart, for with his middle-class prejudices it seemed dreadful to go into a shop; but he shrugged his shoulders, after all what did it matter? and he made up his mind to have a shot at it. He had a queer feeling that by accepting every humiliation, by going out to meet it even, he was forcing the hand of fate. When he presented himself, feeling horribly shy, in the department at nine o'clock he found that many others were there before him. They were of all ages, from boys of sixteen to men of forty; some were talking to one another in undertones, but most were silent; and when he took up his place those around him gave him a look of hostility. He heard one man say:

"The only thing I look forward to is getting my refusal soon enough to give me time to look elsewhere."

The man, standing next him, glanced at Philip and asked:

"Had any experience?"

"No," said Philip.

He paused a moment and then made a remark: "Even the smaller houses won't see you without appointment after lunch."

Philip looked at the assistants. Some were draping chintzes and cretonnes, and others, his neighbour told him, were preparing country orders that had come in by post. At about a quarter-past nine the buyer arrived. He heard one of the men who were waiting say to another that it was Mr. Gibbons. He was middle-aged, short and corpulent, with a black beard and dark, greasy hair. He had brisk movements and a clever face. He wore a silk hat and a frock coat, the lapel of which was adorned with a white geranium surrounded by leaves. He went into his office, leaving the door open; it was very small and contained only an American roll-desk in the corner, a bookcase, and a cupboard. The men standing outside watched him mechanically take the geranium out of his coat and put it in an ink-pot filled with water. It was against the rules to wear flowers in business.

[During the day the department men who wanted to keep in with the governor admired the flower.

"I've never seen better," they said, "you didn't grow it yourself?"

"Yes I did," he smiled, and a gleam of pride filled his intelligent eyes.]

He took off his hat and changed his coat, glanced at the letters and then at the men who were waiting to see him. He made a slight sign with one finger, and the first in the queue stepped into the office. They filed past him one by one and answered his questions. He put them very briefly, keeping his eyes fixed on the applicant's face.

"Age? Experience? Why did you leave your job?"

He listened to the replies without expression. When it came to Philip's turn he fancied that Mr. Gibbons stared at him curiously. Philip's clothes were neat and tolerably cut. He looked a little different from the others.

"Experience?"

"I'm afraid I haven't any," said Philip.

"No good."

Philip walked out of the office. The ordeal had been so much less painful than he expected that he felt no particular disappointment. He could hardly hope to succeed in getting a place the first time he tried. He had kept the newspaper and now looked at the advertisements again: a shop in Holborn needed a salesman too, and he went there; but when he arrived he found that someone had already been engaged. If he wanted to get anything to eat that day he must go to Lawson's studio before he went out to luncheon, so he made his way along the Brompton Road to Yeoman's Row.

"I say, I'm rather broke till the end of the month," he said, as soon as he found an opportunity. "I wish you'd lend me half a sovereign, will you?"

It was incredible the difficulty he found in asking for money; and he remembered the casual way, as though almost they were conferring a favour, men at the hospital had extracted small sums out of him which they had no intention of repaying.

"Like a shot," said Lawson.

But when he put his hand in his pocket he found that he had only eight shillings. Philip's heart sank.

"Oh well, lend me five bob, will you?" he said lightly.

"Here you are."

Philip went to the public baths in Westminster and spent sixpence on a bath. Then he got himself something to eat. He did not know what to do with himself in the afternoon. He would not go back to the hospital in case anyone should ask him questions, and besides, he had nothing to do there now; they would wonder in the two or three departments he had worked in why he did not come, but they must think what they chose, it did not matter: he would not be the first student who had dropped out without warning. He went to the free library, and looked at the papers till they wearied him, then he took out Stevenson's *New Arabian Nights*; but he found he could not read: the words meant nothing to him, and he continued to brood over his helplessness. He kept on thinking the same things all the time, and the fixity of his thoughts made his head ache. At last, craving for fresh air, he went into the Green Park and lay down on the grass. He thought miserably of his deformity, which made it impossible for him to go to the war. He went to sleep and dreamed that he was suddenly sound of foot and out at the Cape in a regiment of Yeomanry; the pictures he had looked at in the illustrated papers gave materials for his fancy; and he saw himself on the Veldt, in khaki, sitting with other men round a fire at night. When he awoke he found that it was still quite light, and presently he heard Big Ben strike seven. He had twelve hours to get through with nothing to do. He dreaded the interminable night. The sky was overcast and he feared it would rain; he would have to go to a lodging-house where he could get a bed; he had seen them advertised on lamps outside houses in Lambeth: Good Beds sixpence; he had never been inside one, and dreaded the foul smell and the vermin. He made up his mind to stay in the open air if he possibly could. He remained in the park till it was closed and then began to walk about. He was very tired. The thought came to him that an accident would be a piece of luck, so that he could be taken to a hospital and lie there, in a clean bed, for weeks. At midnight he was so hungry that he could not go without food anymore, so he went to a coffee stall at Hyde Park Corner and ate a couple of potatoes and had a cup of coffee. Then he walked again. He felt too restless to sleep, and he had a horrible dread of being moved on by the police. He noted that he was beginning to look upon the constable from quite a new angle. This was the third night he had spent out. Now and then he sat on the benches in Piccadilly and towards morning he strolled down to the Embankment. He listened to the striking of Big Ben, marking every quarter of an hour, and reckoned out how long it left till the city woke again. In the morning he spent a few coppers on making himself neat and clean, bought a paper to read the advertisements, and set out once more on the search for work.

He went on in this way for several days. He had very little food and began to feel weak and ill, so that he had hardly enough energy to go on looking for the work which seemed so desperately hard to find. He was growing used now to the long waiting at the back of a shop on the chance that he would be taken on, and the curt dismissal. He walked to all parts of London in answer to the advertisements, and he came to know by sight men who applied as fruitlessly as himself. One or two tried to make friends with him, but he was too tired and too wretched to accept their advances. He did not go anymore to Lawson, because he owed him five shillings. He began to be too dazed to think clearly and ceased very much to care what would happen to him. He cried a good deal. At first he was very angry with himself for this and ashamed, but he found it relieved him, and somehow made him feel less hungry. In the very early morning he suffered a good deal from cold. One night he went into his room to change his linen; he slipped in about three, when he was quite sure everyone would be asleep, and out again at five; he lay on the bed and its softness was enchanting; all his bones ached, and as he lay he revelled in the pleasure of it; it was so delicious that he did not want to go to sleep. He was growing used to want of food and did not feel very hungry, but only weak. Constantly now at the back of his mind was the thought of doing away with himself, but he used all the strength he had not to dwell on it, because he was afraid the temptation would get hold of him so that he would not be able to help himself. He kept on saying to himself that it would be absurd to commit suicide, since something must happen soon; he could not get over the impression that his situation was too preposterous to be taken quite seriously; it was like an illness which must be endured but from which he was bound to recover. Every night he swore that nothing would induce him to put up with such another and determined next morning to write to his uncle, or to Mr. Nixon, the solicitor, or to Lawson; but when the time came he could not bring himself to make the humiliating confession of his utter failure. He did not know how Lawson would take it. In their friendship Lawson had been scatter-brained and he had prided himself on his common sense. He would have to tell the whole history of his folly. He had an uneasy feeling that Lawson, after helping him, would turn the cold shoulder on him. His uncle and the solicitor would of course do something for him, but he dreaded their reproaches. He did not want anyone to reproach him: he clenched his teeth and repeated that what had happened was inevitable just because it had happened. Regret was absurd.

The days were unending, and the five shillings Lawson had lent him would not last much longer. Philip longed for Sunday to come so that he could go to Athelny's. He did not know what prevented him from going there sooner, except perhaps that he wanted so badly to get through on his own; for Athelny, who had been in straits as desperate, was the only person who could do anything for him. Perhaps after dinner he could bring himself to tell Athelny that he was in difficulties. Philip repeated to himself over and over again what he should say to him. He was dreadfully afraid that Athelny would put him off with airy phrases: that would be so horrible that he wanted to delay as long as possible the putting of him to the test. Philip had lost all confidence in his fellows.

Saturday night was cold and raw. Philip suffered horribly. From mid-day on Saturday till he dragged himself wearily to Athelny's house he ate nothing. He spent his last twopence on Sunday morning on a wash and a brush up in the lavatory at Charing Cross.

Chapter CI

WHEN PHILIP RANG A HEAD WAS PUT OUT OF THE WINDOW, AND IN A minute he heard a noisy clatter on the stairs as the children ran down to let him in. It was a pale, anxious, thin face that he bent down for them to kiss. He was so moved by their exuberant affection that, to give himself time to recover, he made excuses to linger on the stairs. He was in a hysterical state and almost anything was enough to make him cry. They asked him why he had not come on the previous Sunday, and he told them he had been ill; they wanted to know what was the matter with him; and Philip, to amuse them, suggested a mysterious ailment, the name of which, double-barrelled and barbarous with its mixture of Greek and Latin (medical nomenclature bristled with such), made them shriek with delight. They dragged Philip into the parlour and made him repeat it for their father's edification. Athelny got up and shook hands with him. He stared at Philip, but with his round, bulging eyes he always seemed to stare. Philip did not know why on this occasion it made him self-conscious.

"We missed you last Sunday," he said.

Philip could never tell lies without embarrassment, and he was scarlet when he finished his explanation for not coming. Then Mrs. Athelny entered and shook hands with him.

"I hope you're better, Mr. Carey," she said.

He did not know why she imagined that anything had been the matter with him, for the kitchen door was closed when he came up with the children, and they had not left him.

"Dinner won't be ready for another ten minutes," she said, in her slow drawl. "Won't you have an egg beaten up in a glass of milk while you're waiting?"

There was a look of concern on her face which made Philip uncomfortable. He forced a laugh and answered that he was not at all hungry. Sally came in to lay the table, and Philip began to chaff her. It was the family joke that she would be as fat as an aunt of Mrs. Athelny, called Aunt Elizabeth, whom the children had never seen but regarded as the type of obscene corpulence.

"I say, what *has* happened since I saw you last, Sally?" Philip began.

"Nothing that I know of."

"I believe you've been putting on weight."

"I'm sure you haven't," she retorted. "You're a perfect skeleton."

Philip reddened.

"That's a *tu quoque*, Sally," cried her father. "You will be fined one golden hair of your head. Jane, fetch the shears."

"Well, he is thin, father," remonstrated Sally. "He's just skin and bone."

"That's not the question, child. He is at perfect liberty to be thin, but your obesity is contrary to decorum."

As he spoke he put his arm proudly round her waist and looked at her with admiring eyes.

"Let me get on with the table, father. If I am comfortable there are some who don't seem to mind it."

"The hussy!" cried Athelny, with a dramatic wave of the hand. "She taunts me with the notorious fact that Joseph, a son of Levi who sells jewels in Holborn, has made her an offer of marriage."

"Have you accepted him, Sally?" asked Philip.

"Don't you know father better than that by this time? There's not a word of truth in it."

"Well, if he hasn't made you an offer of marriage," cried Athelny, "by Saint George and Merry England, I will seize him by the nose and demand of him immediately what are his intentions."

"Sit down, father, dinner's ready. Now then, you children, get along with you and wash your hands all of you, and don't shirk it, because I mean to look at them before you have a scrap of dinner, so there."

Philip thought he was ravenous till he began to eat, but then discovered that his stomach turned against food, and he could eat hardly at all. His brain was weary; and he did not notice that Athelny, contrary to his habit, spoke very little. Philip was relieved to be sitting in a comfortable house, but every now and then he could not prevent himself from glancing out of the window. The day was tempestuous. The fine weather had broken; and it was cold, and there was a bitter wind; now and again gusts of rain drove against the window. Philip wondered what he should do that night. The Athelnys went to bed early, and he could not stay where he was after ten o'clock. His heart sank at the thought of going out into the bleak darkness. It seemed more terrible now that he was with his friends than when he was outside and alone. He kept on saying to himself that there were plenty more who would be spending the night out of doors. He strove to distract his mind by talking, but in the middle of his words a spatter of rain against the window would make him start.

"It's like March weather," said Athelny. "Not the sort of day one would like to be crossing the Channel."

Presently they finished, and Sally came in and cleared away.

"Would you like a twopenny stinker?" said Athelny, handing him a cigar.

Philip took it and inhaled the smoke with delight. It soothed him extraordinarily. When Sally had finished Athelny told her to shut the door after her.

"Now we shan't be disturbed," he said, turning to Philip. "I've arranged with Betty not to let the children come in till I call them."

Philip gave him a startled look, but before he could take in the meaning of his words, Athelny, fixing his glasses on his nose with the gesture habitual to him, went on.

"I wrote to you last Sunday to ask if anything was the matter with you, and as you didn't answer I went to your rooms on Wednesday."

Philip turned his head away and did not answer. His heart began to beat violently. Athelny did not speak, and presently the silence seemed intolerable to Philip. He could not think of a single word to say.

"Your landlady told me you hadn't been in since Saturday night, and she said you owed her for the last month. Where have you been sleeping all this week?"

It made Philip sick to answer. He stared out of the window.

"Nowhere."

"I tried to find you."

"Why?" asked Philip.

"Betty and I have been just as broke in our day, only we had babies to look after. Why didn't you come here?"

"I couldn't."

Philip was afraid he was going to cry. He felt very weak. He shut his eyes and frowned, trying to control himself. He felt a sudden flash of anger with Athelny because he would not leave him alone; but he was broken; and presently, his eyes still closed, slowly in order to keep his voice steady, he told him the story of his adventures during the last few weeks. As he spoke it seemed to him that he had behaved inanely, and it made it still harder to tell. He felt that Athelny would think him an utter fool.

"Now you're coming to live with us till you find something to do," said Athelny, when he had finished.

Philip flushed, he knew not why.

"Oh, it's awfully kind of you, but I don't think I'll do that."

"Why not?"

Philip did not answer. He had refused instinctively from fear that he would be a bother, and he had a natural bashfulness of accepting favours. He knew besides that the Athelnys lived from hand to mouth, and with their large family had neither space nor money to entertain a stranger.

"Of course you must come here," said Athelny. "Thorpe will tuck in with one of his brothers and you can sleep in his bed. You don't suppose your food's going to make any difference to us."

Philip was afraid to speak, and Athelny, going to the door, called his wife.

"Betty," he said, when she came in, "Mr. Carey's coming to live with us."

"Oh, that is nice," she said. "I'll go and get the bed ready."

She spoke in such a hearty, friendly tone, taking everything for granted, that Philip was deeply touched. He never expected people to be kind to him, and when they were it surprised and moved him. Now he could not prevent two large tears from rolling down his cheeks. The Athelnys discussed the arrangements and pretended not to notice to what a state his weakness had brought him. When Mrs. Athelny left them Philip leaned back in his chair, and looking out of the window laughed a little.

"It's not a very nice night to be out, is it?"

Chapter CII

ATHELNY TOLD PHILIP THAT HE COULD EASILY GET HIM SOMETHING TO DO in the large firm of linen-drapers in which himself worked. Several of the assistants had gone to the war, and Lynn and Sedley with patriotic zeal had promised to keep their places open for them. They put the work of the heroes on those who remained, and since they did not increase the wages of these were able at once to exhibit public spirit and effect an economy; but the war continued and trade was less depressed; the holidays were coming, when numbers of the staff went away for a fortnight at a time: they were bound to engage more assistants. Philip's experience had made him doubtful whether even then they would engage him; but Athelny, representing himself as a person of consequence in the firm, insisted that the manager could refuse him nothing. Philip, with his training in Paris, would be very useful; it was only a matter of waiting a little and he was bound to get a well-paid job to design costumes and draw posters. Philip made a poster for the summer sale and Athelny took it away. Two days later he brought it back, saying that the manager admired it very much and regretted with all his heart that there was no vacancy just then in that department. Philip asked whether there was nothing else he could do.

"I'm afraid not."

"Are you quite sure?"

"Well, the fact is they're advertising for a shop-walker tomorrow," said Athelny, looking at him doubtfully through his glasses.

"D'you think I stand any chance of getting it?"

Athelny was a little confused; he had led Philip to expect something much more splendid; on the other hand he was too poor to go on providing him indefinitely with board and lodging.

"You might take it while you wait for something better. You always stand a better chance if you're engaged by the firm already."

"I'm not proud, you know" smiled Philip.

"If you decide on that you must be there at a quarter to nine tomorrow morning."

Notwithstanding the war there was evidently much difficulty in finding work, for when Philip went to the shop many men were waiting already. He recognised some whom he had seen in his own searching, and there was one whom he had noticed lying about the park in the afternoon. To Philip now that suggested that he was as homeless as himself and passed the night out of doors. The men were of all sorts, old and young, tall and short; but every one had tried to make himself smart for the interview with the manager: they had carefully brushed hair and scrupulously clean hands. They waited in a passage which Philip learned afterwards led up to the dining-hall and the work rooms; it was broken every few yards by five or six steps. Though there was electric light in the shop here was only gas, with wire cages over it for protection, and it flared noisily. Philip arrived punctually, but it was nearly ten o'clock when he was admitted into the office. It was three-cornered, like a cut of cheese lying on its side: on the walls were pictures of women in corsets, and two poster-proofs, one of a man in pyjamas, green and white in large stripes, and the other of a ship in full sail ploughing an azure sea: on the sail was printed in large letters "great white sale." The widest side of the office was the back of one of the shop-windows, which was being dressed at the time, and an assistant went to and fro during the interview. The manager was reading a letter. He was a florid man, with sandy hair and a large sandy moustache; from the middle of his watch-chain hung a bunch of football medals. He sat in his shirt-sleeves at a large desk with a telephone by his side; before him were the day's advertisements, Athelny's work, and cuttings from newspapers pasted on a card. He gave Philip a glance but did not speak to him; he dictated a letter to the typist, a girl who sat at a small table in one corner; then he asked Philip his name, age, and what experience he had had. He spoke with a cockney twang in a high, metallic voice which he seemed not able always to control; Philip noticed that his upper teeth were large and protruding; they gave you the impression that they were loose and would come out if you gave them a sharp tug.

"I think Mr. Athelny has spoken to you about me," said Philip.

"Oh, you are the young feller who did that poster?"

"Yes, sir."

"No good to us, you know, not a bit of good."

He looked Philip up and down. He seemed to notice that Philip was in some way different from the men who had preceded him.

"You'd 'ave to get a frock coat, you know. I suppose you 'aven't got one. You seem a respectable young feller. I suppose you found art didn't pay."

Philip could not tell whether he meant to engage him or not. He threw remarks at him in a hostile way.

"Where's your home?"

"My father and mother died when I was a child."

"I like to give young fellers a chance. Many's the one I've given their chance to and they're managers of departments now. And they're grateful to me, I'll say that for them. They know what I done for them. Start at the bottom of the ladder, that's the only way to learn the business, and then if you stick to it there's no knowing what it can lead to. If you suit, one of these days you may find yourself in a position like what mine is. Bear that in mind, young feller."

"I'm very anxious to do my best, sir," said Philip.

He knew that he must put in the sir whenever he could, but it sounded odd to him, and he was afraid of overdoing it. The manager liked talking. It gave him a happy consciousness of his own importance, and he did not give Philip his decision till he had used a great many words.

"Well, I daresay you'll do," he said at last, in a pompous way. "Anyhow I don't mind giving you a trial."

"Thank you very much, sir."

"You can start at once. I'll give you six shillings a week and your keep. Everything found, you know; the six shillings is only pocket money, to do what you like with, paid monthly. Start on Monday. I suppose you've got no cause of complaint with that."

"No, sir."

"Harrington Street, d'you know where that is, Shaftesbury Avenue. That's where you sleep. Number ten, it is. You can sleep there on Sunday night, if you like; that's just as you please, or you can send your box there on Monday." The manager nodded: "Good-morning."

Chapter CIII

Mrs. Athelny lent Philip money to pay his landlady enough of her bill to let him take his things away. For five shillings and the pawn-ticket on a suit he was able to get from a pawnbroker a frock coat which fitted him fairly well. He redeemed the rest of his clothes. He sent his box to Harrington Street by Carter Patterson and on Monday morning went with Athelny to the shop. Athelny introduced him to the buyer of the costumes and left him. The buyer was a pleasant, fussy little man of thirty, named Sampson; he shook hands with Philip, and, in order to show his own accomplishment of which he was very proud, asked him if he spoke French. He was surprised when Philip told him he did.

"Any other language?"

"I speak German."

"Oh! I go over to Paris myself occasionally. *Parlez-vous français?* Ever been to Maxim's?"

Philip was stationed at the top of the stairs in the "costumes." His work consisted in directing people to the various departments. There seemed a great many of them as Mr. Sampson tripped them off his tongue. Suddenly he noticed that Philip limped.

"What's the matter with your leg?" he asked.

"I've got a club-foot," said Philip. "But it doesn't prevent my walking or anything like that."

The buyer looked at it for a moment doubtfully, and Philip surmised that he was wondering why the manager had engaged him. Philip knew that he had not noticed there was anything the matter with him.

"I don't expect you to get them all correct the first day. If you're in any doubt all you've got to do is to ask one of the young ladies."

Mr. Sampson turned away; and Philip, trying to remember where this or the other department was, watched anxiously for the customer in search of information. At one o'clock he went up to dinner. The dining-room, on the top floor of the vast building, was large, long, and well lit; but all the windows were shut to keep out the dust, and there was a horrid smell of cooking. There were long tables covered with cloths, with big glass bottles of water at intervals, and down the centre salt cellars and bottles of vinegar. The assistants crowded in noisily, and sat down on forms still warm from those who had dined at twelve-thirty.

"No pickles," remarked the man next to Philip.

He was a tall thin young man, with a hooked nose and a pasty face; he had a long head, unevenly shaped as though the skull had been pushed in here and there oddly, and on his forehead and neck were large acne spots red and inflamed. His name was Harris. Philip discovered that on some days there were large soup-plates down the table full of mixed pickles. They were very popular. There were no knives and forks, but in a minute a large fat boy in a white coat came in with a couple of handfuls of them and threw them loudly on the middle of the table. Each man took what he wanted; they were warm and greasy from recent washing in dirty water. Plates of meat swimming in gravy were handed round by boys in white jackets, and as they flung each plate down with the quick gesture of a prestidigitator the gravy slopped over on to the table-cloth. Then they brought large dishes of cabbages and potatoes; the sight of them turned Philip's stomach; he noticed that everyone poured quantities of vinegar over them. The noise was awful. They talked and laughed and shouted, and there was the clatter of knives and forks, and strange sounds of eating. Philip was glad to get back into the department. He was beginning to remember where each one was, and had less often to ask one of the assistants, when somebody wanted to know the way.

"First to the right. Second on the left, madam."

One or two of the girls spoke to him, just a word when things were slack, and he felt they were taking his measure. At five he was sent up again to the diningroom for tea. He was glad to sit down. There were large slices of bread heavily spread with butter; and many had pots of jam, which were kept in the "store" and had their names written on.

Philip was exhausted when work stopped at half-past six. Harris, the man he had sat next to at dinner, offered to take him over to Harrington Street to show him where he was to sleep. He told Philip there was a spare bed in his room, and, as the other rooms were full, he expected Philip would be put there. The house in Harrington Street had been a bootmaker's; and the shop was used as a bed-room; but it was very dark, since the window had been boarded three parts up, and as this did not open the only ventilation came from a small skylight at the far end. There was a musty smell, and Philip was thankful that he would not have to sleep there. Harris took him up to the sitting-room, which was on the first floor; it had an old piano in it with a keyboard that looked like a row of decayed teeth; and on the table in a cigar-box without a lid was a set of dominoes; old numbers of *The Strand Magazine* and of *The Graphic* were lying about. The other rooms were used as bedrooms. That in which Philip was to sleep was at the top of the house. There were six beds in it, and a trunk or a box stood by the side of each. The only furniture was a chest of drawers: it had four large drawers and two small ones, and Philip as the new-comer had one of these; there were keys to them, but as they were all alike they were not of much use, and Harris advised him to keep his valuables in his trunk. There was a looking-glass on the chimney-piece. Harris showed Philip the lavatory, which was a fairly large room with eight basins in a row, and here all the inmates did their washing. It led into another room in which were two baths, discoloured, the woodwork stained with soap; and in them were dark rings at various intervals which indicated the water marks of different baths.

When Harris and Philip went back to their bed-room they found a tall man changing his clothes and a boy of sixteen whistling as loud as he could while he brushed his hair. In a minute or two without saying a word to anybody the tall man went out. Harris winked at the boy, and the boy, whistling still, winked back. Harris told Philip that the man was called Prior; he had been in the army and now served in the silks; he kept pretty much to himself, and he went off every night, just like that, without so much as a good-evening, to see his girl. Harris went out too, and only the boy remained to watch Philip curiously while he unpacked his things. His name was Bell and he was serving his time for nothing in the haberdashery. He was much interested in Philip's evening clothes. He told him about the other men in the room and asked him every sort of question about himself. He was a cheerful youth, and in the intervals of conversation sang in a half-broken voice snatches of music-hall songs. When Philip had finished he went out to walk about the streets and look at the crowd; occasionally he stopped outside the doors of restaurants and watched the people going in; he felt hungry, so he bought a bath bun and ate it while he strolled along. He had been given a latch-key by the prefect, the man who turned out the gas at a quarter-past eleven, but afraid of being locked out he returned in good time; he had learned already the system of fines: you had to pay a shilling if you came in after eleven, and half a crown after a quarter-past, and you were reported besides: if it happened three times you were dismissed.

All but the soldier were in when Philip arrived and two were already in bed. Philip was greeted with cries.

"Oh, Clarence! Naughty boy!"

He discovered that Bell had dressed up the bolster in his evening clothes. The boy was delighted with his joke.

"You must wear them at the social evening, Clarence."

"He'll catch the belle of Lynn's, if he's not careful."

Philip had already heard of the social evenings, for the money stopped from the wages to pay for them was one of the grievances of the staff. It was only two shillings a month, and it covered medical attendance and the use of a library of worn novels; but as four shillings a month besides was stopped for washing, Philip discovered that a quarter of his six shillings a week would never be paid to him.

Most of the men were eating thick slices of fat bacon between a roll of bread cut in two. These sandwiches, the assistants' usual supper, were supplied by a small shop a few doors off at twopence each. The soldier rolled in; silently, rapidly, took off his clothes and threw himself into bed. At ten minutes past eleven the gas gave a big jump and five minutes later went out. The soldier went to sleep, but the others crowded round the big window in their pyjamas and night-shirts and, throwing remains of their sandwiches at the women who passed in the street below, shouted to them facetious remarks. The house opposite, six storeys high, was a workshop for Jewish tailors who left off work at eleven; the rooms were brightly lit and there were no blinds to the windows. The sweater's daughter—the family consisted of father, mother, two small boys, and a girl of twenty—went round the house to put out the lights when work was over, and sometimes she allowed herself to be made love to by one of the tailors. The shop assistants in Philip's room got a lot of amusement out of watching the manoeuvres of one man or another to stay behind, and they made small bets on which would succeed. At midnight the people were turned out of the Harrington Arms at the end of the street, and soon after they all went to bed: Bell, who slept nearest the door, made his way across the room by jumping from bed to bed, and even when he got to his own would not stop talking. At last everything was silent but for the steady snoring of the soldier, and Philip went to sleep.

He was awaked at seven by the loud ringing of a bell, and by a quarter to eight they were all dressed and hurrying downstairs in their stockinged feet to pick out their boots. They laced them as they ran along to the shop in Oxford Street for breakfast. If they were a minute later than eight they got none, nor, once in, were they allowed out to get themselves anything to eat. Sometimes, if they knew they could not get into the building in time, they stopped at the little shop near their quarters and bought a couple of buns; but this cost money, and most went without food till dinner. Philip ate some bread and butter, drank a cup of tea, and at half-past eight began his day's work again.

"First to the right. Second on the left, madam."

Soon he began to answer the questions quite mechanically. The work was monotonous and very tiring. After a few days his feet hurt him so that he could hardly stand: the thick soft carpets made them burn, and at night his socks were painful to remove. It was a common complaint, and his fellow "floormen" told him that socks and boots just rotted away from the continual sweating. All the men in his room suffered in the same fashion, and they relieved the pain by sleeping with their feet outside the bed-clothes. At first Philip could not walk at all and was obliged to spend a good many of his evenings in the sitting-room at Harrington Street with his feet in a pail of cold water. His companion on these occasions was Bell, the lad in the haberdashery, who stayed in often to arrange the stamps he collected. As he fastened them with little pieces of stamp-paper he whistled monotonously.

Chapter CIV

THE SOCIAL EVENINGS TOOK PLACE ON ALTERNATE MONDAYS. THERE WAS one at the beginning of Philip's second week at Lynn's. He arranged to go with one of the women in his department.

"Meet 'em 'alf-way," she said, "same as I do."

This was Mrs. Hodges, a little woman of five-and-forty, with badly dyed hair; she had a yellow face with a network of small red veins all over it, and yellow whites to her pale blue eyes. She took a fancy to Philip and called him by his Christian name before he had been in the shop a week.

"We've both known what it is to come down," she said.

She told Philip that her real name was not Hodges, but she always referred to "me 'usband Misterodges"; he was a barrister and he treated her simply shocking, so she left him as she preferred to be independent like; but she had known what it was to drive in her own carriage, dear—she called everyone dear—and they always had late dinner at home. She used to pick her teeth with the pin of an enormous silver brooch. It was in the form of a whip and a hunting-crop crossed, with two spurs in the middle. Philip was ill at ease in his new surroundings, and the girls in the shop called him "sidey." One addressed him as Phil, and he did not answer because he had not the least idea that she was speaking to him; so she tossed her head, saying he was a "stuck-up thing," and next time with ironical emphasis called him Mister Carey. She was a Miss Jewell, and she was going to marry a doctor. The other girls had never seen him, but they said he must be a gentleman as he gave her such lovely presents.

"Never you mind what they say, dear," said Mrs. Hodges. "I've 'ad to go through it same as you 'ave. They don't know any better, poor things. You take my word for it, they'll like you all right if you 'old your own same as I 'ave."

The social evening was held in the restaurant in the basement. The tables were put on one side so that there might be room for dancing, and smaller ones were set out for progressive whist.

"The 'eads 'ave to get there early," said Mrs. Hodges.

She introduced him to Miss Bennett, who was the belle of Lynn's. She was the buyer in the "Petticoats," and when Philip entered was engaged in conversation with the buyer in the "Gentlemen's Hosiery"; Miss Bennett was a woman of massive proportions, with a very large red face heavily powdered and a bust of imposing dimensions; her flaxen hair was arranged with elaboration. She was overdressed, but not badly dressed, in black with a high collar, and she wore black *glacé* gloves, in which she played cards; she had several heavy gold chains round her neck, bangles on her wrists, and circular photograph pendants, one being of Queen Alexandra; she carried a black satin bag and chewed Sen-sens.

"Please to meet you, Mr. Carey," she said. "This is your first visit to our social evenings, ain't it? I expect you feel a bit shy, but there's no cause to, I promise you that."

She did her best to make people feel at home. She slapped them on the shoulders and laughed a great deal.

"Ain't I a pickle?" she cried, turning to Philip. "What must you think of me? But I can't 'elp meself."

Those who were going to take part in the social evening came in, the younger members of the staff mostly, boys who had not girls of their own, and girls who had not yet found anyone to walk with. Several of the young gentlemen wore lounge suits with white evening ties and red silk handkerchiefs; they were going to perform, and they had a busy, abstracted air; some were self-confident, but others were nervous, and they watched their public with an anxious eye. Presently a girl with a great deal of hair sat at the piano and ran her hands noisily across the keyboard. When the audience had settled itself she looked round and gave the name of her piece.

"A Drive in Russia."

There was a round of clapping during which she deftly fixed bells to her wrists. She smiled a little and immediately burst into energetic melody. There was a great deal more clapping when she finished, and when this was over, as an encore, she gave a piece which imitated the sea; there were little trills to represent the lapping waves and thundering chords, with the loud pedal down, to suggest a storm. After this a gentleman sang a song called *Bid me Good-bye*, and as an encore obliged with *Sing me to Sleep*. The audience measured their enthusiasm with a nice discrimination. Everyone was applauded till he gave an encore, and so that there might be no jealousy no one was applauded more than anyone else. Miss Bennett sailed up to Philip.

"I'm sure you play or sing, Mr. Carey," she said archly. "I can see it in your face."

"I'm afraid I don't."

"Don't you even recite?"

"I have no parlour tricks."

The buyer in the "gentleman's hosiery" was a well-known reciter, and he was called upon loudly to perform by all the assistants in his department. Needing no pressing, he gave a long poem of tragic character, in which he rolled his eyes, put his hand on his chest, and acted as though he were in great agony. The point, that he had eaten cucumber for supper, was divulged in the last line and was greeted with laughter, a little forced because everyone knew the poem well, but loud and long. Miss Bennett did not sing, play, or recite.

"Oh no, she 'as a little game of her own," said Mrs. Hodges.

"Now, don't you begin chaffing me. The fact is I know quite a lot about palmistry and second sight."

"Oh, do tell my 'and, Miss Bennett," cried the girls in her department, eager to please her.

"I don't like telling 'ands, I don't really. I've told people such terrible things and they've all come true, it makes one superstitious like."

"Oh, Miss Bennett, just for once."

A little crowd collected round her, and, amid screams of embarrassment, giggles, blushings, and cries of dismay or admiration, she talked mysteriously of fair and dark men, of money in a letter, and of journeys, till the sweat stood in heavy beads on her painted face.

"Look at me," she said. "I'm all of a perspiration."

Supper was at nine. There were cakes, buns, sandwiches, tea and coffee, all free; but if you wanted mineral water you had to pay for it. Gallantry often led young men to offer the ladies ginger beer, but common decency made them refuse. Miss Bennett was very fond of ginger beer, and she drank two and sometimes three bottles during the evening; but she insisted on paying for them herself. The men liked her for that.

"She's a rum old bird," they said, "but mind you, she's not a bad sort, she's not like what some are."

After supper progressive whist was played. This was very noisy, and there was a great deal of laughing and shouting, as people moved from table to table. Miss Bennett grew hotter and hotter.

"Look at me," she said. "I'm all of a perspiration."

In due course one of the more dashing of the young men remarked that if they wanted to dance they'd better begin. The girl who had played the accompaniments sat at the piano and placed a decided foot on the loud pedal. She played a dreamy waltz, marking the time with the bass, while with the right hand she "tiddled" in alternate octaves. By way of a change she crossed her hands and played the air in the bass.

"She does play well, doesn't she?" Mrs. Hodges remarked to Philip. "And what's more she's never 'ad a lesson in 'er life; it's all ear."

Miss Bennett liked dancing and poetry better than anything in the world. She danced well, but very, very slowly, and an expression came into her eyes as though her thoughts were far, far away. She talked breathlessly of the floor and the heat and the supper. She said that the Portman Rooms had the best floor in London and she always liked the dances there; they were very select, and she couldn't bear dancing with all sorts of men you didn't know anything about; why, you might be exposing yourself to you didn't know what all. Nearly all the people danced very well, and they enjoyed themselves. Sweat poured down their faces, and the very high collars of the young men grew limp.

Philip looked on, and a greater depression seized him than he remembered to have felt for a long time. He felt intolerably alone. He did not go, because he was afraid to seem supercilious, and he talked with the girls and laughed, but in his heart was unhappiness. Miss Bennett asked him if he had a girl.

"No," he smiled.

"Oh, well, there's plenty to choose from here. And they're very nice respectable girls, some of them. I expect you'll have a girl before you've been here long."

She looked at him very archly.

"Meet 'em 'alf-way," said Mrs. Hodges. "That's what I tell him."

It was nearly eleven o'clock, and the party broke up. Philip could not get to sleep. Like the others he kept his aching feet outside the bed-clothes. He tried with all his might not to think of the life he was leading. The soldier was snoring quietly.

Chapter CV

THE WAGES WERE PAID ONCE A MONTH BY THE SECRETARY. ON PAY-DAY each batch of assistants, coming down from tea, went into the passage and joined the long line of people waiting orderly like the audience in a queue outside a gallery door. One by one they entered the office. The secretary sat at a desk with wooden bowls of money in front of him, and he asked the employee's name; he referred to a book, quickly, after a suspicious glance at the assistant, said aloud the sum due, and taking money out of the bowl counted it into his hand.

"Thank you," he said. "Next."

"Thank you," was the reply.

The assistant passed on to the second secretary and before leaving the room paid him four shillings for washing money, two shillings for the club, and any fines that he might have incurred. With what he had left he went back into his department and there waited till it was time to go. Most of the men in Philip's house were in debt with the woman who sold the sandwiches they generally ate for supper. She was a funny old thing, very fat, with a broad, red face, and black hair plastered neatly on each side of the forehead in the fashion shown in early pictures of Queen Victoria. She always wore a little black bonnet and a white apron; her sleeves were tucked up to the elbow; she cut the sandwiches with large, dirty, greasy hands; and there was grease on her bodice, grease on her apron, grease on her skirt. She was called Mrs. Fletcher, but everyone addressed her as "Ma"; she was really fond of the shop assistants, whom she called her boys; she never minded giving credit towards the end of the month, and it was known that now and then she had lent someone or other a few shillings when he was in straits. She was a good woman. When they were leaving or when they came back from the holidays, the boys kissed her fat red cheek; and more than one, dismissed and unable to find another job, had got for nothing food to keep body and soul together. The boys were sensible of her large heart and repaid her with genuine affection. There was a story they liked to tell of a man who had done well for himself at Bradford, and had five shops of his own, and had come back after fifteen years and visited Ma Fletcher and given her a gold watch.

Philip found himself with eighteen shillings left out of his month's pay. It was the first money he had ever earned in his life. It gave him none of the pride which might have been expected, but merely a feeling of dismay. The smallness of the sum emphasised the hopelessness of his position. He took fifteen shillings to Mrs. Athelny to pay back part of what he owed her, but she would not take more than half a sovereign.

"D'you know, at that rate it'll take me eight months to settle up with you."

"As long as Athelny's in work I can afford to wait, and who knows, p'raps they'll give you a rise."

Athelny kept on saying that he would speak to the manager about Philip, it was absurd that no use should be made of his talents; but he did nothing, and Philip soon came to the conclusion that the press-agent was not a person of so much importance in the manager's eyes as in his own. Occasionally he saw Athelny in the shop. His flamboyance was extinguished; and in neat, commonplace, shabby clothes he hurried, a subdued, unassuming little man, through the departments as though anxious to escape notice.

"When I think of how I'm wasted there," he said at home, "I'm almost tempted to give in my notice. There's no scope for a man like me. I'm stunted, I'm starved."

Mrs. Athelny, quietly sewing, took no notice of his complaints. Her mouth tightened a little.

"It's very hard to get jobs in these times. It's regular and it's safe; I expect you'll stay there as long as you give satisfaction."

It was evident that Athelny would. It was interesting to see the ascendency which the uneducated woman, bound to him by no legal tie, had acquired over the brilliant, unstable man. Mrs. Athelny treated Philip with motherly kindness now that he was in a different position, and he was touched by her anxiety that he should make a good meal. It was the solace of his life (and when he grew used to it, the monotony of it was what chiefly appalled him) that he could go every Sunday to that friendly house. It was a joy to sit in the stately Spanish chairs and discuss all manner of things with Athelny. Though his condition seemed so desperate he never left him to go back to Harrington Street without a feeling of exultation. At first Philip, in order not to forget what he had learned, tried to go on reading his medical books, but he found it useless; he could not fix his attention on them after the exhausting work of the day; and it seemed hopeless to continue working when he did not know in how long he would be able to go back to the hospital. He dreamed constantly that he was in the wards. The awakening was painful. The sensation of other people sleeping in the room was inexpressibly irksome to him; he had been used to solitude, and to be with others always, never to be by himself for an instant, was at these moments horrible to him. It was then that he found it most difficult to combat his despair. He saw himself going on with that life, first to the right, second on the left, madam, indefinitely; and having to be thankful if he was not sent away: the men who had gone to the war would be coming home soon, the firm had guaranteed to take them back, and this must mean that others would be sacked; he would have to stir himself even to keep the wretched post he had.

There was only one thing to free him and that was the death of his uncle. He would get a few hundred pounds then, and on this he could finish his course at the hospital. Philip began to wish with all his might for the old man's death. He reckoned out how long he could possibly live; he was well over seventy, Philip did not know his exact age, but he must be at least seventy-five; he suffered from chronic bronchitis and every winter had a bad cough. Though he knew them by heart Philip read over and over again the details in his text-book of medicine of chronic bronchitis in the old. A severe winter might be too much for the old man. With all his heart Philip longed for cold and rain. He thought of it constantly, so that it became a monomania. Uncle William was affected by the great heat too, and in August they had three weeks of sweltering weather. Philip imagined to himself that one day perhaps a telegram would come saying that the Vicar had died suddenly, and he pictured to himself his unutterable relief. As he stood at the top of the stairs and directed people to the departments they wanted, he occupied his mind with thinking incessantly what he would do with the money. He did not know how much it would be, perhaps no more than five hundred pounds, but even that would be enough. He would leave the shop at once, he would not bother to give notice, he would pack his box and go without saying a word to anybody; and then he would return to the hospital. That was the first thing. Would he have forgotten much? In six months he could get it all back, and then he would take his three examinations as soon as he could, midwifery first, then medicine and surgery. The awful fear seized him that his uncle, notwithstanding his promises, might leave everything he had to the parish or the church. The thought made Philip sick. He could not be so cruel. But if that happened Philip was quite determined what to do, he would not go on in that way indefinitely; his life was only tolerable because he could look forward to something better. If he had no hope he would have no fear. The only brave thing to do then would be to commit suicide, and, thinking this over too, Philip decided minutely what painless drug he would take and how he would get hold of it. It encouraged him to think that, if things became unendurable, he had at all events a way out.

"Second to the right, madam, and down the stairs. First on the left and straight through. Mr. Philips, forward please."

Once a month, for a week, Philip was "on duty." He had to go to the department at seven in the morning and keep an eye on the sweepers. When they finished he had to take the sheets off the cases and the models. Then, in the evening when the assistants left, he had to put back the sheets on the models and the cases and "gang" the sweepers again. It was a dusty, dirty job. He was not allowed to read or write or smoke, but just had to walk about, and the time hung heavily on his hands. When he went off at half-past nine he had supper given him, and this was the only consolation; for tea at five o'clock had left him with a healthy appetite, and the bread and cheese, the abundant cocoa which the firm provided, were welcome.

One day when Philip had been at Lynn's for three months, Mr. Sampson, the buyer, came into the department, fuming with anger. The manager, happening to notice the costume window as he came in, had sent for the buyer and made satirical remarks upon the colour scheme. Forced to submit in silence to his superior's sarcasm, Mr. Sampson took it out of the assistants; and he rated the wretched fellow whose duty it was to dress the window.

"If you want a thing well done you must do it yourself," Mr. Sampson stormed. "I've always said it and I always shall. One can't leave anything to you chaps. Intelligent you call yourselves, do you? Intelligent!"

He threw the word at the assistants as though it were the bitterest term of reproach.

"Don't you know that if you put an electric blue in the window it'll kill all the other blues?"

He looked round the department ferociously, and his eye fell upon Philip.

"You'll dress the window next Friday, Carey. Let's see what you can make of it."

He went into his office, muttering angrily. Philip's heart sank. When Friday morning came he went into the window with a sickening sense of shame. His cheeks were burning. It was horrible to display himself to the passers-by, and though he told himself it was foolish to give way to such a feeling he turned his back to the street. There was not much chance that any of the students at the hospital would pass along Oxford Street at that hour, and he knew hardly anyone else in London; but as Philip worked, with a huge lump in his throat, he fancied that on turning round he would catch the eye of some man he knew. He made all the haste he could. By the simple observation that all reds went together, and by spacing the costumes more than was usual, Philip got a very good effect; and when the buyer went into the street to look at the result he was obviously pleased.

"I knew I shouldn't go far wrong in putting you on the window. The fact is, you and me are gentlemen, mind you I wouldn't say this in the department, but you and me are gentlemen, and that always tells. It's no good your telling me it doesn't tell, because I know it does tell."

Philip was put on the job regularly, but he could not accustom himself to the publicity; and he dreaded Friday morning, on which the window was dressed, with a terror that made him awake at five o'clock and lie sleepless with sickness in his heart. The girls in the department noticed his shamefaced way, and they very soon discovered his trick of standing with his back to the street. They laughed at him and called him "'sidey."

"I suppose you're afraid your aunt'll come along and cut you out of her will."

On the whole he got on well enough with the girls. They thought him a little queer; but his club-foot seemed to excuse his not being like the rest, and they found in due course that he was good-natured. He never minded helping anyone, and he was polite and even tempered.

"You can see he's a gentleman," they said.

"Very reserved, isn't he?" said one young woman, to whose passionate enthusiasm for the theatre he had listened unmoved.

Most of them had "fellers," and those who hadn't said they had rather than have it supposed that no one had an inclination for them. One or two showed signs of being willing to start a flirtation with Philip, and he watched their manoeuvres with grave amusement. He had had enough of love-making for some time; and he was nearly always tired and often hungry.

Chapter CVI

PHILIP AVOIDED THE PLACES HE HAD KNOWN IN HAPPIER TIMES. THE LITTLE gatherings at the tavern in Beak Street were broken up: Macalister, having let down his friends, no longer went there, and Hayward was at the Cape. Only Lawson remained; and Philip, feeling that now the painter and he had nothing in common, did not wish to see him; but one Saturday afternoon, after dinner, having changed his clothes he walked down Regent Street to go to the free library in St. Martin's Lane, meaning to spend the afternoon there, and suddenly found himself face to face with him. His first instinct was to pass on without a word, but Lawson did not give him the opportunity.

"Where on earth have you been all this time?" he cried.

"I?" said Philip.

"I wrote you and asked you to come to the studio for a beano and you never even answered."

"I didn't get your letter."

"No, I know. I went to the hospital to ask for you, and I saw my letter in the rack. Have you chucked the Medical?"

Philip hesitated for a moment. He was ashamed to tell the truth, but the shame he felt angered him, and he forced himself to speak. He could not help reddening.

"Yes, I lost the little money I had. I couldn't afford to go on with it."

"I say, I'm awfully sorry. What are you doing?"

"I'm a shop-walker."

The words choked Philip, but he was determined not to shirk the truth. He kept his eyes on Lawson and saw his embarrassment. Philip smiled savagely.

"If you went into Lynn and Sedley, and made your way into the 'made robes' department, you would see me in a frock coat, walking about with a *dégagé* air and directing ladies who want to buy petticoats or stockings. First to the right, madam, and second on the left."

Lawson, seeing that Philip was making a jest of it, laughed awkwardly. He did not know what to say. The picture that Philip called up horrified him, but he was afraid to show his sympathy.

"That's a bit of a change for you," he said.

His words seemed absurd to him, and immediately he wished he had not said them. Philip flushed darkly.

"A bit," he said. "By the way, I owe you five bob."

He put his hand in his pocket and pulled out some silver.

"Oh, it doesn't matter. I'd forgotten all about it."

"Go on, take it."

Lawson received the money silently. They stood in the middle of the pavement, and people jostled them as they passed. There was a sardonic twinkle in Philip's eyes, which made the painter intensely uncomfortable, and he could not tell that Philip's heart was heavy with despair. Lawson wanted dreadfully to do something, but he did not know what to do.

"I say, won't you come to the studio and have a talk?"

"No," said Philip.

"Why not?"

"There's nothing to talk about."

He saw the pain come into Lawson's eyes, he could not help it, he was sorry, but he had to think of himself; he could not bear the thought of discussing his situation, he could endure it only by determining resolutely not to think about it. He was afraid of his weakness if once he began to open his heart. Moreover, he took irresistible dislikes to the places where he had been miserable: he remembered the humiliation he had endured when he had waited in that studio, ravenous with hunger, for Lawson to offer him a meal, and the last occasion when he had taken the five shillings off him. He hated the sight of Lawson, because he recalled those days of utter abasement.

"Then look here, come and dine with me one night. Choose your own evening."

Philip was touched with the painter's kindness. All sorts of people were strangely kind to him, he thought.

"It's awfully good of you, old man, but I'd rather not." He held out his hand. "Good-bye."

Lawson, troubled by a behaviour which seemed inexplicable, took his hand, and Philip quickly limped away. His heart was heavy; and, as was usual with him, he began to reproach himself for what he had done: he did not know what madness of pride had made him refuse the offered friendship. But he heard someone running behind him and presently Lawson's voice calling him; he stopped and suddenly the feeling of hostility got the better of him; he presented to Lawson a cold, set face.

"What is it?"

"I suppose you heard about Hayward, didn't you?"

"I know he went to the Cape."

"He died, you know, soon after landing."

For a moment Philip did not answer. He could hardly believe his ears.

"How?" he asked.

"Oh, enteric. Hard luck, wasn't it? I thought you mightn't know. Gave me a bit of a turn when I heard it."

Lawson nodded quickly and walked away. Philip felt a shiver pass through his heart. He had never before lost a friend of his own age, for the death of Cronshaw, a man so much older than himself, had seemed to come in the normal course of things. The news gave him a peculiar shock. It reminded him of his own mortality, for like everyone else Philip, knowing perfectly that all men must die, had no intimate feeling that the same must apply to himself; and Hayward's death, though he had long ceased to have any warm feeling for him, affected him deeply. He remembered on a sudden all the good talks they had had, and it pained him to think that they would never talk with one another again; he remembered their first meeting and the pleasant months they had spent together in Heidelberg. Philip's heart sank as he thought of the lost years. He walked on mechanically, not noticing where he went, and realised suddenly, with a movement of irritation, that instead of turning down the Haymarket he had sauntered along Shaftesbury Avenue. It bored him to retrace his steps; and besides, with that news, he did not want to read, he wanted to sit alone and think. He made up his mind to go to the British Museum. Solitude was now his only luxury. Since he had been at Lynn's he had often gone there and sat in front of the groups from the Parthenon; and, not deliberately thinking, had allowed their divine masses to rest his troubled soul. But this afternoon they had nothing to say to him, and after a few minutes, impatiently, he wandered out of the room. There were too many people, provincials with foolish faces, foreigners poring over guide-books; their hideousness besmirched the everlasting masterpieces, their restlessness troubled the god's immortal repose. He went into another room and here there was hardly anyone. Philip sat down wearily. His nerves were on edge. He could not get the people out of his mind. Sometimes at Lynn's they affected him in the same way, and he looked at them file past him with horror; they were so ugly and there was such meanness in their faces, it was terrifying; their features were distorted with paltry desires, and you felt they were strange to any ideas of beauty. They had furtive eyes and weak chins. There was no wickedness in them, but only pettiness and vulgarity. Their humour was a low facetiousness. Sometimes he found himself looking at them to see what animal they resembled (he tried not to, for it quickly became an obsession), and he saw in them all the sheep or the horse or the fox or the goat. Human beings filled him with disgust.

But presently the influence of the place descended upon him. He felt quieter. He began to look absently at the tombstones with which the room was lined. They were the work of Athenian stone masons of the fourth and fifth centuries before

Christ, and they were very simple, work of no great talent but with the exquisite spirit of Athens upon them; time had mellowed the marble to the colour of honey, so that unconsciously one thought of the bees of Hymettus, and softened their outlines. Some represented a nude figure, seated on a bench, some the departure of the dead from those who loved him, and some the dead clasping hands with one who remained behind. On all was the tragic word farewell; that and nothing more. Their simplicity was infinitely touching. Friend parted from friend, the son from his mother, and the restraint made the survivor's grief more poignant. It was so long, long ago, and century upon century had passed over that unhappiness; for two thousand years those who wept had been dust as those they wept for. Yet the woe was alive still, and it filled Philip's heart so that he felt compassion spring up in it, and he said:

"Poor things, poor things."

And it came to him that the gaping sight-seers and the fat strangers with their guide-books, and all those mean, common people who thronged the shop, with their trivial desires and vulgar cares, were mortal and must die. They too loved and must part from those they loved, the son from his mother, the wife from her husband; and perhaps it was more tragic because their lives were ugly and sordid, and they knew nothing that gave beauty to the world. There was one stone which was very beautiful, a bas relief of two young men holding each other's hand; and the reticence of line, the simplicity, made one like to think that the sculptor here had been touched with a genuine emotion. It was an exquisite memorial to that than which the world offers but one thing more precious, to a friendship; and as Philip looked at it, he felt the tears come to his eyes. He thought of Hayward and his eager admiration for him when first they met, and how disillusion had come and then indifference, till nothing held them together but habit and old memories. It was one of the queer things of life that you saw a person every day for months and were so intimate with him that you could not imagine existence without him; then separation came, and everything went on in the same way, and the companion who had seemed essential proved unnecessary. Your life proceeded and you did not even miss him. Philip thought of those early days in Heidelberg when Hayward, capable of great things, had been full of enthusiasm for the future, and how, little by little, achieving nothing, he had resigned himself to failure. Now he was dead. His death had been as futile as his life. He died ingloriously, of a stupid disease, failing once more, even at the end, to accomplish anything. It was just the same now as if he had never lived.

Philip asked himself desperately what was the use of living at all. It all seemed inane. It was the same with Cronshaw: it was quite unimportant that he had lived;

he was dead and forgotten, his book of poems sold in remainder by second-hand booksellers; his life seemed to have served nothing except to give a pushing journalist occasion to write an article in a review. And Philip cried out in his soul:

"What is the use of it?"

The effort was so incommensurate with the result. The bright hopes of youth had to be paid for at such a bitter price of disillusionment. Pain and disease and unhappiness weighed down the scale so heavily. What did it all mean? He thought of his own life, the high hopes with which he had entered upon it, the limitations which his body forced upon him, his friendlessness, and the lack of affection which had surrounded his youth. He did not know that he had ever done anything but what seemed best to do, and what a cropper he had come! Other men, with no more advantages than he, succeeded, and others again, with many more, failed. It seemed pure chance. The rain fell alike upon the just and upon the unjust, and for nothing was there a why and a wherefore.

Thinking of Cronshaw, Philip remembered the Persian rug which he had given him, telling him that it offered an answer to his question upon the meaning of life; and suddenly the answer occurred to him: he chuckled: now that he had it, it was like one of the puzzles which you worry over till you are shown the solution and then cannot imagine how it could ever have escaped you. The answer was obvious. Life had no meaning. On the earth, satellite of a star speeding through space, living things had arisen under the influence of conditions which were part of the planet's history; and as there had been a beginning of life upon it so, under the influence of other conditions, there would be an end: man, no more significant than other forms of life, had come not as the climax of creation but as a physical reaction to the environment. Philip remembered the story of the Eastern King who, desiring to know the history of man, was brought by a sage five hundred volumes; busy with affairs of state, he bade him go and condense it; in twenty years the sage returned and his history now was in no more than fifty volumes, but the King, too old then to read so many ponderous tomes, bade him go and shorten it once more; twenty years passed again and the sage, old and grey, brought a single book in which was the knowledge the King had sought; but the King lay on his deathbed, and he had no time to read even that; and then the sage gave him the history of man in a single line; it was this: he was born, he suffered, and he died. There was no meaning in life, and man by living served no end. It was immaterial whether he was born or not born, whether he lived or ceased to live. Life was insignificant and death without consequence. Philip exulted, as he had exulted in his boyhood when the weight of a belief in God was lifted from his shoulders: it seemed to him that the last burden of responsibility was taken from him; and for the first time he was utterly free. His insignificance was turned to power, and he felt himself suddenly equal with the cruel fate which had seemed to persecute him; for, if life was meaningless, the world was robbed of its cruelty. What he did or left undone did not matter. Failure was unimportant and success amounted to nothing. He was the most inconsiderate creature in that swarming mass of mankind which for a brief space occupied the surface of the earth; and he was almighty because he had wrenched from chaos the secret of its nothingness. Thoughts came tumbling over one another in Philip's eager fancy, and he took long breaths of joyous satisfaction. He felt inclined to leap and sing. He had not been so happy for months.

"Oh, life," he cried in his heart, "Oh life, where is thy sting?"

For the same uprush of fancy which had shown him with all the force of mathematical demonstration that life had no meaning, brought with it another idea; and that was why Cronshaw, he imagined, had given him the Persian rug. As the weaver elaborated his pattern for no end but the pleasure of his aesthetic sense, so might a man live his life, or if one was forced to believe that his actions were outside his choosing, so might a man look at his life, that it made a pattern. There was as little need to do this as there was use. It was merely something he did for his own pleasure. Out of the manifold events of his life, his deeds, his feelings, his thoughts, he might make a design, regular, elaborate, complicated, or beautiful; and though it might be no more than an illusion that he had the power of selection, though it might be no more than a fantastic legerdemain in which appearances were interwoven with moonbeams, that did not matter: it seemed, and so to him it was. In the vast warp of life (a river arising from no spring and flowing endlessly to no sea), with the background to his fancies that there was no meaning and that nothing was important, a man might get a personal satisfaction in selecting the various strands that worked out the pattern. There was one pattern, the most obvious, perfect, and beautiful, in which a man was born, grew to manhood, married, produced children, toiled for his bread, and died; but there were others, intricate and wonderful, in which happiness did not enter and in which success was not attempted; and in them might be discovered a more troubling grace. Some lives, and Hayward's was among them, the blind indifference of chance cut off while the design was still imperfect; and then the solace was comfortable that it did not matter; other lives, such as Cronshaw's, offered a pattern which was difficult to follow: the point of view had to be shifted and old standards had to be altered before one could understand that such a life was its own justification. Philip thought that in throwing over the desire for happiness he was casting aside the last of his illusions. His life had seemed horrible when it was measured by its happiness, but now he seemed to gather strength as he realised that it might be measured by something else. Happiness mattered as little as pain. They came in, both of them, as all the other details of his life came in, to the elaboration of the design. He seemed for an instant to stand above the accidents of his existence, and he felt that they could not affect him again as they had done before. Whatever happened to him now would be one more motive to add to the complexity of the pattern, and when the end approached he would rejoice in its completion. It would be a work of art, and it would be none the less beautiful because he alone knew of its existence, and with his death it would at once cease to be.

Philip was happy.

Chapter CVII

Mr. Sampson, the buyer, took a fancy to Philip. Mr. Sampson was very dashing, and the girls in his department said they would not be surprised if he married one of the rich customers. He lived out of town and often impressed the assistants by putting on his evening clothes in the office. Sometimes he would be seen by those on sweeping duty coming in next morning still dressed, and they would wink gravely to one another while he went into his office and changed into a frock coat. On these occasions, having slipped out for a hurried breakfast, he also would wink at Philip as he walked up the stairs on his way back and rub his hands.

"What a night! What a night!" he said. "My word!"

He told Philip that he was the only gentleman there, and he and Philip were the only fellows who knew what life was. Having said this, he changed his manner suddenly, called Philip Mr. Carey instead of old boy, assumed the importance due to his position as buyer, and put Philip back into his place of shop-walker.

Lynn and Sedley received fashion papers from Paris once a week and adapted the costumes illustrated in them to the needs of their customers. Their *clientèle* was peculiar. The most substantial part consisted of women from the smaller manufacturing towns, who were too elegant to have their frocks made locally and not sufficiently acquainted with London to discover good dressmakers within their means. Beside these, incongruously, was a large number of music-hall artistes. This was a connection that Mr. Sampson had worked up for himself and took great pride in. They had begun by getting their stage-costumes at Lynn's, and he had induced many of them to get their other clothes there as well.

"As good as Paquin and half the price," he said.

He had a persuasive, hail-fellow well-met air with him which appealed to customers of this sort, and they said to one another:

"What's the good of throwing money away when you can get a coat and skirt at Lynn's that nobody knows don't come from Paris?"

Mr. Sampson was very proud of his friendship with the popular favourites whose frocks he made, and when he went out to dinner at two o'clock on Sunday with Miss Victoria Virgo—"she was wearing that powder blue we made her and I lay she didn't let on it come from us, I 'ad to tell her meself that if I 'adn't designed it with my own 'ands I'd have said it must come from Paquin"—at her beautiful house in Tulse Hill, he regaled the department next day with abundant details. Philip had never paid much attention to women's clothes, but in course of time he began, a little amused at himself, to take a technical interest in them. He had an eye for colour which was more highly trained than that of anyone in the department, and he had kept from his student days in Paris some knowledge of line. Mr. Sampson, an ignorant man conscious of his incompetence, but with a shrewdness that enabled him to combine other people's suggestions, constantly asked the opinion of the assistants in his department in making up new designs; and he had the quickness to see that Philip's criticisms were valuable. But he was very jealous, and would never allow that he took anyone's advice. When he had altered some drawing in accordance with Philip's suggestion, he always finished up by saying:

"Well, it comes round to my own idea in the end."

One day, when Philip had been at the shop for five months, Miss Alice Antonia, the well-known serio-comic, came in and asked to see Mr. Sampson. She was a large woman, with flaxen hair, and a boldly painted face, a metallic voice, and the breezy manner of a comédienne accustomed to be on friendly terms with the gallery boys of provincial music-halls. She had a new song and wished Mr. Sampson to design a costume for her.

"I want something striking," she said. "I don't want any old thing, you know. I want something different from what anybody else has."

Mr. Sampson, bland and familiar, said he was quite certain they could get her the very thing she required. He showed her sketches.

"I know there's nothing here that would do, but I just want to show you the kind of thing I would suggest."

"Oh no, that's not the sort of thing at all," she said, as she glanced at them impatiently. "What I want is something that'll just hit 'em in the jaw and make their front teeth rattle."

"Yes, I quite understand, Miss Antonia," said the buyer, with a bland smile, but his eyes grew blank and stupid.

"I expect I shall 'ave to pop over to Paris for it in the end."

"Oh, I think we can give you satisfaction, Miss Antonia. What you can get in Paris you can get here."

When she had swept out of the department Mr. Sampson, a little worried, discussed the matter with Mrs. Hodges.

"She's a caution and no mistake," said Mrs. Hodges.

"Alice, where art thou?" remarked the buyer, irritably, and thought he had scored a point against her.

His ideas of music-hall costumes had never gone beyond short skirts, a swirl of lace, and glittering sequins; but Miss Antonia had expressed herself on that subject in no uncertain terms.

"Oh, my aunt!" she said.

And the invocation was uttered in such a tone as to indicate a rooted antipathy to anything so commonplace, even if she had not added that sequins gave her the sick. Mr. Sampson "got out" one or two ideas, but Mrs. Hodges told him frankly she did not think they would do. It was she who gave Philip the suggestion:

"Can you draw, Phil? Why don't you try your 'and and see what you can do?"

Philip bought a cheap box of water colours, and in the evening while Bell, the noisy lad of sixteen, whistling three notes, busied himself with his stamps, he made one or two sketches. He remembered some of the costumes he had seen in Paris, and he adapted one of them, getting his effect from a combination of violent, unusual colours. The result amused him and next morning he showed it to Mrs. Hodges. She was somewhat astonished, but took it at once to the buyer.

"It's unusual," he said, "there's no denying that."

It puzzled him, and at the same time his trained eye saw that it would make up admirably. To save his face he began making suggestions for altering it, but Mrs. Hodges, with more sense, advised him to show it to Miss Antonia as it was.

"It's neck or nothing with her, and she may take a fancy to it."

"It's a good deal more nothing than neck," said Mr. Sampson, looking at the *décolletage*. "He can draw, can't he? Fancy 'im keeping it dark all this time."

When Miss Antonia was announced, the buyer placed the design on the table in such a position that it must catch her eye the moment she was shown into his office. She pounced on it at once.

"What's that?" she said. "Why can't I 'ave that?"

"That's just an idea we got out for you," said Mr. Sampson casually. "D'you like it?"

"Do I like it!" she said. "Give me 'alf a pint with a little drop of gin in it."

"Ah, you see, you don't have to go to Paris. You've only got to say what you want and there you are."

The work was put in hand at once, and Philip felt quite a thrill of satisfaction when he saw the costume completed. The buyer and Mrs. Hodges took all the credit of it; but he did not care, and when he went with them to the Tivoli to see Miss Antonia wear it for the first time he was filled with elation. In answer to her questions he at last told Mrs. Hodges how he had learned to draw—fearing that the people he lived with would think he wanted to put on airs, he had always taken the greatest care to say nothing about his past occupations—and she repeated the information to Mr. Sampson. The buyer said nothing to him on the subject, but began to treat him a little more deferentially and presently gave him designs to do for two of the country customers. They met with satisfaction. Then he began to speak to his clients of a "clever young feller, Paris art-student, you know" who worked for him; and soon Philip, ensconced behind a screen, in his shirt-sleeves, was drawing from morning till night. Sometimes he was so busy that he had to dine at three with the "stragglers." He liked it, because there were few of them and they were all too tired to talk; the food also was better, for it consisted of what was left over from the buyers' table. Philip's rise from shop-walker to designer of costumes had a great effect on the department. He realised that he was an object of envy. Harris, the assistant with the queer-shaped head, who was the first person he had known at the shop and had attached himself to Philip, could not conceal his bitterness.

"Some people 'ave all the luck," he said. "You'll be a buyer yourself one of these days, and we shall all be calling you sir."

He told Philip that he should demand higher wages, for notwithstanding the difficult work he was now engaged in, he received no more than the six shillings a week with which he started. But it was a ticklish matter to ask for a rise. The manager had a sardonic way of dealing with such applicants.

"Think you're worth more, do you? How much d'you think you're worth, eh?"

The assistant, with his heart in his mouth, would suggest that he thought he ought to have another two shillings a week.

"Oh, very well, if you think you're worth it. You can 'ave it." Then he paused and sometimes, with a steely eye, added: "And you can 'ave your notice too."

It was no use then to withdraw your request, you had to go. The manager's idea was that assistants who were dissatisfied did not work properly, and if they were not worth a rise it was better to sack them at once. The result was that they never asked for one unless they were prepared to leave. Philip hesitated. He was a little suspicious of the men in his room who told him that the buyer could not do without him. They were decent fellows, but their sense of humour was primitive, and it would have seemed funny to them if they had persuaded Philip to ask for more wages and he were sacked. He could not forget the mortification he had suffered in looking for work, he did not wish to expose himself to that again, and he knew there was small chance of his getting elsewhere a post as designer: there were hundreds of people about who could draw as well as he. But he wanted money very badly; his clothes were worn out, and the heavy carpets rotted his socks and boots; he had almost persuaded himself to take the venturesome step when one morning, passing up from breakfast in the basement through the passage that led to the manager's office, he saw a queue of men waiting in answer to an advertisement. There were about a hundred of them, and whichever was engaged would be offered his keep and the same six shillings a week that Philip had. He saw some of them cast envious glances at him because he had employment. It made him shudder. He dared not risk it.

Chapter CVIII

THE WINTER PASSED. NOW AND THEN PHILIP WENT TO THE HOSPITAL, slinking in when it was late and there was little chance of meeting anyone he knew, to see whether there were letters for him. At Easter he received one from his uncle. He was surprised to hear from him, for the Vicar of Blackstable had never written him more than half a dozen letters in his whole life, and they were on business matters.

DEAR PHILIP—If you are thinking of taking a holiday soon and care to come down here I shall be pleased to see you. I was very ill with my bronchitis in the winter and Doctor Wigram never expected me to pull through. I have a wonderful constitution and I made, thank God, a marvellous recovery.

Yours affectionately,
WILLIAM CAREY

The letter made Philip angry. How did his uncle think he was living? He did not even trouble to inquire. He might have starved for all the old man cared. But as he walked home something struck him; he stopped under a lamp-post and read the letter again; the handwriting had no longer the business-like firmness which had characterised it; it was larger and wavering: perhaps the illness had shaken him more than he was willing to confess, and he sought in that formal note to express a yearning to see the only relation he had in the world. Philip wrote back that he could come down to Blackstable for a fortnight in July. The invitation was convenient, for he had not known what to do with his brief holiday. The Athelnys went hopping in September, but he could not then be spared, since during that month the autumn models were prepared. The rule of Lynn's was that everyone must take a fortnight whether he wanted it or not; and during that time, if he had nowhere to go, the assistant might sleep in his room, but he was not allowed food. A number had no friends within reasonable distance of London, and to these the holiday was an awkward interval when they had to provide food out of their small wages and, with the whole day on their hands, had nothing to spend. Philip had not been out of London since his visit to Brighton with Mildred, now two years before, and he longed for fresh air and the silence of the sea. He thought of it with such a passionate desire, all through May and June, that, when at length the time came for him to go, he was listless.

On his last evening, when he talked with the buyer of one or two jobs he had to leave over, Mr. Sampson suddenly said to him:

"What wages have you been getting?"

"Six shillings."

"I don't think it's enough. I'll see that you're put up to twelve when you come back."

"Thank you very much," smiled Philip. "I'm beginning to want some new clothes badly."

"If you stick to your work and don't go larking about with the girls like what some of them do, I'll look after you, Carey. Mind you, you've got a lot to learn, but you're promising, I'll say that for you, you're promising, and I'll see that you get a pound a week as soon as you deserve it."

Philip wondered how long he would have to wait for that. Two years?

He was startled at the change in his uncle. When last he had seen him he was a stout man, who held himself upright, clean-shaven, with a round, sensual face; but he had fallen in strangely, his skin was yellow; there were great bags under the eyes, and he was bent and old. He had grown a beard during his last illness, and he walked very slowly.

"I'm not at my best today," he said when Philip, having just arrived, was sitting with him in the dining-room. "The heat upsets me."

Philip, asking after the affairs of the parish, looked at him and wondered how much longer he could last. A hot summer would finish him; Philip noticed how thin his hands were; they trembled. It meant so much to Philip. If he died that summer he could go back to the hospital at the beginning of the winter session; his heart leaped at the thought of returning no more to Lynn's. At dinner the Vicar sat humped up on his chair, and the housekeeper who had been with him since his wife's death said:

"Shall Mr. Philip carve, sir?"

The old man, who had been about to do so from disinclination to confess his weakness, seemed glad at the first suggestion to relinquish the attempt.

"You've got a very good appetite," said Philip.

"Oh yes, I always eat well. But I'm thinner than when you were here last. I'm glad to be thinner, I didn't like being so fat. Dr. Wigram thinks I'm all the better for being thinner than I was."

When dinner was over the housekeeper brought him some medicine.

"Show the prescription to Master Philip," he said. "He's a doctor too. I'd like him to see that he thinks it's all right. I told Dr. Wigram that now you're studying to be a doctor he ought to make a reduction in his charges. It's dreadful the bills I've had to pay. He came every day for two months, and he charges five shillings a visit. It's a lot of money, isn't it? He comes twice a week still. I'm going to tell him he needn't come anymore. I'll send for him if I want him."

He looked at Philip eagerly while he read the prescriptions. They were narcotics. There were two of them, and one was a medicine which the Vicar explained he was to use only if his neuritis grew unendurable.

"I'm very careful," he said. "I don't want to get into the opium habit."

He did not mention his nephew's affairs. Philip fancied that it was by way of precaution, in case he asked for money, that his uncle kept dwelling on the financial calls upon him. He had spent so much on the doctor and so much more on the chemist, while he was ill they had had to have a fire every day in his bed-room, and now on Sunday he needed a carriage to go to church in the evening as well as in the morning. Philip felt angrily inclined to say he need not be afraid, he was not going to borrow from him, but he held his tongue. It seemed to him that everything had left the old man now but two things, pleasure in his food and a grasping desire for money. It was a hideous old age.

In the afternoon Dr. Wigram came, and after the visit Philip walked with him to the garden gate.

"How d'you think he is?" said Philip.

Dr. Wigram was more anxious not to do wrong than to do right, and he never hazarded a definite opinion if he could help it. He had practised at Blackstable for five-and-thirty years. He had the reputation of being very safe, and many of his patients thought it much better that a doctor should be safe than clever. There was a new man at Blackstable—he had been settled there for ten years, but they still looked upon him as an interloper—and he was said to be very clever; but he had not much practice among the better people, because no one really knew anything about him.

"Oh, he's as well as can be expected," said Dr. Wigram in answer to Philip's inquiry.

"Has he got anything seriously the matter with him?"

"Well, Philip, your uncle is no longer a young man," said the doctor with a cautious little smile, which suggested that after all the Vicar of Blackstable was not an old man either.

"He seems to think his heart's in a bad way."

"I'm not satisfied with his heart," hazarded the doctor, "I think he should be careful, very careful."

On the tip of Philip's tongue was the question: how much longer can he live? He was afraid it would shock. In these matters a periphrase was demanded by the decorum of life, but, as he asked another question instead, it flashed through him that the doctor must be accustomed to the impatience of a sick man's relatives. He must see through their sympathetic expressions. Philip, with a faint smile at his own hypocrisy, cast down his eyes.

"I suppose he's in no immediate danger?"

This was the kind of question the doctor hated. If you said a patient couldn't live another month the family prepared itself for a bereavement, and if then the patient lived on they visited the medical attendant with the resentment they felt at having tormented themselves before it was necessary. On the other hand, if you said the patient might live a year and he died in a week the family said you did not know your business. They thought of all the affection they would have lavished on the defunct if they had known the end was so near. Dr. Wigram made the gesture of washing his hands.

"I don't think there's any grave risk so long as he—remains as he is," he ventured at last. "But on the other hand, we mustn't forget that he's no longer a young man, and well, the machine is wearing out. If he gets over the hot weather I don't see why he shouldn't get on very comfortably till the winter, and then if the winter does not bother him too much, well, I don't see why anything should happen."

Philip went back to the dining-room where his uncle was sitting. With his skull-cap and a crochet shawl over his shoulders he looked grotesque. His eyes had been fixed on the door, and they rested on Philip's face as he entered. Philip saw that his uncle had been waiting anxiously for his return.

"Well, what did he say about me?"

Philip understood suddenly that the old man was frightened of dying. It made Philip a little ashamed, so that he looked away involuntarily. He was always embarrassed by the weakness of human nature.

"He says he thinks you're much better," said Philip.

A gleam of delight came into his uncle's eyes.

"I've got a wonderful constitution," he said. "What else did he say?" he added suspiciously.

Philip smiled.

"He said that if you take care of yourself there's no reason why you shouldn't live to be a hundred."

"I don't know that I can expect to do that, but I don't see why I shouldn't see eighty. My mother lived till she was eighty-four."

There was a little table by the side of Mr. Carey's chair, and on it were a Bible and the large volume of the Common Prayer from which for so many years he had been accustomed to read to his household. He stretched out now his shaking hand and took his Bible.

"Those old patriarchs lived to a jolly good old age, didn't they?" he said, with a queer little laugh in which Philip read a sort of timid appeal.

The old man clung to life. Yet he believed implicitly all that his religion taught him. He had no doubt in the immortality of the soul, and he felt that he had conducted himself well enough, according to his capacities, to make it very likely that he would go to heaven. In his long career to how many dying persons must he have administered the consolations of religion! Perhaps he was like the doctor who could get no benefit from his own prescriptions. Philip was puzzled and shocked by that eager cleaving to the earth. He wondered what nameless horror was at the back of the old man's mind. He would have liked to probe into his soul so that he might see in its nakedness the dreadful dismay of the unknown which he suspected.

The fortnight passed quickly and Philip returned to London. He passed a sweltering August behind his screen in the costumes department, drawing in his shirt-sleeves. The assistants in relays went for their holidays. In the evening Philip generally went into Hyde Park and listened to the band. Growing more accustomed to his work it tired him less, and his mind, recovering from its long stagnation, sought for fresh activity. His whole desire now was set on his uncle's death. He kept on dreaming the same dream: a telegram was handed to him one morning, early, which announced the Vicar's sudden demise, and freedom was in his grasp. When he awoke and found it was nothing but a dream he was filled with sombre rage. He occupied himself, now that the event seemed likely to happen at any time, with elaborate plans for the future. In these he passed rapidly over the year which he must spend before it was possible for him to be qualified and dwelled on the journey to Spain on which his heart was set. He read books about that country, which he borrowed from the free library, and already he knew from photographs exactly what each city looked like. He saw himself lingering in Cordova on the bridge that spanned the Guadalquivir; he wandered through tortuous streets in Toledo and sat in churches where he wrung from El Greco the secret which he felt the mysterious painter held for him. Athelny entered into his humour, and on Sunday afternoons they made out elaborate itineraries so that Philip should miss nothing that was noteworthy. To cheat his impatience Philip began to teach himself Spanish, and in the deserted sitting-room in Harrington Street he spent an hour every evening doing Spanish exercises and puzzling out with an English translation by his side the magnificent phrases of Don Quixote. Athelny gave him a lesson once a week, and Philip learned a few sentences to help him on his journey. Mrs. Athelny laughed at them.

"You two and your Spanish!" she said. "Why don't you do something useful?"

But Sally, who was growing up and was to put up her hair at Christmas, stood by sometimes and listened in her grave way while her father and Philip exchanged remarks in a language she did not understand. She thought her father the most wonderful man who had ever existed, and she expressed her opinion of Philip only through her father's commendations.

"Father thinks a rare lot of your Uncle Philip," she remarked to her brothers and sisters.

Thorpe, the eldest boy, was old enough to go on the Arethusa, and Athelny regaled his family with magnificent descriptions of the appearance the lad would make when he came back in uniform for his holidays. As soon as Sally was seventeen she was to be apprenticed to a dressmaker. Athelny in his rhetorical way talked of the birds, strong enough to fly now, who were leaving the parental nest, and with tears in his eyes told them that the nest would be there still if ever they wished to return to it. A shakedown and a dinner would always be theirs, and the heart of a father would never be closed to the troubles of his children.

"You do talk, Athelny," said his wife. "I don't know what trouble they're likely to get into so long as they're steady. So long as you're honest and not afraid of work you'll never be out of a job, that's what I think, and I can tell you I shan't be sorry when I see the last of them earning their own living."

Child-bearing, hard work, and constant anxiety were beginning to tell on Mrs. Athelny; and sometimes her back ached in the evening so that she had to sit down and rest herself. Her ideal of happiness was to have a girl to do the rough work so that she need not herself get up before seven. Athelny waved his beautiful white hand.

"Ah, my Betty, we've deserved well of the state, you and I. We've reared nine healthy children, and the boys shall serve their king; the girls shall cook and sew and in their turn breed healthy children." He turned to Sally, and to comfort her for the anti-climax of the contrast added grandiloquently: "They also serve who only stand and wait."

Athelny had lately added socialism to the other contradictory theories he vehemently believed in, and he stated now:

"In a socialist state we should be richly pensioned, you and I, Betty."

"Oh, don't talk to me about your socialists, I've got no patience with them," she cried. "It only means that another lot of lazy loafers will make a good thing out of the working classes. My motto is, leave me alone; I don't want anyone interfering with me; I'll make the best of a bad job, and the devil take the hindmost."

"D'you call life a bad job?" said Athelny. "Never! We've had our ups and downs, we've had our struggles, we've always been poor, but it's been worth it, ay, worth it a hundred times I say when I look round at my children."

"You do talk, Athelny," she said, looking at him, not with anger but with scornful calm. "You've had the pleasant part of the children, I've had the bearing of them, and the bearing with them. I don't say that I'm not fond of them, now they're there, but if I had my time over again I'd remain single. Why, if I'd remained single I might have a little shop by now, and four or five hundred pounds in the bank, and a girl to do the rough work. Oh, I wouldn't go over my life again, not for something."

Philip thought of the countless millions to whom life is no more than unending labour, neither beautiful nor ugly, but just to be accepted in the same spirit as one accepts the changes of the seasons. Fury seized him because it all seemed useless. He could not reconcile himself to the belief that life had no meaning and yet everything he saw, all his thoughts, added to the force of his conviction. But though fury seized him it was a joyful fury. Life was not so horrible if it was meaningless, and he faced it with a strange sense of power.

Chapter CIX

THE AUTUMN PASSED INTO WINTER. PHILIP HAD LEFT HIS ADDRESS WITH Mrs. Foster, his uncle's housekeeper, so that she might communicate with him, but still went once a week to the hospital on the chance of there being a letter. One evening he saw his name on an envelope in a handwriting he had hoped never to see again. It gave him a queer feeling. For a little while he could not bring himself to take it. It brought back a host of hateful memories. But at length, impatient with himself, he ripped open the envelope.

> 7 *William Street,*
> *Fitzroy Square.*
>
> DEAR PHIL—Can I see you for a minute or two as soon as possible. I am in awful trouble and don't know what to do. It's not money.
>
> Yours truly,
> MILDRED

He tore the letter into little bits and going out into the street scattered them in the darkness.

"I'll see her damned," he muttered.

A feeling of disgust surged up in him at the thought of seeing her again. He did not care if she was in distress, it served her right whatever it was, he thought of her with hatred, and the love he had had for her aroused his loathing. His recollections filled him with nausea, and as he walked across the Thames he drew himself aside in an instinctive withdrawal from his thought of her. He went to bed, but he could not sleep; he wondered what was the matter with her, and he could not get out of his head the fear that she was ill and hungry; she would not have written to him unless she were desperate. He was angry with himself for his weakness, but he knew that he would have no peace unless he saw her. Next morning he wrote a letter-card and posted it on his way to the shop. He made it as stiff as he could and said merely that he was sorry she was in difficulties and would come to the address she had given at seven o'clock that evening.

It was that of a shabby lodging-house in a sordid street; and when, sick at the thought of seeing her, he asked whether she was in, a wild hope seized him that she had left. It looked the sort of place people moved in and out of frequently. He had not thought of looking at the postmark on her letter and did not know how many days it had lain in the rack. The woman who answered the bell did not reply to his inquiry, but silently preceded him along the passage and knocked on a door at the back.

"Mrs. Miller, a gentleman to see you," she called.

The door was slightly opened, and Mildred looked out suspiciously.

"Oh, it's you," she said. "Come in."

He walked in and she closed the door. It was a very small bed-room, untidy as was every place she lived in; there was a pair of shoes on the floor, lying apart from one another and uncleaned; a hat was on the chest of drawers, with false curls beside it; and there was a blouse on the table. Philip looked for somewhere to put his hat. The hooks behind the door were laden with skirts, and he noticed that they were muddy at the hem.

"Sit down, won't you?" she said. Then she gave a little awkward laugh. "I suppose you were surprised to hear from me again."

"You're awfully hoarse," he answered. "Have you got a sore throat?"

"Yes, I have had for some time."

He did not say anything. He waited for her to explain why she wanted to see him. The look of the room told him clearly enough that she had gone back to the life from which he had taken her. He wondered what had happened to the baby; there was a photograph of it on the chimney-piece, but no sign in the room that a child was ever there. Mildred was holding her handkerchief. She made it into a little ball, and passed it from hand to hand. He saw that she was very nervous. She was staring at the fire, and he could look at her without meeting her eyes. She was much thinner than when she had left him; and the skin, yellow and dryish, was drawn more tightly over her cheek-bones. She had dyed her hair and it was now flaxen: it altered her a good deal, and made her look more vulgar.

"I was relieved to get your letter, I can tell you," she said at last. "I thought p'raps you weren't at the 'ospital anymore."

Philip did not speak.

"I suppose you're qualified by now, aren't you?"

"No."

"How's that?"

"I'm no longer at the hospital. I had to give it up eighteen months ago."

"You are changeable. You don't seem as if you could stick to anything."

Philip was silent for another moment, and when he went on it was with coldness.

"I lost the little money I had in an unlucky speculation and I couldn't afford to go on with the medical. I had to earn my living as best I could."

"What are you doing then?"

"I'm in a shop."

"Oh!"

She gave him a quick glance and turned her eyes away at once. He thought that she reddened. She dabbed her palms nervously with the handkerchief.

"You've not forgotten all your doctoring, have you?" She jerked the words out quite oddly.

"Not entirely."

"Because that's why I wanted to see you." Her voice sank to a hoarse whisper. "I don't know what's the matter with me."

"Why don't you go to a hospital?"

"I don't like to do that, and have all the stoodents staring at me, and I'm afraid they'd want to keep me."

"What are you complaining of?" asked Philip coldly, with the stereotyped phrase used in the out-patients' room.

"Well, I've come out in a rash, and I can't get rid of it."

Philip felt a twinge of horror in his heart. Sweat broke out on his forehead.

"Let me look at your throat?"

He took her over to the window and made such examination as he could. Suddenly he caught sight of her eyes. There was deadly fear in them. It was horrible to see. She was terrified. She wanted him to reassure her; she looked at him pleadingly, not daring to ask for words of comfort but with all her nerves astrung to receive them: he had none to offer her.

"I'm afraid you're very ill indeed," he said.

"What d'you think it is?"

When he told her she grew deathly pale, and her lips even turned yellow; she began to cry, hopelessly, quietly at first and then with choking sobs.

"I'm awfully sorry," he said at last. "But I had to tell you."

"I may just as well kill myself and have done with it."

He took no notice of the threat.

"Have you got any money?" he asked.

"Six or seven pounds."

"You must give up this life, you know. Don't you think you could find some work to do? I'm afraid I can't help you much. I only get twelve bob a week."

"What is there I can do now?" she cried impatiently.

"Damn it all, you *must* try to get something."

He spoke to her very gravely, telling her of her own danger and the danger to which she exposed others, and she listened sullenly. He tried to console her. At last he brought her to a sulky acquiescence in which she promised to do all he advised. He wrote a prescription, which he said he would leave at the nearest chemist's, and he impressed upon her the necessity of taking her medicine with the utmost regularity. Getting up to go, he held out his hand.

"Don't be downhearted, you'll soon get over your throat."

But as he went her face became suddenly distorted, and she caught hold of his coat.

"Oh, don't leave me," she cried hoarsely. "I'm so afraid, don't leave me alone yet. Phil, please. There's no one else I can go to, you're the only friend I've ever had."

He felt the terror of her soul, and it was strangely like that terror he had seen in his uncle's eyes when he feared that he might die. Philip looked down. Twice that woman had come into his life and made him wretched; she had no claim upon him; and yet, he knew not why, deep in his heart was a strange aching; it was that which, when he received her letter, had left him no peace till he obeyed her summons.

"I suppose I shall never really quite get over it," he said to himself.

What perplexed him was that he felt a curious physical distaste, which made it uncomfortable for him to be near her.

"What do you want me to do?" he asked.

"Let's go out and dine together. I'll pay."

He hesitated. He felt that she was creeping back again into his life when he thought she was gone out of it forever. She watched him with sickening anxiety.

"Oh, I know I've treated you shocking, but don't leave me alone now. You've had your revenge. If you leave me by myself now I don't know what I shall do."

"All right, I don't mind," he said, "but we shall have to do it on the cheap, I haven't got money to throw away these days."

She sat down and put her shoes on, then changed her skirt and put on a hat; and they walked out together till they found a restaurant in the Tottenham Court Road. Philip had got out of the habit of eating at those hours, and Mildred's throat was so sore that she could not swallow. They had a little cold ham and Philip drank a glass of beer. They sat opposite one another, as they had so often sat before; he wondered if she remembered; they had nothing to say to one another and would have sat in silence if Philip had not forced himself to talk. In the bright light of the restaurant, with its vulgar looking-glasses that reflected in an endless series, she looked old and haggard. Philip was anxious to know about the child, but he had not the courage to ask. At last she said:

"You know baby died last summer."

"Oh!" he said.

"You might say you're sorry."

"I'm not," he answered, "I'm very glad."

She glanced at him and, understanding what he meant, looked away.

"You were rare stuck on it at one time, weren't you? I always thought it funny like how you could see so much in another man's child."

When they had finished eating they called at the chemist's for the medicine Philip had ordered, and going back to the shabby room he made her take a dose. Then they sat together till it was time for Philip to go back to Harrington Street. He was hideously bored.

Philip went to see her every day. She took the medicine he had prescribed and followed his directions, and soon the results were so apparent that she gained the greatest confidence in Philip's skill. As she grew better she grew less despondent. She talked more freely.

"As soon as I can get a job I shall be all right," she said. "I've had my lesson now and I mean to profit by it. No more racketing about for yours truly."

Each time he saw her, Philip asked whether she had found work. She told him not to worry, she would find something to do as soon as she wanted it; she had several strings to her bow; it was all the better not to do anything for a week or two. He could not deny this, but at the end of that time he became more insistent. She laughed at him, she was much more cheerful now, and said he was a fussy old thing. She told him long stories of the manageresses she interviewed, for her idea was to get work at some eating-house; what they said and what she answered. Nothing definite was fixed, but she was sure to settle something at the beginning of the following week: there was no use hurrying, and it would be a mistake to take something unsuitable.

"It's absurd to talk like that," he said impatiently. "You must take anything you can get. I can't help you, and your money won't last forever."

"Oh, well, I've not come to the end of it yet and chance it."

He looked at her sharply. It was three weeks since his first visit, and she had then less than seven pounds. Suspicion seized him. He remembered some of the things she had said. He put two and two together. He wondered whether she had made any attempt to find work. Perhaps she had been lying to him all the time. It was very strange that her money should have lasted so long.

"What is your rent here?"

"Oh, the landlady's very nice, different from what some of them are; she's quite willing to wait till it's convenient for me to pay."

He was silent. What he suspected was so horrible that he hesitated. It was no use to ask her, she would deny everything; if he wanted to know he must find out for himself. He was in the habit of leaving her every evening at eight, and when the clock struck he got up; but instead of going back to Harrington Street he stationed himself at the corner of Fitzroy Square so that he could see anyone who came along William Street. It seemed to him that he waited an interminable time, and he was on the point of going away, thinking his surmise had been mistaken, when the door of No. 7 opened and Mildred came out. He fell back into the darkness and watched her walk towards him. She had on the hat with a quantity of feathers on it which he had seen in her room, and she wore a dress he recognised, too showy for the street and unsuitable to the time of year. He followed her slowly till she came into the Tottenham Court Road, where she slackened her pace; at the corner of Oxford Street she stopped, looked round, and crossed over to a music-hall. He went up to her and touched her on the arm. He saw that she had rouged her cheeks and painted her lips.

"Where are you going, Mildred?"

She started at the sound of his voice and reddened as she always did when she was caught in a lie; then the flash of anger which he knew so well came into her eyes as she instinctively sought to defend herself by abuse. But she did not say the words which were on the tip of her tongue.

"Oh, I was only going to see the show. It gives me the hump sitting every night by myself."

He did not pretend to believe her.

"You mustn't. Good heavens, I've told you fifty times how dangerous it is. You must stop this sort of thing at once."

"Oh, hold your jaw," she cried roughly. "How d'you suppose I'm going to live?"

He took hold of her arm and without thinking what he was doing tried to drag her away.

"For God's sake come along. Let me take you home. You don't know what you're doing. It's criminal."

"What do I care? Let them take their chance. Men haven't been so good to me that I need bother my head about them."

She pushed him away and walking up to the box-office put down her money. Philip had threepence in his pocket. He could not follow. He turned away and walked slowly down Oxford Street.

"I can't do anything more," he said to himself.

That was the end. He did not see her again.

Chapter CX

CHRISTMAS THAT YEAR FALLING ON THURSDAY, THE SHOP WAS TO CLOSE FOR four days: Philip wrote to his uncle asking whether it would be convenient for him to spend the holidays at the vicarage. He received an answer from Mrs. Foster, saying that Mr. Carey was not well enough to write himself, but wished to see his nephew and would be glad if he came down. She met Philip at the door, and when she shook hands with him, said:

"You'll find him changed since you was here last, sir; but you'll pretend you don't notice anything, won't you, sir? He's that nervous about himself."

Philip nodded, and she led him into the dining-room.

"Here's Mr. Philip, sir."

The Vicar of Blackstable was a dying man. There was no mistaking that when you looked at the hollow cheeks and the shrunken body. He sat huddled in the arm-chair, with his head strangely thrown back, and a shawl over his shoulders. He could not walk now without the help of sticks, and his hands trembled so that he could only feed himself with difficulty.

"He can't last long now," thought Philip, as he looked at him.

"How d'you think I'm looking?" asked the Vicar. "D'you think I've changed since you were here last?"

"I think you look stronger than you did last summer."

"It was the heat. That always upsets me."

Mr. Carey's history of the last few months consisted in the number of weeks he had spent in his bed-room and the number of weeks he had spent downstairs. He had a hand-bell by his side and while he talked he rang it for Mrs. Foster, who sat in the next room ready to attend to his wants, to ask on what day of the month he had first left his room.

"On the seventh of November, sir."

Mr. Carey looked at Philip to see how he took the information.

"But I eat well still, don't I, Mrs. Foster?"

"Yes, sir, you've got a wonderful appetite."

"I don't seem to put on flesh though."

Nothing interested him now but his health. He was set upon one thing indomitably and that was living, just living, notwithstanding the monotony of his life and the constant pain which allowed him to sleep only when he was under the influence of morphia.

"It's terrible, the amount of money I have to spend on doctor's bills." He tinkled his bell again. "Mrs. Foster, show Master Philip the chemist's bill."

Patiently she took it off the chimney-piece and handed it to Philip.

"That's only one month. I was wondering if as you're doctoring yourself you couldn't get me the drugs cheaper. I thought of getting them down from the stores, but then there's the postage."

Though apparently taking so little interest in him that he did not trouble to inquire what Phil was doing, he seemed glad to have him there. He asked how long he could stay, and when Philip told him he must leave on Tuesday morning, expressed a wish that the visit might have been longer. He told him minutely all his symptoms and repeated what the doctor had said of him. He broke off to ring his bell, and when Mrs. Foster came in, said:

"Oh, I wasn't sure if you were there. I only rang to see if you were."

When she had gone he explained to Philip that it made him uneasy if he was not certain that Mrs. Foster was within earshot; she knew exactly what to do with him if anything happened. Philip, seeing that she was tired and that her eyes were heavy from want of sleep, suggested that he was working her too hard.

"Oh, nonsense," said the Vicar, "she's as strong as a horse." And when next she came in to give him his medicine he said to her:

"Master Philip says you've got too much to do, Mrs. Foster. You like looking after me, don't you?"

"Oh, I don't mind, sir. I want to do everything I can."

Presently the medicine took effect and Mr. Carey fell asleep. Philip went into the kitchen and asked Mrs. Foster whether she could stand the work. He saw that for some months she had had little peace.

"Well, sir, what can I do?" she answered. "The poor old gentleman's so dependent on me, and, although he is troublesome sometimes, you can't help liking him, can you? I've been here so many years now, I don't know what I shall do when he comes to go."

Philip saw that she was really fond of the old man. She washed and dressed him, gave him his food, and was up half a dozen times in the night; for she slept in the next room to his and whenever he awoke he tinkled his little bell till she came in. He might die at any moment, but he might live for months. It was wonderful that she should look after a stranger with such patient tenderness, and it was tragic and pitiful that she should be alone in the world to care for him.

It seemed to Philip that the religion which his uncle had preached all his life was now of no more than formal importance to him: every Sunday the curate came and administered to him Holy Communion, and he often read his Bible; but it was clear that he looked upon death with horror. He believed that it was the gateway to life everlasting, but he did not want to enter upon that life. In constant pain, chained to his chair and having given up the hope of ever getting out into the open again, like a child in the hands of a woman to whom he paid wages, he clung to the world he knew.

In Philip's head was a question he could not ask, because he was aware that his uncle would never give any but a conventional answer: he wondered whether at the very end, now that the machine was painfully wearing itself out, the clergyman still believed in immortality; perhaps at the bottom of his soul, not allowed to shape itself into words in case it became urgent, was the conviction that there was no God and after this life nothing.

On the evening of Boxing Day Philip sat in the dining-room with his uncle. He had to start very early next morning in order to get to the shop by nine, and he was to say good-night to Mr. Carey then. The Vicar of Blackstable was dozing and Philip, lying on the sofa by the window, let his book fall on his knees and looked idly round the room. He asked himself how much the furniture would fetch. He had walked round the house and looked at the things he had known from his childhood; there were a few pieces of china which might go for a decent price and Philip wondered if it would be worthwhile to take them up to London; but the furniture was of the Victorian order, of mahogany, solid and ugly; it would go for nothing at an auction. There were three or four thousand books, but everyone knew how badly they sold, and it was not probable that they would fetch more than a hundred pounds. Philip did not know how much his uncle would leave, and he reckoned out for the hundredth time what was the least sum upon which he could finish the curriculum at the hospital, take his degree, and live during the time he wished to spend on hospital appointments. He looked at the old man, sleeping restlessly: there was no humanity left in that shrivelled face; it was the face of some queer animal. Philip thought how easy it would be to finish that useless life. He had thought it each evening when Mrs. Foster prepared for his uncle the medicine which was to give him an easy night. There were two bottles: one contained a drug which he took regularly, and the other an opiate if the pain grew unendurable. This was poured out for him and left by his bed-side. He generally took it at three or four in the morning. It would be a simple thing to double the dose; he would die in the night, and no one would suspect anything; for that was how Doctor Wigram expected him to die. The end would be painless. Philip clenched his hands as he thought of the money he wanted so badly. A few more months of that wretched life could matter nothing to the old man, but the few more months meant everything to him: he was getting to the end of his endurance, and when he thought of going back to work in the morning he shuddered with horror. His heart beat quickly at the thought which obsessed him, and though he made an effort to put it out of his mind he could not. It would be so easy, so desperately easy. He had no feeling for the old man, he had never liked him; he had been selfish all his life, selfish to his wife who adored him, indifferent to the boy who had been put in his charge; he was not a cruel man, but a stupid, hard man, eaten up with a small sensuality. It would be easy, desperately easy. Philip did not dare. He was afraid of remorse; it would be no good having the money if he regretted all his life what he had done. Though he had told himself so often that regret was futile, there were certain things that came back to him occasionally and worried him. He wished they were not on his conscience.

His uncle opened his eyes; Philip was glad, for he looked a little more human then. He was frankly horrified at the idea that had come to him, it was murder that he was meditating; and he wondered if other people had such thoughts or whether he was abnormal and depraved. He supposed he could not have done it when it came to the point, but there the thought was, constantly recurring: if he held his hand it was from fear. His uncle spoke.

"You're not looking forward to my death, Philip?"

Philip felt his heart beat against his chest.

"Good heavens, no."

"That's a good boy. I shouldn't like you to do that. You'll get a little bit of money when I pass away, but you mustn't look forward to it. It wouldn't profit you if you did."

He spoke in a low voice, and there was a curious anxiety in his tone. It sent a pang into Philip's heart. He wondered what strange insight might have led the old man to surmise what strange desires were in Philip's mind.

"I hope you'll live for another twenty years," he said.

"Oh, well, I can't expect to do that, but if I take care of myself I don't see why I shouldn't last another three or four."

He was silent for a while, and Philip found nothing to say. Then, as if he had been thinking it all over, the old man spoke again.

"Everyone has the right to live as long as he can."

Philip wanted to distract his mind.

"By the way, I suppose you never hear from Miss Wilkinson now?"

"Yes, I had a letter some time this year. She's married, you know."

"Really?"

"Yes, she married a widower. I believe they're quite comfortable."

Chapter CXI

Next day Philip began work again, but the end which he expected within a few weeks did not come. The weeks passed into months. The winter wore away, and in the parks the trees burst into bud and into leaf. A terrible lassitude settled upon Philip. Time was passing, though it went with such heavy feet, and he thought that his youth was going and soon he would have lost it and nothing would have been accomplished. His work seemed more aimless now that there was the certainty of his leaving it. He became skilful in the designing of costumes, and though he had no inventive faculty acquired quickness in the adaptation of French fashions to the English market. Sometimes he was not displeased with his drawings, but they always bungled them in the execution. He was amused to notice that he suffered from a lively irritation when his ideas were not adequately carried out. He had to walk warily. Whenever he suggested something original Mr. Sampson turned it down: their customers did not want anything *outré*, it was a very respectable class of business, and when you had a connection of that sort it wasn't worthwhile taking liberties with it. Once or twice he spoke sharply to Philip; he thought the young man was getting a bit above himself, because Philip's ideas did not always coincide with his own.

"You jolly well take care, my fine young fellow, or one of these days you'll find yourself in the street."

Philip longed to give him a punch on the nose, but he restrained himself. After all it could not possibly last much longer, and then he would be done with all these people forever. Sometimes in comic desperation he cried out that his uncle must be made of iron. What a constitution! The ills he suffered from would have killed any decent person twelve months before. When at last the news came that the Vicar was dying Philip, who had been thinking of other things, was taken by surprise. It was in July, and in another fortnight he was to have gone for his holiday. He received a letter from Mrs. Foster to say the doctor did not give Mr. Carey many days to live, and if Philip wished to see him again he must come at once. Philip went to the buyer and told him he wanted to leave. Mr. Sampson was a decent fellow, and when he knew the circumstances made no difficulties. Philip said good-bye to the people in his department; the reason of his leaving had spread among them in an exaggerated form, and they thought he had come into a fortune. Mrs. Hodges had tears in her eyes when she shook hands with him.

"I suppose we shan't often see you again," she said.

"I'm glad to get away from Lynn's," he answered.

It was strange, but he was actually sorry to leave these people whom he thought he had loathed, and when he drove away from the house in Harrington Street it was with no exultation. He had so anticipated the emotions he would experience on this occasion that now he felt nothing: he was as unconcerned as though he were going for a few days' holiday.

"I've got a rotten nature," he said to himself. "I look forward to things awfully, and then when they come I'm always disappointed."

He reached Blackstable early in the afternoon. Mrs. Foster met him at the door, and her face told him that his uncle was not yet dead.

"He's a little better today," she said. "He's got a wonderful constitution."

She led him into the bed-room where Mr. Carey lay on his back. He gave Philip a slight smile, in which was a trace of satisfied cunning at having circumvented his enemy once more.

"I thought it was all up with me yesterday," he said, in an exhausted voice. "They'd all given me up, hadn't you, Mrs. Foster?"

"You've got a wonderful constitution, there's no denying that."

"There's life in the old dog yet."

Mrs. Foster said that the Vicar must not talk, it would tire him; she treated him like a child, with kindly despotism; and there was something childish in the old man's satisfaction at having cheated all their expectations. It struck him at once that Philip had been sent for, and he was amused that he had been brought on a fool's errand. If he could only avoid another of his heart attacks he would get well enough in a week or two; and he had had the attacks several times before; he always felt as if he were going to die, but he never did. They all talked of his constitution, but they none of them knew how strong it was.

"Are you going to stay a day or two?" he asked Philip, pretending to believe he had come down for a holiday.

"I was thinking of it," Philip answered cheerfully.

"A breath of sea-air will do you good."

Presently Dr. Wigram came, and after he had seen the Vicar talked with Philip. He adopted an appropriate manner.

"I'm afraid it is the end this time, Philip," he said. "It'll be a great loss to all of us. I've known him for five-and-thirty years."

"He seems well enough now," said Philip.

"I'm keeping him alive on drugs, but it can't last. It was dreadful these last two days, I thought he was dead half a dozen times."

The doctor was silent for a minute or two, but at the gate he said suddenly to Philip:

"Has Mrs. Foster said anything to you?"

"What d'you mean?"

"They're very superstitious, these people: she's got hold of an idea that he's got something on his mind, and he can't die till he gets rid of it; and he can't bring himself to confess it."

Philip did not answer, and the doctor went on.

"Of course it's nonsense. He's led a very good life, he's done his duty, he's been a good parish priest, and I'm sure we shall all miss him; he can't have anything to reproach himself with. I very much doubt whether the next vicar will suit us half so well."

For several days Mr. Carey continued without change. His appetite which had been excellent left him, and he could eat little. Dr. Wigram did not hesitate now to still the pain of the neuritis which tormented him; and that, with the constant shaking of his palsied limbs, was gradually exhausting him. His mind remained clear. Philip and Mrs. Foster nursed him between them. She was so tired by the many months during which she had been attentive to all his wants that Philip insisted on sitting up with the patient so that she might have her night's rest. He passed the long hours in an arm-chair so that he should not sleep soundly, and read by the light of shaded candles *The Thousand and One Nights*. He had not read them since he was a little boy, and they brought back his childhood to him. Sometimes he sat and listened to the silence of the night. When the effects of the opiate wore off Mr. Carey grew restless and kept him constantly busy.

At last, early one morning, when the birds were chattering noisily in the trees, he heard his name called. He went up to the bed. Mr. Carey was lying on his back, with his eyes looking at the ceiling; he did not turn them on Philip. Philip saw that sweat was on his forehead, and he took a towel and wiped it.

"Is that you, Philip?" the old man asked.

Philip was startled because the voice was suddenly changed. It was hoarse and low. So would a man speak if he was cold with fear.

"Yes, d'you want anything?"

There was a pause, and still the unseeing eyes stared at the ceiling. Then a twitch passed over the face.

"I think I'm going to die," he said.

"Oh, what nonsense!" cried Philip. "You're not going to die for years."

Two tears were wrung from the old man's eyes. They moved Philip horribly. His uncle had never betrayed any particular emotion in the affairs of life; and it was dreadful to see them now, for they signified a terror that was unspeakable.

"Send for Mr. Simmonds," he said. "I want to take the Communion."

Mr. Simmonds was the curate.

"Now?" asked Philip.

"Soon, or else it'll be too late."

Philip went to awake Mrs. Foster, but it was later than he thought and she was up already. He told her to send the gardener with a message, and he went back to his uncle's room.

"Have you sent for Mr. Simmonds?"

"Yes."

There was a silence. Philip sat by the bed-side, and occasionally wiped the sweating forehead.

"Let me hold your hand, Philip," the old man said at last.

Philip gave him his hand and he clung to it as to life, for comfort in his extremity. Perhaps he had never really loved anyone in all his days, but now he turned instinctively to a human being. His hand was wet and cold. It grasped Philip's with feeble, despairing energy. The old man was fighting with the fear of death. And Philip thought that all must go through that. Oh, how monstrous it was, and they could believe in a God that allowed his creatures to suffer such a cruel torture! He had never cared for his uncle, and for two years he had longed every day for his death; but now he could not overcome the compassion that filled his heart. What a price it was to pay for being other than the beasts!

They remained in silence broken only once by a low inquiry from Mr. Carey.

"Hasn't he come yet?"

At last the housekeeper came in softly to say that Mr. Simmonds was there. He carried a bag in which were his surplice and his hood. Mrs. Foster brought the communion plate. Mr. Simmonds shook hands silently with Philip, and then with professional gravity went to the sick man's side. Philip and the maid went out of the room.

Philip walked round the garden all fresh and dewy in the morning. The birds were singing gaily. The sky was blue, but the air, salt-laden, was sweet and cool. The roses were in full bloom. The green of the trees, the green of the lawns, was eager and brilliant. Philip walked, and as he walked he thought of the mystery which was proceeding in that bed-room. It gave him a peculiar emotion. Presently Mrs. Foster came out to him and said that his uncle wished to see him. The curate was putting his things back into the black bag. The sick man turned his head a little and greeted him with a smile. Philip was astonished, for there was a change in him, an extraordinary change; his eyes had no longer the terror-stricken look, and the pinching of his face had gone: he looked happy and serene.

"I'm quite prepared now," he said, and his voice had a different tone in it. "When the Lord sees fit to call me I am ready to give my soul into his hands."

Philip did not speak. He could see that his uncle was sincere. It was almost a miracle. He had taken the body and blood of his Saviour, and they had given him strength so that he no longer feared the inevitable passage into the night. He knew he was going to die: he was resigned. He only said one thing more:

"I shall rejoin my dear wife."

It startled Philip. He remembered with what a callous selfishness his uncle had treated her, how obtuse he had been to her humble, devoted love. The curate, deeply moved, went away and Mrs. Foster, weeping, accompanied him to the door. Mr. Carey, exhausted by his effort, fell into a light doze, and Philip sat down by the bed and waited for the end. The morning wore on, and the old man's breathing grew stertorous. The doctor came and said he was dying. He was unconscious and he pecked feebly at the sheets; he was restless and he cried out. Dr. Wigram gave him a hypodermic injection.

"It can't do any good now, he may die at any moment."

The doctor looked at his watch and then at the patient. Philip saw that it was one o'clock. Dr. Wigram was thinking of his dinner.

"It's no use your waiting," he said.

"There's nothing I can do," said the doctor.

When he was gone Mrs. Foster asked Philip if he would go to the carpenter, who was also the undertaker, and tell him to send up a woman to lay out the body.

"You want a little fresh air," she said, "it'll do you good."

The undertaker lived half a mile away. When Philip gave him his message, he said:

"When did the poor old gentleman die?"

Philip hesitated. It occurred to him that it would seem brutal to fetch a woman to wash the body while his uncle still lived, and he wondered why Mrs. Foster had asked him to come. They would think he was in a great hurry to kill the old man off. He thought the undertaker looked at him oddly. He repeated the question. It irritated Philip. It was no business of his.

"When did the Vicar pass away?"

Philip's first impulse was to say that it had just happened, but then it would seem inexplicable if the sick man lingered for several hours. He reddened and answered awkwardly.

"Oh, he isn't exactly dead yet."

The undertaker looked at him in perplexity, and he hurried to explain.

"Mrs. Foster is all alone and she wants a woman there. You understood, don't you? He may be dead by now."

The undertaker nodded.

"Oh, yes, I see. I'll send someone up at once."

When Philip got back to the vicarage he went up to the bed-room. Mrs. Foster rose from her chair by the bed-side.

"He's just as he was when you left," she said.

She went down to get herself something to eat, and Philip watched curiously the process of death. There was nothing human now in the unconscious being that struggled feebly. Sometimes a muttered ejaculation issued from the loose mouth. The sun beat down hotly from a cloudless sky, but the trees in the garden were pleasant and cool. It was a lovely day. A bluebottle buzzed against the window-pane. Suddenly there was a loud rattle, it made Philip start, it was horribly frightening; a movement passed through the limbs and the old man was dead. The machine had run down. The bluebottle buzzed, buzzed noisily against the window-pane.

Chapter CXII

JOSIAH GRAVES IN HIS MASTERFUL WAY MADE ARRANGEMENTS, BECOMING BUT economical, for the funeral; and when it was over came back to the vicarage with Philip. The will was in his charge, and with a due sense of the fitness of things he read it to Philip over an early cup of tea. It was written on half a sheet of paper and left everything Mr. Carey had to his nephew. There was the furniture, about eighty pounds at the bank, twenty shares in the A.B.C. company, a few in Allsop's brewery, some in the Oxford music-hall, and a few more in a London restaurant. They had been bought under Mr. Graves' direction, and he told Philip with satisfaction:

"You see, people must eat, they will drink, and they want amusement. You're always safe if you put your money in what the public thinks necessities."

His words showed a nice discrimination between the grossness of the vulgar, which he deplored but accepted, and the finer taste of the elect. Altogether in investments there was about five hundred pounds; and to that must be added the balance at the bank and what the furniture would fetch. It was riches to Philip. He was not happy but infinitely relieved.

Mr. Graves left him, after they had discussed the auction which must be held as soon as possible, and Philip sat himself down to go through the papers of the deceased. The Rev. William Carey had prided himself on never destroying anything, and there were piles of correspondence dating back for fifty years and bundle upon bundle of neatly docketed bills. He had kept not only letters addressed to him, but letters which himself had written. There was a yellow packet of letters which he had written to his father in the forties, when as an Oxford undergraduate he had gone to Germany for the long vacation. Philip read them idly. It was a different William Carey from the William Carey he had known, and yet there were traces in the boy which might to an acute observer have suggested the man. The letters were formal and a little stilted. He showed himself strenuous to see all that was noteworthy, and he described with a fine enthusiasm the castles of the Rhine. The falls of Schaffhausen made him "offer reverent thanks to the all-powerful Creator of the universe, whose works were wondrous and beautiful," and he could not help thinking that they who lived in sight of "this handiwork of their blessed Maker must be moved by the contemplation to lead pure and holy lives." Among some bills Philip found a miniature which had been painted of William Carey soon after he was ordained. It represented a thin young curate, with long hair that fell over his head in natural curls, with dark eyes, large and dreamy, and a pale ascetic face.

Philip remembered the chuckle with which his uncle used to tell of the dozens of slippers which were worked for him by adoring ladies.

The rest of the afternoon and all the evening Philip toiled through the innumerable correspondence. He glanced at the address and at the signature, then tore the letter in two and threw it into the washing-basket by his side. Suddenly he came upon one signed Helen. He did not know the writing. It was thin, angular, and old-fashioned. It began: my dear William, and ended: your affectionate sister. Then it struck him that it was from his own mother. He had never seen a letter of hers before, and her handwriting was strange to him. It was about himself.

My dear William—Stephen wrote to you to thank you for your congratulations on the birth of our son and your kind wishes to myself. Thank God we are both well and I am deeply thankful for the great mercy which has been shown me. Now that I can hold a pen I want to tell you and dear Louisa myself how truly grateful I am to you both for all your kindness to me now and always since my marriage. I am going to ask you to do me a great favour. Both Stephen and I wish you to be the boy's godfather, and we hope that you will consent. I know I am not asking a small thing, for I am sure you will take the responsibilities of the position very seriously, but I am especially anxious that you should undertake this office because you are a clergyman as well as the boy's uncle. I am very anxious for the boy's welfare and I pray God night and day that he may grow into a good, honest, and Christian man. With you to guide him I hope that he will become a soldier in Christ's Faith and be all the days of his life God-fearing, humble, and pious.

Your affectionate sister,
Helen

Philip pushed the letter away and, leaning forward, rested his face on his hands. It deeply touched and at the same time surprised him. He was astonished at its religious tone, which seemed to him neither mawkish nor sentimental. He knew nothing of his mother, dead now for nearly twenty years, but that she was beautiful, and it was strange to learn that she was simple and pious. He had never thought of that side of her. He read again what she said about him, what she expected and thought about him; he had turned out very differently; he looked at himself for a moment; perhaps it was better that she was dead. Then a sudden impulse caused him to tear up the letter; its tenderness and simplicity made it seem peculiarly private; he had a queer feeling that there was something indecent in his reading what exposed his mother's gentle soul. He went on with the Vicar's dreary correspondence.

A few days later he went up to London, and for the first time for two years entered by day the hall of St. Luke's Hospital. He went to see the secretary of the Medical School; he was surprised to see him and asked Philip curiously what he had been doing. Philip's experiences had given him a certain confidence in himself and a different outlook upon many things: such a question would have embarrassed him before; but now he answered coolly, with a deliberate vagueness which prevented further inquiry, that private affairs had obliged him to make a break in the curriculum; he was now anxious to qualify as soon as possible. The first examination he could take was in Midwifery and the Diseases of Women, and he put his name down to be a clerk in the ward devoted to feminine ailments; since it was holiday time there happened to be no difficulty in getting a post as obstetric clerk; he arranged to undertake that duty during the last week of August and the first two of September. After this interview Philip walked through the Medical School, more or less deserted, for the examinations at the end of the summer session were all over; and he wandered along the terrace by the riverside. His heart was full. He thought that now he could begin a new life, and he would put behind him all the errors, follies, and miseries of the past. The flowing river suggested that everything passed, was passing always, and nothing mattered; the future was before him rich with possibilities.

He went back to Blackstable and busied himself with the settling up of his uncle's estate. The auction was fixed for the middle of August, when the presence of visitors for the summer holidays would make it possible to get better prices. Catalogues were made out and sent to the various dealers in second-hand books at Tercanbury, Maidstone, and Ashford.

One afternoon Philip took it into his head to go over to Tercanbury and see his old school. He had not been there since the day when, with relief in his heart, he had left it with the feeling that thenceforward he was his own master. It was strange to wander through the narrow streets of Tercanbury which he had known so well for so many years. He looked at the old shops, still there, still selling the same things; the booksellers with school-books, pious works, and the latest novels in one window and photographs of the Cathedral and of the city in the other; the games shop, with its cricket bats, fishing tackle, tennis rackets, and footballs; the tailor from whom he had got clothes all through his boyhood; and the fishmonger where his uncle whenever he came to Tercanbury bought fish. He wandered along the sordid street in which, behind a high wall, lay the red brick house which was the preparatory school. Further on was the gateway that led into King's School, and he stood in the quadrangle round which were the various buildings. It was just four and the boys were hurrying out of school. He saw the masters in their gowns and mortar-boards, and they were strange to him. It was more than ten years since he had left and many changes had taken place. He saw the headmaster; he walked slowly down from the schoolhouse to his own, talking to a big boy who Philip supposed was in the sixth; he was little changed, tall, cadaverous, romantic as Philip remembered him, with the same wild eyes; but the black beard was streaked with grey now and the dark, sallow face was more deeply lined. Philip had an impulse to go up and speak to him, but he was afraid he would have forgotten him, and he hated the thought of explaining who he was.

Boys lingered talking to one another, and presently some who had hurried to change came out to play fives; others straggled out in twos and threes and went out of the gateway, Philip knew they were going up to the cricket ground; others again went into the precincts to bat at the nets. Philip stood among them a stranger; one or two gave him an indifferent glance; but visitors, attracted by the Norman staircase, were not rare and excited little attention. Philip looked at them curiously. He thought with melancholy of the distance that separated him from them, and he thought bitterly how much he had wanted to do and how little done. It seemed to him that all those years, vanished beyond recall, had been utterly wasted. The boys, fresh and buoyant, were doing the same things that he had done, it seemed that not a day had passed since he left the school, and yet in that place where at least by name he had known everybody now he knew not a soul. In a few years these too, others taking their place, would stand alien as he stood; but the reflection brought him no solace; it merely impressed upon him the futility of human existence. Each generation repeated the trivial round. He wondered what had become of the boys who were his companions: they were nearly thirty now; some would be dead, but others were married and had children; they were soldiers and parsons, doctors, lawyers; they were staid men who were beginning to put youth behind them. Had any of them made such a hash of life as he? He thought of the boy he had been devoted to; it was funny, he could not recall his name; he remembered exactly what he looked like, he had been his greatest friend; but his name would not come back to him. He looked back with amusement on the jealous emotions he had suffered on his account. It was irritating not to recollect his name. He longed to be a boy again, like those he saw sauntering through the quadrangle, so that, avoiding his mistakes, he might start fresh and make something more out of life. He felt an intolerable loneliness. He almost regretted the penury which he had suffered during the last two years, since the desperate struggle merely to keep body and soul together had deadened the pain of living. *In the sweat of thy brow shalt thou earn thy daily bread:* it was not a curse upon mankind, but the balm which reconciled it to existence.

But Philip was impatient with himself; he called to mind his idea of the pattern of life: the unhappiness he had suffered was no more than part of a decoration which was elaborate and beautiful; he told himself strenuously that he must accept with gaiety everything, dreariness and excitement, pleasure and pain, because it added to the richness of the design. He sought for beauty consciously, and he remembered how even as a boy he had taken pleasure in the Gothic cathedral as one saw it from the precincts; he went there and looked at the massive pile, grey under the cloudy sky, with the central tower that rose like the praise of men to their God; but the boys were batting at the nets, and they were lissom and strong and active; he could not help hearing their shouts and laughter. The cry of youth was insistent, and he saw the beautiful thing before him only with his eyes.

Chapter CXIII

AT THE BEGINNING OF THE LAST WEEK IN AUGUST PHILIP ENTERED UPON his duties in the "district." They were arduous, for he had to attend on an average three confinements a day. The patient had obtained a "card" from the hospital some time before; and when her time came it was taken to the porter by a messenger, generally a little girl, who was then sent across the road to the house in which Philip lodged. At night the porter, who had a latch-key, himself came over and awoke Philip. It was mysterious then to get up in the darkness and walk through the deserted streets of the South Side. At those hours it was generally the husband who brought the card. If there had been a number of babies before he took it for the most part with surly indifference, but if newly married he was nervous and then sometimes strove to allay his anxiety by getting drunk. Often there was a mile or more to walk, during which Philip and the messenger discussed the conditions of labour and the cost of living; Philip learned about the various trades which were practised on that side of the river. He inspired confidence in the people among whom he was thrown, and during the long hours that he waited in a stuffy room, the woman in labour lying on a large bed that took up half of it, her mother and the midwife talked to him as naturally as they talked to one another. The circumstances in which he had lived during the last two years had taught him several things about the life of the very poor, which it amused them to find he knew; and they were impressed because he was not deceived by their little subterfuges. He was kind, and he had gentle hands, and he did not lose his temper. They were pleased because he was not above drinking a cup of tea with them, and when the dawn came and they were still waiting they offered him a slice of bread and dripping; he was not squeamish and could eat most things now with a good appetite. Some of the houses he went to, in filthy courts off a dingy street, huddled against one another without light or air, were merely squalid; but others, unexpectedly, though dilapidated, with worm-eaten floors and leaking roofs, had the grand air: you found in them oak balusters exquisitely carved, and the walls had still their panelling. These were thickly inhabited. One family lived in each room, and in the daytime there was the incessant noise of children playing in the court. The old walls were the breeding-place of vermin; the air was so foul that often, feeling sick, Philip had to light his pipe. The people who dwelled here lived from hand to mouth. Babies were unwelcome, the man received them with surly anger, the mother with despair; it was one more mouth to feed, and there was little enough wherewith to feed those already there. Philip often discerned the wish that the child might be born dead or might die quickly. He delivered one woman of twins (a source of humour to the facetious) and when she was told she burst into a long, shrill wail of misery. Her mother said outright:

"I don't know how they're going to feed 'em."

"Maybe the Lord'll see fit to take 'em to 'imself," said the midwife.

Philip caught sight of the husband's face as he looked at the tiny pair lying side by side, and there was a ferocious sullenness in it which startled him. He felt in the family assembled there a hideous resentment against those poor atoms who had come into the world unwished for; and he had a suspicion that if he did not speak firmly an "accident" would occur. Accidents occurred often; mothers "overlay" their babies, and perhaps errors of diet were not always the result of carelessness.

"I shall come every day," he said. "I warn you that if anything happens to them there'll have to be an inquest."

The father made no reply, but he gave Philip a scowl. There was murder in his soul.

"Bless their little 'earts," said the grandmother, "what should 'appen to them?"

The great difficulty was to keep the mothers in bed for ten days, which was the minimum upon which the hospital practice insisted. It was awkward to look after the family, no one would see to the children without payment, and the husband grumbled because his tea was not right when he came home tired from his work and hungry. Philip had heard that the poor helped one another, but woman after woman complained to him that she could not get anyone in to clean up and see to the children's dinner without paying for the service, and she could not afford to pay. By listening to the women as they talked and by chance remarks from which he could deduce much that was left unsaid, Philip learned how little there was in common between the poor and the classes above them. They did not envy their betters, for the life was too different, and they had an ideal of ease which made the existence of the middle-classes seem formal and stiff; moreover, they had a certain contempt for them because they were soft and did not work with their hands. The proud merely wished to be left alone, but the majority looked upon the well-to-do as people to be exploited; they knew what to say in order to get such advantages as the charitable put at their disposal, and they accepted benefits as a right which came to them from the folly of their superiors and their own astuteness. They bore the curate with contemptuous indifference, but the district visitor excited their bitter hatred. She came in and opened your windows without so much as a by your leave or with your leave, "and me with my bronchitis, enough to give me my death of cold"; she poked her nose into corners, and if she didn't say the place was dirty you saw what she thought right enough, "an' it's all very well for them as 'as servants, but I'd like to see what she'd make of 'er room if she 'ad four children, and 'ad to do the cookin', and mend their clothes, and wash them."

Philip discovered that the greatest tragedy of life to these people was not separation or death, that was natural and the grief of it could be assuaged with tears, but loss of work. He saw a man come home one afternoon, three days after his wife's confinement, and tell her he had been dismissed; he was a builder and at that time work was slack; he stated the fact, and sat down to his tea.

"Oh, Jim," she said.

The man ate stolidly some mess which had been stewing in a sauce-pan against his coming; he stared at his plate; his wife looked at him two or three times, with little startled glances, and then quite silently began to cry. The builder was an uncouth little fellow with a rough, weather-beaten face and a long white scar on his forehead; he had large, stubbly hands. Presently he pushed aside his plate as if he must give up the effort to force himself to eat, and turned a fixed gaze out of the window. The room was at the top of the house, at the back, and one saw nothing but sullen clouds. The silence seemed heavy with despair. Philip felt that there was nothing to be said, he could only go; and as he walked away, wearily, for he had been up most of the night, his heart was filled with rage against the cruelty of the world. He knew the hopelessness of the search for work and the desolation which is harder to bear than hunger. He was thankful not to have to believe in God, for then such a condition of things would be intolerable; one could reconcile oneself to existence only because it was meaningless.

It seemed to Philip that the people who spent their time in helping the poorer classes erred because they sought to remedy things which would harass them if themselves had to endure them without thinking that they did not in the least disturb those who were used to them. The poor did not want large airy rooms; they suffered from cold, for their food was not nourishing and their circulation bad; space gave them a feeling of chilliness, and they wanted to burn as little coal as need be; there was no hardship for several to sleep in one room, they preferred it; they were never alone for a moment, from the time they were born to the time they died, and loneliness oppressed them; they enjoyed the promiscuity in which they dwelled, and the constant noise of their surroundings pressed upon their ears unnoticed. They did not feel the need of taking a bath constantly, and Philip often heard them speak with indignation of the necessity to do so with which they were faced on entering the hospital: it was both an affront and a discomfort. They wanted chiefly to be left alone; then if the man was in regular work life went easily and was not without its pleasures: there was plenty of time for gossip, after the day's work a glass of beer was very good to drink, the streets were a constant source of entertainment, if you wanted to read there was *Reynolds'* or *The News of the World*; "but there, you couldn't make out 'ow the time did fly, the truth was and that's a fact, you was a rare one for reading when you was a girl, but what with one thing and another you didn't get no time now not even to read the paper."

The usual practice was to pay three visits after a confinement, and one Sunday Philip went to see a patient at the dinner hour. She was up for the first time.

"I couldn't stay in bed no longer, I really couldn't. I'm not one for idling, and it gives me the fidgets to be there and do nothing all day long, so I said to 'Erb, I'm just going to get up and cook your dinner for you."

'Erb was sitting at table with his knife and fork already in his hands. He was a young man, with an open face and blue eyes. He was earning good money, and as things went the couple were in easy circumstances. They had only been married a few months, and were both delighted with the rosy boy who lay in the cradle at the foot of the bed. There was a savoury smell of beefsteak in the room and Philip's eyes turned to the range.

"I was just going to dish up this minute," said the woman.

"Fire away," said Philip. "I'll just have a look at the son and heir and then I'll take myself off."

Husband and wife laughed at Philip's expression, and 'Erb getting up went over with Philip to the cradle. He looked at his baby proudly.

"There doesn't seem much wrong with him, does there?" said Philip.

He took up his hat, and by this time 'Erb's wife had dished up the beefsteak and put on the table a plate of green peas.

"You're going to have a nice dinner," smiled Philip.

"He's only in of a Sunday and I like to 'ave something special for him, so as he shall miss his 'ome when he's out at work."

"I suppose you'd be above sittin' down and 'avin' a bit of dinner with us?" said 'Erb.

"Oh, 'Erb," said his wife, in a shocked tone.

"Not if you ask me," answered Philip, with his attractive smile.

"Well, that's what I call friendly, I knew 'e wouldn't take offence, Polly. Just get another plate, my girl."

Polly was flustered, and she thought 'Erb a regular caution, you never knew what ideas 'e'd get in 'is 'ead next; but she got a plate and wiped it quickly with her apron, then took a new knife and fork from the chest of drawers, where her best cutlery rested among her best clothes. There was a jug of stout on the table, and 'Erb poured Philip out a glass. He wanted to give him the lion's share of the beefsteak, but Philip insisted that they should share alike. It was a sunny room with two windows that reached to the floor; it had been the parlour of a house which at one time was if not fashionable at least respectable: it might have been inhabited fifty years before by a well-to-do tradesman or an officer on half pay. 'Erb had been a football player before he married, and there were photographs on the wall of various teams in self-conscious attitudes, with neatly plastered hair, the captain seated proudly in the middle holding a cup. There were other signs of prosperity: photographs of the relations of 'Erb and his wife in Sunday clothes; on the chimney-piece an elaborate arrangement of shells stuck on a miniature rock; and on each side mugs, "A present from Southend" in Gothic letters, with pictures of a pier and a parade on them. 'Erb was something of a character; he was a non-union man and expressed himself with indignation at the efforts of the union to force him to join. The union wasn't no good to him, he never found no difficulty in getting work, and there was good wages for anyone as 'ad a head on his shoulders and wasn't above puttin' 'is 'and to anything as come 'is way. Polly was timorous. If she was 'im she'd join the union, the last time there was a strike she was expectin' 'im to be brought back in an ambulance every time he went out. She turned to Philip.

"He's that obstinate, there's no doing anything with 'im."

"Well, what I say is, it's a free country, and I won't be dictated to."

"It's no good saying it's a free country," said Polly, "that won't prevent 'em bashin' your 'ead in if they get the chanst."

When they had finished Philip passed his pouch over to 'Erb and they lit their pipes; then he got up, for a "call" might be waiting for him at his rooms, and shook hands. He saw that it had given them pleasure that he shared their meal, and they saw that he had thoroughly enjoyed it.

"Well, good-bye, sir," said 'Erb, "and I 'ope we shall 'ave as nice a doctor next time the missus disgraces 'erself."

"Go on with you, 'Erb," she retorted. " 'Ow d'you know there's going to be a next time?"

Chapter CXIV

THE THREE WEEKS WHICH THE APPOINTMENT LASTED DREW TO AN END. Philip had attended sixty-two cases, and he was tired out. When he came home about ten o'clock on his last night he hoped with all his heart that he would not be called out again. He had not had a whole night's rest for ten days. The case which he had just come from was horrible. He had been fetched by a huge, burly man, the worse for liquor, and taken to a room in an evil-smelling court, which was filthier than any he had seen: it was a tiny attic; most of the space was taken up by a wooden bed, with a canopy of dirty red hangings, and the ceiling was so low that Philip could touch it with the tips of his fingers; with the solitary candle that afforded what light there was he went over it, frizzling up the bugs that crawled upon it. The woman was a blowsy creature of middle age, who had had a long succession of still-born children. It was a story that Philip was not unaccustomed to: the husband had been a soldier in India; the legislation forced upon that country by the prudery of the English public had given a free run to the most distressing of all diseases; the innocent suffered. Yawning, Philip undressed and took a bath, then shook his clothes over the water and watched the animals that fell out wriggling. He was just going to get into bed when there was a knock at the door, and the hospital porter brought him a card.

"Curse you," said Philip. "You're the last person I wanted to see tonight. Who's brought it?"

"I think it's the 'usband, sir. Shall I tell him to wait?"

Philip looked at the address, saw that the street was familiar to him, and told the porter that he would find his own way. He dressed himself and in five minutes, with his black bag in his hand, stepped into the street. A man, whom he could not see in the darkness, came up to him, and said he was the husband.

"I thought I'd better wait, sir," he said. "It's a pretty rough neighbour'ood, and them not knowing who you was."

Philip laughed.

"Bless your heart, they all know the doctor, I've been in some damned sight rougher places than Waver Street."

It was quite true. The black bag was a passport through wretched alleys and down foul-smelling courts into which a policeman was not ready to venture by himself. Once or twice a little group of men had looked at Philip curiously as he passed; he heard a mutter of observations and then one say:

"It's the 'orspital doctor."

As he went by one or two of them said: "Good-night, sir."

"We shall 'ave to step out if you don't mind, sir," said the man who accompanied him now. "They told me there was no time to lose."

"Why did you leave it so late?" asked Philip, as he quickened his pace.

He glanced at the fellow as they passed a lamp-post.

"You look awfully young," he said.

"I'm turned eighteen, sir."

He was fair, and he had not a hair on his face, he looked no more than a boy; he was short, but thick set.

"You're young to be married," said Philip.

"We 'ad to."

"How much d'you earn?"

"Sixteen, sir."

Sixteen shillings a week was not much to keep a wife and child on. The room the couple lived in showed that their poverty was extreme. It was a fair size, but it looked quite large, since there was hardly any furniture in it; there was no carpet on the floor; there were no pictures on the walls; and most rooms had something, photographs or supplements in cheap frames from the Christmas numbers of the illustrated papers. The patient lay on a little iron bed of the cheapest sort. It startled Philip to see how young she was.

"By Jove, she can't be more than sixteen," he said to the woman who had come in to "see her through."

She had given her age as eighteen on the card, but when they were very young they often put on a year or two. Also she was pretty, which was rare in those classes in which the constitution has been undermined by bad food, bad air, and unhealthy occupations; she had delicate features and large blue eyes, and a mass of dark hair done in the elaborate fashion of the coster girl. She and her husband were very nervous.

"You'd better wait outside, so as to be at hand if I want you," Philip said to him.

Now that he saw him better Philip was surprised again at his boyish air: you felt that he should be larking in the street with the other lads instead of waiting anxiously for the birth of a child. The hours passed, and it was not till nearly two that the baby was born. Everything seemed to be going satisfactorily; the husband was called in, and it touched Philip to see the awkward, shy way in which he kissed his wife; Philip packed up his things. Before going he felt once more his patient's pulse.

"Hulloa!" he said.

He looked at her quickly: something had happened. In cases of emergency the S.O.C.—senior obstetric clerk—had to be sent for; he was a qualified man, and the "district" was in his charge. Philip scribbled a note, and giving it to the husband, told him to run with it to the hospital; he bade him hurry, for his wife was in a dangerous state. The man set off. Philip waited anxiously; he knew the woman was bleeding to death; he was afraid she would die before his chief arrived; he took what steps he could. He hoped fervently that the S.O.C. would not have been called elsewhere. The minutes were interminable. He came at last, and, while he examined the patient, in a low voice asked Philip questions. Philip saw by his face that he thought the case very grave. His name was Chandler. He was a tall man of few words, with a long nose and a thin face much lined for his age. He shook his head.

"It was hopeless from the beginning. Where's the husband?"

"I told him to wait on the stairs," said Philip.

"You'd better bring him in."

Philip opened the door and called him. He was sitting in the dark on the first step of the flight that led to the next floor. He came up to the bed.

"What's the matter?" he asked.

"Why, there's internal bleeding. It's impossible to stop it." The S.O.C. hesitated a moment, and because it was a painful thing to say he forced his voice to become brusque. "She's dying."

The man did not say a word; he stopped quite still, looking at his wife, who lay, pale and unconscious, on the bed. It was the midwife who spoke.

"The gentlemen 'ave done all they could, 'Arry," she said. "I saw what was comin' from the first."

"Shut up," said Chandler.

There were no curtains on the windows, and gradually the night seemed to lighten; it was not yet the dawn, but the dawn was at hand. Chandler was keeping the woman alive by all the means in his power, but life was slipping away from her, and suddenly she died. The boy who was her husband stood at the end of the cheap iron bed with his hands resting on the rail; he did not speak; but he looked very pale and once or twice Chandler gave him an uneasy glance, thinking he was going to faint: his lips were grey. The midwife sobbed noisily, but he took no notice of her. His eyes were fixed upon his wife, and in them was an utter bewilderment. He reminded you of a dog whipped for something he did not know was wrong. When Chandler and Philip had gathered together their things Chandler turned to the husband.

"You'd better lie down for a bit. I expect you're about done up."

"There's nowhere for me to lie down, sir," he answered, and there was in his voice a humbleness which was very distressing.

"Don't you know anyone in the house who'll give you a shakedown?"

"No, sir."

"They only moved in last week," said the midwife. "They don't know nobody yet."

Chandler hesitated a moment awkwardly, then he went up to the man and said: "I'm very sorry this has happened."

He held out his hand and the man, with an instinctive glance at his own to see if it was clean, shook it.

"Thank you, sir."

Philip shook hands with him too. Chandler told the midwife to come and fetch the certificate in the morning. They left the house and walked along together in silence.

"It upsets one a bit at first, doesn't it?" said Chandler at last.

"A bit," answered Philip.

"If you like I'll tell the porter not to bring you any more calls tonight."

"I'm off duty at eight in the morning in any case."

"How many cases have you had?"

"Sixty-three."

"Good. You'll get your certificate then."

They arrived at the hospital, and the S.O.C. went in to see if anyone wanted him. Philip walked on. It had been very hot all the day before, and even now in the early morning there was a balminess in the air. The street was very still. Philip did not feel inclined to go to bed. It was the end of his work and he need not hurry. He strolled along, glad of the fresh air and the silence; he thought that he would go on to the bridge and look at day break on the river. A policeman at the corner bade him good-morning. He knew who Philip was from his bag.

"Out late tonight, sir," he said.

Philip nodded and passed. He leaned against the parapet and looked towards the morning. At that hour the great city was like a city of the dead. The sky was cloudless, but the stars were dim at the approach of day; there was a light mist on the river, and the great buildings on the north side were like palaces in an enchanted island. A group of barges was moored in midstream. It was all of an unearthly violet, troubling somehow and awe-inspiring; but quickly everything grew pale, and cold, and grey. Then the sun rose, a ray of yellow gold stole across the sky, and the sky was iridescent. Philip could not get out of his eyes the dead girl lying on the bed, wan and white, and the boy who stood at the end of it like a stricken beast. The bareness of the squalid room made the pain of it more poignant. It was cruel that a stupid chance should have cut off her life when she was just entering upon it; but in the very moment of saying this to himself, Philip thought of the life which had been in store for her, the bearing of children, the dreary fight with poverty, the youth broken by toil and deprivation into a slatternly middle age—he saw the pretty face grow thin and white, the hair grow scanty, the pretty hands, worn down brutally by work, become like the claws of an old animal—then, when the man was past his prime, the difficulty of getting jobs, the small wages he had to take; and the inevitable, abject penury of the end: she might be energetic, thrifty, industrious, it would not have saved her; in the end was the workhouse or subsistence on the charity of her children. Who could pity her because she had died when life offered so little?

But pity was inane. Philip felt it was not that which these people needed. They did not pity themselves. They accepted their fate. It was the natural order of things. Otherwise, good heavens! otherwise they would swarm over the river in their multitude to the side where those great buildings were, secure and stately; and they would pillage, burn, and sack. But the day, tender and pale, had broken now, and the mist was tenuous; it bathed everything in a soft radiance; and the Thames was grey, rosy, and green; grey like mother-of-pearl and green like the heart of a yellow rose. The wharfs and store-houses of the Surrey Side were massed in disorderly loveliness. The scene was so exquisite that Philip's heart beat passionately. He was overwhelmed by the beauty of the world. Beside that nothing seemed to matter.

Chapter CXV

PHILIP SPENT THE FEW WEEKS THAT REMAINED BEFORE THE BEGINNING OF the winter session in the out-patients' department, and in October settled down to regular work. He had been away from the hospital for so long that he found himself very largely among new people; the men of different years had little to do with one another, and his contemporaries were now mostly qualified: some had left to take up assistantships or posts in country hospitals and infirmaries, and some held appointments at St. Luke's. The two years during which his mind had lain fallow had refreshed him, he fancied, and he was able now to work with energy.

The Athelnys were delighted with his change of fortune. He had kept aside a few things from the sale of his uncle's effects and gave them all presents. He gave Sally a gold chain that had belonged to his aunt. She was now grown up. She was apprenticed to a dressmaker and set out every morning at eight to work all day in a shop in Regent Street. Sally had frank blue eyes, a broad brow, and plentiful shining hair; she was buxom, with broad hips and full breasts; and her father, who was fond of discussing her appearance, warned her constantly that she must not grow fat. She attracted because she was healthy, animal, and feminine. She had many admirers, but they left her unmoved; she gave one the impression that she looked upon love-making as nonsense; and it was easy to imagine that young men found her unapproachable. Sally was old for her years: she had been used to help her mother in the household work and in the care of the children, so that she had acquired a managing air, which made her mother say that Sally was a bit too fond of having things her own way. She did not speak very much, but as she grew older she seemed to be acquiring a quiet sense of humour, and sometimes uttered a remark which suggested that beneath her impassive exterior she was quietly bubbling with amusement at her fellow-creatures. Philip found that with her he never got on the terms of affectionate intimacy upon which he was with the rest of Athelny's huge family. Now and then her indifference slightly irritated him. There was something enigmatic in her.

When Philip gave her the necklace Athelny in his boisterous way insisted that she must kiss him; but Sally reddened and drew back.

"No, I'm not going to," she said.

"Ungrateful hussy!" cried Athelny. "Why not?"

"I don't like being kissed by men," she said.

Philip saw her embarrassment, and, amused, turned Athelny's attention to something else. That was never a very difficult thing to do. But evidently her mother spoke of the matter later, for next time Philip came she took the opportunity when they were alone for a couple of minutes to refer to it.

"You didn't think it disagreeable of me last week when I wouldn't kiss you?"

"Not a bit," he laughed.

"It's not because I wasn't grateful." She blushed a little as she uttered the formal phrase which she had prepared. "I shall always value the necklace, and it was very kind of you to give it me."

Philip found it always a little difficult to talk to her. She did all that she had to do very competently, but seemed to feel no need of conversation; yet there was nothing unsociable in her. One Sunday afternoon when Athelny and his wife had gone out together, and Philip, treated as one of the family, sat reading in the parlour, Sally came in and sat by the window to sew. The girls' clothes were made at home and Sally could not afford to spend Sundays in idleness. Philip thought she wished to talk and put down his book.

"Go on reading," she said. "I only thought as you were alone I'd come and sit with you."

"You're the most silent person I've ever struck," said Philip.

"We don't want another one who's talkative in this house," she said.

There was no irony in her tone: she was merely stating a fact. But it suggested to Philip that she measured her father, alas, no longer the hero he was to her childhood, and in her mind joined together his entertaining conversation and the thriftlessness which often brought difficulties into their life; she compared his rhetoric with her mother's practical common sense; and though the liveliness of her father amused her she was perhaps sometimes a little impatient with it. Philip looked at her as she bent over her work; she was healthy, strong, and normal; it must be odd to see her among the other girls in the shop with their flat chests and anaemic faces. Mildred suffered from anaemia.

After a time it appeared that Sally had a suitor. She went out occasionally with friends she had made in the work-room, and had met a young man, an electrical engineer in a very good way of business, who was a most eligible person. One day she told her mother that he had asked her to marry him.

"What did you say?" said her mother.

"Oh, I told him I wasn't over-anxious to marry anyone just yet awhile." She paused a little as was her habit between observations. "He took on so that I said he might come to tea on Sunday."

It was an occasion that thoroughly appealed to Athelny. He rehearsed all the afternoon how he should play the heavy father for the young man's edification till he reduced his children to helpless giggling. Just before he was due Athelny routed out an Egyptian tarboosh and insisted on putting it on.

"Go on with you, Athelny," said his wife, who was in her best, which was of black velvet, and, since she was growing stouter every year, very tight for her. "You'll spoil the girl's chances."

She tried to pull it off, but the little man skipped nimbly out of her way.

"Unhand me, woman. Nothing will induce me to take it off. This young man must be shown at once that it is no ordinary family he is preparing to enter."

"Let him keep it on, mother," said Sally, in her even, indifferent fashion. "If Mr. Donaldson doesn't take it the way it's meant he can take himself off, and good riddance."

Philip thought it was a severe ordeal that the young man was being exposed to, since Athelny, in his brown velvet jacket, flowing black tie, and red tarboosh, was a startling spectacle for an innocent electrical engineer. When he came he was greeted by his host with the proud courtesy of a Spanish grandee and by Mrs. Athelny in an altogether homely and natural fashion. They sat down at the old ironing-table in the high-backed monkish chairs, and Mrs. Athelny poured tea out of a lustre teapot which gave a note of England and the countryside to the festivity. She had made little cakes with her own hand, and on the table was home-made jam. It was a farm-house tea, and to Philip very quaint and charming in that Jacobean house. Athelny for some fantastic reason took it into his head to discourse upon Byzantine history; he had been reading the later volumes of the *Decline and Fall*; and, his forefinger dramatically extended, he poured into the astonished ears of the suitor scandalous stories about Theodora and Irene. He addressed himself directly to his guest with a torrent of rhodomontade; and the young man, reduced to helpless silence and shy, nodded his head at intervals to show that he took an intelligent interest. Mrs. Athelny paid no attention to Thorpe's conversation, but interrupted now and then to offer the young man more tea or to press upon him cake and jam. Philip watched Sally; she sat with downcast eyes, calm, silent, and observant; and her long eye-lashes cast a pretty shadow on her cheek. You could not tell whether she was amused at the scene or if she cared for the young man. She was inscrutable. But one thing was certain: the electrical engineer was good-looking, fair and clean-shaven, with pleasant, regular features, and an honest face; he was tall and well-made. Philip could not help thinking he would make an excellent mate for her, and he felt a pang of envy for the happiness which he fancied was in store for them.

Presently the suitor said he thought it was about time he was getting along. Sally rose to her feet without a word and accompanied him to the door. When she came back her father burst out:

"Well, Sally, we think your young man very nice. We are prepared to welcome him into our family. Let the banns be called and I will compose a nuptial song."

Sally set about clearing away the tea-things. She did not answer. Suddenly she shot a swift glance at Philip.

"What did you think of him, Mr. Philip?"

She had always refused to call him Uncle Phil as the other children did, and would not call him Philip.

"I think you'd make an awfully handsome pair."

She looked at him quickly once more, and then with a slight blush went on with her business.

"I thought him a very nice civil-spoken young fellow," said Mrs. Athelny, "and I think he's just the sort to make any girl happy."

Sally did not reply for a minute or two, and Philip looked at her curiously: it might be thought that she was meditating upon what her mother had said, and on the other hand she might be thinking of the man in the moon.

"Why don't you answer when you're spoken to, Sally?" remarked her mother, a little irritably.

"I thought he was a silly."

"Aren't you going to have him then?"

"No, I'm not."

"I don't know how much more you want," said Mrs. Athelny, and it was quite clear now that she was put out. "He's a very decent young fellow and he can afford to give you a thorough good home. We've got quite enough to feed here without you. If you get a chance like that it's wicked not to take it. And I daresay you'd be able to have a girl to do the rough work."

Philip had never before heard Mrs. Athelny refer so directly to the difficulties of her life. He saw how important it was that each child should be provided for.

"It's no good your carrying on, mother," said Sally in her quiet way. "I'm not going to marry him."

"I think you're a very hard-hearted, cruel, selfish girl."

"If you want me to earn my own living, mother, I can always go into service."

"Don't be so silly, you know your father would never let you do that."

Philip caught Sally's eye, and he thought there was in it a glimmer of amusement. He wondered what there had been in the conversation to touch her sense of humour. She was an odd girl.

Chapter CXVI

DURING HIS LAST YEAR AT ST. LUKE'S PHILIP HAD TO WORK HARD. HE WAS contented with life. He found it very comfortable to be heart free and to have enough money for his needs. He had heard people speak contemptuously of money: he wondered if they had ever tried to do without it. He knew that the lack made a man petty, mean, grasping; it distorted his character and caused him to view the world from a vulgar angle; when you had to consider every penny, money became of grotesque importance: you needed a competency to rate it at its proper value. He lived a solitary life, seeing no one except the Athelnys, but he was not lonely; he busied himself with plans for the future, and sometimes he thought of the past. His recollection dwelled now and then on old friends, but he made no effort to see them. He would have liked to know what was become of Norah Nesbit; she was Norah something else now, but he could not remember the name of the man she was going to marry; he was glad to have known her: she was a good and a brave soul. One evening about half-past eleven he saw Lawson, walking along Piccadilly; he was in evening clothes and might be supposed to be coming back from a theatre. Philip gave way to a sudden impulse and quickly turned down a side-street. He had not seen him for two years and felt that he could not now take up again the interrupted friendship. He and Lawson had nothing more to say to one another. Philip was no longer interested in art; it seemed to him that he was able to enjoy beauty with greater force than when he was a boy; but art appeared to him unimportant. He was occupied with the forming of a pattern out of the manifold chaos of life, and the materials with which he worked seemed to make preoccupation with pigments and words very trivial. Lawson had served his turn. Philip's friendship with him had been a motive in the design he was elaborating: it was merely sentimental to ignore the fact that the painter was of no further interest to him.

Sometimes Philip thought of Mildred. He avoided deliberately the streets in which there was a chance of seeing her; but occasionally some feeling, perhaps curiosity, perhaps something deeper which he would not acknowledge, made him wander about Piccadilly and Regent Street during the hours when she might be expected to be there. He did not know then whether he wished to see her or dreaded it. Once he saw a back which reminded him of hers, and for a moment he thought it was she; it gave him a curious sensation: it was a strange sharp pain in his heart, there was fear in it and a sickening dismay; and when he hurried on and found that he was mistaken he did not know whether it was relief that he experienced or disappointment.

* * *

At the beginning of August Philip passed his Surgery, his last examination, and received his diploma. It was seven years since he had entered St. Luke's Hospital. He was nearly thirty. He walked down the stairs of the Royal College of Surgeons with the roll in his hand which qualified him to practice, and his heart beat with satisfaction.

"Now I'm really going to begin life," he thought.

Next day he went to the secretary's office to put his name down for one of the hospital appointments. The secretary was a pleasant little man with a black beard, whom Philip had always found very affable. He congratulated him on his success, and then said:

"I suppose you wouldn't like to do a locum for a month on the South coast? Three guineas a week with board and lodging."

"I wouldn't mind," said Philip.

"It's at Farnley, in Dorsetshire. Doctor South. You'd have to go down at once; his assistant has developed mumps. I believe it's a very pleasant place."

There was something in the secretary's manner that puzzled Philip. It was a little doubtful.

"What's the crab in it?" he asked.

The secretary hesitated a moment and laughed in a conciliating fashion.

"Well, the fact is, I understand he's rather a crusty, funny old fellow. The agencies won't send him anyone anymore. He speaks his mind very openly, and men don't like it."

"But d'you think he'll be satisfied with a man who's only just qualified? After all I have no experience."

"He ought to be glad to get you," said the secretary diplomatically.

Philip thought for a moment. He had nothing to do for the next few weeks, and he was glad of the chance to earn a bit of money. He could put it aside for the holiday in Spain which he had promised himself when he had finished his appointment at St. Luke's or, if they would not give him anything there, at some other hospital.

"All right. I'll go."

"The only thing is, you must go this afternoon. Will that suit you? If so, I'll send a wire at once."

Philip would have liked a few days to himself; but he had seen the Athelnys the night before (he had gone at once to take them his good news) and there was really no reason why he should not start immediately. He had little luggage to pack. Soon after seven that evening he got out of the station at Farnley and took a cab to Doctor South's. It was a broad low stucco house, with a Virginia creeper growing over it. He was shown into the consulting-room. An old man was writing at a desk. He looked up as the maid ushered Philip in. He did not get up, and he did not speak; he merely stared at Philip. Philip was taken aback.

"I think you're expecting me," he said. "The secretary of St. Luke's wired to you this morning."

"I kept dinner back for half an hour. D'you want to wash?"

"I do," said Philip.

Doctor South amused him by his odd manner. He got up now, and Philip saw that he was a man of middle height, thin, with white hair cut very short and a long mouth closed so tightly that he seemed to have no lips at all; he was clean-shaven but for small white whiskers, and they increased the squareness of face which his firm jaw gave him. He wore a brown tweed suit and a white stock. His clothes hung loosely about him as though they had been made for a much larger man. He looked like a respectable farmer of the middle of the nineteenth century. He opened the door.

"There is the dining-room," he said, pointing to the door opposite. "Your bedroom is the first door you come to when you get on the landing. Come downstairs when you're ready."

During dinner Philip knew that Doctor South was examining him, but he spoke little, and Philip felt that he did not want to hear his assistant talk.

"When were you qualified?" he asked suddenly.

"Yesterday."

"Were you at a university?"

"No."

"Last year when my assistant took a holiday they sent me a 'Varsity man. I told 'em not to do it again. Too damned gentlemanly for me."

There was another pause. The dinner was very simple and very good. Philip preserved a sedate exterior, but in his heart he was bubbling over with excitement. He was immensely elated at being engaged as a locum; it made him feel extremely grown-up; he had an insane desire to laugh at nothing in particular; and the more he thought of his professional dignity the more he was inclined to chuckle.

But Doctor South broke suddenly into his thoughts.

"How old are you?"

"Getting on for thirty."

"How is it you're only just qualified?"

"I didn't go in for the medical till I was nearly twenty-three, and I had to give it up for two years in the middle."

"Why?"

"Poverty."

Doctor South gave him an odd look and relapsed into silence. At the end of dinner he got up from the table.

"D'you know what sort of a practice this is?"

"No," answered Philip.

"Mostly fishermen and their families. I have the Union and the Seamen's Hospital. I used to be alone here, but since they tried to make this into a fashionable seaside resort a man has set up on the cliff, and the well-to-do people go to him. I only have those who can't afford to pay for a doctor at all."

Philip saw that the rivalry was a sore point with the old man.

"You know that I have no experience," said Philip.

"You none of you know anything."

He walked out of the room without another word and left Philip by himself. When the maid came in to clear away she told Philip that Doctor South saw patients from six till seven. Work for that night was over. Philip fetched a book from his room, lit his pipe, and settled himself down to read. It was a great comfort, since he had read nothing but medical books for the last few months. At ten o'clock Doctor South came in and looked at him. Philip hated not to have his feet up, and he had dragged up a chair for them.

"You seem able to make yourself pretty comfortable," said Doctor South, with a grimness which would have disturbed Philip if he had not been in such high spirits.

Philip's eyes twinkled as he answered.

"Have you any objection?"

Doctor South gave him a look, but did not reply directly.

"What's that you're reading?"

"*Peregrine Pickle*. Smollett."

"I happen to know that Smollett wrote *Peregrine Pickle*."

"I beg your pardon. Medical men aren't much interested in literature, are they?"

Philip had put the book down on the table, and Doctor South took it up. It was a volume of an edition which had belonged to the Vicar of Blackstable. It was a thin book bound in faded morocco, with a copper-plate engraving as a frontispiece; the pages were musty with age and stained with mould. Philip, without meaning to, started forward a little as Doctor South took the volume in his hands, and a slight smile came into his eyes. Very little escaped the old doctor.

"Do I amuse you?" he asked icily.

"I see you're fond of books. You can always tell by the way people handle them."

Doctor South put down the novel immediately.

"Breakfast at eight-thirty," he said and left the room.

"What a funny old fellow!" thought Philip.

He soon discovered why Doctor South's assistants found it difficult to get on with him. In the first place, he set his face firmly against all the discoveries of the last thirty years: he had no patience with the drugs which became modish, were thought to work marvellous cures, and in a few years were discarded; he had stock mixtures which he had brought from St. Luke's, where he had been a student, and had used all his life; he found them just as efficacious as anything that had come into fashion since. Philip was startled at Doctor South's suspicion of asepsis; he had accepted it in deference to universal opinion; but he used the precautions which Philip had known insisted upon so scrupulously at the hospital with the disdainful tolerance of a man playing at soldiers with children.

"I've seen antiseptics come along and sweep everything before them, and then I've seen asepsis take their place. Bunkum!"

The young men who were sent down to him knew only hospital practice; and they came with the unconcealed scorn for the General Practitioner which they had absorbed in the air at the hospital; but they had seen only the complicated cases which appeared in the wards; they knew how to treat an obscure disease of the suprarenal bodies, but were helpless when consulted for a cold in the head. Their knowledge was theoretical and their self-assurance unbounded. Doctor South watched them with tightened lips; he took a savage pleasure in showing them how great was their ignorance and how unjustified their conceit. It was a poor practice, of fishing-folk, and the doctor made up his own prescriptions. Doctor South asked his assistant how he expected to make both ends meet if he gave a fisherman with a stomach-ache a mixture consisting of half a dozen expensive drugs. He complained too that the young medical men were uneducated: their reading consisted of *The Sporting Times* and *The British Medical Journal*; they could neither write a legible hand nor spell correctly. For two or three days Doctor South watched Philip closely, ready to fall on him with acid sarcasm if he gave him the opportunity; and Philip, aware of this, went about his work with a quiet sense of amusement. He was pleased with the change of occupation. He liked the feeling of independence and of responsibility. All sorts of people came to the consulting-room. He was gratified because he seemed able to inspire his patients with confidence; and it was entertaining to watch the process of cure which at a hospital necessarily could be watched only at distant intervals. His rounds took him into low-roofed cottages in which were fishing tackle and sails and here and there mementoes of deep-sea travelling, a lacquer box from Japan, spears and oars from Melanesia, or daggers from the bazaars of Stamboul; there was an air of romance in the stuffy little rooms, and the salt of the sea gave them a bitter freshness. Philip liked to talk to the sailor-men, and when they found that he was not supercilious they told him long yarns of the distant journeys of their youth.

Once or twice he made a mistake in diagnosis (he had never seen a case of measles before, and when he was confronted with the rash took it for an obscure disease of the skin); and once or twice his ideas of treatment differed from Doctor South's. The first time this happened Doctor South attacked him with savage irony; but Philip took it with good humour; he had some gift for repartee, and he made one or two answers which caused Doctor South to stop and look at him curiously. Philip's face was grave, but his eyes were twinkling. The old gentleman could not avoid the impression that Philip was chaffing him. He was used to being disliked and feared by his assistants, and this was a new experience. He had half a mind to fly into a passion and pack Philip off by the next train, he had done that before with his assistants; but he had an uneasy feeling that Philip then would simply laugh at him outright; and suddenly he felt amused. His mouth formed itself into a smile against his will, and he turned away. In a little while he grew conscious that Philip was amusing himself systematically at his expense. He was taken aback at first and then diverted.

"Damn his impudence," he chuckled to himself. "Damn his impudence."

Chapter CXVII

PHILIP HAD WRITTEN TO ATHELNY TO TELL HIM THAT HE WAS DOING A locum in Dorsetshire and in due course received an answer from him. It was written in the formal manner he affected, studded with pompous epithets as a Persian diadem was studded with precious stones; and in the beautiful hand, like black letter and as difficult to read, upon which he prided himself. He suggested that Philip should join him and his family in the Kentish hop-field to which he went every year; and to persuade him said various beautiful and complicated things about Philip's soul and the winding tendrils of the hops. Philip replied at once that he would come on the first day he was free. Though not born there, he had a peculiar affection for the Isle of Thanet, and he was fired with enthusiasm at the thought of spending a fortnight so close to the earth and amid conditions which needed only a blue sky to be as idyllic as the olive groves of Arcady.

The four weeks of his engagement at Farnley passed quickly. On the cliff a new town was springing up, with red brick villas round golf links, and a large hotel had recently been opened to cater for the summer visitors; but Philip went there seldom. Down below, by the harbour, the little stone houses of a past century were clustered in a delightful confusion, and the narrow streets, climbing down steeply, had an air of antiquity which appealed to the imagination. By the water's edge were neat cottages with trim, tiny gardens in front of them; they were inhabited by retired captains in the merchant service, and by mothers or widows of men who had gained their living by the sea; and they had an appearance which was quaint and peaceful. In the little harbour came tramps from Spain and the Levant, ships of small tonnage; and now and then a windjammer was borne in by the winds of romance. It reminded Philip of the dirty little harbour with its colliers at Blackstable, and he thought that there he had first acquired the desire, which was now an obsession, for Eastern lands and sunlit islands in a tropic sea. But here you felt yourself closer to the wide, deep ocean than on the shore of that North Sea which seemed always circumscribed; here you could draw a long breath as you looked out upon the even vastness; and the west wind, the dear soft salt wind of England, uplifted the heart and at the same time melted it to tenderness.

One evening, when Philip had reached his last week with Doctor South, a child came to the surgery door while the old doctor and Philip were making up prescriptions. It was a little ragged girl with a dirty face and bare feet. Philip opened the door.

"Please, sir, will you come to Mrs. Fletcher's in Ivy Lane at once?"

"What's the matter with Mrs. Fletcher?" called out Doctor South in his rasping voice.

The child took no notice of him, but addressed herself again to Philip.

"Please, sir, her little boy's had an accident and will you come at once?"

"Tell Mrs. Fletcher I'm coming," called out Doctor South.

The little girl hesitated for a moment, and putting a dirty finger in a dirty mouth stood still and looked at Philip.

"What's the matter, Kid?" said Philip, smiling.

"Please, sir, Mrs. Fletcher says, will the new doctor come?"

There was a sound in the dispensary and Doctor South came out into the passage.

"Isn't Mrs. Fletcher satisfied with me?" he barked. "I've attended Mrs. Fletcher since she was born. Why aren't I good enough to attend her filthy brat?"

The little girl looked for a moment as though she were going to cry, then she thought better of it; she put out her tongue deliberately at Doctor South, and, before he could recover from his astonishment, bolted off as fast as she could run. Philip saw that the old gentleman was annoyed.

"You look rather fagged, and it's a goodish way to Ivy Lane," he said, by way of giving him an excuse not to go himself.

Doctor South gave a low snarl.

"It's a damned sight nearer for a man who's got the use of both legs than for a man who's only got one and a half."

Philip reddened and stood silent for a while.

"Do you wish me to go or will you go yourself?" he said at last frigidly.

"What's the good of my going? They want you."

Philip took up his hat and went to see the patient. It was hard upon eight o'clock when he came back. Doctor South was standing in the dining-room with his back to the fireplace.

"You've been a long time," he said.

"I'm sorry. Why didn't you start dinner?"

"Because I chose to wait. Have you been all this while at Mrs. Fletcher's?"

"No, I'm afraid I haven't. I stopped to look at the sunset on my way back, and I didn't think of the time."

Doctor South did not reply, and the servant brought in some grilled sprats. Philip ate them with an excellent appetite. Suddenly Doctor South shot a question at him.

"Why did you look at the sunset?"

Philip answered with his mouth full.

"Because I was happy."

Doctor South gave him an odd look, and the shadow of a smile flickered across his old, tired face. They ate the rest of the dinner in silence; but when the maid had given them the port and left the room, the old man leaned back and fixed his sharp eyes on Philip.

"It stung you up a bit when I spoke of your game leg, young fellow?" he said.

"People always do, directly or indirectly, when they get angry with me."

"I suppose they know it's your weak point."

Philip faced him and looked at him steadily.

"Are you very glad to have discovered it?"

The doctor did not answer, but he gave a chuckle of bitter mirth. They sat for a while staring at one another. Then Doctor South surprised Philip extremely.

"Why don't you stay here and I'll get rid of that damned fool with his mumps?"

"It's very kind of you, but I hope to get an appointment at the hospital in the autumn. It'll help me so much in getting other work later."

"I'm offering you a partnership," said Doctor South grumpily.

"Why?" asked Philip, with surprise.

"They seem to like you down here."

"I didn't think that was a fact which altogether met with your approval," Philip said drily.

"D'you suppose that after forty years' practice I care a twopenny damn whether people prefer my assistant to me? No, my friend. There's no sentiment between my patients and me. I don't expect gratitude from them, I expect them to pay my fees. Well, what d'you say to it?"

Philip made no reply, not because he was thinking over the proposal, but because he was astonished. It was evidently very unusual for someone to offer a partnership to a newly qualified man; and he realised with wonder that, although nothing would induce him to say so, Doctor South had taken a fancy to him. He thought how amused the secretary at St. Luke's would be when he told him.

"The practice brings in about seven hundred a year. We can reckon out how much your share would be worth, and you can pay me off by degrees. And when I die you can succeed me. I think that's better than knocking about hospitals for two or three years, and then taking assistantships until you can afford to set up for yourself."

Philip knew it was a chance that most people in his profession would jump at; the profession was overcrowded, and half the men he knew would be thankful to accept the certainty of even so modest a competence as that.

"I'm awfully sorry, but I can't," he said. "It means giving up everything I've aimed at for years. In one way and another I've had a roughish time, but I always had that one hope before me, to get qualified so that I might travel; and now, when I wake in the morning, my bones simply ache to get off, I don't mind where particularly, but just away, to places I've never been to."

Now the goal seemed very near. He would have finished his appointment at St. Luke's by the middle of the following year, and then he would go to Spain; he could afford to spend several months there, rambling up and down the land which stood to him for romance; after that he would get a ship and go to the East. Life was before him and time of no account. He could wander, for years if he chose, in unfrequented places, amid strange peoples, where life was led in strange ways. He did not know what he sought or what his journeys would bring him; but he had a feeling that he would learn something new about life and gain some clue to the mystery that he had solved only to find more mysterious. And even if he found nothing he would allay the unrest which gnawed at his heart. But Doctor South was showing him a great kindness, and it seemed ungrateful to refuse his offer for no adequate reason; so in his shy way, trying to appear as matter of fact as possible, he made some attempt to explain why it was so important to him to carry out the plans he had cherished so passionately.

Doctor South listened quietly, and a gentle look came into his shrewd old eyes. It seemed to Philip an added kindness that he did not press him to accept his offer. Benevolence is often very peremptory. He appeared to look upon Philip's reasons as sound. Dropping the subject, he began to talk of his own youth; he had been in the Royal Navy, and it was his long connection with the sea that, when he retired, had made him settle at Farnley. He told Philip of old days in the Pacific and of wild adventures in China. He had taken part in an expedition against the head-hunters of Borneo and had known Samoa when it was still an independent state. He had touched at coral islands. Philip listened to him entranced. Little by little he told Philip about himself. Doctor South was a widower, his wife had died thirty years before, and his daughter had married a farmer in Rhodesia; he had quarrelled with him, and she had not come to England for ten years. It was just as if he had never had wife or child. He was very lonely. His gruffness was little more than a protection which he wore to hide a complete disillusionment; and to Philip it seemed tragic to see him just waiting for death, not impatiently, but rather with loathing for it, hating old age and unable to resign himself to its limitations, and yet with the feeling that death was the only solution of the bitterness of his life. Philip crossed his path, and the natural affection which long separation from his daughter had killed—she had taken her husband's part in the quarrel and her children he had never seen—settled itself upon Philip. At first it made him angry, he told himself it was a sign of dotage; but there was something in Philip that attracted him, and he found himself smiling at him he knew not why. Philip did not bore him. Once or twice he put his hand on his shoulder: it was as near a caress as he had got since his daughter left England so many years before. When the time came for Philip to go Doctor South accompanied him to the station: he found himself unaccountably depressed.

"I've had a ripping time here," said Philip. "You've been awfully kind to me."

"I suppose you're very glad to go?"

"I've enjoyed myself here."

"But you want to get out into the world? Ah, you have youth." He hesitated a moment. "I want you to remember that if you change your mind my offer still stands."

"That's awfully kind of you."

Philip shook hands with him out of the carriage window, and the train steamed out of the station. Philip thought of the fortnight he was going to spend in the hopfield: he was happy at the idea of seeing his friends again, and he rejoiced because the day was fine. But Doctor South walked slowly back to his empty house. He felt very old and very lonely.

Chapter CXVIII

It was late in the evening when Philip arrived at Ferne. It was Mrs. Athelny's native village, and she had been accustomed from her childhood to pick in the hop-field to which with her husband and her children she still went every year. Like many Kentish folk her family had gone out regularly, glad to earn a little money, but especially regarding the annual outing, looked forward to for months, as the best of holidays. The work was not hard, it was done in common, in the open air, and for the children it was a long, delightful picnic; here the young men met the maidens; in the long evenings when work was over they wandered about the lanes, making love; and the hopping season was generally followed by weddings. They went out in carts with bedding, pots and pans, chairs and tables; and Ferne while the hopping lasted was deserted. They were very exclusive and would have resented the intrusion of foreigners, as they called the people who came from London; they looked down upon them and feared them too; they were a rough lot, and the respectable country-folk did not want to mix with them. In the old days the hoppers slept in barns, but ten years ago a row of huts had been erected at the side of a meadow; and the Athelnys, like many others, had the same hut every year.

Athelny met Philip at the station in a cart he had borrowed from the public-house at which he had got a room for Philip. It was a quarter of a mile from the hop-field. They left his bag there and walked over to the meadow in which were the huts. They were nothing more than a long, low shed, divided into little rooms about twelve feet square. In front of each was a fire of sticks, round which a family was grouped, eagerly watching the cooking of supper. The sea-air and the sun had browned already the faces of Athelny's children. Mrs. Athelny seemed a different woman in her sun-bonnet: you felt that the long years in the city had made no real difference to her; she was the country woman born and bred, and you could see how much at home she found herself in the country. She was frying bacon and at the same time keeping an eye on the younger children, but she had a hearty handshake and a jolly smile for Philip. Athelny was enthusiastic over the delights of a rural existence.

"We're starved for sun and light in the cities we live in. It isn't life, it's a long imprisonment. Let us sell all we have, Betty, and take a farm in the country."

"I can see you in the country," she answered with good-humoured scorn. "Why, the first rainy day we had in the winter you'd be crying for London." She turned to Philip. "Athelny's always like this when we come down here. Country, I like that! Why, he don't know a swede from a mangel wurzel."

"Daddy was lazy today," remarked Jane, with the frankness which characterised her, "he didn't fill one bin."

"I'm getting into practice, child, and tomorrow I shall fill more bins than all of you put together."

"Come and eat your supper, children," said Mrs. Athelny. "Where's Sally?"

"Here I am, mother."

She stepped out of their little hut, and the flames of the wood fire leaped up and cast sharp colour upon her face. Of late Philip had only seen her in the trim frocks she had taken to since she was at the dressmaker's, and there was something very charming in the print dress she wore now, loose and easy to work in; the sleeves were tucked up and showed her strong, round arms. She too had a sun-bonnet.

"You look like a milkmaid in a fairy story," said Philip, as he shook hands with her.

"She's the belle of the hop-fields," said Athelny. "My word, if the Squire's son sees you he'll make you an offer of marriage before you can say Jack Robinson."

"The Squire hasn't got a son, father," said Sally.

She looked about for a place to sit down in, and Philip made room for her beside him. She looked wonderful in the night lit by wood fires. She was like some rural goddess, and you thought of those fresh, strong girls whom old Herrick had praised in exquisite numbers. The supper was simple, bread and butter, crisp bacon, tea for the children, and beer for Mr. and Mrs. Athelny and Philip. Athelny, eating hungrily, praised loudly all he ate. He flung words of scorn at Lucullus and piled invectives upon Brillat-Savarin.

"There's one thing one can say for you, Athelny," said his wife, "you do enjoy your food and no mistake!"

"Cooked by your hand, my Betty," he said, stretching out an eloquent forefinger.

Philip felt himself very comfortable. He looked happily at the line of fires, with people grouped about them, and the colour of the flames against the night; at the end of the meadow was a line of great elms, and above the starry sky. The children talked and laughed, and Athelny, a child among them, made them roar by his tricks and fancies.

"They think a rare lot of Athelny down here," said his wife. "Why, Mrs. Bridges said to me, I don't know what we should do without Mr. Athelny now, she said. He's always up to something, he's more like a schoolboy than the father of a family."

Sally sat in silence, but she attended to Philip's wants in a thoughtful fashion that charmed him. It was pleasant to have her beside him, and now and then he glanced at her sunburned, healthy face. Once he caught her eyes, and she smiled quietly. When supper was over Jane and a small brother were sent down to a brook that ran at the bottom of the meadow to fetch a pail of water for washing up.

"You children, show your Uncle Philip where we sleep, and then you must be thinking of going to bed."

Small hands seized Philip, and he was dragged towards the hut. He went in and struck a match. There was no furniture in it; and beside a tin box, in which clothes were kept, there was nothing but the beds; there were three of them, one against each wall. Athelny followed Philip in and showed them proudly.

"That's the stuff to sleep on," he cried. "None of your spring-mattresses and swansdown. I never sleep so soundly anywhere as here. *You* will sleep between sheets. My dear fellow, I pity you from the bottom of my soul."

The beds consisted of a thick layer of hopbine, on the top of which was a coating of straw, and this was covered with a blanket. After a day in the open air, with the aromatic scent of the hops all round them, the happy pickers slept like tops. By nine o'clock all was quiet in the meadow and everyone in bed but one or two men who still lingered in the public-house and would not come back till it was closed at ten. Athelny walked there with Philip. But before he went Mrs. Athelny said to him:

"We breakfast about a quarter to six, but I daresay you won't want to get up as early as that. You see, we have to set to work at six."

"Of course he must get up early," cried Athelny, "and he must work like the rest of us. He's got to earn his board. No work, no dinner, my lad."

"The children go down to bathe before breakfast, and they can give you a call on their way back. They pass The Jolly Sailor."

"If they'll wake me I'll come and bathe with them," said Philip.

Jane and Harold and Edward shouted with delight at the prospect, and next morning Philip was awakened out of a sound sleep by their bursting into his room. The boys jumped on his bed, and he had to chase them out with his slippers. He put on a coat and a pair of trousers and went down. The day had only just broken, and there was a nip in the air; but the sky was cloudless, and the sun was shining yellow. Sally, holding Connie's hand, was standing in the middle of the road, with a towel and a bathing-dress over her arm. He saw now that her sun-bonnet was of the colour of lavender, and against it her face, red and brown, was like an apple. She greeted him with her slow, sweet smile, and he noticed suddenly that her teeth were small and regular and very white. He wondered why they had never caught his attention before.

"I was for letting you sleep on," she said, "but they would go up and wake you. I said you didn't really want to come."

"Oh, yes, I did."

They walked down the road and then cut across the marshes. That way it was under a mile to the sea. The water looked cold and grey, and Philip shivered at the sight of it; but the others tore off their clothes and ran in shouting. Sally did everything a little slowly, and she did not come into the water till all the rest were splashing round Philip. Swimming was his only accomplishment; he felt at home in the water; and soon he had them all imitating him as he played at being a porpoise, and a drowning man, and a fat lady afraid of wetting her hair. The bathe was uproarious, and it was necessary for Sally to be very severe to induce them all to come out.

"You're as bad as any of them," she said to Philip, in her grave, maternal way, which was at once comic and touching. "They're not anything like so naughty when you're not here."

They walked back, Sally with her bright hair streaming over one shoulder and her sun-bonnet in her hand, but when they got to the huts Mrs. Athelny had already started for the hop-garden. Athleny, in a pair of the oldest trousers anyone had ever worn, his jacket buttoned up to show he had no shirt on, and in a wide-brimmed soft hat, was frying kippers over a fire of sticks. He was delighted with himself: he looked every inch a brigand. As soon as he saw the party he began to shout the witches' chorus from *Macbeth* over the odorous kippers.

"You mustn't dawdle over your breakfast or mother will be angry," he said, when they came up.

And in a few minutes, Harold and Jane with pieces of bread and butter in their hands, they sauntered through the meadow into the hop-field. They were the last to leave. A hop-garden was one of the sights connected with Philip's boyhood and the oast-houses to him the most typical feature of the Kentish scene. It was with no sense of strangeness, but as though he were at home, that Philip followed Sally through the long lines of the hops. The sun was bright now and cast a sharp shadow. Philip feasted his eyes on the richness of the green leaves. The hops were yellowing, and to him they had the beauty and the passion which poets in Sicily have found in the purple grape. As they walked along Philip felt himself overwhelmed by the rich luxuriance. A sweet scent arose from the fat Kentish soil, and the fitful September breeze was heavy with the goodly perfume of the hops. Athelstan felt the exhilaration instinctively, for he lifted up his voice and sang; it was the cracked voice of the boy of fifteen, and Sally turned round.

"You be quiet, Athelstan, or we shall have a thunderstorm."

In a moment they heard the hum of voices, and in a moment more came upon the pickers. They were all hard at work, talking and laughing as they picked. They sat on chairs, on stools, on boxes, with their baskets by their sides, and some stood by the bin throwing the hops they picked straight into it. There were a lot of children about and a good many babies, some in makeshift cradles, some tucked up in a rug on the soft brown dry earth. The children picked a little and played a great deal. The women worked busily, they had been pickers from childhood, and they could pick twice as fast as foreigners from London. They boasted about the number of bushels they had picked in a day, but they complained you could not make money now as in former times: then they paid you a shilling for five bushels, but now the rate was eight and even nine bushels to the shilling. In the old days a good picker could earn enough in the season to keep her for the rest of the year, but now there was nothing in it; you got a holiday for nothing, and that was about all. Mrs. Hill had bought herself a pianner out of what she made picking, so she said, but she was very near, one wouldn't like to be near like that, and most people thought it was only what she said, if the truth was known perhaps it would be found that she had put a bit of money from the savings bank towards it.

The hoppers were divided into bin companies of ten pickers, not counting children, and Athelny loudly boasted of the day when he would have a company consisting entirely of his own family. Each company had a bin-man, whose duty it was to supply it with strings of hops at their bins (the bin was a large sack on a wooden frame, about seven feet high, and long rows of them were placed between the rows of hops); and it was to this position that Athelny aspired when his family was old enough to form a company. Meanwhile he worked rather by encouraging others than by exertions of his own. He sauntered up to Mrs. Athelny, who had been busy for half an hour and had already emptied a basket into the bin, and with his cigarette between his lips began to pick. He asserted that he was going to pick more than anyone that day, but mother; of course no one could pick so much as mother; that reminded him of the trials which Aphrodite put upon the curious Psyche, and he began to tell his children the story of her love for the unseen bridegroom. He told it very well. It seemed to Philip, listening with a smile on his lips, that the old tale fitted in with the scene. The sky was very blue now, and he thought it could not be more lovely even in Greece. The children with their fair hair and rosy cheeks, strong, healthy, and vivacious; the delicate form of the hops; the challenging emerald of the leaves, like a blare of trumpets; the magic of the green alley, narrowing to a point as you looked down the row, with the pickers in their sun-bonnets: perhaps there was more of the Greek spirit there than you could find in the books of professors or in museums. He was thankful for the beauty of England. He thought of the winding white roads and the hedgerows, the green meadows with their elm-trees, the delicate line of the hills and the copses that crowned them, the flatness of the marshes, and the melancholy of the North Sea. He was very glad that he felt its loveliness. But presently Athelny grew restless and announced that he would go and ask how Robert Kemp's mother was. He knew everyone in the garden and called them all by their Christian names; he knew their family histories and all that had happened to them from birth. With harmless vanity he played the fine gentleman among them, and there was a touch of condescension in his familiarity. Philip would not go with him.

"I'm going to earn my dinner," he said.

"Quite right, my boy," answered Athelny, with a wave of the hand, as he strolled away. "No work, no dinner."

Chapter CXIX

PHILIP HAD NOT A BASKET OF HIS OWN, BUT SAT WITH SALLY. JANE THOUGHT it monstrous that he should help her elder sister rather than herself, and he had to promise to pick for her when Sally's basket was full. Sally was almost as quick as her mother.

"Won't it hurt your hands for sewing?" asked Philip.

"Oh, no, it wants soft hands. That's why women pick better than men. If your hands are hard and your fingers all stiff with a lot of rough work you can't pick near so well."

He liked to see her deft movements, and she watched him too now and then with that maternal spirit of hers which was so amusing and yet so charming. He was clumsy at first, and she laughed at him. When she bent over and showed him how best to deal with a whole line their hands met. He was surprised to see her blush. He could not persuade himself that she was a woman; because he had known her as a flapper, he could not help looking upon her as a child still; yet the number of her admirers showed that she was a child no longer; and though they had only been down a few days one of Sally's cousins was already so attentive that she had to endure a lot of chaffing. His name was Peter Gann, and he was the son of Mrs. Athelny's sister, who had married a farmer near Ferne. Everyone knew why he found it necessary to walk through the hop-field every day.

A call-off by the sounding of a horn was made for breakfast at eight, and though Mrs. Athelny told them they had not deserved it, they ate it very heartily. They set to work again and worked till twelve, when the horn sounded once more for dinner. At intervals the measurer went his round from bin to bin, accompanied by the booker, who entered first in his own book and then in the hopper's the number of bushels picked. As each bin was filled it was measured out in bushel baskets into a huge bag called a poke; and this the measurer and the pole-puller carried off between them and put on the wagon. Athelny came back now and then with stories of how much Mrs. Heath or Mrs. Jones had picked, and he conjured his family to beat her: he was always wanting to make records, and sometimes in his enthusiasm picked steadily for an hour. His chief amusement in it, however, was that it showed the beauty of his graceful hands, of which he was excessively proud. He spent much time manicuring them. He told Philip, as he stretched out his tapering fingers, that the Spanish grandees had always slept in oiled gloves to preserve their whiteness. The hand that wrung the throat of Europe, he remarked dramatically, was as shapely and exquisite as a woman's; and he looked at his own, as he delicately picked the hops, and sighed with self-satisfaction. When he grew tired of this he rolled himself a cigarette and discoursed to Philip of art and literature. In the afternoon it grew very hot. Work did not proceed so actively and conversation halted. The incessant chatter of the morning dwindled now to desultory remarks. Tiny beads of sweat stood on Sally's upper lip, and as she worked her lips were slightly parted. She was like a rosebud bursting into flower.

Calling-off time depended on the state of the oast-house. Sometimes it was filled early, and as many hops had been picked by three or four as could be dried during the night. Then work was stopped. But generally the last measuring of the day began at five. As each company had its bin measured it gathered up its things and, chatting again now that work was over, sauntered out of the garden. The women went back to the huts to clean up and prepare the supper, while a good many of the men strolled down the road to the public-house. A glass of beer was very pleasant after the day's work.

The Athelnys' bin was the last to be dealt with. When the measurer came Mrs. Athelny, with a sigh of relief, stood up and stretched her arms: she had been sitting in the same position for many hours and was stiff.

"Now, let's go to The Jolly Sailor," said Athelny. "The rites of the day must be duly performed, and there is none more sacred than that."

"Take a jug with you, Athelny," said his wife, "and bring back a pint and a half for supper."

She gave him the money, copper by copper. The bar-parlour was already well filled. It had a sanded floor, benches round it, and yellow pictures of Victorian prize-fighters on the walls. The licencee knew all his customers by name, and he leaned over his bar smiling benignly at two young men who were throwing rings on a stick that stood up from the floor: their failure was greeted with a good deal of hearty chaff from the rest of the company. Room was made for the new arrivals. Philip found himself sitting between an old labourer in corduroys, with string tied under his knees, and a shiny-faced lad of seventeen with a love-lock neatly plastered on his red forehead. Athelny insisted on trying his hand at the throwing of rings. He backed himself for half a pint and won it. As he drank the loser's health he said:

"I would sooner have won this than won the Derby, my boy."

He was an outlandish figure, with his wide-brimmed hat and pointed beard, among those country-folk, and it was easy to see that they thought him very queer; but his spirits were so high, his enthusiasm so contagious, that it was impossible not to like him. Conversation went easily. A certain number of pleasantries were exchanged in the broad, slow accent of the Isle of Thanet, and there was uproarious laughter at the sallies of the local wag. A pleasant gathering! It would have been a hard-hearted person who did not feel a glow of satisfaction in his fellows. Philip's eyes wandered out of the window where it was bright and sunny still; there were little white curtains in it tied up with red ribbon like those of a cottage window, and on the sill were pots of geraniums. In due course one by one the idlers got up and sauntered back to the meadow where supper was cooking.

"I expect you'll be ready for your bed," said Mrs. Athelny to Philip. "You're not used to getting up at five and staying in the open air all day."

"You're coming to bathe with us, Uncle Phil, aren't you?" the boys cried.

"Rather."

He was tired and happy. After supper, balancing himself against the wall of the hut on a chair without a back, he smoked his pipe and looked at the night. Sally was busy. She passed in and out of the hut, and he lazily watched her methodical actions. Her walk attracted his notice; it was not particularly graceful, but it was easy and assured; she swung her legs from the hips, and her feet seemed to tread the earth with decision. Athelny had gone off to gossip with one of the neighbours, and presently Philip heard his wife address the world in general.

"There now, I'm out of tea and I wanted Athelny to go down to Mrs. Black's and get some." A pause, and then her voice was raised: "Sally, just run down to Mrs. Black's and get me half a pound of tea, will you? I've run quite out of it."

"All right, mother."

Mrs. Black had a cottage about half a mile along the road, and she combined the office of postmistress with that of universal provider. Sally came out of the hut, turning down her sleeves.

"Shall I come with you, Sally?" asked Philip.

"Don't you trouble. I'm not afraid to go alone."

"I didn't think you were; but it's getting near my bed-time, and I was just thinking I'd like to stretch my legs."

Sally did not answer, and they set out together. The road was white and silent. There was not a sound in the summer night. They did not speak much.

"It's quite hot even now, isn't it?" said Philip.

"I think it's wonderful for the time of year."

But their silence did not seem awkward. They found it was pleasant to walk side by side and felt no need of words. Suddenly at a stile in the hedgerow they heard a low murmur of voices, and in the darkness they saw the outline of two people. They were sitting very close to one another and did not move as Philip and Sally passed.

"I wonder who that was," said Sally.

"They looked happy enough, didn't they?"

"I expect they took us for lovers too."

They saw the light of the cottage in front of them, and in a minute went into the little shop. The glare dazzled them for a moment.

"You are late," said Mrs. Black. "I was just going to shut up." She looked at the clock. "Getting on for nine."

Sally asked for her half-pound of tea (Mrs. Athelny could never bring herself to buy more than half a pound at a time), and they set off up the road again. Now and then some beast of the night made a short, sharp sound, but it seemed only to make the silence more marked.

"I believe if you stood still you could hear the sea," said Sally.

They strained their ears, and their fancy presented them with a faint sound of little waves lapping up against the shingle. When they passed the stile again the lovers were still there, but now they were not speaking; they were in one another's arms, and the man's lips were pressed against the girl's.

"They seem busy," said Sally.

They turned a corner, and a breath of warm wind beat for a moment against their faces. The earth gave forth its freshness. There was something strange in the tremulous night, and something, you knew not what, seemed to be waiting; the silence was on a sudden pregnant with meaning. Philip had a queer feeling in his heart, it seemed very full, it seemed to melt (the hackneyed phrases expressed precisely the curious sensation), he felt happy and anxious and expectant. To his memory came back those lines in which Jessica and Lorenzo murmur melodious words to one another, capping each other's utterance; but passion shines bright and clear through the conceits that amuse them. He did not know what there was in the air that made his senses so strangely alert; it seemed to him that he was pure soul to enjoy the scents and the sounds and the savours of the earth. He had never felt such an exquisite capacity for beauty. He was afraid that Sally by speaking would break the spell, but she said never a word, and he wanted to hear the sound of her voice. Its low richness was the voice of the country night itself.

They arrived at the field through which she had to walk to get back to the huts. Philip went in to hold the gate open for her.

"Well, here I think I'll say good-night."

"Thank you for coming all that way with me."

She gave him her hand, and as he took it, he said:

"If you were very nice you'd kiss me good-night like the rest of the family."

"I don't mind," she said.

Philip had spoken in jest. He merely wanted to kiss her, because he was happy and he liked her and the night was so lovely.

"Good-night then," he said, with a little laugh, drawing her towards him.

She gave him her lips; they were warm and full and soft; he lingered a little, they were like a flower; then, he knew not how, without meaning it, he flung his arms round her. She yielded quite silently. Her body was firm and strong. He felt her heart beat against his. Then he lost his head. His senses overwhelmed him like a flood of rushing waters. He drew her into the darker shadow of the hedge.

Chapter CXX

PHILIP SLEPT LIKE A LOG AND AWOKE WITH A START TO FIND HAROLD TICKling his face with a feather. There was a shout of delight when he opened his eyes. He was drunken with sleep.

"Come on, lazy bones," said Jane. "Sally says she won't wait for you unless you hurry up."

Then he remembered what had happened. His heart sank, and, half out of bed already, he stopped; he did not know how he was going to face her; he was overwhelmed with a sudden rush of self-reproach, and bitterly, bitterly, he regretted what he had done. What would she say to him that morning? He dreaded meeting her, and he asked himself how he could have been such a fool. But the children gave him no time; Edward took his bathing-drawers and his towel, Athelstan tore the bed-clothes away; and in three minutes they all clattered down into the road. Sally gave him a smile. It was as sweet and innocent as it had ever been.

"You do take a time to dress yourself," she said. "I thought you was never coming."

There was not a particle of difference in her manner. He had expected some change, subtle or abrupt; he fancied that there would be shame in the way she treated him, or anger, or perhaps some increase of familiarity; but there was nothing. She was exactly the same as before. They walked towards the sea all together, talking and laughing; and Sally was quiet, but she was always that, reserved, but he had never seen her otherwise, and gentle. She neither sought conversation with him nor avoided it. Philip was astounded. He had expected the incident of the night before to have caused some revolution in her, but it was just as though nothing had happened; it might have been a dream; and as he walked along, a little girl holding on to one hand and a little boy to the other, while he chatted as unconcernedly as he could, he sought for an explanation. He wondered whether Sally meant the affair to be forgotten. Perhaps her senses had run away with her just as his had, and, treating what had occurred as an accident due to unusual circumstances, it might be that she had decided to put the matter out of her mind. It was ascribing to her a power of thought and a mature wisdom which fitted neither with her age nor with her character. But he realised that he knew nothing of her. There had been in her always something enigmatic.

They played leap-frog in the water, and the bathe was as uproarious as on the previous day. Sally mothered them all, keeping a watchful eye on them, and calling to them when they went out too far. She swam staidly backwards and forwards while the others got up to their larks, and now and then turned on her back to float. Presently she went out and began drying herself; she called to the others more or less peremptorily, and at last only Philip was left in the water. He took the opportunity to have a good hard swim. He was more used to the cold water this second morning, and he revelled in its salt freshness; it rejoiced him to use his limbs freely, and he covered the water with long, firm strokes. But Sally, with a towel round her, went down to the water's edge.

"You're to come out this minute, Philip," she called, as though he were a small boy under her charge.

And when, smiling with amusement at her authoritative way, he came towards her, she upbraided him.

"It is naughty of you to stay in so long. Your lips are quite blue, and just look at your teeth, they're chattering."

"All right. I'll come out."

She had never talked to him in that manner before. It was as though what had happened gave her a sort of right over him, and she looked upon him as a child to be cared for. In a few minutes they were dressed, and they started to walk back. Sally noticed his hands.

"Just look, they're quite blue."

"Oh, that's all right. It's only the circulation. I shall get the blood back in a minute."

"Give them to me."

She took his hands in hers and rubbed them, first one and then the other, till the colour returned. Philip, touched and puzzled, watched her. He could not say anything to her on account of the children, and he did not meet her eyes; but he was sure they did not avoid his purposely, it just happened that they did not meet. And during the day there was nothing in her behaviour to suggest a consciousness in her that anything had passed between them. Perhaps she was a little more talkative than usual. When they were all sitting again in the hop-field she told her mother how naughty Philip had been in not coming out of the water till he was blue with cold. It was incredible, and yet it seemed that the only effect of the incident of the night before was to arouse in her a feeling of protection towards him: she had the same instinctive desire to mother him as she had with regard to her brothers and sisters.

It was not till the evening that he found himself alone with her. She was cooking the supper, and Philip was sitting on the grass by the side of the fire. Mrs. Athelny had gone down to the village to do some shopping, and the children were scattered in various pursuits of their own. Philip hesitated to speak. He was very nervous. Sally attended to her business with serene competence, and she accepted placidly the silence which to him was so embarrassing. He did not know how to begin. Sally seldom spoke unless she was spoken to or had something particular to say. At last he could not bear it any longer.

"You're not angry with me, Sally?" he blurted out suddenly.

She raised her eyes quietly and looked at him without emotion.

"Me? No. Why should I be?"

He was taken aback and did not reply. She took the lid off the pot, stirred the contents, and put it on again. A savoury smell spread over the air. She looked at him once more, with a quiet smile which barely separated her lips; it was more a smile of the eyes.

"I always liked you," she said.

His heart gave a great thump against his ribs, and he felt the blood rushing to his cheeks. He forced a faint laugh.

"I didn't know that."

"That's because you're a silly."

"I don't know why you liked me."

"I don't either." She put a little more wood on the fire. "I knew I liked you that day you came when you'd been sleeping out and hadn't had anything to eat, d'you remember? And me and mother, we got Thorpy's bed ready for you."

He flushed again, for he did not know that she was aware of that incident. He remembered it himself with horror and shame.

"That's why I wouldn't have anything to do with the others. You remember that young fellow mother wanted me to have? I let him come to tea because he bothered so, but I knew I'd say no."

Philip was so surprised that he found nothing to say. There was a queer feeling in his heart; he did not know what it was, unless it was happiness. Sally stirred the pot once more.

"I wish those children would make haste and come. I don't know where they've got to. Supper's ready now."

"Shall I go and see if I can find them?" said Philip.

It was a relief to talk about practical things.

"Well, it wouldn't be a bad idea, I must say. . . . There's mother coming."

Then, as he got up, she looked at him without embarrassment.

"Shall I come for a walk with you tonight when I've put the children to bed?"

"Yes."

"Well, you wait for me down by the stile, and I'll come when I'm ready."

He waited under the stars, sitting on the stile, and the hedges with their ripening blackberries were high on each side of him. From the earth rose rich scents of the night, and the air was soft and still. His heart was beating madly. He could not understand anything of what happened to him. He associated passion with cries and tears and vehemence, and there was nothing of this in Sally; but he did not know what else but passion could have caused her to give herself. But passion for him? He would not have been surprised if she had fallen to her cousin, Peter Gann, tall, spare, and straight, with his sunburned face and long, easy stride. Philip wondered what she saw in him. He did not know if she loved him as he reckoned love. And yet? He was convinced of her purity. He had a vague inkling that many things had combined, things that she felt though was unconscious of, the intoxication of the air and the hops and the night, the healthy instincts of the natural woman, a tenderness that overflowed, and an affection that had in it something maternal and something sisterly; and she gave all she had to give because her heart was full of charity.

He heard a step on the road, and a figure came out of the darkness.

"Sally," he murmured.

She stopped and came to the stile, and with her came sweet, clean odours of the countryside. She seemed to carry with her scents of the new-mown hay, and the savour of ripe hops, and the freshness of young grass. Her lips were soft and full against his, and her lovely, strong body was firm within his arms.

"Milk and honey," he said. "You're like milk and honey."

He made her close her eyes and kissed her eyelids, first one and then the other. Her arm, strong and muscular, was bare to the elbow; he passed his hand over it and wondered at its beauty; it gleamed in the darkness; she had the skin that Rubens painted, astonishingly fair and transparent, and on one side were little golden hairs. It was the arm of a Saxon goddess; but no immortal had that exquisite, homely naturalness; and Philip thought of a cottage garden with the dear flowers which bloom in all men's hearts, of the hollyhock and the red and white rose which is called York and Lancaster, and of love-in-a-mist and Sweet William, and honeysuckle, larkspur, and London Pride.

"How can you care for me?" he said. "I'm insignificant and crippled and ordinary and ugly."

She took his face in both her hands and kissed his lips.

"You're an old silly, that's what you are," she said.

Chapter CXXI

WHEN THE HOPS WERE PICKED, PHILIP WITH THE NEWS IN HIS POCKET that he had got the appointment as assistant house-physician at St. Luke's, accompanied the Athelnys back to London. He took modest rooms in Westminster and at the beginning of October entered upon his duties. The work was interesting and varied; every day he learned something new; he felt himself of some consequence; and he saw a good deal of Sally. He found life uncommonly pleasant. He was free about six, except on the days on which he had out-patients, and then he went to the shop at which Sally worked to meet her when she came out. There were several young men, who hung about opposite the "trade entrance" or a little further along, at the first corner; and the girls, coming out two and two or in little groups, nudged one another and giggled as they recognised them. Sally in her plain black dress looked very different from the country lass who had picked hops side by side with him. She walked away from the shop quickly, but she slackened her pace when they met, and greeted him with her quiet smile. They walked together through the busy street. He talked to her of his work at the hospital, and she told him what she had been doing in the shop that day. He came to know the names of the girls she worked with. He found that Sally had a restrained, but keen, sense of the ridiculous, and she made remarks about the girls or the men who were set over them which amused him by their unexpected drollery. She had a way of saying a thing which was very characteristic, quite gravely, as though there were nothing funny in it at all, and yet it was so sharp-sighted that Philip broke into delighted laughter. Then she would give him a little glance in which the smiling eyes showed she was not unaware of her own humour. They met with a handshake and parted as formally. Once Philip asked her to come and have tea with him in his rooms, but she refused.

"No, I won't do that. It would look funny."

Never a word of love passed between them. She seemed not to desire anything more than the companionship of those walks. Yet Philip was positive that she was glad to be with him. She puzzled him as much as she had done at the beginning. He did not begin to understand her conduct; but the more he knew her the fonder he grew of her; she was competent and self-controlled, and there was a charming honesty in her: you felt that you could rely upon her in every circumstance.

"You are an awfully good sort," he said to her once *à propos* of nothing at all.

"I expect I'm just the same as everyone else," she answered.

He knew that he did not love her. It was a great affection that he felt for her, and he liked her company; it was curiously soothing; and he had a feeling for her which seemed to him ridiculous to entertain towards a shop-girl of nineteen: he respected her. And he admired her magnificent healthiness. She was a splendid animal, without defect; and physical perfection filled him always with admiring awe. She made him feel unworthy.

Then, one day, about three weeks after they had come back to London as they walked together, he noticed that she was unusually silent. The serenity of her expression was altered by a slight line between the eyebrows: it was the beginning of a frown.

"What's the matter, Sally?" he asked.

She did not look at him, but straight in front of her, and her colour darkened.

"I don't know."

He understood at once what she meant. His heart gave a sudden, quick beat, and he felt the colour leave his cheeks.

"What d'you mean? Are you afraid that . . . ?"

He stopped. He could not go on. The possibility that anything of the sort could happen had never crossed his mind. Then he saw that her lips were trembling, and she was trying not to cry.

"I'm not certain yet. Perhaps it'll be all right."

They walked on in silence till they came to the corner of Chancery Lane, where he always left her. She held out her hand and smiled.

"Don't worry about it yet. Let's hope for the best."

He walked away with a tumult of thoughts in his head. What a fool he had been! That was the first thing that struck him, an abject, miserable fool, and he repeated it to himself a dozen times in a rush of angry feeling. He despised himself. How could he have got into such a mess? But at the same time, for his thoughts chased one another through his brain and yet seemed to stand together, in a hopeless confusion, like the pieces of a jig-saw puzzle seen in a nightmare, he asked himself what he was going to do. Everything was so clear before him, all he had aimed at so long within reach at last, and now his inconceivable stupidity had erected this new obstacle. Philip had never been able to surmount what he acknowledged was a defect in his resolute desire for a well-ordered life, and that was his passion for living in the future; and no sooner was he settled in his work at the hospital than he had busied himself with arrangements for his travels. In the past he had often tried not to think too circumstantially of his plans for the future, it was only discouraging; but now that his goal was so near he saw no harm in giving away to a longing that was so difficult to resist. First of all he meant to go to Spain. That was the land of his heart; and by now he was imbued with its spirit, its romance and colour and history and grandeur; he felt that it had a message for him in particular which no other country could give. He knew the fine old cities already as though he had trodden their tortuous streets from childhood, Cordova, Seville, Toledo, Leon, Tarragona, Burgos. The great painters of Spain were the painters of his soul, and his pulse beat quickly as he pictured his ecstasy on standing face to face with those works which were more significant than any others to his own tortured, restless heart. He had read the great poets, more characteristic of their race than the poets of other lands; for they seemed to have drawn their inspiration not at all from the general currents of the world's literature but directly from the torrid, scented plains and the bleak mountains of their country. A few short months now, and he would hear with his own ears all around him the language which seemed most apt for grandeur of soul and passion. His fine taste had given him an inkling that Andalusia was too soft and sensuous, a little vulgar even, to satisfy his ardour; and his imagination dwelled more willingly among the wind-swept distances of Castile and the rugged magnificence of Aragon and Leon. He did not know quite what those unknown contacts would give him, but he felt that he would gather from them a strength and a purpose which would make him more capable of affronting and comprehending the manifold wonders of places more distant and more strange.

For this was only a beginning. He had got into communication with the various companies which took surgeons out on their ships, and knew exactly what were their routes, and from men who had been on them what were the advantages and disadvantages of each line. He put aside the Orient and the P. & O. It was difficult to get a berth with them; and besides their passenger traffic allowed the medical officer little freedom; but there were other services which sent large tramps on leisurely expeditions to the East, stopping at all sorts of ports for various periods, from a day or two to a fortnight, so that you had plenty of time, and it was often possible to make a trip inland. The pay was poor and the food no more than adequate, so that there was not much demand for the posts, and a man with a London degree was pretty sure to get one if he applied. Since there were no passengers other than a casual man or so, shipping on business from some out-of-the-way port to another, the life on board was friendly and pleasant. Philip knew by heart the list of places at which they touched; and each one called up in him visions of tropical sunshine, and magic colour, and of a teeming, mysterious, intense life. life! That was what he wanted. At last he would come to close quarters with life. And perhaps, from Tokyo or Shanghai it would be possible to tranship into some other line and drop down to the islands of the South Pacific. A doctor was useful anywhere. There might be an opportunity to go up country in Burma, and what rich jungles in Sumatra or Borneo might he not visit? He was young still and time was no object to him. He had no ties in England, no friends; he could go up and down the world for years, learning the beauty and the wonder and the variedness of life.

Now this thing had come. He put aside the possibility that Sally was mistaken; he felt strangely certain that she was right; after all, it was so likely; anyone could see that Nature had built her to be the mother of children. He knew what he ought to do. He ought not to let the incident divert him a hair's breadth from his path. He thought of Griffiths; he could easily imagine with what indifference that young man would have received such a piece of news; he would have thought it an awful nuisance and would at once have taken to his heels, like a wise fellow; he would have left the girl to deal with her troubles as best she could. Philip told himself that if this had happened it was because it was inevitable. He was no more to blame than Sally; she was a girl who knew the world and the facts of life, and she had taken the risk with her eyes open. It would be madness to allow such an accident to disturb the whole pattern of his life. He was one of the few people who was acutely conscious of the transitoriness of life, and how necessary it was to make the most of it. He would do what he could for Sally; he could afford to give her a sufficient sum of money. A strong man would never allow himself to be turned from his purpose.

Philip said all this to himself, but he knew he could not do it. He simply could not. He knew himself.

"I'm so damned weak," he muttered despairingly.

She had trusted him and been kind to him. He simply could not do a thing which, notwithstanding all his reason, he felt was horrible. He knew he would have no peace on his travels if he had the thought constantly with him that she was wretched. Besides, there were her father and mother: they had always treated him well; it was not possible to repay them with ingratitude. The only thing was to marry Sally as quickly as possible. He would write to Doctor South, tell him he was going to be married at once, and say that if his offer still held he was willing to accept it. That sort of practice, among poor people, was the only one possible for him; there his deformity did not matter, and they would not sneer at the simple manners of his wife. It was curious to think of her as his wife, it gave him a queer, soft feeling; and a wave of emotion spread over him as he thought of the child which was his. He had little doubt that Doctor South would be glad to have him, and he pictured to himself the life he would lead with Sally in the fishing village. They would have a little house within sight of the sea, and he would watch the mighty ships passing to the lands he would never know. Perhaps that was the wisest thing. Cronshaw had told him that the facts of life mattered nothing to him who by the power of fancy held in fee the twin realms of space and time. It was true. *Forever wilt thou love and she be fair!*

His wedding present to his wife would be all his high hopes. Self-sacrifice! Philip was uplifted by its beauty, and all through the evening he thought of it. He was so excited that he could not read. He seemed to be driven out of his rooms into the streets, and he walked up and down Birdcage Walk, his heart throbbing with joy. He could hardly bear his impatience. He wanted to see Sally's happiness when he made her his offer, and if it had not been so late he would have gone to her there and then. He pictured to himself the long evenings he would spend with Sally in the cosy sitting-room, the blinds undrawn so that they could watch the sea; he with his books, while she bent over her work, and the shaded lamp made her sweet face more fair. They would talk over the growing child, and when she turned her eyes to his there was in them the light of love. And the fishermen and their wives who were his patients would come to feel a great affection for them, and they in their turn would enter into the pleasures and pains of those simple lives. But his thoughts returned to the son who would be his and hers. Already he felt in himself a passionate devotion to it. He thought of passing his hands over his little perfect limbs, he knew he would be beautiful; and he would make over to him all his dreams of a rich and varied life. And thinking over the long pilgrimage of his past he accepted it joyfully. He accepted the deformity which had made life so hard for him; he knew that it had warped his character, but now he saw also that by reason of it he had acquired that power of introspection which had given him so much delight. Without it he would never have had his keen appreciation of beauty, his passion for art and literature, and his interest in the varied spectacle of life. The ridicule and the contempt which had so often been heaped upon him had turned his mind inward and called forth those flowers which he felt would never lose their fragrance. Then he saw that the normal was the rarest thing in the world. Everyone had some defect, of body or of mind: he thought of all the people he had known (the whole world was like a sick-house, and there was no rhyme or reason in it), he saw a long procession, deformed in body and warped in mind, some with illness of the flesh, weak hearts or weak lungs, and some with illness of the spirit, languor of will, or a craving for liquor. At this moment he could feel a holy compassion for them all. They were the helpless instruments of blind chance. He could pardon Griffiths for his treachery and Mildred for the pain she had caused him. They could not help themselves. The only reasonable thing was to accept the good of men and be patient with their faults. The words of the dying God crossed his memory:

Forgive them, for they know not what they do.

Chapter CXXII

HE HAD ARRANGED TO MEET SALLY ON SATURDAY IN THE NATIONAL Gallery. She was to come there as soon as she was released from the shop and had agreed to lunch with him. Two days had passed since he had seen her, and his exultation had not left him for a moment. It was because he rejoiced in the feeling that he had not attempted to see her. He had repeated to himself exactly what he would say to her and how he should say it. Now his impatience was unbearable. He had written to Doctor South and had in his pocket a telegram from him received that morning: *"Sacking the mumpish fool. When will you come?"* Philip walked along Parliament Street. It was a fine day, and there was a bright, frosty sun which made the light dance in the street. It was crowded. There was a tenuous mist in the distance, and it softened exquisitely the noble lines of the buildings. He crossed Trafalgar Square. Suddenly his heart gave a sort of twist in his body; he saw a woman in front of him who he thought was Mildred. She had the same figure, and she walked with that slight dragging of the feet which was so characteristic of her. Without thinking, but with a beating heart, he hurried till he came alongside, and then, when the woman turned, he saw it was someone unknown to him. It was the face of a much older person, with a lined, yellow skin. He slackened his pace. He was infinitely relieved, but it was not only relief that he felt; it was disappointment too; he was seized with horror of himself. Would he never be free from that passion? At the bottom of his heart, notwithstanding everything, he felt that a strange, desperate thirst for that vile woman would always linger. That love had caused him so much suffering that he knew he would never, never quite be free of it. Only death could finally assuage his desire.

But he wrenched the pang from his heart. He thought of Sally, with her kind blue eyes; and his lips unconsciously formed themselves into a smile. He walked up the steps of the National Gallery and sat down in the first room, so that he should see her the moment she came in. It always comforted him to get among pictures. He looked at none in particular, but allowed the magnificence of their colour, the beauty of their lines, to work upon his soul. His imagination was busy with Sally. It would be pleasant to take her away from that London in which she seemed an unusual figure, like a cornflower in a shop among orchids and azaleas; he had learned in the Kentish hop-field that she did not belong to the town; and he was sure that she would blossom under the soft skies of Dorset to a rarer beauty. She came in, and he got up to meet her. She was in black, with white cuffs at her wrists and a lawn collar round her neck. They shook hands.

"Have you been waiting long?"

"No. Ten minutes. Are you hungry?"

"Not very."

"Let's sit here for a bit, shall we?"

"If you like."

They sat quietly, side by side, without speaking. Philip enjoyed having her near him. He was warmed by her radiant health. A glow of life seemed like an aureole to shine about her.

"Well, how have you been?" he said at last, with a little smile.

"Oh, it's all right. It was a false alarm."

"Was it?"

"Aren't you glad?"

An extraordinary sensation filled him. He had felt certain that Sally's suspicion was well-founded; it had never occurred to him for an instant that there was a possibility of error. All his plans were suddenly overthrown, and the existence, so elaborately pictured, was no more than a dream which would never be realised. He was free once more. Free! He need give up none of his projects, and life still was in his hands for him to do what he liked with. He felt no exhilaration, but only dismay. His heart sank. The future stretched out before him in desolate emptiness. It was as though he had sailed for many years over a great waste of waters, with peril and privation, and at last had come upon a fair haven, but as he was about to enter, some contrary wind had arisen and drove him out again into the open sea; and because he had let his mind dwell on these soft meads and pleasant woods of the land, the vast deserts of the ocean filled him with anguish. He could not confront again the loneliness and the tempest. Sally looked at him with her clear eyes.

"Aren't you glad?" she asked again. "I thought you'd be as pleased as Punch."

He met her gaze haggardly.

"I'm not sure," he muttered.

"You are funny. Most men would."

He realised that he had deceived himself; it was no self-sacrifice that had driven him to think of marrying, but the desire for a wife and a home and love; and now that it all seemed to slip through his fingers he was seized with despair. He wanted all that more than anything in the world. What did he care for Spain and its cities, Cordova, Toledo, Leon; what to him were the pagodas of Burma and the lagoons of South Sea Islands? America was here and now. It seemed to him that all his life he had followed the ideals that other people, by their words or their writings, had instilled into him, and never the desires of his own heart. Always his course had been swayed by what he thought he should do and never by what he wanted with his whole soul to do. He put all that aside now with a gesture of impatience. He had lived always in the future, and the present always, always had slipped through his fingers. His ideals? He thought of his desire to make a design, intricate and beautiful, out of the myriad, meaningless facts of life: had he not seen also that the simplest pattern, that in which a man was born, worked, married, had children, and died, was likewise the most perfect? It might be that to surrender to happiness was to accept defeat, but it was a defeat better than many victories.

He glanced quickly at Sally, he wondered what she was thinking, and then looked away again.

"I was going to ask you to marry me," he said.

"I thought p'raps you might, but I shouldn't have liked to stand in your way."

"You wouldn't have done that."

"How about your travels, Spain and all that?"

"How d'you know I want to travel?"

"I ought to know something about it. I've heard you and Dad talk about it till you were blue in the face."

"I don't care a damn about all that." He paused for an instant and then spoke in a low, hoarse whisper. "I don't want to leave you! I can't leave you."

She did not answer. He could not tell what she thought.

"I wonder if you'll marry me, Sally."

She did not move and there was no flicker of emotion on her face, but she did not look at him when she answered.

"If you like."

"Don't you want to?"

"Oh, of course I'd like to have a house of my own, and it's about time I was settling down."

He smiled a little. He knew her pretty well by now, and her manner did not surprise him.

"But don't you want to marry *me?*"

"There's no one else I would marry."

"Then that settles it."

"Mother and Dad will be surprised, won't they?"

"I'm so happy."

"I want my lunch," she said.

"Dear!"

He smiled and took her hand and pressed it. They got up and walked out of the gallery. They stood for a moment at the balustrade and looked at Trafalgar Square. Cabs and omnibuses hurried to and fro, and crowds passed, hastening in every direction, and the sun was shining.

THE MOON AND SIXPENCE

Chapter I

I CONFESS THAT WHEN FIRST I MADE ACQUAINTANCE WITH CHARLES STRICKland I never for a moment discerned that there was in him anything out of the ordinary. Yet now few will be found to deny his greatness. I do not speak of that greatness which is achieved by the fortunate politician or the successful soldier; that is a quality which belongs to the place he occupies rather than to the man; and a change of circumstances reduces it to very discreet proportions. The Prime Minister out of office is seen, too often, to have been but a pompous rhetorician, and the General without an army is but the tame hero of a market town. The greatness of Charles Strickland was authentic. It may be that you do not like his art, but at all events you can hardly refuse it the tribute of your interest. He disturbs and arrests. The time has passed when he was an object of ridicule, and it is no longer a mark of eccentricity to defend or of perversity to extol him. His faults are accepted as the necessary complement to his merits. It is still possible to discuss his place in art, and the adulation of his admirers is perhaps no less capricious than the disparagement of his detractors; but one thing can never be doubtful, and that is that he had genius. To my mind the most interesting thing in art is the personality of the artist; and if that is singular, I am willing to excuse a thousand faults. I suppose Velasquez was a better painter than El Greco, but custom stales one's admiration for him: the Cretan, sensual and tragic, proffers the mystery of his soul like a standing sacrifice. The artist, painter, poet, or musician, by his decoration, sublime or beautiful, satisfies the aesthetic sense; but that is akin to the sexual instinct, and shares its barbarity: he lays before you also the greater gift of himself. To pursue his secret has something of the fascination of a detective story. It is a riddle which shares with the universe the merit of having no answer. The most insignificant of Strickland's works suggests a personality which is strange, tormented, and complex; and it is this surely which prevents even those who do not like his pictures from being indifferent to them; it is this which has excited so curious an interest in his life and character.

It was not till four years after Strickland's death that Maurice Huret wrote that article in the *Mercure de France* which rescued the unknown painter from oblivion and blazed the trail which succeeding writers, with more or less docility, have followed. For a long time no critic has enjoyed in France a more incontestable authority, and it was impossible not to be impressed by the claims he made; they seemed extravagant; but later judgments have confirmed his estimate, and the reputation of Charles Strickland is now firmly established on the lines which he laid down. The rise of this reputation is one of the most romantic incidents in the history of art. But I do not propose to deal with Charles Strickland's work except in so far as it touches upon his character. I cannot agree with the painters who claim superciliously that the layman can understand nothing of painting, and that he can best show his appreciation of their works by silence and a cheque-book. It is a grotesque misapprehension which sees in art no more than a craft comprehensible perfectly only to the craftsman: art is a manifestation of emotion, and emotion speaks a language that all may understand. But I will allow that the critic who has not a practical knowledge of technique is seldom able to say anything on the subject of real value, and my ignorance of painting is extreme. Fortunately, there is no need for me to risk the adventure, since my friend, Mr. Edward Leggatt, an able writer as well as an admirable painter, has exhaustively discussed Charles Strickland's work in a little book* which is a charming example of a style, for the most part, less happily cultivated in England than in France.

Maurice Huret in his famous article gave an outline of Charles Strickland's life which was well calculated to whet the appetites of the inquiring. With his disinterested passion for art, he had a real desire to call the attention of the wise to a talent which was in the highest degree original; but he was too good a journalist to be unaware that the "human interest" would enable him more easily to effect his purpose. And when such as had come in contact with Strickland in the past, writers who had known him in London, painters who had met him in the cafés of Montmartre, discovered to their amazement that where they had seen but an unsuccessful artist, like another, authentic genius had rubbed shoulders with them there began to appear in the magazines of France and America a succession of articles, the reminiscences of one, the appreciation of another, which added to Strickland's notoriety, and fed without satisfying the curiosity of the public. The subject was grateful, and the industrious Weitbrecht-Rotholz in his imposing monograph[†] has been able to give a remarkable list of authorities.

The faculty for myth is innate in the human race. It seizes with avidity upon any incidents, surprising or mysterious, in the career of those who have at all distinguished themselves from their fellows, and invents a legend to which it then attaches a fanatical belief. It is the protest of romance against the commonplace of life. The incidents of the legend become the hero's surest passport to immortality. The ironic philosopher reflects with a smile that Sir Walter Raleigh is more safely inshrined in the memory of mankind because he set his cloak for the Virgin Queen

---

A Modern Artist: Notes on the Work of Charles Strickland, by Edward Leggatt, A.R.H.A. Martin Secker, 1917.

†*Karl Strickland: sein Leben und seine Kunst*, by Hugo Weitbrecht-Rotholz, Ph.D. Schwingel und Hanisch. Leipzig, 1914.

to walk on than because he carried the English name to undiscovered countries. Charles Strickland lived obscurely. He made enemies rather than friends. It is not strange, then, that those who wrote of him should have eked out their scanty recollections with a lively fancy, and it is evident that there was enough in the little that was known of him to give opportunity to the romantic scribe; there was much in his life which was strange and terrible, in his character something outrageous, and in his fate not a little that was pathetic. In due course a legend arose of such circumstantiality that the wise historian would hesitate to attack it.

But a wise historian is precisely what the Rev. Robert Strickland is not. He wrote his biography* avowedly to "remove certain misconceptions which had gained currency" in regard to the later part of his father's life, and which had "caused considerable pain to persons still living." It is obvious that there was much in the commonly received account of Strickland's life to embarrass a respectable family. I have read this work with a good deal of amusement, and upon this I congratulate myself, since it is colourless and dull. Mr. Strickland has drawn the portrait of an excellent husband and father, a man of kindly temper, industrious habits, and moral disposition. The modern clergyman has acquired in his study of the science which I believe is called exegesis an astonishing facility for explaining things away, but the subtlety with which the Rev. Robert Strickland has "interpreted" all the facts in his father's life which a dutiful son might find it inconvenient to remember must surely lead him in the fullness of time to the highest dignities of the Church. I see already his muscular calves encased in the gaiters episcopal. It was a hazardous, though maybe a gallant thing to do, since it is probable that the legend commonly received has had no small share in the growth of Strickland's reputation; for there are many who have been attracted to his art by the detestation in which they held his character or the compassion with which they regarded his death; and the son's well-meaning efforts threw a singular chill upon the father's admirers. It is due to no accident that when one of his most important works, *The Woman of Samaria*,† was sold at Christie's shortly after the discussion which followed the publication of Mr. Strickland's biography, it fetched £235 less than it had done nine months before when it was bought by the distinguished collector whose sudden death had brought it once more under the hammer. Perhaps Charles Strickland's power and originality would scarcely have sufficed to turn the scale if the remarkable mythopoeic faculty of mankind had not brushed aside with impatience

---

Strickland: The Man and His Work, by his son, Robert Strickland. Wm. Heinemann, 1913.

†This was described in Christie's catalogue as follows: "A nude woman, a native of the Society Islands, is lying on the ground beside a brook. Behind is a tropical landscape with palm-trees, bananas, etc. 60 in. x 48 in."

a story which disappointed all its craving for the extraordinary. And presently Dr. Weitbrecht-Rotholz produced the work which finally set at rest the misgivings of all lovers of art.

Dr. Weitbrecht-Rotholz belongs to that school of historians which believes that human nature is not only about as bad as it can be, but a great deal worse; and certainly the reader is safer of entertainment in their hands than in those of the writers who take a malicious pleasure in representing the great figures of romance as patterns of the domestic virtues. For my part, I should be sorry to think that there was nothing between Anthony and Cleopatra but an economic situation; and it will require a great deal more evidence than is ever likely to be available, thank God, to persuade me that Tiberius was as blameless a monarch as King George V. Dr. Weitbrecht-Rotholz has dealt in such terms with the Rev. Robert Strickland's innocent biography that it is difficult to avoid feeling a certain sympathy for the unlucky parson. His decent reticence is branded as hypocrisy, his circumlocutions are roundly called lies, and his silence is vilified as treachery. And on the strength of peccadillos, reprehensible in an author, but excusable in a son, the Anglo-Saxon race is accused of prudishness, humbug, pretentiousness, deceit, cunning, and bad cooking. Personally I think it was rash of Mr. Strickland, in refuting the account which had gained belief of a certain "unpleasantness" between his father and mother, to state that Charles Strickland in a letter written from Paris had described her as "an excellent woman," since Dr. Weitbrecht-Rotholz was able to print the letter in facsimile, and it appears that the passage referred to ran in fact as follows: *God damn my wife. She is an excellent woman. I wish she was in hell.* It is not thus that the Church in its great days dealt with evidence that was unwelcome.

Dr. Weitbrecht-Rotholz was an enthusiastic admirer of Charles Strickland, and there was no danger that he would whitewash him. He had an unerring eye for the despicable motive in actions that had all the appearance of innocence. He was a psycho-pathologist, as well as a student of art, and the subconscious had few secrets from him. No mystic ever saw deeper meaning in common things. The mystic sees the ineffable, and the psycho-pathologist the unspeakable. There is a singular fascination in watching the eagerness with which the learned author ferrets out every circumstance which may throw discredit on his hero. His heart warms to him when he can bring forward some example of cruelty or meanness, and he exults like an inquisitor at the *auto da fé* of an heretic when with some forgotten story he can confound the filial piety of the Rev. Robert Strickland. His industry has been amazing. Nothing has been too small to escape him, and you may be sure that if Charles Strickland left a laundry bill unpaid it will be given you *in extenso*, and if he forebore to return a borrowed half-crown no detail of the transaction will be omitted.

Chapter II

WHEN SO MUCH HAS BEEN WRITTEN ABOUT CHARLES STRICKLAND, IT may seem unnecessary that I should write more. A painter's monument is his work. It is true I knew him more intimately than most: I met him first before ever he became a painter, and I saw him not infrequently during the difficult years he spent in Paris; but I do not suppose I should ever have set down my recollections if the hazards of the war had not taken me to Tahiti. There, as is notorious, he spent the last years of his life; and there I came across persons who were familiar with him. I find myself in a position to throw light on just that part of his tragic career which has remained most obscure. If they who believe in Strickland's greatness are right, the personal narratives of such as knew him in the flesh can hardly be superfluous. What would we not give for the reminiscences of someone who had been as intimately acquainted with El Greco as I was with Strickland?

But I seek refuge in no such excuses. I forget who it was that recommended men for their soul's good to do each day two things they disliked: it was a wise man, and it is a precept that I have followed scrupulously; for every day I have got up and I have gone to bed. But there is in my nature a strain of asceticism, and I have subjected my flesh each week to a more severe mortification. I have never failed to read the Literary Supplement of *The Times*. It is a salutary discipline to consider the vast number of books that are written, the fair hopes with which their authors see them published, and the fate which awaits them. What chance is there that any book will make its way among that multitude? And the successful books are but the successes of a season. Heaven knows what pains the author has been at, what bitter experiences he has endured and what heartache suffered, to give some chance reader a few hours' relaxation or to while away the tedium of a journey. And if I may judge from the reviews, many of these books are well and carefully written; much thought has gone to their composition; to some even has been given the anxious labour of a lifetime. The moral I draw is that the writer should seek his reward in the pleasure of his work and in release from the burden of his thought; and, indifferent to aught else, care nothing for praise or censure, failure or success.

Now the war has come, bringing with it a new attitude. Youth has turned to gods we of an earlier day knew not, and it is possible to see already the direction in which those who come after us will move. The younger generation, conscious of strength and tumultuous, have done with knocking at the door; they have burst in and seated themselves in our seats. The air is noisy with their shouts. Of their elders some, by imitating the antics of youth, strive to persuade themselves that their day is not yet over; they shout with the lustiest, but the war cry sounds hollow in their mouth; they are like poor wantons attempting with pencil, paint and powder, with shrill gaiety, to recover the illusion of their spring. The wiser go their way with a decent grace. In their chastened smile is an indulgent mockery. They remember that they too trod down a sated generation, with just such clamour and with just such scorn, and they foresee that these brave torch-bearers will presently yield their place also. There is no last word. The new evangel was old when Nineveh reared her greatness to the sky. These gallant words which seem so novel to those that speak them were said in accents scarcely changed a hundred times before. The pendulum swings backwards and forwards. The circle is ever travelled anew.

Sometimes a man survives a considerable time from an era in which he had his place into one which is strange to him, and then the curious are offered one of the most singular spectacles in the human comedy. Who now, for example, thinks of George Crabbe? He was a famous poet in his day, and the world recognised his genius with a unanimity which the greater complexity of modern life has rendered infrequent. He had learned his craft at the school of Alexander Pope, and he wrote moral stories in rhymed couplets. Then came the French Revolution and the Napoleonic Wars, and the poets sang new songs. Mr. Crabbe continued to write moral stories in rhymed couplets. I think he must have read the verse of these young men who were making so great a stir in the world, and I fancy he found it poor stuff. Of course, much of it was. But the odes of Keats and of Wordsworth, a poem or two by Coleridge, a few more by Shelley, discovered vast realms of the spirit that none had explored before. Mr. Crabbe was as dead as mutton, but Mr. Crabbe continued to write moral stories in rhymed couplets. I have read desultorily the writings of the younger generation. It may be that among them a more fervid Keats, a more ethereal Shelley, has already published numbers the world will willingly remember. I cannot tell. I admire their polish—their youth is already so accomplished that it seems absurd to speak of promise—I marvel at the felicity of their style; but with all their copiousness (their vocabulary suggests that they fingered Roget's *Thesaurus* in their cradles) they say nothing to me: to my mind they know too much and feel too obviously; I cannot stomach the heartiness with which they slap me on the back or the emotion with which they hurl themselves on my bosom; their passion seems to me a little anaemic and their dreams a trifle dull. I do not like them. I am on the shelf. I will continue to write moral stories in rhymed couplets. But I should be thrice a fool if I did it for aught but my own entertainment.

Chapter III

But all this is by the way.

I was very young when I wrote my first book.

By a lucky chance it excited attention, and various persons sought my acquaintance.

It is not without melancholy that I wander among my recollections of the world of letters in London when first, bashful but eager, I was introduced to it. It is long since I frequented it, and if the novels that describe its present singularities are accurate much in it is now changed. The venue is different. Chelsea and Bloomsbury have taken the place of Hampstead, Notting Hill Gate, and High Street, Kensington. Then it was a distinction to be under forty, but now to be more than twenty-five is absurd. I think in those days we were a little shy of our emotions, and the fear of ridicule tempered the more obvious forms of pretentiousness. I do not believe that there was in that genteel Bohemia an intensive culture of chastity, but I do not remember so crude a promiscuity as seems to be practised in the present day. We did not think it hypocritical to draw over our vagaries the curtain of a decent silence. The spade was not invariably called a bloody shovel. Woman had not yet altogether come into her own.

I lived near Victoria Station, and I recall long excursions by bus to the hospitable houses of the literary. In my timidity I wandered up and down the street while I screwed up my courage to ring the bell; and then, sick with apprehension, was ushered into an airless room full of people. I was introduced to this celebrated person after that one, and the kind words they said about my book made me excessively uncomfortable. I felt they expected me to say clever things, and I never could think of any till after the party was over. I tried to conceal my embarrassment by handing round cups of tea and rather ill-cut bread and butter. I wanted no one to take notice of me, so that I could observe these famous creatures at my ease and listen to the clever things they said.

I have a recollection of large, unbending women with great noses and rapacious eyes, who wore their clothes as though they were armour; and of little, mouse-like spinsters, with soft voices and a shrewd glance. I never ceased to be fascinated by their persistence in eating buttered toast with their gloves on, and I observed with admiration the unconcern with which they wiped their fingers on their chair when they thought no one was looking. It must have been bad for the furniture, but I suppose the hostess took her revenge on the furniture of her friends when, in turn, she visited them. Some of them were dressed fashionably, and they said they couldn't for the life of them see why you should be dowdy just because you had written a novel; if you had a neat figure you might as well make the most of it, and a smart shoe on a small foot had never prevented an editor from taking your "stuff." But others thought this frivolous, and they wore "art fabrics" and barbaric jewelry. The men were seldom eccentric in appearance. They tried to look as little like authors as possible. They wished to be taken for men of the world, and could have passed anywhere for the managing clerks of a city firm. They always seemed a little tired. I had never known writers before, and I found them very strange, but I do not think they ever seemed to me quite real.

I remember that I thought their conversation brilliant, and I used to listen with astonishment to the stinging humour with which they would tear a brother-author to pieces the moment that his back was turned. The artist has this advantage over the rest of the world, that his friends offer not only their appearance and their character to his satire, but also their work. I despaired of ever expressing myself with such aptness or with such fluency. In those days conversation was still cultivated as an art; a neat repartee was more highly valued than the crackling of thorns under a pot; and the epigram, not yet a mechanical appliance by which the dull may achieve a semblance of wit, gave sprightliness to the small-talk of the urbane. It is sad that I can remember nothing of all this scintillation. But I think the conversation never settled down so comfortably as when it turned to the details of the trade which was the other side of the art we practised. When we had done discussing the merits of the latest book, it was natural to wonder how many copies had been sold, what advance the author had received, and how much he was likely to make out of it. Then we would speak of this publisher and of that, comparing the generosity of one with the meanness of another; we would argue whether it was better to go to one who gave handsome royalties or to another who "pushed" a book for all it was worth. Some advertised badly and some well. Some were modern and some were old-fashioned. Then we would talk of agents and the offers they had obtained for us; of editors and the sort of contributions they welcomed, how much they paid a thousand, and whether they paid promptly or otherwise. To me it was all very romantic. It gave me an intimate sense of being a member of some mystic brotherhood.

Chapter IV

No one was kinder to me at that time than Rose Waterford. She combined a masculine intelligence with a feminine perversity, and the novels she wrote were original and disconcerting. It was at her house one day that I met Charles Strickland's wife. Miss Waterford was giving a tea-party, and her small room was more than usually full. Everyone seemed to be talking, and I, sitting in silence, felt awkward; but I was too shy to break into any of the groups that seemed absorbed in their own affairs. Miss Waterford was a good hostess, and seeing my embarrassment came up to me.

"I want you to talk to Mrs. Strickland," she said. "She's raving about your book."

"What does she do?" I asked.

I was conscious of my ignorance, and if Mrs. Strickland was a well-known writer I thought it as well to ascertain the fact before I spoke to her.

Rose Waterford cast down her eyes demurely to give greater effect to her reply.

"She gives luncheon-parties. You've only got to roar a little, and she'll ask you."

Rose Waterford was a cynic. She looked upon life as an opportunity for writing novels and the public as her raw material. Now and then she invited members of it to her house if they showed an appreciation of her talent and entertained with proper lavishness. She held their weakness for lions in good-humoured contempt, but played to them her part of the distinguished woman of letters with decorum.

I was led up to Mrs. Strickland, and for ten minutes we talked together. I noticed nothing about her except that she had a pleasant voice. She had a flat in Westminster, overlooking the unfinished cathedral, and because we lived in the same neighbourhood we felt friendly disposed to one another. The Army and Navy Stores are a bond of union between all who dwell between the river and St. James's Park. Mrs. Strickland asked me for my address, and a few days later I received an invitation to luncheon.

My engagements were few, and I was glad to accept. When I arrived, a little late, because in my fear of being too early I had walked three times round the cathedral, I found the party already complete. Miss Waterford was there and Mrs. Jay, Richard Twining and George Road. We were all writers. It was a fine day, early in spring, and we were in a good humour. We talked about a hundred things. Miss Waterford, torn between the aestheticism of her early youth, when she used to go to parties in sage green, holding a daffodil, and the flippancy of her maturer years, which tended to high heels and Paris frocks, wore a new hat. It put her in high spirits. I had never heard her more malicious about our common friends. Mrs. Jay, aware that impropriety is the soul of wit, made observations in tones hardly above a whisper that might well have tinged the snowy tablecloth with a rosy hue. Richard Twining bubbled over with quaint absurdities, and George Road, conscious that he need not exhibit a brilliancy which was almost a by-word, opened his mouth only to put food into it. Mrs. Strickland did not talk much, but she had a pleasant gift for keeping the conversation general; and when there was a pause she threw in just the right remark to set it going once more. She was a woman of thirty-seven, rather tall and plump, without being fat; she was not pretty, but her face was pleasing, chiefly, perhaps, on account of her kind brown eyes. Her skin was rather sallow. Her dark hair was elaborately dressed. She was the only woman of the three whose face was free of make-up, and by contrast with the others she seemed simple and unaffected.

The dining-room was in the good taste of the period. It was very severe. There was a high dado of white wood and a green paper on which were etchings by Whistler in neat black frames. The green curtains with their peacock design, hung in straight lines, and the green carpet, in the pattern of which pale rabbits frolicked among leafy trees, suggested the influence of William Morris. There was blue delft on the chimneypiece. At that time there must have been five hundred dining-rooms in London decorated in exactly the same manner. It was chaste, artistic, and dull.

When we left I walked away with Miss Waterford, and the fine day and her new hat persuaded us to saunter through the Park.

"That was a very nice party," I said.

"Did you think the food was good? I told her that if she wanted writers she must feed them well."

"Admirable advice," I answered. "But why does she want them?"

Miss Waterford shrugged her shoulders.

"She finds them amusing. She wants to be in the movement. I fancy she's rather simple, poor dear, and she thinks we're all wonderful. After all, it pleases her to ask us to luncheon, and it doesn't hurt us. I like her for it."

Looking back, I think that Mrs. Strickland was the most harmless of all the lion-hunters that pursue their quarry from the rarefied heights of Hampstead to the nethermost studios of Cheyne Walk. She had led a very quiet youth in the country, and the books that came down from Mudie's Library brought with them not only their own romance, but the romance of London. She had a real passion for reading (rare in her kind, who for the most part are more interested in the author than in his book, in the painter than in his pictures), and she invented a world of the imagination in which she lived with a freedom she never acquired in the world of every day. When she came to know writers it was like adventuring upon a stage which till then she had known only from the other side of the footlights. She saw them dramatically, and really seemed herself to live a larger life because she entertained them and visited them in their fastnesses. She accepted the rules with which they played the game of life as valid for them, but never for a moment thought of regulating her own conduct in accordance with them. Their moral eccentricities, like their oddities of dress, their wild theories and paradoxes, were an entertainment which amused her, but had not the slightest influence on her convictions.

"Is there a Mr. Strickland?" I asked

"Oh yes; he's something in the city. I believe he's a stockbroker. He's very dull."

"Are they good friends?"

"They adore one another. You'll meet him if you dine there. But she doesn't often have people to dinner. He's very quiet. He's not in the least interested in literature or the arts."

"Why do nice women marry dull men?"

"Because intelligent men won't marry nice women."

I could not think of any retort to this, so I asked if Mrs. Strickland had children.

"Yes; she has a boy and a girl. They're both at school."

The subject was exhausted, and we began to talk of other things.

Chapter V

During the summer I met Mrs. Strickland not infrequently. I went now and then to pleasant little luncheons at her flat, and to rather more formidable tea-parties. We took a fancy to one another. I was very young, and perhaps she liked the idea of guiding my virgin steps on the hard road of letters; while for me it was pleasant to have someone I could go to with my small troubles, certain of an attentive ear and reasonable counsel. Mrs. Strickland had the gift of sympathy. It is a charming faculty, but one often abused by those who are conscious of its possession: for there is something ghoulish in the avidity with which they will pounce upon the misfortune of their friends so that they may exercise their dexterity. It gushes forth like an oil-well, and the sympathetic pour out their sympathy with an abandon that is sometimes embarrassing to their victims. There are bosoms on which so many tears have been shed that I cannot bedew them with mine. Mrs. Strickland used her advantage with tact. You felt that you obliged her by accepting her sympathy. When, in the enthusiasm of my youth, I remarked on this to Rose Waterford, she said:

"Milk is very nice, especially with a drop of brandy in it, but the domestic cow is only too glad to be rid of it. A swollen udder is very uncomfortable."

Rose Waterford had a blistering tongue. No one could say such bitter things; on the other hand, no one could do more charming ones.

There was another thing I liked in Mrs. Strickland. She managed her surroundings with elegance. Her flat was always neat and cheerful, gay with flowers, and the chintzes in the drawing-room, notwithstanding their severe design, were bright and pretty. The meals in the artistic little dining-room were pleasant; the table looked nice, the two maids were trim and comely; the food was well cooked. It was impossible not to see that Mrs. Strickland was an excellent housekeeper. And you felt sure that she was an admirable mother. There were photographs in the drawing-room of her son and daughter. The son—his name was Robert—was a boy of sixteen at Rugby; and you saw him in flannels and a cricket cap, and again in a tail-coat and a stand-up collar. He had his mother's candid brow and fine, reflective eyes. He looked clean, healthy, and normal.

"I don't know that he's very clever," she said one day, when I was looking at the photograph, "but I know he's good. He has a charming character."

The daughter was fourteen. Her hair, thick and dark like her mother's, fell over her shoulders in fine profusion, and she had the same kindly expression and sedate, untroubled eyes.

"They're both of them the image of you," I said.

"Yes; I think they are more like me than their father."

"Why have you never let me meet him?" I asked.

"Would you like to?"

She smiled, her smile was really very sweet, and she blushed a little; it was singular that a woman of that age should flush so readily. Perhaps her naïveté was her greatest charm.

"You know, he's not at all literary," she said. "He's a perfect philistine."

She said this not disparagingly, but affectionately rather, as though, by acknowledging the worst about him, she wished to protect him from the aspersions of her friends.

"He's on the Stock Exchange, and he's a typical broker. I think he'd bore you to death."

"Does he bore you?" I asked.

"You see, I happen to be his wife. I'm very fond of him."

She smiled to cover her shyness, and I fancied she had a fear that I would make the sort of gibe that such a confession could hardly have failed to elicit from Rose Waterford. She hesitated a little. Her eyes grew tender.

"He doesn't pretend to be a genius. He doesn't even make much money on the Stock Exchange. But he's awfully good and kind."

"I think I should like him very much."

"I'll ask you to dine with us quietly sometime, but mind, you come at your own risk; don't blame me if you have a very dull evening."

Chapter VI

BUT WHEN AT LAST I MET CHARLES STRICKLAND, IT WAS UNDER CIRCUMstances which allowed me to do no more than just make his acquaintance. One morning Mrs. Strickland sent me round a note to say that she was giving a dinner-party that evening, and one of her guests had failed her. She asked me to stop the gap. She wrote:

It's only decent to warn you that you will be bored to extinction. It was a thoroughly dull party from the beginning, but if you will come I shall be uncommonly grateful. And you and I can have a little chat by ourselves.

It was only neighbourly to accept.

When Mrs. Strickland introduced me to her husband, he gave me a rather indifferent hand to shake. Turning to him gaily, she attempted a small jest.

"I asked him to show him that I really had a husband. I think he was beginning to doubt it."

Strickland gave the polite little laugh with which people acknowledge a facetiousness in which they see nothing funny, but did not speak. New arrivals claimed my host's attention, and I was left to myself. When at last we were all assembled, waiting for dinner to be announced, I reflected, while I chatted with the woman I had been asked to "take in," that civilised man practises a strange ingenuity in wasting on tedious exercises the brief span of his life. It was the kind of party which makes you wonder why the hostess has troubled to bid her guests, and why the guests have troubled to come. There were ten people. They met with indifference, and would part with relief. It was, of course, a purely social function. The Stricklands "owed" dinners to a number of persons, whom they took no interest in, and so had asked them; these persons had accepted. Why? To avoid the tedium of dining *tête-à-tête*, to give their servants a rest, because there was no reason to refuse, because they were "owed" a dinner.

The dining-room was inconveniently crowded. There was a K.C. and his wife, a Government official and his wife, Mrs. Strickland's sister and her husband, Colonel MacAndrew, and the wife of a Member of Parliament. It was because the Member of Parliament found that he could not leave the House that I had been invited. The respectability of the party was portentous. The women were too nice to be well dressed, and too sure of their position to be amusing. The men were solid. There was about all of them an air of well-satisfied prosperity.

Everyone talked a little louder than natural in an instinctive desire to make the party go, and there was a great deal of noise in the room. But there was no general conversation. Each one talked to his neighbour; to his neighbour on the right during the soup, fish, and entree; to his neighbour on the left during the roast, sweet, and savoury. They talked of the political situation and of golf, of their children and the latest play, of the pictures at the Royal Academy, of the weather and their plans for the holidays. There was never a pause, and the noise grew louder. Mrs. Strickland might congratulate herself that her party was a success. Her husband played his part with decorum. Perhaps he did not talk very much, and I fancied there was towards the end a look of fatigue in the faces of the women on either side of him. They were finding him heavy. Once or twice Mrs. Strickland's eyes rested on him somewhat anxiously.

At last she rose and shepherded the ladies out of the room. Strickland shut the door behind her, and, moving to the other end of the table, took his place between the K.C. and the Government official. He passed round the port again and handed us cigars. The K.C. remarked on the excellence of the wine, and Strickland told us where he got it. We began to chat about vintages and tobacco. The K.C. told us of a case he was engaged in, and the Colonel talked about polo. I had nothing to say and so sat silent, trying politely to show interest in the conversation; and because I thought no one was in the least concerned with me, examined Strickland at my ease. He was bigger than I expected: I do not know why I had imagined him slender and of insignificant appearance; in point of fact he was broad and heavy, with large hands and feet, and he wore his evening clothes clumsily. He gave you somewhat the idea of a coachman dressed up for the occasion. He was a man of forty, not good-looking, and yet not ugly, for his features were rather good; but they were all a little larger than life-size, and the effect was ungainly. He was clean-shaven, and his large face looked uncomfortably naked. His hair was reddish, cut very short, and his eyes were small, blue or grey. He looked commonplace. I no longer wondered that Mrs. Strickland felt a certain embarrassment about him; he was scarcely a credit to a woman who wanted to make herself a position in the world of art and letters. It was obvious that he had no social gifts, but these a man can do without; he had no eccentricity even, to take him out of the common run; he was just a good, dull, honest, plain man. One would admire his excellent qualities, but avoid his company. He was null. He was probably a worthy member of society, a good husband and father, an honest broker; but there was no reason to waste one's time over him.

Chapter VII

THE SEASON WAS DRAWING TO ITS DUSTY END, AND EVERYONE I KNEW WAS arranging to go away. Mrs. Strickland was taking her family to the coast of Norfolk, so that the children might have the sea and her husband golf. We said good-bye to one another, and arranged to meet in the autumn. But on my last day in town, coming out of the Stores, I met her with her son and daughter; like myself, she had been making her final purchases before leaving London, and we were both hot and tired. I proposed that we should all go and eat ices in the park.

I think Mrs. Strickland was glad to show me her children, and she accepted my invitation with alacrity. They were even more attractive than their photographs had suggested, and she was right to be proud of them. I was young enough for them not to feel shy, and they chattered merrily about one thing and another. They were extraordinarily nice, healthy young children. It was very agreeable under the trees.

When in an hour they crowded into a cab to go home, I strolled idly to my club. I was perhaps a little lonely, and it was with a touch of envy that I thought of the pleasant family life of which I had had a glimpse. They seemed devoted to one another. They had little private jokes of their own which, unintelligible to the outsider, amused them enormously. Perhaps Charles Strickland was dull judged by a standard that demanded above all things verbal scintillation; but his intelligence was adequate to his surroundings, and that is a passport, not only to reasonable success, but still more to happiness. Mrs. Strickland was a charming woman, and she loved him. I pictured their lives, troubled by no untoward adventure, honest, decent, and, by reason of those two upstanding, pleasant children, so obviously destined to carry on the normal traditions of their race and station, not without significance. They would grow old insensibly; they would see their son and daughter come to years of reason, marry in due course—the one a pretty girl, future mother of healthy children; the other a handsome, manly fellow, obviously a soldier; and at last, prosperous in their dignified retirement, beloved by their descendants, after a happy, not unuseful life, in the fullness of their age they would sink into the grave.

That must be the story of innumerable couples, and the pattern of life it offers has a homely grace. It reminds you of a placid rivulet, meandering smoothly through green pastures and shaded by pleasant trees, till at last it falls into the vasty sea; but the sea is so calm, so silent, so indifferent, that you are troubled suddenly by a vague uneasiness. Perhaps it is only by a kink in my nature, strong in me even in those days, that I felt in such an existence, the share of the great majority, something amiss. I recognised its social values, I saw its ordered happiness, but a fever in my blood asked for a wilder course. There seemed to me something alarming in such easy delights. In my heart was a desire to live more dangerously. I was not unprepared for jagged rocks and treacherous shoals if I could only have change—change and the excitement of the unforeseen.

Chapter VIII

ON READING OVER WHAT I HAVE WRITTEN OF THE STRICKLANDS, I AM CONscious that they must seem shadowy. I have been able to invest them with none of those characteristics which make the persons of a book exist with a real life of their own; and, wondering if the fault is mine, I rack my brains to remember idiosyncrasies which might lend them vividness. I feel that by dwelling on some trick of speech or some queer habit I should be able to give them a significance peculiar to themselves. As they stand they are like the figures in an old tapestry; they do not separate themselves from the background, and at a distance seem to lose their pattern, so that you have little but a pleasing piece of colour. My only excuse is that the impression they made on me was no other. There was just that shadowiness about them which you find in people whose lives are part of the social organism, so that they exist in it and by it only. They are like cells in the body, essential, but, so long as they remain healthy, engulfed in the momentous whole. The Stricklands were an average family in the middle class. A pleasant, hospitable woman, with a harmless craze for the small lions of literary society; a rather dull man, doing his duty in that state of life in which a merciful Providence had placed him; two nice-looking, healthy children. Nothing could be more ordinary. I do not know that there was anything about them to excite the attention of the curious.

When I reflect on all that happened later, I ask myself if I was thick-witted not to see that there was in Charles Strickland at least something out of the common. Perhaps. I think that I have gathered in the years that intervene between then and now a fair knowledge of mankind, but even if when I first met the Stricklands I had the experience which I have now, I do not believe that I should have judged them differently. But because I have learned that man is incalculable, I should not at this time of day be so surprised by the news that reached me when in the early autumn I returned to London.

I had not been back twenty-four hours before I ran across Rose Waterford in Jermyn Street.

"You look very gay and sprightly," I said. "What's the matter with you?"

She smiled, and her eyes shone with a malice I knew already. It meant that she had heard some scandal about one of her friends, and the instinct of the literary woman was all alert.

"You did meet Charles Strickland, didn't you?"

Not only her face, but her whole body, gave a sense of alacrity. I nodded. I wondered if the poor devil had been hammered on the Stock Exchange or run over by an omnibus.

"Isn't it dreadful? He's run away from his wife."

Miss Waterford certainly felt that she could not do her subject justice on the curb of Jermyn Street, and so, like an artist, flung the bare fact at me and declared that she knew no details. I could not do her the injustice of supposing that so trifling a circumstance would have prevented her from giving them, but she was obstinate.

"I tell you I know nothing," she said, in reply to my agitated questions, and then, with an airy shrug of the shoulders: "I believe that a young person in a city tea-shop has left her situation."

She flashed a smile at me, and, protesting an engagement with her dentist, jauntily walked on. I was more interested than distressed. In those days my experience of life at first hand was small, and it excited me to come upon an incident among people I knew of the same sort as I had read in books. I confess that time has now accustomed me to incidents of this character among my acquaintance. But I was a little shocked. Strickland was certainly forty, and I thought it disgusting that a man of his age should concern himself with affairs of the heart. With the superciliousness of extreme youth, I put thirty-five as the utmost limit at which a man might fall in love without making a fool of himself. And this news was slightly disconcerting to me personally, because I had written from the country to Mrs. Strickland, announcing my return, and had added that unless I heard from her to the contrary, I would come on a certain day to drink a dish of tea with her. This was the very day, and I had received no word from Mrs. Strickland. Did she want to see me or did she not? It was likely enough that in the agitation of the moment my note had escaped her memory. Perhaps I should be wiser not to go. On the other hand, she might wish to keep the affair quiet, and it might be highly indiscreet on my part to give any sign that this strange news had reached me. I was torn between the fear of hurting a nice woman's feelings and the fear of being in the way. I felt she must be suffering, and I did not want to see a pain which I could not help; but in my heart was a desire, that I felt a little ashamed of, to see how she was taking it. I did not know what to do.

Finally it occurred to me that I would call as though nothing had happened, and send a message in by the maid asking Mrs. Strickland if it was convenient for her to see me. This would give her the opportunity to send me away. But I was overwhelmed with embarrassment when I said to the maid the phrase I had prepared, and while I waited for the answer in a dark passage I had to call up all my strength of mind not to bolt. The maid came back. Her manner suggested to my excited fancy a complete knowledge of the domestic calamity.

"Will you come this way, sir?" she said.

I followed her into the drawing-room. The blinds were partly drawn to darken the room, and Mrs. Strickland was sitting with her back to the light. Her brother-in-law, Colonel MacAndrew, stood in front of the fireplace, warming his back at an unlit fire. To myself my entrance seemed excessively awkward. I imagined that my arrival had taken them by surprise, and Mrs. Strickland had let me come in only because she had forgotten to put me off. I fancied that the Colonel resented the interruption.

"I wasn't quite sure if you expected me," I said, trying to seem unconcerned.

"Of course I did. Anne will bring the tea in a minute."

Even in the darkened room, I could not help seeing that Mrs. Strickland's face was all swollen with tears. Her skin, never very good, was earthy.

"You remember my brother-in-law, don't you? You met at dinner, just before the holidays."

We shook hands. I felt so shy that I could think of nothing to say, but Mrs. Strickland came to my rescue. She asked me what I had been doing with myself during the summer, and with this help I managed to make some conversation till tea was brought in. The Colonel asked for a whisky-and-soda.

"You'd better have one too, Amy," he said.

"No; I prefer tea."

This was the first suggestion that anything untoward had happened. I took no notice, and did my best to engage Mrs. Strickland in talk. The Colonel, still standing in front of the fireplace, uttered no word. I wondered how soon I could decently take my leave, and I asked myself why on earth Mrs. Strickland had allowed me to come. There were no flowers, and various knick-knacks, put away during the summer, had not been replaced; there was something cheerless and stiff about the room which had always seemed so friendly; it gave you an odd feeling, as though someone were lying dead on the other side of the wall. I finished tea.

"Will you have a cigarette?" asked Mrs. Strickland.

She looked about for the box, but it was not to be seen.

"I'm afraid there are none."

Suddenly she burst into tears, and hurried from the room.

I was startled. I suppose now that the lack of cigarettes, brought as a rule by her husband, forced him back upon her recollection, and the new feeling that the small comforts she was used to were missing gave her a sudden pang. She realised that the old life was gone and done with. It was impossible to keep up our social pretences any longer.

"I daresay you'd like me to go," I said to the Colonel, getting up.

"I suppose you've heard that blackguard has deserted her," he cried explosively.

I hesitated.

"You know how people gossip," I answered. "I was vaguely told that something was wrong."

"He's bolted. He's gone off to Paris with a woman. He's left Amy without a penny."

"I'm awfully sorry," I said, not knowing what else to say.

The Colonel gulped down his whisky. He was a tall, lean man of fifty, with a drooping moustache and grey hair. He had pale blue eyes and a weak mouth. I remembered from my previous meeting with him that he had a foolish face, and was proud of the fact that for the ten years before he left the army he had played polo three days a week.

"I don't suppose Mrs. Strickland wants to be bothered with me just now," I said. "Will you tell her how sorry I am? If there's anything I can do, I shall be delighted to do it."

He took no notice of me.

"I don't know what's to become of her. And then there are the children. Are they going to live on air? Seventeen years."

"What about seventeen years?"

"They've been married," he snapped. "I never liked him. Of course he was my brother-in-law, and I made the best of it. Did you think him a gentleman? She ought never to have married him."

"Is it absolutely final?"

"There's only one thing for her to do, and that's to divorce him. That's what I was telling her when you came in. 'Fire in with your petition, my dear Amy,' I said. 'You owe it to yourself and you owe it to the children.' He'd better not let me catch sight of him. I'd thrash him within an inch of his life."

I could not help thinking that Colonel MacAndrew might have some difficulty in doing this, since Strickland had struck me as a hefty fellow, but I did not say anything. It is always distressing when outraged morality does not possess the strength of arm to administer direct chastisement on the sinner. I was making up my mind to another attempt at going when Mrs. Strickland came back. She had dried her eyes and powdered her nose.

"I'm sorry I broke down," she said. "I'm glad you didn't go away."

She sat down. I did not at all know what to say. I felt a certain shyness at referring to matters which were no concern of mine. I did not then know the besetting sin of woman, the passion to discuss her private affairs with anyone who is willing to listen. Mrs. Strickland seemed to make an effort over herself.

"Are people talking about it?" she asked.

I was taken aback by her assumption that I knew all about her domestic misfortune.

"I've only just come back. The only person I've seen is Rose Waterford."

Mrs. Strickland clasped her hands.

"Tell me exactly what she said." And when I hesitated, she insisted. "I particularly want to know."

"You know the way people talk. She's not very reliable, is she? She said your husband had left you."

"Is that all?"

I did not choose to repeat Rose Waterford's parting reference to a girl from a tea-shop. I lied.

"She didn't say anything about his going with anyone?"

"No."

"That's all I wanted to know."

I was a little puzzled, but at all events I understood that I might now take my leave. When I shook hands with Mrs. Strickland I told her that if I could be of any use to her I should be very glad. She smiled wanly.

"Thank you so much. I don't know that anybody can do anything for me."

Too shy to express my sympathy, I turned to say good-bye to the Colonel. He did not take my hand.

"I'm just coming. If you're walking up Victoria Street, I'll come along with you."

"All right," I said. "Come on."

Chapter IX

"THIS IS A TERRIBLE THING," HE SAID, THE MOMENT WE GOT OUT INTO THE street."

I realised that he had come away with me in order to discuss once more what he had been already discussing for hours with his sister-in-law.

"We don't know who the woman is, you know," he said. "All we know is that the blackguard's gone to Paris."

"I thought they got on so well."

"So they did. Why, just before you came in Amy said they'd never had a quarrel in the whole of their married life. You know Amy. There never was a better woman in the world."

Since these confidences were thrust on me, I saw no harm in asking a few questions.

"But do you mean to say she suspected nothing?"

"Nothing. He spent August with her and the children in Norfolk. He was just the same as he'd always been. We went down for two or three days, my wife and I, and I played golf with him. He came back to town in September to let his partner go away, and Amy stayed on in the country. They'd taken a house for six weeks, and at the end of her tenancy she wrote to tell him on which day she was arriving in London. He answered from Paris. He said he'd made up his mind not to live with her anymore."

"What explanation did he give?"

"My dear fellow, he gave no explanation. I've seen the letter. It wasn't more than ten lines."

"But that's extraordinary."

We happened then to cross the street, and the traffic prevented us from speaking. What Colonel MacAndrew had told me seemed very improbable, and I suspected that Mrs. Strickland, for reasons of her own, had concealed from him some part of the facts. It was clear that a man after seventeen years of wedlock did not leave his wife without certain occurrences which must have led her to suspect that all was not well with their married life. The Colonel caught me up.

"Of course, there was no explanation he could give except that he'd gone off with a woman. I suppose he thought she could find that out for herself. That's the sort of chap he was."

"What is Mrs. Strickland going to do?"

"Well, the first thing is to get our proofs. I'm going over to Paris myself."

"And what about his business?"

"That's where he's been so artful. He's been drawing in his horns for the last year."

"Did he tell his partner he was leaving?"

"Not a word."

Colonel MacAndrew had a very sketchy knowledge of business matters, and I had none at all, so I did not quite understand under what conditions Strickland had left his affairs. I gathered that the deserted partner was very angry and threatened proceedings. It appeared that when everything was settled he would be four or five hundred pounds out of pocket.

"It's lucky the furniture in the flat is in Amy's name. She'll have that at all events."

"Did you mean it when you said she wouldn't have a bob?"

"Of course I did. She's got two or three hundred pounds and the furniture."

"But how is she going to live?"

"God knows."

The affair seemed to grow more complicated, and the Colonel, with his expletives and his indignation, confused rather than informed me. I was glad that, catching sight of the clock at the Army and Navy Stores, he remembered an engagement to play cards at his club, and so left me to cut across St. James Park.

Chapter X

A DAY OR TWO LATER MRS. STRICKLAND SENT ME ROUND A NOTE ASKING IF I could go and see her that evening after dinner. I found her alone. Her black dress, simple to austerity, suggested her bereaved condition, and I was innocently astonished that notwithstanding a real emotion she was able to dress the part she had to play according to her notions of seemliness.

"You said that if I wanted you to do anything you wouldn't mind doing it," she remarked.

"It was quite true."

"Will you go over to Paris and see Charlie?"

"I?"

I was taken aback. I reflected that I had only seen him once. I did not know what she wanted me to do.

"Fred is set on going." Fred was Colonel MacAndrew. "But I'm sure he's not the man to go. He'll only make things worse. I don't know who else to ask."

Her voice trembled a little, and I felt a brute even to hesitate.

"But I've not spoken ten words to your husband. He doesn't know me. He'll probably just tell me to go to the devil."

"That wouldn't hurt you," said Mrs. Strickland, smiling.

"What is it exactly you want me to do?"

She did not answer directly.

"I think it's rather an advantage that he doesn't know you. You see, he never really liked Fred; he thought him a fool; he didn't understand soldiers. Fred would fly into a passion, and there'd be a quarrel, and things would be worse instead of better. If you said you came on my behalf, he couldn't refuse to listen to you."

"I haven't known you very long," I answered. "I don't see how anyone can be expected to tackle a case like this unless he knows all the details. I don't want to pry into what doesn't concern me. Why don't you go and see him yourself?"

"You forget he isn't alone."

I held my tongue. I saw myself calling on Charles Strickland and sending in my card; I saw him come into the room, holding it between finger and thumb:

"To what do I owe this honour?"

"I've come to see you about your wife."

"Really. When you are a little older you will doubtless learn the advantage of minding your own business. If you will be so good as to turn your head slightly to the left, you will see the door. I wish you good-afternoon."

I foresaw that it would be difficult to make my exit with dignity, and I wished to goodness that I had not returned to London till Mrs. Strickland had composed her difficulties. I stole a glance at her. She was immersed in thought. Presently she looked up at me, sighed deeply, and smiled.

"It was all so unexpected," she said. "We'd been married seventeen years. I never dreamed that Charlie was the sort of man to get infatuated with anyone. We always got on very well together. Of course, I had a great many interests that he didn't share."

"Have you found out who"—I did not quite know how to express myself—"who the person, who it is he's gone away with?"

"No. No one seems to have an idea. It's so strange. Generally when a man falls in love with someone people see them about together, lunching or something, and her friends always come and tell the wife. I had no warning—nothing. His letter came like a thunderbolt. I thought he was perfectly happy."

She began to cry, poor thing, and I felt very sorry for her. But in a little while she grew calmer.

"It's no good making a fool of myself," she said, drying her eyes. "The only thing is to decide what is the best thing to do."

She went on, talking somewhat at random, now of the recent past, then of their first meeting and their marriage; but presently I began to form a fairly coherent picture of their lives; and it seemed to me that my surmises had not been incorrect. Mrs. Strickland was the daughter of an Indian civilian, who on his retirement had settled in the depths of the country, but it was his habit every August to take his family to Eastbourne for change of air; and it was here, when she was twenty, that she met Charles Strickland. He was twenty-three. They played together, walked on the front together, listened together to the nigger minstrels; and she had made up her mind to accept him a week before he proposed to her. They lived in London, first in Hampstead, and then, as he grew more prosperous, in town. Two children were born to them.

"He always seemed very fond of them. Even if he was tired of me, I wonder that he had the heart to leave them. It's all so incredible. Even now I can hardly believe it's true."

At last she showed me the letter he had written. I was curious to see it, but had not ventured to ask for it.

My dear Amy—I think you will find everything all right in the flat. I have given Anne your instructions, and dinner will be ready for you and the children when you come. I shall not be there to meet you. I have made up my mind to live apart from you, and I am going to Paris in the morning. I shall post this letter on my arrival. I shall not come back. My decision is irrevocable.

Yours always,
CHARLES STRICKLAND

"Not a word of explanation or regret. Don't you think it's inhuman?"

"It's a very strange letter under the circumstances," I replied.

"There's only one explanation, and that is that he's not himself. I don't know who this woman is who's got hold of him, but she's made him into another man. It's evidently been going on a long time."

"What makes you think that?"

"Fred found that out. My husband said he went to the club three or four nights a week to play bridge. Fred knows one of the members, and said something about Charles being a great bridge-player. The man was surprised. He said he'd never even seen Charles in the card-room. It's quite clear now that when I thought Charles was at his club he was with her."

I was silent for a moment. Then I thought of the children.

"It must have been difficult to explain to Robert," I said.

"Oh, I never said a word to either of them. You see, we only came up to town the day before they had to go back to school. I had the presence of mind to say that their father had been called away on business."

It could not have been very easy to be bright and careless with that sudden secret in her heart, nor to give her attention to all the things that needed doing to get her children comfortably packed off. Mrs. Strickland's voice broke again.

"And what is to happen to them, poor darlings? How are we going to live?"

She struggled for self-control, and I saw her hands clench and unclench spasmodically. It was dreadfully painful.

"Of course I'll go over to Paris if you think I can do any good, but you must tell me exactly what you want me to do."

"I want him to come back."

"I understood from Colonel MacAndrew that you'd made up your mind to divorce him."

"I'll never divorce him," she answered with a sudden violence. "Tell him that from me. He'll never be able to marry that woman. I'm as obstinate as he is, and I'll never divorce him. I have to think of my children."

I think she added this to explain her attitude to me, but I thought it was due to a very natural jealousy rather than to maternal solicitude.

"Are you in love with him still?"

"I don't know. I want him to come back. If he'll do that we'll let bygones be bygones. After all, we've been married for seventeen years. I'm a broadminded woman. I wouldn't have minded what he did as long as I knew nothing about it. He must know that his infatuation won't last. If he'll come back now everything can be smoothed over, and no one will know anything about it."

It chilled me a little that Mrs. Strickland should be concerned with gossip, for I did not know then how great a part is played in women's life by the opinion of others. It throws a shadow of insincerity over their most deeply felt emotions.

It was known where Strickland was staying. His partner, in a violent letter, sent to his bank, had taunted him with hiding his whereabouts: and Strickland, in a cynical and humourous reply, had told his partner exactly where to find him. He was apparently living in an hotel.

"I've never heard of it," said Mrs. Strickland. "But Fred knows it well. He says it's very expensive."

She flushed darkly. I imagined that she saw her husband installed in a luxurious suite of rooms, dining at one smart restaurant after another, and she pictured his days spent at race-meetings and his evenings at the play.

"It can't go on at his age," she said. "After all, he's forty. I could understand it in a young man, but I think it's horrible in a man of his years, with children who are nearly grown-up. His health will never stand it."

Anger struggled in her breast with misery.

"Tell him that our home cries out for him. Everything is just the same, and yet everything is different. I can't live without him. I'd sooner kill myself. Talk to him about the past, and all we've gone through together. What am I to say to the children when they ask for him? His room is exactly as it was when he left it. It's waiting for him. We're all waiting for him."

Now she told me exactly what I should say. She gave me elaborate answers to every possible observation of his.

"You will do everything you can for me?" she said pitifully. "Tell him what a state I'm in."

I saw that she wished me to appeal to his sympathies by every means in my power. She was weeping freely. I was extraordinarily touched. I felt indignant at Strickland's cold cruelty, and I promised to do all I could to bring him back. I agreed to go over on the next day but one, and to stay in Paris till I had achieved something. Then, as it was growing late and we were both exhausted by so much emotion, I left her.

Chapter XI

During the journey I thought over my errand with misgiving. Now that I was free from the spectacle of Mrs. Strickland's distress I could consider the matter more calmly. I was puzzled by the contradictions that I saw in her behaviour. She was very unhappy, but to excite my sympathy she was able to make a show of her unhappiness. It was evident that she had been prepared to weep, for she had provided herself with a sufficiency of handkerchiefs; I admired her forethought, but in retrospect it made her tears perhaps less moving. I could not decide whether she desired the return of her husband because she loved him, or because she dreaded the tongue of scandal; and I was perturbed by the suspicion that the anguish of love contemned was alloyed in her broken heart with the pangs, sordid to my young mind, of wounded vanity. I had not yet learned how contradictory is human nature; I did not know how much pose there is in the sincere, how much baseness in the noble, nor how much goodness in the reprobate.

But there was something of an adventure in my trip, and my spirits rose as I approached Paris. I saw myself, too, from the dramatic standpoint, and I was pleased with my rôle of the trusted friend bringing back the errant husband to his forgiving wife. I made up my mind to see Strickland the following evening, for I felt instinctively that the hour must be chosen with delicacy. An appeal to the emotions is little likely to be effectual before luncheon. My own thoughts were then constantly occupied with love, but I never could imagine connubial bliss till after tea.

I enquired at my hotel for that in which Charles Strickland was living. It was called the Hôtel des Belges. But the concierge, somewhat to my surprise, had never heard of it. I had understood from Mrs. Strickland that it was a large and sumptuous place at the back of the Rue de Rivoli. We looked it out in the directory. The only hotel of that name was in the Rue des Moines. The quarter was not fashionable; it was not even respectable. I shook my head.

"I'm sure that's not it," I said.

The concierge shrugged his shoulders. There was no other hotel of that name in Paris. It occurred to me that Strickland had concealed his address, after all. In giving his partner the one I knew he was perhaps playing a trick on him. I do not know why I had an inkling that it would appeal to Strickland's sense of humour to bring a furious stockbroker over to Paris on a fool's errand to an ill-famed house in a mean street. Still, I thought I had better go and see. Next day about six o'clock I took a cab to the Rue des Moines, but dismissed it at the corner, since I preferred to walk to the hotel and look at it before I went in. It was a street of small shops subservient to the needs of poor people, and about the middle of it, on the left as I walked down, was the Hôtel des Belges. My own hotel was modest enough, but it was magnificent in comparison with this. It was a tall, shabby building, that cannot have been painted for years, and it had so bedraggled an air that the houses on each side of it looked neat and clean. The dirty windows were all shut. It was not here that Charles Strickland lived in guilty splendour with the unknown charmer for whose sake he had abandoned honour and duty. I was vexed, for I felt that I had been made a fool of, and I nearly turned away without making an enquiry. I went in only to be able to tell Mrs. Strickland that I had done my best.

The door was at the side of a shop. It stood open, and just within was a sign: *Bureau au premier.* I walked up narrow stairs, and on the landing found a sort of box, glassed in, within which were a desk and a couple of chairs. There was a bench outside, on which it might be presumed the night porter passed uneasy nights. There was no one about, but under an electric bell was written *Garçon.* I rang, and presently a waiter appeared. He was a young man with furtive eyes and a sullen look. He was in shirt-sleeves and carpet slippers.

I do not know why I made my enquiry as casual as possible.

"Does Mr. Strickland live here by any chance?" I asked.

"Number thirty-two. On the sixth floor."

I was so surprised that for a moment I did not answer.

"Is he in?"

The waiter looked at a board in the *bureau.*

"He hasn't left his key. Go up and you'll see."

I thought it as well to put one more question.

"Madame est là?"

"Monsieur est seul."

The waiter looked at me suspiciously as I made my way upstairs. They were dark and airless. There was a foul and musty smell. Three flights up a woman in a dressing-gown, with touzled hair, opened a door and looked at me silently as I passed. At length I reached the sixth floor, and knocked at the door numbered thirty-two. There was a sound within, and the door was partly opened. Charles Strickland stood before me. He uttered not a word. He evidently did not know me.

I told him my name. I tried my best to assume an airy manner.

"You don't remember me. I had the pleasure of dining with you last July."

"Come in," he said cheerily. "I'm delighted to see you. Take a pew."

I entered. It was a very small room, overcrowded with furniture of the style which the French know as Louis Philippe. There was a large wooden bed-stead on which was a billowing red eiderdown, and there was a large wardrobe, a round table, a very small wash-stand, and two stuffed chairs covered with red rep. Everything was dirty and shabby. There was no sign of the abandoned luxury that Colonel MacAndrew had so confidently described. Strickland threw on the floor the clothes that burdened one of the chairs, and I sat down on it.

"What can I do for you?" he asked.

In that small room he seemed even bigger than I remembered him. He wore an old Norfolk jacket, and he had not shaved for several days. When last I saw him he was spruce enough, but he looked ill at ease: now, untidy and ill-kempt, he looked perfectly at home. I did not know how he would take the remark I had prepared.

"I've come to see you on behalf of your wife."

"I was just going out to have a drink before dinner. You'd better come too. Do you like absinthe?"

"I can drink it."

"Come on, then."

He put on a bowler hat much in need of brushing.

"We might dine together. You owe me a dinner, you know."

"Certainly. Are you alone?"

I flattered myself that I had got in that important question very naturally.

"Oh yes. In point of fact I've not spoken to a soul for three days. My French isn't exactly brilliant."

I wondered as I preceded him downstairs what had happened to the little lady in the tea-shop. Had they quarrelled already, or was his infatuation passed? It seemed hardly likely if, as appeared, he had been taking steps for a year to make his desperate plunge. We walked to the Avenue de Clichy, and sat down at one of the tables on the pavement of a large café.

Chapter XII

THE AVENUE DE CLICHY WAS CROWDED AT THAT HOUR, AND A LIVELY FANCY might see in the passers-by the personages of many a sordid romance. There were clerks and shopgirls; old fellows who might have stepped out of the pages of Honoré de Balzac; members, male and female, of the professions which make their profit of the frailties of mankind. There is in the streets of the poorer quarters of Paris a thronging vitality which excites the blood and prepares the soul for the unexpected.

"Do you know Paris well?" I asked.

"No. We came on our honeymoon. I haven't been since."

"How on earth did you find out your hotel?"

"It was recommended to me. I wanted something cheap."

The absinthe came, and with due solemnity we dropped water over the melting sugar.

"I thought I'd better tell you at once why I had come to see you," I said, not without embarrassment.

His eyes twinkled.

"I thought somebody would come along sooner or later. I've had a lot of letters from Amy."

"Then you know pretty well what I've got to say."

"I've not read them."

I lit a cigarette to give myself a moment's time. I did not quite know now how to set about my mission. The eloquent phrases I had arranged, pathetic or indignant, seemed out of place on the Avenue de Clichy. Suddenly he gave a chuckle.

"Beastly job for you this, isn't it?"

"Oh, I don't know," I answered.

"Well, look here, you get it over, and then we'll have a jolly evening."

I hesitated.

"Has it occurred to you that your wife is frightfully unhappy?"

"She'll get over it."

I cannot describe the extraordinary callousness with which he made this reply. It disconcerted me, but I did my best not to show it. I adopted the tone used by my Uncle Henry, a clergyman, when he was asking one of his relatives for a subscription to the Additional Curates Society.

"You don't mind my talking to you frankly?"

He shook his head, smiling.

"Has she deserved that you should treat her like this?"

"No."

"Have you any complaint to make against her?"

"None."

"Then, isn't it monstrous to leave her in this fashion, after seventeen years of married life, without a fault to find with her?"

"Monstrous."

I glanced at him with surprise. His cordial agreement with all I said cut the ground from under my feet. It made my position complicated, not to say ludicrous. I was prepared to be persuasive, touching, and hortatory, admonitory and expostulating, if need be vituperative even, indignant and sarcastic; but what the devil does a mentor do when the sinner makes no bones about confessing his sin? I had no experience, since my own practice has always been to deny everything.

"What, then?" asked Strickland.

I tried to curl my lip.

"Well, if you acknowledge that, there doesn't seem much more to be said."

"I don't think there is."

I felt that I was not carrying out my embassy with any great skill. I was distinctly nettled.

"Hang it all, one can't leave a woman without a bob."

"Why not?"

"How is she going to live?"

"I've supported her for seventeen years. Why shouldn't she support herself for a change?"

"She can't."

"Let her try."

Of course there were many things I might have answered to this. I might have spoken of the economic position of woman, of the contract, tacit and overt, which a man accepts by his marriage, and of much else; but I felt that there was only one point which really signified.

"Don't you care for her anymore?"

"Not a bit," he replied.

The matter was immensely serious for all the parties concerned, but there was in the manner of his answer such a cheerful effrontery that I had to bite my lips in order not to laugh. I reminded myself that his behaviour was abominable. I worked myself up into a state of moral indignation.

"Damn it all, there are your children to think of. They've never done you any harm. They didn't ask to be brought into the world. If you chuck everything like this, they'll be thrown on the streets."

"They've had a good many years of comfort. It's much more than the majority of children have. Besides, somebody will look after them. When it comes to the point, the MacAndrews will pay for their schooling."

"But aren't you fond of them? They're such awfully nice kids. Do you mean to say you don't want to have anything more to do with them?"

"I liked them all right when they were kids, but now they're growing up I haven't got any particular feeling for them."

"It's just inhuman."

"I daresay."

"You don't seem in the least ashamed."

"I'm not."

I tried another tack.

"Everyone will think you a perfect swine."

"Let them."

"Won't it mean anything to you to know that people loathe and despise you?"

"No."

His brief answer was so scornful that it made my question, natural though it was, seem absurd. I reflected for a minute or two.

"I wonder if one can live quite comfortably when one's conscious of the disapproval of one's fellows? Are you sure it won't begin to worry you? Everyone has some sort of a conscience, and sooner or later it will find you out. Supposing your wife died, wouldn't you be tortured by remorse?"

He did not answer, and I waited for some time for him to speak. At last I had to break the silence myself.

"What have you to say to that?"

"Only that you're a damned fool."

"At all events, you can be forced to support your wife and children," I retorted, somewhat piqued. "I suppose the law has some protection to offer them."

"Can the law get blood out of a stone? I haven't any money. I've got about a hundred pounds."

I began to be more puzzled than before. It was true that his hotel pointed to the most straitened circumstances.

"What are you going to do when you've spent that?"

"Earn some."

He was perfectly cool, and his eyes kept that mocking smile which made all I said seem rather foolish. I paused for a little while to consider what I had better say next. But it was he who spoke first.

"Why doesn't Amy marry again? She's comparatively young, and she's not unattractive. I can recommend her as an excellent wife. If she wants to divorce me I don't mind giving her the necessary grounds."

Now it was my turn to smile. He was very cunning, but it was evidently this that he was aiming at. He had some reason to conceal the fact that he had run away with a woman, and he was using every precaution to hide her whereabouts. I answered with decision.

"Your wife says that nothing you can do will ever induce her to divorce you. She's quite made up her mind. You can put any possibility of that definitely out of your head."

He looked at me with an astonishment that was certainly not feigned. The smile abandoned his lips, and he spoke quite seriously.

"But, my dear fellow, I don't care. It doesn't matter a twopenny damn to me one way or the other."

I laughed.

"Oh, come now; you mustn't think us such fools as all that. We happen to know that you came away with a woman."

He gave a little start, and then suddenly burst into a shout of laughter. He laughed so uproariously that people sitting near us looked round, and some of them began to laugh too.

"I don't see anything very amusing in that."

"Poor Amy," he grinned.

Then his face grew bitterly scornful.

"What poor minds women have got! Love. It's always love. They think a man leaves only because he wants others. Do you think I should be such a fool as to do what I've done for a woman?"

"Do you mean to say you didn't leave your wife for another woman?"

"Of course not."

"On your word of honour?"

I don't know why I asked for that. It was very ingenuous of me.

"On my word of honour."

"Then, what in God's name have you left her for?"

"I want to paint."

I looked at him for quite a long time. I did not understand. I thought he was mad. It must be remembered that I was very young, and I looked upon him as a middle-aged man. I forgot everything but my own amazement.

"But you're forty."

"That's what made me think it was high time to begin."

"Have you ever painted?"

"I rather wanted to be a painter when I was a boy, but my father made me go into business because he said there was no money in art. I began to paint a bit a year ago. For the last year I've been going to some classes at night."

"Was that where you went when Mrs. Strickland thought you were playing bridge at your club?"

"That's it."

"Why didn't you tell her?"

"I preferred to keep it to myself."

"Can you paint?"

"Not yet. But I shall. That's why I've come over here. I couldn't get what I wanted in London. Perhaps I can here."

"Do you think it's likely that a man will do any good when he starts at your age? Most men begin painting at eighteen."

"I can learn quicker than I could when I was eighteen."

"What makes you think you have any talent?"

He did not answer for a minute. His gaze rested on the passing throng, but I do not think he saw it. His answer was no answer.

"I've got to paint."

"Aren't you taking an awful chance?"

He looked at me. His eyes had something strange in them, so that I felt rather uncomfortable.

"How old are you? Twenty-three?"

It seemed to me that the question was beside the point. It was natural that I should take chances; but he was a man whose youth was past, a stockbroker with a position of respectability, a wife and two children. A course that would have been natural for me was absurd for him. I wished to be quite fair.

"Of course a miracle may happen, and you may be a great painter, but you must confess the chances are a million to one against it. It'll be an awful sell if at the end you have to acknowledge you've made a hash of it."

"I've got to paint," he repeated.

"Supposing you're never anything more than third-rate, do you think it will have been worthwhile to give up everything? After all, in any other walk in life it doesn't matter if you're not very good; you can get along quite comfortably if you're just adequate; but it's different with an artist."

"You blasted fool," he said.

"I don't see why, unless it's folly to say the obvious."

"I tell you I've got to paint. I can't help myself. When a man falls into the water it doesn't matter how he swims, well or badly: he's got to get out or else he'll drown."

There was real passion in his voice, and in spite of myself I was impressed. I seemed to feel in him some vehement power that was struggling within him; it gave me the sensation of something very strong, overmastering, that held him, as it were, against his will. I could not understand. He seemed really to be possessed of a devil, and I felt that it might suddenly turn and rend him. Yet he looked ordinary enough. My eyes, resting on him curiously, caused him no embarrassment. I wondered what a stranger would have taken him to be, sitting there in his old Norfolk jacket and his unbrushed bowler; his trousers were baggy, his hands were not clean; and his face, with the red stubble of the unshaved chin, the little eyes, and the large, aggressive nose, was uncouth and coarse. His mouth was large, his lips were heavy and sensual. No; I could not have placed him.

"You won't go back to your wife?" I said at last.

"Never."

"She's willing to forget everything that's happened and start afresh. She'll never make you a single reproach."

"She can go to hell."

"You don't care if people think you an utter blackguard? You don't care if she and your children have to beg their bread?"

"Not a damn."

I was silent for a moment in order to give greater force to my next remark. I spoke as deliberately as I could.

"You are a most unmitigated cad."

"Now that you've got that off your chest, let's go and have dinner."

Chapter XIII

I DARESAY IT WOULD HAVE BEEN MORE SEEMLY TO DECLINE THIS PROPOSAL. I think perhaps I should have made a show of the indignation I really felt, and I am sure that Colonel MacAndrew at least would have thought well of me if I had been able to report my stout refusal to sit at the same table with a man of such character. But the fear of not being able to carry it through effectively has always made me shy of assuming the moral attitude; and in this case the certainty that my sentiments would be lost on Strickland made it peculiarly embarrassing to utter them. Only the poet or the saint can water an asphalt pavement in the confident anticipation that lilies will reward his labour.

I paid for what we had drunk, and we made our way to a cheap restaurant, crowded and gay, where we dined with pleasure. I had the appetite of youth and he of a hardened conscience. Then we went to a tavern to have coffee and liqueurs.

I had said all I had to say on the subject that had brought me to Paris, and though I felt it in a manner treacherous to Mrs. Strickland not to pursue it, I could not struggle against his indifference. It requires the feminine temperament to repeat the same thing three times with unabated zest. I solaced myself by thinking that it would be useful for me to find out what I could about Strickland's state of mind. It also interested me much more. But this was not an easy thing to do, for Strickland was not a fluent talker. He seemed to express himself with difficulty, as though words were not the medium with which his mind worked; and you had to guess the intentions of his soul by hackneyed phrases, slang, and vague, unfinished gestures. But though he said nothing of any consequence, there was something in his personality which prevented him from being dull. Perhaps it was sincerity. He did not seem to care much about the Paris he was now seeing for the first time (I did not count the visit with his wife), and he accepted sights which must have been strange to him without any sense of astonishment. I have been to Paris a hundred times, and it never fails to give me a thrill of excitement; I can never walk its streets without feeling myself on the verge of adventure. Strickland remained placid. Looking back, I think now that he was blind to everything but to some disturbing vision in his soul.

One rather absurd incident took place. There were a number of harlots in the tavern: some were sitting with men, others by themselves; and presently I noticed that one of these was looking at us. When she caught Strickland's eye she smiled. I do not think he saw her. In a little while she went out, but in a minute returned and, passing our table, very politely asked us to buy her something to drink. She sat down and I began to chat with her; but, it was plain that her interest was in Strickland. I explained that he knew no more than two words of French. She tried to talk to him, partly by signs, partly in pidgin French, which, for some reason, she thought would be more comprehensible to him, and she had half a dozen phrases of English. She made me translate what she could only express in her own tongue, and eagerly asked for the meaning of his replies. He was quite good-tempered, a little amused, but his indifference was obvious.

"I think you've made a conquest," I laughed.

"I'm not flattered."

In his place I should have been more embarrassed and less calm. She had laughing eyes and a most charming mouth. She was young. I wondered what she found so attractive in Strickland. She made no secret of her desires, and I was bidden to translate.

"She wants you to go home with her."

"I'm not taking any," he replied.

I put his answer as pleasantly as I could. It seemed to me a little ungracious to decline an invitation of that sort, and I ascribed his refusal to lack of money.

"But I like him," she said. "Tell him it's for love."

When I translated this, Strickland shrugged his shoulders impatiently.

"Tell her to go to hell," he said.

His manner made his answer quite plain, and the girl threw back her head with a sudden gesture. Perhaps she reddened under her paint. She rose to her feet.

"Monsieur n'est pas poli," she said.

She walked out of the inn. I was slightly vexed.

"There wasn't any need to insult her that I can see," I said. "After all, it was rather a compliment she was paying you."

"That sort of thing makes me sick," he said roughly.

I looked at him curiously. There was a real distaste in his face, and yet it was the face of a coarse and sensual man. I suppose the girl had been attracted by a certain brutality in it.

"I could have got all the women I wanted in London. I didn't come here for that."

Chapter XIV

During the journey back to England I thought much of Strickland. I tried to set in order what I had to tell his wife. It was unsatisfactory, and I could not imagine that she would be content with me; I was not content with myself. Strickland perplexed me. I could not understand his motives. When I had asked him what first gave him the idea of being a painter, he was unable or unwilling to tell me. I could make nothing of it. I tried to persuade myself than an obscure feeling of revolt had been gradually coming to a head in his slow mind, but to challenge this was the undoubted fact that he had never shown any impatience with the monotony of his life. If, seized by an intolerable boredom, he had determined to be a painter merely to break with irksome ties, it would have been comprehensible, and commonplace; but commonplace is precisely what I felt he was not. At last, because I was romantic, I devised an explanation which I acknowledged to be far-fetched, but which was the only one that in any way satisfied me. It was this: I asked myself whether there was not in his soul some deep-rooted instinct of creation, which the circumstances of his life had obscured, but which grew relentlessly, as a cancer may grow in the living tissues, till at last it took possession of his whole being and forced him irresistibly to action. The cuckoo lays its egg in the strange bird's nest, and when the young one is hatched it shoulders its foster-brothers out and breaks at last the nest that has sheltered it.

But how strange it was that the creative instinct should seize upon this dull stockbroker, to his own ruin, perhaps, and to the misfortune of such as were dependent on him; and yet no stranger than the way in which the spirit of God has seized men, powerful and rich, pursuing them with stubborn vigilance till at last, conquered, they have abandoned the joy of the world and the love of women for the painful austerities of the cloister. Conversion may come under many shapes, and it may be brought about in many ways. With some men it needs a cataclysm, as a stone may be broken to fragments by the fury of a torrent; but with some it comes gradually, as a stone may be worn away by the ceaseless fall of a drop of water. Strickland had the directness of the fanatic and the ferocity of the apostle.

But to my practical mind it remained to be seen whether the passion which obsessed him would be justified of its works. When I asked him what his brother-students at the night classes he had attended in London thought of his painting, he answered with a grin:

"They thought it a joke."

"Have you begun to go to a studio here?"

"Yes. The blighter came round this morning—the master, you know; when he saw my drawing he just raised his eyebrows and walked on."

Strickland chuckled. He did not seem discouraged. He was independent of the opinion of his fellows.

And it was just that which had most disconcerted me in my dealings with him. When people say they do not care what others think of them, for the most part they deceive themselves. Generally they mean only that they will do as they choose, in the confidence that no one will know their vagaries; and at the utmost only that they are willing to act contrary to the opinion of the majority because they are supported by the approval of their neighbours. It is not difficult to be unconventional in the eyes of the world when your unconventionality is but the convention of your set. It affords you then an inordinate amount of self-esteem. You have the self-satisfaction of courage without the inconvenience of danger. But the desire for approbation is perhaps the most deeply seated instinct of civilised man. No one runs so hurriedly to the cover of respectability as the unconventional woman who has exposed herself to the slings and arrows of outraged propriety. I do not believe the people who tell me they do not care a row of pins for the opinion of their fellows. It is the bravado of ignorance. They mean only that they do not fear reproaches for peccadillos which they are convinced none will discover.

But here was a man who sincerely did not mind what people thought of him, and so convention had no hold on him; he was like a wrestler whose body is oiled; you could not get a grip on him; it gave him a freedom which was an outrage. I remember saying to him:

"Look here, if everyone acted like you, the world couldn't go on."

"That's a damned silly thing to say. Everyone doesn't want to act like me. The great majority are perfectly content to do the ordinary thing."

And once I sought to be satirical.

"You evidently don't believe in the maxim: Act so that every one of your actions is capable of being made into a universal rule."

"I never heard it before, but it's rotten nonsense."

"Well, it was Kant who said it."

"I don't care; it's rotten nonsense."

Nor with such a man could you expect the appeal to conscience to be effective. You might as well ask for a reflection without a mirror. I take it that conscience is the guardian in the individual of the rules which the community has evolved for its own preservation. It is the policeman in all our hearts, set there to watch that we do not break its laws. It is the spy seated in the central stronghold of the ego. Man's desire for the approval of his fellows is so strong, his dread of their censure so violent, that he himself has brought his enemy within his gates; and it keeps watch over him, vigilant always in the interests of its master to crush any half-formed desire to break away from the herd. It will force him to place the good of society before his own. It is the very strong link that attaches the individual to the whole. And man, subservient to interests he has persuaded himself are greater than his own, makes himself a slave to his taskmaster. He sits him in a seat of honour. At last, like a courtier fawning on the royal stick that is laid about his shoulders, he prides himself on the sensitiveness of his conscience. Then he has no words hard enough for the man who does not recognise its sway; for, a member of society now, he realises accurately enough that against him he is powerless. When I saw that Strickland was really indifferent to the blame his conduct must excite, I could only draw back in horror as from a monster of hardly human shape.

The last words he said to me when I bade him good-night were:

"Tell Amy it's no good coming after me. Anyhow, I shall change my hotel, so she wouldn't be able to find me."

"My own impression is that she's well rid of you," I said.

"My dear fellow, I only hope you'll be able to make her see it. But women are very unintelligent."

Chapter XV

When I reached London I found waiting for me an urgent request that I should go to Mrs. Strickland's as soon after dinner as I could. I found her with Colonel MacAndrew and his wife. Mrs. Strickland's sister was older than she, not unlike her, but more faded; and she had the efficient air, as though she carried the British Empire in her pocket, which the wives of senior officers acquire from the consciousness of belonging to a superior caste. Her manner was brisk, and her good-breeding scarcely concealed her conviction that if you were not a soldier you might as well be a counter-jumper. She hated the Guards, whom she thought conceited, and she could not trust herself to speak of their ladies, who were so remiss in calling. Her gown was dowdy and expensive.

Mrs. Strickland was plainly nervous.

"Well, tell us your news," she said.

"I saw your husband. I'm afraid he's quite made up his mind not to return." I paused a little. "He wants to paint."

"What do you mean?" cried Mrs. Strickland, with the utmost astonishment.

"Did you never know that he was keen on that sort of thing."

"He must be as mad as a hatter," exclaimed the Colonel.

Mrs. Strickland frowned a little. She was searching among her recollections.

"I remember before we were married he used to potter about with a paint-box. But you never saw such daubs. We used to chaff him. He had absolutely no gift for anything like that."

"Of course it's only an excuse," said Mrs. MacAndrew.

Mrs. Strickland pondered deeply for some time. It was quite clear that she could not make head or tail of my announcement. She had put some order into the drawing-room by now, her housewifely instincts having got the better of her dismay; and it no longer bore that deserted look, like a furnished house long to let, which I had noticed on my first visit after the catastrophe. But now that I had seen Strickland in Paris it was difficult to imagine him in those surroundings. I thought it could hardly have failed to strike them that there was something incongruous in him.

"But if he wanted to be an artist, why didn't he say so?" asked Mrs. Strickland at last. "I should have thought I was the last person to be unsympathetic to—to aspirations of that kind."

Mrs. MacAndrew tightened her lips. I imagine that she had never looked with approval on her sister's leaning towards persons who cultivated the arts. She spoke of "culchaw" derisively.

Mrs. Strickland continued:

"After all, if he had any talent I should be the first to encourage it. I wouldn't have minded sacrifices. I'd much rather be married to a painter than to a stockbroker. If it weren't for the children, I wouldn't mind anything. I could be just as happy in a shabby studio in Chelsea as in this flat."

"My dear, I have no patience with you," cried Mrs. MacAndrew. "You don't mean to say you believe a word of this nonsense?"

"But I think it's true," I put in mildly.

She looked at me with good-humoured contempt.

"A man doesn't throw up his business and leave his wife and children at the age of forty to become a painter unless there's a woman in it. I suppose he met one of your—artistic friends, and she's turned his head."

A spot of colour rose suddenly to Mrs. Strickland's pale cheeks.

"What is she like?"

I hesitated a little. I knew that I had a bombshell.

"There isn't a woman."

Colonel MacAndrew and his wife uttered expressions of incredulity, and Mrs. Strickland sprang to her feet.

"Do you mean to say you never saw her?"

"There's no one to see. He's quite alone."

"That's preposterous," cried Mrs. MacAndrew.

"I knew I ought to have gone over myself," said the Colonel. "You can bet your boots I'd have routed her out fast enough."

"I wish you had gone over," I replied, somewhat tartly. "You'd have seen that every one of your suppositions was wrong. He's not at a smart hotel. He's living in one tiny room in the most squalid way. If he's left his home, it's not to live a gay life. He's got hardly any money."

"Do you think he's done something that we don't know about, and is lying doggo on account of the police?"

The suggestion sent a ray of hope in all their breasts, but I would have nothing to do with it.

"If that were so, he would hardly have been such a fool as to give his partner his address," I retorted acidly. "Anyhow, there's one thing I'm positive of, he didn't go away with anyone. He's not in love. Nothing is farther from his thoughts."

There was a pause while they reflected over my words.

"Well, if what you say is true," said Mrs. MacAndrew at last, "things aren't so bad as I thought."

Mrs. Strickland glanced at her, but said nothing. She was very pale now, and her fine brow was dark and lowering. I could not understand the expression of her face. Mrs. MacAndrew continued:

"If it's just a whim, he'll get over it."

"Why don't you go over to him, Amy?" hazarded the Colonel. "There's no reason why you shouldn't live with him in Paris for a year. We'll look after the children. I daresay he'd got stale. Sooner or later he'll be quite ready to come back to London, and no great harm will have been done."

"I wouldn't do that," said Mrs. MacAndrew. "I'd give him all the rope he wants. He'll come back with his tail between his legs and settle down again quite comfortably." Mrs. MacAndrew looked at her sister coolly. "Perhaps you weren't very wise with him sometimes. Men are queer creatures, and one has to know how to manage them."

Mrs. MacAndrew shared the common opinion of her sex that a man is always a brute to leave a woman who is attached to him, but that a woman is much to blame if he does. *Le coeur a ses raisons que la raison ne connait pas.*

Mrs. Strickland looked slowly from one to another of us.

"He'll never come back," she said.

"Oh, my dear, remember what we've just heard. He's been used to comfort and to having someone to look after him. How long do you think it'll be before he gets tired of a scrubby room in a scrubby hotel? Besides, he hasn't any money. He must come back."

"As long as I thought he'd run away with some woman I thought there was a chance. I don't believe that sort of thing ever answers. He'd have got sick to death of her in three months. But if he hasn't gone because he's in love, then it's finished."

"Oh, I think that's awfully subtle," said the Colonel, putting into the word all the contempt he felt for a quality so alien to the traditions of his calling. "Don't you believe it. He'll come back, and, as Dorothy says, I daresay he'll be none the worse for having had a bit of a fling."

"But I don't want him back," she said.

"Amy!"

It was anger that had seized Mrs. Strickland, and her pallor was the pallor of a cold and sudden rage. She spoke quickly now, with little gasps.

"I could have forgiven it if he'd fallen desperately in love with someone and gone off with her. I should have thought that natural. I shouldn't really have blamed him. I should have thought he was led away. Men are so weak, and women are so unscrupulous. But this is different. I hate him. I'll never forgive him now."

Colonel MacAndrew and his wife began to talk to her together. They were astonished. They told her she was mad. They could not understand. Mrs. Strickland turned desperately to me.

"Don't *you* see?" she cried.

"I'm not sure. Do you mean that you could have forgiven him if he'd left you for a woman, but not if he's left you for an idea? You think you're a match for the one, but against the other you're helpless?"

Mrs. Strickland gave me a look in which I read no great friendliness, but did not answer. Perhaps I had struck home. She went on in a low and trembling voice:

"I never knew it was possible to hate anyone as much as I hate him. Do you know, I've been comforting myself by thinking that however long it lasted he'd want me at the end? I knew when he was dying he'd send for me, and I was ready to go; I'd have nursed him like a mother, and at the last I'd have told him that it didn't matter, I'd loved him always, and I forgave him everything."

I have always been a little disconcerted by the passion women have for behaving beautifully at the deathbed of those they love. Sometimes it seems as if they grudge the longevity which postpones their chance of an effective scene.

"But now—now it's finished. I'm as indifferent to him as if he were a stranger. I should like him to die miserable, poor, and starving, without a friend. I hope he'll rot with some loathsome disease. I've done with him."

I thought it as well then to say what Strickland had suggested.

"If you want to divorce him, he's quite willing to do whatever is necessary to make it possible."

"Why should I give him his freedom?"

"I don't think he wants it. He merely thought it might be more convenient to you."

Mrs. Strickland shrugged her shoulders impatiently. I think I was a little disappointed in her. I expected then people to be more of a piece than I do now, and I was distressed to find so much vindictiveness in so charming a creature. I did not realise how motley are the qualities that go to make up a human being. Now I am well aware that pettiness and grandeur, malice and charity, hatred and love, can find place side by side in the same human heart.

I wondered if there was anything I could say that would ease the sense of bitter humiliation which at present tormented Mrs. Strickland. I thought I would try.

"You know, I'm not sure that your husband is quite responsible for his actions. I do not think he is himself. He seems to me to be possessed by some power which is using him for its own ends, and in whose hold he is as helpless as a fly in a spider's web. It's as though someone had cast a spell over him. I'm reminded of those strange stories one sometimes hears of another personality entering into a man and driving out the old one. The soul lives unstably in the body, and is capable of mysterious transformations. In the old days they would say Charles Strickland had a devil."

Mrs. MacAndrew smoothed down the lap of her gown, and gold bangles fell over her wrists.

"All that seems to me very far-fetched," she said acidly. "I don't deny that perhaps Amy took her husband a little too much for granted. If she hadn't been so busy with her own affairs, I can't believe that she wouldn't have suspected something was the matter. I don't think that Alec could have something on his mind for a year or more without my having a pretty shrewd idea of it."

The Colonel stared into vacancy, and I wondered whether anyone could be quite so innocent of guile as he looked.

"But that doesn't prevent the fact that Charles Strickland is a heartless beast." She looked at me severely. "I can tell you why he left his wife—from pure selfishness and nothing else whatever."

"That is certainly the simplest explanation," I said. But I thought it explained nothing. When, saying I was tired, I rose to go, Mrs. Strickland made no attempt to detain me.

Chapter XVI

What followed showed that Mrs. Strickland was a woman of character. Whatever anguish she suffered she concealed. She saw shrewdly that the world is quickly bored by the recital of misfortune, and willingly avoids the sight of distress. Whenever she went out—and compassion for her misadventure made her friends eager to entertain her—she bore a demeanour that was perfect. She was brave, but not too obviously; cheerful, but not brazenly; and she seemed more anxious to listen to the troubles of others than to discuss her own. Whenever she spoke of her husband it was with pity. Her attitude towards him at first perplexed me. One day she said to me:

"You know, I'm convinced you were mistaken about Charles being alone. From what I've been able to gather from certain sources that I can't tell you, I know that he didn't leave England by himself."

"In that case he has a positive genius for covering up his tracks."

She looked away and slightly coloured.

"What I mean is, if anyone talks to you about it, please don't contradict it if they say he eloped with somebody."

"Of course not."

She changed the conversation as though it were a matter to which she attached no importance. I discovered presently that a peculiar story was circulating among her friends. They said that Charles Strickland had become infatuated with a French dancer, whom he had first seen in the ballet at the Empire, and had accompanied her to Paris. I could not find out how this had arisen, but, singularly enough, it created much sympathy for Mrs. Strickland, and at the same time gave her not a little prestige. This was not without its use in the calling which she had decided to follow. Colonel MacAndrew had not exaggerated when he said she would be penniless, and it was necessary for her to earn her own living as quickly as she could. She made up her mind to profit by her acquaintance with so many writers, and without loss of time began to learn shorthand and typewriting. Her education made it likely that she would be a typist more efficient than the average, and her story made her claims appealing. Her friends promised to send her work, and took care to recommend her to all theirs.

The MacAndrews, who were childless and in easy circumstances, arranged to undertake the care of the children, and Mrs. Strickland had only herself to provide for. She let her flat and sold her furniture. She settled in two tiny rooms in Westminster, and faced the world anew. She was so efficient that it was certain she would make a success of the adventure.

Chapter XVII

IT WAS ABOUT FIVE YEARS AFTER THIS THAT I DECIDED TO LIVE IN PARIS FOR A while. I was growing stale in London. I was tired of doing much the same thing every day. My friends pursued their course with uneventfulness; they had no longer any surprises for me, and when I met them I knew pretty well what they would say; even their love affairs had a tedious banality. We were like tram-cars running on their lines from terminus to terminus, and it was possible to calculate within small limits the number of passengers they would carry. Life was ordered too pleasantly. I was seized with panic. I gave up my small apartment, sold my few belongings, and resolved to start afresh.

I called on Mrs. Strickland before I left. I had not seen her for some time, and I noticed changes in her: it was not only that she was older, thinner, and more lined; I think her character had altered. She had made a success of her business, and now had an office in Chancery Lane; she did little typing herself, but spent her time correcting the work of the four girls she employed. She had had the idea of giving it a certain daintiness, and she made much use of blue and red inks; she bound the copy in coarse paper, that looked vaguely like watered silk, in various pale colours; and she had acquired a reputation for neatness and accuracy. She was making money. But she could not get over the idea that to earn her living was somewhat undignified, and she was inclined to remind you that she was a lady by birth. She could not help bringing into her conversation the names of people she knew which would satisfy you that she had not sunk in the social scale. She was a little ashamed of her courage and business capacity, but delighted that she was going to dine the next night with a K.C. who lived in South Kensington. She was pleased to be able to tell you that her son was at Cambridge, and it was with a little laugh that she spoke of the rush of dances to which her daughter, just out, was invited. I suppose I said a very stupid thing.

"Is she going into your business?" I asked.

"Oh no; I wouldn't let her do that," Mrs. Strickland answered. "She's so pretty. I'm sure she'll marry well."

"I should have thought it would be a help to you."

"Several people have suggested that she should go on the stage, but of course I couldn't consent to that. I know all the chief dramatists, and I could get her a part tomorrow, but I shouldn't like her to mix with all sorts of people."

I was a little chilled by Mrs. Strickland's exclusiveness.

"Do you ever hear of your husband?"

"No; I haven't heard a word. He may be dead for all I know."

"I may run across him in Paris. Would you like me to let you know about him?"

She hesitated a minute.

"If he's in any real want I'm prepared to help him a little. I'd send you a certain sum of money, and you could give it him gradually, as he needed it."

"That's very good of you," I said.

But I knew it was not kindness that prompted the offer. It is not true that suffering ennobles the character; happiness does that sometimes, but suffering, for the most part, makes men petty and vindictive.

Chapter XVIII

IN POINT OF FACT, I MET STRICKLAND BEFORE I HAD BEEN A FORTNIGHT IN Paris.

I quickly found myself a tiny apartment on the fifth floor of a house in the Rue des Dames, and for a couple of hundred francs bought at a second-hand dealer's enough furniture to make it habitable. I arranged with the concierge to make my coffee in the morning and to keep the place clean. Then I went to see my friend Dirk Stroeve.

Dirk Stroeve was one of those persons whom, according to your character, you cannot think of without derisive laughter or an embarrassed shrug of the shoulders. Nature had made him a buffoon. He was a painter, but a very bad one, whom I had met in Rome, and I still remembered his pictures. He had a genuine enthusiasm for the commonplace. His soul palpitating with love of art, he painted the models who hung about the stairway of Bernini in the Piazza de Spagna, undaunted by their obvious picturesqueness; and his studio was full of canvases on which were portrayed moustachioed, large-eyed peasants in peaked hats, urchins in becoming rags, and women in bright petticoats. Sometimes they lounged at the steps of a church, and sometimes dallied among cypresses against a cloudless sky; sometimes they made love by a Renaissance well-head, and sometimes they wandered through the Campagna by the side of an ox-wagon. They were carefully drawn and carefully painted. A photograph could not have been more exact. One of the painters at the Villa Medici had called him *Le Maître de la Boîte à Chocolats*. To look at his pictures you would have thought that Monet, Manet, and the rest of the Impressionists had never been.

"I don't pretend to be a great painter," he said, "I'm not a Michael Angelo, no, but I have something. I sell. I bring romance into the homes of all sorts of people. Do you know, they buy my pictures not only in Holland, but in Norway and Sweden and Denmark? It's mostly merchants who buy them, and rich tradesmen. You can't imagine what the winters are like in those countries, so long and dark and cold. They like to think that Italy is like my pictures. That's what they expect. That's what I expected Italy to be before I came here."

And I think that was the vision that had remained with him always, dazzling his eyes so that he could not see the truth; and notwithstanding the brutality of fact, he continued to see with the eyes of the spirit an Italy of romantic brigands and picturesque ruins. It was an ideal that he painted—a poor one, common and shop-soiled, but still it was an ideal; and it gave his character a peculiar charm.

It was because I felt this that Dirk Stroeve was not to me, as to others, merely an object of ridicule. His fellow-painters made no secret of their contempt for his work, but he earned a fair amount of money, and they did not hesitate to make free use of his purse. He was generous, and the needy, laughing at him because he believed so naïvely their stories of distress, borrowed from him with effrontery. He was very emotional, yet his feeling, so easily aroused, had in it something absurd, so that you accepted his kindness, but felt no gratitude. To take money from him was like robbing a child, and you despised him because he was so foolish. I imagine that a pickpocket, proud of his light fingers, must feel a sort of indignation with the careless woman who leaves in a cab a vanity-bag with all her jewels in it. Nature had made him a butt, but had denied him insensibility. He writhed under the jokes, practical and otherwise, which were perpetually made at his expense, and yet never ceased, it seemed wilfully, to expose himself to them. He was constantly wounded, and yet his good-nature was such that he could not bear malice: the viper might sting him, but he never learned by experience, and had no sooner recovered from his pain than he tenderly placed it once more in his bosom. His life was a tragedy written in the terms of knockabout farce. Because I did not laugh at him he was grateful to me, and he used to pour into my sympathetic ear the long list of his troubles. The saddest thing about them was that they were grotesque, and the more pathetic they were, the more you wanted to laugh.

But though so bad a painter, he had a very delicate feeling for art, and to go with him to picture-galleries was a rare treat. His enthusiasm was sincere and his criticism acute. He was catholic. He had not only a true appreciation of the old masters, but sympathy with the moderns. He was quick to discover talent, and his praise was generous. I think I have never known a man whose judgment was surer. And he was better educated than most painters. He was not, like most of them, ignorant of kindred arts, and his taste for music and literature gave depth and variety to his comprehension of painting. To a young man like myself his advice and guidance were of incomparable value.

When I left Rome I corresponded with him, and about once in two months received from him long letters in queer English, which brought before me vividly his spluttering, enthusiastic, gesticulating conversation. Sometime before I went to Paris he had married an Englishwoman, and was now settled in a studio in Montmartre. I had not seen him for four years, and had never met his wife.

Chapter XIX

I HAD NOT ANNOUNCED MY ARRIVAL TO STROEVE, AND WHEN I RANG THE BELL of his studio, on opening the door himself, for a moment he did not know me. Then he gave a cry of delighted surprise and drew me in. It was charming to be welcomed with so much eagerness. His wife was seated near the stove at her sewing, and she rose as I came in. He introduced me.

"Don't you remember?" he said to her. "I've talked to you about him often." And then to me: "But why didn't you let me know you were coming? How long have you been here? How long are you going to stay? Why didn't you come an hour earlier, and we would have dined together?"

He bombarded me with questions. He sat me down in a chair, patting me as though I were a cushion, pressed cigars upon me, cakes, wine. He could not let me alone. He was heart-broken because he had no whisky, wanted to make coffee for me, racked his brain for something he could possibly do for me, and beamed and laughed, and in the exuberance of his delight sweated at every pore.

"You haven't changed," I said, smiling, as I looked at him.

He had the same absurd appearance that I remembered. He was a fat little man, with short legs, young still—he could not have been more than thirty—but prematurely bald. His face was perfectly round, and he had a very high colour, a white skin, red cheeks, and red lips. His eyes were blue and round too, he wore large gold-rimmed spectacles, and his eyebrows were so fair that you could not see them. He reminded you of those jolly, fat merchants that Rubens painted.

When I told him that I meant to live in Paris for a while, and had taken an apartment, he reproached me bitterly for not having let him know. He would have found me an apartment himself, and lent me furniture—did I really mean that I had gone to the expense of buying it?—and he would have helped me to move in. He really looked upon it as unfriendly that I had not given him the opportunity of making himself useful to me. Meanwhile, Mrs. Stroeve sat quietly mending her stockings, without talking, and she listened to all he said with a quiet smile on her lips.

"So, you see, I'm married," he said suddenly; "what do you think of my wife?"

He beamed at her, and settled his spectacles on the bridge of his nose. The sweat made them constantly slip down.

"What on earth do you expect me to say to that?" I laughed.

"Really, Dirk," put in Mrs. Stroeve, smiling.

"But isn't she wonderful? I tell you, my boy, lose no time; get married as soon as ever you can. I'm the happiest man alive. Look at her sitting there. Doesn't she make a picture? Chardin, eh? I've seen all the most beautiful women in the world; I've never seen anyone more beautiful than Madame Dirk Stroeve."

"If you don't be quiet, Dirk, I shall go away."

"*Mon petit choux,*" he said.

She flushed a little, embarrassed by the passion in his tone. His letters had told me that he was very much in love with his wife, and I saw that he could hardly take his eyes off her. I could not tell if she loved him. Poor pantaloon, he was not an object to excite love, but the smile in her eyes was affectionate, and it was possible that her reserve concealed a very deep feeling. She was not the ravishing creature that his love-sick fancy saw, but she had a grave comeliness. She was rather tall, and her grey dress, simple and quite well-cut, did not hide the fact that her figure was beautiful. It was a figure that might have appealed more to the sculptor than to the costumier. Her hair, brown and abundant, was plainly done, her face was very pale, and her features were good without being distinguished. She had quiet grey eyes. She just missed being beautiful, and in missing it was not even pretty. But when Stroeve spoke of Chardin it was not without reason, and she reminded me curiously of that pleasant housewife in her mob-cap and apron whom the great painter has immortalised. I could imagine her sedately busy among her pots and pans, making a ritual of her household duties, so that they acquired a moral significance; I did not suppose that she was clever or could ever be amusing, but there was something in her grave intentness which excited my interest. Her reserve was not without mystery. I wondered why she had married Dirk Stroeve. Though she was English, I could not exactly place her, and it was not obvious from what rank in society she sprang, what had been her upbringing, or how she had lived before her marriage. She was very silent, but when she spoke it was with a pleasant voice, and her manners were natural.

I asked Stroeve if he was working.

"Working? I'm painting better than I've ever painted before."

We sat in the studio, and he waved his hand to an unfinished picture on an easel. I gave a little start. He was painting a group of Italian peasants, in the costume of the Campagna, lounging on the steps of a Roman church.

"Is that what you're doing now?" I asked.

"Yes. I can get my models here just as well as in Rome."

"Don't you think it's very beautiful?" said Mrs. Stroeve.

"This foolish wife of mine thinks I'm a great artist," said he.

His apologetic laugh did not disguise the pleasure that he felt. His eyes lingered on his picture. It was strange that his critical sense, so accurate and unconventional when he dealt with the work of others, should be satisfied in himself with what was hackneyed and vulgar beyond belief.

"Show him some more of your pictures," she said.

"Shall I?"

Though he had suffered so much from the ridicule of his friends, Dirk Stroeve, eager for praise and naïvely self-satisfied, could never resist displaying his work. He brought out a picture of two curly-headed Italian urchins playing marbles.

"Aren't they sweet?" said Mrs. Stroeve.

And then he showed me more. I discovered that in Paris he had been painting just the same stale, obviously picturesque things that he had painted for years in Rome. It was all false, insincere, shoddy; and yet no one was more honest, sincere, and frank than Dirk Stroeve. Who could resolve the contradiction?

I do not know what put it into my head to ask:

"I say, have you by any chance run across a painter called Charles Strickland?"

"You don't mean to say you know him?" cried Stroeve.

"Beast," said his wife.

Stroeve laughed.

"Ma pauvre chèrie." He went over to her and kissed both her hands. "She doesn't like him. How strange that you should know Strickland!"

"I don't like bad manners," said Mrs. Stroeve.

Dirk, laughing still, turned to me to explain.

"You see, I asked him to come here one day and look at my pictures. Well, he came, and I showed him everything I had." Stroeve hesitated a moment with embarrassment. I do not know why he had begun the story against himself; he felt an awkwardness at finishing it. "He looked at—at my pictures, and he didn't say anything. I thought he was reserving his judgment till the end. And at last I said: 'There, that's the lot!' He said: 'I came to ask you to lend me twenty francs.' "

"And Dirk actually gave it him," said his wife indignantly.

"I was so taken aback. I didn't like to refuse. He put the money in his pocket, just nodded, said 'Thanks,' and walked out."

Dirk Stroeve, telling the story, had such a look of blank astonishment on his round, foolish face that it was almost impossible not to laugh.

"I shouldn't have minded if he'd said my pictures were bad, but he said nothing—nothing."

"And you *will* tell the story, Dirk," said his wife.

It was lamentable that one was more amused by the ridiculous figure cut by the Dutchman than outraged by Strickland's brutal treatment of him.

"I hope I shall never see him again," said Mrs. Stroeve.

Stroeve smiled and shrugged his shoulders. He had already recovered his good-humour.

"The fact remains that he's a great artist, a very great artist."

"Strickland?" I exclaimed. "It can't be the same man."

"A big fellow with a red beard. Charles Strickland. An Englishman."

"He had no beard when I knew him, but if he has grown one it might well be red. The man I'm thinking of only began painting five years ago."

"That's it. He's a great artist."

"Impossible."

"Have I ever been mistaken?" Dirk asked me. "I tell you he has genius. I'm convinced of it. In a hundred years, if you and I are remembered at all, it will be because we knew Charles Strickland."

I was astonished, and at the same time I was very much excited. I remembered suddenly my last talk with him.

"Where can one see his work?" I asked. "Is he having any success? Where is he living?"

"No; he has no success. I don't think he's ever sold a picture. When you speak to men about him they only laugh. But I *know* he's a great artist. After all, they laughed at Manet. Corot never sold a picture. I don't know where he lives, but I can take you to see him. He goes to a café in the Avenue de Clichy at seven o'clock every evening. If you like we'll go there tomorrow."

"I'm not sure if he'll wish to see me. I think I may remind him of a time he prefers to forget. But I'll come all the same. Is there any chance of seeing any of his pictures?"

"Not from him. He won't show you a thing. There's a little dealer I know who has two or three. But you mustn't go without me; you wouldn't understand. I must show them to you myself."

"Dirk, you make me impatient," said Mrs. Stroeve. "How can you talk like that about his pictures when he treated you as he did?" She turned to me. "Do you know, when some Dutch people came here to buy Dirk's pictures he tried to persuade them to buy Strickland's? He insisted on bringing them here to show."

"What did *you* think of them?" I asked her, smiling.

"They were awful."

"Ah, sweetheart, you don't understand."

"Well, your Dutch people were furious with you. They thought you were having a joke with them."

Dirk Stroeve took off his spectacles and wiped them. His flushed face was shining with excitement.

"Why should you think that beauty, which is the most precious thing in the world, lies like a stone on the beach for the careless passer-by to pick up idly? Beauty is something wonderful and strange that the artist fashions out of the chaos of the world in the torment of his soul. And when he has made it, it is not given to all to know it. To recognise it you must repeat the adventure of the artist. It is a melody that he sings to you, and to hear it again in your own heart you want knowledge and sensitiveness and imagination."

"Why did I always think your pictures beautiful, Dirk? I admired them the very first time I saw them."

Stroeve's lips trembled a little.

"Go to bed, my precious. I will walk a few steps with our friend, and then I will come back."

Chapter XX

DIRK STROEVE AGREED TO FETCH ME ON THE FOLLOWING EVENING AND take me to the café at which Strickland was most likely to be found. I was interested to learn that it was the same as that at which Strickland and I had drunk absinthe when I had gone over to Paris to see him. The fact that he had never changed suggested a sluggishness of habit which seemed to me characteristic.

"There he is," said Stroeve, as we reached the café.

Though it was October, the evening was warm, and the tables on the pavement were crowded. I ran my eyes over them, but did not see Strickland.

"Look. Over there, in the corner. He's playing chess."

I noticed a man bending over a chess-board, but could see only a large felt hat and a red beard. We threaded our way among the tables till we came to him.

"Strickland."

He looked up.

"Hulloa, fatty. What do you want?"

"I've brought an old friend to see you."

Strickland gave me a glance, and evidently did not recognise me. He resumed his scrutiny of the chess-board.

"Sit down, and don't make a noise," he said.

He moved a piece and straightway became absorbed in the game. Poor Stroeve gave me a troubled look, but I was not disconcerted by so little. I ordered something to drink, and waited quietly till Strickland had finished. I welcomed the opportunity to examine him at my ease. I certainly should never have known him. In the first place his red beard, ragged and untrimmed, hid much of his face, and his hair was long; but the most surprising change in him was his extreme thinness. It made his great nose protrude more arrogantly; it emphasised his cheek-bones; it made his eyes seem larger. There were deep hollows at his temples. His body was cadaverous. He wore the same suit that I had seen him in five years before; it was torn and stained, threadbare, and it hung upon him loosely, as though it had been made for someone else. I noticed his hands, dirty, with long nails; they were merely bone and sinew, large and strong; but I had forgotten that they were so shapely. He gave me an extraordinary impression as he sat there, his attention riveted on his game—an impression of great strength; and I could not understand why it was that his emaciation somehow made it more striking.

Presently, after moving, he leaned back and gazed with a curious abstraction at his antagonist. This was a fat, bearded Frenchman. The Frenchman considered the position, then broke suddenly into jovial expletives, and with an impatient gesture, gathering up the pieces, flung them into their box. He cursed Strickland freely, then, calling for the waiter, paid for the drinks, and left. Stroeve drew his chair closer to the table.

"Now I suppose we can talk," he said.

Strickland's eyes rested on him, and there was in them a malicious expression. I felt sure he was seeking for some gibe, could think of none, and so was forced to silence.

"I've brought an old friend to see you," repeated Stroeve, beaming cheerfully.

Strickland looked at me thoughtfully for nearly a minute. I did not speak.

"I've never seen him in my life," he said.

I do not know why he said this, for I felt certain I had caught a gleam of recognition in his eyes. I was not so easily abashed as I had been some years earlier.

"I saw your wife the other day," I said. "I felt sure you'd like to have the latest news of her."

He gave a short laugh. His eyes twinkled.

"We had a jolly evening together," he said. "How long ago is it?"

"Five years."

He called for another absinthe. Stroeve, with voluble tongue, explained how he and I had met, and by what an accident we discovered that we both knew Strickland. I do not know if Strickland listened. He glanced at me once or twice reflectively, but for the most part seemed occupied with his own thoughts; and certainly without Stroeve's babble the conversation would have been difficult. In half an hour the Dutchman, looking at his watch, announced that he must go. He asked whether I would come too. I thought, alone, I might get something out of Strickland, and so answered that I would stay.

When the fat man had left I said:

"Dirk Stroeve thinks you're a great artist."

"What the hell do you suppose I care?"

"Will you let me see your pictures?"

"Why should I?"

"I might feel inclined to buy one."

"I might not feel inclined to sell one."

"Are you making a good living?" I asked, smiling.

He chuckled.

"Do I look it?"

"You look half starved."

"I am half starved."

"Then come and let's have a bit of dinner."

"Why do you ask me?"

"Not out of charity," I answered coolly. "I don't really care a twopenny damn if you starve or not."

His eyes lit up again.

"Come on, then," he said, getting up. "I'd like a decent meal."

Chapter XXI

I LET HIM TAKE ME TO A RESTAURANT OF HIS CHOICE, BUT ON THE WAY I bought a paper. When we had ordered our dinner, I propped it against a bottle of St. Galmier and began to read. We ate in silence. I felt him looking at me now and again, but I took no notice. I meant to force him to conversation.

"Is there anything in the paper?" he said, as we approached the end of our silent meal.

I fancied there was in his tone a slight note of exasperation.

"I always like to read the *feuilleton* on the drama," I said.

I folded the paper and put it down beside me.

"I've enjoyed my dinner," he remarked.

"I think we might have our coffee here, don't you?"

"Yes."

We lit our cigars. I smoked in silence. I noticed that now and then his eyes rested on me with a faint smile of amusement. I waited patiently.

"What have you been up to since I saw you last?" he asked at length.

I had not very much to say. It was a record of hard work and of little adventure; of experiments in this direction and in that; of the gradual acquisition of the knowledge of books and of men. I took care to ask Strickland nothing about his own doings. I showed not the least interest in him, and at last I was rewarded. He began to talk of himself. But with his poor gift of expression he gave but indications of what he had gone through, and I had to fill up the gaps with my own imagination. It was tantalising to get no more than hints into a character that interested me so much. It was like making one's way through a mutilated manuscript. I received the impression of a life which was a bitter struggle against every sort of difficulty; but I realised that much which would have seemed horrible to most people did not in the least affect him. Strickland was distinguished from most Englishmen by his perfect indifference to comfort; it did not irk him to live always in one shabby room; he had no need to be surrounded by beautiful things. I do not suppose he had ever noticed how dingy was the paper on the wall of the room in which on my first visit I found him. He did not want arm-chairs to sit in; he really felt more at his ease on a kitchen chair. He ate with appetite, but was indifferent to what he ate; to him it was only food that he devoured to still the pangs of hunger; and when no food was to be had he seemed capable of doing without. I learned that for six months he had lived on a loaf of bread and a bottle of milk a day. He was a sensual man, and yet was indifferent to sensual things. He looked upon privation as no hardship. There was something impressive in the manner in which he lived a life wholly of the spirit.

When the small sum of money which he brought with him from London came to an end he suffered from no dismay. He sold no pictures; I think he made little attempt to sell any; he set about finding some way to make a bit of money. He told me with grim humour of the time he had spent acting as guide to Cockneys who wanted to see the night side of life in Paris; it was an occupation that appealed to his sardonic temper and somehow or other he had acquired a wide acquaintance with the more disreputable quarters of the city. He told me of the long hours he spent walking about the Boulevard de la Madeleine on the look-out for Englishmen, preferably the worse for liquor, who desired to see things which the law forbade. When in luck he was able to make a tidy sum; but the shabbiness of his clothes at last frightened the sight-seers, and he could not find people adventurous enough to trust themselves to him. Then he happened on a job to translate the advertisements of patent medicines which were sent broadcast to the medical profession in England. During a strike he had been employed as a house-painter.

Meanwhile he had never ceased to work at his art; but had soon tired of the studios, entirely by himself. He had never been so poor that he could not buy canvas and paint, and really he needed nothing else. So far as I could make out, he painted with great difficulty, and in his unwillingness to accept help from anyone lost much time in finding out for himself the solution of technical problems which preceding generations had already worked out one by one. He was aiming at something, I knew not what, and perhaps he hardly knew himself; and I got again more strongly the impression of a man possessed. He did not seem quite sane. It seemed to me that he would not show his pictures because he was really not interested in them. He lived in a dream, and the reality meant nothing to him. I had the feeling that he worked on a canvas with all the force of his violent personality, oblivious of everything in his effort to get what he saw with the mind's eye; and then, having finished, not the picture perhaps, for I had an idea that he seldom brought anything to completion, but the passion that fired him, he lost all care for it. He was never satisfied with what he had done; it seemed to him of no consequence compared with the vision that obsessed his mind.

"Why don't you ever send your work to exhibitions?" I asked. "I should have thought you'd like to know what people thought about it."

"Would you?"

I cannot describe the unmeasurable contempt he put into the two words.

"Don't you want fame? It's something that most artists haven't been indifferent to."

"Children. How can you care for the opinion of the crowd, when you don't care twopence for the opinion of the individual?"

"We're not all reasonable beings," I laughed.

"Who makes fame? Critics, writers, stockbrokers, women."

"Wouldn't it give you a rather pleasing sensation to think of people you didn't know and had never seen receiving emotions, subtle and passionate, from the work of your hands? Everyone likes power. I can't imagine a more wonderful exercise of it than to move the souls of men to pity or terror."

"Melodrama."

"Why do you mind if you paint well or badly?"

"I don't. I only want to paint what I see."

"I wonder if I could write on a desert island, with the certainty that no eyes but mine would ever see what I had written."

Strickland did not speak for a long time, but his eyes shone strangely, as though he saw something that kindled his soul to ecstasy.

"Sometimes I've thought of an island lost in a boundless sea, where I could live in some hidden valley, among strange trees, in silence. There I think I could find what I want."

He did not express himself quite like this. He used gestures instead of adjectives, and he halted. I have put into my own words what I think he wanted to say.

"Looking back on the last five years, do you think it was worth it?" I asked.

He looked at me, and I saw that he did not know what I meant. I explained.

"You gave up a comfortable home and a life as happy as the average. You were fairly prosperous. You seem to have had a rotten time in Paris. If you had your time over again would you do what you did?"

"Rather."

"Do you know that you haven't asked anything about your wife and children? Do you never think of them?"

"No."

"I wish you weren't so damned monosyllabic. Have you never had a moment's regret for all the unhappiness you caused them?"

His lips broke into a smile, and he shook his head.

"I should have thought sometimes you couldn't help thinking of the past. I don't mean the past of seven or eight years ago, but further back still, when you first met your wife, and loved her, and married her. Don't you remember the joy with which you first took her in your arms?"

"I don't think of the past. The only thing that matters is the everlasting present."

I thought for a moment over this reply. It was obscure, perhaps, but I thought that I saw dimly his meaning.

"Are you happy?" I asked.

"Yes."

I was silent. I looked at him reflectively. He held my stare, and presently a sardonic twinkle lit up his eyes.

"I'm afraid you disapprove of me?"

"Nonsense," I answered promptly; "I don't disapprove of the boa-constrictor; on the contrary, I'm interested in his mental processes."

"It's a purely professional interest you take in me?"

"Purely."

"It's only right that you shouldn't disapprove of me. You have a despicable character."

"Perhaps that's why you feel at home with me," I retorted.

He smiled dryly, but said nothing. I wish I knew how to describe his smile. I do not know that it was attractive, but it lit up his face, changing the expression, which was generally sombre, and gave it a look of not ill-natured malice. It was a slow smile, starting and sometimes ending in the eyes; it was very sensual, neither cruel nor kindly, but suggested rather the inhuman glee of the satyr. It was his smile that made me ask him:

"Haven't you been in love since you came to Paris?"

"I haven't got time for that sort of nonsense. Life isn't long enough for love and art."

"Your appearance doesn't suggest the anchorite."

"All that business fills me with disgust."

"Human nature is a nuisance, isn't it?" I said.

"Why are you sniggering at me?"

"Because I don't believe you."

"Then you're a damned fool."

I paused, and I looked at him searchingly.

"What's the good of trying to humbug me?" I said.

"I don't know what you mean."

I smiled.

"Let me tell you. I imagine that for months the matter never comes into your head, and you're able to persuade yourself that you've finished with it for good and all. You rejoice in your freedom, and you feel that at last you can call your soul your own. You seem to walk with your head among the stars. And then, all of a sudden you can't stand it anymore, and you notice that all the time your feet have been walking in the mud. And you want to roll yourself in it. And you find some woman, coarse and low and vulgar, some beastly creature in whom all the horror of sex is blatant, and you fall upon her like a wild animal. You drink till you're blind with rage."

He stared at me without the slightest movement. I held his eyes with mine. I spoke very slowly.

"I'll tell you what must seem strange, that when it's over you feel so extraordinarily pure. You feel like a disembodied spirit, immaterial; and you seem to be able to touch beauty as though it were a palpable thing; and you feel an intimate communion with the breeze, and with the trees breaking into leaf, and with the iridescence of the river. You feel like God. Can you explain that to me?"

He kept his eyes fixed on mine till I had finished, and then he turned away. There was on his face a strange look, and I thought that so might a man look when he had died under the torture. He was silent. I knew that our conversation was ended.

Chapter XXII

I SETTLED DOWN IN PARIS AND BEGAN TO WRITE A PLAY. I LED A VERY REGULAR life, working in the morning, and in the afternoon lounging about the gardens of the Luxembourg or sauntering through the streets. I spent long hours in the Louvre, the most friendly of all galleries and the most convenient for meditation; or idled on the quays, fingering second-hand books that I never meant to buy. I read a page here and there, and made acquaintance with a great many authors whom I was content to know thus desultorily. In the evenings I went to see my friends. I looked in often on the Stroeves, and sometimes shared their modest fare. Dirk Stroeve flattered himself on his skill in cooking Italian dishes, and I confess that his *spaghetti* were very much better than his pictures. It was a dinner for a King when he brought in a huge dish of it, succulent with tomatoes, and we ate it together with the good household bread and a bottle of red wine. I grew more intimate with Blanche Stroeve, and I think, because I was English and she knew few English people, she was glad to see me. She was pleasant and simple, but she remained always rather silent, and I knew not why, gave me the impression that she was concealing something. But I thought that was perhaps no more than a natural reserve accentuated by the verbose frankness of her husband. Dirk never concealed anything. He discussed the most intimate matters with a complete lack of self-consciousness. Sometimes he embarrassed his wife, and the only time I saw her put out of countenance was when he insisted on telling me that he had taken a purge, and went into somewhat realistic details on the subject. The perfect seriousness with which he narrated his misfortunes convulsed me with laughter, and this added to Mrs. Stroeve's irritation.

"You seem to like making a fool of yourself," she said.

His round eyes grew rounder still, and his brow puckered in dismay as he saw that she was angry.

"Sweetheart, have I vexed you? I'll never take another. It was only because I was bilious. I lead a sedentary life. I don't take enough exercise. For three days I hadn't . . ."

"For goodness sake, hold your tongue," she interrupted, tears of annoyance in her eyes.

His face fell, and he pouted his lips like a scolded child. He gave me a look of appeal, so that I might put things right, but, unable to control myself, I shook with helpless laughter.

We went one day to the picture-dealer in whose shop Stroeve thought he could show me at least two or three of Strickland's pictures, but when we arrived were told that Strickland himself had taken them away. The dealer did not know why.

"But don't imagine to yourself that I make myself bad blood on that account. I took them to oblige Monsieur Stroeve, and I said I would sell them if I could. But really—" He shrugged his shoulders. "I'm interested in the young men, but *voyons*, you yourself, Monsieur Stroeve, you don't think there's any talent there."

"I give you my word of honour, there's no one painting today in whose talent I am more convinced. Take my word for it, you are missing a good affair. Someday those pictures will be worth more than all you have in your shop. Remember Monet, who could not get anyone to buy his pictures for a hundred francs. What are they worth now?"

"True. But there were a hundred as good painters as Monet who couldn't sell their pictures at that time, and their pictures are worth nothing still. How can one tell? Is merit enough to bring success? Don't believe it. *Du reste*, it has still to be proved that this friend of yours has merit. No one claims it for him but Monsieur Stroeve."

"And how, then, will you recognise merit?" asked Dirk, red in the face with anger.

"There is only one way—by success."

"Philistine," cried Dirk.

"But think of the great artists of the past—Raphael, Michael Angelo, Ingres, Delacroix—they were all successful."

"Let us go," said Stroeve to me, "or I shall kill this man."

Chapter XXIII

I SAW STRICKLAND NOT INFREQUENTLY, AND NOW AND THEN PLAYED CHESS with him. He was of uncertain temper. Sometimes he would sit silent and abstracted, taking no notice of anyone; and at others, when he was in a good humour, he would talk in his own halting way. He never said a clever thing, but he had a vein of brutal sarcasm which was not ineffective, and he always said exactly what he thought. He was indifferent to the susceptibilities of others, and when he wounded them was amused. He was constantly offending Dirk Stroeve so bitterly that he flung away, vowing he would never speak to him again; but there was a solid force in Strickland that attracted the fat Dutchman against his will, so that he came back, fawning like a clumsy dog, though he knew that his only greeting would be the blow he dreaded.

I do not know why Strickland put up with me. Our relations were peculiar. One day he asked me to lend him fifty francs.

"I wouldn't dream of it," I replied.

"Why not?"

"It wouldn't amuse me."

"I'm frightfully hard up, you know."

"I don't care."

"You don't care if I starve?"

"Why on earth should I?" I asked in my turn.

He looked at me for a minute or two, pulling his untidy beard. I smiled at him.

"What are you amused at?" he said, with a gleam of anger in his eyes.

"You're so simple. You recognise no obligations. No one is under any obligation to you."

"Wouldn't it make you uncomfortable if I went and hanged myself because I'd been turned out of my room as I couldn't pay the rent?"

"Not a bit."

He chuckled.

"You're bragging. If I really did you'd be overwhelmed with remorse."

"Try it, and we'll see," I retorted.

A smile flickered in his eyes, and he stirred his absinthe in silence.

"Would you like to play chess?" I asked.

"I don't mind."

We set up the pieces, and when the board was ready he considered it with a comfortable eye. There is a sense of satisfaction in looking at your men all ready for the fray.

"Did you really think I'd lend you money?" I asked.

"I didn't see why you shouldn't."

"You surprise me."

"Why?"

"It's disappointing to find that at heart you are sentimental. I should have liked you better if you hadn't made that ingenuous appeal to my sympathies."

"I should have despised you if you'd been moved by it," he answered.

"That's better," I laughed.

We began to play. We were both absorbed in the game. When it was finished I said to him:

"Look here, if you're hard up, let me see your pictures. If there's anything I like I'll buy it."

"Go to hell," he answered.

He got up and was about to go away. I stopped him.

"You haven't paid for your absinthe," I said, smiling.

He cursed me, flung down the money and left.

I did not see him for several days after that, but one evening, when I was sitting in the café, reading a paper, he came up and sat beside me.

"You haven't hanged yourself after all," I remarked.

"No. I've got a commission. I'm painting the portrait of a retired plumber for two hundred francs."*

"How did you manage that?"

"The woman where I get my bread recommended me. He'd told her he was looking out for someone to paint him. I've got to give her twenty francs."

"What's he like?"

"Splendid. He's got a great red face like a leg of mutton, and on his right cheek there's an enormous mole with long hairs growing out of it."

Strickland was in a good humour, and when Dirk Stroeve came up and sat down with us he attacked him with ferocious banter. He showed a skill I should never have credited him with in finding the places where the unhappy Dutchman was most sensitive. Strickland employed not the rapier of sarcasm but the bludgeon of invective. The attack was so unprovoked that Stroeve, taken unawares, was

---

*This picture, formerly in the possession of a wealthy manufacturer at Lille, who fled from that city on the approach of the Germans, is now in the National Gallery at Stockholm. The Swede is adept at the gentle pastime of fishing in troubled waters.

defenceless. He reminded you of a frightened sheep running aimlessly hither and thither. He was startled and amazed. At last the tears ran from his eyes. And the worst of it was that, though you hated Strickland, and the exhibition was horrible, it was impossible not to laugh. Dirk Stroeve was one of those unlucky persons whose most sincere emotions are ridiculous.

But after all when I look back upon that winter in Paris, my pleasantest recollection is of Dirk Stroeve. There was something very charming in his little household. He and his wife made a picture which the imagination gratefully dwelt upon, and the simplicity of his love for her had a deliberate grace. He remained absurd, but the sincerity of his passion excited one's sympathy. I could understand how his wife must feel for him, and I was glad that her affection was so tender. If she had any sense of humour, it must amuse her that he should place her on a pedestal and worship her with such an honest idolatry, but even while she laughed she must have been pleased and touched. He was the constant lover, and though she grew old, losing her rounded lines and her fair comeliness, to him she would certainly never alter. To him she would always be the loveliest woman in the world. There was a pleasing grace in the orderliness of their lives. They had but the studio, a bedroom, and a tiny kitchen. Mrs. Stroeve did all the housework herself; and while Dirk painted bad pictures, she went marketing, cooked the luncheon, sewed, occupied herself like a busy ant all the day; and in the evening sat in the studio, sewing again, while Dirk played music which I am sure was far beyond her comprehension. He played with taste, but with more feeling than was always justified, and into his music poured all his honest, sentimental, exuberant soul.

Their life in its own way was an idyl, and it managed to achieve a singular beauty. The absurdity that clung to everything connected with Dirk Stroeve gave it a curious note, like an unresolved discord, but made it somehow more modern, more human; like a rough joke thrown into a serious scene, it heightened the poignancy which all beauty has.

Chapter XXIV

SHORTLY BEFORE CHRISTMAS DIRK STROEVE CAME TO ASK ME TO SPEND THE holiday with him. He had a characteristic sentimentality about the day and wanted to pass it among his friends with suitable ceremonies. Neither of us had seen Strickland for two or three weeks—I because I had been busy with friends who were spending a little while in Paris, and Stroeve because, having quarrelled with him more violently than usual, he had made up his mind to have nothing more to do with him. Strickland was impossible, and he swore never to speak to him again. But the season touched him with gentle feeling, and he hated the thought of Strickland spending Christmas Day by himself; he ascribed his own emotions to him, and could not bear that on an occasion given up to good-fellowship the lonely painter should be abandoned to his own melancholy. Stroeve had set up a Christmas-tree in his studio, and I suspected that we should both find absurd little presents hanging on its festive branches; but he was shy about seeing Strickland again; it was a little humiliating to forgive so easily insults so outrageous, and he wished me to be present at the reconciliation on which he was determined.

We walked together down the Avenue de Clichy, but Strickland was not in the café. It was too cold to sit outside, and we took our places on leather benches within. It was hot and stuffy, and the air was grey with smoke. Strickland did not come, but presently we saw the French painter who occasionally played chess with him. I had formed a casual acquaintance with him, and he sat down at our table. Stroeve asked him if he had seen Strickland.

"He's ill," he said. "Didn't you know?"

"Seriously?"

"Very, I understand."

Stroeve's face grew white.

"Why didn't he write and tell me? How stupid of me to quarrel with him. We must go to him at once. He can have no one to look after him. Where does he live?"

"I have no idea," said the Frenchman.

We discovered that none of us knew how to find him. Stroeve grew more and more distressed.

"He might die, and not a soul would know anything about it. It's dreadful. I can't bear the thought. We must find him at once."

I tried to make Stroeve understand that it was absurd to hunt vaguely about Paris. We must first think of some plan.

"Yes; but all this time he may be dying, and when we get there it may be too late to do anything."

"Sit still and let us think," I said impatiently.

The only address I knew was the Hôtel des Belges, but Strickland had long left that, and they would have no recollection of him. With that queer idea of his to keep his whereabouts secret, it was unlikely that, on leaving, he had said where he was going. Besides, it was more than five years ago. I felt pretty sure that he had not moved far. If he continued to frequent the same café as when he had stayed at the hotel, it was probably because it was the most convenient. Suddenly I remembered that he had got his commission to paint a portrait through the baker from whom he bought his bread, and it struck me that there one might find his address. I called for a directory and looked out the bakers. There were five in the immediate neighbourhood, and the only thing was to go to all of them. Stroeve accompanied me unwillingly. His own plan was to run up and down the streets that led out of the Avenue de Clichy and ask at every house if Strickland lived there. My commonplace scheme was, after all, effective, for in the second shop we asked at the woman behind the counter acknowledged that she knew him. She was not certain where he lived, but it was in one of the three houses opposite. Luck favoured us, and in the first we tried the concierge told us that we should find him on the top floor.

"It appears that he's ill," said Stroeve.

"It may be," answered the concierge indifferently. "*En effet,* I have not seen him for several days."

Stroeve ran up the stairs ahead of me, and when I reached the top floor I found him talking to a workman in his shirt-sleeves who had opened a door at which Stroeve had knocked. He pointed to another door. He believed that the person who lived there was a painter. He had not seen him for a week. Stroeve made as though he were about to knock, and then turned to me with a gesture of helplessness. I saw that he was panic-stricken.

"Supposing he's dead?"

"Not he," I said.

I knocked. There was no answer. I tried the handle, and found the door unlocked. I walked in, and Stroeve followed me. The room was in darkness. I could only see that it was an attic, with a sloping roof; and a faint glimmer, no more than a less profound obscurity, came from a skylight.

"Strickland," I called.

There was no answer. It was really rather mysterious, and it seemed to me that Stroeve, standing just behind, was trembling in his shoes. For a moment I hesitated to strike a light. I dimly perceived a bed in the corner, and I wondered whether the light would disclose lying on it a dead body.

"Haven't you got a match, you fool?"

Strickland's voice, coming out of the darkness, harshly, made me start.

Stroeve cried out.

"Oh, my God, I thought you were dead."

I struck a match, and looked about for a candle. I had a rapid glimpse of a tiny apartment, half room, half studio, in which was nothing but a bed, canvases with their faces to the wall, an easel, a table, and a chair. There was no carpet on the floor. There was no fire-place. On the table, crowded with paints, palette-knives, and litter of all kinds, was the end of a candle. I lit it. Strickland was lying in the bed, uncomfortably because it was too small for him, and he had put all his clothes over him for warmth. It was obvious at a glance that he was in a high fever. Stroeve, his voice cracking with emotion, went up to him.

"Oh, my poor friend, what is the matter with you? I had no idea you were ill. Why didn't you let me know? You must know I'd have done anything in the world for you. Were you thinking of what I said? I didn't mean it. I was wrong. It was stupid of me to take offence."

"Go to hell," said Strickland.

"Now, be reasonable. Let me make you comfortable. Haven't you anyone to look after you?"

He looked round the squalid attic in dismay. He tried to arrange the bed-clothes. Strickland, breathing laboriously, kept an angry silence. He gave me a resentful glance. I stood quite quietly, looking at him.

"If you want to do something for me, you can get me some milk," he said at last. "I haven't been able to get out for two days."

There was an empty bottle by the side of the bed, which had contained milk, and in a piece of newspaper a few crumbs.

"What have you been having?" I asked.

"Nothing."

"For how long?" cried Stroeve. "Do you mean to say you've had nothing to eat or drink for two days? It's horrible."

"I've had water."

His eyes dwelt for a moment on a large can within reach of an outstretched arm.

"I'll go immediately," said Stroeve. "Is there anything you fancy?"

I suggested that he should get a thermometer, and a few grapes, and some bread. Stroeve, glad to make himself useful, clattered down the stairs.

"Damned fool," muttered Strickland.

I felt his pulse. It was beating quickly and feebly. I asked him one or two questions, but he would not answer, and when I pressed him he turned his face irritably to the wall. The only thing was to wait in silence. In ten minutes Stroeve, panting, came back. Besides what I had suggested, he brought candles, and meat-juice, and a spirit-lamp. He was a practical little fellow, and without delay set about making bread-and-milk. I took Strickland's temperature. It was a hundred and four. He was obviously very ill.

Chapter XXV

Presently we left him. Dirk was going home to dinner, and I proposed to find a doctor and bring him to see Strickland; but when we got down into the street, fresh after the stuffy attic, the Dutchman begged me to go immediately to his studio. He had something in mind which he would not tell me, but he insisted that it was very necessary for me to accompany him. Since I did not think a doctor could at the moment do any more than we had done, I consented. We found Blanche Stroeve laying the table for dinner. Dirk went up to her, and took both her hands.

"Dear one, I want you to do something for me," he said.

She looked at him with the grave cheerfulness which was one of her charms. His red face was shining with sweat, and he had a look of comic agitation, but there was in his round, surprised eyes an eager light.

"Strickland is very ill. He may be dying. He is alone in a filthy attic, and there is not a soul to look after him. I want you to let me bring him here."

She withdrew her hands quickly, I had never seen her make so rapid a movement; and her cheeks flushed.

"Oh no."

"Oh, my dear one, don't refuse. I couldn't bear to leave him where he is. I shouldn't sleep a wink for thinking of him."

"I have no objection to your nursing him."

Her voice was cold and distant.

"But he'll die."

"Let him."

Stroeve gave a little gasp. He wiped his face. He turned to me for support, but I did not know what to say.

"He's a great artist."

"What do I care? I hate him."

"Oh, my love, my precious, you don't mean that. I beseech you to let me bring him here. We can make him comfortable. Perhaps we can save him. He shall be no trouble to you. I will do everything. We'll make him up a bed in the studio. We can't let him die like a dog. It would be inhuman."

"Why can't he go to a hospital?"

"A hospital! He needs the care of loving hands. He must be treated with infinite tact."

I was surprised to see how moved she was. She went on laying the table, but her hands trembled.

"I have no patience with you. Do you think if you were ill he would stir a finger to help you?"

"But what does that matter? I should have you to nurse me. It wouldn't be necessary. And besides, I'm different; I'm not of any importance."

"You have no more spirit than a mongrel cur. You lie down on the ground and ask people to trample on you."

Stroeve gave a little laugh. He thought he understood the reason of his wife's attitude.

"Oh, my poor dear, you're thinking of that day he came here to look at my pictures. What does it matter if he didn't think them any good? It was stupid of me to show them to him. I daresay they're not very good."

He looked round the studio ruefully. On the easel was a half-finished picture of a smiling Italian peasant, holding a bunch of grapes over the head of a dark-eyed girl.

"Even if he didn't like them he should have been civil. He needn't have insulted you. He showed that he despised you, and you lick his hand. Oh, I hate him."

"Dear child, he has genius. You don't think I believe that I have it. I wish I had; but I know it when I see it, and I honour it with all my heart. It's the most wonderful thing in the world. It's a great burden to its possessors. We should be very tolerant with them, and very patient."

I stood apart, somewhat embarrassed by the domestic scene, and wondered why Stroeve had insisted on my coming with him. I saw that his wife was on the verge of tears.

"But it's not only because he's a genius that I ask you to let me bring him here; it's because he's a human being, and he is ill and poor."

"I will never have him in my house—never."

Stroeve turned to me.

"Tell her that it's a matter of life and death. It's impossible to leave him in that wretched hole."

"It's quite obvious that it would be much easier to nurse him here," I said, "but of course it would be very inconvenient. I have an idea that someone will have to be with him day and night."

"My love, it's not you who would shirk a little trouble."

"If he comes here, I shall go," said Mrs. Stroeve violently.

"I don't recognise you. You're so good and kind."

"Oh, for goodness sake, let me be. You drive me to distraction."

Then at last the tears came. She sank into a chair, and buried her face in her hands. Her shoulders shook convulsively. In a moment Dirk was on his knees beside her, with his arms round her, kissing her, calling her all sorts of pet names, and the facile tears ran down his own cheeks. Presently she released herself and dried her eyes.

"Leave me alone," she said, not unkindly; and then to me, trying to smile: "What must you think of me?"

Stroeve, looking at her with perplexity, hesitated. His forehead was all puckered, and his red mouth set in a pout. He reminded me oddly of an agitated guinea-pig.

"Then it's No, darling?" he said at last.

She gave a gesture of lassitude. She was exhausted.

"The studio is yours. Everything belongs to you. If you want to bring him here, how can I prevent you?"

A sudden smile flashed across his round face.

"Then you consent? I knew you would. Oh, my precious."

Suddenly she pulled herself together. She looked at him with haggard eyes. She clasped her hands over her heart as though its beating were intolerable.

"Oh, Dirk, I've never since we met asked you to do anything for me."

"You know there's nothing in the world that I wouldn't do for you."

"I beg you not to let Strickland come here. Anyone else you like. Bring a thief, a drunkard, any outcast off the streets, and I promise you I'll do everything I can for them gladly. But I beseech you not to bring Strickland here."

"But why?"

"I'm frightened of him. I don't know why, but there's something in him that terrifies me. He'll do us some great harm. I know it. I feel it. If you bring him here it can only end badly."

"But how unreasonable!"

"No, no. I know I'm right. Something terrible will happen to us."

"Because we do a good action?"

She was panting now, and in her face was a terror which was inexplicable. I do not know what she thought. I felt that she was possessed by some shapeless dread which robbed her of all self-control. As a rule she was so calm; her agitation now was amazing. Stroeve looked at her for a while with puzzled consternation.

"You are my wife; you are dearer to me than anyone in the world. No one shall come here without your entire consent."

She closed her eyes for a moment, and I thought she was going to faint. I was a little impatient with her; I had not suspected that she was so neurotic a woman. Then I heard Stroeve's voice again. It seemed to break oddly on the silence.

"Haven't you been in bitter distress once when a helping hand was held out to you? You know how much it means. Couldn't you like to do someone a good turn when you have the chance?"

The words were ordinary enough, and to my mind there was in them something so hortatory that I almost smiled. I was astonished at the effect they had on Blanche Stroeve. She started a little, and gave her husband a long look. His eyes were fixed on the ground. I did not know why he seemed embarrassed. A faint colour came into her cheeks, and then her face became white—more than white, ghastly; you felt that the blood had shrunk away from the whole surface of her body; and even her hands were pale. A shiver passed through her. The silence of the studio seemed to gather body, so that it became an almost palpable presence. I was bewildered.

"Bring Strickland here, Dirk. I'll do my best for him."

"My precious," he smiled.

He wanted to take her in his arms, but she avoided him.

"Don't be affectionate before strangers, Dirk," she said. "It makes me feel such a fool."

Her manner was quite normal again, and no one could have told that so shortly before she had been shaken by such a great emotion.

Chapter XXVI

NEXT DAY WE MOVED STRICKLAND. IT NEEDED A GOOD DEAL OF FIRMNESS and still more patience to induce him to come, but he was really too ill to offer any effective resistance to Stroeve's entreaties and to my determination. We dressed him, while he feebly cursed us, got him downstairs, into a cab, and eventually to Stroeve's studio. He was so exhausted by the time we arrived that he allowed us to put him to bed without a word. He was ill for six weeks. At one time it looked as though he could not live more than a few hours, and I am convinced that it was only through the Dutchman's doggedness that he pulled through. I have never known a more difficult patient. It was not that he was exacting and querulous; on the contrary, he never complained, he asked for nothing, he was perfectly silent; but he seemed to resent the care that was taken of him; he received all inquiries about his feelings or his needs with a jibe, a sneer, or an oath. I found him detestable, and as soon as he was out of danger I had no hesitation in telling him so.

"Go to hell," he answered briefly.

Dirk Stroeve, giving up his work entirely, nursed Strickland with tenderness and sympathy. He was dexterous to make him comfortable, and he exercised a cunning of which I should never have thought him capable to induce him to take the medicines prescribed by the doctor. Nothing was too much trouble for him. Though his means were adequate to the needs of himself and his wife, he certainly had no money to waste; but now he was wantonly extravagant in the purchase of delicacies, out of season and dear, which might tempt Strickland's capricious appetite. I shall never forget the tactful patience with which he persuaded him to take nourishment. He was never put out by Strickland's rudeness; if it was merely sullen, he appeared not to notice it; if it was aggressive, he only chuckled. When Strickland, recovering somewhat, was in a good humour and amused himself by laughing at him, he deliberately did absurd things to excite his ridicule. Then he would give me little happy glances, so that I might notice in how much better form the patient was. Stroeve was sublime.

But it was Blanche who most surprised me. She proved herself not only a capable, but a devoted nurse. There was nothing in her to remind you that she had so vehemently struggled against her husband's wish to bring Strickland to the studio. She insisted on doing her share of the offices needful to the sick. She arranged his bed so that it was possible to change the sheet without disturbing him. She washed him. When I remarked on her competence, she told me with that pleasant little smile of hers that for a while she had worked in a hospital. She gave no sign that she hated Strickland so desperately. She did not speak to him much, but she was quick to forestall his wants. For a fortnight it was necessary that someone should stay with him all night, and she took turns at watching with her husband. I wondered what she thought during the long darkness as she sat by the bed-side. Strickland was a weird figure as he lay there, thinner than ever, with his ragged red beard and his eyes staring feverishly into vacancy; his illness seemed to have made them larger, and they had an unnatural brightness.

"Does he ever talk to you in the night?" I asked her once.

"Never."

"Do you dislike him as much as you did?"

"More, if anything."

She looked at me with her calm grey eyes. Her expression was so placid, it was hard to believe that she was capable of the violent emotion I had witnessed.

"Has he ever thanked you for what you do for him?"

"No," she smiled.

"He's inhuman."

"He's abominable."

Stroeve was, of course, delighted with her. He could not do enough to show his gratitude for the whole-hearted devotion with which she had accepted the burden he laid on her. But he was a little puzzled by the behaviour of Blanche and Strickland towards one another.

"Do you know, I've seen them sit there for hours together without saying a word?"

On one occasion, when Strickland was so much better that in a day or two he was to get up, I sat with them in the studio. Dirk and I were talking. Mrs. Stroeve sewed, and I thought I recognised the shirt she was mending as Strickland's. He lay on his back; he did not speak. Once I saw that his eyes were fixed on Blanche Stroeve, and there was in them a curious irony. Feeling their gaze, she raised her own, and for a moment they stared at one another. I could not quite understand her expression. Her eyes had in them a strange perplexity, and perhaps—but why?—alarm. In a moment Strickland looked away and idly surveyed the ceiling, but she continued to stare at him, and now her look was quite inexplicable.

In a few days Strickland began to get up. He was nothing but skin and bone. His clothes hung upon him like rags on a scarecrow. With his untidy beard and long hair, his features, always a little larger than life, now emphasised by illness, he had an extraordinary aspect; but it was so odd that it was not quite ugly. There was something monumental in his ungainliness. I do not know how to express precisely the impression he made upon me. It was not exactly spirituality that was obvious, though the screen of the flesh seemed almost transparent, because there was in his face an outrageous sensuality; but, though it sounds nonsense, it seemed as though his sensuality were curiously spiritual. There was in him something primitive. He seemed to partake of those obscure forces of nature which the Greeks personified in shapes part human and part beast, the satyr and the faun. I thought of Marsyas, whom the god flayed because he had dared to rival him in song. Strickland seemed to bear in his heart strange harmonies and unadventured patterns, and I foresaw for him an end of torture and despair. I had again the feeling that he was possessed of a devil; but you could not say that it was a devil of evil, for it was a primitive force that existed before good and ill.

He was still too weak to paint, and he sat in the studio, silent, occupied with God knows what dreams, or reading. The books he liked were queer; sometimes I would find him poring over the poems of Mallarmé, and he read them as a child reads, forming the words with his lips, and I wondered what strange emotion he got from those subtle cadences and obscure phrases; and again I found him absorbed in the detective novels of Gaboriau. I amused myself by thinking that in his choice of books he showed pleasantly the irreconcilable sides of his fantastic nature. It was singular to notice that even in the weak state of his body he had no thought for its comfort. Stroeve liked his ease, and in his studio were a couple of heavily upholstered arm-chairs and a large divan. Strickland would not go near them, not from any affectation of stoicism, for I found him seated on a three-legged stool when I went into the studio one day and he was alone, but because he did not like them. For choice he sat on a kitchen chair without arms. It often exasperated me to see him. I never knew a man so entirely indifferent to his surroundings.

Chapter XXVII

TWO OR THREE WEEKS PASSED. ONE MORNING, HAVING COME TO A PAUSE IN my work, I thought I would give myself a holiday, and I went to the Louvre. I wandered about looking at the pictures I knew so well, and let my fancy play idly with the emotions they suggested. I sauntered into the long gallery, and there suddenly saw Stroeve. I smiled, for his appearance, so rotund and yet so startled, could never fail to excite a smile, and then as I came nearer I noticed that he seemed singularly disconsolate. He looked woebegone and yet ridiculous, like a man who has fallen into the water with all his clothes on, and, being rescued from death, frightened still, feels that he only looks a fool. Turning round, he stared at me, but I perceived that he did not see me. His round blue eyes looked harassed behind his glasses.

"Stroeve," I said.

He gave a little start, and then smiled, but his smile was rueful.

"Why are you idling in this disgraceful fashion?" I asked gaily.

"It's a long time since I was at the Louvre. I thought I'd come and see if they had anything new."

"But you told me you had to get a picture finished this week."

"Strickland's painting in my studio."

"Well?"

"I suggested it myself. He's not strong enough to go back to his own place yet. I thought we could both paint there. Lots of fellows in the Quarter share a studio. I thought it would be fun. I've always thought it would be jolly to have someone to talk to when one was tired of work."

He said all this slowly, detaching statement from statement with a little awkward silence, and he kept his kind, foolish eyes fixed on mine. They were full of tears.

"I don't think I understand," I said.

"Strickland can't work with anyone else in the studio."

"Damn it all, it's your studio. That's his lookout."

He looked at me pitifully. His lips were trembling.

"What happened?" I asked, rather sharply.

He hesitated and flushed. He glanced unhappily at one of the pictures on the wall.

"He wouldn't let me go on painting. He told me to get out."

"But why didn't you tell him to go to hell?"

"He turned me out. I couldn't very well struggle with him. He threw my hat after me, and locked the door."

I was furious with Strickland, and was indignant with myself, because Dirk Stroeve cut such an absurd figure that I felt inclined to laugh.

"But what did your wife say?"

"She'd gone out to do the marketing."

"Is he going to let her in?"

"I don't know."

I gazed at Stroeve with perplexity. He stood like a schoolboy with whom a master is finding fault.

"Shall I get rid of Strickland for you?" I asked.

He gave a little start, and his shining face grew very red.

"No. You'd better not do anything."

He nodded to me and walked away. It was clear that for some reason he did not want to discuss the matter. I did not understand.

Chapter XXVIII

THE EXPLANATION CAME A WEEK LATER. IT WAS ABOUT TEN O'CLOCK AT night; I had been dining by myself at a restaurant, and having returned to my small apartment, was sitting in my parlour, reading. I heard the cracked tinkling of the bell, and, going into the corridor, opened the door. Stroeve stood before me.

"Can I come in?" he asked.

In the dimness of the landing I could not see him very well, but there was something in his voice that surprised me. I knew he was of abstemious habit or I should have thought he had been drinking. I led the way into my sitting-room and asked him to sit down.

"Thank God I've found you," he said.

"What's the matter?" I asked in astonishment at his vehemence.

I was able now to see him well. As a rule he was neat in his person, but now his clothes were in disorder. He looked suddenly bedraggled. I was convinced he had been drinking, and I smiled. I was on the point of chaffing him on his state.

"I didn't know where to go," he burst out. "I came here earlier, but you weren't in."

"I dined late," I said.

I changed my mind: it was not liquor that had driven him to this obvious desperation. His face, usually so rosy, was now strangely mottled. His hands trembled.

"Has anything happened?" I asked.

"My wife has left me."

He could hardly get the words out. He gave a little gasp, and the tears began to trickle down his round cheeks. I did not know what to say. My first thought was that she had come to the end of her forbearance with his infatuation for Strickland, and, goaded by the latter's cynical behaviour, had insisted that he should be turned out. I knew her capable of temper, for all the calmness of her manner; and if Stroeve still refused, she might easily have flung out of the studio with vows never to return. But the little man was so distressed that I could not smile.

"My dear fellow, don't be unhappy. She'll come back. You mustn't take very seriously what women say when they're in a passion."

"You don't understand. She's in love with Strickland."

"What!" I was startled at this, but the idea had no sooner taken possession of me than I saw it was absurd. "How can you be so silly? You don't mean to say

The Moon and Sixpence

you're jealous of Strickland?" I almost laughed. "You know very well that she can't bear the sight of him."

"You don't understand," he moaned.

"You're an hysterical ass," I said a little impatiently. "Let me give you a whisky-and-soda, and you'll feel better."

I supposed that for some reason or other—and Heaven knows what ingenuity men exercise to torment themselves—Dirk had got it into his head that his wife cared for Strickland, and with his genius for blundering he might quite well have offended her so that, to anger him, perhaps, she had taken pains to foster his suspicion.

"Look here," I said, "let's go back to your studio. If you've made a fool of yourself you must eat humble pie. Your wife doesn't strike me as the sort of woman to bear malice."

"How can I go back to the studio?" he said wearily. "They're there. I've left it to them."

"Then it's not your wife who's left you; it's you who've left your wife."

"For God's sake don't talk to me like that."

Still I could not take him seriously. I did not for a moment believe what he had told me. But he was in very real distress.

"Well, you've come here to talk to me about it. You'd better tell me the whole story."

"This afternoon I couldn't stand it anymore. I went to Strickland and told him I thought he was quite well enough to go back to his own place. I wanted the studio myself."

"No one but Strickland would have needed telling," I said. "What did he say?"

"He laughed a little; you know how he laughs, not as though he were amused, but as though you were a damned fool, and said he'd go at once. He began to put his things together. You remember I fetched from his room what I thought he needed, and he asked Blanche for a piece of paper and some string to make a parcel."

Stroeve stopped, gasping, and I thought he was going to faint. This was not at all the story I had expected him to tell me.

"She was very pale, but she brought the paper and the string. He didn't say anything. He made the parcel and he whistled a tune. He took no notice of either of us. His eyes had an ironic smile in them. My heart was like lead. I was afraid something was going to happen, and I wished I hadn't spoken. He looked round for his hat. Then she spoke:

" 'I'm going with Strickland, Dirk,' she said. 'I can't live with you anymore.'

"I tried to speak, but the words wouldn't come. Strickland didn't say anything. He went on whistling as though it had nothing to do with him."

Stroeve stopped again and mopped his face. I kept quite still. I believed him now, and I was astounded. But all the same I could not understand.

Then he told me, in a trembling voice, with the tears pouring down his cheeks, how he had gone up to her, trying to take her in his arms, but she had drawn away and begged him not to touch her. He implored her not to leave him. He told her how passionately he loved her, and reminded her of all the devotion he had lavished upon her. He spoke to her of the happiness of their life. He was not angry with her. He did not reproach her.

"Please let me go quietly, Dirk," she said at last. "Don't you understand that I love Strickland? Where he goes I shall go."

"But you must know that he'll never make you happy. For your own sake don't go. You don't know what you've got to look forward to."

"It's your fault. You insisted on his coming here."

He turned to Strickland.

"Have mercy on her," he implored him. "You can't let her do anything so mad."

"She can do as she chooses," said Strickland. "She's not forced to come."

"My choice is made," she said, in a dull voice.

Strickland's injurious calm robbed Stroeve of the rest of his self-control. Blind rage seized him, and without knowing what he was doing he flung himself on Strickland. Strickland was taken by surprise and he staggered, but he was very strong, even after his illness, and in a moment, he did not exactly know how, Stroeve found himself on the floor.

"You funny little man," said Strickland.

Stroeve picked himself up. He noticed that his wife had remained perfectly still, and to be made ridiculous before her increased his humiliation. His spectacles had tumbled off in the struggle, and he could not immediately see them. She picked them up and silently handed them to him. He seemed suddenly to realise his unhappiness, and though he knew he was making himself still more absurd, he began to cry. He hid his face in his hands. The others watched him without a word. They did not move from where they stood.

"Oh, my dear," he groaned at last, "how can you be so cruel?"

"I can't help myself, Dirk," she answered.

"I've worshipped you as no woman was ever worshipped before. If in anything I did I displeased you, why didn't you tell me, and I'd have changed. I've done everything I could for you."

She did not answer. Her face was set, and he saw that he was only boring her.

She put on a coat and her hat. She moved towards the door, and he saw that in a moment she would be gone. He went up to her quickly and fell on his knees before her, seizing her hands: he abandoned all self-respect.

"Oh, don't go, my darling. I can't live without you; I shall kill myself. If I've done anything to offend you I beg you to forgive me. Give me another chance. I'll try harder still to make you happy."

"Get up, Dirk. You're making yourself a perfect fool."

He staggered to his feet, but still he would not let her go.

"Where are you going?" he said hastily. "You don't know what Strickland's place is like. You can't live there. It would be awful."

"If I don't care, I don't see why you should."

"Stay a minute longer. I must speak. After all, you can't grudge me that."

"What is the good? I've made up my mind. Nothing that you can say will make me alter it."

He gulped, and put his hand to his heart to ease its painful beating.

"I'm not going to ask you to change your mind, but I want you to listen to me for a minute. It's the last thing I shall ever ask you. Don't refuse me that."

She paused, looking at him with those reflective eyes of hers, which now were so different to him. She came back into the studio and leaned against the table.

"Well?"

Stroeve made a great effort to collect himself.

"You must be a little reasonable. You can't live on air, you know. Strickland hasn't got a penny."

"I know."

"You'll suffer the most awful privations. You know why he took so long to get well. He was half starved."

"I can earn money for him."

"How?"

"I don't know. I shall find a way."

A horrible thought passed through the Dutchman's mind, and he shuddered.

"I think you must be mad. I don't know what has come over you."

She shrugged her shoulders.

"Now may I go?"

"Wait one second longer."

He looked round his studio wearily; he had loved it because her presence had made it gay and home-like; he shut his eyes for an instant; then he gave her a long look as though to impress on his mind the picture of her. He got up and took his hat.

"No; I'll go."

"You?"

She was startled. She did not know what he meant.

"I can't bear to think of you living in that horrible, filthy attic. After all, this is your home just as much as mine. You'll be comfortable here. You'll be spared at least the worst privations."

He went to the drawer in which he kept his money and took out several bank-notes.

"I would like to give you half what I've got here."

He put them on the table. Neither Strickland nor his wife spoke.

Then he recollected something else.

"Will you pack up my clothes and leave them with the concierge? I'll come and fetch them tomorrow." He tried to smile. "Good-bye, my dear. I'm grateful for all the happiness you gave me in the past."

He walked out and closed the door behind him. With my mind's eye I saw Strickland throw his hat on a table, and, sitting down, begin to smoke a cigarette.

Chapter XXIX

I KEPT SILENCE FOR A LITTLE WHILE, THINKING OF WHAT STROEVE HAD TOLD me. I could not stomach his weakness, and he saw my disapproval.

"You know as well as I do how Strickland lived," he said tremulously. "I couldn't let her live in those circumstances—I simply couldn't."

"That's your business," I answered.

"What would *you* have done?" he asked.

"She went with her eyes open. If she had to put up with certain inconveniences it was her own lookout."

"Yes; but, you see, you don't love her."

"Do you love her still?"

"Oh, more than ever. Strickland isn't the man to make a woman happy. It can't last. I want her to know that I shall never fail her."

"Does that mean that you're prepared to take her back?"

"I shouldn't hesitate. Why, she'll want me more than ever then. When she's alone and humiliated and broken it would be dreadful if she had nowhere to go."

He seemed to bear no resentment. I suppose it was commonplace in me that I felt slightly outraged at his lack of spirit. Perhaps he guessed what was in my mind, for he said:

"I couldn't expect her to love me as I loved her. I'm a buffoon. I'm not the sort of man that women love. I've always known that. I can't blame her if she's fallen in love with Strickland."

"You certainly have less vanity than any man I've ever known," I said.

"I love her so much better than myself. It seems to me that when vanity comes into love it can only be because really you love yourself best. After all, it constantly happens that a man when he's married falls in love with somebody else; when he gets over it he returns to his wife, and she takes him back, and everyone thinks it very natural. Why should it be different with women?"

"I daresay that's logical," I smiled, "but most men are made differently, and they can't."

But while I talked to Stroeve I was puzzling over the suddenness of the whole affair. I could not imagine that he had had no warning. I remembered the curious look I had seen in Blanche Stroeve's eyes; perhaps its explanation was that she was growing dimly conscious of a feeling in her heart that surprised and alarmed her.

"Did you have no suspicion before today that there was anything between them?" I asked.

He did not answer for a while. There was a pencil on the table, and unconsciously he drew a head on the blotting-paper.

"Please say so, if you hate my asking you questions," I said.

"It eases me to talk. Oh, if you knew the frightful anguish in my heart." He threw the pencil down. "Yes, I've known it for a fortnight. I knew it before she did."

"Why on earth didn't you send Strickland packing?"

"I couldn't believe it. It seemed so improbable. She couldn't bear the sight of him. It was more than improbable; it was incredible. I thought it was merely jealousy. You see, I've always been jealous, but I trained myself never to show it; I was jealous of every man she knew; I was jealous of you. I knew she didn't love me as I loved her. That was only natural, wasn't it? But she allowed me to love her, and that was enough to make me happy. I forced myself to go out for hours together in order to leave them by themselves; I wanted to punish myself for suspicions which were unworthy of me; and when I came back I found they didn't want me—not Strickland, he didn't care if I was there or not, but Blanche. She shuddered when I went to kiss her. When at last I was certain I didn't know what to do; I knew they'd only laugh at me if I made a scene. I thought if I held my tongue and pretended not to see, everything would come right. I made up my mind to get him away quietly, without quarrelling. Oh, if you only knew what I've suffered!"

Then he told me again of his asking Strickland to go. He chose his moment carefully, and tried to make his request sound casual; but he could not master the trembling of his voice; and he felt himself that into words that he wished to seem jovial and friendly there crept the bitterness of his jealousy. He had not expected Strickland to take him up on the spot and make his preparations to go there and then; above all, he had not expected his wife's decision to go with him. I saw that now he wished with all his heart that he had held his tongue. He preferred the anguish of jealousy to the anguish of separation.

"I wanted to kill him, and I only made a fool of myself."

He was silent for a long time, and then he said what I knew was in his mind.

"If I'd only waited, perhaps it would have gone all right. I shouldn't have been so impatient. Oh, poor child, what have I driven her to?"

I shrugged my shoulders, but did not speak. I had no sympathy for Blanche Stroeve, but knew that it would only pain poor Dirk if I told him exactly what I thought of her.

He had reached that stage of exhaustion when he could not stop talking. He went over again every word of the scene. Now something occurred to him that he had not told me before; now he discussed what he ought to have said instead of what he did say; then he lamented his blindness. He regretted that he had done this, and blamed himself that he had omitted the other. It grew later and later, and at last I was as tired as he.

"What are you going to do now?" I said finally.

"What can I do? I shall wait till she sends for me."

"Why don't you go away for a bit?"

"No, no; I must be at hand when she wants me."

For the present he seemed quite lost. He had made no plans. When I suggested that he should go to bed he said he could not sleep; he wanted to go out and walk about the streets till day. He was evidently in no state to be left alone. I persuaded him to stay the night with me, and I put him into my own bed. I had a divan in my sitting-room, and could very well sleep on that. He was by now so worn out that he could not resist my firmness. I gave him a sufficient dose of veronal to insure his unconsciousness for several hours. I thought that was the best service I could render him.

Chapter XXX

BUT THE BED I MADE UP FOR MYSELF WAS SUFFICIENTLY UNCOMFORTABLE TO give me a wakeful night, and I thought a good deal of what the unlucky Dutchman had told me. I was not so much puzzled by Blanche Stroeve's action, for I saw in that merely the result of a physical appeal. I do not suppose she had ever really cared for her husband, and what I had taken for love was no more than the feminine response to caresses and comfort which in the minds of most women passes for it. It is a passive feeling capable of being roused for any object, as the vine can grow on any tree; and the wisdom of the world recognises its strength when it urges a girl to marry the man who wants her with the assurance that love will follow. It is an emotion made up of the satisfaction in security, pride of property, the pleasure of being desired, the gratification of a household, and it is only by an amiable vanity that women ascribe to it spiritual value. It is an emotion which is defenceless against passion. I suspected that Blanche Stroeve's violent dislike of Strickland had in it from the beginning a vague element of sexual attraction. Who am I that I should seek to unravel the mysterious intricacies of sex? Perhaps Stroeve's passion excited without satisfying that part of her nature, and she hated Strickland because she felt in him the power to give her what she needed. I think she was quite sincere when she struggled against her husband's desire to bring him into the studio; I think she was frightened of him, though she knew not why; and I remembered how she had foreseen disaster. I think in some curious way the horror which she felt for him was a transference of the horror which she felt for herself because he so strangely troubled her. His appearance was wild and uncouth; there was aloofness in his eyes and sensuality in his mouth; he was big and strong; he gave the impression of untamed passion; and perhaps she felt in him, too, that sinister element which had made me think of those wild beings of the world's early history when matter, retaining its early connection with the earth, seemed to possess yet a spirit of its own. If he affected her at all, it was inevitable that she should love or hate him. She hated him.

And then I fancy that the daily intimacy with the sick man moved her strangely. She raised his head to give him food, and it was heavy against her hand; when she had fed him she wiped his sensual mouth and his red beard. She washed his limbs; they were covered with thick hair; and when she dried his hands, even in his weakness they were strong and sinewy. His fingers were long; they were the capable, fashioning fingers of the artist; and I know not what troubling thoughts they excited in her. He slept very quietly, without a movement, so that he might have been dead, and he was like some wild creature of the woods, resting after a long chase; and she wondered what fancies passed through his dreams. Did he dream of the nymph flying through the woods of Greece with the satyr in hot pursuit? She fled, swift of foot and desperate, but he gained on her step by step, till she felt his hot breath on her neck; and still she fled silently, and silently he pursued, and when at last he seized her was it terror that thrilled her heart or was it ecstasy?

Blanche Stroeve was in the cruel grip of appetite. Perhaps she hated Strickland still, but she hungered for him, and everything that had made up her life till then became of no account. She ceased to be a woman, complex, kind and petulant, considerate and thoughtless; she was a Mænad. She was desire.

But perhaps this is very fanciful; and it may be that she was merely bored with her husband and went to Strickland out of a callous curiosity. She may have had no particular feeling for him, but succumbed to his wish from propinquity or idleness, to find then that she was powerless in a snare of her own contriving. How did I know what were the thoughts and emotions behind that placid brow and those cool grey eyes?

But if one could be certain of nothing in dealing with creatures so incalculable as human beings, there were explanations of Blanche Stroeve's behaviour which were at all events plausible. On the other hand, I did not understand Strickland at all. I racked my brain, but could in no way account for an action so contrary to my conception of him. It was not strange that he should so heartlessly have betrayed his friends' confidence, nor that he hesitated not at all to gratify a whim at the cost of another's misery. That was in his character. He was a man without any conception of gratitude. He had no compassion. The emotions common to most of us simply did not exist in him, and it was as absurd to blame him for not feeling them as for blaming the tiger because he is fierce and cruel. But it was the whim I could not understand.

I could not believe that Strickland had fallen in love with Blanche Stroeve. I did not believe him capable of love. That is an emotion in which tenderness is an essential part, but Strickland had no tenderness either for himself or for others; there is in love a sense of weakness, a desire to protect, an eagerness to do good and to give pleasure—if not unselfishness, at all events a selfishness which marvellously conceals itself; it has in it a certain diffidence. These were not traits which I could imagine in Strickland. Love is absorbing; it takes the lover out of himself; the most clear-sighted, though he may know, cannot realise that his love will cease; it gives body to what he knows is illusion, and, knowing it is nothing else, he loves it better than reality. It makes a man a little more than himself, and at the same time a little less. He ceases to be himself. He is no longer an individual, but a thing, an instrument to some purpose foreign to his ego. Love is never quite devoid of sentimentality, and Strickland was the least inclined to that infirmity of any man I have known. I could not believe that he would ever suffer that possession of himself which love is; he could never endure a foreign yoke. I believed him capable of uprooting from his heart, though it might be with agony, so that he was left battered and ensanguined, anything that came between himself and that uncomprehended craving that urged him constantly to he knew not what. If I have succeeded at all in giving the complicated impression that Strickland made on me, it will not seem outrageous to say that I felt he was at once too great and too small for love.

But I suppose that everyone's conception of the passion is formed on his own idiosyncrasies, and it is different with every different person. A man like Strickland would love in a manner peculiar to himself. It was vain to seek the analysis of his emotion.

Chapter XXXI

NEXT DAY, THOUGH I PRESSED HIM TO REMAIN, STROEVE LEFT ME. I OFFERED to fetch his things from the studio, but he insisted on going himself; I think he hoped they had not thought of getting them together, so that he would have an opportunity of seeing his wife again and perhaps inducing her to come back to him. But he found his traps waiting for him in the porter's lodge, and the concierge told him that Blanche had gone out. I do not think he resisted the temptation of giving her an account of his troubles. I found that he was telling them to everyone he knew; he expected sympathy, but only excited ridicule.

He bore himself most unbecomingly. Knowing at what time his wife did her shopping, one day, unable any longer to bear not seeing her, he waylaid her in the street. She would not speak to him, but he insisted on speaking to her. He spluttered out words of apology for any wrong he had committed towards her; he told her he loved her devotedly and begged her to return to him. She would not answer; she walked hurriedly, with averted face. I imagined him with his fat little legs trying to keep up with her. Panting a little in his haste, he told her how miserable he was; he besought her to have mercy on him; he promised, if she would forgive him, to do everything she wanted. He offered to take her for a journey. He told her that Strickland would soon tire of her. When he repeated to me the whole sordid little scene I was outraged. He had shown neither sense nor dignity. He had omitted nothing that could make his wife despise him. There is no cruelty greater than a woman's to a man who loves her and whom she does not love; she has no kindness then, no tolerance even, she has only an insane irritation. Blanche Stroeve stopped suddenly, and as hard as she could slapped her husband's face. She took advantage of his confusion to escape, and ran up the stairs to the studio. No word had passed her lips.

When he told me this he put his hand to his cheek as though he still felt the smart of the blow, and in his eyes was a pain that was heartrending and an amazement that was ludicrous. He looked like an overblown schoolboy, and though I felt so sorry for him, I could hardly help laughing.

Then he took to walking along the street which she must pass through to get to the shops, and he would stand at the corner, on the other side, as she went along. He dared not speak to her again, but sought to put into his round eyes the appeal that was in his heart. I suppose he had some idea that the sight of his misery would touch her. She never made the smallest sign that she saw him. She never even changed the hour of her errands or sought an alternative route. I have an idea that there was some cruelty in her indifference. Perhaps she got enjoyment out of the torture she inflicted. I wondered why she hated him so much.

I begged Stroeve to behave more wisely. His want of spirit was exasperating.

"You're doing no good at all by going on like this," I said. "I think you'd have been wiser if you'd hit her over the head with a stick. She wouldn't have despised you as she does now."

I suggested that he should go home for a while. He had often spoken to me of the silent town, somewhere up in the north of Holland, where his parents still lived. They were poor people. His father was a carpenter, and they dwelt in a little old red-brick house, neat and clean, by the side of a sluggish canal. The streets were wide and empty; for two hundred years the place had been dying, but the houses had the homely stateliness of their time. Rich merchants, sending their wares to the distant Indies, had lived in them calm and prosperous lives, and in their decent decay they kept still an aroma of their splendid past. You could wander along the canal till you came to broad green fields, with windmills here and there, in which cattle, black and white, grazed lazily. I thought that among those surroundings, with their recollections of his boyhood, Dirk Stroeve would forget his unhappiness. But he would not go.

"I must be here when she needs me," he repeated. "It would be dreadful if something terrible happened and I were not at hand."

"What do you think is going to happen?" I asked.

"I don't know. But I'm afraid."

I shrugged my shoulders.

For all his pain, Dirk Stroeve remained a ridiculous object. He might have excited sympathy if he had grown worn and thin. He did nothing of the kind. He remained fat, and his round, red cheeks shone like ripe apples. He had great neatness of person, and he continued to wear his spruce black coat and his bowler hat, always a little too small for him, in a dapper, jaunty manner. He was getting something of a paunch, and sorrow had no effect on it. He looked more than ever like a prosperous bagman. It is hard that a man's exterior should tally so little sometimes with his soul. Dirk Stroeve had the passion of Romeo in the body of Sir Toby Belch. He had a sweet and generous nature, and yet was always blundering; a real feeling for what was beautiful and the capacity to create only what was commonplace; a peculiar delicacy of sentiment and gross manners. He could exercise tact when dealing with the affairs of others, but none when dealing with his own. What a cruel practical joke old Nature played when she flung so many contradictory elements together, and left the man face to face with the perplexing callousness of the universe.

Chapter XXXII

I DID NOT SEE STRICKLAND FOR SEVERAL WEEKS. I WAS DISGUSTED WITH HIM, and if I had had an opportunity should have been glad to tell him so, but I saw no object in seeking him out for the purpose. I am a little shy of any assumption of moral indignation; there is always in it an element of self-satisfaction which makes it awkward to anyone who has a sense of humour. It requires a very lively passion to steel me to my own ridicule. There was a sardonic sincerity in Strickland which made me sensitive to anything that might suggest a pose.

But one evening when I was passing along the Avenue de Clichy in front of the café which Strickland frequented and which I now avoided, I ran straight into him. He was accompanied by Blanche Stroeve, and they were just going to Strickland's favourite corner.

"Where the devil have you been all this time?" said he. "I thought you must be away."

His cordiality was proof that he knew I had no wish to speak to him. He was not a man with whom it was worthwhile wasting politeness.

"No," I said; "I haven't been away."

"Why haven't you been here?"

"There are more cafés in Paris than one, at which to trifle away an idle hour."

Blanche then held out her hand and bade me good-evening. I do not know why I had expected her to be somehow changed; she wore the same grey dress that she wore so often, neat and becoming, and her brow was as candid, her eyes as untroubled, as when I had been used to see her occupied with her household duties in the studio.

"Come and have a game of chess," said Strickland.

I do not know why at the moment I could think of no excuse. I followed them rather sulkily to the table at which Strickland always sat, and he called for the board and the chessmen. They both took the situation so much as a matter of course that I felt it absurd to do otherwise. Mrs. Stroeve watched the game with inscrutable face. She was silent, but she had always been silent. I looked at her mouth for an expression that could give me a clue to what she felt; I watched her eyes for some tell-tale flash, some hint of dismay or bitterness; I scanned her brow for any passing line that might indicate a settling emotion. Her face was a mask that told nothing. Her hands lay on her lap motionless, one in the other loosely clasped. I knew from what I had heard that she was a woman of violent passions; and that injurious blow that she had given Dirk, the man who had loved her so devotedly, betrayed a sudden temper and a horrid cruelty. She had abandoned the safe shelter of her husband's protection and the comfortable ease of a well-provided establishment for what she could not but see was an extreme hazard. It showed an eagerness for adventure, a readiness for the hand-to-mouth, which the care she took of her home and her love of good housewifery made not a little remarkable. She must be a woman of complicated character, and there was something dramatic in the contrast of that with her demure appearance.

I was excited by the encounter, and my fancy worked busily while I sought to concentrate myself on the game I was playing. I always tried my best to beat Strickland, because he was a player who despised the opponent he vanquished; his exultation in victory made defeat more difficult to bear. On the other hand, if he was beaten he took it with complete good-humour. He was a bad winner and a good loser. Those who think that a man betrays his character nowhere more clearly than when he is playing a game might on this draw subtle inferences.

When he had finished I called the waiter to pay for the drinks, and left them. The meeting had been devoid of incident. No word had been said to give me anything to think about, and any surmises I might make were unwarranted. I was intrigued. I could not tell how they were getting on. I would have given much to be a disembodied spirit so that I could see them in the privacy of the studio and hear what they talked about. I had not the smallest indication on which to let my imagination work.

Chapter XXXIII

Two or three days later Dirk Stroeve called on me.

"I hear you've seen Blanche," he said.

"How on earth did you find out?"

"I was told by someone who saw you sitting with them. Why didn't you tell me?"

"I thought it would only pain you."

"What do I care if it does? You must know that I want to hear the smallest thing about her."

I waited for him to ask me questions.

"What does she look like?" he said.

"Absolutely unchanged."

"Does she seem happy?"

I shrugged my shoulders.

"How can I tell? We were in a café; we were playing chess; I had no opportunity to speak to her."

"Oh, but couldn't you tell by her face?"

I shook my head. I could only repeat that by no word, by no hinted gesture, had she given an indication of her feelings. He must know better than I how great were her powers of self-control. He clasped his hands emotionally.

"Oh, I'm so frightened. I know something is going to happen, something terrible, and I can do nothing to stop it."

"What sort of thing?" I asked.

"Oh, I don't know," he moaned, seizing his head with his hands. "I foresee some terrible catastrophe."

Stroeve had always been excitable, but now he was beside himself; there was no reasoning with him. I thought it probable enough that Blanche Stroeve would not continue to find life with Strickland tolerable, but one of the falsest of proverbs is that you must lie on the bed that you have made. The experience of life shows that people are constantly doing things which must lead to disaster, and yet by some chance manage to evade the result of their folly. When Blanche quarrelled with Strickland she had only to leave him, and her husband was waiting humbly to forgive and forget. I was not prepared to feel any great sympathy for her.

"You see, you don't love her," said Stroeve.

"After all, there's nothing to prove that she is unhappy. For all we know they may have settled down into a most domestic couple."

Stroeve gave me a look with his woeful eyes.

"Of course it doesn't much matter to you, but to me it's so serious, so intensely serious."

I was sorry if I had seemed impatient or flippant.

"Will you do something for me?" asked Stroeve.

"Willingly."

"Will you write to Blanche for me?"

"Why can't you write yourself?"

"I've written over and over again. I didn't expect her to answer. I don't think she reads the letters."

"You make no account of feminine curiosity. Do you think she could resist?"

"She could—mine."

I looked at him quickly. He lowered his eyes. That answer of his seemed to me strangely humiliating. He was conscious that she regarded him with an indifference so profound that the sight of his handwriting would have not the slightest effect on her.

"Do you really believe that she'll ever come back to you?" I asked.

"I want her to know that if the worst comes to the worst she can count on me. That's what I want you to tell her."

I took a sheet of paper.

"What is it exactly you wish me to say?"

This is what I wrote:

DEAR MRS. STROEVE—Dirk wishes me to tell you that if at any time you want him he will be grateful for the opportunity of being of service to you. He has no ill-feeling towards you on account of anything that has happened. His love for you is unaltered. You will always find him at the following address.

Chapter XXXIV

BUT THOUGH I WAS NO LESS CONVINCED THAN STROEVE THAT THE CONNECtion between Strickland and Blanche would end disastrously, I did not expect the issue to take the tragic form it did. The summer came, breathless and sultry, and even at night there was no coolness to rest one's jaded nerves. The sun-baked streets seemed to give back the heat that had beat down on them during the day, and the passers-by dragged their feet along them wearily. I had not seen Strickland for weeks. Occupied with other things, I had ceased to think of him and his affairs. Dirk, with his vain lamentations, had begun to bore me, and I avoided his society. It was a sordid business, and I was not inclined to trouble myself with it further.

One morning I was working. I sat in my pyjamas. My thoughts wandered, and I thought of the sunny beaches of Brittany and the freshness of the sea. By my side was the empty bowl in which the concierge had brought me my *café au lait* and the fragment of *croissant* which I had not had appetite enough to eat. I heard the concierge in the next room emptying my bath. There was a tinkle at my bell, and I left her to open the door. In a moment I heard Stroeve's voice asking if I was in. Without moving, I shouted to him to come. He entered the room quickly, and came up to the table at which I sat.

"She's killed herself," he said hoarsely.

"What do you mean?" I cried, startled.

He made movements with his lips as though he were speaking, but no sound issued from them. He gibbered like an idiot. My heart thumped against my ribs, and, I do not know why, I flew into a temper.

"For God's sake, collect yourself, man," I said. "What on earth are you talking about?"

He made despairing gestures with his hands, but still no words came from his mouth. He might have been struck dumb. I do not know what came over me; I took him by the shoulders and shook him. Looking back, I am vexed that I made such a fool of myself; I suppose the last restless nights had shaken my nerves more than I knew.

"Let me sit down," he gasped at length.

I filled a glass with St. Galmier, and gave it to him to drink. I held it to his mouth as though he were a child. He gulped down a mouthful, and some of it was spilled on his shirt-front.

"Who's killed herself?"

I do not know why I asked, for I knew whom he meant. He made an effort to collect himself.

"They had a row last night. He went away."

"Is she dead?"

"No; they've taken her to the hospital."

"Then what are you talking about?" I cried impatiently. "Why did you say she'd killed herself?"

"Don't be cross with me. I can't tell you anything if you talk to me like that."

I clenched my hands, seeking to control my irritation. I attempted a smile.

"I'm sorry. Take your time. Don't hurry, there's a good fellow."

His round blue eyes behind the spectacles were ghastly with terror. The magnifying-glasses he wore distorted them.

"When the concierge went up this morning to take a letter she could get no answer to her ring. She heard someone groaning. The door wasn't locked, and she went in. Blanche was lying on the bed. She'd been frightfully sick. There was a bottle of oxalic acid on the table."

Stroeve hid his face in his hands and swayed backwards and forwards, groaning.

"Was she conscious?"

"Yes. Oh, if you knew how she's suffering! I can't bear it. I can't bear it."

His voice rose to a shriek.

"Damn it all, you haven't got to bear it," I cried impatiently. "She's got to bear it."

"How can you be so cruel?"

"What have you done?"

"They sent for a doctor and for me, and they told the police. I'd given the concierge twenty francs, and told her to send for me if anything happened."

He paused a minute, and I saw that what he had to tell me was very hard to say.

"When I went she wouldn't speak to me. She told them to send me away. I swore that I forgave her everything, but she wouldn't listen. She tried to beat her head against the wall. The doctor told me that I mustn't remain with her. She kept on saying, 'Send him away!' I went, and waited in the studio. And when the ambulance came and they put her on a stretcher, they made me go in the kitchen so that she shouldn't know I was there."

While I dressed—for Stroeve wished me to go at once with him to the hospital—he told me that he had arranged for his wife to have a private room, so that she might at least be spared the sordid promiscuity of a ward. On our way he explained to me why he desired my presence; if she still refused to see him, perhaps she would see me. He begged me to repeat to her that he loved her still; he would reproach her for nothing, but desired only to help her; he made no claim on her, and on her recovery would not seek to induce her to return to him; she would be perfectly free.

But when we arrived at the hospital, a gaunt, cheerless building, the mere sight of which was enough to make one's heart sick, and after being directed from this official to that, up endless stairs and through long, bare corridors, found the doctor in charge of the case, we were told that the patient was too ill to see anyone that day. The doctor was a little bearded man in white, with an offhand manner. He evidently looked upon a case as a case, and anxious relatives as a nuisance which must be treated with firmness. Moreover, to him the affair was commonplace; it was just an hysterical woman who had quarrelled with her lover and taken poison; it was constantly happening. At first he thought that Dirk was the cause of the disaster, and he was needlessly brusque with him. When I explained that he was the husband, anxious to forgive, the doctor looked at him suddenly, with curious, searching eyes. I seemed to see in them a hint of mockery; it was true that Stroeve had the head of the husband who is deceived. The doctor faintly shrugged his shoulders.

"There is no immediate danger," he said, in answer to our questioning. "One doesn't know how much she took. It may be that she will get off with a fright. Women are constantly trying to commit suicide for love, but generally they take care not to succeed. It's generally a gesture to arouse pity or terror in their lover."

There was in his tone a frigid contempt. It was obvious that to him Blanche Stroeve was only a unit to be added to the statistical list of attempted suicides in the city of Paris during the current year. He was busy, and could waste no more time on us. He told us that if we came at a certain hour next day, should Blanche be better, it might be possible for her husband to see her.

Chapter XXXV

I SCARCELY KNOW HOW WE GOT THROUGH THAT DAY. STROEVE COULD NOT bear to be alone, and I exhausted myself in efforts to distract him. I took him to the Louvre, and he pretended to look at pictures, but I saw that his thoughts were constantly with his wife. I forced him to eat, and after luncheon I induced him to lie down, but he could not sleep. He accepted willingly my invitation to remain for a few days in my apartment. I gave him books to read, but after a page or two he would put the book down and stare miserably into space. During the evening we played innumerable games of piquet, and bravely, not to disappoint my efforts, he tried to appear interested. Finally I gave him a draught, and he sank into uneasy slumber.

When we went again to the hospital we saw a nursing sister. She told us that Blanche seemed a little better, and she went in to ask if she would see her husband. We heard voices in the room in which she lay, and presently the nurse returned to say that the patient refused to see anyone. We had told her that if she refused to see Dirk the nurse was to ask if she would see me, but this she refused also. Dirk's lips trembled.

"I dare not insist," said the nurse. "She is too ill. Perhaps in a day or two she may change her mind."

"Is there anyone else she wants to see?" asked Dirk, in a voice so low it was almost a whisper.

"She says she only wants to be left in peace."

Dirk's hands moved strangely, as though they had nothing to do with his body, with a movement of their own.

"Will you tell her that if there is anyone else she wishes to see I will bring him? I only want her to be happy."

The nurse looked at him with her calm, kind eyes, which had seen all the horror and pain of the world, and yet, filled with the vision of a world without sin, remained serene.

"I will tell her when she is a little calmer."

Dirk, filled with compassion, begged her to take the message at once.

"It may cure her. I beseech you to ask her now."

With a faint smile of pity, the nurse went back into the room. We heard her low voice, and then, in a voice I did not recognise the answer:

"No. No. No."

The nurse came out again and shook her head.

"Was that she who spoke then?" I asked. "Her voice sounded so strange."

"It appears that her vocal cords have been burnt by the acid."

Dirk gave a low cry of distress. I asked him to go on and wait for me at the entrance, for I wanted to say something to the nurse. He did not ask what it was, but went silently. He seemed to have lost all power of will; he was like an obedient child.

"Has she told you why she did it?" I asked.

"No. She won't speak. She lies on her back quite quietly. She doesn't move for hours at a time. But she cries always. Her pillow is all wet. She's too weak to use a handkerchief, and the tears just run down her face."

It gave me a sudden wrench of the heart-strings. I could have killed Strickland then, and I knew that my voice was trembling when I bade the nurse good-bye.

I found Dirk waiting for me on the steps. He seemed to see nothing, and did not notice that I had joined him till I touched him on the arm. We walked along in silence. I tried to imagine what had happened to drive the poor creature to that dreadful step. I presumed that Strickland knew what had happened, for someone must have been to see him from the police, and he must have made his statement. I did not know where he was. I supposed he had gone back to the shabby attic which served him as a studio. It was curious that she should not wish to see him. Perhaps she refused to have him sent for because she knew he would refuse to come. I wondered what an abyss of cruelty she must have looked into that in horror she refused to live.

Chapter XXXVI

THE NEXT WEEK WAS DREADFUL. STROEVE WENT TWICE A DAY TO THE HOSpital to inquire after his wife, who still declined to see him; and came away at first relieved and hopeful because he was told that she seemed to be growing better, and then in despair because, the complication which the doctor had feared having ensued, recovery was impossible. The nurse was pitiful to his distress, but she had little to say that could console him. The poor woman lay quite still, refusing to speak, with her eyes intent, as though she watched for the coming of death. It could now be only the question of a day or two; and when, late one evening, Stroeve came to see me I knew it was to tell me she was dead. He was absolutely exhausted. His volubility had left him at last, and he sank down wearily on my sofa. I felt that no words of condolence availed, and I let him lie there quietly. I feared he would think it heartless if I read, so I sat by the window, smoking a pipe, till he felt inclined to speak.

"You've been very kind to me," he said at last. "Everyone's been very kind."

"Nonsense," I said, a little embarrassed.

"At the hospital they told me I might wait. They gave me a chair, and I sat outside the door. When she became unconscious they said I might go in. Her mouth and chin were all burnt by the acid. It was awful to see her lovely skin all wounded. She died very peacefully, so that I didn't know she was dead till the sister told me."

He was too tired to weep. He lay on his back limply, as though all the strength had gone out of his limbs, and presently I saw that he had fallen asleep. It was the first natural sleep he had had for a week. Nature, sometimes so cruel, is sometimes merciful. I covered him and turned down the light. In the morning when I awoke he was still asleep. He had not moved. His gold-rimmed spectacles were still on his nose.

Chapter XXXVII

THE CIRCUMSTANCES OF BLANCHE STROEVE'S DEATH NECESSITATED ALL manner of dreadful formalities, but at last we were allowed to bury her. Dirk and I alone followed the hearse to the cemetery. We went at a foot-pace, but on the way back we trotted, and there was something to my mind singularly horrible in the way the driver of the hearse whipped up his horses. It seemed to dismiss the dead with a shrug of the shoulders. Now and then I caught sight of the swaying hearse in front of us, and our own driver urged his pair so that we might not remain behind. I felt in myself, too, the desire to get the whole thing out of my mind. I was beginning to be bored with a tragedy that did not really concern me, and pretending to myself that I spoke in order to distract Stroeve, I turned with relief to other subjects.

"Don't you think you'd better go away for a bit?" I said. "There can be no object in your staying in Paris now."

He did not answer, but I went on ruthlessly:

"Have you made any plans for the immediate future?"

"No."

"You must try and gather together the threads again. Why don't you go down to Italy and start working?"

Again he made no reply, but the driver of our carriage came to my rescue. Slackening his pace for a moment, he leaned over and spoke. I could not hear what he said, so I put my head out of the window; he wanted to know where we wished to be set down. I told him to wait a minute.

"You'd better come and have lunch with me," I said to Dirk. "I'll tell him to drop us in the Place Pigalle."

"I'd rather not. I want to go to the studio."

I hesitated a moment.

"Would you like me to come with you?" I asked then.

"No; I should prefer to be alone."

"All right."

I gave the driver the necessary direction, and in renewed silence we drove on. Dirk had not been to the studio since the wretched morning on which they had taken Blanche to the hospital. I was glad he did not want me to accompany him, and when I left him at the door I walked away with relief. I took a new pleasure in the streets of Paris, and I looked with smiling eyes at the people who hurried to and fro. The day was fine and sunny, and I felt in myself a more acute delight in life. I could not help it; I put Stroeve and his sorrows out of my mind. I wanted to enjoy.

Chapter XXXVIII

I DID NOT SEE HIM AGAIN FOR NEARLY A WEEK. THEN HE FETCHED ME SOON after seven one evening and took me out to dinner. He was dressed in the deepest mourning, and on his bowler was a broad black band. He had even a black border to his handkerchief. His garb of woe suggested that he had lost in one catastrophe every relation he had in the world, even to cousins by marriage twice removed. His plumpness and his red, fat cheeks made his mourning not a little incongruous. It was cruel that his extreme unhappiness should have in it something of buffoonery.

He told me he had made up his mind to go away, though not to Italy, as I had suggested, but to Holland.

"I'm starting tomorrow. This is perhaps the last time we shall ever meet."

I made an appropriate rejoinder, and he smiled wanly.

"I haven't been home for five years. I think I'd forgotten it all; I seemed to have come so far away from my father's house that I was shy at the idea of revisiting it; but now I feel it's my only refuge."

He was sore and bruised, and his thoughts went back to the tenderness of his mother's love. The ridicule he had endured for years seemed now to weigh him down, and the final blow of Blanche's treachery had robbed him of the resiliency which had made him take it so gaily. He could no longer laugh with those who laughed at him. He was an outcast. He told me of his childhood in the tidy brick house, and of his mother's passionate orderliness. Her kitchen was a miracle of clean brightness. Everything was always in its place, and nowhere could you see a speck of dust. Cleanliness, indeed, was a mania with her. I saw a neat little old woman, with cheeks like apples, toiling away from morning to night, through the long years, to keep her house trim and spruce. His father was a spare old man, his hands gnarled after the work of a lifetime, silent and upright; in the evening he read the paper aloud, while his wife and daughter (now married to the captain of a fishing smack), unwilling to lose a moment, bent over their sewing. Nothing ever happened in that little town, left behind by the advance of civilisation, and one year followed the next till death came, like a friend, to give rest to those who had laboured so diligently.

"My father wished me to become a carpenter like himself. For five generations we've carried on the same trade, from father to son. Perhaps that is the wisdom of life, to tread in your father's steps, and look neither to the right nor to the left. When I was a little boy I said I would marry the daughter of the harness-maker who lived next door. She was a little girl with blue eyes and a flaxen pigtail. She would have kept my house like a new pin, and I should have had a son to carry on the business after me."

Stroeve sighed a little and was silent. His thoughts dwelt among pictures of what might have been, and the safety of the life he had refused filled him with longing.

"The world is hard and cruel. We are here none knows why, and we go none knows whither. We must be very humble. We must see the beauty of quietness. We must go through life so inconspicuously that Fate does not notice us. And let us seek the love of simple, ignorant people. Their ignorance is better than all our knowledge. Let us be silent, content in our little corner, meek and gentle like them. That is the wisdom of life."

To me it was his broken spirit that expressed itself, and I rebelled against his renunciation. But I kept my own counsel.

"What made you think of being a painter?" I asked.

He shrugged his shoulders.

"It happened that I had a knack for drawing. I got prizes for it at school. My poor mother was very proud of my gift, and she gave me a box of water-colours as a present. She showed my sketches to the pastor and the doctor and the judge. And they sent me to Amsterdam to try for a scholarship, and I won it. Poor soul, she was so proud; and though it nearly broke her heart to part from me, she smiled, and would not show me her grief. She was pleased that her son should be an artist. They pinched and saved so that I should have enough to live on, and when my first picture was exhibited they came to Amsterdam to see it, my father and mother and my sister, and my mother cried when she looked at it." His kind eyes glistened. "And now on every wall of the old house there is one of my pictures in a beautiful gold frame."

He glowed with happy pride. I thought of those cold scenes of his, with their picturesque peasants and cypresses and olive-trees. They must look queer in their garish frames on the walls of the peasant house.

"The dear soul thought she was doing a wonderful thing for me when she made me an artist, but perhaps, after all, it would have been better for me if my father's will had prevailed and I were now but an honest carpenter."

"Now that you know what art can offer, would you change your life? Would you have missed all the delight it has given you?"

"Art is the greatest thing in the world," he answered, after a pause.

He looked at me for a minute reflectively; he seemed to hesitate; then he said:

"Did you know that I had been to see Strickland?"

"You?"

I was astonished. I should have thought he could not bear to set eyes on him. Stroeve smiled faintly.

"You know already that I have no proper pride."

"What do you mean by that?"

He told me a singular story.

Chapter XXXIX

When I left him, after we had buried poor Blanche, Stroeve walked into the house with a heavy heart. Something impelled him to go to the studio, some obscure desire for self-torture, and yet he dreaded the anguish that he foresaw. He dragged himself up the stairs; his feet seemed unwilling to carry him; and outside the door he lingered for a long time, trying to summon up courage to go in. He felt horribly sick. He had an impulse to run down the stairs after me and beg me to go in with him; he had a feeling that there was somebody in the studio. He remembered how often he had waited for a minute or two on the landing to get his breath after the ascent, and how absurdly his impatience to see Blanche had taken it away again. To see her was a delight that never staled, and even though he had not been out an hour he was as excited at the prospect as if they had been parted for a month. Suddenly he could not believe that she was dead. What had happened could only be a dream, a frightful dream; and when he turned the key and opened the door, he would see her bending slightly over the table in the gracious attitude of the woman in Chardin's *Benedicité*, which always seemed to him so exquisite. Hurriedly he took the key out of his pocket, opened, and walked in.

The apartment had no look of desertion. His wife's tidiness was one of the traits which had so much pleased him; his own upbringing had given him a tender sympathy for the delight in orderliness; and when he had seen her instinctive desire to put each thing in its appointed place it had given him a little warm feeling in his heart. The bed-room looked as though she had just left it: the brushes were neatly placed on the toilet-table, one on each side of the comb; someone had smoothed down the bed on which she had spent her last night in the studio; and her night-dress in a little case lay on the pillow. It was impossible to believe that she would never come into that room again.

But he felt thirsty, and went into the kitchen to get himself some water. Here, too, was order. On a rack were the plates that she had used for dinner on the night of her quarrel with Strickland, and they had been carefully washed. The knives and forks were put away in a drawer. Under a cover were the remains of a piece of cheese, and in a tin box was a crust of bread. She had done her marketing from day to day, buying only what was strictly needful, so that nothing was left over from one day to the next. Stroeve knew from the enquiries made by the police that Strickland had walked out of the house immediately after dinner, and the fact that Blanche had washed up the things as usual gave him a little thrill of horror. Her methodicalness made her suicide more deliberate. Her self-possession was frightening. A sudden pang seized him, and his knees felt so weak that he almost fell. He went back into the bed-room and threw himself on the bed. He cried out her name.

"Blanche. Blanche."

The thought of her suffering was intolerable. He had a sudden vision of her standing in the kitchen—it was hardly larger than a cupboard—washing the plates and glasses, the forks and spoons, giving the knives a rapid polish on the knife-board; and then putting everything away, giving the sink a scrub, and hanging the dish-cloth up to dry—it was there still, a grey torn rag; then looking round to see that everything was clean and nice. He saw her roll down her sleeves and remove her apron—the apron hung on a peg behind the door—and take the bottle of oxalic acid and go with it into the bed-room.

The agony of it drove him up from the bed and out of the room. He went into the studio. It was dark, for the curtains had been drawn over the great window, and he pulled them quickly back; but a sob broke from him as with a rapid glance he took in the place where he had been so happy. Nothing was changed here, either. Strickland was indifferent to his surroundings, and he had lived in the other's studio without thinking of altering a thing. It was deliberately artistic. It represented Stroeve's idea of the proper environment for an artist. There were bits of old brocade on the walls, and the piano was covered with a piece of silk, beautiful and tarnished; in one corner was a copy of the *Venus of Milo,* and in another of the Venus of the Medici. Here and there was an Italian cabinet surmounted with Delft, and here and there a bas-relief. In a handsome gold frame was a copy of Velasquez' *Innocent X,* that Stroeve had made in Rome, and placed so as to make the most of their decorative effect were a number of Stroeve's pictures, all in splendid frames. Stroeve had always been very proud of his taste. He had never lost his appreciation for the romantic atmosphere of a studio, and though now the sight of it was like a stab in his heart, without thinking what he was at, he changed slightly the position of a Louis XV table which was one of his treasures. Suddenly he caught sight of a canvas with its face to the wall. It was a much larger one than he himself was in the habit of using, and he wondered what it did there. He went over to it and leaned it towards him so that he could see the painting. It was a nude. His heart began to beat quickly, for he guessed at once that it was one of Strickland's pictures. He flung it back against the wall angrily—what did he mean by leaving it there?—but his movement caused it to fall, face downwards, on the ground. No matter whose the picture, he could not leave it there in the dust, and he raised it; but then curiosity got the better of him. He thought he would like to have a proper look at it, so he brought it along and set it on the easel. Then he stood back in order to see it at his ease.

He gave a gasp. It was the picture of a woman lying on a sofa, with one arm beneath her head and the other along her body; one knee was raised, and the other leg was stretched out. The pose was classic. Stroeve's head swam. It was Blanche. Grief and jealousy and rage seized him, and he cried out hoarsely; he was inarticulate; he clenched his fists and raised them threateningly at an invisible enemy. He screamed at the top of his voice. He was beside himself. He could not bear it. That was too much. He looked round wildly for some instrument; he wanted to hack the picture to pieces; it should not exist another minute. He could see nothing that would serve his purpose; he rummaged about his painting things; somehow he could not find a thing; he was frantic. At last he came upon what he sought, a large scraper, and he pounced on it with a cry of triumph. He seized it as though it were a dagger, and ran to the picture.

As Stroeve told me this he became as excited as when the incident occurred, and he took hold of a dinner-knife on the table between us, and brandished it. He lifted his arm as though to strike, and then, opening his hand, let it fall with a clatter to the ground. He looked at me with a tremulous smile. He did not speak.

"Fire away," I said.

"I don't know what happened to me. I was just going to make a great hole in the picture, I had my arm all ready for the blow, when suddenly I seemed to see it."

"See what?"

"The picture. It was a work of art. I couldn't touch it. I was afraid."

Stroeve was silent again, and he stared at me with his mouth open and his round blue eyes starting out of his head.

"It was a great, a wonderful picture. I was seized with awe. I had nearly committed a dreadful crime. I moved a little to see it better, and my foot knocked against the scraper. I shuddered."

I really felt something of the emotion that had caught him. I was strangely impressed. It was as though I were suddenly transported into a world in which the values were changed. I stood by, at a loss, like a stranger in a land where the reactions of man to familiar things are all different from those he has known. Stroeve tried to talk to me about the picture, but he was incoherent, and I had to guess at what he meant. Strickland had burst the bonds that hitherto had held him. He had found, not himself, as the phrase goes, but a new soul with unsuspected powers. It was not only the bold simplification of the drawing which showed so rich and so singular a personality; it was not only the painting, though the flesh was painted with a passionate sensuality which had in it something miraculous; it was not only the solidity, so that you felt extraordinarily the weight of the body; there was also a spirituality, troubling and new, which led the imagination along unsuspected ways, and suggested dim empty spaces, lit only by the eternal stars, where the soul, all naked, adventured fearful to the discovery of new mysteries.

If I am rhetorical it is because Stroeve was rhetorical. (Do we not know that man in moments of emotion expresses himself naturally in the terms of a novelette?) Stroeve was trying to express a feeling which he had never known before, and he did not know how to put it into common terms. He was like the mystic seeking to describe the ineffable. But one fact he made clear to me; people talk of beauty lightly, and having no feeling for words, they use that one carelessly, so that it loses its force; and the thing it stands for, sharing its name with a hundred trivial objects, is deprived of dignity. They call beautiful a dress, a dog, a sermon; and when they are face to face with Beauty cannot recognise it. The false emphasis with which they try to deck their worthless thoughts blunts their susceptibilities. Like the charlatan who counterfeits a spiritual force he has sometimes felt, they lose the power they have abused. But Stroeve, the unconquerable buffoon, had a love and an understanding of beauty which were as honest and sincere as was his own sincere and honest soul. It meant to him what God means to the believer, and when he saw it he was afraid.

"What did you say to Strickland when you saw him?"

"I asked him to come with me to Holland."

I was dumbfounded. I could only look at Stroeve in stupid amazement.

"We both loved Blanche. There would have been room for him in my mother's house. I think the company of poor, simple people would have done his soul a great good. I think he might have learnt from them something that would be very useful to him."

"What did he say?"

"He smiled a little. I suppose he thought me very silly. He said he had other fish to fry."

I could have wished that Strickland had used some other phrase to indicate his refusal.

"He gave me the picture of Blanche."

I wondered why Strickland had done that. But I made no remark, and for some time we kept silence.

"What have you done with all your things?" I said at last.

"I got a Jew in, and he gave me a round sum for the lot. I'm taking my pictures home with me. Beside them I own nothing in the world now but a box of clothes and a few books."

"I'm glad you're going home," I said.

I felt that his chance was to put all the past behind him. I hoped that the grief which now seemed intolerable would be softened by the lapse of time, and a merciful forgetfulness would help him to take up once more the burden of life. He was young still, and in a few years he would look back on all his misery with a sadness in which there would be something not unpleasurable. Sooner or later he would marry some honest soul in Holland, and I felt sure he would be happy. I smiled at the thought of the vast number of bad pictures he would paint before he died.

Next day I saw him off for Amsterdam.

Chapter XL

For the next month, occupied with my own affairs, I saw no one connected with this lamentable business, and my mind ceased to be occupied with it. But one day, when I was walking along, bent on some errand, I passed Charles Strickland. The sight of him brought back to me all the horror which I was not unwilling to forget, and I felt in me a sudden repulsion for the cause of it. Nodding, for it would have been childish to cut him, I walked on quickly; but in a minute I felt a hand on my shoulder.

"You're in a great hurry," he said cordially.

It was characteristic of him to display geniality with anyone who showed a disinclination to meet him, and the coolness of my greeting can have left him in little doubt of that.

"I am," I answered briefly.

"I'll walk along with you," he said.

"Why?" I asked.

"For the pleasure of your society."

I did not answer, and he walked by my side silently. We continued thus for perhaps a quarter of a mile. I began to feel a little ridiculous. At last we passed a stationer's, and it occurred to me that I might as well buy some paper. It would be an excuse to be rid of him.

"I'm going in here," I said. "Good-bye."

"I'll wait for you."

I shrugged my shoulders, and went into the shop. I reflected that French paper was bad, and that, foiled of my purpose, I need not burden myself with a purchase that I did not need. I asked for something I knew could not be provided, and in a minute came out into the street.

"Did you get what you wanted?" he asked.

"No."

We walked on in silence, and then came to a place where several streets met. I stopped at the curb.

"Which way do you go?" I enquired.

"Your way," he smiled.

"I'm going home."

"I'll come along with you and smoke a pipe."

"You might wait for an invitation," I retorted frigidly.

"I would if I thought there was any chance of getting one."

"Do you see that wall in front of you?" I said, pointing.

"Yes."

"In that case I should have thought you could see also that I don't want your company."

"I vaguely suspected it, I confess."

I could not help a chuckle. It is one of the defects of my character that I cannot altogether dislike anyone who makes me laugh. But I pulled myself together.

"I think you're detestable. You're the most loathsome beast that it's ever been my misfortune to meet. Why do you seek the society of someone who hates and despises you?"

"My dear fellow, what the hell do you suppose I care what you think of me?"

"Damn it all," I said, more violently because I had an inkling my motive was none too creditable, "I don't want to know you."

"Are you afraid I shall corrupt you?"

His tone made me feel not a little ridiculous. I knew that he was looking at me sideways, with a sardonic smile.

"I suppose you are hard up," I remarked insolently.

"I should be a damned fool if I thought I had any chance of borrowing money from you."

"You've come down in the world if you can bring yourself to flatter."

He grinned.

"You'll never really dislike me so long as I give you the opportunity to get off a good thing now and then."

I had to bite my lip to prevent myself from laughing. What he said had a hateful truth in it, and another defect of my character is that I enjoy the company of those, however depraved, who can give me a Roland for my Oliver. I began to feel that my abhorrence for Strickland could only be sustained by an effort on my part. I recognised my moral weakness, but saw that my disapprobation had in it already something of a pose; and I knew that if I felt it, his own keen instinct had discovered it, too. He was certainly laughing at me up his sleeve. I left him the last word, and sought refuge in a shrug of the shoulders and taciturnity.

Chapter XLI

WE ARRIVED AT THE HOUSE IN WHICH I LIVED. I WOULD NOT ASK HIM TO come in with me, but walked up the stairs without a word. He followed me, and entered the apartment on my heels. He had not been in it before, but he never gave a glance at the room I had been at pains to make pleasing to the eye. There was a tin of tobacco on the table, and, taking out his pipe, he filled it. He sat down on the only chair that had no arms and tilted himself on the back legs.

"If you're going to make yourself at home, why don't you sit in an arm-chair?" I asked irritably.

"Why are you concerned about my comfort?"

"I'm not," I retorted, "but only about my own. It makes me uncomfortable to see someone sit on an uncomfortable chair."

He chuckled, but did not move. He smoked on in silence, taking no further notice of me, and apparently was absorbed in thought. I wondered why he had come.

Until long habit has blunted the sensibility, there is something disconcerting to the writer in the instinct which causes him to take an interest in the singularities of human nature so absorbing that his moral sense is powerless against it. He recognises in himself an artistic satisfaction in the contemplation of evil which a little startles him; but sincerity forces him to confess that the disapproval he feels for certain actions is not nearly so strong as his curiosity in their reasons. The character of a scoundrel, logical and complete, has a fascination for his creator which is an outrage to law and order. I expect that Shakespeare devised Iago with a gusto which he never knew when, weaving moonbeams with his fancy, he imagined Desdemona. It may be that in his rogues the writer gratifies instincts deep-rooted in him, which the manners and customs of a civilised world have forced back to the mysterious recesses of the subconscious. In giving to the character of his invention flesh and bones he is giving life to that part of himself which finds no other means of expression. His satisfaction is a sense of liberation.

The writer is more concerned to know than to judge.

There was in my soul a perfectly genuine horror of Strickland, and side by side with it a cold curiosity to discover his motives. I was puzzled by him, and I was eager to see how he regarded the tragedy he had caused in the lives of people who had used him with so much kindness. I applied the scalpel boldly.

"Stroeve told me that picture you painted of his wife was the best thing you've ever done."

Strickland took his pipe out of his mouth, and a smile lit up his eyes.

"It was great fun to do."

"Why did you give it him?"

"I'd finished it. It wasn't any good to me."

"Do you know that Stroeve nearly destroyed it?"

"It wasn't altogether satisfactory."

He was quiet for a moment or two, then he took his pipe out of his mouth again, and chuckled.

"Do you know that the little man came to see me?"

"Weren't you rather touched by what he had to say?"

"No; I thought it damned silly and sentimental."

"I suppose it escaped your memory that you'd ruined his life?" I remarked.

He rubbed his bearded chin reflectively.

"He's a very bad painter."

"But a very good man."

"And an excellent cook," Strickland added derisively.

His callousness was inhuman, and in my indignation I was not inclined to mince my words.

"As a mere matter of curiosity I wish you'd tell me, have you felt the smallest twinge of remorse for Blanche Stroeve's death?"

I watched his face for some change of expression, but it remained impassive.

"Why should I?" he asked.

"Let me put the facts before you. You were dying, and Dirk Stroeve took you into his own house. He nursed you like a mother. He sacrificed his time and his comfort and his money for you. He snatched you from the jaws of death."

Strickland shrugged his shoulders.

"The absurd little man enjoys doing things for other people. That's his life."

"Granting that you owed him no gratitude, were you obliged to go out of your way to take his wife from him? Until you came on the scene they were happy. Why couldn't you leave them alone?"

"What makes you think they were happy?"

"It was evident."

"You are a discerning fellow. Do you think she could ever have forgiven him for what he did for her?"

"What do you mean by that?"

"Don't you know why he married her?"

I shook my head.

"She was a governess in the family of some Roman prince, and the son of the house seduced her. She thought he was going to marry her. They turned her out into the street neck and crop. She was going to have a baby, and she tried to commit suicide. Stroeve found her and married her."

"It was just like him. I never knew anyone with so compassionate a heart."

I had often wondered why that ill-assorted pair had married, but just that explanation had never occurred to me. That was perhaps the cause of the peculiar quality of Dirk's love for his wife. I had noticed in it something more than passion. I remembered also how I had always fancied that her reserve concealed I knew not what; but now I saw in it more than the desire to hide a shameful secret. Her tranquillity was like the sullen calm that broods over an island which has been swept by a hurricane. Her cheerfulness was the cheerfulness of despair. Strickland interrupted my reflections with an observation the profound cynicism of which startled me.

"A woman can forgive a man for the harm he does her," he said, "but she can never forgive him for the sacrifices he makes on her account."

"It must be reassuring to you to know that you certainly run no risk of incurring the resentment of the women you come in contact with," I retorted.

A slight smile broke on his lips.

"You are always prepared to sacrifice your principles for a repartee," he answered.

"What happened to the child?"

"Oh, it was still-born, three or four months after they were married."

Then I came to the question which had seemed to me most puzzling.

"Will you tell me why you bothered about Blanche Stroeve at all?"

He did not answer for so long that I nearly repeated it.

"How do I know?" he said at last. "She couldn't bear the sight of me. It amused me."

"I see."

He gave a sudden flash of anger.

"Damn it all, I wanted her."

But he recovered his temper immediately, and looked at me with a smile.

"At first she was horrified."

"Did you tell her?"

"There wasn't any need. She knew. I never said a word. She was frightened. At last I took her."

I do not know what there was in the way he told me this that extraordinarily suggested the violence of his desire. It was disconcerting and rather horrible. His life was strangely divorced from material things, and it was as though his body at times wreaked a fearful revenge on his spirit. The satyr in him suddenly took possession, and he was powerless in the grip of an instinct which had all the strength of the primitive forces of nature. It was an obsession so complete that there was no room in his soul for prudence or gratitude.

"But why did you want to take her away with you?" I asked.

"I didn't," he answered, frowning. "When she said she was coming I was nearly as surprised as Stroeve. I told her that when I'd had enough of her she'd have to go, and she said she'd risk that." He paused a little. "She had a wonderful body, and I wanted to paint a nude. When I'd finished my picture I took no more interest in her."

"And she loved you with all her heart."

He sprang to his feet and walked up and down the small room.

"I don't want love. I haven't time for it. It's weakness. I am a man, and sometimes I want a woman. When I've satisfied my passion I'm ready for other things. I can't overcome my desire, but I hate it; it imprisons my spirit; I look forward to the time when I shall be free from all desire and can give myself without hindrance to my work. Because women can do nothing except love, they've given it a ridiculous importance. They want to persuade us that it's the whole of life. It's an insignificant part. I know lust. That's normal and healthy. Love is a disease. Women are the instruments of my pleasure; I have no patience with their claim to be helpmates, partners, companions."

I had never heard Strickland speak so much at one time. He spoke with a passion of indignation. But neither here nor elsewhere do I pretend to give his exact words; his vocabulary was small, and he had no gift for framing sentences, so that one had to piece his meaning together out of interjections, the expression of his face, gestures and hackneyed phrases.

"You should have lived at a time when women were chattels and men the masters of slaves," I said.

"It just happens that I am a completely normal man."

I could not help laughing at this remark, made in all seriousness; but he went on, walking up and down the room like a caged beast, intent on expressing what he felt, but found such difficulty in putting coherently.

"When a woman loves you she's not satisfied until she possesses your soul. Because she's weak, she has a rage for domination, and nothing less will satisfy her. She has a small mind, and she resents the abstract which she is unable to grasp. She is occupied with material things, and she is jealous of the ideal. The soul of man wanders through the uttermost regions of the universe, and she seeks to imprison it in the circle of her account-book. Do you remember my wife? I saw Blanche little by little trying all her tricks. With infinite patience she prepared to snare me and bind me. She wanted to bring me down to her level; she cared nothing for me, she only wanted me to be hers. She was willing to do everything in the world for me except the one thing I wanted: to leave me alone."

I was silent for a while.

"What did you expect her to do when you left her?"

"She could have gone back to Stroeve," he said irritably. "He was ready to take her."

"You're inhuman," I answered. "It's as useless to talk to you about these things as to describe colours to a man who was born blind."

He stopped in front of my chair, and stood looking down at me with an expression in which I read a contemptuous amazement.

"Do you really care a twopenny damn if Blanche Stroeve is alive or dead?"

I thought over his question, for I wanted to answer it truthfully, at all events to my soul.

"It may be a lack of sympathy in myself if it does not make any great difference to me that she is dead. Life had a great deal to offer her. I think it's terrible that she should have been deprived of it in that cruel way, and I am ashamed because I do not really care."

"You have not the courage of your convictions. Life has no value. Blanche Stroeve didn't commit suicide because I left her, but because she was a foolish and unbalanced woman. But we've talked about her quite enough; she was an entirely unimportant person. Come, and I'll show you my pictures."

He spoke as though I were a child that needed to be distracted. I was sore, but not with him so much as with myself. I thought of the happy life that pair had led in the cosy studio in Montmartre, Stroeve and his wife, their simplicity, kindness, and hospitality; it seemed to me cruel that it should have been broken to pieces by a ruthless chance; but the cruellest thing of all was that in fact it made no great difference. The world went on, and no one was a penny the worse for all that wretchedness. I had an idea that Dirk, a man of greater emotional reactions than depth of feeling, would soon forget; and Blanche's life, begun with who knows what bright hopes and what dreams, might just as well have never been lived. It all seemed useless and inane.

Strickland had found his hat, and stood looking at me.

"Are you coming?"

"Why do you seek my acquaintance?" I asked him. "You know that I hate and despise you."

He chuckled good-humouredly.

"Your only quarrel with me really is that I don't care a twopenny damn what you think about me."

I felt my cheeks grow red with sudden anger. It was impossible to make him understand that one might be outraged by his callous selfishness. I longed to pierce his armour of complete indifference. I knew also that in the end there was truth in what he said. Unconsciously, perhaps, we treasure the power we have over people by their regard for our opinion of them, and we hate those upon whom we have no such influence. I suppose it is the bitterest wound to human pride. But I would not let him see that I was put out.

"Is it possible for any man to disregard others entirely?" I said, though more to myself than to him. "You're dependent on others for everything in existence. It's a preposterous attempt to try to live only for yourself and by yourself. Sooner or later you'll be ill and tired and old, and then you'll crawl back into the herd. Won't you be ashamed when you feel in your heart the desire for comfort and sympathy? You're trying an impossible thing. Sooner or later the human being in you will yearn for the common bonds of humanity."

"Come and look at my pictures."

"Have you ever thought of death?"

"Why should I? It doesn't matter."

I stared at him. He stood before me, motionless, with a mocking smile in his eyes; but for all that, for a moment I had an inkling of a fiery, tortured spirit, aiming at something greater than could be conceived by anything that was bound up with the flesh. I had a fleeting glimpse of a pursuit of the ineffable. I looked at the man before me in his shabby clothes, with his great nose and shining eyes, his red beard and untidy hair; and I had a strange sensation that it was only an envelope, and I was in the presence of a disembodied spirit.

"Let us go and look at your pictures," I said.

Chapter XLII

I DID NOT KNOW WHY STRICKLAND HAD SUDDENLY OFFERED TO SHOW THEM to me. I welcomed the opportunity. A man's work reveals him. In social intercourse he gives you the surface that he wishes the world to accept, and you can only gain a true knowledge of him by inferences from little actions, of which he is unconscious, and from fleeting expressions, which cross his face unknown to him. Sometimes people carry to such perfection the mask they have assumed that in due course they actually become the person they seem. But in his book or his picture the real man delivers himself defenceless. His pretentiousness will only expose his vacuity. The lathe painted to look like iron is seen to be but a lathe. No affectation of peculiarity can conceal a commonplace mind. To the acute observer no one can produce the most casual work without disclosing the innermost secrets of his soul.

As I walked up the endless stairs of the house in which Strickland lived, I confess that I was a little excited. It seemed to me that I was on the threshold of a surprising adventure. I looked about the room with curiosity. It was even smaller and more bare than I remembered it. I wondered what those friends of mine would say who demanded vast studios, and vowed they could not work unless all the conditions were to their liking.

"You'd better stand there," he said, pointing to a spot from which, presumably, he fancied I could see to best advantage what he had to show me.

"You don't want me to talk, I suppose," I said.

"No, blast you; I want you to hold your tongue."

He placed a picture on the easel, and let me look at it for a minute or two; then took it down and put another in its place. I think he showed me about thirty canvases. It was the result of the six years during which he had been painting. He had never sold a picture. The canvases were of different sizes. The smaller were pictures of still-life and the largest were landscapes. There were about half a dozen portraits.

"That is the lot," he said at last.

I wish I could say that I recognised at once their beauty and their great originality. Now that I have seen many of them again and the rest are familiar to me in reproductions, I am astonished that at first sight I was bitterly disappointed. I felt nothing of the peculiar thrill which it is the property of art to give. The impression that Strickland's pictures gave me was disconcerting; and the fact remains, always to reproach me, that I never even thought of buying any. I missed a wonderful chance. Most of them have found their way into museums, and the rest are the treasured possessions of wealthy amateurs. I try to find excuses for myself. I think that my taste is good, but I am conscious that it has no originality. I know very little about painting, and I wander along trails that others have blazed for me. At that time I had the greatest admiration for the Impressionists. I longed to possess a Sisley and a Degas, and I worshipped Manet. His *Olympia* seemed to me the greatest picture of modern times, and *Le Déjeuner sur l'Herbe* moved me profoundly. These works seemed to me the last word in painting.

I will not describe the pictures that Strickland showed me. Descriptions of pictures are always dull, and these, besides, are familiar to all who take an interest in such things. Now that his influence has so enormously affected modern painting, now that others have charted the country which he was among the first to explore, Strickland's pictures, seen for the first time, would find the mind more prepared for them; but it must be remembered that I had never seen anything of the sort. First of all I was taken aback by what seemed to me the clumsiness of his technique. Accustomed to the drawing of the old masters, and convinced that Ingres was the greatest draughtsman of recent times, I thought that Strickland drew very badly. I knew nothing of the simplification at which he aimed. I remember a still-life of oranges on a plate, and I was bothered because the plate was not round and the oranges were lop-sided. The portraits were a little larger than life-size, and this gave them an ungainly look. To my eyes the faces looked like caricatures. They were painted in a way that was entirely new to me. The landscapes puzzled me even more. There were two or three pictures of the forest at Fontainebleau and several of streets in Paris: my first feeling was that they might have been painted by a drunken cabdriver. I was perfectly bewildered. The colour seemed to me extraordinarily crude. It passed through my mind that the whole thing was a stupendous, incomprehensible farce. Now that I look back I am more than ever impressed by Stroeve's acuteness. He saw from the first that here was a revolution in art, and he recognised in its beginnings the genius which now all the world allows.

But if I was puzzled and disconcerted, I was not unimpressed. Even I, in my colossal ignorance, could not but feel that here, trying to express itself, was real power. I was excited and interested. I felt that these pictures had something to say to me that was very important for me to know, but I could not tell what it was. They seemed to me ugly, but they suggested without disclosing a secret of momentous significance. They were strangely tantalising. They gave me an emotion that I could not analyse. They said something that words were powerless to utter. I fancy that Strickland saw vaguely some spiritual meaning in material things that was so strange that he could only suggest it with halting symbols. It was as though he found in the chaos of the universe a new pattern, and were attempting clumsily, with anguish of soul, to set it down. I saw a tormented spirit striving for the release of expression.

I turned to him.

"I wonder if you haven't mistaken your medium," I said.

"What the hell do you mean?"

"I think you're trying to say something, I don't quite know what it is, but I'm not sure that the best way of saying it is by means of painting."

When I imagined that on seeing his pictures I should get a clue to the understanding of his strange character I was mistaken. They merely increased the astonishment with which he filled me. I was more at sea than ever. The only thing that seemed clear to me—and perhaps even this was fanciful—was that he was passionately striving for liberation from some power that held him. But what the power was and what line the liberation would take remained obscure. Each one of us is alone in the world. He is shut in a tower of brass, and can communicate with his fellows only by signs, and the signs have no common value, so that their sense is vague and uncertain. We seek pitifully to convey to others the treasures of our heart, but they have not the power to accept them, and so we go lonely, side by side but not together, unable to know our fellows and unknown by them. We are like people living in a country whose language they know so little that, with all manner of beautiful and profound things to say, they are condemned to the banalities of the conversation manual. Their brain is seething with ideas, and they can only tell you that the umbrella of the gardener's aunt is in the house.

The final impression I received was of a prodigious effort to express some state of the soul, and in this effort, I fancied, must be sought the explanation of what so utterly perplexed me. It was evident that colours and forms had a significance for Strickland that was peculiar to himself. He was under an intolerable necessity to convey something that he felt, and he created them with that intention alone. He did not hesitate to simplify or to distort if he could get nearer to that unknown thing he sought. Facts were nothing to him, for beneath the mass of irrelevant incidents he looked for something significant to himself. It was as though he had become aware of the soul of the universe and were compelled to express it. Though these pictures confused and puzzled me, I could not be unmoved by the emotion that was patent in them; and, I knew not why, I felt in myself a feeling that with regard to Strickland was the last I had ever expected to experience. I felt an overwhelming compassion.

"I think I know now why you surrendered to your feeling for Blanche Stroeve," I said to him.

"Why?"

"I think your courage failed. The weakness of your body communicated itself to your soul. I do not know what infinite yearning possesses you, so that you are driven to a perilous, lonely search for some goal where you expect to find a final release from the spirit that torments you. I see you as the eternal pilgrim to some shrine that perhaps does not exist. I do not know to what inscrutable Nirvana you aim. Do you know yourself? Perhaps it is Truth and Freedom that you seek, and for a moment you thought that you might find release in Love. I think your tired soul sought rest in a woman's arms, and when you found no rest there you hated her. You had no pity for her, because you have no pity for yourself. And you killed her out of fear, because you trembled still at the danger you had barely escaped."

He smiled dryly and pulled his beard.

"You are a dreadful sentimentalist, my poor friend."

A week later I heard by chance that Strickland had gone to Marseilles. I never saw him again.

Chapter XLIII

Looking back, I realise that what I have written about Charles Strickland must seem very unsatisfactory. I have given incidents that came to my knowledge, but they remain obscure because I do not know the reasons that led to them. The strangest, Strickland's determination to become a painter, seems to be arbitrary; and though it must have had causes in the circumstances of his life, I am ignorant of them. From his own conversation I was able to glean nothing. If I were writing a novel, rather than narrating such facts as I know of a curious personality, I should have invented much to account for this change of heart. I think I should have shown a strong vocation in boyhood, crushed by the will of his father or sacrificed to the necessity of earning a living; I should have pictured him impatient of the restraints of life; and in the struggle between his passion for art and the duties of his station I could have aroused sympathy for him. I should so have made him a more imposing figure. Perhaps it would have been possible to see in him a new Prometheus. There was here, maybe, the opportunity for a modern version of the hero who for the good of mankind exposes himself to the agonies of the damned. It is always a moving subject.

On the other hand, I might have found his motives in the influence of the married relation. There are a dozen ways in which this might be managed. A latent gift might reveal itself on acquaintance with the painters and writers whose society his wife sought; or domestic incompatability might turn him upon himself; a love affair might fan into bright flame a fire which I could have shown smouldering dimly in his heart. I think then I should have drawn Mrs. Strickland quite differently. I should have abandoned the facts and made her a nagging, tiresome woman, or else a bigoted one with no sympathy for the claims of the spirit. I should have made Strickland's marriage a long torment from which escape was the only possible issue. I think I should have emphasised his patience with the unsuitable mate, and the compassion which made him unwilling to throw off the yoke that oppressed him. I should certainly have eliminated the children.

An effective story might also have been made by bringing him into contact with some old painter whom the pressure of want or the desire for commercial success had made false to the genius of his youth, and who, seeing in Strickland the possibilities which himself had wasted, influenced him to forsake all and follow the divine tyranny of art. I think there would have been something ironic in the picture of the successful old man, rich and honoured, living in another the life which he, though knowing it was the better part, had not had the strength to pursue.

The facts are much duller. Strickland, a boy fresh from school, went into a broker's office without any feeling of distaste. Until he married he led the ordinary life of his fellows, gambling mildly on the Exchange, interested to the extent of a sovereign or two on the result of the Derby or the Oxford and Cambridge Race. I think he boxed a little in his spare time. On his chimney-piece he had photographs of Mrs. Langtry and Mary Anderson. He read *Punch* and the *Sporting Times*. He went to dances in Hampstead.

It matters less that for so long I should have lost sight of him. The years during which he was struggling to acquire proficiency in a difficult art were monotonous, and I do not know that there was anything significant in the shifts to which he was put to earn enough money to keep him. An account of them would be an account of the things he had seen happen to other people. I do not think they had any effect on his own character. He must have acquired experiences which would form abundant material for a picaresque novel of modern Paris, but he remained aloof, and judging from his conversation there was nothing in those years that had made a particular impression on him. Perhaps when he went to Paris he was too old to fall a victim to the glamour of his environment. Strange as it may seem, he always appeared to me not only practical, but immensely matter-of-fact. I suppose his life during this period was romantic, but he certainly saw no romance in it. It may be that in order to realise the romance of life you must have something of the actor in you; and, capable of standing outside yourself, you must be able to watch your actions with an interest at once detached and absorbed. But no one was more single-minded than Strickland. I never knew anyone who was less self-conscious. But it is unfortunate that I can give no description of the arduous steps by which he reached such mastery over his art as he ever acquired; for if I could show him undaunted by failure, by an unceasing effort of courage holding despair at bay, doggedly persistent in the face of self-doubt, which is the artist's bitterest enemy, I might excite some sympathy for a personality which, I am all too conscious, must appear singularly devoid of charm. But I have nothing to go on. I never once saw Strickland at work, nor do I know that anyone else did. He kept the secret of his struggles to himself. If in the loneliness of his studio he wrestled desperately with the Angel of the Lord he never allowed a soul to divine his anguish.

When I come to his connection with Blanche Stroeve I am exasperated by the fragmentariness of the facts at my disposal. To give my story coherence I should describe the progress of their tragic union, but I know nothing of the three months during which they lived together. I do not know how they got on or what they talked about. After all, there are twenty-four hours in the day, and the summits of emotion can only be reached at rare intervals. I can only imagine how they passed the rest of the time. While the light lasted and so long as Blanche's strength endured, I suppose that Strickland painted, and it must have irritated her when she saw him absorbed in his work. As a mistress she did not then exist for him, but only as a model; and then there were long hours in which they lived side by side in silence. It must have frightened her. When Strickland suggested that in her surrender to him there was a sense of triumph over Dirk Stroeve, because he had come to her help in her extremity, he opened the door to many a dark conjecture. I hope it was not true. It seems to me rather horrible. But who can fathom the subtleties of the human heart? Certainly not those who expect from it only decorous sentiments and normal emotions. When Blanche saw that, notwithstanding his moments of passion, Strickland remained aloof, she must have been filled with dismay, and even in those moments I surmise that she realised that to him she was not an individual, but an instrument of pleasure; he was a stranger still, and she tried to bind him to herself with pathetic arts. She strove to ensnare him with comfort and would not see that comfort meant nothing to him. She was at pains to get him the things to eat that he liked, and would not see that he was indifferent to food. She was afraid to leave him alone. She pursued him with attentions, and when his passion was dormant sought to excite it, for then at least she had the illusion of holding him. Perhaps she knew with her intelligence that the chains she forged only aroused his instinct of destruction, as the plate-glass window makes your fingers itch for half a brick; but her heart, incapable of reason, made her continue on a course she knew was fatal. She must have been very unhappy. But the blindness of love led her to believe what she wanted to be true, and her love was so great that it seemed impossible to her that it should not in return awake an equal love.

But my study of Strickland's character suffers from a greater defect than my ignorance of many facts. Because they were obvious and striking, I have written of his relations to women; and yet they were but an insignificant part of his life. It is an irony that they should so tragically have affected others. His real life consisted of dreams and of tremendously hard work.

Here lies the unreality of fiction. For in men, as a rule, love is but an episode which takes its place among the other affairs of the day, and the emphasis laid on it in novels gives it an importance which is untrue to life. There are few men to whom it is the most important thing in the world, and they are not very interesting ones; even women, with whom the subject is of paramount interest, have a contempt for them. They are flattered and excited by them, but have an uneasy feeling that they are poor creatures. But even during the brief intervals in which they are in love, men do other things which distract their mind; the trades by which they earn their living engage their attention; they are absorbed in sport; they can interest themselves in art. For the most part, they keep their various activities in various compartments, and they can pursue one to the temporary exclusion of the other. They have a faculty of concentration on that which occupies them at the moment, and it irks them if one encroaches on the other. As lovers, the difference between men and women is that women can love all day long, but men only at times.

With Strickland the sexual appetite took a very small place. It was unimportant. It was irksome. His soul aimed elsewhither. He had violent passions, and on occasion desire seized his body so that he was driven to an orgy of lust, but he hated the instincts that robbed him of his self-possession. I think, even, he hated the inevitable partner in his debauchery. When he had regained command over himself, he shuddered at the sight of the woman he had enjoyed. His thoughts floated then serenely in the empyrean, and he felt towards her the horror that perhaps the painted butterfly, hovering about the flowers, feels to the filthy chrysalis from which it has triumphantly emerged. I suppose that art is a manifestation of the sexual instinct. It is the same emotion which is excited in the human heart by the sight of a lovely woman, the Bay of Naples under the yellow moon, and the *Entombment* of Titian. It is possible that Strickland hated the normal release of sex because it seemed to him brutal by comparison with the satisfaction of artistic creation. It seems strange even to myself, when I have described a man who was cruel, selfish, brutal and sensual, to say that he was a great idealist. The fact remains.

He lived more poorly than an artisan. He worked harder. He cared nothing for those things which with most people make life gracious and beautiful. He was indifferent to money. He cared nothing about fame. You cannot praise him because he resisted the temptation to make any of those compromises with the world which most of us yield to. He had no such temptation. It never entered his head that compromise was possible. He lived in Paris more lonely than an anchorite in the deserts of Thebes. He asked nothing from his fellows except that they should leave him alone. He was single-hearted in his aim, and to pursue it he was willing to sacrifice not only himself—many can do that—but others. He had a vision.

Strickland was an odious man, but I still think he was a great one.

Chapter XLIV

A CERTAIN IMPORTANCE ATTACHES TO THE VIEWS ON ART OF PAINTERS, AND this is the natural place for me to set down what I know of Strickland's opinions of the great artists of the past. I am afraid I have very little worth noting. Strickland was not a conversationalist, and he had no gift for putting what he had to say in the striking phrase that the listener remembers. He had no wit. His humour, as will be seen if I have in any way succeeded in reproducing the manner of his conversation, was sardonic. His repartee was rude. He made one laugh sometimes by speaking the truth, but this is a form of humour which gains its force only by its unusualness; it would cease to amuse if it were commonly practised.

Strickland was not, I should say, a man of great intelligence, and his views on painting were by no means out of the ordinary. I never heard him speak of those whose work had a certain analogy with his own—of Cezanne, for instance, or of Van Gogh; and I doubt very much if he had ever seen their pictures. He was not greatly interested in the Impressionists. Their technique impressed him, but I fancy that he thought their attitude commonplace. When Stroeve was holding forth at length on the excellence of Monet, he said: "I prefer Winterhalter." But I daresay he said it to annoy, and if he did he certainly succeeded.

I am disappointed that I cannot report any extravagances in his opinions on the old masters. There is so much in his character which is strange that I feel it would complete the picture if his views were outrageous. I feel the need to ascribe to him fantastic theories about his predecessors, and it is with a certain sense of disillusion that I confess he thought about them pretty much as does everybody else. I do not believe he knew El Greco. He had a great but somewhat impatient admiration for Velasquez. Chardin delighted him, and Rembrandt moved him to ecstasy. He described the impression that Rembrandt made on him with a coarseness I cannot repeat. The only painter that interested him who was at all unexpected was Brueghel the Elder. I knew very little about him at that time, and Strickland had no power to explain himself. I remember what he said about him because it was so unsatisfactory.

"He's all right," said Strickland. "I bet he found it hell to paint."

When later, in Vienna, I saw several of Peter Brueghel's pictures, I thought I understood why he had attracted Strickland's attention. Here, too, was a man with a vision of the world peculiar to himself. I made somewhat copious notes at the time, intending to write something about him, but I have lost them, and have now only the recollection of an emotion. He seemed to see his fellow-creatures grotesquely, and he was angry with them because they were grotesque; life was a confusion of ridiculous, sordid happenings, a fit subject for laughter, and yet it made him sorrowful to laugh. Brueghel gave me the impression of a man striving to express in one medium feelings more appropriate to expression in another, and it may be that it was the obscure consciousness of this that excited Strickland's sympathy. Perhaps both were trying to put down in paint ideas which were more suitable to literature.

Strickland at this time must have been nearly forty-seven.

Chapter XLV

I HAVE SAID ALREADY THAT BUT FOR THE HAZARD OF A JOURNEY TO TAHITI I should doubtless never have written this book. It is thither that after many wanderings Charles Strickland came, and it is there that he painted the pictures on which his fame most securely rests. I suppose no artist achieves completely the realisation of the dream that obsesses him, and Strickland, harassed incessantly by his struggle with technique, managed, perhaps, less than others to express the vision that he saw with his mind's eye; but in Tahiti the circumstances were favourable to him; he found in his surroundings the accidents necessary for his inspiration to become effective, and his later pictures give at least a suggestion of what he sought. They offer the imagination something new and strange. It is as though in this far country his spirit, that had wandered disembodied, seeking a tenement, at last was able to clothe itself in flesh. To use the hackneyed phrase, here he found himself.

It would seem that my visit to this remote island should immediately revive my interest in Strickland, but the work I was engaged in occupied my attention to the exclusion of something that was irrelevant, and it was not till I had been there some days that I even remembered his connection with it. After all, I had not seen him for fifteen years, and it was nine since he died. But I think my arrival at Tahiti would have driven out of my head matters of much more immediate importance to me, and even after a week I found it not easy to order myself soberly. I remember that on my first morning I awoke early, and when I came on to the terrace of the hotel no one was stirring. I wandered round to the kitchen, but it was locked, and on a bench outside it a native boy was sleeping. There seemed no chance of breakfast for some time, so I sauntered down to the water-front. The Chinamen were already busy in their shops. The sky had still the pallor of dawn, and there was a ghostly silence on the lagoon. Ten miles away the island of Murea, like some high fastness of the Holy Grail, guarded its mystery.

I did not altogether believe my eyes. The days that had passed since I left Wellington seemed extraordinary and unusual. Wellington is trim and neat and English; it reminds you of a seaport town on the South Coast. And for three days afterwards the sea was stormy. Grey clouds chased one another across the sky. Then the wind dropped, and the sea was calm and blue. The Pacific is more desolate than other seas; its spaces seem more vast, and the most ordinary journey upon it has somehow the feeling of an adventure. The air you breathe is an elixir which prepares you for the unexpected. Nor is it vouchsafed to man in the flesh to know aught that more nearly suggests the approach to the golden realms of fancy than the approach to Tahiti. Murea, the sister isle, comes into view in rocky splendour, rising from the desert sea mysteriously, like the unsubstantial fabric of a magic wand. With its jagged outline it is like a Monseratt of the Pacific, and you may imagine that there Polynesian knights guard with strange rites mysteries unholy for men to know. The beauty of the island is unveiled as diminishing distance shows you in distincter shape its lovely peaks, but it keeps its secret as you sail by, and, darkly inviolable, seems to fold itself together in a stony, inaccessible grimness. It would not surprise you if, as you came near seeking for an opening in the reef, it vanished suddenly from your view, and nothing met your gaze but the blue loneliness of the Pacific.

Tahiti is a lofty green island, with deep folds of a darker green, in which you divine silent valleys; there is mystery in their sombre depths, down which murmur and plash cool streams, and you feel that in those umbrageous places life from immemorial times has been led according to immemorial ways. Even here is something sad and terrible. But the impression is fleeting, and serves only to give a greater acuteness to the enjoyment of the moment. It is like the sadness which you may see in the jester's eyes when a merry company is laughing at his sallies; his lips smile and his jokes are gayer because in the communion of laughter he finds himself more intolerably alone. For Tahiti is smiling and friendly; it is like a lovely woman graciously prodigal of her charm and beauty; and nothing can be more conciliatory than the entrance into the harbour at Papeete. The schooners moored to the quay are trim and neat, the little town along the bay is white and urbane, and the flamboyants, scarlet against the blue sky, flaunt their colour like a cry of passion. They are sensual with an unashamed violence that leaves you breathless. And the crowd that throngs the wharf as the steamer draws alongside is gay and debonair; it is a noisy, cheerful, gesticulating crowd. It is a sea of brown faces. You have an impression of coloured movement against the flaming blue of the sky. Everything is done with a great deal of bustle, the unloading of the baggage, the examination of the customs; and everyone seems to smile at you. It is very hot. The colour dazzles you.

Chapter XLVI

I HAD NOT BEEN IN TAHITI LONG BEFORE I MET CAPTAIN NICHOLS. HE CAME IN one morning when I was having breakfast on the terrace of the hotel and introduced himself. He had heard that I was interested in Charles Strickland, and announced that he was come to have a talk about him. They are as fond of gossip in Tahiti as in an English village, and one or two enquiries I had made for pictures by Strickland had been quickly spread. I asked the stranger if he had breakfasted.

"Yes; I have my coffee early," he answered, "but I don't mind having a drop of whisky."

I called the Chinese boy.

"You don't think it's too early?" said the Captain.

"You and your liver must decide that between you," I replied.

"I'm practically a teetotaller," he said, as he poured himself out a good half-tumbler of Canadian Club.

When he smiled he showed broken and discoloured teeth. He was a very lean man, of no more than average height, with grey hair cut short and a stubbly grey moustache. He had not shaved for a couple of days. His face was deeply lined, burned brown by long exposure to the sun, and he had a pair of small blue eyes which were astonishingly shifty. They moved quickly, following my smallest gesture, and they gave him the look of a very thorough rogue. But at the moment he was all heartiness and good-fellowship. He was dressed in a bedraggled suit of khaki, and his hands would have been all the better for a wash.

"I knew Strickland well," he said, as he leaned back in his chair and lit the cigar I had offered him. "It's through me he came out to the islands."

"Where did you meet him?" I asked.

"In Marseilles."

"What were you doing there?"

He gave me an ingratiating smile.

"Well, I guess I was on the beach."

My friend's appearance suggested that he was now in the same predicament, and I prepared myself to cultivate an agreeable acquaintance. The society of beach-combers always repays the small pains you need be at to enjoy it. They are easy of approach and affable in conversation. They seldom put on airs, and the offer of a drink is a sure way to their hearts. You need no laborious steps to enter upon familiarity with them, and you can earn not only their confidence, but their gratitude, by turning an attentive ear to their discourse. They look upon conversation as the great pleasure of life, thereby proving the excellence of their civilisation, and for the most part they are entertaining talkers. The extent of their experience is pleasantly balanced by the fertility of their imagination. It cannot be said that they are without guile, but they have a tolerant respect for the law, when the law is supported by strength. It is hazardous to play poker with them, but their ingenuity adds a peculiar excitement to the best game in the world. I came to know Captain Nichols very well before I left Tahiti, and I am the richer for his acquaintance. I do not consider that the cigars and whisky he consumed at my expense (he always refused cocktails, since he was practically a teetotaller), and the few dollars, borrowed with a civil air of conferring a favour upon me, that passed from my pocket to his, were in any way equivalent to the entertainment he afforded me. I remained his debtor. I should be sorry if my conscience, insisting on a rigid attention to the matter in hand, forced me to dismiss him in a couple of lines.

I do not know why Captain Nichols first left England. It was a matter upon which he was reticent, and with persons of his kidney a direct question is never very discreet. He hinted at undeserved misfortune, and there is no doubt that he looked upon himself as the victim of injustice. My fancy played with the various forms of fraud and violence, and I agreed with him sympathetically when he remarked that the authorities in the old country were so damned technical. But it was nice to see that any unpleasantness he had endured in his native land had not impaired his ardent patriotism. He frequently declared that England was the finest country in the world, sir, and he felt a lively superiority over Americans, Colonials, Dagos, Dutchmen, and Kanakas.

But I do not think he was a happy man. He suffered from dyspepsia, and he might often be seen sucking a tablet of pepsin; in the morning his appetite was poor; but this affliction alone would hardly have impaired his spirits. He had a greater cause of discontent with life than this. Eight years before he had rashly married a wife. There are men whom a merciful Providence has undoubtedly ordained to a single life, but who from wilfulness or through circumstances they could not cope with have flown in the face of its decrees. There is no object more deserving of pity than the married bachelor. Of such was Captain Nichols. I met his wife. She was a woman of twenty-eight, I should think, though of a type whose age is always doubtful; for she cannot have looked different when she was twenty, and at forty would look no older. She gave me an impression of extraordinary tightness. Her plain face with its narrow lips was tight, her skin was stretched tightly over her bones, her smile was tight, her hair was tight, her clothes were tight, and the white drill she wore had all the effect of black bombazine. I could not imagine why Captain Nichols had married her, and having married her why he had not deserted her. Perhaps he had, often, and his melancholy arose from the fact that he could never succeed. However far he went and in howsoever secret a place he hid himself, I felt sure that Mrs. Nichols, inexorable as fate and remorseless as conscience, would presently rejoin him. He could as little escape her as the cause can escape the effect.

The rogue, like the artist and perhaps the gentleman, belongs to no class. He is not embarrassed by the *sans gêne* of the hobo, nor put out of countenance by the etiquette of the prince. But Mrs. Nichols belonged to the well-defined class, of late become vocal, which is known as the lower-middle. Her father, in fact, was a policeman. I am certain that he was an efficient one. I do not know what her hold was on the Captain, but I do not think it was love. I never heard her speak, but it may be that in private she had a copious conversation. At any rate, Captain Nichols was frightened to death of her. Sometimes, sitting with me on the terrace of the hotel, he would become conscious that she was walking in the road outside. She did not call him; she gave no sign that she was aware of his existence; she merely walked up and down composedly. Then a strange uneasiness would seize the Captain; he would look at his watch and sigh.

"Well, I must be off," he said.

Neither wit nor whisky could detain him then. Yet he was a man who had faced undaunted hurricane and typhoon, and would not have hesitated to fight a dozen unarmed niggers with nothing but a revolver to help him. Sometimes Mrs. Nichols would send her daughter, a pale-faced, sullen child of seven, to the hotel.

"Mother wants you," she said, in a whining tone.

"Very well, my dear," said Captain Nichols.

He rose to his feet at once, and accompanied his daughter along the road. I suppose it was a very pretty example of the triumph of spirit over matter, and so my digression has at least the advantage of a moral.

Chapter XLVII

I HAVE TRIED TO PUT SOME CONNECTION INTO THE VARIOUS THINGS CAPTAIN Nichols told me about Strickland, and I here set them down in the best order I can. They made one another's acquaintance during the latter part of the winter following my last meeting with Strickland in Paris. How he had passed the intervening months I do not know, but life must have been very hard, for Captain Nichols saw him first in the Asile de Nuit. There was a strike at Marseilles at the time, and Strickland, having come to the end of his resources, had apparently found it impossible to earn the small sum he needed to keep body and soul together.

The Asile de Nuit is a large stone building where pauper and vagabond may get a bed for a week, provided their papers are in order and they can persuade the friars in charge that they are workingmen. Captain Nichols noticed Strickland for his size and his singular appearance among the crowd that waited for the doors to open; they waited listlessly, some walking to and fro, some leaning against the wall, and others seated on the curb with their feet in the gutter; and when they filed into the office he heard the monk who read his papers address him in English. But he did not have a chance to speak to him, since, as he entered the common-room, a monk came in with a huge Bible in his arms, mounted a pulpit which was at the end of the room, and began the service which the wretched outcasts had to endure as the price of their lodging. He and Strickland were assigned to different rooms, and when, thrown out of bed at five in the morning by a stalwart monk, he had made his bed and washed his face, Strickland had already disappeared. Captain Nichols wandered about the streets for an hour of bitter cold, and then made his way to the Place Victor Gélu, where the sailor-men are wont to congregate. Dozing against the pedestal of a statue, he saw Strickland again. He gave him a kick to awaken him.

"Come and have breakfast, mate," he said.

"Go to hell," answered Strickland.

I recognised my friend's limited vocabulary, and I prepared to regard Captain Nichols as a trustworthy witness.

"Busted?" asked the Captain.

"Blast you," answered Strickland.

"Come along with me. I'll get you some breakfast."

After a moment's hesitation, Strickland scrambled to his feet, and together they went to the Bouchée de Pain, where the hungry are given a wedge of bread, which they must eat there and then, for it is forbidden to take it away; and then to the Cuillère de Soupe, where for a week, at eleven and four, you may get a bowl of thin, salt soup. The two buildings are placed far apart, so that only the starving should be tempted to make use of them. So they had breakfast, and so began the queer companionship of Charles Strickland and Captain Nichols.

They must have spent something like four months at Marseilles in one another's society. Their career was devoid of adventure, if by adventure you mean unexpected or thrilling incident, for their days were occupied in the pursuit of enough money to get a night's lodging and such food as would stay the pangs of hunger. But I wish I could give here the pictures, coloured and racy, which Captain Nichols' vivid narrative offered to the imagination. His account of their discoveries in the low life of a seaport town would have made a charming book, and in the various characters that came their way the student might easily have found matter for a very complete dictionary of rogues. But I must content myself with a few paragraphs. I received the impression of a life intense and brutal, savage, multicoloured, and vivacious. It made the Marseilles that I knew, gesticulating and sunny, with its comfortable hotels and its restaurants crowded with the well-to-do, tame and commonplace. I envied men who had seen with their own eyes the sights that Captain Nichols described.

When the doors of the Asile de Nuit were closed to them, Strickland and Captain Nichols sought the hospitality of Tough Bill. This was the master of a sailors' boarding-house, a huge mulatto with a heavy fist, who gave the stranded mariner food and shelter till he found him a berth. They lived with him a month, sleeping with a dozen others, Swedes, negroes, Brazilians, on the floor of the two bare rooms in his house which he assigned to his charges; and every day they went with him to the Place Victor Gélu, whither came ships' captains in search of a man. He was married to an American woman, obese and slatternly, fallen to this pass by Heaven knows what process of degradation, and every day the boarders took it in turns to help her with the housework. Captain Nichols looked upon it as a smart piece of work on Strickland's part that he had got out of this by painting a portrait of Tough Bill. Tough Bill not only paid for the canvas, colours, and brushes, but gave Strickland a pound of smuggled tobacco into the bargain. For all I know, this picture may still adorn the parlour of the tumbledown little house somewhere near the Quai de la Joliette, and I suppose it could now be sold for fifteen hundred pounds. Strickland's idea was to ship on some vessel bound for Australia or New Zealand, and from there make his way to Samoa or Tahiti. I do not know how he had come upon the notion of going to the South Seas, though I remember that his imagination had long been haunted by an island, all green and sunny, encircled by a sea more blue than is found in Northern latitudes. I suppose that he clung to Captain Nichols because he was acquainted with those parts, and it was Captain Nichols who persuaded him that he would be more comfortable in Tahiti.

"You see, Tahiti's French," he explained to me. "And the French aren't so damned technical."

I thought I saw his point.

Strickland had no papers, but that was not a matter to disconcert Tough Bill when he saw a profit (he took the first month's wages of the sailor for whom he found a berth), and he provided Strickland with those of an English stoker who had providentially died on his hands. But both Captain Nichols and Strickland were bound East, and it chanced that the only opportunities for signing on were with ships sailing West. Twice Strickland refused a berth on tramps sailing for the United States, and once on a collier going to Newcastle. Tough Bill had no patience with an obstinacy which could only result in loss to himself, and on the last occasion he flung both Strickland and Captain Nichols out of his house without more ado. They found themselves once more adrift.

Tough Bill's fare was seldom extravagant, and you rose from his table almost as hungry as you sat down, but for some days they had good reason to regret it. They learned what hunger was. The Cuillère de Soupe and the Asile de Nuit were both closed to them, and their only sustenance was the wedge of bread which the Bouchée de Pain provided. They slept where they could, sometimes in an empty truck on a siding near the station, sometimes in a cart behind a warehouse; but it was bitterly cold, and after an hour or two of uneasy dozing they would tramp the streets again. What they felt the lack of most bitterly was tobacco, and Captain Nichols, for his part, could not do without it; he took to hunting the "Can o' Beer," for cigarette-ends and the butt-end of cigars which the promenaders of the night before had thrown away.

"I've tasted worse smoking mixtures in a pipe," he added, with a philosophic shrug of his shoulders, as he took a couple of cigars from the case I offered him, putting one in his mouth and the other in his pocket.

Now and then they made a bit of money. Sometimes a mail steamer would come in, and Captain Nichols, having scraped acquaintance with the timekeeper, would succeed in getting the pair of them a job as stevedores. When it was an English boat, they would dodge into the forecastle and get a hearty breakfast from the crew. They took the risk of running against one of the ship's officers and being hustled down the gangway with the toe of a boot to speed their going.

"There's no harm in a kick in the hindquarters when your belly's full," said Captain Nichols, "and personally I never take it in bad part. An officer's got to think about discipline."

I had a lively picture of Captain Nichols flying headlong down a narrow gangway before the uplifted foot of an angry mate, and, like a true Englishman, rejoicing in the spirit of the Mercantile Marine.

There were often odd jobs to be got about the fish-market. Once they each of them earned a franc by loading trucks with innumerable boxes of oranges that had been dumped down on the quay. One day they had a stroke of luck: one of the boardingmasters got a contract to paint a tramp that had come in from Madagascar round the Cape of Good Hope, and they spent several days on a plank hanging over the side, covering the rusty hull with paint. It was a situation that must have appealed to Strickland's sardonic humour. I asked Captain Nichols how he bore himself during these hardships.

"Never knew him say a cross word," answered the Captain. "He'd be a bit surly sometimes, but when we hadn't had a bite since morning, and we hadn't even got the price of a lie down at the Chink's, he'd be as lively as a cricket."

I was not surprised at this. Strickland was just the man to rise superior to circumstances, when they were such as to occasion despondency in most; but whether this was due to equanimity of soul or to contradictoriness it would be difficult to say.

The Chink's Head was a name the beach-combers gave to a wretched inn off the Rue Bouterie, kept by a one-eyed Chinaman, where for six sous you could sleep in a cot and for three on the floor. Here they made friends with others in as desperate condition as themselves, and when they were penniless and the night was bitter cold, they were glad to borrow from anyone who had earned a stray franc during the day the price of a roof over their heads. They were not niggardly, these tramps, and he who had money did not hesitate to share it among the rest. They belonged to all the countries in the world, but this was no bar to good-fellowship; for they felt themselves freemen of a country whose frontiers include them all, the great country of Cockaine.

"But I guess Strickland was an ugly customer when he was roused," said Captain Nichols, reflectively. "One day we ran into Tough Bill in the Place, and he asked Charlie for the papers he'd given him."

" 'You'd better come and take them if you want them,' says Charlie.

"He was a powerful fellow, Tough Bill, but he didn't quite like the look of Charlie, so he began cursing him. He called him pretty near every name he could lay hands on, and when Tough Bill began cursing it was worth listening to him. Well, Charlie stuck it for a bit, then he stepped forward and he just said: 'Get out, you bloody swine.' It wasn't so much what he said, but the way he said it. Tough Bill never spoke another word; you could see him go yellow, and he walked away as if he'd remembered he had a date."

Strickland, according to Captain Nichols, did not use exactly the words I have given, but since this book is meant for family reading I have thought it better, at the expense of truth, to put into his mouth expressions familiar to the domestic circle.

Now, Tough Bill was not the man to put up with humiliation at the hands of a common sailor. His power depended on his prestige, and first one, then another, of the sailors who lived in his house told them that he had sworn to do Strickland in.

One night Captain Nichols and Strickland were sitting in one of the bars of the Rue Bouterie. The Rue Bouterie is a narrow street of one-storeyed houses, each house consisting of but one room; they are like the booths in a crowded fair or the cages of animals in a circus. At every door you see a woman. Some lean lazily against the side-posts, humming to themselves or calling to the passer-by in a raucous voice, and some listlessly read. They are French, Italian, Spanish, Japanese, coloured; some are fat and some are thin; and under the thick paint on their faces, the heavy smears on their eyebrows, and the scarlet of their lips, you see the lines of age and the scars of dissipation. Some wear black shifts and flesh-coloured stockings; some with curly hair, dyed yellow, are dressed like little girls in short muslin frocks. Through the open door you see a red-tiled floor, a large wooden bed, and on a deal table a ewer and a basin. A motley crowd saunters along the streets—Lascars off a P. and O., blond Northmen from a Swedish barque, Japanese from a man-of-war, English sailors, Spaniards, pleasant-looking fellows from a French cruiser, negroes off an American tramp. By day it is merely sordid, but at night, lit only by the lamps in the little huts, the street has a sinister beauty. The hideous lust that pervades the air is oppressive and horrible, and yet there is something mysterious in the sight which haunts and troubles you. You feel I know not what primitive force which repels and yet fascinates you. Here all the decencies of civilisation are swept away, and you feel that men are face to face with a sombre reality. There is an atmosphere that is at once intense and tragic.

In the bar in which Strickland and Nichols sat a mechanical piano was loudly grinding out dance music. Round the room people were sitting at table, here half a dozen sailors uproariously drunk, there a group of soldiers; and in the middle, crowded together, couples were dancing. Bearded sailors with brown faces and large horny hands clasped their partners in a tight embrace. The women wore nothing but a shift. Now and then two sailors would get up and dance together. The noise was deafening. People were singing, shouting, laughing; and when a man gave a long kiss to the girl sitting on his knees, cat-calls from the English sailors increased the din. The air was heavy with the dust beaten up by the heavy boots of the men, and grey with smoke. It was very hot. Behind the bar was seated a woman nursing her baby. The waiter, an undersized youth with a flat, spotty face, hurried to and fro carrying a tray laden with glasses of beer.

In a little while Tough Bill, accompanied by two huge negroes, came in, and it was easy to see that he was already three parts drunk. He was looking for trouble. He lurched against a table at which three soldiers were sitting and knocked over a glass of beer. There was an angry altercation, and the owner of the bar stepped forward and ordered Tough Bill to go. He was a hefty fellow, in the habit of standing no nonsense from his customers, and Tough Bill hesitated. The landlord was not a man he cared to tackle, for the police were on his side, and with an oath he turned on his heel. Suddenly he caught sight of Strickland. He rolled up to him. He did not speak. He gathered the spittle in his mouth and spat full in Strickland's face. Strickland seized his glass and flung it at him. The dancers stopped suddenly still. There was an instant of complete silence, but when Tough Bill threw himself on Strickland the lust of battle seized them all, and in a moment there was a confused scrimmage. Tables were overturned, glasses crashed to the ground. There was a hellish row. The women scattered to the door and behind the bar. Passers-by surged in from the street. You heard curses in every tongue, the sound of blows, cries; and in the middle of the room a dozen men were fighting with all their might. On a sudden the police rushed in, and everyone who could made for the door. When the bar was more or less cleared, Tough Bill was lying insensible on the floor with a great gash in his head. Captain Nichols dragged Strickland, bleeding from a wound in his arm, his clothes in rags, into the street. His own face was covered with blood from a blow on the nose.

"I guess you'd better get out of Marseilles before Tough Bill comes out of hospital," he said to Strickland, when they had got back to the Chink's Head and were cleaning themselves.

"This beats cock-fighting," said Strickland.

I could see his sardonic smile.

Captain Nichols was anxious. He knew Tough Bill's vindictiveness. Strickland had downed the mulatto twice, and the mulatto, sober, was a man to be reckoned with. He would bide his time stealthily. He would be in no hurry, but one night Strickland would get a knife-thrust in his back, and in a day or two the corpse of a nameless beach-comber would be fished out of the dirty water of the harbour. Nichols went next evening to Tough Bill's house and made enquiries. He was in hospital still, but his wife, who had been to see him, said he was swearing hard to kill Strickland when they let him out.

A week passed.

"That's what I always say," reflected Captain Nichols, "when you hurt a man, hurt him bad. It gives you a bit of time to look about and think what you'll do next."

Then Strickland had a bit of luck. A ship bound for Australia had sent to the

Sailors' Home for a stoker in place of one who had thrown himself overboard off Gibraltar in an attack of delirium tremens.

"You double down to the harbour, my lad," said the Captain to Strickland, "and sign on. You've got your papers."

Strickland set off at once, and that was the last Captain Nichols saw of him. The ship was only in port for six hours, and in the evening Captain Nichols watched the vanishing smoke from her funnels as she ploughed East through the wintry sea.

I have narrated all this as best I could, because I like the contrast of these episodes with the life that I had seen Strickland live in Ashley Gardens when he was occupied with stocks and shares; but I am aware that Captain Nichols was an outrageous liar, and I daresay there is not a word of truth in anything he told me. I should not be surprised to learn that he had never seen Strickland in his life, and owed his knowledge of Marseilles to the pages of a magazine.

Chapter XLVIII

IT IS HERE THAT I PURPOSED TO END MY BOOK. MY FIRST IDEA WAS TO BEGIN IT with the account of Strickland's last years in Tahiti and with his horrible death, and then to go back and relate what I knew of his beginnings. This I meant to do, not from wilfulness, but because I wished to leave Strickland setting out with I know not what fancies in his lonely soul for the unknown islands which fired his imagination. I liked the picture of him starting at the age of forty-seven, when most men have already settled comfortably in a groove, for a new world. I saw him, the sea grey under the mistral and foam-flecked, watching the vanishing coast of France, which he was destined never to see again; and I thought there was something gallant in his bearing and dauntless in his soul. I wished so to end on a note of hope. It seemed to emphasise the unconquerable spirit of man. But I could not manage it. Somehow I could not get into my story, and after trying once or twice I had to give it up; I started from the beginning in the usual way, and made up my mind I could only tell what I knew of Strickland's life in the order in which I learned the facts.

Those that I have now are fragmentary. I am in the position of a biologist who from a single bone must reconstruct not only the appearance of an extinct animal, but its habits. Strickland made no particular impression on the people who came in contact with him in Tahiti. To them he was no more than a beach-comber in constant need of money, remarkable only for the peculiarity that he painted pictures which seemed to them absurd; and it was not till he had been dead for some years and agents came from the dealers in Paris and Berlin to look for any pictures which might still remain on the island, that they had any idea that among them had dwelt a man of consequence. They remembered then that they could have bought for a song canvases which now were worth large sums, and they could not forgive themselves for the opportunity which had escaped them. There was a Jewish trader called Cohen, who had come by one of Strickland's pictures in a singular way. He was a little old Frenchman, with soft kind eyes and a pleasant smile, half trader and half seaman, who owned a cutter in which he wandered boldly among the Paumotus and the Marquesas, taking out trade goods and bringing back copra, shell, and pearls. I went to see him because I was told he had a large black pearl which he was willing to sell cheaply, and when I discovered that it was beyond my means I began to talk to him about Strickland. He had known him well.

"You see, I was interested in him because he was a painter," he told me. "We don't get many painters in the islands, and I was sorry for him because he was such a bad one. I gave him his first job. I had a plantation on the peninsula, and I wanted a white overseer. You never get any work out of the natives unless you have a white man over them. I said to him: 'You'll have plenty of time for painting, and you can earn a bit of money.' I knew he was starving, but I offered him good wages."

"I can't imagine that he was a very satisfactory overseer," I said, smiling.

"I made allowances. I have always had a sympathy for artists. It is in our blood, you know. But he only remained a few months. When he had enough money to buy paints and canvases he left me. The place had got hold of him by then, and he wanted to get away into the bush. But I continued to see him now and then. He would turn up in Papeete every few months and stay a little while; he'd get money out of someone or other and then disappear again. It was on one of these visits that he came to me and asked for the loan of two hundred francs. He looked as if he hadn't had a meal for a week, and I hadn't the heart to refuse him. Of course, I never expected to see my money again. Well, a year later he came to see me once more, and he brought a picture with him. He did not mention the money he owed me, but he said: 'Here is a picture of your plantation that I've painted for you.' I looked at it. I did not know what to say, but of course I thanked him, and when he had gone away I showed it to my wife."

"What was it like?" I asked.

"Do not ask me. I could not make head or tail of it. I never saw such a thing in my life. 'What shall we do with it?' I said to my wife. 'We can never hang it up,' she said. 'People would laugh at us.' So she took it into an attic and put it away with all sorts of rubbish, for my wife can never throw anything away. It is her mania. Then, imagine to yourself, just before the war my brother wrote to me from Paris, and said: 'Do you know anything about an English painter who lived in Tahiti? It appears that he was a genius, and his pictures fetch large prices. See if you can lay your hands on anything and send it to me. There's money to be made.' So I said to my wife: 'What about that picture that Strickland gave me? Is it possible that it is still in the attic?' 'Without doubt,' she answered, 'for you know that I never throw anything away. It is my mania.' We went up to the attic, and there, among I know not what rubbish that had been gathered during the thirty years we have inhabited that house, was the picture. I looked at it again, and I said: 'Who would have thought that the overseer of my plantation on the peninsula, to whom I lent two hundred francs, had genius? Do you see anything in the picture?' 'No,' she said, 'it does not resemble the plantation and I have never seen coconuts with blue leaves; but they are mad in Paris, and it may be that your brother will be able to sell it for the two hundred francs you lent Strickland.' Well, we packed it up and we sent it to my brother. And at last I received a letter from him. What do you think he said? 'I received your picture,' he said, 'and I confess I thought it was a joke that you had played on me. I would not have given the cost of postage for the picture. I was half afraid to show it to the gentleman who had spoken to me about it. Imagine my surprise when he said it was a masterpiece, and offered me thirty thousand francs. I daresay he would have paid more, but frankly I was so taken aback that I lost my head; I accepted the offer before I was able to collect myself.' "

Then Monsieur Cohen said an admirable thing.

"I wish that poor Strickland had been still alive. I wonder what he would have said when I gave him twenty-nine thousand eight hundred francs for his picture."

Chapter XLIX

I LIVED AT THE HÔTEL DE LA FLEUR, AND MRS. JOHNSON, THE PROPRIETRESS, had a sad story to tell of lost opportunity. After Strickland's death certain of his effects were sold by auction in the market-place at Papeete, and she went to it herself because there was among the truck an American stove she wanted. She paid twenty-seven francs for it.

"There were a dozen pictures," she told me, "but they were unframed, and nobody wanted them. Some of them sold for as much as ten francs, but mostly they went for five or six. Just think, if I had bought them I should be a rich woman now."

But Tiaré Johnson would never under any circumstances have been rich. She could not keep money. The daughter of a native and an English sea-captain settled in Tahiti, when I knew her she was a woman of fifty, who looked older, and of enormous proportions. Tall and extremely stout, she would have been of imposing presence if the great good-nature of her face had not made it impossible for her to express anything but kindliness. Her arms were like legs of mutton, her breasts like giant cabbages; her face, broad and fleshy, gave you an impression of almost indecent nakedness, and vast chin succeeded to vast chin. I do not know how many of them there were. They fell away voluminously into the capaciousness of her bosom. She was dressed usually in a pink Mother Hubbard, and she wore all day long a large straw hat. But when she let down her hair, which she did now and then, for she was vain of it, you saw that it was long and dark and curly; and her eyes had remained young and vivacious. Her laughter was the most catching I ever heard; it would begin, a low peal in her throat, and would grow louder and louder till her whole vast body shook. She loved three things—a joke, a glass of wine, and a handsome man. To have known her is a privilege.

She was the best cook on the island, and she adored good food. From morning till night you saw her sitting on a low chair in the kitchen, surrounded by a Chinese cook and two or three native girls, giving her orders, chatting sociably with all and sundry, and tasting the savoury messes she devised. When she wished to do honour to a friend she cooked the dinner with her own hands. Hospitality was a passion with her, and there was no one on the island who need go without a dinner when there was anything to eat at the Hôtel de la Fleur. She never turned her customers out of her house because they did not pay their bills. She always hoped they would pay when they could. There was one man there who had fallen on adversity, and to him she had given board and lodging for several months. When the Chinese laundryman refused to wash for him without payment she had sent his things to be washed with hers. She could not allow the poor fellow to go about in a dirty shirt, she said, and since he was a man, and men must smoke, she gave him a franc a day for cigarettes. She used him with the same affability as those of her clients who paid their bills once a week.

Age and obesity had made her inapt for love, but she took a keen interest in the amatory affairs of the young. She looked upon venery as the natural occupation for men and women, and was ever ready with precept and example from her own wide experience.

"I was not fifteen when my father found that I had a lover," she said. "He was third mate on the *Tropic Bird*. A good-looking boy."

She sighed a little. They say a woman always remembers her first lover with affection; but perhaps she does not always remember him.

"My father was a sensible man."

"What did he do?" I asked.

"He thrashed me within an inch of my life, and then he made me marry Captain Johnson. I did not mind. He was older, of course, but he was good-looking too."

Tiaré—her father had called her by the name of the white, scented flower which, they tell you, if you have once smelt, will always draw you back to Tahiti in the end, however far you may have roamed—Tiaré remembered Strickland very well.

"He used to come here sometimes, and I used to see him walking about Papeete. I was sorry for him, he was so thin, and he never had any money. When I heard he was in town, I used to send a boy to find him and make him come to dinner with me. I got him a job once or twice, but he couldn't stick to anything. After a little while he wanted to get back to the bush, and one morning he would be gone."

Strickland reached Tahiti about six months after he left Marseilles. He worked his passage on a sailing vessel that was making the trip from Auckland to San Francisco, and he arrived with a box of paints, an easel, and a dozen canvases. He had a few pounds in his pocket, for he had found work in Sydney, and he took a small room in a native house outside the town. I think the moment he reached Tahiti he felt himself at home. Tiaré told me that he said to her once:

"I'd been scrubbing the deck, and all at once a chap said to me: 'Why, there it is.' And I looked up and I saw the outline of the island. I knew right away that there was the place I'd been looking for all my life. Then we came near, and I seemed to recognise it. Sometimes when I walk about it all seems familiar. I could swear I've lived here before."

"Sometimes it takes them like that," said Tiaré. "I've known men come on shore for a few hours while their ship was taking in cargo, and never go back. And I've known men who came here to be in an office for a year, and they cursed the place, and when they went away they took their dying oath they'd hang themselves before they came back again, and in six months you'd see them land once more, and they'd tell you they couldn't live anywhere else."

Chapter L

I HAVE AN IDEA THAT SOME MEN ARE BORN OUT OF THEIR DUE PLACE. ACCIDENT has cast them amid certain surroundings, but they have always a nostalgia for a home they know not. They are strangers in their birthplace, and the leafy lanes they have known from childhood or the populous streets in which they have played, remain but a place of passage. They may spend their whole lives aliens among their kindred and remain aloof among the only scenes they have ever known. Perhaps it is this sense of strangeness that sends men far and wide in the search for something permanent, to which they may attach themselves. Perhaps some deep-rooted atavism urges the wanderer back to lands which his ancestors left in the dim beginnings of history. Sometimes a man hits upon a place to which he mysteriously feels that he belongs. Here is the home he sought, and he will settle amid scenes that he has never seen before, among men he has never known, as though they were familiar to him from his birth. Here at last he finds rest.

I told Tiaré the story of a man I had known at St. Thomas's Hospital. He was a Jew named Abraham, a blond, rather stout young man, shy and very unassuming; but he had remarkable gifts. He entered the hospital with a scholarship, and during the five years of the curriculum gained every prize that was open to him. He was made house-physician and house-surgeon. His brilliance was allowed by all. Finally he was elected to a position on the staff, and his career was assured. So far as human things can be predicted, it was certain that he would rise to the greatest heights of his profession. Honours and wealth awaited him. Before he entered upon his new duties he wished to take a holiday, and, having no private means, he went as surgeon on a tramp steamer to the Levant. It did not generally carry a doctor, but one of the senior surgeons at the hospital knew a director of the line, and Abraham was taken as a favour.

In a few weeks the authorities received his resignation of the coveted position on the staff. It created profound astonishment, and wild rumours were current. Whenever a man does anything unexpected, his fellows ascribe it to the most discreditable motives. But there was a man ready to step into Abraham's shoes, and Abraham was forgotten. Nothing more was heard of him. He vanished.

It was perhaps ten years later that one morning on board ship, about to land at Alexandria, I was bidden to line up with the other passengers for the doctor's examination. The doctor was a stout man in shabby clothes, and when he took off his hat I noticed that he was very bald. I had an idea that I had seen him before. Suddenly I remembered.

"Abraham," I said.

He turned to me with a puzzled look, and then, recognising me, seized my hand. After expressions of surprise on either side, hearing that I meant to spend the night in Alexandria, he asked me to dine with him at the English Club. When we met again I declared my astonishment at finding him there. It was a very modest position that he occupied, and there was about him an air of straitened circumstance. Then he told me his story. When he set out on his holiday in the Mediterranean he had every intention of returning to London and his appointment at St. Thomas's. One morning the tramp docked at Alexandria, and from the deck he looked at the city, white in the sunlight, and the crowd on the wharf; he saw the natives in their shabby gabardines, the blacks from the Soudan, the noisy throng of Greeks and Italians, the grave Turks in tarbooshes, the sunshine and the blue sky; and something happened to him. He could not describe it. It was like a thunderclap, he said, and then, dissatisfied with this, he said it was like a revelation. Something seemed to twist his heart, and suddenly he felt an exultation, a sense of wonderful freedom. He felt himself at home, and he made up his mind there and then, in a minute, that he would live the rest of his life in Alexandria. He had no great difficulty in leaving the ship, and in twenty-four hours, with all his belongings, he was on shore.

"The Captain must have thought you as mad as a hatter," I smiled.

"I didn't care what anybody thought. It wasn't I that acted, but something stronger within me. I thought I would go to a little Greek hotel, while I looked about, and I felt I knew where to find one. And do you know, I walked straight there, and when I saw it, I recognised it at once."

"Had you been to Alexandria before?"

"No; I'd never been out of England in my life."

Presently he entered the Government service, and there he had been ever since.

"Have you never regretted it?"

"Never, not for a minute. I earn just enough to live upon, and I'm satisfied. I ask nothing more than to remain as I am till I die. I've had a wonderful life."

I left Alexandria next day, and I forgot about Abraham till a little while ago, when I was dining with another old friend in the profession, Alec Carmichael, who was in England on short leave. I ran across him in the street and congratulated him on the knighthood with which his eminent services during the war had been rewarded. We arranged to spend an evening together for old time's sake, and when I agreed to dine with him, he proposed that he should ask nobody else, so that we could chat without interruption. He had a beautiful old house in Queen Anne Street, and being a man of taste he had furnished it admirably. On the walls of the dining-room I saw a charming Bellotto, and there was a pair of Zoffanys that I envied. When his wife, a tall, lovely creature in cloth of gold, had left us, I remarked laughingly on the change in his present circumstances from those when we had both been medical students. We had looked upon it then as an extravagance to dine in a shabby Italian restaurant in the Westminster Bridge Road. Now Alec Carmichael was on the staff of half a dozen hospitals. I should think he earned ten thousand a year, and his knighthood was but the first of the honours which must inevitably fall to his lot.

"I've done pretty well," he said, "but the strange thing is that I owe it all to one piece of luck."

"What do you mean by that?"

"Well, do you remember Abraham? He was the man who had the future. When we were students he beat me all along the line. He got the prizes and the scholarships that I went in for. I always played second fiddle to him. If he'd kept on he'd be in the position I'm in now. That man had a genius for surgery. No one had a look in with him. When he was appointed Registrar at Thomas's I hadn't a chance of getting on the staff. I should have had to become a G.P., and you know what likelihood there is for a G.P. ever to get out of the common rut. But Abraham fell out, and I got the job. That gave me my opportunity."

"I daresay that's true."

"It was just luck. I suppose there was some kink in Abraham. Poor devil, he's gone to the dogs altogether. He's got some twopenny-halfpenny job in the medical at Alexandria—sanitary officer or something like that. I'm told he lives with an ugly old Greek woman and has half a dozen scrofulous kids. The fact is, I suppose, that it's not enough to have brains. The thing that counts is character. Abraham hadn't got character."

Character? I should have thought it needed a good deal of character to throw up a career after half an hour's meditation, because you saw in another way of living a more intense significance. And it required still more character never to regret the sudden step. But I said nothing, and Alec Carmichael proceeded reflectively:

"Of course it would be hypocritical for me to pretend that I regret what Abraham did. After all, I've scored by it." He puffed luxuriously at the long Corona he was smoking. "But if I weren't personally concerned I should be sorry at the waste. It seems a rotten thing that a man should make such a hash of life."

I wondered if Abraham really had made a hash of life. Is to do what you most want, to live under the conditions that please you, in peace with yourself, to make a hash of life; and is it success to be an eminent surgeon with ten thousand a year and a beautiful wife? I suppose it depends on what meaning you attach to life, the claim which you acknowledge to society, and the claim of the individual. But again I held my tongue, for who am I to argue with a knight?

Chapter LI

Tiaré, when I told her this story, praised my prudence, and for a few minutes we worked in silence, for we were shelling peas. Then her eyes, always alert for the affairs of her kitchen, fell on some action of the Chinese cook which aroused her violent disapproval. She turned on him with a torrent of abuse. The Chink was not backward to defend himself, and a very lively quarrel ensued. They spoke in the native language, of which I had learned but half a dozen words, and it sounded as though the world would shortly come to an end; but presently peace was restored and Tiaré gave the cook a cigarette. They both smoked comfortably.

"Do you know, it was I who found him his wife?" said Tiaré suddenly, with a smile that spread all over her immense face.

"The cook?"

"No, Strickland."

"But he had one already."

"That is what he said, but I told him she was in England, and England is at the other end of the world."

"True," I replied.

"He would come to Papeete every two or three months, when he wanted paints or tobacco or money, and then he would wander about like a lost dog. I was sorry for him. I had a girl here then called Ata to do the rooms; she was some sort of a relation of mine, and her father and mother were dead, so I had her to live with me. Strickland used to come here now and then to have a square meal or to play chess with one of the boys. I noticed that she looked at him when he came, and I asked her if she liked him. She said she liked him well enough. You know what these girls are; they're always pleased to go with a white man."

"Was she a native?" I asked.

"Yes; she hadn't a drop of white blood in her. Well, after I'd talked to her I sent for Strickland, and I said to him: 'Strickland, it's time for you to settle down. A man of your age shouldn't go playing about with the girls down at the front. They're bad lots, and you'll come to no good with them. You've got no money, and you can never keep a job for more than a month or two. No one will employ you now. You say you can always live in the bush with one or other of the natives, and they're glad to have you because you're a white man, but it's not decent for a white man. Now, listen to me, Strickland.' "

Tiaré mingled French with English in her conversation, for she used both languages with equal facility. She spoke them with a singing accent which was not unpleasing. You felt that a bird would speak in these tones if it could speak English.

" 'Now, what do you say to marrying Ata? She's a good girl and she's only seventeen. She's never been promiscuous like some of these girls—a captain or a first mate, yes, but she's never been touched by a native. *Elle se respecte, vois-tu.* The purser of the *Oahu* told me last journey that he hadn't met a nicer girl in the islands. It's time she settled down too, and besides, the captains and the first mates like a change now and then. I don't keep my girls too long. She has a bit of property down by Taravao, just before you come to the peninsula, and with copra at the price it is now you could live quite comfortably. There's a house, and you'd have all the time you wanted for your painting. What do you say to it?"

Tiaré paused to take breath.

"It was then he told me of his wife in England. 'My poor Strickland,' I said to him, 'they've all got a wife somewhere; that is generally why they come to the islands. Ata is a sensible girl, and she doesn't expect any ceremony before the Mayor. She's a Protestant, and you know they don't look upon these things like the Catholics.'

"Then he said: 'But what does Ata say to it?' 'It appears that she has a *béguin* for you,' I said. 'She's willing if you are. Shall I call her?' He chuckled in a funny, dry way he had, and I called her. She knew what I was talking about, the hussy, and I saw her out of the corner of my eyes listening with all her ears, while she pretended to iron a blouse that she had been washing for me. She came. She was laughing, but I could see that she was a little shy, and Strickland looked at her without speaking."

"Was she pretty?" I asked.

"Not bad. But you must have seen pictures of her. He painted her over and over again, sometimes with a *pareo* on and sometimes with nothing at all. Yes, she was pretty enough. And she knew how to cook. I taught her myself. I saw Strickland was thinking of it, so I said to him: 'I've given her good wages and she's saved them, and the captains and the first mates she's known have given her a little something now and then. She's saved several hundred francs.'

"He pulled his great red beard and smiled.

" 'Well, Ata,' he said, 'do you fancy me for a husband.'

"She did not say anything, but just giggled.

" 'But I tell you, my poor Strickland, the girl has a *béguin* for you,' I said.

" 'I shall beat you,' he said, looking at her.

" 'How else should I know you loved me,' she answered."

Tiaré broke off her narrative and addressed herself to me reflectively.

"My first husband, Captain Johnson, used to thrash me regularly. He was a man. He was handsome, six foot three, and when he was drunk there was no holding him. I would be black and blue all over for days at a time. Oh, I cried when he died. I thought I should never get over it. But it wasn't till I married George Rainey that I knew what I'd lost. You can never tell what a man is like till you live with him. I've never been so deceived in a man as I was in George Rainey. He was a fine, upstanding fellow too. He was nearly as tall as Captain Johnson, and he looked strong enough. But it was all on the surface. He never drank. He never raised his hand to me. He might have been a missionary. I made love with the officers of every ship that touched the island, and George Rainey never saw anything. At last I was disgusted with him, and I got a divorce. What was the good of a husband like that? It's a terrible thing the way some men treat women."

I condoled with Tiaré, and remarked feelingly that men were deceivers ever, then asked her to go on with her story of Strickland.

" 'Well,' I said to him, 'there's no hurry about it. Take your time and think it over. Ata has a very nice room in the annexe. Live with her for a month, and see how you like her. You can have your meals here. And at the end of a month, if you decide you want to marry her, you can just go and settle down on her property.'

"Well, he agreed to that. Ata continued to do the housework, and I gave him his meals as I said I would. I taught Ata to make one or two dishes I knew he was fond of. He did not paint much. He wandered about the hills and bathed in the stream. And he sat about the front looking at the lagoon, and at sunset he would go down and look at Murea. He used to go fishing on the reef. He loved to moon about the harbour talking to the natives. He was a nice, quiet fellow. And every evening after dinner he would go down to the annexe with Ata. I saw he was longing to get away to the bush, and at the end of the month I asked him what he intended to do. He said if Ata was willing to go, he was willing to go with her. So I gave them a wedding dinner. I cooked it with my own hands. I gave them a pea soup and lobster *à la portugaise,* and a curry, and a coconut salad—you've never had one of my coconut salads, have you? I must make you one before you go—and then I made them an ice. We had all the champagne we could drink and liqueurs to follow. Oh, I'd made up my mind to do things well. And afterwards we danced in the drawing-room. I was not so fat, then, and I always loved dancing."

The drawing-room at the Hôtel de la Fleur was a small room, with a cottage piano, and a suite of mahogany furniture, covered in stamped velvet, neatly arranged around the walls. On round tables were photograph albums, and on the walls enlarged photographs of Tiaré and her first husband, Captain Johnson. Still, though Tiaré was old and fat, on occasion we rolled back the Brussels carpet, brought in the maids and one or two friends of Tiaré's, and danced, though now to the wheezy music of a gramaphone. On the verandah the air was scented with the heavy perfume of the tiaré, and overhead the Southern Cross shone in a cloudless sky.

Tiaré smiled indulgently as she remembered the gaiety of a time long passed.

"We kept it up till three, and when we went to bed I don't think anyone was very sober. I had told them they could have my trap to take them as far as the road went, because after that they had a long walk. Ata's property was right away in a fold of the mountain. They started at dawn, and the boy I sent with them didn't come back till next day.

"Yes, that's how Strickland was married."

Chapter LII

I SUPPOSE THE NEXT THREE YEARS WERE THE HAPPIEST OF STRICKLAND'S LIFE. Ata's house stood about eight kilometres from the road that runs round the island, and you went to it along a winding pathway shaded by the luxuriant trees of the tropics. It was a bungalow of unpainted wood, consisting of two small rooms, and outside was a small shed that served as a kitchen. There was no furniture except the mats they used as beds, and a rocking-chair, which stood on the verandah. Bananas with their great ragged leaves, like the tattered habiliments of an empress in adversity, grew close up to the house. There was a tree just behind which bore alligator pears, and all about were the coconuts which gave the land its revenue. Ata's father had planted crotons round his property, and they grew in coloured profusion, gay and brilliant; they fenced the land with flame. A mango grew in front of the house, and at the edge of the clearing were two flamboyants, twin trees, that challenged the gold of the coconuts with their scarlet flowers.

Here Strickland lived, coming seldom to Papeete, on the produce of the land. There was a little stream that ran not far away, in which he bathed, and down this on occasion would come a shoal of fish. Then the natives would assemble with spears, and with much shouting would transfix the great startled things as they hurried down to the sea. Sometimes Strickland would go down to the reef, and come back with a basket of small, coloured fish that Ata would fry in coconut oil, or with a lobster; and sometimes she would make a savoury dish of the great land-crabs that scuttled away under your feet. Up the mountain were wild orange-trees, and now and then Ata would go with two or three women from the village and return laden with the green, sweet, luscious fruit. Then the coconuts would be ripe for picking, and her cousins (like all the natives, Ata had a host of relatives) would swarm up the trees and throw down the big ripe nuts. They split them open and put them in the sun to dry. Then they cut out the copra and put it into sacks, and the women would carry it down to the trader at the village by the lagoon, and he would give in exchange for it rice and soap and tinned meat and a little money. Sometimes there would be a feast in the neighbourhood, and a pig would be killed. Then they would go and eat themselves sick, and dance, and sing hymns.

But the house was a long way from the village, and the Tahitians are lazy. They love to travel and they love to gossip, but they do not care to walk, and for weeks at a time Strickland and Ata lived alone. He painted and he read, and in the evening, when it was dark, they sat together on the verandah, smoking and looking at the night. Then Ata had a baby, and the old woman who came up to help her through her trouble stayed on. Presently the granddaughter of the old woman came to stay with her, and then a youth appeared—no one quite knew where from or to whom he belonged—but he settled down with them in a happy-go-lucky way, and they all lived together.

Chapter LIII

"TENEZ, *VOILÀ LE CAPITAINE BRUNOT,*" SAID TIARÉ, ONE DAY WHEN I WAS FITting together what she could tell me of Strickland. "He knew Strickland well; he visited him at his house."

I saw a middle-aged Frenchman with a big black beard, streaked with grey, a sunburned face, and large, shining eyes. He was dressed in a neat suit of ducks. I had noticed him at luncheon, and Ah Lin, the Chinese boy, told me he had come from the Paumotus on the boat that had that day arrived. Tiaré introduced me to him, and he handed me his card, a large card on which was printed *René Brunot,* and underneath, *Capitaine au Long Cours.* We were sitting on a little verandah outside the kitchen, and Tiaré was cutting out a dress that she was making for one of the girls about the house. He sat down with us.

"Yes; I knew Strickland well," he said. "I am very fond of chess, and he was always glad of a game. I come to Tahiti three or four times a year for my business, and when he was at Papeete he would come here and we would play. When he married"—Captain Brunot smiled and shrugged his shoulders—"*enfin,* when he went to live with the girl that Tiaré gave him, he asked me to go and see him. I was one of the guests at the wedding feast." He looked at Tiaré, and they both laughed. "He did not come much to Papeete after that, and about a year later it chanced that I had to go to that part of the island for I forgot what business, and when I had finished it I said to myself: '*Voyons,* why should I not go and see that poor Strickland?' I asked one or two natives if they knew anything about him, and I discovered that he lived not more than five kilometres from where I was. So I went. I shall never forget the impression my visit made on me. I live on an atoll, a low island, it is a strip of land surrounding a lagoon, and its beauty is the beauty of the sea and sky and the varied colour of the lagoon, and the grace of the coconut-trees; but the place where Strickland lived had the beauty of the Garden of Eden. Ah, I wish I could make you see the enchantment of that spot, a corner hidden away from all the world, with the blue sky overhead and the rich, luxuriant trees. It was a feast of colour. And it was fragrant and cool. Words cannot describe that paradise. And here he lived, unmindful of the world and by the world forgotten. I suppose to European eyes it would have seemed astonishingly sordid. The house was dilapidated and none too clean. Three or four natives were lying on the verandah. You know how natives love to herd together. There was a young man lying full length, smoking a cigarette, and he wore nothing but a *pareo.*"

The *pareo* is a long strip of trade cotton, red or blue, stamped with a white pattern. It is worn round the waist and hangs to the knees.

"A girl of fifteen, perhaps, was plaiting pandanus-leaf to make a hat, and an old woman was sitting on her haunches smoking a pipe. Then I saw Ata. She was suckling a new-born child, and another child, stark naked, was playing at her feet. When she saw me she called out to Strickland, and he came to the door. He, too, wore nothing but a *pareo*. He was an extraordinary figure, with his red beard and matted hair, and his great hairy chest. His feet were horny and scarred, so that I knew he went always bare foot. He had gone native with a vengeance. He seemed pleased to see me, and told Ata to kill a chicken for our dinner. He took me into the house to show me the picture he was at work on when I came in. In one corner of the room was the bed, and in the middle was an easel with the canvas upon it. Because I was sorry for him, I had bought a couple of his pictures for small sums, and I had sent others to friends of mine in France. And though I had bought them out of compassion, after living with them I began to like them. Indeed, I found a strange beauty in them. Everyone thought I was mad, but it turns out that I was right. I was his first admirer in the islands."

He smiled maliciously at Tiaré, and with lamentations she told us again the story of how at the sale of Strickland's effects she had neglected the pictures, but bought an American stove for twenty-seven francs.

"Have you the pictures still?" I asked.

"Yes; I am keeping them till my daughter is of marriageable age, and then I shall sell them. They will be her *dot*."

Then he went on with the account of his visit to Strickland.

"I shall never forget the evening I spent with him. I had not intended to stay more than an hour, but he insisted that I should spend the night. I hesitated, for I confess I did not much like the look of the mats on which he proposed that I should sleep; but I shrugged my shoulders. When I was building my house in the Paumotus I had slept out for weeks on a harder bed than that, with nothing to shelter me but wild shrubs; and as for vermin, my tough skin should be proof against their malice.

"We went down to the stream to bathe while Ata was preparing the dinner, and after we had eaten it we sat on the verandah. We smoked and chatted. The young man had a concertina, and he played the tunes popular on the music-halls a dozen years before. They sounded strangely in the tropical night thousands of miles from civilisation. I asked Strickland if it did not irk him to live in that promiscuity. No, he said; he liked to have his models under his hand. Presently, after loud yawning, the natives went away to sleep, and Strickland and I were left alone. I cannot describe to you the intense silence of the night. On my island in the Paumotus there is never at night the complete stillness that there was here. There is the rustle of the myriad animals on the beach, all the little shelled things that crawl about ceaselessly, and there is the noisy scurrying of the land-crabs. Now and then in the lagoon you hear the leaping of a fish, and sometimes a hurried noisy splashing as a brown shark sends all the other fish scampering for their lives. And above all, ceaseless like time, is the dull roar of the breakers on the reef. But here there was not a sound, and the air was scented with the white flowers of the night. It was a night so beautiful that your soul seemed hardly able to bear the prison of the body. You felt that it was ready to be wafted away on the immaterial air, and death bore all the aspect of a beloved friend."

Tiaré sighed.

"Ah, I wish I were fifteen again."

Then she caught sight of a cat trying to get at a dish of prawns on the kitchen table, and with a dexterous gesture and a lively volley of abuse flung a book at its scampering tail.

"I asked him if he was happy with Ata.

" 'She leaves me alone,' he said. 'She cooks my food and looks after her babies. She does what I tell her. She gives me what I want from a woman.'

" 'And do you never regret Europe? Do you not yearn sometimes for the light of the streets in Paris or London, the companionship of your friends, and equals, *que sais-je?* for theatres and newspapers, and the rumble of omnibuses on the cobbled pavements?'

"For a long time he was silent. Then he said:

" 'I shall stay here till I die.'

" 'But are you never bored or lonely?' I asked.

"He chuckled.

" '*Mon pauvre ami,*' he said. 'It is evident that you do not know what it is to be an artist.' "

Capitaine Brunot turned to me with a gentle smile, and there was a wonderful look in his dark, kind eyes.

"He did me an injustice, for I too know what it is to have dreams. I have my visions too. In my way I also am an artist."

We were all silent for a while, and Tiaré fished out of her capacious pocket a handful of cigarettes. She handed one to each of us, and we all three smoked. At last she said:

"Since *ce monsieur* is interested in Strickland, why do you not take him to see Dr. Coutras? He can tell him something about his illness and death."

"*Volontiers,*" said the Captain, looking at me.

I thanked him, and he looked at his watch.

"It is past six o'clock. We should find him at home if you care to come now."

I got up without further ado, and we walked along the road that led to the doctor's house. He lived out of the town, but the Hôtel de la Fleur was on the edge of it, and we were quickly in the country. The broad road was shaded by pepper-trees, and on each side were the plantations, coconut and vanilla. The pirate birds were screeching among the leaves of the palms. We came to a stone bridge over a shallow river, and we stopped for a few minutes to see the native boys bathing. They chased one another with shrill cries and laughter, and their bodies, brown and wet, gleamed in the sunlight.

Chapter LIV

As we walked along I reflected on a circumstance which all that I had lately heard about Strickland forced on my attention. Here, on this remote island, he seemed to have aroused none of the detestation with which he was regarded at home, but compassion rather; and his vagaries were accepted with tolerance. To these people, native and European, he was a queer fish, but they were used to queer fish, and they took him for granted; the world was full of odd persons, who did odd things; and perhaps they knew that a man is not what he wants to be, but what he must be. In England and France he was the square peg in the round hole, but here the holes were any sort of shape, and no sort of peg was quite amiss. I do not think he was any gentler here, less selfish or less brutal, but the circumstances were more favourable. If he had spent his life amid these surroundings he might have passed for no worse a man than another. He received here what he neither expected nor wanted among his own people—sympathy.

I tried to tell Captain Brunot something of the astonishment with which this filled me, and for a little while he did not answer.

"It is not strange that I, at all events, should have had sympathy for him," he said at last, "for, though perhaps neither of us knew it, we were both aiming at the same thing."

"What on earth can it be that two people so dissimilar as you and Strickland could aim at?" I asked, smiling.

"Beauty."

"A large order," I murmured.

"Do you know how men can be so obsessed by love that they are deaf and blind to everything else in the world? They are as little their own masters as the slaves chained to the benches of a galley. The passion that held Strickland in bondage was no less tyrannical than love."

"How strange that you should say that!" I answered. "For long ago I had the idea that he was possessed of a devil."

"And the passion that held Strickland was a passion to create beauty. It gave him no peace. It urged him hither and thither. He was eternally a pilgrim, haunted by a divine nostalgia, and the demon within him was ruthless. There are men whose desire for truth is so great that to attain it they will shatter the very foundation of their world. Of such was Strickland, only beauty with him took the place of truth. I could only feel for him a profound compassion."

"That is strange also. A man whom he had deeply wronged told me that he felt a great pity for him." I was silent for a moment. "I wonder if there you have found the explanation of a character which has always seemed to me inexplicable. How did you hit on it?"

He turned to me with a smile.

"Did I not tell you that I, too, in my way was an artist? I realised in myself the same desire as animated him. But whereas his medium was paint, mine has been life."

Then Captain Brunot told me a story which I must repeat, since, if only by way of contrast, it adds something to my impression of Strickland. It has also to my mind a beauty of its own.

Captain Brunot was a Breton, and had been in the French Navy. He left it on his marriage, and settled down on a small property he had near Quimper to live for the rest of his days in peace; but the failure of an attorney left him suddenly penniless, and neither he nor his wife was willing to live in penury where they had enjoyed consideration. During his seafaring days he had cruised the South Seas, and he determined now to seek his fortune there. He spent some months in Papeete to make his plans and gain experience; then, on money borrowed from a friend in France, he bought an island in the Paumotus. It was a ring of land round a deep lagoon, uninhabited, and covered only with scrub and wild guava. With the intrepid woman who was his wife, and a few natives, he landed there, and set about building a house, and clearing the scrub so that he could plant coconuts. That was twenty years before, and now what had been a barren island was a garden.

"It was hard and anxious work at first, and we worked strenuously, both of us. Everyday I was up at dawn, clearing, planting, working on my house, and at night when I threw myself on my bed it was to sleep like a log till morning. My wife worked as hard as I did. Then children were born to us, first a son and then a daughter. My wife and I have taught them all they know. We had a piano sent out from France, and she has taught them to play and to speak English, and I have taught them Latin and mathematics, and we read history together. They can sail a boat. They can swim as well as the natives. There is nothing about the land of which they are ignorant. Our trees have prospered, and there is shell on my reef. I have come to Tahiti now to buy a schooner. I can get enough shell to make it worthwhile to fish for it, and, who knows? I may find pearls. I have made something where there was nothing. I too have made beauty. Ah, you do not know what it is to look at those tall, healthy trees and think that every one I planted myself."

"Let me ask you the question that you asked Strickland. Do you never regret France and your old home in Brittany?"

"Someday, when my daughter is married and my son has a wife and is able to take my place on the island, we shall go back and finish our days in the old house in which I was born."

"You will look back on a happy life," I said.

"*Evidemment,* it is not exciting on my island, and we are very far from the world—imagine, it takes me four days to come to Tahiti—but we are happy there. It is given to few men to attempt a work and to achieve it. Our life is simple and innocent. We are untouched by ambition, and what pride we have is due only to our contemplation of the work of our hands. Malice cannot touch us, nor envy attack. Ah, *mon cher monsieur,* they talk of the blessedness of labour, and it is a meaningless phrase, but to me it has the most intense significance. I am a happy man."

"I am sure you deserve to be," I smiled.

"I wish I could think so. I do not know how I have deserved to have a wife who was the perfect friend and helpmate, the perfect mistress and the perfect mother."

I reflected for a while on the life that the Captain suggested to my imagination.

"It is obvious that to lead such an existence and make so great a success of it, you must both have needed a strong will and a determined character."

"Perhaps; but without one other factor we could have achieved nothing."

"And what was that?"

He stopped, somewhat dramatically, and stretched out his arm.

"Belief in God. Without that we should have been lost."

Then we arrived at the house of Dr. Coutras.

Chapter LV

Mr. Coutras was an old Frenchman of great stature and exceeding bulk. His body was shaped like a huge duck's egg; and his eyes, sharp, blue, and good-natured, rested now and then with self-satisfaction on his enormous paunch. His complexion was florid and his hair white. He was a man to attract immediate sympathy. He received us in a room that might have been in a house in a provincial town in France, and the one or two Polynesian curios had an odd look. He took my hand in both of his—they were huge—and gave me a hearty look, in which, however, was great shrewdness. When he shook hands with Capitaine Brunot he enquired politely after *Madame et les enfants*. For some minutes there was an exchange of courtesies and some local gossip about the island, the prospects of copra and the vanilla crop; then we came to the object of my visit.

I shall not tell what Dr. Coutras related to me in his words, but in my own, for I cannot hope to give at second-hand any impression of his vivacious delivery. He had a deep, resonant voice, fitted to his massive frame, and a keen sense of the dramatic. To listen to him was, as the phrase goes, as good as a play; and much better than most.

It appears that Dr. Coutras had gone one day to Taravao in order to see an old chiefess who was ill, and he gave a vivid picture of the obese old lady, lying in a huge bed, smoking cigarettes, and surrounded by a crowd of dark-skinned retainers. When he had seen her he was taken into another room and given dinner—raw fish, fried bananas, and chicken—*que sais-je*, the typical dinner of the *indigène*—and while he was eating it he saw a young girl being driven away from the door in tears. He thought nothing of it, but when he went out to get into his trap and drive home, he saw her again, standing a little way off; she looked at him with a woebegone air, and tears streamed down her cheeks. He asked someone what was wrong with her, and was told that she had come down from the hills to ask him to visit a white man who was sick. They had told her that the doctor could not be disturbed. He called her, and himself asked what she wanted. She told him that Ata had sent her, she who used to be at the Hôtel de la Fleur, and that the Red One was ill. She thrust into his hand a crumpled piece of newspaper, and when he opened it he found in it a hundred-franc note.

"Who is the Red One?" he asked of one of the bystanders.

He was told that that was what they called the Englishman, a painter, who lived with Ata up in the valley seven kilometres from where they were. He recognised

Strickland by the description. But it was necessary to walk. It was impossible for him to go; that was why they had sent the girl away.

"I confess," said the doctor, turning to me, "that I hesitated. I did not relish fourteen kilometres over a bad pathway, and there was no chance that I could get back to Papeete that night. Besides, Strickland was not sympathetic to me. He was an idle, useless scoundrel, who preferred to live with a native woman rather than work for his living like the rest of us. *Mon Dieu*, how was I to know that one day the world would come to the conclusion that he had genius? I asked the girl if he was not well enough to have come down to see me. I asked her what she thought was the matter with him. She would not answer. I pressed her, angrily perhaps, but she looked down on the ground and began to cry. Then I shrugged my shoulders; after all, perhaps it was my duty to go, and in a very bad temper I bade her lead the way."

His temper was certainly no better when he arrived, perspiring freely and thirsty. Ata was on the look-out for him, and came a little way along the path to meet him.

"Before I see anyone give me something to drink or I shall die of thirst," he cried out. "*Pour l'amour de Dieu*, get me a coconut."

She called out, and a boy came running along. He swarmed up a tree, and presently threw down a ripe nut. Ata pierced a hole in it, and the doctor took a long, refreshing draught. Then he rolled himself a cigarette and felt in a better humour.

"Now, where is the Red One?" he asked.

"He is in the house, painting. I have not told him you were coming. Go in and see him."

"But what does he complain of? If he is well enough to paint, he is well enough to have come down to Taravao and save me this confounded walk. I presume my time is no less valuable than his."

Ata did not speak, but with the boy followed him to the house. The girl who had brought him was by this time sitting on the verandah, and here was lying an old woman, with her back to the wall, making native cigarettes. Ata pointed to the door. The doctor, wondering irritably why they behaved so strangely, entered, and there found Strickland cleaning his palette. There was a picture on the easel. Strickland, clad only in a *pareo*, was standing with his back to the door, but he turned round when he heard the sound of boots. He gave the doctor a look of vexation. He was surprised to see him, and resented the intrusion. But the doctor gave a gasp, he was rooted to the floor, and he stared with all his eyes. This was not what he expected. He was seized with horror.

"You enter without ceremony," said Strickland. "What can I do for you?"

The doctor recovered himself, but it required quite an effort for him to find his voice. All his irritation was gone, and he felt—*eh bien, oui, je ne le nie pas*—he felt an overwhelming pity.

"I am Dr. Coutras. I was down at Taravao to see the chiefess, and Ata sent for me to see you."

"She's a damned fool. I have had a few aches and pains lately and a little fever, but that's nothing; it will pass off. Next time anyone went to Papeete I was going to send for some quinine."

"Look at yourself in the glass."

Strickland gave him a glance, smiled, and went over to a cheap mirror in a little wooden frame, that hung on the wall.

"Well?"

"Do you not see a strange change in your face? Do you not see the thickening of your features and a look—how shall I describe it?—the books call it lion-faced. *Mon pauvre ami*, must I tell you that you have a terrible disease?"

"I?"

"When you look at yourself in the glass you see the typical appearance of the leper."

"You are jesting," said Strickland.

"I wish to God I were."

"Do you intend to tell me that I have leprosy?"

"Unfortunately, there can be no doubt of it."

Dr. Coutras had delivered sentence of death on many men, and he could never overcome the horror with which it filled him. He felt always the furious hatred that must seize a man condemned when he compared himself with the doctor, sane and healthy, who had the inestimable privilege of life. Strickland looked at him in silence. Nothing of emotion could be seen on his face, disfigured already by the loathsome disease.

"Do they know?" he asked at last, pointing to the persons on the verandah, now sitting in unusual, unaccountable silence.

"These natives know the signs so well," said the doctor. "They were afraid to tell you."

Strickland stepped to the door and looked out. There must have been something terrible in his face, for suddenly they all burst out into loud cries and lamentation. They lifted up their voices and they wept. Strickland did not speak. After looking at them for a moment, he came back into the room.

"How long do you think I can last?"

"Who knows? Sometimes the disease continues for twenty years. It is a mercy when it runs its course quickly."

Strickland went to his easel and looked reflectively at the picture that stood on it.

"You have had a long journey. It is fitting that the bearer of important tidings should be rewarded. Take this picture. It means nothing to you now, but it may be that one day you will be glad to have it."

Dr. Coutras protested that he needed no payment for his journey; he had already given back to Ata the hundred-franc note, but Strickland insisted that he should take the picture. Then together they went out on the verandah. The natives were sobbing violently.

"Be quiet, woman. Dry thy tears," said Strickland, addressing Ata. "There is no great harm. I shall leave thee very soon."

"They are not going to take thee away?" she cried.

At that time there was no rigid sequestration on the islands, and lepers, if they chose, were allowed to go free.

"I shall go up into the mountain," said Strickland.

Then Ata stood up and faced him.

"Let the others go if they choose, but I will not leave thee. Thou art my man and I am thy woman. If thou leavest me I shall hang myself on the tree that is behind the house. I swear it by God."

There was something immensely forcible in the way she spoke. She was no longer the meek, soft native girl, but a determined woman. She was extraordinarily transformed.

"Why shouldst thou stay with me? Thou canst go back to Papeete, and thou wilt soon find another white man. The old woman can take care of thy children, and Tiaré will be glad to have thee back."

"Thou art my man and I am thy woman. Whither thou goest I will go, too."

For a moment Strickland's fortitude was shaken, and a tear filled each of his eyes and trickled slowly down his cheeks. Then he gave the sardonic smile which was usual with him.

"Women are strange little beasts," he said to Dr. Coutras. "You can treat them like dogs, you can beat them till your arm aches, and still they love you." He shrugged his shoulders. "Of course, it is one of the most absurd illusions of Christianity that they have souls."

"What is it that thou art saying to the doctor?" asked Ata suspiciously. "Thou wilt not go?"

"If it please thee I will stay, poor child."

Ata flung herself on her knees before him, and clasped his legs with her arms and kissed them. Strickland looked at Dr. Coutras with a faint smile.

"In the end they get you, and you are helpless in their hands. White or brown, they are all the same."

Dr. Coutras felt that it was absurd to offer expressions of regret in so terrible a disaster, and he took his leave. Strickland told Tané, the boy, to lead him to the village. Dr. Coutras paused for a moment, and then he addressed himself to me.

"I did not like him, I have told you he was not sympathetic to me, but as I walked slowly down to Taravao I could not prevent an unwilling admiration for the stoical courage which enabled him to bear perhaps the most dreadful of human afflictions. When Tané left me I told him I would send some medicine that might be of service; but my hope was small that Strickland would consent to take it, and even smaller that, if he did, it would do him good. I gave the boy a message for Ata that I would come whenever she sent for me. Life is hard, and Nature takes sometimes a terrible delight in torturing her children. It was with a heavy heart that I drove back to my comfortable home in Papeete."

For a long time none of us spoke.

"But Ata did not send for me," the doctor went on, at last, "and it chanced that I did not go to that part of the island for a long time. I had no news of Strickland. Once or twice I heard that Ata had been to Papeete to buy painting materials, but I did not happen to see her. More than two years passed before I went to Taravao again, and then it was once more to see the old chiefess. I asked them whether they had heard anything of Strickland. By now it was known everywhere that he had leprosy. First Tané, the boy, had left the house, and then, a little time afterwards, the old woman and her grandchild. Strickland and Ata were left alone with their babies. No one went near the plantation, for, as you know, the natives have a very lively horror of the disease, and in the old days when it was discovered the sufferer was killed; but sometimes, when the village boys were scrambling about the hills, they would catch sight of the white man, with his great red beard, wandering about. They fled in terror. Sometimes Ata would come down to the village at night and arouse the trader, so that he might sell her various things of which she stood in need. She knew that the natives looked upon her with the same horrified aversion as they looked upon Strickland, and she kept out of their way. Once some women, venturing nearer than usual to the plantation, saw her washing clothes in the brook, and they threw stones at her. After that the trader was told to give her the message that if she used the brook again men would come and burn down her house."

"Brutes," I said.

"*Mais non, mon cher monsieur*, men are always the same. Fear makes them cruel. . . . I decided to see Strickland, and when I had finished with the chiefess asked for a boy to show me the way. But none would accompany me, and I was forced to find it alone."

When Dr. Coutras arrived at the plantation he was seized with a feeling of uneasiness. Though he was hot from walking, he shivered. There was something hostile in the air which made him hesitate, and he felt that invisible forces barred his way. Unseen hands seemed to draw him back. No one would go near now to gather the coconuts, and they lay rotting on the ground. Everywhere was desolation. The bush was encroaching, and it looked as though very soon the primeval forest would regain possession of that strip of land which had been snatched from it at the cost of so much labour. He had the sensation that here was the abode of pain. As he approached the house he was struck by the unearthly silence, and at first he thought it was deserted. Then he saw Ata. She was sitting on her haunches in the lean-to that served her as kitchen, watching some mess cooking in a pot. Near her a small boy was playing silently in the dirt. She did not smile when she saw him.

"I have come to see Strickland," he said.

"I will go and tell him."

She went to the house, ascended the few steps that led to the verandah, and entered. Dr. Coutras followed her, but waited outside in obedience to her gesture. As she opened the door he smelt the sickly sweet smell which makes the neighbourhood of the leper nauseous. He heard her speak, and then he heard Strickland's answer, but he did not recognise the voice. It had become hoarse and indistinct. Dr. Coutras raised his eyebrows. He judged that the disease had already attacked the vocal chords. Then Ata came out again.

"He will not see you. You must go away."

Dr. Coutras insisted, but she would not let him pass. Dr. Coutras shrugged his shoulders, and after a moment's rejection turned away. She walked with him. He felt that she too wanted to be rid of him.

"Is there nothing I can do at all?" he asked.

"You can send him some paints," she said. "There is nothing else he wants."

"Can he paint still?"

"He is painting the walls of the house."

"This is a terrible life for you, my poor child."

Then at last she smiled, and there was in her eyes a look of superhuman love. Dr. Coutras was startled by it, and amazed. And he was awed. He found nothing to say.

"He is my man," she said.

"Where is your other child?" he asked. "When I was here last you had two."

"Yes; it died. We buried it under the mango."

When Ata had gone with him a little way she said she must turn back. Dr. Coutras surmised she was afraid to go farther in case she met any of the people from the village. He told her again that if she wanted him she had only to send and he would come at once.

Chapter LVI

THEN TWO YEARS MORE WENT BY, OR PERHAPS THREE, FOR TIME PASSES IMperceptibly in Tahiti, and it is hard to keep count of it; but at last a message was brought to Dr. Coutras that Strickland was dying. Ata had waylaid the cart that took the mail into Papeete, and besought the man who drove it to go at once to the doctor. But the doctor was out when the summons came, and it was evening when he received it. It was impossible to start at so late an hour, and so it was not till next day soon after dawn that he set out. He arrived at Taravao, and for the last time tramped the seven kilometres that led to Ata's house. The path was overgrown, and it was clear that for years now it had remained all but untrodden. It was not easy to find the way. Sometimes he had to stumble along the bed of the stream, and sometimes he had to push through shrubs, dense and thorny; often he was obliged to climb over rocks in order to avoid the hornet-nests that hung on the trees over his head. The silence was intense.

It was with a sigh of relief that at last he came upon the little unpainted house, extraordinarily bedraggled now, and unkempt; but here too was the same intolerable silence. He walked up, and a little boy, playing unconcernedly in the sunshine, started at his approach and fled quickly away: to him the stranger was the enemy. Dr. Coutras had a sense that the child was stealthily watching him from behind a tree. The door was wide open. He called out, but no one answered. He stepped in. He knocked at a door, but again there was no answer. He turned the handle and entered. The stench that assailed him turned him horribly sick. He put his handkerchief to his nose and forced himself to go in. The light was dim, and after the brilliant sunshine for a while he could see nothing. Then he gave a start. He could not make out where he was. He seemed on a sudden to have entered a magic world. He had a vague impression of a great primeval forest and of naked people walking beneath the trees. Then he saw that there were paintings on the walls.

"*Mon Dieu*, I hope the sun hasn't affected me," he muttered.

A slight movement attracted his attention, and he saw that Ata was lying on the floor, sobbing quietly.

"Ata," he called. "Ata."

She took no notice. Again the beastly stench almost made him faint, and he lit a cheroot. His eyes grew accustomed to the darkness, and now he was seized by an overwhelming sensation as he stared at the painted walls. He knew nothing of pictures, but there was something about these that extraordinarily affected him. From floor to ceiling the walls were covered with a strange and elaborate composition. It was indescribably wonderful and mysterious. It took his breath away. It filled him with an emotion which he could not understand or analyse. He felt the awe and the delight which a man might feel who watched the beginning of a world. It was tremendous, sensual, passionate; and yet there was something horrible there, too, something which made him afraid. It was the work of a man who had delved into the hidden depths of nature and had discovered secrets which were beautiful and fearful too. It was the work of a man who knew things which it is unholy for men to know. There was something primeval there and terrible. It was not human. It brought to his mind vague recollections of black magic. It was beautiful and obscene.

"*Mon Dieu,* this is genius."

The words were wrung from him, and he did not know he had spoken.

Then his eyes fell on the bed of mats in the corner, and he went up, and he saw the dreadful, mutilated, ghastly object which had been Strickland. He was dead. Dr. Coutras made an effort of will and bent over that battered horror. Then he started violently, and terror blazed in his heart, for he felt that someone was behind him. It was Ata. He had not heard her get up. She was standing at his elbow, looking at what he looked at.

"Good Heavens, my nerves are all distraught," he said. "You nearly frightened me out of my wits."

He looked again at the poor dead thing that had been man, and then he started back in dismay.

"But he was blind."

"Yes; he had been blind for nearly a year."

Chapter LVII

AT THAT MOMENT WE WERE INTERRUPTED BY THE APPEARANCE OF Madame Coutras, who had been paying visits. She came in, like a ship in full sail, an imposing creature, tall and stout, with an ample bust and an obesity girthed in alarmingly by straight-fronted corsets. She had a bold hooked nose and three chins. She held herself upright. She had not yielded for an instant to the enervating charm of the tropics, but contrariwise was more active, more worldly, more decided than anyone in a temperate clime would have thought it possible to be. She was evidently a copious talker, and now poured forth a breathless stream of anecdote and comment. She made the conversation we had just had seem far away and unreal.

Presently Dr. Coutras turned to me.

"I still have in my *bureau* the picture that Strickland gave me," he said. "Would you like to see it?"

"Willingly."

We got up, and he led me on to the verandah which surrounded his house. We paused to look at the gay flowers that rioted in his garden.

"For a long time I could not get out of my head the recollection of the extraordinary decoration with which Strickland had covered the walls of his house," he said reflectively.

I had been thinking of it, too. It seemed to me that here Strickland had finally put the whole expression of himself. Working silently, knowing that it was his last chance, I fancied that here he must have said all that he knew of life and all that he divined. And I fancied that perhaps here he had at last found peace. The demon which possessed him was exorcised at last, and with the completion of the work, for which all his life had been a painful preparation, rest descended on his remote and tortured soul. He was willing to die, for he had fulfilled his purpose.

"What was the subject?" I asked.

"I scarcely know. It was strange and fantastic. It was a vision of the beginnings of the world, the Garden of Eden, with Adam and Eve—*que sais-je?*—it was a hymn to the beauty of the human form, male and female, and the praise of Nature, sublime, indifferent, lovely, and cruel. It gave you an awful sense of the infinity of space and of the endlessness of time. Because he painted the trees I see about me every day, the coconuts, the banyans, the flamboyants, the alligator-pears, I have seen them ever since differently, as though there were in them a spirit and a mystery which I am ever on the point of seizing and which forever escapes me. The colours were the colours familiar to me, and yet they were different. They had a significance which was all their own. And those nude men and women. They were of the earth, and yet apart from it. They seemed to possess something of the clay of which they were created, and at the same time something divine. You saw man in the nakedness of his primeval instincts, and you were afraid, for you saw yourself."

Dr. Coutras shrugged his shoulders and smiled.

"You will laugh at me. I am a materialist, and I am a gross, fat man—Falstaff, eh?—the lyrical mode does not become me. I make myself ridiculous. But I have never seen painting which made so deep an impression upon me. *Tenez*, I had just the same feeling as when I went to the Sistine Chapel in Rome. There too I was awed by the greatness of the man who had painted that ceiling. It was genius, and it was stupendous and overwhelming. I felt small and insignificant. But you are prepared for the greatness of Michael Angelo. Nothing had prepared me for the immense surprise of these pictures in a native hut, far away from civilisation, in a fold of the mountain above Taravao. And Michael Angelo is sane and healthy. Those great works of his have the calm of the sublime; but here, notwithstanding beauty, was something troubling. I do not know what it was. It made me uneasy. It gave me the impression you get when you are sitting next door to a room that you know is empty, but in which, you know not why, you have a dreadful consciousness that notwithstanding there is someone. You scold yourself; you know it is only your nerves—and yet, and yet . . . In a little while it is impossible to resist the terror that seizes you, and you are helpless in the clutch of an unseen horror. Yes; I confess I was not altogether sorry when I heard that those strange masterpieces had been destroyed."

"Destroyed?" I cried.

"*Mais oui*; did you not know?"

"How should I know? It is true I had never heard of this work; but I thought perhaps it had fallen into the hands of a private owner. Even now there is no certain list of Strickland's paintings."

"When he grew blind he would sit hour after hour in those two rooms that he had painted, looking at his works with sightless eyes, and seeing, perhaps, more than he had ever seen in his life before. Ata told me that he never complained of his fate, he never lost courage. To the end his mind remained serene and undisturbed. But he made her promise that when she had buried him—did I tell you that I dug his grave with my own hands, for none of the natives would approach the infected house, and we buried him, she and I, sewn up in three *pareos* joined together, under the mango-tree—he made her promise that she would set fire to the house and not leave it till it was burned to the ground and not a stick remained."

I did not speak for a while, for I was thinking. Then I said:

"He remained the same to the end, then."

"Do you understand? I must tell you that I thought it my duty to dissuade her."

"Even after what you have just said?"

"Yes; for I knew that here was a work of genius, and I did not think we had the right to deprive the world of it. But Ata would not listen to me. She had promised. I would not stay to witness the barbarous deed, and it was only afterwards that I heard what she had done. She poured paraffin on the dry floors and on the pandanus-mats, and then she set fire. In a little while nothing remained but smouldering embers, and a great masterpiece existed no longer.

"I think Strickland knew it was a masterpiece. He had achieved what he wanted. His life was complete. He had made a world and saw that it was good. Then, in pride and contempt, he destroyed, it."

"But I must show you my picture," said Dr. Coutras, moving on.

"What happened to Ata and the child?"

"They went to the Marquesas. She had relations there. I have heard that the boy works on one of Cameron's schooners. They say he is very like his father in appearance."

At the door that led from the verandah to the doctor's consulting-room, he paused and smiled.

"It is a fruit-piece. You would think it not a very suitable picture for a doctor's consulting-room, but my wife will not have it in the drawing-room. She says it is frankly obscene."

"A fruit-piece!" I exclaimed in surprise.

We entered the room, and my eyes fell at once on the picture. I looked at it for a long time.

It was a pile of mangoes, bananas, oranges, and I know not what; and at first sight it was an innocent picture enough. It would have been passed in an exhibition of the Post-Impressionists by a careless person as an excellent but not very remarkable example of the school; but perhaps afterwards it would come back to his recollection, and he would wonder why. I do not think then he could ever entirely forget it.

The colours were so strange that words can hardly tell what a troubling emotion they gave. They were sombre blues, opaque like a delicately carved bowl in lapis lazuli, and yet with a quivering lustre that suggested the palpitation of mysterious life; there were purples, horrible like raw and putrid flesh, and yet with a glowing, sensual passion that called up vague memories of the Roman Empire of Heliogabalus; there were reds, shrill like the berries of holly—one thought of Christmas in England, and the snow, the good cheer, and the pleasure of children—and yet by some magic softened till they had the swooning tenderness of a dove's breast; there were deep yellows that died with an unnatural passion into a green as fragrant as the spring and as pure as the sparkling water of a mountain brook. Who can tell what anguished fancy made these fruits? They belonged to a Polynesian garden of the Hesperides. There was something strangely alive in them, as though they were created in a stage of the earth's dark history when things were not irrevocably fixed to their forms. They were extravagantly luxurious. They were heavy with tropical odours. They seemed to possess a sombre passion of their own. It was enchanted fruit, to taste which might open the gateway to God knows what secrets of the soul and to mysterious palaces of the imagination. They were sullen with unawaited dangers, and to eat them might turn a man to beast or god. All that was healthy and natural, all that clung to happy relationships and the simple joys of simple men, shrunk from them in dismay; and yet a fearful attraction was in them, and, like the fruit on the Tree of the Knowledge of Good and Evil they were terrible with the possibilities of the Unknown.

At last I turned away. I felt that Strickland had kept his secret to the grave.

"*Voyons, René, mon ami,*" came the loud, cheerful voice of Madame Coutras, "what are you doing all this time? Here are the *apéritifs*. Ask *Monsieur* if he will not drink a little glass of Quinquina Dubonnet."

"*Volontiers,* Madame," I said, going out on to the verandah.

The spell was broken.

Chapter LVIII

THE TIME CAME FOR MY DEPARTURE FROM TAHITI. ACCORDING TO THE GRAcious custom of the island, presents were given me by the persons with whom I had been thrown in contact—baskets made of the leaves of the 'coconut-tree, mats of pandanus, fans; and Tiaré gave me three little pearls and three jars of guava-jelly made with her own plump hands. When the mail-boat, stopping for twenty-four hours on its way from Wellington to San Francisco, blew the whistle that warned the passengers to get on board, Tiaré clasped me to her vast bosom, so that I seemed to sink into a billowy sea, and pressed her red lips to mine. Tears glistened in her eyes. And when we steamed slowly out of the lagoon, making our way gingerly through the opening in the reef, and then steered for the open sea, a certain melancholy fell upon me. The breeze was laden still with the pleasant odours of the land. Tahiti is very far away, and I knew that I should never see it again. A chapter of my life was closed, and I felt a little nearer to inevitable death.

Not much more than a month later I was in London; and after I had arranged certain matters which claimed my immediate attention, thinking Mrs. Strickland might like to hear what I knew of her husband's last years, I wrote to her. I had not seen her since long before the war, and I had to look out her address in the telephone-book. She made an appointment, and I went to the trim little house on Campden Hill which she now inhabited. She was by this time a woman of hard on sixty, but she bore her years well, and no one would have taken her for more than fifty. Her face, thin and not much lined, was of the sort that ages gracefully, so that you thought in youth she must have been a much handsomer woman than in fact she was. Her hair, not yet very grey, was becomingly arranged, and her black gown was modish. I remembered having heard that her sister, Mrs. MacAndrew, outliving her husband but a couple of years, had left money to Mrs. Strickland; and by the look of the house and the trim maid who opened the door I judged that it was a sum adequate to keep the widow in modest comfort.

When I was ushered into the drawing-room I found that Mrs. Strickland had a visitor, and when I discovered who he was, I guessed that I had been asked to come at just that time not without intention. The caller was Mr. Van Busche Taylor, an American, and Mrs. Strickland gave me particulars with a charming smile of apology to him.

"You know, we English are so dreadfully ignorant. You must forgive me if it's necessary to explain." Then she turned to me. "Mr. Van Busche Taylor is the distinguished American critic. If you haven't read his book your education has been shamefully neglected, and you must repair the omission at once. He's writing something about dear Charlie, and he's come to ask me if I can help him."

Mr. Van Busche Taylor was a very thin man with a large, bald head, bony and shining; and under the great dome of his skull his face, yellow, with deep lines in it, looked very small. He was quiet and exceedingly polite. He spoke with the accent of New England, and there was about his demeanour a bloodless frigidity which made me ask myself why on earth he was busying himself with Charles Strickland. I had been slightly tickled at the gentleness which Mrs. Strickland put into her mention of her husband's name, and while the pair conversed I took stock of the room in which we sat. Mrs. Strickland had moved with the times. Gone were the Morris papers and gone the severe cretonnes, gone were the Arundel prints that had adorned the walls of her drawing-room in Ashley Gardens; the room blazed with fantastic colour, and I wondered if she knew that those varied hues, which fashion had imposed upon her, were due to the dreams of a poor painter in a South Sea island. She gave me the answer herself.

"What wonderful cushions you have," said Mr. Van Busche Taylor.

"Do you like them?" she said, smiling. "Bakst, you know."

And yet on the walls were coloured reproductions of several of Strickland's best pictures, due to the enterprise of a publisher in Berlin.

"You're looking at my pictures," she said, following my eyes. "Of course, the originals are out of my reach, but it's a comfort to have these. The publisher sent them to me himself. They're a great consolation to me."

"They must be very pleasant to live with," said Mr. Van Busche Taylor.

"Yes; they're so essentially decorative."

"That is one of my profoundest convictions," said Mr. Van Busche Taylor. "Great art is always decorative."

Their eyes rested on a nude woman suckling a baby, while a girl was kneeling by their side holding out a flower to the indifferent child. Looking over them was a wrinkled, scraggy hag. It was Strickland's version of the Holy Family. I suspected that for the figures had sat his household above Taravao, and the woman and the baby were Ata and his first son. I asked myself if Mrs. Strickland had any inkling of the facts.

The conversation proceeded, and I marvelled at the tact with which Mr. Van Busche Taylor avoided all subjects that might have been in the least embarrassing, and at the ingenuity with which Mrs. Strickland, without saying a word that was untrue, insinuated that her relations with her husband had always been perfect. At last Mr. Van Busche Taylor rose to go. Holding his hostess' hand, he made her a graceful, though perhaps too elaborate, speech of thanks, and left us.

"I hope he didn't bore you," she said, when the door closed behind him. "Of course it's a nuisance sometimes, but I feel it's only right to give people any information I can about Charlie. There's a certain responsibility about having been the wife of a genius."

She looked at me with those pleasant eyes of hers, which had remained as candid and as sympathetic as they had been more than twenty years before. I wondered if she was making a fool of me.

"Of course you've given up your business," I said.

"Oh, yes," she answered airily. "I ran it more by way of a hobby than for any other reason, and my children persuaded me to sell it. They thought I was over-taxing my strength."

I saw that Mrs. Strickland had forgotten that she had ever done anything so disgraceful as to work for her living. She had the true instinct of the nice woman that it is only really decent for her to live on other people's money.

"They're here now," she said. "I thought they'd like to hear what you had to say about their father. You remember Robert, don't you? I'm glad to say he's been recommended for the Military Cross."

She went to the door and called them. There entered a tall man in khaki, with the parson's collar, handsome in a somewhat heavy fashion, but with the frank eyes that I remembered in him as a boy. He was followed by his sister. She must have been the same age as was her mother when first I knew her, and she was very like her. She too gave one the impression that as a girl she must have been prettier than indeed she was.

"I suppose you don't remember them in the least," said Mrs. Strickland, proud and smiling. "My daughter is now Mrs. Ronaldson. Her husband's a Major in the Gunners."

"He's by way of being a pukka soldier, you know," said Mrs. Ronaldson gaily. "That's why he's only a Major."

I remembered my anticipation long ago that she would marry a soldier. It was inevitable. She had all the graces of the soldier's wife. She was civil and affable, but she could hardly conceal her intimate conviction that she was not quite as others were. Robert was breezy.

"It's a bit of luck that I should be in London when you turned up," he said. "I've only got three days' leave."

"He's dying to get back," said his mother.

"Well, I don't mind confessing it, I have a rattling good time at the front. I've made a lot of good pals. It's a first-rate life. Of course war's terrible, and all that sort of thing; but it does bring out the best qualities in a man, there's no denying that."

Then I told them what I had learned about Charles Strickland in Tahiti. I thought it unnecessary to say anything of Ata and her boy, but for the rest I was as accurate as I could be. When I had narrated his lamentable death I ceased. For a minute or two we were all silent. Then Robert Strickland struck a match and lit a cigarette.

"The mills of God grind slowly, but they grind exceeding small," he said, somewhat impressively.

Mrs. Strickland and Mrs. Ronaldson looked down with a slightly pious expression which indicated, I felt sure, that they thought the quotation was from Holy Writ. Indeed, I was unconvinced that Robert Strickland did not share their illusion. I do not know why I suddenly thought of Strickland's son by Ata. They had told me he was a merry, light-hearted youth. I saw him, with my mind's eye, on the schooner on which he worked, wearing nothing but a pair of dungarees; and at night, when the boat sailed along easily before a light breeze, and the sailors were gathered on the upper deck, while the captain and the supercargo lolled in deck-chairs, smoking their pipes, I saw him dance with another lad, dance wildly, to the wheezy music of the concertina. Above was the blue sky, and the stars, and all about the desert of the Pacific Ocean.

A quotation from the Bible came to my lips, but I held my tongue, for I know that clergymen think it a little blasphemous when the laity poach upon their preserves. My Uncle Henry, for twenty-seven years Vicar of Whitstable, was on these occasions in the habit of saying that the devil could always quote scripture to his purpose. He remembered the days when you could get thirteen Royal Natives for a shilling.

About the Author

WILLIAM SOMERSET MAUGHAM (1874-1965) WAS BORN IN PARIS ON JANUARY 25, 1874, and moved to England after the death of his parents when he was ten. He attended the University of Heidelberg in Germany and studied medicine at St. Thomas's Hospital in London. Although Maugham passed his medical exams, he was more interested in becoming a writer, and he published his first novel, *Liza of Lambeth*, in 1897. Other novels followed, including *The Hero* (1901) and *Mrs. Craddock* (1902), both of which offered strong criticism of contemporary English society and its values. Maugham concentrated on playwriting in the years before World War I, but alternated dramas with novels. He drew lightly on aspects of his own life and the feelings of alienation and loneliness he had experienced in youth for *Of Human Bondage* (1915), a very successful novel that vaulted him to the front ranks of contemporary novelists in Britain. Maugham volunteered for ambulance service in France during World War I. After the war he traveled extensively, including to the United States, where he married. His honeymoon in Tahiti inspired him to write *The Moon and Sixpence* (1919), a fictionalized biography of the artist Paul Gauguin. Maugham would achieve his greatest renown as a novelist with *The Razor's Edge* (1944), based on his travels to India in 1938. His first collection of short fiction, *Orientations*, had appeared in 1899 and Maugham would write short stories throughout his career, eventually earning recognition as a master of the form with volumes including *The Trembling of a Leaf* (1921), *Ashenden* (1928), and *Creatures of Circumstance* (1947). He also wrote numerous books on travel, and collections of literary essays and sketches. He died in Nice, France on December 16, 1965.